ANTHONY
ADVERSE

Books by HERVEY ALLEN

PROSE

· Toward the Flame: A War Diary
Israfel: The Life and Times of Edgar Allan Poe
Poe's Brother (*with Thomas Ollive Mabbott*)
Anthony Adverse

POETRY

Wampum and Old Gold
Carolina Chansons (*with DuBose Heyward*)
The Bride of Huitzil: An Aztec Legend
The Blindman
Earth Moods and Other Poems
Songs for Annette
Sarah Simon
New Legends

ANTHONY ADV
By
Hervey Allen

Decorations by Allan McNab

New York
Farrar and Rinehart, Inc.
On Murray Hill
1933

"There is something in us that can be without us, and will be after us, though indeed it hath no history of what it was before us, and cannot tell how it entered into us."

—SIR THOMAS BROWNE.

TO

EDNA ALLEN RICKMERS

CONTENTS

VOLUME ONE

THE ROOTS OF THE TREE

BOOK I—IN WHICH THE SEED FALLS IN THE ENCHANTED FOREST

PAGE

I. The Coach 3
II. The Little Madonna 16
III. At the "Golden Sheaf" 29
IV. The Enchanted Forest 40
V. A Pastoral Interlude 54
VI. The Muse of Tragedy 65
VII. The Fly Walks In 81
VIII. A Hole in the Wall 96

BOOK II—IN WHICH THE ROOTS OF THE TREE ARE EXPOSED

IX. The Convent of Jesus the Child 111
X. The Chick Emerges 140
XI. Between Two Worlds 151
XII. Casa da Bonnyfeather 158
XIII. The Evidence of Things Unseen 170
XIV. Reality Makes a Bid 185
XV. The Shadows of Faith 202
XVI. Pagan Mornings 212
XVII. Philosophical Afternoons 219
XVIII. Bodies in the Dark 231
XIX. The Numbers of the Virgin 237

BOOK III—IN WHICH THE ROOTS OF THE TREE ARE TORN LOOSE

XX. Apples and Ashes 247
XXI. Adventures of a Shepherdess 266
XXII. Icons and Iconoclasts 291
XXIII. Farewells and Epitaphs 312

CONTENTS

VOLUME TWO

THE OTHER BRONZE BOY

BOOK IV—IN WHICH SEVERAL IMAGES TRAVEL TOGETHER

		PAGE
XXIV.	The Table of the Sun	331
XXV.	The Villa Brignole	349
XXVI.	The Street of the Image Makers	361
XXVII.	The Pillars of Hercules	373
XXVIII.	The Seed of a Miracle	389

BOOK V—IN WHICH THE NECESSARY ALLOY IS ADDED

XXIX.	The House of Silenus	409
XXX.	The Miracle in the Chapel of St. Paul, Regla	427
XXXI.	A Decent Mammalian Philosophy	441
XXXII.	Honour Among Thieves	454
XXXIII.	A Mantilla Intrudes	469
XXXIV.	Through a Copy of Velasquez	476
XXXV.	The Temporary Sequestration of the *Ariostatica*	496

BOOK VI—IN WHICH THE BRONZE GOES INTO THE FIRE

XXXVI.	A Gradual Approach to Africa	519
XXXVII.	The Crew Go Ashore	542
XXXVIII.	A Whiff of Grapeshot	557
XXXIX.	Viewed from Gallegos	567
XL.	The Master of Gallegos	573
XLI.	A Glimpse into the Furnace	593
XLII.	The Vision of Light	618
XLIII.	The Image Begins to Melt	635
XLIV.	The Hard Metal Runs	643
XLV.	The Bronze Is Sublimed	656
XLVI.	The *Unicorn* Charges Home	680

CONTENTS

VOLUME THREE

THE LONELY TWIN

Book VII—In Which a Worldly Brother Is Acquired

PAGE

XLVII. Reverberations 703
XLVIII. Old Friends Grown Older 715
XLIX. What Banking Is About 726
L. Don Luis Reflects by Candlelight 742
LI. The Coach and the Berlin 756
LII. Over the Crest 783
LIII. The Force of Gravity 805
LIV. The Plains of France 816
LV. The Little Man at Great Headquarters 830

Book VIII—In Which Prosperity Enforces Loneliness

LVI. A Metallic Standard Is Resumed 863
LVII. Your Humble Obedient Servant 888
LVIII. *Gloria Mundi* 927
LIX. The Swan-song of Romance 948
LX. *Panem et Circenses* 970
LXI. Shoes and Stockings 990
LXII. The Prince of the Peace Beyond the Pyrenees 1015

Book IX—In Which the Tree Is Cut Down

LXIII. By the River of Babylon 1063
LXIV. The Snake Changes Its Skin 1098
LXV. The People of the Bear 1142
LXVI. The Pilgrimage of Grace 1163
LXVII. The Prison of St. Lazarus 1193
LXVIII. The Stone in the Heart of the Tree 1209
Epilogue 1221

VOLUME ONE

The Roots of the Tree

BOOK ONE

*In Which the Seed Falls
in the Enchanted
Forest*

CHAPTER ONE

THE COACH

BETWEEN the villages of Aubière and Romagnat in the ancient Province of Auvergne there is an old road that comes suddenly over the top of a high hill. To stand south of this ridge looking up at the highway flowing over the skyline is to receive one of those irrefutable impressions from landscape which requires more than a philosopher to explain. In this case it is undoubtedly, for some reason, one of exalted expectation.

From the deep notch in the hillcrest where the road first appears, to the bottom of the valley below it, the fields seem to sweep down hastily for the express purpose of widening out and waiting by the way. From the low hills for a considerable distance about, the stone farm buildings all happen to face toward it, and although most of them have stood thus for centuries their expressions of curiosity remain unaltered.

Somewhat to the east the hill of Gergovia thrusts its head into the sky, and continually stares toward the notch as if speculating whether

3

Celtic pedlars, Roman legionaries, Franks, crusaders, or cavaliers will raise the dust there.

In fact in whatever direction a man may look in this particular vicinity his eyes are led inevitably by the seductive tracery of the sky-line to the most interesting point in all that countryside, the place where the road surmounts the hill. Almost anything might appear there suddenly against the empty sky, fix itself upon the memory, and then move on to an unknown destination.

Perhaps the high hill of Gergovia where heroic events have taken place in the remote past now misses a certain epic grandeur in the rhythms of mankind. For ages past tribes have ceased to migrate and armies to march over the highway it looks down upon. Caval-cades, or companies of pilgrims have rarely been seen upon it for some centuries now. Individual wayfaring has long been the rule. Even by the last quarter of the eighteenth century it had long been apparent what the best way of travelling the roads of this world is when one has a definite, personal object in view. Such, indeed, was then the state of society that the approach of a single individual, if he hap-pened to belong to a certain class, might cause as much consternation to a whole countryside as the advance of a hostile army.

It was this condition of affairs, no doubt, that accounted for the alarm upon the faces of several peasants as they stood waiting uneasily in the late afternoon sunshine one spring day in the year 1775. They were gazing apprehensively at the deep notch in the hill just above them where the road, which they had been mending, surmounted the ridge. Indeed, a grinding sound of wheels from the farther side of the crest had already reached the ears of the keenest some moments before.

Presently there was the loud crack of a whip, the shouts of a pos-tilion, and the heads of two horses made their appearance prick-eared against the sky. The off-leader, for there were evidently more horses behind, was ridden by a squat-bodied little man with abnormally short legs. A broad-brimmed felt hat with the flap turned up in front served, even at considerable distance, to accentuate under its dingy green cockade an unusual breadth of countenance. The ridge at the apex is very steep. The first team had already begun to descend before immediately behind it appeared the second straining hard against the breast straps. Then the coach, a "V"-shaped body with the powdered heads of two footmen in cocked hats peering over its slightly curved roof, outlined itself sharply in the bright notch of the road and seemed for an instant to pause there.

As soon as it hove in full sight a babble of relieved exclamation arose from the group of watching peasants. It was *not* the coach of M. de Besance.

As to whose coach it might be, there was small time for speculation. The problem rapidly began to solve itself. The coach was heavy and the hill was steep. Suddenly, at a cry from the little postilion, who began to use his whip like a demon, the horses stretched themselves out. An immense cloud of dust arose and foamed about the wheels.

The black body of the coach was now seen coming down the road like a log over a waterfall. Oaths, cries, shouts from the white-faced footmen, the squall and moan of brakes, and a frantic drumming of hoofs accompanied its descent. Four horses and the carriage flashed as one object through the spray of a little stream at the foot of the hill. There was a nautical pitch as the vehicle mounted violently upon a brief length of causeway that led to the ford. But so great was the momentum which it had accumulated and the terror of the horses that the postilion was unable to check them even with the attempted assistance of the peasants.

A large hole full of water on one side of the little causeway now became horribly apparent to him. With a quick jerk on the bridle and a firm hand the clever little driver dragged his horses around it. The front wheels missed it by a fraction. But there had not been time to turn the trick entirely. For an instant the left hind wheel hung spinning. Then to the accompaniment of a shrill feminine scream from the interior of the coach it sank with a sickening jar and gravelly crunch into the very centre of the pit. Nevertheless, the rear of the carriage finally rose to the level of the causeway as the horses once more struggled forward. A high water mark showed itself upon the yellow stockings of the petrified footmen. The coach lurched again violently, rocked, and stopped.

Scarcely had the coach body ceased to oscillate in its slings when from the window projected a claret-coloured face surmounted by a travel-stained wig much awry. A hand like a lion's paw flourished a gold-headed cane furiously, and from the mouth of its entirely masculine owner, which vent can only be described as grim, proceeded in a series of staccato barks and lion-like roars a masterpiece of Spanish profanity. It began with God the Father and ranged through the remainder of the Trinity. It touched upon the apostles, not omitting Judas; skipped sulphurously through a score or two of saints, and ended with a few choked bellows caused by twinges of violent pain, on Santiago of Compostela. During the entire period of this soul-shaking address, and for several speechless seconds after, a small, intensely black, forked beard continued to flicker like an adder's tongue through the haze of words surrounding it. Somewhat exhausted, its owner now paused.

Those who thought his vocabulary exhausted, however, were sadly mistaken.

The gentleman looking out of the coach window owned estates both in Spain and in Italy. From both he drew copious revenues not only of rents but of idiom. He was of mixed Irish, Spanish, and Tuscan ancestry, and his fluency was even thrice enhanced. He now gripped his cane more firmly and lapsed into Italian.

"You mule's bastard," roared he, twisting his head around with an obvious grin of pain to address the little man sitting astride the lead horse, "Come here, I say. Come here till I break your back. I'll . . ." The rest was cut short by a second grimace of agony and a whistling sound from the cane.

The recipient of this alluring invitation climbed down from his saddle rather slowly, but with no further signs of hesitation walked imperturbably past his four quivering horses toward the door of the coach. His legs, which already appeared small when astride a horse, were now seen to be shorter than ever and crooked. Yet he moved with a certain feline motion that was somehow memorable. As he turned to face the door of the coach and removed his cocked hat, two tufts of mouse-coloured hair just over his ears, and a long, black whip thrust through his belt till it projected out of his coat tails behind, completed for the peasants, who were now crowding as close as they dared, the illusion that they were looking, not at a man, but at an animal vaguely familiar.

The door of the coach was now pushed open by the gold-headed cane revealing to those by the roadside a glimpse of the sumptuous interior of a nobleman's private carriage. Its owner had been riding with his back to the horses. As the door opened wider a long, white object projecting across the aisle toward the rear disclosed itself as a human leg disguised by a plethora of bandages and resting upon a "T"-shaped stand contrived out of a couple of varnished boards. On this couch the ill member with its swathed foot seemed to repose like a mummy. On the rear seat could be caught a glimpse of a brocaded skirt the folds of which remained motionless.

The claret-coloured face now appeared again and the cane was once more flourished as if about to descend upon the back of the unfortunate postilion waiting hat in hand just beyond its reach. But the gentleman had now reached the limit of his field of action. He was the owner of the mummified limb on the "T"-shaped stand, a fact of which he was just then agonizingly reminded, and a torrent of several languages that seemed to start at his waist literally leapt out of his mouth.

To the surprise of all but the footmen, who were thoroughly inured to such scenes, the little man in the road ventured to reply. He purred in a soft Spanish patois accompanied by gestures that provided a perfect pantomime. Due to his eloquent motions towards the peasants in the ditch and the hole in the road, it was not necessary to understand his dialect in order to follow his argument. With this the gentleman, who had meanwhile violently jerked his wig back into place, seemed inclined to agree.

Seeing how things were going, a tall fellow somewhat more intelligent than his companions now stepped forward.

"It is to be hoped. that monsieur will overlook the existence of the terrible hole which has caused him such discomfort . . ."

"Overlook its existence, you scoundrel, when it nearly bumped me into purgatory!" roared the gentleman. "What do you mean?"

"Ah, if we had only known monsieur was coming this way so soon it should have been filled in before this. It is very difficult now to get these rascals to come to the corvée. We were informed you would not arrive until day after tomorrow. I can tell you, sir," continued he, turning an eye on his miserable companions which they did not seem to appreciate, "I can tell you they were just now in a fine sweat when they heard monsieur's coach ascending the hill. If it had been that of M. le Comte de Besance . . . oh, if it had been M. le Comte himself!"

"M. de Besance? Ah, then we are already upon his estates!" interrupted the gentleman in the coach. "Do you hear that, my dear?" Seemingly placated, and as if the incident were drawing to a close, he began to close the door. Noticing the crest on the outside panel for the first time, the man by the road licked his lips and hastened to correct himself.

"But yes, monseigneur," he gasped, "the Château de Besance is scarcely half an hour's drive. One goes as far as the cross-roads at Romagnat and then turns to the left by the little wood. And the road from here on monseigneur will find in excellent shape. For a week now we have laboured upon it even in·wheat sowing time."

Mollified at finding himself so near the end of a long and painful journey the gentleman's face relaxed somewhat from its unrelenting scowl. A few pale blotches began to appear through its hitherto uniform tint of scarlet. Encouraged by this the unfortunate bailiff essayed further.

"By special order we have smoothed the road from Romagnat for the illustrious guest expected at the château; but not until day after tomorrow." Here he bowed. "Yet an hour later and this accurséd hole would have been filled. A little more willingness on the part of these"—a grim smile of understanding on the face of the nobleman here transported the bailiff—"a little more skill on the part of monseigneur's coachman . . ."

Scarcely had these words left the man's mouth, however, before a hail of rocks and mud set him dodging and dancing. The small postilion who had all this time been waiting in the road hat in hand was galvanized into instant action. On all fours, he dashed about snatching up every clod and stone that came ready to his paws. The whip flickered tail-like over his back, his grey-green eyes blazed brilliantly, and he spat and squalled out a stream of curses that might have done credit to his master. One of the peasants began to mutter something about the evil eye, and all began to draw back from the coach.

"Are we all right?" shouted the master to his footmen.

"Yes, Your Excellency," they replied as if with one voice.

"Drive on then, Sancho, you devil's cat," roared the gentleman now grinning with enjoyment at the grotesque scene before him and with satisfaction at finding that neither his leg nor his coach was irreparably damaged.

But at the word "cat" the little postilion fairly bounded into the air. His hair seemed to stand on end. Those outside the coach appeared to be fascinated. They continued to stand and stare until with an impatient gesture the gentleman on the inside pulled a tasselled cord. A small bell hung in a yoke on the roof tinkled musically, and the horses long accustomed to the signal moved forward.

Finding himself about to be left alone on the highroad in a hopeless minority, the postilion with a final snarl turned, picked up his hat, clapped it on his head, and in a series of panther-like leaps, for his legs were far too short to run, gained the lead horse already some yards ahead and vaulted into the saddle.

"A cat! A cat!" shrieked the peasants. The four horses broke into a trot, and the coach and its passengers rocked and rolled along the road that had been so carefully "smoothed" to the Château de Besance.

But rumour preceded it in the person of a peasant runner who took a short cut across the fields. The servants at the château were warned of the unexpectedly sudden approach of visitors. Even before the coach reached the cross-roads at Romagnat that entire village was agog. For nothing except scandal spreads so fast as an apt nickname. The two indeed are frequently related, and in this case as long as he remained in that part of Auvergne Don Luis Guzman Sotoymer y O'Connell, conde de Azuaga in Estremadura, Marquis da Vincitata in Tuscany, and Envoy Extraordinary to the Court of France from that grand duchy, was invariably associated with his feline postilion, Sancho, and referred to over the entire countryside as Monsieur le Marquis de Carabas and his cat.

Compared with the surface of the royal highway the recently smoothed road upon the estates of M. de Besance was as a calm harbour to the Bay of Biscay. Both Don Luis and his leg thus began to experience considerable benefit from the comparative ease with which the coach now rolled along. The end of a ten days' journey from

Versailles was almost in sight, and the marquis began to contemplate the bandages in the vicinity of his big toe—from which only a faint, blue light now seemed to emanate—if not with entire satisfaction at least with considerable relief. As he did so his eyes happened to stray past his carefully cherished foot into the deep recess formed by the rear seat, thus serving to remind him of what he was at times somewhat prone to forget.

The ample rear seat of the coach upholstered in a smooth velvet of a light rose colour was deep enough to form, with its painted side panels and the arched roof above it, what seemed from the front seat, where the marquis was now leaning back, to be a deep alcove. Sunk in the luxurious cushions of the seat, and reclining against the back of the coach with her head directly under an oval window was what appeared to be the body of a young girl scarcely eighteen years of age. Her form was completely relaxed. Her long sensitive hands, upon one finger of which was a wedding ring, lay with startling and weblike whiteness against the rose of the cushions. Two waxen arms disappeared at the elbows into the folds of a grey silk travelling scarf wrapped about her shoulders like a Vigée-Lebrun drapery. She sat with one leg crossed over the other so that her skirt, stiffly brocaded in a heavy heliotrope and gold pattern, fell in a sharp-edged fold that might have been moulded in porcelain to one white-slippered foot.

Used as he was to an almost selfless yielding in his girl-wife which constantly expressed itself in his presence in her relaxed physical attitudes, there was, as he now looked at her across the aisle of the coach, something in her posture which caused Don Luis to glance hastily and uneasily at her face. Her small, rather neat head lay drooped to one side. Since Bourges, which they had left hastily after the death of her maid by plague, she had been unable to accomplish an elaborate powdered coiffure. Consequently her own hair of a pure saffron colour seldom seen in the south of Europe, burst, rather than was combed back, into a high Grecian knot held precariously by one gold-knobbed pin. Across her wide, clear forehead, above carefully pencilled and minutely pointed arcs of eyebrows, and blowing out from the temples before and around two finely chiselled ears, sprang a delightful hedge of ringlets and tiny silken wires. These in the rays of the western sun, which darted now and again through the oval window behind, were touched along with a thousand dust motes that danced in the semi-darkness of the coach, into a sudden blaze and aura of golden glory. A straight nose, and a rather small, pursed mouth, whose corners were nevertheless drawn out enough to be turned down toward an obstinate little chin, completed a countenance with a bisque complexion like that of a miniature. It needed only that the eyes should be wide open and staring directly at you out of

the shadows to give the impression that you were actually in the presence of some dream-like and helpless doll. But her eyes were now
closed, or almost so. As her husband looked at them with their long,
brown lashes disclosing only a blue polished glimmer of the pupils
beneath, while the lids remained perfectly motionless, it calmly occurred
to him that she might have fainted.

Yet this realization even when it became a certainty did not suggest
to Don Luis any necessity for immediate action. Before everything
else the marquis was a connoisseur, an appreciator of rare and accidental patterns of beauty in nature, and of their successful imitation
or creation in art. The picture before him was a combination of both.
The wide-flung frame of the upholstered seat, the delicate rose-leaf
tint of the background, the perspective of the alcove, and the unusual
arrangement of its lights and shadows were, so it happened, in exact
harmony with the central and somewhat tragic figure of the portrait.
There was even a high light in precisely the proper place, for a large
emerald breast pin concentrated the stray beams of sunlight and
deflected them in a living grey-green shaft across the folds of the
girl's scarf.

Don Luis was delighted. For the time being he felt that his con-
descension and his trouble in marrying this young woman had been
rewarded. And where had he seen that exact arrangement of head-
dress and features, accidental to be sure, but quite purely classic in
effect? Ah, it was on a coin of Faustine; or was it Theodora? Perhaps a combination of both. One's mind played tricks like that. His
artistic imagination no doubt! Yes, there was something a little
Byzantine here, and yet quite Grecian behind with the knot, of course.
Well, he would look again in that cabinet in the Pitti next time he
was in Florence. He knew the exact spot where it stood. Just next
to that vile medallion of Guido. . . . But a slight trembling of his
wife's eyelids reminded him that some more direct attention to the
subject of so admirable a reverie was now in order.

"Maria," said he, leaning forward and feeling along her arms as
if she were a doll whose limbs might have been accidentally broken,
"listen, I am speaking to you."

Recalled thus from somewhere else by a command not to be disregarded, she slowly opened her eyes, wide, and very blue, upon him.
Scarcely had full consciousness returned to her look before she hastened to disengage her arms from his grasp and to whisper, "Better
now. It was that last jolt. I was sure we should all be killed. I
prayed to her all the way down the hill. I dreamed I was with her
now." A haze suffused itself over her eyes as if she had been looking
at the little hills of a child's paradise with the morning mist still
gathered upon them.

For a moment he remained silent. There was one crack, however, in his otherwise turtle-like armour. Glancing toward a statuette of the Madonna, which at his wife's entreaty had been set in a niche in the side of the coach, he crossed himself fervently. The upholstery had been cut away to allow the insertion of this figure and its little shrine, and for some time he kept his eyes fixed in its direction with an expression at once conventionally pious and fearfully sincere. Only a boyhood in Spain could have achieved it. But while it lasted and his lips moved, the girl remained still. A look of mixed jealousy and chagrin as if she were loath to share some personal possession with him hardened her eyes and brought her chin a little further forward while his devotions went on. At last, seeing that his gaze had shifted to the window again, she ventured to ask, "What happened?"

"Nothing," said he. The coach rolled on a short distance.

Settling back he pulled up a square flap in the cushion and produced from a locker in the seat a bottle and a small, silver travelling mug. "Nothing, fortunately," he repeated, "but drink this and you will soon feel better. Shall I tell you now? It was a deep hole in the road. A few minutes later and it would have been filled. No doubt it did jar you badly sitting directly over the wheel, but the coach of monseigneur is undoubtedly a good one. We shall not be delayed."

Without spilling any of the wine which he offered her, she managed to sip it down and wipe the scarlet stain from her lips with a wisp of a handkerchief. Seeing how steady were her hands, Don Luis congratulated her and proceeded to follow up his panacea for all earthly ills, as he put the bottle back in the seat, with a little cheering chat.

"It is really too bad that both of the mishaps of the journey have fallen upon you, my dear," said he, wiping his own lips. "I could complain to M. de Besance about this last one and make it lively for those lazy peasants. He is said to prefer the high justice to the low, but it is not quite so easy in these disturbed times to take the high hand as it used to be. Hanging or driving away a tenant is not to be thought of nowadays, especially when one's luck at cards has been of the sorriest. They say some of these fellows in the country are getting impatient at sending all their rents to Versailles. The fields here look in condition though," he exclaimed, "fine, well-tilled acres!"

She nodded wearily.

"So they didn't expect us so soon," he chuckled, "otherwise that hole would not have 'existed.' Well, Sancho paid them back in their own loose dirt." He proceeded to relate the incident, at which she succeeded in smiling faintly.

"No, we are decidedly before-hand with them. If you had not insisted on delaying at Bourges to be sure that maid would die, we

might have been here two days sooner. That delay was a sheer waste
of time. Oh! it has been difficult with your hair, I am sure. But do
you know I admire you as you are. There is a certain classic air about
you. They told me you were quite the rage at the Petit Trianon in a
milkma'd's smock. It was really clever of you to manage that. To
be commanded to the dairy by the queen herself, twice!"

A slight tinge of colour began to suffuse her cheeks.

"Still you should never have let them find out that you really did
know how to milk," he went on. "That was a faux pas, a decidedly
peculiar accomplishment for the wife of an envoy extraordinary. It
is not real simplicity they want. You should have merely pretended
to be learning rapidly. But to have finished milking before Madame!
It was fatal! I can tell you our stock dropped after that. I felt like
M. Law himself. If it had not been for my luck in the Œil-de-Bœuf
and that night at de Guémené's soirée we should have been nowhere,
nowhere at all. Even the mission might have failed. But when I won
M. d'Orléans' new coach from him at écarté, and drove off in it with
the lilies on the door! Ha! That was something, even if one's wife
did know how to milk." He looked at her, stroking his beard with
satisfaction.

The coach rolled on while the shadows deepened. In the depths of
the seat he could not see the tears in the eyes of his young wife. The
world outside glimmered before her.

A red ray of sunset dashed itself against the rose-coloured cushions
and glanced into the shimmering pools of her eyes. Reflected there
she saw the Palace of Love at the Petit Trianon; the torchlight on the
pool before it. A dust mote became a boat gliding past in the red
glow. Ghosts of music began to sound in her ears. The trees whispered outside like the park forest.

Suddenly the vision became intensely clear. Up the little steps of
the temple sprang a young soldier in a white and gold uniform. He
was putting roses on the altar before the god of love. She leaned
forward now to see his face—and found herself gazing directly into
the eyes of her husband.

His lips parted slowly in a completely self-possessed smile. She
gasped slightly. The vision had been so clear! She was almost afraid
he must have seen it, too. But Don Luis was not given to visions.
The gouty leg had unaccountably stopped pulsing and its owner now
felt inclined to talk.

"M. le Comte de Besance did not come off so well in his bets with
me either." His smile widened. "Five hundred louis against my
living on his estates till my leg is cured! All of these fellows are so
sure of their provincial springs. No one can dispute with them. It is
like arguing with a country priest about a local miracle. Por Dios,

how he leered over that fine hand he held. I almost believe he wanted
to lose just to have me try his spa. Else how could he have played
so ill? So I shall take my time here. It is due my good luck. And
I like the air already. None the less that there are no handsome Irish
captains of the guard to breathe it. Mark that! O'Connell was my
great-grandfather's name. That is all the Irish you will get. We
shall say no more about that fellow, but"—and he leaned forward
clutching her knee—"*remember!*"

Having delivered this ultimatum he sat back again for some time
in silence. At last one of the footmen absent-mindedly began to drum
upon the roof. "Leave off that," roared his master. Outside the man
snatched his hand back as if he had suddenly found it resting on a hot
stove. Don Luis continued.

"You can rest here and forget all about it. They say the Château
de Besance is a pleasant enough place. The last M. de Besance but
one spent some time in Italy and even journeyed to see the Grand
Turk. The rugs are said to be remarkable, and there are some good
Venetian pieces. Besides, the place is not too large to be comfortable.
I shall get you another maid, somehow, and you can indulge your
cursed English taste for driving about the country."

"Scotch, you mean," the girl said softly, "my father . . ."

"It is all the same," said he, a little impatient at the interruption.
"Doubtless there is a small carriage in the count's stables. But no
jaunting about in peasants' carts! That was bad enough at Livorno
when you were a girl. Remember!"

He had an unpleasant way of trilling the phrase in Italian, an accent
that might have accompanied a sneer. She always felt it and winced.
Yet seldom was he so talkative or so amiable as now. Despite an
occasional sardonic fall in his tones, without which he could scarcely
have expressed himself, for the first time in her married life of about
a year he was verging upon the affable. Sensing the state of his feelings as well as their ephemeral nature, she decided to pick flowers
while the sun shone.

"At the château—could I have a dog?" she asked. Her quick reading of the human barometer and her instant grasp of opportunity
tickled his shrewd fancy. In the mood he was in he consented with
an ease that astonished himself.

"At the château, yes. But it must not come into the coach. I will
not be having the cushions made for royalty itself ruined."

She laughed. The very thought of a companion who could give
and receive affection revived her. Leaning forward she looked out
of the window and let the breeze play on her forehead. They were
just approaching a village.

Presently the coach and four wheeled sharply around a well-curb

at the forks of the road.   A weather-beaten cross stood above the
town fountain, and the usual crowd of women drawing water at that
time of day put their pitchers down or slipped the bucket yokes from
their shoulders at the sound of horses.   Almost everyone in the village
who could find an excuse to be away, and there were few who could
not, stood waiting to stare curiously but silently at the coach.   The
only sound was the *clopping* of hoofs and the occasional snarl of the
more vicious village curs carefully held back from barking.   Dogs
which barked at guests on the estates of M. le Comte de Besance
invariably failed to return to their owners.

"To the château?" cried Sancho, drawing up and flourishing his
whip.

One of the horses began to crane its neck and sniff toward the
fountain.   The crowd gaped and began to murmur something among
themselves about a cat.   "But, yes, certainly, a cat!"   There seemed
a humorous difference of opinion.   Sancho began to jabber.   The bell
on the top of the coach tapped twice with unusual emphasis, and he
swung the horses to the left.

"That fool!" exclaimed the marquis, "he would stop at every village
well to start a brawl.   An end must be put to that!   If he fights with
everyone who howls 'cat' after him between here and the Alps, I shall
be needing a new coachman long before we get to Italy.   Besides, the
man does look like a cat!   You can see, my love, it would never do
to have a dog in the coach with Puss-in-Boots on the box, never!"
Don Luis actually leaned out of the window and laughed at his own
joke.   In town he would never have thought of doing so.   It was the
first time she had ever heard him laugh heartily and something in the
tone of it startled her.

They were ascending a long rise now between a pleasant park-like
wood on one side and a carefully pruned vineyard on the other.   A few
bunches of grapes smaller than berries as yet showed here and there.
An all but imperceptible perfume was in the air.   Maria breathed
deeply and lay back with her eyes closed.   The scent was delightfully
familiar, suggestive even in its intangibility, and she allowed herself,
as she relaxed into the cushions, the unexpected boon of indulging to
the full an overpowering illusion that she was returning home.

After all, perhaps the Château de Besance might have its compensations.   She would play that she was coming home anyway.   It would
make the arrival at another strange place more bearable.   The faint
tinge of colour brightened in her cheeks.   Even the illusion made her
heart beat faster.

Her husband was looking out over the vineyards, wide and peculiarly mellow in the last, long rays of full daylight.   If only that
countenance with its pointed beard, the cheeks forever a dark wine

colour, the hard black eyes, and the mouth like a trap,—if only *he* were not here now to spoil her dream! A small breeze blowing across the aisle of the coach fanned her cheeks and brought a more pungent whiff as of the vineyards about Livorno. Shutting her eyes tight she breathed more deeply, then she turned away from him and opened them wide.

From the little niche in the side of the coach the madonna was looking at her. The girl began to pray to her silently. The face of the Virgin was very familiar. The little statuette was the one memento which she had been allowed to keep that still reminded her of home. Her lips moved imperceptibly, her nostrils widened to the breeze, her eyes remained fixed upon the face of the statue. For a few wretched and blessed moments she was back again in her own room in her father's house.

Don Luis had no idea of what was going on in his wife's mind. He saw that she was praying and that seemed natural enough. But he did not care how, when, where, or to what a woman prayed. Just now he was nowhere in particular himself. His leg had stopped hurting and left him pleasantly vacant of mind; in an easy, almost garrulous mood. He leaned out of the window still farther and noticed they were nearly at the top of the hill. Hadn't the bailiff in charge of the peasants said the château was just over the top of the rise? The memory of that unfortunate fleeing in a hail of mud again caused Don Luis to laugh aloud.

The little postilion turned about in his saddle and looked back at his master. An amused grin spread from his whiskers along his jaws. A knowing wink passed between the master and his man. Just then the horses began to descend.

"What can you see ahead?" shouted the marquis.

But the reply of the postilion was lost in the sudden grinding of brakes.

CHAPTER TWO

THE LITTLE MADONNA

THE peasants working on the corvée of M. de Besance had just completed filling the hole in the causeway and were gathering up their tools to depart for a well-earned night's rest, when the sound of galloping hoofs once more fell upon their ears.

There was a short cessation of the sound. Then without any further warning a man mounted on a spirited bay horse darkened the notch at the top of the hill. Picking his way rapidly down the steep slope, he splashed at a sharp clip through the ford and cantered onto the causeway. A certain military precision lurked in the folds of a blue cloak that fell from his shoulders in trim, straight lines. As he came opposite the group of peasants he reined up his horse sharply, and at the first glance as if his judgment was seldom at a loss, picked out the bailiff in charge of the work although the man's clothes were still bespattered by the dirt with which his friend the postilion had recently favoured him. The stranger beckoned to him, but somewhat suspicious from his recent experience the man hesitated to step forward as smartly as before. Nor did two large pistols in the holsters of a military saddle, and the brass clover of a rapier scabbard projecting below the newcomer's riding cloak add to the bailiff's sense of self-possession.

"Come here," said the horseman, seeing how matters stood, in a voice that was not to be denied. With some visible hesitation the bailiff advanced.

"Have you seen a gentleman on a black gelding pass this way recently?"

"No, sir, he has not come by this road," replied the man.

The stranger's horse refreshed from its recent plunge in the ford danced about uneasily and pawed the dust. "*Ha,* Solange, you witch you, *ho,* girl!" he cried, reining her about in a semi-circle with a sure hand and bringing her back again as he called over one shoulder, "How do you know that?"

"Because, monsieur," replied his informant, "we have been working here all day and no one has passed southward except the coach of monsieur . . . pardon, I mean monseigneur, the guest of M. le Comte."

"Monseigneur!" said the stranger raising his eyebrows. "Why do you say that?"

16

"The crest, sir, the lilies were on the door!"

"Are you sure of it?"

"Am I likely to forget it? Dieu! am I not covered from head to foot by the filth which that devil, his cat of a postilion, threw at me. Look!" and the bailiff turned to exhibit the state of his back.

He was immediately struck by another missile, but this time of a more welcome kind. As he stooped to pick up the coin, he saw the limbs of the mare suddenly gathered under her as she felt the spur. By the time he had picked up the money and bitten it, both horse and rider were fifty yards away.

"Monsieur is in a hurry," he muttered, as he pocketed the piece and prepared to go home.

It was easy enough to follow the coach. In the newly smoothed highway the broad wheel tracks of the great vehicle were as plainly to be seen as if it had just been driven over a field of virgin snow. Yet the coach itself was nowhere visible. Behind the top of a little rise above the village the stranger dismounted and made sure of this before urging his mount onto the level open ground below. He was about to gallop on when a low cloud of dust at the top of a hill across the valley caught his eye.

The coach was just emerging from a patch of woodland and going over the skyline. From where he stood he could even see someone lean from the window to speak to the postilion while the latter turned in his saddle to reply. Then the whole equipage disappeared over the ridge.

Clapping spurs to his horse the stranger galloped down the road, leaped over a low hedge, and taking an open short cut across some meadows, found himself in a trice back on the road again. The village, which he had thus avoided, lay between the highways at the "V" of the cross-roads, and he was now passing rapidly uphill with a wood on one hand and vineyards on the other. Just short of the hillcrest he again dismounted suddenly and threw the reins over the mare's neck. She stood patiently, precisely where she had been left. Muffling his cloak well about him, he strode rapidly forward a few yards, stooping low. He then left the road, and taking shelter behind a convenient shrub, looked down into the valley beyond.

Before him lay a low valley, a wide, cultivated landscape stretching away in the softly brilliant afterglow of a French sunset. In the foreground was the park of Besance. A statue gleamed here and there amid the wide-armed trees like an ivory high light. The road wound through the groves in a vague "S"-shaped curve up to the château itself, an old building with candle snuffer towers. But there was a new wing in front with high, arched renaissance windows and a row of conical trees in tubs. It was one of those minor Versailles which

during the last two reigns had sprung up all over Europe.   As he
watched, a fountain began to play on the terrace and the downstairs
windows gleamed with a saffron light as someone flitted from room to
room lighting chandeliers.   The coach now emerged ʻfrom between a
wall of hedges, made the half-circle before the entrance, and drew up
before the door.   In the lens-like air, as the footmen leaped to let down
the steps, he could even see their brass buttons.   After some little
delay the coach moved out and trotted around to the rear.

A scene of considerable bustle was now revealed on the steps of the
château.   Four lackeys bearing a man with a white object that stuck
out straight before him were swaying up the stairs, marshalled by a
bustling major-domo.   A woman stood waiting for them at the top
while various bags and valises in charge of other servants disappeared
through the door.   Even at that distance he could still make out the
peculiar heliotrope shade of her skirt, and that she was carrying something in her hand.   "By God!" said he in English, and with an emotion
so violent that it found vent in immediate action.   With a determined
and almost desperate gesture he plucked a handful of leaves off the
bush which concealed him, and scattered them angrily.

The four men bearing their human burden now began to shuffle on
the last ascent to the door.   Evidently what they had in hand was no
light matter.   At the very top someone stumbled.   The whole group
began to sway perilously.   Then, as the invalid's cane began to play
over their heads and along their backs viciously, they fairly precipitated themselves into the gaping mouth of the door.   Only the woman
now remained, apparently looking out over the landscape where the
shadows were beginning to gather.   In the excitement attending the
entrance of the baggage and the gentleman it seemed as if she stood
there forgotten.

The watcher behind the bush had never hoped for such a stroke of
good fortune.   She might have been looking directly at him.   With a
deft bound he gained a large rock that stood squarely upon the crest
behind which he had been hiding.   He held his cloak out wide, and
tossed it.   Then he began to caper and wave his hat.

For a moment the little figure on the steps stood as if transfixed.
Then she too threw out her arms wildly and began to wave whatever
it was she was holding in her hands.   For a few seconds these mutual
signals continued.   Then the woman turned suddenly and hurried into
the house.   To the man standing on the rock it seemed as though she
had taken the daylight with her.

He instantly recovered himself, however, and hurried downhill to
his horse.   A glow far more lasting than his exercise on the rock could
have produced suffused him.   He felt bursting with good nature and
kindliness.   Plucking some small bunches of grass he rubbed down the

mare, and fondled her soft nose. The grass was next applied to a pair
of long, very fine military boots. A finely worked handkerchief flicked
the dust from a cocked hat whence, to judge by the shading, a braid-
edging and cockade had recently been removed. The stranger as if
from mere military habit then looked at the priming of his pistols,
tightened the girth, and patting his horse affectionately but heartily on
the flank, sprang into the saddle and trotted off at a brisk pace toward
the village.

In the great hall of the Château de Besance Don Luis sat under a
chandelier, propped up in a huge chair nursing his leg. The pain of
having been let down upon it did not subside for some time. Immediately upon being brought in he had done full justice to the occasion,
and his shattered malacca cane that lay beside him on the parqueterie
was a mute witness that the man who stumbled would have good reason to recollect his misfortune. No one, indeed, had escaped wholly.
Even Maria upon suddenly hastening in to help him had been ordered
to let his bandages alone. He told her to go upstairs and dress for
dinner, in a way which made even the servants wince. Not that the
marquis had been impolite. It was merely his tone. There was a
crushing viciousness in it which made his young wife's solicitude wilt
like a flower caught in the cloven hoof of a bull. In her agitation she
had all but fled the room, leaving the little object which she had been
carrying like a favourite doll lying forgotten upon a near-by table.

The major-domo of M. de Besance was wondering how he could fill
the place of the caned lackey whose arm would be useless for a week.
Well, he would have to wait upon the table himself. Monsieur was
undoubtedly a hard case, and perhaps it would be better to take no
chances. M. de Besance had sent strict orders for the careful entertainment of these guests. The accident was terrible! He must make
amends for it. He glanced at the face of the sufferer. A restorative
perhaps, something unusual. He bowed and retired, to return presently with a small, squat, greenish-black bottle.

The marquis' expression changed. He watched the cork-drawing
with the eye of an expert and could find nothing at which to cavil.
The man's precise mixture of art and ritual was impeccable. A divine
odour as of a basket of fresh, ripe peaches left in the sun filled the
room. With good care and a steady hand the butler decanted the
upper inch of the liquid into a glass that had been carefully wiped, and
handed it to Don Luis. The latter inhaled the bouquet and a look of
understanding passed between the two men. It was an occasion.

"Of the year of Malplaquet, Your Excellency," said the man bowing.

The marquis drank slowly. Old toper as he was he was scarcely
prepared for the surcharged flavour. It would have been cloying had
it not been accompanied by a fiery glow that might have made a sala-

mander start. The marquis just succeeded in not choking, and finished
the glass. His eyes shone. He was surprised that such a beverage
existed. It was worth having come from Paris just to sniff the
bouquet. A genial glow miraculously combined with a delightful
languor swam through his veins. His leg ceased to stab. When the
mist of pain and the dullness of fatigue cleared from his eyes as though
someone had washed a dusty window, he now saw that he was seated
in an apartment furnished with an exquisite but somewhat outmoded
taste.

"Monsieur need not move," said the butler. He lit a fire of resinous
wood which instantly began to crackle and throw lambent shadows
about the brass andirons and white marble mantelpiece where two
satyrs grinned at each other through a tracery of leaves and grapes.

It was not the first nobleman the old servant had treated for the
gout with brandy. The great thing to do was to keep them still. "Hot
water and a valet will be here instantly, Your Excellency. You shall
be made comfortable." He covered the bottom of the glass again.
"Supper will also be served here, and I shall have an apartment prepared for monsieur on the ground floor. The stairs are unnecessary.
I did not know of His Excellency's affliction or the chamber on this
floor should have been ready upon his arrival. Another accident for
monsieur is unthinkable! The new room will take some few moments.
After dinner it will be ready. Monsieur can retire then, if he desires,
without going upstairs."

The man waited without seeming to do so for a sign of approval.
Don Luis knew when he was being well served. A major-domo of the
old school was rare in this degenerate reign. He raised his hand in a
gesture of assent and let it fall back to the stem of his glass. The man
retired. His queue, the precisely horizontal bow, and every line of his
back were at once respectful and correct. As he turned to close the
door silently he saw the guest of his master sitting dreamfully with
his nose poised like a beak just over the rim of the glass. In his eyes
there was an expression of great content.

Don Luis finished the rest of the peach brandy and sat gazing into
the fire. Below the waist he seemed to have vanished. One of those
rare moments of heightened consciousness and clear vision was upon
him. He felt himself to be all eyes. The combination of spirits and
fatigue had been precisely right. Without moving his head he permitted his glance to wander about the room. It passed with keen
relish from one stately bit to another and finally came to rest on the
object which his wife had left on the table. It was the little madonna
which she had carried from the coach to take to her room. In the
state that he was in, his hands reached for it somewhat mechanically.
For the first time he began to examine it closely, dreamfully.

It was very old, evidently the work of several distinct and widely separated historical epochs. He turned the little shrine in which the figure stood to and fro. The shrine itself was certainly ancient Byzantine work. No Gothic artist could have conceived those wide, flat arches at the top. What a vast dome had been conveyed in-little by that curious, buttressed hood over the Virgin's head! And that sky, and those stars! Don Luis grunted and took out a small pocket glass. The secret of that heavenly blue must have been lost.

The figure, though small, was posed with immense dignity against a background of night. With some fusing of sepia, cobalt, and ebony the artist had contrived to convey that living blue of heaven on a summer evening which opens out through vast antres of atmosphere to the milky shimmer of stars beyond. Spread out and over this, like the far and near points in a crushed net, was a galaxy of golden stars. These, as he moved them to a better perspective, scintillated with the true zodiacal fire. In the top of the dome he was delighted to recognize the arrangement of the constellation Virgo, and to note, as he brought them closer again, a light dash of silver in the rays of what would otherwise have been too yellow a fire. The consummate brushwork of some painter upon ceramics had wrought that. In some mysterious way the whole background had been given a universal lustre which by reverberated reflections all but cancelled out the shadow of the figure that stood before it. "It was a cunning device," thought Don Luis. He looked more closely. "By heaven, it was glaze!"

From this sea of stars the face of the Virgin swam up to him somehow vaguely familiar. It was as if he had seen it in life. Or, was it a kind of universal human memory?—something learned so far back in childhood, perhaps from the face of his mother, or before, that it had been consciously forgotten? The expression of the features was so deeply brooding, and yet so universal, that it had produced in him that distinct and unplaceable sensation of having often seen them somewhere else. Those clear brows, those wide-open eyes, the slightly distended nostrils and the archaic smile; there was a hint of something sphinx-like, yes, distinctly Egyptian about it. And yet the poise of the head was Greek. He was at a loss at first to place it. Now he looked more closely at the stiff, jewelled robe.

It was made of small pieces of coloured stones with the glint of a jewel-chip here and there. It was set with seed pearls about the hems, and ennobled with a gilt pattern of some papyrus-like plant. Florentine mosaic work before the grand dukes, early Medici! He could also see it was attached to the statue by minute, extended silver wires; a new coat given to her by some pious owner long ago. It rose out and away from her body, to fall lower down into a stiff, jewelled skirt such as medieval royalties once wore. He could even see behind the robe, for it stood out from her like a herald's tabard. Beneath the bodice her breasts sloped down in pointed ovals that suggested sleep, and dreaming there, in utter peace, held in the crook of her arm was the infant. He thought of Dionysius on the arm of Apollo at first. And yet, as he peered again, almost fearfully now, since the thing had become so real, there was something too intimate and tender about this child in its mother's arms to be pagan. No, it was undoubtedly the Christ-child on Mary's breast. It must have been modelled in Alexandria an age ago, the statue itself. It would have taken a Christian born a pagan to have done it, an Egyptian Greek, some artist who could combine various old gods and humanity into something new; something old but something new.

It had always been a theory of the marquis that it is in the miniature masterpieces, those which can be put into a glass cabinet, that the arts of civilization culminate. First come your gigantic architecture and your monoliths; then something more human, more livable, realism, perhaps, gradually becoming beautifully conventional; then medallions, engravings, miniatures, cameos, and statuettes. And here was a nice illustration of the thing, he liked to think. He stroked his beard.

In Byzantium this single shrine would have been part of a triptych. He could still see that the right side of it had once fitted on to something else. He put it back on the table and slipped the glass into his pocket. The gilded sun-burst, that almost imperial sun-crown upon the head of the Virgin; that had Constantinople written all over it. Some devout Arian had once owned it. He leaned back and let his imagination supply the two missing panels:—God the Father most elevated in the middle, on one side of Him the dove descending out of the clouds from the Father's bosom, on the other the little shrine he held in his hands. The triptych was perfect again. How easily he had restored it! But was it necessary?

This shrine he actually held—why, it alone represented the entire Trinity and humanity, too! The cosmos for that matter; there were the stars. Had not the Holy Ghost descended upon the woman? The Son of God and man was in her arms. And the Father?—why *He* was there by necessary implication, invisible as always, but the creator of all. How huge, how universal was this little symbol he could hold in one hand. For a moment he was humble before it. He came as near to worship as he could. Then his natural pride reasserted itself. His logical and theological mind laughed in his skull to think that out of that Arian triptych only this remained. How literal and how elaborate was heresy! The other panels had been unnecessary. Only the Catholic symbol was required and everything essential was there. Ah, a nice point! Something even the Jansenists could scarcely refute. A fit subject for a monograph.

And yet artistically *was* the statue perfect? Weren't those fluted mother-of-pearl inlays about her feet a little tawdry; about 1700, no doubt. But no, narrow your eyes and you could see the eternal stars mirrored in them. She was standing before the universe at the pearly gates. Seventeen centuries had contrived to make something perfect. Don Luis conferred upon them the greatest compliment of his own. Drawing a small gold box from his waistcoat he sprung back the lid, tapped his fingers lightly in a kind of salutation, and took a large pinch of snuff.

The resulting sneeze so startled a valet who had just entered the room that the marquis laughed. It would never do to have all these servants afraid of him. Fear could make an antelope awkward. The marquis bade the man good evening and began to ask questions about the château. Presently the valet was at his ease and the work of revamping Don Luis proceeded comfortably enough. A small silver basin filled with hot water served to refresh him as, with the wig and cravat removed, a warm sponge was passed over his shaven head and neck. He soaked his hands in the water. A fresh, lace jabot was then wound about his neck and the frill carefully made to stand out from his shirt. A larger and more comfortable bag wig was taken out of its box and slipped onto his head. It was scarcely necessary to use the brush at all, and the bow on the queue was kept clean of powder. To Don Luis that was the test. No whisking off afterward! He preferred to beat servants rather than be beaten by them, if it came to that. A small dash of verbena on his handkerchief, and with the cushions carefully, even solicitously rearranged on the leg stand by the butler himself, the marquis felt at home, ready for dinner in fact.

The man threw a few more logs on the fire, drew up a table before Don Luis, carefully avoiding his bandaged limb, and began to lay covers for two. The napery was ivory-smooth, the candles were carefully shaded, and the plate was not only good but positively inviting. "If the chef can do the appointments justice," thought Don Luis, "I am prepared to be convinced that M. de Besance was not merely trying to cure his homesickness by a vicarious visit in my person to his ancestral halls." He preferred to remain cynical, however. Nevertheless the variety and nice arrangement of the wine glasses tended to confirm the claims of his absent host. The butler now lit a small lamp under a brazier and announced that dinner was ready when madame should be announced. "Tell her," said the marquis.

The logs crackled in the grate and in some distant part of the house a clock began to chime. The room was a large one. The table was set under the last chandelier next to the fireplace. The candlelight from the sconces and chandeliers reflected themselves and their crystals with long splashes of yellow light on the polished floor. As Maria entered the apartment from the opposite door, it seemed to her that the little table was at an immense distance. The silver and glass twinkled upon it like stars caught in a fleecy cloud, and over the edge of it, looking like the moon itself, shone the scarlet face of her husband. To a light splashing of silk she seemed to float to him over the lake of the floor in her wide panniered skirts, moving her feet invisibly like those of a swan. "Madame la Marquise." The man with the injured arm should have been at the door to announce. With some well-concealed embarrassment the butler also hastened forward to seat her.

"Bravo, my dear," said her husband, "such a toilette in so short a time is a marvel! You know the lamentable reason which keeps me from rising to the occasion." To her relief she saw him smile. She began to talk rather hastily.

"I have a maid, a woman from Fontanovo, that M. de Besance sent here some days ago. You cannot imagine how pleasant it is to hear Tuscan again. It is almost as welcome as English." She checked herself and coloured deeply. The marquis overlooked the reference to home.

"While we were in Paris I thought it best to use nothing but French, but we can now speak Italian," said he, changing into that tongue. "It is certainly charming of M. de Besance to have sent an Italian maid, probably one of his household he picked up while in Florence recently."

"She is returning to Italy and hopes to go back with us."

"Ah, that explains it then. But not altogether. Besance has been the best of fellows. Paris would have been quite a different place without him. That little journey of congratulation to the Duchess of Parma—I was able to help him with that, and we were compatible. It is not often one makes such a friend after forty. Do you suppose he would really have turned his château over to us on a bet at cards? No, he is genuinely anxious to see me cured, and his enthusiasm about the waters at Royat was really catching. I hear of many cures there, too. By the way," said he turning to the man, "Henri? Jacques?"

"Pierre, Your Excellency."

"Pierre, then. How far is it to the baths?"

"About an hour's drive, monsieur, by way of Clermont. And there is, if monsieur desires to stay overnight, an excellent inn."

The prospect seemed to cheer Don Luis greatly. Since some time before his marriage his leg had kept him little better than an invalid, and a round of high living at Paris and Versailles was not calculated to help the gout. The very thought of getting rid of his discomfort and being active again made him feel like rising from his chair then and there. Indeed, for the first time in his life the state of his health had for a year past caused him to give it some thought.

Newly married to the daughter of a Scotch merchant of Leghorn who had some vague Jacobean claim to nobility, the marquis had from the first been swept off his feet by the strange beauty of the young girl who now sat across the table from him. He had first seen her, accidentally, while settling a matter of business at her father's establishment. As he happened to be the owner of the buildings in which her father's concern did business, it was not difficult for him to find the way of gaining a swift consent to his suit. That is not to say that the marquis' method of approach was crass; on the contrary, it was adroit.

The good merchant was a widower up in years and anxious to see his only child well and securely bestowed. To that end a very considerable dowry was her portion. In fact, the old man was prepared to embarrass himself, and did so. Although Don Luis was a quarter of a century older than his bride, still in the eyes of the world, and to her father, the match had seemed a fortunate one. The marquis condescended, no doubt, but the dowry was worth stooping for, and to do him justice, in his own way Don Luis loved the girl. He held wide fiefs from both the Grand Duke of Tuscany and the Crown of Spain, and was much employed in delicate diplomatic affairs from time to time. To Maria's father in particular the marquis had seemed like a god from the machine come to snatch his daughter back to the high Olympus of court life to which in some sort she belonged. From that realm an invincible attachment to the unfortunate house of Stuart on the part of her ancestors and her father's consequent necessitous lapse into trade had effectually banished her.

The girl herself had been too young and inexperienced to realize the full implications of what her father pressed upon her in the most favourable light. Even her maid, a girl about her own age, and her one human confidante, had abetted the scheme as a wise young woman should. There had been no one else to turn to but the little madonna. From her she received comfort but no advice. The girl's heart had continued to shiver in a premonitory way at the sight of her prospective husband. But obedience and love for her father, who she knew parted with her only because he thought he was setting her feet upon a fortunate path, sealed her lips. Yet dutiful as she was, even after her marriage there was one thing for which she could not bring herself to pray. It was for the restoration of her husband's health. The thought of physical contact, the mere touch of his hand, indeed, turned her to stone.

With Don Luis it was far, far otherwise. He had in one sense been starved for some time, and his touch was therefore too hungry to note anything but its own temperature. Yet he had deliberately starved himself. For if he was in love with his wife, he was also in love with himself, and that self was possessed of an enormous sense

of the ludicrous. In the rôle of husband and lover he saw himself,
not young and handsome—for he was too wise and too candid to suppose the opposite of what his own mirror disclosed—but forceful;
not to be denied; a master of life upon important occasions and possessed of some dignity withal. A man of the world, he had no illusion
about bed-time intimacies. There was only one way to maintain a
manly dignity there. Hence he did not intend to approach his marriage bed for the first time on crutches, with a bandaged foot and
debilitated—lights or no lights. Besides it *might* be painful. The
thought of it made him grin and wince at the same time. He was
anxious for an heir, too. But so far he had deferred to circumstances.

The meal continued. The potage paysan might have been a bit flat
but the rye bread in it had been toasted and imparted that nut-like
flavour in which the marquis delighted. A dish of trout in butter, a
mushroom patty, an endive salad with chives together with some excellent wines from the count's cellar composed a light meal for which
Pierre apologized profusely. A fresh cheese cool from the spring
house, and a firm, white loaf caught in a silver clamp provided with a
small steel saw in the shape of a dragon's head with teeth amused
Maria.

By the time the marquis had sampled his host's liqueurs he was prepared to remain all summer. No doubt the cure *would* take that long.
He was tired after Paris anyway. He rattled on about his recovery.
"Have the coach ready at nine o'clock tomorrow. Tell that man of
mine," said he to Pierre, "and don't allow him anything but table wine
tonight. I shall go to the springs first thing in the morning. My
dear, I shall soon be well! I feel sure of it. A man you have not
yet met in fact!" He looked across the shaded candles at his wife
eagerly.

Her eyes opened wide and the colour left her cheeks. She felt like
one trying to thrust off a nightmare. Then the vision of the figure
waving to her from the rocks came to comfort her. Watching her
closely, her husband leaned back and laughed. Certain visions also
flashed across his mind. He had never seen her look so well. It
would all be well enough shortly. The child might come in the spring,
after they were in Florence. That would fill her life for her, and
bind her to him. He need not worry about cavaliers after that. Not
that the young Irishman at Versailles would ordinarily have caused
him a second thought. A beautiful, young wife would have admirers,
of course. But under the circumstances! No, it had been just as
well to leave a little sooner. He was a dashing fellow and the uniform of the guard was a handsome one. It was better not to put too
much strain on a young girl's sense of duty. He looked at her again.
Her eyes had wandered past him and her lips were moving. Follow-

ing her glance he saw that her gaze was fixed on the madonna still standing on a near-by table. She looked up again a bit startled.

"You forgot her when you went upstairs, you know. I was examining her while you were dressing. She is quite a precious work of art. Where did you get her, by the way? Let me see her again."

She rose obediently and brought the figure in its little shrine to him. He put down his glass and took the relic in his hands.

"Where did you say you got her?"

"From my maid at home. It had been in her family for a long time. She was a Scotch girl."

"Scotch!" said he, "this at least did not come from Scotland."

"Her father was a Greek or of a Greek strain at least, a Greco-Florentine. His name was Paleologus."

"What a strange combination," he smiled. "I remember her now, I think. She wanted to come along with you."

"Yes, Faith Paleologus," she turned the syllables over in her mouth as if they were somehow unpleasantly reminiscent.

"Did you ever notice this, Maria?" he asked, turning the statue sideways. Taking a knife he pointed behind the mosaic work.

It had never occurred to her to look under the Virgin's robe. She had always thought of it as part of her. Following the glittering point of the knife she now saw the little silver wires holding the stiff dress out from the statue like a herald's tabard before it. Underneath was the figure of a naked woman with a child at her breast! Small jewelled lights glinting through the tiny bits of glass and chips of gems in her robe played upon the shadows and curves of her exquisite body. But the knife was pointing coldly at a fracture. At some remote time the statue had evidently been broken off below the knees and mended again cunningly. To the mind of the young girl, who was scarcely more than an idolater, the whole thing came as a shock. With a gasp she reached down, took the madonna from her husband's hands, and as if the knife threatened it, caught it to her breast as though it were alive.

"Be careful," he said. But she crushed it the harder. A look of extreme happiness glimmered on her face. Then suddenly becoming aware of him again she stiffened.

"You are tired," said he, "take a good rest. I shall be leaving early tomorrow for the springs. You will have the whole day at the château to yourself. Why not arrange for a drive? That new maid can go with you." Taking her free hand he kissed it and looked up at her. The hand fell back into place. "Good night, Maria."

She recollected herself and swept him a curtsy. The shrine remained cuddled in her arms like a doll. Like a doll she carried it from the room and turning just at the door looked at him. With a little movement almost fierce in its intensity she clasped her precious thing even closer and disappeared up the stairs. "What a child she is," thought he, "what a child!" He looked around. The bell-pull on the wall was too far to reach. He struck a goblet with a knife. Pierre appeared.

"Bed," said the marquis, "and mind how you get me there!"

The man disappeared. He returned a few moments later with two sturdy assistants carrying long poles. These were lashed securely under Don Luis' chair. Placing themselves between the ends of the staffs before and behind, the men lifted the burden easily and in this improvised sedan he was carried out of the room. Pierre, holding a lighted candelabrum above his head, led the way.

The marquis smiled grimly. He saw himself proceeding down the marble hall like a Roman consul. No, it was like a bridegroom carried to his chamber with the torch before him. The fancy tickled him. There was something in the omen he liked. He seated himself upon his bed with some difficulty and began with the tenderest solicitude to unwrap the bandages from his foot. The valet with equal care aided him to remove his clothes, then the wig.

Presently a shaggy, powerful man with a closely shaved head, a thick chest, one swollen foot and large stubby hands was seen sitting on the edge of the bed. The candlelight glittered on his scalp. He slipped a long flannel sack over his head. It fell in folds about his waist. He tied on a night-cap and had a small calf-bound volume brought him as he settled himself, not without grievances, in the huge bed. The valet arranged the light. "At what hour, monsieur?" "Eight," replied the marquis in a far-away voice. The man bowed and retired. The marquis read on:

Now, my masters, you have heard a beginning of the horrific history of Pantagruel. You shall have the rest, and then you shall see how Panurge was married, and made a cuckold within a month of his wedding. How Pantagruel found out the philosopher's stone, the manner how he found it, and the way to use it. How he passed over the Caspian mountains, and how he sailed through the Atlantick sea, defeated the cannibals, and conquered the isle of Perles. How he fought against the devil, ransacked the great black chamber and threw Proserpine in the fire. How he visited the regions of the moon, and a thousand other little merriments. All veritable. These are brave things truly. Good night gentlemen. . . .

Upstairs the light from his wife's bedroom turned her window that looked toward the village into a bright yellow square.

CHAPTER THREE

AT THE "GOLDEN SHEAF"

FROM the rock on the hill where the stranger had exchanged signals with Maria to the village below it was nearly a mile. The mare at that time of the evening expected oats not far ahead and needed no urging. Indeed, as he rode into the little town of Romagnat her rider was forced to pull her up at the cross-roads with a firm rein. She stamped impatiently and pretended to shy at the grey figure of an old woman drawing water in the twilight. He heard the bucket splash in the well. It was supper time and the streets appeared deserted. Except for a few lights here and there and an occasional murmur of voices or cry of a child he might have been alone. The bucket now reappeared on the well and the woman turned toward him.

"Can you tell me, mother," said he, "where the inn is?"

"It is there, monsieur," she replied, pointing toward a dim light at the end of the street leading back in the general direction of the chateau, "at the lantern, where the door is opening now." Some distance up the hill a glow of firelight flooded out and vanished. "But the great hostel is at Clermont about a league from here," continued the old woman hoping for a reward.

"Thank you, I am only wanting supper." He automatically fumbled in his pocket, but then thought better of it. The less cause for being remembered the better. His disappointed informant disappeared, and he turned toward the light.

It was a dim and smoky one hung under what at first appeared to be a suspended mass of rubbish, but as he drew closer this resolved itself into a sheaf of wheat tied over a sign. *La Gerbe d'Or* could still be faintly traced in faded characters as the lantern swung gently to and fro. He stood for a moment studying the building and its surroundings carefully like an old campaigner, then he turned through a low brick archway and rode into the courtyard of the inn. The delighted whinny of the mare brought out an ostler.

"Send me your master, my lad, and be quick about it!"

The man in the door, munching a large sponge-like fragment of black bread, took a look at the long, lithe figure on the horse and disappeared. A few moments later he came back with a lantern and a round, shiny-faced little man in a white apron.

"I want a room for the night and supper," said the horseman.

"Certainly, if monsieur will descend, the request is not *very* unusual."

The face of the clown with the lantern began to prepare itself for a laugh at the stranger's expense.

"Come here, my host," said the man on the horse who did not show any intention as yet of descending. Somewhat abashed the fat man came and stood by the saddle. The horseman now leaned over and began to talk in low impressive tones. He was an adept at assuming that confidential air which by taking one into a secret both flatters and impresses. The boor with the lantern had not been included and to the innkeeper he represented the gaping world.

"Look, my friend," said the gentleman dismounting and bringing an ardent and commanding countenance close to that of the round-faced man, "I am here on the king's business, and I do not want the world to hear of it. Do you understand?" A small, yellow coin with the countenance of the king upon it passed hostward between them. A convulsive grasp of the fingers and a look of understanding were simultaneous. "Yes, monsieur," whispered the fat man like a conspirator.

"Well then," said the gentleman, "can you give me a room and serve my supper in it quietly without having half the village in to gape at me? And how about your wife's tongue?"

"I will serve you supper myself, monsieur, and my poor wife's tongue has been silent these two years." The fat man choked. The stranger laid his hand upon his host's shoulder. "She is in heaven, my friend," said he, "never doubt!"

"Ah, monsieur, you are very kind, but I am sure of it. Come this way and you shall have what you want. It shall be the private chamber upstairs. Here, François, give me your lantern and get the other from the settle." Unlocking a narrow door that opened into the court the innkeeper led the way.

They ascended a circular stone stairway and came out into a small, blunt hall. The host rattled his keys again and presently threw open a door, standing aside for his guest to enter. The room ran clear across the house. On one side was a window looking out upon the court and on the other a long, leaded casement through which penetrated a faint glow from the street. The fat man advanced and opening the lantern took out the candle and kindled the fire. A bright blaze sprang up from a pile of dry faggots revealing a low apartment with ceiling beams, a high four-poster bed in the corner, a table, two chests, and several chairs. On the rough mortar wall was a black crucifix immediately over the bed, and on the chimney a faded print of what had once been meant for a likeness of "Louis the Well-Beloved"

—some fifty years before. The host looked at his guest inquiringly.

"Excellent," said the latter.

"It was our own room before my wife died," continued the fat man lighting the sconces, "I sleep downstairs now to keep an eye on the servants. I hope monsieur will find himself comfortable. Supper will be served directly."

"The sooner the better," replied his guest. "Have that ostler bring up my saddle and bags, and see that my horse gets a full measure. No drenched chaff, mind you. A good rub-down, too. But send the man up to me."

The fat man bustled out puffing with importance. It was some time since he had had a guest who did not haggle over terms. Presently the ostler was heard ascending the stairs. His ungainly form filled the door of the room as he deposited the saddle and its heavy bags on the floor with a bump.

"Look out for the pistols, François," said the gentleman.

The man stared blankly.

"In the holsters, you know, you had better unstrap them."

The man did so, bringing them gingerly to the table and laying them down carefully. The weight of the weapons and the silver crown on the flaps filled him with awe for their possessor. The gentleman, very tall and straight, now stood before the fireplace and was holding aside his cloak to warm himself thus revealing a long rapier with a plain brass hilt. His eyes glittered with a hard steel-blue under a mass of brown curls that had escaped from the bow and queue in which he had in vain attempted to confine them. A long, straight nose with thin, quivering nostrils over a firm bow of a mouth and a stronger chin completed a countenance which with extraordinary mobility could flash from an expression of grim determination to one of extreme charm. He appeared to be about thirty years old.

"Take good care of the mare, 'Solange.' She answers to that. Fill her nose-bag full, she will not eat from a strange manger. Mind she doesn't nip you, but rub her down, and make a good deep bed."

"Yes, monsieur," said the man, "Maître Henri has already told me."

"Do it, then!" snapped out the gentleman. He snapped him a coin which fell onto the floor. The man groped for it and stood up to find himself even nearer to the stranger whose nostrils expanded. He fumbled for his cap which he had forgotten. He took it off.

"And, François."

"Yes, monsieur!"

"Do not come up here again, you bring the smell of the stable with you."

"No, monsieur," said the man letting his hands fall humbly with a ponderous despair as if he had been reminded of something fatal.

Suddenly a smile of vivid brightness irradiated the face of the stranger. His white teeth seemed like a flash of sunshine in the light of which the heart of the man before him became happily warm as he stood clutching his cap in one hand and the piece of silver in the other.

"François," said the gentleman continuing to smile, "would you like to earn a piece like that again tomorrow?"

"But yes, monsieur," gasped the ostler.

"Then remember this, do not say a word to anyone about my being here. Nothing, you understand?" The face suddenly became grim again, "It might be dangerous!"

"Nothing, monsieur, nothing," but now the ostler was somehow again looking at the face with a smile on it. His own expanded into a loutish grin with snagged teeth left here and there in ponderous gums. An idea slowly hatched itself. "Monsieur," said he bowing like a mountain in pain, "has never arrived. I cannot remember him —even in my prayers!"

"Precisely," said the gentleman. "Go now."

A peal of boyish laughter followed him down the stairs. "Whew!" said the gentleman, and threw open the window that looked into the street.

It was a clear starlit night. He could see for some little distance over a tract of open country beside the hill from which he had just ridden down. Far to the right the giant, sphinx-like curve of a demi-mountain shouldered itself into the constellations. In the valley shone the brilliant windows of the château. He drew a chair up and watched. She was taking supper there now. A look of longing came over his face. Then it suddenly turned white with fury. "With him!"

He sat for a while with an exceedingly grim expression in a reverie so absorbing that he temporarily lost all count of time. Gradually, as if he were dwelling on something more pleasant in the past or some bright hope of the future, a faint smile began to play about his lips. Even with this, however, the look of determination remained. Presently his host knocked and entered bearing a tray piled high with supper. The gentleman was hungry and peculiarly sensitive to odours, and the odour which now filled the room was highly satisfactory to both his nose and his appetite.

"It is the best I could do for monsieur at short notice," said the innkeeper.

He began to lay the table. A bowl of soup, a steaming ragout of rabbit and carrots, white rolls, and a bottle of wine discovered themselves.

"Excellent!" said the stranger, as he settled himself with evident satisfaction to the repast. "Indeed, I was prepared for something worse than this." He filled his glass and after a preliminary sip tossed it off without further doubt. Nevertheless, the innkeeper continued to stand before him clasping and unclasping his hands in the folds of his white apron in considerable perturbation.

"Excellent," repeated the gentleman, polishing off the soup and sampling the ragoût. The man, however, continued as before. "Well?" said the gentleman, raising his eyebrows interrogatively but with a slight tinge of annoyance. "Oh, I see," and he reached for his purse, stretching his long legs out under the table to do so.

"No, no!" said the innkeeper deprecatingly. "Monsieur mistakes me. I have no doubt of his ability to pay—when he departs. It is this. It is the law that I must report the arrival and the names of strangers who stop here together with a declaration of their business to the mayor-postmaster. They must, in fact, show their papers within twelve hours. Otherwise I shall be heavily fined." Here his hands locked themselves underneath the apron. "The times are troubled ones, you know, monsieur, the roads . . ."

"Do you take me for a brigand?" demanded the gentleman with the stern look which he was able to assume instantly. "Besides, I have not yet been here twelve hours."

"Forgive me, monsieur, but it is not so simple as that," said his host. "My brother is the mayor-postmaster. He is even now downstairs and knows that you have arrived. He has seen supper brought to your room."

The stranger paused for a moment over his ragout while the flame of the two candles on the table continued to mount steadily. There was no expression whatever on his face now. His legs continued stretched out under the table in a nonchalant manner. Suddenly he drew them up under him determinedly, and leaning forward with a quizzical grin as though he anticipated something amusing, remarked, "Show him up."

"Monsieur will not come down? My brother, the postmaster . . ."

"Postmaster be damned!" snapped the gentleman. "Who do you think *I* am?"

With a deprecatory gesture, the innkeeper disappeared. There was the sound of a short colloquy downstairs, a door opened, and two pairs of heavy feet stumbled up the stairs. The gentleman addressed himself unconcernedly to his ragout. The footfalls came down the hall and ceased. The gentleman helped himself to a particularly savoury morsel, swallowed it slowly, and looked up as if his thoughts were elsewhere.

Standing in the door, with the broad, white expanse of the innkeeper behind him, was an almost equally rotund personage with a wide, stupidly cunning face. A huge cocked hat with a moth-eaten

cockade was pressed down importantly upon his brow to which it
managed to impart by wrinkling the rolls of fat a portentous and
official frown. There was in the man's manner a combination of
obsequiousness and truculence either of which was ready to triumph
over the other as events might decide. To the gentleman at the table
there was no doubt as to which attitude was going to win the day,
however. His spurred boot shot out swiftly from beneath the cloth.
Catching a chair deftly, he kicked it precisely into the middle of the
room.

"Sit down," said he.

The man advanced somewhat gingerly and sat, only to find himself
looking directly into the stranger's face. Seeing the latter eyeing his
hat with surprise and disapproval, after an evident inward debate, he
removed it and laid it on his fat knees.

"Monsieur, the innkeeper's brother, I believe," said the stranger
looking at him with the ghost of a twinkle. "No one could doubt
that at least."

"And the mayor-postmaster," began the little man puffing out his
cheeks.

"How am I to be sure of *that?*" asked the stranger leaning back and
looking at the man grimly. "Have you your documents with you?"

The pompous look upon the face of the astonished official collapsed
from his cheeks as if they had been a child's balloon pricked by a pin.
He squinted anxiously from his ferret eyes and began to feel his
pockets dubiously. "Not *with* me," he admitted, still fumbling. Then
his hands sank back onto his hat again. The situation was unprece-
dented. Already he was almost convinced that he was falsely im-
personating himself.

"Extraordinary!" said the gentleman regarding him doubtfully.

"But, but, I *am* the mayor, the postmaster. All the village knows
it! Is it not true, Henri?" he demanded appealing desperately to his
brother.

"Indeed, monsieur, it is," replied the innkeeper. "The curé lives
but a few doors above and can verify it. Surely . . ."

"Well, well," replied the stranger, "I am inclined to believe you."
He raised a hand to deprecate the need of the curé.

"See," cried the mayor-postmaster with a flash of inspiration on his
dull face, "here is my cockade!" He shifted his hat suddenly and
turned that dingy mark of office toward his doubter. "Monsieur has
been looking at the wrong side! He did not see the cockade when I
entered."

"Ah, that *is* different," smiled the gentleman. "Can you blame me
—when I was looking at the *wrong* side?"

"Certainly not, monsieur," both voices replied together.

"In that case I shall be glad to show my own papers." He reached in his pocket and drew out a long folded sheet. "You see," continued he frowning, "I always carry my identification about me. And it would be well," he added, fixing the flustered man before him with a cold stare while rapping the knuckles of his extended hand with the edge of the document, "if you would do the same when you demand the credentials of a military gentleman."

The shot went home. With a flushed face and far from steady hand the fat man took the extended paper. He unfolded it nervously and began to read. He was almost afraid to find whom he had offended.

It was a special leave of absence issued by the Minister of War and dated from Versailles permitting M. Denis Moore, subject of His Most Christian Majesty, captain-interpreter attached to the first regiment of the royal horseguard, to travel upon private affairs in all the kingdom of France during the space of four months. Upon the expiration of leave he was to report back for duty at Versailles. The script was in the beautiful, round hand of a clerk of the war office, yet the eyes of the mayor moved over it slowly while his lips spelled out the words. At the bottom of the document, however, much to his relief, he came upon a block of good solid print. There, along with such other exalted personages as the intendants of provinces and the mayors of cities, he thought he found himself included amongst "all loyal subjects of the king" as bound to render aid, protection and assistance to the said Captain Denis Moore in all his lawful designs whatsoever. Nor as an officer of the royal household was the captain to be hindered, taxed, prevented, or delayed in his going to and fro on pain of the explicit displeasure of the king himself. "And of this ye shall take good heed."

"It is the Minister of War," said the captain, pointing to a signature whose many flourishes the poor man was in vain trying to decipher. Face to face with the signature of so great a man as the Minister of War the mayor-postmaster felt himself to be something less than dust. He also felt himself in the distinguished presence of an unusual man. Under the circumstances, it would be best to waive the usual small fee for examination. No, he would say nothing about it! He folded the paper carefully and handed it back. "Monsieur the captain will excuse the interruption I hope," he said, preparing to leave the room with evident relief.

"Without doubt," said the captain, "but sit down. I have something further to consult about with you. Come in," said he to the innkeeper, "and kindly close the door. Can we be overheard?"

"By no one!"

"You will both understand," continued the captain. "that what I am about to say to you is the king's business and goes no further than this room." He glanced significantly at both of them. While their voluble reassurances continued to flow, he again unfolded the paper.

"You will note," said he, pointing to the line upon which the phrase occurred, "that I am on 'private business.' " The mayor nodded sagely. "Now follow me"—his finger ran on down the page—"and that you are 'bound to render aid, assistance, and protection.' It is that, monsieur the mayor, which I am now about to ask of you. Draw your chairs up closer while I explain." It was not long before the three heads were so close together over the table that a fly could scarcely have crawled between them.

In a lower voice than he had been using, and with that confidential air of being about to impart a matter of capital import, the captain continued. "There arrived today at the Château de Besance a certain gentleman, the Marquis da Vincitata. He is on his way back to Genoa. He was sent last year on a special diplomatic mission by the Grand Duke of Tuscany to the court of Versailles. The matter was one of such extreme importance that you will understand I cannot possibly discuss it with you at all."

The innkeeper was already too flattered at having been made a confidant in affairs of state even to attempt to reply. His brother, however, managed to gasp out a deprecatory noise at the very idea of a complete revelation, waving his fat hand as if to brush away so ridiculous a thought. Fearful that the swelling pomposity of the mayor might become apoplectic, the captain paused for a moment before he went on.

"The marquis has certain letters in his possession." He now lowered his voice to a whisper. "I am following him. It is my mission to obtain them, and it is in this that I shall require the assistance of you both as loyal subjects, but especially of you, monsieur the mayor."

"Certainly, in any way, but . . ."

"It will be quite simple. I have already taken the first steps to ingratiate myself with the marquis' wife. She is young and pretty, and he is old." A look of extreme knowingness and worldly wisdom appeared on the faces of both worthies as they gazed with open-mouthed admiration at the captain. Scarcely able to stifle his laughter he condescended to enlighten them further. "From her I have already learned that the marquis intends to linger here for some time while taking the waters at Royat. It is my hope before the gentleman is cured to persuade the lady . . ."

"To steal the papers," mumbled the mayor.

"Exactly," said the captain, actually patting him on the arm. "I see you are able to think quickly." The combined smiles of the delighted parties now seemed to illuminate the room.

"But to do that I must have a quiet place where I can stay, reasonably close to the château, and one—mind you—where the news of my being there will not leak out. One idle word carried to the ear of the marquis and the game is up. Do you understand? One word! —and can you help me?"

Confronted by his first problem in statecraft, the mayor sat thinking ponderously. One could almost hear the wheels turn. The innkeeper finally came to his assistance by whispering something in his ear.

"Why, the very thing, why didn't I think of it?" cried his brother. "The farm of Jacques Honneton! He is my brother-in-law, a widower, and his place is quite close to the château."

"Not too close?" inquired the captain.

"No, no, monsieur, about a mile or so. And you can be quite comfortable there."

"I shall, of course, be glad to pay liberally," interrupted the captain, "in a case of this kind the government . . . You can see," said he turning to the innkeeper, "that under the circumstances I cannot remain *here*."

"It will all be in the family anyway," said the innkeeper.

"And," said the captain taking the words out of his host's mouth and bringing his fist down on the table, "it must stay there! Men have been broken on the wheel for a slip of the tongue in a case like this. I remember . . ."

"Never fear, my captain," cried the mayor already white to the gills. "I will take it upon myself . . ."

"Then we understand each other thoroughly I take it, and I can leave the arrangements at the farm with you." The captain inclined his head slightly, indicating that the interview was at an end. With the air of two conspirators upon whom the burden of portentous things rested heavily, the innkeeper and his brother the mayor-postmaster left the room. The latch clicked. Snatching the napkin up hastily the captain crammed it in his mouth. For some seconds what might have been mistaken for a choking noise escaped through the folds.

Rising after a few minutes, he blew out the supper candles, noticing with an amused smile that in the midst of the conspiracy the innkeeper had forgotten to remove the tray. "How dramatic even the simplest person can become," thought he. "The man has been completely transported by his new rôle." The captain wondered whether the dramatic sense was not on the whole a weakness in human nature. It depended on who produced the play, he supposed. "Now in the army your great generals . . ." He strolled over to the window again.

The lights in the lower story of the château were being extinguished.

Finally only one remained.   Suddenly a single upstairs window shone
out brilliantly.   The captain grinned.   "Separate rooms, eh!   No
stairs for a one-legged man.   Vive the gout!"   His theory about the
two lighted windows at opposite ends of the château pleased him immensely.   "So the marquis imagined I was calmly going to be left
behind at Versailles mounting guard.   It will be much easier here with
him away at the springs most of the day."   He looked at the lights
in the upper window again.   A strong tremor shook him.   "Maria,"
he cried between his teeth, "Maria!"   If he could see her tonight!
No, that would be mere folly.   It might spoil all.   If he could only
send her a message, though.   God!   She was going to bed alone down
there less than a mile away!

He leaned half-way out of the window and for some moments
continued to fill his lungs with the cool spring air that was at once
refreshing and provocative.   A sensuous odour of vineyards in bloom
came to his nostrils as a love song might have drifted to his ears.
When he drew himself back into the room again the innkeeper was
removing the remains of supper.

"Pardon, monsieur," said he, "I knocked, you did not answer, and
I thought you had gone downstairs."

A sudden idea flashed across the captain's mind.   This man must
know some people at the château.   "Could you get a message to the
lady at the château, my friend?" he blurted out, "tonight!"

"Not tonight, mon capitaine, it is much too late, but early tomorrow
morning without doubt.   The cook's sister . . ."

"I do not care how, that is for you to settle.   Only of this be sure.
Employ no fools.   I shall pay your messenger well and the message
must be delivered to the marquise, not to her husband.   To the marquise herself, quietly, mind you, and without fail.   I shall hold you
responsible for this."   He slipped a gold piece on the tray.   "You can
arrange the messenger's wages yourself, you know."

"It shall be done as you say, monsieur," said the innkeeper with
eyes shining.   "No one will ever be the wiser.   We have our own
ways of getting news to and fro about the château even when M. le
Comte is home."

"Doubtless you have," replied the captain, looking keenly at the
wine bottle.

"From the château vineyards, monsieur, but not from the count's
cellars.   Ma foi . . ."

"I said nothing," interrupted his guest.   "But here is the message."   He took a scrap of paper from his dispatch box and sat down.
For a moment his crayon hung poised above it.   On the whole it
would be better to write nothing.   He began to sketch rapidly.

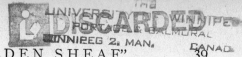

Presently he handed the folded paper to the landlord. "Tomorrow before breakfast, to the lady, and to no one else!"

"Without fail, monsieur." The man took up the tray and went downstairs wishing his guest a hearty good night. Arrived in the kitchen he began to set the dishes aside to be washed next morning. Finally nothing remained on the tray but the folded note and the gold piece. He took them up and listened. Above his head the beams creaked reassuringly. Nevertheless, it was with some hesitation even when in his own room that he finally opened the note and spread out the paper before a dim rush light.

Before him lay no writing but a vivid little street scene sketched with an economy of line which it is safe to say was entirely wasted upon the pair of small eyes now examining it. Their owner, however, had no difficulty in recognizing instantly the peculiar gabled front of his own inn. And if there had been any doubt of it, the sheaf of wheat, the sign, and the lantern swinging beneath, left nothing vague as to the place or the artist's intention. There was the brick arch, too. But with the budding critical spirit of a true connoisseur, Maître Henri noted with considerable satisfaction that the arrangement of the chimney pots was decidedly wrong. If this detail had not escaped him, it was with both surprise and indignation that he next surveyed the strange equipage which appeared to be passing before his door. It was a coach to which, with an apt stroke or two, the artist had somehow managed to give the outlines of a classical chariot. Its prancing steeds were driven by a cat. Vulcan, or some other infernal lame god with a crutch, lolled back in it. Behind him in the guise of a footman stood Mercury with a small shameless Cupid on his shoulders. The latter was shooting into the upstairs window of the inn. The arrow pointed straight toward it with a message attached.

Certainly no such vehicle had ever troubled the streets of Romagnat. Of that Maître Henri was sure. Nor did he entirely relish the half-tipsy air which the artist had managed to convey to the inn. His was a respectable place. Above all that shirt flapping from the window was a libel. The wash was always hung in the court! Bursting with indignation he hurried out to make sure, crossed the narrow street, and turned to survey the front of his establishment. The light in the captain's window was out, but certainly there was a shirt flapping there over the sill as if hung out to dry. "Mort Dieu! What was the place coming to?"

CHAPTER FOUR

THE ENCHANTED FOREST

THE captain was awakened next morning by his friend the innkeeper. Despite his chagrin at the shirt, which he noticed was
still fluttering at the window, the good man was once more obviously in the rôle of conspirator. Nor did the fact that he came bearing
a tray with a bowl of coffee and rolls prevent him from walking as
though a burden of state still rested upon his shoulders. Between his
half-closed eyelids Denis Moore surveyed him as he arranged the table,
and permitted an inward smile to escape as an audible yawn. Finding
his guest awake, the innkeeper turned and bade him good morning.

"The message was safely delivered, monsieur. The cook's sister
has returned, two hours ago."

"Any reply?" yawned the captain stretching himself, but with a
throb of pulses under the covers.

"No, monsieur, you said nothing about that. Did . . .?"

"I did *not* expect one."

"Oh!" said the innkeeper.

"At least not till later, you know. And what do we hear from the
mayor-postmaster?"

"All has been arranged as I—as he said. There will be a room
prepared for you at the farm we spoke of. You can go this morning
if you like. François can drive you over in the cart with the cover.
If monsieur will not mind sitting in the back, on a truss of straw, no
one will see him there as he goes through the village."

"And the mare?" inquired the captain.

"She can be taken over this evening after it is dark."

The captain was visibly pleased. "I am bound to say that you have
both done very well, you and your brother, the mayor-postmaster. I
shall see that your services are properly mentioned in my report," he
added, sitting up officially, and drawing on his shirt. "All that is
needed now is a closed mouth. You can leave the rest to me."

The innkeeper bowed and puffed out his cheeks. In his mind's eye
he beheld a document heavy with seals and loaded with encomiums
winging its official way to Paris. What an honour for the family
Gervais to be mentioned to the Minister of War! "Monsieur is indeed
very kind," he murmured. With some difficulty he returned to his

40

rôle in actual life. "Is there anything . . . is the breakfast satisfactory?"

His guest surveyed it somewhat skeptically. "A flask of whisky, perhaps." The host stared blankly. "Eau de vie, then." With incredulity upon his face the man vanished to returned a few minutes later with the desired liquid. "Bon Dieu!" said he as the captain emptied a considerable portion of it into his cup and tossed it off raw. "In the morning, monsieur!"

The captain laughed. "It is a family custom, my friend. Several generations in France have not changed it. We still drink to the King of France whenever we can in Irish whisky, as my grandfather, the great O'Moore, once drank to King James." He looked at the flask wistfully. "Lacking whisky, brandy is the next best thing."

"But in the morning, monsieur!"

"It is a fine loyal way to begin the day. Will you join me?"

Not daring to refuse, the innkeeper gulped down a fiery potion poured out by his host, and retired gasping. "Exit," thought the captain, "I shall now be left in peace at least for some time. But what a slander on the O'Moore's. Brandy before breakfast! One would think us to be Russians." Labouring under great excitement as he was, he had craved the drink.

It might be hours before he heard from the château. Hours? Days! Perhaps not at all! But he dismissed that from his mind. Underneath he could hear the morning activities of the inn already well under way. Judging by the clatter in the stable, François was currying down the mare and being nipped at for his pains. He looked out into the littered courtyard. It was a beautiful, clear day and the smoke from Maître Henri's two chimneys rose straight into the air. Then he crossed to the other window and standing back some little way so as to remain unobserved from the street, glanced toward the château. An exclamation of surprise escaped him. On the road leading to the village a cloud of dust could be seen coming his way rapidly. There was no time to lose.

He turned back into the room and from an inner flap of his saddlebag extracted a square object carefully packed in a fragment of blanket. Unwrapping this rapidly he took out a fair sized mirror which it contained. Again hastening to the window he propped the glass on the window-sill almost at right angles to the street. Drawing up a chair some distance within the room, he seated himself, adjusted the mirror once or twice and waited.

Like many old buildings the inn did not front squarely on the road. Even the slight angle at which it was offset plus the overhang of the casement enabled the scene outside to be thrown upon the glass in a bright little miniature of that portion of the village street which the

captain was most anxious to see without being seen. Despite his
anxiety, the situation and his secret view amused him.

A few yards below him two women in white caps could be seen gossiping and gesturing violently. Their shrill voices came in through
the window. He noticed the peculiar "well-what-could-one-do-about-
it" gesture of one of the women as she seemed to let the bad luck she
was relating pour back onto the spine of Providence. A black goat
switching a long lily stalk in its teeth wandered across the street.
"What kind of an omen is that?" thought the captain, who was now
amused to imagine himself a crystal gazer. Undoubtedly a great deal
of fate was concentrated in the mirror. He could not help feeling that
way about it. Suddenly the women turned and both gazed in the
same direction. There was the distant crack of a whip and a rumble.
He could hear feet running to the door downstairs. A small blur
appeared in the glass that grew rapidly, almost terrifyingly swiftly
into a coach and four. He caught a glimpse of a squat, cat-faced
postilion riding the right lead horse, and the two tall footmen behind.
In the distortion of the glass there was something diabolical about
them. Then horses, coach and footmen seemed to vanish uphill across
the mirror into nothing. The next instant the cocked hats, white wigs
and profiles of the two footmen appeared close to and on an exact
level with the window. Their heads and a small part of the coach
roof seemed to glide along the sill miraculously. He caught the flash
of a yellow glove. There was a sharp crack, and the captain swore
automatically. The mirror, shivered into a hundred jagged fragments,
had tinkled musically to the floor.

He was on his knees now. He wondered if the missile had
bounded back into the street. Inadvertently he had miscalculated the
height of his room above the road. It had not been quite so easy to
reach it as he had expected. Then he gave a relieved exclamation and
rose with the desired object in his hands. In a few seconds the piece
of paper was disengaged from the small stone about which it had
been tightly wrapped, and opened out on the table before him. He
bent over it, for the writing though clear was exceedingly minute.

> He will be gone all day. This afternoon early, the road to
> Beaumont by the mill at the first bridge. Driving. The maid
> can be trusted. Till then Dieu te garde—*and always.*

"And always"—his lips moved as if in prayer and sank to the paper
in Amen. All his frame flushed with happiness. He felt his throat
beating in the collar that was suddenly too tight for him. No, he had
never known how much he needed her. The tumult and the longing
of his body surprised his mind out of thought. There could be only

one meaning to the note. She had decided at last then. It had been impossible finally to bid him good-bye. Those days at Versailles had won against all her scruples at last. Or, could she only be flattered that he had followed her? But this was not the court! He ran to the window to reassure himself. No, no this was Auvergne. Miles of pastoral landscape, vineyards, fields, forests, and meadows rolled up and away to the heights of Gergovia. Sound, odour, and sight swept up to him bringing a sudden access of peace, conviction, and determination. The quest for which he had been prepared to devote his summer was about to end. He turned and threw himself upon the bed in an ecstasy that shook him. For a moment he gave himself up to a sensation of unmitigated happiness. He breathed deeply and lay still. When he arose some minutes later he noticed that he was still only in his stockings. And he had been walking about heedlessly amid the shattered fragments of the mirror that lay scattered about the floor.

In the heightened emotional state in which he found himself, the accident to the glass worried him more than he would have thought possible. An unusual sensitivity in which he became painfully aware of the strangeness of his surroundings flooded in upon him. It was like homesickness; the only remedy was to be with her wherever she was. Yet he found a positive fear of going out, of meeting strange faces, possessed him. After the moment of ecstasy he was now at the nadir of that state, and a conviction of impending tragedy overpowered him. "How could such an affair turn out well? Suppose, yes, suppose *that* . . . what would they do then?" He reached out almost unconsciously and took a pull at the brandy. A feeling of relief and of normal assurance gradually returned. He felt better, confident. He walked about, pulled on his boots, dressed with great care, slung his rapier carefully under the arranged folds of his cloak, and tied back his hair, missing his broken glass sorely. "Damn that piece of luck!" But he would forget. He rapped on the floor and brought up the landlord.

"Monsieur must be careful or he will give himself away. Lucky that no one else heard him."

In the mood he was now in, it didn't matter. Yet he realized the man was right.

"How soon can François be ready with the wagon? I must leave for the farm as soon as possible."

"In a few minutes," replied the innkeeper. "Watch from the window. When I come out into the court without my apron all will be clear and you can come down. But do not delay, sir. People are about now all the time." The man went downstairs while the captain watched impatiently. François hitched a mule to the wagon. Presently the fat host appeared in his vest. Snatching up his holsters and saddle-bags the captain dashed downstairs and bundling his stuff hurriedly into the cart leaped in behind. It was a high, two-wheeled wagon with a kind of bulging tent over it which when drawn behind effectually concealed its burden.

"Good-bye, Maître Henri, and thank you," said the passenger to the innkeeper. "Give me your hand to clinch the bargain."

The fat man cried out at the grip he received from the gentleman under the cover. But on withdrawing his hand he found that within it which caused him to bid his guest, as he rattled out of the court, an all but affectionate farewell.

A few minutes later and the captain was safely ensconced at the farm of Jacques Honneton. By his manner and the elaborate precautions in the reception of his guest, that well-to-do peasant had evidently not failed to be filled up with the importance and peculiar requirements of his charge. The mayor-postmaster must have been more than usually impressive. Best of all, the window of his room, Denis noticed, had a clear and uninterrupted view across the park and of the entire front of the château. That fact, he thought, might have strategic possibilities. He proceeded to make himself comfortable and to inquire from his new host as to the road to Beaumont.

"Là-bas, monsieur," said Honneton, pointing out a streak across the landscape that about a mile away disappeared into a dense mass of ancient greenery.

At the château that morning Maria was strangely happy. It was the first fully happy day she remembered since her marriage. Despite the cold fear which had crept along her spine the night before at supper as the marquis chatted so hopefully of his recovery—and all that it implied—the sensation of coming home, which had begun with her in the coach the afternoon before, had continued. Against the sanguine prophecy of Don Luis as to his health, she had, although she tried not to permit herself to do so, set off the glimpse of the figure waving from the rock. Without realizing that she had unconsciously leaped toward him as an alternative with all of her being, she consciously thought of the near presence of Denis as a protection. Someone to appeal to in case—in case one needed someone to whom to appeal. Then the maid was a dear, a merry and understanding person about thirty but seemingly much younger. They had already confessed their ages, while the golden childish ringlets over which the older woman leaned in unfeigned admiration were being brushed just before bed the night before.

"Ah, madame was so young—and to be married to the old monsieur, already a year!" It seemed impossible. The talk ran on in the eager Tuscan that completed for Maria the illusion that she was being put to bed again at Livorno by Faith Paleológus. Without realizing it she began to talk of her maid, her father's house, of Italy, of all the old life, a forbidden subject, or practically so, for Don Luis would hear none of it.

"You are now in a new world, my dear, forget the old one," he would say, and look dubiously on the frequent letters from home. Once a month she could reply. And he must read and correct her letter when it was finally done with many sighs and not a few blots. Always it must be rewritten. "A marquise, you know, must at least be correct in her correspondence." How she hated it—and him.

Now she could talk at her ease. A flood of delightful, childish chatter was soon joined in by the maid as she brushed and brushed, and watched the bright, beautiful face tilted back at her in child-like confidence, and relief, and ease. They went to sleep whispering. At midnight Lucia found she was relating the story of her life to her mistress who was asleep. The last details of a romantic affair with the butler of M. de Besance died away with a sigh as the final candle in a corner sconce guttered and went out.

Then in the morning had come the wonderful picture from Denis. No, he had not been wrong. Of course, she understood. Perhaps without Lucia she could not have puzzled it out so quickly. And what else could she do but reply? That tallest footman had carried some notes for her before to Denis at Versailles. And Denis remembered! After all she could write a good letter; say a great deal on such a little space of paper. How surprised Don Luis would be if he read that. But heaven forbid! She could trust Lucia, though. Yes, she was sure of that. It had all taken only a few moments. And she would see him this afternoon—at that mill in the forest that Lucia knew about. What a jewel she was, and how much she knew about the château and the country around after arriving only a few days ago.

To Lucia what seemed more natural than that madame should have a cavalier. One could not expect an ogre to fill the heart of a goddess. Besides she herself must get back to Italy and it would be well to ingratiate herself with madame, to make herself indispensable. With a certain amount of knowledge one need never be discharged at all. She had learned that much at Paris. One did not leave the hotel of M. de Besance with two fair-sized shoes full of gold pieces merely for dusting off the chairs. But before all she was a woman, an Italian, and the cry of youth to youth was as natural to her and as little to be cavilled at as the sunlight streaming through the window. So the drive that afternoon was arranged, and the letter, carefully wrapped about the stone, which so thoroughly shattered the captain's reflections, was dispatched.

Hence, at half past one of that beautiful spring afternoon the pony and the little landaulet painted with wreaths of roses and blue ribbons, that Mlle. de Besance now secretly pined for even in the family great coach at Versailles, was waiting at the door. Since madame herself was going to drive, the small bell on the bridle must be silenced. It would never do to have the pony shying at it, Lucia insisted. Maria pouted at this, but a knowing glance from her companion reminded her that it would never do. "No, no, it must be taken off." There was a slight delay while the offending chime was removed and then they were off, taking the great circle of the drive, the straight road through the hedges, and then a swift turn to the right and on to the road for Beaumont.

The horse was a well-behaved but eager little beast. For some time now he had been little used and he travelled the road briskly. The red tassel on the whip began to bend back into the wind and the wheels on level spaces grew dim. Maria laughed with sheer exhilaration. The sunlight drenched the rows of vines, and as if she had already extracted from it that quality that would soon be pressed out as wine, her cheeks glowed and her eyes sparkled. From the heights about looked down upon her old ruined towers, white villages, and little chapels whence the distant bells rang out now and again in what seemed like a chime to the trot and time of the horse. Always over this country of Auvergne there was the sound of bells. At that season the vines had already been tended weeks before. In the vine-yards they passed through they saw no one.

Suddenly as if a cloud had passed over their heads they were in the forest. It was damp and cool. Great beeches covered with green moss on the southern side threw level arms across the road. The sound of the pony's hoofs was muffled in loam and leaves. The wheels swished through them like the prow of a boat moving rapidly through water. Their eyes grew wide in the watery, green light. The silence seemed prophetic. Bright golden patches shimmered and chequered the road ahead. Down the long, cool glades they saw the pronged antlers of the deer disappearing amid the trees and blending into the shadows of branches. It was an enchanted country. Only the forlorn and distant sound of a hunter's horn durst disturb it. No one else ever came there, no one but themselves. Then as she threw her head back to drink in the wonder of it, and to taste the essence of spring that seemed to flow from the tips of the beech buds trembling in the heat on the highest branches, her whole being for the first time partook of life to the full. She was in that hour and in that green virgin place a woman, full grown.

The old merchant's daughter was a girl, a memory moving pathetically, only half-alive it seemed now, about a gloomy house in Livorno. Her father's voice, that careful, wise and knowing voice, was far, far off, talking to someone else that had once been she, but was so no more. And the girl-wife? Ah, Madre mia!—what had *that* man to do with *her?*

The horse sped on as if he would take her away from Don Luis forever, leaving the cold about her heart and the fear behind. A robin flicked across the road in a patch of sunlight. Against the tender green of the leaves his breast seemed to burn like scarlet. As if he had flashed a message from the heart of that enchanted forest, rushed upon her the remembrance, the knowledge, and the full conviction that she was going to meet her lover.

There could be no holding back now. Had he not followed her all the way from Paris? After the crushing of all hope by her marriage, after a year of foreboding and life in death, to find this full cup of life held out to her, waiting as it were just around the next turn in the road, intoxicated her, thrilled her through every fibre and flamed up with a sudden blaze and hope of fulfilment in the very core of her being. "Yes, yes, yes—and never again no," that was what the voices amid these trees, and whispers in the night all the way from Paris—she knew it now—that was what they had all been saying.

She flicked the horse with her whip, half amazed at her own sureness and firmness of grasp. The little carriage darted along under the tunnel of great branches even faster. Lucia with surprise and fear in her eyes grasped the sides of the vehicle tighter. The road began now in a series of long even curves to descend. The speed increased. They could hear the pony breathing. A sparkle of water glittered through the leaves ahead, then some weathered stonework. They wheeled out onto an open green over which the road twisted to a high arched bridge, and drew up before a long abandoned, stone building. The singing voice of a small, rapid river talking to itself filled the air of the deserted valley in which the ruin lay.

"It is the mill, madame," said Lucia. "That way," she pointed to a squat doorway from which stairs overgrown with ferns descended to some green region below. Maria looked. A huge root writhing like a serpent had ages ago taken charge of and embraced that threshold so that nothing could now make it let go short of steel and fire. "Watch," said Maria, handing the reins to her companion who looked down at her almost enviously. A wave of colour swept over the young girl's face, tingeing for a moment her neck and shoulders. Then she turned, and stepping over the threshold lightly, disappeared into the green shadows of the door.

For a moment it seemed to Maria that she was descending into darkness. The steps made a complete turn. She felt her way in the uncertain shadows. The wall grew smooth. Then, almost as soon as she became aware of the light ahead and below, her hand began to brush over the cool and lacy texture of ferns that grew ever more luxuriantly from the damp stone. When she emerged again into the daylight the whole tunnel of the ancient stairs of the mill tower was a vault of faintly vibrant green.

She now found herself almost on a level with the stream. Behind her rose the mill a whole story to the level of the road to which it served as an embankment. Before her stretched a short natural terrace bounded on the side of the stream by the abandoned mill race choked with water-lilies and on the other by a high bank crowned with huge trees. The place was still dewy and smelt of mallows. From the road its existence, to any casual traveller, must remain unsuspected unless he came by the stairs or cut his way through the great trees and undergrowth that now flourished on the top of the ruined dam. The miller of times past, whoever he had been, had chosen his site well.

It seemed to Maria stepping out upon the smooth, natural lawn of this sequestered coign that by some magic she had suddenly succeeded in leaving the world behind. Surely neither man nor beast came here. Those delicate white flowers, tossing themselves in hazy sprays above the grass, were meant for magic feet. The sound of the river bubbled itself monotonously into her ears. She stood, she did not know how long, listening to it. The sensation of having reached a spot where time had ceased slowly grew upon her. She remembered some dim, old Scotch story of a maid who had strayed into a place like this and come back still young. But the names of the gravestones of her generation had weathered away. Then she saw him.

He had been waiting by the bank under an overhanging branch of a pine, watching her. As long as he lived he would never forget her standing there listening to the stream, gazing into another world.

There are certain expressions at times upon the faces of some women that utterly confute the doctrine of original sin but confirm predestination. Such glances of the soul are to be overtaken only when it does not know it is being watched and reveals itself unconsciously as one of the elect, sprung from love and naturally and innocently bound for it again. Whatever else circumstances may do to such a soul that has no part with evil, they can never alter the essence of its being. It remains clear as a flame does even when fed by and consuming the most dreadful refuse. Such a clear glance from the depths of the young girl's being Denis Moore had just had the good fortune of seeing. It was not lost upon him. He had both sensitivity and experience enough to understand. When he stepped out from behind the branch which had concealed him, he had already abandoned utterly the very simple rôle of the hunter. It would never be sufficient merely to bring that beautiful body to the ground. Now he had seen who it was that lived within it. He must live with her, alive, all of her. That glance of hers had revealed to him a kindred thing within himself which he had forgotten. It caused him to remember the clean fire of his youth before he had begun to choke it with ashes. It was that which he desired to blend with her. Some spiritual breeze seemed to have blown the ashes away.

Perhaps on the whole it would have been better for them both if this had not been so. Better if she had found merely a cavalier waiting for her. Then they might have met, parted, and let pass. For there was one thing that the experience of the captain had not taught him. The flame kindled by the mere clashing of two bodies together is usually a flash; the fire engendered by the fusing of souls consumes the body and cannot be put out. Such things, however, are not ordered by merely worldly coincidence. They are kindled by the great urge and turn out as they may. So it was not a cavalier who stepped out into the sunlight to meet Maria, but Denis Moore stripped of all worldly regimentals, and reduced to a man quivering like a boy.

It was thus that she saw him as he was for the first time.

For a moment they stood gazing at each other. Then as if a magnet drew them together the faster as they approached, they moved toward each other, cries rather than words on their lips.

"Maria!" "Denis!"—and a long silence while he wrapped his cloak about them both. Then too overcome to speak he led her to the edge of the mill race where on the green they sat down. She bent forward and put down her face amid the cool leaves of water-lilies, bathing her forehead and cheeks with one hand, for he would not let go of the other. She had not realized what would happen in her when he actually held her in his arms. For her it was the discovery of a whole new continent of the emotions; to him a new aspect of shores that he had long thought familiar. She touched her own lips, reflected in the water, affectionately, and drank. When she looked at him again she was cool and white.

Now that she had surrendered unconditionally, womanlike, she began to plead with him and to try to make terms. So long and gallant a defence of the heart's city as hers had been, implied, she thought, that the garrison should withdraw with the honours of war. At least she had not been taken by storm. She would never admit that.

"Is it," she said leaning her head against him, "is it for always?"

"Always," he replied after her as if exchanging vows.

"And you will never leave, never go away?"

"Never!"

"You will take me away from him? Away—" Her voice trailed out.

He had not thought of that. He had not thought of her as his wife, until now. How could he? How did he know that it would turn out like this? He would have to leave France, the army. A tremendous vista of change suddenly opened up before him. Yet how could it turn out any other way if he was to be what he knew himself to be? He did not shrink from the change that yawned before him. He was not sorry that the adventure had turned into a great quest with the lady won. He was merely taken by surprise. It remained only to carry her off.

She grasped the hem of his cloak almost tearfully. "In whose arms was she folded?" He read the question in her eyes.

"Yes!" he answered pressing his lips on hers, "I swear it."

"By the Madonna?" she whispered.

"By Mary, the Mother of God, by . . ."

She put her hand over his mouth. It was enough. In her mind's eye she saw him holding his hand out over the figure in her little shrine. No oath could be holier than that. From that moment she felt herself to be his. If the holy ones had registered those other vows, how could they help hearing these? Her lips moved and the tears came into her eyes.

"Denis, Denis," she said, as if she had added him to her pantheon.

A moment of beatific oblivion enfolded them both.

Presently they were walking up and down by the little mill race, talking. There was so much to tell. All the journey down from Paris. The terrible time at Bourges with the plague. The new maid at the château. How he had followed them. His "conspiracy" of the night before at the inn. She clapped her hands. And so they were safe here for a while! No one would carry the news to Don Luis. The officials, the mayor-postmaster himself—she pouted the title delightfully—were on their side. "Oh, how clever of you, Denis— and that wonderful note!"—and how she had understood it right away. "But I was so glad! I did not know I could be so glad to see you waving that evening." The memory of the supper that night returned and brought a cloud on her sunshine. That cloud that even now she felt was just over the horizon. She trembled, and again he must repeat his promises to take her away. "Before—before Don Luis was well!" She told him her worst fear. He comforted her and promised, delighted to find that she might still be his as he might have dreamed. Her very confusion over it exalted him.

"But when, but where shall we go?" she kept asking now.

"You must trust me, Maria, I shall find a way. It will take much planning. Your . . . the marquis has powerful friends. We must make sure. It would never do to fail."

"No, no!" she gasped pale at the very thought.

"But let us leave that till again, till the next time," he hastened to say. "There will be many days now to talk it all over. Let be just for now. I did not know before, could not be sure, you know, that I must plan for this."

Seeing his face become troubled, she threw herself into his arms. They would be happy now for this hour and in this place. Let all else go. What more did she need than his assurance? All would go well with them—all would go well.

The afternoon fled away before they knew it. They must tell each other of all the things they had thought and felt since they had met. When they had first begun to love. Of how wonderful it had been that evening of the fête at the Court of Love at Versailles. Of how she had known, how she had *guessed,* whom the roses were for that he had laid on the altar. How she had dared then in her own mind, but not admitted it. Of how Don Luis' suspicions had first made certain to her that "the Irish captain" was her cavalier. He had actually made her happy in her pain. She knew that now. They smiled over it together. He at Don Luis, and she at the little girl from Livorno.

How long ago it seemed. How this afternoon had changed everything. It was almost gone! The sun was behind the forest. It was getting cool. There was the voice of Lucia calling anxiously. "Madame, Maa-*dame!*" They must part. It seemed impossible. She must go back to the other world and away from him.

There was a hurried consultation. Unconsciously they talked in whispers now. Yes, she understood the arrangement of lights in her window. "*One* when Don Luis was going the next morning to the springs, *two* when she could not see Denis next day. *Three* would bring him to her immediately if need be, no matter what."

"*Madame!*" there was an almost frantic note in the maid's voice now.

He made her cry out. Then she had broken away and vanished up the stairs. There was the sound of voices, a neigh from the pony, and the dwindling grit of wheels. He turned and flung himself down on the grass. When he rose again the stars had begun to shine through the branches.

He wrapt his cloak about him and took the road back through the beechwood. Despite the late twilight it was dark there and he did not arrive at the farm Honneton till quite late. When he did so a cheery fire, most unusual for that time of year, and a good supper awaited him. Afterward he went and sat in his room looking out of the window at a landscape that about ten o'clock began to grow bright under the face of a waning moon.

It was May in Auvergne. The scent of the vineyards drifted up to him as they had the night before, but this time with a seductive softness he would scarcely have thought possible. A peace greater than he had ever known filled his heart and soul. There was not a doubt in his mind or body that he had found that without which happiness would be impossible. He was glad the die was cast. Nothing could alter it now. Over the road through the notch in the hill, they would ride off together, some day, soon. He would think of that tomorrow. America, perhaps, or Ireland, he had relatives there. But tonight let there be nothing, nothing to spoil his dream.

He leaned out again into the fragrant night. The lights in the château were still burning. But none upstairs. An hour or two passed. He did not know it. Then the light in her window blazed up. Presently he could see the dot of one flame placed near the casement. He watched breathlessly. It remained, burning steadily. So it was to be tomorrow then. He got up, stumbled about headlong, found the tinder box and lit a candle. He brought it to the window and raised the flame up and down. Across the fields the candle in her window repeated the motion of his own. "Good night, good night, my lover," said the two lights. Then the candle at the château went out. He extinguished his likewise and tumbled into bed. Without knowing it he had been chilled sitting at the window—for how long? He looked at the moon. She was riding high now. The sleep of an infant engulfed him.

Don Luis had been carried to bed in the same state as the night before. The soaking in the hot water at Royat had relaxed him. And he had never seen Maria so gay as she had been tonight at supper. Almost too gay! He wondered if she could be acting, but dismissed the idea. Doubtless the château was a delight to her. She had been driving, too, and had had a good time. It was lucky Besance had sent that maid down, otherwise he would have had to drag Maria back and forth to the springs, and amuse her. Oh, yes, and there was the dog. They were going to look for that tomorrow, she said. Well, he must get better now. Two or three months the physicians insisted, and no wine. That was a long time, at best. He moved his leg impatiently and was rewarded promptly by the proper twinge. Why not begin by staying a week at the springs and get a good start? An excellent idea! He pulled the bell cord.

"Jean," said he, "pack my portmanteau tomorrow for several days' stay. Have it ready early, and tell madame I shall be gone for a week. If I need anything I can send the coach back."

The thought of not making the still painful Royat drive twice a day was an immense relief. Later on it would be easy enough. He wondered he had not thought of it immediately. He took up his book. While the two candles nodded to each other across the moonlit fields, Don Luis nodded to *Rabelais* over the counterpane.

CHAPTER FIVE

A PASTORAL INTERLUDE

EARLY the next morning after dashing a bucket of cold water over himself in the courtyard to the amazement of the stable boy, and looking after the comfort of Solange, who was now comfortably ensconced in Maître Honneton's largest stall, Denis proceeded to dress in his room with unusual care. The time he spent on shaving and the arrangement of his hair while looking at the bottom of Maître Honneton's most highly scoured milk pan would have satisfied a professional macaroni. As he was giving the ruffles of his finest shirt the final touch he had the ineffable satisfaction of seeing the coach of Monsieur le Marquis de Carabas, with Puss-in-Boots on the lead horse as usual, swing around the great drive of the château and take the road for Royat.

So the field was clear! Of course, it would be the mill again. He had forgotten to say so, he remembered now. But surely she would know. He went out and saddled Solange, in the meanwhile questioning Honneton.

"Yes, monsieur, you can reach the woods that way," said the farmer walking out with him to the brow of the hill on which the farm stood. He pointed to a rut across the landscape lined by old walls and hedges, more like a ditch than a highway. "It is a very ancient lane, mon capitaine, used only by the hay carts in summer-time, and not much for that now since the fields have been put to vines. You will meet no one. Nor, unless one stands on the height here, could a person see you pass. We still occasionally use it ourselves when the salt carts from Beaumont wish to dodge the gabelle, but that is only at night," and his eyes twinkled.

"Thank you, Honneton," replied Denis mounting, "you will not forget how important it is that no one . . ." "Have no fear, monsieur. There are none but men here, except Marie, the cook, and—" he extended a sabot significantly, and laughed. The captain gave rein to his mare and disappeared a few minutes later into the mouth of the dark walls of hedge.

The lane, almost a tunnel under its sturdy hedges, extended across the landscape like a ruled line. Here and there the green way stretched before him on a straight level and he gave the mare full head. She sprang forward under him, quivering with the joy of the morning, and would have whinnied had he not checked her with his voice. "A bad habit, girl," he warned her, striking her across the neck with his glove, a punishment she danced under. On a steep slope her shoes rang on a bit of hard pavement where the turf had washed off. He saw the regular cut flagstone. A Roman road! Some of Caesar's work about Gergovia? Presently, as he had expected, the way opened out on the top of the hill into an old camp, an oblong court of green in which a few sheep were straying. Where the praetorium must have been, a young lamb was nuzzling his mother. He dismounted and ran up on the wall.

The old fossa was only a faint hollow now, filled with daisies, but he was much higher here than he had expected. He could look directly across to the hill of Gergovia. The roof of the château lay far below him in the trees. On the other side the beech forest began, and tumbled in waves of hills down to the river. The clear, cool, morning air, the glittering sunlight on miles of new leaves, the height, and the silence except for a continual undercurrent of faint birdsong from the woods, flooded him with a sensation of fresh and ardent well-being, a sense of youth and of being new-born in strength that almost caused him to shout. How triumphant to be alive, to have found his mate, to be above and beyond fear! It was a sheerly masculine experience. The small fountains of life stirred within him filling his frame with premonitory thrills of the ecstasies to come. He beat his gloves on his arm till it tingled. Wrapping his cloak about him in semi-bravado he strode along the parapet like Caesar himself. Down there, down there in the forest, he was going to meet her at the old mill.

He whistled to Solange who was sniffing uneasily at the sheep. A few seconds later and the forest had engulfed them. The mystery of the place closed about him. He missed his own shadow. The hoofs of the mare fell noiselessly on the moss. He might be a ghost riding under the branches. Who knew after all the end of the errand upon which he was bound? He wondered about his own father—when and where? Presently the mare was hobbled in a glade in the forest and he was in the sunlight again on the little green by the mill. But it had been rather eery descending the old stairs, and the place was lonely, without her. He wished that she would come now. How slowly the time passed here! It was so still except for the river. Did it after all move?

When Maria came down the stairs and stepped out onto the little terrace she was terribly startled to see the white body of a young god flashing and swimming about in the mill race. For a minute her heart was in her mouth. It was as if she had surprised the youthful spirit of all these spring woods sporting in his secret pool. But the head thrust up through the lily pads was that of Denis. For a minute they

both looked at each other with horrified surprise, and then burst into
a laugh. The blood rushed to his face. "Wait in the tunnel," he cried,
"I shall only be a moment." He could hear her laughter echoed from
the fern-clad walls while he frantically slipped into his clothes. "I did
not expect you so soon!" he called. "I should hope not, mon capitaine." The laughter continued. What a fool he had been, after
dressing so carefully, too! Now look, there was mud on the ruffles
of his shirt. And his hair!

But she loved his damp curls when she came to him at last. He
could not hold her close enough. "Let me go, Denis!" she gasped at
length. "You goose, I have something to tell you. Such news," she
cried flinging her arms about him again, and whispering into his
"driest ear." "He is going to be away for a week, for a whole week!
I shall be all alone, and my own mistress at the château. It will be
like a honeymoon. Let us call it that," and she clapped her hands
like a child as she always did when pleased and excited. "Lucia and I
have packed luncheon and brought it along. She thought of it. We
might have supper here, too. He will be gone, gone all today, and
tomorrow."

"And the day after that!" added Denis.

Her eyes grew large at the vista of endless happiness that was about
to ensue. They began to plan out the time together, interrupting one
another. He drew a little calendar in a patch of sand. Tomorrow
they would drive out to a farm that Lucia knew of and get the puppy.
"And the next day?" She faltered bewildered by the endless possibilities.

"We will go up on the high hill of Gergovia. It is a wonderful
place that," and he began to tell her. The old story of the brave Gauls
took on a new lease of life.

"And after that to the old tower on the hill I can see from the
château."

"Why not?" he said. "Anywhere, anywhere with you! We can
arrange it each evening and meet the next day. Only we must not
be seen together anywhere. That would cause talk and might get
back to the château. Remember after all a week is *not* so long."

How short, how terribly short it suddenly seemed. She had pictured him riding by the side of the little landaulet. It would have been
so romantic. She could look back at him and drop her glove. He
would dismount and bring it to her, and kiss her hand. The tableau
enchanted her. It was not often she could imagine a scene so clearly
as that. It was like something out of *Paul and Virginia,* more real
than life and somehow more beautiful.

"It will be better to be very careful now, and so have many days
all through the summer," he was saying.

So he was *not* planning to take her away with him soon. But why not now, this week, while Don Luis was away? They could be gone for days before he knew, she said.

"No, no, that would never do." He began to explain. "He would get the news in a few hours at most after she was missed." They must have some place to go to. He was writing a merchant at Marseilles about a ship. It would take some days, a week or so perhaps to hear. He had thought of Ireland, but America would be better on the whole. He had heard those who had campaigned there and knew the country. He began to tell her about it. By noon they were still lost in an idyll of forest life beyond the seas when Lucia called from the world above and reminded them of lunch.

She brought it down in a little basket; was charmed with monsieur, with his gift also. A brave gentleman, indeed! Her interest in the affair became quite enthusiastic. She laid the luncheon out on a white cloth under the trees and went back to keep watch. "I have mine in the cart, you know. Not many pass this way but it will be well to be with the pony. Monsieur will know what to do if I call—and madame? Ah, she is picking water-lilies!" She gathered a few, placed them in the empty lunch basket by the side of the race and departed to the world above.

They sat down under the trees and ate together. It was their first meal. In her heart she thought of it as a kind of lovers' sacrament. She said a little grace closing her eyes, while he looked on fascinated and remembered to cross himself just in time.

"Ah, it will be like this in America, will it not, Denis? We shall eat out in the woods this way often. And you will not let the savages nor the great beasts come near me?"

He protested again and again that he would not. The tears came into his eyes as he thought of what must be ahead of her in hardships, of the long journey, the ship, a strange land, nowhere to turn, and he a poor man. For a moment his heart failed him. Could he ask that of her? She was so daintily lovely here, so fragile it seemed to him now; almost artificially beautiful with her face like a cameo against the dark convolutions of the roots in the bank before which she sat. Those little rosebuds and garlands embroidered on the clear silk of her gown, what would become of them in Canada? Could he after all? Ah, could he not!

That delightful little golden head! He was mad about that, the face that looked up at him with so much wonder and appeal, so much hope, and innocence and abandon. He must have that near him in the future, forever. The future? Why, here he was dreaming when she was near him now! Who could tell about the far-off days to come? God held them in fee. But this *now*, this was his, and she was near him. As if he were drawing her back from the shadows of the unknown and would save her from all that his mind might forebode but could not certainly form, he suddenly caught her to him. She saw that he had been weeping. An access of wonder, and unreasoning pity overcame her. She comforted him for she knew not what, for some sorrow that lay within her, too. A great tenderness engulfed them both. Of all the doors by which love enters pity is the widest. Passion, the incendiary, is always waiting close by in the disguise of an importunate beggar to glide over the threshold and set fire to the house.

The afternoon shadows slowly lengthened over the grass. The river fled away forever modulating a monotone. The dead windows of the mill with little pine trees on the sills looked out at nothing. A small bird flitted back and forth over the white table-cloth on the grass. He looked doubtfully at the two figures by the bank under the pine trees. They did not stir. Finally he lit upon a thin stemmed glass and tilting back his little head drank delicately. It was a light, sweet wine but it made him a bad, bold bird. He began to scatter the fragments of Maria's cake wantonly. Finally he put his head under his wing in broad daylight and went to sleep. Under the pine branches there was nothing to show that the two who lay there were alive except the long, slow rise and fall of their breasts. The wind tangled their curls together as it would if they had both been dead. Caught in the full tide of spring they drifted closer and closer together through the long afternoon.

When Denis rode home through the starlit forest that evening it was as if he had discovered himself as an entirely new person. He was inherently one of those rare but strong and natural people in whom the realities of passion actually experienced invariably transcend expectancy. Nor was this due to a lack of imagination. It was merely that his mind could not remember with a thought vivid enough to compass the actual feel of the flesh.

For the first time as he went home that evening he began to realize that he was in a predicament. He had already been caught in the eddy of a current that flowed through him and possessed him. Once in the main stream of it he could neither control nor direct. As his imagination had been unequal to his capabilities, so his will might be found inadequate to the unexpected strain. "Might be?" He knew it would. It came upon him like fate. Yet what could he do? He could not go away now. By every tie that his heart and soul knew he was bound to her. Yes, even despite her marriage, by every tie of an honourable mind. That her father had sold her with good intentions was no reason why he should recognize the bargain. Society, the society he knew, would scoff at such scruples. Her marriage was a circumstance to be circumvented. He would do that. He would make her, so far as the world knew, honourable amends. Beyond the sea they would be man and wife. That last small remnant of his grandfather's estate and the sale of his commission would enable him to . . . oh, yes, that was all quite possible, a matter of correspondence and some little time.

Time, that was it! Could he control himself, tomorrow, or the next day? They had been so near the verge this afternoon. He knew it now. But he did not care when he was with her. He had become for a time, what? Putty in the hands of some outside force that might mould him as it desired, not as he willed. But he would summon his self-control again. He ground his teeth together and gripped the mare with his knees so that she started forward.

They came up out of the forest into the old camp again. He forced the horse onto the rampart and stood looking back. A low chattering of night birds and hooting of little owls trembled up to him through the night. The moon was just rising and a light breeze that seemed to follow the path she laid over the miles of new leaves rippled the forest like a lake. The breeze increased in intensity and pressed against him. It was warm, damp, and fragrant, moulding itself into every fold and hollow of his body. Wisps of it blew like hair across his lips and the smooth hands of the mistral caressed his cheek. He was holding her in his arms again. For an instant the spell of the afternoon recurred in full force. Every nerve of his body shuddered toward her. The past and the future were forgotten. His entire consciousness became aware of the meaning, blent with, and seemed to pass on into the languorous longing of the spring night.

When he came to again, the mare, as if she had seen a ghost, was shivering under him in the moonlight, and the last fringes of the mistral had passed over the ramparts. The wood which the wind had passed through was strangely silent. He rode home with a fear and doubt of himself knocking at his heart. Of the young man who strode so confidently along those ramparts that very morning nothing but a vague memory remained. There was only one thing that was stronger than his fear and that was his longing. When he got to his room the single candle was burning in the window at the château. He lit his own and signalled. But there was no answer. Maria had evidently gone to bed.

And, indeed, she had. Lucia had seen to it. It was only by the exertion of some tact and will power that she had prevailed on her mistress not to go down to supper in the great hall. With the quick instinct of her kind she had realized that the girl was in a state that might well attract the not unobservant eyes of Pierre. Hence the evening dress, which with great trouble and some impatience had been put on, was now with evident relief and no trouble whatever taken off. Supper was served in the room. A complete lethargy seemed now to have fallen upon Maria. She had resigned herself into the hands of Lucia as if it were a relief to have someone else make even the smallest decisions for her.

The older woman had now long passed the point where she was striving to make herself agreeable from pure self-interest. All her motherly instincts had been aroused, and it was plain from every little motion and attitude as she waited upon Maria that she was actuated by strong affection for her. Indeed, she had been completely captivated by her young mistress whom she now pitied, admired and loved with all her heart. The affair of madame had consequently taken on for Lucia a new aspect. It had become a vicarious experience of her own. She had not expected that it would be so serious and absorbing either to Maria or to herself. Denis was exactly the kind of person she would have chosen for Maria, and with the sudden turn of the affair she was at once delighted with the present and fearful for the future. Absorbed in the fate of the lovers, she scarcely paused to consider what might happen to her should a crisis of any kind occur. Her first loyalty was to her mistress, beside that any other duty as a member of the marquis' household was too pale and abstract to engage her attention. She was one of those persons whose actions were controlled purely by likes or dislikes. She loved her mistress and she disliked Don Luis.

Being of a somewhat bovine temperament herself, it was a surprise to Lucia to note the effect of an afternoon spent in the presence of her lover upon the highly strung young girl whom she was now trying in vain to soothe. That this was not the effect of surrender but of being tremendously aroused without full satisfaction, she was wise enough in the ways of her own sex to know. The result of having for the first time been stirred to the depths of her being was to Maria like the after effects of a strong and over-stimulating drug. She was now completely unnerved. Had she been a weak character she would have been hysterical. She had come away in a daze. Her body and spirit were now in an indescribable tumult. Nowhere could she find rest or satisfaction. The sense of the physical absence of her lover was devastating. At the thought of him she experienced a longing for which there seemed no adequate human control. She threw herself on her knees before the madonna, but it was in vain. The very passivity of the statue and her own attitude was an aggravation. It was now like a final twist of the rack that the thought of Don Luis intruded itself upon her mind. For the first time she fully understood what that meant. A spiritual nausea and darkness overwhelmed her. She cast herself on the bed and then leaped from it in loathing. Finally she took to walking up and down the room repeating, "Denis, Denis, where are you? Denis!"

"Hush, madame, hush, the servants will hear you." Lucia strove to engage her attention. "See, I shall put the candle in the window for him. It is a single one. You will see him tomorrow."

The girl took the candle from her and rushed to the window with it herself. She raised the light up and down several times, but there was no answer. Then she turned and burst into tears.

"Do you love him so much?" said the maid stroking her hair.

"Oh, Lucia, Lucia," cried Maria.

A few minutes later she had been put to bed and was asleep. Lucia bent over her. Except for a faint spasm now and then in the throat muscles, she was calm again, worn out. Presently she sighed and lay utterly still.

It was Lucia who managed next day that they should see each other only for a short time, and then not alone. In the morning she drove into the country with Maria and they returned with a puppy which was instantly taken home to the young girl's heart. It was at least a living and responsive being upon which she could pour out some of the affection that now constantly overwhelmed her. They stopped at the mill for luncheon where Denis was walking up and down distractedly. He had been there since early morning. But the good woman by the exercise of much harmless ingenuity contrived not to leave them alone. Long before sunset Denis had to watch the two women disappear along the road into the forest with Maria looking back, her scarf waving in the wind, and the small, brown face of the little dog peering over her shoulder. He was forced to admit to himself that Lucia was both right and understanding. Nevertheless, an indignation overcame him and a sick longing as they drove away and he found himself alone again without having taken Maria in his arms. Tomorrow, tomorrow, despite himself, despite Lucia, he would feel those lips on his. That hope alone made the night supportable.

Nor was he disappointed. Before noon the next day they had climbed the high hill of Gergovia and were standing alone together upon its top looking down upon all that part of Auvergne. It was the first hot day of the season and from the valleys already the warmth shimmered up to them to lose itself in the crystal heights. These in turn glowed up and away into a vault of deepest blue blown clear of clouds, quivering and sparkling.

Up here the red volcanic nature of the soil was apparent. From the rows in the vineyards below, where the grass had been stripped, emanated an almost violet hue. The domes of ancient volcanoes and little breast-like hills rolled all about them, dotted with white villages caught in a network of roads. From these came faintly but clearly the thin voices of bells. A large amphitheatre of hills covered with masses of vineyards and forest stretched southward and upward to the Puy-de-Dôme. Even from Gergovia they looked up to see the ruined temple of the Gallic sun god overlooking his ancient domain.

The entire bowl of surrounding mountains seemed to be catching the sunlight and flinging it back at them. Over the flat meadow on the top of the shoulder, where they were now standing, and where the town of the Gauls had once stood, the bees were greedy amid the clover as if they preferred the wild, clean sweetness of the flowers on that great height to the more cloying honey of the blossoms in the valley below. Indeed, from this place still exhaled the faint memory of a fresher fragrance as if the dawn had lingered there before moving westward to the lesser steeps. But now that whole hilltop was murmurous with wings, and vibrant with a passion of light and heat.

The arms of Denis closed about the body of Maria. Had anyone looked over the slight rim of that hollow mountain meadow to the very centre of which they had wandered, so that it enclosed them with a complete circle from all but the sky, he would have seen but one figure apparently, so close were they standing. Denis bent over Maria, while her hands, as if they were tapping at the door of his heart, fumbled at his breast. They stood for an instant with the spring concentrated in them. Then he picked her up and carried her over the rim of the slope.

A jumble of huge stones, once a gate tower that had hurled back the legions of Rome, lay scattered along the brow of the hill. He picked his way amid these rapidly. Where the foundations still remained they now leaned outward, overhung with brush or vines, and sheltering a ledge-like hollow filled with last autumn's leaves. A short distance below, the shoulder of the hill fell away at a tremendous angle. It was a place where in the winter the shepherds of the neighbourhood remembered to look for lost lambs sheltering themselves from the blast. Brushing aside the long, trailing tendrils like a veil, Denis laid Maria softly in the nest of dry ferns and leaves behind them. The veil fell again. To the curious sheep cropping near by it seemed as if the man and his burden had vanished into the old wall. Soon their bells continued to sound again gently.

Only once more during that noontide were they disturbed; this time by a soft, tremulous cry.

On the meadow above, the sound of the bees' wings continued growing a little deeper in tone as the heat of the day advanced. By far the majority of these honey gatherers were of the ordinary neuter and domestic kind for whom work was an end in itself. Here and there, however, amid this host of humble workers, who took good care to avoid so dangerous a neighbourhood, cruised a large male bumble-bee like a pirate or gentleman adventurer covered with the gold dust of the treasuries he had robbed. These for the most part seemed to have their nests or robber lairs about the tumbled stones of the old tower where a kind of white cornflower trailed through the grass.

From a fracture in the stone immediately above the little ledge where the lovers had hidden themselves a peculiarly beautiful specimen of this blossom had put forth. But a large black spider, who had also fixed on the same cranny in the rock for his abode, had fastened on this bud as a support for his web and had succeeded in dragging it to the ground. In the shadow of the rock, the flower, which could open fully only in the brightest sunshine, still lay even after the noon had passed with the small green tip of its maidenhead fastening its petals at the end of the pod.

Attracted by so lovely and virginal a store of honey, a bumble-bee lit upon this blossom and after stroking its petals for some time as if he were in love, began to tear away the small green membrane that still defended it from his assault. The petals opened slightly and began to curl. Settling back as it were upon his haunches, and raking his body back and forth over this small opening the bee finally succeeded in inserting himself into the flower. Here, as if in ecstasy, he dashed himself about. The flower opening ever wider, trembled, and drooped upon its stem. At this moment the spider, suddenly becoming aware of what was happening, emerged from his nook and began to weave his web again across the bee.

Some hours after this lilliputian tragedy had occurred, Denis and Maria emerged from their place of concealment. All considerations except that of each for the other were now banished from their minds. The clear peace of the great height and the quiet of the late afternoon woods through which they began to descend found an answering echo in their own natures. Strangely enough it was this walk down the ancient road that approaches the plateau of Gergovia from its least precipitous side which formed for them the crowning experience of their love. The same cool mood of completion and benign contentment after having fulfilled the plan of creation that breathed from the panorama of landscape before them as the day verged toward its close, was for a few blessed moments their own. For a half mile perhaps, certainly no farther, they walked together in utter unity with each other and in complete harmony with the world without. It is this rare mood which perhaps more than any other deserves to be called "happiness." And it was this which they afterwards remembered and desired to return to and perpetuate rather than that "agony of pleasure," which, while it convulses the body, cancels the mind.

To Lucia, who had long been watching anxiously as the sun dropped toward the western hills, the lovers appeared to be subdued as they came down the forest road. It was difficult for the good woman to refrain from a smile as she noticed the subtle air of possession with which Maria now leaned against and held Denis' arm. The frantic welcome with which the young dog would have greeted her was hushed by his mistress as out of keeping with her mood and the place. Upon her face the colour now began to show.

In Denis' manner, however, there was no sign of embarrassment. Taking it as a matter of course that the maid must be in all their secrets from now on, he turned to her, and with a smile the undeniable charm of which was in itself a powerful appeal, confided Maria again to her charge.

"You will take good care of madame, will you not, Lucia?" he asked. Despite himself and to his surprise, his voice trembled.

"As if she were my own child! Oh, monsieur, do not doubt me," responded the woman deeply moved, "I love her, too."

"I am sure of it, sure of it," he replied, and added in a low tone, "You will trust me, also?"

She gave him a warm grasp of her hand.

Turning he clasped Maria to him murmuring, "Good-bye, good-bye." They stood together for a moment by the little carriage and would have parted with tears had not the dog in her arms insisted on trying to lick both their faces at once. His comfortable assurance that all was meant for him tipped the scales of their emotion into merriment.

"Oh, he *is* a dear, Denis, isn't he?" said she as he helped her into the cart. Under the guidance of Lucia the pony started forward. Riding for an instant on the step he had just time enough to snatch a kiss. Maria turned and tossed something back at him. He picked it up. It was a white cornflower whose petals, although it was now nearly evening, were not yet fully blown. As he raised it to his lips there floated from it the wings of a bee.

He picked both of them up out of the grass and folded them carefully along with the petals of the flower in his pocketbook. That night when he looked out of the window in his room at the farm there were two lights burning in the upper room of the château.

CHAPTER SIX

THE MUSE OF TRAGEDY

THE marquis had returned unexpectedly. From half-way up the heights of Gergovia Lucia had caught sight of the great coach coming over the ridge from Clermont. By urging the little horse it had been possible to reach the château about half an hour before Don Luis arrived. Maria came down to meet Don Luis with the puppy in her arms and noted with consternation that he was able with only a cane to negotiate the front steps alone. She had, however, presence of mind enough to welcome him with congratulations on his improvement. To her surprise he seemed almost childishly pleased. Even the little dog received a reassuring pat. But that sagacious young animal from the start evinced a very evident doubt as to the good intentions of the man with the cane.

Sitting in the hot springs at Royat with a half dozen other invalids, after three days the marquis had become enormously bored. He had actually begun to miss his young wife and to long for her company. Immensely cheered by his remarkable progress in so short a time, he had somewhat overrated his powers of locomotion and visualized himself as already walking about the gardens of the spa and sitting with her in the various pavilions. Not exactly a thrilling existence after Paris, he admitted, but perhaps not so completely rustic as the château. After all, Clermont was a considerable place for the provinces, and they might meet some of the local noblesse. It was not in vain that he drove in state with two footmen and the big coach. Without doubt the impression already made was a good one. With a pretty young wife by his side in a court gown of the latest mode, several doors might soon be open. Hence he had returned to fetch her back the next morning.

"A stay of a week, my dear." She could not wholly conceal her disappointment at leaving, but of course acquiesced. Under the rouge which Lucia had wisely applied she turned pale, but managed to summon a smile. Somehow she must get word tonight to Denis. Don Luis noticed her hesitation. He was somewhat nettled, but glad on the whole that she had found the château so pleasant. At the best she would have to spend considerable time there, he thought. Perhaps most of the summer. That night they packed for the stay at Royat.

Once in her room Maria could not refrain from tears. She could not see Denis at the mill tomorrow; she would be driving to Royat in that horrible coach. For a moment she had an impulse to put three candles in the window. Lucia restrained her. To do so might have fatal results. She reasoned with Maria. "There is no need to bring Monsieur Denis here tonight, madame. No danger threatens. You will return in a few days and he will still be here."

"But how will he know what has happened?" the girl cried desperately, lighting the second candle and placing it on the sill with tears in her eyes. "Ah, if it had only been one!" The answering signal seemed only to increase her woe. At last it was arranged that Lucia should carry Denis a note. She slipped out without difficulty and made her way to the farm. To Maria lying in bed listening it seemed Lucia would never return. When she did, it was with good news.

"I spoke to him through the window, madame. His light was out, but I tapped on the frame. Monsieur is so grand wrapped in a blanket! He does not even wear a night-cap." She rattled on while the girl sighed. "He will wait for you till you return again no matter how long, he said. When you do, put the candle in the window as before. Also he said, madame, that if anything went wrong to address to Maître Honneton at the farm in care of the mayor-postmaster at Romagnat. He will arrange that with the postmaster. After you fold the letter put a cross on the *outside,* too." Lucia giggled. "But do not write unless you must. No news will be good news, and he will wait." She paused.

"Was that all he said?" asked the girl after a little. "Come, Lucia, was that all?" She stamped her foot as the maid smiled provokingly. "Lucia!"

"No, madame, that was not all. He sent you this."

It was a small chamois skin bag with a cord from it like a scapula. She went to the window and by the light of the two candles opened it with eager fingers. Inside was a gold ring worn thin.

The two women laughed and cried themselves to sleep. Lucia's merriment was taking, yet in reality she did not feel as much as she expressed. She was by no means a fool, and the possibilities of the situation were more vividly before her than she cared to indicate. Come what might, madame must be kept calm and collected. A repetition of the emotional transports of the evening before might be difficult to explain to the marquis. From her trundle bed beside her mistress, Lucia continued in a tender way to rally and to soothe Maria until the deep breathing of the girl gave place to her last sleepy answers. Lucia now arose, took a candle and looked at her. The new ring was on her finger—she must remember to take *that* off!—and there was a smile on her lips which the woman, turning to the madonna, prayed might remain.

Early the next morning the dust rolled behind the coach as it dashed along the highway toward the springs. Don Luis was buoyant but Maria had little to say. Had the marquis looked very closely he might have found that the rather ponderous wedding ring which he had conferred upon his wife in Livorno had just below it a narrow, worn, gold band. On that point alone Maria would not listen to Lucia. She had been obdurate. But Don Luis did not notice. He was not thinking just then of wedding rings.

From the brow of the hill on which the farm Honneton was situated Denis looked down gloomily. A violet thunder storm later on in the day served to relieve his feelings by expressing his mood in a larger language than he could command. That evening he sent for the mayor-postmaster and, as he expressed it, "perfected the plot." But no letter with a cross came. A week dragged by. The captain was forced to take his exercise at night. He swam at the mill. Yet to be there without her was torture.

It was now ten days since! He was about to saddle Solange and ride over to Royat for news, when on the tenth night the candle, and only a single one, glowed in the window at the château. Maître Honneton was somewhat surprised to be aroused after midnight by his guest who forced him to swallow an enormous quantity of brandy. When the farmer awoke it was late in the morning and the captain had already been gone several hours.

Maria had returned and left the marquis at the springs. As early as possible without causing comment she had taken the little carriage and driven over to the mill. Denis, however, had been there a long time before. The feel of her heart throbbing against his own caused him to lean back against a tree so that he might not seem to stagger with her. The sight of his mother's ring on her finger as he kissed her hands moved him greatly.

"You will always wear it?"

"Always," she whispered. "To the grave, and beyond."

"Hush! Do not say that, Maria."

She looked up at him with a trust and adoration that went to his heart. He cursed the ten days that they had been parted. Otherwise . . .

He began to tell her of his plan.

"I have been thinking while you have been away. We must lose no more time, after . . ."

"Yes?" she said.

"After what has happened." He held her closer. "I must go back to Paris, make my arrangements, which will take some days, and then come back for you."

"O Denis," she cried, "oh, you are not going away, going to leave me now! No, not for even a little while! I need you here. I must have you. I . . ." Her hands were beating at his breast again.

He explained, and even argued. "It is necessary. We shall require money. I cannot desert! I am an officer. I must sell my commission, make all our plans. We shall need money to leave France. Can't you see?"

"You can have my jewels," she said, "all but this," and she clasped the ring.

"Ah, that would not do, my little love. One may run off with a man's wife and still remain a gentleman, but one does not also make off with his jewels. Is it not so? You must come with me even in the gown which I shall give you."

"What colour will it be?" she asked trying to laugh.

"White, like the cornflower you gave me," he said and kissed her. "But can't you see that it is as I say?"

To his surprise she could not. The very thought of his leaving reduced her to nervous despair.

"A week then," he said, "then I *must* go. Must, or the summer will be over before we know it. And we must leave from here. In the cities as an ambassador the marquis would have every assistance. Here, the simple officials are on my side. You see how it is? I am coming back, coming back to take you away forever." He took her again and held her close in his arms.

So they had their week. The new moon came again, and with it, for the season strode rapidly that year, not only days but long, warm nights. Then he had ridden off for Paris and the marquis was back again at the château.

Don Luis made the trip to Royat every day now. With the rapid subsidence of all pain in his leg, he enjoyed it. For the new coach he bought some superb horses from M. de Polignac. It had provided him with as fine a turnout as the province had ever seen. So he dashed back and forth in fine style and every day or so took Maria along with him. There was little else talked about over the countryside than the Marquis de Carabas with his enchanting Puss-in-Boots for a postilion, and the adorable little wife. To the wives of the petty noblesse, and to those unfortunate great ones who could not afford to be at Versailles, the presence of Don Luis and all that was his was a positive boon. A round of suppers and small garden fêtes began. The marquise, it was whispered, was not of high birth. But after all with Puss-in-Boots in the saddle Cinderella might well ride in the coach. Undoubtedly too, her foot was small. Several eyes noted that, and not since the Chevalier de Boufflers had come that way had anyone heard such conversation as Don Luis'. What if his wife were silent? She herself was a golden little mouse.

Maria was, indeed, silent. It was now well on into July and Denis was not yet back. At last there was a letter. The arrangements at Paris had taken much longer than he supposed. He might even have to go to Havre to arrange about the ship. *"Patience, I love you. All will be well."*

The days slipped by. The motion of the rapidly driven coach began to make her seasick. Lucia began to be anxious. She questioned madame. She observed. Yes, there could be no doubt of it. There was already the difference of one eyelet in lacing. Kneeling on the floor dressing her, she clasped the girl about the knees and looking up with tears told her. Maria blanched.

But to Lucia's surprise a look of joy and triumph then irradiated her face. It was as if suddenly while looking up Maria had caught the gleam of some bright vision looking down at her. Her eyelids drooped. Behind them there stood in the green haze of an illimitable wilderness a log hut. A woman with a golden-haired child in her arms came to the door. The blood crackling in Maria's ears rang like the sound of an axe in the forest. "Denis, Denis," she whispered. She saw him coming, running toward her.

"It is our child," she cried aloud throwing up her arms, "ours!" Presently she was sitting by the window again at the château. She began to pray to the madonna to bless her baby.

Three months ago she would not have been able to meet Don Luis under such a burden of anxiety without collapsing. Despite the anxiety of Denis' continued absence and the perplexities and risks of the future, she found herself in her now fast growing maturity pos-sessed of a fund of firmness and strength she had never known before. The delicate lines of girlhood had already begun to alter in her counte-nance subtly. From her eyes no longer looked a shy and virginal spirit. The glance, the widened archness of the eyes, the chin and throat, but above all the breasts began to proclaim the woman. Nor was this change entirely physical. Come what might she had deter-mined to bear her child. Her longing for Denis had also altered. It was now more tender, deeper, but not so necessitous. Nor could even the fear of the steady recovery of her husband entirely quell the fierce joy which surged over her. At the springs, and at the evening affairs at various châteaux she began to take a part in the conversation, drop-ping her shawl over one shoulder and letting it fall loosely as she talked, instead of holding it with one hand tightly before her bosom and answering questions respectfully as she had before.

Don Luis was delighted. Without analysing it, he noted the change with satisfaction. She was growing up. His marriage after all would hold elements of companionship to which he had scarcely dared look forward. With him she determined to be gay. And she succeeded with an ease which astonished her. He could in certain moods be fascinating. She began to understand him and to evoke them. It was Lucia who was now subdued and fearful. Only at nights a blind fear would settle upon Maria. She would think she heard her husband coming to her room. Lucia would do her best to console her. But for the most part Maria would lie at those times with her eyes wide open staring into the gloom. Here was a burden which she knew she would after all have to bear alone. Every night, and every night they looked for the candle in Denis' window. There were no more letters. It seemed aeons since she had seen him. It was beginning to be difficult now for her to recall his features when awake. In her dreams they came clearer than ever and left her weak and distrait in the morning.

Don Luis was now walking about without a cane at times, still limping, but visibly recovering mentally and physically. He would come home in the evenings, lead her out to a seat in the garden and caress her. At these times sheer terror made her passive. The strength of his hands made even his lightest touch seem threatening. "O God! If Denis would only come and take her away!"

It was well on into August when one midnight as she sat by the window while Lucia slept the candle suddenly burned again in Denis' window. A great trembling came over her. It was some time before she could kindle her own. For a minute the two lights fairly danced. He had scarcely hoped to find her awake. Then she remembered. There were to be guests at the château next day! Still trembling she lit another candle and placed it beside the first one. It was with difficulty that she refrained from lighting a third. She might bring him to her. In a few minutes he might be in her arms. She took the third taper in her hand. Then she threw it away and wakened the maid. While she dressed, Maria poured out her heart in a note to Denis.

He must meet her at the mill as soon as it was safe. She had something of all importance to tell him. But wait for the signal. She could not come to him tomorrow, would tell him why later. "Oh you are back again, back again," rang her constant refrain. The pen kept saying it over and over. She did not realize how often. Lucia took the paper and disappeared. It was almost morning when she returned. The great dog at the farm had kept baying. "If monsieur had not come at last, come to meet her . . ." But Maria did not hear Lucia. She was reading Denis' letter, the long absence was explained. All was well.

The guests at the château stayed for several days. Denis had come back on a Monday. It was not until Thursday morning that Don Luis finally departed for Royat, somewhat disgruntled that Maria's head-

aches prevented her from going with him. She was becoming necessary to him. He would send the coach over for her next day. He
even thought of deferring his own departure until then. Her solicitude that he should not miss his regular treatment at the springs
secretly touched him. Well, it should not be long now. She would
soon find him all that a husband ought to be. She was right about
the cure. He would follow his regimen closely from now on. He
would soak himself for half a day in the hot water. Sancho was
surprised how alertly and easily he mounted into the coach. In his
own mind Don Luis was already well. It was nearly noon when he
drove off at last.

At the mill Denis waited for her from early morning, pacing up
and down uneasily. "What was this 'all important thing' she had to
tell him? It was?—if it was *that*—it would enormously complicate
their plans."

It was the wait at some seaport that he feared. They must if possible so time their departure as to arrive when, and not before, the
ship sailed. Otherwise he would have to go ahead and make arrangements. Don Luis would stir officialdom to its depths. He had the
means of doing so. They must arrive ahead of the posts. Give him
no time for warning. Be gone and beyond recall. The long journey
made the northern ports impossible. It must be Marseilles. If she
had risked all, so had he. Given up his post at Versailles, his whole
past, wiped it out. All that represented it now was in his saddle-bags.
Heavy enough to gall the mare. Poor lass, he would miss her. Suddenly he realized with wakeful keenness like one aroused from a dream
that he was leaving forever all that he knew. The thought overpowered him as if he had been suddenly told by a physician of the
certainty of immediate death. It was poignant, it was undeniable.
He fell into an hour of reverie listening to the stream. A foreboding
note in its many voices that he had not heard before kept recurring.
Then her face glimmered up from the water-lilies as it had that morning when she had stooped to drink. He stretched out his arms to the
vision. It was some time before he realized that she was really standing above him looking down.

They had both imagined the transports of this reunion but it was
not so. They were too near together when once in each other's arms
to strive any closer. She leaned back and looked up at him in great
peace. The new strength in her face, seen now for the first time after
his absence, amazed and thrilled him. Her lips began to move silently
so that he leaned closer.

"Do you know what it is that I have to tell you, Denis, my Denis?"

Something of her own great tenderness as she told him overcame
him, too.

Through the valley the stream rushed on as if madly prophetic in an unknown tongue. Sometimes merely colloquial, giggling, flashing into a low laugh of sheer joy, always unintelligible, this child of the mist which came apparently out of nothing, hurried headlong to the limitless sea. Beyond its gamut of musical tones that expressed so often for those who listened the moods which most moved them, moods for which there were no words, was now an undertone and now an overtone of mystery, as if in the course of geological ages the river had learned something of eternity which it was trying to reverberate amid the stones.

"Does it understand?" whispered Maria. "No," said Denis, "but we hear."

The next day she was at the springs with Don Luis again. Denis had ridden off headlong at night for Marseilles. He would be back again as soon as he could arrange a passage for America and horses for the trip down. The next time his light burned in the window she was to leave the château, come over to the farm, and they would be gone. That would give them at least six hours' start, even a full day probably. It would take the marquis some time at best to discover which way they had gone. The mayor could also be counted upon temporarily to put him on the wrong track. In the meantime the days passed swiftly. It was now the end of August.

Maria received one letter from Denis. There was a ship sailing from Marseilles for New Orleans the second Monday in September. He had arranged a cabin on board for "his wife and maid." So it was finally settled that Lucia was to go. "I shall be back on the night of the third. Watch!" Maria packed a few things in a small bag, not forgetting the little madonna. Lucia with the aid of her mistress wrote a long letter. She would never see her parents again. Both women wept. The calendar slipped over into September.

On the first Don Luis rode horseback to the springs and felt the better for it. It was with some difficulty that Maria persuaded him to allow her to follow in the coach instead of riding with him. On the second she was still trying to be gay outwardly with the wives of the invalids at the spa. On the morning of the third she sat alone in one of the pavilions half distracted with anxiety. Would they return in time to meet Denis? If not, what then?

Don Luis sat all that morning with the water above his knees. Over a small iron table set in a shallow part of the pool he and M. d'Ayen indulged in a hand of loo while the bubbles came up through their toes. The place was hot, the cards stuck to the damp table, and the game progressed slowly. The duke was a dabbler in chemistry and began to discuss the properties of the waters, the history of the baths, water clocks, time measure, classical music, and the opera of which he was a devotee. He was known as an "amiable conversationalist." Opera was a pet aversion of the marquis'.

The morning thus wore away rapidly in a spirited discussion as to whether or not opera could be regarded as a separate art. According to Don Luis opera was a mere pot-pourri of music, painting, and bad drama. The libretto was a poor fly of poetry buzzing in the transparent web of the plot. D'Ayen on the other hand maintained that, given a fine performance with great artists, all the arts employed blent into a unity of effect which in itself was unique in artistic experience. The degree of beauty, because it was compounded from so many sources, was the greatest known. Theories of aesthetics were thus involved.

M. d'Ayen had started to explain his own at great length when Lucia appeared at the railing and announced that it was long past the hour of luncheon. Madame had been waiting in the pavilion outside and was faint. The two rose from the water and hastened to dress. They were much pleased with each other. It was not to have been expected that at a place like Royat such a morning of talk could be found. They met at the door going out with mutual compliments. Maria was still seated in the pavilion some little way down the path. The duke looked at her keenly.

"Monsieur is not only to be congratulated on his present wonderful recovery but for an event of the future, I see. Allow me to anticipate the usual felicitations. There is a certain expression of the face in women, you know! I happen to be familiar with it. Tomorrow, then. We shall finish our discussion?"

"I hope so!" replied Don Luis so emphatically that the other bowed. "Au revoir."

Don Luis turned to his wife.

That these remarks had greatly disturbed him, he could not deny. He studied her carefully as she came toward him. She flushed under his steady and appraising glance. But the marquis was not so simple as to suppose that every blush was a confession of guilt. With her heightened colour, standing in a simple gown under the shade of the trellis she appeared more beautiful to him than he had ever known her. How mature she had grown! That was all, he thought with relief, a little more mature. Doubtless d'Ayen thought himself as great an authority on women as on the opera. He had felt angry with him for a moment. Yet the remark had been well meant. He now forgave him. How much—how much he wished it were *true*. Well . . .

"What were you two talking about so long?" she said. "I am nearly dead with hunger sitting here. Was it a religious discussion?"

"Hardly that, my dear," said he, "although M. d'Ayen did venture to assume the rôle of prophet and foretell a miracle. By the aid of man it may come true." He took her arm and held it closely. They walked up on the terrace together and had lunch. They were returning to the château that night.

On the way home that evening the marquis galloped on ahead of the coach like a veritable cavalier. The regimen at the springs had made him vigorous again. What with a careful diet, no liqueurs after supper, the hot water, and exercise regularly adhered to for many weeks, he was not only recovered but actually felt younger than he had for years. A good bout with the foils tomorrow would have been pleasant to anticipate. How he missed that! When he arrived home he would have his old fencing-master up from the garrison at Florence. That raising of the hilt that seemed to lower the point, the fatigued retreat, and the sudden clever rally; that was a movement worth knowing. And the fellow had other tricks in his bag that he could teach as well. Like a good pedlar he had always one more.

Don Luis galloped up to the château a mile ahead of the coach and dismounted with a spring. He hurried to his room, and calling the valet had himself shaved for the second time that day. It was already past the usual hour for dinner before his wig was properly adjusted. A white satin suit with gold frogs and lacing caused him to glitter under the chandeliers and candlelight.

To Maria, who had been awaiting him for some time, his now almost jovial presence seemed to pervade the room. She could scarcely bring herself to realize that this was to be the last meal with him. There was now an assurance and robustness in his mien and gestures, a certain sardonic vigour in his locution that made it seem impossible she should ever dare to think of casting him off. Yet even as the courses proceeded she knew that Lucia was putting the last things for the journey that night in her servant's reticule. It must be small enough to go on a pillion, Denis had said. They would ride as far as Issoire tonight and take coach at three in the morning. She thought of him waiting for her now at the farm and the colour leaped to her face and her heart began to beat strangely. Ah, tomorrow, and tomorrow, and tomorrow!

Don Luis was saying something to her. She became aware now that he was also looking at her piercingly, that he must have been doing so during her entire reverie. Her heart seemed to empty itself and become dry. Far off she heard him saying: "After you have retired tonight dismiss the maid. Tell her to go to her own room and not to disturb you till morning. Do not be alarmed," he said, taking her hand which was stone cold, "you will not be sleeping alone."

The supper proceeded in silence. She ate nothing. Don Luis gradually became angry. He had expected some shrinking, perhaps. But his wife's face over the candles was now a clear, transparent white, and he found himself looking into a pair of eyes so shadowed with an agony of fear that they reminded him of a dying deer's. He had often cut their throats that way—after the chase was over. This one was. He smiled.

As she left the room, he leaned forward in his chair to watch her. She turned as usual at the door to say good night, then stood there as if in a daze. "Remember," he said in his peculiar way.

His mind flashed back to the last time he had said that to her, in the coach just before their arrival here. That young captain! The remark of M. d'Ayen recurred to him again. He started uneasily. "No, no, impossible! Nothing had occurred at Versailles!" But he sat thinking. Pierre waited silently to remove the glasses. Finally he poured out some more wine. But the marquis sat abstracted. Unconsciously he played with his coffee spoon. A certain grim tenseness began to lift the black tuft of his beard and tighten the lines of his close-shaven jaws. Finally his teeth clicked and his mouth took on the appearance of a closed trap. "Pierre," said he, turning around upon the man almost violently.

"Monsieur!" said the man startled.

"Send Sancho to me immediately. I shall be in my own room."

A few minutes later that worthy knocked at his master's door. The voice of the marquis could be heard within for some moments giving earnest and emphatic instructions. At the end of that time the servant reappeared. Holding a candle before his curious countenance, the man walked down the corridor with a light noiseless tread. As he did so his animal-like shadow sneaked after him along the wall.

Once beyond the paralysing presence of her husband, Maria's first impulse was to flee immediately. She came up the stairs on the wings of fear and sped to her room. Had the maid been there they might have left instantly and have been gone into the night. But Lucia had gone to supper. As Maria closed the door calling her, and no answer came, an access of terror and trembling overcame her and she was forced for a moment to sit down. The dim light of one candle left burning before the mirror on the dresser served only to deepen the gloom of walls and curtains, and the young girl saw her haggard face peering at her from the glass with an expression of horror. The absence of Lucia, upon whom she was so dependent, temporarily deprived Maria of will power. She felt it impossible to leave without her. At any moment Lucia might return. But the thought that at any moment Don Luis also might appear made her sick and faint.

A low cry escaped her and she gasped. Her state of indecision was more than she could sustain. At last she seized the bell tassel and pulled it violently. But Lucia did not answer. A conviction of fatality amounting to despair overcame Maria. Then she rallied. Without Lucia then!

For a moment she was all activity.

She seized the candle and rushing to the window held it there waiting beat by beat of her pulses for an answering light. But there was no light whatever at the farm. Where was Denis? Not in his room! Perhaps he was already waiting at the cross-roads below the farm with the horses. Hardly yet, though. It was still early and they were not to leave the château till after midnight.

No, she knew he was not waiting at the cross-roads. That was the desperate prompting of false hope. It had all been *so* well understood. They were to go to the farm and leave from there. In no other way could the horses be so well concealed. And they were to change into their new clothes there before the fire, and ride off. It was all so easy. But he had promised to answer the last night—not till later, of course. If she could only make him see now! Where was he? She waved the candle to and fro excitedly. It went out. In the darkness she stood pressing her forehead to the window. Above the edge of the hill where the farm loomed darkly came only the cold glitter of stars.

Nevertheless, she could not stay here. She lit the candle again with shaking hands. Then she hastily tore open the bag which Lucia had packed and extricating from it the statue of the madonna and a dark riding cloak, she threw the latter over herself concealing her white dress. The bag was now nearly empty and seemed to gape at her widely. Then she tiptoed to the door, opened it gently, listened, and stepped out.

The long, gloomy corridor was empty. Except for the slight beam of light through her own keyhole and a thin radiance from either end of the hall it was almost black. At regular intervals the tall, white, locked doors of the château guest chambers glimmered duskily like the portals of so many vaults. She hesitated. To her left the corridor led to the main staircase of the château; to the right to the servants' stairs. It was from these two stairways that the light glimmered up at either end.

Pierre would have locked the front door by now, and the marquis' room was in that direction. She might meet him coming up! Her scalp crept at the thought. She had never been in the servants' wing, but they were probably quiet now. She might slip out that way. She might still find Lucia there. At any rate *he* was not that way. She turned to the right and crept slowly and softly down the corridor holding the small shrine in her arms like a doll. Presently she found herself by the railing of the servants' stairs. From a lamp placed on a table in the hall below a faint glow was cast upward throwing grotesque shadows. Very carefully she peeped over. The stairs were circular and it appeared to her that she was looking down a deep well with a lantern at the bottom.

She put her foot on the first tread and started to descend noiselessly. Then she was arrested in mid-air by the sound of a yawn and a scraping noise. She looked down through the banisters. Curled up in the shadow on the last step was Sancho. He was scratching himself under the arm with a peculiarly persistent motion. His head with the curious, dark grey tufts behind his ears was now and then projected into the light and she caught a green glint from his eyes. No mouse ever crept back more stealthily into the shadow than Maria. So that was why Lucia did not come! There could be no doubt about it. The man was watching. She must get back to her room instantly.

But it was not so easy to find. There were many doors down the long corridor. She started trying the handles. In her desperate haste she must have passed her own. Somehow she was too far down toward the main hall. She must go back, be methodical, and miss none. She listened for an instant. Someone was coming up the big stairs. She turned scarcely able to stifle a scream. She saw a candle-glow through the keyhole of the next room. She opened her own door, and darted in. For one second only she stood in the faint light before she closed the door softly. She even remembered not to let the latch click.

For a few instants excitement sustained her and cleared her mind. For the first time in her life her movements became precise and of lightning rapidity. She tore the cloak off, wrapped the statue in it, thrust the bundle into the open bag, and the bag under the bed. Gathering three candlesticks from her stand and dresser she placed them in the window. She lit them from the one already kindled and threw that into the fireplace. Then she turned facing the door with her back to the wall against a long yellow curtain. Her hands were clasped behind her. For an entire minute no one came. It was that delay which at last shattered her.

Don Luis had turned into the corridor just as Maria was closing the door. Against the opposite wall he had seen a dim square of light and a shadow there like that of a cloaked woman carrying a child. It vanished like a spectre. Don Luis was carrying a candle himself. The hall beyond was dark, silent. He could not be certain. It was a very old house. He was not superstitious. But he was sufficiently startled to stop where he was for a full minute. Then he too saw the ray of light from the keyhole of his wife's room. A solution

of the spectre dawned upon him. He strode forward angrily and
flung open the door. . . .

While the marquis had for a moment been stayed by a shadow,
Denis three leagues away at Le Crest was knocking persistently and
hallooing at the door of a blacksmith who presently stuck a frowsy
head through an upstairs window and inquired with sleepy insolence
what was wanted. A short interchange of views on the subject of
shoeing horses at night decided the point of whether the smith should
come down or wait for the gentleman to come up and fetch him at
the point of a pistol. Under the double impetus of threats and promised rewards the man made what he considered to be haste. Monsieur
meant business, there was no doubt about it! But it was almost an
hour before the fellow could blow up his fire, take the shoe off the
foot which had gone lame, and fit a new one. Denis watched the man
working over the cherry-coloured iron while the time passed mercilessly. In his terrible anxiety the dark shed seemed like a prison
chamber and the smith some black-browed jailer who was about to
put him to the question. Would he, when the iron was thrust into
him, be able to remain firm? He was half dead with fatigue as it was.
The smith passed close to him with the sizzling metal and he felt the
heat through his sleeve and flinched. "How much pain could a man
stand before he would tell?" he wondered. Tired and nervous as he
was, he felt how weak he might be. He roused himself. He had
almost gone to sleep. Solange had gone lame early that afternoon.
He was hours late. Tossing the man a full day's wage, he spurred
out of the town striking sparks from the cobbles. . . .

Don Luis stepped through the door and looked at his wife standing
with her back to the wall. Her attitude was so tragic, her background
of the yellow curtain with the three candles burning in the window so
theatrical, that he thought for a moment she was staging a scene.
He drew a chair up between his knees with the back before him and
sat regarding her.

"The illumination I take it is in honour of the event?" Her lips
moved but no words followed. "I cannot say I ever heard so ringing
a line," he sneered. "Come, come, don't you think this is rather a
cold welcome for your husband? The Muse of Tragedy, the three
lamps, curtain and all. Magnificent! But—considering the scene to
follow—aren't you perhaps a little over-costumed? I expected to find
you in bed."

Her eyes rested on him for an instant like those of an accused
person seeing the state tormentor approach for the first time. He
became aware that there was no art in this. He was looking at the
face of terror in nature. Why was it?

"Come here!" he said softly.

She flattened herself against the wall as if waiting for him to spring. It was provocative. A gust of fury lifted him from the chair. With one stroke he ripped her gown from neck to heel. She clung desperately to the curtain. It came away, falling over both of them. The candles wavered. He had not expected her to fight him. She cried out once bitterly. He wrapped her head and arms in the curtain, and stripped her like an Indian husking maize. Then he carried her to the bed and threw her down there. She had ceased struggling now. She did not know anyone could be so strong. She felt and looked like a bird blown on to a ship by a hurricane. Her breast rose and fell quickly, but at intervals. Between breaths she lay as if dead. Only her eyelids quivered.

The last vestige of pity had vanished from the breast of Don Luis. His wig had been torn off and he had happened to see himself in the glass while he was struggling with Maria. So this was the dignified approach to the marriage bed he had so fondly planned! Marriage bed? He looked at her lying under the shadow of the canopy. It was quite dark in that end of the room. He crossed to the window and taking one of the candles came back and stood beside her. Holding it above his head so that the yellow light washed over the pale body of the girl, he studied her carefully for some time. Then with a terrific imprecation he dashed the light to the floor. The two candles remaining on the sill continued to burn softly.

Presently she became aware that he was sitting on the bed beside her. She opened her eyes slightly and saw that her own hands were completely lost in his. His huge fingers curved around her arm again reminded her of the paw of some monumental lion. He was holding her hands so gently though that she almost felt sorry for him. A little harder now. She opened her eyes as the clasp became firmer and found herself looking into his very close to her face. She felt him breathe.

"His name?" said Don Luis whose grasp now began to hurt her. She looked at him again and bit her lip. Her fingers began to ache intolerably.

"His name?" repeated her husband.

She closed her eyes and braced herself. Her hands now seemed on fire. She lost all sense of anything except the intolerable pain that began to shoot up her arms to her shoulders. Had the pain been less she might have answered, but her whole mind was now preoccupied with it. The reiterated demand of the insistent voice became only a senseless buzz. Then she fainted.

Don Luis had not meant to carry it quite as far as that. He dashed water in her face. It startled him to see the print of his own fingers on hers, which she kept contracting spasmodically. Finally he bathed

them in a bowl of cold water. At that she came to, but remained in a
kind of daze. She was now lying as if not only her hands but her
entire body had been crushed in his grasp. Indeed, from that moment on he never saw her in any other attitude. Those masterful
hands had done their work more thoroughly than he intended.

He sat down and began to ponder. A long time passed. He was
annoyed with himself for having allowed his rage to reduce him to so
rudimentary a procedure. He had forgotten how fragile youth was.
How sensitive he had been as a boy! Pshaw! That was a long time
ago now. Well, he had forgotten. He looked at her again. The
cold of the hours before dawn was beginning to penetrate the chamber. He started to cover her with the counterpane, but paused. She
was like the living dream, the pale counterfeit of which the sculptor
occasionally detains in stone. By that body he intended to have an
heir. What had happened should not swerve him from his goal.
Also, it would be the most exquisite revenge possible. He would bide
his time. In the meantime—this thing which she held from him?
He could arrange about that! Don Luis covered her up as if putting
something away for safe keeping. He sat down again and in a calm,
methodical manner perfected his new plans. There was only one link
still missing in a carefully welded chain. Even the pressure of his
hands had not been able to forge that, as yet. But patience! There
were other more subtle ways.

Toward morning she grew feverish and sat up. Her eyes did not
seem to see anything in the room. She choked and clutched her
throat. He began to fan her. Then he threw open the window. It
was almost dawn and deathly silent. Suddenly as if a drum were
beating, the sound of hoofs at a furious gallop came in a sharp staccato over the fields. "Denis, Denis!" cried Maria, and fell back on
the pillow. "Ah!" said Don Luis exhaling a long breath.

Denis galloped into the courtyard of the farm, threw a blanket over
his trembling horse, and rushed to his window. In the upstairs room
of the château he saw two candles. They burned steadily. So all
his haste had been in vain then. Something had interfered. Well,
he would hear from Lucia tomorrow. There was no message yet or
Honneton would have given it to him. Whatever it was he would
soon know. Probably a late return from the springs had interfered.
He lay back for an instant on his bed without taking off his boots and
was instantly asleep. Since morning he had ridden long leagues.

CHAPTER SEVEN

THE FLY WALKS IN

VERY early next morning the coach drew up before the door of the château and the two footmen began loading luggage. Don Luis sat in the library writing a letter of fervent appreciation to his friend the Comte de Besance. He could see the two footmen strapping on the leather trunks and putting bags in the hampers. Presently Lucia with a white, scared face ran down with something that had evidently been overlooked. It was a small, black bag which she hurriedly put in the coach. At her appearance Sancho stuck his nose in the air and began to whistle softly. She gave him a vindictive look and went back. The marquis' pen marched rapidly.

Not only have I to thank you, dear friend, for the hospitality of your delightful roof which conceals, as I have discovered, an excellent cellar, but for the restoration of my health. I am now entirely recovered. At this moment I could take a creditable part in an affair of honour, nor do I mean as a second, or with pistols.

All that you claimed for your springs here at Royat was true. Their effect upon me has been one of rejuvenation. Indeed, I am almost superstitious about them. I am forced to attribute even to their vicinity a life-invoking quality.

Our stay here would have been even longer had not my wife, whom you so much admired, unfortunately dislocated one of the small joints in her finger which will probably require the attentions of a chirurgeon. One of that profession I hope will be found at the first large town on our way down.

We pass by Marseilles to Florence, but leisurely. I have purchased four magnificent horses from your neighbour M. de Polignac and we shall make as many detours as we list, thus seeing much of your beautiful country. I am in no haste. Do not, I pray you, concern yourself unduly about madame. The accident is a slight one and will soon be remedied.

He closed the letter with a host of salutations and a flourished signature, sanded it, sealed it, and rang for Pierre.

"Send this to Paris by the count's agent. I understand he leaves

81

with the rents shortly? Good! He will travel faster than the post, I think."

"Yes, monsieur. May I say," said Pierre respectfully, "that I . . . that *we* regret monsieur is leaving so soon. He has been most generous."

"It is only on account of this accident to madame that we are hastened. Otherwise we should have stayed some days longer. You have been very attentive. I have said so in my letter to M. de Besance." Pierre looked relieved and pleased.

It was not the intention of the marquis to have any but the best rumours of his visit at the Château de Besance emanate to the world. Even the man he had caned now considered himself lucky. No one but Lucia knew anything of what had occurred through the summer or of the night before. "And I am keeping her with madame!" thought the marquis. "It will be a pity if anything leaks out." He smiled sardonically at Pierre disappearing with the letter to M. de Besance.

Don Luis opened the window and called to Sancho. Some conversation in a low tone took place between them after which the marquis handed him the gold-headed walking stick which he no longer needed, his sword, his great coat, and a small strong box to put in the coach. He then walked upstairs and saw Maria and Lucia down to the door. No words were exchanged between them. The suggestion of something doll-like had again returned to Maria. She walked like a marionette. Even to herself her life seemed only a semblance and her actions corresponded. They were both apathetic and mechanical. As she passed between the lines of bowing servants at the door many of them noted how pale she looked. The face of Lucia was more anxious than the slight sling in which her mistress carried one hand might seem to warrant. Don Luis saw to it that Lucia had no opportunity to explain.

"Au revoir, monsieur le marquis, grand merci et bon voyage," cried the servitors, genuinely sorry at the departure of a guest who had proved so liberal. "Adieu," replied the marquis with the ghost of a smile. He helped his wife into the coach lifting her under the arms. Then he took his sword from the seat, buckled it on, and climbed in. Lucia followed. The footman folded up the little stairs. "Ready, your Excellency?"

Don Luis grasped one side of the seat firmly and waved his hat out of the window. There was a report like a pistol from the whip of Sancho. The four horses started forward so violently that the front seat upon which Don Luis had motioned the two women to seat themselves was nearly drawn out from under them. A silent "Oh" formed itself upon the lips of Maria. She caught an amused gleam in her husband's eye. "It will be hard on the harness. Fortunately it is new and strong." Lucia broke out weeping. "Leave off that!" said Don Luis fingering his cane. The woman turned deathly white and swallowed her sobs.

Don Luis was like an old general who after taking all the necessary care to bring a campaign to a successful issue had been betrayed to the enemy by his adjutant. His surprise and defeat had consequently been complete. But he was also a general who never abandoned the field. Annihilation was the only way to deal with him, as it was his own method whether in advance toward or retreat from an enemy. He was now seemingly in retreat after disaster. But what might have seemed to the ordinary man an irretrievable misfortune was to him merely a blow of fate to be circumvented, or even taken advantage of in any direction that remained.

Sitting by his wife's bedside the night before, the furnace of his soul had burnt at white heat under the enormous pressure of a will that never relaxed. The result of this incandescence was a hard, clear diamond of unadulterated hate at the core of his being. Such jewels are rare as the moulds which produce them. With them a few names have been etched permanently on the window panes of the house of fame. Don Luis' diamond was for private use only.

His original purpose of enjoying Maria and of having an heir on her body remained unaltered. Indeed, it was now fixed, in the diamond, as it were. The elements of pleasure had merely been transmuted. His enjoyment would now be that of hate instead of love. This fixity of purpose had been announced to himself the night before when he had looked into the glass the second time and put his wig back into place. What had been put askew by emotional circumstance was now rearranged. The wig did not at first feel the same as before, but it looked it. No one would ever know, presently not even the man who wore it.

While adjusting his wig Don Luis had also readjusted circumstances. This he had done to his own satisfaction. Every revolution of the wheels of the coach, he imagined, was still taking him toward his goal. It remained merely to dispose of the contents of the vehicle and to ward off possible interference from the outside.

About a half mile beyond the château the coach was overtaken by Maria's little dog which had been left behind. In the extremity of the departure she had not even remembered it. Having seen its mistress enter the coach it had followed as fast as its short legs would permit. As the vehicle lumbered up a short hill, the dog appeared, barking and whining. It kept leaping for the iron step and falling off. In hopes the wheel would take care of it in a natural way, Don Luis sat for some time ignoring it. Seeing, however, that it would surely follow them through the next village, at the top of the hill he opened the door. Maria could not keep from calling it.

With a supreme effort the animal again made the step and started to wriggle into the coach, wagging its tail. With tremendous force the marquis closed the door on its back. The one sharp cry that pierced the morning expressed so well for Maria her own agony that she remained passive. The coach was now moving too swiftly downhill for the footmen to leave. They expected it to stop at the bottom on account of the dog but in this they were disappointed. Sancho evidently had his instructions. Over the worst ruts and cobbles, through the long white villages, past the low, truncated hills covered with vineyards they rushed southward into the valley of the Allier. The whip cracked and the splendid horses leaped. The two men behind hung on grimly to their straps. The two women on the small front seat shot from side to side and collided with each other. Don Luis sat back in the deep, rose-coloured upholstery and hummed an air from Italian opera. As M. d'Ayen would have phrased it, from one of those "perfect scenes." Occasionally he treated himself to a pinch of Batavian snuff.

When Denis finally awoke the sun was high and streaming into the room. He was still staring up at the ceiling with his body flung across the bed and his booted feet on the floor just as he had gone to sleep. He found himself stiff and unrefreshed. In the hard boots in which they had been encased for nearly two days his feet were chafed and sore. It was some time before he could recollect himself. As soon as he did so he went out to find the farmer.

It was the beginning of the grape harvest and his host was at a neighbour's farm some distance away helping to tread out the first vat. It was almost an hour before he and the boy who had been sent to find him returned. Maître Honneton seemed surly at having been thus interrupted. He stood gloomily before Denis. His bare ankles where they protruded above his long sabots were dyed a rich, red purple as if he had been treading in blood.

"Monsieur sent for me?"

"The message that came this morning!" said Denis eagerly.

"Message? But there was no message, monsieur."

"What! Are you sure? Didn't the maid bring one?"

"No, monsieur, and if it was to come from the château, surely monsieur knows that the marquis and his family have left."

"Left? Gone!" cried Denis all in a breath. "Why didn't you tell me? You mean they have driven off to the springs?" His voice rose with hope as this easy solution occurred to him.

"No, no, monsieur, by the road to Issoire, very early this morning. From the vineyards we saw them pass with all the luggage strapped on. There were small-trunks on the roof. It was for a journey. They are gone."

"Oh, why, why didn't you tell me?" Denis kept asking. Maître Honneton had not thought it necessary. Monsieur had left no instructions. He knew Denis was tired after so long a journey. He had heard him return late.

They walked back to the farm together while the good man's apologies continued to flow. Distracted as he was, Denis could not help but be touched by his simple solicitude. He sat down by the well-curb for a moment to gather his wits.

He was tired, desperately tired. The trip to Marseilles had nearly done him out. There had been a thousand arrangements to make; the ship, the relays of horses. They should be on their way by now. The mare's going lame yesterday had ruined it all. And that signal of two candles last night! What had that meant? To leave without a word to him—it looked bad. The disappointment and anxiety added to his fatigue made him feel sick. And he had slept all those precious hours away! God! he must do something. Not sit here like a fool. He took the mare from the stable. At any other time her gentle protests at being saddled when still footsore and weary would have touched him to the heart. Now he pulled the saddle girth tighter and swore. Honneton stood looking on blankly. He scarcely knew monsieur. "He who had been so debonair."

Denis ran to his room for his sword and pistols. He renewed the priming. One curtain he noticed was blowing out of her window at the château. It seemed to be waving him farewell. He knew he would never see this place again. He took his things out into the courtyard and mounted. Pressing a purse into the hand of the farmer, he said, "Remember, should anyone ever ask about me, you know nothing." He clasped the man's hand warmly. The sadness of all farewells came upon them both. What had he done that as the man's hand left his own Denis seemed to have lost touch with life! He felt older and alone. He rode down over the slope.

It had rained the night before and there was a pool by the gate. As the mare passed she left one footprint. The water and sand began to fill it in. Maître Honneton stood looking down at it. Presently the faint, smiling curve of the horseshoe disappeared. The man hefted the weight of the purse in his hand with satisfaction. Here was something tangible. "But how long would even that last?"

With the motion of the horse and the fresh breeze in his face Denis began to recover his powers of decision. A thought struck him. "Perhaps the marquis had remained at the château and sent the

two women on ahead." If so, he had better find out. He turned the
head of the mare toward the towers. Then as he came to the cross-
roads where the way branched to the south he saw the broad tracks
of the well-known wheels. For a moment he was at a loss. The wheel
tracks drew him like a magnet. He took after the coach and hesitated no longer.

So far he had seemed in a dream. Now he was thoroughly awake.
His entire nature responded to the need for action. Only in action
could he find relief. Who had blundered? Had she? Lucia? What
had happened? He must know! Solange felt the spurs and loped on,
in the opposite direction but along the same road over which she had
galloped so furiously the night before. She was still slightly lame.
No matter, what was a horse to him now?

At the top of the hill he found the dog by the road. At first he
thought the coach had passed over it, but as he looked down at it,
shaken by a tempest of memories, something in its forlorn attitude
caused him to dismount and examine the little animal. How that un-
responsive thing had once welcomed him and quivered at his touch!
At hers! But the coach had not passed over it. It was not crushed!
Yet what an attitude, not fit to be seen! He began to kick a hole in
the bank with his boot. Presently he forced himself to pick the thing
up. Its back had been broken. By a blow, a cane! Whose, he thought
he knew. His mind obligingly presented him with a scene. Murmuring something which choked him he covered the puppy up. The hollow bank caved in and he stamped the turf down. He was surprised
to find how rage weakened him. His knees trembled as he swung into
the saddle.

What a fool he had been! He cursed himself. He had been too
careful. He should have taken time by the bridle and ridden off with
Maria two months ago. He might have known what kind of a man
he was dealing with in Don Luis. Well, he knew now. Yet, would
she have gone with him at first after all? Ah, the enchanted forest,
the magic pool by the mill, that day on the hill! It was springtime
in this volcanic country that had detained them. They had been bewitched. The thought of her in his arms swept away regrets. It was
an answer even to his self-reproaches. At worst he had tried to plan
too well. But what *had* happened?

He hoped to find them at Issoire but they had passed through hours
before. This brought him to himself again. He must husband his
own strength and that of his horse. He saw to her himself; unsad-
dled her, gave her a rest. He took a cup of wine and forced himself to eat. Through the afternoon he nursed the mare along with a
hundred little attentions that a cavalryman knows. He walked up the
hills, loosened the girth, rubbed her down, gave her a little water

carefully. It was now near sunset and the wheel tracks, those broad unmistakable tracks, still led forward relentlessly. It was a problem of one tired horse and a heavy man against four tired horses and a heavy coach. At last he topped a rise from which several miles of country beyond could be seen. The mare stood with her head hanging down while Denis looked eagerly ahead. The road was empty and led straight away for some distance. Then it disappeared amid clumps of trees, the remains of a wood. Fatigue and disappointment overcame him.

———————————

It was just after sunset when the coach at Don Luis' command pulled up before an inn. It had been passing through a deserted strip of country for some time; for the last mile or so between isolated clumps of trees that were gradually closing in to form a wood. The long, rambling buildings of the inn with smoke and sparks pouring out of the chimney against the darkness of the forest beyond was the only habitation they had seen for some time. Don Luis regarded it with evident satisfaction and sent a man for the innkeeper. When that worthy appeared the marquis stepped out of the coach and proceeded to arrange matters to suit himself.

He saw Maria and Lucia upstairs into a room overlooking the courtyard. He gave it a brief inspection, and remarking that supper would follow shortly, locked the door, pocketed the key, and walked downstairs. He held a short, emphatic conversation with the innkeeper, but in a voice which was too low to be overheard either by the servants or the lonely young guest in the worn garb of a curé who sat by the fire turning a capon on the spit. Greeting the curé with the respect for the Church which a Spanish upbringing made instinctive, Don Luis returned to the courtyard.

Sancho had already driven in and was preparing to feed his horses when Don Luis approached him. The master and man talked together earnestly while a number of heads appeared at various windows and loungers at the doors. The curious little man with the tail was already causing comment. Then to the surprise of the onlookers he mounted the lead horse, swung the coach in a circle, and drove off up the road toward the forest. Don Luis returned and sat down by the fire. The young priest was just taking the fowl from the spit as he entered.

"Monsieur will do me the great favour of sharing with me?" he asked. "It is a gift from one of my flock and if shared with a stranger will make a truly Christian feast." The man smiled and arranged a bowl of salad and a cup of wine invitingly. The accent of a gentleman and the face of a youthful ascetic allured Don Luis. He thought he knew the type. He would see if he had been correct—there

was time yet—and he sat down. The simple feast proceeded. To Don
Luis' surprise so did the conversation.

He was a young man who evidently knew something of the great
world and had enjoyed it, yet he had bound himself out as a parish
priest in this remote spot. Who was he? Don Luis wondered. Influence might have done better for him than this. But the priest was
now talking of his parishioners, unconsciously answering the questions
which the marquis could not ask. The annals of his quiet neighbourhood lived and took on a pastoral form; peasants, and his life among
them, became an idyll of primitive Christianity. "Such a delightful
homily," thought Don Luis, "would make the man's fortune at court,
an antique style." And how the man's face lit up as he spoke of his
poor. But he was not asking for money. He was pleading that men
of our rank—the "our" slipped out unconsciously—should follow
Christ and come down and help their brethren. "Then they would
know what the love of God meant, because they would feel as Our
Lord had felt in his own heart. So they would be like him."

Don Luis felt himself comfortable despite the man's earnestness.
The sermon was therefore a triumph. He also caught himself thinking that he would not care to hear a rebuke from the curé's earnest lips.

"It is not liberty about which the philosophers are all talking that
men need," the young priest was saying. "Even fraternity is not
enough. That is an idea. It must be a feeling, love. Love of each
for his neighbour. Love, I say, kindled by God. That will make us
equal. That will raise us all at the same time into one highest rank."

"And the Church and State when we are all of the same rank—
what will become of them?" asked Don Luis. He had heard of men
like this. The times were uneasy. The priest's face lit with the reflected glow of the millennium. For a moment it seemed near. "The
Church will then be universal and there will be no need for the State.
God will be our king."

The Marquis pondered and took a pinch of snuff. By God, he
would have to feed the starving then! The women upstairs must be
hungry. This religious glow had made him forget them. He rose
and listened. From some distance up the road came the sound of a
trotting horse.

"I trust I have not bored, monsieur," said the priest. "A thousand
pardons. I have not meant . . ."

"Not at all," said Don Luis, "quite the contrary." He gave the
man a reassuring smile. "But I have cause to think that the person
approaching may be a former acquaintance of mine whom I may wish
to avoid. If monsieur the curé would be so kind as *not* to call attention to my presence?" The marquis quietly pushed his own plate
under that of the priest, and bowed.

"Certainly," said the curé with a mild look of surprise.

Don Luis retired to a dark corner opposite the chimney and sat down. Presently a horse was heard on the cobbles. Solange stood there with her head hanging down.

Denis had seen the track of the wheels where the coach had turned in, but he had also seen them still leading beyond. So he understood they had been there and had gone. He could force himself farther but not the horse. Well, he might get another horse here and press on. At least he would ask. He must rest and eat, too. He turned in and calling for the host began to question him.

The host was a glib little man. In the story which Don Luis had paid him to tell he was quite pat. Yes, the coach and persons that monsieur described had been there that afternoon but had departed about four o'clock. It was a pity. Yes, he was sure it was as long ago as that. No, there were no horses to be had until one came to St.-Pierre—four leagues! Would monsieur care to be made comfortable for the night?

Denis was not sure about that yet, but he would take supper. After that he would see. At this last disappointment, fatigue and despair descended upon him like a pall. He had not thought they were so far ahead of him. It seemed impossible. Perhaps they had left the château earlier than he thought. He opened the door and stepped into the public room.

He was too tired even to glance about the place. He stood before the fire and warmed himself. From his dark corner Don Luis inspected him closely. He saw with great satisfaction the look of fatigue and trouble on the countenance of the young man, and the fact that he now limped slightly as if his boots chafed him. He noted his long reach as Denis dragged a chair up to the chimney, and the style of his rapier. The disarming nick on the hilt did not escape him. A handsome young dog and one sufficiently difficult to deal with, he was forced to admit. At least she had had the good sense to choose a man. So this was the hero who had undertaken to provide an heir for the Marquis da Vincitata! Very quietly the possessor of that ancient title loosened his own sword in its scabbard. For something like eleven generations his family had known how, where, and when to draw. Don Luis was not going to be the exception. His cause was the best; the place was opportune.

But he was in no instant hurry. He had in fact hoped that Maria would have seen Denis from her window as he rode into the inn courtyard. In that case he had intended to tackle him on the stairs. But if that plan fell through, as it had, he intended to detain him at the inn and take his measure exactly as he was doing now. But there was something more than this. A certain element of the spider in Don

Luis permitted him to enjoy vastly the opportunity of sitting back in his dark corner and watching the fly walk in. Thoroughly a Latin, he was not only an actor in, but an author-spectator of his own drama. Circumstances were now collaborating with him to his huge satisfaction.

The priest meanwhile noticed the haggard look upon the features of the newcomer. The young cure was already familiar with misery in all its various guises. He was aware that the young man across the fire from him was in great agony of soul. He longed to comfort him, but the inimical and secret presence of his recent guest effectually restrained him. Naturally sensitive, and by contact with the primal substratum of life unconsciously, if not preternaturally aware of the atmosphere attending emotion, the room to the good cure had suddenly become unbearably tense. He felt as if he were sitting waiting for an execution. So strong was this irrational feeling that he began to reason himself out of it.

Of all this Denis was totally oblivious. So far a reasonable hope had buoyed him up. But his mind and his body had now sunk temporarily into a lethargy. The comfortable warmth of the embers made his fatigue more apparent to himself, and yet relaxed him. Supper was long in coming. His eyelids began to droop despite the efforts of his will. To keep himself from being overtaken by oblivion he called for wine. There was set before him a clear glass decanter containing a liquid alleged to be burgundy. He removed the stopper and held the bottle up to the light suspiciously. Instantly he saw a red liquid sphere through which drifted, tumbling and eddying, shifting clouds of sediment. There was a certain hypnotic effect about thus gazing into those bloody depths which, tired as he was, his mind did not instantly overcome. For some seconds he continued to gaze with a blank expression. It was only for an instant or so but—

Through the wine a figure seemed to grow and advance upon him. An oval pot-shaped body began to shoot forth arms and legs that wriggled up and down the sides of the bottle. A face with a black horn below the mouth grinned at him. The grin expanded clear across the bottle in a devilishly implacable smile surrounded by familiar features. Denis turned with the speed of thought and dashed the contents of the bottle into the face of the man who had stolen upon him.

"Death for that," said the marquis. "You fool!"

For some seconds they stood facing each other. They heard the wine dripping onto the floor. The consternation on Denis' face faded into relieved joy. So they had *not* escaped him after all.

He laughed like a boy. "For *that*, monsieur? Are you sure?"

"Draw!" blazed Don Luis. His sword flashed.

As the steel flickered in the firelight there was a loud crash of crockery at the door and the falsetto voice of the innkeeper began to scream, "Not in the house, messieurs; messieurs, for the love of God, not in the house!" He ran back into the court crying for help where a babblement arose while the wreck of Denis' supper smoked on the threshold.

"For the love of God, not anywhere," cried the priest, rising up now and laying hold of Don Luis' sword arm. Thus beset and hindered, the marquis beside himself with rage stood choking. The wine trickled down his face and bubbled on his lips as he strove to speak.

"It is useless to try to interfere, father," said Denis in a calm dry tone. "You must have seen the insult which monsieur has just received from me."

"The edicts, the ordinance of 'twenty-three! Have a care, gentlemen!" cried the priest.

The marquis shook the man off with some difficulty. Had he not been a priest he would have hurled him into the fire.

"Come," said he to Denis, "we shall settle this in the court."

Protesting, the curé followed them to the door where he remained to look on with gloomy anticipation.

It had been comparatively dark in the long, low public room, but outside there still lingered the late, white European twilight. It was that hour when the sky reflects and completely suffuses the last western rays, when very small objects in nature such as men cast no shadow at all, when a certain eeriness as of the meads of the departed settles down over buildings and landscape. The sounds of life are subdued. To some melancholy temperaments it is the most tolerable hour of the day.

In this calm light the two men in their shirt sleeves stood facing each other a few paces apart on a short space of closely cropped green near the center of the court. The litter which surrounded it marked off its limits in a roughly oval boundary. The servants and hangers-on about the inn had already crowded into the court at the cries of the landlord whose anxiety that his place would be closed for harbouring brawlers led him up until the last moment to beseech someone to interfere.

No one, however, had cared to intrude upon the two determined gentlemen who burst out of the door. The red wine upon Don Luis' face and clothes looked as if first blood had already been drawn. That more was to follow none could doubt. Doors, windows, wheelbarrows, dunghills, and other points of vantage were now at a premium.

"I think, monsieur the captain," said Don Luis in a low tone, "that under the circumstances we can omit all formalities." Denis nodded. "Since there are no seconds, do you give the word to draw, I shall simply count three and engage. The present distance is satisfactory? The end you understand?"

"Draw," said Denis.

"Monsieur the curé," cried the marquis aloud, "I call on you to witness that all is fair and understood between us here."

They fell on guard.

"One, two, three!"

Their blades rasped and hissed together. The clash of steel, the stamp of feet, and the heavy breathing of the two men filled the court-yard. There was nearly a full minute of sword play in which no very earnest attacks were made while each tried to feel out the other's school of fence.

Denis' was a simple combination of the short sword fence at which any gentleman about the court was more or less an adept, and of the onslaught and mêlée taught in barracks for the heavier military rapier. It was simple but dangerous. But there was a lack of economy in his recoveries and a waste of motion in his attacks which betrayed to the marquis that the arm behind the point which now so persistently menaced him remembered the sabre. It was upon this that he counted.

So far Don Luis had in no way betrayed himself as a subtle swords-man. To Denis' riposte and remise his counter-riposte and reprise had followed, a trifle slow Denis thought. It was that upon which *he* counted. The marquis, however, although he was no believer in the bottes secrets of the old school of fence, had learned as a boy from an ancient Spaniard, one of the last of the "Captains of Complements" de la cienca de las armas, a mathematical pedant of the sword. Nor had the supple and baffling wrist movements of the Italian school been neglected by Don Luis in his later manhood in Tuscany.

Thinking it time now to bring matters to a conclusion Denis burst upon his opponent with a furious assault, hoping by sheer speed and energy to get past the guard of the "slower" man. For a moment the air about the marquis was full of the darting tongues of Denis' sword. But to the surprise of the young man, the older by slight but deft motions of his body, which Denis had never seen before, avoided the swiftest thrusts. At the last Denis was not quite quick enough in recovering. The blood dyed his left arm from the shoulder down. To his joy, however, Don Luis now began to give ground.

An expectant gasp went up from the lookers-on.

The marquis stepped back with a peculiar motion of the feet as if they were being planted on exact chalked circles and squares, move-ments that forced Denis, if he was to continue the attack, to move to one side and the other of his opponent in order to find openings for his thrusts. For with each motion of his feet the blade of the marquis assumed the exact line which at once guarded his body and advanced his point. They had moved thus with lightning rapidity to the other end of the green before Denis realized that he was being led instead of pursuing. He must change his tactics. "God!"

He was almost exhausted . . . the long ride . . .

Suddenly the marquis straightened up from the knees and leaned forward. His left hand, so far held behind him as usual, now began to move forward as he parried, as if it too would thrust Denis' blade aside. Gathered up in, and holding a heavy cuff, this was precisely what it did.

Fence with two hands, sword and dagger, had long been forgotten in France. Denis was sure his adversary was failing and could no longer keep his balance. He rallied his own last resources and changing to a kind of half sabre cut, and half rapier thrust, endeavoured to beat down this ridiculous new guard of his enemy and to strike home. The marquis lowered his hilt and retreated swiftly.

To Denis, whose eye followed rejoicing, it seemed as if the marquis' point were falling. "So it was the end!"

He raised his own arm, unconsciously now that of a charging cavalryman wielding a sabre. The impulse to thrust left his brain. He thought his hand leapt forward. And so it did. But the sword fell out of it.

Passing one foot in front of the other as fast as the beat of a duck's wing, and at the same time lunging forward from the waist, the marquis had thrust Denis through the heart. Almost two hundred seconds had elapsed since he had counted "three."

Denis did not move. Two spinning black discs collapsed into whirling funnels of darkness in his eyes.

A blank silence for an instant held everyone in the courtyard. Then the young curé ran forward and turned Denis over on his back. He listened to his heart and a few seconds later looked up at the marquis with an expression in which the emotion of a woman and the indignation of a strong man struggled for mastery. From the upstairs windows came a long, muffled, shuddering cry. Two white, despairing hands were beating on the sill.

"Ah," said the marquis, wiping his sword, "Helen has come upon the wall to see!"

"Monsieur," said the young priest, his face turning scarlet, "God has also seen."

In the room above someone came and took the white face away from the window.

"The provocation was mortal," replied Don Luis looking at the priest as if he had suddenly remembered an unpleasant fact.

"And the sin also," said the curé, letting Denis' hand fall. Don Luis' eyes hardened.

"Monsieur, monsieur," cried the priest, rising up and facing the nobleman, " 'Thou shalt not kill!' It is you and men like you that are bringing a doom upon yourselves and your class." His face worked. "Hear me, Holy Father, I witness against this man. Hear me, ye saints . . ."

Don Luis sheathed his sword and walked away. The voice of the priest continued for some time. From the stable Solange could be heard neighing. No one had yet brought her her oats.

The courtyard had by now cleared itself as if by magic. It was some minutes before Don Luis could find the landlord, and a quarter of an hour at least before he could drive "sense" into his head. The edicts against duelling were enforced mercilessly in France. It was not the intention of Don Luis to have to fall back upon diplomatic immunity in order to avoid being hanged upside down in chains. He had other plans. He took the man roughly by the shoulder and convinced him that the less said about the matter the better. "If you want to keep your inn open, tell your people to keep their faces shut, and do likewise yourself!"

"But if there are inquiries, monsieur?"

"Refer them to the curé and hand the horse and the dead man over to him. Get him out of sight now. This is not your fault, and anyway you can do nothing about it."

The presence of the marquis' two tall footmen made this fact glaringly apparent. The innkeeper decided to make the best of a bad affair. Ten gold pieces were in his pocket; the intendant was at Clermont. Parbleu! what could a poor man do? He shrugged his shoulders.

Don Luis went upstairs. One of the footmen went out to the road and waved a lantern. Presently the jingling of harness was heard. The coach returned, made a wide circle, and drew up again before the inn.

Maria's room was almost dark. After a little Don Luis could make her out lying on the bed. Lucia crouched by her side. He called out for the man with the lantern. "We leave immediately," he said to Lucia. There was no reply. Presently the lantern came. "Take this woman and the things downstairs," he said, "and see them into the coach. Leave the lantern."

Her room seemed empty and silent now. Outside a tree stirred in the night breeze and tapped at the pane. He went to the bed and held the lantern over Maria. Looking down, he beheld her utterly bloodless face with wide, still eyes staring out of dark circles. Looking up, she saw his scarlet stained features apparently glaring out of the ceiling from a circle of light.

He set the lantern down and took her hands to raise her. Her mouth that reminded him now of his grandmother's in her coffin twitched slightly. He leaned down to listen.

"I will tell you. His name is Denis," she whispered, and went limp. He carried her to the coach.

Before the inn the bulk of the coach loomed up against the feathery background of the dark forest like a hearse with plumes. About it twinkled several lanterns. The curé and the innkeeper stood by silently as Don Luis consigned his burden to Lucia and climbed in himself. The footmen began to fold up the stairs.

"Pardon, monsieur," said the footman, "but there is blood on your face."

"Get water," said Don Luis calmly. He had forgotten. "Bring a bucket." He got out again and washed himself by the road. The young priest continued to look at him, holding his lantern so as to throw the light upon him. Don Luis was annoyed.

"Have the goodness to recollect, monsieur the curé, that this is wine not blood."

"I see blood," replied the priest.

"Where?" asked Don Luis.

"On your soul, monsieur." The curé turned on his heel and went into the inn.

Despite himself Don Luis suddenly went cold. One of the horses whinnied. From the stable came the answering neigh of the lonely mare. "Drive on, Sancho, you simpleton!" cried the marquis.

"If monsieur will get into the coach?" replied the man. It was the first time he had ever known his master to be confused. "Reason enough, too," thought Sancho. "It will be a terrible night and the horses are nearly foundered." His whip cracked viciously. "Who knows what will happen now?"

CHAPTER EIGHT

A HOLE IN THE WALL

THE coach rolled and pitched along. The road through the forest was bad and the darkness of a moonless midnight engulfed it. The two dim driving lanterns danced and swayed across the inky landscape like fox-fires. Sancho used his whip mercilessly. At St.-Pierre early next morning two of the beasts were ready to die. A wheel was strained and had to be replaced. Don Luis was forced to pause while men, women, animals, and material, as he put it, "renewed themselves." He himself was blithe. He drove a flinty bargain with the keeper of the post relays for some heavier horses. He left his own, not without apprehension, and pressed on. He was sorry for the horses.

Don Luis could not know that Denis had severed all connections, that no one would be expecting his return. He supposed that after the death of a king's officer there would sooner or later be some hue and cry. For the purely legal offence of killing a man in a duel the marquis cared nothing. At worst he could get out of it. That Denis had first dashed wine in his face might prove fortunate in case . . . He ground his teeth at the thought of explaining away his honour. A Spaniard before a foreign tribunal! His honour required that the real cause of that duel should under no circumstances ever become known.

No, he preferred to let the innkeeper, or the curé, answer questions, should there be any to answer, and to dissever himself and all that was his utterly and forever from the man he had left lying in the courtyard of the inn. As for the child that was with Maria, he would somehow take care of *that!*

After his own child came, later, he would eventually take Maria to Spain. She should live and die secluded there. In Estremadura hidalgos did not inquire after the health or happiness of one's wife. All this might take several years. In the meantime she might see reason, reconcile herself. In the meantime he had both private and diplomatic affairs to settle before leaving Italy. He intended to arrive there ostensibly in the same condition as he had set out. He had already satisfied his honour, now he would have the use of her body. It would provide him with an heir and a means of punishing her. He might even repeat it. As he thought about it he knew now that he preferred it that way. There was a certain zest. He looked across

96

the aisle at her where she lay in the arms of Lucia. She did not move. So these were the two women who had thought to play the fool with him. A fine clever pair! There was a little surprise coming to Lucia, too. He drooped his lids and smiled. Sancho was heading due east into the Montagnes du Forez.

If they looked for him at all it would be by the roads down the valley of the Allier or in the passes of the Cévennes. No one but a crazy man would take a great coach like this through the Montagnes du Forez. But at a little hamlet in the foothills they stopped and purchased mules from the charcoal burners. The smith spent the afternoon forging two heavy chains. At evening the long clouds draped themselves against the massif and crept down into the valley. The wolves howled. At dawn the coach started upward.

Sancho rejoiced as only a Spaniard can at finding himself on the back of a mule. The whip snapped damply in the morning mist. The coach advanced upward foot by foot. The torrent beside the road deepened into a dark gorge. Where a waterfall could be heard roaring below they hurled down the heavy luggage. The two footmen walked behind putting their shoulders to the spokes at especially bitter spots.

By noon the coach had disappeared from the plains below as if it had flown into the clouds. Indeed, for much of the time a grey mist actually wrapped it. Three weeks later it descended with chained wheels into the valley of the Rhône. Sancho licked his whiskers. He would be able to indulge in fresh fish and cream again. They galloped south along the post road, pausing only for relays, and trundled over the bridge into Avignon. Here the marquis was out of French territory in the enclave and had friends. One of the towers on the walls had for some ages past been used as a dwelling. An old washerwoman lived there. It tickled the marquis' fancy and suited his purpose. He sent Maria and Lucia to the turret room. In the evenings Lucia could walk on the ramparts. Sancho followed her. At night he slept by the stairs and watched.

The conscience of the Marquis da Vincitata was a curious blend of himself, particular circumstances, and the times. Had he been a simple-hearted or romantic person certain short cuts to an immediate oblivion for his recent and present difficulties might have been found available. They had, of course, occurred to him, but only that. He regarded such promptings as crude, open to possible embarrassments later on, and beneath him. In short, he was not a murderer by direct action. As far as a man could, he merely intended to shape events. It was here that his conscience came in.

Whether he was religious or only fundamentally superstitious might provide matter for argument. Probably he was a blend of both. At least he had been piously brought up. The words of the curé had therefore made an impression upon him which that good man would have been the last to credit. But as a matter of fact Don Luis already considered the "blood on his soul" as a burden. His code approved, but his religion disapproved. Thus he was able to balance one load exactly, but he would not add to the weight against him. Above all he was in both religion and ethics a child of his own class and the century in which he was born, that is, purely conventional. In his ideals of conduct any analysis of motive was lacking. Hence his actions were merely an application in unfailing practice of a technique acceptable to his equals in rank. In short, his conscience was a code of honour tempered by some fear of the supernatural. In this precarious balance hung the fate of the unborn child.

In fact the balance was so very delicate that the marquis had come to a temporary halt at Avignon merely to readjust the scales in which he had undertaken to weigh out his own justice. True, he had already given them every chance of tipping in the direction which he desired by throwing in the weight of the coach for good measures; by driving over as heartbreaking mountain roads as he could find. The results, however, had not been so satisfactory as he had hoped. At present it seemed as if Maria would lose her mind instead of the child. A demented wife was not in the scope of his plans. Hence, there was to be a sufficient interval of quiet.

The opportunity of torturing several wives and so of improving gradually upon the method, does not occur frequently to many men. Don Luis was neither a widower nor a Bluebeard, hence his method with his first wife was not above criticism. The numbing mental shock of having seen her lover done to death before her eyes was greater than the physical misery which the violent motion of the coach could confer. It was from mental shock that she had nearly succumbed, and it was here that her husband had miscalculated. The extreme physical exhaustion of the trip over the mountains in addition to what she had already suffered reduced her to a state of apathy in which for a time she could remember nothing at all.

This condition provided sufficient respite to allow Maria to survive. Left utterly alone, except for the constant and now tender ministrations of Lucia, she gradually regained a grasp on herself. Her memory returned, but with it came the strength to bear it. After some weeks went by she began to sit in a chair on the ramparts overlooking the placid landscape that sloped away from the walls of Avignon. The bravery of a great despair filled her, and she determined, as she sat feeling the babe stir within her, to match her own strength, her determination, and if need be her life, against the will that strove to possess her body and soul. Despite Don Luis, she would bring this child of her love into the world. Its future she must place in the hands of God. She could do no more. The statue of the Virgin came forth from the black bag again. Placing it in a little hole in the battlements where the coping had dropped away and made room for a flowering plant with long green leaves, she sat facing it, praying quietly through the long afternoons.

Every evening when the old woman returned to her tower she found the young girl sitting with sorrow and rapture in her face before the madonna. That Maria's sorrow was a tragedy which only heaven could heal, she understood. She pitied her. She brought her small bowls of fresh goat milk, mushrooms from the pastures beyond the walls, and wild flowers for her room. Only once was this blessed solitude interrupted—by the visit of a physician at Don Luis' behest. The kindly old man would scarcely have discovered in the subsequent proceedings of his generous employer the results of medical advice.

Don Luis had been engaged for some time in working out a mate in five moves with the governor of the town who was a devotee of chess. He had also completed sundry alterations both in the body and in the chassis of the coach which were not without a certain sinister significance. The body was painted a dull black, the lilies of monseigneur were removed from the door and a blank escutcheon substituted. Heavier axles and wheels with larger hubs were prepared. The sling straps were removed, the springs reinforced, and the body of the vehicle hung from chains. Save that there were no barred gratings at the windows, from the outside the coach now resembled nothing so much as one of those vehicles in which the unfortunate objects of a lettre de cachet were transported from fortress to fortress. No one would have recognized it for the graceful equipage which had left Versailles in May.

The cat-like postilion who drove the mules with a secret and malicious joy was the only thing which remained unchanged. For Don Luis' conversations with the governor had not been entirely confined to theories of chess. About the end of October the frigate *Hermione* sailing from Marseilles with replacements for the Indies was joined by his two erstwhile footmen who had unexpectedly changed the livery of the Marquis da Vincitata for that of the King of France. Whatever stories they might have to tell of their late employer would scarcely intrigue the natives of Malabar. When the days were growing visibly much shorter the coach and its four passengers set out for the Alps. The endless wanderings of one of them were thus precariously renewed.

Had someone from a great height been able to observe the progress of the coach over the network of little roads spun like gossamer across the landscape below, he would have been convinced that the owner of the equipage was possessed of a vacillating if not a captious mind.

For many weeks it appeared to advance and retreat, to seek the most unlikely of byways, to make long detours and excursions, and to pause briefly at the most remote and sequestered spots. By a series of preposterous zigzags and circumlocutions it drew slowly near to, when it did not seem to be retreating from, the pinnacles of the Maritime Alps.

The exact state of "circumstances" which Don Luis thus hoped as he told himself "to achieve" had, however, not come about. Although he had indeed weighed his fist heavily in the scale, an unexpected strength in the powers of nature implicit in the endurance of his wife had prevented him. Without imitating Nero he could not get rid of that which he hated and retain what he desired. It was now nearly the end of December. He must be in Italy early in the new year. An occasional scream from Maria which she could no longer forbear and the indignation of Lucia that fear no longer entirely controlled were also annoying him. It would not do to have scenes even in the smallest towns, and he must retain some degree of hold on the maid. The last was now most essential in any event. The delay at Avignon had been too long. He had defeated himself. As they began to enter Liguria the calendar convinced him. He gave the order and headed directly over the best roads for the pass.

Maria had long ere this lost all consciousness of place or time. She seemed to herself to be tossing endlessly on a pitiless ocean, always in misery and discomfort varied only by crests of agony and valleys of pain as the waves passed under her uneasy vessel. Lucia had woven and fitted her secretly at night with a small harness made out of the strips of a blanket. The traditions of generations of peasant women expectant of lifting and ploughing till their time was fulfilled, informed her fingers. It was this simple contrivance which had so far proved a life-saver in the midst of prolonged and premeditated shipwreck.

The coach began to mount toward the clouds again, this time on a road engineered by ancient skill. The slowness and steadiness of the first degrees of the ascent brought to Maria a freedom from pain to which she had long been a stranger. Leaning against the shoulder of Lucia she looked out of the coach window and beheld the pleasant villages of the world slumbering in the sunshine of the plains below. The fields and hills of Liguria unrolled behind them like a painted map. From the mouth of the gloomy gorge upon which they were just entering it seemed like a glimpse into that toy paradise of which she had so often dreamed.

She no longer knew where she was, or remembered what had happened. The man who sat across from her was a stranger. What a fine coat he wore! She would like some of the long lace drooping over his hands for the skirt of her doll. Her tired body seemed to be floating in air. She was a great distance from it. She was a sleepy little girl. She had been lost.

"Thank you, signore," she said suddenly, with a smile in which all her radiant beauty seemed to shine again from her face as from a revived flower, "thank you for taking me home." Then her features sank. She drooped and wilted into Lucia's arms.

So deeply was the marquis immersed in his own opaque nature that for a while he thought she had been ironical.

They had left the summer below far behind now. Through the high pass as they slowly mounted swept the white, swirling skirts of December storms. The frozen fingers of sleet trailed over them and flapped against the glass. The road grew slippery and Sancho, as if he were loath to wet his feet, went slinking through the snow leading the mules. Far above them in a coign of the cliff to which the road staggered was a mountain hamlet. Once the clouds parted and far above the village flashed amid the shining atmosphere a sheer and breathless pinnacle of glittering ice.

Inside the coach it grew bitterly cold. Even Don Luis began to regret his temerity. Travellers at this season of the year had been known to set out by this road and to fail fatally. Maria began to utter at more and more frequent intervals a sharp spasmodic cry. Her eyes were closed and she seemed to hear nothing. Lucia wrapped her as it grew ever colder in her own cloak. The marquis finally got out and walked.

It was a question now whether they would make the village ahead of them. In the gorge it would soon be dark. Even the mules seemed to understand. They strained ahead desperately. As the last sombre twilight reflected itself down upon them they began to pass through a region of vast, purgatorial rocks. Don Luis shivered and re-entered the coach. Sancho began as a last resort to ply his whip again. The now constant wailing of the woman within was answered by strange voices from the winds without. Slowly the coach struggled around a huge buttress onto another incline. The lights of the village came in sight. An hour later they arrived in darkness and in icy storm. A thousand feet above them the wind from Italy raved over the crest of the pass.

Roused by the yammering of Sancho, and the thuds of the marquis' stick on the door of the largest house the reluctant portal finally opened after considerable parley. Maria was carried in and laid on a bed in an inner room, a kind of cave-like place, the rear wall of which was the living stone of the mountain. Through a partition the champing and lowing of cattle could be heard in the stable beyond as Sancho made place for the mules. A few lanterns began to flit about through the storm and the women to gather as the news of the arrival and the predicament of the travellers spread from house to house. Presently an old woman with a nose like an owl's and tangled hair through which her eyes glared piercingly arrived with a large copper kettle in her hand. It was filled with snow and put on the fire to thaw and boil.

The chimney, indeed, was the one comfortable feature of the establishment. It was wide and deep and fed by great logs. Few travellers stopped here and when they did, only by necessity. There was not even a professional welcome. Don Luis was forced to content himself with some porridge, tough goat's flesh, and a stoop of vile wine. He sat in the only chair with a bare table before him and Sancho curled up at his feet. The latter was fast asleep as near the fire as he could get. His damp coat steamed while he snored with a kind of continuous purr. Outside the tumult of the wind was incredible.

The old woman with several others had gone into Maria's room with Lucia. He could hear their feet moving about in the lulls of the storm as if they were stamping upon something. Sometimes it sounded as if they were being chased by mice. Maria's cries had ceased now. Presently the pot boiled over and threatened to quench the fire. He took it off and shouted. The old woman came out again. She jabbered at him in a dialect he could not understand. Her nose seemed about to touch her chin. He laughed at her, and she cursed him. "Of what use are men!" She spat into the pot, made the sign of the cross over it, and threw in a bundle of dried leaves. Presently the pure snow-water turned a cloudy green. Taking the kettle with her, she disappeared into the room again. He grew tired waiting. If the child was born it had not cried yet. Perhaps after all . . .

He wrapped himself in his cloak and stretched out on the table with his feet to the fire and his head on a small valise. Hours passed. It was after midnight. He dozed fitfully. The table was hard. The wind had gradually died away. Once he heard the women whispering together as the door opened and someone came out. They seemed to be quarrelling over what to do. Let them! He turned over. Finally he slept. Maria was lying in the next room staring up at the ceiling. The old woman was piling hot stones wrapped in cloth about her extremities. Despite these measures her feet were slowly turning cold.

Lucia had come out into the room and was now sitting on the chair which the marquis had lately occupied. On her lap was a man child which she now and then held up and turned over in the warmth of the blaze. He moved feebly and breathed. A red darkness like a shadow on his face began to fade. Towards morning he gave a few feeble cries. Don Luis awoke and looked at him but said nothing. He lay for some time thinking. Lucia wrapped the child up and settled it across her knees. It was sleeping now. She herself soon fell into an exhausted slumber.

Don Luis rose quietly and went into his wife's room. He was startled to see candles burning at the foot of her bed. She lay very quiet. There could be no doubt of it. Circumstances had again defeated him.

He turned suddenly at a slight noise. The old woman was standing beside him holding out her hand.

The marquis smiled grimly. So he must pay for it, too! He began to fumble in his pocket. Then a thought struck him. He reached down, and taking the wedding ring from Maria's finger dropped it into the outstretched palm of the ancient crone. There was a worn, gold band on Maria's finger underneath her ring which he had never seen before. Some childish trinket, he supposed. The iciness of his wife's hand seemed to remain in the palm of Don Luis. Even the ring had been cold.

The old crone rushed out into the morning light to look at it. A heavy snow had fallen in the night and under the first rays of the dawn there was in that high, snowy atmosphere a frosty, pale blue like the hue in the depths of a cold lake. As she held the ring up to the east its single stone seemed to have concentrated in it a spark of fire that was surrounded but not quenched by blue ice. She clutched it to her breast and trudged up the road with the dry snow blowing like dust about her. Jesù-Maria! She was rich!

Don Luis strolled over to the fire to warm his hands. Lucia was sleeping deeply, her face marked with the heavy lines of sad fatigue. Her mouth drooped. The child lay utterly still, its web-like hands to its face.

The marquis very quietly pushed two logs closer together and continued to warm himself looking down at the pair. His face retained a single inscrutable expression like a mask. Behind it he was solving what he considered to be the final problem of a disastrous episode. The two persons before him were in question. Should he drive quietly on and leave them sleeping there? Should he take them both, or take only the child? It must be baptized as soon as possible. It might not live long. He did not care to have that on his soul in addition to . . . his hands clenched uneasily.

A log burned through and fell in the fireplace behind him.

If this woman ever followed him, he would know how to take care of *her*. The story must die, be buried here with the lovely and faithless dust in the next room. He hoped the glaciers would cover it. He had seen mountain churchyards like that—the ice wall overhanging the tombs, moving slowly. His was a great and honourable name. Woe to those who hissed against it! He looked at Lucia narrowly again. Well, it would be wiser to give her the opportunity to forget completely. He stirred Sancho with his foot. In the silent room they whispered together for a while.

The silence of a great height and a heavy winter morning after snowfall now wrapped the whole village. The tired women who had toiled so long and desperately the night before had gone home for a brief rest before returning. Even the cattle in the shed behind lay quiet, glad of their own warmth. Sancho had given them hay and their usual morning bawling was stayed. Through the partition came only occasionally the faint jingle of chains as if someone had cast down a silver coin on marble. With great stealth and skill Sancho was harnessing the mules while they ate. Presently he tiptoed into the room with a small brass receptacle filled with charcoal. He dropped a few coals into it and blew them up. Don Luis nodded approval, and raised his eyebrows inquiringly. The man nodded and left his master alone.

Unlocking the small portmanteau which had served the night before as his pillow, Don Luis drew from it an unusually long, tasselled purse. It was half full. After a little search he found a small bag and untying it proceeded without any noise to transfer from it a sufficient quantity of gold pieces to stuff the purse like a sausage. At the top he placed a tightly folded note that he scrawled, and pulled the strings tight. He now opened the portmanteau wide and placed it beside Lucia. It was too small.

He closed it again, walked out to the coach, and returned with the larger black bag which had belonged to Maria. All this stealthily. He now put the bag in the same place beside Lucia which his own had just occupied and opened it. It gaped widely. Inside were a few silver toilet articles and on the bottom Maria's black riding cloak. The toilet articles he deposited in the white heat of the fire and then stooped down to rearrange the folds of the cloak. A hard object which he felt underneath the cloth he pushed impatiently to one side. He then rose and bent over Lucia. She still continued in the sleep of exhaustion. One hand clutched that part of the blanket nearest to the baby's head.

With great care Don Luis slowly withdrew the folds of the cloth from the woman's fingers and gently laid across her palm the tasselled purse. She stirred slightly while her fingers slowly closed around it. Don Luis smiled and remained standing before her for some minutes till her breathing again became regular. In the fire the backs of Maria's silver brushes began to melt. White drops of metal began to course down the faces of Cupids to mingle with small bullet-like lumps of metal that had once been festoons of grapes. They now lay in the ashes.

Very swiftly, but equally as lightly, Don Luis lifted the child from the knees of Lucia and lowered it into the bag. He closed it, and avoiding giving it the slightest jar, tiptoed to the door. He turned on the doorstep to look back. Lucia was asleep. Only the top of her high comb showed over the back of her chair. In the other room the candles still burned at the foot of Maria's bed. As he closed the door the draught blew them out. Moving silently through the deep snow he lifted the bag into the coach, climbed up, and closed himself in.

Sancho put the mules in motion. Through the silent drifts where even the iron hoofs were muffled they moved upward toward the crest of the pass. Presently the sun, which had already for some hours been looking at the plains of Tuscany, dazzled their eyes. Sancho leaned forward gazing with his hand to his forehead. The morning clouds had not yet lifted. All that was going on upon the busy plains below still remained withheld from him by their ghostly veil. To one passenger of the coach at least the future was equally mysterious. He was still riding as he had been for many months before, completely in the dark. Indeed, it was not until many hours later that the marquis was disturbed by the faint voice in the bag. Don Luis also slept soundly. The small charcoal footstove imparted a somnolent warmth to the coach. It had in fact slightly tainted the air. But it was now burnt out, and they had long left the regions of snow behind them. By the time they began to pass through the villages in the foothills the protests of the young gentleman in the bag were too strenuous to be much longer ignored.

At Aulla the marquis was forced to descend to attend to several vital necessities. They remained till next day, the marquis at the inn, and the child with a wet nurse. She found the baby nursed vigorously, tended him, and wrapped him about with long bands after the manner of her kind. Some hours of the morning were passed procuring four decent horses. The marquis had no intention of entering his own country drawn by mules. Hearing the child reported thriving, Don Luis decided to chance deferring its baptism for some hours.

Indeed, as they rapidly approached his own feudal domains his self-confidence returned apace. His bodily movements became more confident, his gestures more imperious, and he no longer worried much about his soul. As they crossed the bridge over the Arno the obsequiousness of the officer in charge of the Tuscan troops at the little guardhouse reminded Don Luis forcefully not only where, but who he was. In short the Marquis da Vincitata was himself again. The experience through which he had passed had shaken him more than he cared to admit. But for that reason his mind all the more began to thrust the memory into oblivion. Every revolution of the wheels left it further in the past.

Into the future, to which every revolution of the same wheels were also carrying him and the child, Don Luis did not need to look very far. After a few miles he would take care that their respective paths in life should never be the same again. And he would continue to see to that. Should they ever meet it would always be at right angles, and on different levels. The marquis felt sure of his own. But the probability of their meeting was, he assured himself, and for excellent reasons, extremely remote. When the cries of the baby annoyed him he closed the bag.

They turned south at Pontedera from the main route to Florence and took the road to Livorno. Don Luis had two small items of business to transact there before returning to the main highway from which, he told himself, he had been turned aside after all only temporarily.

Towards nightfall of an evening unusually warm for that time of year the coach came to a standstill on a lonely piece of road on the hills overlooking Livorno. Presently it drove on for a little and halted again. But to the eyes of its driver, who could see remarkably well in the dark, it was plain that a figure had emerged from it at the first halting place carrying something in one hand. The man with the bag turned down a quiet lane bordered by poplars and proceeded rapidly through the dusk as if the place were familiar to him. Presently he was passing along the high white wall of some ecclesiastical establishment.

The Convent of Jesus the Child was indeed familiar to Don Luis, for his family had aided greatly in its establishment. Of its present financial condition he was not aware. There was apparently no· gate into the lane. The straight lines of the stone walls continued for some distance. At last he came to what was in fact merely a hole in the wall. He placed the bag upon the sill and fumbling about in the blackness finally felt a cold metal handle and pulled it. At a seemingly vast distance within arose the jangle of a small bell. He retreated some way off and stood listening in the darkness.

The child began to cry. In the tense silence of the last twilight its feeble voice continued minute· after minute in a thin wail. He was about to return and pull the bell again when the noise of a sliding shutter prevented him. A light stabbed out from the wall and across the lane. The bar of it remained for some seconds as if suspended in darkness. Then it was withdrawn as suddenly as it came. With it the cries of the child were also extinguished. For some minutes Don Luis listened intently. A bell tolled calling the nuns within to prayer. He sighed unconsciously and turned away. It was, he knew, a custom of the pious souls who thus received unfortunate orphans to baptize them immediately. A great weight was now lifted from him.

He returned to Sancho in a cheerful mood. "You can light the lamps now," said he, and continued speaking, while the lanterns were being kindled, in low, familiar tones.

"Sí, sí, señor, I understand," said the curious little man coming to the door and laying his hand sympathetically on his master's arm. "Always I shall serve you." His whip cracked and they drove away.

Don Luis leaned back and closed his eyes. His hand felt the hollow in the cushions where Maria had once sat beside him. It would not be easy to break the news of the death of an only daughter to her father. "Buried in the Alps, buried do you understand?" he said, "buried!" He repeated it aloud as though rehearsing a scene in which he would soon have to take a difficult part.

Only Sancho remained. One faithful servant! But what more could a man expect of life? He shrugged his shoulders. The sound of hoofs and the grinding noise of the wheels died away in the darkness toward Livorno.

The child in the convent awoke and cried out as the bag was opened and the light dazzled it. At the sight of a raw male infant one of the nuns screamed and caught her breath.

What was to be done with it?

END OF BOOK ONE

BOOK TWO

In Which the Roots of the Tree
Are Exposed

CHAPTER NINE

THE CONVENT OF JESUS THE CHILD

IN THE Convent of Jesus the Child, Contessina, the lay portress, moved about the central courtyard of the place as quietly as her wooden pattens would permit. She came every morning and evening to perform certain tasks for the nuns, and she was now as busy as usual about the hour of matins. Since she was the only able-bodied person in attendance upon ten querulous old women and a boy infant her work was exacting enough and would have exhausted the patience of several men.

But to the young peasant woman, who had children of her own at home, and had no inclination to question her lot, her acceptable labours seemed merely a form of natural service in an immutable scheme. Her position as "lay portress" was hereditary. It went with the land upon which she dwelt. The convent had always been on the little hill in the valley; her husband's broad vineyards lay just below it, and as long as anyone could remember there had always been a wife or daughter from the white house in the vine-lands to serve as a maid-of-all-work to the sisterhood on the hill.

Nor did it ever occur to Contessina to trouble herself that her labours were somewhat monotonous. On the contrary, she instinctively felt a decided satisfaction in their unchanging round. Change, indeed, was the last thing that anyone would immediately associate with the Convent of Jesus the Child. The very approach to it served to convey even to the most casual passer-by a sense of antiquity, security, and somnolence.

It was situated in the exact centre of a small, oval valley planted with vineyards that looked westward over the city of Livorno, the hills opening in that direction toward a wide vista of wine-coloured sea. The buildings, for there were several that rambled into a rough rectangle, were themselves built upon a little eminence in the dale, and were to be approached on all sides only by a series of deeply sunken lanes. From the high banks of these ancient, grassy tracks cropped out here and there, especially after heavy spring rains, fragments of marble masonry; the drum of an antique pillar or a mottled festoon of ivy on shattered stone.

In fact, the whole hill or mound upon which the convent stood must have been seething under its turf-covered waves and trellised terraces with the dim animal and vegetable forms of the pagan past. Perhaps there were even gods and giants, heroes and demigods with all their half-human, half-divine progeny buried there, the lost-children of the ineffably beautiful and calm classic dream. If so, they remained now in a conceivably pregnant darkness, earthy spirits affecting the roots of things, while from the low tower of the convent on the hill above them fell the sound of the chapel bell tolling away by matins, angelus, and vespers the slowly passing hours of the Christian era. These had for innumerable generations been regularly marked not only by the prayers of the nuns in the chapel itself but by the bowed heads of the labourers in the vineyards below.

Yet despite the calm and serenity which undoubtedly surrounded the convent, it was still evident, to any eye used to looking below the surface of things, that even here the restless forces of change had been at their usual work, albeit somewhat more calmly and with less of a tendency to become visible in violent breaks and shattered outlines than elsewhere. Here the forms of objects and the profiles of eras had quietly flowed; had simply mouldered one into the other, while to each generation that beheld only a little of this constant flux and weathering all things appeared to have remained the same.

No one except a curious and perhaps pedantic antiquary would have recognized in sections of the convent's whitewashed walls the dim entablatures of a pagan temple or have paused to wonder about certain fragments of friezes that emerged here and there into the sunlight only to disappear again behind more recently erected portions of the buildings or beneath ancient cloisters of vaulted stone. Here, as everywhere else in the vicinity, one thing melted calmly into another; only in the convent itself the process had been arrested and had congealed, if one cared to look closely.

The place where the running handwriting of time was most plainly visible and carefully preserved was in the most ancient and central courtyard or cloister. Here burst forth with a continual humorous lament, like the ironical laughter of Nature herself, a clear fountain whose source was either forgotten or unknown.

Above it rose an immense plane tree that overlooked the red tiles of the convent and all the countryside toward Livorno and the sea. Its top was the home of a flock of bronze-coloured pigeons, fed and regarded with secret superstition and reverence by the peasants for miles about. The huge, mossy roots of the tree, knotted and writhing like a cascade of gigantic serpents, overflowed the brink of the fountain, embraced the wide bowl of it, and disappeared with static, muscular convulsions into the fertile soil of the hill under the pavement.

Just at the foot of this eternal and apparently changeless tree there had stood for many ages looking down into the fountain the antique, bronze statues of the twins Castor and Pollux. In that anciently remote portion of Italy the change from paganism to Christianity had been a gradual one, and in the course of time the church had seen fit to consecrate a place which had never ceased to be venerated. The worship of the offspring of Leda and the Swan was discreetly discouraged while another legend more orthodox in its implications was fitted upon the statues. The bronze twins were said to be the youthful Saviour and his brother St. John, both in a state of boyish innocence. A church known as the Chapel of the Holy Children was constructed out of fragments of the temple and devoted to their worship. The clergy attached to it had in primitive times taken an active part in the harmless semi-pagan festivals of the neighbourhood; immersing catechumens in the fountain, and blessing the nobly responding vines.

Then, in some dim foray following the age of Charlemagne, "St. John" had been carried hence upon a galley of Byzantium into parts unknown.

The loss was a severe one. For some time the vogue of the shrine on the little hill had languished. But the ingenuity of the clergy was again equal to the occasion. The name of the chapel was now changed to that of Jesus the Child, while the illiterate memory of the countryside was encouraged to forget that the bronze boy who remained alone by the fountain had ever had a brother.

How the Chapel of Jesus the Child was afterward turned into a nunnery of perpetual adoration, how that in turn became an orphanage, and toward the end of the eighteenth century a convent school for fashionable young girls, was only the final addition of its quiet history, every chapter of which had left its mark in some indelible manner upon the venerable pile.

The tree, the fountain, and the bronze statue alone remained unchanged. Their natural and pagan outlines were quite undisguised. But the pillars of the court which had once formed the façade of the temple of Castor and Pollux were now the supports of the convent's inmost cloister.

The rest of the buildings clustered about it, a maze of corridors and cells now for the most part long disused and in various stages of desolation and decay. The girls' school was kept in a more modern wing at the extreme end of the building, and the chapel alone was now used for worship. Even the ancient custom of a bride's strewing flowers upon the pool before the statue of Jesus the Child on the night before her marriage had been given up. The courtyard was now exclusively the abode of a number of superannuated sisters whose cells gave upon the place. And it was no wonder that Contessina, who clattered about in her wooden shoes merrily enough at home, felt constrained to walk quietly there—for upon this cloistered refuge of old age and antiquity there actually brooded a serene and immemorial quiet, a green patina of light and leaf-shade, a sequestered placidity that it was sacrilege to disturb.

The main impression of the place was a vision of light; a kind of trembling and watery iridescence, a flow of leaf-shadows and brilliant sunshine that filtered through the quivering leaves of the plane tree only to be reflected from the broad basin of the fountain and washed in turn along the marble walls. That, and the stream of water perpetually rushing into the fountain, lent to the whole cloister a soft, molten voice and a golden-liquid colour that endowed it with a kind of mysteriously cheerful life; with a vague and yet an essentially happy personality.

The tree, probably the last of a sacred grove, and the well or spring were long thought to have been endowed with miraculous powers. Even the conversation of the pigeons was once held to be salubrious for young married women to hear. But since the arrival of the nuns all that had been forgotten. Only the water, which came from no one knew where, continued to fall with a sleepy noise into a dateless, green, marble fountain hewn from a single vast block. The jet seemed to be wrung from the spongy mouth of a battered sea-monster whose face, scoured dim by the ages, had once stood between the bronze statues of the twins. The bronze boy who still remained was a naked child with a time-worn smile and eyes that appeared to have gone blind from contemplating for centuries the shifting changelessness of the pool.

In the very monotony of the changes which the bright fountain so constantly mirrored was a certain hypnotic fascination. All those who entered the courtyard were forced by a subtle trick of architectural perspective to look at the pool before noticing the roots of the tree. Perhaps the constant interplay of light and shadow upon the water accounted for the fixed and dreamless expression upon the face of the bronze boy, who had watched it since the gods began. Indeed, it was hard to tell, after regarding them steadily even for a few moments at a time, whether the changes in the fountain arose internally or were caused by something working upon it from without. In this its waters might be said to resemble the flowing stream of events themselves. To be sure, it shadowed forth a perpetual interplay of reflected patches of blue Etruscan sky and the verdant glooms and gleams of the plane tree soaring above. But the tree itself was obviously the prime example of still-life in eternity. And then the water, which at a first glance appeared to be stagnant in its green basin, was soon seen and heard to be flowing away at a rapid rate.

To anyone coming suddenly out of the gloom of the cloisters into the honeyed light of the courtyard the huge trunk of the tree was not at first to be discovered in the comparative darkness of its own central shadow. Raise the eyes above the line of its roots, and the tree seemed to be let down into the place; positively to be hanging in atmosphere as though aerially supported on the great fanlike vanes of its own wide-spreading foliage, or drooping from the flaring parachute of leaves at the top. It was this effect in particular which gave to the whole courtyard that peculiar, paradoxical aspect of something immutable forever occurring without cause or reason, which is as near perhaps to a true vision of reality as the eyes of man can attain.

Most people were merely momentarily confused or idly amused by these manifestations, but during the course of centuries one or two sages and several simple-minded persons who had entered the courtyard had been suddenly shocked back into their own original and naturally mystical vision by their first glimpse of the place. All the habitual nonsense by which their minds forced them to construct a reasonable basis for reality was shattered at one blow by the amazing miracle of the hanging tree.

Yet the world remained; the fountain giggled, and the tree hung.

For a lucky moment or two only, they saw it wholly with their own eyes again. It was as if like gods, or infants, they had stumbled suddenly into a cloudy nursery where the forms of matter were toyfully assuming various astounding outlines for the amusement of the inmates.

And it was exactly in that mood or condition that a pair of eyes, hung on a convenient wall peg, were looking at the courtyard on a certain morning while Contessina walked about it quietly, hanging up some baby clothes which she had just finished washing.

The pair of eyes in question were very bright ones in the head of a boy something over a year old who was hanging strapped in swaddling clothes to a back-board suspended from a peg in the wall under an arch of the cloister. He was quite used to hanging there for hours at a time. And as no one had ever paid any attention either to his cries of indignation or wails of boredom—except at precise and stated intervals when he was taken down—he had already learned the futility of protest in an indifferent universe composed apparently of vast, glimmering faces and shifting light and shade.

The world as he found it nevertheless permitted him to exist rather satisfactorily. With considerable internal discomfort at times it was true, but then he was not as yet much cursed with either memory or anticipation. And he had early discovered, was in fact fascinated by, the remarkable manifestations in the region of his eyes.

He already used those valuable organs well; that is to say, he used them both together. Through them the world was already accurately focused upon him, and he upon it; and he must, even in the course of a few hundred days since his emergence from the waters of darkness, have made many more profound inferences about it than some adult philosophers would be prepared to admit. His eyes no longer merely followed something moving or stared, they were, as often as not, directed from within and in such a manner as to indicate that he felt *he* was in the courtyard and not *it* in him. In fact, he was already quite sure of it.

It had taken several months and certain alterations in the shape of his eyes to enable him to arrive at this stupendous and not entirely logical conclusion.

The light and shade had at first been wholly in him. He was submerged in it. Then the light had brightened. As he hung on the wall and opened his eyes from the blank of infancy it was the first thing that had awakened his mind. And it had awakened it accompanied with a sense of well-being and joy. The golden trembling of the leaf-filtered light in the courtyard had washed in ripples of happiness over the closed head-of-consciousness while it had responded slowly like the submerged bud of a water-lily in a clear, sunny lake. That bud had at last come to the surface, differentiated itself from the surrounding waters, and opened its matured and sensitive flower to find what was in the light.

At first there were only shadows that moved in it like clouds over the waters of chaos. Then greyly, gigantic static outlines began to loom up in the mist. The mist itself became mottled. Patches of colours stood out; mysteriously and disappointingly disappeared. Spots of light dazzled; moved here and there like beams of a torch on a wall; vanished. Darkness resumed. He slept. Then the process would go on again—always a little farther removed; each day more distinct; not quite so deeply inside him.

And all these sights were for the most part accompanied by noises in the head, taps and thumps as shadows approached and withdrew, gurglings, chortlings, hisses, and strings of vowels. An occasional stupendous roaring or crash made him cry out. Then, lapped in his own voice, everything dissolved in sound. As he hung day after day under the arch he began to know that with the sunlight other things always happened or were part of it. These were a continuous low gurgling sound, and warmth. Sometimes the gurglings grew louder and were accompanied by certain white flutterings. This excited him pleasantly and he imitated the sound. As for all the sensations that alternately soothed or tortured him, as the wheel of life upon which he was bound and destined to be broken began to revolve, there are no names for them except legion.

Suddenly—for the instrument having prepared itself, he now blundered upon the use of it as if by accident—all this chaos was swiftly resolved. His eyes came to a focus one day as he hung on the wall. And there lay the courtyard before him, basking in the sunlight, awash with shade. The fountain glittered and the tree hung. The pigeons fluttered. Contessina, whose voice he recognized, and other forms in white moved to and fro accompanied by sound. Once having realized space, the directions of sounds next attracted his notice. Time began to glimmer upon him. Meanwhile the world beyond was every day more glittering, fresh, and beautiful. He lapsed into sleep regretfully and returned to the light with joy. He lived only in the light. Let there be light and there was light. Out of it all the forms of things had also been created from chaos for him as his own act of creation recapitulated the great original. The baby and the fountain sang together in the beautiful first morning of life.

For months this sound of pure human joy like the distant crowing of roosters had from time to time echoed from the walls of the courtyard to be re-echoed apparently by the fountain and carried off. Contessina and the nuns had unconsciously thrilled to it. It was a voice they had forgotten but still recognized. For the second time since the child had come to them the great plane tree was in full leaf again.

Contessina finished tying the clothes on a line and walked over to the baby. She was passionately fond of it. She had three of her own at home but they were all dark little girls with brown eyes. The golden hair and blue-grey pupils of the man child hanging on the wall seemed to her to belong to another and better world. She made certain feminine sounds to the baby, the elliptical grammar of which conveyed to him a sense of her complete approval and a decided encouragement to continue to exist. In his own manner he replied. Contessina then walked away again.

He held out his arms to her but only tentatively. For he had already learned that affection was not always returned.

Contessina on her part was waiting for the nuns to depart to the chapel for matins. A number of the old women garbed in white with wide head-dresses were now sitting upon a marble bench in the sunlight pattering and murmuring their morning prayers with a sound as eternal as the waterspout itself.

Presently the convent bell rang. The nuns rose, formed in procession, and disappeared down a corridor in the direction of the chapel, raising a quavering morning chant. The pigeons resettled about the fountain and began to walk and talk expectantly. More and more kept coming down out of the air with the sound of tearing silk. The child cried out with delight.

Contessina now took him down from the wall, and unwrapping him from the board, carried him over to the brim of the fountain upon which she sat holding him upon her knee.   He stretched and moved his limbs gratefully.   The pigeons gathered about her, lit on her shoulders and covered the pavement with a plaque of iridescent bronze.

She produced a bag from her skirt and began to toss them some barley.   Waves of excitement ran through the living metal.   Contessina and the baby laughed.   He began to seek her breasts.   She opened her dress and gave him suck.   The sound of the falling water and the soft talk of the pigeons filled the courtyard as with one contented voice.

Contessina looked at the bronze boy on the other side of the basin under the tree and began to make a little conversational prayer to him in her heart.   Her lips did not move and into her features crept the same eternal, blind expression that slept on the face of the statue.

> "Dear Christ who also fed the pigeons when thou wast a boy, thou wast also once a baby, as thou art now in the chapel lying upon blessed Mary's breast, Contessina is poor and can bring to thine altar only a little wine from Jacopo's vineyards.   Nevertheless, it is blessed by Father Xavier and becomes thy blood. Have mercy upon me.   Accept also the milk of thy maid-servant's breast, which I share now between my own baby and this thine orphan.   Remember them, thy helpless children.   Remember also my old mother who Father Xavier says is still in purgatory and who suckled nine.   Ah, dear Child, for thy own mother's sweet sake remember her."

Contessina's eyes filled with tears.   She removed the baby from her breast, crossed herself, and dashed some water on her face.

The child was still hungry.

From the same bag in which she kept the grain for the pigeons she now brought out a little cloth package and spread it out on the rim of the fountain.   The pigeons which now approached she drove away. The cloth contained some fragments of sausage boiled tender, some goat's cheese seethed with flour, mashed pieces of carrots, garlic and parsley all made into a kind of cake.   She crumbled these finely, and mixing the meal with the fountain water in a clean hollow of the stone to the consistency of sticky gruel, she let it warm for a while in the sun.   Then she fed it to the baby with her finger.   It was a dangerous food.   On it most of Caesar's veterans had been fed in infancy as a supplement to what flowed naturally from the teats of the Roman wolf.

Contessina now returned to her more usual tasks.   She laid the baby on a pile of dirty clothes in the sun where he soon went to sleep. The nuns always remained out of the courtyard till about noon. Contessina pounded their linen garments with a paddle and soused them in the fountain till they were spotless. Then she laid them out in the sun to dry. By the time she came to the pile on which the baby still lay asleep she was hot and tired, and it was almost time for the old women to return.

She took the child up in her arms and went over to the fountain. Glancing hastily at the shadow on the wall-dial, to be sure she would not be disturbed, she slipped hastily into the pool with the child in her arms and sank slowly into the shell-shaped bowl. The water displaced by her body rose and overflowed. The baby gasped and clung to her. Then he relaxed and splashed comfortably as the liquid atmosphere washed delightfully over his frame. The pigeons, the woman, and the child all made similar noises. After a minute or two Contessina hastily resumed her clothes while the baby dried off in the sun. She then wrapped him in clean linen bandages, binding him to his back-board as far up as his chest. Only his arms remained free. When the nuns returned he was hanging under the arch on the wall again.

From the refectory the nuns brought him a piece of bacon on a string which they tied to his wrist. They took care of him through the afternoon until Contessina returned in the evening. She then fed him again and put him to bed.

As he grew older he began to creep about the courtyard. He played with pebbles and twigs in the sunlight. He began to stand up and dabble in the fountain. He shouted at the bronze boy across the pool. But that taciturn youth continued staring into the basin and made no reply. The days of the little boy who stood looking up at him so hopefully flowed away like the water with an unbroken joyous monotony.

Contessina would have liked to take the child home with her to the farm. As he grew older she saw that he was lonely. And she would have liked nothing better than to have had him trotting around the farmyard with her baby daughter during the afternoons. But her diffident suggestions were firmly vetoed by the mother superior.

Several curious circumstances had combined both for good and for evil to keep the boy, who had arrived so mysteriously and inopportunely, confined to the cloister. Indeed, it was largely his own doing that he finally escaped at all and acquired a worldly name.

The first thing he could distinctly remember was seeing his own face in the fountain. Someone like himself had at last come to play with him. He followed the "other boy" around and around the basin.

"Anthony," said one of the old nuns who had smiled and stopped to watch him in passing. So the boy in the fountain became "Anthony," his best, and for a while his only friend. The boy in the court watched the boy in the water and spent hours talking to him.

It was more successful than trying to talk to the bronze boy whose expression never changed. The lips of the boy in the water moved, and he laughed back at you. He was alive.

Presently when the child in the courtyard moved his own lips he said nothing aloud. "Anthony" in the pool was talking. Anthony in the court listened. And it was not long before he distinctly heard what the voice of the boy in the fountain had to say. They talked about everything. Their conversations continued for hours. They would even laugh together, a long rippling laughter.

The old nuns who sat in the court turning their breviaries or doing embroidery nudged each other and smiled. Their own conversation was always more subdued than that of the water. Unconsciously, in order to be heard, they had fallen into a lower register than the constant babble of the fountain. Occasionally the pigeons and the water accidentally harmonized like a musical accompaniment.

How long these talks by the fountain with the other boy went on it would be hard to tell. At last what Anthony had always fondly wished for occurred. The bronze boy joined in, too.

It was now possible, since Anthony knew a great many words and had heard stories from both Contessina and the nuns, to continue and to make variations upon the most enchanting themes. In all these "Anthony" in the pool and the "Bronze Boy" now began to take an active part.

Then there were the children of the ring who went dancing about the rim of the fountain carrying a festoon of ivy. They were somewhat confusing, because they were all the same and it made him dizzy to look at them. If he looked at them for a long while they seemed to blend into a misty ring as if they were on a wheel going at great speed. It was hard to stop them. And it was hard to play with them. For if he once began to single them out he never knew where to leave off. He kept going around and around the fountain because he could never tell with which of the marble children he had started. They worried him even in his dreams. They kept spinning and dancing around in his head till he woke up and shouted at them to stop.

Sister Agatha would come in and look at him when he shouted. She said, "Say your prayers to the Madonna." And there was some comfort in that, because *she* was always standing in exactly the same place.

He saw the madonna when he went to bed at night. And when he woke up in the morning she was still looking at him from the little niche in the wall where she stood just at the foot of his bed. It was best to lie, he thought, so he could see her and be seen. Then he was sure just where she was when he wanted to talk to her in the dark. Perhaps she had brought him here? If not, how had he come here? "Here" was the courtyard. It was bright and sunny, the centre of all things. On all sides of it extended corridors, long, dark, silent. He had once lost himself down one of these. He had been gone for a whole half-day. Contessina at last found him silent and white, shuddering in an old cell. There was a high window there and he was crouching in its shaft of sunlight. After that he knew what being "lost" meant. You were left alone with yourself in darkness. You couldn't get back to the light. And there was no madonna to talk to in the corridors. She lived in his room, by the bed.

All the world beyond the courtyard must be made up of these endless, dark corridors and abandoned rooms. They went on and never stopped. After a while he learned that there were other courtyards. Sometimes he was taken there for a walk by the nuns.

But the other courtyards were strange. There was no bronze boy, no tree and fountain there. Only arches. Only his own courtyard was home. A universe of endless corridors leading into strange hostile courtyards surrounded him.

It was Contessina who told him about "heaven." Heaven was up there at the top of the tree where the pigeons went at night. It was in the sky into which the tree climbed. He began to lie under the tree in a bowl of its great roots near the bronze boy and look up. Sometime, he made up his mind, he would get out of the courtyard into heaven. He would climb the tree. The nuns stopped him now for fear he would fall. He began to wait until they were absent in order to try climbing.

The nuns were kindly enough. They were all fond of the child. Through the long afternoons they talked; they even played with him. They taught him his prayers. They made him clothes out of their old linen, stitched with the exquisite needlework that only they could do. He sat watching their embroidery growing on the frames. He learned to help work a little hand loom for them. They made him a doll.

But Father Xavier, the confessor of the convent, who would occasionally come into the courtyard, had taken that away. He brought him a wooden horse, a ball, some coloured stones and a broken abacus instead. With these the child was rich. His life now seemed crowded. Through all his life ran the rhythm of the convent hours; the times to eat, to pray, to rise and to go to bed. It did not occur to him that this routine of existence could be varied. The bell that marked its periods was as much a part of nature to him as was the rising and setting sun.

Some of the old women in the courtyard died and were buried. To Sisters Agnes, Agatha, and Ursula he clung all the closer. For the first time he became aware of mutability and a growing loneliness. The occasional visits of Father Xavier, who took a growing interest in the boy, were now attended with an excitement that the good priest took care to restrain. He pitied the child, whom he admired for his intense vigour and eager intelligence. He was at some pains to improve his speech. And he determined to speak to the mother superior about his education when the time arrived. In the meanwhile, he made friends with him. There was little difficulty about that. Even the careful Jesuit found it pleasant to be an oracle and a hero.

On the whole, however, the best times little Anthony spent were his mornings with Contessina. For several hours after matins he was left alone with her. From her came many of his rugged phrases in hill-Tuscan that so amused Father Xavier. And she seldom stopped him from doing what he pleased. "Young rabbits will play," she said.

She would let him plunge into the fountain and paddle about. The old women would never allow that. And it was pleasant especially on hot summer mornings to splash naked in the pool. In the centre it was deep enough for him to swim like a dog. Afterwards he would curl up in the roots of the tree and go to sleep in the sun. Contessina always wakened him before the nuns returned. She had long given up bathing in the pool herself. For a time he dimly remembered going into the pool in her arms. Then it seemed only one of his dreams of some vanished playmate who had haunted the fountain long ago. Soon he thought of it no more.

He was now able to climb up to the first low branch of the tree and to crawl out on it and look down into the water. From there he could see the little school of minnows in a patch of sunlight all with their heads toward the spout, breathing. He and the fish seemed to be bathed in the same golden atmosphere. It was from the limb that he talked to all of the dream playmates he had summoned from the deep.

They were as real to him now as any other people who came into the court. All he had to do was to think about them and they appeared; "Anthony" in the pool, the Bronze Boy, and the children from the stone ring who danced so gayly about. The pigeons were literally his bosom friends. They *all* came and talked with him. The dream-boy in the water would now come out of the pool. Sometimes when he himself was in the court he could see him lying out on the limb of the tree watching the minnows. The sunlight glimmered about him in the leaves. He would talk with him in a low tone of voice like the water.

"Anthony," he would call, "Anthony." And the boy in the tree would reply.

Most of these talks ranged about the wonderful fact that they both had the same name. Presently the bronze boy would join in. A story conducted in the terms of an endless conversation would go on for hours. His visions had become real. The Bronze Boy promised him that he should be able to climb the tree. At night he talked to the madonna in his room. She remained there. Sometimes he heard her voice coming down to him through the leaves. But he could never see her. She was the image in his room.

On the whole he preferred "Anthony" in the pool to anyone else. The stone children dancing in the ring were still confusing. He marked one of them with a scratch and that stopped them dancing. Now they stood still. He had killed them himself. He looked for the boy in the pool again. Decidedly he was the best of all. He must play with someone. A year-long reverie about the boy in the pool began. It was delightful, unending. Anthony was at the same time himself and the boy in the pool.

When he was a little more than three years old his world, which had by this time become a hopeless confusion of reality and dreams, was enlarged considerably by his being taken to chapel. Father Xavier celebrated mass there. You walked down several corridors; you crossed another court, and went into the church. In some of the courts there were other things besides fountains and churches. He kept his ears open now and heard about these things surreptitiously. But he could make no pictures for the words.

Livorno? He heard often about Livorno. People went there sometimes. Livorno was in another court, then. But what was "a Livorno"? The Madonna was in the chapel, too. The same as the little madonna in his room. He asked about her. "Yes, she was the same," they said. But larger in the chapel. She grew larger when she went there. So did Father Xavier. He was much taller in his robes, very long ones, when saying mass.

At first the child was intensely interested in the service but after a while it grew monotonous. He had no part in it, so he began to make stories in chapel, too. It was easy now, no matter where he was, to escape. All he had to do was to close his eyes and think. In the chapel he would lean against one of the stone pillars even when on his knees, and be somewhere or somebody else.

He would be the bronze boy looking at the water. He would even smile like that lonely heavenly-twin. The young lips had somehow caught the trick of the ancient, metal ones. Looking down at him, old Sister Ursula thought him rapt in childish adoration with his eyes fixed on the altar.

But to Anthony the incense was water spouting from the altar. The marble of the chancel shimmering with candles was the pool in the court, a more miraculous one. Father Xavier moving about was the shadow of the plane tree. And he, Anthony, he himself was swimming without effort in the mist. The boy in the pool would flash down amid the fishes naked as the child in bronze. How they dashed about! How cool, how beautiful it was there. Then a bell would ring and his own little miracle would be ended. He would be back in the chapel again.

It was in the mist above this miraculous pool in the chapel that he first began to see the face of the madonna. The business of church was, he knew, in some way vaguely connected with her. Now and again during the responses he heard her name repeated. From now on she began to join the company of his dreams. She herself, of course, stood looking down at him always from her niche in his own room.

It was a small, square, whitewashed chamber. Besides a straw bed, a few clothes on pegs, and a crucifix, there was nothing there but "his madonna." He understood that she in some peculiar way belonged to him and he to her. Before he could remember the madonna had brought him there, Sister Ursula said. Her image dominated the place from its niche in the wall. For many years she was the last thing that glimmered in his sight as he went to sleep and the first thing he beheld when waking. All night she had been watching him, he knew. On long summer evenings when he seemed to go to bed too early her white face faded slowly into the twilight. Then the gold sun-burst above her features burned a little longer before it too went out. For a long time he said his only prayers to her. Then she became someone to talk to. He spoke to her. His lips moved slightly as though reading to himself, whispering in the dusk.

After he had once seen her in the chapel she came to join him with the water-child in the court. He saw her there now in the sunlight. The three of them began to talk to one another. The babble of the water falling into the fountain moulded itself easily in his ears into soft voices and heavenly replies. The other child lay in the arms of the great tree half lost in the gloom. The leaf shadows washed over him. Only his beautiful face stood out clearly. For many months these singular triangular conversations sufficed. The Madonna had thus more than answered Anthony's most urgent prayer. She had finally come into the courtyard herself.

No one would listen to his stories of the "other boy" without laughing, no one except Father Xavier. He seemed to take the matter seriously. He even shook his head. Finally he pointed out that the boy in the pool was only a shadow, like the dark one on the ground. Anthony had not noticed the shadow before. That followed, too!

Everywhere except to bed. So it must be true about the boy in the pool. You could see for yourself.

But you did not need to see for yourself. Everything that Father Xavier said *was* true. The child parted unwillingly from his first friend. The image still came to play with him, but its face was somehow sorrowful now. That was because it knew itself to be a shadow. Now the real boy was lonely again. For a while there was no one to play with.

Then at last he found a way. He began to make "real" stories to himself about all the children of the pool. The children were imaginary, but the stories were real. After a while, if you made good stories, and did not ask Father Xavier about them, the children became real, too. If you sat very still they would even come out to play with you again.

There was no one to tell Anthony that there were any real children in the world besides himself. Everyone, of course, took it for granted that he knew. Yet how could he know? He took the world as he found it, and he had never been taken beyond the convent walls.

In absolutely forbidding Contessina or anyone else to take the child Anthony outside of the convent the mother superior had her own excellent reasons. It was not that she wished to be harsh or was narrowly bigoted; she had a duty to perform to the institution of which she was the responsible head. Both she and the boy confided to her care were, like everybody else in the world, to some extent the victims of circumstances.

Many years before Anthony had been thrust through the hole in the wall by the tender solicitude of Don Luis, the Medici had turned the little fishing village of Livorno, only a few miles below the convent, into the privileged port which has since become known to the world as "Leghorn."

The news of the "Livornina," as the grand duke's decree of free trade and religious toleration was called, penetrated into remote regions. English Catholics, Flemings fleeing from Alva, Huguenots, Turks and Jews found refuge at Livorno in great numbers. The town grew cosmopolitan and prosperous. The country around shared in the benefits. But not wholly or enthusiastically. Over the orthodox hills that looked down on the thriving seaport, where the wicked flourished according to Scripture, passed a suppressed but holy shudder.

The decree of Ferdinand was not to be gainsaid. Yet to snatch some brands from the burning of the heretical bonfire that blazed so merrily would assuredly be a work of merit.

Several pious, petty nobles of the hinterland combined in the good work urged on by the local clergy. Among them was a maternal ancestor of Don Luis. Endowments and legacies were soon forthcoming, and the ancient Chapel of Jesus the Child, which had almost languished away under an order of nuns devoted to perpetual, silent adoration, was reconstituted as an orphanage under the Sisters of Mercy. The purpose of the charitable endowment was to save souls, and the method of receiving orphans was simplicity itself.

Anyone, without let or hindrance, might leave at the hole in the convent wall provided for that purpose an otherwise unwelcome infant. They might ring the bell, also provided, and go away serene in the knowledge that the sliding panel would open and the child vanish inwards, to be baptized, nourished, and brought up in the Catholic faith.

The sisters devoted to this charity had toiled faithfully. Leghorn had become a great seaport. The bell rang more and more frequently. The numbers of the motley flock of orphans over whom the nuns watched bore ample evidence that the reasonable hope of the founders of the institution had not only been realized but greatly surpassed. Gifts consequently continued to be forthcoming, and the convent flourished according to its needs. All might have continued to go well had not the Queen of Spain insisted upon finding some spare dominions for her favourite younger son. In consequence of her maternal solicitude, one Christmas Day some fifty years before Anthony was born, the combined English and Spanish fleets had descended upon Livorno.

In the troubled times of the occupation that followed troops had been quartered in the convent. For a long time the sisters and their flock had been hopelessly scattered. When a remnant of the nuns finally returned in their old age it was to find their house dilapidated, their lands seized upon by tenacious hands, and their lambs, who might have been grateful, scattered as lost sheep.

Lawsuits had further harassed them. They lacked earthly guidance. There was nothing to do but pray. The place had been almost forgotten and the bell seldom rang. The few children who did come were hastily sent elsewhere in sheer desperation. Word of this went about the streets of the town and for some years the bell had finally ceased to ring at all. It looked as if the last of the sisterhood would soon depart in peace and poverty, when the Convent of Jesus the Child suddenly took on a new lease of life and service through the unexpected arrival of Sister Marie José.

She was not only very much younger than the other nuns, but capable, ambitious, and full of energy. What her former history had been no one at Livorno ever knew. She had been sent to rehabilitate the convent, and she prevailed against great odds. From the first by sheer force of character and circumstances she had been recognized by the remnant of the sisterhood as superior in fact. With the death of the ancient head of the house she had also become mother superior in name.

After some cogitation, her solution for the difficulties that already surrounded the convent was to avoid importing any more into it. That is to say, she tacitly abandoned the scheme of continuing it as an orphanage, which in fact no longer existed. Instead she started a convent school for prosperous young girls.

The license of the ecclesiastical authorities had not, under the circumstances, been difficult to obtain. Mother Marie José had even succeeded in awakening their languid interest. She was an educated woman herself, and she had been ably seconded in her efforts by Father Xavier, a Jesuit, who upon the suppression of his order had been removed from the court of the Duchess of Parma and had gone to reside quietly near Livorno.

Father Xavier combined simple but cultivated manners with an odour of sanctity and the smell of the lamp. He was, in short, a gentleman, a priest, and a scholar. As he had acted circumspectly, he was permitted to continue at Livorno, nominally as confessor to the convent, while his real work took him into certain cosmopolitan circles in the city that both required and appreciated diplomacy and the watchful presence of an able and educated man.

In the new school at the convent he had felt a powerful spiritual lever fall into his hands. Largely through his efforts the daughters of some of the best families of the town and neighbourhood had been obtained as pupils. Even some of the Protestant English merchants in Livorno sent their daughters to "The School on the Hill." Five new sisters had been lately received to teach. These, together with the revenues which were again ponderable, sufficed to conduct the establishment and to take care of the ancient women of the old régime who still survived but whose duties were purely nominal.

Over all this Father Xavier kept a constant and watchful eye. In most things he and Mother Marie José moved as one. But the mother superior was justly proud of the new school as her own creation and jealous of its reputation. It might in a few years come to rank with those which received none but the daughters of the rich and the nobility. Such was her ambition.

It was, therefore, with no little consternation that on a certain January evening in the year 1776 she was suddenly disturbed by the unwelcome jangling of the long disused orphans' bell.

One of the nuns upon whom the habits of former years were firmly

fixed had answered it automatically. A few minutes later Mother
Marie José was looking down into the gaping mouth of a black bag
in which lay a boy baby loudly lamenting his fate. Besides the baby
and his meagre clothes, the bag contained the rich, dark riding-cloak
of a lady, an ancient figurine of the Madonna and Child in a curiously
worked shrine, and ten Spanish gold pieces. There was nothing else
whatever.

Mother Marie José was now faced by a serious dilemma. According to the legal requirements of the founders of the convent she was
bound to receive the child. On the other hand, she was now engaged
in running a fashionable girls' school the reputation of which could
never survive a revival of the orphanage. The two were utterly
incompatible, and the baby was a boy.

It was also evident from the contents of the bag that the child was
by no means a mere stray brat from the town streets. Persons of
quality were somehow involved. The convent had already suffered
at the hands of the civil law, and this made Mother Marie José doubly
wary of a possible test case. It seemed especially suspicious that sufficient money for a year's nurture had been provided.

Besides, the statue of the Madonna that accompanied the child had
thrown about him from the time of his arrival a certain glamour and
protection. The pious old nuns, who secretly looked with somewhat
hostile eyes upon the new school, regarded this orphan as their sacred
charge from the first. If he were not received, trouble within and
without the walls of the establishment might reasonably be expected
to follow.

The mother superior consulted Father Xavier. A policy of caution
and silence was agreed upon. The boy was duly baptized "Anthony,"
the saint's name day of his arrival. He was then relegated to the
most sequestered parts of the building to be looked after by the old
nuns skilled in the care of foundlings.

In another part of the establishment Mother Marie José and the
new sisters continued to teach school without mentioning their involuntary charity. Except for Father Xavier, Contessina, and the few
old sisters whose cells abutted on the courtyard, his existence remained
unknown. No more unwelcome orphans came to trouble Mother Marie
José. After a full year had passed from Anthony's arrival she
obtained the necessary formal permission; the bell was silenced forever, and the hole in the wall bricked up. The metamorphosis of the
Convent of Jesus the Child was complete. What to do about the
young orphan who remained over from the old order of things was
put off from time to time. The problem was not yet urgent. It
seemed better and easier to let it alone.

Meanwhile the boy had begun his education.

One day Father Xavier unexpectedly came into the courtyard and took out of Anthony's hands some yarn which he had been holding up for Sister Agatha to wind.

"My son," said he, "from now on you are through with woolly things and the distaff. Come with me."

He led him down one of the long corridors and unlocked a little door at the end of it. They stepped out together into the bright sunshine of the world beyond the walls. The boy raised his little nose and sniffed the breeze. This for some reason or other caused Father Xavier to laugh.

Even here though there was nothing much to be seen of the great world outside. They had merely emerged into a deep, walled lane behind the convent. They continued down it a little way.

Overhead Anthony could see the same sky that he saw from the court. There were other trees there. He was somewhat surprised by that. So many of them! But he was still too small to see over the top of the high banks. The lane, he told himself, was merely a corridor without a roof. That was at least amusing. By and by, still chatting, they came to the door of a little house and passed through it into a marvellous room.

There was a charcoal brazier in one corner that kept the place pleasantly warm. A small window on one side looked into a court. Another court with new things in it! Birds huger than any he had ever seen were pecking about and dusting themselves. Pigeons were not to be compared with them. There were some old, high-backed, red velvet chairs against the walls. He could never admire the frayed and dusty tassels of these enough. Upon one of them he was actually permitted to sit. Father Xavier, a spare man in a tight, black gown, sat opposite to him, smilingly hospitably. He would answer all questions. He gave Anthony a small glass of something clear and sweet. Compared to this all else to drink was milk or water. Anthony could not find words to express himself. Finally he cried.

The narrow face of the priest worked with a surprised pity. He could, luckily for the boy, understand the fetters of the avid young mind so overwhelmed by images without words. The starved vocabulary that Anthony had picked up from Contessina and the nuns in the courtyard broke down even in this barely furnished room. The priest began to touch things and name them. They went to the window and saw "chickens." A cat Anthony knew, but not a goat. Holy Mother! what a miracle was a goat!

Here was a real interest in life for the priest. Father Xavier, whose story was a tragic one, was somewhat ennuied at his present post so different from his last, so dull. He began to freshen in the pristine glamour shed by the young mind just released in his room and beating

itself about the walls like a dazzled moth going for the light.   Here
at least was something he could catch with his own hands and pin
down, even if he had failed elsewhere. He would do it. The boy
should come often. That day both his worldly and his spiritual education began. "It is fortunate," thought Father Xavier, "that they can
be combined."

Father Xavier, who as a young man had once been counted one of
the ablest instructors of youth in an order devoted to teaching, had
long since, by his varied experience at the court of Parma and the
world in general, acquired wisdom as well as knowledge. He could
now look back upon his own career with discerning eyes and see what
was worth dividing in order to teach, as well as how to divide it.

The suppression by the pope of the order to which he belonged
had caused him to do a good deal more thinking for himself than he
might otherwise have found either advisable or necessary. He was
devoted to rehabilitating the Society of Jesus, but not blindly so. He,
and the party to which he belonged, believed that new conditions
required other methods of propaganda. Above all they desired an
infusion of new blood and a number of ardent young men capable of
coping with the modern world as they should find it.

In the orphan, whom adverse circumstances had so opportunely
deposited in the courtyard of his convent, Father Xavier thought he
saw a providential opportunity. He was not at all sure that the boy
would develop into the kind of man, who, as he phrased it, would be
worthy of taking up the cross. That would remain to be seen; "in
the hands of God." But he might begin the good work by laying the
basis of a broad and general foundation in which he determined that
languages should play the principal part. Not, of course, that he meant
to neglect the child's soul.

"For what," said he to Leucosta, his ancient housekeeper, whom he
was wont to address for confirmation of his own opinions, "what is
it at the present time we most need in the face of the breaking up of
the old order? This oncoming generation is going to be confronted,
mind you, Leucosta, by society in a state of flux. Why, then we
need—self-realization accompanied by great self-control, a genial outward humility accompanied by a sustaining spiritual pride, and—a
knowledge of the fundamental moral tenets of Christ's religion instead
of a mere sentimental respect or romantic adoration for its founder."

Knowing that the father was always talkative during Sunday dinner
after chapel, Leucosta, who was stone deaf, hastened to clear off the
table and bring a bottle of crusty port which Mr. Udney, the English
consul at Leghorn, had sent to Father Xavier. Mr. Udney was much
"obleeged" to him in a certain matter. The priest sampled the wine

with approval. "Fit for the orthodox," he said, and poured out a glass for the old woman as well.

Not the fecund imagination of John Knox could have surmised that Father Xavier was mentally encroaching on his vows in the direction of Leucosta.

"She looked like a mummy of the Cumaean Sibyl preserved in vinegar," said Mr. Udney to his wife, after returning from an interview with the priest preliminary to entering his young daughter Florence at the convent school. "As for the priest himself, he is the personification of geniality and wise diplomacy. My Protestant scruples were, I admit, set at rest rather too easily. I advise *you* to be watchful, however." The port had followed a month later and had something to do with mental reservations and an oath of allegiance taken to King George by an old Jacobite merchant at Leghorn. Father Xavier sipped it, reflecting.

"It will probably be a dangerous experiment and I must prepare myself to be disappointed," he said aloud. "But you agree with me, Leucosta, that it will be best to keep this boy uncontaminated by the world for some time yet. I wish a virgin field for the sowing of the seed, and the rooting up of tares is always confusing and wastes the time of the gardener. *Of course,* you will agree with me! That is the reason I keep a deaf housekeeper. You will recollect, my good woman, that one of the chief virtues of the Romans was that they consulted the Fates merely to have their own opinions decently confirmed. A deaf Sibyl is invaluable. It promotes the capacity for action, and that is the only way in which any opinion can finally be tested. In the end the Fates do answer. Thou, Leucosta, art an invaluable one."

He waved to the old crone to bring him his hat while he continued to address her.

"And what after all could we do better for the boy? A love-child, and as lusty a young pagan as I ever saw bathing in a heathen fountain. He is like the Angles that Augustine sent to Hildebrand. Or let us hope that he will be. Shall I turn that fine pair of arms and delicate hands over to Pietro the blacksmith as a human attachment to his bellows? No. There are more fitting ones in the village below. Or, shall I, as Monsieur Rousseau tends to advise, turn him loose into nature to become the wolf-boy of Tuscany like the little fellow in M. what's-his-name's pamphlet? No, no. One or two intellects who dwelt about this middle-sea of ours have thought of things that are worth propounding to the barbarians. And every new generation, *you* will recollect, Leucosta, is a fresh invasion of savages. Well, what can a poor teacher do then, my belle of three generations past, thou fate of all mankind? Why, I read it in thy wrinkled face. Even as all teachers have always done from the beginning of things; the best they can, under wicked and adverse circumstances. Now give me my hat, mother. That is right, brush it. The nap went years ago, but the conventions of respectability are thus observed."

And Father Xavier walked off down the closed lane to seize his young pupil by his "delicate" hand.

They slowly began to educate each other. They began first with manners and personal behaviour. One must know how to eat and drink decently. What words to say upon entering and leaving a room. When to stand up and bow, and when to sit down. There was, it appeared, a kind of being in the world called a "gentleman." Father Xavier said there were not many of them. One must learn to think and feel correctly about other people in order to become one. Manners were a sign of this. There was a certain ritual in the house for men and women as there was for *Deo* in the chapel. One must also be clean, silent, and pay attention. When you did not pay attention Father Xavier took the lobe of your ear between his sharp finger-nails and pinched. He finally left a mark there.

"Is that the mark of a gentleman?" asked Anthony looking in a small glass.

"In a way it is," said Father Xavier. "It is also *ad majoram Dei gloriam*. It would be better to have a small piece of your ear drop off than never to learn what both of them are hung on your head for. They are meant to listen with when someone wiser than yourself is talking."

In the course of several years the mark became permanent along with the lesson it conveyed.

"You see, my son, I do not talk to you very long at a time," said Father Xavier. "And when you play I do not interrupt you. You must do the same by me."

They understood each other well enough. Words began to expand into languages as the "talks" became longer. Anthony spent nearly all his afternoons at the priest's house. Languages began to expand into literature, literature into understanding and enlightenment. The old abacus had been repaired. It merged slowly from numbers into the beginning of the science of them. Along with all this went a growth of mutual respect and affection. Father Xavier had scarcely allowed for the latter. It troubled his ascetic heart sometimes as he came home to find the bright young head bent over the copying sheets or peering out of the door waiting for him to turn the corner of the walled lane by the little iron gate. Perhaps he was coming to set too much store by it. He searched his heart. No, he must not waver. Surely in this case the end *did* justify the means. If there were incidental rewards of human companionship the Lord might still call

Samuel and remember Eli. "My son," he would say gently in Latin, and "Welcome to this house, father," would come the reply.

About the outside world, which he now began to apprehend lay around, but still beyond him, Anthony could never ask enough or be tired of talking. Forced to defend himself from the minutiae of every particular in the creation, Father Xavier took refuge in generalities when Anthony was six years old. He purchased a second-hand globe from some defunct scholar's library and began to talk about "the earth." Before he had even seen a field Anthony was aware of the major divisions of the planet. As long as he lived a large crack of leaking plaster extended the length of Africa from Capetown to Cairo. Soon he was reading animal fables and saints' lives in Latin and helping Father Xavier as a bare-legged little acolyte in the chapel.

The perforated incense pot which he swung there bore some resemblance to the many-nostrilled beast that spouted into the fountain in the court. At first he played he was the animal behind it throwing spray into the pool. He loved to make the smoke ripple over the smooth floor of the chancel which reflected the lights as if it were water. Then he began to learn, and to understand, what the responses meant. He began to realize someone within himself, who, as a being apart from his body, addressed words to some unseen Presence who remained a mystery. He was also taught the proper words to say to the Madonna, and he preferred always to speak to her.

For was she not visible, and real? Did she not actually live with him in his own room, not a mystery and a spirit, but close, and familiarly beloved? The thing they talked to before the altar remained unknown, a name made of three black letters in a book. But a name for which there was no image on earth, only a word. So it went for many a day with the good priest acting as father indeed. The rest of the boy's silent life was passed timelessly among the old women pacing slowly up and down the corridors with faintly rustling gowns and high, starched head-dresses. Or he was in his room, or playing in the court, or going every day down the "roofless hall" to the priest's house. Here only he expanded and lived abundantly.

How many, many times was he to recall in all the countless things that were touched upon there, and later revived in memory, Father Xavier's gentle, patient, and yet insistent voice. How many facts and fancies lived forever for him in those tones alone. Only of the reason that he must not go forth to wander and see for himself, of that alone, the priest would never treat. He must not, and that was all. Nor was this as yet a burdensome denial. The time for his release would come, he knew that. Lacking means of comparison, the boy's life seemed to him full enough.

Sweet are the uses of adversity and always unforeseen. The careful shaping which Father Xavier had provided for the waif left in the courtyard was not to be devoted to the end by which he had justified the means. Old Leucosta, if she had not been deaf, might have told him so. The resources of the mind and soul of Father Xavier were considerable, but his foresight was by no means infallible. In the field he had so carefully fenced-in he had overlooked something. It was the giant plane tree which grew in the midst thereof, which from ancient times had overlooked both the pagan temple and the Christian convent.

———————

Half-way up, until it topped the roofs of the convent, the tree, sheltered from all winds, was a dense mass of foliage. For a long time Anthony had confined his exploits to these lower regions and pretended to himself that he was satisfied. But it was a half satisfaction only, clambering about these lower limbs. The best he could do was to lie out on the branches like his friend the dream boy and peer down into the shadows of the pool. But even this was tantalizing, for in the pool itself were to be caught now and then reflected glimpses of the open sky. Gradually as he became expert with practice, and more fearless, the boy enlarged the extent of his arboreal kingdom.

No one could find him there. Even Father Xavier had come into the court looking for him and had gone away. Anthony was at first surprised. He thought the priest would surely know. So it *was* possible to escape after all, if you desired. The sense of the possession of a secure retreat, a world all his own above the regions of the convent, aroused in the boy a feeling of independence and adventure which was the most delightful and strongest impression he had ever known. He cherished it night and day as his greatest and only private possession until it became, and remained, a passion. Behind it, gathered up now into an intensity which was equivalent to the stored force of an explosive, was a curiosity whose power could scarcely be calculated. This was impelling him farther upwards day by day.

As his skill in climbing increased, the bare, giant limbs that soared away from him to break into a second green country in the sky above appeared continually to lure him on. He thought of them for weeks. One day after matins, and an extra prayer to the madonna in his own room, he set out after making sure that the courtyard was deserted before he crossed it. Taking off his shirt, for the day was already hot, he left the ground and swung himself like a young ape onto the lowest branch of the tree.

The first familiar stages were easily accomplished. He was soon in the great centre bole of the tree and on a level with the gutters. The leafy, sheltered area that shaded the courtyard spread out below him like a cracked, green saucer through which gleamed glints of the pool below. He was utterly alone now, dangling his feet above this flat top of polished leaves.

From here, like an inverted tripod, three great trunks split the main stem, one of which, more upright than the others, might be said to be a continuation of the tree below. It rose grandly, with here and there a few stumps of branches sheered off by the winds above the roof line, to a second and higher fork. Even beyond that it could still be traced, provided now with a more shaggy coat of shorn branches, and rising like a handle to support the dark ribs of the leafy umbrella which floated triumphantly above. Beyond that were the clouds.

The boy began to climb toward the upper fork. He did not seem like a monkey now. The sense of the importance of his own predicament had lent a very human caution to his movements. The slight angle of the tree helped. He hauled himself upward, placing his feet in the holes left by vanished branches and clutching the stubs and leaf clumps which remained. It was breathless. From the corner of his eyes he could see the red tile roofs glimmering below him, receding vastly at every higher step. Presently with his breast scratched and bleeding he lay panting in the last fork. The handle of the parasol now rose straight above. He looked up.

He did not dare look out or down. Should he go on, or return? After all he had come to where the tree finally forked. That was something. He might go back safely to the comfortable, sheltered life of the walls below and remain there—always—or, he might go on and see what he should see. The boy sat for some time with his head in his hands, wrestling with himself. He prayed to the madonna again. At last he was able to look down without falling.

Along the edge of the roof trotted a cat with a dove in its mouth. "So that was where they went!" he thought. "They came and took what they wanted and went away. They climbed up as he was doing."

The cat looked over the edge of the gutter at old Sister Ursula who was tottering across the court on her cane. Through the maze of leaves below him, Anthony could hear her clicking across the flagstones. That the picture of the court was in his imagination made it the brighter. He watched the cat watching the nun. The sound of the cane passed. The cat turned, took a firmer hold of the dead bird, and trotted on over the ridge of the roof. Anthony laughed and again began to climb.

The sun beat on the back of his neck, and his chest and belly hurt him as he clasped the trunk. But it was easier than he thought. One hitch at a time, then the next. He planned each move carefully. Suddenly, before he expected it, he was safe amid the ribs of the parasol. The pigeons, which he had often fed in the courtyard below, now began to discuss his arrival in doubtful and puzzled tones. Presently the conclave, since he remained quiet, decided in his favour. A few cautious dissenters departed. He lay resting and listening to their tones, the very language of the air.

Presently he wriggled up the last stout branches and thrust his head through the final fabric of the leaves. The spread of them just below him cut off his dizzy height from the ground. On the top of his gigantic umbrella he crooked his elbows and knees in the last branches and looked out and beyond.

At that instant his eyes were probably the only pair in Europe which beheld the world precisely as it was, a miracle of beauty beyond rapture, hung in mystery, and smiling back at the miraculous skies.

It was the colours of the world that most amazed him. He had expected to find it like the pictures in books, white and grey. In a state of pleasant rest after the exhausting climb he hung there in the boughs for a brief period of ecstasy, the greatest he was ever to know; time suspended, and all expectations surpassed.

Gradually he became conscious of himself again as the cool wind played on his face and rocked him. He began to fit pieces of things together.

The view coalesced surprisingly well. He could understand most of it in the large; the sun flashing enormously on the sea to the west; the dim blue outline that was an island; the far wavering coasts hemmed with white where they met the sea; the white roads all tumbling down to the town below. He could never see enough of it! He longed to be able to fly; to swoop down and examine things intimately like the pigeons; to cross over that blue line where the water met the sky.

Already his mood of complete happiness had vanished. A cosmic curiosity overwhelmed him and made him unhappy. He was like a starving man with food dangled before his eyes. He reached out as if to clutch all that lay below. The small pattern of his own hand blotted out half the view. He almost lost his balance, and burst into tears.

That night he was back in his room again, worn out with fatigue and excitement, but no longer a child. Like the cats he would keep this means of escape to himself. Some day, soon, he would get out and keep going, always. He would see it all. He would take no one with him, no one!

The face of the madonna glimmered from the wall. After the great height and uncertainty it was pleasant to be back with her again. She had brought him here, they said. He began to ponder and altered his plan. He would take her along when he went away. It would be better not to be entirely alone. There should be someone to talk to. He began to tell her about the world beyond, softly, so no one but she could hear. It was a relief thus to share his secret. He slept.

Once having discovered the way to such a vantage point Anthony returned again and again. To the visits to Father Xavier's room, to the hours of reading and talking with the priest, there were now added long periods of observation in the treetop. The tree was used to supplement and as a check upon the more formal instruction received in the realms below. But from the day he first climbed it the dream companions in the courtyard below betook themselves into the limbo of memory. The boy by the spout retired with an archaic smile into the bronze; the dancing children in stone remained as if frozen forever by the chill world of reality.

Had the madonna not remained constantly in his room it is possible that she too might have followed the others into the land whence only the burning wand of passion or fever could afterward summon them. She stood fixed there, however, day and night. Unforgettable, immovable, part of the living furniture of his existence. For he was taught and commanded to speak with her; to bring his troubles before her as a good and helpful act. In the life about him he saw others doing likewise and heard her name spoken by living lips. The madonna was not like the others of his dreams. His dream of her was accepted by other people as a reality. It seemed to be the same as reality. The madonna had the advantage of still possessing a cult. That of the bronze boy and his brother had disappeared from the memory of men ages before. So the madonna remained.

With Anthony she had already become a habit of thought. There were paths in his brain which belonged to her. Strapping her carefully on his back, he took her with him one day to the top of the tree as if to tempt her with the kingdoms of the world. Her silence in regard to them when he went to sleep that night was a distinct disappointment.

As time went on he began, as he lay in the treetop day after day, to learn much of the life of the neighbourhood. The houses and the people that lived in them, the horses, asses, and oxen that plied in and out to Livorno or from village to village became known to him. The very creaking of the carts as they passed by took on an individuality. It was in this way that he became aware of the presence of other real children in the convent besides himself as one morning he watched a small fleet of carriages bringing the pupils to Mother Marie José's school.

A small cloud of them emerged about the same time along the road from the town just before the convent bell rang, he observed. Once in the lane by the convent wall he could not see what became of them. Before long he became familiar, nevertheless, with the passengers of every carriage. Every morning they were always the same. It was seldom that he missed watching at that time.

So far he had kept his vantage point an utter secret. The joy of sole possession, the example of the cats, and an instinctive feeling of defensive reticence combined to seal his lips. Yet above all things he longed to speak with these other children who were now, he knew, so close to him. Even to ask about them would, he also knew, serve to betray himself. But he pondered the problem, nevertheless, day by day. He had almost come to a dangerous conclusion about the matter. He was going to wave to them from the tree, when with the approach of summer the school stopped.

For a long, dreary time Anthony considered himself to have been left alone. He moped. Why did they not come back? It was often upon the tip of his tongue to ask. He began to approach it obliquely with Father Xavier, plying him with questions about the world without which seemed to the priest to be surprisingly knowing ones. But the boy dared not come to the point and would fall into silence and sulk.

Father Xavier felt that the time had come to settle something about Anthony. He had his own plans. He would have liked to prepare the boy for entrance to a seminary near Rome. He must begin by taking him about with him outside. There was something about the cast of the boy's mind which he did not altogether like. His avid questionings and the things which moved him most reminded the priest too frequently of the idle curiosity of the age without the walls. He had tried to protect his charge from this in a way, and yet perhaps he had also been to blame for awakening it. Under the circumstances though . . . He spoke to Mother Marie José about it. She agreed with him.

By all means the boy should be given his first sight of life beyond the walls in the company of his ghostly tutor. How better could it first be brought home to him? In fact she had almost forgotten about Anthony. She was very busy now about several things. It might be better, too, to wait until the pupils for the coming term were secured before parading the unwelcome presence of this orphan about the town. Undoubtedly, that would be talked about. She sent for Anthony. In her formal presence the boy froze within himself. Her voice from long hours of instruction was unintentionally harsh. Anthony remained silent. She could find nothing in him of the qualities Father Xavier had enlarged upon. The misplaced enthusiasm of the childless priest, she thought. This could wait. Anthony was remanded to the courtyard. Indeed he fled there in relief. He climbed the tree and Father Xavier could not find him.

Another summer slipped by punctuated only by escape into the cool heights of the boughs, the droning of the pigeons and of Father Xavier.

CHAPTER TEN

THE CHICK EMERGES

IT WAS a great day for Anthony when in the late autumn he once more saw the dust of the approaching vehicles and the children returned. Reality was once more brought home to him. There were several new girls. One, who arrived nearly always a little late in a car behind a lazy, fat pony, especially delighted him. She was about his own size and her wriggles were noteworthy. He could not quite make out her features. The cart always disappeared when he was just about to catch a full glimpse of her face into the lane behind the wall. It was impossible to look closer for the edge of the roof cut off his view. He tried to imagine her into the court but she had no face. Somehow, too, he had lost the trick of evoking vivid dreams. The reality was now so much plainer. The glimpses of her enchanting arrivals and departures grew more and more tantalizing. See her face, speak to her, he must.

He began to investigate the plan of the corridors beyond the huge, half-vacant wing of the convent that he already knew. He soon discovered an important fact. While the children were present, all the nuns in the other part of the building were absent from their rooms. This gave him courage. He began to explore more thoroughly.

On the third day, he found the corridor that led to the door. Breathless and on tiptoe, more frightened even than when he had climbed the tree, he ventured to the threshold and looked out. The world lay before him on its own level. All he had to do was to put his feet upon it and walk out. He did so cautiously, then brazenly. As the shadow of the roof passed from his head and the full sunlight burst upon him, he ceased from half-crouching and stood up manfully. At last, and forever, he knew himself to be free. The spell of the place had been broken conclusively. No one had led him. He had found the way out himself.

Even now, however, he still found himself in a lane with the convent on one side and a high wall on the other. In both directions it made a slight curve and he could not see beyond. He turned to the right and started to walk. He passed a place in the wall of the convent that was filled up with new bricks of a brighter colour than the rest, a blind window. Then the trees started to meet overhead and became vaguely familiar. Suddenly he found himself before the door of the priest's house. "Come in," said Father Xavier's voice.

Anthony walked in and sat down. He felt weak with apprehension. It was some minutes before he could bring himself to believe that the priest had not noticed the unusual direction of his approach. Not to have been found out upon this occasion gave him a confidence which he never lost. That afternoon Father Xavier began to talk to Anthony about his future. To the priest's suggestion of the seminary the boy made no comment. He sat silent, puzzling over the direction of the lane. "In a few years if you are attentive and do well, you can go to Rome," Father Xavier was saying. Anthony was wondering where the lane led when you turned the other way. The next day he found out for himself.

It was lucky, thought Anthony, that the little girl whose face he could not see always came late. He watched her one morning from the tree approaching after all the others had arrived. The pony took considerable persuading. The boy slithered to the ground and darting through the corridors ran out and placed himself in an offset of the wall until she drove up. A half-grown Italian lad held the reins. Anthony was dressed in nothing but a long, ragged cassock that flapped about his bare feet. It had once belonged to Father Xavier and the row of rusty buttons ran from the neck to the ground. The boy had a good view of the little girl. Under a mop of brown hair, she had a fair, chubby face and blue eyes. Anthony lounged close to the wall and said nothing. Neither the little girl nor her driver paid any attention to him beyond giving him a glance. The sight of acolytes lounging about near chapels was not novel to them. The little girl took her satchel and went into school. Beyond making a face at Anthony when he drove away even the driver ignored him.

Morning after morning, whenever circumstances would permit him to leave the court without being noticed, and regardless of the weather, Anthony continued to wait by the same nook in the wall. Some time during the second week he was rewarded by a smile. A little later he ventured to hold the pony while she left the cart, and to strike up a friendship with the lad who drove her. Anthony was now rewarded with a "good morning" to which after some days he ventured to reply. Secretly, to both children, the sound of their own voices thus exchanged was thrilling, but especially to Anthony. The little girl was proud that he came to hold her pony. No one did so for the other girls. Knowing that she would be teased about it if she said anything, she held her tongue.

From Angelo the driver, Anthony gradually learned all there was to know about his "puella." The older boy laughed at his queer jargon of convent Latin and Italian, correcting him loftily. Anthony had the good sense to be humble before this older boy and thus lived in his good graces. He, Angelo, worked for *Meester* Udney, the English consul at Livorno. *Mees* Florence was the consul's daughter. The Udneys had two great houses and were very rich. All of the Inglese were rich. Most of them were heretics. Angelo crossed himself. He lived in great fear of the evil eye. It was from the villa that they drove every day, only sometimes in town. The pony was slow, and they had permission from the mother superior to be late—when necessary. It was always necessary. Angelo grinned. Miss Florence, it appeared, usually had her own way.

One morning Anthony presented her with some pigeon eggs in a little nest of woven leaves which he had made. The gift was acceptable. About Totnes she had once hunted for birds' eggs with her cousins. Here at Livorno it was not permitted. She was the consul's daughter! The eggs were adorable. In return she brought Anthony a pair of shoes. They were too short for him but he cut out the toes and after that refrained from meeting her in entirely bare feet.

He told her about the pigeons and how he had first seen her from the tree where the birds lived. The restraint gradually wore off from their brief morning talks. Every day they had some childish news to exchange, usually about animals. Anthony about his pigeons and the cats; the girl about her pets at home. Before the term was over it was arranged between them that Anthony should come to see her rabbits. There were also several puppies that had become the heroes of an animal epic recounted from day to day.

Angelo demurred to this plan at first. Anthony would have to ride to the villa in the pony cart. It appeared slightly irregular. Orders had been given by Mr. Udney that no one should be given rides in the cart. Miss Florence stamped her foot, however, and argued her case. After several days of appeal, cajolery, and threats Angelo succumbed. Anthony was to lie in the back of the cart with a wrap thrown over him. How he was to return did not concern either himself or the other conspirators—as yet.

One afternoon he borrowed Father Xavier's hat and whisking himself to the end of the lane stood waiting patiently till the rumble of the departing carriages ceased. Some minutes later the pony cart with Angelo and Florence passed by slowly as had been arranged. Climbing into it hastily, Anthony wriggled under the rug in the back, and they were off.

It was a marvellous sensation bumping along by the efforts of someone else. Miss Florence was bubbling with suppressed excitement and laughter. Angelo put the pony through what paces it might be said to have had. He succeeded at least in making it wheeze. It is doubtful if Elijah enjoyed the triumph of his chariot journey to Heaven as keenly as did Anthony his trip in the pony cart to the modest villa of Mr. Udney. Both were a transit to paradise. But to be able to peep out from the blanket and to see the scenes which he had so often observed from the tree actually passing before his eyes, to catch a glimpse now and then of a laughing face, a real one, smiling down at him—what were the rewards of a mere prophet compared to all this? Besides, the speed, particularly downhill, was prodigious. He could scarcely believe he was not dreaming when he closed his eyes under the blanket. The very pain of the bumps gave him pleasure. They were so reassuring. Presently they turned into an avenue lined with poplars. Anthony was commanded to cover up and keep still. After some delay, strange voices, and the smell of a strange place, Angelo uncovered him and the boy found himself in the stable yard of the villa. He was being shown the horses, huge beasts he thought, when Florence came out and joined him. She had changed out of her school dress and was in a long, blue frock with ribbons. She was more beautiful than anything Anthony had ever seen. Miss Florence was a very small girl but she was not too young to enjoy being admired even by a ragged acolyte. After giving him more than sufficient time to recover his breath, they went to see her rabbit hutch.

Confronted by such an ideal beast as a rabbit for the first time; actually permitted to hold one in his hands, Anthony was reduced to tears. He could not help himself. It was too much.

"They *are* lovely," whispered Florence. "I like the white ones best."

He nodded sympathetically, wiping his eyes on Father Xavier's best hat. They both agreed that the tweaking nose of the largest rabbit was a miracle of rare device. From the rabbits they passed out into the rear courtyard which, it appeared, was the abode of the pups.

By this time Anthony had forgotten his entire past, and the future did not yet exist. Lost solely in each other, and in the animal riot about their feet, the sylvan voices of the two children laughing uncontrollably at the comical pranks of dogdom floated into the library window to the ears of Mrs. Udney. She crossed the room to look out, stood for a minute amazed, and then turned her head to say in a half whisper, "Come here, Henry." Mr. Udney—who was perusing a document the last line of which averred, "your petitioner will ever pray"—was glad to be recalled to life. He dropped the paper on the floor and joined his wife. It was a singular scene upon which they now looked down.

Standing in the middle of the yard was their daughter Florence with her frock in the most admired disorder. She was looking up with an expression of extreme happiness into the face of a figure whose grotesqueness passed belief.

Presented to the view of Mr. and Mrs. Udney was the back of a huge triangular priest's hat clapped upon the invisible head of a young body in a long, black, clerical gown that fell in one sheer line from neck to bare, brown calves. One point of the hat, which was worn at the angle of a shed roof, was exactly between a pair of shoulder blades that appeared through the gown as did two elbows from their ragged sleeves. The effect upon the spectator was that of having been suddenly presented with the eye of Don Quixote, or, that Lazarus had taken orders. While the Udneys gasped, the laughter in the court continued till the stable arches rang.

The laughter was the least bit hysterical now. Mrs. Udney giggled. "My dear," said she, "where do you suppose she found him?" "I'll be demned!" said Mr. Udney, changing the sound of one vowel out of deference to his spouse. "Let us have them up." He cleared his throat in a preparatory manner—"Florence!" Laughter in the court ceased. The children felt they were seen. Anthony felt an impulse to run, mastered it, and turned toward the direction of the voice. "Take off your hat," whispered the little girl, "it's mother." The boy removed his hat with an unavoidable flourish owing to its size and tucked it like a picture frame under his arm. He looked up.

The removal of the hat did not disclose an ecclesiastical gnome but the fair face of an English boy rather deeply tanned, yet still unmistakable, under delicate ringlets of yellow hair. His features were more than usually aquiline. There was a firm little jaw, a broad brow, and grey-blue eyes. If anything, the face was perhaps a little too thin. But this not unpleasant hint of keenness was tempered by far-looking eyes and half-parted lips into the expression of one not fully awakened yet from a remembered dream. The head sat upon a firm neck, while the narrow-waisted, black gown with its long row of buttons made the boy look taller than he actually was. In the afternoon's sunlight he seemed to radiate a certain indescribable lustre like the leaves of a fresh plant after rain. Mrs. Udney, who had no son as yet, felt her bodice move. Her husband laughed unconsciously. "Upon my word!" he said. "Florence," he called, "bring up your prince of the church for tea." He turned away from the window chuckling.

"How do you suppose a face like that got to Italy?" he asked his wife. "Leghorn is a peculiar place. King George seems to have lost a subject somehow." The consul in him felt a dim impulse to inquire —at which Mr. Udney smiled. His wife remained by the window. Their cogitations upon different lines were now interrupted by the arrival of one Signore Terrini, a dandified young painter, whose tailor aped English styles in an Italian way.

Florence took Anthony by the hand not engaged with the hat and led him up to the library. The boy could never forget that room; the long white curtains rippling in and out through the shaft of sunlight, the warm, brown rows of calf-bound volumes, Mr. Udney's desk heaped with papers, the ink, sand, and black seals. The smell of sealing wax forever after served to summon it to view. There was Mrs. Udney in a soft, white, low-bosomed dress, seated by the tea table, the silver, the sound of low, happy voices within, that of poplar trees without. That such places existed, he had no inkling. He had never seen a lady. He stood entranced and showed it.

They were talking Italian to the artist to whom Anthony was now introduced. Mrs. Udney took the boy by both hands, looked in his face, and declared he was an angel. He blushed, but liked it. Florence was enormously proud of her acquisition who was soon seated on a chaise longue eating a raspberry tart and drinking weak tea, neither of which delights he had ever tasted before. A mist came over his eyes. He experienced the sensation of being at home.

Terrini leaned forward. He would give anything to catch that expression for a copy of the young St. John he was doing. The face of the original he worked from was blurred. The slight plumpness of the lower part of the fingers and back of the hands—one should remember that in portraits of little boys. The children of merchants were the artist's chief subject and stock in trade. What a model! One could repeat it indefinitely. He began to ask Anthony about himself.

Miss Florence broke in and was permitted to help explain. She did so with giggles which were contagious. The atmosphere grew even easier. They were gay at no one's expense. Soon Anthony was talking about himself. His queer jargon of obsolete Tuscan interspersed with learned and stilted phrases from Latin and French amazed and secretly convulsed them. In this lingo the brief annals of his quiet existence were soon told. Mr. Udney became interested and led Anthony about the room talking to him. The avid mind and the starved curiosity of the boy were at once apparent to him. The audience looked on quietly, amazed at the lad's exclamations over the ordinary furniture of domestic life and his familiarity with classics. A lecture on the use of the library globes, which Mr. Udney's encouragement drew forth, was inimitable. The gentleman was "demned" again.

From the standpoint of the British consul the whole exhibition was a confirmation of his own opinion as to the wrong-headed education provided by the Romish clergy. Probably his own daughter was having much the same kind of stuff driven into her head by the nuns. It was a sore point between him and his wife. To be sure, there was no other school, but . . . He would have enlarged on the subject to her had it not been for the presence of the Italian artist who was, of course, of the "opposite persuasion." Besides it occurred to him again, as he looked at Anthony sidewise, that the boy *did* look English. His own son, if he ever had one, might look like that, he flattered himself.

Mrs. Udney, on the other hand, was quietly scheming behind the teacups to have Anthony remain for the night. Instinctively she wanted him in the house. By these vague prejudices and emotions passing unrecorded through the hearts and brains of strangers the future of the boy was irrevocably shaped.

Mrs. Udney advanced her proposition only tentatively, but she was heartily seconded by Florence. To her surprise, her husband seemed amused and easily consented. Even Signore Terrini entered into the spirit of the occasion, as he always made a point of doing, and sketched Anthony with his hat on while Mr. Udney wrote a note. A charming sketch of Florence followed as a slight hint of what might be done. This with a magnificent flourish the artist signed "Terrini, Livorno, 1785," and handed to Mrs. Udney. As for Anthony, he was invited forthwith to late dinner which proved to be the climax of a clearly miraculous day.

Mother Marie José was considerably disturbed when she was informed about an hour before vespers that Anthony was missing. It annoyed her to find that old Sister Agatha was more worried about the child than the consequences which might follow his disappearance. The woman was too venerable, weak, and frightened to be disciplined any longer. The mother superior blamed herself for not having acted promptly upon Father Xavier's recommendation of some months before. After another thorough search of the convent she sent for the priest. They agreed that if Anthony did not appear shortly, inquiry should be made next day leading to his return. There was a difference of opinion between them as to how he should then be disposed of. Father Xavier was for continuing his instructions at the convent until he could send him to Rome. Mother Marie was for placing him with some honest tradesman as an apprentice.

In the continued presence of Anthony at the convent she saw many and increasing difficulties. Above all she hoped that he might now return without having caused any talk. Her school was in too flourishing a condition to be blown upon by gossip. She recollected that the boy was now ten years old and this worried her. On the other hand, she was infinitely indebted to Father Xavier. Without him she could scarcely have obtained her more fashionable hopefuls. The priest's securing of the English consul's daughter had been especially satisfactory. The patronage of the English element in the town was essential.

It was with some reluctance, therefore, after carefully weighing the matter, that she finally consented to the priest's plea, and then only with the understanding that he would make himself responsible for the boy's whereabouts and good behaviour if he continued to remain at the convent. Father Xavier was surprised to find how relieved and happy he was at this outcome. He had become more interested in the child than he had realized.

Such was the state of affairs when Mr. Udney's groom arrived with a note for the mother superior. The messenger desired an answer. Mother Marie turned pale. The note was the confirmation of her worst fears. In her agitation she saw the work of a decade about to tumble about her ears.

> . . . Kindly carry my compliments to Father Xavier and inform him that his hat has been very much admired here . . .

Mr. Udney had not quite been able to restrain himself.

Mother Marie did not understand. She was scandalized she should be asked to "convey compliments" from one man to another. At the thought of the ragged orphan riding "concealed in a carriage" with the daughter of one of her most valued patrons the roots of her hair crept. It outraged every convention of a hard training and an unimaginative soul. She forgot the children were very small. Mr. Udney's "explanation" had only made matters worse. She changed her mind on the instant. Anthony would have to go.

Father Xavier had never seen her so vehement. He was secretly somewhat afraid of Mother Marie. It would never do to oppose her now. He could see that. If he was going to do anything for the boy, prevent him from being turned into a peasant or a carpenter, for instance, he would have to act promptly. He would have to act that night! So he agreed with the mother superior.

"And this note?" she groaned.

"Allow me to carry the answer myself," he suggested. "I shall call on Mr. Udney immediately—to get my hat."

"Your hat!" cried she indignantly.

"But I shall also take the opportunity," continued Father Xavier, "of explaining matters there. I can do so I am sure. Also," he hurried on, seeing her look of doubt still lingering, "when I return I shall have disposed of your orphan. I am well known to Signore Udney, you know." He spread his hands out appealingly, and with a hint of caution. "You will be well advised I think if you leave the matter to me." She nodded. "It is a lonely life we lead, sometimes, my sister, is it not? We orphans, you know," he said as he passed out. She nodded again. "Yes, sometimes," he heard her reply in a low voice. "Do as you wish with him." But he did not hear that. He had gone.

She sat in a mist of recollection longer than she knew. For the first time in ten years they waited for her at vespers. Before she rose from her knees she had changed her mind again. Father Xavier should keep his pupil.

The priest in the meanwhile in his best gown but hatless was being driven to Mr. Udney's. He arrived there when they were half through dinner to be welcomed warmly by all including Anthony whose cup was now running over with happiness.

"I have come for my hat and for the young rascal who took it," Father Xavier declared as he sat down.

"In the meantime let this refurbish you internally as well," said Mr. Udney loading his plate. He was fond of the priest who did not insist on his cloth. "A wise and kindly man," thought the Englishman cutting him a choice slice of mutton. They had in fact been able to help each other on several occasions. It was not the first time Mr. Udney had carved for the priest. Over the wine—while Mrs. Udney, Signore Terrini and the children gathered about her spinet in the next room—Father Xavier related all that he knew of the story of Anthony to Mr. Udney . . .

"And so, my good friend," he ended,—the genuine eloquence of affection having already lent wings to his plea,—"I would I could say my co-religionist, I want your assistance in this matter, just as you lately were in want of mine." Mr. Udney held up his hand.

"Have you any plans?" he asked.

"There is the Casa da Bonnyfeather. I had thought of that." Mr. Udney smiled at the priest's evident familiarity with lay affairs in the town.

"Yes, I could help you there. Old Bonnyfeather is, or was a Jacobite, yet in his trading here, and everywhere, he needs his British protection. You see I made certain concessions about his oath of allegiance. Nothing really irregular, you know," he added hastily. The priest smiled.

"I also made certain concessions."

"Ah, he is of your persuasion then. You are his confessor?" Mr. Udney did not press that point. The father sipped his port.

"In other words, if both of us should call on him, say, tomorrow," continued Mr. Udney, "he might find room in his establishment for a promising orphan. It would be difficult to resist both the temporal and ecclesiastical authorities combined. Would it not, father?"

"Impossible, I think," smiled the priest. "But why not tonight?"

"Why not?" echoed his host. "Mr. Bonnyfeather will not be busy."

They came out and sat in the hall looking into the big room. Mrs.

Udney was touching the keys while Signore Terrini twittered through an aria in an affected tenor. The children were sitting close together, Anthony's bare toes gleaming out of his shoes. They seemed to be reflecting the warmth of his expression of happiness. Suddenly they started to dance. Mrs. Udney had caught sight of her audience in the hall and cutting off Signore Terrini rather mercilessly, had broken into the stirring strains of "Malbrouk s'en va-t-en guerre." The notes rang and the face of the boy became exalted. Mrs. Udney managed to beckon to her husband who came near. A smile passed between them quietly as they looked at the rapt face of Anthony. "Does he really stay tonight, then?" she asked. "Yes," said he stooping lower, watching her hands flutter over the keyboard. "Father Xavier and I are making final arrangements for him, I trust. Mr. Bonnyfeather!"

"Good," said she. "Splendid! I knew you would do something."

He rejoined Father Xavier in the hall.

Presently the sound of wheels was heard above the tune. The music ceased and Anthony returned to this world to find a strange little girl seated beside him. Mrs. Udney rose and took the children to their rooms.

Between the cool, lavender-scented sheets, a totally new experience for Anthony, his body seemed to be floating in the smooth water of the pool. From somewhere down the hall came the silvery voice of a little girl wishing him good night. As he sank deeper into the complete rest of tired happiness, he looked in vain for the face of the madonna over the foot of his bed. Presently a soft glow suffusing the white wall of his chamber, and the habit of his mind combined to place her there where she belonged. He began his prayer. His lips moved making a sound like the trees outside, and like that dying away into the peace of the night.

Father Xavier and Mr. Udney trotted rapidly down the winding road to Livorno. The moon was rising. The water and air about it became visible and blent together in a pervading white shimmer. In this the whiter buildings of the town and the long harbour mole seemed to swim. The coloured lights of the shipping were caught like fire-flies in a dark web of tangled rigging and masts. The streets were silent, but from a Maltese ketch some distance out came the ecstatic agony of a pulsing stringed instrument punctuated by the beating of feet on deck. An occasional weird cry arose. In the light warm air the music was alternately loud and soft.

"The boy is in good hands tonight at least," said Father Xavier softly. "I wish . . ."

"It is curious," remarked Mr. Udney, "that no men are too savage to be affected by moonlight. It is the same to us all. Like imagination it presents a familiar world in a new light." Mr. Udney was privately given to this kind of semi-profundity. He hoped Father Xavier would be impressed.

"I am wondering," said the latter, "how Mr. Bonnyfeather will take the proposal of receiving so young a lad into his establishment. Since the death of his daughter . . ."

"Tush, man! That was a decade or so ago, wasn't it? Never fear. Secretly he may be glad to have this boy. A Scot, though, would never say so, you know."

They drew up before a long building whose arches looped along the water front, and were soon knocking loudly at a high double gate. The echo boomed through the emptiness beyond. In the sombre archway a streak of lantern light suddenly flowed under the gate.

"Wha be ye poondin' at sic a rate oot there?" grumbled a voice to itself while a chain rattled. A small grille opened and a head in a red night-cap peered through.

"It's Mr. Udney, Sandy," said that gentleman reassuringly. "And Father Xavier," he added as the lantern was flashed on them both suspiciously.

"Losh, mon, come in, come in!" replied the voice as the bolts were shot back. "To think I hae kepit the Breetish consul, and the faither durlen withoot. Mind ye dinna trrip ower the besom the noo."

Mr. Udney chuckled as their footfalls wakened the stones of the court.

Mr. Bonnyfeather was at home.

CHAPTER ELEVEN

BETWEEN TWO WORLDS

ANTHONY was driven back to the convent the next morning in the cart with Florence. He was received with tears by Sister Agatha. There was a message for him to report to the mother superior. She had already relented and had made up her mind to give the boy only a sharp lesson and allow him to continue with Father Xavier. That the priest had already made other arrangements for bestowing the lad, she did not yet know.

His room and the court seemed warm and pleasantly familiar to Anthony. It was home after all. He was glad to see the madonna, but it was with a sinking sensation in the pit of his stomach that he threaded the maze of long corridors leading to the mother superior's room. One was not summoned there for trifles. Already the outside world seemed distant and ineffectual. His feet raised stony echoes that might call a dangerous attention to himself. He began to walk on tiptoe.

Mother Marie José's cheek band had been illy laundered. It was rough and chafed her under the chin. She had removed it and was changing her head-dress when Anthony appeared silently and unexpectedly at the door. Looking in, the boy saw a perfectly smooth-shaven head shining like a skull, a face unexpectedly broad with two glittering, brown eyes staring out of it, and a birthmark that flowed down over the woman's chin into the breast of her black gown. Between the chin and the eyes the face seemed terribly vacant by contrast. It was an almost supernatural countenance. A comet seemed passing beneath two burning stars. Intense fear and horror contorted the face of the boy. Mother Marie José gave a faint scream and snatched at her head-dress which covered the secret of her life. From its broad, linen band only her fine wide forehead and her statuesque profile now showed. She had indeed taken the veil again, but from her eyes there still darted an intensely feminine fire. She approached Anthony deliberately and laid hold of his arm.

"Never tell what you saw," she said through her teeth. The grasp tightened. "Do you understand, you boy!" She began to shake him. Her face drew nearer. With a sudden desperate jerk he tore his arm free and dashed down the corridor. He flashed headlong into his room and stood there while a mixture of rage, fear, indignation, and

151

surprise clutched his throat in dry, hard sobs.   Presently he saw the
calm face of the madonna through his tears.   He snatched her to him
from her niche and peeped out of the door.   Old Sister Agatha had
gone from the court.   He took the statue, climbed with it into the
tree, and hid himself.

Mother Marie José was also trembling with conflicting emotion in
which anger and fear predominated.   She rang her bell and sent
urgently for Father Xavier.   She spoke to him imperatively when he
appeared.   Her one idea now was to get Anthony away.

"I am sorry he has been impudent to you," he replied.

She accepted his unconscious explanation eagerly.

"Take him to your house until you have made your arrangements
for him.   I will not permit him to stay here.   It is impossible.   Not
an hour.   I . . ."

"Recollect yourself, madam," said the priest.

She saw she had gone too far.   "Do as I ask you then," she said
beseechingly.   "I will send his belongings and a certificate of character
to you shortly, but get him beyond these walls."

The priest looked at her sorrowfully and turned away.   No matter
what had occurred, he thought her haste petulant to say the least.   He
was surprised that she should show such feeling.   One never knew
what a woman would do.   He had intended to take Anthony to town
tomorrow.   So it must be today, then!   Today?   His heart sank.   He
tried to shut the image of the child out of his mind.   It would never
do to torture himself for a whole day longer.   Now, it must be now.

Anthony was not in his room.   Father Xavier bundled a few of the
child's pitiful belongings into a pillow case.   A broken wooden horse
smote his eyes dim.   He turned to the door and called.

The boy did not answer at first.   Then he saw that Father Xavier
was weeping.   "I am here, father," he called.   His bright hair and
face peered out of the leaves half-way up the tree.

"Come down, my son, I have something to tell you that you must
hear."   He kept trying to smile.   The boy climbed down and approached him bravely.

"You are to come with me," said Father Xavier, and took him by
the hand.   They went down the lane to the house together silently.
Anthony was still holding fast to the statue of the madonna.

The priest had intended to keep the lad with him all afternoon.   He
had carefully prepared in his own mind the things which he most
wished to impress upon Anthony, a last and memorable lesson as it
were, and he had also counted upon explaining some of the things
which would be required of the boy in the strange, new world where
he would shortly find himself.   Faced by the actual fact of parting,
and shaken by the unexpected violence of Mother Marie José, the

heart and nerves of the man had combined to drive his excellent little
homily from his head. A genuine ascetic, Father Xavier was also
shocked to find himself yearning over this orphan whom chance had
thrown in his way as if he had been a child of his own flesh. "The
flesh is indeed weak," he told himself. Affection shown at leave-tak-
ing would be weakening with himself. To save himself from that, he
knew that he might become stern. He did not want to do that. He
could not be sure of himself either way. Plainly it would never do to
prolong things. He had intended to send out for a decent suit for the
boy. Well, he would have to go in his ragged cassock now. The
priest walked up and down keeping his face from Anthony. "How
long would the Mother Superior take with her certificate and the other
things? One might think a prince was departing with paraphernalia.
Did she know she was torturing him?" Presently the portress came
with a black, mildewed bag.

"Is that all?" said Father Xavier.

"There was a statue of the madonna in his room which is also his.
It is to go too, the mother superior said," replied the woman. "Here
is the certificate. You will please be sure to have this receipt signed
for all of his things, father. I was told to be sure not to forget to tell
you that."

The priest nodded, and pointed to the madonna lying on the chair.
"All here," he said. The good Contessina turned to go. Anthony
was sitting by the window watching the chickens. Suddenly he found
himself in the woman's arms. She was crying over him, hugging him.

"The saints be with you, my bright little pigeon. May you fly far.
Mary go with you!—my God! Good-bye, good-bye!" Then she was
gone. A natural phenomenon had dimmed the scene from Father
Xavier's eyes. Pretending not to notice, he busied himself by putting
the madonna into the bag. He now closed it and looked up. Anthony
was standing with a blank face.

"I am going away?" he asked

"Yes."

"Now?"

The priest nodded slowly.

"Because of what I have done?"

"No," said the man in spite of himself.

"Tell me, then!" cried the boy. A sudden hope leaped into his eyes.
"Is it to Signore Udney? Ma donna there is not like . . ."

"Like whom?"

The boy faltered. "Thou knowest," he said finally.

"Come," said Father Xavier. "I shall tell you as we go." He took
the bag from the table and led the boy from the room. As they passed

down the lane a certain bricked-up window in the wall gaped at them like a mouth that had been stopped with clay.

It was a good two miles to Livorno, a hot day, and a dusty road. The stones of the highway hurt the feet of the boy used only to the smooth courts of the convent. He limped, but he listened so intently to what Father Xavier was telling him that he scarcely had time to notice his feet.

The priest's voice was once more calm. In affectionate tones he was creating for Anthony a new vista in life. "Apprenticed"—Father Xavier had to explain what that meant. Yes, he had arranged it all the night before. "While I was sleeping at Signore Udney's," thought Anthony. He looked back. Nothing was to be seen now of the convent except its red roofs and the pigeons circling about the top of his tree. They swooped down and disappeared. Contessina was feeding them then. So, they could get along without him! He pondered the fact. "But I shall come several times a week, my son," the father's voice was saying, "to continue your instruction—for at least a while." The man sighed. "Then, who knows?" Anthony looked up as the tones faltered again. "Often?" he asked. The priest nodded with a determined look. The boy smiled. "I am glad," he said.

They walked on in silence. Anthony did not look back again. It was a relief when he felt the warm, smooth flagstones of the approach to the Porta Pisa under his feet. There was a throng of country carts lined up there from which two Austrian soldiers in glistening, white uniforms, with muskets slung behind them, were collecting small copper coins. Anthony stared. They passed by the striped sentry boxes with the grand ducal arms, and turned toward the water front. The whirl and colour of a seaport dizened itself into his eyes. For a moment it threatened to engulf him.

He had never imagined there were so many people in the world, or so many tongues. Along the rivers of the streets poured in both directions a mass of vehicles; wheelbarrows piloted by whistling, bawling porters; creaking oxcarts. Donkeys with huge barrels slung on either side crowded pedestrians to the wall and swept all before them triumphantly. Army wagons like canal boats on wheels, laden with wine and forage for the garrison, jolted toward the Castello Vecchio. They often seemed to dam up the whole street. As they turned the corner of the Piazza d'Arme a flood of low-hung drays piled with bales, or loaded with live cattle and poultry swept past them, whips cracking.

Father Xavier and Anthony stood back against the wall to avoid the whisking tails of horses and mules that slithered by with ears laid back. The dust rolled, streaked with pencilled sunlight at the cross streets. Porters jostled them, and merchants in laced coats laughed.

Anthony could scarcely repress an impulse to take refuge in the dark, cool alleyways, or to dart into one of the many courtyards filled with bright, fluttering clothes.   At times he seemed lost in a forest of legs, knee breeches, and the flapping trousers of British tars.   Above his head their black glazed hats sailed past, a yard of ribbon fluttering behind.   He tripped over a beggar who cursed him horribly.   The stench of everything-at-once overpowered him, and clutched at his throat.   Suddenly they turned a corner and came out on the long cobble-paved water front of the minor, inner port or Darsena.

As long as he lived Anthony never forgot that moment.   There was a vividness about it which was, at the time, more than he could appreciate.   For the first time the lenses of his senses now came to a completely clear and perfectly blent focus.   Into the still bare, and somewhat misty room of his mind burst the glorious, light-flooded vision of reality.   There was not still-life only as heretofore.   On this crowded water front there was motion and song.   He lifted his head to drink it all in.   He felt his heritage as one of the swarm fully conferred upon him.   The vision beyond and the beholder for the first time lost themselves in each other and became one.

For years it was impossible, except at rare moments, or by the aid of closed eyelids to separate them again.   That, as he came to know afterwards, was both the reward and the stumbling-block of a good mind in a healthy body.

But this first impression of Livorno was his awakening.   As he thought of it years later, it seemed to him that at the convent his vision of life had taken place mysteriously in the camera obscura of a child's mind.   Indeed, as he looked back, there was even a kind of charm about it, a rather dark, melancholy tinge with bright tufts of colour standing out beautifully.   Looking at a street scene reflected in a black, polished stone in a jeweller's window at Paris many years afterward, he was forcibly reminded again of his days at the convent.   Things grew and disappeared in the black mirror in a vista without reason.   They moved by a totally disconnected motion with a volition all their own.   One could be a polytheist in a world like that.   It was lovely, dimly god-like and beautiful, but entirely unreal.

The one exception to this had been his first vision from the treetop.

Now—now as he stood at the street corner just where the land met the sea—life became more than a mere proper focus of several clear lenses.   It seemed as if the windows of his soul had suddenly been thrown wide open.   He felt the air, he heard a clangour, the light streamed in and flooded the room.   Whimsical circumstance decreed that all this wealth of the senses, the very odour of it, should forever be carried for him in a Fortunatus purse of orange peel.

For in the quay opposite, a felucca from Sardinia was unloading.

Piles of oranges lay heaped upon its deck. Some had been crushed beneath the feet of the crew and the air reeked with them. Father Xavier held up his hand and a dark sailor in a red jacket tossed him a yellow globe. As the two stood at the corner sharing it, Anthony's eyes continued to wander along the water front.

Landwise stretched an apparently endless row of long, white buildings facing the harbour. Between them and the quays was a broad, cobble-paved way crawling with jolting, roaring drays, piled with sea stores and merchandise. On the water side sharp bows, gilded figureheads, and bowsprits pierced and overhung the roadway, while a geometrical forest of dark masts, spars, and cordage swept clear around and bordered the inner port. Amid this, like snowdrifts caught here and there in the boughs of a leafless wood, hung drying sails. The sun twinkled at a thousand points on polished brass. It seemed to Anthony that each ship was alive, looking at him narrowly out of its eyelike hawseholes. Farther off was the flashing water beyond the molo, or outer harbour, with a glimpse of the white tower on the breakwater and the dark purple of the sea beyond.

Father Xavier also stood looking at it. While he finished his half of the orange he unconsciously permitted himself a few moments of purely sensuous enjoyment by beholding the view as if through the boy's eyes. The spell was broken as a ship's bell suddenly clanged out. The strokes were instantly taken up and swept the harbour front in a gust of molten sound. The priest threw his orange away, picked up the bag, and grasping Anthony by the hand continued along the narrow sidewalk.

It was somewhat difficult now to make way there. The sound of the ship's bells had been the signal releasing a throng of clerks and apprentices. They poured out of a hundred doors and gates laughing, bawling out, and chaffing one another. Besides that, certain Italian urchins of the crowd began to attach themselves to Father Xavier and his charge. In the tall, thin-waisted priest with the huge hat who carried a peculiar black bag, in the tow-headed acolyte whose ragged cassock flapped about his bare calves there was something rare and too earnest, an air of visitors from another world bound upon some destiny that smacked of strangeness and drama. Despite all they could do to hurry on, a small procession began to form behind the backs of Father Xavier and Anthony. It grew like a snowball, but moved like a queue to the accompaniment of whistles and catcalls. At last they began to pass under the cool arcade of a long, low building whose arches looped for some distance along the water front.

Just above the head of Anthony large, oval windows heavily barred peered out from under a heavy parapet like a row of eyes under the shaded brim of a monstrous hat. Under the arches these eyes seemed to be staring through gigantic spectacles. The total expression of the house was one of annoyed surprise. Since it had commenced life as a nobleman's palace and ended as a warehouse, there was some reason for that. Indeed, what had once been known as the Palacio Gobo now bore shamefacedly along its entire forehead, as if it had been caught in the act and branded, a scarlet legend that could be read afar from the decks of ships, CASA DA BONNYFEATHER. Yet an air of ill-used magnificence still continued to haunt it doubtfully as if loath to depart. It succeeded in concealing itself somehow and eluded the passers-by in the deep grooves and convolutions of the rusticated marble front.

Before the central bronze gates of this peculiar edifice, upon which some vestiges of gilding could still be traced, Father Xavier and his charge came to a sudden halt. The crowd of youngsters following became expectantly silent but finally hooted when after some time no one came. In the meanwhile Anthony peered through the grille.

Beyond the dark, tunnelled archway of the entrance, he could see a sun-flooded courtyard. There was a dilapidated fountain in pie-crust style, and behind that a broad flight of steps led up rather too grandly to a great double door only one leaf of which was open. As he leaned forward to peer in, someone from behind tweaked his cassock violently. It ripped up the back exuberantly. There was a shout of delight. Another urchin laid hold of him.

"Cosa volete, birbante?" yelled Father Xavier shaking the culprit.

Matters were obviously approaching a crisis when one of the crowd shouted that the facchino was coming, and a Swiss porter opened the gate. Holding his torn skirt about him, Anthony stepped through after Father Xavier.

He was not quite quick enough, however. There was a sudden rush behind him and his cassock was this time ripped clear off his back and whisked away. A shower of rubbish followed him as the gate clanged. He ran a little distance down the archway and stood shivering. Father Xavier's face was still red, but both he and the porter now started to laugh heartily.

It was thus, naked as when he was born, that Anthony first found shelter in the Casa da Bonnyfeather.

CHAPTER TWELVE

CASA DA BONNYFEATHER

THEY turned to the left through a door half-way down the vaulted tunnel of the entrance and found themselves in a vestibule provided with black marble benches. It had evidently once been the guard-room of the palace. Against the wall there was a rack for halberds now occupied by a couple of mops and a frayed broom. Anthony found the benches too cold to sit upon. He stood disconsolately in the middle of the apartment with mosaic dolphins sporting about his cold feet. The porter departed to inform the Capo della Casa of the unexpected guests. Father Xavier reflected with some alarm that the present costume of his charge was not that proper to the introduction of an apprentice to his master. Suddenly he remembered something, and with great eagerness opened the bag.

From it he extracted a lady's riding cloak moth-eaten along the folds. He shook it dubiously. Several small spiders scampered away and the dried petals of a white flower lilted to the floor. It would have to do—under the circumstances. He dropped it over the boy's shoulders who gathered it about him eagerly, holding it with crossed hands. Presently the porter returned and beckoned to Father Xavier to follow him. The priest told Anthony to wait.

To Anthony standing alone in the centre of the vestibule, it seemed as if he had been left in a limbo between two worlds. The chill of the stone made his feet ache and crept up his spine like a cold iron. Somewhere, in another world, he could hear a clock ticking. It went on and on. Presently he could stand it no longer. The old silk cloak rustled eerily when he moved, and smelt mouldy. He followed where the others had led, mounted several steps, and stepped through a doorway.

At the end of what seemed to be a vast apartment, Father Xavier was talking to an elderly gentleman in black who was seated behind a desk in a high-backed chair. Anthony remembered now that Father Xavier had told him to wait. He therefore stopped and gathered the old cloak about him holding it close at the breast. He was afraid to go back now. If he moved they might see him.

What daunted the boy most was the fact that the portion of the room where the two men were talking was raised several feet above the rest of the apartment like the quarter-deck of a ship. It even had

158

a rail across it. Before the old gentleman, who wore an immense, old-fashioned wig, was a large bronze inkstand full of quills. From the railing to Anthony stretched a long aisle lined on either side by a perspective of empty desks piled high with ledgers and copy books. The clerks had all left. In either wall a row of big oval windows admitted bars of sunlight. Father Xavier and the gentleman continued talking. They were talking in English. Anthony knew that. He heard his own name several times. It grew tiresome. He looked up.

In an oval panel in the ceiling a number of people in cloudy costumes were gathered banqueting about a huge man with a beard. Anthony was peculiarly intrigued by a slim figure with wings on his heels. "How convenient," the boy thought, "but how small the wings are!" He pondered with his chin in the air.

"You will understand, then, what has happened," Father Xavier was saying. "The mother superior was most insistent. I had not intended to bring the boy to you until tomorrow, as we had arranged, but under the circumstances—" He spread out his hands in a comprehensive gesture. "Were it not for her request I should not bother you about signing this receipt. There is nothing in the bag of any value I am quite sure except the ten gold pieces. We have never quite fathomed this case, apparently one of desertion by people of means. The boy has some of the earmarks of gentle blood. For that reason, in view of possible influential complications later on, it seems best to be able to show that not only did the convent care for the orphan as its foundation on the old status required, but restored him to the world with the best of prospects—I am sure!—and with every item of his property intact. Bag and baggage complete for his earthly journey, you see."

"But a not too extensive wardrobe as I gather," interpolated the gentleman smiling quizzically.

"My dear Mr. Bonnyfeather," replied Father Xavier, "you will not only gain merit for having sheltered the orphan, but for clothing the naked as well. A rare opportunity, I assure you. Now, as to the receipt? Shall I get the bag first?"

"Tut, tut, man, of course I'll sign it. You act as if you suspected me of thinking you had spent the money for drink on the way down." Mr. Bonnyfeather leaned forward to dip his pen, but never touched it. His fingers remained extended pointing at the door. A look of astonished recognition and extreme fear worked in his countenance.

"Who . . . who is that?" he finally rasped.

Father Xavier turned hastily and saw Anthony contemplating the ceiling with a seraphic look.

"Why, that is the young gentleman of whom we have just been

speaking," exclaimed the priest. "He seems to be admiring your frescoes. I told him to wait in the vestibule!"

"The benches are hard there," observed Mr. Bonnyfeather, regaining his self-control with an obvious effort, "we save them for our minor creditors." He laughed half-heartedly. "The truth is," he hurried on in an uncontrollable and unusual burst of confidence, "the truth is, standing there with his face just in that position he reminded me forcibly just now of—my daughter." The phrase passed his lips for the first time in ten years. It aroused a thousand silent echoes of emotion in the merchant's empty heart. He wiped his forehead. The priest remained silent for some time.

"Perhaps you will speak with the boy now?" he said at last. Mr. Bonnyfeather nodded.

"Come here, Anthony," said Father Xavier a little sternly. The boy advanced slowly holding his cape about him. Mr. Bonnyfeather's mind flashed back to a night ten years before. In the chair now occupied by the priest sat a bulky nobleman with a florid face and black-pointed beard. "Buried in the Alps," he was saying, "both of them. Buried! Do you understand?" The black beard punctuated the remark emphatically. Through the haze of this vision, as if in warm denial, the bright, serious face of the boy intervened. The priest was speaking again.

"Shake hands with your benefactor, my son. You are fortunate in having so kindly and sheltering an arm extended to you." Father Xavier was in reality congratulating himself on a good piece of work. Mr. Bonnyfeather now recollected himself and took the small palm extended to him out of the folds of the faded cloak with a kindly pressure. The boy's face still troubled him. He cleared his throat.

"Do you think you will like it here, my boy?"

"I cannot tell yet, signore," replied Anthony gravely.

"That is right," said the merchant evidently gratified. "Be frank and we shall have no difficulty in getting along. *Hummmm!* I shall arrange for some other—for some clothes for you directly." Anthony coloured.

"Thank you," he said.

As if the matter were concluded satisfactorily, Mr. Bonnyfeather now reached down, carefully read, and signed the receipt. "The indentures will be ready tomorrow, father. You can stop in for them then or the next time you come to town. It will be best I think to have our own notary. No one outside need then know that the convent has had anything to do with this case. You yourself can witness the mother superior's signature."

The priest bowed in assent. "May I," said he, "attempt to thank you again? To me it is more than . . ."

Mr. Bonnyfeather held up his hand and rose from his chair.

They walked down the room together, Anthony trailing behind. "That is the bag," said the priest as they came into the vestibule. "Not a very heavy one, I see," replied Mr. Bonnyfeather. "It is hard to tell what there might be in it, though." The old man's eyes twinkled. A small lock of grey hair had escaped from under his wig on one side. It conferred upon his rather austere and regular face a decided touch of benignity. "Will you be staying for supper with us?" The priest shook his head. "No, it is time to go—now." A misty look came into his eyes.

"I shall be back to continue your lessons, you know," he said to Anthony trying to be casual, and added softly, "my son." The boy flung up his arms. Father Xavier stopped short for an instant, hesitated, then seized his hat and almost fled through the door. Mr. Bonnyfeather whose heart had for a long time kept the same beat as the clock which regulated his establishment felt a slight internal pause in time as he looked at Anthony.

"Come," he said, "let us have a look at your new home." They walked down the archway together into the courtyard.

Seated before the fountain with her back toward them while she was milking a goat, was the largest woman in Italy. She had flaming hair, and from where they were standing her figure appeared to be that of a huge pear with a ripe cherry on top of the pear. A small keg under her seemed to provide ridiculous support, and for every quiver of her frame as she milked, the goat bobbed its tufted tail. Anthony laughed till he had to clutch at his cape to keep it from falling off. At this sound the pear rose from the bucket, and pivoting on what appeared to be two mast stumps ending in dumplings, took hold of a green petticoat and quivered a curtsy to Mr. Bonnyfeather.

"Angela," said he, "this is Master Anthony, the new apprentice. Will you look after him in the kitchen till after supper? I may change my mind about his sleeping in the clerks' dormitory. You might lend him some of your son's clothes, temporarily. He has suffered a mishap."

The face of the woman of a fine olive complexion beamed broadly upon the small figure before her.

"Benvenuto, signore," she said. "I shall attend to your clothes, sir, as soon as I milk. Saints! The goat has gone!"

She started after the animal much in the manner of a mountain pursuing a flea, but holding up her skirt. The goat had taken refuge in some defunct garden-beds, the graceful stone outlines of which on either side of the court now enclosed nothing but heaps of rubbish. As the mountain approached, the flea merely hopped away and the process repeated itself. Finally it shifted to the other flower-bed.

Mr. Bonnyfeather, although he had emitted no unseemly noises, was in no shape to aid even had he been so inclined. He was, however, still able to nod to Anthony who now joined in the hunt. The mountain was thus aided in its pursuit of the flea by a small, flapping blackbird with white, gawky legs. Mr. Bonnyfeather could no longer restrain his guffaws. Anthony now approached. The goat lowered her horns, and the boy flapped his cloak. At this ill omen, Capricorna departed nimbly up a staircase to the flat roof. Its bearded, female countenance appeared shortly afterward peering solemnly over the low parapet.

"*M-a-a-a-a*, my friends."

The challenge was accepted and the chase moved heavenward. The small boy preceded the huge woman up the narrow staircase toward the roof. Suddenly, the goat appeared at the top. Her pursuers paused thoughtfully in mid-air, but not for long. Gathering her feet under her like a bird in flight, the goat descended upon those below in the manner of an ancient battering ram. Two sounds marked the whizzing return of her body to the earth below; a small puff when it hit Anthony, and a grunt like a startled sow when Anthony hit Angela. The goat passed over them. They both rolled to the bottom of the stairs where they were met by Mr. Bonnyfeather who was trying to laugh and cry at the same time.

For a few breathless moments the mountain appeared to be in travail. Then it wheezed, groaned, arose, and departed to the kitchen feeling itself below the timber line for broken bones. An enormous clattering of pots and pans later ensued.

Anthony had luckily been saved serious injury by being driven into a soft place on the mountain. Nevertheless, he was in a miserable enough state. Mr. Bonnyfeather carried his limp form into the house and sat down with him by a table near the door. The boy's face was chalky and his white eyelids trembled. He gasped occasionally and there was blood on his lips.

"Welcome, indeed!" thought Mr. Bonnyfeather, "puir little laddie!" He sat for a minute wondering what he could do.

"Faith, Faith," he called at last. There was no answer. "Drat the woman, she'll be oot wi the clarks, brisket bonny, nae doot." His indignation rose with his anxiety. The whole establishment had availed themselves of his permission to go to a carnival performance. Gianfaldoni was to dance. Only the cook, who had no interest in that art any longer, remained in the courtyard. Mr. Bonnyfeather reflected with some bitterness that even Faith Paleologus, his trusted housekeeper of a decade or more, would desert him to see a mere ballerino. Alone with the hurt child in his arms in a huge, dusty, old ballroom seething with mouldy frescoes and hung with cobwebbed chandeliers, he felt as if fate had played him a scurvy trick.

It was in this baroque scene of departed grandeur that the merchant habitually ate and entertained visiting ship captains. As he looked about it now in the fast-fading light, the moth-eaten splendours of the high-roofed and too ample apartment seemed to be mocking his loneliness. There was not a human sound in the generally thronged courtyard. An occasional suppressed bleat from the goat only served to lend a slightly demoniac quality to the unusual quiet. It was suddenly borne in upon Mr. Bonnyfeather sitting in the silence and the twilight that every living thing had deserted him—that life would leave him alone thus a helpless and childless old man. He looked down at the pallid face of the boy and sighed.

It was some thirty years now since he had held a child in his arms who resembled this one. The similarity of their features was undoubted. It troubled him. It stirred, and not vaguely, a sorrow so deep as to be tearless, a grief lapped as it were in deep, damp stone, but one from which great pressure or a sudden shattering blow might still extort drops of moisture. It was in this deep vein that he was now penetrated. It came upon him that even the cloak looked familiar. But all women's cloaks look the same. Pooh! He was a foolish old man alone in the dark, aegri somnia. Stop dreaming! He must do something for this child who was ill, who had been flung as it seemed into his arms by the Church—and that devil of a goat, Auld Hornie himself.

Well, he *would* do something about it. He *was* lonely. He could cheat the devil at least. As if he had come to a sudden and irrevocable resolution Mr. Bonnyfeather rose determinately and laid Anthony on the big oak table putting an old leather cushion under his head. The boy stirred weakly, and half opening his eyes closed them again with a shiver.

The great ballroom of the Palacio Gobo had once extended the entire length of the lower floor, but in its second incarnation as the Casa da Bonnyfeather this painted scene of much ancient, ceremonious gayety had been divided like Gaul. Stone partitions had been thrown across either end and the space behind them divided in turn into several smaller rooms. Of the two new apartments, thus laid off at either end of the old, one was occupied by the cook with a numerous family, and the other by Mr. Bonnyfeather himself.

It was toward his own particular section of the building that the merchant now made his way. Taking a large bunch of keys from his bulging pockets, he unlocked the door in the partition.

Before him was a long hall floored with a carpet of deep pile upon which his feet fell noiselessly. In the daytime this corridor was lighted from above by a skylight. That, however, was only a glimmer now above his head where a few stars appeared as if peering through a hole in the roof. All that part of the building would now have been entirely dark had it not been for a subdued radiance that escaped from a small Chinese lamp on a gilt stand at the extreme end of the hall.

Set beside the wide, white door of Mr. Bonnyfeather's room, the gilded and carved lintel of which it invested with important shadows, the light of this oriental lantern seemed to percolate its jade screen statically as if determined to tinge even the shadows upon which it now shone with its own quiet serenity. Behind the partition he had reared, and amid these shadows, the merchant had attempted to build for himself a refuge from the world. Once over the threshold of these precincts, Mr. Bonnyfeather shook off the rather staid man of business that the world knew and became a mere man. He unbent and moved now, not only more at ease, but more gracefully, as if he had cast off the habits of half a lifetime and returned to those of his youth.

Besides his own room at the end of the corridor, there were two others on each side of it as he passed down. The two on the left were empty and had been so for years. One had belonged to his wife who had died in childbirth, and the other to the daughter she had borne. The rooms on the right, which looked into the court, were those of Faith Paleologus, the housekeeper, and Sandy McNab, the chief clerk.

On this evening, while the living were absent, as he stepped into the corridor the place seemed to Mr. Bonnyfeather unbearably quiet. The sense of loneliness which he had experienced so vividly a few moments earlier was now reinforced and increased severalfold, and this time with a kind of stealthy eeriness inherent in the close quarters and the silent carpet underfoot.

As he passed the long-locked doors on his left, there arose in him a strong impression that the rooms behind them were still occupied. The memory of voices, footfalls, and faces once familiar to them surged up in him toward reality again. They suddenly threatened to force conviction upon him. They succeeded. A blind terror overcame him and stopped him sweating before the last door on the left. His keys tinkled in his hand. He had heard a sound in there! Had he? He listened intently again. A minute passed. "Maria?" he called.

At the sound of his own voice his self-possession flooded back. Nevertheless, to reassure himself, he tried the handle of the door immediately across the hall on the right. It was that of his housekeeper. It too was locked. He had hoped after all she might be in. He mumbled something and stood baffled. "Drat the woman! Cauld she no trust the maister wi his ain linen!" The dialect rasped in his head when he grew excited. He had intended to put the boy in there for a while.

But how long it had been since there were any sounds of life in the room across the hall! If he *was* going to hear things there—they had better be real ones. Besides, that child was still lying out in the big room ill in the dark. Well, he *could* do it. Open Maria's room alone? But who was there left to open it with him, now? No one. He would put somebody alive in there. It needed the familiar face of that young stranger. Something gay there, laughter, life! And he would do it before Faith returned.

He strode into his own room and dashed a shower of sparks into the tinder box. Presently a number of candles were blazing, all that he had. He felt reassured. Their sudden cheerfulness seemed to beam approval on his plan. Taking a candelabrum with no less than six tapers in it, he came back into the hall again, set it down on the floor, and with determined fingers thrust a rusty key into the lock of his daughter's room. He winced as the ward rasped, but steeled himself. He turned the knob boldly, thrust back the door on its faintly complaining hinges, and faced the past.

It was not so poignant as he had expected. Through a window set high in the wall at the other end came lively noises from the street beyond. A horse trotted by. The empty bed under an empty niche in one corner of the wall had dust upon it. That was all. There was a dressing table with a cloth hung over its mirror. He removed the cloth and set the candle before the glass as rapidly as possible. The room seemed to glare then. Some faded, girlish dresses hanging in an open wardrobe he did not try to look at. He dusted the bed off, returned to his room, and came back again with covers taken from his own couch. These he disposed rapidly in a comfortable way putting the pillow at the foot of the bed. Then he took a candle and went for Anthony.

The boy had opened his eyes and was trying to remember where he was. His belly and his ribs hurt him. He felt sick. The effort of recollection was just now too much. Presently there was a gleam of light on the ceiling. He looked up dizzily and saw the outline of a chariot drawn by plunging horses disappearing into a dark bank of clouds. The face of the driver had dropped out of the plaster. Then he saw the old merchant leaning over him and felt himself being gathered into the man's arms. He remembered now. But where was he being taken? If Father Xavier were only here! "Father," he called. He felt the man who carried him tremble.

As he neared the door with the boy in his arms, Mr. Bonnyfeather saw a lantern crossing the court. Suddenly its owner tripped over something and began to swear. The language was Protestant and from north of the Tweed. Ignoring all intercessors, the man, who was now trying to relight his lantern, addressed himself exclusively to God Almighty.

"Come in, Sandy mon, I want ye," said Mr. Bonnyfeather. "It's argint," he called as he passed through the door with Anthony. A few seconds later, the boy was lying on the bed which had been prepared for him. Sandy McNab's florid countenance was soon staring in at the proceedings of Mr. Bonnyfeather with astonishment.

"I'll no deny that it gave me a jert to see the licht from her door the noo. I couldna faddom it. Mon, yon laddie looks forfairn!" he exclaimed as his eyes fell on Anthony.

"You'd no be feelin' so gawsy yoursel' if you'd had the hourns of a gait aneath your breastie, atwell," replied Mr. Bonnyfeather.

"Whaws bairn is he?" asked Sandy, ignoring the rebuke implied in the merchant's tone of voice. "I dinna ken thot—aiblins," replied the merchant. "He's the new apprentice." Mr. McNab whistled and grinned. "Haud your fissle," said the merchant with some heat, "rin and fetch me a ship's doctor. The first ye can find aboot the dock. Dinna ye see the laddie's in a vera bad wa?"

"Ye maun busk him," countered the irrepressible McNab.

Mr. Bonnyfeather arose. "Will ye stand there and bleeze the nicht awa?" he asked icily.

"Barlafumble!" cried Sandy. "I'll no try to argle-bargle wi ye aughtlins. Ye ken I'm too auld-farrant for thot. But it's een blank— new to a blinkie o' a clark like mysel' to find the maistre o' this estab- lishment singin' balow-baloo to a bit breekless apprentice. It gars me a' mixty-maxty. You're a' the guid mon agin."

"Bletheration!" said his master, laughing in spite of himself. That was exactly what the man at the door had hoped for. It was unusual for Mr. Bonnyfeather to become excited. It was several years now since the chief clerk had seen the merchant's high cheek bones with that faint flush on them and his eyes shining. Something more important than appeared on the surface was toward, he thought. Besides, in this room! He noticed that Mr. Bonnyfeather's hands trembled. He needed company. That was evident. The boy on the bed began to gasp.

"Mind yoursel' he's aboot to bock!" cried Sandy. Lacking anything better he snatched off his hat into which Anthony "bocked." "Puir bairn, you maun be corn't wi crappit head. You're donzie, but wha will reimbarse me for your clappin' my headpiece like a coggie. Dinna coghle ower it so. I'm na feelin' sae cantie and chancy mysel'. Coomin' ower the coort, ye ken, I trippet ower yon clatch of a bag and was like to clout oot me brain pan. Wha would ken a dorlach cauld cleek-it a mon by the foot?"

Mr. McNab took his hat to the window gingerly, opened the window, and somewhat regretfully threw out the hat. "I hope they keep to the crown o' the causey oot there the nicht," he opined. "And noo I'll rin for the physeecian." Glancing at his master with more anxiety than at the boy, he sauntered out, indicating the offending bag with his foot. Mr. Bonnyfeather nodded helplessly. For the second time that day, he wanted to laugh and cry at the same time. He placed the bag on the dresser and sat down close by the bedside. The silence of the house was once more audible.

Anthony alternately dozed and awoke fitfully. When he opened his eyes now, he seemed to be back in his room at the convent. The place had somehow altered. There was a very bright light. The window had shifted its place and altered its shape. The niche in the wall was there, but the statue had vanished from it. That troubled him. He closed his eyes once more and tried to collect himself. When he opened them again they inevitably fell on the vacant niche. The process repeated itself and grew irritating. He muttered about it to himself; talked as though in his sleep. Mr. Bonnyfeather leaned over him rearranging the covers. He wished McNab would come back with the doctor, or that Faith would return. The boy seemed out of his head. What was all this talk about the Madonna? It was some little time before the merchant could make out that "the madonna" was missing from her niche. Then he remembered the receipt he had signed that afternoon. Perhaps the thing was in the bag. He also remembered vaguely that there had once been a saint's image or something in the niche when it was her room.

There was some difficulty with the bag. It seemed reluctant to open after Sandy had tripped over it. The old catch was bent. The boy cried out something and Mr. Bonnyfeather's hand slipped. Inadvertently he ripped the old leather while tugging at it. The bag fell open and gaped like a mouth that had nothing more to say. Out of it Mr. Bonnyfeather extracted a long red purse like a tongue—and the madonna. The sun-burst on her head had been bent a little. He straightened it gingerly and put the statue in the niche where the boy evidently wanted it. Somehow it too seemed vaguely familiar. He tried to remember. But all madonnas were alike, more or less. Yet she did seem to belong there, to fit nicely. It was as if she had been there before.

The boy's eyes opened again and now found what they had sought. An expression like that of a little girl whose lost doll has been found just at bedtime flitted over his face. His eyes caressed the statue and closed happily. He began to breathe more easily. Some colour crept into his cheeks as he slept.

After a while Mr. Bonnyfeather ventured to wipe the blood from

Anthony's mouth. He saw now that it had come from a small cut in the boy's lip. He sat by the bed and waited. An hour slipped by. As he gazed steadily at the lad's quiet face, the conviction of his first impression of it again attained the feeling of certainty. He felt as though he were being haunted. Below the nostrils the resemblance certainly weakened. There was a firmer and broader chin. He placed his hands across the boy's mouth so as to shield it from his view. Instantly from the pillow the face of his daughter looked up at him. The merchant sat down overcome. His head dropped forward into his hands.

His thoughts were still in a whirl when McNab came back with a ship's surgeon. Searching along the dock, it had taken him some time to find one. The doctor was an orderly soul and it irked him to find the patient's head placed at the foot of the bed. He forthwith shifted Anthony about and Mr. Bonnyfeather was forced to see the boy's face just where he had tried to avoid placing it. The doctor's examination disclosed no broken bones. He removed the old cloak, and despite the fact that Anthony cried out, went over him thoroughly. Lacking his instruments for bleeding, the surgeon prescribed rest. He departed with the chief clerk after having received one of the gold pieces from the purse that had come in the bag. It was a large fee. Mr. McNab began to recollect audibly that his hat recently sacrificed in the same good cause was of the best quality. Mr. Bonnyfeather, however, was obtuse. In a short while he was left alone again.

This time the face of the boy was exactly where that of the last occupant of the bed had been. In the mind of the man watching, the two faces were already confused or combined. It was hard to tell which. Only his reason refused to consent. He began to go over word by word the nocturnal interview with Don Luis of ten years before. The words, the very gestures of the marquis, precise, formal, not to be evaded, came back now across the warmth of his new yearning like a wind from glacial peaks. He heard the heavy wheels of the coach rolling away again into the night leaving him standing dazed. "Buried in the Alps."

His own wife had died in childbed, too. It had been like that with Maria! If only her child had lived! Whether it had been a boy or girl he did not know. Don Luis had done all the talking. Futile to ask! The man seemed to be in a white rage that night about something. Not a word for Maria. Only the cold facts, and a final farewell. Disappointment, no doubt. Well, he could understand that. Don Luis had never married again either. Gone to Spain. Nothing had passed between him and the marquis afterwards—nothing but the rent. Ought he to write now? About what? A facial resemblance? Cer-

tainly not like Don Luis.   Mr. Bonnyfeather thought of something
and started.   Impossible!

Impossible any way you looked at it.   Why, he would have to begin
by doubting the marquis' word.   What a letter that would be.   And
what a reply!   He winced.

He must collect himself.   The events of the past few hours were
not sufficient to explain the state in which he now found himself.   He
should not have stayed here alone looking at the boy's face, nor should
he have opened her room.   That was a mistake after all.   If the housekeeper had only not been out.   "Damn the woman, would she never
come home!"   It must be nearly midnight.   He drew out his watch.
In doing so he became aware that someone was standing in the doorway.   He turned about swiftly, terribly startled in spite of himself.

CHAPTER THIRTEEN

THE EVIDENCE OF THINGS UNSEEN

A COUNTENANCE so regular and aquiline as to suggest a bird of prey in forward flight was looking into the chamber where Mr. Bonnyfeather sat grasping his watch convulsively. The face was so pallid and so deep-set in a round straw bonnet that the light from the jade lamp cast a positively greenish hue upon it. It had a broad, low forehead under masses of thick, blue-black hair, a rouged mouth that would have been passionate had it not now been contorted into a grimace of terror and surprise, and a pair of black-brown eyes. These seemed to have something staring through them from behind like those painted on an Egyptian mummy case. The folds of the dress were in obscurity, and a high furbelow from the bonnet seemed to run up like a plume into the night beyond. Mr. Bonnyfeather's grip on his watch tightened. Several seconds, answered by heart beats which he felt throbbing in his hand, passed slowly before he recognized in the plan of the shadows the familiar lineaments of his housekeeper, Faith Paleologus.

"Creest, woman!" said he, "why do ye creep up like that on a body? It's fearsome." He was glad to hear his own voice and continued to talk as he slipped his watch into his pocket allowing the heavy seals to dangle heedlessly. "Whar hae ye been? It's long past midnight, ye ken. Wha hae ye been doin' wee yoursel' the nicht?" She knew he must be excited to question her thus and to lapse into Scotch, to be so direct and familiar. His voice stiffened her. She resented it.

"I'm not so old yet but that I still like a bit of a fling now and then. It was carnival, you know, and I danced. Do you really want to know where?"

"Naw . . . no," he replied, recollecting himself. "But if you had been here I should not have had to put him in this room."

"Who is *he* then?" she asked. "I saw the light from this room as I came in. You wonder I made no noise? It's over ten years agone, you know, since . . ."

"Yes, but . . ."

"You opened it then?"

He nodded unwillingly.

"Why?"

He pointed to the boy on the bed.

170

"John Bonnyfeather," she whispered, "who is it that has come back with her face?"

"Orr-h! You saw it, too?" He went forward and shaded the boy's chin with his hand.

"Saw it! Do you think I need to have you do that? When I looked in here, I thought I was looking at the past again. And I am," she added moving forward so rapidly as to startle him. "Here is a piece of it come back." She snatched the madonna from the niche and bore it to the light. "It is the same, I know." They bent over it together. "Do you think I could ever mistake that? Look!" Under the candles she showed him the almost invisible fracture in the statue to which the knife of the marquis had once pointed so unerringly.

"I gave it to her years ago, here, in this room, long before she left!" The old man reached out for the madonna like a child assuring itself of the reality of an object by touch. But his hands trembled so that she kept the statue and looking at him meaningly returned it to its niche. "How did *that* come here?" she again flung at him.

"I dinna ken!" said Mr. Bonnyfeather mopping himself where the edge of his wig met his brow. Trying to explain things to himself, he recounted to her all that he knew of Anthony together with the events of the afternoon. They whispered to each other for half an hour by the boy's bedside.

". . . and that's all I know and the rest is uncanny," he finally ended. A short silence ensued between them.

"An orphan, eh, and from the old place on the hill?" she said. He nodded dubiously.

"I'll have to sleep on it," he sighed rising. "I'm worn out, watching, and waiting for you. You can take your turn now at being a nurse again. For a lad this time."

"He'll be staying on in this room?" she asked, laying her hand on his arm so eagerly that he looked surprised.

"Yes," he said.

"Wait, then. I'll mix some hot milk and wine for you. You'll need it."

He sat down again and waited while she crossed the big hall to the kitchen and returned. As he looked at the boy Mr. Bonnyfeather's satisfaction with his decision increased. His eyes travelled from the figure on the bed to the figure in the niche. He crossed himself and remained for some minutes in prayer.

Faith returned with the posset cup. He drank silently.

"You'll leave this light here?" she asked as he rose again. "I'll get some more candles. He's sleeping soundly enough now."

The old man nodded and left. A few seconds later she heard his door close. The woman took off her bonnet and gathering her wrap closer about her began her vigil.

The candles were still blazing brightly in Mr. Bonnyfeather's room. He looked about him with keen satisfaction. A certain pride and hauteur was visible in his countenance as he did so. If, when he entered the corridor which led to this retreat, he dropped the merchant and became the man; when he finally crossed the threshold of his own chamber and closed the door, a further transformation took place. He then, in his own mind at least, became a nobleman. Nor was this a mere aberration on his part. If Prince Charles Edward Stuart had only been able to pass on from Derby to London and had his father proclaimed at Westminster as well as at Holyrood, Mr. John Bonnyfeather, merchant, would have been the Marquis of Aberfoil. Since George and not James III or his son was now king, all that was left of the hypothetical Marquisate of Aberfoil was a proud memory in an old man's heart, and a room in a mouldering palace in Italy.

Unlike the other chambers in Mr. Bonnyfeather's immediate apartment, his own room had been originally part of the old building. It extended clear across the end of the ancient ballroom and had once been used as a retiring room. At one end there was an immense monumental fireplace where several hundred cupids went swarming through the Carrara helping themselves to several thousand bunches of gilded grapes. The fruit appeared to be dripping like gilded icicles from the mantelpiece itself. Just above this, propped out at a considerable angle to avoid a fat satyr carved on the chimney behind, was a large oil portrait of James II in periwig, sword, and very high-heeled shoes. It had been done at St.-Germain's in the latter days of the monarch when he had become a "healing saint." The lines by the nose were almost cavernous, the corners of the mouth turned down, and the eyes looked puzzled and weary. At the apartment before him, King James squinted with an implacably sullen and gloomy look. Nevertheless, the picture was cherished by Mr. Bonnyfeather. It had been given to his grandfather who had followed his king into exile.

On the mantel itself there was nothing but a handsomely wrought silver casket immediately below the portrait with a heavy candelabrum at either side. In these were exceptionally large wax candles that burned with a fine, clear light. In the mind of Mr. Bonnyfeather, here was the family hearth of his castle in Scotland. It, with the portrait, the casket, and the candles, had attained in his inherited affections and loyalties the status of a lay shrine. Nor was the shrine without its relics. In the casket before the picture reposed his grand-father's useless patent of nobility, a miniature of his daughter as a little girl, and an ivory crucifix. When Mr. Bonnyfeather prayed, as he still did occasionally, he placed the crucifix against the casket and knelt down on the hearth.

The rest of the room had somehow taken on the air of that chamber in nowhere that it actually was. It was furnished with a kind of blurred magnificence. In one corner there was a painted bed with a canopy over it. There had at one time even been a railing about it, but as this had caused amusement to the servants, Mr. Bonnyfeather had had it removed. Next to the bed was an immense wardrobe, the panelled doors of which led upward like a cliff to an urn on the top.

Seen from the door, set off by the gilded parallelogram of the base of the vanished railing, the bed and the wardrobe resembled nothing so much as a catafalque waiting beside the closed doors of a family tomb.

Certain lugubrious, and ludicrous, aspects of this bedroom had in early years impinged themselves even upon the mind of Mr. Bonny-feather to whom it was home. For one thing a heaven full of adipose goddesses romping with cupids through a rack of plaster clouds had been ruthlessly scraped from the ceiling, and the oval, to which for some esoteric reason their sporting had been confined, had been painted a deep blue. As a consequence, at night the centre of the room seemed to rise into a dome. The walls which had once been the scene of dithyrambic landscapes had also been painted over. But this coat was now wearing thin and the original, wild pastoral vistas were faintly visible in outline and subdued colour as if seen through a light Scotch mist. The effect was to exaggerate greatly the size of the apartment. It was like looking in the morning into the vanishing dreams of the night before.

In this mysterious and all but mystical atmosphere, the old merchant nourished his dreams both of the past and of the future. In the day-time with the bright, Tuscan sun streaming through the high, oval windows, not unlike the portholes of some gargantuan ship, the place was warm, dimly green, with half-obliterated forests and cascades slumbering on the wall; glinting with old gilt, and withal cheerful. But with the descent of night all this was changed. The catafalque of the bed seemed to thrust itself forward. The dome rose into the ceil-ing again. King James glowered. And the family tomb in the corner seemed waiting determinedly for John Bonnyfeather, the last of his race. It was not without a shudder that he could prevail upon him-self to hang his breeches there after eight o'clock at night.

To offset the Jacobean melancholy that threatened to engulf the place at dusk, the old man had many years before covered the floor with a bright red, Turkey carpet. He set cheerful brass firedogs to ramping in the fireplace under piles of old ship timbers always ready to blaze merrily, and provided himself with several mirrors and an endless number of silver candlesticks, candelabra of noble proportions, and sconces. Since the death of his daughter he might be said to have developed a passion for light. Mr. Bonnyfeather's weekly consumption of candles would have furnished forth a requiem mass for a grandee of Spain. This room with its nightly illumination together with some fiery old port which produced the same result constituted the chief indulgences of his amiable soul.

Here he retired, laid aside his wig, and put on a velvet dressing gown. Here he pored over his accounts spread out on a huge teakwood desk under a ship's lantern; planned out a profitable voyage for one of his several ships, or answered especially important correspondence. A large globe which he turned often, running his keen Scotch eye with a canny glance over many seas and lands, stood by the desk. There was a drawer for maps and charts. There were compasses and dividers apt to his hand, and down one side of the room a long bookcase was insufficient to hold his tomes. Atlases, almanacs, and port guides of recent dates had begun to accumulate in little towers along the floor.

To stand at the door, as he was doing now, and to run his eyes over the apartment with the candles burning, always had about it the elements of a cheerful surprise. The change from the dimly lit corridor was an abrupt one. A wash of silver light reflected by mirrors, sconces, and other silver objects flooded from the walls of the room. The George flashed on the breast of King James. The comfortable, large, gilt furniture and the books twinkled. Only in the corner the bed remained in mysterious shadow with his slippers beside it like two crouching cats.

The merchant began to undress. He hung his clothes on an old pair of antlers, all that remained of feudal rights in Scotland, put on his wrapper, and drew up a comfortable chair before the fire. He was quite chilled through by his wait in Anthony's room, and the last discovery of Faith Paleologus had shaken him quite as much as his first sight of Anthony's face. He had decided already to keep the boy in the house but upon purely instinctive and emotional grounds. An explanation that would provide him adequate reason for so serious a change in his fixed household habits at first seemed to him an absolute necessity. More important still, the status of the boy was not clear to him. By his actions it seemed as though the old man were trying to extract the answer to these questions by poking hollow places in the fire or by repeated applications to the bottle of port.

But the longer he thought the less likely it seemed that any reasonable and satisfactory explanation could be arrived at. If the marquis had been hiding anything, it was something which he desired to hide. It would be useless, and it would certainly be dangerous even to attempt to follow things up there. That last interview was meant to be a final one. Mr. Bonnyfeather knew that. Mr. Bonnyfeather could not see himself accusing Don Luis of abandoning his own child—even if he had had one that lived—which he had denied. "And if it had not been his child . . . if it had been Maria's!"

The old man's own conscience, his honour, stopped him here. His daughter was dead. The vista opened up for him an instant in a certain direction was one from which he recoiled a second time that night in sheer horror. All the pride, all the intense loyalty and belief in his own blood and family cherished through generations almost to the point of monomania precluded for him further explorations in that direction. With what felt like an actual muscular action in his head, he closed the door against even this suspicion.

He meant to shut it out entirely. But thought is swifter than honour. He had only succeeded in imprisoning the impression, perhaps an intuition, in the cells of his brain.

So he would not inquire any further, at the convent, or at any other place. Whatever was mysterious about this happening might, so far as he was concerned, remain so—far better so. He checked himself again. "Buried in the Alps!" The words came back to him now in the cold accents of Don Luis with a positive comfort. They must be final.

The old man now reproached himself even for his thoughts. How lovely and how innocent that daughter had been! It was a long time since he had looked at the girl in the miniature. He would look at her again tonight. The pain that her likeness never failed to inflict upon him should tonight be his penance. Its beauty and delicacy should also be his comfort and assurance.

He unlocked the casket and took out the locket. He snapped it open. Save for certain subtle feminine contours, there looked up at him from the oval frame the face of the boy on the bed in the next room. Mr. Bonnyfeather grew weak and leaned with his head against the mantel. He *felt* now beyond all reasonable doubt what he would never admit to himself he wanted to know.

A small chiming clock on his desk struck four as he climbed into bed. It was answered by the town chimes and echoed by all the ships' bells in the harbour. Mr. Bonnyfeather felt at peace with himself, his Maker, and the past over the decision he had finally made while resting his head against the mantel. Characteristically for him, it was compounded out of an emotional conviction and a reasonable doubt. It took the middle way between the horns of a dilemma. The boy who had come into his house that night should be received and

brought up *as if* he were akin, but never acknowledged. The tie between them that he felt to be there but could not understand should
remain without a name. That would solve the question by not asking
it. It would, it should suffice.

The merchant took a deep breath of relief. From the cellar below
the odour of tea and spices permeated his room. He breathed it in
with satisfaction. For one who proved himself capable and deserved
it, there might be a good inheritance in the vaults of the Casa da
Bonnyfeather. "And so we shall see," he thought, "what we shall
see."

"God be praised. But you especially, Merciful Virgin, who have
had this child in your holy and mysterious keeping, and have brought
comfort to an old man's heart."

Outside the last of the ships' bells had just ceased to ring as drowsiness fell upon him.

The same bells which had rung Mr. Bonnyfeather across the borders
of sleep had awakened Faith Paleologus in the next room. She had
not meant to go to sleep, but she was tired after the carnival. It was
only a few minutes after Mr. Bonnyfeather's door had closed before
she had forgotten herself entirely. She awoke now with her bonnet
at a drunken angle, her clothes disarranged, and her body slumped
down in her chair. Her first thought was that she must look a mess.
Her second that the boy might see her.

She stole a look at him furtively. He was sleeping soundly. The
rosy tinge of healthy slumber had returned to his cheeks. For some
time her eyes continued to drink at this fountain of youth. There
was no chance of her being seen doing so. Finally one of the candles
guttered. She rose silently, straightened her bonnet, and renewed the
candles from the pile she had brought from the kitchen earlier. Then
she took the candelabrum and tiptoed into her own room. There was
a long mirror.

Before this she took off her bonnet and let down her hair. It fell
in a dense black mass about her knees. She brushed it and combed
it carefully, plaited it in two long, thick coils, and wound them around
her head. The ends, after a manner all her own, she pulled up through
the loops of the coils and bound them tight with black tape. They
stood up over her forehead like two small horns. She next rubbed
her face with a soft camel-hair brush dipped in lemon juice, patted her
cheeks with a soft towel and noted the effect. She bathed her eyes
with cold water. Then she unloosed her clothes about the shoulders
and slipped them all, with one simple movement, to the floor. From
the middle of this pile, she stepped out of her shoes entirely naked.

The carefully demure housekeeper lay behind her heaped on the floor with the toes of her shoes turned in.

The rather splendid moth that had thus emerged from its best silk cocoon now flew across the room to one corner where on the stone floor reposed a ship's water cask that had been sawed in half. It was four feet high and two-thirds full of cold water. Without any change of facial expression the woman stepped into it and crouched down until the liquid met over her shoulders. She remained there for about half a minute as if her head floating free from her body were regarding the room. Then she rose without splashing, dried herself hastily, and began to move quietly but rapidly about. Every trace of fatigue had vanished. There was a certain panther-like sureness, an inevitable grace to her movements that was admirable. At that moment, upon emerging from the cool water which at once soothed her nerves and stimulated her muscles, her brain was like that of a dancer, preoccupied with physical motion but thinking about nothing at all.

Faith Paleologus was tall and appeared to be slender. Her shoulders if one looked carefully were too wide. But so superb was the bosom that rose up to support them that this blemish, if blemish it were, was magnificently disguised. A sculptor of the old school might have seen in her an Artemis to the breasts and above that some relation of the Niké of Samothrace. Perhaps the latter was also suggested by her straight profile that seemed to cleave the element through which it moved as if she were standing on the bow of a ship. Yet there was something too strange about her to name as a guilty one the quality that was uniquely hers. She seemed designed by the inscrutable for a use that was incomplete; for a purpose doomed to defeat by finding an end in itself. It was her hips. They were not those of a woman but of something else. A lemure's perhaps. Exquisitely capable for the relief of lovers they were inadequate for anything more. In their image was implicit an obstruction to life.

Her presence in the house of so honourable, and in the final analysis so religious, a person as Mr. Bonnyfeather was by no means the enigma which this glimpse into the privacy of his housekeeper's room might indicate. The implications of her body were offset and to some extent controlled by a cautious and clever mind.

On the stage of life Faith Paleologus was a consummate actress. Her rôle was a minor one, during the daytime, but it was subtly conceived. When she resumed her clothes in the morning and prepared to move about the precincts of the Casa da Bonnyfeather, her carefully chosen costume, and it was nothing more, her motions, her attitude, and the very tones of her voice proclaimed the staid virgin of uncertain age. In a household predominantly one of male contacts her face afforded no opportunities for amorous speculation. By a stroke which fell little short of genius she had contrived an artfully repulsive bustle to cover her inviting hips. Furthermore, she was never seen outside, even in the courtyard, without her bonnet, a long, perfectly smooth cylinder of black straw. It was worn sufficiently tilted up, and was tied under the chin with a dull bow of such miraculous precision as to cause every honest British seaman she passed to touch his cap with an automatic and nostalgic respect. She had, in short, learned by art the basest note in the cheap scale of respectability. "Never commit an indiscretion at home."

Yet it would be a genuine mistake to suppose that Faith Paleologus was one of the numerous and familiar who regard themselves as a means of gain and find the marketing pleasant. There were several gentlemen in sundry places who congratulated themselves on still being alive to regret having made that error. Her need was as deep as the gulf out of which it arose. It might, if she had cared to make it do so, have carried her far. But for her own always immediate purposes, she found Livorno an ideal place.

It was composed, at the time she trod the boards there, of several physical neighbourhoods socially an astronomical distance apart. Along the water front wandered avidly a cosmopolitan flux, keen eyes, ardent souls, and bodies from many shores. During the daytime Faith chose to hide herself from this; to live within the precincts of an orderly mercantile establishment, and to conduct the simple domestic affairs of its owner and his resident clerks. But on some evenings, especially about the full of the moon, she left it, bonneted, and bound ostensibly upon some domestic errand. A few minutes later would find her not only in other precincts but in other purlieus.

There she laid aside her respectable bonnet and received in privacy a male member of the world flux that she had chosen, and summoned as she well knew how, up from the water front. During such interviews her face darkened and took on the rapt expression of some sibyl brooding upon far distant events. The brown iris of her eyes contorted, the black pupils narrowed into an inhuman and almost oblong shape as if she were threading a needle. Then suddenly they widened and grew clearer and calm again. Whether it was some impassioned spirit temporarily appeased or merely a satisfied animal that now looked through them it would be hard to tell.

A young poet, an outcast who had once tarried with her, thought that he had recognized in her face, when the disguise of the bonnet was removed for him, a portrait of that Fate who sits at the gates of first beginnings and tangles the threads of life. He had wondered if this personage could be loose and wandering about the plains of earth. He had returned to Faith again and again, fascinated, trying to read her secret, until she cast him off tired of his impotent curiosity.

But she was respected and even feared at the Casa da Bonnyfeather. Her work was not all "acting." It provided her sufficient scope for the exercise of other abilities. In a town where all save the German and English mercantile establishments were notorious for their clattiness and confusion, she maintained her employer's as a model of order and cleanliness. The private apartments of Mr. Bonnyfeather, into which no guest was ever summoned since the death of his wife, were not only spotless but bordered on the luxurious. Nothing was lacking which at any time Mr. Bonnyfeather or she herself really needed. The one exception to this was the room of Sandy McNab, which was Spartan. He slept there and nothing more.

The master's table, which was always served in the old ballroom exactly under the skeleton of the huge central chandelier immediately opposite the main door, was provided with an abounding plenty. This was more a matter of business acumen than anything else. Mr. Bonnyfeather himself was rather abstemious of both food and drink. Scarcely a day passed, however, without one or two guests, generally ship captains, factors, a brother merchant, or a traveller of note and distinction who bore letters of introduction or of credit to the house. In addition, most men of affairs, bankers, and even priests and artists in Livorno made it a point to drop in occasionally upon Mr. Bonnyfeather both for the good cheer and for the conversation.

From the table talk that went on about his board the merchant gathered not only entertainment but a curious and valuable knowledge of affairs in general, from world politics to how the tides ran in the Bay of Fundy, or why the pilot fees were so high on the River Hoogli. Many a profitable enterprise and many a shrewd deal had its inception or consummation here. There were few rumours adrift on the trade winds of the world which passed him by. The conversation was polyglot. A stray Russian had so far been the only guest who had been forced to discuss nothing but his soup. Even ships with cargoes consigned to his rivals found their captains dining in a garrulous frame of mind with Mr. Bonnyfeather.

This notable table was catered to by Angela, the fat cook, one of the best in town. The dishes proceeded in an orderly manner through a hole in the kitchen wall. Thence they were wheeled steaming on a small wagon with manifold trays by Tony Guessippi, the cook's husband. He was a kind of wizened male spider whose function in life was to convey the dishes which his wife concocted to their ultimate destination and to beget children on her body. A flock of eleven semi-naked youngsters and an equally lavish technique with knife and ladle testified that Destiny had not been mistaken this time in her choice

On fine days both leaves of the great central door leading into the old ballroom were thrown open. At the top of the wide, low steps which now swept up with a uselessly superb flare, Mr. Bonnyfeather and his guests were to be seen dining under the swathed chandelier. The old merchant enjoyed this. In his secret heart he was the laird of Aberfoil dispensing feudal hospitality to more illustrious guests. Something of that feeling overflowed into his mien and conversation and served to flavour the meal with both the salt and pepper of an old-world courtesy.

In all this Faith Paleologus was essential to Mr. Bonnyfeather. Not only did she oversee the smooth and profitable abundance of his own board, but the more simple comforts of the rest of the establishment as well. The merchant conducted his business in many languages, and there were no less than nine resident clerks, four Swiss porters, and several messengers and draymen who both ate and slept in rooms that overlooked the courtyard. On one side of this was a kind of small barracks for the "gentlemen writers." A ship's cook and two boys sufficed for them. The scrubwomen, five of whom appeared every morning, also made up the beds. When the master's own ships were in harbour the pursers were provided with their rooms and table, and there were generally transient guests of the establishment who came with some legitimate claim on its hospitality.

Such was the "factory" as it was called of the House of Bonnyfeather in which the housekeeper held unrelenting sway. Over the cellar, the warehouse, the stables, and the office itself hovered the eagle eye of Mr. Sandy (William) McNab.

The one spot in the place exempt from all authority was the purlieus of the kitchen. Here in gargantuan disorder and simian anarchy rioted the clan Guessippi; boys, girls, chickens, cats, and goats. No dogs had been able to survive. It was only when Faith herself appeared there at some crisis of uproar that silence and dismay brought about a specious appearance of order. At such times all the children fled either into or under the family bed. Tony departed to the wine cellar leaving his wife alone with her own bulk. It was well known throughout the neighbourhood that Faith had the evil eye. For that reason no spoons were ever missing, and the scrubwomen invariably reported early. One angry glance, and you might wither away; a stare, and the Virgin herself might not be able to help you.

To a certain degree the authority of Faith had been inherited. Inheritance indeed might account for much else that was peculiar in her. Her father had been a Florentine of Greek extraction. The family tree led back to Constantinople. They were workers in mosaic and had, with the extinction of the Medici, their patrons, fallen upon evil times. The last of them, a boy with a face like a hawk and the mad lusts of a leopard, had fallen in with a Scotchwoman in the house of Mr. Bonnyfeather's father at Livorno. She, Eliza McNab, was one of several who had followed the fortunes of the Bonnyfeathers into exile. She was a true daughter of the heather. After a while the young Paleologus disappeared to assemble mosaics in parts unknown. He left his wife with a flower-like pattern of bruises, a baby daughter, and the statue of the madonna. It was this daughter who had become the maid of Mr. Bonnyfeather's only child Maria, and it was she, Faith, who had succeeded in due time to the keys of his house.

At half past four on the morning after Anthony arrived the Casa da Bonnyfeather lay wrapt in the profound quiet which precedes the first stir of dawn. The last of the clerks had returned from the carnival. The only light to be seen in the courtyard was the faint, downward ray cast from the lattice of Faith Paleologus. Presently, it disappeared. She had crossed the corridor and gone into Anthony's room again. She placed the candles on the table and sat down. It was not her intention to remain watching for the rest of the night. The boy was sleeping utterly quietly and could need no further attention. But she, too, desired to study his face again. She had already formed conclusions of her own. In her case there was no point of honour beyond which speculation was taboo. Quite the contrary. The maid of Maria had no doubts about the family resemblance. She concluded that Mr. Bonnyfeather knew more than he cared to tell. Else why had the boy been placed in this room? Then there was the madonna, of course. To Faith that was simply a confirmation of what she had already surmised. Well, she would find out some day. She had lived long enough to know that one of the best ways to get to the bottom of a mystery is to hold your own tongue. Others invariably wagged theirs sooner or later. Someone's long ears usually wagged at the same time.

She wondered about Don Luis. What was his connection with all this? Of many who came to the Casa da Bonnyfeather he had been the only one who had read her with a glance. "What are *you* doing here?" he had said. But he also could hold his tongue. She had admired him for that, and other things. Their one night together had been memorable. It had been her hope that he would take her away with him along with Maria. For that reason she had urged the marriage on the girl.

So her pretty young charge had given the marquis the slip after all! She would never have given her credit for that. Don Luis was no simpleton. It aroused Faith's reluctant admiration for Maria for whom even when a girl she had felt little else than a well-concealed envy that amounted almost to jealousy. Maria had been beautiful. Faith had been glad to see her leave the house.

So by hook or crook this boy had come back for *her* to look after—with the Paleologus madonna. She did not like that. She had an impulse to destroy the thing. But she checked herself. No, that would be to give herself away; to cause questions to be asked. She looked up at the statue and glowered. What had been its rôle in all this? Nothing, of course, nothing! It was only a statue, an old one at that. Her eyes sank to the boy's face again.

There was the same unassailable loveliness. How she had envied it once in Maria. It was the opposite with which her nature was ever trying to unite. In this present young masculine mould in which it had been returned to her, it seemed possible that she might yet come to possess it after all, to possess it even for an instant in the only way she knew how, by the only approach to strength and beauty which she had. She was only thirty-two.

Presently her face darkened and her eyes contorted.

She rose silently, took the candles, and approached the bed. She listened, and bent over Anthony with an attitude infinitely stealthy. Her breathing deepened. Her hands trembled unexpectedly and a drop of hot wax splashed on his breast. He moved convulsively and opened his eyes. She snatched the candles away and began tucking him in again. But she had not been quite quick enough. In the sudden glare of light as he first wakened the boy had seen her eyes.

"This place is full of them!" he cried out. He remembered where he was now. Then he saw her standing beside him.

"Who are you?" he asked.

"The housekeeper. I'm here to make you comfortable." She smiled at him.

"It was you who covered me up just now?"

"Yes, the sheets had slipped off and you looked cold."

He pondered the information as if it had great importance. "Doubtfully," she thought a little apprehensively. He rubbed his eyes.

"It's funny, but do you know just now I thought I saw that old goat looking down at me again."

"You must have dreamed it," she said. "Can't you see the door's closed? It can't get in here."

"No," he admitted doubtfully. The impression had been a strong one. The door was closed, however. He could see that for himself. He gave it up.

"What's your name?" he finally asked. Then as if in a hurry to make a fair exchange—"mine is Anthony."

"Faith."

"Faith!" He pondered that, too. Then as if to himself, "Father Xavier said faith was the evidence of things unseen."

"And who is Father Xavier?" she asked, an unconscious twinge of contempt creeping into her voice. She loathed priests.

"He is my friend," said Anthony, "and," he added, sensitive to the tone of her voice, "I shall be lonely without him. He is coming here to see me again often." He flung this as a kind of challenge. Then as if to placate her, "You stay here?"

"I live here. I shall be near you all the time."

"Oh," he said. The conversation paused. He closed his eyes again.

She waited for a long time now as if to pose her new question to what lay so deep within him that it must answer truthfully when spoken to. But she must not let him go to sleep entirely. Time passed. She spoke to him dreamfully.

"Do you remember any other good friend?"

"Yes, I remember," he whispered.

Instinctively she chose now a tone just sufficient to reach him and no more. She leaned nearer carefully.

"Who?"

But the effect was exactly the opposite of what she had hoped for. He suddenly aroused himself, sat up and began to look about in a puzzled way as if he missed someone.

"I thought I saw her here, last night," he said.

"I wonder who *she* was?" thought Faith. "The old man said nothing about her."

The boy's eyes continued to search through the room. He remembered it vaguely from the night before, but he was confused by having been turned around on the bed by the doctor. Presently he twisted himself completely about.

"There!" he said triumphantly, pointing to the madonna in her niche. "There she is."

"If she had only destroyed that statue last night! That would have been the time," she thought. It was always a mistake not to act on a deep prompting like that, to reason herself out of it. One should listen to one's voices. But it was too late now. The boy evidently set great store by the thing. It, "she," she caught herself saying, was a "close friend." He thought he had seen her here last night! A convent child with visions! Priest-bred, bah! He would have to get over that. Nevertheless, she felt herself balked in some way or other. Her first approach had been frustrated. She cursed herself for having given the statue to Maria. "I might have known it would come back to haunt me. It brought ill luck to my mother." In spite of herself she went cold.

"Well, is there anything you want?" she asked preparing to go.

He shook his head and settled back under the covers. It was a comfortable bed. Like the one at Signora Udney's, he thought. He closed his eyes. Outside a cock began to crow.

Faith slipped back to her own room. She must catch a wink of sleep herself before her day began. Silence wrapped the Casa da Bonnyfeather for another hour. Whatever moved then through its dilapidated corridors stole through them as silently as the dawn that was just breaking.

CHAPTER FOURTEEN

REALITY MAKES A BID

NEXT morning Mr. Bonnyfeather "communicated" his decision of the night before to Faith. She said nothing, but she approved. Both of them were aware that considerable comment might be expected in and about the Casa da Bonnyfeather. Positions were eagerly sought after there, and the arrival of so young an apprentice and his immediate translation to the sacred apartment of the Capo della Casa would tickle curiosity. Both of them sat at breakfast thinking of this.

"*Hum-um!*" said Mr. Bonnyfeather. "How is he this morning?"

"A little dizzy yet, but quite all right again. Three eggs for breakfast," she replied.

"Keep him by you, in the room for several days," he went on. "Tell them he was badly shaken up. You can stretch a point. It will then be natural enough that you should be taking care of him under the circumstances."

"I had thought of it," she said.

"I knew you *had*," he smiled. "But what after that?"

"You can tell McNab he is too young yet to be in the dormitory with the grown men. They will be glad enough not to have him about carrying tales. It would be miserable for him and them. Also say that no one's position has been filled or is threatened by his coming here. It is just a case of charity for Father Xavier. Most of the trouble here starts over fears or petty jealousies, you know. After a while it will seem perfectly natural for him to keep on staying where he is. It will also just have happened. Trust McNab to spread news."

"Exactly," said Mr. Bonnyfeather. He was somewhat surprised by having his own schemes put so eloquently. His housekeeper generally held her tongue. "But it is natural enough," he thought, "she was Maria's maid." He was relieved and grateful to find that he would not have to try to explain to her what he must never explain to himself. "This is just another orphan to whom we are giving a start. As you say, 'pure charity.'" He looked at her significantly. She nodded and waited. "Do you think anyone else might notice the—his face?"

"McNab, perhaps. He was here before Maria left. He remembers her. All the rest are new."

"Have the barber in and crop the boy's hair close. It will make it easier for me, too, in a way." He sighed. "Also, get him clothes. Out of your household account. I'll not ask you to save there. One good suit. For a gentleman's son."

"Or a merchant's grandson?" she asked suddenly. She saw his cheek bones flush.

"Woman," he said, "dinna propose it in words. I dinna ken mysel'. Let the dead stay buried!" His face worked.

"Peace to you. I'm no gossip. Could you think that after all these years? I'll not whisper it this side of my shroud."

"It's not that," he said, calmer now. "I wouldn't have you think . . ."

"I think nothing," she said, "except that this is a new day and it's time to begin it."

She walked over to a chest, unlocked it, and drew forth two flags which she laid over his arm. "Leave the boy to me now. I'll see to him." He looked relieved and climbed to the roof intent on what amounted to a daily ritual.

Arrived there he hoisted the two flags each on a separate pole. One was the Union Jack and the other his house flag, a red pennant with a black thistle. In addition to this he always addressed a short prayer to some member of the Holy Trinity. He then unlocked the small chest set into the parapet and took out a telescope. From the roof of the house the entire inner and outer harbour and a long vista down the coast was visible. Steadying the glass on a little bronze tripod, it was his custom every morning by this means to study both the molo and the Darsena carefully and to sweep the horizon. In half an hour he would be thoroughly familiar with what was going on at Livorno; what ships were coming and going, and what business they were bound upon. The glass was a good one. He could even recognize faces at a considerable distance. It aided greatly in eliminating from his affairs the disconcerting element of surprise. It would now be seven o'clock.

At precisely that instant Mr. Bonnyfeather could always be seen descending the stairs from the roof. At the foot of the stairs Simon, the porter, handed him his gold-headed cane and a freshly filled snuff box. A large ship's bell which hung in the courtyard rang out. The gates were thrown open into the street. The drays began to rumble and the clerks to write. The Casa da Bonnyfeather was open for business.

On the morning after Anthony's arrival, Mr. Bonnyfeather was forced to make one minor change in the ritual. No one else knew it. He took the telescope out and swept the harbours as usual. His thoughts, however, were not upon the various swarming decks which he passed in review but in the room just under his feet. Through the corridor skylight, which was opened every fine morning like a ship's hatch, came the snipping of scissors and clear bursts of laughter. The barber was using his most humorous blandishments while removing Anthony's hair. Faith had lost no time about it.

Mr. Bonnyfeather smiled and turned his glass on the horizon. A cloud of mist seemed to cut off his view on a clear day. "Dampness in the glass!" He unscrewed the eyepiece and wiped it assiduously, likewise the large lens. He looked again. It was still dimmer. Forced to admit the fact in spite of himself, he furtively wiped his own eyes. When he levelled the glass again the horizon stood out startlingly clear.

Into a patch of brilliant sunlight sailed a full-rigged ship. The field of the glass covered her exactly. He could see the figurehead leaning forward and the slow rise and fall of the bows as the waves whitened under the fore-chains. Suddenly the ship hesitated, the sails fluttered, and then filled out on the other tack. All the shadows on them now lay serenely on the other side. In the crystal atmosphere of the glass the ship seemed to be manœuvring with supernatural ease in a better world. It was his own ship, long overdue, that was thus so calmly coming home again. He descended the stairs in the rested mood that often follows tears.

"Tell the draymen," said he, as the porter handed him his cane, "that the *Unicorn* is coming in after all. Be ready at the docks."

"A lucky day, sir," said Simon.

"*Very,*" replied Mr. Bonnyfeather. His hand shook a little as he took the cane.

In the corridor under the skylight the last of Anthony's ringlets had just fallen to the floor. Faith led him to Maria's mirror. "I am a man now," said he fiercely. A very tall and slim, and a very young, young gentleman dressed in a pair of plain, bow shoes and a decent, dark green suit with buckles at the knees was trying to frown back at him from the glass. Even Anthony thought him to be good-looking. It annoyed him vastly to find that the barber was taking all the credit for it as a result of his handiwork. "I grew these all myself," said the boy, turning upon the man angrily and running his hand through his crisply shorn locks. There was a ripple of laughter from the door. "Are you sure of it?" said Faith Paleologus. The barber clashed his shears and departed.

Three mornings later Anthony emerged from his seclusion to take up his duties in the world of men. He was anxious to do so. An overpowering curiosity, and a new, vivid sense of reality, totally submerged any shrinking from the unknown which his temperament might ordinarily have provided. He accompanied Mr. Bonnyfeather to the roof and was there permitted to raise the house flag which he was given to understand was henceforth to be his first daily task. Below him the mules were being hitched to the dray. Big Angela and her progeny were drawing water at the fountain. The clerks were making for the office. Amid the garden-beds wandered his friend the goat. Mr. Bonnyfeather busied himself with the telescope. Presently Sandy McNab beckoned to Anthony. "Come down here, laddie," said he. Leaving the old man on the roof, Anthony descended.

"How are you now?" said McNab in Italian, seeing that the boy had understood only his gestures. He also shook him by the hand with so firm a clasp as to make him wince. "Quite well, sir," replied Anthony bravely. Mr. McNab studied him for a minute. "You'll do now I guess," he said. He looked at the short hair approvingly. "Hold your chin up when you go about, and look out for goats." He grinned. "But not so high as that," he cautioned, shoving the boy's nose down with his thumb. "I mean take your own part and don't be afraid of anybody. You understand? That's what 'hold your chin up' means." Anthony nodded. "Come on now, you're to eat breakfast with the clerks. The other meals you take with the master. And that's lucky for you," he added, taking the boy roughly but not unkindly by the hand. "There is a world of difference in victuals." He led the way across the broad flagstones of the courtyard to the office which they entered together in company with several clerks.

It was the big room where Anthony had first met Mr. Bonnyfeather. But it was now a scene of great animation. Down the aisle between the desks had appeared as if by magic a long table at which were seated a crowd of about twenty men varying in years from youth to middle age. They ate steadily and heartily of dishes strange to Anthony. No time, it appeared, was to be lost. At the extreme end of the apartment Mr. Bonnyfeather's desk rose impressively behind its railing, majestic but lonely.

To the boy's surprise and delight little attention was paid to him when he came in. Those near by looked up and nodded perfunctorily at McNab who sat at the head of the table near the door. He drew a stool up for Anthony next to him and rearranged some plates. "This will be your place now every morning," he said. "Help yourself."

He set the example by pouring himself a large basin of tea and heaping his plate with fish and scrambled eggs. Out of the coagulated mass a mackerel looked up at Anthony with a desperate purple eye. For a moment he could feel again where the goat had hit him. He turned his eyes up to the frescoed ceiling and for some moments allowed them to remain there. Just above him his friend with the

winged heels was taking off from a cloud, leaving the banquet of the
gods behind. Perhaps he, too, felt dizzy.

"I see you are a man of sensibility," said a pleasant voice in French
next to Anthony. Anthony took his eyes from the ceiling and turned
to find himself looking into a keen, youngish face with sparkling
brown eyes. "I myself," continued the stranger smiling in a friendly
way upon him, "have upon several mornings preferred to contemplate
the banquet of the gods in the ceiling rather than this breakfast of
the English upon the floor." Anthony summoned his small stock of
French to mind and replied with immense precision, "Is it that in the
ceiling they are not eating fish?"

"Never," cried his new-found friend fiercely, "never a fish!" He
waved confirmatively toward a Bacchus just above him. "Have you
not noticed," he rattled on, "the terrible Medusa-like stare of the
mackerel? It produces in the pit of the stomach the sensation of
stone." Anthony agreed. He could not follow it all, but he felt called
upon to make a counter-reply.

"But at the breakfast of the English the food is real," he managed
to string together. "True," cried his new friend, "your observation
does you credit, monsieur, it is a just one. You have named the chief
advantage the English have over the gods. But consider, it is only
a temporary one. By tonight this breakfast will have become food
for an idea. It will have become an idea. That is the end of break-
fasts. And think," said he, suddenly whisking about on the bench so
that he sat astride of it with his hands on his hips, "think what kind
of an idea that mackerel will become which is even now going into
the head of Meester McNab."

Mr. McNab's eyes bulged out with indignation. For a moment he
seemed doubtful himself as to the destination of the fish and choked.
"Hauld your clack," he mumbled, and then turned to Anthony. "Eat
your bun, my boy," said he, "and sop it in your tea. Toussaint there
is a Frenchman and a philosopher. If you listen to him you'll have
naught but an ideal breakfast in your little basket when the bell rings."
As if in premonition of famine and as an example to the young, Mr.
McNab, after clearing his own plate with a piece of bread in spiral
motion, departed for his desk. Anthony, who was embarrassed at
thus finding himself the centre of a debate, was relieved to see McNab
grinning over his shoulder at Toussaint who laughed back. The latter
now continued to regard him with his arms akimbo.

"I can see that we shall get along famously," he said. "You speak
French beautifully"—Anthony blushed with delight—"and you dislike
mackerel. It is the basis for a firm, philosophic friendship. You look
like a northerner. Where have you been civilized? You do not speak
English?" Anthony shook his head.

"I would advise you to learn it," his friend rattled on. "It is the language out of which realities proceed, fish, tea, gold, raiment—and finally power. It will help you here greatly, for that is the kind of thing they are after." The boy nodded as if he knew. "Father Xavier has already said so," he interpolated. "Ah, yes, of course, the Jesuit. He would know. But he has already taught you other things, I suppose?" "Yes, monsieur, Latin, French, and I know Italian. I have read *The Divine Comedy.*"

"Excellent," cried the philosopher. "You have begun. I myself will continue your education, in French." He held up a warning finger. "But say nothing about it. Your desk is to be next to mine. Monseigneur McNab has in a way turned you over to me. You see I know where you come from." For some reason the boy felt his cheeks glow.

"Tut, tut, it is a great advantage. You're not handicapped by a mother. It is *they* who make the world civilized and that is what is the matter with it. They want you for themselves. Congratulate yourself. Also we shall circumvent Mr. McNab. I am supposed to teach you about invoices. They are easy. Afterwards we shall put them by in a drawer and converse"—he pointed upwards dramatically —"in the language which is useful up there. You see those nine women dancing about the gentleman with the lyre?" Anthony nodded. "We shall meet them," said he. "Possibly even the gentleman himself. In the meantime, let me recommend to you the conduct of this one, in so far as you see it portrayed there," he added hastily, and pointed to the figure of a boy standing behind the couch of Jove. From the cup which he bore, the page was slyly taking a drink behind the other man's back. "Do you understand, mon ami?" asked Toussaint looking down into Anthony's face.

Anthony nodded, "I think so," he replied. "At least I shall learn French."

"At the very least!" replied Toussaint. "And now I shall prove to you that McNab is wrong." He pulled a fine gold watch out of his bright yellow waistcoat and looked at it. "You have seven minutes before the bell rings to finish your breakfast. You shall now see what it is to be a natural philosopher."

He assembled some plates rapidly under the fascinated stare of Anthony, placed upon them a fried egg with an unbroken yolk, a piece of thin bacon beside it, a light, white roll and a piece of butter which he cut into a square. Then he poured out some tea carefully straining out the leaves. "It *is* a little cold," said he, "due to my causerie, but you see what makes it inviting is that it is the combination of food and an idea. It is déjeuner and not merely the breaking of a fast.

Eat while you still have time." They both broke into a laugh together. The first of many.

"Five minutes till the bell rings," said Mr. McNab with his eyes upon them from the other end of the room. He was already at work. Toussaint made a grimace. Anthony stuffed himself. Presently the bell rang.

Instantly, all those who were still lingering arose. The porters seized the loose planks of which the tables were composed and carried them out bodily with the remains of the breakfast upon them. The stools upon which the planks rested were each claimed by a clerk who carried it to his desk and sat down upon it forthwith, opened his ledger, and began to indite. A man with a broom swept the fragments down the aisle. In a short time a complete silence save for the scratching of divers pens reigned unbroken.

The sun streamed through the windows and only the gods in the ceiling continued to dine. Beneath them the figures of the gentlemen writers bent over the desks, adding up columns or writing letters. Decorum from a niche in the corner smiled. About five minutes later the ferrule of a cane was heard clicking on the mosaics in the vestibule. Mr. McNab left his desk and took his place by the door.

"Good morning, sir," said he as Mr. Bonnyfeather came through the door.

"Good morning, Mr. McNab, good morning, gentlemen," said Mr. Bonnyfeather. A respectful murmur of welcome ensued without interrupting the pens. Mr. Bonnyfeather advanced one more step, took off his hat, and hung it over the face of a dilapidated satyr whose horns were worn giltless by this use. From under the cocked hat it grinned helplessly. Mr. Bonnyfeather, the step, and the simultaneous removal of the hat in the same place at the same time each morning never failed. It had gone on for thirty years. The Frenchman Toussaint Clairveaux was fascinated. He had watched it for seven. The satyr was slowly becoming respectable. There could be no doubt about it. Mr. Bonnyfeather now took a pinch of snuff and advanced to his desk. On this particular morning he made an announcement.

"I shall need all hands at the quay this afternoon to take stock of cargo. The *Unicorn* has at last been released by the customs." A buzz of excitement followed. All knew that it was a rich Eastern cargo and premiums might follow. Mr. Bonnyfeather believed in prize money in peace as well as in war.

"He is a remarkable man, a gentleman, an honest spirit," said Toussaint to Anthony who was now seated on a high stool near him. The boy looked up to meet an encouraging smile from Mr. Bonnyfeather sitting at the big desk. He felt encouraged. Just then McNab came along and bade him follow. They went over into the corner to the chief clerk's bureau. Mr. McNab took out a heap of papers, spread them out, and looked at Anthony. "These are your indentures," he vouchsafed. "You sign them here." He handed a pen to the boy. At the place which McNab indicated the lad wrote very carefully, *Anthony.*

"Anthony what?" asked McNab peering down at him. The boy looked puzzled. "Your last name?" The boy shook his head slowly. It had never occurred to him that he needed one. Other people had them, of course. Mr. McNab grunted and began to look through the papers.

"A deposition by the Mother Superior of the Convent of Jesus the Child situate in this Our Grand Duchy of Tuscany." McNab grunted. "In the name of the Father the Son and the Holy Ghost, greeting." Grunt. The rest was in Latin.

The chief clerk paused for a minute, gripped the paper more firmly, and gave it a shake. The text, however, remained in the same language. He cleared his throat and looked at Anthony.

"Can *you* read this?" he asked, handing the paper to Anthony. The boy looked at him uneasily.

"Let's see if you can," suggested Mr. McNab in a doubtful tone of voice. "Read it aloud." As if reciting to Father Xavier, Anthony began.

It was a simple recital of the facts of his own arrival at the convent. He had been, it appeared, "but newly born, a perfect man child with a sore navel." Why was that? he thought. The contents of the black bag were then enumerated, himself included. He became intensely interested and pressed on. The corridors of the convent at night with Sister Agatha walking along them carrying a bundle through the shadows leaped out from the bare recital on the page. He knew every turn she would take, the whole scene. The deposition in bad, bare, legal Latin took on for the boy the fascination of a literary masterpiece of which he was the hero. "And on the next day following the said male infant, parents unknown, was baptized Anthony . . ."

"Go on," said McNab.

"According to the rite of the Holy . . ."

"You have no last name," interrupted the man sternly.

"No, sir," said Anthony meekly.

"Also you seem to have entered the world in great adversity," continued his tormentor. He drummed on the desk. "Have you any suggestions?" Anthony shook his head.

"—and to have arrived here under still more adverse circumstances!" Mr. McNab's eyes twinkled. "Well," said he, "why not catch up your past misfortunes into a name and give your good luck a chance? Wait a minute."

He went over to Mr. Bonnyfeather and for some minutes held him in conversation. Anthony could see them looking his way now and then and laughing. He felt uncomfortable. Why was it curious not to have a last name? Finally, Mr. Bonnyfeather took up his largest, plumed pen and wrote something with a flourish on a small piece of paper. He held it up before him considering it. Then he nodded as if satisfied and handed it still smiling to Mr. McNab. The clerk returned to his bureau and thrust the paper under the boy's nose. On it was written—

Anthony Adverse

"*That,*" said Mr. McNab with a Mede and Persian gesture, "is your name." And it was. Mr. McNab pronounced it, "Advarse." It was thus that Anthony always thought of it.

The signing of the papers was now completed and Toussaint called as witness. Anthony watched anxiously to see if his friend would laugh at the new name. He remained perfectly serious. The clerk now drew up a small document of his own. It was a draft on Anthony's pay for nine shillings for a hat, payable to Mr. William McNab. This also the boy signed. Mr. McNab was now satisfied. He stuck the quill pen behind his ear and looked at Anthony.

"There is only one advantage," he said, "in having a name. It prevents you signing other peoples' names to papers. But as in everything else this advantage is outweighed by a corresponding disadvantage." The boy opened his eyes as the man was evidently in earnest. A certain grim kindness now lurked about the folds of McNab's heavy jowl which Anthony had not noticed before. "A corresponding disadvantage," continued McNab. "You have to sign your own name! Do so as little as possible. And never sign any paper without thinking it over three separate times." The boy blinked. "For example, this paper which you have just signed will cost you two months' pay. No, not quite. Sixty days from now you will receive one shilling. You understand, sixty days! If you had not signed it, you would have received ten shillings. . . . Come with me," said McNab, "and I will show you."

He took Anthony over to a large iron till which he unlocked. From a drawer he drew out ten shillings and placed them in the boy's hand. "All of these would have been yours, *but* you signed a paper, didn't you? Hence," growled McNab, "these are mine." He counted nine shillings out of the boy's palms back into his own. The one remaining seemed to Anthony to have no weight at all. The clerk let the lightness of it sink home. "Sixty days from now," he said, and put the single shilling back in the till with the fatal paper. The other nine pieces he poured into his waistcoat pocket where they seemed to chime. He pointed Anthony to his own desk and walked away.

Pondering over the responsibility of having a name and the enormous difference between one and ten shillings, the boy climbed back on his stool. The tears welled up in his eyes. He was afraid they might drop on the desk so that Toussaint would see them. The latter was writing. Anthony looked up at the ceiling again. Presently his eyes dried leaving them hard and clear. He was soon lost amid the painted clouds.

The young gentleman with the winecup was also a "perfect man child." His navel, however, was not sore. Anthony noticed that. The other things were all there too. On the lady sitting next to the big man with the beard they were missing. You longed to provide them. His own, for instance. The thought appealed to him as an original one. He cherished it carefully. The group amid the frescoes began to move. A faint glow began to steal up his back. The stool under him grew pleasantly warm. "What if . . . that woman who had helped dress him and bathe him when he had been ill. How soft her hands had been." It was the same feeling. He trembled. Toussaint was shaking him by the elbow and laughing. All the blood in Anthony's body seemed to rush to his face.

"Come, come," said his new-found friend in a kindly way. "Do you want to turn into one of those?" He pointed to the satyr under Mr. Bonnyfeather's hat. "There are lots of them around here like that."

"I could never be like that!" Anthony flung back indignantly, irritated at finding his thoughts so easily read. His face no doubt had betrayed him. He must be careful then in this place where there were so many sharp eyes about. It was not like the convent where you could sit and let the shadows come and go through your eyes with no one to see them. No, no, he must never betray himself by his expression again. His face became so grimly determined that Toussaint laughed again.

"Now, you look like Monsieur McNab," he said.

"Oh, dear," thought Anthony, "that is impossible, too." But he had no time to protest further, for Toussaint was spreading out before him a number of blank forms. On each one of them was engraved a small black ship in full sail with something printed underneath several times over in as many languages.

Take notice: the good ship..............of...............,
God willing, proposes to sail from.............this..........
day of............ 17... with the following cargo; to wit, item:

There now unrolled about a foot of paper with ditto marks under
"item" and a long line opposite each ditto. On each of these lines
Anthony was shown how to copy the list of a ship's cargo from forms
already filled out by Toussaint. The forms were duplicates and the
work must be accurate. Each line must correspond exactly. It was
to be checked later at the customs. At first, no matter how careful
he was, he kept making mistakes. Barrels of sugar insisted on inserting themselves upon lines meant exclusively for barrels of pork.
Whereupon Toussaint tore up the form. At last Anthony managed
to complete a set exactly and felt elated. Another was immediately
shoved under his nose. He continued to write all morning. His hands
grew cramped and his body tired. Toussaint permitted him to slip
down once or twice from his stool and to look on.

"Tell me," said Anthony, pointing to the phrase "God willing" on
the form, "what has God got to do with all this?"

"It is a pious word for wind," said Toussaint.

"Oh," said Anthony, "and God makes it blow? Is that it?"

"I suppose so," said Toussaint.

"But he does, of course."

"Perhaps; copy these."

But the boy stopped in the middle of the form. "Who does then?"

"No one," replied Toussaint without allowing his pen to pause.

Anthony had never thought of that. The mistakes multiplied. His
world was shivering. Toussaint tore up so many forms that Mr.
McNab snorted.

Various visitors came in to see Mr. Bonnyfeather from time to
time. You could hear them talking at the desk, but it was better not to
look. The room gradually grew hotter. Anthony felt himself getting
hungry. Finally, the bell in the courtyard chimed once. A thunder
of closing ledgers followed and the clerks rushed out. Anthony and
Toussaint were left alone.

From a cubbyhole in the desk, the Frenchman drew forth one of
several small, calf-bound volumes. Here he cherished a microscopic
library, shifting, trading, and even buying second-hand books from
time to time. In the course of seven years much literature had passed
through the cubbyhole but tarried in his head. The Frenchman had a
memory for the printed word as though his brain contained an acid
which bit the reflection of the page on the surface of a mirror.

"You are hungry now," he said to Anthony, "I know. But it is
half an hour yet till dinner and if you will give me that half hour

every day, I shall be glad to share it with you. I do not think I shall be wasting my time—or yours. What do you say?"

The man's eyes glowed softly as if within him a banked fire had begun to break through the ashes. He saw the reflection of it in the face of the boy before him. "It is a bargain, then!" he cried. "See, I shall clinch it with this to remind you of it always." He opened up the little book excitedly, crossed out his own name, and wrote Anthony's. Then he handed it to the boy with a noble gesture. "Open it," he said, "let us lose no time." It was a copy of La Fontaine's *Fables* with little engravings.

They turned to "Le Corbeau et le Renard" and began. They translated carefully into Italian, and when this was not precise enough, into Latin. Then Toussaint began to correct Anthony's accent. Again and again he repeated the French. The boy was delighted. Here were more words, and such words! After his flat Jesuit's Latin and soft Tuscan, his tongue seemed at last to have found itself. Finally, Toussaint recited the whole poem. The clean music of it, the caressing stroke of the rhyme, and the charm of the story held Anthony on the stool as if he were looking at a play. He stared up into Toussaint's face with parted lips.

"Anthony," said a kindly voice from the other end of the room. It was Mr. Bonnyfeather. They both rose instinctively.

"We were just having a little French lesson, monsieur," said Touissaint apprehensively.

"Splendid," replied the older man, "but we are waiting dinner."

"I am sorry, indeed . . ." began Toussaint.

"You do not need to be, perhaps later on . . ." Mr. Bonnyfeather drew for a moment with his cane on the ground. "Well, we can let that wait. In the meantime by all means go on here as you have begun." He nodded approvingly. By this time Anthony had joined him and they went out of the door together, the little book in the boy's hand.

Toussaint Clairveaux remained leaning on his desk and dreaming. He saw a small garden running down to the River Loire, a bridge, across the river, a white castle on a hill, and broad steps leading up the steep street of Blois. At a small pond in the garden a man with a scholar's gown thrown over his arm was helping an urchin sail a boat. It drifted out of reach. The man let it go after a few half-hearted efforts to recover it. The wind stranded it amid the reeds. The child began to cry. "Ah, mon cher," said a woman's soft voice behind them, "it has always been like that." The man shifted uncomfortably but said nothing. Presently he took a book out of the pocket of his gown, leaned back, and began to read. The woman picked up the boy and comforted him. He snuggled in her dress. She began to recite "Le Corbeau et le Renard."

Tears ran down the face of Toussaint Clairveaux and splashed upon his desk. How delightful, how dear! Oh how heavenly ravishing were those accents! Would to Christ he could listen to them again if only for another instant now! O fields of asphodel, over which that woman's sad face is now looking, under what sunless rays do you ripple and toss? Are they as beautiful as that glimpse from the garden across the Loire?—the washerwomen along the banks of the river under the willows, the white château in a haze of green buds, a bird singing? He choked.

"Jean-Jacques Rousseau, it was you who tempted me to leave all that, to go vagabonding for Arcadia," he cried aloud, raising his hands dramatically to the ceiling as if appealing to all-seeing Jove feasting away up there. "You made me an émigré before the Revolution began, an émigré to nowhere. And now, I am caught here." He looked about him desperately. He swept the papers off his desk onto the floor.

"I am lost in a prison where a merchant's hat is wearing the horns off a satyr," he shrieked. "I shall never find the country of the beautiful savages!"

By this time the poor man was nervously striding up and down before the rail of Mr. Bonnyfeather's desk, gesticulating at the empty desks below. At every one of them sat a useless regret or a vain desire. That was his senate.

"Ah, if I could have reached those wild American forests I should have suffused my soul as a true poet and have blent you all into one." He shook his fist at the nine separate muses who paid no attention. "All into one! I should have charmed the savages. It was that woman with the great eyes who kept me here. Ah, yes! Ah, it was not you, Jean-Jacques, after all. The spirit of man is truly noble as you say, as mine was. Yes, I believe that. This boy, I shall lead into your beautiful pages. He shall later cross the sea and find that natural country for himself, unspoiled. He shall see how beautiful are the minds and bodies of men when left to themselves with nature. He shall feast like you up there in the ceiling. I, I cannot go, I am lost, bewitched. And sacred blood of a bitch!" he snorted, returning to what after all was his chief grievance, "ever since I have followed that Paleologus to this place she will not even speak to me."

Mr. McNab looked in and saw a little Frenchman apparently going mad. He grinned. The bell in the court rang twice. "To eat or not to eat, that is the question," the Scot called cupping his hand. Toussaint Clairveaux cursed him, stuffed a copy of *La Nouvelle Héloïse* into his pocket, and raced for his dinner with McNab. The mercurial Frenchman was now laughing, too. Despite the gulf between them, the two men had learned to admire each other. They were both capable of utter concentration on the matter at hand and were completely sincere. Over the desk they ceased to clash.

Anthony and Mr. Bonnyfeather were ascending the steps into the big hall just as the last prolonged resonance of the bell in the courtyard died away. The table under the muffled chandelier was set for four.

The guest for dinner that day was Captain Bittern of the *Unicorn*. He was a very thin man with a hatchet face and a perfectly horizontal, thin-lipped mouth. His hat from being perpetually jammed down on his forehead in a high wind had left a permanent red streak in the oily tan of his hide. Deep-set in cavernous sockets, his clear, cold, blue eyes looked out from behind puckered lids past the vertical, bony ridge of a long nose. It was a face which seemed even in the mouldy stillness of the old ballroom to be facing into a high wind. Anthony sat directly opposite it.

He felt instinctively that it would be impossible to disobey or to discount any command or statement that proceeded from those absolutely positive, horizontal lips. During the course of about thirty years several thousand nautical men and "natives" in various parts of the world had agreed with Anthony. One expected to hear a bass voice boom out, but the captain's pitch was a perfectly self-possessed falsetto. The effect of this from such a countenance was startling. The voice piped away steadily, monotonously, unexhausted, like a constant gale keening through taut rigging. It never rumbled. In the man's ears were two very small gold rings. He had risen from the fo'c'sle to the quarter-deck. The rings remained.

The meal began by Captain Bittern tilting a plate of soup into his transverse cavern at one fell motion. The lips simply widened toward the ears, and the soup, still on a perfect level, disappeared. The act, if such it could be called, was so irrevocable as to be almost ridiculous. Had it not been for the captain's eyes still looking out over the horizon of the bowl as if in search of distant icebergs, Anthony must have laughed. Mr. Bonnyfeather remembered that he had once seen a shark swallow a child's coffin like that in the China sea. Nothing could be done about it. The captain never laughed. It was impossible to imagine that the corners of those lips should ever be turned either up or down.

Nevertheless, the merchant treated him with great respect. He was the oldest and most dependable of the four captains of the fleet of the house. The single horn of his ship's figurehead pointed into far and dangerous seas, and pointed home again. He was just back from Singapore and the Islands, four months overdue. The account he gave of his cargo made Mr. Bonnyfeather rub his hands. Several long tumblers of raw rum innocent of any water followed the captain's soup. At every return to port Captain Bittern preserved himself in the genial fluid. In transit he abstained. Rum had absolutely no effect upon him except to embalm his body and to heighten the eloquence of his falsetto. He now began, after a series of gastronomic vanishing acts performed with both liquids and solids, to relate the story of his voyage. He took not the slightest notice of Mr. Bonnyfeather, Anthony, or Faith Paleologus. It was exactly as if he were reciting a portion of his memoirs for the benefit of the cosmos while in his cabin at sea.

Anthony longed now to understand English. He resolved to lose no time in learning it. From the tones of the captain's voice and a few words here and there he caught the emotional drift. When the captain was bargaining he did so with his hands. Over one successful deal, he squeaked. He almost broke the spell he cast by that. Anthony started when he felt Faith grip him by the knee. She managed to get him to lean closer to her and began in her low liquid voice to translate what the captain was saying.

The typhoon which had forced Captain Bittern to refit completely at Mauritius was epochal. The low voice of Faith beside him seemed to transmit to Anthony's eyes rather than to his ears the picture of the *Unicorn* dismasted, staggering, with the little beast at the bow waving his horn at the scudding clouds and then plunging for the bottom, while ribbons of split canvas streamed from the futile jury-mast rigged forward. The captain's voice became the constant piping and fluting of the wind. For the first time some conception of the power of the elements was projected into the boy's imagination. Anthony felt a mountain snatched away from under the ship, and gasped as he slid with the vessel into a molten, lead-covered abyss. The effect of wind was intolerable. By a peculiar reversal of effect the storm which the captain seemed to be facing now flowed out along with his words from his elemental face. The voice of the man piped like the wind; the voice of the woman flowed and leaped with excitement like the sea. The two mated in the boy's mind and became one experience.

A large chest and a desk in the captain's cabin started suddenly to slide about and enter into a monstrous combat with each other. The desk burst open and its insides gushed out as the chest leaped upon it. The bilge water and the paper were slowly ground into pulp as the chest continued to celebrate its victory drunkenly. The white paste produced by this milling of water and paper gathered in the panels between the beams. The cabin lamp went out. The stern windows dazzled with blue lightning. The sea rushed in. It went on for days. He went up on deck with the captain and saw an albatross sucked across the sky down into the funnel of the west where the sun plunged drawing the atmosphere after him. Suddenly it was calm again. The crew came on deck like ants out of the earth after rain, and crawled about jagged stumps of masts. Presently Anthony was tasting oranges and drinking from cocoanuts in Mauritius. In memory of the long drought during the six weeks' calm which had followed that storm, Captain Bittern allowed a fourth tumbler of rum to trickle soothingly through his teeth. He smacked his lips. Mr. Bonnyfeather sighed. It was this kind of thing, he thought, that made it profitable for a nobleman to have become a merchant.

That afternoon on the dock Anthony was able to understand why the hull of the *Unicorn* looked so aged and battered while aloft all was new with a varnished spick-and-spanness. He fell in love with the trim ship from the romping little horned-horse that sprang out of her bows to the faded gilt of the taffrail. From the yawning hatches streamed up an endless succession of bales, chests, and long mummy-like packages. The odour of preserved fruit, spices, sandalwood, and tar blent with all the rank smells of Christendom along the docks. He had never thought there could be so many different kinds of things in the world. Toussaint and the clerks kept calling them off to one another hour after hour. The odours and the weight of materials and objects seemed to press inward upon Anthony, to weigh upon his chest. He breathed deeply to free himself of the impression but could not do so. It was there, it was real. It was as real as he was. Even more so, harder and firmer.

What a fine thing it must be to own all of this, actually to possess all of these things. He glanced with a new respect and understanding at Mr. Bonnyfeather who was laughing and talking with some other merchants on the quarter-deck. They were congratulating him; already beginning to chaffer and bargain. Various bales went their way from time to time. The railing of the quarter-deck stretched between Anthony and their world just as it did between him and Mr. Bonnyfeather's desk. There was a difference then between men, which had something to do with all of these things.

He looked about him once more. Nothing belonged to him. He had only his dreams. He was a poor boy, an orphan. He understood that now. In sixty days he would have only one shilling. He had lost nine by the first use of his name. He looked at Mr. McNab standing by the capstan with a pile of papers on it. Toussaint was checking off. Mr. McNab was wearing his new hat. "God willing," thought Anthony, "I shall follow both their advices. I will not write my name on papers, and I shall certainly learn English." He began to listen to the English words for things. His chest expanded. In the days to come he would prove himself.

He went over to the group by the capstan and began to help Toussaint to check the invoices. McNab nodded approvingly. Anthony felt himself suddenly in the main current of real life. The quiet pool of the convent courtyard lay far behind him. "Where was the drift taking him?" he wondered.

"Attention," said Toussaint, "thirty-four bolts of prime Manila hemp." "Thirty-four," said Anthony. "Check," said McNab.

CHAPTER FIFTEEN

THE SHADOWS OF FAITH

ANTHONY was not detained very long by the copying out of invoices and manifests. His first promotion in the world of affairs was to the desk of the correspondents or gentlemen writers. A copperplate hand that had been conferred upon him by Father Xavier, and his proficiency in languages were responsible. The arid years in the convent were now to a certain extent a positive advantage. He could never get enough of the life about him. He absorbed it at a remarkable rate, in gulps.

No thirstier horse had ever been led to water. So avid was he of the words and the experiences, emotions, and facts which he acquired through words that he was scarcely conscious of the barriers between languages. Words were simply the coins minted by the tongues of men with which realization could be purchased. Whether they were English, French, Spanish, or Italian he cared little. All of these, with an infinite variety of dialect, he heard in daily use all about him. The quays, the streets, the counting houses of Livorno, and even the Casa da Bonnyfeather itself were in a state of babel.

For a while language remained for him nothing but the common tongue of mankind. It was not until some months had passed that he began to understand differences. Now, without thinking about it, he instinctively tasted the various savour of words and through them life. He found it good.

Slowly English began to displace in his thought his strange jargon of hill-Tuscan and ecclesiastical Latin. He heard English talked constantly in the office. It was dinned into his ears at the table and in the house. It corresponded to the new and real experiences he was having. It was also an advantage, he found, to use it when employed as a messenger about the docks or to ship's officers. It got you instant attention. He began to realize that his physical appearance corresponded with it. He began to use it when he had some important problem to think out. He spoke it with a slight Scotch tang and a softening of the vowels. The burr had been softened to a purr. The combined effect was musical and rather arresting. It was impossible to tell whence he hailed. His verbal messages seemed to come from some self-cultivated Arcadian nowhere.

Toussaint was a potent force in all this. Mr. Bonnyfeather had been quick to see the advantage of French lessons. They did not long continue to occupy only the half hour before lunch. Before long they were removed to the old ballroom after dinner had been cleared away, and they went on in the afternoon.

Soon Toussaint and Anthony were reading books together. Some writing followed as a matter of course. Later Toussaint put Anthony to copying out correspondence with French firms. In a year he was able to answer letters that required no more than a perfunctory reply. Spanish followed.

At the table Anthony listened carefully. He had learned when in doubt how to resort to a grammar or a dictionary. In the section of correspondence in the office he would pass from stool to stool. Of the several gentlemen writers each was glad to find the boy by his side for the sake of his young and happy presence and for the chance to impress upon him the superlative importance of a particular department. That Anthony was under the special eye of the Capo della Casa all of them knew.

But Mr. Bonnyfeather was most careful about that. He never permitted Anthony to take advantage of it. It was a nice piece of tact. On one or two occasions the merchant had condescended to explain to the boy. There he learned something valuable.

"See and hear everything, but be careful what you do and say," admonished the old man. "Do not tell me that Garcia sleeps at his desk, I know it, I see him nod. If he thought you knew it, he would hate you. Knowledge which threatens anyone's bread and butter should be concealed if you wish to get on."

But there was something more to it than just that. Out of the several occasions when Anthony had been thus admonished he began to understand Mr. Bonnyfeather's careful, masculine sense of honour, the indignity of eavesdropping to all concerned, the pettiness of tattle. In short, that to mind his own business meant he must first possess his own tongue in dignity and peace. A discretion rather beyond his years was thus thrust upon him.

Once he had blurted out something he had heard at the big table while he was walking along the street with McNab. It was about the unexpected arrival of a ship from Smyrna laden with oil consigned to Mr. Bonnyfeather. A smartly dressed young lad standing on the corner had turned immediately and made his way through the crowd into the near-by door of a counting house.

"Did you see yon laddie gang off wi' your tidings?" asked Sandy. "He's Maister Nolte, the nevvy of a German marchant. In ten minutes they'll be sellin' oot a' their oil at the present prices. If you're no keerfu' you'll be takin' your victuals in the kitchen, laddie." They walked on, Anthony's cheeks burning.

"You'll not say anything to Mr. Bonnyfeather, McNab?" he ventured.

"I always hold my tongue," was the reply. It was a matter-of-fact statement with no scorn in it. But the boy wilted.

"And I'll tell ye this," added McNab. "It's not only statements ye maun be keerfu' aboot, it's questions, too. Ye ask a warld too mony. Watch wi' yer ain eyes and see what happens. Then draw your ain concloosions. Dinna pay attention after ye ken what is gangin' on to what every zany may have to say."

They entered a warehouse and went to the desk of the shipping clerk. Anthony noticed that McNab let the clerk do all the talking, using only an apt prod now and then to his volubility. In five minutes the man had contradicted himself twice and proved himself in the wrong. McNab collected his bill and left.

"Ye see?" said he, peering down at Anthony. The boy never forgot. Mr. McNab blew his nose loudly into a scarlet handkerchief large enough to muffle a horn. That afternoon to the sound of his bugling they collected seventeen bills.

Distance had worked its inevitable negative magic with Father Xavier. For the first six weeks he had come rather regularly two or three times a week. Then for one reason or another his visits became irregular, the instruction desultory. It was finally dropped. The priest had done all he could. He felt that himself. New influences which he could not fully control were impinging upon his pupil's mind. The lives of saints, church history, Latin fables seemed enormously remote to Anthony now. Like the fountain in the convent courtyard they sounded in his ears as something speaking from a dream. Finally he saw Father Xavier only when Mr. Bonnyfeather confessed. This was not often. Then he heard that Father Xavier had gone to Naples. He received a letter and answered it. Another, and he forgot to reply.

Mr. Bonnyfeather's father had changed his religion to suit the Cardinal of York. Something of the old Calvinistic independence remained in the son. Secretly Mr. Bonnyfeather perused some of his grandfather's books on theology. The doctrine of predestination fascinated him. It was with a distinct struggle he persuaded himself that he had laid it aside. Several times he had been on the point of asking Father Xavier about it. Then he thought better of it.

The old man was growing a little rheumatic now. He was often cold and his feet went blue at night. The fireplace which caused so much astonishment to the servants—its like was not in the vicinity— roared constantly on cold, damp nights, which are not unknown at Livorno. Occasionally he would take supper in his room. The warmth and the blaze of the many candles were preferable to the chill and shadows in the great hall. At such times he began to call Anthony in to dine. Over the cover the story of Mr. Bonnyfeather's family began to take shape in the boy's mind. The sudden flight from the old estate by the Scotch laird and his family to King James at St.-Germain's, the long, loyal service at the toy court of the exiles, the hope deferred, the honourable poverty—all this was with Mr. Bonnyfeather a favourite theme.

Then there was the merchant's father, "the second marquis," as the old man loved to call him. He had been invaluable to the Stuarts, a great stirrer-up of Jacobite intrigues. Louis the Great had settled a pension upon him. "Ah, those were great days!" As a very little boy Mr. Bonnyfeather remembered Versailles.

As a lad he had been dragged about the Highlands during the "'45." William McNab had come back with him then. The McNabs were faithful to the old lairds; had always sent the rent. They were family retainers. Mr. Bonnyfeather extolled them. Faith was half Greek, to be sure, but her mother's blood would tell. And then he would tell over again of how his father had fought at Culloden and barely escaped at Prestonpans. His face would light up with the old hope of the victory. Or his eyes would flash as he told how it felt to be the oldest son of a nobleman on his father's estates hunting the stag. At the last, fishermen had rowed them out to a French ship with Cumberland's dragoons sweeping along behind them over the reaches of a misty beach. That was their last glimpse of Scotland. He would sigh and take another glass of port.

"And now," he would say, placing both hands on his breast in agitation, "you see me here, the third marquis—in trade!" He would hasten on as if explanation were essential.

"It came about in this way. When the prince returned again to France my father still followed him. He had become a Catholic in all but name. Then Charles Edward died. We came to Italy to be near the last of the house of Stuart. My father was received into the church with all his family. He held a small place as chamberlain to the Cardinal of York. There he was still called marquis. His title and a small pittance from the cardinal was all that he had. The French pension was no longer paid. I should not forget the crucifix which the pope sent him. I saw how things were going and wrote to some of my Whig relatives in England. One, my mother's brother, smoothed the path for me. I alienated my father, however, by taking advantage of my uncle's offer. I went to England and attended college at Exeter.

"There I met the son of a cloth merchant, Francis Baring, whose friendship has been invaluable and abiding. You will see in this Protestant Bible where he has written a number of things which we then thought profound. And it was he who drew these three clasped hands on the flyleaf. The third hand was for John Henry Nolte, now a merchant at Hamburg. We were inseparable and it is not often that three people get on so well together. Years later, just before my daughter was married"—Mr. Bonnyfeather paused—"the three of us took a long journey together through England and Scotland. I saw then for the last time the estate of which there will be no fourth marquis. But I was nobly entertained by both John and Francis Baring in London. I have since prospered greatly as a merchant myself by remembering as a nobleman what a king once said, 'L'exactitude est la politesse des rois!' You should remember that, too."

Mr. Bonnyfeather invariably ended his oft-repeated story in that way. Something in the intonation of the last phrase, something in the man's attitude and expression as he rehearsed it, looking at the boy over the candles with a supreme earnestness, gradually impressed upon Anthony that for some reason or other here was a tradition he was expected to follow. Further than that Mr. Bonnyfeather dared not permit himself to go. Anthony remained silent. They would get up at last and go over by the fire.

It was at such times over his port that Mr. Bonnyfeather became most genial. He then jumped all doubts and scruples and secretly permitted himself the luxury of feeling that he was talking to his grandson. He had been lonely for years and to have so pleasant and bright a companion as young Anthony sitting before the fire sped their association mightily. He wrapped the boy in a haze of carefully concealed affection, but as time went on gradually opened his heart.

The intimacy and remote ramifications of his business and of the personalities connected with it were discussed as if Anthony had been years older and were the heir of the house. The boy sat and listened gravely. But upon occasion Anthony could also delight with a well-timed question, a smile of understanding, or a surprising reply. The voyages of ships were traced out on the map and globe. Anthony gradually became familiar with most of the great harbours of the world; what was to be had in them, the names and personalities of the merchants, market conditions; what, in a general sense, from politics to planting, was afoot in Europe and America. Nor was it a hardship to listen. With Mr. Bonnyfeather, he became lost in it. The little hectic spots glowed on the old man's cheek bones and the boy talked too, or listened with open lips and glowing eyes. An hour of this after supper, and they would sit down to write the letters resulting from the talk. These were of such a character that Mr. Bonnyfeather did not desire them to go across the desks of the clerks.

Thus Anthony rapidly stepped into being the old man's secretary. As time went on he was able and not afraid to suggest a better phrase here and there or a more trenchant approach. He strove always to see the men to whom the letters were addressed. He learned all he could about them from the captains who had dealt with them, or from the files of correspondence in the vault. There was a roomful. But before he was sixteen he had read nearly all of it. The net which the firm of Bonnyfeather and those that it dealt with cast over the waters of the world was surprisingly well integrated in his mind. Helping always to weave the meshes firmer and closer was the constant talk of the harbour front that daily flooded his ears. But it was not all business by any means which occupied these evenings.

In Mr. Bonnyfeather's room were his books. They were a strange assortment. The intellectual, political, and spiritual adventures of his family might be read in their titles. The Covenanters as well as the Jacobites were represented. The conversion of Mr. Bonnyfeather's father to Catholicism had not prevented his son from bringing back from Exeter a collection at which the *Librorum Prohibitorum* would have shied.

Anthony pored over these. He became lost in the maze of the *Faërie Queene*. The illustrations, and afterwards the text of Fox's *Book of Martyrs* first gave him some conception of the Protestant side of the controversy. He was amazed to discover it at all. Baxter's *Saints' Rest* scared him sick. It required Toussaint to reassure him. Father Xavier might have been amazed, to say the least, to have seen the pastures in which his pupil was not only wandering but feeding. Mr. Bonnyfeather had considerable Shakespeare by heart and was given to a little rodomontade in its recitation, especially of the first part of *Henry IV*, and *The Merchant of Venice*. It served to turn the trick for the boy who would scarcely otherwise have been able to understand at first the nature of the stage. The lonely island in *The Tempest* haunted him. Somehow he thought Mr. Bonnyfeather in his black velvet suit, leaning over the globe and conjuring forth cargoes, was like Prospero.

Before he left Livorno Anthony had whole passages of *Religio Medici* by heart. Milton's Italian poems first attracted him, then the Latin. It seemed perfectly natural to the polyglot nature of the boy that a poet should write in many tongues. As the music of English became more audible to him he went on to *L'Allegro* and *Il Penseroso*. *Paradise Lost* made him drunk. His own experience of visions and dreams at the convent made the scenes and images of the poem rise up for him as if fixed on his retina. The incandescent light, the lambent glooms of the blind poet's dramatic universe peopled by even brighter gods and darker heroes remained for Anthony always the supreme banquet of words in any tongue. There was nothing like the sound of it anywhere else, that great, perfectly controlled, almighty organ vibrating and filling with oceanic and cosmic harmony the cathedral of the mind. It made the Italian operas which he later went to hear at Livorno with Vincent Nolte seem ridiculous. Sometimes the contrast would come across him as he watched a romantic little cockchafer in red tights warbling and strutting melodramatically before his trilling ladybird while brigands supplied harmony. Or he thought of it when the meretricious, saccharine roar of the finale sounded. Then he would laugh, and Vincent, whose syrupy German soul was congealing into sweet crystals and beer, would hiccough with indignation.

Milton and Dante dramatized theology for Anthony. For him it could never be abstract. Even the Holy Ghost had personality. He had a comforting smile.

It was with this life-endowing quality of the mind that Anthony passed on from the poets and vivifiers of language to the necromancers of words. On the middle shelf was a long and daunting array of Catholic and Protestant polemics, theological treatises, works of piety and religion. Anthony had made up his mind to read all the books in the room. So he read these, too; Augustine to Calvin, Athanasius, Chrysostom, Origen, and the Reverend Adonijah Parkhurst. He strained his eyes over Kerson's *Practical Cathechisme,* plunged into Bishop Burton, and heard the remote noise of the sectaries through the years of James I to Charles II arguing somewhere in space. All were totally disconnected in time. They merely occurred on the shelf. All were in words, all were therefore about something.

A universe landscaped with the strange heavens of religious utopiasters; full of maimed souls thrillingly rescued from or delivered to the devil burst on his view. Innocent and inane first parents in delightful, tropical paradises; shining battlements of the City of God on hills clouded by lightning gleamed like oases amid the dark deserts of limbo, where old gentlemen with wigs like Mr. Bonnyfeather's and terrific names gibbered and twittered moral aphorisms and definitions while pouring dust on their own heads. Or they threw worm-eaten tomes at one another. Underneath, always underneath, were the hot, the cold, and the dry, the wet, the noisy, the silent hells. These he could see were logical pictures of indignant devices invented to punish in the other world ghastly extremes of conduct in this. In short, on the middle shelf of Mr. Bonnyfeather's bookcase was a fair cross-section of the Western mind which having lost its own religion was trying to confer Greek order on Semitic nonsense. All of these books were obsessed by one thought. They were perfectly sure that one God controlled everything. Yet Anthony read in one Nicole, "Dieu est la Diable, c'est là toute la religion."

Fortunately for him, most of this curious babble was lost on the boy. Yet his mind retained queer snatches of it, voices that later on would shout advice about his conduct out of limbo. It seemed to him as if a troop of these disembodied theologians followed his earthly experience arguing. Occasionally some louder voice would make itself intelligible, shouting a distinct message to him out of the disputing crowd. In the meantime the gods and demons, the troops of angels, seraphim, and the apocalyptic landscapes were certainly fascinating.

Lowest of all on the shelves, but in big volumes like foundations of the edifice which they in fact supported, were the classics. They were all in Latin for Mr. Bonnyfeather read no Greek. Something in his accurate and precise Scotch mind loved Latin. But he was not scholar enough to carry this to a pedantic extreme. Roman life did not come to an end for him when Cicero ceased to fulminate. It and Mr. Bonnyfeather went on.

In his old age he had come to like Claudian better than Virgil. The hills of Sicily rolling their flowers close down to the sea, but always in a "wildly cultivated" manner, the absurd panegyrics of contemptible tyrants and defeated generals, which yet retained the method of true praise; all this seemed to him as he read Claudian to speak not only of Rome but of his own time. He too could feel the tang of something magnificent coming to an end with confusion to follow. The barbarians were so near.

In the pages of Ammianus Marcellinus the groans and weariness of the great Roman machine rumbling to its end were audible. Yet how great were those heroes and emperors who repaired its disintegrations with the bones of their bodies and the virtue of their souls! How terrible were the selfish tyrants feasting in the midst of catastrophe! Mr. Bonnyfeather would stride up and down reading from the great book, intoning it, while Anthony leaned forward. The story of Julian fascinated them. Ah! how much Europe needed someone like that now, someone to thrust out the sick new things and bring back the strong old gods as they were. Prussian Frederick could not do it, said the merchant. But there was this man Buonaparte. Some people thought . . . at any rate from the roof they had seen the cannon flashing one night over the horizon and ships on fire. The English did not want him. The old man shook his head. Perhaps they are wrong, those islanders. "I, you see, have had my feet on the mainland for some time now," he would say. Then he would end by reading an ancient description of the valley of the Moselle:

Immemorial vines embower the pleasant, white villas. The cup of the valley receives the bounty of the sun god, the gratitude of man rises in pious incense from the hills. The dead are honoured in the households of the living, and the spirit of the distant emperors in the towns. The magistrates punish vice with the approval of the many virtuous. The rich desire no roses in January; they enjoy them with the peasants in the spring. In the amphitheatres the extreme rage of the barbarian provides spectacles for the multitude and laughter for the cultivated; in the fields his chained vigour enhances the crops. The songs of the tenants are heard upon the estates of great landlords. Fortune is seldom invoked, for no change is desired. Through all the valley winds the River Moselle in three reflecting curves.

Anthony understood from the tones of Mr. Bonnyfeather's voice that he was yearning for something he had lost, trying to find a country where he could be fully alive and at ease at the same time. The book of Marcellinus and that of Jean-Jacques Rousseau which he and Toussaint were reading both placed that country in the past. It was also there in the Bible and in the theologians—that happy garden! Everybody seemed to have lost it and to be trying to get back to it. He himself at times already regretted the convent garden.

The madonna had come from there. He had brought her along with him. She was still in his room. He could return to her at night as an orphan wanderer from the old convent courtyard, or like an exile from the garden or the valley of the Moselle—or whatever it was he lost in the daytime—and be at peace again. The madonna understood. She listened to him. He could tell her of his troubles during the day. Books could not take her away from him, let them say whatever they might. All those crowds of people talking about God stayed outside in the desert. Those who argued could not enter this oasis. He knew! They spent the night howling outside, pouring dust on their own heads. As though from the living boughs of paradise he felt the bright face of the madonna looking down upon him while he slept.

Faith would invariably be waiting for him when he left Mr. Bonnyfeather's room and crossed the hall to go into his own. It was part of her routine to see that the house was closed and that all were asleep. At night she felt better and more awake than in the daytime. To watch all the others retire, leaving her to darkness, gave her a sense of superiority and freedom in which she revelled. She prowled, silently. She picked over a chicken and sipped a glass of wine in the kitchen. The embers of the dying charcoal looked at her with small red eyes. She sat in corners and contemplated.

Anthony would find her sitting just behind her own door which was opposite his. He did not see her. He became aware of her. The darkness there was slightly disarranged. Its folds seemed to blend, as the jade lamp burnt dimly, with the distorted shadows of the wings and hour-glass carved above the lintel of Mr. Bonnyfeather's door. Whether she watched him or not he did not know.

After he had gone to bed. she would come in, fold up his clothes, rearrange the covers and bid him good night. There was a hint of affection when she touched him, as she did often, which he felt it wrong to repulse but from which he almost shrank. In the balance he remained passive. From the time she had nursed him just after his arrival, she had thus speciously kept the key of his room as it were in her apron pocket. Sometimes she would sit down by the candles on his dresser and talk.

There was a smooth quality in her voice that soothed him. As she talked, always of personalities about the office and yard, he would watch a curious finger-play of shadows that took place at the foot of his bed on the white wall. Perhaps it was the shadow of the curtain or the flow of the candle. He and the madonna looked at it. Long, black fingers, semi-transparent here and there, kept twitching wantonly at an inflamed point of light. As this went on and her voice accompanied it, he would slowly drift into sleep. Sometimes he would awake a little after she had gone, rise, and close the door to be alone with the madonna. Another presence interfered. He found it necessary to keep it out. As the months slipped by and all became a matter of habit, he grew less sensitive to such feelings. He began to take the real world to bed with him. Only the lashes when they at last rested on his cheeks finally allowed nothing real to pass.

In the cope over the madonna's head the little stars twinkled as the great ones did above the house. The madonna kept looking past the child in her arms into the shadows and darkness of the room as if something were there. Anthony had not noticed that yet. To discover it, her expression must be carefully studied in the light as Don Luis had once done. Don Luis had understood how to use light and shadow only too well.

What was in the darkness bided its time silently.

CHAPTER SIXTEEN

PAGAN MORNINGS

EARLY in the morning, long before the flags were flying from
the roof of the Casa da Bonnyfeather, Angela, the cook, drove
out in her high-wheeled cart to collect fresh delicacies for the
merchant's table from all the country around.

The cart was nothing more than a strong, framed platform resting
on a high axle with an underslung rack behind it long enough to lie
down upon. The rack with its dangling ropes was really for wine
kegs. The shafts, which also formed the beams of the wagon platform, ranged straight forward parallel with the ground but pointed
toward each other at the ends—as Anthony thought, like parallel lines
becoming intimate near infinity. Between them there was just room
enough for the lean shoulders and fat rump of a happy little mule.

To the animal's plump sides the padded shafts of the cart were
lashed by looped ropes that passed criss-cross over a yellow pack-
saddle. The pack-saddle rested in turn upon a broad scarlet pad. A
brown leather collar resembling a huge horseshoe engaged bronze
rings on the shaft ends with two brass hooks. It seemed to envelop
the forward part of the animal hopelessly. Indeed, from this encum-
brance the head of the mule projected like a mounted hunting trophy.
But its eyes were shielded by beaded straw blinders, it wore a plaited
hair bridle, and before its smooth chest dangled an object like a small,
brass umbrella shedding strings of parachutes. These were bells.

To meet Angela and her cart in the early morning upon the country
roads about Livorno was a spontaneously exhilarating experience. As
the cart approached in a light cloud of dust and a swirl of leaves, a
mad rhythm shaking its bells, there was something Dionysian about
it. One of the small Christian chapels of the neighbouring hill country might, it seemed, have suffered a pagan relapse during the grape
harvest and be revelling along on a heathen pilgrimage at a scandalous
rate.

The clean, polished heels of the little mule kicked the pebbles out
behind him in a lateral hail. The grey, olive-wood spokes were frequently all but invisible. Behind the mule, the car seemed to float
horizontally, or to be falling forward downhill in a mist of speed. It
looked as if the mule were pursued by it. And on the platform sat

212

Angela, a fat, abundant Earth Mother, leaning back against a wine cask.

Her scarlet slippers, her bright green dress, her flashing smile under her brilliant red hair matched the colour and design of the ribbed canvas hood overhead embroidered with horseshoes, suns, and shooting stars. Her whip cracked merrily, and stung. But no less so than the pungent Tuscan drolleries with which she was given to favour passing travellers and acquaintances on the road. Franciscan fathers would by sheer instinct, and at the very first glimpse of the cart, hitch the rope about their waist a little tighter, and cross themselves as she passed.

"Christ may have died in vain," said Toussaint to himself one morning, as he halted in the courtyard and ran his stick over the spokes which gave out a muted harplike sound, "but here is a perfect pagan thing made by the hand of man and acceptable to God." Of course Anthony was wild to ride in it.

It was not difficult to assume an invitation. He would simply excuse himself from the flag-raising ceremony or deputize Toussaint in his place. Then having risen very early, he would crawl into the wine rack under the cart and wait while Tony hitched the mule and the family Guessippi performed its ablutions in the court.

This early morning cleansing was the only orderly procedure in the riotous routine of their day. Washing had been rigorously decreed by Faith herself. It was therefore enforced by the fear of the evil eye and regarded by the juvenile Guessippis as a malign decree of fate, without reason but inevitable.

As soon as the courtyard was thoroughly light the tribe emerged from the kitchen door in that state in which it had pleased God to deliver them to their parents. They were lined up before the fountain in the order tall to small, the younger ones whimpering in a subdued manner. Angela, the eldest, with an imperturbable expression on her bright, olive face, then soused them each with a bucket of cold water. One muffled whoop apiece was permitted. Just before the water descended Angela called aloud the name of the victim. After each baptism "M" or "N" was permitted to depart immediately for the kitchen to dress.

Thus were daily cleansed and brought to physical grace and the communion of men Arnolfo, Maria, Nicolò, Beatrice, Claudia, Federigo, Pietro, Innocenza, and Jacopo Guessippi. Luigi the infant was mercifully permitted to remain in his cradle stewing comfortably in his own juice near the kitchen fire.

After the last bucketful had descended upon the smallest, young Angela herself would glide behind the clump of snarled tritons composing the central group of the fountain, drop her frock, slip in as deep as her firm, little, pearlike breasts, and wriggle out again. Then after a few moments' mystery with an old towel and snaggled comb she would reappear, climb into the back of the cart on the wine-rack, settle herself comfortably into the straw, and smile at Anthony.

As often as possible especially in the spring and summer, Anthony made it a point to drive out with Angela and to attend this lay baptismal rite of the early morning. The rigmarole of the children's names captivated him. The soft vowels and consonants fell as liquidly from the lips of little Angela as did the water from the bucket which followed them. "Arnolfo—*swish,* Maria—*swish,* Nicolò, Beatrice, Claudia, Federigo—*swish.*"

As time went on these names burned themselves upon Anthony's memory. He would mumble over them at his desk like a priest at prayer. In the mornings he began to call them out with Angela. It added a new zest to the occasion. They chanted them together. Years afterwards he had but to repeat the formula and the scene would rise before him.

There was to him something mysterious about it. The early morning shapes of the things about, the characters that composed it, the event itself took on a meaning in another world beside reality. It was like an ancient ritual the function of which had been forgotten. Life was full of things like that for Anthony, happenings that seemed to hide their true significance in a mist of impersonal memory always about to be clear.

If he could only remember what he had forgotten! For a long while he kept trying to do so. Gradually as he grew older the feeling wore away. Then at times it would overcome him as if he were homesick again. Something would remind him of something better somewhere else. Perhaps in this case it was the repetition of the scene in precisely the same terms, its inevitableness, that made it take on an importance which could not be accounted for merely by common sense.

The nine naked children lined up before the little girl—he should have done something to lessen their discomfort, but he could not. Their dismal expectation of the inevitable aroused his pity, and yet it was ludicrous. Gradually he came to understand how he could remain merely a spectator. It was because these children were suffering what was to them mysteriously ordained, what was the common lot of all of them. It was in their different methods of confronting the bucket of cold water that the interest lay.

The stoical Arnolfo thrust out his already faintly hairy chest and allowed fate to run off him as from a roof. Innocenza shivered, the thin-legged Claudia wept, plump Beatrice pleaded, the sullen Pietro dodged. As spectator Anthony was each in turn. He enjoyed where the actors could not, but he also felt with them that fate was unavoidable. When their names were called the water descended from on high. It stifled the howls. It descended upon those forked, naked things, on Nicolò, on Maria, even upon the tiny Jacopo who retired with a pair of cherubic buttocks twinkling under a bucket that engulfed his head and shoulders. From it floated back faintly musical lamentations.

Unknown to himself, before that fountain in the courtyard of the Casa da Bonnyfeather, Anthony lost most of his idle sensations about and tendencies to dream curiously over the human form. His curiosity was surfeited, he saw that humanity was a shape, repeated endlessly with minor variations, and that these minor variations were unimportant in themselves. All one could tell by them was the way that certain kinds of people might act when the cold water descended. Thin people, he saw, acted differently from the fat ones. There was not so much difference between boys and girls. He learned this from what he saw rather than from what he thought.

Now he saw why the stone children that had danced around the fountain at the convent had all been made the same. They were children of one idea and not each one a variation upon it. They were like the idea from which they sprang, all beautiful and happy. But to sympathize with the Guessippi children he must in turn be Tom, Dick, and Harry. Only part of him was in them at any one time. All of him had danced with the stone children.

How long ago that seemed! How old were the stone children? Oh very old! He did not feel new. He felt older than most people in the world about him. At least he thought so, lying in the cart waiting for little Angela.

So he thought too lying in his room at night looking at the madonna. She remained. She and he remained as they always had been. All that went on during the day passed in a space between them which they both overlooked at night. Some time he would creep back whence he had come. He would go back and be close to her like that other child in her arms. Other children ran back to their mothers. He longed sometimes to do that, too. It was a need, a desire he did not question.

As for the Guessippi children he made them tolerable to himself by imagining them to be like the stone children in the ring. All alike, beautiful, dancing under the cold water. Now he could be happy with such beautiful things. Their little individual differences had vanished. He did not have to sympathize with each in turn.

As for little Angela she certainly belonged to the children of the stone ring—to that time. She had only stepped out of it into now. He could see how smooth, how delightful and graceful, how self-

contained she was. Impersonal. Her being was equivalent to affectionate and caressing sounds, coolness and softness thought of warmly.
"Maea," he called her secretly. This word simply bubbled out of the
feeling of the fifteen-year-old boy as he lay in the "perfectly pagan"
wine cart.

He was envied secretly by Toussaint who passed by with his basin
in the early morning with tired eyes to dash cold water upon those
windows of his disappointed soul. He too would have liked to ride
in that cart back into Arcady with little Angela. He would wink
knowingly, conveying by merely assuming it as adults do his own immense experience and prophetic insight to Anthony.

Anthony would wink back, but it was with him only a greeting.
He was not thinking about Toussaint. He was waiting for little Angela to finish her bath behind the fountain and to join him in the cart.

There was an assurance, a complete and happy naturalness about
"Angela Maea" that he liked from the first. From the vast mass of
her mother she had sprouted like an unexpected, delicate bud from a
log. The bud had grown into a slim, young branch. When she
joined Anthony in the cart, drops from her bath in the fountain would
still be glittering in her hair. Her breath was sweet and her face was
brown and firm with dark red lips. It seemed as if she had just been
passing over a meadow gathering mushrooms before sunrise. Her
brown eyes appraised him frankly and liked him. Before the cart
would start they would lie and look at each other with quiet delight.

Then Angela the great would ascend the cart. Looking up from
the little rack in which they lay at the enormous proportions of the
woman before and above them they would both laugh. How different
from themselves! "Angela," they would both whisper together as if
still calling the roll of those about to be cleansed before the fountain.
The vision evoked convulsed them.

Then the whip would crack, then the mule would clatter along
through the still deserted streets, through the gate as the morning gun
was fired from the Castell' Vecchio—and out onto the long, white
road to Pisa. It was that way they nearly always took. Anthony
abandoned himself on the hills to the sensation of speed. He was
going somewhere. He felt free. The hills of the world were before
him. Of them he could never see enough. The pungent smell of
burning olive wood, of myrtles, or of a slope of vineyards in blossom
seemed to fill his head. It was good. Somehow it was often strangely
familiar. There was dew on the new-mown hay. The drops of moisture in Angela's hair drew rainbows. From the farmyards as they
passed came the shrill cry of chanticleers that ran over the hills into

one far-off, continuous song of morning. They answered the birds in shrill mockery together. Great Angela never looked back. Her back was far too broad even to try to see all that went on behind it. Big Angela knew the countryside like a cookbook: where the best oil was to be had, who had the fattest ducks, the farm where the freshest cress grew, the most luscious broccoli. As she made stop after stop for bargain and purchase, they drew farther and farther back into the hills.

To the sound of endless chaffer and the clink of small bronze or silver coins the cart took on more and more the aspect of a bit of the hanging market gardens of Babylon on wheels. The small casks behind were filled with wine, the hampers under the fat woman's elbows grew loud with cacklings and quacks. From between the wicker bars thrust forth the snake-like, hissing heads of geese. In his muffled basket a cock hailed a false dawn. Bunches of beets, garlic, onions, heads of lettuce, fruit were suspended from the roof. A small pig twisted on the floor bound by the heels.

On top of all this like a figure of plenty with the harvest about her sat the mountainous woman, a flower thrust into her flaming hair. From behind, the happy faces of Angela and Anthony seemed to mock at famine and the passer-by. Sometimes they drove out far enough to look down into the valley of the Arno with the river twisting through the white villages and grey olive orchards that swept away with it to the sea. They could see the little people tending their vines between the living posts of the mulberry tree. White oxen ploughed and lowed plaintively. Always to the west was the blue flash from tables of sea. Returning, Anthony could look north where the Apennines shouldered away vaguely into the light and haze, growing clearer and greener as the day gained on itself.

Once down a byroad he saw the red roofs of the convent. His pigeons were still circling about the tree. How far off was that, how long ago! At the city gate there was always an argument about the amount of the tax. Then they would be home, cries of hungry acclamation following them along the street. In the noisy drive through the town streets he and little Angela kept close. In the courtyard they slipped away from each other quietly. She to the kitchen, he to the office.

Mr. Bonnyfeather condoned these excursions, enjoyed them secretly. McNab frowned. Toussaint smiled. A small package of cheese was usually his share and a whispered description of the trip. Then the pens would scratch on.

Faith did not approve of these morning adventures, but she said

nothing. Anthony, she thought, spent too much time with the Guessippis. She began to find work for little Angela whenever she could.
The games of hide-and-seek, the romps with the children in the kitchen
wing grew somewhat more difficult and further between. Anthony
was fast growing up. Somehow Faith made him feel this. Her effect upon him was something of a paradox. In her presence he felt
older, less embarrassed, yet she continued to put him to bed like a child.

CHAPTER SEVENTEEN

PHILOSOPHICAL AFTERNOONS

Toussaint CLAIRVEAUX, Gentleman Writer,

Monsieur:—It is my desire that you will undertake the instruction of the young clerk, Anthony Adverse, now apprenticed to me, with the end in view of founding him in the following specific things, to wit: *Easy and Legible Penmanship* for both Letters and Accounts (I provide you with models of the letters and figures I wish him to use), *facility in Arithmetic* with particular application to the accounts of this firm, *Geometry* with application to hoisting machinery, tackles, and navigation, *Geography* (he already knows the Globes), let him memorize the entire list of names of places, natural features; in short the principal legend on the set of English great-charts with which I shall provide you, *Natural History* in all branches so that he may have a knowledge of the first origins of various products and the localities from which they come, a *history of trade* sufficient to understand the origin and meaning of commercial regulations, agreements, usages, and the laws of trade and exchange now generally in force, a knowledge of the *different classes and qualities of manufactured and natural goods, products and materials* (for this you will call in the assistance of Mr. William McNab for three hours a week in the storeroom, Monday, Wednesday and Friday. Do not neglect this. Let the boy be able to tell the qualities of cloth by the feel of them in the dark. Let him educate his taste and smell in teas, wines, and spices. It is my desire that you supplement his practice in commercial letter writing in French, English, Spanish and Italian by instruction in the grammar of these tongues, calling in assistance when necessary). I shall myself oversee his Latin. You may draw on the chief clerk for buying what books you deem necessary, first looking upon my own shelves to ascertain that you do not duplicate unnecessarily.

Knowing you to be a man of liberal education and wide reading, albeit somewhat unfortunate in your private financial ventures, I have nevertheless confided A.A. to your charge. Conduct your instruction so far as possible in French. Act (confidentially), on the supposition that you are preparing this boy for the situation in life of a gentleman-merchant. In addition to this I recommend to bring to his attention such works of the Modern Encyclopaedists, Philosophers, and Savants as you can best present yourself, having regard to the tender years of your pupil. I exclude Voltaire.

You are to regard yourself in authority as the boy's tutor. The afternoons are made over to you until further notice. Both you and your pupil will be released from the office from dinner time to five o'clock post meridian. Waste not the time yourself nor permit the boy to do so. Your salary is increased during the time in which you instruct him by twenty-five scudos the month and you will take your noon meal at the big table. Fear nothing in letting me know wherein you cannot fulfil that I may call in aid. I trust you with much, a mind, and perhaps a soul.

May the Holy Trinity guide you,

JOHN BONNYFEATHER.

So day after day and year by year the instruction went on. The maps crinkled on the big table while in imagination Anthony sailed out through all the world. "Pass from Hamburg to Pondicherry," Toussaint would say and the boy would begin. "But you arrive first off the coast of Coromandel," Toussaint would remark afterwards with a slight hint of reproach as if a breach in etiquette had been committed by Anthony's omission. Then the Frenchman would start in to talk of the countries, the towns, the cities, and the rivers; their history, who traded there for what. If there was a classical legend or story about any blur of colour on the map which they passed in these mythical voyages, Toussaint rehearsed it. To many of these places in the course of his hopeless search for Arcadia he had been himself.

"At Malacca are settled many old Chinese merchants who sit smoking opium by their lily ponds or sipping little cups of rice wine. There is good quail hunting in the country behind. In Cochin China they allow fish to rot upon the roofs and from this they make sauce for their dishes. The liquor is brown and put in the center compartment of the divided dish. Only pretend to dip your bamboo shoots in it when you dine with these merchants. Make a delectable noise when you eat. It is good manners. The charts of the northern coast of Van Diemen's Land are cartographers' dreams, *Terra Australis Incognita*. Stand off from Bermuda ten miles and burn flares for a pilot. Nothing is to be had there but onions, oranges, yellow fever, and trouble with the admiral. At Malta the drinking water is all brought from Africa and stinks. Since the Reformation most of the knights are French. They choose only old men as grand masters in order to keep things in their own hands and have frequent elections which are profitable. St. Paul himself was wrecked there. The inhabitants are really Phoenicians. There is a bad fever peculiar to the place."

Thus the maps took on reality, and what Toussaint did not know Anthony heard sooner or later at the Big Table or in talking with Mr. Bonnyfeather at night.

For two years the boy kept a set of ships' account books for Mc-Nab. It was for the *Unicorn*. At the end of that time Anthony attempted to balance them with the hatchet-faced Captain Bittern. In January of the year before he found the captain had made a mistake. The captain himself pointed it out to him. It was serious. After four hours' continuous talk on the subject of Bottomry and agents' commissions Anthony saw what was wrong, but he did not feel sorry.

Bottomry, indeed, was the boy's bête noire. There was a young lawyer in Livorno by the name of Baldasseroni who was an expert in this terrible subject. Assurance in general was his hobby. For several months he came once a week at Mr. Bonnyfeather's request and lectured for hours at a time on the theory and practice of Bottomry. Toussaint finally tried to get rid of him by engaging him in an argument as to the desirability of old age pensions as lately suggested by the republican writer Thomas Paine. In trying to work out a scheme for the Island of Corsica the two quarrelled over the possible number of old people in the island. "Before the French came," said Toussaint, "the feuds prevented anyone from reaching old age." The lawyer became enraged at this insult to Italians and challenged Toussaint to a duel.

There was no way of getting out of it. So one afternoon with McNab as Toussaint's second they rode out to a lonely beach and shot at each other. Anthony was so thrilled as to be delighted. The bullet of Toussaint passed through the haunches of Signore Baldasseroni. McNab plugged him up with his handkerchief, for he threatened to bleed to death. Nevertheless, the laughter of the Scot was Homeric. " 'Twas an aspect of Bottomry the signore had no confarred suffeecint thoct upon you maun say," he remarked to Mr. Bonnyfeather who smiled grimly and dropped the subject from the "curriculum."

Toussaint strutted about like a peacock for days. He felt himself to be a gentleman again. Signore Baldasseroni meditated for some weeks on the bottom he had neglected to insure. Anthony was relieved. Yet the primary facts of marine and other assurance remained in the boy's mind flavoured with a curious reminiscent humour and human connotations.

To a romantic like Toussaint assurance was a road to Utopia, for the selfish and ruthless it was a method of cashing in on old ships and drowned sailors. This was what Mr. Bonnyfeather said about it.

To most Latins it was a form of the lottery.   Therefore, you assured ships with honest, literal, and unimaginative persons.   The British were best.   "The kind of people that meet in the little room at Lloyds, for instance," said the old man.   "I once went there with Francis Baring.   Those people were able to read figures without lying to themselves or each other about them."   "This," thought Anthony, "is the final value of arithmetic.   It is why McNab and not Toussaint, who is a much more brilliant mathematician, is chief clerk."   Anthony had already begun to see around the Frenchman a little.   Against the background of many others he began to stand out in relief.   It was possible to see already that behind him were certain shadows.

All that the boy learned, no matter how abstract, remained for him in the terms of men.   Even the stars came down out of their spheres to assume human meaning.

John Peel Williams, ex-mate of the ship *Lion,* living on his own scanty savings and the bounty of Mr. Bonnyfeather, came down from his garret in the slums once a week to give practical instruction in the use of the instruments of navigation.   He had huge, steady hands and the voice of a hoarse sea lion.   While the old house shook to his rumbling and grumbling, the abstract geometry of Toussaint was snatched down out of nowhere and suddenly became the earth and other spheres around it.   Outlines of terrestrial and celestial circles, zeniths and nadirs, of small ships crawling through angles and degrees displayed themselves in blue chalk on the floor of the ballroom from Friday to Monday when they were finally washed away.   Navigation had been Mr. Williams' only intellectual escape from his own dull soul.   His emotional exit was by way of alcohol.   The first was his God and the second his demon.   A subtle combination of both evoked in him the inspired teacher.

He had read extensively in "navigation" but in nothing else.   His admiration for the universe was due solely to his own comment upon it, oft, and eternally repeated, "I tell you the stars cannot lie."   Mr. Williams proceeded by the method of the elimination of negatives. He showed Anthony that all other methods than the particular one he proposed were wrong.   Thus with immense gusto he orated into limbo the astrolabe.   He disposed vigorously of the cross-staff with profound pity for those who had been forced to discover new worlds by its doubtful aid.   He frowned upon the half-arc, and he finally with enormous and dramatic emphasis produced his sextant out of a shining leather case, extolled it with infinite explanations, and ascending to the roof, roaring like a bull in springtime, shot the astonished sun. So much for latitude.

As to longitude there was still great difficulty. "Owing," said Mr. Williams, "not to the stars, which cannot lie, but to our own unfortunate position on the earth. The English Admiralty has long offered a prize for the best method of solving it. The log of the day's run and the careful knowledge of drift due to winds, currents, and the ship's habits are the best we can as yet do. But that is guess-work, the rule of thumb. I hear that the comparison of clocks has been suggested, but I myself am at work on a bi-focal mirror, two mirrors and an hemisphere. With mirror '1' you take the sun at sunrise, with mirror '2' you take the moon at moonrise. You mark the path of their rays as extended upon the hemisphere. The place," said Mr. Williams, leaning forward and lowering his voice to half a gale, "the place where these rays intersect, will, if properly calculated from the data provided by my table, that I am preparing slowly, very slowly, and the degrees marked on the hemisphere, give you your longitude. The chief difficulty is owing to the shifty nature of the moon. However, let me show you this astonishing instrument."

They ascended together the five pairs of stairs of his lodging. At the top floor a door across the hall half opened. An old woman looked out expectantly. Seeing the mate she shoved the door shut again. "She is a decayed gentlewoman," said he in a whisper not audible more than four floors away, "who makes her living by astrology on the fifth floor and keeping girls on the first. She has written a book. In it are all the old lies about the stars." His voice growled with indignation. He picked up a poor, cheaply bound volume and commenced to read like a tremulous cannon.

> It is said by savants that the angles of the three great pyramids denote a shifting in the position of the North Star. There will come a time when Polaris will no longer mark the extension of the axis from the northern pole of the earth.

Anthony saw the door across the hall open slightly and the head of the old woman protrude listening. She saw him, and put her finger on her lips.

"Think of it, think of it!" roared the mate. "Here is an old woman who has written a book denying the whole truth of the beautiful and eternal science of navigation. She would have the pole star itself shift. What then would become of all the books and tables founded upon the fact that Polaris remains forever fixed? What would become of them, I say?" His rage was extreme. The door across the hall closed again. The mate bellowed on now like a wounded animal. The book shook in his hand.

The stars of the Dipper outline the womb of our universe. Out of the tail of the Great Bear were born the sun and the seven planets that we see. The ancient religions of the earth preserve this essential tradition. The era of Christianity itself can be read in the dial of the stars. We are now entering upon the last phase of an epoch when man has worshipped himself. God is about to become matter. Nature, God and man will be taken for one. All things will then become confused. Words themselves will come to have no meaning. Babel will ensue. When the sun enters upon the region of the Water Carrier a new spiritual man will arrive. The soul will again recognize itself. The cycle is repeating itself. . . .

The mate broke off and hurled the volume into the corner.

"Come up on the roof," said he, "and see my instrument. It is a waste of time to read such words."

They climbed up a ladder to a trap door. On the tiles, resting on a light platform was a half globe covered with quicksilver and marked with degrees around the edge. Two mirrors on rods shifted about it.

"Now," said the mate, "we are getting back to facts again! But I will tell you something. It is my own discovery. Latitude and longitude are the same thing! With these two mirrors I shall prove it to you." He proceeded to manipulate them. Small suns glittered on the quicksilver globe. He became fascinated. His voice boomed on as he continued for a full half hour to confuse the astonished boy who tried to follow him. Anthony could make nothing of it. The tone of the man's voice reminded him of Toussaint's when he was reading or talking about Rousseau. It was what Mr. Bonnyfeather called "enthusiasm—an emotion without a sufficient cause."

"How can anybody really get excited about quicksilver globes?" thought Anthony.

His own instinct for words came to his rescue. No one could ever get anywhere, he saw, who thought that latitude and longitude were the same thing. He sat for a while apparently listening respectfully, but swinging his feet over the edge of the roof and looking out over Livorno.

The water he saw was exactly separated from the shore. Hills were the opposite of valleys. The sky was not the earth. On the horizon they seemed to meet, but he knew when you got there there was a gulf between.

After a while he crawled back down the ladder without disturbing the mate. Above him the stentorian voice rolled on. As he slipped down the hall the old woman looked out again. She was laughing. As he passed by she thrust her book into his hand. A red card fell out.

Signora Bovino
Explains the Past,
and
Elucidates the Future,
Casts Horoscopes, and Reads Palms.
Her Art is Invulnerable
on the Fifth Floor
Strada Calypso
───────
Satisfactory Amatory Entertainment
on the First.

Anthony looked up again but the door had closed noiselessly.

He went home and tried to read the book. A new meaning to religion dawned on him as he turned its pages. But between strange visions of the past which the book suggested, shrieked out a shrill feminine babel of nonsense in print. His head spun. He had had enough of stars.

For a while Anthony had been induced to believe by Mr. Williams that the stars could not lie. It was impossible for him to believe, however, that the art of Signora Bovino was invulnerable, even on the fifth floor. Yet Mr. Bonnyfeather who was now the final appeal in most things confirmed the fact that the North Star actually was shifting. The news caused something to crack in Anthony's head. He blinked. So there *was* something in the old woman after all! Both her art and the art of navigation were partly right. You could not trust anything too far, then. Curious!

He began to wonder about Father Xavier, but that was past now. It was difficult to question what he had heard from him, very difficult. He had accepted it as truth for so long. And then there was Toussaint. Perhaps Rousseau, then, was only Toussaint's enthusiasm. On the days when they walked out into the country and read *La Nouvelle Héloïse* together Anthony began to listen with his own ears rather than those which the eloquence of his tutor would have provided for him.

They used to climb the hills back of the town on hot days and sit down under the trees. There was one place which Toussaint particularly affected. It was a small valley with a nondescript ruin in it which peculiarly moved the soul of the Frenchman. They would lie down by a spring while the grasshoppers chirped in the grass and Toussaint or Anthony read aloud. In his excitement Toussaint would occasionally mount upon a rock and give vent to his feelings at some passage that aroused his enthusiasm. Under the spell of his eloquence the little valley became a charming glade in an antique world.

Toussaint waved his hand. He struck an attitude with his cloak falling from his arm like a toga, and pointed dramatically to the pile of stones covered with vines across the little valley that lay before him.

"Do you see that ruin?" he cried. Anthony could see it plainly. "I shall cause it to rise before your eyes; to become once more the home of simple and happy folk uncontaminated by the vices which a cruel society would now thrust upon them. I am about to show you humanity walking alone, upright, free and noble; the beautiful body and soul of man unfettered by the cruel irons of the fatal social contract. Religion has not been invented. There is only the force of nature reverently and happily worshipped. There is no fear. All is love. There is nothing but the beautiful earth and the most beautiful thing on it, man. The more I think of him the nobler he becomes." With a single and simultaneous gesture of one foot and two hands the philosopher now disposed of the entire Christian era.

"Roll back, you dull ages of slavery, pass three thousand years. I see before me a charming wattled hut. It is near nightfall. In the doorway sits a woman with a distaff. She manipulates the wool, while her naked and beautiful children, while the lambs and kids bound about her threshold. The father returns. Over that hill, out of the beech forest, he appears, huge, noble, but graceful. A slaughtered deer is thrown over his shoulders. A bow is in his hand. The dogs bark. The woman and children run to meet him. Their embraces are unrestrained. The deer is roasted before the fire. Baked roots are raked from the ashes; a simple cake or two. The power of nature is thanked in a simple prayer. The family quenches its thirst at the spring. They leap in the pool and swim in the moonlight. They admire each other. They are unashamed. They lie down to undisturbed rest. There is no care for the morrow. Nature will provide. There are no priests except the father, no taxes, no false manners, no conventions, no neighbours to impose upon them or to be impressed, no books, no lessons except that of husbandry, no, no, no . . ." Toussaint swept away everything with a final gesture.

After these outbursts Anthony was surprised to see that even the ruin remained. It had, he observed, after the mist of oratory cleared away, an obstinate faculty of remaining a heap of stones covered by vines.

Toussaint would then walk about a little. Then he would throw himself down in the grass again and eagerly begin to thumb over the pages of some book which he had brought with him. It was usually one of Rousseau's. He was especially fond of chanting these lines by heart until he found the place he was looking for, whatever it might be:

Emile was filled with love of Sophie. And what were her charms that bound him to her? They were tenderness, virtue, the love of honour. But what most moved the heart of Sophie? Those feelings that were of the very nature of her love : respect for goodness, for moderation, simplicity, for generous disinterestedness, a contempt for splendour and luxury.

Frequently in their walks while admiring the beauties of nature their pure and innocent hearts were exalted to their Creator. But they did not fear His presence, before Him they uncovered themselves to each other. Then they saw their own perfection in all its beauty, then they loved each other most and conversed charmingly on the subjects that the virtuous most appreciated. Often they shed tears that were purer than the dews of heaven.

For some reason or other the recital of these paragraphs nearly always brought tears to the eyes of Toussaint. It brought a scene to his mind as if Watteau had gone sketching in Japan.

It was also during these afternoon walks, readings and "recitations" by Toussaint that the news of the French Revolution had first been brought to Anthony's ears. At first Toussaint had been its prophet, if one could believe him. As the boy listened to him he thought at first his friend was talking about the Kingdom of God which seemed close at hand. Every day now was to be a little better than the day before. Things from now on were to go that way, for some reason. Because that was the way they went. Anthony had read a great deal about the Kingdom in the theological books on Mr. Bonnyfeather's shelves. Toussaint's kingdom was to be a Republic. But it was never clear to Anthony, no matter how much Toussaint explained the "difference," what was the difference between the Republic that the Revolution was to bring and the far-off Kingdom of God, the reign of Christ and all his saints.

"But man will bring about his own perfect state by reason. Can't you see!" Toussaint would cry. "What has God got to do with that?"

"Stuff and nonsense," said Mr. Bonnyfeather one night when Anthony questioned him about all this. "You are quite right. The old books were talking about the same thing. Perfection is nothing new. It is just an old dream that had been forgotten for a while. Now they are talking about it again with new words. It is the spirit of just men made perfect. Don't you see if reason is to make just men perfect, then reason must be God? It is only a new word for the Almighty. If not, if it is human reason they are talking about, how can an imperfect thing make a perfect one? Besides," grumbled the old man, "find the just men. Where are they? . . .

"I will tell you something about all this talk of perfection, of constant progress that is going on everywhere now," said the merchant getting up and walking up and down. "It is popular because it is flattering. And there is one great idea under it all that I am convinced from both my own experience and my reading is wrong. It is this man Rousseau that your tutor is always reading to you from, and talking to you about, who is mainly responsible. Listen, this is it. It is the idea that human nature is naturally good; that by pulling on its own bootstraps it can raise itself to God. Do not believe that. If you do you are lost."

The pit seemed to open at Anthony's feet. He looked at his patron amazed, not so much for what he said as for the earnest way he said it. Anthony had never seen him so determined before.

"No, no, the Church is right," cried the old merchant. "I have lived long enough to find that out. Men are not so good as they pretend to be, or like to think they are. They are in fact evil. Besides, I do not know anyone by the name of 'man.' I meet and deal only with men and women. They are evil. They do evil in spite of themselves even when trying to do good. You must be humble in spirit to believe that. That is what humility means. You must not be too proud to ask for help for your evil self from the outside; to pray, to try to commune. It is the people who are always trying to make the world better that are proud. They have no need of God. Those who know they have a fatal lack in themselves will not try to make others perfect. They will only be sorry for themselves and for others; perhaps they will be kind, decent, affable if they can be. They will hope that others will find out how helpless and how liable to do evil they are, too. A thousand citizens like that gathered together in one place would make a good town to live in. You will never find it. Do not look for that town. It is too much to expect on earth. It is the City of God.

"Remember it is only by a miracle that a man can escape from himself. By the power of something more than human. That is what our religion means with all its faults. For it, too, is partly made by man. Can you understand?"

"I can follow what you say," said Anthony.

"You will feel it some time, you will understand it, after you are vile enough, then you will know. Now, good night."

The boy rose to go.

"Am I so evil?" he asked.

The old man stopped suddenly and came over to the door. He put his hands on Anthony's shoulders and drew him toward him. He drew his head back and looked down into his face.

"Not yet," he said. For an instant he held the lad close to him. "God keep you!" he murmured.

During the entire time in which Anthony remained under the roof

of the Casa da Bonnyfeather this was the sole positive manifestation
of affection which he received from the old merchant. Sometimes he
felt restrained in the old man's presence. Of Mr. Bonnyfeather's
great affection for him the boy was of course by this time aware. At
first he had accepted it with the calm, egotistic assurance of a boy.
Naturally, people would like him! But as he grew older he realized
that Mr. Bonnyfeather was, as he expressed it to himself, "his earthly
father." Between them, though no words had passed on the subject,
it was understood that Anthony should some day succeed to the old
merchant's place. A hundred little expressions and phrases that the
old man used showed it was that of which he was thinking. Then,
too, his constant urging of the boy's ambition and the careful preparation and planning of his instruction all pointed that way. Yet there
was a reserve in each which the other respected. Mr. Bonnyfeather
alluded frequently to his own past. Anthony was finally able to piece
most of it together. But the boy's past he never even touched upon.
"It is to save me embarrassment," thought Anthony. Of the lost
daughter the merchant said nothing. Faith had once talked of her
one night while the shadows danced, but carefully. The boy had no
cause to connect himself with her. Rather than ask about something
which he knew might give Mr. Bonnyfeather pain, he would have cut
off his own hand.

So they sat together in the merchant's room at night talking, reading, going over business affairs. There was in that room as time went
on a complete feeling of confidence and ease between them. The dim
figures in the wall seemed to Anthony to be in his past, the lost country
out of which he had mysteriously come. From that company of
dreams he had merely removed as it were into the clearer, into the
very clear and precise atmosphere of Mr. Bonnyfeather's room in the
bright candlelight. He was now sitting with the man who was a father
to him, having the world as it actually is explained and made understandable. Some day he, Anthony, would sit at that desk planning
out the voyages of the firm's ships, but not for a long while. No, he
would not, could not bear to think of that. But in the room he nevertheless felt himself to be heir apparent. Outside in the court, in the
counting house, and in the city there was a subtle difference in their
attitude to each other. Mr. Bonnyfeather, he could see, did not care
to make plain to everybody what was understood between them when
they were alone. And with this tacit arrangement the boy fell in line
and acted his part. That was perhaps the crux of the situation.
Anthony was sensitive and understanding enough to accept it and not
to presume.

Only once or twice in later years had that earlier feeling of restraint
fallen upon them. It came at times when Mr. Bonnyfeather seemed

about to say something that weighed much on his mind. He would stand looking down into Anthony's face while he was talking. Then a silence would overtake him for a minute as if his tongue had been stopped by an overpowering thought. Anthony felt sure at such times that he was about to hear something of peculiar importance. Then, as if Mr. Bonnyfeather had changed subjects with himself, he would lower his eyes and go on just where he had left off.

Of all these things the boy thought as he went to sleep at night, particularly after Faith had gone. Then he would creep out and draw close enough to the madonna to be able to see her in the faint light that beat in from the hall. He was thankful that he seemed to have found an earthly father. She herself, the statue, had now become two things in one to him, things gathered up out of all the dreams and experiences of his past. She was that woman who might take a child in her arms and comfort him, even a big lad, when, as he went to bed again, he felt like a child in the dark, helpless and alone; alone as the spirit of every man must be when he attempts to commune with himself. But she had also become that power-beyond of which Mr. Bonnyfeather had spoken, something to which he might appeal, which in his very efforts to talk with it seemed to dictate its own reply within him.

So, creeping close to her by the wall in the warm Italian night, the slim figure of the orphan out of habitude from old times came close to the Virgin to whisper to her of that chaos of thought and feeling that was already burning in his body and mind. For a while, crouched by the wall in the moonlight, he was at home again. He had returned to the heart of that mystery from which he had come.

CHAPTER EIGHTEEN

BODIES IN THE DARK

TOUSSAINT had, as Anthony grew tall and took on the promise of an early manhood, begun to talk to him of love. It was always of "love" and seldom of women. Of women Anthony had heard much in a coarse and generally good-natured way about the port.

Sailors who followed girls; clerks related their experiences. These were sometimes strange or drôle enough. Usually they were merely muddled. For a long time they had seemed to Anthony adventures and experiences that could only happen to others, things which could not, and need not, affect him. Indeed, he felt a little superior about it all. He felt that he should pretend an interest, yet secretly glad that he really cared so little.

But the stories of Garcia, the Spanish clerk, were graphic. Indeed, that young correspondent was occasionally given to using the firm's best stationery to draw pictures upon in which the attitudes of human bodies when united with each other were so accurately and intimately portrayed as to leave no room for imagination between them. It was for that very reason that Anthony, who was allowed the privilege of looking at these *graphti* from time to time, was, despite a few natural burning throbs, finally disappointed. There were too many of these pictures for him. It was being too prodigal with something rare. You also saw somewhat the same thing in farmyards when you drove out into the country. No one paid much attention to it there. Why draw pictures about it in town? Big Angela could drive a flinty bargain for sour wine while it was going on in the stables. Only children stared.

Nevertheless, from the Spanish clerk and anatomist the boy learned certain intimate phrases and idioms which even the books of Castilian grammar omitted by pure consent. McNab had given the final quietus to the drawing lessons by leaning over Garcia and Anthony one day during a more than usually erective bit.

"Mon," said McNab suddenly extracting the paper from under the artist's pencil and holding it up, "if you're in that state of mind I'll lend you a hae crown mysel'." Cornering Anthony later he had remarked with a lift to his nostrils, " 'Twas bad enough gazin' at the ceilin' when ye first came. Now you're crawlin' under and lookin' up." The lad wilted. Then he felt sick. After that he confined himself and Garcia to letters in Spanish and nothing more. Behind

231

his desk McNab looked at the pictures, laughed and threw them in the waste bin.

The passage about Emile and Sophie did not move Anthony. He said so. Toussaint was hurt. According to him "love" was allowing the soul to expand. It was important to find someone with the qualities of soul with which one could—expand. Emile and Sophie had been able to expand together, he pointed out. Together their souls had filled the whole world for them and made it beautiful. Yes, they had loved each other's bodies. The human body was beautiful and pure. "Notice," said the philosopher, "when they revealed themselves to each other, when on those charming walks they were naked and lay down in the grass together,—it was then that from the sight of their beautiful bodies their souls most caught fire. Then they had the most beautiful and truly virtuous thoughts. The finest things were said then, their purest tears would flow."

"Why was that?" asked Anthony.

This irritated Toussaint. A Gallic wriggle of his shoulders was really his best answer. To find words to explain it, he was forced again to hunt some place in the pages of Rousseau which was peculiarly "expansive." There it was all clear. One felt that it *must* be so, he insisted. One could weep and be pure with those lovers in the book. In reading the book Toussaint seldom thought about Faith Paleologus. The book and she belonged to two different worlds. He preferred not to confuse them. Yet sometimes . . .

"All those children in the stone ring about the fountain were beautiful," thought Anthony. "Bodies in most books and some pictures are also like that, especially in novels and poems. But real bodies are not all beautiful. Some are disgusting. Not all those Guessippi children are beautiful. Innocenza, she is like a double radish under a smooth little onion. And there is Arnolfo. No, certainly he is not ugly, but he is not beautiful. What could you think about Arnolfo?" There was something about Arnolfo which Anthony would like to have talked about with Toussaint. But Toussaint was always reading from a book. This was about something that had really happened.

Arnolfo had taken Anthony upstairs one day into the warm, empty room over the kitchen. Then he had closed the door mysteriously and locked it. Then he had let down his clothes. "Look," said Arnolfo, "Look! I can do that." After a few fascinating moments he proved that he could.

"Can *you?*" he asked.

"Could he?"—Anthony wondered. Arnolfo was both triumphant and incredulous. The boy was smaller than Anthony. Anthony felt inclined to lie to him or to boast. He mumbled something, sweating. "I don't think English clerks *can,*" sneered Arnolfo. "Straw hair!"

So phrased it was now a dilemma of embarrassments. He must either retire or prove himself. Besides, could he, *could* he? Something must be done. In behalf of himself, his race, and his class Anthony accepted the challenge.

There were a few moments of terrible doubt.

Then he forgot Arnolfo. The walls of the room and the glimmering window retreated to a vast distance. He was left alone, absolutely alone with a new and enchanted self. It seemed as if someone else were touching him; he and himself.

A vision of the fountain in the courtyard at the convent appeared to him. It became clearer and clearer. The water in the pool was bubbling. The bronze boy was capering along the rim like a monkey. The stone children beneath were dancing madly around and around. Suddenly they blurred into a misty ring of speed. The water rose of itself, overflowed, and engulfed the bronze boy. He saw the roots of the great tree entirely exposed. Then it was over. He wilted. The mist cleared.

He was back in the mean, hot little room again. He, Anthony Adverse, awfully naked! Arnolfo was laughing at him!

That little monkey knew it was the first time! He had been with him, peeping at the fountain in the temple. He had seen it! Another great emotion surged over Anthony bringing his strength back to him again. It was anger. His leg shot out by itself. The foot on the end of it kicked Arnolfo soundly. Arnolfo had laughed!

In the face of the elements the Italian boy collapsed and lay white and still. He saw tears of fury in the steely eyes of the boy above him, who, he felt sure, was going to kill him. Arnolfo kept very quiet. His legs and arms relaxed and quivered like the limbs of a sleeping rabbit. His olive skin blanched. Anthony looked down at him.

He understood now the meaning of the form of Arnolfo. It was like a little animal. What had happened to it did not matter. Arnolfo had never found himself. Arnolfo was "lost." What he did to himself was purely physical. It did not concern anyone else nor did it concern anything living in Arnolfo. But to Anthony, ah, to Anthony! He drew his belt tightly about his waist and rushed downstairs out into the cool air and light.

But reminiscent twinges of ecstasy and hot glows of anger continued to flow up and down his spine. For the first time in his life he loathed himself. He ran back through the hallway and peered into Faith's room. She had gone out. The big ship's tub in the corner stood alluringly with its circle of water gleaming. He locked the door, dragged off his clothes, and plunged in.

There, that was better now! It was good to wash yourself, to come out clean and cool. How wonderful water was! He felt that somehow he had been, forgiven by it.   He went back into his own room and lay down.

Many things suddenly became clear to him in the light of this tremendous experience.   Now, he knew.   By finding out about himself he understood so much more about others.   No, it was not all bad, this experience.   Not by any means.   Love must be something like that. So this was what it was all about.   He forgave Arnolfo.   He would make up for having kicked him.   Yes, it was very pleasant.   It was wonderful.

Then an alarming thought occurred to him.   Perhaps, after all, he might be like Arnolfo.   No, he did not look like Arnolfo—that little beast—and yet how like him, too.   After a while he fell into a dreamless sleep.   Faith came and looked at him but he did not know it. She saw he had been using her water.   The marks of his feet had not yet dried from her floor.

The fascination of this experience did not overwhelm Anthony. That was because in his inmost thoughts he never felt himself entirely alone.   It was that with which he spoke intimately, particularly at night.   When he called it anything at all it was "the madonna."   God as yet was something remote.   He was the spirit which Father Xavier had addressed, the force of nature which Toussaint talked about, the creator of everything ages ago, but hardly present now, hardly something intimate.

But the madonna was always there in his room.   She always had been there.   She was a habit.   She had a shape and a locality.   In addition to her form visible in the statue, which he had long understood to be only a representation, only a statue of her, there was an actual presence of her in his mind which from early time he had been able to evoke in dreams.   Lately she had become more of a voice.   He would pray to her in the dark.   It was not necessary to light a candle before her any more to see her.   It was rather helpful not to have a candle.   You addressed her first in the regular prayer, Ave Maria. Then you talked to her.   When you did wrong she talked to you. When he became like Arnolfo, for instance, when he did that, he lost her.   He was left alone with himself.   He was afraid.   He could not bear to be utterly alone.   That was what it meant to be lost.   It was like that time long ago before anybody had come to play with him, dark, terrible.   He prayed to her to stay with him, to help him.   Sometimes she did so.   Sometimes he drove her away.   Then he could not find her again for days.   And on those days he was unhappy, he was miserable.   He sulked.

At last he made a discovery.   When you did nothing but feel you were left alone.   It was only your body you had then.   The voice lived only in your mind.   "She" was there.   To the orphan this voice, which had the form of a woman who cherished a child in her arms, was a necessary comfort. He was completely miserable without her. He instinctively felt that he could not speak to Mr. Bonnyfeather about this trouble that was sometimes stronger than he was himself. As for Arnolfo, he could only feel. He saw that boy was all body, he was like an animal. That was why they said animals did not have a soul. He understood it now. They had no voices in them.

Anthony did not want to be "like an animal." He was afraid too that his own body might come to look like Arnolfo's. Undoubtedly after such times when you looked in the glass your face had changed. Others might not be able to see it, but you could see it yourself. He began to take great trouble with himself. He would disguise that. The clerks noticed that "Mr. Adverse" as they half humorously, half affectionately called him, was getting to be a bit of a dude. They wondered who the girl was and twitted him about her. His pride was aroused. Everybody had a girl or said they had. He believed them. What would they think of him if they really knew! After a long struggle, by the help of the voice and the opinion of the outside world, he was able to remain a man. And he was so proud of it, happy about it. He was master of himself. He longed to tell someone that he was, Toussaint, for instance. But how could he go about that? Yet his triumph became visible.

A new and manly confidence showed in his speech, in the way he carried himself, acted and moved. He felt himself at home now in the world of men. He was almost grateful to Arnolfo. He could be kind to him when he saw him now. He, Anthony, knew, and he had triumphed. "No," he thought, "I am not evil, not as evil as Mr. Bonnyfeather thinks. I am strong. I have proved it." He did not always feel it necessary now to talk with the madonna as he went to bed. He was so firm in his own new-found strength. No, he did not really need her—any more. Only sometimes. The crisis had passed, he thought.

Besides, he would soon be a full-grown man now. It troubled him a little that at the age of sixteen his soul still seemed to be the same as the one he had always had. Would that never grow up? The child inside of him! His body now was tall, broad in the shoulders, long in the legs. His face was keen. He was proud of that strong, merry yet thoughtful fellow who looked out of his eyes. And it was something to be able to control that body now. It was no longer the soft, fragile, tender thing it had once been. It was swift, eager, warm, strong, and overflowing. He was master of this glorious animal, he, the child inside of him. He was proud of it. Hence the swagger.

Also he knew a thing or two, he thought. Toussaint had a hard time of it in arguments. It seemed doubtful at times if Anthony were going to be an apostle of Rousseau, an Emile to be matched with some glorious Sophie, as the little Frenchman so ardently hoped.

"Ah, if Faith had only had the mind of a Sophie," thought Toussaint, "with that glorious body of hers how happy Toussaint and Faith might have been together!" Even now from the body of this death of his love, from the living tomb of his hope, he could not bear to be parted. He must be near her. It was some comfort to see even the embodiment of his disappointment. His eyes followed her. She never looked at him. Her eyes were elsewhere.

As she sat in Anthony's room now at night her eyes seemed to be resting upon that curious shadow-play at the foot of the boy's bed. If it had not been physically impossible it might have seemed that it was her eyes that somehow caused these shadows to shift and dance. In her deep inexpressive pupils, had you looked closely under the sunbonnet even by daytime, the same mysterious kind of ghostly nothings might be seen at play. Anthony had noticed that.

The eyes of this woman were often upon him, he began to discover. He had been uncomfortable under her scrutiny at first, but now in his new-found strength he felt superior to her. He was a man. Then what she had to say at night gradually grew more and more interesting. She began to tell him revealing little bits of the biographies of those who moved under the same roof as he did. They could laugh together now over certain foibles of others which they discussed. Some of the facts of life were revealed to them in the same way. He would lie watching the shadows and listening to her talk. The tones of her voice, he discovered, thrilled him. They did not send him to sleep any more. It was a new kind of companionship. Physically, she served him in endless ways. She knew his bodily habits uncommonly well and catered to them. She had also been there a long time. She began to recount some stories of the women about the place. It was flattering to know that he as a man could understand. Also it was quite all right to close the door so that Mr. Bonnyfeather need not be disturbed by their voices. Indeed, he never had been. He did not know.

It was now that a series of events occurred for which even long afterwards Anthony was unable to fix the blame. He could not tell whether they were due to Fate, the Virgin, Faith, or what.

"Chance," said Toussaint. "The auld deil," said McNab without hesitation. "Human nature," said Mr. Bonnyfeather. But none of these gentlemen ever knew *all* the story or they might have been as perplexed as Anthony.

CHAPTER NINETEEN

THE NUMBERS OF THE VIRGIN

ANTHONY had made up his mind he was in love with little Angela. It was high time, he thought, that he should have a girl. It was not very difficult to persuade yourself that you were in love with Angela, who, heaven knows, was good-looking enough. Anyway, he did not as yet really know any other girl sufficiently well even to pretend to himself that he could be in love with her. "Angela Maea" he still called Angela. It was close enough to Angela *mia* to pass muster when whispering to her without causing him to explain how much deeper than that the name really went.

It was not quite so easy, however, to make Angela understand that you were in love with her; in love, that is, in a really formal way, a situation to be publicly, although very quietly, made apparent to everybody. Angela merely preferred to like you, to be fond of you, and not to be formal about it. In other words, you had such a good time with her, you enjoyed being with her so much, it was difficult to remember to stop to make love to her in the proper way by talking about it as Emile did to Sophie; by letting your soul "expand" as Toussaint had explained.

When you made a speech to her almost as fine as those in the books she would never take you seriously. In fact, she did not seem to know what you were talking about. She laughed. You saw it was funny and you had to laugh, too. That was hardly fair. It stopped your love-making. If you continued, and insisted you were serious about it she finally sulked. Then you had to put your arm around her and explain. After a while she would kiss and make up, but only after a long while. No, it was simply impossible to make love to Angela.

But the kisses of Angela—how cool they were! How happy, and yet how calm! How you forgot yourself when you kissed her! How soft, and friendly, and comfortable were her brown arms about your neck! Oh, how Anthony was to remember them afterwards, those kisses, in thirsty, and hot, and bitter places! Maea's kisses of peace he called them. The cool haze near snowbanks in the spring where the first flowers began to grow—that was to remind him afterwards of the kisses of little Angela.

So if she would not really be his in a way that he could flaunt before the whole clerks' row in the counting house, still it was pleasant, it was delightful, to drive with her back into the hill country in the early morning. Big Angela was glad to let them have the cart now. It was more and more difficult for her to climb into it, for impossible as it might seem, as she grew older she grew even larger. The plump mule was also delighted. These tall, slim youngsters who drove behind him and shook the reins on the hills were nothing to pull. He sped along gayly, shaking the loud bells merrily to the peals of laughter from the cart.

Little Angela remembered all the old places to call and the dainties with which to load the cart. Its advent now in various farmyards was more the signal for gayety than for bargaining. What the two young people who drove it lacked in powers of haggling they made up in the sense of youth and happiness they carried with them. The country gossip they picked up and their talk of the town were vastly appreciated. They learned to retail this gossip with considerable skill and not a little collaboration. The new vintages would be brought out, the new-born lambs exhibited, or they must taste of the most remarkable sausages and cheeses. Boys and girls always gathered around wherever the cart stopped as well as the old people, and Anthony would orate to them of the latest news from the French wars. Then they would drive on to the next place.

Yes, decidedly, even the pleasure of bargaining could be dispensed with for the joy these young people brought, thought the farmers' wives. You could afford to be a little generous in the light of such eyes, the blue ones of the tall, gay, golden-haired English lad who spoke your own language so uncannily well; of the brown-eyed and statuesque girl with the ringing laugh. The hampers that returned to the Casa da Bonnyfeather did not suffer although old Angela pretended to grumble. The geese, she said, were never fat enough and the prices were extortionate, she insisted. Yet secretly in her heart, like all the other wives of the countryside, she blessed the cart and those who now rode upon it.

Then these pagan mornings were suddenly ended. It was when only three of the Guessippi children still remained small enough to be doused in front of the fountain before the cart left. Now it was only, "Innocenza, Jacopo, Luigi." The other names remained, but only as part of the ritual. Just at this particular time it pleased God to make Papa Tony Guessippi, the waiter, rich. As usual Providence moved mysteriously.

In the first place, one morning as Anthony climbed down from the cart on returning from an especially enjoyable drive with Angela, out of sheer braggadocio and exuberance he kissed her. He hoped somebody would see him, and someone did. It was Faith. After that, but not too soon afterward, Faith began to make it her business to look after things in the kitchen herself. They were, so she said, not going to her satisfaction. Big Angela was scarcely to be moved by anything but an earthquake, but little Angela and Tony found it quite difficult to bear her presence. Do what they would, they could not avoid the eyes of Faith. She was there in the kitchen often. They shivered and crossed themselves secretly.

Thus matters stood when, secondly, there was a great thunderstorm and a bolt of lightning fell in the street just behind the Casa da Bonnyfeather. No less than nine copper pans were fused in Angela's kitchen. In Anthony's room the madonna herself was thrown to the floor.

The consternation produced by these events had hardly died away when, thirdly, Count Spanocchi, the Governor of Livorno, in order to repair the defences of the city, announced by proclamation the establishment of an official lottery with several very large prizes. It was already rumoured that the French were coming. That, however, really did not worry anybody very much except the English merchants. Little else was talked of day after day in the streets except the best numbers to bet upon. Everything, even an event, has numbers. But which were the lucky ones?

Big Angela remembering that nine saucepans had been destroyed by lightning bet 9. Now 10 is the number of lightning. So the good woman squandered nearly all her savings in procuring ten tickets upon each one of which 9 appeared in some combination. Speechless at the cleverness of his wife in reading omens, Tony sat down in the corner of the kitchen and gave vent to his jealous spleen.

"It was not for you to have done that, Angela," said he. "You should have told me and allowed your husband to bet upon those numbers. He is a man and has more money than you will ever have to risk in the lottery."

This was a sore point with Angela. Despite her great bulk and herculean labours, Tony, the insignificant, received more for carrying the dishes to the table than she did for preparing them. He was a man, was he? She determined to dispute that.

"You, a man!" she shouted. "You are a worthless, hot little mouse. Get out!" She descended upon him with the remaining pan. Faith watched without comment, but she followed Tony out. Fixing him with her eyes she said something to him in a low voice that Angela could not overhear. The huge cook was much troubled. Bad luck would follow, she felt sure.

A little later Tony approached Anthony hat in hand. "Is it true, Signore Adverso," he asked in suppressed excitement, "that the madonna in your room was also struck by lightning?"

"Also?" said Anthony puzzled. "Oh—yes, it is true. That is she was not struck. She was merely thrown to the floor and not even broken."

The man crossed himself. A look of great relief shone on his face. "Ah, then," he said, "I will do it!"

"Do what?" asked Anthony.

"You shall see," he said. "If I win you shall share in my luck."

That evening in the crowd before the counting house of Franchetti adjoining the mayoralty, Tony spent all he had and all he could borrow on the numbers of lightning, saucepans, and the Virgin. The tickets he finally displayed were numbered 10, 9, 6, 8, 15. In order to obtain these he had to do some costly trading with other ticket holders in the crowd. But he was happy. He had plunged for the cinquina.

He left nothing undone in order to win. He said the Crielleisonne; he said thirteen Ave Marias in as many churches, he invoked Baldassare, Gasper, and Marchionne, the three wise men. Then he went home and quarrelled with his wife. She told him he was "peini di superba, debiti, e pidocchi." After this he went outside without answering back. This is hard to do, but it is almost bound to bring good luck.

Even little Angela bet. She dreamed her mother was dead. Nevertheless she played that number, 52. The lottery had been heavily subscribed. It was not only popular, but patriotic.

Two days of terrible, breathless waiting now followed. Then delirium descended upon the Casa da Bonnyfeather. "Signore Antonio Guessippi" had won 40,000 scudi.

The news came in the morning. Before noon it was necessary to shut the street gates to keep out the acclaiming populace. Poor Tony was beside himself. At luncheon he was drunk. Little Angela had to wait on the table in his place. While she brought the dishes her father's head was thrust through the serving window from time to time alternately bidding Mr. Bonnyfeather a tearful farewell and exulting over him.

"Not once again will I, Tony, bring the soup to thee, thou greyheaded old man. It is I now who am rich. Many persons will henceforth bring soup to me." Just then he was snatched back into the kitchen.

A noise of struggling, the smashing of dishes, and big Angela's remonstrances convulsed those sitting about the table. But it was incredible to Tony that a man so rich as he should any longer be dominated by his wife. His head, somewhat the worse for wear, reappeared through the window. He was weeping now.

"Thou knowest what I have suffered, O best of patrons. It is over now. It is not from thee I would part but from that huge hill, that mountain to which I am married. It is not I who would have had all these children. I could not help myself. I . . ." Here he was pulled into the kitchen again and a pail shoved down over his head. He sat weeping under it, shouting that he was rich. When he attempted to move, his wife held him down. After a while he gave up the struggle and sat quiet.

He seemed to have gone into eclipse under the pail, but it was not so. In its serene darkness bright visions of freedom and affluent grandeur glowed intensely. The money he knew would make him more power-ful than his wife. He would leave this scene of his lifelong defeat immediately. Tonight! He would snatch his entire family out of this ignominious kitchen, her field of victory. He would return to Pisa, the scene of his illustrious nativity and the home of his ancestors, in unimaginable triumph. There should be a coach for every single mem-ber of his family—except for her. A coach even for Bambino Luigi, who was a prince now. As for fat Angela—that mountain—she should ride with him and watch him throw his money out of the win-dow to the crowd. It would kill her. Not a stick or a dish would they take away of their poverty, nothing but the clothes on their backs. He would bury her in things, choke her with pearls, hire cooks for her— that was a master thought. And he would have a small thin mistress. Never would he be held down on that hill again, never! They would leave tonight, with cavalry! He would ask the governor for an escort.

Seeing him sit so quietly Angela removed the pail and smiled at him. He looked at her with baleful eyes. "Thy home is no more, woman," he said, and spat at her.

She was amazed. It did not seem to be her husband that she had uncovered. Who was this little man who gibbered at her? The day had been too much to bear anyway. She began to cry out and wring her hands. Presently she was surrounded by her brood all weeping hysterically except little Angela. They could feel their world dis-solving.

At three o'clock McNab took Tony in hand and went to receive the purse from the governor. Tony could not be trusted alone, of course. A flowery speech of presentation by His Excellency dressed in his gala uniform of a white coat with red vest and breeches, the huzzaing and pandemonium of the crowd completed the nervous devastation of Tony. It was only by the grace of God, McNab, and the hired coach that he got home with the money. It was promptly locked up in the strong room. The rich man's wife did not get a scudo. A few minutes later Tony was gone again, having taken a considerable sum along with him. Big Angela cooked supper as if nothing had hap-pened, as if she were not the wife of a rich man. Little Angela served it. Anthony could see she had been weeping. He managed to press her hand as she took his plate. Faith smiled.

In the middle of the meal a tremendous clamour arose at the gate. An enormous crowd in carnival mood was serenading its lucky hero who was returning in state from the mayoralty. There were shouts, the indecent sounds of wind instruments, the trampling of many horses. The courtyard was invaded by twelve coaches and the guard of honour which had been furnished by the helpless governor. The troopers had some difficulty in keeping the mob back.

In the first coach, the most sumptuous that could be hired in Livorno, sat Tony. A case of fine Florentine wine was opened before him, and he was smoking a tremendous cigar. He was now in a thoroughly truculent state.

"I have come for my wife, my children, and my money," shouted he at Mr. Bonnyfeather who was standing on the steps with Anthony and Faith beside him.

"Scotch woman, with the evil eye, my good fortune will save us from you. Do not envy us at *this* hour." He crossed himself. Then he began to demand his money in an insufferable manner from Mr. Bonnyfeather who stood looking on rather shocked. The corks popped in the coach and Tony raved out of the window.

"You had best let him go, sir, I think," said McNab working his way through the crowd. "He has been to the governor again and got an escort for as far as Pisa. You had better clear the whole family out now. There is a carriage for everyone, you see, even for little Luigi."

The crowd outside which was peering through the gate thought there was some dispute about the money and began to howl. Without waiting for further orders McNab began to carry the bags out of the strong room and to put them in the coach. As each one appeared a roar followed. Presently Angela and her brood were brought out by Faith. The younger children were weeping, carrying a few broken toys. Tony shouted to them to throw them away. Luigi clutched his dirty doll.

"Good-bye, Anthony," said a quiet voice behind him. He turned, startled, from watching the silly scene below. It was little Angela. Angela was going! Maea would not be near him any more. He stood stunned. He could not say anything. Where?—Why? She stood for a moment waiting for him to speak to her but he could not. Then she turned away wearily and marshalled the preposterous brood of her parents down the steps. In the courtyard for the last time she began to call their names.

At this unexpected element of order in the scene of riot and confusion, a sudden silence settled on the crowd and the apprentices and clerks looking on. For the first time, as if by general consent, it seemed to be realized by all present that there was an element of tragedy in the farce.

"Arnolfo, Maria, Nicolò, Beatrice, Claudia, Federigo, Pietro, Innocenza, Jacopo, Luigi," chanted the soft, clear, sane voice. Anthony's lips followed mechanically. But now the water did not descend. As each name was called, that child was bundled into a separate coach. Into the last crept little Angela and burst into tears. Her father and mother were already quarrelling in the first carriage.

"No!" shouted Tony to his wife, "no!"

Suddenly with surprising agility, the huge woman descended again, and despite her husband's veto, seized her goat which was innocently looking on. A struggle followed. Cries, screams, acclamations, and the bleatings of the animal rent the air. The goat was dragged into the carriage and the door closed. Then its head appeared at the window looking out beside that of Tony who was now too far gone to object. He mouthed at Mr. Bonnyfeather with a foolish grin.

"Get them gone, Sandy," said the merchant to McNab, "there is something obscene about this."

"Aye," said McNab and signalled violently to the sergeant in charge of the troopers to move on. The procession, long remembered in Livorno, started.

There was, as Mr. Bonnyfeather had said, something obscene about it. A kind of evil grotesqueness, as if the twelve carriages were the happy funeral of an idiot, endeared it to the mob. From the first carriage, where sat the mountainous woman with flaming hair, and from the window of which peered a bleating goat, a madman was flinging out coins. Scrambles, shrieks, fights, and hard-breathing riots, as if society were disintegrating before it, marked the progress of this vehicle of prodigality with its attendant soldiers down the streets. Behind followed a procession of scared gnomes with small, pinched faces against the gawdy upholstery of their grand carriages. The passengers dwindled in size until the now frantic little Jacopo and Luigi passed. In the last vehicle was a young girl sobbing her heart out.

Big Angela did not dare to restrain her husband. The rain of silver continued. Every coin lost filled her with despair. She groaned aloud. It was thus that the procession finally passed through the Porta Pisa and disappeared into the darkness beyond.

In the courtyard of the Casa da Bonnyfeather Anthony sat alone on the dark steps with his head in his hands. He had been sitting there for over an hour. It was very quiet now. The noise of the riot had long died away. Under the shed he could just make out the outline of the cart. Its shafts seemed to be extended up to the stars like empty, beseeching arms. He choked. He could scarcely understand the feeling of tight, dry despair that hindered his breathing. What was it that had happened? Something over which none of them had any control. For the first time an arrow had penetrated his soul. Angela was gone.

He turned and blundered up the steps blindly. There was a light in the kitchen. From old habit his heart leaped out to it. Angela used to be there. He looked. Faith was preparing something hot. The place was in frightful disorder. Amid the broken dishes, cast-off clothes and fragments of food she moved calmly, even a little triumphantly, while the charcoal watched her expectantly with its small, red eyes.

He went in and threw himself down on his bed.

END OF BOOK TWO

BOOK THREE

In which the Roots of the Tree
Are Torn Loose

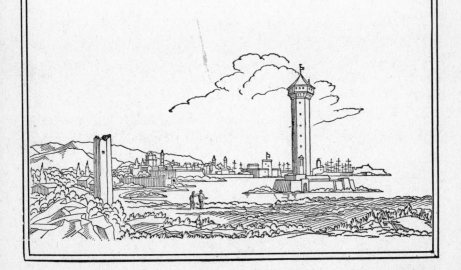

CHAPTER TWENTY

APPLES AND ASHES

IT WAS a warm night. A faint streak of moonlight came through Anthony's window and fell across the foot of his bed, splashing itself against the wall. He lay with his eyes wide open in the darkness. An occasional shout from passers-by returning from the crowds that had followed the procession echoed in his vaulted chamber. These calls grew fewer and finally ceased at last to have individual significance. They blent themselves with the general, low, musical monotone of the city's life that murmured now as if mankind were at last getting what it desired under the full moon while the trees sighed about it doubtfully. On the wall at the foot of the bed, as the moon climbed higher, a faint outline of the shadow-play began. Anthony looked at it wearily and closed his eyes.

He had never felt so lonely. The realization of all that Angela meant to him grew upon him. He longed for her intensely. He wanted to have her now in his arms, to press her firm little breasts against his chest, to fondle and comfort her, to be boy and girl together. That was what "being in love" meant! But he had always kept putting that out of his mind about Angela,—because of Arnolfo, perhaps. But she was different. It would be right with her. He had seen her once when she went behind the fountain. There had seemed to be a light about her. He would like to see her that way again— now! He would make her come back by dreaming her into his room. He opened his eyes to find her. In the full gust of a now manly passion, strangely enough, his strong childhood faculty of evoking vivid visions returned.

For a minute he saw Angela lying beside him in the moonlight. There was a faint, tender smile on her parted lips. Her eyes looked at him wide, and solemnly, as they had sometimes done when she sat on the seat of the cart beside him. She loved him! Why had he not known that before? For an instant her whole form glimmered into a bright, ivory light, glistening. He trembled toward her, the light, quick fire of his youth's desire flowing so that it possessed him. He half sat up and stretched out his hands to touch her. A mist began to curl about her ankles. It seemed to rush up her limbs and vanished with her like smoke into the moonlight.

Suddenly on the other side of the room he saw the table clearly standing against the wall.

He felt as if he were falling and dropped back on the pillow. An agony of grief, disappointment, and insufferable sorrow filled him and overflowed from his eyes. And he had not even spoken to her the last time! "Good-bye, Anthony." It rang through his brain. He put his hands over his ears.

What a dolt of a boy he had been to let all that time go by without . . . to let Toussaint persuade him by words out of a book what being in love meant! He tore at his clothes as he thought of that. He shifted uneasily. One thing though, the self, the thing that lived in his body was growing up. After tonight he was not a boy; the life inside him was not childish any more. How fierce and determined it was. How it *would* have its way. He could hardly imagine denying it now. How could you? It owned you. The voice seemed to have gone. He listened. It had nothing to say. Faintly, perhaps. So faintly you could not be sure. But what was it compared to this thing within him that demanded and clamoured and burned? Nothing! Something to be dismissed.

And he had thought he could tell Angela how to make love like Emile and Sophie! To *tell* her that! And so she had laughed at him. She had known. Had she? How did she know? Just as he did now. Now, after it was too late. She had known all along! He understood now why it was that he had been so happy with her when she had looked at him like *that*. *That* was being in love. They had been. They were! And he had thought it had something to do with words.

There was only one kind of words that could give him any satisfaction now—oaths. He had always shrunk from them a little when he heard them along the docks. They had secretly hurt him, the terrible, coarse ones particularly. Now he needed them. A string of them rolled out of his brain through his lips. He whispered them huskily in his throat. He cursed himself. It was a relief. He shifted his head onto his other arm. That cheek was not wet. It felt hot against his muscles. How cool and smooth his arm was.

Then he heard Faith coming down the hall. He forgot everything for a moment but her footsteps. Would she come in? He hoped not. He did not want her to see that he had been in torment, weeping. She would understand. He knew she would. What was it she had whispered to Tony about the madonna? But how could she know those numbers would win, that Angela would have to go? How could she? But would she come in? He hoped not.

Her footsteps passed down the corridor to Mr. Bonnyfeather's door. He heard her knock and give the merchant his hot, night drink. The door closed. Faith returned to the kitchen again. After all she might have come in. He might have liked to talk to her—in the dark. How hot it was! He was clammy. Even the bedclothes were drenched with perspiration. He began to throw off his clothes now. The thought of the tub of cool water in the room just across the hall occurred to him. Quick! He would run across and cool himself off before Faith returned. On noiseless, bare feet he sped through the door.

The reflection of the full moon from the courtyard turned the walls of Faith's apartment into a dull, silvery grey. The various familiar objects of her furniture seemed to be faintly luminous. What a night it was! He could see the disk of the water in the cask faintly gleaming around the edge. There seemed to be a film of quicksilver on it. He discarded his last garment to step in. At that instant a crisp rustling sound as if someone were drawing a silk drapery over stone, the very faintest of hisses, caused him to turn.

In a patch of moonlight near the door stood a naked woman. He was just in time to see the folds of her dress rustle down from her knees into coils about her feet. She stood poised there for a moment, with her head drawn back, before she stepped out of them. He saw she was beautiful. For some seconds he did not realize that it was Faith. Then he gasped.

In the moonlight she was another person. She continued to look at him. He could feel that and looked down. Then he looked at her again. He stood still, rooted. The faint aroma of her body floated to him. A sudden tide of passion dragged at his legs. He could not help it. He swayed slightly, away from her. Then he felt her arms wind around him in the dark. They were smooth and cool, smoother than his own. Her hand pressed his head onto her breast.

He was half blind, and speechless now. All his senses had merged into one feeling. She seemed to be carrying him somewhere. As he stepped through the moony darkness his legs had lost the sensation of weight. "I shall think it is Angela," he said to himself. But he soon forgot all about Angela. He could remember nothing but himself.

To lie face downward on smooth, soft water with warmth lapping you about, that had always been delightful. How easily your arms and legs moved in such an element. The whole surface of the body felt its soft, exquisite touch. To be supported and yet possessed by an ocean of unknown blue depths below you and to cease to think! Yes, it was something like swimming on a transcendent summer night.

Although his eyes were tightly closed, he was looking into dim, moonlit depths where blue and green flashes of light and long silver shafts wavered down to the darker depths below him. On the subliminal floor of this ocean in which he was now submerged, the same shadow-play that had haunted the walls of his room seemed to be going on. Translucent monsters, giant growths dimly opaque, were alive and moving down there.

Now he began to rise and fall with the waves that washed over him and yet lifted and lowered him, carrying with them as they passed a tide of tingling feeling from his neck to his heels. After a while he was just drifting in a continuous, rippling current of ecstasy that penetrated him as if he were part of the current in which he lay. He was completely alone again, but happy, completely happy. "Are you?" something from beyond him seemed to ask. "Yes," he answered, "be quiet . . . not thinking now . . . let me alone."

He drifted on with the current. Wherever it might be going he would go with it. It was moving fast now. He was being borne along more swiftly. Faster yet. The entire ocean was rushing down a slope. He was being whirled around and around, dying with a delicious giddiness that drew on his brain. He was in a whirlpool. He was being drawn into the centre of it.

There began to be something just a little terrifying in the pleasure of the descent. The sensation divided. "Be careful!" He opened his eyes and thrust up his head like one stretched on an exquisite rack. In the blur of moonlight and darkness a vision shaped itself. He saw he was not in the ocean but swimming in the pool under the tree. He was moving around with the water in it.

The water in the pool was bubbling and whirling at enormous speed. It was shrinking down into a funnel-shape toward the middle. He would be drawn into that. A curious, dim, white animal could be seen at play as the water shoaled toward the floor of the pool. He looked beneath himself. The monster with a pale, smooth belly lay looking up at him. Its eyes were terrible. He began to struggle to avoid it but his limbs were possessed by the lethargy of a dream. He saw that his own movements were reflected in every motion by the bronze boy that stood at the edge of the pool. There was a terrible, mad pleasure that convulsed that boy by more than pain.

There was something in the hollow statue causing that. He must get rid of it; fill up the hollow in the pool and rest again! The bronze boy grew still, trembled. Suddenly from the mouth of the beast below him a flood burst forth and filled up the pool. It overflowed gently now and washed Anthony clear over the brim.

He was lying on his back now looking up at the moonlight filtered through the leaves of the great tree. All was well.

He lay, for how long he did not know, in a timeless trance of relief and release. When he opened his eyes he saw that Faith Paleologus was lying beside him. Her bosom rose and fell softly. Then he remembered Angela.

He was sorry he had forgotten her. As the lethargy passed he made a little mourning within himself for the memory that had been Angela. But he saw that it was for a memory, an ideal, not for Angela herself. Perhaps after a few days that ideal would return. The desire would return and he would dream of it as Angela. He looked at Faith who lay there breathing as if she were asleep. He did not blame her. No feeling of rage overcame him as it had that day in the room with Arnolfo. Yet this was a much more important thing that had happened. It had merely happened to him, there could be no doubt of that. Yet not because of some person, not because of Faith. It was the blind, overpowering feeling that had come upon them both. That was what had done it. A slight noise from the courtyard disturbed his half-dreamful, easy reverie.

He began to become fully conscious of who and where he was. He had better not stay here any longer. He looked at the woman beside him again. She did not open her eyes. There was a blank look of relaxation on her face that the grey moonlight accentuated. Somehow it was a little funny to see a countenance completely the slave of feeling. A mouth should not register mere contentment; be so relaxed. Something inside should make the muscles behave and hold it shut at least. He laughed silently.

Then he was completely aroused. He noticed he did not care whether he had any clothes on or not. What if she did see him now? There was no bravado about it. He simply did not care. It was purely a matter of indifference. Come, this was getting dull. It was over. What he wanted now was a wide bed to himself and a sleep. He stretched himself. He felt completely well and indifferent about things in general. What a relief it was not to be so sensitive about everything. Well, why should he care, or say anything to Faith? She understood.

He got up quietly and walked across the hall into his own bedroom. Then he suddenly remembered he had left his clothes in Faith's room. Some of the possible practical implications of the affair now thrust themselves upon him. It would not always be dark and private as it was now. In the daytime people awoke. They went about seeing and saying things. His shirt was still lying by the water butt in the housekeeper's room. He stopped before his bed. He would like another bath, too, more than before. What should he do about it?

On her bed Faith stirred slightly and put out her arms in the semi-darkness. Her young lover was gone. The shock of the disappointment aroused her. She sat up. Her many experiences with men ashore after a long voyage had destroyed in her a certain subtlety of apprehension which she had once possessed. She now expected the comforting embraces of the aftermath of the first time to verge into the return of warmth of the second. She had forgotten it was not always so. For a moment a sense of loss overwhelmed her. To solace herself she began to think about what had just occurred. From this she derived comfort; over certain details an immense satisfaction.

He had, she felt, belonged to her completely for a few moments. It was the fruit of years of planning. As the boy had grown into a youth, blossomed into first manhood, his presence had obsessed her. He possessed that curious freshness, an aloof beauty that seemed to her to be the essence of innocence in itself, the very tag of it. He was like his mother in that. It was what she had always desired, needed. In Maria it had of course been unapproachable. It was that of which she had been jealous. Now she had possessed it, she felt; crawled within the circle that fenced it off, made it a part of her. She felt she had triumphed over the dead woman, too, the girl who had been carried off by Don Luis.

Ah, *there* would have been a mate for her! There was something hard, unbreakable, unconquerable about that man. She pressed her breasts back upon themselves, her virginal breasts, and trembled. They could bear a great weight. The thought of it possessed her. Her eyes narrowed in the moonlight. Just then a light footfall disturbed her. She looked up. Anthony was coming into the room again.

He passed her bed without a glance, and calmly and methodically, so as to make no noise, stepped into the water cask and immersed himself. Even his head went under. The water overflowed and ran sparkling in patches of moonlight over the floor. He emerged, dried himself, and picked up his clothes.

"Now," she thought, "he will come to me again." As though she did not exist he started for the door.

It was more than she could bear. Before he reached it her arms were about him again. He kept going. She threw herself down and clasped him about the knees. "Stay with me," she begged him, her mouth writhing in a whisper, "I will make you die with pleasure."

He reached down and seizing her by the wrists, unclasped her fingers with a strength that she had not suspected in him. His hands were like a man's. She fell forward on the floor with the palms of her hands on his feet. He withdrew them as if her touch hurt him. She lay there alone for a long time. When she finally looked up the full moon already grey with the opposing dawn was looking in at her. Its mouth seemed to be drawn down like her own.

It was some time before Anthony could orient himself to all that this experience implied. Most of his attitude about it was instinctive. For a long time he did not even care to look at the madonna. She was still in his room. He felt her there. But there was nothing to be said between them. He had trusted himself too far. He was essentially weak. That was plain. Yet he could not bring himself to ask for help.

Indeed, it was a curious kind of self-balance which he now attained. Mr. Bonnyfeather might be right after all. Perhaps he, Anthony, was essentially sinful, but in the light of that fact he would act with caution. He would not allow himself to be surprised again. With possible pitfalls revealed to him, he walked circumspectly, and yet more confidently and with a new completeness of knowledge. The swagger disappeared, but he stood upright like a man, looking around him, aware and beware. Into the life about him he entered as one initiated.

What indignation he came to feel over the occurrence was gradual rather than of sudden growth and quick ebb. He disliked Faith more and more as time went on. He would not let her come into his room any more, and he resented her eyes which he now felt upon him. That she had long lain in wait for him was plain. He shivered at that. There was something puma-like in her patience, he saw. Yet it was not entirely unpleasant to have been desired. Only he did not want her to desire him any longer. He did not belong to her. That was all. He could not. When he had been with her he had been left alone. He desired someone that he could share himself with. There must be two. The trouble with what Arnolfo had taught him was that when you did that you tore yourself apart. You became two, divided. You were trying to be you and yourself. You touched you. It was a strain, a rending of the person. What you should love, your own dear body, you ended by loathing. That he had found out would never do. You would end by hating yourself, be unhappy, desperate.

Even with Faith it had been better. Not entirely wrong, he thought. But he had still found himself alone. Then there was something too simply avid and sheerly physical about her. What lived inside of her you could not really meet. Was it there at all? With Angela it would have been different. With her he felt he would not have been left alone. He longed for her more now. He continued to miss her as the full significance of his loss became apparent. It was on that account that he finally came to hate Faith. She, he felt in his bones, had arranged the departure of Angela. It was Faith who had put that idea of the numbers of the madonna into Tony's foolish head.

Even his madonna, he felt, had something to do with it. He was still unconsciously idolater enough to feel that. It was one of the reasons he delayed returning to her; why the voice was stilled for so long. A hush had fallen upon it. Sometimes at night he was frightened by this. Yes, it was all very complicated. He longed to talk to someone about it. Never could he approach Mr. Bonnyfeather about it all. His solution would be one of action, to dismiss Faith. That would accomplish nothing for Anthony.

And then, added to all this, was the knowledge that in what had happened he had not at all directed himself. He had not willed it. It had merely come upon him. The woman had known that. The male in him rebelled. He should have taken the lead. Yet he did not hold Faith directly responsible. She, he saw, had merely taken advantage of the way the world was arranged. She had merely caught him up in the force which she personified. That was what he must be careful of, the blind force. So he began to avoid her, even to avoid the house. The whole Casa da Bonnyfeather began to become irksome at times, dangerous through familiarity with what lurked there. He began to go out and to be about the town more and more.

For the first time the afternoons with Toussaint, and the lessons with various other people began to pall on him. He struck up a vivid friendship with young Vincent Nolte, the nephew of a Hamburg merchant at Livorno. A rather heedless round of gadding about and tasting life as it offered itself began. It was soon necessary to draw on some small savings from his clerk's salary. They were soon gone. McNab looked serious when he asked for a month's advance. "Gang and ask it o' the maister," he said.

Somewhat diffidently Anthony approached Mr. Bonnyfeather. In a rush of embarrassed confidence he explained the new turn his interests had taken. To Anthony's surprise Mr. Bonnyfeather not only took it as a matter of course but looked pleased. He refused to advance Anthony anything on his "salary." Instead he provided him with a generous allowance from his purse. Of this Anthony was to say nothing. The old man was glad to hear that Anthony was waking up, as he expressed it. He had even thought of hastening the process, it appeared. But he had let well enough alone. Anthony squirmed to think what that "well enough" had been. But he was able to obtain what leisure he desired.

"After the noon bell, then, your time will now be your own," said Mr. Bonnyfeather. "It is harder to spend time and get full value for it than for money," the old merchant continued somewhat sententiously. "You do not believe that now, but you will soon find it true. I shall expect you, however, to go on with your studies, particularly mathematics. You should by this time begin to be interested enough in some subject to begin to pursue it and to plan your work yourself. What would you think of going to England to complete your schooling as I did? To Exeter, say. I still have connections there. It would unify what you already know mighty well. You would also be acquiring the idiom which is your birthright." The old merchant stopped him-self suddenly.

Anthony scarcely noticed his expression. He was thinking of the opera that night with Vincent and some companions. He only aroused himself sufficiently from the dream of affluence which his new allow-ance evoked to promise to consider Exeter.

How often afterwards he wondered with what a different die his life might have been stamped if he had really considered that offer seriously. How different would his path have been? As it was, he considered it only briefly, only with his lips.

Toussaint was hurt to find his pupil straying away. He had re-garded him already as a silent convert to Rousseau and the new doc-trines. It was especially important to hold him, he felt, now that the Revolution was about to descend upon Italy. Nevertheless, their afternoons together grew fewer although more intimate and intense. For Toussaint realized he was not talking to a boy any longer. He began to open his last reserve. As he looked at Anthony his heart beat with pride, his face glowed with affection. There was an emotion now about their meetings over the table or by the ruin as though each time were to be the last class.

But from Toussaint's intense monologues and exhortations Anthony would now break away with a feeling of relief as soon as he decently could. The little man's great enthusiasm was often funny to him now. Anthony could not share in this intense emotion over abstractions. Above all he disliked having his own feelings probed and made reason-able. The Revolution and the Rights of Man were all well enough, he supposed, but what did Toussaint think about a woman? How would he feel about Faith, for instance? Several times as he listened to some philosophical exhortation it was on the tip of his tongue to say something about Faith, or even about Angela. Toussaint might really know something important after all. At least it would be inter-esting to find out and to watch his expression. Yet from embarrass-ment he still refrained from asking. As time went on, however, the temptation grew.

If Toussaint would only let him say something sometimes! He wanted to explain but he got no chance. The other's voice went on. Anthony would fling out exasperated at last to find amusement and distraction where he could beyond the now irksome walls of the Casa da Bonnyfeather.

He took to fencing after a while with a little Spaniard who kept a place near the Porta Colonella. But he did not care much for it. The polite conventions of the art bored him. Then he and Vincent Nolte with some other youths hired a retired Austrian lieutenant to teach them the pistol. That went well for Anthony. But Vincent was awkward. He could never get over shying at the report. He finally dropped out while Anthony kept on. In six months Anthony developed into a fair shot with several types of handguns. He learned not only their use but how to care for them. Then the bottom fell out of pistol practice, too. Nothing was so pleasant at last as going about town with Vincent. The dandy state was upon them both. They idled magnificently in new clothes along the Corso. They patronized an English tailor and met other young bloods. A pistol, Anthony soon found, was the only thing that Vincent was shy about.

Vincent Nolte was, as McNab once remarked, "a little too large for his size." He had very light, curly, brown hair that he was conscious of as his chief attraction, and an open, rather sweet countenance. He had light-blue eyes and a firm chin under large, pink, sensual lips. His nose was keen and straight. But it flared out so much at the nostrils as to make the beak of it seem to be just about to recover from a flattening blow. His ears were very small, a little ridiculous, and somewhat porcine. But you seldom saw them. Indeed, if anything, it was their absence you felt.

It was only when Vincent turned his back to you that you saw that his neck and the back of his head formed one and the same plane. It was a racial peculiarity in Vincent accentuated that lent him a fascination. On the pivot of his spine, his head, a little bulging at the brows and crowned with its flaring mass of curls, turned with an unreasonable majesty. His was a pride that could scarcely be allowed in one so young. Still it was impossible to escape the keen, blue darts of his glances.

Yet despite the fact that nature seemed to have tried to make a masterpiece of Vincent Nolte and had then marred it and tweaked it out of proportion at every turn, despite that, the boy had an undeniable charm. There was, for instance, his warm, clear German voice, and there were the bright things and incidents with which he continually managed to surround himself. In their innumerable and unexpected combinations the delight of him lay.

He was the son of a Hamburg merchant, the same with whom Mr. Bonnyfeather and Francis Baring had wandered through Scotland years before. It was for that reason at first, and later on for himself, that the young man in spite of his harum-scarum escapades was constantly welcomed at the table of the Casa da Bonnyfeather. Besides, he was the nephew of Otto Frank, or rather of *Otto Frank & Company,* a most successful German firm in Livorno. At one time they had been a dangerous rival of the House of Bonnyfeather. But since Mr. Bonnyfeather had outdistanced them many years before he could now afford to look upon them complacently enough.

He could even be glad to see, as he secretly told himself, with an eye to possible future advantages and mutual understandings, the heirs of the two houses dining together and a friendship growing up between them. With the French army liable to swoop down at any time on the town it was quite possible that the business of all the English firms at Livorno might be wiped out at one stroke. In that case an intimate connection with the branch of a neutral Hamburg house might be invaluable.

In fact the canny old merchant was already pulling in his financial horns, transferring large credits to his friends the Barings in England and Holland, and trying to collect long outstanding debts. He was simply quietly putting his affairs in order in case the avalanche that had already slipped down into Lombardy should suddenly dam the rivers of trade in Tuscany.

Part of his policy consisted in shifting what business he still carried on overseas into the names of German merchants. Now and then he also began to employ a Yankee ship. The new gridiron ensign had lately begun to appear with a surprising frequency in the Mediterranean. He had sometimes even thought of transferring his still reluctant and purely practical allegiance to King George to the Grand Duke Francis and of flying the flag of Tuscany from the roof of his commercial stronghold. But his long connection with the English was notorious. The subterfuge would have been too transparent. There were not wanting in Livorno those who would have been base enough to point it out if the French did come. The presence of the British fleet near by still heartened the old man, and he continued to hoist the Union Jack every morning as of old, but more thoughtfully and prayerfully as the war clouds thickened about him.

He called in Signore Baldasseroni, by now the best commercial lawyer in Livorno, and made his will. He remitted to the marquis in Spain two years' rent, renewed his lease in advance, and registered it with a notary. Above all he feared being turned out of his beloved rooms in the Casa da Bonnyfeather in his old age. He desired to die there even if it were necessary to close out his business entirely. He kept the *Unicorn* and faithful Captain Bittern close by in case of emergencies, sending the vessel only on short coasting voyages that followed the movements of the British fleet and convoys.

In short, as might have been expected, Mr. Bonnyfeather acted wisely and circumspectly; secretly, and with great forethought. In this scheme an increased allowance conferred upon Anthony to enable him to go about with Vincent Nolte was only one item in his general fiscal policy. It was not, had Anthony only known it, conferred for purely sentimental reasons. None the less Anthony spent the money merrily. In this way the time went on well enough, it seemed; whole months of it.

For to all outward appearances the placid pool of Anthony's existence continued to reflect unbrokenly the animated but essentially unchanging scenes about him. Of the shifting shadows in its depths the surface at least showed nothing. Only the gentlest of winds seemed so far to have rippled it pleasantly. Perhaps it was this light, animated change playing over deeply troubled waters like breezes and sunlight on the surface of a geyser waiting to erupt that lent the latter days in Livorno all the diversity and fascination which they had. Suddenly, however, the smooth surface of the pool was broken as if by the plunge of a meteor. It was a long time before the rings of so violent a disturbance spread themselves out and calm reflections returned. The meteor was a quarrel with Toussaint. It came, instantly, as if out of the blue.

It all happened because he had overcome his reluctance to speak to Toussaint about Faith. In the little meadow, while they sat together looking down at the ruin one afternoon, the meteor fell.

It had been very warm. They had taken a bottle of light claret along and consumed it. Toussaint had talked for a long time about a perfect state. All Europe was to be included. How heavenly would it be in the halcyon future just ahead to withdraw to some earthly paradise with a beloved, with a perfect woman. In words that glowed with a faintly golden, poetic tinge through the soporific mist of their mutual afternoon laziness, and the wine, Toussaint painted the scenes of an ideal, platonic honeymoon on the shores of Lake Léman. No place was quite so beautiful as Lake Léman, he said.

". . . the reflections of snow peaks in water!—but do you hear me?" he asked, looking at Anthony, who was leaning back against the trunk of a tree with his eyes closed.

"Yes," said Anthony. It was not exactly a lie. He *had* heard him over the chirp of the grasshoppers. He had even seen himself going out in a skiff on Toussaint's beautiful lake—with Angela. They would row out together to an island where no one could talk to them— no one! Be alone!

In the mind of Toussaint a woman with the conversational powers of Madame de Staël and the body of Faith Paleologus was gathering flowers with him in a meadow by Lake Léman. The white, cool mountains towered above them. They looked at the lake and talked. "If that Paleologus were only . . . if she only would . . ."

"Yes," said Anthony, "I heard you."

Both their dreams were shattered. They looked at each other and laughed. Somehow they understood what each was thinking.

"Who would you take with you?" said Toussaint, for the first time dropping completely his rôle of mentor and speaking man to man.

For an instant it was on the tip of Anthony's tongue to say "Angela." Yet he could not. Toussaint was laughing a little. Toussaint evidently enjoyed the embarrassment of the lad before him who sat against the tree blushing. That was obvious. Then it occurred to Anthony that this was his opportunity. He would ask Toussaint about Faith. He would get the advice and comfort of a friend. He wanted that. He wanted to get it off his mind. He began in an awkward and blundering way. It was hard to break down his own reserve. Finally he blurted out the story baldly enough.

It seemed more terrible now that he had put it into sound. Perhaps it was a mistake after all to have let it slip into words. They sounded bad. During the misery of this recital he kept his eyes on the ground. Now he raised them to the face of his friend. There would be sympathy there at least—wouldn't there?

Over his tightly wound stock the face of Toussaint glared at him as if he were being choked by his own neckwear. It was convulsed and livid with fury. He put his fingers up to his neck. Suddenly he leaned forward and without an instant's warning struck Anthony in the face. A stroke of lightning could not have been more unexpected. For an instant Anthony put his hand to his cheek in a kind of dumb surprise. Then he felt the sharp smart of the insulting fingers. Blinding tears spurted from his eyes. With a roar of rage he threw himself upon the little Frenchman and shook him unmercifully.

Toussaint made no resistance. He seemed paralysed by what he had done. Anthony stopped after a while, frightened by his own strength. What was it that had happened? Why? He leaned back against the tree again, exhausted by rage.

"Mon Dieu!" said Toussaint, reassembling himself painfully on the ground, "vous m'avez tué." He groaned, weeping. Anthony looked at him now in silent misery.

"I love her," shouted Toussaint at him suddenly. "I love her—and it was you! You boy! Meldrun!" He began to get up. "Go away! Leave me!"

Anthony snatched his hat and ran. He got to the Casa da Bonnyfeather breathless. Toussaint came in later much the worse for wear. His coat was tattered. They said nothing. They passed each other and went on as strangers. They both hid it from all the others. They were outwardly polite. But both were heartsick at what had happened. There were no more meetings by the ruin now. In the afternoons Anthony went out. Faith, he saw, had guessed. Damn her! Her eyes smiled. The place was growing unbearable, especially at meal times. It was better at the Franks'.

So Anthony was often at Otto Frank's dining with Vincent Nolte.

The counting room and apartments of "Otto Franco," as he was called, were in the great house of the Franchetti on the Piazza della Comunità at the corner of the Piazza d'Arme. From the door of it and from its street windows there was an excellent view of the piazza, where the troops of the garrison occasionally paraded, and of the town hall or mayoralty close by. It was the official centre of both commercial and governmental activities of the town. Something was always going on there. There were sights to be seen, news, and rumours to be picked up. After several years of the life along the docks Anthony was intrigued by the piazza. It was the opposite face of the life of Livorno. To him a new one that he was glad to look upon. He began to go nearly every noon as soon as the work at the office was over to dine with Vincent Nolte.

He would make some purely formal excuse to Toussaint about not being able to spend that afternoon "as usual," hastily change into a new, bottle-green suit, dampen his curls, and dash out of the gate.

To the right of the Casa da Bonnyfeather a long alley led directly from the quays along the Darsena through a maze of high tenements to emerge finally on the wide Strada Ferdinanda. After threading his way over refuse piles, under flapping multi-coloured clothes, past goats, and long strings of spaghetti hung out to dry, Anthony would thus emerge suddenly as if coming out of a shadowed tunnel into the brilliant sunlight of the strada.

By this short cut he had left the world of ships and the sea behind him. By it he seemed to have become at once and at one stride the citizen of a more sophisticated world.

The Strada Ferdinanda ran in a direct line from the Porta Pisa to the Porta Colonella. Alone among the streets of the town at that time it was swept daily. A double line of poplars ran down the middle of it, and it was lined with white marble fronts and bright, stone houses where considerable brasswork twinkled in the sun.

Here the officers of the garrison exercised their horses. Governor Spanocchi was frequently to be glimpsed rolling along in his high-backed equipage of state with gilded harness, outriders, and an escort of cavalry. The landaus and phaetons of the well-to-do dashed back and forth. About noon the gigs of merchants brought them home for the day, the flower vendors from the country made their last desperate effort to dispose of their fast wilting wares, and a golden dust hung in the air from one gate of the city to the other. The flag could then be seen drooping on its staff at the castle. Exactly at a quarter after twelve the diligence from Pisa flashed down the long street with a tooting horn and four horses, to draw up on the piazza before the mayoralty. Here the passports of travellers were examined while a crowd gathered to view the arrivals of the day. The Pisa diligence was probably the only one in Italy that made a point of leaving and arriving on time. So far at least had the influence of English travellers prevailed over the native indifference to the clock. The entire city was nevertheless proud of this daily miracle of punctuality elsewhere unknown.

Anthony always timed himself by the infallible diligence. If it had arrived before he turned into the Strada he could consider himself late for the noon meal. If not, he was sure to find Vincent's uncle, "Otto Franco," at the corner of the Piazza d'Arme strutting up and down before his office entirely bareheaded.

The singular little man would be without a cravat, his linen shirt open so as to allow the breezes to wave the hair on his chest. His morning gown flapped in the breeze. In a pair of huge, red, crescent-shaped, Turkish slippers he slithered along the sidewalks while he gesticulated violently. He was followed by a train of goods and money-brokers and a few clerks from his own establishment ready to grab and carry the luggage of strangers. The reason for this bizarre show was to advertise the importance of the Capo della Casa to the strangers just dismounting from the diligence across the street. There a hired runner announced the merits of his master in several languages and pointed him out to travellers desirous of changing their money or of obtaining passage for themselves or their goods to other lands. And it was seldom that someone was not thus inveigled into his net. Nor did they ever have cause to regret it, for Otto Frank was both able and honest. He differed from his rivals only in not hiding his light under a bushel of dignity. Others who had tried his methods had failed. As he himself explained it, they lacked the courage of Turkish slippers and a naked breast.

When Anthony passed this personage he would invariably receive a loud invitation to dinner. The entire menu was always loudly re-hearsed. He would hide his amusement and accept respectfully, going into the counting room where Vincent was usually to be found at his desk looking gloomy enough. For as long as Uncle Otto continued to drum trade in this manner the social aspirations of Signore Vincent Nolte as the representative of a dignified merchant firm were kept in dark eclipse. Vincent's father, Herr Johann Nolte of Hamburg, was, indeed, the head of the house and supplied the capital for Uncle Otto. The uncle's noisy advertising was therefore the more difficult for the son of a long line of Hanseatic merchants to swallow. Nevertheless, there were compensations. Vincent's position in the house gave him considerable freedom. As he grew older more and more of the busi-ness of the firm was being concentrated in his hands by Hamburg. Vincent was no fool. Even though his uncle was still consul for Ham-burg at Livorno and wore the red coat with one silver epaulette, his nephew was already beginning to rule the roost. In reality it was Vincent's invitation to dine which Anthony accepted.

Vincent would put his hand on his friend's shoulder and tow him upstairs to the long dining-room where the family ate. Although the windows gave onto the Piazza d'Arme the room was in Germany. There was a great Nuremberg stove at one end, a long rack with steins and cannikins against one wall and little, carved hanging-shelves on the other. The table was long and massive, supported by wooden Corinthian columns ending in claws. Set about it were dark, high-backed, Gothic chairs with a wealth of meticulous carving in which a frieze of bears pursued by men in medieval costume armed with cross-bows predominated. For some reason or other the pursuit of the bears was not occasionally interrupted by an angel blowing a trumpet out of a wooden cloud.

The effect of this room and of the chairs in particular was peculiar. Anthony had never seen anything like it. It was astonishing to see a Corinthian column ending in claws. Evidently things beyond the Rhine rested upon a different pediment. It was somehow like the German language. His Latin, all the past he knew, did not help him much here. Also there was a peculiar cheerfulness and cleanliness about the apartment.

Under the windows, in which a hundred brilliant flowers bloomed in boxes, sat a pale-faced little girl in a kirtle, with straw-coloured hair peeping out under her white, starched cap. She was knitting, although she was only about eleven years old, like any hausfrau. Beside her a doll sat looking at her with large china eyes. The name of the little mädchen was Anna. She was Vincent's cousin. When the two young men entered the room she would come forward, curtsy, and put up her cool little cheek to be kissed. Anthony was charmed with her. While the servants were laying the long, white table-cloth he would sit down on the floor beside her and listen to her talk. At first it was all in Italian but as time went on and he began to understand her she lapsed gradually into broad Hamburg Deutsch.

German, indeed, was the chief thing which Anthony acquired from his long intimacy with Vincent and the Franks. That he should pick up another language without thinking about it was merely a continuation of the normal order of his existence. Little else but German was spoken at the table in the Frank establishment and Anthony could soon join in boldly. Occasionally he aroused a good-natured laugh and Anna would correct him. From her he learned most of the German he knew, and he never heard it spoken without recalling the gentle tones of her voice.

While Vincent was donning some gorgeous attire for the afternoon sally, Anthony listened to stories of Hamburg from Anna; to tales of a never-to-be-forgotten visit to Helgoland in the company of one Tante Rachel Rickmers of Bremerhaven. White cliffs were there. How green the pastures were above them! The sea gnawed at the land like a bone! Vincent had once taken her to the Gymnasium of Professor Carl F. Hipp. She herself had actually sat on his august knee while he "with condescending illustrious eyeshine" talked to so small a girl. Ach, how beautiful were those days! When would they be going back to Germany?

Meanwhile she was feeding her birds, and dressing her doll for dinner. Meanwhile Uncle Otto had appeared at the door, kicked off his Turkish slippers and roared for a stein of beer, which he drank at a gulp to cut the Italian dust out of his throat. "In hot countries the best brew lacks zest," he would exclaim, spit, and dive into his own chamber to change into bright raiment which like his nephew he particularly affected, or, if guests were expected, into his consular uniform of which he was inordinately proud.

After a short Lutheran grace, in which it seemed strange to Anthony that no one crossed himself, the meal began, usually with a buttermilk soup with boiled cherries floating in it of which Uncle Otto was very fond. The smell of beer and sauerkraut would always have penetrated the apartment. There were various pickled meats, Rhine wines, sausages and pfannkuchen, boiled vegetables with vinegar on them, and, as a slight concession to the locality, always a smoking dish of spaghetti with liver sauce. There was about this German meal a certain acid tang which Anthony had not met elsewhere. At first he disliked it, but it was not long before both its quantity and its bitter-sweet flavours often rendered the food which he had been used to somewhat insipid. Still he could never really like sour things nor control his face when he met them. Anna laughed. For this her mother never failed to reprove her.

It was truly remarkable the quantity of beer which the firm of *Otto Frank & Company,* both uncle and nephew, could stow away. At least a shipload a year, thought Anthony. He looked at them with astonishment.

"The most profound difference between men on the continent of Europe," said Uncle Otto, wiping the foam from his lips, "is between wine drinkers and beer guzzlers. Religion is nothing to be compared to it. Religions change; beer and wine remain. Make up your mind before you are forty where you intend to spend your declining years, whether in a beer or in a wine land. It will make all the difference between a vivacious and a complacent old age."

"What are you going to do with that vivacious wardrobe of yours then, Uncle Otto, if you go back to Germany?" asked Vincent. "It would only be tolerated on an old man in a wine-drinking place. It is,

I should say, decidedly a product of the joyous grape; to be conceived of only by an Italian tailor in his cups."

"Ach!" replied his uncle. "Herr Gott! I am not old yet, neither have I gone back to Germany already to beer alone. Besides, when that time comes it will be so distant as to make all these fine costumes out of date."

"Fine costumes, indeed!" continued Vincent who knew that the vainglory of his uncle's raiment was a weak point in his armour. "You should see them, Anthony, the glories of our Capo della Casa; six embroidered and laced coats from azure to sunset-glow, a bottle-green, gold-frogged wedding coat, satin breeches to match, rhinestone buckles in filigree, a sword with a snakeskin hilt and an emerald. Du Lieber! and all of French make, all out of fashion already."

Here his uncle fairly snarled at him.

"I told you so," continued the incorrigible nephew, "I told you that the English cut was coming in. If you had only taken my advice and had your tailor copy the wardrobes of some of the young milords who dine at your own table you would now be in the swim as I am."

Here he leaned back and displayed his London watch fob, his neat but gorgeous vest, the broad, double-breasted coat that was just coming into style. Herr Frank roared at him. All that Vincent had said was true.

It generally took the soft voice of Frau Elisabeth to smooth over these occasions. To her this mere ruffling of the surface of her husband's complacency was a stirring of her own depths. Her voice was like oil. Presently Uncle Otto would tell his one and only joke. Something about a Dutchman who swallowed peaches whole and complained that the stones hurt his throat. They would all laugh at him, and pleased at the success of his joke he would rise smiling.

A bell was struck, the servants cleared the remains of the meal rapidly. Another cover was laid. Frau Frank again took her place at the head of the table for the "second cover," and as Uncle Otto, Vincent, and Anthony walked out the paying guests of the establishment trooped in. Anthony would look back. The face of the German woman would be solemn with a silent grace, the heads of the travellers, mostly English, bowed, and little Anna would be sitting in her chair again knitting, with the birds hopping about above her.

Uncle Otto would lead the way to his desk. "Do, my good nephew, have a look at this correspondence," he would say. "I need your advice about it—and thine too, Herr Adverso, the Spanish is difficult." Then he would go away leaving Vincent to settle all the pressing problems of the day.

The two young men would work together over the letters. Vincent's trust in Anthony was absolute. There was no question here of the old rivalry of the two commercial houses. Knotty problems were discussed on their merits, as if confidences could never be betrayed, and in the process both of them learned respect for each other's experience and powers of decision. After the replies to the piles of correspondence had been written and various directions noted, they would look up at each other and laugh to think how helpless and pompous Uncle Otto was in the face of the simplest difficulties—and how able they were themselves. How pitiable was the vain old man! Vincent would shoot the ledgers back into their racks. Then they would both take up their hats and gloves, give each other a whisking, take a last reassuring glimpse into a small bit of mirror, and sally forth into the Strada Ferdinanda canes in hand.

CHAPTER TWENTY-ONE

ADVENTURES OF A SHEPHERDESS

IT WAS fashionable to walk in the strada from half past three to five o'clock. But you must appear to be going somewhere, about to make a call, or at least prepared to meet up with friends to make supper engagements and rendezvous for the evening. All the world made it a point to know just exactly where it was bound for while walking on the Strada Ferdinanda between half past three and five. Hence, if you did not have an engagement you assumed one.

At first Anthony would have had to assume one had it not been for Vincent. But with that popular young gentleman's arm linked in his own he was always sure of a supper engagement before the castle clock struck five. For there was no one more certain of getting a promising party of young bloods together for the evening than Vincent Nolte. At worst you could always turn up at the galleries of Signore Terrini, the painter, now grown prosperous and fat, surrounded by the phlegmatic portraits of the purse-proud or the originals of them eating cakes and sipping wine. Signore Terrini was now the only painter in Italy who could still make his nudes look absolutely naked. "True to life" in every particular. For that he was admired by the foreign merchants who composed his clientele, and his studio, which contrived to hint of naughtiness, with some canvases turned to the wall, yet remained at the hour of cake and claret, or gooseberry wine, "elegant." In Livorno it was even taken for a salon.

Here on any afternoon two well-dressed young men introduced by "the master" were sure of not being permitted to look forward to a lonely evening. This was an unfailing resource. But after a while it was unnecessary. Social prestige like any other ponderous body when once set in motion acquires momentum. Attracted into the orbit of Vincent, sometimes an eccentric one, Anthony was soon whirling by his own proper motion. It was pleasant, he found, thus to glide along.

Several of the impressive doorways along the strada were in a few months' time quite familiar. It was soon evident to both Vincent and Anthony that the daughters of bankers provided not only the most substantial collations but the most luxurious transportation to the opera. To call on anyone whose father did not at least keep a coach was soon, unless other attractions were unusual, voted beneath their mutual dignity. Theatre nights particularly were those upon which they chose to shine.

When there was a company at the opera or a band of actors in town, *that* afternoon they would only walk the length of the street once merely to be in good form. Then they would turn back to the piazza. There one of them would stand in line for a few minutes chatting with other young dandies while waiting for the half-blind clerk at the little booth like a sentry box to make out their opera tickets.

The old clerk wrote a beautiful hand but naturally very slowly. It was also necessary to mark down every assignment to the boxes in a book and to call out the name of the purchaser. Thus it was possible to take exception to anyone who was not qualified. There had at one time been duels over certain seats. But times were changing now. The old clerk merely carried out a ritual. A great many people now were vulgar and rich enough merely to send a footman for the pink slip. Knowing and ardent young gentlemen, however, still saw to it that they got a box due their rank.

"The Stall of the Angels, tonight, Signore Adverso." How it thrilled Anthony to be unexceptionable as he folded the long, pink slip three times precisely, counted his change into his tasselled purse, and stepped aside with a slight bow and flourish. Provided, of course, that the next in line was a gentleman. If it was a footman you held your place and permitted a gentleman to step up. Of late there had been a good deal of grumbling about that from the lackeys. Like a first rumbling of revolution among the lower orders there seemed to be some tendency among these fellows to combine. The gentlemen, of course, became even more punctilious. Buying a ticket was now like attending a Spanish levée. At last one afternoon a burly Swiss footman was positively insolent and required a touch of Vincent's cane to settle the matter while Anthony held his place. There was to be a double bill that night and the queue was a long one.

"The Revolution has not yet arrived here, my fine fellow," said Vincent.

"But soon," muttered the Swiss rubbing his arm. His fellow servants seemed about to make the prophecy come true. The young bucks gathered about Vincent. He laughed and stood the man off while Anthony coolly bought the tickets and handed his place over to Luigi Pontrovo, the bishop's secretary. After that there was no more trouble. But class feeling was already beginning to run high. The story of even so trivial an incident spread. That day the names of Anthony and Vincent were passed about from lip to lip on the Corso.

That evening they were pointed out in the Stall of the Angels sitting with Maddalena Strozzi, the daughter of a Florentine banker, and her friend Mlle. de Rhan visiting her from Nantes. In the sconces at the side of the stall, and in the two high candelabra provided extra, burned the best French beeswax candles which the Casa da Bonnyfeather imported. It was considered by all present to be an extravagant and nice little attention to the young ladies. The tallow dips provided by the management in the other stalls guttered in drafts and dripped sadly. One had to be careful how one used one's fan with only a tallow dip just above. In the Stall of the Angels the fans fluttered merrily and carelessly as fans should, and from the front of the box shimmered a peculiarly clear, yellow light. Farther back in the shadows sat Donna Anna Montefeltro, the duenna of the banker's daughter. Her fat, powdered face like a white mask had a huge laced and ribboned coiffure above it that disappeared into the darkness of the box curtain. Her eyes, which never seemed to take time off even to wink, glittered like brown, polished wood.

The bill that night was a double one, *La Veillée et la Matinée Villageoise* out of compliment to the large number of French émigrés in the audience, followed by Schröder's comedy of *Die Unglückliche Ehe aus Delicatessen*. The latter was given at the request of a number of German merchants who had not often in Livorno the opportunity of hearing a play in their own tongue.

Vincent was forced to translate the German for the two girls and Donna Montefeltro. "From too much refinement come unhappy matches," he whispered, touching Maddalena on the arm when he thought no one was watching, and looking wise. She looked at him with mock surprise over her fan. The powder creases in Montefeltro's face assumed a conventional, shocked design.

"There is no chorus I hope to this German play with the revolting title, Signore Nolte," she said. "Maddalena is not permitted to view the ballet as yet. You promised me, you know." Vincent hastened to reassure her.

"There will be little or no dancing, signora. You know this is not the local staff on the stage this evening but the company which has been thrust out of Brussels and is on its travels. They will go by way of Vienna to Hamburg, avoiding Buonaparte. Nothing could be more genteel than that. In addition all the chief figures in the plays tonight are men. You see I have even been too careful. But Mees and Bergamis are both famous actors. The main event, indeed, is the fact that Debrülle who acts Count Klingsberg in the German comedy has borrowed my uncle's uniform coat for the part and it will undoubtedly be recognized. My uncle and his wife are sitting just across from us there. Watch the fun." Vincent bowed to his uncle who somewhat pompously replied.

Uncle Otto was not aware that his coat had been "borrowed." He sat bored enough beside his frau through the rather short performance in French which came first. He looked somewhat puzzled at the polite applause which followed and from which he refrained. Not having been able to find his consul's uniform that evening had made him a bit glum. He sat waiting for the German play to begin, sullenly, dressed in his most gorgeous, pink, French costume.

Already he was conscious that what his nephew had said about his clothes was true. In the long, frogged paletot and knee-breeches he already felt somehow a little out-of-age. Secretly it was as if he were going about in a dressing gown and drawers. He looked over the audience for consolation. About half of it was still in wigs and velvets, the more distinguished half, of course! What was coming over the world? All these young men in their own hair, wide-breasted coats, and breeches half-way down their calves! And the women with those thin, Greek night-gowns, a tight ribbon under their breasts! Uncle Otto snorted.

A vague feeling of uneasiness, of unexpected and undesired change in all the ways of life and the familiar habiliments of things sent him suddenly cold. He wished he were back in Hamburg; that he had on his consul's uniform, the long, red coat with the gold buttons and the silver epaulette on one shoulder. In that he looked like a British general. The feeling of authority and position which it gave him would have warmed his heart. Where was it? He turned again to his wife, who was breathing heavily in her stays, to renew his reproaches. At least she might keep his wardrobe in order! The dispute grew loud enough to amuse those sitting near by. Across the theatre Uncle Otto could see young Vincent whispering into the ear of the banker's daughter. What did that young dog care in his high choker and loud, English watch fob. The thing flashed in your eyes clear across the pit. Wax candles for the mädchens, moonstone cuff-links! He leaned back and fanned his purple cheeks. The curtain went up for the entr'acte.

For Anthony this proved to be the event of the evening. It was one of those little plotless pieces in which poetry, moonlight, sentiment, and music waked the old court tradition of shepherdesses and the sylvan village in the background to a brief charming life. Something just a little old-fashioned about it now gave it a hint of yearning. This was announced by the low, full-throated overture of the fiddles and the baritone singer Debrülle. He, dressed as a shepherd, warbled a melodious reveille to his love still asleep in a village wrapped—behind a gauze curtain—in the mists of morning.

A low, happy reply of girls' voices, the high, feminine note of the violins, and the clever imitation of a cock's crowing brought a ripple of pleasure and amusement from the audience. Anthony had managed to secure Mlle. de Rhan's hand and an electric thrill from the returned pressure of his fingers caused him to breathe deeply. The gauze curtain was withdrawn. A few more candles in rose-coloured lanterns contrived to throw on the painted, rustic village, now plainly revealed backstage, the illusion of sunrise. The music quickened into dance-time with the theme of a song emerging. Anthony leaned forward.

The great apron of the stage swept out into the semi-darkness of the audience, ringed round by its half-mystic, mellow candle footlights. The little hood for the head of the leader of the orchestra cast a wide fan-like shadow across it. Down there you could dimly see the white, upturned faces of the audience, wigs, and the flutter of a fan, the twinkle of women's jewels. Debrülle was standing in the middle of the stage with outstretched arms, pleading in a rich baritone for his love to

> "Come forth, come forth,
> Into the morning light,
> The dew is on the rose,
> The rose, the birds begin . . ."

when from the preposterously bucolic houses on each side of the grass-painted street emerged a troop of milkmaids in green stockings and red bodices. Half of them carried milking stools and the others bright, silver buckets. They advanced now, clicking their heels, and performing various evolutions with the stools and buckets in that kind of a dance which it is well known that all milkmaids indulge in just at sunrise.

> "The dew is on the rose,
> The birds begin, begin,
> The milkmaids rise . . ."

Insisted the now impatiently impassioned voice of the baritone—

> "But where is she, the charm—
> The charming shepherdess
> My morning love . . ."

It seemed as if the music had reached the crest of yearning.

"Ah, where indeed?" thought Anthony. He had forgotten her for a moment. Where had she gone, his dear, little girl? The very word "girl" sent a thrill through him. He lingered over it as if it tasted sweet. Would there never be any answer to all his useless inquiries? She had driven through the Porta Pisa—and disappeared into the great world beyond. Would he never see Angela, Angela, Angela again?

The trembling fibres of his fresh, boyish body stretched to the last, high, pathetic fall of the shop-worn chords.

How much greater his sorrow for her loss, his need of her, had been than he had ever known before! The music opened new depths in him. It was all dark and lonely there. The strange, pallid memory of Faith moved slippery about there in the shadow-play. He shuddered. "Angela!" Angela could save him.

In a little village like that they might have had a house together; be happy forever. Why not? He could forget everything there, even the madonna. He would have Angela. Have her! He choked. Unknown to him the poetry of his own longing had transposed the cheap little scene before him into the most exquisite art. How beautiful it was! "The dew is on the rose." He could smell it; feel it on his own bare feet as on the grass those lost, lovely mornings out on the road. In love with Angela! "Gone, gone, lost, *lala, lala la-a,*" the fiddles wailed. "O God, even a poor convent child can pray to you! Listen to me." There were tears in his eyes for himself. He could not see Uncle Otto over there any more. He dropped Mlle. de Rhan's hand to dash them away furtively. Her lips curled in surprise.

Then the violins, as violins do, surpassed themselves. What had seemed the summit of ecstasy proved only an overture after all. They went up and up into a madrigal of pure happiness. The baritone paused.

The boy was beside himself now. The warm air and perfumes from the stalls below poured up and intoxicated him. Someone just underneath must be crushing lime leaves in her hand. His temples and wrists throbbed to the music. From behind the wings came a girl's voice, fresh, but rich and full-throated as a song from the orange groves of Sicily heard far up on the slopes in the early morning.

A little shepherdess with her crook, in red, high-heeled shoes and a short apron-skirt, now advanced down-stage answering with high thrilling notes the amative welcome of her swain. Their mutual warblings moved the audience to applause. But Anthony could only *see* that. In his own ears the blood was crackling. That voice, the way she pointed her toes, the movements of her limbs were deliciously familiar. Could it be . . .? He felt the sweat running down his back under his coat.

She was wearing an absurd little straw hat, wide-brimmed at one side, curved up archly at the other. As yet he could not see under it. Then she turned her face upward into the light. It was Angela.

He was afraid it was a dream. It would escape him. His knees fell apart and he leaned further forward clear over the front of the box. He would have called out to her but his voice failed. Then he remembered where he was. Surely she would see him. She was looking directly at him now. He made his arm move. Someone else's hand on the end of it seemed to take out his handkerchief and shake it. Presently in the middle of the dream he became aware that Angela was lifting up her arms toward him and singing at the box. Oh, yes, he and Vincent—and the other girls were in it. It was real! He smiled and moved his lips in their old formula. He knew she would hear what he was saying. He laughed aloud.

Some of the faces in the audience now began to be turned toward the Stall of the Angels. It was plain that between the young shepherdess on the stage and the young man hanging over the railing with a trembling handkerchief in his hand there was an understanding. The baritone gladly took up the local lead and the song was finished off obviously addressed to the good-looking young folks in the box with the clear wax candles.

Anthony sat back dizzy with happiness and lax with relief. She had come back to him out of the country where she had been for a while. In that delightful little village. . . . Of course! How could he have ever doubted it? He had found her again. Angela had come back! Far down on the stage he saw two white hands toss him a kiss. The handkerchief replied. The curtain fell on a round of laughter and applause. People kept looking up. Now for the first time Anthony felt terribly embarrassed.

Across the pit Mrs. Udney raised her glasses to examine the box which had been receiving so much attention. She was sitting with her husband the English consul, her daughter Florence, and a young Scotch merchant, David Parish, the scion of a rising commercial house at Antwerp. David, she hoped, was the young man to be. Mrs. Udney smiled as she watched the obviously fluttered party opposite and started somewhat as her focus finally fixed upon Anthony. She thought she had never seen a face so completely happy. And yet where had she seen it before? Just then Anthony happened to look up, a streak of light gilding his hair. Mrs. Udney suddenly remembered him looking up at her from under a priest's hat while she stood at her library window years before.

"My dear," she exclaimed giggling with excitement, "look who is in the box there!" She handed her glasses to Florence. "Do you recognize your prince of the church? An old sweetheart of Florence's," she continued, smiling on David Parish and touching him on the arm with her fan. It suited her plans quite well to claim a fashionably dressed young man in a box with two bankers' daughters as her own daughter's first conquest. Florence looked. Her small chin took on a serious angle for a minute under the binoculars. She blushed.

"Yes, I remember." She might have said more, her mother thought.

Mr. Parish and Mr. Udney had each his turn. The former smiled complacently.

"My word!" exclaimed Mr. Udney, "Father Xavier and I made no mistake. Mr. Bonnyfeather has certainly done well by his appren—" a tight squeeze from his wife stopped him—"ahem, by his ward."

"Decidedly," chimed in Mrs. Udney. "We must have him in to tea again," she looked sidewise at Parish. "What do you think, Florence?"

"Certainly, mother. Will he sleep in the spare bedroom this time?" asked Florence seemingly out of a reverie. Her mother could have pinched her. The consul chuckled. Mr. Parish looked at him a little uncomfortably. The curtains went up on *Too Much Refinement Makes Unhappy Matches*—in German.

Anthony sat in a trance through the comedy. He had even forgotten that Mlle. de Rhan had a hand, that she existed. Mademoiselle felt her throat tighten a little with jealous chagrin. She would scarcely have credited the young creature in mouse-grey who sat next to her with having known an actress. He was deeper than she had supposed. Donna Montefeltro was outwardly scandalized and inwardly pleased. The box of her charges had been pleasantly prominent that night. It might pay to cultivate this young Englishman. How innocent he looked. She grinned over her fan, remembering.

With Vincent, Anthony's stock had soared. The young dog! and never to say a word about it! He pawed his friend excitedly but was only shaken off. Presently he and Signorina Strozzi were leaning forward breathlessly waiting for the cue when Uncle Otto's coat should appear. Presently "Count Klingsberg" strutted out. For a few minutes nothing happened. Then someone giggled. A whisper began to run about. "The coat of El Signore Consolino di Amburgo, ah!" Then Uncle Otto became aware of it. He snorted and shook his stick. His nephew bowed back. Even those who could not understand German could understand this. Gusts of applause shook the house. The actor played up to it. The curtain went down on a great hit—and the audience filed out laughing and talking.

Vincent's friends waved at him. The boy's little ears tingled with excitement. He and Anthony had contrived to be the most popular young men in Livorno that night. The girls fluttered their fans in the gay light of public approval and looked pleased and excited, even a little impressed.

As they filed out Anthony looked down on the crowd surging toward the door below. A long poke bonnet with a prim, black bow was for a second turned up toward him. At the bottom of it, as if at the end of a shadowed tunnel, he saw the face of Faith. It was pale, he noticed. Always she seemed to be looking out from shadows. He went cold for an instant. Too bad *she* had to spoil an otherwise perfect evening! But how wonderful it had been. Angela!

On the way out he forgot Faith. The Udneys stopped him. He saw Florence standing behind her mother. How lovely and fragile she had grown! Only the brown, golden hair and the deep grey eyes of the plump little girl remained. "Anthony, mother is asking you to tea." She laughed as she withdrew her hand. It was true. And she had called him by his first name. He drew himself together to reply in almost too perfect English. Vincent was now included in the invitation. "This is Mr. David Parish," said Florence.

"How do you do, *Mr.* David Parish?" said Anthony. Everybody laughed except Parish. "Yes, indeed, they would both come."

"Delighted," added Vincent, telling the literal truth and looking with rapturous approval at Anthony. His friend seemed to know everybody. The English consul's daughter! Vincent whistled under his breath as he drew on his gloves.

They went out and bowed Maddalena and Mlle. de Rhan into their carriage. Donna Anna was by this time completely persuaded of the eligibility of the two young men. The English consul's wife was impeccable. Yes, they might call on the two signorinas tomorrow. The carriage rolled away.

Anthony and Vincent turned to join the crowd of young men standing behind them. There was considerable chaffing to be endured. "Who was she?" "How did Anthony know her?" After some minutes of hearty German backslapping and heavy jokes, they managed to put them off. The two were left alone at last standing on the curb.

Anthony clutched Vincent's sleeve. "How can I speak to her— now?" he cried. Vincent laughed. After all there were some things this English friend of his did not know.

"That's easy enough," he exclaimed, "follow me." He led the way toward the dim lantern over the stage door. Moonlight pricked out the pictures and messages scrawled upon the bricks of the old theatre. It was a warm, calm night. The noise of carriage wheels died away through the streets. By this time everybody would be taking the air on the Corso.

Vincent would have liked to be walking there, too. By this time the news of the doings of the theatre would be noised about and it would be pleasant to be greeted knowingly by acquaintances. But this adventure of Anthony was also alluring, worth following up just to see what would happen. Anthony was proving to be somewhat mysterious he felt. Nevertheless, one would like to walk on the Corso, be in two places at the same time. Besides it would never do to go home till Uncle Otto had cooled down about the coat. No, he would have to make a night of it.

They gave a small coin to the man at the door and went in. Behind the curtain the theatre seemed vast and dark. A few lanterns hung here and there in the wings lighting up bits of stacked scenery like autumnal glimpses of a valley seen through the clouds. The wreck of the little village lay strewn about. They stumbled over a pile of the milkmaids' buckets making a ferocious din. Finally someone emerged from the wings shouting, "This way, this way, messieurs," and led the way down a narrow, brick stairs in the wall to the cell-like dressing-rooms. A door opened letting out a wash of light and revealing a man standing there stripped to the waist and washing the grease paint off his face with a coarse towel. It was Debrülle himself.

"Come in," he half shouted, "I thought you would come for it." He handed Vincent his uncle's coat with the silver epaulette. "I am a thousand times obliged to you, my dear fellow," he hurried on, "it was the hit of the evening. Ah, your friend! The young man in the box." The actor murmured his pleasure. "We are also greatly indebted to you, signore,—I suppose," he added seemingly not as enthusiastic over Anthony's part as he was over the coat. He continued to address himself to Vincent. A flat, stale smell of old cigars, sloe gin, and damp cellar permeated everything.

"Can you tell me, sir, where I can find Angela?" said Anthony after a while, unable to refrain any longer.

"Angela? Ah! the little shepherdess, I suppose?" said Debrülle. "No," he continued dubiously, "she has gone to her lodgings by this time. We are a very genteel company, *very* strict, you know." He winked at Vincent. Anthony could not hide his disappointment. So she had not left him any message and it would not do to inquire. "They were very strict." Presently Vincent rose to leave. Debrülle shook hands with Anthony with an amused gleam in his eyes.

"It was a great pleasure, sir, to hear you sing tonight," the young man gasped. He was sincere enough in this and he had to say something.

The face of the actor lit up radiantly. "I am glad to hear you say so, my dear boy," said he. "It is not often we receive a compliment so genuine, after teasing our admirers—and so well deserved," he added laughing again. "Of course, she left something for you. Unless the girls go home early, you know, they are bothered to death. Here it is." He rustled about among his paint pots and cigar stubs and produced a small red card. Anthony grasped it blushing.

They stumbled up the brick steps together, Uncle Otto's coat on Vincent's arm. There was a ripping sound. "Heavens!" said Debrülle striking a spark, "you have tramped off the epaulette." It was true. Vincent turned a little pale. "Gott! I shall be sued by your uncle, the consul, now. I do not envy you either." Debrülle went on up, laughing, his voice rumbling through the wings. At the door he stopped under the smoking lantern and scribbled something on a card.

"There," he said, handing it to Vincent, "come to the matinée tomorrow. Thanks again! I wish you both luck. You with your uncle and the coat, and you, monsieur, with—a happy pastoral night!" He flourished his gold-headed stick and went clicking down the sidewalk toward the Corso. A stave of the song to the shepherdess drifted back through the moonlight. The gin made him place his feet carefully. He stopped to look back once and raised his hand. It looked like a blessing. They both laughed.

Chez Signora Bovino

"But what *am* I going to do about it?" asked Vincent, anxiously examining the coat from the shoulder of which the epaulette drooped disconsolately. To Anthony the predicament of his friend seemed trivial. He went close to the lantern and by its smoky light examined the little red card.

Signora Bovino
Explains the Past
and
Elucidates the Future,
Casts Horoscopes, and Reads Palms.
Her Art is Invulnerable
on the Fifth Floor
Strada Calypso
————
Satisfactory Amatory Entertainment
on the First.

Underneath was a dainty sketch of a small shepherdess with angel's wings and a ribboned crook. Anthony laughed. He thought of the longitude machine on the roof at Signora Bovino's. Well, he would take care not to waken Mr. Williams. Doubtless he would be taking the moon. Let him. His pupil would have a different use for it tonight "on the first floor." A recklessness and warmth intoxicated the boy as he stood looking at the card. It was his first adventure— all his own. A faint haze came between the card and his eyes. He felt suddenly competent, by "the art of Madame Bovino," to foretell the immediate future. He grasped Vincent by the arm.

"Come on," he said. "Forget that small trouble." Vincent kept fingering the rent in the coat. "I'll tell you what we'll do. Tomorrow we will take it to a tailor and have *two* epalettes sewed on it. You can tell your uncle it is a compliment from his friend the actor who knows what the uniform of a consul ought to be." He linked his arm in Vincent's sweeping him along by his own recklessness. In the moonlight it was as if they were both a little drunk. Anything seemed possible. Vincent felt his friend to be inspired. Recklessness was always the mood most contagious for Vincent.

"I think there might be someone waiting for you, too," whispered Anthony excitedly as they swept along. "I know it!" He had completely taken the lead now. Vincent gave a low whistle. He felt the warmth and tenseness of his friend's arm. The two hastened even faster.

As they turned into the street, of high, narrow houses with flat roofs where Anthony had so often come by day to work out his problems with the stertorous ex-mate, he looked upward by habit. Sure enough, on the house of Signora Bovino the outline of the old sailor could be seen against the skyline "shooting the moon." Anthony cautioned Vincent and they began to walk softly. It would never do to have that enormous voice hail them from the roof. They crossed the street quietly, and keeping close to the wall arrived safely at the door. A few lights glimmered from the lower shutters, but the door was barred and the house was silent. It would not do to arouse the mate by using the bell pull. He would be peering over the parapet instantly. Vincent tapped at the lowest shutter. He was beginning to take the lead again. After another tap it was opened. A white hand came forth. Vincent slipped something into it. "The signora," he said.

"Have you been here before?" asked Anthony feeling indignant.

"No, no, it is always the way, you know," answered his friend offhand while tossing the consul's uniform over his shoulder nonchalantly. "When you see a hand, put something in it." A mischievous smile pre-empted Vincent's lips. "I have a notion to put Uncle Otto's coat on."

"Oh, don't, Vincent, you are in trouble enough with your uncle," whispered Anthony.

Just then the door swung back noiselessly, revealing Signora Bovino in a loose, linen wrapper. She started to laugh, but Anthony put his finger on his lips, and pointed upward. She nodded and beckoned them in.

"So you have come for a lesson in navigation, Meester Adverso. No! What can it be, then?"

Anthony looked so confused that she laid her hand on his arm. A senile giggle escaped her. "Come, I know. She has told me. Madre Maria! I do not blame you. She is a dear piece, and in the best front chamber. Clean linen! And she will let no one else come up now these two nights since she came. A lady! But your friend here. Is he with you?"

"Yes, oh, *no!*" said Anthony seeing what she meant. "I thought perhaps you could . . . at least . . ."

"But yes! The whole troupe is staying here. You know, signore, I do not keep a regular house, though." A look of fierce respectability stiffened her. "Only transients. They usually have their own gentlemen." She held up the candle inspecting Vincent. The epaulette caught her eye. She looked pleased. "Ah, of the military I see." Vincent swaggered. "You do not need to be afraid, sir, and hide it. Everything here is of the greatest discretion. I merely tell fortunes." She winked. They went upstairs very quietly. A smell of garlic and perfume permeated the passage. Presently the old woman swung her candle up.

"Her room," she said to Anthony. "Good night, Meester—" she laid her finger on her lips and laughed. In the dying candlelight as she led Vincent down the corridor Anthony could see there was no paint on the panels. Could this be the door to happiness? It was dark now in the hall, but there was moonlight flowing under the threshold. He leaned against the door-post, a lump in his throat. How long it had been! He took a deep breath.

"Angela!"

There was the sound of someone stirring but no answer. Silence. He tapped lightly on the door. The sound of padding feet.

"Who is it?—you?"

He leaned close to the panel whispering, "Arnolfo, Maria, Nicolò, Beatrice, Claudia—Angela Maea." Someone caught her breath. The door opened suddenly. He stumbled forward into the moonlight and found himself in her arms.

"Oh, I thought I had lost you, Angela Maea!"

"Then you *did* care, you never forgot me," she cried low, clinging to him. "Anthony, how you are trembling! Let me see you." She led him to the window. "Oh, yes, it is you, *you*. I thought I might never see you again." She looked up at him in the moonlight with a half-doubt and trouble in her face.

"What is it?" he whispered. "Aren't you really glad to see me?"

"I am only half as happy as I expected to be," she said, hiding her face against his shoulder, "I cannot see you for the tears." Her thin night-gown fluttered about her and he wrapped her closer.

They went over to the bed and sat down. She lay back, breathing dreamfully and contentedly with her hands under her head, looking up at him. In the moony twilight of the room it was like a dream to both of them.

"Let me come behind the fountain to you, Angela. I saw you that way once. Did you know? Both of us that way now! There is no one else but you and me now."

"No one," she sighed. "You are all that is left of those days. They are all gone but you, did you know that?" He felt her tears again. "Only 'Anthony' and 'Angela.' There is no use saying the other names any more. No one will answer."

"Angela!"

He felt himself overcome by an access of pity for her. It merged into passive tenderness, then into a kind of wild weeping passion for what he did not know, something he felt through her. Presently they were utterly quiet. A deep, pagan peace slowly and surely enveloped them. He closed his eyes.

Down an immense vista as if a poke bonnet had been elongated into a straw telescope he saw the gloomy face of Faith Paleologus looking at him hungrily out of the shadows. It was an immense shock, the reverberations of which echoed through Angela.

"Tell me, tell me! Anthony, what is it?"

He raised his head from her breast. "That woman, Faith! She is here in the room. The night after you left. Angela!" He was crying to her for help. She soothed him, smoothing the disturbing vision away with her soft hands, putting her mouth to his. Her breath permeated him. It was well again. Only Angela could do that, he knew, only Angela. With her he could forget everything. And she was his now, forever. His strength flooded back at the thought. An undisturbed and perfect pleasure of both the inner life and the body perfectly shared, all else forgotten, rest, and comfort as of a divine blessing freely imparted and necessarily given engulfed them both. Outside the moonlight died from the street and slowly paled into day. On the bed the youth and the young girl slept as one in being, their curls and legs tangled together as if they lay on an island beach washed by the ocean of Nirvana. Towards morning he began to dream.

He saw a wave run up a beach, leaving a faint, lacy trace on the sand. Then another, and another. Each destroyed the trace of the one preceding and left its own. All the outlines they left on the sand were different. Yet they were all the same, all pictures of the wave of waves. It went on forever.

Then the noise of the waves merged slowly into the murmur of the leaves on the great plane tree in the court of the convent. He was lying in the pool of that place, looking up into the moonlit branches of the tree. The pigeons were faintly awake. Like the blood murmuring in his ears he could hear their sleepy love-making. He lay and floated, happy in an ecstasy of calm. The waters were troubled no more.

Then in the shadows he saw that both the bronze boy and his lost brother were there. The lost twin had come back! Their limbs seemed to melt into the roots of the tree in a quiescent embrace. The madonna was there, too. She emerged slowly out of the light of the tree. It was the woman of the statue he knew so well, her features and her grace, but much younger, naked. Her hair seemed caught in the net of leaves and of the stars behind them, and the smile on her lips was without sorrow. There was no child in her arms. Slowly she merged herself in the pool. The water rose and he felt himself washed over the brink. But he could still see himself there. He looked down upon himself over the brim as he had when a child. His own utterly happy face came up to meet him as it used to do—the eyes wide with a dream, the hair burning and golden, laughing, dazzling.

He opened his eyes to see the vision better. The sun was streaming in through a chink in the shutter. Angela lay beside him brown and rosy, covered with little glints of the dawn as if the sun were shining on her through the leaves of the great tree. He drew her even more closely to him. She looked at him out of innumerable centuries with his own completely happy smile. For an hour they lay so. Then the noise in the streets began.

Someone in the room below them began to stir. They could hear the mumble of talk, movings around, slaps, small outcries, and laughter. Presently the door banged and a man with heavy boots departed. A bed creaked once again and all was silent. Then there were funny little snores.

They laughed themselves, and began to talk in low voices. How easy it was to talk to Angela, like having thoughts with another self. Half of the things you said were already answered. She asked eagerly about the Casa da Bonnyfeather. He told her all that had happened, also about Faith.

"I knew last night," she said.

The quarrel with Toussaint, Mr. Bonnyfeather, the new friend Vincent, the life about town—how clear and meaningful it all seemed now as he told it to her.

"But you, Angela, where have *you* been? Here I have been telling you all about myself." She tossed her curls at him.

"Even you, Anthony. They always do."

"They, who are *they?*" he asked.

"Men," she said whimsically, "all of them."

It was the first shock of disillusion after the dream. So she had known others before him then! His mouth went hard . . .

"But you had Faith," she said.

"No," he replied indignantly, "she had me. I . . ." he stopped, colouring and ashamed. It was true. She drew him down to her again.

"Listen, I will tell you," she whispered. "Do not blame me. I loved you. But I thought I would never see you again when we drove through the Porta Pisa that night. You remember! We had not gone five miles before the carriages stopped in a lonely place. It was dark by then. One of the soldiers came back and took all of us children up to the front carriage. They had dragged father out on the grass and he was lying there shivering and singing. Then they began to take out the money bags and divide them up. Mother tried to fight them but they tied her hands behind her back, and a rag around her face. We were too frightened to say anything. She sat by father rolling her eyes. Some of the soldiers and drivers started to quarrel over the money but the sergeant drew his pistol and made them take what he gave them.

"'If you come back to Livorno,' the sergeant said, 'you will get this.' He gave Arnolfo a terrible kick and pointed his pistol at mother's head! 'The guards at the gate understand. Do you see!' He threw one small purse in mother's lap. Then he herded us all into one carriage and made that man drive off with us toward Pisa, swearing he would cut our throats if we made a noise.

"After about an hour the new coachman stopped and made us all get out again. He took the small purse from mother that the sergeant had given her. She begged and held up Luigi, but he only laughed. 'Pisa is there, not far,' he said, and whipped up his horses back to Livorno. Father was dead drunk.

"We got mother's hands untied and waited till morning. We started toward Pisa. Arnolfo and I tried to carry father. He became violent. We could see he was not drunk now but out of his mind. He cursed mother for hours. Finally some men with hay carts came along and took us into the market at Pisa. They had to tie father. We arrived at the door of my grandparents weeping, hungry, and without a scudo. They are very poor. My father who still thought he was rich had to be locked in the cellar. A few days later some men with staves and irons came for him. He shrieked and called out. We did not see him again. He is always going to be mad.

"My grandmother went to her priest about it. After a while he told us that word had come back from Livorno that our story wasn't true. It was the governor, I guess. He and the sergeant. We could do nothing and we were very hungry."

Angela put her hands over her face as if to shut out the memory. He saw tears trickle through her fingers.

"There is more yet. Shall I go on?" He nodded. She waited a while before she could begin.

"At Pisa the smallpox came. Luigi, all the younger ones, died. They would not let us leave the house and there was nothing to eat. One goat. After a while we ate her. Big Angela—her loose skin hung around her like rags! Arnolfo got out one night and ran away.

"At last no one but my grandmother and two of the girls were there. One day the old woman took a broom and beat me with it! 'Go out, big girl, and bring us some money,' she said. 'We starve!' I could not give myself to the soldiers. I was afraid. I begged only enough to keep us alive. My grandmother continued to give me many blows. At last one day I was sitting on the steps of the Duomo when Debrülle, the singer, came along. I went with him. Do you see how it was?"

Anthony lay stretched out going hot and cold. He was dry-eyed now. So it *had* been that big German with the baritone voice. "I hate him," he said simply.

"Do not. He has been very kind to me. He took me to Milan with him, bought me some clothes, put me on the stage with his company as a flower girl. He taught me to sing. Anthony, I have a lovely voice, they say. I am the shepherdess now. I shall be a great actress some day. The lights, the people! I shall have beautiful clothes, jewels, and see the world. No, he is very good to me, Debrülle, he has been like a father."

"Do you love him?" he asked.

She shook her head. "Not like that, you know. He, he is not with me often," she whispered. "I bear him."

"Then you will not marry me, Angela?" he said. He looked at her with a terrified determination and drew her to him.

"Once," she said, "but not now. It is too late."

"But what are you going to do?" he cried.

"I am going on," she said. "Now I have had you, I am going on." A smile of triumph and tenderness lit her face.

He pleaded with her, but she merely turned her head away and closed her eyes. "Come," she said after awhile, "lie on my breast again." Thus they strove to forget together.

Later in the morning the signora knocked at their door. She finally put her head inside the room. "Pardon, last night I forgot to bring you the napkins of pleasure. Here they are now. When you dress yourselves come up to my room. There is a charming breakfast there. Your friend, the man with the great voice, has had it brought in. And you are to come, too, Meester Adverso. Ah! how generous is the noble singer to his shepherdess! Yes, I have heard about you both from his lips. It is true love then. You will bring luck to my house.

Come, I will tell your fortunes for nothing. Jesù! how beautiful you are." Her eyes rested on them burning with admiration and regret. "Do not be ashamed," she said. "I was young once. Now there is nothing left but the pleasure of the eyes." She closed the door reluctantly and went upstairs sighing.

They lingered for a while but presently from upstairs the full-chested tones of Debrülle rolled down to them:

> "The dew is on the rose,
> The birds begin, begin,
> The milkmaids rise,
> But where is she, the charm—
> The charming shepherdess,
> My morning love?"

And there was something so whole-hearted and good-natured about those tones that they hastened in spite of themselves to rise and dress.

"You will like him, you see if you don't!" said Angela. Anthony shook his head.

"Yes, yes, you will. For my sake anyway, promise!" She pouted and kissed him. They moved toward the door and opened it. A great pencil of sunlight washed down the stairs. The smell of German coffee and frying sausages rolled down to them. They heard a gay laugh and a cork popped loudly in the apartment of Signora Bovino. The colour heightened in her cheeks. They stood for a minute at the threshold. He caught her to him madly.

"Good-bye, Angela, my own Angela Maea. Oh, you do not know how I love you!"

> "But where is she, the charm—
> The charming . . . my morning love?"

trolled from upstairs. It was from that voice that he would hold her fast forever.

"You do not know."

"But I do, Anthony, dear, I know. I have found out. I love you. I thank the Virgin I found you again. And now we shall always be like this." She flung her arms around him choking, giving him a long kiss. "Boy, mine, dearest always, some time you will know, too."

"But where is she . . ." began the voice again upstairs.

"Coming, coming, papa mio," she cried; dashed the tears out of her eyes and dragged Anthony over the threshold. The wind banged the door behind them. She ran laughing up the stairs to Debrülle.

She had thanked the Virgin. Well, so would he, the beautiful young Virgin without the child who had come to him last night in the dream. To her then! He stretched out his hands to her. A great peace and calm of completion was on him. He could have, or be, no more than that no matter how long he lived. With or without Angela then! He blew a kiss back at the closed door. Then he went up the stairs.

The apartment of Signora Bovino was a great surprise. It was awash with sunlight that fell through a skylight now wide open. Bright, blooming plants waved in the windows and a far door led out onto the roof where there were tubbed flowers. A great yellow cat lay spread-eagled in the sun out there. And there was a table set with a snowy cloth that flapped lazily. In one corner the signora busied herself over a small charcoal stove. In the other sat Vincent looking happy and foolish with a large German girl on his knees. Debrülle was doing some dance steps and humming to Angela as she copied him, one foot after the other, daintily. The whole room hailed Anthony with a shout. It was impossible not to accept such a welcome. The last bit of ice left for Debrülle thawed under his ardent captivating humour. He clapped Anthony on the back with an undeniable affection.

"You, my prince charming, and your shepherdess have nearly starved us. Didn't you hear me singing to you? In another moment the sausages would have been in flames. Come now, not a minute longer. Herr Nolte, fräulein . . .? ahem."

"Anthony, Anthony, it is to be *our* breakfast," cried Angela, dancing up. "You and I are to sit at the head of the table." Her eyes were still shining like skies after a rain. She led them all out and they sat down. The old woman beaming and grinning, rapidly set the dishes.

"When you have finished, signora, be pleased to sit down with us," Debrülle said. "Thou, too, wast once a lady I see." From somewhere in the past she summoned a grand curtsy. They all applauded.

"Ladies and gentlemen," said Debrülle, pausing and looking around for anybody who might dare to contradict him, *"Ladies and gentlemen*—This is a kind of impromptu and unofficial wedding breakfast for the charming couple at the head of the table. It is the best under the circumstances," he continued, looking at Anthony significantly, "that we can do. May they always be as happy as they were last night. Always,"· he added as if by an afterthought—"wherever they are."

They drank with a shout. Over his steaming bowl of coffee Debrülle broke into a German love song that clutched them all by the heart. At the second chorus Vincent chimed in, carried away by the sheer, rank sentiment of it.

> "One night at least a wandering knight may have,
> Though disinherited from all the past,
> And bear the memory of that burning love—
> And bear that memory with him to the last."

The high, clear voice of Angela trilled in. The boy next to her felt his breath pause as if that moment were too poignant and clear to require an earthly atmosphere to live it.

> "And bear that memory with him to the last."

All their voices blent in a long, sentimental, drawn out, dying chord that left them sitting astonished with their own harmony. Indeed, it seemed as if they had not made it themselves. It had been drawn upon an unexpectedly rich account of pleasure, a draft that left happiness undiminished.

Debrülle now opened small brown jugs of Asti Spumonti that foamed like Normandy cider. It was clearer and lighter than champagne, a noble morning drink, bringing a glow of joy without heat or thirst. Anthony could see by the way he looked at Angela that Debrülle loved her; loved her with a kind of fatherly pity as if care of her happiness had been conferred on him as his part in life. Anthony understood now the expression on the actor's face the night before in the dressing-room. It was his greater knowledge and his pity, a wise generosity beyond a purely possessive male instinct that had allowed Debrülle to let Angela have her young lover. And this gayety now? It was partly to drown regret, regret that Debrülle was not the same age, was not Anthony. And yet there was wine and music and happiness this morning! It was as if Debrülle had shared in the joy of the night before by some occult transference. Angela and Anthony would have to take him in. He was there. How strange! How could he have ever imagined an association like this?

Anthony shook his head. He had possessed her completely, and she him, yet somehow he was going to lose her again. He looked at her now beside him putting a little flower into her hair, joyous and cool. He thought of the young madonna in the dream who had slowly blent herself with the cool water. Perhaps Angela was like that— something that overflowed, that ran away like cool, clear water, a natural thing that one could not possess by clutching with hands. One could only be in it a while and be washed over the brink when it overflowed—and look back upon one's own happy face, glorious like the sun beating across the parapet through the green cool leaves of Signora Bovino's plants. He walked over to them a minute to be alone.

The calm and deep joy of the night before leaving his blood cool and his limbs relaxed in well-being, the present gayety and sunny happiness, the harmony of dear voices searching his soul, the strange premonitory loneliness of the days to come without Angela,—all blent and existed simultaneously within him in a mood so far beyond thought that he stood for a minute like a god among the leaves lost in an indescribable flood of bright, imageless feeling. Then they called him back.

The instinct of aloofness on his part made the occasion become even a little gayer if possible. It was as if the others in order to confirm their own mood became more abandoned so as to take him along. Not the least element of a spectator could be tolerated. Nor was it now hard for them to prevail. Now that he understood it all; had thrust it down past words and argument and resolved it into pure feeling, he let himself go. The wine helped.

Presently he was singing too, whenever he could, with a better voice than he ever had thought he had. After even the professional reper- toire of Debrülle was exhausted, Vincent's girl proved to be able to make convulsing faces. All the past was forgotten now. Only the present existed. Then Signora Bovino began to tell fortunes.

She cast their horoscopes and they bent breathless over her books and queer charts where zodiacal animals swarmed amid the stars.

"You have an immense fortune in diamonds coming to you," she promised Angela. Debrülle would never have any children. He clapped his hand tragically to his forehead. Vincent would be rich but would die poor. A long life but a merry one! A hard dark man with a huge beard was to be the lot of the fräulein. " 'Küche, kochen, und kinder.' Ach!" The fräulein sulked. For some reason the signora had left Anthony to the last. She now turned her piercing eyes upon him and began her formula again.

"What day and hour were you born?"

He had sat suddenly frozen when she began to ask the others that. The mood of the morning passed. The wine died in him. A look of embarrassed misery now crept into his features.

"I do not know, signora, I—you see . . . ."

He coloured to the brows. In the name of God, who was he?

There was a moment of silence. Then the kindly Debrülle stepped in. He sneezed and made them laugh. "Doubtless the illustrious signora," he went on with the tears of the sneeze still in his eyes, "has other methods of foretelling the future."

"Oh, yes, holy saints and angels!" There were other ways. "Yes indeed!"

How much did Debrülle know? Anthony wondered. How much had Angela told him?

The signora opened an old, black box and took out the ancient shoulder blades of sheep, and a black veil embroidered with faded stars. She sat down at the table and throwing the veil over her head began to click the sheep bones mysteriously behind it. An ancient Tuscan chant with gibberish come down from the days of Etruria mumbled from her gums. They looked at her, awed in spite of themselves. The dark veiled head now had the outlines of a sibyl and the power to stir something in them, they knew not what. *Click, click,* went the bones. A voice began.

"You were born at midnight between a lucky and an unlucky day. I see many ships. A crucifix is speaking. You will see the King of the World and serve him. There is a great fire by night. I cannot make this out. There is a veiled woman, a mountain very far away, a great tree, stars." She threw off the veil and looked at Anthony with interest and surprise. "I am only sure of two things," she said, "you will travel far, the earth turned under you; and you must beware of cold steel. You will not always be very happy, my son." She looked at his palm and nodded confirmingly. "Now," she said, "put something in mine."

It occurred to Anthony, as he felt in his pocket, that Signora Bovino might be performing a function which the world could not do without and yet would never acknowledge. One should pay well for that. He would owe her a great memory.

"And bear that memory with him to the last."

The stave seemed to sing itself for him. He gave her his best gold coin. Debrülle and Vincent pressed forward. The old woman soon had cause to be pleased and showed it. Seeing her auspicious expression the fräulein thrust her palm under the signora's nose.

"Have you nothing better to tell me?" she asked wistfully.

A long line extended right across the girl's hand like the hinge of a leather box. Her fingers closed on her wrist like a lid. There were no vertical lines from the wrist. The old woman looked at it.

"Go along with you," she said, throwing the girl's hand aside like an object. "You are not one of us. Your grandfather must have been a Chinaman."

It was true, the whole room burst into laughter. They had not noticed it before, but there was something Mongolian about this girl; an almond creep to her eyes.

Debrülle rose and took his cape. Angela hurriedly got her things together. "The matinée, you know," he said, and held out his hand. Anthony took it and paused. He owed the man much. "Thank you, I know, now. Thank you! Take care of Angela," he whispered.

The man caught both his hands and squeezed them hard. "By God, I will." He went out first.

With a low cry Angela ran across the room and flung her arms about Anthony. For one instant he felt her warm cheek beating against his. He crushed her lips with a cry. Then she had gone.

He was left standing in a universe deserted, alone beyond all sounds, undone. He could see nothing. "Madonna, sweet Mother of God, come to me now!"

As if his inner life were a plant that flourished in the soil of his body he felt it sicken down to the most remote and delicate roots. The nerve tips which are always in motion bathed by the rich liquor of the blood upon which they draw for nourishment and warmth ceased for a moment to move and became numb. He felt them dimly loosen. He grew cold. Then the heart throbbed again overcoming the shock as if by sheer energy. But living was for a little a great misery.

Another aspect of life had confronted Anthony. Existence might be painful! For the first time the thought flashed upon him that escape from it might be a relief. There was a gate out of this. How dark the garden of the world could suddenly become, how scentless the flowers. The clear, sheer joyous morning light was over. What would hot noon be like? Thus the man's soul was first torn loose within him. He stood leaning on the table with one hand. He tottered a little. The figures of things had become confused. A cool sweat burst out just above his eyebrows. He looked ill.

The old woman, mumbling something kindly, thrust him into a chair and gave him a fiery drink. When he could see clearly again the German girl was projected before him just across the table, sitting there with tears in her eyes still looking hopelessly at her palm. Poor soul! Life was sad for her, too! Something had happened to her before she was born. A pity overflowed the boy, warming him again. For the first time he understood what it was to be a simple child, a lost angel caught in a body without hope. A look of understanding passed between them. There was comfort in it.

"Come, come," said Vincent, who did not understand exactly what had happened, but could see that his friend looked white. "If you are ill, I will go home with you. It is time to leave anyway, I guess." He picked up his uncle's torn coat. They went out onto the landing. A door opened across the hall.

"Ahoy there," said a voice in a tone that was just now to Anthony ghastly with heartiness. "Do you think you can get away from me like that? I have been listening to you all morning." It was the navigating Mr. Williams. They both stopped helplessly. He came down to them with his sextant in a bag. "I'll go over to the casa with you now," he roared. "We can work out that new way of plotting the longitude this afternoon." He followed them like fate.

"Oh, my God!" said Vincent, "he's coming!"

Anthony felt too far-off to resist. They turned up the street together. The immense voice boomed on, causing cart drivers to stare. It was warm and sticky outside after the cool breezes of the roof.

"I tell you the stars cannot lie . . . they . . ."

Yes, it was true. That was the worst of it. If you could only decide these things for yourself. Then . . . then Debrülle would not go off with Angela, for instance. But there was something else, something beyond your own will and desire, that did the deciding. All your plans were as nothing to that. He, Anthony, had felt it at work this morning, fate, something beyond appeal. Things had happened. The little cottage with the garden around it would never rise from Toussaint's old ruin as he had pictured to himself. Never! It would remain a heap of stones.

Toussaint was a fool, a fool! Mentally Anthony took out his grief that now lapsed into anger on that little man. It was foolish and sentimental, he knew. But he had been hurt, sickened. Someone must be at fault. Would that great ass of an ex-mate never stop roaring at him? He was sick of them all. Of every one of them. Of the casa, of Mr. Bonnyfeather, of Faith. Damn her! He couldn't stand her any more. To take his boy's body that night!

"The admiralty is right after all. They will have to agree on a line of longitude and keep one clock to that time. Then you will have another clock that . . ."

"Christ deliver us!"

They turned into the vaulted archway of the Casa da Bonnyfeather. The three pairs of feet echoed hollowly. The bell rang releasing the clerks for luncheon. They streamed across the yard, glad to escape. So would he be, he thought. He was tired of it all, the whole familiar scene. There was no one by the fountain either. Angela! After a while as though at a distance he saw they were all sitting down to lunch. Vincent was trying to be merry as usual. Toussaint was still looking sorry. Mr. Williams rumbled. The old merchant sat more quietly than usual as if there was something troubling him. It all went on. How hot the day was. Suddenly he felt someone's hand under the table laid on his knee. Even through silk it felt cool, but it trembled slightly. With her other hand Faith was fingering a spoon.

"Let me alone," he cried leaping up so that they all stared at him.

"What is it?" said Faith.

"You . . ." He turned and ran to his room.

"Anthony is a bit ill today," said Vincent after an awkward pause. "We had . . . er, a rather—somewhat of a go last night."

"Does he need a leech, do you think?" asked Mr. Bonnyfeather.

"I'm thinkin' ye can spare yoursel' the expanse," said McNab, looking at Faith. So was Toussaint. For the first time she turned slightly pale.

Once in his room Anthony locked himself in. He paid no attention when Vincent came to the door later. He was dry-eyed now. He wished only to be left alone. He walked up and down. Then at last he cast himself down on the bed before the madonna. Of what good was the outside world? It intruded upon your own only to give pain. It had taken years, but now, now at last he could open his heart up to the madonna again. She and he were left alone as they had been when he first came there.

CHAPTER TWENTY-TWO

ICONS AND ICONOCLASTS

IN TIMES of great change it is a question whether the restlessness of the human heart is due more to individual dissatisfaction with experience than to the drag and flux of the age. The two play upon each other, reverberate, and are inextricably intermingled. In this interplay there is no rest to be found anywhere. No adjustment suffices. Few can attain equilibrium. The pendulum of the time is felt trembling at one extreme, high above all heads, and threatening them. Men dash about underneath it like disturbed ants.

Yet every rational being desires a "home" of some kind for body and mind. Men cannot act spasmodically for ever. They finally gather together about some standard bearer and press in some definite direction always labelled "Forward." No matter what the vista ahead may be they must come to some decision at some place, be it a battlefield marked by graves. Here at least is a rest, an end. Perhaps, who knows, a beginning. The normal symptom of such times is the feeling of the approach of war. Usual things, moods, modes, interests, and passions, even lusts, lose their zest. The familiar becomes unreal. Foundations hitherto taken as eternal begin to crumble.

In the last days which Anthony spent in Livorno he was intensely possessed by, if not wholly conscious of, the sensation of something new impending. Remembering it afterwards, his attitudes and actions —which then and for some time later seemed inexplicable—became plainer to him. He could see that along with the vast majority he had unconsciously temporarily suspended his own will in order to drift with a new tide in the affairs of men. Whither he did not seem to care. It was a relief; easier just to watch and see what would happen to him. Who could expect to direct, control, or even understand so titanic a thing as the European current? The frantic outbreak of gambling in society everywhere, which overflowed into the very streets of the town and obstructed the gutters with card players and dicers, was one expression of this. "Let fate decide." The universe was thrown back to its original state. The Guessippis had been merely some of the first lambs to be shorn. The crowds roared now every night before the lottery. The governor became ridiculously rich and the government bankrupt.

Against this background the patient habits of mercantile industry as a gainful occupation began to appear silly and to disintegrate. Minor firms began to close their doors as if by premonition.

Almost alone, in a scene that was already trembling toward chaos, the sedate Mr. Bonnyfeather continued calmly to hang his hat on the horns of the satyr every morning. The counting house hummed. To some plan, to which he and McNab alone were privy, the store-rooms began to empty themselves. At Nantes, Hamburg, Rotterdam, and London the accounts of *"John Bonnyfeather, merchant,"* began to show snug balances. The grim Captain Bittern came and went with the *Unicorn* upon mysterious errands under the protecting guns of Nelson's fleet.

Anthony worked over a flood of papers, which seemed to him to have lost all vital interest. He made his eyes and hands do things. He answered and filed mechanically only to escape at noon with Vincent Nolte. Sometimes he looked at Toussaint working beside him. They no longer exchanged anything but necessary words. He too was feeling the electric weather of the time.

The face of Toussaint Clairveaux had become a military and political barometer. As the news of the successes of the French continued to arrive, as he felt the "glorious revolution" approaching, his countenance became more and more radiant. He seemed to have secret sources of information. At the thought of seeing the personification of all his hopes and ideals, the invincible Buonaparte in the streets of Livorno, he glowed with an almost ethereal enthusiasm. Even Faith was temporarily forgotten. He thought he did not care what might become of himself or her when Mr. Bonnyfeather should no longer hang his hat on the horns of the satyr. The new age would have arrived before it was too late.

He looked at the satyr. A small remnant of gilding still glimmered on its horns. It might not be too late after all. Anthony he now regarded as lost. Rousseau, Toussaint now saw, was merely a John the Baptist. The messiah of the age was about to enter Jerusalem in the person of Buonaparte, on a war horse. Anthony had been worshipping Venus. He would not be among the elect. His one favourite pupil! How he yearned over him. "Ah, he had failed there —that woman again!" He sighed. He longed to talk with Anthony. He was utterly alone.

The French émigrés who had settled at Milan and Florence now began to troop through Livorno, lingering a little before going elsewhere. English families came and embarked. Otto Franco did a roaring business. Some of the beaten Austrian battalions hustled onto transports with the grand duke's treasure. The town throbbed with drums. In the night the garrison departed. License revelled by moonlight while the watch tactfully proclaimed that all was well. Provided with letters of marque from Mr. Udney, the *Unicorn* departed from the now empty quay before the Casa da Bonnyfeather, "bound for Gibraltar." The dray mules were sold at public auction. On the old courtyard a strange silence had fallen. The clerks soon wondered what they were going to do.

It was now that Mr. Bonnyfeather began to employ Anthony on constant trips to Mr. Udney for the execution of various documents. Among these was a copy of his will which had been carefully drawn just before the final departure of the *Unicorn*. It was witnessed by McNab and Captain Bittern. It was the old merchant's care to register it with both the local and British authorities.

Had Anthony known the contents of the document the sudden renewed cordiality of the British consul might not have caused him so much personal satisfaction as it did. Mr. Udney was a practical man. The prospect of property in a young man's future by no means darkened it for the Englishman. After the will was filed a slight shade of deference crept into his attitude toward Anthony, which, if inexplicable to that young gentleman, was none the less flattering.

He and Vincent had of course long ago availed themselves of the invitation to come to tea at the Udneys'. It was not at the old villa but at the consul's rooms over his *case*. The Union Jack on a staff and the gilded royal arms over the door gave it a certain "dash." Upstairs, due to the participation of the consul in the recent satisfactory condemnations of certain prizes, the apartment was furnished in the latest Parisian style. Amid the heavy travesties of Greece and Rome, shining brass wreaths and republican fasces, Mrs. Udney's old English spinet remained with both the voice and the appearance of a charming ghost. Here, seated on a great "X"-shaped chair that might have supported the bulk of Tully, from a huge urn surmounted by a Roman eagle she poured tea.

It was the first almost English tea that Anthony had seen, or drunk. David Parish, who still remained constant and took Miss Florence driving every day with her mother, passed the gingerbread, Mrs. Udney's specialty after a youthful sojourn in Jamaica. She talked of the island often. It and Nevis were the nicest places in the world. Florence argued for the country about Totnes in Devon while Mr. Udney, consuming bowls of hyson from the bottom of the urn, nodded his approval.

He loved his moors. Please God, he would soon see them again! He was fifty-three and all his teeth were out. It was time Florence was marrying. This chap Parish was attentive enough, good prospects, too. Yet there was something about Anthony that attracted him. Evidently the boy had crept into old Bonnyfeather's heart. To a good tune at that! Unknown origin, of course. But good stuff, look at him. Well, well, things would have to take their own way, he supposed—or his wife's. Unconsciously she and fate had become for him, in his domestic affairs at least, synonymous.

They had never had a son. He had given it up. It made him too tired now. He remembered that day at the villa years ago when Florence had brought Anthony. How the boy had moved his heart— and that priest's, poor fellow! They had both done well by the boy. It was those secret impulses that counted. They shaped the world; made plans. He looked at Florence talking to Anthony with a mixture of pride and happiness. Oh, well, let *her* have a son. He turned to his wife. "My dear, another cup of tea, from the lees, strong."

"Why, Mr. Udney, since when did you start to take it off the lees?"

"A long time since," he replied firmly with the immense capacity for self-pity of the older male in his voice.

Florence was all of girlhood that Anthony had missed. The kind of person from the kind of family that he felt somehow he belonged to and had been robbed of. How easy it was to talk to her. It was something like talking that night to Angela but less intense, more assured, more casually satisfactory. Her frocks were so fashionable— neat and clean, *not* like Angela's—softly unusual he thought. She was wearing a white, high-waisted gown of the new Greek cut with a cross-ribbon binding in her waist under her breasts. There were little ribboned puffs on the sleeves which covered her arms just halfway to the elbow. She was not too plump any more. Long, and slim, and cool with firm legs. Those white sandals! One could see her pink toes through the thin net stockings and straps.

Florence was "Miss Udney," too. Someone to be proud of knowing. One's equal—or more? A new, a right, and a nice experience, safe from the dark magic of Faith. His kind!

In addition, unbelievable as it might seem, Miss Udney had eyes, nose, and lips. And it was probable that she continued under her dress. But he did not care to think of that just now. She used a faint violet perfume. From her emanated a fragrant coolness as of a lush spot about a thawing spring in early April. It was that which caused him to lean near her and to talk in a hushed way. And it was difficult, he felt, for both of them not to keep on looking at each other's eyes. Parish evidently did not care much for this. He kept passing the gingerbread a little too frequently.

They talked of England, mostly. Florence had been home to school for several years since she had seen Anthony. Her description of Devon made him "homesick." He felt the same way about Florence's country as Mr. Bonnyfeather felt about the valley of the Moselle. It was dreamland and Utopia, only real. England was on the map. He and Florence were often there together, alone. It was a comfort to know that Angela could not come there. No one could disturb them as they played under the huge stones of the bridge at Post Bridge, or looked for white heather where the moor ponies fed above Widde-combe and watched the rabbits playing about the tors. Florence was more graphic than she knew. He could see it all. Together they lingered over it in conversational dreams. Florence found it pleasant and effortless to talk with such a listener. With Anthony she talked about what interested her; with Parish about what was supposed to be interesting. She sighed. Yet she had come to make herself like Parish. He was touchingly attentive, generous, and in love. Her mother liked him too, she felt.

Mrs. Udney was secretly a little alarmed now over the arrival of Anthony. She almost wished she had not brought him around. Parish was getting too restive. She had merely meant to spur him on. He might shy off. She wished Anthony would join in the talk more generally. Finally she would go to the spinet and looking back at them both, touch the chords of "Malbrouk s'en va-t-en guerre." That tune always brought the colour to Anthony's face. He felt a boy again and awkward. Yet it touched a chord of sympathy. Flor-ence remembered, too. So for a good many afternoons it went on.

Vincent had dropped out entirely. The plump, Florentine banker's daughter was more to his mind. She had surrendered to him fur-tively. Taking tea to Vincent now seemed a waste of time. Anthony had gone to the Strozzi's once or twice, too. He found Mlle. de Rhan quite intriguing. But she had soon gone back to Nantes. He had promised to write and he did so once. Vincent's intimate details about Maddalena began to revolt him. One did not care to think of Vincent that way. There was something between the pig and the rabbit about the German. He was kin to Arnolfo, Anthony thought. Smooth! He remembered the big blonde at Signora Bovino's crying. So they saw less of each other. Vincent was troubled about this separation. What had happened?—he wondered. He intended to speak to Anthony about it.

But upon all this stirring about of tea leaves in cups, and drifting of rose petals in casual breezes blew the strong wind of war.

One afternoon Florence had seemed particularly gay and attractive. Her face shone from some inner excitement. Mrs. Udney had been careful to thump the spinet more than usual. She gathered them all around her and made them sing. As Anthony left Mr. Udney entered suddenly and beckoned to him.

"Give this to your guardian," he said. It was a sealed letter. "Be *sure* not to forget," he called. "It is urgently important, hurry home!"

That was the last Saturday of June 1796 when Mr. Udney's letter apparently began to act as a solvent on the world which Anthony had known as "Livorno" and the "Casa da Bonnyfeather."

Mr. Bonnyfeather opened the letter with his carving knife when Anthony came in late to supper. "As I expected," he muttered. He sent the waiter out and leaned forward a little pale. McNab, Toussaint, Faith, and Anthony sat waiting.

"The French are at Florence, the consul informs me," he finally said. "Buonaparte will certainly be here by Tuesday if not sooner. That gives us about forty-eight hours to close this factory." He paused painfully. The happy excitement on the face of Toussaint died out. They were all looking at the old merchant with pity now. A slight flush tinged his high cheek bones as he went on.

"Not a word of this to anyone. I shall want you, Mr. McNab, Toussaint, and Anthony, with me in my own quarters tonight. The clerks must all be gone by Monday. Everyone—but those present," said Mr. Bonnyfeather. "Keep the cook and one porter. Make your arrangements accordingly, Faith, and no delay."

They ate hurriedly.

"May I tell Vincent and the Franks?" asked Anthony as they rose.

"That is well thought of. They should know," said Mr. Bonnyfeather. "But hurry back." The Franks were enormously grateful for the tip.

By the time Anthony returned the lights were burning in the old merchant's room. Piles of papers and cash bags were on the table with McNab and Toussaint hard at work. They made out a discharge and a letter of recommendation for each employee, counted out the total due each clerk plus a quarter's pay, and made a pile of the coin. Mr. Bonnyfeather answered any queries while he burned correspondence steadily. They worked all night.

Early next morning rioting broke out in the piazza. The lottery was closed and the money gone. Rumours of the French advance flew about. The town throbbed. At noon the British fleet anchored off the molo under Commodore Nelson. Save for the now frantic activity of English departure along the docks of the Darsena the town lay quiet under the British guns. In the court of the Casa da Bonnyfeather all hands gathered after lunch looking rather glum. Mr. Bonnyfeather appeared on the steps. The little crowd below him uncovered. He began haltingly but then went on gallantly enough.

"Gentlemen, Buonaparte will be in this town in a few hours. Although England and France are not apparently at war, all British property will undoubtedly be confiscated. Trade is at an end. The gates of this establishment will never be opened again in my time for business. The Casa da Bonnyfeather has ceased to exist. I have retired." He paused with all eyes upon him.

"I have not forgot any of you. You will receive immediately from
Mr. McNab your full pay plus a quarter's salary gratis, also letters
of recommendation to other mercantile firms, and your passports.
Those of you who are British subjects had best go aboard the fleet
tonight. Do not on any pretext delay. There are many things I
would say now but cannot. This sudden decision is due to the act
of a tyrant who comes proclaiming liberty. I have done all I can for
you who have served me faithfully. Receive my thanks, and may
God be with you!"

There was a moment's dead silence. Then the English gave a cheer.
There was a rush to pack belongings. In a few hours the place was
as quiet as the courtyard of a ruined castle. Outside only the slap
of a brush on the front of the establishment as a sailor white-washed
carefully over the legend "Casa da Bonnyfeather" disturbed the silence
of its now deserted quay. Mr. Bonnyfeather beckoned to Anthony.
They went up on the roof and hauled down both the flags together.
"My son," said he with emotion as they locked them in the chest,
"if anyone ever raises them again it must be you." He snapped the
lock. Anthony stood by feeling a lump in his throat.

"And what shall we do now?" he asked.

"I shall talk about that with you later," the old man replied. "Just
now—" He broke off and went to his room.

For some moments Anthony stood there. The past seemed locked
in the chest. Then he remembered the present and hastened over to
the Udneys'. The consulate downstairs was in an uproar but Mrs.
Udney, Florence, and Parish were upstairs.

"Oh, I am so glad *you* came," Florence cried. "We are leaving
tomorrow with the fleet." She checked herself suddenly colouring to
the eyes. "I did want to say good-bye, you know."

Of course, *they* would be going! He knew that, and yet until the
last moment he had hoped not. How much he had hoped he was
aware of only now as he looked at her standing so near him. So
Florence was going away, too.

"All the world is going away!" he blurted out looking miserable
and depressed before he could recollect himself. "I wish you were
staying. Is it England?"

Her eyes suffused with tears. "No," she said, "Rotterdam!"

"Rotterdam!" he mumbled.

"I think you had better tell Mr. Adverse, my dear," broke in her
mother. "Florence, don't turn your back on us that way. It isn't
polite."

"Good-bye," said the lips of Florence to Anthony though no sound
was heard. When she turned to her mother and Parish she was gay
again with bright colour in her cheeks.

"Isn't she a little goose about it, David?" said Mrs. Udney. "Florence wants to tell you, Anthony, that she and Mr. Parish are engaged. It will be announced shortly." She looked at him keenly. But his face did not change now.

"Rather wooden," thought Mrs. Udney.

"I hope you will like Rotterdam as well as Totnes, Miss Florence," he managed to say.

"Believe me, she will," said Parish sitting down beside her with the air of a proprietor. "It is a fine town with lots of English and Scotch merchants."

Anthony nodded. He sat on his chair with his knees straight out before him and drank his tea alone. For the life of him he could not think of anything to say. He felt unaccountably sad. Parish talked on confidently. As soon as he could Anthony bade them all good-bye. On the way down he met Mr. Udney coming up. Anthony was surprised by the heartiness of his good-bye. "Good luck, my boy, write us. I want to hear from you!" He caught him by the arm as if to keep him.

"Mr. Udney, I have a great deal to thank you for. I . . . I shall miss you sadly. It will be very lonely . . . with all the English gone . . . very . . . I——"

"Cheer up, my boy, we English always come back, you know. You are staying on with your guardian I suppose?"

"No, I am leaving!" said Anthony, and looked shocked. It seemed as if someone else had made the decision. But he was sure of it, sure!

"Hadn't you better consider your . . ." began the consul.

"No, sir, *I am leaving Livorno!*" He flung out of the door.

"Humph!" said Mr. Udney and went upstairs to his wife, who was alone now.

"Our young friend seems to be badly cut up over the recent trend of events here."

"Does he?" she said doubtfully.

"Yes, he is going to leave. I should think he would stay on and look after Mr. Bonnyfeather's interests—and his own."

"His *own?*" she put down the teacup.

"Yes, didn't you know he is Bonnyfeather's heir?"

"Henry!" she cried. "Why didn't you tell me? Oh, you . . . you old fool!"

She turned and began to play violently on the spinet.

"Well, I'll be damned!" muttered Mr. Udney.

Just as Anthony turned the corner of the street the strains of "Malbrouk s'en va-t-en guerre" reached him faintly like an echo from a past life. He winced and clenched his fist. Mrs. Udney might have spared him that. *That* settled it. He *was* going.

With a heave of his shoulders as if he had cast off a load, he raced to Otto Frank's. They had a merry supper there. That night they watched the post-chaises and carriages dashing away southward. Everybody, everybody was going.

About one o'clock there was a ringing bugle call at the Porta Pisa. A few minutes later the high, clear, thrilling strain burst out at the end of the long street. Down the Strada Ferdinanda with a clicking of sabres, sparks streaming from under their horses' hoofs, and the wind whipping in their pennons streamed a squadron of French cavalry. The old days were done. Only the English finished loading goods under the guns of the fleet.

In the great hall of the mayoralty the French major swore. Cavalry was no good on the sea. That had not occurred to the major before. He was a cavalryman. He could do nothing to stop the British. But he began to arrest people right and left as a relief to his own feelings and as a proof of his zeal.

Uncle Otto was led off protesting, in his uniform coat despite the two epaulettes now sewed on it. Thus was the neutrality of Hamburg wantonly outraged. With many other important merchants of Livorno Uncle Otto spent a miserable night locked up in an old banquet hall at the mayoralty. But on the lists of merchants taxable, which the French officer conveniently used for arrests, the name of John Bonnyfeather no longer appeared. He had retired and was now listed as "widower tenant of the Marquis da Vincitata, age 76, one female housekeeper, and four servants." The French were not arresting "widower tenants." Mr. Bonnyfeather slept at home.

He and Anthony lingered long over their breakfast next morning. It was pleasant in the cool of the summer morning with the great door wide open, with the long shadows in the court and the murmur of the fountain now plainly audible in the strange quiet. Everyone else but he and Anthony had left earlier to watch for the arrival of the main body of the French.

Mr. Bonnyfeather was pleased to find himself contented and relieved at having "retired." He would never have been able to do so himself without the aid of circumstances. He would have died in harness. Now he would have the beds in the court planted with flowers, keep a carriage and pair and drive out when the French departed. He would rest his soul and die in peace here. He had plenty, well secured. He would have in a few old friends to very, very special little dinners and play chess. Ah, he had never permitted himself the time for that. He must get out his notes on combinations again. McNab and Toussaint could stay on a little and look after the few loose ends of things that remained, discreetly of course. The faintest premonitions of physical and spiritual lethargy were pleasant this first, lovely summer morning of his retirement. He relaxed, stretching, with his feet under the table and musing. A rooster in the old mule stables crowed dreamfully. Mr. Bonnyfeather looked at Anthony.

The lad was musing, too, but with a troubled face. "What a strong, lithe, young blade he had grown to be," thought the old man. "And how much, how much he still looked like Maria! Ah, he would forget that now, it was long ago. Let the dead bury their dead." He started. With his business gone this youth was the only vital concern he still had. Well, he would not have to conceal that any longer, now that he was alone. He put his hand gently on Anthony's.

"You look troubled, my son."

"Yes," said Anthony looking up with the expression of frank affection and confidence that had long been customary between them in privacy, "I am greatly troubled. I do not seem to be able to find any comfort anywhere."

"At your age I was restless, too. It is in the blood."

"No, it is not exactly that. I hardly know how to begin to tell you. I have been thinking . . . I have been troubled by things that have been happening to me. I do not know just what I should do, where I should go. You see . . ."

"If it is about the future you need not be greatly troubled about that. I have made sure provision for you there, and in the meanwhile. This has been your home since . . ."

"Do you know anything before that?" Anthony asked by an impulse he could no longer restrain. "Who am I, where did I come from? I do not even know my birthday! My father!"

The old man withdrew his hand suddenly.

"Oh, do not think me ungrateful, please, sir, do not think it. It can never be told you in words what I feel. I know I was a miserable orphan, a— You have been my father. I have read those convent records, the day I got my last name, you remember. But is that all? Don't you know—anything?" His voice trailed off. Mr. Bonnyfeather sat looking into the distance.

"I have been thinking about it a great deal lately," Anthony plunged on. "I didn't used to, but now lately. I will tell you why."

Before he knew it he had plunged into the story of the horoscope at Signora Bovino's, the whole story of Angela, the loss of Florence, his decision to leave Livorno, even the quarrel with Toussaint. The world seemed crumbling about him. If he did not know who he was he must go out and become somebody. He even spoke of his comfort in the madonna that seemed to link him with a past. "To give me some roots as if I had not just happened, been an original creation. I have never told anybody all this. No one, only you. I needed to tell you. Don't you see? That is all. There is nobody else who would understand me, man or woman." He then remembered Faith and stopped.

How did he instinctively know that she would understand? He had not thought of that before. The thought reminded him that he not only disliked her but feared her. She knew, evilly! No, he could not speak to her, or of her. No one should ever know about that, only himself and the madonna. Toussaint! Too many knew already. He looked at the old man anxiously. What they saw in each other's faces now made them both pale.

Mr. Bonnyfeather leaned forward, pondering long. At last he spoke.

"I will show you something," said he. Then after another long pause—"but you must promise me on the honour of your soul, as a gentleman—you must know what I mean by that now—never to ask me any more questions or to try to inquire further. Nay, I *must* ask you something more, for my own sake. If you are grateful to me and love my honour, do not, even if in the future you should accidentally find out more than I can tell you, permit your discovery to be known. Keep it close. Die with it safe." An expression of fiery pride, that for a few seconds made Mr. Bonnyfeather look years younger, quickened him.

"Will honour be equal to the fundamental curiosity I have aroused? Do you understand what you promise, Anthony? Give me your hand." They looked at each other steadily.

"I promise you," said Anthony.

"Come," said the old merchant, and rising from the table he gravely led the way to his room.

Under the picture of the exiled James he opened the little casket with some difficulty. It was years now since he had looked there, he reflected. In fact not since that night when Anthony had been brought to him. He took out the miniature of his daughter and holding it cupped in his hands looked at it again. It was almost like having her come back from the dead. A tremor shook him.

Whatever might come now, he reflected, he had protected her memory. Even her son, if son of hers he was, should never know, should never try to find out. Perhaps it was a cruel promise to exact from the boy, but he had exacted it of himself, and kept his promise even in secret thought. The Bonnyfeathers had preferred ruin to disloyalty, always. This boy— The boy owed him much. This should be the price, the test of loyal gratitude. And he had tried to teach him what "honour" was—the honour of a Bonnyfeather.

He gazed with avid eyes on the face of his child and bowed to kiss the picture as sometimes in the night, when he knelt by the dying ashes of his fire, he kissed the crucifix. And by the rigid code of his feudal soul he had no doubt but that he was doing right, now, and to the past. The name of Bonnyfeather was going out. Let it die in honour—and rest. He turned with his icon in his hand.

"My son," he said, "come here. I am putting our honour in your hands."

He laid the picture in Anthony's palms.

"I believe," said he, "that she was your mother. I am not certain, but I think so. That is all I can say."

Looking up at him from the locket Anthony beheld the same face that he had seen reflected from the fountain of his dreams. It seemed to him as if he were peering down again as a child upon his other self. It was the same face that had gazed back at him that night with Angela when the young madonna came to bathe in the pool, his own face, and yet more lovely, tender and hazily radiant. That was the way his soul thought of itself, if the world would only let it be. As if a shadow had fallen on the water the image glimmered away from him still laughing innocently through his tears.

"Mother, beautiful mother. I know what I am like now. Let me not forget."

It was for that reason that he did not turn with an inevitable and instinctive, "Who was she?" on his lips, despite his promise. It seemed to him that he already knew her as he knew himself.

He gave the picture back again, silently.

"Wait for me outside," said Mr. Bonnyfeather. "I wish to be alone for a little."

From the ashes he began to rake together a few bits of unconsumed branches to make a small fire. Presently by the aid of the bellows the coals became white hot. He did not look at the picture again. "Farewell, Maria, may it be soon." He stooped low and half closed his eyes. The bellows sighed; the gold melted.

When Mr. Bonnyfeather returned to the old ballroom the only material likeness of Maria which existed was that which was still traceable to a knowing eye in Anthony's face. The eyes which could best trace it there were already growing dim.

"So much for the past," said the old gentleman gallantly. "Have I answered your question?"

"You have given me your best gift, I know it," said Anthony. Mr. Bonnyfeather felt his old blood warm him again.

"That was understandingly said, I think," he replied. "I am repaid. We are even! In the future you will remember that whatever you may do for me will be in your own interest as well. Do you understand me?"

"It has always been so before, sir!"

"It is a little more certain now." Yet some shreds of his long reticence were so firmly rooted in precaution that Mr. Bonnyfeather could not bring himself to mention his will. He preferred to delegate the bald mention of it to another.

"Ahem . . . if I were you I would not let these youthful love affairs make me melancholy," he went on. "It is very seldom that one finds happiness that way. Our loves are both our joy and our undoing. Remember, it is that way life is evoked, and life is both happy and full of sorrow. In youth we think only of the pleasure. I did. I was undeceived. Do not think that these first light shades can darken your soul. You are restless, too. The times are disturbed. I have thought of that. You need to change this place for another, to go out and prove yourself on the world."

"I should not care to go to England, to college, just now," said Anthony—thinking that Florence would not be there.

"No, I have thought of a better school than that for you. I mean the age itself. Also I need you now. It so happens that you are the only one left who may be able to carry out a certain plan of mine successfully. Neither McNab nor Toussaint will do. It is the collection of a large sum of money long due me, about nine thousand pounds. It will take you to Cuba. What do you think?"

Anthony leaned forward too eagerly to permit his interest to be doubted.

"It is like this," continued the merchant, "you may have noticed from our Spanish correspondence that with the firm of *Don Carlos Gallego & Son* in Havana we have long had extensive dealings. Owing to the nature of our transactions, which were somewhat peculiar, their payments have been in kind as well as in cash. We would ship them, for instance, cargoes of brass wire, calicoes, toys, millinery, Brummagem muskets, chain shot and handcuffs, together with horse beans, German beads, Manchester cottons, gewgaws, and kegs of Austrian thalers coined under Maria Theresa. It is that last item in particular which has been costly. Such things, you are aware, are eventually destined for trade in Africa, and there can be no doubt but that the firm of Gallego conducts slave operations, both hunting and selling, on a large scale. They in their turn send us cargoes of palm oil, ivory, various fine woods, and so forth. They also remit at various times bills to our credit. Thus, although we were forced to extend a large credit to these people and to carry them for long terms, the profits in the end were so high as to warrant even the risk of the loss of an entire cargo by pirates or guarda costas.

"As matters now stand it so happens that we have in the last three years shipped them three cargoes and received only one in return. A debt of an unusual amount is therefore due us, the largest remaining on our books. With the disturbed conditions now existing on the high seas, and this port in the hands of the French, it will be impossible for the Gallegos to ship us any more ivory. We must collect from them in cash or by bills on France or Spain, or not at all.

"Furthermore, for over a year we have had no answer to our correspondence, although I know our letters were delivered at Havana. The old Señor Gallego is honest by long proof. He is very old, and it is possible that he may have lately died. Of his son I know nothing, nor of the present condition of the firm. There is no way at present in Havana to collect this large debt legally. Spain forbids all direct trade with her colonies. Everything, therefore, depends on the attitude of the colonial officials, frankly upon our finesse in bribery, if we are to realize even our own outlay. You will therefore have to act as a private diplomat on a ticklish mission rather than as an aggrieved creditor. But you speak and write Spanish, you have been instructed carefully in the ways of trade according to my own plans, and I think I do not flatter myself in having confidence in your intelligence, ability, and eventual success. A reasonable accommodation would do. I should expect to dispatch you with funds, and letters to my agent in Havana. He is an Italian, one Carlo Cibo, amply capable of instructing you in all the villainous indirections necessary to conduct honest business in a Spanish colonial capital. The temptations of the place are said to be curious—" Mr. Bonnyfeather then added as if by afterthought, raising his eyebrows and twinkling—"something like Livorno it would seem. Do you care to hazard yourself in the enterprise?"

"It will be a dream coming true, sir. I could not imagine anything more to my mind."

"Perhaps?" said the old man. "Well, well, prepare yourself for the journey. Consult McNab about what you will take. He knows Havana from old times. We shall take the first opportunity of getting you off. A neutral ship would be best now if one happens along. The neutrals will profit by these troubles. But we shall see. Here comes your friend Vincent bubbling with news."

Vincent was indeed afire with excitement. The French were entering the town in full force now.

"They expect Buonaparte directly. I thought you might both like to come over and watch from our windows when he arrived. Uncle Otto has been released but he has been badly scared and is in bed."

Mr. Bonnyfeather would not go, however.

"I shall not go so far as to imitate your uncle but it will be wisest for me to stay here. You go, Anthony." He waved them out and remained sitting in his chair while Vincent and Anthony hastened to Otto Franco's. The streets and the piazza were thronged.

Mr. Bonnyfeather took a book from the sleeve of his wadded dressing gown and began to read.

Britannia Rediviva

A Poem on the Birth of the Prince, Born on the
tenth of June, 1688.

How different it would have been for John Bonnyfeather, for instance, if that prince had reigned. The old Jacobite, a compound of feudal sentimentality and commercial acumen, read on, allowing his dreams of what might have been to warm his heart with ghostly comfort in the silence of the deserted house. Suddenly the pomp of the courtly verse seemed to take on for him a peculiarly personal meaning. A good omen for Anthony's voyage, he thought, a light on the past. He lingered over the lines:

> Departing spring could only stay to shed
> Her blooming beauties on her genial bed,
> But left the manly Summer in her stead,
> With timely fruit the longing land to cheer,
> And to fulfil the promise of the year.
> Betwixt the seasons came the auspicious heir,
> This age to blossom, and the next to bear.

Well, he had seen the blossom. And he would not have to bear the next age. Thanks to the Virgin that would rest on other, younger shoulders! "Anthony, my son, my son."

The thunder of the cannon of the departing British fleet saluting the Tuscan flag still flying on the castle startled him and made him drop *Dryden* to the floor. So they were going! All safe. The pulse of the French drums could be heard answering coming through the Porta Pisa.

Half an hour later there was a roar from the crowd. The tricolour had taken the place of the grand duke's ensign. But John Bonnyfeather had not heard that. He was sleeping peacefully an old man's nap in the afternoon sun. Only the echoes of the outside world whispered in the Casa da Bonnyfeather. On the shadowed wall behind the merchant a faded Sisyphus was trying to roll a huge rock up an impossible hill while various imps were laughing at him. About two o'clock the gate clicked and Faith came stealthily across the court in her bonnet. She looked down at the old merchant sardonically, smiled, and passed on to her room noiselessly.

Meanwhile from the upper windows of the Casa da Franco Anthony, Vincent, Toussaint, and the Franks, with the exception of Uncle Otto, were watching the arrival of the French. When the castle was seized Governor Spanocchi had been found there and was now brought to the mayoralty at his own urgent request under guard. The crowd howled at him for its lottery money, which he was shrewdly enough thought to have shipped off with the town treasure chests. About two o'clock the cannon from the castle were heard firing vainly at a few English ships just steering out of the roads.

Shortly afterwards a column of French cavalry came galloping down the Strada Ferdinanda with a magnificent horseman at their head. He was at first taken for General Buonaparte and was cheered by a radical mob. It was Murat. He dismounted and began to arrange a fitting reception for the conqueror.

The governor and his staff were forced to get into gala uniform. The various foreign consuls were assembled. Uncle Otto was made to get out of bed and put on his official coat. His pallor was extreme. It took a great deal of beer and the reassurances of both Vincent and Anthony to get him across the narrow street. Amid the crestfallen group of city officials and important merchants dragged out for the occasion and standing uneasily on the steps of the mayoralty just opposite, his shoulders sloped most disconsolately. His nephew waved to him from the window, but in vain.

As usual with all military occasions an interminable delay now took place. The crowd grew restive, insolent, and was squeezed against the walls by the French horses for its trouble. Cries and curses arose, the screams of a child. Presently a little girl was carried away gasping and moaning. She had been trampled by a horse. Toussaint looked down pale and shocked. He could not bear the noise the child had made. Just then the police knocked at the door ordering every house to illuminate that night. "Liberty" had officially arrived. One must rejoice now or go to prison.

Anthony laughed and began to quote Rousseau at Toussaint. Then he was ashamed of himself for his thoughtless cruelty. The face of his old tutor was haggard with disappointment. For the first time in months Anthony took him by the hand and with quiet remorse begged his pardon. He could see that it was a real crisis for the idealistic little Frenchman.

"Toussaint, mon maître, you who were so sweet to me when I was a little boy—how could I be so cruel! Do you not know I love you? What has just happened, do not think of it. The child! It was a cruel accident. The hero is yet to arrive. Be yourself, a philosopher as always."

The little man looked up at him with so great a thankfulness in his face as to touch Anthony infinitely. He could never forget that bland, sweet look. How foolish their misunderstanding had been. About what? About Faith!

"You forgive me that blow, then, mon vieux?" Toussaint asked.

Anthony reached over and rumpled the short curls on the little man's head.

"There," he said, "an insult for an insult! Now we are even." They walked back to the window again arm in arm.

The drums in the piazza had begun to roll. A sharp command could be heard. As they looked out together a thousand sabres flashed out as one. In the late afternoon sunlight it seemed as if the arrival of Jove were being announced by a steel lightning and thunder. A noise of galloping horses and wheels was heard in the distance. The world craned its neck.

Down the Strada Ferdinanda a plain carriage drawn by grey horses and followed by a few mud-splashed guards careened into sight. It was moving at great speed. A small, hatless, pale man with his lank hair blowing in the wind was leaning back in the middle of the rear seat reading a book. He paid no attention whatever to the roars of the crowd. As the carriage turned into the piazza the heavy, rear artillery wheels with which it had been fitted described a quarter circle on the cobbles, grating hideously. The man in the carriage sat up at the same instant and tossed his book out into the street. Some urchins scrambled for a treatise on ballistics which fluttered and fell among them like a hurt butterfly. Another flash of lightning, the sabres came to salute. The carriage stopped with a jerk before the mayoralty.

The pale young man, who now seemed as he sat bolt upright to occupy not only the entire carriage but the piazza as well, put on his hat and saluted. Flash, flash, and the sabres grated back in their scabbards. The men sat at attention like ragged, equestrian statues with bronze faces. Murat came down the steps to meet Buonaparte.

"Well, general," said a high clear voice which would have been feminine had it not been so crisp and accusatory. "So you were too late!"

"The ships had already gone, mon général . . ." began Murat when he was cut short.

From the carriage an accusatory finger pointed at the group on the steps. It was fixed on Uncle Otto.

"Is that an English uniform I see?"

"No, padrone," moaned the terrified little German. "No! Questa è l'uniforma di Amburgo!"

Even the troopers grinned with their general. *"Padrone!"*

"Hamburg!" said Buonaparte as if he had already abolished the

place, and got out of the carriage. He ran up the steps and took the governor's sword which was held out to him like a bodkin.

"I shall expect you to provide my troops with ration, fodder, clothing and shoes, especially shoes," shouted the little man looking at Spanocchi like a small eagle. "That is what you exist for now. See to it that the requisitions are filled."

"The dearth is extreme, Highness," faltered the poor man used only to addressing Austrian superiors. "The prices . . ."

"Tut, tut! Omelettes are inflated due to the extreme scarcity of eggs. You talk like a merchant, now *go!* Hullin," said he turning to a tall major of grenadiers, "I appoint you city major. Comb out the place. Do not be such a simpleton as you were at Pisa. If they have let the English go, make them pay. Money! Take the shoes off their feet. Court-martial the governor. Act as if you were still taking the Bastille again."

He swept his eyes about the piazza as though noting who was there to see and hear. For ten seconds or more he seemed to be looking directly into the Franks' window at Anthony and at Toussaint whose face worked with emotion. He whispered something to Hullin, who glanced up and shook his head.

"A fine welcome you give me here," he continued turning now on the quaking merchants. From the window across the narrow street Anthony and Vincent could see him clearly and hear every word. His voice rose to a high pitch.

"Do not doubt it. I shall give the English a final lesson. I march on Vienna and then northwards. Hamburg, every hiding place of these water rats shall be ferreted out, swept clean. Then their island next." He beat his left leg with his gauntlets. The leg trembled. Livorno was a bitter disappointment. He had seen the sails of Nelson glimmering away as he entered. Beckoning to an adjutant he reseated himself in the carriage.

To Toussaint it seemed as if Buonaparte had turned on the crowd the unseeing glance of a mummy. There was no speculation in those eyes. Only dull flashes as from the fires of Stromboli over the horizon at night. He was pallid, yellow. His long, sleek, jet-black hair dangled around his face like the locks of a Seminole Indian threading the swamp. He sat there diminutive, youthful, in a worn simple uniform with gloom on his brow.

"No light," thought Toussaint. "Bon Dieu! no light!"

The sabres flashed only lightning once more. Hullin stood on the carriage steps in an attitude of profound respect listening to some last muttered admonitions. Then as suddenly as he had come, and with the same ominous rumble of wheels, Buonaparte was gone.

To Anthony looking down from the window, watching all this,

there had come that inexplicable feeling that his own fate had some-how been laid in the hands of the little man whom he had watched getting in and out of his carriage. How and why? Out of what immense ramifications of events had the threads of his own existence been laid in those hands? One thin thread to be sure, but it was bound up and woven into that thick rope of Europe, those millions of other gossamers tangled into a strong strand by which the world was to be towed along for a while; towed out of stagnant waters into new.

It was a curious thing, but of all the thousands of eyes that had looked on Buonaparte that day in·Livorno there was scarcely a pair but took this for granted. For a few moments Anthony had actually watched a section of that strand running through those nervous, white hands. It was a relief to have them gone. He felt as if he had to recapture the skein of his own life again. He did not know where it might lead, but at least he could follow it now himself, even if blindly. "To Havana," Mr. Bonnyfeather said. Anywhere, as long as it led away from Livorno.

For months past all the threads in the town had been warped out of the normal blocks and·pulleys through which they ran. All the world now seemed out of gear. His own thread had slipped clear off the familiar pulley where it had been running in what might have become a ceaseless round. Now it flapped free, was hurtling off into the unknown. He was glad of that. It would not be his hands only that would rig it to the tackle of life again. No, there was a strong mysterious drag on it, he felt. He would see the world now. Never could he see enough of it. The void of his first ten years was still deep as a well. One lifetime was not sufficient to fill it. He turned from the window with an unconscious gesture of hail and farewell to find himself in the Franks' room with Toussaint sitting on the sill beside him. The little man sighed.

"It was the gloomy face of a tyrant, Anthony," he said.

Uncle Otto came in trying to recover face and exclaiming "Bir-bante!" His wife and the little girl and Vincent did their best to soothe him. The small ego of Uncle Otto had met something so cosmic that he looked shattered.

Anthony and Toussaint walked home together, the latter gloomy. But that night at supper Faith began to talk with Toussaint and actu-ally smiled at him. Sunlight burst in upon the little man and shone again from his face. To Anthony there was something sinister about it all. Yet he was surprised to find that much as he disliked Faith he did not care to have her kind to Toussaint. He was enraged with himself at this. What strange unknown depths were in him? Actu-ally he could not tell himself what kind of person he was. What would he do under new circumstances in other worlds? Who and what was he?

He sat half-undressed on the edge of his bed pondering. Now he knew why Mr. Bonnyfeather had said, "God keep you." You did not even know who you were yourself. The face in the miniature came back to him now with comfort. That was what he wanted to be like. Only this morning he had felt he was like that, his mother! Part of him. Who and what was the other part? He wondered. But he could never ask now. His father!

"*Father, mother, father, mother,*" he kept saying the words over again trying to give them some reality, shape, and memory. He was somebody's son. He would some day be a father. Angela might have a child! He had not thought of that. What did it all mean? These human words had always had a sound of prayer about them, still had.

"Mother, son, father—Holy mother," he turned to the Madonna on the wall. The old formulas sprang to his lips full of new meanings. It was a relief to be able to pray that way again! He had not been able to do so for so long. Not until the other day. Whatever he might do he was not to be left alone. The misery, restlessness, and youthful despairs of the past hectic months rushed from his lips in a whispered confession to the Virgin. All doubt had vanished with the blessed relief. Was she not there, on the wall, in heaven, as always! Had she not come to him in his dream with Angela, young and beautiful? He and the Virgin were very old, very old together. He had seen her that night as his soul remembered her, looking back through ancient doors of birth and death made transparent by the light of eternal passion breaking through them. Before, now, and forever, he had seen her merging with the waters at the root of the great tree as he remembered her in the springtime of the world.

"Ah, they called her mother, mother of sorrows. But she was mother of joy as well. Yes, he believed that. She was sitting there now, as always, with the child in her arms. But in the dream there were two of them. The other heavenly twin had come back. Who was he, that lost one? Was he like Anthony lost for a while on earth? Was he Anthony? Anthony who could return to her knees, in dreams? Ah God! if he could only lay his head on her breast! Be rocked to sleep there as he never had been, forget and forget, already he would forget."

He drew near to her in a dreamful mood in which the life within him seemed to leave his body sitting breathing, while he drew closer to her against the wall. He laid his head there and kneeled looking at her head lost among the stars. Silence and peace and silence. To be and not to think, only to know and feel. Ecstasy.

At last he opened his eyes again and found that he really was kneeling against the wall. By the dim light that burned before her, very dim, except about the little shrine, he seemed to see her now more clearly than ever before. His eyes were wide awake and rested. They were made to peer into far spaces. It was not necessary even to wink. He looked steadily and easily at the statue.

It seemed to him as he saw her there now as the madonna of his dreams, but older, sweeter, with something more tender, more human, the mystic woman of the fountain touched and wafted by some ineffable experience into a being far more beautiful, sympathetic, and divine. And it seemed now to him, too, that for the first time he saw she was holding the child out to him as if he should draw near and touch it. He had been like that once. Was he now? Partly perhaps. The child was her son. Father Xavier had told him the story. Born in the rocky stable amid the oxen under the stars. And there had been more to that story. It was about the babe after he became a man. He had thought very little about that. Perhaps he should think more. Why did she hold him out that way? Should he really draw near and touch him? He put out his hand. Then he saw that the child was still sleeping on her breast. He dared not awaken him. Not yet. "After a while," he thought. It was as though his lips went on speaking another's words. "After a while when you find him again."

Late in the night he awakened cold. He was still leaning against the wall, but the light had gone out. It was dark now. He slipped, half dressed as he was, under the covers and slept exhausted. Next morning the room for the first time for months seemed washed with a happy light as he woke.

"There will not be many more mornings here," he thought. How quiet and how home-like it was. He pressed his cheek against the pillow enjoying it and whistling softly. How wonderful, and after all how happy his days had been here! A light tap sounded on his door.

"Anthony, are you awake yet, my boy?" said the kindly voice of Mr. Bonnyfeather. "Get up and dress yourself. I have news for you."

Anthony smoothed out the dent on the pillow where his head had been and put on his clothes. In the big room they were already at breakfast. The court lay quiet and serene in the morning sun with the shadows withdrawing from it as if by magic.

CHAPTER TWENTY-THREE

FAREWELLS AND EPITAPHS

"YOUR ship has come in, Anthony," said Mr. Bonnyfeather. "At least I hope it has," he added hastily, smiling at the involuntarily prophetic nature of the remark.

"Nolte sent word this morning. It is an American brig and he and his precious uncle will be taking advantage of this neutral to get rid of some of their anxious travellers. Frau Frank must have had her hands full feeding a dozen or more at once. You and McNab go down and look her over. If it is necessary you might ask her captain to supper tonight. I might persuade him to make your voyage direct. But be careful, arrange everything if you can, yourselves. We do not want to attract notice here just now. So far the French have ignored us. You will have to avoid all clearance papers."

The old man turned to his latest London newspaper which he scanned anxiously. A month ago war seemed inevitable, he noted anxiously—over his chop.

Anthony and McNab hurried through breakfast and went down to the quay at the lower end of the Darsena. A trim little brig was warped in close to the dock but not into the slip. She had springs on her cables, and running his eye aloft McNab noted that, while to an unprofessional glance the canvas might seem snugly furled, it was stowed so as to be let go if necessary with a run.

Anthony liked the ship. He had never met anything quite like her. She appeared a little more frail and bird-like than any other craft he had seen. From her sharp bows blew back the carved eagle feathers of an Indian chief's head-dress. His hooked nose seemed to snuff the surges. The masts raked aft at a sharp angle and were stayed so tautly that the standing rigging hummed in the morning breeze. Her deck was spotless. Between the two masts was a "long tom" carefully covered with canvas. Aft, the box over the captain's cabin rose above the quarter-deck. Even in port her hatches were battened down. Except for these, and her polished wheel and hooded binnacle, there seemed nothing else on deck.

"All a-tanto and not a soul aboard?" grunted McNab.

They walked down past the brig a little farther giving their eyes a sailor's treat. The wind whipped the ensign out over the water. It flowed out into the breeze curling with long tiger streaks. On a blue field a circle of stars seemed whirling about nothing. It was the first time Anthony had seen the Stars and Stripes. Then, just around the corner of the galley, they saw what ever afterwards he thought of as the spirit of the ship.

Seated in a sea-chair lashed to two large wooden half-moons sat rocking contentedly, and with an air of self-possession that only she herself could convey, a prim, bony woman with extraordinarily pointed lips. She was knitting a positively gigantic stocking with the heaviest yarn imaginable, and for every stitch and click of her needles she twisted the extreme tips of her lips. It looked as if she silently whistled. At the distance of a few yards they stood looking at her over the water as at an apparition. On McNab and Anthony she did not bestow a glance. For a while they watched time being destroyed while the stocking grew.

"Ahoy, the brig there," said McNab at last tentatively.

"*Ee*-lisha," said the woman without missing a stitch and continuing to rock, "Ee-*lisha!*"

"Comin' on deck," said a deep voice from the cabin with a restraint so abject as to make McNab grin. A red-faced man with an iron-grey beard and cold blue eyes stuck his head through the aft sliding hatch and looked at them.

"Ahoy, the brig," said McNab again.

"Ahoy, the dock there," said the man and glowered. The woman continued to knit. It seemed to Anthony as if they had reached an impasse. McNab cleared his throat.

"If you'll waft us a wee bit o' a skiff, captain," said he, "I'll put that in your lug will belike warm your pocket."

"*Aye?*" said the man. "Philly!"

A darky stuck his head out of the galley.

"Fetch the gentlemen."

"The crew are ashore," he bawled. "Ye won't mind having the cook get ye, I hope," he continued, evidently to Anthony, who was dressed like a merchant's clerk.

"Not at all," said Anthony, "if he's a good cook."

"Best 'tween here and Boston," replied the captain.

"He ain't," said the woman.

The little boat sculled by the negro danced to them over the few yards of harbour.

"It's na miracle the French hae no seized yon brig," said McNab as they were ferried across. "Yon carline wi' her knittin' needles would stand off Buonaparte I'm thinkin'."

WAMPANOAG
Providence, R. I.

gleamed across the duck-like stern as they passed. They climbed up the dangling ladder and found themselves on deck in the tremendous white light that beat about the rocking chair.

"Good morning, ma'm," said McNab touching his hat, despite himself a little sneakily.

The woman missed one stitch. "Ee-*lisha*," she said.

"Come below," roared the captain.

At the foot of the ladder they found themselves standing in the most peculiar captain's cabin imaginable. It was neither a ship's cabin nor a New England parlour. It was both. There were four bunks built into the ribs of the ship. Two of these like Dutch beds were provided with folding shutters. The two, round stern windows were curtained with an effeminate lace. Under each of these eyes was a chest painted pure white, labelled respectively "Jane" and "Elisha." Between the two chests the great keel beam of the ship curved out like a nose and widened toward the floor as if it were trying to expand its bolted nostrils.

The effect of all this was to give the aft end of the cabin with its half-curtained eyes the appearance of a peculiarly bestial face trying to be coquettish in a lace night-cap. As he looked at the two chests standing out like white, bared tusks from the cheeks of this sinister countenance, Anthony felt as Red Riding-hood must have when she first began to realize that her grandmother was a wolf.

But if the cabin was sinister toward the stern it made up for it by being safely domestic forward. Lashed to the ship's ribs by a perverse puzzle of beautifully intricate knots was a mahogany sideboard of undoubtedly genteel lineage. Its gracefully curved limbs seemed straining outward. The lady was plainly being held there against her will—facing the wolf. A sturdy, manly sea-desk near by watched this perpetual crisis indifferently. It was stuffed with ship's papers to the point of self-importance and it wore a plume pen in its inkstand hat with an air of "business or nothing."

Anthony and McNab sat down upon two chairs spiked to the deck while the captain seemed to preside from the chest labelled "Elisha."

"Captain Ee-lisha Adonijah Jorham of Providence Plantations, New England," said the red-faced man looking at them with level eyes. "Gentlemen, at yer service. She," he continued jabbing upward with one thumb, "is my wife, Mrs. Jorham. She was a Putnam—*once.*" He lowered his voice slightly.

Having no means of controverting this McNab and Anthony introduced themselves. It was not long before the captain and McNab had taken each other's measure. Yankee had met Scot. Both were interested in each other and fenced carefully. Ten minutes went by and neither had learned anything.

"I'm thinkin'," said McNab, "that the deil will soon be dizzy gangin' aroond the bush. Let's talk till the point."

Captain Elisha opened his chest and took out a bottle of rum. As he did so, as if by prearrangement, his wife came down the ladder and stood knitting. She would not sit down. The captain sighed. Nevertheless, the discussion went on.

After an hour it appeared that the captain would be glad to consider a voyage to Havana on charter terms, provided he was allowed to make certain ports of call on the way. Yes, he knew of course of Mr. Bonnyfeather, and of the conditions at Livorno. On their mutual dislike of the French he and McNab almost clinched the bargain. Then the captain sheered off. He would prefer to sign with Mr. Bonnyfeather himself.

But there were to be no papers, reminded McNab. It would not do now. Mr. Bonnyfeather was no longer in business. It might compromise him. This was to be a purely private affair. Merely to take the young gentleman to Havana. It could all be arranged verbally.

All the more reason then for seeing the merchant personally, said the captain. It was McNab's turn to sigh. Mr. Bonnyfeather, he knew, would not drive so close a bargain as might be. Nevertheless, he was forced to play his last card and invite the captain that night to dinner. In the presence of the lady Anthony thoughtfully added her to the invitation.

"What do you say, Mrs. Jorham?" asked the captain. All realized it was a final appeal.

"I won't mind some shore fixin's—if they're turned out right," she added noncommittally. "Ye might send Philadelphy along with that Bank tartle to help out. I'm plum worn out watchin' the critter tryin' to get away."

"Like the sideboard, ma'm?" said Anthony unable to restrain himself. The captain laughed.

"Young man," said she icily, "where might *ye* be expectin' to spend etarnity?" Her mouth pointed.

"Wall, wall," cried the captain trying to move them out before the threatened gale could break. "At eight then, after dark. I'll mind the patrols. So long now." He looked with an approving but anxious eye at Anthony. The knitting had stopped and his wife was watching.

"I don't care if I do," said McNab pouring himself a drink from the square bottle and tossing it off. "A wee doch-an-dorris, noo . . ."

But no sooner had his hand left the bottle the first time than it was seized by Mrs. Jorham and deposited in the chest marked "Jane." It was the first drop that had passed, and the last for any of them. A parched twinge wrinkled the lips of Captain Elisha, but he waved them out as his wife locked the chest. They went.

"A watched bottle never gurgles," said McNab as they went down the ship's side. In the cabin the typhoon had burst.

" 'Twas an ill jest o' yours, laddie. If you sail in yon ship you're no like to hae heard the last o' it. Losh!"

The captain, his face more fiery than before, was hailing them.

"I'll send the nigger with the tartle," he shouted at the dock. Then he must have heard the voice of his mate calling him, for he dived below.

―――――

The dinner for the Jorhams was to be an unusual feast; one not for business alone. Indeed, McNab had been instructed to return to the brig and to arrange for Anthony's passage on the captain's terms. He had done so. He and Philadelphia had returned with the turtle which was killed in the courtyard amidst immense curiosity. Dinner was to be a memorable, final feast.

Mr. Bonnyfeather had planned it with a double motive. As a farewell to Anthony it was to be a merry one. He would spare Anthony the sadness of a sorrowful parting and he would also spare himself the lonely, private agony of a good-bye that he scarce dared to face. "The last, the dear last of us all," he thought looking at the boy's golden head. They sat in his room together talking, making last arrangements, pausing, and reverting to familiar topics as one goes back to look at something for the last time.

Faith was very busy outside packing Anthony's chests. They could hear her moving about in the hall.

"I suppose you will be taking the madonna with you, Mr. Anthony," she said coming in suddenly.

"Oh," said he getting up. He had almost forgotten her. "*Yes,* wrap her up carefully. Put her in the big chest."

Faith nodded. So she would see the last of *that,* she thought. She turned the thing face downward and closed the lid. "Farewell to the bad luck of a Paleologus!"

In the room Anthony and Mr. Bonnyfeather sounded very merry. But it seemed to both of them at times that the misty landscapes on the wall were hazier than usual. The old man lighted his candles. He wiped his spectacles and put them on again several times. Thus they both talked through the long twilight as if they would always be able to do so till evenings were no more. At eight o'clock the guests arrived.

It fell to Anthony that evening to do the honours. He found Captain Elisha and Mrs. Jorham, the latter assisted gingerly by Philadelphia, climbing down in the court from a high-wheeled cab. The captain was dressed in a homespun suit so tight that it gave him the

cherubic outlines of an overgrown cupid.   Mrs. Jorham trailed behind
her a long sea-green skirt of a mid-century, colonial vintage.   Into
this ocean of faded velvet a pointed bodice thrust violently like the
bow of a ship.   Above it her head rose like a teak figurehead.   She
carried a canvas umbrella with whalebone ribs and what appeared to
be a spar for a handle.   On the end of the spar was a yellow ivory ball
like a doll's head.   The whole affair, which had a belligerent air about
it, flapped about the point, bulged in the middle, where its hips might
have been, and was tied about the waist with a rope.   As Mrs. Jorham
stood in the court holding it maternally close to the folds of her skirt
it appeared to be her bashful replica in miniature and might have been
her female child.

"Philly," said she, "take my umbreller."   The captain laid his pea-
jacket over the darky's other arm.   Holding these objects majestically
before him, Philadelphia ushered them up the steps.

The Americans seemed to have learned from the Indians the savage
custom of shaking hands.   They shook hands with Mr. Bonnyfeather,
with Anthony, with McNab, with Faith, solemnly and with malice of
forethought.   It looked as if Captain Elisha would shake hands with
himself when his eye fell upon the dinner-table already set with many
glasses.   He and Mr. Bonnyfeather disappeared to talk business while
Anthony was left alone with Mrs. Jorham and the umbrella.

They sat facing each other on two heavy gilt chairs.   Seemingly at
a vast distance from them in the great apartment the white round of
the table, much enlarged for the occasion, lay in a cheerful glow.   But
by contrast all the rest of the room was in darkness.   The folds of the
angular woman's skirt swept around her and into the shadows.   Above
them in the twilight gleamed the bony ribs and the pale ivory knob of
the umbrella.   She seemed to emanate a kind of masterful, yet mater-
nally-virtuous disapproval of everything, whose only softening influence was a touch of lugubrious woe.   Having said "how" to this
chieftainess in whalebone, Anthony was now at a loss.   He could not
shake hands again.   At the very thought he started to smile.   The
woman's lips pointed indignantly.

"I trust," said she, "that ye haven't spent the arternoon jokin'.
Ye seemed in an idle mood this mornin'.   It was not that I object to
what ye said about my sideboard!   It was yer levity in comparin' it
to a woman."

"I have been getting ready to leave home all afternoon, Mrs. Jorham.   I can assure you there was not much levity in that, and I was
not idle."

Mrs. Jorham looked somewhat mollified but nevertheless shook her
head doubtfully.   "Mere earthly consarns are not sufficient.   You
should cast your eyes above."   Anthony looked surprised.   "Unless

you have devoted some time during the day to prayer you may consider it wasted, you know." She laid her umbrella across her knees and folded her hands in her lap.

Embarked thus on the pursuit of her favourite quarry, the soul, she began to feel more congenial. In the semi-darkness her outline lost much of its rigidity. She cuddled the umbrella. It no longer seemed likely that she might open it in the twilight and flit off on the wings of a bat. There might even be shelter under it for two. Anthony wondered about the captain.

"Whenever I'm fixin' to make a v'y'ge," snapped Mrs. Jorham, "I go in for extensive prayer. V'y'ges are solemn things. Ye can never tell. I pack my duds in the mornin', all but the scriptures, and I usually goes to the ta-own churchyards in the arternoon and takes the good book along for reference. There's nothing like a few chice epitaphs and a little solemn scripture to put you in a frame of mind fit to go to sea. It makes your petitions gin-uine, the kind that goes straight through to the marcy seat. I tell ye I know it. Have ye any clever graveyards here?" she inquired suggestively.

"Several," said Anthony, "but most of the clever epitaphs are in Latin."

"That's the way in heathen parts," she went on. "I am glad to tell that it's dyin' out at home. I must say Latin's Greek to me, although I was a Putnam."

"Do the Putnams speak Latin like the Jesuits?" asked Anthony. He wondered if they were tonsured, too.

"Nope, they don't need it to git along in Bosting, and most of my family round Nuburyport went in for rum and ile. But all of 'em got fine epitaphs. Granite stones, too. Not a soapstone in the lot. No, siree." The lady paused triumphantly.

"Ye ever been to my pa-arts?"

Anthony shook his head regretfully.

"Well, sir, there's a fine parcel o' ta-owns in New England. A feast for Christian eyes with white churches and neat houses. The snow comes regular and kills off the roaches. We don't have critters except what comes in ships from Jamaiky and other foreign pa-arts. But the best thing about the ta-owns is the clever graveyards. I've seen a sight of 'em all up and da-own the cyoast. But they Southern planters sleeps too proud o' their own private plots! You'd think Gabriel was goin' to call ra-ound and give some souls a separate toot. No, sir, there'll be just one long, common blast, and them that sleeps late'll fry. One o' the slickest churchyards I ever see was at Bridgewater, Mass. I spent a hull week there. Visitin'! I got them inscriptions pat. Some of 'em was poetry. Here's one: 'Here lies buried Mrs. Martha Alden, the wife of Mr. Eleazer Alden, who died 6 January, 1769, aged 69 years.' " Mrs. Jorham broke into song.

> "The resurrection day will come,
> And Christ's strong voice will burst the tume;
> The sleeping dead, we trust, will rise
> With joy and pleasure in her eyes,
> And ever shine among the wise.
>
> A-men."

The nasal tune twanged its way about the mouldering frescoes. It seemed to curl up among the clouds that had once been rosy with a false dawn but were now like rolling billows of blue and grey smoke through which the chariots of the gods plunged in a growing twilight.

"It'll do the heathens good," said Mrs. Jorham rolling her eyes aloft and askance. "And that naked man rolling his barrel in hell. Well, I cala-late their clothes *would* singe off, but it don't seem right. I wouldn't allow even the damned to expose themselves."

Anthony sat silent in sheer amazement. The woman was evidently having a good time. He remembered having read about persons like this in Mr. Bonnyfeather's Protestant books. There was, for instance, "The female Saint of Wimbledon." What was it, that phrase the old author used, a classical scholar, he was, oh, yes, "That chaste Diana of endangered souls,"—something, something, rolls—

> "The heat of pious ardour lit her face
> As through the wood of error roared the chase,
> Acteon-like the heretic was torn
> While scornfully she wound her Christian horn."

And so on ad infinitum.

O lord! he wished Vincent would come. He could hear the snatch of harmony at Signora Bovino's ringing out now as if his mind were defending itself automatically. Undoubtedly he was being chased.

> "In memory of Capt. Seth Alden—
> The corpse in silent darkness lies
> Our friend is gone, the captain dies . . ."

"Thar she spa-outs, and thar she bla-ows," roared the voice of Captain Elisha who emerged just then from the corridor with Mr. Bonnyfeather. They had clinched their bargain over a bottle of rum, at least the captain had, and he was not what might be termed his better self.

"Has that old cachalot been spa-outin' dirges to ye, young man? I'm sorry for ye, plum sorry!" He clapped Anthony on the back. "A little sea-vility, a little sea-vility is what you Putnams need to larn, Jane. I allers said so. I'm the man to larn yer. The idear. I kin smell them tumes right through the tartle soup."

"Ee-lisha, ye've been drinkin'," said his wife sniffing something else than turtle soup.

"I hev. And what's more I'm goin' right on for the rest of the evenin' and ye can belay yer temperance drip and *mo*-lasses." He looked approvingly at the table. "Philly, is that potage perfected?"

"It air, suh!"

The captain made a gesture which in its generous expansiveness included the more remote members of the solar system. "Come on," said he, and led Mr. Bonnyfeather by the arm to his own table.

"Mr. Adverse," said Mrs. Jorham in a voice now so subdued that Anthony felt sorry for her, "don't forget what I have been tellin' ye. Do a graveyard or two, before . . ."

"Belay them sepelchrees, Jane," called her husband.

But Anthony promised and saw that he had made a friend. Slipping her arm in his they advanced to the table.

"Madame," said Mr. Bonnyfeather escaping, "you will also permit *me* to do some of the honours." He seated her on his right. All the gentlemen now took their chairs, and with this display of manners Mrs. Jorham was obviously touched. She permitted herself a dab at her eyes.

"Ye make me feel at home," she said to Mr. Bonnyfeather.

"I regard that," said he, "as a touching compliment."

Mrs. Jorham began to rally and to remember who she had once been. "I do miss the fixin's sometimes," she sighed running her eye over the glass and silver and fingering the tablecloth. "And land's sake the napkins! We do live like Injuns on the *Wampanoag*! I often says to Elisha, says I . . ." but the captain was looking at her. "Anyway it's nice to be settin' with gentlemen and a respectable female again!"

"I'll say it is," slipped in the captain, also looking with approval at Faith.

Suddenly an electric thrill ran through him. He had seen Faith flutter her eye at him. There could be no doubt of it. It hadn't happened to him for years.

"Woman," said he, tossing off a glass of wine to her with a loud smack, "it's a tarnation wonder someone didn't marry ye years ago.

Years ago! I say." He banged his fist on the table so that the soup jumped.

Mrs. Jorham's eyes narrowed. The landscape did not seem so respectable as she had thought a moment before.

"There's some things a woman can wait too long to change her mind about," she said dryly. Faith's throat rippled. There was an awkward pause. Toussaint jumped into the breach gallantly.

"Madame, I can assure you it has not been for lack of opportunities, or want of a philosopher to persuade mademoiselle that she remains a . . . er, single. Monsieur," said he catching Mr. Bonnyfeather's eye, "may I be the first to propose a toast—*To the Ladies.*"

"Gaud bless 'em," added McNab with a sardonic twist looking at the two women glaring at each other. "What would we do without them?" The crisis might have continued but just then Vincent dashed in late shaking the rain off his curls.

"Well! Elisha, I told ye it would rain," said Mrs. Jorham.

"Aye, ye're a clever barometer, I'll give ye that," said the captain.

"Vera sansitive to dampness in any form," muttered McNab to Faith. But Faith was proposing the return toast.

"I propose something we can all drink to," she said smiling at Mrs. Jorham, "and I with as much hope as any of you, perhaps more, who knows? 'The future.'"

"But not without faith," amended Mr. Bonnyfeather who could not avoid the obvious.

Mrs. Jorham hesitated. She had been trapped.

"Come on, Jane," said Captain Elisha appreciating the housekeeper's finesse.

"I'm a temperance woman," she snapped.

"Madame," said Mr. Bonnyfeather, "allow me. A very light wine, a remedy for the climate, never intoxicating, in small doses. The custom of the country." He bowed, his eyes twinkling, and from a decanter filled Mrs. Jorham's glass with a fiery burgundy. He stood waiting.

Mrs. Jorham arose with a stiff yet coy reluctance. She hesitated but finally clinked her glass against Mr. Bonnyfeather's as if she had already been seduced and nothing could be done about it.

"The future," she murmured, her cheeks tingling at her inconceivable abandon. Then she swallowed the burgundy with a gulp.

"The auld deil," whispered McNab to Anthony.

She sat down slowly. Her hands remained spread out on the table as if placed on a faintly pleasant electric contact.

"Well, darn my mother's socks!" said the captain.

Everybody laughed and broke out talking at once. The ice had been broken.

Anthony glanced at Mr. Bonnyfeather. He was sitting with a look of great satisfaction at the success of his ruse. As for Mrs. Jorham there was no doubt that she was wrapt in a deep spiritual experience. The end of her nose was slowly beginning to glow.

Vincent was as full of news and as merry as ever. "Have you heard the new song the gamins are singing? It throws the French out of step when they pass." He broke out with his full tenor.

"Io cledevo di veder fla pochino,
Che se n'andasser via questi blicconi:
Dia Saglata! ne vien ogni tantino
Quasi, quasi dilei, Dio mi peldoni!
O che anche Clisto polta il palticcino,
O che i Soplani son tanti minchioni!"

The happy, careless voice transported Anthony again to the molten hours they had wasted delightfully together along the Corso. In the gay mocking lilt was concentrated the life of the streets of Livorno. How he loved it all. Now that he was going, how homesick for it he was already. Could it, could it be possible that so much happiness, and dear sorrow, could pass? "The future?" What was it? Let them always sit listening about a table like this. The voice ceased. The silence seemed unbearable.

"Sing again, Vincent, sing again. The song we sang that morning together, do you remember?"

Vincent burst out with it. Anthony joined in. On the surge of his own notes he recovered himself. His voice rang out clearly. He could blend it with Vincent's beautifully. For another moment he was gayly happy. But this time with a new poignance.

He looked at Mr. Bonnyfeather. With the music and the words he poured out his boundless gratitude and at the end reached over and filled his glass to the old man. They all understood and drank with a shout. The table rose, Captain Jorham grunting.

The bright red flush appeared on the merchant's cheek bones. He was much moved. The young voices had gone home. He rose slowly and held out his glass with an air that the world had already forgotten.

"Anthony, my dear boy, God bless you."

They drank it silently. Anthony caught Faith's eye. He was aware that behind her serious expression she was amused at all this. A minute ago he could almost have forgiven her. But not now, not ever. It would be war between them to the last. Poor Toussaint! He wished Faith would make up her mind to leave Leghorn. They were sitting down now. He would have to reply.

Heavens, what was that strange noise?

Captain Jorham had also been moved by the occasion, and his pota-
tions, to the point of song. His face glowed like a bonfire. A husky
roar proceeded from his chest.

> "Yankee skipper comin' down the river
>   Yankee skipper, *HO* . . ."

He had forgotten the rest of the words. He hummed the tune, rumbling like a cart going downhill. Then a look of inspiration came into
his eyes. He had remembered the last line just in time.

> "Yankee skipper comin' down the river."

He ended triumphantly, gurgling. Then he filled his glass till it spilled
and slopped over as he raised it.

"To the v'y'ge!"

The success of the toast was disturbed by a sound as of dry sticks
crackling. It proceeded from Mrs. Jorham. Mr. Bonnyfeather was
about to pat her on the back when it became evident that she was
laughing.

"Why, Jane," said her husband, "ye ain't gorn off that way since
ye was a Putnam."

"Ain't I?" she spat back. "How do ye know?"

For some reason, perhaps because a small bright bead seemed about
to leave the fiery tip of Mrs. Jorham's nose but miraculously did not,
they all laughed. She joined in heartily. A whole brush-fire seemed
to be alight, crackling and snapping. Suddenly in the middle of it a
hen was disturbed and went off cackling. Wine is a marvellous play-
fellow. They all lay back and roared. McNab nearly split his tight
waistcoat. At this he suddenly looked serious and they went off again.
Captain Jorham was still standing like a nonplussed colossus with his
glass poised questioningly. He glanced at his buttons uneasily. They
were all right.

"Whar's the joke?" he rumbled.

Then they all wondered. Something, something that nobody could
quite remember now had been so funny. Anthony still wheezed but it
was purely physical. His stomach seemed to have collapsed with the
joke. A cold voice stilled them all.

"Elisha, be ye fixin' to go to Havaner?" demanded Mrs. Jorham.
She seemed to have accused him of a crime. They all looked at him.
How would he defend himself? He put his glass down defiantly.

"I be," he said.

"Then," said she, "who's goin' to do the navigatin'? That's what
I want to know."

She looked at them all appealingly.

"The last time we come over we started for London. Do ye know where we fetched up at? Lisbon!" she shouted. "Lisbon!"

"Woman," he said sitting down heavily, "I forbid ye."

She had touched him to the quick. For the past two years something terribly wrong had overtaken the navigation of Captain Elisha Jorham. He could not fathom it. Secretly he had taken to coasting from port to port picking up what he called "cargoes of notions." He had turned many a lucky penny. But the cargoes of the *Wampanoag* had become as eccentric as her course when she took to the high seas. He had hoped to conceal his difficulties. Only Mr. Bonnyfeather's exceptional offer of an hour before had finally screwed his resolution to the point of heading for deep blue water again. That Lisbon landfall had shaken him terribly, and now his wife had betrayed him.

He sat looking crushed, shaking his head at her.

"Ye've taken the bread out of yer own mouth," he muttered, "I *know* the way back."

"I'm sure you do, captain," said Mr. Bonnyfeather, "besides Mr. Adverse here is by now an excellent navigator in theory. All he needs is some actual practice. You and he can work your reckoning together. You can give him his final polish in the art. Just what he needs."

Captain Jorham looked much mollified and relieved.

"When do you plan to get under way?" continued the merchant.

"Thar's a strong land breeze usually picks up about dawn on these coasts," said the captain in his own element again. "If Mr. Adverse can come aboard at about two bells we'll leave first thing in the mornin'. Better not delay and risk trouble with the authorities."

Mr. Bonnyfeather looked at Anthony. A glance of understanding passed between them.

"Get your chests down while it's dark and then keep below till you are out of the Darsena. Your passports might be an awkward question now with Mr. Udney's visa.

"Vincent," he added, "I regret to interfere with any of your uncle's plans, but I'm afraid your aunt will have to entertain some of her refugees a few days longer. I have engaged Captain Jorham to take Anthony to Havana. He goes north to Genoa first to pick up cargo. There is nothing for him here, as you know. If Genoa suits any of your travellers' plans, they will have to be aboard tonight."

"I'm only sorry for one thing, sir," said Vincent.

He put his arm around Anthony.

"Aye," said the old man, "we're a grieten sair o'er that! And noo let's hae a stirrup cup tigether for the last time, and no more good-byes, for I canna bide them."

All their cups touched. Anthony felt very proud and tall and straight. Excitement he knew would now lend him wings to clear the threshold. He thought of his old friend Mercury taking off from the cloud with the banquet behind him.

They broke away from the table. Anthony looked up just in time to see Mr. Bonnyfeather vanish into the door of his corridor. He did not look back. The door closed.

"Faith," said Anthony, "will you do me a favour?"

"Yes, Signore Adverso," she said trying to look through him it seemed. He met her glance. "Certainly."

"Fetch my hat and cape and the small bag on the table from my room. I do not care to go back there any more."

"I'll take care o' the chests," said McNab.

"Good night, Captain Jorham, I'll see you directly," he called after him. It helped thus to be doing ordinary things. Vincent still sat at the table turning a glass about in his hand. Their eyes met affectionately.

"Good night," bellowed the captain from the court. "Two bells, mind ye. The tide won't wait. A clever evenin' it was, fine and dandy. Philly."

"Yes, suh."

"*On* them chests!"

"I'll swan if it ain't rainin'!" said Mrs. Jorham. She raised the immense umbrella over them. They disappeared under it.

"Yankee skipper comin' down the river," trilled the captain. The echoes awoke in the old court in a kind of jargon.

"Land's sake, 'Lisha, ye'll wake the dead," they heard his wife say.

"Anthony," said Vincent turning to him. "Is it all right between us? Lately I have thought, sometimes, you know . . . I didn't want you to leave without being sure. I . . ." he choked.

All that was best in his nature shone in his face.

Anthony grasped his hands.

"Yes, yes, all right for always, Vincent."

"Let's swear it," said the German looking dramatic and sentimental but earnest as ever.

"The same old Vincent," said Anthony laughing. Then he grew silent. "But we'll call it an oath." They exchanged grips again.

Just then Faith returned. She also smiled. The little bag was very heavy and as she gave it to Anthony she said, "I see you are leaving with more than you brought."

"Are you sorry?" he asked.

"No," she said. She brought her hands up half-way to her breast tensely and then let them fall.

"No, I'll tell you something. It belongs to you!" Then she turned and began to gather the silver together on the table. It bore the Bonny-feather mark.

He saw his chests go out. "Did you put the madonna in, Faith?" he asked just to be sure. She had always looked after his things. His voice suddenly sounded boyish again.

"In the big one with the books."

For an instant he caught her eyes burning at him over the table like wells of night. Then she blew out the candles.

He and Vincent stumbled down the steps together. The rain was over but clouds were still scudding across the moon. The courtyard was awash with writing shadows. He stood looking at it for the last time. The fountain dripped musically like a faint bell. As he and Vincent turned into the street the only light in all the harbour was on the *Wampanoag*. It moved very quietly. They were bringing her up to her anchor.

Anthony remembered the Darsena that day that he and Father Xavier had first come to the Casa da Bonnyfeather. All the busy life of the place, the bells, the voices, and the ships had departed. Something had dragged them away as if upon an invisible tide. The tide was ebbing from these shores. He, too, felt it tonight. It clutched him strongly. He was going out with it. He would not remain here looking at the past. It and Mr. Bonnyfeather would remain closed up together in the room with the misty walls.

Here just on this corner he had stood as a little boy first looking at the bright, new world. Right here Father Xavier had caught the orange that he had shared with him. How sweet it had tasted then. Now he would catch the whole orange for himself, the whole round world of it, press it to his lips and drain it dry. It was only the rind of it that was bitter. "Golden fruit of the Hesperides growing in the west, I shall find the bough." On the quay he parted with Vincent.

Two bearded Yankee sailors rowed him out to the *Wampanoag*. They looked at him curiously, sitting in the stern sheets with a coat-of-many-capes falling over his shoulders. He had bought a knitted cap for the voyage and under this his hair, now just beginning to turn brown, struggled out about his cheeks. His eyes looked widely into the darkness and his lips were parted with happy expectation. He had seemed very tall and straight as he stood for a moment on the thwart. There was something pleasant and strong about him. Something of the sweetness that had been Maria and the passionate strength of Denis Moore, a wide, clear, Scotch forehead and a provoking Irish smile. The man at the stroke oar winked at him as they shoved off.

"Be you the young gentleman we're takin' to Havaner?" he asked.

"Yes, do you want to go there?"

The man laughed and spat over the side.

"Not that we're ever axed. But westward bound *is* homeward bound, and that suits *me*." He brought the boat around with a long sweep under the stern.

"Ho, it does, does it?" said Captain Jorham looking over the taffrail and lowering a lantern so that it cast a smudge of light on the black water. "Wall then, lay forward with ye, and bring the anchor to the peak. Stand by to cast loose on the jibs. Did ye slush them blocks like I told ye? Belay your jaw tackle now, and no stampin' and cater-waulin' round the capstan. Pipe down and a quiet getaway. Pass the word for that again. Mind *ye*, Collins."

"Aye, aye," muttered the sailor, and went forward.

"Ye'd best go below now for a while," said the captain to Anthony. "Yer dunnage hez been stowed in the cabin and Jane's made the star-board bunk up for ye. Ye'll be snug enough. Don't mind her. She do snore."

Anthony went below. A lantern was burning and cast a dim radiance over the place. His chests were already neatly lashed to the stanchions. He started to hang up some things. Just then over the chest marked "Jane" one panel of the closed bunk opened and the head of Mrs. Jorham in a night-cap looked out. She pointed her lips.

"That's right," she said, "that's yours. Elisha sleeps over there behind tother shutters. This is mine. But don't mind me. I'm used to it. I'm glad to have you with us." She beamed on him, pointed her lips, and closed the panel.

He sat down and laughed silently. She reminded him of a picture of a toucan he had once seen, "extraordinary female bird walled in." What a beak it was! The thought of Elisha and Jane billing and cooing through that panel sent him off again. He lay back and enjoyed himself thoroughly. He felt the anchor thump gently. Ropes dragged on deck. Then through the side of the ship came mysteriously the low laughter of ripples as she began to glide. He laid his ear to the planks rejoicing in that hushed, half-merry and semi-sad chantey of farewell. "Good-bye, Livorno." Feet stamped over his head.

Half an hour later his now sleepy reverie was disturbed by Captain Jorham lighting a rank pipe at the lantern.

"Ye can come on deck now. We're out o' the Darsena and passin' the molo. Now's the rub." He stumped on deck with Anthony. The brig was slipping along very quietly in a following wind with nothing but her jibs set.

"They don't stand out like a squaresail against the sky," said the captain, eyeing the molo with its row of cannon and the flagstaff still bare before sunrise. "In ten minutes we'll be by. The tide's with us."

Suddenly Philadelphia emerged from the galley beating a pan. "Breakfus is re-ady!"

"God *dang* ye!" howled the captain plunging at him and smothering the pan. They watched the shore breathlessly. There was a spurt of fire on the sea wall by the molo . . .

"*One, two, three, four, five, six,*" counted the captain.

Bang, drifted to them the report of the sentry's musket.

"Make sail," he ordered. "Over two thousand yards. We'll make it, Mr. Adverse."

The *Wampanoag* surged forward. Both her masts were now blossoming out sail after sail. As yet there was nothing more from the fort. Then they saw some lanterns glimmer behind the embrasures in the morning twilight. The captain gave the ship a sudden wide yaw to port.

Flash, flash, flash. Along the molo smoke and thunder. The round shot smacked just to starboard and astern. Captain Elisha whistled as he twisted the spokes of the big wheel again and brought the *Wampanoag* back on her course.

"The trick is not to spill more'n half your wind," said he calmly.

"They are old Spanish pieces, captain," said Anthony.

"Aye, aye," said he, "and sleepy gunners behind 'em."

Flash, bang, smack.

"Kind o' vicious about it, be'n't they? But the stern of a ship ain't much to hit at nigh a mile in the glimmerin' dawn. Tide hasn't half ebbed yet and we'll keep our backside pinted at 'em clear over the bar."

"Lay aloft and douse them sails down, all hands. Philly, God dang ye, buckets, buckets!"

"The canvas is still wet from the rain last night, sir, isn't it?" asked Anthony.

"Yep," said the captain looking not too pleased. Then he laughed. "By God, ye're right, young man, ye're a cool one! . . . Belay that," he bellowed. "Collins, h'ist the grand old gridiron, let 'em see what they're shootin' at."

Well out from the lee of the land, the ship gathered way rapidly as she flashed down the roads with a bone in her teeth and the morning light tingeing her topsails. It was a long and lucky shot that would catch her now! But the French were evidently annoyed and continued to burn powder.

Thus with the fort thundering behind her and the Stars and Stripes snapping at her peak the *Wampanoag* rushed forward into the open sea.

END OF VOLUME ONE

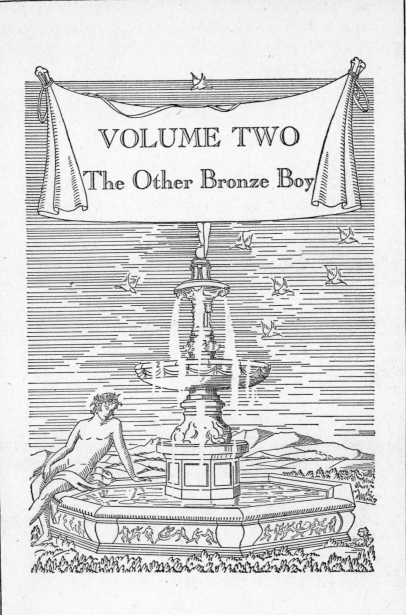

VOLUME TWO

The Other Bronze Boy

VOLUME TWO

The Other Bronze Boy

BOOK FOUR

*In Which Several Images
Travel Together*

CHAPTER TWENTY-FOUR

THE TABLE OF THE SUN

THAT great continental knee that curves southward to thrust the leg of Europe into the boot of Italy also encloses its gulf with a twinkling garter of mountains. These are not always clearly to be seen, but once glimpsed are provocative beyond most vistas, even if the traveller is an experienced one. In winter and other doubtful seasons the gulf hides itself in rain, or mists which sweep down like the swirling skirts of cosmic dancers from the slopes of the Maritime Alps.

But in early summer before a sirocco blows it is quite another thing. Then the sky over the gulf is turquoise, and the Mediterranean Homeric blue. By night the planets appear to lower themselves and burn nearer to the earth, and the stars to march higher as they do in tropic latitudes. Dawn comes from Italy, and if you are so lucky or so wise as to be on deck at that early hour, you need have no fear of an anticlimax in your destination, for before you lies Genoa rising unbelievable, white marble terrace above white marble; red tiles, churches, towers, villas, orchards, and castles ringed in by a noble amphitheatre of hills.

It was thus that Anthony Adverse first beheld it from the deck of the *Wampanoag* one summer morning while the ship's cutwater slipped contentedly through the untroubled seas. Never since his first bright sight of the world from the top of the tree at the convent had he seen anything quite so beautiful. Something of that first, fresh exaltation now returned to him as he leaned over the rail, gazing his eyes full.

They were tacking in slowly against a land breeze, now on a wide reach to port and now close hauled to windward, while the crew slowly took in sail. The sweet, heavy scent of orange groves and the intangible coolness of jasmine and new-mown grass rolled to him across the water. Only now, after nearly an hour of light, the olive orchards were beginning to stand out greyly amid the brighter green of the pink-topped oleanders.

The light widened and the sea grew bluer. Just a few minutes before it had been dark violet. How could he ever sleep; miss a moment of it? Why did men have to die and leave a world like this? Life could not be long enough on a star so beautiful. He wondered if Captain Jorham, who was at the wheel while the steersman helped take in sail, saw or felt anything similar.

Philadelphia called them below to breakfast.

Anthony had slept like a child every night since leaving Livorno. His senses were keen, yet soothed and washed limpid by the clear sea air. There was a tang and a zest about everything—about the movements of his arms, of his hands and fingers. He could feel the most delicate surface texture of things. In the quiet ship he could hear the slightest sound. Captain Jorham looked at him and grinned.

"Feelin' pretty keen, eh? I used ter myself. Glad to get away?"

Anthony had to admit that he was. All the little objects of furniture, houses; people that had annoyed him; the pain of familiarity with a thousand things that he wished instinctively to avoid but that had possessed some irksome claim upon him had vanished. He was no longer accountable to them. He need be sorry for nothing. Just now he was too happy to regret even those he loved—had loved! What a magical thing was this, the mere transporting of the body!

He within, he felt, remained the same. He himself had not moved. It was merely the outside world that had shifted. The encumbrances about him had vanished.

So he sat in the cabin that morning inhaling his coffee slowly, feeling the surprisingly healthy warmth of it, watching the green water slip by outside the porthole and enjoying one of the noblest of illusions immensely. Travel had set him free.

The blocks rattled on the deck as the ship came about again. Mrs. Jorham galvanized by the smell of coffee opened her panel and thrust her head, dressed in brown curl-papers and a night-cap, through the narrow aperture. Captain Jorham, seating himself upon the chest marked "Jane," began to feed his wife biscuits and bacon. From the biscuits from time to time he gallantly knocked out the weevils. It was a sign that he was in the best of good humour.

"'Strordinary female bird walled in," thought Anthony.

The lips of Mrs. Jorham pointed, came out of the slot, and surreptitiously pecked her husband on his leather cheek. Then she looked at Anthony and rearranged her cap. Properly embarrassed by such intimate domestic details and endearments before a stranger, she smiled, pecked her husband once again, and closed the panel with an overpowering air of virtue and dignity. Throughout the entire meal her manner had been that of a lady-Putnam. That was it. She was not a toucan, she was a Putnam! Anthony saw that even on shipboard, in the intimate presence of strangers and of the ocean itself, Mrs. Jorham contrived to remain elegant and refined. It was a perfection which knocked out the weevils in their own dust. It was "Putnamism." Captain Jorham, who participated in it distantly by marriage, was proud of it, too. He set down the mess-kid in which only the wriggling weevils remained, triumphantly.

After Philadelphia cleared the board the captain took some papers from his desk and spreading them out on the table with a knowing air, dipped his pen, and beckoned to Anthony. As he sat down beside him he noticed that Captain Jorham not only reeked of tobacco but was also redolent of rum.

"Sign here," said the captain, without previous palaver.

Anthony leaned over the paper, which he found to be a roster of the crew. The captain's stubby finger pointed to the vacant line marked *mate*.

"Died o' smallpox at Lisbon," vouchsafed Captain Jorham.

But Anthony still hesitated with McNab's first lesson in mind.

"It's all fair and above board," continued Captain Jorham a little anxiously. "Didn't yer old man tell ye about it before ye left? He and I arranged it all before supper that night. Ye're to be carried as second mate. That'll keep the Frenchies from askin' any questions about ye at Genoway. I'll tell ye how it is. It's mighty ticklish work these days bein' a neutral and tryin' to make ports and pick up cargoes with the French lordin' it on land and the king's navee on the water. It all depends pretty much on what cargo ye carry. But if I can git a nice cargo of fryin' ile over to Havaner it'll sell high. That's what I'm pushin' into Genoway fer. There's a sight of it piled up there now. Cost nothin'! It's worth the chance. It would go plum against the grain to run empty to Havaner. I'm layin' to pick up some fine blocks of marble for ballast, tew. I expect even the British ul have a hard time calalatin' *that* as contraband. And the French 'll let us clear all right if we don't have English refugees aboard. Na-ow if ye just sign on as mate, between ye and me sort of *ex-officio*—no wages, of course,—ye can pass tolerable fer Yankee born. Better say Virginny, though. Your talk's a lot more like that. Ye don't use your nose proper to Bosting way. I'll tell ye another thing, tew, if the British board us at sea it may save yer bein' pressed, ye bein' a mate. Look here!"

He pointed out on the roll the names of six seamen with the notation, "Pressed at Sea off Ushant, February 6, 1796, by H.M.S. Ariadne."

"A fast frigate or she'd never have done it. Most chasers we just sink in the blue, but there's a few on 'em can overhaul us with a followin' wind. That leaves us six hands forward to git home on. Old 'uns all. That English snotty that boarded us did know how to pick his men. Even the babies now have practice in that, dang 'em! Still it ain't such a bad berth bein' a mate on board with a lady in the cabin."

More than convinced by this time Anthony signed. The captain looked pleased and relieved. He opened up "Elisha" and taking out a bottle poured out a double tot.

"Wall, *mister*," he said with a twinkle, "here's luck to ye, and a fast first run."

The panel opened slightly as the lady-Putnam sniffed through the orifice.

Anthony saw trouble come into the woman's eyes. Her mouth trembled a little, but she said nothing. At last with a look of unhappy resignation she closed herself in again.

The captain drew his hand across his mouth and went on deck. As the ship beat in toward the harbour he descended twice again for a spiritual interview with "Elisha." Before they passed the Molo Vecchio he was in a genially prophetic humour and moved with a superbly confident roll. It was in this semi-rapt condition that the skipper felt himself most able to cope with a bargaining world. "Well iled." But the precise amount of lubricant necessary to fill the *Wampanoag* with a profitable cargo was hard to gauge. There was one curious thing about it, however. Liquor had brought the captain luck. A cargo of parrots once proved remunerative beyond all sober expectation. He gave a slight hitch to his trousers.

"Goin' ashore, *mister?*" he asked with a grin. That a young gentleman like Anthony should be his mate tickled him immensely. In his present mood the joke seemed colossal. "Get yer togs on."

Anthony dived into his chest hastily to get his purse and coat. As he opened the chest for the first time since leaving, he found a letter addressed to him in the engraved strokes of Mr. Bonnyfeather. He opened it very impatiently now and read hastily. He reproached himself for this, but with the early morning noises of the new city coming through the port he could not control his impatience.

It was a prolix letter of instruction how to proceed about the collection of the debt. Mr. Bonnyfeather had apparently foreseen all possible contingencies. They were under nine heads. Bother! This could wait till Havana. How coldly it was written. The old man addressed him as if he were nothing but an agent. There were several enclosures, some drafts on Spanish bankers, and two other letters.

Il Signore Carlo Cibo, Regla, Habana, Cuba.

That could wait, too. How cramped the old man's signature was getting now. Well, his hand . . . Then his eyes fell on a postscript.

> P. S.   I have not cast this epistle in terms of affection lest I should have no eyes left to see with as I write it. Wherever you are when you read this, remember the hand of him who writ it is (as ever in the past) extended to you in blessing (and even from the grave). I have put this in your chest myself. Do you look under your great-coat for further remembrance, my son. Thine,
> J. B.

He sat down on his bunk holding the letter which swam grey before him. How had it been possible for him to forget all past benefits in a few hours? He felt he should like to stab himself to make the hard heart in his breast capable of feeling as it should.

Yet, perhaps gratitude was like sorrow, you could not feel it all at once or it would overwhelm you. He looked at the open chest. He could see the madonna wrapped up there in something that made her look like a mummy. Preserved, eh? So the past was still with him. But he would not disturb her now. And he would look under the great-coat later on. He could not bear to receive anything more from that hand "extended even from the . . ." Oh, for just one day without any past behind it and no future before! The old man must still be well in Livorno.

Livorno? Where was that? Was there such a place? It was the noise and smell of Genoa that were coming in through the port.

He roused himself. In order to act it would be necessary to shake off the past, to remember it only in its proper place. Be grateful, yes! But not now, not this morning—in Genoa. He closed the lid of the chest with a bang right on the nose of the madonna and all the rest.

But he had forgotten his purse. He had to open the chest again for *that*. As he put back Mr. Bonnyfeather's letter which he had unconsciously clutched in one hand all the while, the other enclosure fell out before him.

To the Reverend Father Claude Aquaviva Xavier, S.J.
At the Palazzo Brignole, Genoa.

A.A., Deliver this in person. 'Tis the old summer school of the
Jesuits in the suburb Albaro. Fail not in this if time permit.

So Father Xavier was in Genoa! Here was the past with a vengeance. How long it had been since he had thought of him! He had
sent him his last childish letter to Naples years ago, and he had not
answered the last from the priest. Meant to, of course. Naples?
These priests of the suppressed Jesuits moved about now from pillar
to post. Probably Father Xavier had had no easy time of it. His
heart smote him. He might have written him. But it was just after
Faith . . . damn it all! How much there was in that chest! Well,
he would try to see him. The direction was in Mr. Bonnyfeather's
hand, his last request as it were. This time he closed the chest deliberately and locked it, clapped on his hat and went on deck. Captain
Jorham eyed him.

"It ain't sea-vility for the mate to keep the captain waitin', mister,"
he said as they stepped into the boat.

Philadelphia, grinning and sweating, rowed them through the
crowded shipping of the old semi-circular harbour. Looking up,
Anthony saw the tricolour waving on the massive Fortress of Sperone
towering above them on Monte Peraldo. Bugle calls floated down
faintly. Here and there along the miles of walls inland the sun glinted
on cannon or flashed on bayonets. All the churches were built of black
and white marble. There seemed to be any number of their striped
façades and towers.

They landed at the Porta Lanterna and it was four mortal hours
before the French officers in charge of the port were finished examining papers and quizzing Anthony who had to translate for the
captain.

It was not easy to convince the military authorities that a neutral
ship was not a legitimate prize of war. They rowed out and made
sure she was empty. But they looked disappointed. Captain Jorham
had cause to be grateful for his "mate." Finally with his papers
reluctantly signed permitting him to purchase "ship's stores, olive-oil,
marble, and statuary," he was allowed to go.

"Stat-*uary*," rumbled the captain, "stat*oo*-ary?"

Anthony laughed. The French had been slow to understand about
the marble blocks for ballast. Statuary was made out of marble,
marble was statuary. Meldrun! let them buy them both, neither was
contraband. The captain kept looking at the document.

"By God, mister, I got an idear!" he suddenly roared.

It was some minutes before Anthony's back stopped stinging between the shoulders as they walked along.

Genoa was a welter of small, crooked streets with narrow, high houses, hunchbacked, twisted, and set at all angles. A perpetual dank shadow lived here as if at the bottom of an old well. Even the stones seemed to be rotten. An odour as of old cheese wrapped in a goatskin weighed on the senses.

The streets swarmed with half-naked urchins, women with baskets of fish or equally redolent dirty clothes on their heads. Soldiers slouched by on unmilitary errands, and every fifth or sixth person was a dark, scurvy-looking priest with a sallow, grimy countenance. Here, about the Porto Franco, where their errands lay that morning, Anthony could scarcely believe that he was really within the walls of the noble city set in green hills that he had seen from the ship.

They passed under endless arcades where the plaster walls had turned black with ages of grime. Festering piles of rubbish and garbage, rag piles, and unspeakable refuse piled against the walls. Yet between the outward-facing arches along the curb the merchants of macaroni and polenta kept their stalls, especially where the sword-like streaks of sunlight descended upon their heads.

The quantity of oil which the captain desired seemed unheard of. Even with his new mate to do the talking, the bargaining took them well past noon. The Ligurian dialects were often difficult, and the Genoese laughed at Anthony's Tuscan. When at last all was completed it took another hour or two to assemble carts to haul the jars to the quay. Captain Jorham was too wise to take his eyes off his purchases for a minute, or to pay until the last jar wrapped in straw ropes was safely deposited in the official confines of the Porto Franco. Then he was forced to see that the custom officials there had good cause to remember him.

But even at that the captain could rub his hands with satisfaction. Since the French had come, trade in Genoa was at a standstill. For that reason he was able to purchase supplies and provisions for the voyage at less than cost. His eyes sparkled, and to Anthony's alarm he showed some signs of being about to clap his newly acquired mate on the back for the second time that day.

Under ordinary circumstances Captain Elisha would have now returned to the ship to take his grub and save his pennies, but the liquor he had taken that morning was already dying out in him by noon. And he had secretly embarked on a long sipping wassail which engaged him for about four months every three years, when he began to hear the stealthy approach of certain footsteps overtaking him out of the past. It was his peculiar habit during the approach of the shadow feet, to mix wine with rum and porter into a potion known as "A Dog's Nose" for the reason that there are no whiskers on it and it drips. Rum and porter he had, but little or no wine.

Also he desired to purchase marble for ballast and to sell that usually unprofitable item at Havana for tombstones. It could be replaced there by ordinary stones, said to be abundant in Cuba. As a cautious measure he desired holes to be drilled in those marble blocks to secure them when once aboard. Then he was pleased with his "mate" for slinging the lingo so well. He intended to use such abilities further.

For above all there was the great "idear."

This was nothing less than to take full advantage of the permission to purchase statuary, so accidentally conferred upon him that morning, and to fill the vacant bunks in the fo'c'sle of the *Wampanoag* with "idols," to wit: various examples of life-size ecclesiastical statuary, saints, madonnas, and bambinos manufactured at Genoa in vast quantities cheaply, and hence doubtless salable at substantial profit to the less-artistic faithful in Havana. Indeed, the churches in Cuba, as Captain Elisha assured himself, although his data was based on only a few visits of irreverent curiosity, were lamentably bare of "idols." Some Protestant qualms assailed him, but the idea he felt was truly inspired.

Standing on a sunny corner he mopped his brow with a green duster while all this passed rapidly and somewhat confusedly through his troubled old mind. He was hungry, likewise he was very thirsty. Mrs. Jorham was safely "on board." Well, he would get her a present. He would get himself plenty of wine, see the ta-own and make his macaroni mate do the talking.

"Come on, mister, let's find victuals and drink. Lead the way. Captain's and owner's charges."

Anthony was willing. He had been afraid they would go back to the ship. Now he might be able to get time off to see the town—and Father Xavier.

He hailed a French officer passing across the way, an amiable fellow, who led them gayly along a decent, little side street under wrought-iron balconies into a trellised courtyard covered by one huge vine. A party of French officers sat at a big stone table in the centre, their sabretaches, swords and sashes heaped up like tangled trophies on the stone benches. There was a litter of bottles, half-devoured salads, cheeses, loaves, and the remnant of a fine ham garnished with cloves on the wine-stained table-cloth. Corks popped and flew about with oaths. They raised a shout when their comrade appeared. Captain Elisha's eyes brightened. He sensed distraction.

He and Anthony sat down in a corner. A woman with a red petticoat flapping about her bare calves came and placed a small wooden table before them. On this she set a bowl of grape vinegar, a dish of fresh young garlic, salt and a brown loaf.

"Onions," remarked Captain Jorham, "are a *sovran* remedy for scurvy."

He forthwith fell to and proceeded to eat the entire bowl of garlic, dipping each pearl-like bulb in the vinegar, sprinkling a little salt on it, and then plumping it into his mouth where it disappeared slowly, wagging its green tail nearly to the end. But just before the end, each tail was bitten off at precisely the same distance and spat out upon the floor. After the "onions" he inserted a piece of bran bread off the edge of his knife and rammed it home as if to keep the bullets in place. He looked about him complacently and noted that he was sitting in the centre of a demi-lune of tender garlic tips all pointing outward. He counted them; one to forty-three.

"Scurvy's an awful thing if it gets to you," he said, "makes your fangs loosen." He spat experimentally through his own front teeth again. They were firm. Still he looked a little uneasy about something.

"Liquor, mister," he said, "somethin' hot and stirrin'! I feel them onions prominent in my midst. *Ugh!* that's better!" The captain plugged with his spoon thoughtfully. "I heard of a schooner from Bermudy what started oncet with a cargo of cedar casks and onions for the whalin' grounds off the South-Shetlands. Them onions was sealed in they casks to keep. That was where trouble started. Afore that ship reached Jamaiky the casks swelled up like a cargo o' new-fangled French balloons. Onion gas! The ship went skiddin' along on her side. They couldn't tack her. They had to stave in them casks or they'd a floated clear o' the water and made leeway clear to Afriky. Well, sir, I'm beginnin' to feel like that schooner now. *Whiroosh!*"

One of the French officers, a man with a long, red beard smeared with salad oil and particles of cheese, looked at him in disgust.

"I'm floatin'," said Captain Elisha, "I'm risin' like bakers' bread. I'm like a bloater when he's tickled, a dead cachalot in the sun. Nothin' but strong cordial will belay it." He reached for the vinegar. Anthony stopped him alarmed. Just then the woman returned with a jug and a large smoking dish. Captain Elisha applied himself to the jug. His throat rippled.

"Coolin'," he said, "but nigh as sour as vinegar." He put it down. Anthony tasted the wine. It was Lachryma Christi. His teeth went on edge. He ordered the sweetest thing available, Mountain-Malaga. The captain gulped a glass of it. He still rumbled but looked more comfortable.

"That's the antidote, mister, now let's sample the grub. I'm blown up fer full capacity."

It was a large basin of rice and boiled chicken. They polished this off between them. It was enough for Anthony. He ordered some muscat of which he was very fond. The captain was captivated with it. After two bottles he looked around on a new world. The "onions" were hopelessly buried.

"Na-ow I allow I'm beginnin' to be hungry." He looked at the empty dish regretfully and at his mate expectantly. Anthony called the woman and ordered further refreshment. Having now some gauge upon the captain's capacity and being enthusiastic with burgundy himself, he commanded a feast.

The captain cut himself a large quid of tobacco, which he stuffed into a round place in his cheek, while he continued to look on approvingly. The woman somewhat awed departed. They heard her giving excited directions in the kitchen. Meanwhile the captain extracted what solace he could from the tobacco, evolving in the process great quantities of saliva. Presently he had attracted the notice of the party of French officers who began to bet on his aim.

At some distance on the pavement before Captain Jorham a small lizard was basking innocently in the sun. The captain's front teeth were bared from time to time and immediately afterward the universe of the lizard dissolved in brown juice. It moved each time like a flash. The eye could not follow it. At a distance of about four feet nearer the wall, and farther away from the captain, another and browner lizard seemed to appear. It was about twenty feet to the wall.

The bets began to become interesting. At each saurian remove the stakes became higher and the odds against the captain rose. But the major with the red beard and salad oil, looking at the mahogany tinge of the captain's teeth, bet a meagre fortune upon him. The major was an artilleryman. Two more shifts of the devastated lizard confirmed the major's faith touchingly. He now staked his watch and placed it on the table. The trajectory he hastily calculated was then about four and a half metres, allowing for the curve of the parabola. It was a long chance. But the captain fetched the lizard. The unfortunate, and by now suspicious, animal paused once more, but this time near a hole in the wall. Whatever happened it had only two inches to flinch, and it was now nearly twenty feet away from the captain. The latter ruminated slowly, accumulating ammunition with a lacklustre look. The stakes were by this time reckless even from a military standpoint. Captain Elisha straightened himself, every eye upon him. Suddenly the lizard was washed into its hole. A yellow rainbow had collapsed accurately upon it.

The consequent enthusiasm was loud and prolonged. The major, who had won a month's pay, insisted that the captain should join him and his companions in celebrating so remarkable an event. The artillery, he maintained, had been gloriously upheld. Anthony participated in the reflected glory. The whole party gathered about the big stone table while Anthony translated for the captain the round of congratulatory toasts that followed. Outwardly unperturbed but inwardly ravished, Captain Jorham sat grey and bleak as Plymouth Rock in a gale of laughter. Nevertheless he was adequate to the international occasion.

"Confusion to the British."

The table roared back at him with delight. The major would have embraced him but even Captain Jorham renigged at the salad oil beard. Instantly he was more popular with the others, captains and lieutenants who had only moustaches. In the offing much more food now appeared. The captain resumed his seat and began to feed. Between dishes they plied him with wine. He drank all and everything, setting down his empty glass each time with obvious regret. For the first time in his life, surrounded by enthusiastic friends, he became entirely gay. Into the frozen swamp of his feelings burst a warm April light. He began to croak and to bellow

"Yankee skipper comin' down the river
Ho, ho, ho, ho *HO*."

"Incroyable, magnifique! Allons, enfants de la patrie!"

The little courtyard rocked with song. Taking the cue from his mate the captain waved his glass, too. The woman in red petticoats stood by loyally. Shouting something to a mysterious "Batcheetcha" in the kitchen she produced a stage thunder there amid the pans. Things were pounded in a pestle. The two timbres of sizzling denoting roasting and frying arose simultaneously. Chickens died noisily several times. The major was a generous man. Cloths whisked and dishes clicked. Everybody began to eat and drink all over again as if their stomachs had expanded as the generous wine enlarged their souls.

They ate tagliarini, they ate ravioli, they ate cocks' combs and sheep-kidney minced with mutton chops and liver. They imbibed tender pieces of shredded veal fried and heaped upon a vast platter like a miraculous draught of shrimps. They ate chickens and spaghetti and mushrooms and ducks. When all the others were satiated Captain Jorham continued. He polished off a heap of sausages fried with garlic, topped that with a dish of green figs, and washed it all into place like a glacial drift that finds the worst is over and warmer times have come again—with waves of Madeira.

A happy silence compounded of satiety and pure human affability settled down upon the party. They looked at one another with complete approval and admiration. A Gascoigne major whose forefathers had been petty, brawling, and carousing nobles gazed into the eyes of Captain Elisha whose grandfather was an English regicide, and belched little nothings into his ear.

"Surely," thought Anthony, looking at a rat-like quartermaster opposite him, "no more gallant band of heroes has ever assembled to do honours to strong souls from the sea like Captain Jorham and his mate."

It mattered not that nothing which Captain Jorham said could be understood intellectually. What was the intellect? Indeed, where was it? The very sounds the old sailor made were enormously popular. He who had overwhelmed the lizard! Mark you, at six metres! When he told a joke and laughed, the courtyard howled. Two brown, dirty little boys sat in a crook of the great vine looking down from the pergola above. They chattered like little monkeys with their arms about each other watching a feast of lions. Yet even they, Anthony felt, and all the rest he thought felt with him, were part of this pleasant perfect society. To be approved, included, and considered. Yes, everything was perfect. Everybody was delightful. He was. They all were.

He had never drunk quite so much or enjoyed it so greatly before. Wine ran in his blood. He was absolved from all responsibility. The world, though slightly hazy, sparkled like a thicket in the sunshine. The pattern of vine leaves and the shadows on the floor under the trellis were revealed to him as beautiful beyond hope of imitation.

For the first few bottles he had still felt himself as a spectator, at times even a disapproving one. Then, as he had returned again and again to the scarlet glass, he seemed to emerge completely into another atmosphere. Delight, warmth, a delicious lightness and a complete identification with a perfect world ensued. He was convinced that this was the way things really were. A sober vision simply did not reveal them or put one in touch. Everything now became very clear, a little enlarged. The edges of things were framed in amber and the vistas beyond became supernal; bathed in auriferous light. Never had he felt so at home with his fellows as with these men in this courtyard. All of these people, all of them, men that he had never seen before today, were friends. The capacity for trouble had been removed from the universe. He was one in a brotherhood of a paradisiacal company.

Wine, the sun and vines had done this. The sun? He looked up at the sun through the vine leaves. This delicious wash of grape shade and shifting light under the trellis was like being at the bottom of a lake, a lake of air. So he was! He remembered that now. And it was in this kind of light under the plane tree that he had first come to life. No one could remember original darkness. He remembered the full, simple, unquestioning joy of light now. The clear light and the warmth and joy that had become part of him, that was still in him. Nothing could ever destroy that. It was what he was. Like the face in the miniature, that face! He crowed like a child again, moving his hands and feet slowly, feeling them. He thought; he dreamed.

It was the sun that brought all of this food and wine and joy out of the earth. That gave light, that made the eyes live. In that light moved shadows, men and things that ordinarily seemed to be to the light what shadows were, projections of something else. You could never quite understand what was throwing these shadows when you were sober. You forgot the origin of them and so you did not see things, and men themselves. But now, now he felt near to these fellow beings and things at last. He could see them as they actually were. You could draw close and know them. The darkness between them was gone. In the sunlight all were of one substance. All were part of this glory of heat and light beating down into the little court-yard. The very food and wine they had eaten came from it. They ate it and it became part of them. All were of one substance, men and things. All of it came out of the light.

Everybody was always eating and drinking everywhere. He longed to tell them about it but he could not. It was the sun that laid this daily table around which humanity gathered. Or something that made the sun. . . . He rose to his feet overpowered by so sublime a thought, striving for words. Only thick, lowing sounds came from his lips. He could not tell them. They shouted back at him but he did not understand. He felt sad. He wandered off somewhere. The world seemed to open out before him. The light became brighter. It flashed; streamed.

A vast table whose gleaming cloth stretched out like a white road to the horizon lay spread out before him thronged by all the nations of men. He could see them coming and going. Beyond the horizon there was nothing, nothing but clouds rising out of an abyss. He too could draw near to the table and partake with everybody. He dragged his feet a few steps farther and seemed to be standing on the table himself. He sat down on it. The table-cloth shone like the sun on water, dazzled.

He did not want to eat after all. He felt dizzy. He put his hand to his head and leaned against something. An hour passed, another. After a while the horizon cleared enough to see again. The monster table of the sun had vanished. He was sitting on the curb before the door of the restaurant looking up the Strada Balbi, long, white, blinding and silent in the late, hot afternoon.

Oh, yes, he knew now where he was. It was Genoa! He had been thinking about something. About a sacrament? Something like that.

An ancient love feast? Oh, well, nonsense! How long had he been sitting here? Where was the captain? They had something to do. What day was it now? But what did he care about time! He turned and walked back into the courtyard steadying himself. He had a great drink of water. It tasted flat. The woman was laughing at him. Everything was clearer now. He must have slept a long time. Only a sense of tremendous well-being and a little irresponsibility remained. After a while the floor grew steady. Bon!

Captain Jorham lay sleeping, leaning back in a chair propped against the wall. A fly was crawling over his bald head slowly.

Those princes, those best of all good fellows, where were they? Vanished. Yet there was something tangible about them. The major had paid the bill. " 'For the honour of the French Army,' signore, he said," thus the woman pocketing Anthony's coin. He felt relieved. All that for a tip! Now he knew he was sober.

Inside the skull over which the fly was crawling the captain was not really asleep. His brain had merely slipped the cogs of time backward some twenty years and transported him hence. He was sitting on a bench before his door in Scituate, Massachusetts. Just across the bay over there was Abner Lincoln's house and mill by the stream. The mill wheel was turning. The swallows dipped and left rings in the shallows. It was sunset. Overhead Jane was putting their child to bed. He could hear her singing and the feet of the child padding about on the floor. Now his wife was humming and rocking the baby monotonously. A note of foreboding crept into her voice. Suddenly the mill across the stream started to grind. It seemed to be uttering the letter "R" for minutes at a time. It was grinding up something. His child! Run, do something about it! If only he could move his feet. *"Rrrrrr."* He reached up and brushed the fly out of his ear.

Better! The mill had stopped. Dreaming? Why wake up? How happy he and Jane had been until . . . . let him hear the child's feet again. Dead! Oh, yes, he had forgotten! He was afraid he *might* hear them again, at night. No, no, not dead! Yes, *dead!* Good lord! "Do not cry, Jane. We will go to the cemetery tomorrow." But it is already tomorrow. "Come, you can take your knitting." He started for the cemetery, and woke with his feet slipping. After a few minutes he remembered. The child was dead years ago. Poor little baba! But he must forget that, not hear the feet, on the deck, anywhere. . . . Shove it down, put the lid on it, live only now. "Remember, Elisha, it is pleasant here now, better now, better *now*," insisted one part of him to the other. "You can always take a drink and make it *now*. Take a drink, take a drink!" Captain Jorham arose from his chair roaring for liquor.

"This is the way I put soft shoes on my baby's feet, mister," he said as he downed a glass. "Can't hear 'em then." Anthony was sure the captain was still very drunk. Yet he looked sober.

They stayed the rest of the afternoon at the Café of St. Lawrence the Martyr. They had another little nap while it rained. Felt better, all well. The time seemed to have come to sally forth. The captain, Anthony was relieved to find, was now in a gracious Madeiran mood.

At six o'clock of a particularly fine June evening the City of Genoa was already beginning to bestir itself smoothly for the moonlight night that was to follow. After the shower it was very clear, cool. Long, deepening shadows lay across the streets. Yet the sky was suffused with the red light of the approaching sunset. The air was blue and sparkling, just exhilarating and soothing enough to be grateful as an aftermath to the wine which still warmed them. Responsibility had nobly died.

Scarcely caring where they were going, they threaded their way through a maze of streets so narrow that no vehicles could pass. It was far too late to think of going after the marble blocks. In the mood in which he found himself Captain Jorham was willing to go anywhere and readily fell in with Anthony's suggestion that they should visit Father Xavier in the suburbs. Afterwards they could have supper, more wine, return late, or make a night of it. Yes, the marble and statuary could go till tomorrow. Everything could wait until tomorrow. Just at present they were like two fish swimming indolently and without particular direction, suspended, and suspiring in a golden, liquid atmosphere.

Bell-jingling strings of mules going home, sedan chairs for hire, painted private chairs for the nobility preceded through the dark tunnels of streets by carriers with linen lanterns on poles, passed and crossed and recrossed each other in all directions as if a festa were going on. Tall, narrow houses frescoed in glowing colours with pictures of saints, gods, and angels rose all about them, flinging their balconies half-way across the street. Beneath streamed a medley of motley costumes whose weird, cloaked fashions and screaming colours blent with the voluble soft voices and grotesque street cries into the total spectacle of the life that thronged and flowed, gathered and dispersed, gestured and hurried onward.

It was with some difficulty that Anthony prevented the captain from climbing into a gorgeous but lousy sedan whose bearers kept turning up at every corner and offering themselves. God knows where they would have got to in that. He linked his arm through the captain's. He occasionally wobbled a little yet. Keeping a sharp eye on their pockets, they passed on. Suddenly they left behind them the zone of premature evening in the narrow streets and emerged by pure chance on the Strada Nuova where day was dying brilliantly.

The endless street stretched on up into the hills above, narrow, clean, lined with rows of marble fronts where a few lights were already beginning to twinkle on the balconies. The long rays of light struck along it like a cañon. Only illustrious people could live on a street like that. Beggars were out of place there even in Genoa.

They shook off a man with sore eyes who had followed them holding his inflamed lids apart. Calling a gay little carriage drawn by two mules with pompons and bells they left the beggar toiling and cursing after. The fat driver on the tasselled box was in no more hurry than his team. They trotted on indolently inland toward Albaro, rising every moment a little higher and gradually leaving the crowded port behind. It was now that to his great joy Anthony rediscovered the noble city which he had seen from the ship like a happy morning dream. All day he had lost it amid the narrow streets of the stinking water front.

Although the approach to the suburb of Albaro itself is through ribbon-like lanes giving entrance to long, silent villas painted with vast frescoes which the sea air has dimmed—subjects holy, profane, and grim—yet there are many spaces where the main road passes in an arc over crests and opens upon sweeping vistas of the heights above and the sea below.

It was a little after sunset when the mules and driver as if by mutual consent came to a halt at one of these spots. The breathing of the animals, gradually becoming more regular after the labour of the ascent, as they slowly and more slowly inhaled the restful quiet of the evening air, finally seemed to die away altogether and to become one with the silence of the evening. All in the carriage were in unconscious sympathy with this relaxing rhythm, and the process continued to penetrate even further into their minds as they looked about them.

Lofty hills with fortresses on their crags from which banners of evening mist were already flowing leapt above them. On the lower slopes white villas smouldered in the sunset, set deeply in an ever darkening green intaglio of gardens and lawns. The twelve miles of the city's defences streamed and tumbled like the wall of China across the heights. In the valleys of the Bsagnio and Polcevera an opalescent fog had already begun to gather. Out of it flowed the dark rivers under their bridges into the still flashing bay.

Genoa, the wide far-flung city, lay there at their feet, encircling the light-twinkling harbour with the beautiful curve of its white arms, gathering the ships to its breast from the ruined Chapel of S. Giovanni Battista on the rocky seashore to the Porta Lanterna. Beyond all this, limitless and smooth with distance, stretched the violet tables of the open sea. Westward it glowed with submarine fires that reflected themselves upon the sky, and as they cooled and went out, blotched the long horizon with glazed patches of floating scarlet veiled by narrow clouds touched by the lingering pencils of the sun. Slowly even these melted showing stars behind. It seemed now as if everything earthly were dissolving into the sky. It was like the hood over the Virgin's head, thought Anthony. Even the hills slowly expanded and blended into the same engulfing shadow that was swallowing the sea.

At the centre of all this dying world sat Anthony. Only the mules, the dim outline of the driver on the box above, and the captain beside him still remained outside of his mind as another reality. The wheels had for a while been holding him up, he felt, but soon he knew himself just to be floating in the body of the carriage on a sea of twilight. Then no carriage. He and the outside world merged. Or he held it all within him as a slowly darkening image. The place where his eyes ended and the world began had again been swept away. It was a timeless, spaceless levitation . . .

Only a moment ago his being extended thus had felt limitless. Now as darkness grew he was slowly withdrawing himself again into a point bounded by stars as they came out one by one and grew clearer. Soon he would be back within his head again. Something already had begun to remain outside.

The mules stirred. The carriage moved forward a few inches on solid ground. He looked down and saw his own hand on his knee and felt it. He looked around at the face of the captain. He also had lost himself Anthony could see.

His face had grown wide and peaceful, glimmering. The lines of stress and hard care and sorrow were relaxed on his forehead and cheeks. His lips framed themselves wonderfully about the smile of a younger man. Much had been forgotten and caressed away as though Elisha Jorham had once participated in vivid happiness and the vision remained, one which he only needed to be reminded of to resume.

"This is Elisha himself," thought Anthony. "I hope that he can see me as I am, too." He moved slightly. They looked at each other long and silently in the low twilight. They were both at home with, and comforted by the unspoiled glory of the world. That was an important discovery for friendship. Then the captain suddenly resumed the mask which experience had provided him. His face hardened.

"Well," said he, "what little thing happens next, mister? I'm trustin' my events to you now, see?"

"Nothing that matters much, sir, I suppose," replied Anthony shaking the stars out of his head.

"Wall, na-ow ye never can be sartain I calalate. Let's make sail anyway. We've got to be goin' somewhere."

The captain was getting sleepy. He began to nod shortly afterwards. A quarter of a mile farther brought them to the door of a small inn.

"I'll turn in here while you drive on and see yer friend," said Captain Elisha. "It's bed and not victuals I want now. But be sure to call fer me in the mornin' even if you make a night of it. That's orders, mister. Don't leave me stranded, mate," he added anxiously, "I can't swing the lingo, you know."

Anthony reassured him. He would call him for an early breakfast.

"Good! It's marble and statoo-ary tomorrow, and that may take longer than buyin' ile. They're never in any hurry around cemeteries." The captain yawned. "But you can't live that way; do business."

Anthony left him comfortable enough in a bedroom under the eaves where the moonlight was already beginning to filter through the tiles.

"Looks like one of Jane's crazy-quilts," murmured the captain fingering the covers dreamfully. "Say, mister . . . ."

But Anthony had already driven on.

CHAPTER TWENTY-FIVE

THE VILLA BRIGNOLE

HALF a mile across the valley from the inn Anthony was driving along the endless garden wall of the Palazzo Brignole. It had once been a summer school of the Jesuits but was long since deserted, as most of that suppressed order had fled to Russia or Poland. The hoofs of the mules echoed against the cracked and peeling stucco of the outbuildings in the empty moonlight. The driver turned in reluctantly enough through a rusty iron gate, and unhitching under a shed, began to make himself and his team as comfortable as the fleas would permit. Supper seemed remote. He was heard to wish fervently that il signore would not be long.

"An hour or two at most," replied Anthony, who then began to pick his way gingerly across a weedy terrace, fingering the letter to Father Xavier. The address upon it now seemed improbable, for in the moonlight he stumbled over piles of rubbish and old stable litter while tribes of owl-eyed cats fled wailing before him.

Even in Genoa Father Xavier could scarcely have found another dwelling which expressed so well the departed grandeur and the present desolation of his order. The vast uncompromising façade of the Palazzo Brignole stretched itself before Anthony on the crest of a series of terraces. Its flat face looked blindly at the moon as if it too were oblivious to change. Its lower apertures were stopped with rubbish like gagged mouths. From its upper windows the cracked and wrinkled shutters, like so many grey cataracts over innumerable eyes, told of nothing but seething darkness in the cells behind them. Two ruined arcades, extending from the house at right angles, stumbled with collapsing arches down the giant steps of the terraces and enclosed within their shattered arms the long approach that had once been a landscaped garden but was now a melancholy wilderness.

It seemed to Anthony as he looked up at the great house, from which not a light shone nor a sound emanated, that the garden was rushing down upon him over its arcades in tangled masses of shrubbery and flowing outlines of serpentine vines. It was a river of dark vegetation in sinister spate. What made it worse was that it had once been meant to be as artificial as a canal and neat as a priest with a new tonsure. It was some moments before he could force himself to follow the cats and plunge into its moon-shadowed mazes toward the house itself. At this hour it was a garden fit only for those that could see in the dark.

He tripped over roots that had forced their way through an old pavement cracked in a thousand directions. At other places the walks gave oozily under his feet. Everything was overgrown with weeds, gaunt, or blackly flamboyant. Frogs croaked in the stagnant stone basins, and as he rose turn after turn up the ruined steps, statues with mossy faces started out at him from their vine-tangled niches or lay prone with leprous spots upon them as if dead in the moonlight. Once he thought he saw a lantern gleaming far before him. But it was only a solitary firefly signalling vainly for an answer. The house remained pale and lampless, and grew even huger and more lonely as he approached it.

At last he stood upon the last pleasance, peering in through an open portal whose doors had long lost their hinges and were now leaning drunkenly against the pilasters of the cavern-like vestibule. Into this he did not care to venture. Indeed, he would have ended his mission here had it not been that now for the first time his ears were saluted by a sound other than that made by frogs and crickets.

At first he thought it was water dripping musically into some abandoned well, but as he stood listening intently the ghost of a tune emerged. Someone was negligently touching the strings of a harp. The sound grew louder. It seemed to emanate from the silent, wandering barracks before him. For a while it had come from nowhere, and the effect of the soft music in the moonlight had been so eery as to halt him where he stood. But to the notes of the harp were now added the slightly flat tones of a feminine voice practising the bravura. One, the highest note, was a dismal failure and made him laugh. It was an entirely human anticlimax. He strode through the vestibule eagerly and almost immediately found himself in the inevitable littered courtyard beyond.

From a porter's lodge in one corner of the quadrangle came a few gleams of light and the sound of the harp although the heavy shutters were closed. There were even heavy bars on the windows. He walked over and knocked at the door but there was no reply. The music had stopped instantly. He heard a few stealthy footfalls behind the shutters and the light went out. At first he was inclined to be angry at this reception, but then he could not help but grin. He knocked again. Silence.

After a long interval a queer voice said softly, "I am not at home. I went away years ago. Let me alone."

"Signora, or ma donna," he said, "I am not a brigand, I do not wish to disturb you. I am looking for a priest, Father Xavier. Do you know him?" He waited anxiously but still there was no reply. Some time passed. Then he knocked again, this time impatiently.

"You must call for him in the court. Call loudly," said the tired voice within. "He is getting a little deaf I think. He no longer cares for my music." That was all. After a while the light reappeared and the harp resumed.

He turned away again. The four walls of the high villa frowned down upon him with tightly-barred windows. The moon looked over one corner of the roof a little tilted. Best do as he had been told!

"Father Xavier, oh, Father Xavier!"

"*Ier, ier, ier,*" mocked the echoes, dying away into a solemn gibberish. The harp dripped and tinkled, and the flat voice in the lodge ran through an eery, windy bar or two again. Somewhere in the shadows a chorus of cats began insultingly. He felt enormously irritated. It was warm and damp here, too. He was sweating. The place was decidedly . . . decidedly so!

"Father Xavier!" he roared again in a sane determined tone.

"What is it, my son?" said a familiar voice so close to his shoulder that he wheeled about, startled in spite of himself.

A few feet away stood a slight, emaciated figure with a black robe fluttering in the night breeze that sighed through the archway. There was a small crucifix hanging from its belt. This, and a shining tonsure of thin, grey locks glinted in the moon. Only the face was the same. At the sight of those familiar features, which standing out above the shadows seemed to be glowing with a quiet light from within, Anthony was transported by the fascination of fond memory into the past. He seemed to be standing again in the court of the Convent of Jesus the Child. Each looked at the other searchingly.

"My father, is it possible you do not know me?" said Anthony.

"Anthony, my son, my son!" cried Father Xavier. "I would rather see you here tonight than an archangel. Where have *you* fallen from?"

He came forward and put his hands on Anthony's shoulders and looked up into his face.

"I used to look down at you. You remember?"

Anthony could feel how old his hands were. A feeling of pity swept over him. An irritating cadenza of the woman's voice interrupted them. Suddenly he felt embarrassed.

"I have a letter from Mr. Bonnyfeather for you," he said awkwardly.

Father Xavier laughed. "A formal introduction I trust—'Anything you may be able to do to further the fortunes of so estimable and prepossessing a young gentleman will be esteemed as a service rendered to your obedient servant'—eh? So, we are on the formal basis of manhood. Come, my son, I shall receive you as I am sure you deserve, letter or no letter."

He laid his hand on Anthony's arm and led him across the court to a little door with a grille in it, a door so narrow as to be successfully concealed behind a large pillar. Taking a candle from the niche where he had left it, Father Xavier extended a shielding hand before the flame and they began to ascend a series of narrow stairs.

The ramifications of the old house were unimaginable. A thousand closed doors loomed mysteriously on a hundred corridors going nowhere. Anthony suddenly felt an overpowering sensation that he had been here before. It seemed improbable that the priest could ever find the way to his own room again. The silence was oppressive, but somehow as they went higher it was not so hostile as it had been on the ground floor. Inside, the house was merely asleep, not dead. People could come back here and be happy again. It was not like the garden. In summer the house was warm and dry, dusty.

They had both unconsciously fallen into their old step as if sauntering again through the corridors of the convent. Father Xavier walked as though he had a child beside him. Anthony's steps became shorter and faster. He did not notice it but the priest did. The light from the candle made the enlarged, blue veins on Father Xavier's hands stand out in knots. A still, porcelain light filtered through his thin, shielding fingers and fell upon his face as if the glow upon it were from within.

As they walked on through endless corridors and up confusing flights of well-like stairs, Father Xavier gave the impression that with all this paraphernalia of the building about him—with the glimpses of frayed frescoes starting up before the candle and dying away into the darkness like the gliding fringes of a delirious dream—the priest had nothing whatever to do. He alone, in all the passing phantasmagoria of vaguely glimpsed scenes of nature and the works of man, held the light which revealed them—and let them go again. Only his face shining as from within remained. Yes, Father Xavier looked that way tonight. Anthony wondered what such impressions might mean.

At last they paused before a door apparently no different from a hundred others they had passed but to which Father Xavier unhesitatingly applied his iron key.

It swung open upon a small apartment under the leads. The moonlight poured in through a dormer window. Beyond was a glimpse of a few pale stars. Even with only one candle and a little moonlight Anthony felt at home in the place immediately. Father Xavier motioned him to a shadowy chair, and when some more candles were lit, he saw it was one of the old, red ones with tassels that had so intrigued him as a child at the convent. Through what vicissitudes had it been since then, he wondered, to come here?

It was marvellous how with the closing of the door the very memory of the labyrinthian chaos of a house that was below and around them had vanished. They might have been in a comfortably furnished, opaque bubble hung somewhere in space, utterly safe from and independent of the outside universe. A few embers from the faggots which had cooked the priest's supper still glowed and made the place, if anything, too warm. Father Xavier threw the window wider and they heard the notes of the harp at a great distance below them.

The priest turned and touched his forehead significantly.

"She is composing an opera which will never be sung," he said. "An old cousin of the Brignoles who has been permitted to live on here in the lodge these ten years now. It *is* a little weird at times. Let us close it out tonight. What do you say?"

He shut the window again and going over to the fire poured some water on the embers. As the last hissing died away he extended his arms along the mantelpiece, leaning back and looking at Anthony.

"Do you remember my old room in the little house?"

"I now feel as if I had never left it, father."

"Here are some of *your* books, the ones with the pictures in them," said Father Xavier smiling and running his hands affectionately over the backs of the leather bindings, without turning to look at them. "That was where your world began, was it not? Ah, those were good times at the convent after all. Better than we knew. And now, to think of it, we have ten years or more to talk away between us. Why, a life-time would not be long enough for that! Have you not found it so, Anthony?"

"I remember some days I think it would take ten years to tell about. I do not think I shall live long enough to find out what really happened in some of them, father. And yet looking at you now it all seems as though I had only dreamed them all. I could almost imagine that harp down there was our old fountain in the court splashing away under the plane tree. That sound of water comes often at night. I hear it then."

"So, does it go that way with you? Yes, we often return to ourselves at night, to what we were, or are. Tell me all about yourself, my son. It is long since we have had a good talk. Do!"

He took down a long pipe from the mantel. "Do you smoke? No? I do. It is one benign, fleshly indulgence to which I have finally succumbed."—He began to rummage around in various curious receptacles for another pipe, carrying his guest's attention from one thing to another, but giving him no chance to speak.—"You must inure yourself to the weed before its true virtues can be evoked. Try this.

Just one or two whiffs at first, if you do not really care for it. Real
Virginia, very light and sweet. Old. I keep it in this jar with a
little damp sponge." He lifted the pipe rapidly and brought a lighter.
The stem was in Anthony's mouth and he was drawing in the sweet
smoke almost before he knew it.

"I *am* a little cold after all," said Father Xavier, looking at the fire
regretfully. "A second till I change into my wool." His voice now
came floating in from his little bedroom just beyond. "I am quite
luxurious here you see," he added as he secretly put on a stole under
his gown.

Anthony had taken a few whiffs of the pipe. The first few were
pleasant but he did not care to go on. He felt himself to be floating
just a little free in space, his feet not quite on the floor. It was not
dizziness but the beginning of levitation. He was no longer connected with anything in space—with nothing except Father Xavier's
voice. That was the only reality—and himself.

"Now tell me about yourself, as you said you would," said Father
Xavier coming back into the room and seating himself opposite with
an air of one who has come to listen to a moving story. He wrapped
the loose gown a little closer over his chest. "Tell me everything.
What *did* happen that day I brought you to the Casa? You had an
encounter with a goat, didn't you? I remember something about that."

"Ah yes, the goat!" Anthony began, and without being aware of it
launched forth into what gradually and surely grew into the minute
autobiography of the years since he had left the convent. If there
was anything that he omitted he could not remember it. All the
people, the house, the books, the benign and sedate Mr. Bonnyfeather,
Toussaint, Faith, and Angela crowded into the little room under the
eaves of the Villa Brignole where Father Xavier sat with two fingers
across his breast holding his woollen gown. At which two fingers
somehow Anthony could not help but look as he went on and on.

At first he was aware only of a certain pleasure in the sheer narrative of his own affairs with so good and trusted a listener. Then
a kind of exaltation overtook him on the wings of which his story
began to move, but always inward toward the core of his being. He
was scarcely conscious of the little exclamations, encouragements, and
an occasional query from Father Xavier. Their voices seemed to
blend, and it seemed to have been suggested to Anthony that he should
ask certain questions of himself rather than that he might answer another person's. He even took a certain vague pleasure in inflicting
pain upon himself as he related his struggles and doubts, or discussed
the perplexing books on Mr. Bonnyfeather's shelves, the curious philosophy of Toussaint, that day in the room with Arnolfo. Now,
strangely enough, he could tell everything, even the burning of that

night with Faith. It was a relief. Somehow it did not seem so terrible now that he had told it. Father Xavier said nothing disturbing. So he could tell him of his love for Angela too, and the vision afterward.

As he began to speak of the madonna, *his* madonna, he began to understand that all he said, all his story of the days he had lived and the nights he had dreamed, were bound up and made one intelligible thing to himself by the feeling about a picture of her that he carried within him. It was inexplicable but it was so. She was the one permanent thing he had known. How could words compass it? It was not the little statue. That was only his particular familiar image of her, an inheritance from childhood. Into what had she grown? How could he tell it to Father Xavier?

"You see what she is lives in me, yet that is what I can speak to when I must speak to something beyond me—or be left alone—or die I guess. Shall I say that in her I, and the world, and what she is meet? At her feet! That is not it, but it is how words put it. It seems to me now I came here just to tell you that. I know it now! I came up from the sea, and through that evil, tangled garden with the dead statues, and into the court tonight. And I heard the music of the mad woman, and then I called to you, and you were there. We are not alone in this deserted house, are we? Tell me we two are not alone, my father. There is something beyond us and yet in us and with us. I believe you know. It is not all like walking up through those meaningless corridors tonight, my father. Thou knowest?"

His voice ceased and the candles burned steadily upright. There was not a sound except the *tick* and *tock* of the pendulum over the mantel.

Then he saw the two fingers on Father Xavier's breast move. His hand was moving in the air and his lips in absolution. His gown fell apart where the fingers had been holding it, revealing the stole. Neither said anything for a while. On both of them had fallen a great peace. It seemed to Anthony that now he was free of the past forever. But the clock went on. It was after midnight. It was the morning of July 14, 1796. The clock and the calendar both said so. But in the souls of the priest and the young man it was no time at all.

After a while Father Xavier got up and going over to a cupboard took out some white wine. Anthony now remembered he had had no supper. They both felt stiff. A small blaze in the grate and some wine and bread brought them back to the warm room again and the present.

Father Xavier then made up a pallet in one corner of the chamber and insisted that Anthony should lie down. He pulled up a chair close to the fire, and wrapping his gown about him again, stuck his slippers up before the little blaze.   Propped upon one elbow Anthony watched the firelight glancing across the priest's strong but sensitive profile.   There was something exquisite and smooth about it, but a strength there that might be stern.   His eyes were a little sunken and the grey locks of the tonsure gave him the look of a venerable youth.

"I am sure," said Father Xavier at last, "that we are *not* alone." The clock seemed to interrupt him again.

"You must tell me about yourself, father," said Anthony.   "Here I have taken up the whole long evening about my own precious affairs." The priest smiled a little sadly.

"I have been busy upon the errands of my order.   For a while at Naples, then in Sicily.   A starving time there.   These are very sad days for us.   We Jesuits no longer whisper into the ears of kings.   It is very difficult to bear the scorn of the world and to reconcile the bull of the Holy Father against us with obedience to the order—and the service of Jesus Christ.   It is difficult in practice, that is.   I have stayed in Italy, but I have been hunted at times.   Indeed, I lately have been very ill, sick in body and mind."   He leaned his head on his hand.

"I was educated in this house, before I went to Rome.   Did you know that, Anthony?   In the old days it was the summer school for the novices.   Please God, it may be so again!"   He seemed to be seeing things in the coals and went on in a lower tone.

"Many years ago in the days of the Colonnas it was the Villa Brignole.   My mother was one of that family.   Now that the Jesuits have been driven out it has fallen into their hands again.   I have relatives here.   They have let me stay on in these rooms quietly until I am stronger and times are better.   Since the French have come things are so disturbed I need hide no longer.   There is food, an old servant, and my books.   I am writing one myself about our holy martyrs for the faith.   It has meant more than I can tell you to have you come here tonight.   Most of the work of my life seems to have crumbled.   But I take courage in you as I see you now."

"Then so do I, father," said Anthony.   "You first encouraged me. Indeed, without you . . ."   He could not go on.

They were both silent a little again.

"Perhaps, you had better give me the letter from Mr. Bonnyfeather now," said Father Xavier smiling.

"I had forgotten all about it!   Forgive me.   I seem to have been interested only in myself tonight.   Believe me, it is not entirely so."

Father Xavier reassured him.   "You can in part blame me for that tonight.   But give Mr. Bonnyfeather some of the credit for having brought us together again," he added as he broke the seal and began to read.

As he read further his brows wrinkled.   It was as he had thought.

All had gone well with Anthony in the matters of this world. More than well. But Mr. Bonnyfeather was in doubt as to his ghostly state of mind. "I have not neglected it," wrote the old man, "I have done what I could, but my ignorance is great and in your absence I have, alas, felt myself somewhat helpless. Sir, you will forgive me, but I am old. Some things have fallen through my hands. Perhaps I should blame myself for having turned the boy over to the Frenchman.

"Perhaps? Yet I would have you remember, too, that he was to be prepared for the world, and that is not a seminary . . . . In the matter of first communion I have been most remiss. He is going on the long journey I mentioned above, so to your care and wisdom I leave the matter. Also in the matter of the will I would have your wisdom exercised as to whether he is to be told now the full extent of his benefits. Do as you think best." So the priest read on for several pages. "And this enclosure to you is only an earnest in advance of that other money matter of which I have spoken." Father Xavier sat pondering for some time.

"Anthony!" said he.

"Yes," replied Anthony sleepily, "sir?"

"Rouse yourself. I have some things I must talk to you about. How long will you be in Genoa?"

"Not over a day or so at most. The ship must sail . . ."

"Yes, I see," said Father Xavier. "Then you must take the sacrament at my hands tomorrow. At least I am still an ordained priest," he added with a proud melancholy half to himself. "I know a chapel where we can go together."

Anthony was sitting up now clasping his knees and thoroughly awake. Somehow he felt a little reluctant. He was not sure. It seemed hurried. He recoiled somewhat.

"I have never taken the wafer, father,—you know?"

The priest nodded and tapped the letter. "So I am told."

"I must pick up the captain too at an inn near here. We have much to do tomorrow—and my confession?"

"It was tonight, have you forgotten already?" Anthony winced. No, he had not forgotten. That was it. Somehow he felt that the confession had been drawn from him. It was unpremeditated—and yet?

"I would not put pressure on you, Anthony—but you are going on a long journey," said Father Xavier looking into the fire. His expression was very sad. He continued after a while. "God knows I would give you more preparation. There are many things I would talk about with you. There is one thing I must say to you tonight lest in my weakness I forget it. There is God and His son as well as the Madonna. No, I would not disturb you in what I may call your faith, in the comfort she has brought you. Continue, but let it lead you on. I would put it this way for your peculiar case. Do you from now on consider that which she holds in her arms." He paused to consider his own phrases. "So Christ came into the world, but so did he not go out of it."

Their concentration on each other was again intense.

"Tomorrow early then," said Anthony after a little, and felt himself relax. He lay back gladly again.

Father Xavier rose. "You have made me very happy," he said. He put a little crucifix on the table and left a candle by it. "There is a piece of worldly news which I was also bidden by Mr. Bonnyfeather to convey to you if I thought it wise to do so." He snuffed the candle carefully. "Well, I *do* think it wise. You are to be his heir." He stayed a minute looking fixedly at Anthony. Then he turned and went into his bedroom. The candle remained burning by the crucifix.

After a while Anthony got up and put it out. He found it impossible to do anything more than say a Pater Noster. He was in a sleepy tumult within. The night had been an exhausting one. He tried to feel grateful in his heart—and went to sleep.

They were awakened next morning by the lusty bellowing in the court below of the man who had driven Anthony the night before. He was much worried about the disappearance of his fare. Anthony stuck his head out of the window and a hearty exchange of divergent views as to the advantage of spending a supperless night in an abandoned shed went on.

"But you always sleep in your carriage," remonstrated Anthony; "why should I pay you extra for it?"

"Si, signore, but always under a dry archway and with wine in my own belly, and hay for the mules. Last night there was famine, fleas, and fog. The cushions are soaked with dew and I in agony from rheumatism. I shall catch the miasmic fever, I shall die. My wife and ten children, my aged mother, my two aunts . . ."

Anthony laughed and tossed something down to him. "I hire you for all day, with meals at restaurants, wine included," he said.

The man picked up the coin and kissed his hand toward the window. "Pardon, signore, I did not understand I was retained by a nobleman. I remain then till you appear." He looked ridiculous bowing there in the court so far below. An obsequious mouse, Anthony laughed again.

"Will it all go as easily as that did? The heir is feeling generous this morning, eh!" said Father Xavier from the next room.

"Very," said Anthony, "and awfully hungry."

"I am afraid you have forgotten something, my son," smiled Father Xavier, standing by the door with his hat under his arm. "We could not eat now, you know. There is holy food for us this morning."

An inexplicable reluctance swept over Anthony. His promise!

"I am sorry. In the joy of the bright morning, after last night, after finding you, I felt like a boy again. I had forgotten."

They emerged into the court and took their way rapidly to the garden. Along the lower terraces a few wisps of mist were still smoking. The rest of the place lay flashing with dewy laurel thickets, flower-beds a riot of colour, and living green steeples of cypresses pointing up through the tangled vines. The sunlight glinted from a hundred little ponds and rain-filled basins. Down at the far gate tossed the scarlet pompons on the mules' bridles.

Anthony stopped and took a deep breath of the cool air just beginning to be tinged with the heat of the coming day. It was, he felt, right, and a fortunate thing to be alive this morning; just to be alive. Then he remembered their errand again and looked a little guiltily at Father Xavier.

"Rejoice," said the priest, "it is not sinful to be gay and happy. We are not bound on a sorrowful errand. Do you not suppose that I am happy about it too? Ah, yes! I am afraid from Mr. Bonnyfeather, and from those books of his you have imbibed a sombre tinge about the matter. The northern races, you know, do not have a talent for religion. It is, after all, an affair of the heart, liable either to sour or to effervesce if it goes too much to the head. It is between the heart and the head that the church mediates. But come! You would not have me making a homily to you here with that shattered Calypso grinning at us from the grass!"

They began to descend the sweeping steps of the approach. Through the gaping gateway behind them came the distant notes of the harp. Father Xavier shook his head. Anthony wondered if she had been playing all night.

"Sometimes for two days and nights at a time, then she sleeps—and so do I," said Father Xavier.

It was a little uncomfortable, thought Anthony, to have his thoughts replied to this way out of the thin air. There was something in the tone of the harp that had reminded him of the garden the night before, damp moon shadows and dripping moss.

"But very beautiful here this morning," continued Father Xavier, "in full day or by the light of memory it can be very lovely even in its ruin. And I remember it when it was kept to the old marchesa's taste. I spent my childhood here and by a curious chance my novitiate, too, after the fathers took it over, years ago. A long time ago now it seems."

They had descended somewhat into the shades of the vegetation and dense paths.

"To that little pool over there I can remember coming with my mother and sailing a toy boat, a divine little *Argo,* I assure you. And it was in this grotto I spent a year alone as a novice. You see, Anthony, this is my—my convent." He lifted a heavy branch and they stepped through into a space of open green with an artificial grotto in the rocks behind it.

Before this cave staggered pitifully enough even though in dull green bronze a large figure of a water carrier. Once from the mouth of his receptacle had gushed a refreshing stream into the basin before him. But that now lay cracked and empty with a few plants struggling in its many fissures, dependent for their sustaining moisture solely upon the accidents of heaven. Already in the growing heat of the morning they were beginning to droop. Yet the eye scarcely noticed their small and ordinary tragedy. It was inevitably fixed by the terrible predicament of the water carrier himself. Above his patient human limbs the empty, lead pipe that had once conducted his secret supply was now uprooted and writhing like a snake determined to trip him.

They stood for a minute looking at this. Father Xavier picked a small flower from the basin and put it in his pocket. His lips moved. Then they went on along the terrace and down a flight, along another terrace and down, and still another—and climbed into the carriage at the gate.

CHAPTER TWENTY-SIX

THE STREET OF THE IMAGE MAKERS

THE hard road, dustless with the damp of night still on it, and shining before them, clicked cheerfully under the wheels. Under the spell of the exhilarating miracle of motion an enchanted sea-scape opened itself before them. The Mediterranean sparkling from headland to headland rolled away northward toward France. The still, white town at the foot of the distant hills with the sun upon it might have been an eternal one. For a moment the mood of the day-before possessed Anthony again. He could apprehend the vision of the table. He could not see it any longer, but he felt that he was united again with all men in the bounty of that feast. The feast of the sun and wine! "It was an affair of the heart." The words recurred to him with startling clearness. The head had nothing to do with it. Why meditate?

What was this that Father Xavier was trying to tell him about the holy communion as they drove along over these ineffable hills? What of sorrow and pain and mercy; of the meaning of certain words? It was true that he could not really hear them. Meaning should be attached to words like these. What was it he was about to do? Something for Father Xavier! It would be his pupil who would do it then; who would take the wafer. Not Anthony, not Anthony Adverse. He would not do it. No, that was it, that was it exactly. He, Anthony, would *not* do it. Presently he would have to tell Father Xavier that he would not. That was going to be hard. He sat back for a minute against the seat and felt the grit of the road crunch reassuringly under the wheels. *Clip, clop, clip, clop,* rang the iron shoes on reality.

"Thus the communion of saints . . ." said Father Xavier.

"Father," said Anthony suddenly, interrupting him, "I must talk to you now. I must tell you that I cannot take the wafer this morning. It is impossible. It would not be I. You would merely be giving it to me. Don't you see, it would be neither the head nor the heart? Not now at least." His eyes widened. "Not now . . ."

Father Xavier had gone grey. He looked as if something within him had crumbled. He sat very still.

"In the house," he thought, "in the house, before we left this morning. Now it is too late. I had prayed for this but it is not to be given to me. The work of my own hands . . ."

They were climbing a hill again, with no visible ending. The mules began to walk dragging the weight behind them slowly upward.

"Will it always be like this, I wonder?" thought the priest—and then bit his own tongue.

"Forgive me, forgive me, my father. I am sorry to have given you pain," said Anthony. "I would not be so sudden in telling you but . . ."

"In God's time and not mine," replied the priest. The colour slowly came back to his face. "Let us say no more about it. Now where are you going today? Perhaps I can help you. At least I know something about Genoa." He smiled, still quite pale.

It was not until many years later that Anthony understood that he had been present at a miracle that morning after all—a miracle of self-control.

At the top of the hill he unexpectedly found himself driving past the inn where he had left the captain the night before. A hearty "Avast there, mister," apprised him of the fact and revealed Captain Elisha gesticulating from the door with a napkin, while wiping egg from his moustache.

There was something about his portly figure, poised on its thick legs like a tree that has gripped the rocks and withstood tempests, which caused Father Xavier to appraise the mariner with approval, nor did a slightly puzzled twinkle in the captain's steady blue eyes escape him. He had seen a deeply concealed but unsolved trouble effervesce in humour like that before.

Captain Elisha on his part soon ceased to regard the kindly priest as a "foreigner." Anthony was more relieved than anyone. It had been impossible for him to imagine upon what grounds these two could meet. It was simply to be as man to man over the breakfast table. Their legs were soon under it.

"I swan to Jesus, mister," said Captain Jorham pouring a little coffee into his rum, "ye're the first mate I ever did have servin' under me that spent his shore leave with the clergy. Beggin' yer pardon, father. Not that I have any pecoolar objectshune. There's wus ways of killin' time I heard tell on. Didn't know Mr. Adverse was of the persuasion." He grew more offhand as he felt himself getting into deeper water.

"You see, Mr. Adverse was a pupil of mine a good many years ago," vouchsafed Father Xavier, "I used to teach him geography and Latin."

"Wall now then," said the captain glad of so naturalistic an explanation of his mate's intimacy with the priesthood, "I did hear him tell ye was by way of bein' an old friend. Sort of a reunion, then eh?"

"Exactly," said Father Xavier.

"I met a priest in Canton oncet that had a whole school o' Chinee orphans. He was a good man for all they might say at home. Heard he was murdered afterwards. One of them slow demises they devils goes in for. Begin with yer fingers and toes and work in." He began to cut up a piece of potato graphically. "It's wonderful how little holdin' ground the soul needs. I've seen a Chinee shaped like an egg and his eyes still bright. Fact! . . Course it's different with children. They just up anchor and goes." He looked troubled.

"What was the priest's name?" asked Father Xavier.

Captain Elisha could not remember but Father Xavier did. It had been one of his own order. "I have his story in my book."

"Wall, I swan—to man!" said the captain. He began to tell them about his voyages to Canton. They all felt at ease with one another. "Seemed like that poor fellow died jes' to make us better acquaint," he averred finally.

"That has been one remote result," said Father Xavier half to himself. "Who knows?"

Anthony observed that the captain was doing well with his "coffee." The mood of the evening before seemed likely to continue. After a while they got up and smoked a pipe outside. Anthony indulged in one, too. He did not care much for it yet. But after the experience of the night before he had made up his mind to go in for tobacco. It might pay to investigate it as well as wine. He felt just a little light in the knees as they climbed into the carriage. The captain had Anthony interpret while he paid his bill.

"And you might ask the woman," he said, "if they have a child in the house."

"Si, signore, just learning to walk. I trust its cries were not disturbing. She is very little yet."

The captain looked relieved. " 'Taint the cryin'," he said. His face seemed to forbid curiosity about his inquiry.

Soon they drove on, merrily enough, it seemed to Anthony. He glanced at Father Xavier curiously. All seemed well there, too. But it had been profane food that morning after all.

"Is your hunger fully satisfied, my son?" said Father Xavier quietly in Anthony's ear. His face did not change. Anthony did not answer.

Not one to neglect any aspect of opportunity, Captain Jorham had been quick to see in the accidental presence of the priest that morning an expert aide and adviser in the purchase of church statuary. As they drove down the hills back to Genoa he began without further ado, or any sense of embarrassment, to unfold his scheme for improving the condition of the church in Cuba.

Somewhat to Anthony's surprise Father Xavier consented to serve in an advisory capacity. Indeed, as the priest listened to the captain's rather remarkable plan unfold an amused smile seemed to be hiding itself in the deep shadows under his eyes. But his mouth remained grave.

Yes, he could undoubtedly aid the captain in making the proper purchases. "It is in the Street of the Image Makers that you will find what you are looking for, I think. As to the marble blocks—I do not know whether I can help you, but I suggest that you ask some of the masons and sculptors at the place that I spoke of. Do you want to go there now?"

Captain Jorham assured him that he did. The less delay the better. Father Xavier directed the driver.

Just where the Albaro Road approaches the city gate they passed a small chapel with a fresco upon its outside walls so striking as to cause Captain Jorham to stop and descend to examine it. Outside the door there was a little money box for the benefit of souls in purgatory. Just above it on either side of the grated portal, behind which an altar could be seen, was an enormous picture of souls frying in hell. The sympathy of the artist had evidently been with the devils who were undoubtedly enjoying themselves. A small baby for the extreme trespass of not having been baptized had had both its thumbs cut off and could find nothing but a hot coal to put in its mouth. This seemed to hold the captain, although the main exhibit was an old-man-soul with a grey moustache and carefully parted hair who was being put feet first into a furnace vomiting flames. Various minor activities of a somewhat frank and painful nature were being carried on in the background. These occasionally caused Captain Jorham to "swan to man." He paused for some minutes, thoughtfully.

"I hope, father," said Anthony taking the opportunity while they were left sitting in the carriage, "that you are not shocked at the captain's scheme for taking the saints to Cuba. I am not responsible, you know."

Father Xavier smiled. "Far from it," he rejoined. "I regard Captain Jorham, and men like him, as respectable means to higher ends. Sailors, soldiers, shopkeepers, and the like are usually commendable in themselves. One should consider what is using them and why. In this case I have my own idea that the end may be a worthy one. But let us say no more, he is returning." They heard a small coin fall in the box. The captain climbed in tilting the carriage slightly. For some distance he seemed inclined to get the priest's views on infant baptism. From these he could derive small comfort.

"Er—na-ow that picture," he went on, "is that your idee of the hereafter?"

Father Xavier was non-committal though not reassuring.

"I'll tell ye some o' the parsons on the Cape could get p'inters from it," he resumed. "It would fill a church down Truro way every Sunday. It's not wasted here I guess. Nope! Do you know I calalate we're all like to be surprised by the way etarnity really is. Nearest I ever come to it was oncet off the Andamans when a bolt of fire fell into the sea right plumb off'n the starboard quarter. Left me blind for a week, it did." He paused dreamfully as if remembering something, closing his eyes.

"What did you see on the other side of the lightning, Captain Jorham?" asked Father Xavier very quietly.

The captain opened his eyes and looked at him. "I'm not giving away etarnal information for nothin' ara-ound here," said the captain. The thought of the coin he had dropped in the box for the baby remained with him. With it he had secretly bought a little comfort and was now indignant at himself for having done so.

They were now well within the town again driving through crowded streets. A seemingly endless number of twists and turns finally landed them in front of an apothecary shop that was built into the side of a hill. They told the driver to wait and entered.

As they did so a number of shabby men who were waiting near the door hurried forward to meet them. "We want medicines only," said Father Xavier. Whereupon these physicians, for such they were, sank back disconsolately into their chairs.

They left the light of the street behind them and continued to walk along a bottle-lined passageway that gradually grew darker.

It was some seconds before Anthony's eyes became used to the deepening shadows or comprehended the meaning of a bright patch of sunlight some distance ahead. The air became dank and cool. They ascended a few rock steps, where some white mushrooms flourished, and then suddenly came out of the long tunnel into a drench of sunshine just beyond.

"This," said Father Xavier, "is the Street of the Image Makers. Without me, my son, I do not think you could have come even so far."

"Swan to man, if we ain't come clean through the hill into a lot of old stone quarries," exclaimed the captain shoving his hat back. "Thar's the sky."

The captain was correct. The Street of the Image Makers descended straight before them into a huge, rocky pocket in the hill which had once been an immense stone quarry. From the surrounding white cliffs tall, forbidding houses turned their bleak backs upon it, and from dizzy ledges goats looked down indulgently upon the place. In fact, the only entrance, that through which they had just come, had been mined in ancient times. Hence, where the tunnel ended the street began. It was merely a gash in the living stone, a gradually widening continuation of the tunnel now open to the sky like the bed of a dry canal.

In the walls of this marble prism shops and dwellings had been hollowed out from time to time, and their fronts carved in the various styles which the caprices of the owners had dictated. Before several doors an arcade rested upon Ionic pillars, one solid piece of stone. Another shop affected a classic façade with a temple-like entablature resembling a rock tomb. Some had severely plain fronts pierced by doors and windows only, but even around these openings skilful chisels had traced wreaths of flowers and vines. Farther on the street widened away and descended into the heart of the abandoned quarry, where at the end of its gleaming vista sparkled a dark blue pond.

Completely removed from the noise and sweaty confusion of the city, the first impression of this little community was that of a sepulchral place set apart from the living interests of mankind. It seemed to brood upon its peculiar affairs exclusively, as if the inner moods of its troglodytical inhabitants were reflected by the single eye of the pool in the marble at the end of their curious avenue.

"This is where most of the holy images, shrines, and ecclesiastical carvings in this part of Italy are made," said Father Xavier. "Look, that is a forge over there." He pointed to a hole in the rock topped by a little chimney pot from which smoke and flames were issuing. "There are also several small potteries scattered about. Sculptors work here in both stone and wood. Those who apply colour are a separate fraternity and live farther down the street. I would not be surprised if the images of the gods had been made here when Genoa was a Roman town. Some of these places you can see from the weathered carvings escape the memory of man."

The priest's remarks had by now brought them before the arcaded shops. From these a continuous muffled thudding proceeded. Looking in, they saw a number of workmen with wooden mallets beating upon chamois skins. Stepping to the first window Father Xavier called loudly for "Messer Stefano." An artisan in a leather apron appeared at the door. Tall, thin, and very dark, there was something Egyptian about the man, as he stood peering out into the sunlight with hawklike eyes, small gold earrings, and a short leather apron.

"Stefano, I have brought you some customers," said Father Xavier. The man hastened to lay aside his tools.

"This is the potentate of the whole street," whispered the priest to

Anthony. "A rather remarkable fellow. You will have to do all your bargaining through him. Humour him. He regards himself with some justice as an artist and a philosopher."

The thudding in the shop had ceased. Only from the forge down the street a thin troll-like clinking could still be heard. As Father Xavier explained the nature of their errand to Messer Stefano at some length it seemed as though not only the padrone but the place itself was listening.

"Go on with your work in there," said Stefano after a while. The hammers of the gold beaters resumed.

"Since the captain here speaks nothing but English," concluded Father Xavier, "you will have to conduct your negotiations with Signore Adverso. You will find him not without a natural insight in this affair, a young gentleman of honour and sensibility, a former pupil of mine." The workman bowed slightly.

"And now," said Father Xavier, turning to Anthony unexpectedly and with a smile that was almost tremulous, "you see I have brought you as far as I can. It is time to say good-bye. Let it be here then."

"To see you again, and when, my father?"

Father Xavier wrung Anthony's hands and hurried up the street. At the mouth of the tunnel he turned. Anthony raised his hand in farewell. He saw that the priest was blessing him. Then he disappeared into the shadow of the tunnel behind.

"If the signori care to, I will show them about the street," said the voice of Stefano smooth but not obsequious. He led the way into the shop.

"All the shops here are now under my direction," the man continued a little proudly, "but the gold leaf is my special care. Would you like to see?"

He drew aside a chamois skin revealing the beautiful, yellow metal underneath spreading out from a lump in the middle in one shining sheet. He showed them the process. "Under a skilful hammer, you see, there will be no holes."

The captain was much impressed. "Wall, sir, I used to think my dad could make gold spread further than any living man. It would have hurt his pride to see this. He was pretty talented though. When I was nine years old he brought me a penny after a successful v'y'ge to Nassau. Sir, I had to show him that coin every Thanksgivin' for ten years. I've kept it so durned long I larned the only Latin off it I ever knowed. *'Expulsis piratus, resti-too-shia commercia.'* Kick out the pirates and reopen the stores," he translated, flushed with his own learning. "And that penny was only copper, and here it is."

Stefano had managed to catch the Latin. "We are not pirates

here," he said grievously displeased. Anthony was forced to explain.
The man summoned a vague laugh from somewhere and laying down
his hammer led them out again.

"You will find each little place given up to its own specialty, signore," he explained. "Trade in images has not been very good for
nearly a hundred years. My grandfather remembered a better time.
With the makers of holy images it now goes hard. War, it is always
war! Few churches or shrines are being built. No one makes vows.
It is mostly the women and antiquarians who buy now. I have been
forced to control things here in Genoa. I buy up even the old figures
and retouch them. Only a few of the most popular blesséd ones still
sell. In here we make nothing but bambinos."

He threw open a door for them at the side of the street. Inside
a number of boys and girls were preparing plaster and pouring it into
moulds. From a drying kiln at one end of the room a girl returned
with a tray full of white baby dolls and laid them before an old man
who sat with brushes and various paints before him. They watched
him a while.

"Do *not* vary the smile, Pietro," said their guide. "How often
must I tell you? It is that one beatific expression of Buonarrotti's
which I desire you to repeat. What do you know of ecstasy?"

"Si, si, padrone," said the artist deprecatingly as he retouched a few
cherubic lips. "But memory plays me tricks with these smiles. I
once had children of my own. You should have let me stay moulding
resignation into holy hands. I was good at that."

"Not so good as you think," said Stefano as they went out.

"It is very difficult to have to make these artists always do the most
perfect thing and keep repeating it," he continued as they went along
further. "So many of them have their own ideas. And that would
be well enough, signore, if this street were given over to secular art.
But you see, in my case, in what *I* have undertaken to do here, the
perfect examples both in life and art have already been given. It is
restraint therefore and imitation that are needed . . .

"Si, I have thought much and often as to the effect of these statues
upon those who will acquire them. They are to bring to mind the
very image of the holy one whose intercession is sought or whose
example is to be followed. In that, as in everything, a certain
technique is necessary. Have you ever thought of that, signore?
Without a technique, a bodily method for faith, morality, religion itself would perish. Without the church as one immortal corporation,
without the methodology which it inculcates and even turns into a
habit, the memory of divine things would be lost. Or it would be left
in the minds of women to be told to babies. It is true most vital
things *are* remembered that way from generation to generation. But

our religion is not so simple as that. There must ever be images, concrete moulds into which it can be poured." He flung up his hands excitedly. "But, pardon me, I do not wish to bore you. You see this is my life work, my enthusiasm, this small street. It is not altogether that I live by it. I live *in* it." He checked himself somewhat embarrassed.

"Tell me what you think," said Anthony. "It is seldom that people will do so. I have often thought about what you are speaking of. Tell me, you would not have them worship the image itself?"

"I would not stop them," said Stefano. "What can you do with such minds as that but give them something outside themselves to adore? Let them play in their divine doll house. Let them dress their saints and be happy. Those who plague such people with abstract ideas about God are foolish. Is it not better to leave them with an image which may lead to something beyond?

"I am not speaking of philosophers and savants, my friend. They are idolaters of ideas. With them both the image and the technique of the ways of life they would inculcate are always lacking. Hence their dreams must be renewed every generation in adults, by the few who can read and understand. God forgive me, I hope I utter no heresy," he crossed himself, "but I have often thought it is not such a mystery after all that God should have embodied himself in human form. Otherwise he would have remained to us unknown, imageless, a vague voice in the winds, mystery in the landscape, the theory of some teacher, or the beautiful dream of an artist in some idol ugly or beautiful as sin. In Christ he became a body, the way, and the life. I believe; I know that." He wiped his brow with his sleeve.

"What is the man saying?" asked Captain Jorham, a little alarmed at being left out so long.

"He is talking about the image of God," said Anthony with secret enjoyment.

"Holy smoke, *resti-too-shia commercia,* let's be gettin' on!" snapped the captain.

"I see that your friend does not fully understand," said Stefano.

"What I was trying to tell *you,* signore," he hurried on in a lower voice, "is that in all my images here I have, for reasons that you can now surmise, tried to embody nothing but the most perfect attitudes and gestures. I have studied the works of the old artists in the days of great faith, and have chosen for each saint or bambino or madonna, even for Christ himself, those features which have been found to have the most appeal. Each one of these images is a lasting and a silent preacher. Come, let me show you something wonderful now."

He took out the key for the door before which they now stood. "These are too precious to be worked on except under supervision.

The model here is of great value. It is part of the French spoil from Milan. Not now, not of this Buonaparte, but of the French kings many generations ago." He threw open the door.

"Only I and my assistant work here," he said. "All of these models are from my hands. See, here is the original." He pulled a cloth off an almost life-sized figure in the centre of the room where the light fell upon it from the door.

It was a Virgin and Child carved in some soft grained stone. Just the head and bust of a peasant woman wrapped in an ample medieval garment. The stone had been coloured and gilded and a great blue fold of the virgin's cloak swept down over her breast. In the folds of the deep hollow slept the child. It could not be seen from the front. It was completely concealed in the hollow. Only the folds of the cloak and the position of the woman's hands conveyed the fact that something infinitely precious was concealed there.

Stefano pointed to the hands and paid them the compliment of saying nothing at all. Then he turned to the models.

"You see we could not afford to reproduce this in stone," he said. "These are clay replicas. When they are first baked the colour is a little garish but if properly placed in the shadow the effect of the lines and the whole figure is admirable. I think we have caught what those hands are saying . . . and the wonderful sweeping fold!" He ran his hand over the bulge of the blue scarf with satisfaction.

"It is well reproduced, Messer Stefano," said Anthony, "but not so durable as the original I suppose."

"No, signore, but light, even porous, and easy to transport," said Stefano lifting one of the images. "See!"

"The biggest thing we've seen yet," said Captain Jorham. "You might start with one of these, mister." He peered over the edge of the fold. "Just as I thought, she's got a baby, too! The hul thing's complete. Better start in and make your dicker now. This is the kind of thing we want. Nothing small and cheap. How about some o' they life-sized figurines?"

With some censoring of the text Anthony translated.

"If it is large figures," said Stefano, "come this way."

He led them directly across the street and up a few steps into a kind of stone lean-to with its rear wall in the rock itself. Here standing in solemn tiers were twenty or thirty life-sized figures of saints and a large thorn-crowned Christ with the conventional anatomy of the bleeding heart exposed. Its expression of agony was so intense as to make a large St. Lawrence stretched out on his gridiron over terra cotta flames comparatively genial.

"That's the stuff," said Captain Jorham. "Some of them are a little cracked, too. They ought to be knocked down reasonable. Git busy, mister. Why not the hul lot?"

Stefano was surprised at the wholesale gusto of his customer. A little disgusted, too, Anthony could see. For that reason he began by bargaining for one of the fine clay figures of the Virgin they had just seen across the street. The man seemed somewhat mollified by this. After all the young gentleman did understand the pride of an artist.

"As your masterpiece," said Anthony, "we will give you for the model ten crowns less than you ask. And that, as you know, is more than meeting your expectations. For that reason, and because we shall be taking all of this old stock, you must make me, on worn figures at least, a more reasonable rate."

After an hour and a half of chaffering, by which time the captain's hat was shoved clear back on his head and his hands deep in his pockets, an agreement was in sight. Another half hour and it was agreed that Stefano should retouch and repaint where necessary. All of the "old holy ones" were to be made bright and new. It would take two days for the paint and gilding to dry. Anthony would call for them then and take them to the *Wampanoag*. It was also arranged that they should be transported in carriages. "Every respect must be shown them," explained Stefano. The excitement in the streets at so extensive a flitting of saints would undoubtedly be considerable. After some demur Captain Jorham agreed. He had once seen a religious riot at Lisbon.

"Tell him we'll even put 'em to bed when we get 'em aboard," he said. "I mean it. It won't do to have any of these people breakin' loose in the hold. Besides somethin' might shatter 'em if the cargo shifted. Now how about them marble blocks for ballast?"

But this could not be arranged. It would take weeks to drill the holes.

"Never thought of that," said Captain Elisha. "Ask him about some plain marble slabs. I can batten them down I calalate. We want weight, weight! There ain't profit in water ballast. The crew drinks it."

It was possible to arrange for the slabs. Captain Elisha looked very pleased. The total outlay had not been large and he had obtained more statuary than he had thought possible. They adjourned to Stefano's hut and sealed the bargain over a bottle of bad wine. By sunset they were back on board the brig.

"And a couple of days will just give us time to load stores, water the ship, and do a little calkin' along the water line where that Portegee bumboat rammed her," mouthed the captain through a mouthful of Philadelphia's grub, "and lay in a few kegs of wine," he added looking his wife in the eye. "Say, Jane, don't 'e look solemn about that.

Wait till you see who's comin' aboard to keep you company. Taews-
day mornin'. Whew!" He paused for a minute with his fork and
knife held bolt upright.

"Right on that Putnam sideboard is going to be a heathen idol—
with a baby. It's the prize o' the hul lot. It goes to Havaner in the
cabin!" He cut a piece of salt pork at one blow. "As for the rest of
'em, there's five empty bunks in the fo'c'sle. I'd like to see the British
come aboard now with a press gang. They'd have to prove Jesus
Christ was born in Sussex. Still," said he rapping on wood, "some of
them post captains could do that all right. It ud take God A'mighty
to stop 'em. That it would." He poured some hot water into his rum.

"Mister, you're a macaroni mate and you can't hand, reef, nor
steer. But you're goin' to have a hul starboard watch with haloes, and
a cargo of tombstones for ballast. There's only one thing I got to say
to you as captain of this *holy* ship. I don't want no miracles occurrin'
when I'm below. Do you hear? *That goes!*" He left the fork
quivering in the table.

"Now you get your charts and we'll lay out the course."

The lines about Captain Jorham's mouth began to be a little more
drawn as he imbibed a large pitcher of "dog's nose." He gradually
became silent and morose as the evening wore away and his wife
knitted and knitted.

"More baby clothes?" said the captain at ten o'clock by the chronometer when they prepared to turn in. She nodded and closed the panel.
The captain drew off his heavy boots.

"Mister," said he, "*you'll* do the navigatin'? You kin?" He looked
anxious.

Anthony felt sure of it. He took out his new sextant that Mr.
Bonnyfeather had given him. The latest London make, he noted.
By degrees and by degrees he would soon be slipping over into new
latitudes. He went on deck for a while and looked again at the city.

In his room at the Palazzo Brignole, Father Xavier fumbling in his
pocket for his pipe found the flower he had picked from the empty
basin in the garden that morning. It seemed to him as it lay in his
palm that he had also permitted that to wither. His hand shook
slightly. But what could one do with wild flowers? Leave them to
the winds of God? A sorry argument about predestination failed to
comfort his soul. His dreams were sorrowful.

On the *Wampanoag* next morning they began to bend on a suit of
new sails.

CHAPTER TWENTY-SEVEN

THE PILLARS OF HERCULES

CAPTAIN JORHAM had miscalculated. Nearly a week passed before the *Wampanoag* could put to sea. Much against his better judgment, because he was so short-handed, he was forced to ship some "Spanish riff-raff" and a few "select" British deserters hanging about the docks at Genoa. The latter, after they sobered up, proved willing hands enough. At least they could be counted on to keep a weather-eye peeled for king's ships. And above all else Captain Elisha was anxious to give British cruisers a wide berth.

At last the brig was watered and her cargo stowed. Five saints were lashed in the fo'c'sle bunks and the grumbling men told to swing hammocks. Late one afternoon they hoisted the anchor merrily enough and a few hours later sunk the peaks which gird in the Gulf of Genoa under the northern horizon.

Under a complete suit of new sails the ship bowled along famously. Philadelphia, happy with an ample supply of olive wood, his favourite fuel, sang at the door of his little galley now surrounded by chicken coops. Forward, two pigs, a milch goat and her kids, and a number of ducks and geese swelled a bucolic chorus that sang of good fare to come.

Captain Jorham had reverted to a kind of man-o'-war discipline for his now motley crew, a discipline with which as an ex-privateersman he was familiar. One Jeb Collins, a middle-aged down-easter with iron-grey hair and a rasping voice, had been appointed "quartermaster" with the authority but not the wages of a second mate. Under the press of sail which the brig was carrying, both of the watches were kept pretty constantly on deck. Captain Jorham had not seen fit to appoint Anthony to either. He took one himself and gave the other to Collins. In the strong and continually freshening breeze pouring out of the east he carried sail till the weather shrouds sang a higher note.

Mrs. Jorham was the only member of the crew who persistently kept below. She sat in her cabin and contemplated with an indignation which only she could control the large terra cotta figure of the Virgin Mary that now occupied the place of her copper coffee urn on the Putnam sideboard. A little less than life-sized, the statue seemed to have thrust aside the urn, which was Mrs. Jorham's chief pride, in wanton intrusion. It occurred to Mrs. Jorham that the Virgin kept wrapping the folds of her ample, blue cloak about her with a calm aloofness that amounted to provocative disdain.

It was only an added exasperation to the captain's wife to find that in the deep fold over the statue's right shoulder a baby lay concealed. Aside from sectarian scruples about "idols," she had also certain personal reasons which made even the statue of a woman with a child in her arms, especially when it was snugly ensconced in her own cabin, peculiarly hard to bear. Besides, as she continued to look at it—and she could scarcely avoid doing so—in the atmosphere of her lonely reveries the thing began to take on the elements of a living personality. She caught herself giving it from time to time a caustic piece of her mind.

That her husband had inflicted this reminder upon her seemed a piece of deliberate cruelty and reproach. Her only consolation was, if he had not been drinking he would not have done so. But in the obstinate state which the captain had now reached, and took care to increase from day to day, remonstrance would be useless. His only reply would be to mix himself another dog's nose. Furthermore, with the primary cause of her husband's drinking Mrs. Jorham was to some extent forced to sympathize. Indeed, she reproached herself in a Biblical manner with having been responsible for it.

Up until now the captain had kept the deck. But the delay at Genoa had advanced his potable calendar considerably, and she foreboded his early and complete retirement to the cabin in no very complacent mood. Meanwhile she sat there reduced to silence, minding her knitting, and brushing away an occasional mist of stinging tears. Under these circumstances she felt it would have been some company and no little protection to have had the new mate keep to the cabin more than he did.

Anthony, however, kept the deck early and late. He was anxious to pick up every item of nautical lore that might come his way, and that in as short a time as possible. His position on the ship was, he realized himself, somewhat ridiculous. To the crew as well as to the captain he was already known as the "macaroni mate." Neither the captain nor the men paid much attention to him at first. He was, as Captain Jorham had said, strictly *"ex-officio."* He had been inclined to accept this position more or less, but during a dog watch at Genoa Collins, the quartermaster, had leaned over the bulwarks with him one evening while they watched the lights of the city coming out one by one, and unburdened his mind.

"Before we git into the trades, Mr. Adverse, you'll find yourself in real charge," said the quartermaster. "I know the skipper, and he ain't d-ue to last tew long as things are going na-ow. Ye're mate on the roster, and ye'll find that mate ye'll have to be. Na-ow I'll dew all *I* can, but you might keep that in mind. Authority's authority, and ye either are, air ye ain't."

So Anthony kept it in mind. To be lost on the Atlantic with a ship and crew—to be lost there! It haunted his dreams. He could only pray that Captain Jorhan would last. But wishes soon became ridiculous. Already it was a miracle how Captain Elisha could keep going as he did.

"He counts on gittin' us through the Straits," said Collins. "And then——"

"Ah, and then!" thought Anthony. He was glad he had spent his life more or less about ships around the docks at Livorno. The nomenclature and the lingo were familiar. He began now to memorize commands. But above all he began to furbish up his navigation. He even wished he had listened to the mad Mr. Williams' theory of lunar longitude. The *Wampanoag's* chronometer was obviously a joke. He made a few friends among the older members of the crew. Once at sea he went up on the yards to shake out or take in sail. Collins at least was for him. That was one comfort. And he had learned the ship from trucks to keelson at Genoa while she was lading. After a week he felt the men respected him even if they laughed. He laughed with them, and kept the deck. The first noon out he brought up his sextant but the captain would have none of it.

"Lay off that, mister, till I give the word. I don't need that contraption to tell where we're at na-ow."

"The old man's awful techy about shootin' the sun," whispered Collins. "He'll try to go by dead reckonin' when he kin."

So the new sextant went back to the cabin. But the men had seen it, and some of the old hands who had sailed with Captain Jorham before looked pleased.

The captain's method of navigation, since his faith had been shattered some years before in his pet sextant, was, although he did not condescend to explain it, abundantly plain. In the Mediterranean it consisted in coasting from one well-known landfall to another. In wider, ampler oceans of late years his progress had become truly wonderful. Each voyage had rivalled that of Columbus in view of the possible mysteries ahead. One grand fact had consoled him. Sailing east from *Amurakee* one was bound to reach *U-rup*. Undoubtedly the converse might also be true. At any rate he was about to put it to a pragmatic test. In the meantime in a comparatively small place like the Mediterranean he felt at home. With two ex-whalers for lookouts he continued to crack on sail unmercifully.

Once the bend in the coast by Genoa was out of sight he took a long southern slant till he raised the peaks of Corsica. A day later the fishing boats making for Ajaccio allowed him to mark himself down as about 42 N. and 8 E. After that it was comparatively easy going for a while. The east wind, which held and continued to freshen a little every day, suited him well. On that tack the *Wampanoag* was at her best. He merely squared away a little to be sure to pass to leeward of Asinara and then ran down the coast of Sardinia as far as S. Pietro.

"Call it thirty-nine North," said Captain Elisha. "Gib is just thirty-six and away, and away west."

But he frowned a little as he looked at the chart. The bulge in the coast of Africa was somewhat confusing. He wanted to give Port Mahon and the Balearics a wide berth on account of British cruisers. To make, as he put it, "a good southing" before he squared away before the wind for the Straits. Part of Africa, however, appeared to be in the way. And Algiers was an unhealthy neighbourhood. Between the horns of this dilemma, Algiers and Minorca, he lingered over the chart for an hour or two. The application of a third dog's nose he was glad to see had straightened out the coast of Africa. "Well, he would hold on south; take a good plenty south." And he did so.

Next day the wind showed every sign of freshening to a blow. With some difficulty Collins got permission to reduce sail and finally to send down the royal and t'gallant masts. Not only the ship but its new mate now rode much easier. Watching the yards roll against the sky while the spars came down had given Anthony his first serious qualms. Nothing, however, could persuade the captain to follow the example of several other ships and head west. Collins was obviously worried at this obstinacy.

"Git a sight today if ye kin, Mr. Adverse," he managed to say while the men were lashing the lower topmasts to the shrouds with extra precautions. "This here weather looks like a little patch o' clear before a big blow. For God's sake take advantage of it. I'll try to keep the skipper below at noon. Seems like I could smell Afriky."

When Anthony came up with his sextant a few hours later both the deck and the horizon were momentarily clear. Taking advantage of a patch of clear sky just at noon, when the scud which had been driving for some hours luckily opened out overhead, he made his first observation at sea.

When he worked out his position he made it to be much farther south than the captain's longest guess would admit. Africa must be not far over the southern horizon. He said so, but somewhat too diffidently.

Ordinarily Captain Elisha would have given heed and taken the credit to himself. Under influences more potent than the calculations of his merely titular mate he now argued and held on. He was con-

vinced at dawn by a frantic voice from the masthead and a not too
distant glimpse of a long beach dead ahead where breakers bared their
fangs and endless sand dunes smoked in the gale. For a few hours
he was somewhat sobered. The ship was instantly put before the
wind which swept her westward. The trend of the coast soon caused
them to man the port braces and give the brig a safe northern slant.
After that they all breathed easier.

"Drunken man's luck it wasn't a lee shore," muttered Collins to
Anthony. "We'll git more wind sure before tonight."

The incident proved a fortunate one for Anthony. In the estimation of all hands he advanced considerably. A certain subdued humorous tolerance with which he had so far been treated now gave
way to a more serious acceptance and respect. From that time on his
appearance on deck with a sextant was hailed by the older members of
the crew in particular with a secret sigh of relief. The vagaries of the
captain's navigation even when sober were only too well known. It
was not long before Anthony discovered the cause.

The captain's sextant, he found after a little checking, had once
been repaired and its angle altered. Evidently it had had a fall some
time prior to the American Revolution. Consequently the more accurate the observation the more certain the error. It was only a few
seconds—but at the end of a voyage! To amuse himself he worked
out a table of compensation.

But of all this he determined for the time being to say nothing.
In the captain's present mood it would do no good. And knowledge
was power. Excellent seaman as Captain Jorham ordinarily was,
should the mixing of dogs' noses continue, Anthony was by no means
certain how much responsibility might not yet rest on the inexperienced
shoulders of his mate. It would be well to keep safe what little claim
to authority he had. With this Mrs. Jorham and the now greatly perturbed Collins agreed.

Indeed, from the time of their brief glimpse of Africa dead ahead
Anthony worked out the course daily with the aid of the quartermaster. The captain was already moving in spheres without parallels, a
diviner ether and an ampler air. The cabin itself had begun to take
on a peculiar air of unreality which Anthony could scarcely account
for. In this both the captain and his wife seemed to have an equal
share. He took the charts out of this realm of speculation into the
more sober and ecclesiastical fo'c'sle.

"Necessity makes strange bedfellows, indeed," Anthony thought as
he and Jeb Collins fumbled over the charts, laying out the compass
bearings for the day while surrounded by several bunks full of Christian martyrs and saints. The whale-oil lamp overhead swung with the
motion of the ship causing murky shadows to chase over the face of

the map like little clouds over a miniature landscape. The face of
St. Lawrence who was lashed on his gridiron to the forward bulkhead
grew alternately dark and pale. Beneath him the terra cotta flames
continued to flicker. Someone, Anthony noticed, had put a tarpaulin
over Christ. St. Catherine's wheel was hung with oilskins and gear.

"It's a turrible time on this little ship when the skipper begins wal-
lerin' in grog," remarked Collins looking about a little apprehensively.
"Luck's usually with him even then, I dew allow, but it don't seem
right to tempt it tew far by lashin' all these heathen people in a Christian fo'c'sle. 'Sides, 'tain't shipshape. I kivered that awful bleedin'
heart myself. Looked like murder and mutiny on board."

He turned to the chart again with a distinct look of relief.

"Lay it a good deal north of west, Mr. Adverse. Ye'll be wantin'
to give them Sallee rovers a wide berth and yet not nose tew near
Minorca. Call it nor'west by north, that's about right till tomorrow
allowin' fer what you said the variation is. She logs about ten knots
in this breeze. Ye can see where that ul git you tomorrow noon.
Hope ye can git the sun then. Maybe? But as I've been sayin' all
erlong it's comin' on to bla-ow. We're not far enough off the coast
yet to suit me."

They went up on deck together. Astern, between the low slate-
coloured cloud that covered them like the roof of a cave, and the leaden
floor of the sea below, was a long bright streak, green, intensely clear,
and apparently gaining on them fast. A flock of gulls streamed past
screaming, going downwind. Beyond the clear streak Anthony thought
he could see land. A long range of sombre hills wrought with a freedom that only ruthless nature could attain were lifting sullen, tortured
peaks above the horizon. Suddenly a hellish glow of sunset flashed
redly from peak to peak. As if returning an answer their dark battlements lightened and winked with sheets of internal flame. Their pinnacles started to wither away. From beneath them endless lines of
mad cavalry with white tossing manes came galloping down on the
ship. The rumble of distant artillery rang around the horizon, a volley
of bullet-like hail spattered the sails and deck.

"Land O," roared the lookout.

As if warned by instinct Captain Elisha instantly appeared on the
quarter-deck.

"Ready about, take your stations for stays," he roared through his
speaking trumpet.

"Stations!" howled Collins. "Git 'em up, Mr. Adverse, don't lose
no time. There's no chance to strip her now." His whistle shrilled.

"Put the helm da-own," bellowed the captain.

The *Wampanoag* shot around into the wind her canvas slatting and
thundering. Warned by the pother overhead as much as by Collins'

now profane encouragements the men were at their stations before the ship teetered into the eye of the wind. As if she had received a sudden blow from a furious fist the *Wampanoag* was taken aback.

"Haul taut! Mainsail haul!" bellowed the enormous trumpet. The aft sails moved around together and filled with a loud report. The yards were braced up. "Let go and haul," commanded the trumpet. Anthony saw the foreyards come round and the canvas bellow out. The jibs were sheeted home. With a great bound under the first full impulse of the gale the brig dashed off on the opposite tack. The men went about coiling up ropes as if nothing had happened.

The cause of all this had been a glimpse of Cape Carthage to leeward. The manœuvre was repeated again several times that night. The captain remained on deck for hours until he had worked well out to the northward into the open sea.

Under the outward buffeting of the elements and the internal refreshment with which Philadelphia constantly supplied him, the captain seemed that night to surpass the usual limits of human personality. He stood behind the steersman with his legs braced far apart in what appeared to Anthony to be seven league sea boots. The foam and spume streamed off his oilskins that fluttered in occasional wild glimpses of moonlight like infernal rags. As the night wore on his voice took on more and more of a brazen quality. He drove his crew and his ship hour by hour clawing off the coast of Africa, thrashing along now on a short, mad stretch to leeward, and now beating up into the teeth of the wind. The rigging shrieked and the bows of the *Wampanoag* thundered and foamed. In the tireless figure on the quarter-deck at home in the storm, Anthony thought he could glimpse a more colossal emanation of the man who had been at one with the world when he sat in the carriage at Genoa watching the sunset. It was the curious quality of this man that he seemed during the night to grow in stature, to be an antidote for fear. Perhaps it was the immense brazen voice from the trumpet that all obeyed. Perhaps? When the dawn broke Anthony was surprised to see again that Captain Jorham was really not so tall. A rather short figure if you looked closely.

About dawn the brig was put before the wind again. From now on it would be a straight run for the Straits. During the night she had been stripped of canvas and was driving with nothing but a reefed foresail, a spanker, and a jib to keep her from yawing. There were two men at the wheel, for the seas were now coming on so fast from behind as to kick her stern at times almost clear of the water. The drag when she settled back again was terrific. Four arms on the spokes were none too many. They shook out a reef in the foresail but it was not enough—another. She continued to plunge more determinedly.

"It'll never do to broach to na-ow," shouted the captain in Anthony's ear as an unusually large wave rose and combed just aft of the taff-rail only to break and go hissing by.

"Na-ow's the time to get a little more drag on her for'd. Do you see, mister?" he roared, pointing to some of the crew busy rigging preventer stays to the foretopmast, "I'm going to give her a double reefed foretops'l."

Presently there was a report as if a small cannon had been fired and streams of ripped canvas whipped about frantically, beating the crew off the yard. Collins drove them back and made them cut it loose. It was snatched to leeward.

"The old sail," said the captain. "Thought we'd try that first. Na-ow watch. Ye might have to do this sometime."

He went forward banging on the scuttle for the other watch who came tumbling up. The new sail was hoisted and bent on slowly with extra lashings. When it opened out they let it blow away clear of the lower yard. For a moment it stood out flat and clear like a horizontal banner streaming forward. At that instant the captain roared and it was sheeted home to the lower yard with an even pull on both tackles.

The brig leaped ahead. The men at the wheel wrestled with the spokes over a brief "S"-shaped course that soon flattened out into a clear wake of bubbles left straight behind. Aft, the waves still rose now as before, followed, but fell astern. Captain Jorham returned to the quarter-deck and spat over the side. He cupped his hands to shout. "Never let 'em slat back on ye. Ye hev to sheet home *jes'* so. If ye let the blocks whip back and tangle, ye're gorn!"

They stood together a while watching the ship tear through the crests and race down into the hollows beyond as if in mad pursuit of some invisible prey. But she rose now and seemed to be lifted ahead, the sails booming as they came up out of the valleys of water into the full force of the wind.

Under the pressure of her increased canvas the *Wampanoag* was whipped forward at startling speed. Anthony could feel transferred to his own body her wild desire to twist and lay-to which the men at the wheel constantly checked. It must be certain, he thought, that something would go. In reality it was only a good hearty gale, but to his inexperience it seemed a hurricane. When the gusts came he waited for an ominous crack overhead, having no adequate idea of the relative strength of yards, cordage, and ship's timbers. So he stood for hours, watching, but nothing happened. The ship had been made for this, he had to admit at last.

The bell was struck with the spray and rain streaming off it. The men at the wheel and the watches were relieved regularly. Old Collins heaved the log. The wind keened through the rigging, and the turmoil of waters raced by. As the sun sank at last in a red mist and the horizon narrowed to the ship's dimensions he began to feel confident again. Soon even the ship disappeared except for a few feet of deck and a dim tracery aloft. He was alone in the universe standing on something. A few feet aft the bearded face of a sailor smoking a pipe seemed to be floating without a body over the feeble glow of the binnacle. Only when the ship rolled could you sense the man's body eclipsing a few misty stars. A faint glimmer from the stern windows followed and followed over the tossing wake. The sound of hissing and foaming was muffled by monotony. An endless, meaningless story told in a mad liquid tongue, it was. Its constant narrative was unimportant, only its cessation or a complete change of tone could be significant. It was the same with the sails. They would go on that way and go on—till the wind changed. He turned and went below.

As he slid the scuttle hood over his head and descended into the cabin the piping of the gale and the song of the rigging was suddenly cut off and made infinitely remote. It was a relief to escape it. Then the curious face at the aft end of the cabin was looking at him. He paused half-way on the ladder listening, missing the noise of wind and water, only to become aware gradually of the internal life of the ship.

It was a kind of suspended motion accompanied by muffled cracklings, strainings and squeaks, groans and the hushed swishing of water under the keel. The floor of the cabin tilted always to another angle, poised, tilted again, slid, and climbed. A long gurgle of bilge water bubbled and stopped like a drowned flute at every subsidence. Clothes suspended from hooks pointed to the middle of the floor only to find the ship's sides nuzzling them. *They* had not moved. And to all of this there was a kind of inexpressible rhythm, a repetition which no one could predict or remember. But it went on.

Yet the main impression of the cabin bathed in its smoky yellow light was that those who sat there were waiting for something inevitable to happen. As Anthony stood on the ladder and looked about him he was instantly aware of it. Yet he could not account for it at all. It was like listening behind a closed door for someone he knew was there but who made no sign. Mrs. Jorham was knitting. She did not even look up. Philadelphia was laying the table, noiselessly. Captain Jorham was nodding with his mouth open. Yet they were waiting—not for him. The shadows slipped slowly from side to side. The lamp hummed as if a moth were in it. The Virgin wrapped her cloak about her and looked in its folds. He came down slowly, peeled off his heavy wet coat and sat in his bunk. The air was not so fresh down here. He was tired and perhaps a little dizzy.

The same impression that he had going to Genoa came over him. He was not moving at all. The sea outside, the shadows, the events in the cabin were all coming out of somewhere and going past him. He, watching this vague panorama, remained still. Yes, the long corridors in Father Xavier's house with all the frescoes in the wall had gone past him. It was all like walking in a treadmill. The convent, the days at the Casa and the streets of Livorno, Faith, Angela, Vincent, Genoa—tonight in the cabin was going by like that. It had all come out of the darkness into the light of his eyes and returned into the darkness again. Dreams of it remained in memory. There was more, more to come. You could not stop it. You walked to the last rung in the treadmill—and then? Travel! He laughed silently as the side of the ship pressed itself against him.

Mrs. Jorham beckoned for him to come and eat but he could not. He felt decidedly dizzy and tired after the long day. He wished the ship would stay still. It kept moving about *him* as the centre of everything, sickeningly. He began to talk to Mrs. Jorham in a low voice through which now and then over his own monotone he could catch the loud ticks of the clumsy chronometer. It sounded like a treadmill. What she replied he could not remember. After a while he went on deck again. In the darkness—he was glad of the darkness—he was very sick.

The fit passed. For a day or two he was dizzy, then very clear again. The motion of the ship no longer troubled him. He was going with it now. He forgot it although the wind had increased if anything. Captain Jorham had added a storm staysail in the teeth of it and the brig rode steadier.

Anthony often wondered what would have happened to them if Captain Jorham had taken to his bunk before they were clear of the Straits. For days now it had not been possible to get a sight of the sun. The ship had been swept steadily westward in a smother of spume half the time with a pall of rolling, dark clouds driving over her and billowing down so low sometimes as to seem about to touch the masts. Through all this pother of the elements Captain Elisha carried his ship by dead reckoning and sea instinct. To him the currents, the tides, the very colour of the water were guides. They scarcely had a glimpse of the stars. At last there were some signs of a break in the gale. The men in the tops watched eagerly for a landfall.

It came suddenly, and unexpectedly to starboard. One day at noon the pall overhead lightened, the sun struggled through. Before them the wind seemed to be tearing the clouds to rags. Without the least warning, as if a curtain had been raised, long lines of snow-capped mountains were seen marching on their right. Sixty miles inland the wild hills of the Sierra Nevadas rose above the brown plains of

Granada with continental fragments of dark cloud-bank breaking against them, clouds rolling up in white mist, filing through the passes, and being driven and harried westward along the slopes. An interplay of swiftly moving titanic shadows turned the long coasts of Spain fading away before them to the southeast into a Satanic country lit inland by infernal gleams.

"That's Cape Gata," said Captain Jorham, indicating a point of land with a few white houses and a fierce surf leaping up about a small, stone battery. "And it's darn lucky if there ain't a British frigate anchored under its lee." He gave the *Wampanoag* a sharp sheer to the south. "We're too far north this time. Sartin we *did* miss Algiers all right, by about two hundred miles, and there's a nasty current along here that helps the British right up to Port Mahon. We'll jes' hev to run for it now. Gib is about a day's sail away."

He turned and whistled loudly through his fingers.

"Lord send this wind holds. Mister, do you know what gettin' through the Straits means? Sounds simple na-ow, doesn't it? Wall, sir, in 'ninety-two I was hangin' out at Luff's boarding house at Gib with five other skippers, mostly British, for six 'tarnal weeks while the west wind bla-ew and bla-ew. There's alers a five to six knot current settin' in through the Straits but a long westerly bla-ow makes it worse. There's eddies then that jes' swallers fishers and small craft. Wall, the seventh week I says to myself, ' 'Lisha, you're gittin' barnacles on the sole o' your trousers,' says I. So I ups anchor and in two days I beats out after p'intin' back and forth between Tarifa and Tangier till I thought I'd wear out the gudgeons. Y' see I knowed all o' them five other skippers was up on O'Hara's Folly with glasses lawfin' like loons. Y' see? Na-ow somethin' happened to the current and one arternoon I jes' sailed up to Trafalgar. Nor that ain't all. I got a cargo at Cadiz and took it round to Lisbon. 'N I filled up with wine and shoes there for the garrison and come back on the same wind, and there was all five o' them Britishers still settin' ra-ound the table at Luff's with corns on their tails. *'Officer, give me one penny for de bread, I say, officer, give me one penny for de bread,'* says I, stickin' my knot in over the geraniums. Wall, *sir,* there was enough crockery come through that winder to furnish an admiral's galley. And that's true, and that's the Straits." He whistled again through his fingers shrilly. Collins laughed.

Next morning Calpe and Abyla, the two immortal pillars, rose superbly before them towering above the surrounding mountains. The gale was blowing itself out. But there was a choppy sea tossing in the Straits. They passed a British ship of the line wallowing drunkenly into Gibraltar with her topmasts housed and only her courses set. The great rollers swept her sides, now exposing her gleaming copper and now leaping to her third line of gun ports, smothering her in spray from time to time. The *Wampanoag* fled past her and down the narrow gulf with a line of mountains on either side and the strong wind behind. The topmasts were being sent up again. Before the Rock lay behind them the brig was once more a tall ship.

They burst out into the Atlantic with long curtains of rain overtaking them as the gale finally blew itself out in a succession of dying squalls. A rare display of rainbows grew and withered, arching away into the hills toward Tangier. Land birds came and perched on the masts. Gulls cried peevishly behind till a fierce lanner came and drove them away.

"Golondrina, señor," said a Spanish sailor to Anthony, scooping up a tired bird from the deck and warming him in his hands. "From my country, over there." The man had a young, ardent face and sensitive fingers that trembled over the bird. Anthony felt sorry for him. The sailor stood leaning over the bulwarks gazing at the white villages among the mountains. Suddenly he pointed toward a lighthouse with a small, red-roofed town clustered about it; orange trees, and barren hills behind. He took off his red, tasselled cap and his eyes shone.

"My town," he cried, "Tarifa! Pardon, señor. Ah, the girls of *my* town! They have the true gracia. Have you seen the Andalusian women yet? No! Your eyes have not yet then been completed!" He leaned over the bird in his hand. "See, its head is small but it has true wisdom there, señor. It knows enough to fly home. El saber nunca ocupa lugar. Fly, golondrina, to the little house under the tower," he whispered. Anthony could not hear the rest. The man smiled and cast it into the air. It circled and made off for Spain. "The last point of Europe!" the sailor cried stretching out his arms, "my town! You return, swallow, and I, I, Juan Garcia, I go to Cuba and there are no graciosas there. Ah, adiós, hermosa, bendita sea la tierra que tu pesas."

"It *is* a beautiful place," said Anthony looking after the departing bird, "Europe, old and noble."

"Sí, sí, señor, sí, sí!" The young sailor's face glowed.

"Pipe down, onion," shouted Collins from the wheel, glaring with his cold, blue eyes.

The man's face darkened. He turned with a magnificent gesture to Anthony. "Señor mío, le beso a usted la mano; y sí hay algo en que le puedo servir tiene usted—aquí!"

"Belay that," thundered the voice. But the youth stalked forward ignoring the quartermaster.

"Don't let 'em hornswaggle ye, Mr. Adverse," warned Collins. "I'm tellin' ye. A louse like him has enough garlic on his breath to start a kippered herring fer home let alone a bird. For a peso he'd stick a knife in your back."

"It's a beautiful morning, isn't it, Collins?" said Anthony suddenly, and looking him in the eye. "I'm proud to be the first officer of a ship on such a day. Did you ever hear this, Collins?

> 'Loud uttering satire, day and night, on each
> Succeeding race and little pompous work
> Of man.'

That you, Collins?"

"Not egg-*zactly*, sir, not day and night, sir. I wouldn't say that." The man shifted his quid. "Sartainly not to the *first* officer on a beautiful mornin'."

He twisted his lock. They looked at each other and laughed.

"All right, then," said Anthony, "all *right!*"—and went below. Collins gave a slight whistle, but not for more wind. They were in the Atlantic now and the only man on board who could use a sextant was to be respected. A little later Captain Jorham came up with his glasses and swept the horizon. His legs were behaving independently and that was a bad sign.

Another bad sign was the topsails of a great English convoy coming down from the direction of Cadiz. Captain Jorham had no desire to bring down some fast sloops of war to investigate his intentions. He soon lost the convoy by cracking on every yard of canvas the *Wampanoag* could carry.

The little brig bloomed out sail after sail till she towered from deck to royalmasts with everything that would draw. The stu'nsail booms were got up and rigged. The jibs were guyed out. Above the royals were skysails. A balloon sail was the skipper's especial pet. It fluttered now and then when she luffed a little. The skipper sat on the bulwarks and kept his eye on it and, "Ease her, ease her," and "now a rap full," he would say to the man at the wheel, "and hold her there."

"Aye, aye," muttered the hand, nervously turning his quid.

"Yankee skipper, comin' down the river," hummed the captain to himself, unconsciously patting the ship's rail.

"Now you're walking out like a flea onto the belly of the world, old gel.

"There's nothin' but blue water between here and Bermudy. Mister, it's clearin' fine," he said, turning suddenly to Anthony. "You can take all the sights you want to na-ow. That there promontory to the south is Cape Spartel, and yonder north over the convoy is Barbate. We're just about the middle o' the entrance to the Straits and that's so nigh exactly thirty-six North and six East that you can mark that off on the chart and take it as your jumpin' off place for the v'y'ge. Na-ow lay a course for jes' west o' the Azores, say, thirty-two—forty. You might sight Corva. Keep nor'west of it if you do. You'll pick up the Northeast Trade thereaba-outs this time of year, and from then on it's plain dumb-fool sailin' to the Indies. You jes' let the wind push you. Run from any sail ye see and don't borrow no trouble. Me—I've got a good deal of trouble on my mind. Na-ow I'm goin' below, and don't you call me unless you're chased or it comes on to bla-ow. Short of suthin', call it nothin', and *leave me with God!*"

He collapsed his telescope with a final snap, and hitching a little sideways scuttled below like a crab.

"Sounds to me like Old Stormalong's resignin'," said Collins as the captain's shoulders disappeared into the cabin followed soon after by Philadelphia with a steaming pot of coffee. "But it'll take more than coffee and a dog's nose to sniff us safe past the Azores unless we want to fetch up on one o' them palmy isles. I remember oncet in the Pacific, when the skipper went off on a long spell like this. We jes' drifted round like the ark for a month, and no doves never came back neither. What do you Noah about that?" chuckled the quartermaster closing one eye solemnly. "Wall, he finally sobered up and brought her round the Horn.

"Mr. Adverse, if I know the signs of the skipper's weather, 'n I ort to, arter sailin' with him since 'eighty-two," continued Collins hemming and hawing a little at having to discuss his captain's vagaries, "it's goin' to be right wet from here to Havaner. And that leaves it pretty well up to you and me." He took a turn or two considering.

"Na-ow," he took another turn and hitched his trousers.

"Na-ow, how would it be if you left the deck to me and I left the navigatin' to you, 'cept fer heavin' the log and markin' up the slate and sich like. I'm askin' you since you're mate now *o*-fficially."

"Is it orders you want?" asked Anthony admiring the wise little bantam of a man with a black silk handkerchief knotted dapperly about his tanned neck and a silver whistle thrust in his pocket.

The quartermaster nodded.

"Very well then, take charge of the deck," said Anthony. "I think I can find out where we are. I have my own sextant, you know."

"That's *one* blessin'," said Collins. He tugged at his forelock. "I'm glad you realize the sitooation, Mr. Adverse. But I wonder if you dew? Let's git rid of ears yonder and I'll partikilarize."

He went to the wheel, and sending the man there forward, began to con the ship himself, running his eyes over the sails constantly and taking advantage of every puff and slant to get the most out of her. Presently he had Anthony in his place, directing him with one hand on the wheel himself.

"Ye have to develop a feel for the thing and that comes slowly. Steady na-ow, bear da-own, sir. Ye keep a kind o' constant balance against the pull. It would never do to be taken aback carryin' everything as we are now. It might yank all the sticks out of her. Ye have to watch like a hawk for squalls, tew. A small cloud on the horizon and white water comin' down fast, that's trouble! I'm going to strip some of the canvas off soon as we're sure the skipper and the Almighty are tetertate like he indicated they would be soon. Less hurry the more speed when ye're short-handed like we are. The old hooker's a fast one though!"

Feeling the ship as it were in his grasp, Anthony stood fascinated but with every sense alive, watching her sway over the long grey seas; hearing the wash and gurgle about the rudder behind. To the quiet voice of Collins which continued in his ears the sea was providing a half-musical accompaniment.

"Na-ow as I was sayin', when I sent the man for'd—every sailor has ears and eyes in the back of his head, ye know—as I was sayin', our sitooation *ain't* comical. It's like this. The skipper's off again. He usually goes on till he has the *squeegees*. That may take two weeks, or yet a month. 'Tain't snakes. It's his dead baby what comes back. He hears her. Na-ow it won't do to let the crew get wind o' that, cause they'd *see* her. Ye see I know. This here is my 'steenth v'y'ge with the cap'n.

"He's a kind o' curious one. There ain't a better skipper afloat. He made a fortune or two on some Canton runs. Then he married him a wife—below now—and built a fa-ine house at Scituate, lookout and all. Meant to settle down. Wall, they lost their only little gal. About three years old, she was. And after that he started to go to pot on land. They dew say his house was baby-haunted. Nobody won't live there since. But I dunno. Anyway him and his wife up and cleared out. He left her to home for one v'y'ge and it was then I heard tell her baby came back. Anyway the Missus wouldn't stay on, and he'd drunk up his money or lost it on some venture or other. The *Wampanoag* is all he's got, for the house can't be sold or rented. There's lots of skippers laughs at him for havin' his Missus aboard, but believe me, he needs her, and I'll say she *dew* look after him wonderful. Besides, she never said it, but I'm sure she's scairt to stay behind.

"Wall, you see how it is. I said fer ye to look after the sun and the charts, but you'll have the cabin on yer hands too, Mr. Adverse. That won't be easy. *Ye got to keep the old man below.* Give him liquor and humour him. Git him over it. If he gits on deck there'll be hell to pay. Wait till he begins to hear that baby walkin'. Paddlin' footsteps on the deck, Mr. Adverse! Mrs. Jorham'll do the rest. She knows how to peter off after the horrors. A little less every day. As

fer me na-ow, I'll get the ship to Havaner if ye can give me some
notion where we are every day or so. Na-ow then I'll take her over,
I expect."

He resumed the wheel and squared his shoulders as if he felt the
mantle of authority settling on them.

"Coil that loose end up, you swab," he roared at one of the Britishers
who was sitting on a pail near the galley. "And git for'd. Step lively.
Ye're dead from yer ankles up and yer feet are asleep. Do you think
ye can put yer bum on a bucket and let it *draw* barnacles on this ship?
Send that man aft to the wheel again."

The sailor slunk off shuffling his bare feet uncomfortably. Anthony
went below. Already the cabin seemed more eery. Now he knew
what they were waiting for.

When he came on deck some hours later to take the sun Collins had
already reduced sail considerably. The skysail and royals were gone
and the balloon sail had vanished. It was a clear day and he managed
to get a good sight.

"I forgot to tell ye that the nigger knows about things in the cabin,"
said Collins looking on over the figures. "He's been with 'em fer ten
years. They own him. I don't want yer to mistake me, Mr. Adverse,
in sayin' what I did about the skipper. Ye won't, will ye? I'm no
sea-lawyer, ye know." The man looked at him with some doubt and
.anxiety in his honest eyes.

"You can depend on it I understand, Collins," said Anthony.

"Then we'll say no more unless we have tew. Na-ow where do ye
make it today?" They fell to over the chart with perfect understanding of each other.

The seriousness and sheer necessity of the work they were doing
and the manifest trust and regard of the seasoned old sailor caused
Anthony to ponder a little as he went below to check over his figures
again and again. This was the first bit of work he had ever done
which seemed vitally important, for a moment an end in itself as well
as a means. Over that little sheaf of figures he had completely forgotten everything else. There was not anywhere even a little rainbow
of play lurking about it. On that basis, then, he and Collins had met.
Here was a platform that he could stand on with many an honest man.
"With many another honest man," he corrected himself.

He was a man. "By God," he thought, "I've grown up! What a
lucky thing Mr. Bonnyfeather put that sextant in the chest. What a
gift!" Suddenly he saw that old gentleman from an entirely new
angle. He *had* worked. "I am his heir." He made sundry good
resolutions. On the chart of the Atlantic Ocean he marked down the
exact spot where he had overtaken his majority.

CHAPTER TWENTY-EIGHT

THE SEED OF A MIRACLE

THE passing of time on a long voyage Anthony soon discovered was not announced to the inner-self by bells, chronometers, or even by days and nights. He could apprehend its duration only as a succession of varying moods superinduced by the weather and the latitude. And in these moods, he also noticed, the ship herself, as a positive personality with a certain will of her own, one to be humoured rather than baldly controlled, seemed to participate.

The mood on starting from Genoa, for instance, had been a briskly busy one gradually relaxing into routine and habit until the gale had overtaken them. Then from somewhere off the coast of Tripoli to a spot in the Atlantic southwest of Gibraltar they had been harried by the storm. It was true they had profited in distance by that harrying but the sky had been leaden and down-billowing, the ship had been plunging and wallowing; rain, spray, and green water had delayed them. No one could be comfortable for a moment. A kind of business-like melancholy and glum endurance punctuated by anxiety had gripped all alike.

But as they turned northward for the region of the trades, an entirely new mood held the whole ship. The wind piped only a little, and quite merrily. The brig still swept along but paused now and then to dance a bit and to dash a capful of spray back playfully. The air was cool and the sun was bright. Melancholy had vanished. A certain active ease and happy relief could have been noted in the *Wampanoag's* log. This, as they pressed west, and the air became gradually hotter, lost its mercurial quality and threatened to end in a vague feeling of sloth. The wind faltered. Off the Azores in late July one moved like the ship—reluctantly. As yet they were not in the refreshing track of the trades. A sticky south wind came in puffs over the port bow.

Meanwhile—the time consisted mostly of meanwhiles—with no direct responsibility for the ship, and with the course for the day agreed upon, Anthony found time to ransack his chest from top to bottom and to improvise a splendid, solitary mode of existence which was so pleasing to his natural soul that it eventually caused him alarm. He left the madonna swaddled just as Faith had packed it. Under the great-coat where Mr. Bonnyfeather had asked him to look was a tight canvas roll containing one hundred guineas. There was also a large box of beautiful calfskin quartos which Mr. Bonnyfeather had had newly bound for him. These he proceeded to devour from Addison to Zeno.

Now he was able to read what, when, and as long as he wanted to, and to think things out even if it took half the day. With an almost complete cessation of events, and with no new people to meet and adjust himself to, he had opportunity to think over his whole existence; to arrange and to classify; to trace cause and effect; and to evaluate.

His entire past now lay behind him in a distant perspective out of which he could pick and choose. In it he thought he saw himself as he actually was. Out of it he began to reconstruct himself as he thought he would like to be. Hence resolutions and resolves, heart burnings and yearnings, regrets, hopes, a few tears and not a little laughter as he lay in the shadow of a boat; lulled by the slow motion of the ship, the sound of the wind and water, and the disappearance of time. All the sorrows and delights of comparative solitude had become his.

Of a few things in his own nature he became acutely aware. He no longer merely accepted them as unchangeable. Some things he would change. There was, for instance, his difficulty in seeing clearly the difference between his own visions and the outside world. Was this because his senses laid hold of things so fiercely and yet so delicately that the images of them were burned into and transformed by his own nature into something else? If so, how did that world, that something else always becoming within him, correspond to events without? On what basis of reality could he proceed? Which world should he accept? Was there a working compromise that he could find?

So far there seemed only one place where the two worlds met. It was in that ideal, or state of being, which was represented to him by the madonna. He could see now that it was a personal accident that she, his particular image of her, had become his visualization of the being in which both inner and outer worlds met and by which they were controlled. Something must control both life and reality, he saw, vision and fact, man and nature. To that something he felt akin as if some portion of it were in him. Yet *he* was also in nature; yet the material world lay without! It was not only the motion of the ship which now caused him to reel as he tried to understand all this.

He would not worry himself any more over the fact that his private image of that in which his own nature and the world met was wrapped up in a rag in his chest. That might be absurd, or it might not. It was convenient to have some image of this necessity. He did not have to be literal about it; he could accept it as his habit, as an aid—and, as Father Xavier had suggested, the image might hold in its arms further developments.

It was a very ancient image that men had found pregnant for millenniums. If he tried to make a new one it might become mathematical, he felt, and he feared that. Why? he wondered. Figures represented thoughts only. There was more to life than thought. Feelings! A figure of a figure—zero was that! So a mathematical madonna would be more ridiculous than a clay madonna. He could not apply even a pronoun to a mathematical image. A word?

Could he make it a word? Perhaps *the* Thing *was* a word. "In the Beginning was the Word." Ah! he had almost forgotten that. The Word, eh? But a man had written that? Had God written it? Suppose he had, what would be the difference in understanding it? A man would have to understand it. And a word must stand for something. This word then had no Image. *The* Word had no Image! Why had it been said that way? "In the Beginning was the Word and the word was light." What did, what could light have to do with it? In the shadow of the boat he stood up and prayed to be able to see. He groped, drawn by a great necessity to try to know all things; all things in one.

All things in one! In that idea there was some glimmering of hope, he thought. In his mind he marshalled what he had already thought. He tried to put it together and go on. Suddenly in his intensity of feeling he felt that he had ceased to think by stages, logically, one thing after another. All of this process was collapsing; telescoping as it were into one, a toneless, colourless state of apprehension in which he understood without making sentences for himself why the Word had no image. In it objects and what reflects them meet. "IT IS" is alive, it is "I AM."

An intense feeling of exaltation accompanied the process of this discovery and then a flashing shock. He stood leaning against the boat, tired, with his eyes closed. Dazzling fire images chased themselves over his darkened eyeballs as if he had been looking at the sun. "Some minute copy of this force that resolved both the inner and the outer world into one must be inside myself. Or I am indeed undone," his lips moved. The fire streaks on his retina began to arrange themselves into a pattern like that of the sunburst behind the madonna's head. "That image again, always that!" He opened his eyes and looked at the sea to rest them.

"If the light hurts yer eyes ye ought to wear a sunshade," said Mrs. Jorham, who, he now discovered, was sitting near and watching him. He had been absorbed in himself, he knew, but she must have brought her rocking chair on deck almost noiselessly. She must have been sitting there a good while. He resented it.

"It's *not* the sun," he said.

"Oh!" She stopped rocking a minute to look at him. "Jes' seein' things, eh? Didn't know ye was troubled that way."

"Well, I am, Mrs. Jorham," he replied a little tartly.

"Um!" she mumbled.

He hated to be questioned this way. "Good Lord!"

"Wait till ye *hear* 'em," she said suddenly, dropping her knitting. Oh, yes, *she* heard things. The woman had her troubles. He remembered now. She took up her knitting again.

"I find a lot of comfort in this." She held up the big socks with the needles in it. "It's kind o' like makin' the sheep go over the stile, ye know. Ye jes' keep countin'. I'm sorry for ye, Mr. Adverse, 'deed I am."

"Oh, thank you, Mrs. Jorham," said Anthony. But she would not be repulsed.

"Want to come and hold the yarn?" she said. He shook his head.

"It's real bad then? But sakes alive, I know something better than this. Come on down and I'll show ye my sewing."

At first he thought he could not, but she turned and looked at him expectantly. He laughed at himself and went. After all why should he, Anthony Adverse, be so superior? Wasn't it only last night that he had seen himself climbing into a bed with Miss Florence Udney? She had been there perfectly plainly. Florence! He had touched her on the hips. Round and smooth. He could still feel her by him today. Very soft, well— Perhaps he could afford after all to look at Mrs. Jorham's sewing. Anyway she was getting it out of the basket.

"How wonderful women were!" The basket was full of beautiful things: A quilt cover all puzzled together out of little triangles of silk stitched microscopically; baby clothes; a fragment of lace work on pins, showing a spider spinning its web. What a design, very delicate, quite spidery! "Made with rows of single Brussels' stitches," said Mrs. Jorham. More baby clothes, a small cap embroidered with tiny violets; that must be for a doll. You could hardly say. Some babies were very small. Table things worked with blood-red roses and tawny leaves. Doll clothes, undoubtedly doll clothes, hemmed. They must have been hemmed in Lilliput. And Captain Jorham's shirts having buttonholes worked in them and a big "E. J." on the neck.

"Marvellous!" What a good way this was to forget God. "In the beginning was the Word . . ." his mind seemed to echo. Oh, bother! Look at the sewing.

Mrs. Jorham put a worn, silver thimble on her finger and began to select various needles and coloured threads out of her neat little basket where ribbons and the eyes of four pairs of scissors stared at one from the lid. She laid out some square patches and began a sort of mono-

logue to herself about the art of sewing which Anthony was allowed
to overhear. A man could be interested in it if he wanted to be. . . .
"And the Word was God." Ah, yes, he had forgotten *that!* "The
Word was God." That was where a personality, an image for the
Word, came in. It was God said, "Let there be light. And there was
light." What did light have to do with it? For goodness' sake,
Anthony, can't you listen to the poor woman? She's talking. Listen
you . . . you . . .

"Sewin' is kinda like playin' on the harpsichord. Ye got to get
yer fingers used to it jes' by plain practice. There's the needle and
there's the thread. Some of the stitches ye make look like notes.
After a while ye can run 'em together without thinkin' about it, and
that's when ye begin to enjoy it. That's when ye begin to play
whole tunes. Looks like a melody, doesn't it?" She held up a pillow
cover. "Larned that out Canton way. Them butterflies are the same
both sides. This here vine's done on linen with flax flourishin' thread.
Land, ye'd think that vine was growin' there, wouldn't ye? I used
to do samplers, but that's too easy. Straight-stitch embroidery on
tammy-cloth's nice. But it's appliqué work I like, flat stitch and outlining with back-stitch. A few corded outlines and fancy stitches, or
the ground with back-stitch settin' in. Some uses a goose or a weighted
cushion but I jes' hold my hands like this. See!" She made the
needle fly and the flower began to grow. . . .

"But what *did* light have to do with it?" the obstinate voice demanded. "Hell's fire, wait and find out," he answered himself. "Mrs.
Jorham is doing the talking."

"Did ye ever think how many kinds of stitches there are? Look
here, I'll show ye some on these patches. Here's a plain running-
stitch. Everybody tries that, even children. Next is back-stitchin'.
You take up six threads, draw it out, then you go three threads back
and pull it through six beyond. Real fast! This way!" Her needle
seemed to devour the cloth. "Right to left, of course, only crazy
people and Chinee go contrary. Then there's hemming. You have
to know how to fold the cloth. There's plain hems, and ornamental
hems what runs along the edges and in and out zigzagging over the
sides, and then stitches with a loop. And you ought to know how to
fasten threads off-and-on. That patch is done for. Now give me two
more. This is sewing.

"An antique seam, and an open work seam, and you can make an
open-hemmed-double-seam. Now let me have a big patch. Gathering
is what I like." She wrinkled the cloth and flashed the needle through
the little waves on the patch so fast he could see only a darting point
of light with the thread following. "Na-ow ye pull it together.
Ain't that nice? *Whee!* Now if ye want ye can just pick out yer

crinkles into couples or fours and start smockin' 'em. I used to make curtains for doll houses that a way; made some for . . ." She stopped. "Land sakes, I've bruk the needle! Give me another, the big one. I'll show ye how to galloon, but first here's whipping. . . ."

"Whipping?" said the voice of Captain Elisha who raised his head from the table where he had apparently been asleep. "Whipping is what ye ought to have. It's ye that's temptin' her aboard this ship na-ow with all yer makin' of doll clothes. I know! She'd never have followed us if ye hadn't come along. It's her mother she wants. Y're turnin' this cabin into a nursery. Can't fool me. I know y' aren't makin' them baby clothes for Abner's brats. It's for her. Where's that doll?"

He got up and began to hunt around peevishly.

"Elisha, ye go and lay da-own. It's bad enough without havin' ye on my hands, *tew*. Ye know very well ye asked and begged me to come. And I told ye what would happen. I told ye. Didn't I?"

"Yes, woman, I ain't blamin' ye for losin' her. But ye oughtn't to be temptin' her on with that doll. It's waitin' for her to come fer it that does me in. Give me a drink.

"God!" said he freezing to the spot where he stood. "What's that on deck now?"

"Only a rope end, Captain Jorham," said Anthony. There was a stir up above. They heard the sheet and its tackle drag across the stern bar.

"Sounds as if the wind's shiftin'," said Captain Elisha. He started for the door and then shrank back. "*Ye* go up and take charge, mister. Get on with ye. Ye're in the trades now. I got real trouble da-own here." He collapsed into his chair. In a great hurry Mrs. Jorham began to mix him a drink. Anthony left the atmosphere of terror which had momentarily gripped him too and gladly ran on deck. It was true. The ship had already come about and was headed due west with a steady, sweeping breeze behind her. The trade winds at last!

"There's nothing ahead of us now but blue water for days and days," said Collins coming up looking relieved. "We can sort of settle da-own now. It's wonderful how different jes' a few minutes of these breezes makes a man feel! A few minutes ago my shirt was stickin' to my back, now look—" he let it billow out behind as he stood looking astern with satisfaction. "The old slant jes' petered out. I saw the jibs flap, and the next minute she was all a-flutter. Just had enough way on her to pay off. Wall, the skipper was about right. We picked 'em up south a bit o' where he said. I'll lay her dead west till ye get yer sight tomorrow and we can set the new course then.

If this wind holds, Mr. Adverse, we won't have to start a rope till we git nigh to Barbados." He lowered his voice. "How's things in the cabin?"

Anthony told him.

"'Pears to me like it's comin' on sooner that I expected. So she's givin' him liquor, eh! Only does that when he's right nigh the wust. Ye can expect that baby aboard almost any day now I'd say. Don't let it wear ye da-own. Las' time I got so I was listenin' for her myself. Near the Andamans that was. And a crack of lightnin', tew. Oh, the skipper told ye, did he? Wall, ye can stay on deck most of the time and 'jes' keep an eye down the companion. He's about paralysed na-ow I s'pose. Na-ow I'll go and git all sail set. We can crack it on right."

Under the urge of Collins' voice the *Wampanoag* began to burgeon again with stu'nsails and royals. The jet before the cutwater leaped high and higher as each new sail was flung out. The brig swept forward with a swift even motion. All noises blent to an even monotone. They had entered upon the long, stable mood of the western passage.

Collins had been too sanguine. The captain showed few signs of having reached a crisis. He slept, awoke, grumbled; pretended to turn a few pages of a large Bible laid open before him; drank again, and laid his head on his arms. A low sound like a saw in difficulties drifted up the cabin ladder all day long. Mrs. Jorham knitted her sixth pair of socks and waited with a fixed, blue fear in her eyes. Before the heels of the next pair were woven she expected a visitor. When no one was looking she went to a drawer in the sideboard, unlocked it, and took out a diaphanous doll. On its clothes she had lavished the last scintilla of her skill as a needlewoman. She hid it in her bunk and resumed knitting slowly.

To escape the tenseness of the cabin Anthony now spent most of his time on deck. He had a mattress brought up and slept by the cabin door. A good deal of the time he took the wheel.

It was a joy to con the ship over the smooth tables of sea towards the dark line that receded ever before her. There was scarcely any perceptible motion to the water. He became aware of the movement of the ocean now as a rhythm felt rather than movement seen. The earth itself might have been breathing and the ship rising and falling on her breast. A mile ahead a long field of weed would slowly rise and then sink again. Many minutes later the ship would answer in her turn as the horizon like a vast disk tilted slightly. For days a great, white bird, whose name Anthony did not know, followed them on motionless pinions hour after hour, as if it knew the future and were waiting for something momentous to happen to the ship. One evening with a strange cry it departed swiftly over the edge of the world in answer to a call.

As they drove westward the patches of weed increased. Then there would be great lakes of clear, blue water twinkling with a cobalt light across which the ship seemed to hurry faster. Out of one of these virgin spaces, like motes out of an eye of space, a school of porpoises suddenly rose one morning and began leaping in a succession of infinite arches before the bow. Jolly fellows with mottled bellies, they preceded the vessel like heralds of her happy royal progress across the depths.

When Anthony looked at the weed-patches with the small-glass he saw crabs and strange urchins gesticulating there like fiddlers of the ship's transit through their unknown realms. All seemed calm and happy in these latitudes. A tunny that one of the men gaffed from the chains, as though he had speared the spirit of these seas, died in spasms of rainbow colours as if its fishy ghost could only manifest itself exquisitely even in departure. All day the flying-fish scudded before them. At night he heard them flop in the water or fall with a bony clatter on the deck. When someone with a boathook fished up a branch of tree with nuts on it, it seemed to be the herbage of another planet. So far behind them now, so infinitely remote before them was even the dream of land.

But if the ocean was beautiful beyond Anthony's utmost capacity to feel, it yet furnished only half the mood of that super-equatorial aisle of the earth-star. Above them and above rose and towered the unthinkable limpid and liquid with its lights appointed; glowing; darkening; ever shifting against sameness, the impalpable womb of clouds. Islands of shadow, glittering groves of slanting rain shot with rainbows appeared and vanished; shifted and melted on the level, molten plains around about. Once a waterspout trailed its smoking skirts uncomfortably near, only to go spinning away to leeward like some cosmic dervish weaving its wasp-like waist up into the dark funnel of the pall above it. Then there would be days of intolerable blue with only wisps of cloud at dawn and nothing but the noise of the sails and the whisper of the sea punctuated startlingly by the clang of the ship's bell.

The men sat about the decks picking oakum or spinning rope yarn, washing damp bundles of old clothes and hanging them up to dry, singing now and then brief snatches, and talking in subdued lazy tones. Even Collins could not find enough for them to do. All the old sails were patched. All the boats and bulwarks were painted, the brasses polished, and the anchor chain made rustless. The standing rigging was slushed down. And still they were only a little over half-way across.

A small fiddle was permitted to squall away in the fo'c'sle and even to come on deck. But after a week it gave up. The presence of the vast silence through which the ship was moving made it too absurd to be tolerated. A game of banker began under the lee of the galley and went on. To Anthony at the wheel eddied back now and then a whiff of burning olive wood from the galley fire, bringing mornings in the cart with Angela vividly to mind. Indeed, the plains about Pisa sometimes seemed to mirage themselves before him when the smoke was strong. Mixed with it were vivid whiffs of tobacco from the sailors' pipes. In that weed he now began to find a solitary solace himself. Tobacco made his body content to be still.

The intolerable vastness of things was now eating itself into his mind. At first it had been oppressive but now he began to feel as if there were a window in the top of his skull that gave on irreducible nothing. A certain element of terror accompanied this. In the vision of the universe which it opened up there was a gaunt possibility of madness, a terror of space, that had drawn a little too near. He could not quite close it off. He had once made the mistake of climbing into the maintop and looking up too long at the stars. Suddenly direction had vanished and he found himself clutching the mast. The circles and circles beyond circles of his geometry had for a while been a comfort. But now he could no longer bound nothing with a compass. Always there was the maw of more and more. No compass opened wide enough.

The constant taking of observations and the necessity to think in terms of arcs and spheres gave him, as he watched the horizon before him, a palpable sense of the huge ball across which the ship was slowly crawling. That was tremendous enough. But to recollect that this frightful sphere was hurtling eastward, and that he was going with it at a speed really beyond thought, made him feel like clinging at times to the wheel, waiting as it were to be thrown off into space like a drop of water from a grindstone. Once under the rising full moon as he looked astern he thought he saw the long, silver streak of water racing; streaming steadily east into the very mouth of the dead planet. Slowly it rose above the line of ocean, serene, but terrible. And then he was being hurled along under it going around again toward the sun.

That night he took a lunar for longitude. Despite all he could do he could not divest himself of a sense of horror as the disk of the moon swept down over the fixed star he had chosen. Through the glass he saw the edge of the moon was sawtoothed. There was something about the motion of all these bodies in the sky, especially at night, that was a little mentally sickening. Strive as he would he could not divest himself of an emotion about them even when, as he had to assure himself, it was merely mathematics he was practising. Even to take a shy look at the infinite seemed to cut him off from the entire ship's company. To glimpse the mood of it even for a few hours had, he felt, changed him somehow permanently. Something within him that he had not known was imprisoned there had been fed with the raw meat of heaven. It was now aroused and clamouring for more. Along with this went a sudden increase in his apprehension of geometrical problems. Theorems which he had once been forced to prove to himself ponderously now suddenly became axiomatic. He became ambitious as a navigator and determined to check his longitude by an observation of Jupiter's satellites. This was a matter of some little difficulty as it was necessary to rig an improvised tripod for the captain's little telescope and to wait for a perfectly calm night.

Collins accomplished the tripod. But it was harder to persuade the captain to let him have the glass, a good one once taken from a prize. He did so only after considerable cajoling. Captain Jorham had not been sleeping lately. He was now very restless. From time to time that day Anthony had heard him and his wife talking. When he came into the cabin they always stopped. There was an air of great tension about both of them, Anthony noticed. But he was now so engrossed in his own little experiment on deck that he paid no particular attention to it. Matters had gone on so long in the cabin he had come at last to take them for granted. Besides—tonight it was calm! And tonight he was going to observe the immersion of Jupiter's inner satellite. How grand that sounded! As he began to focus the glass the nice intricate reasoning behind the observation and the way to use the tables kept running through his head.

The planet hung like a distant lamp half-way to the zenith. In the glass at first he saw nothing but black, then a few sparks of stars. Now he was on it! It was a great, grey, moon-shaped thing. Out of focus of course! He twisted the eye-piece toward him. Now! There it was, the whole beautiful system! An intensely shining, little disk with three bright sparks arranged in a line to the right. If the ship would only stay perfectly still! That was a little better now, clearer. There was the other spark on the left. Much farther out than he had thought. God! How beautiful they were, silver, but silver that was alive. Calm, orderly, perpetually reordering themselves in repetition endlessly repeated and shining that way forever, glorious, lovely— calm! He could never drink in enough of that light. Let it keep sliding into his eyes and become part of him. This was mental drink.

He let Collins look. "Four of 'em, eh! Four moons! That doesn't seem right, does it?" He went back and unlashed the wheel again.

It would take almost an hour yet before that little moon would touch the planet's disk, if his calculations were anywhere near right. He began to walk up and down the deck stopping once in a while to refocus. "Why not hurry it up and be done with it?" something prompted him. "You fool," someone else replied. He laughed. Yet his little moon evidently was moving. And the sea was very, very calm. Almost no wind tonight. The sails flapped. She was just keeping way on her. That was lucky. They had had only a few really calm nights. This was one. Very silent too. He rearranged the screened light near the chronometer so that he could see the hands better.

Philadelphia went by carrying some hot water to the cabin, spilling a little as he passed. Anthony saw him return to the galley later. He was sitting there with his hands on his knees, shaking a little as if with a chill. A big fire was going. Two lanterns were burning. He was sorry for the darky. The captain was wicked enough in speech these days. The man looked positively yellow, Anthony thought. As he passed the cabin door he heard Mrs. Jorham crying monotonously; subdued. She had not done that before. Perhaps he had better take a look. But he would try not to disturb them. He went around and looked through the starboard light. No sounds came to him there, only movement below in the clear lamplight, a picture in a glow. There was something cosmic about this one, too.

The old man seemed to be up to some mischief. He was going about looking for something. Evidently he could not find it. Mrs. Jorham slid into her bunk and closed the panel as if she were afraid. What was it all about? Mere drunken folly? Now he was rearranging the things in the cabin meticulously. All the plates on the rail. Exactly, just so. He stood back to admire the effect. Now he put the tea canister on the sideboard in front of the Virgin and bowed. "Was the drunken ass saying his prayers to her or making fun of her?" You could hardly tell which. He made sacerdotal gestures. It was funny and horrible at the same time. Now he was peeping over the Virgin's cloak. He was talking to the baby! Somehow he had recaptured the very look of a proud young father. His face had gone smooth. He snapped his fingers and bent down tenderly. It seemed terrible enough now, poor old devil! Better not spy on him. But just then the whole implication of the scene below shifted. Captain Jorham had lifted his face out of the big fold of the clay cloak with a look of preternatural cunning. This was the man who could sell Spaniards their own tombstones at a profit.

He looked about him like a cat about to jump on the table and lap cream.

Then with an elaborate drunken cunning that would have defeated itself if Mrs. Jorham had been peeping out of instead of crying in her bunk, he tiptoed over to "Elisha" and took out of that chest a long, narrow bottle of red wine. He grinned knowingly at its ruby flash as he crossed the cabin, reeling. Good Lord, he was going to smash the statue with it! No, he was going to give it to the baby! He slid the bottle down into the deep fold of the Virgin's cloak. It was completely concealed. Once again that evening Captain Jorham stepped back with his head on one side to admire his nice arrangements. Then his real motive emerged. With a look of grim triumph he turned and shook his fist at the closed panel of his wife's bunk.

Anthony could only laugh now. He wondered if Captain Jorham would remember that bottle when his wife began to cut down on his liquor after the spree. Hardly. Perhaps it was just drunken cunning? Then his grin suddenly faded. The observation!

He ran to the telescope and began to readjust it frantically. But it was too late. While he had been watching Captain Jorham hide a bottle in the bosom of the Virgin another equally important event in the cosmos had taken place. The inner satellite of Jupiter had immersed.

"You'll make a good first mate yet," said Collins with a touch of admiration in his voice as he listened to Anthony's remarks. "What was that last language, Portegee?"

Anthony closed up the telescope and reduced his meticulous preparations to debris. He did not deign to reply.

"As for immersion," Collins went on, conning the ship elaborately as a brief puff bellied out the sails, "I never did hold by it nohow. Nor feet washin' neither. My family was Antipoedabaptists and I sucked the milk o' pure doctrine from my mother's knee. Better not kick the chronometer, sir."

A loud crackling sound came from the cabin. The captain was evidently demolishing something brittle. They listened forebodingly.

"I expect tonight's the night," whispered Collins. "Na-ow I'll send the watch for'd and ye hold the cabin da-own, Mr. Adverse. 'Tain't helpful to discipline fer the crew to see the skipper bein' chased. Yep, I'll keep the wheel. Philly can help if he has to."

Anthony gathered his paraphernalia and went below. How important it had seemed, and how serious about it he had been! He could chuckle now.

Fragments of a chair were scattered about the cabin but the captain had disappeared. Anthony stood looking about him. The cabin was absolutely silent. The ship was just drifting before the lightest of airs. He heard the ripple along her keel as she picked up for a moment. Then it died away in subterranean gurgles. Suddenly his heart almost stopped. A growling beast was trying to bite his leg.

From between the legs of the table the captain's head projected and

he was now barking like a dog. It was an eerily perfect performance.
Captain Jorham *was* a dog. It went on for a while and ended in three
long death howls.

Despite himself Anthony's flesh crept. With some ado he finally
enticed the captain to his feet again. The commander of the *Wam-panoag* now began to walk about shuffling and reeling, doing a nervous,
spasmodic little clog each time he turned the corner of the table. He
was trying to catch Anthony to see who he was. His face twitched
and his limbs jerked. An endless stream of talk flowed from his mouth,
now drawn to one side, as if all he said were an aside to someone
invisible. Finally he captured his mate and insisted on shaking hands.
The ugly gleam in his pupils vanished.

"Swan ef it ain't Captain Jorham's macaroni mate! Ye're a ri,
ye a - a - a - *ri*." Anthony dodged the gargantuan fluke which was
about to descend on his back. The captain staggered and reeled over
into his bunk.

"Thank God for that," thought Anthony.

"Polly wants a cracker, polly wants, wants, polly—l'olly, dolly.
Janie wants a dolly. Little Jane wants her dolly. Mrs. Jorham, do
ye hear, do ye hear? Little Jane wants her dolly. She's comin'
fer it, comin' *abooord!* Janie, baba!" He waved and then began
to whisper. The hulk of him quivered and twitched.

"Listen!"

Something gurgled under the keel. The man's scalp crinkled up
into a point pulling his forehead smooth.

Mrs. Jorham opened her panel. "Give him drink and get it over
with tonight. Philly, Philly, some hot water!"

The darky descended warily. He took in the situation at one glance
and scrambled out of the cabin as soon as he could.

"*Give* me that doll," said the captain making a sudden drunken dash
at his wife. She closed the panel in his face. With some difficulty
Anthony got him back to his bunk where he sat sweating. He mixed
him some hot grog and got him to lie down. After a while he seemed
to sleep uneasily. Anthony dimmed the light and crawled into his own
bunk. He meant to stay awake. The light flickered and went out soon
but he did not know it.

When he opened his eyes again it was absolutely dark and he was
instantly aware of being bathed in an atmosphere of inexplicable terror.
Someone had called Philly again, he thought. But no, it was Captain
Jorham talking.

"Listen, do ye hear that?" he whispered.

"Hush!" said his wife's voice. "*Ssh!*"

The captain's voice was pleading now. "Give it to her, Jane. Let
her have it."

A swift horrible scream tore the darkness. It was impossible to hear it and not to partake of a fear that went like cold to the marrow.

"Listen!"

No one did anything else.

Now for the first time Anthony began to understand that Mrs. Jorham might believe her child really was there. It was her breathing. He lay with eyes wide open in the dark, listening. He could hear now as he had never heard before. Furthermore, he gradually became sure himself that there was something at the door. Despite all he could do to reassure himself, he broke out in a sweat. Something *was* there. He could hear it.

"God!" said the captain.

They were evidently sitting together over there in the captain's bunk. Presently he heard one of them moving. It was Mrs. Jorham. She crept past him slowly on her hands and knees in her white night-dress. Now she was going up the little ladder. He heard her gasp. Something was tossed out onto the deck. Mrs. Jorham was lying prone there at the top of the cabin ladder.

Then Anthony had the shock of his life. In the darkness overhead he heard bare feet stirring very softly on the cabin roof. Immediately afterwards Mrs. Jorham fled back to her bunk and closed herself in.

This was more than he could stand. Jumping up he wrapped a blanket around him and went on deck. No one was there except Collins looking grim over the binnacle.

"Did you see anything?" asked Anthony.

Collins quietly pointed to the galley. In there a bright fire was still going. He went forward and looked through the door. The stove was glowing cherry-red under one lid. He lifted the grate and saw the remains of Mrs. Jorham's doll twisting in the flames. A smell of burning cloth and hair pervaded the place. Philadelphia was not there. As he came out again Anthony saw the outline of the darky's figure against the stars in the shrouds forward as far away from the galley as he could get. He sauntered forward and looked up at him a while. The cook was cowering there all hunched up. They kept looking at each other.

"Lil missee gone?" the man finally whispered.

"All gone," said Anthony.

Even then the negro came down slowly and sat on the bulwark for a while.

"Why did you burn it, Philly?" asked Anthony.

"She go way den." He ran his sleeve over his forehead. "Tell you I allus knows troubles comin', Mr. Adverse, when I see dat ooman gwine fer to dress a doll. She start 'bout a month ago now. Wish

I didn't b'long to folks wid a baby hant. It jes' about done ruin my kidneys." He hitched himself uneasily.

"This is not the first time then?"

"No, *suh*. I done burn foh dollies!"

Anthony went aft and got the man a drink. It must have taken great courage, he thought, to creep up and get the doll. So it was real to them all. Not until long after the fire had completely burned out in the galley did Philadelphia return.

"I wouldn't mind a little myself, Mr. Adverse," said Collins. He looked at Anthony over the pannikin. "Well, what do ye think of it na-ow?" he asked.

"What do you stick by the ship for, Collins?" countered Anthony.

"Ye don't know the skipper, sir. He's a grand man," replied Collins wiping his lips. "He'll be himself na-ow, ye see if he ain't. Everybody has their own funny places ye know, in here." He tapped his head. "Ye can't tell how real they are neither. Na-ow . . ."

But Anthony did not care to listen, any more than he cared to return to the cabin. He flopped down on some spare canvas; smoked.

One thing—he was not going to be dressing any more dolls himself! The madonna could stay in the chest. And he was glad he had taken the stand he had with Father Xavier. Toussaint had once laughed at him for being superstitious. And these people on board were Protestants, too. "Heretics." But what was he? A reasonable man, a man of facts and figures, a navigator! No more nonsense from now on—by God!—his pipe went out and he failed to relight it—no more childish nonsense! He would strangle his dreams, his dolls. A philosopher-scientist. Write Toussaint and tell him. These new ideas he had from looking at the stars, sailing the wide earth under the sky had opened up his mind. But mystery was there. Of course it was. Something to do with time—or was it space? He couldn't remember now. It was hard to think about that. You seemed to touch the bottom of things there—or the top. Oh, yes, that time on the masthead looking up, he had lost all sense of direction. What was that idea he had had then? Other things besides men, *things*. Yes, supposing I was a thing, or supposing a thing knew itself as "I." Oh, this is it. The "I" of a thing could have no sense of direction. Say, the sun. It would not know east or west or up or down. "I" felt that on the masthead looking at the stars. What of it? This is an essential thought, I am certain of it. It might lead to something—something, but not now, not now. I must rest. How long, how long life is! The end far-off and I am sleepy now. Alone. Here . . . He saw the moon's disk again sweeping down dragon-toothed over a star. Alone here in this terrible vast desert of stars. This cold-and-fiery endless place! Where are you, living one? I am lost here. I cannot find you. I am cold.

He moved uneasily and began to murmur something on the verge of sleep. Philadelphia came out of the cabin and threw a blanket on him, seeing the dew on his face.

"Ah, warm again! In bed at last! Good night, then. Good night to you." From the wall above him her face was looking down. "Of course she was always there. I am glad. Now she is talking to me."

"What have you been doing all day, little boy?"

"Climbing the big tree. I am tired."

"Did you reach the top?"

"Yes."

"What did you see there?"

"The stars, Mother I-am, the stars."

"What of them, child?"

"I looked among them and dreamed I had lost you. I lost myself."

"But now that you are awake again you see I am here . . ."

What has become of the ship, the Atlantic Ocean and the stars above it? They, he, have vanished into something without space and time. What is it breathing under the blanket? . . .

The man in the lookout thought he saw some stars setting in the "west." They touched the water like lights and went under; disappeared. He was quite sure of it. In the "east" several more came up. He saw them with his own eyes. Presently they were followed by a great light. The man now saw a cloud before him on the horizon. It looked far away, very silvery and stood up from the sea like a cone. Suddenly he saw a forest and three little white houses in the middle of it. The cloud rent opened up and the land turned into a mountain with long scarves of mist trailing away from it. It certainly *was* a mountain.

"Land O," he roared.

"Belay that bellerin'," Collins roared back at him. "That's Nevis, and I seen it a half hour ago from the deck. Get a pillow, ye lubber, and turn over on yer other side. Come da-own out o' that. Philly, pass the word to the captain."

"Yes, suh," said that worthy delighted at the discomfiture of the lookout. "An' I'll jes' tote him a basin o' gruel." He winked.

A considerable stir now went on and Anthony woke up.

"Landfall sooner than we expected, Mr. Adverse," said Collins pointing. "Yer latitude was exact but ye're way out on your longitude. *I've* been expectin' it watchin' the landbirds for three days now. And I'm right glad, for I'm nigh tuckered out with double tricks at the wheel. The skipper ul carry on na-ow. He comes back marvellous."

Anthony climbed the shrouds and sat feasting his eyes on his first glimpse of tropical foliage. A beautiful mountain, gleaming, dark-green, strung with savannas and forests with here and there a bright flash from a waterfall lay some miles ahead off the port bow. A long scarf of mist perpetually dissolving to leeward trailed from the top. He could see a cluster of white houses in a town at its foot. The crew stood about or lined the bulwarks in small groups looking at it, too. Suddenly they scattered. Captain Jorham had come on deck.

He had a chair brought for him and sat on the quarter-deck with a blanket around his knees and a speaking trumpet in his hand. Philadelphia kept bringing him hot coffee every few minutes.

Mrs. Jorham emerged once from the cabin with her curl-papers still on, and going to the stern threw a lot of bottles into the sea. Captain Jorham did not turn his head. Anthony saw the bottles go bobbing astern. A large shark turned lazily on one side and swallowed one. Anthony laughed. He knew of another bottle in safe keeping. Forgotten, he felt sure. "On the knees of the gods!"

Nevis began to sink into the ocean astern. Only a few days now and they would be in Havana. The new world at last. He raised his right hand holding the palm open in expectation.

END OF BOOK FOUR

BOOK FIVE

In Which the Necessary
Alloy is Added

BOOK FIVE

In Which the Necessary Alloy is Added

CHAPTER TWENTY-NINE

THE HOUSE OF SILENUS

D OWN the long, blue coasts of Cuba sailed the *Wampanoag*
with her mate in the shrouds gazing inland as often and
as long as the August sun on the Tropic of Cancer would
permit.

In the mornings, when he first heard the men begin to holystone
the decks and swish water about, he would go aloft with the small-
glass sticking out of his coat pocket. Then crooking a knee about one
of the stays and steadying himself, he took deep lungfuls of the rich
land-breeze which lulled through the sails at that hour.

It was full of a thousand lush and exotic odours from the beaches,
lagoons, and high plateaus; Sargossa weed, juniper and lantana; the
fragrant quiebrahacha, tamarind, and rotting mastic leaves. A rank,
musty sweetness rolled out from the sugar plantations and ferment-
ing lowlands. His land-hungry nose seemed to taste rather than to
smell it. In his mouth his tongue moved and became moister as if
in anticipation of a feast.

By the last hours of starlight the brig would always have drifted
close to the land. The sea-breeze lasted all night, but as the airs grew
lighter she would make more and more leeway, until at last the distant whisper of beaches was audible on deck. It sounded as though
the tropical night were about to reveal its secret; a softly sinister one.
Then suddenly the sails would flutter, the yards would be braced
around, and the land-breeze would fatten the canvas out on the starboard tack.

It was at this moment that the fish bit most frantically. A ferocious barracuda or two, or a young shark would always be slapping
and slamming themselves on the wet deck. But after the first few
mornings in the West Indies Anthony paid small attention to that,
for by the miracle of dawn in those regions smell, hearing, and sight
were in turn assaulted and overcome.

As soon as the warm odours of the land-breeze began to fan over
the deck the wind also brought with it a distant and mysterious cry
from the dark island beyond. It was continuous; strangely sustained.
It seemed to come in waves out of the east and to scatter itself like
spiritual rumours of good news discussed and re-echoed here and
there faintly and more faintly down into the west. To Anthony hang-

ing in the rigging, rapt, looking out over the dark ruffling water, it expressed perfectly his own deep and eery joy at being alive on this star.

The first time he heard this half-harmonic chorus he was non-plussed. No other song was like it. With a constant lyric stream, in which no individual notes could be distinguished, all the roosters in Cuba were blending their voices. The king-cock of them, he thought, with a million jubilant minions must be chanting somewhere in the as yet invisible island hills. This then was the characteristic sound of land—of all habitable land. He remembered it on those mornings in Italy in the cart with Angela. But this was a more magnificent chorus. It had the quality of laughter transposed into some unknown scale, musical, but non-human. At the first hint of grey the paean rose to a kind of harmonized scream of joy.

Then the parrots began, *"chat-chat, chat-chat, chatter-chatter."* They seemed to wake an applause to accompany the cock-crow as if they had been started somewhere by a single handclap. The half-heard thunder of billions of insects tuned in. The morning voice of Cuba swept into a crescendo. It reached a climax that maintained itself, a distant pandemonium that rapidly grew fainter as the ship drew out to sea.

Meanwhile his eyes must also be at work. The stars paled. The planets burned out like melting globes. In a white furnace-glow astern the morning star disappeared moltenly. At one leap the light climbed half-way to the zenith. The inevitable bank of low clouds along the eastern horizon, as if they were in rapid combustion, turned from black to dull red; to crimson; to transparent, white gold. Hot pencils of light thrust rods through them and they suddenly sublimed. A bright track of sea could be seen racing eastward toward an incandescent spot.

Then the incredible forehead of the sun lifted itself out of the water. Red globules of mist ran down his fat cheeks. The world glared from rim to rim. It was turning over. For an instant, as the sun's squat globe swam up from the water, the sea seemed to be drawn after him into a huge bloody bead. Then the black line of the horizon cut through it. It fell back, and you could no longer look that way. Already waves of heat were beating up into Anthony's face. After a while he would open his eyes again, after the blindness passed, and look at the long coasts marching either way into the intolerable, blue distance.

It was a mighty view. He was never tired of sweeping his little glass over it; now at some palm fronded headland or long reaching cayo; now at a purple shadowed vale in the mountains, or a little sunny patch with a peon's hut. He felt like some poor sailor standing in the rigging of the *Niña* or the *Pinta*, shading his eyes for a glimpse of gold-roofed temples on that first, memorable voyage.

They passed a hundred little, palm-lined rivers each with its savannaed delta and a bar creaming at its blue mouth. Where the bluffs came down to the sea these streams cut back into the hills mysteriously. A light mist hung over them in the morning till the sun looked directly at it. He could even see, with a very clear focus, a wilderness of ferns lining their gorges. Once there was a waterfall and a canoe under it fishing. From the woods near by rose a long feather of smoke. And this was the new world!

To him it was *his* new world. He had discovered it for himself. And he knew now how vast the earth was; how wide its oceans. Had he not crossed a sea of space to get here? Why must the ship always go creeping out to sea as soon as the sun rose? How long would it be till he was walking the groves of this island? "Use the glass, Anthony, use the glass—*Cuba, gloria del mundi!*"

One step inland beyond the beaches salt-pans flashing like mirrors. Then a wide, low plain, sandy, grassy; then trees; then a glorious burst of palms and pines, plumed and festooned forest that swept up over the hills into the blue mountains, gentle, rolling from peak to peak with cloud shadows, feathered with giant royal palms standing in groves or lonely, perpendicular, looking down on everything else. Cuba and the royal palm, the tall, wide-blowing royal palm—he could imagine them rustling coolly in the trade wind. The sun burned his already brown face to black olive as he stood thus in the rigging, sweeping his glass inland a hundred and a thousand times to be rewarded at every trial by glows and glooms and vistas of what had once rightly been taken to be Paradise. The sun bleached the ends of his hairs and the roots where they rose out of his forehead until he looked like a grizzled, gilded youth with a bronze body.

"Although," said a book of travels he had in his chest, "Europeans have now pre-empted the soil of Cuba for three centuries, much of the interior of the island has never been mapped and its precise geography is vague." Looking day after day at the wilderness of hills and coastal islands that marched with the *Wampanoag,* he could believe that. Reluctantly, as the sun grew intolerable, he would climb down at last.

At noon the sails drooped. They ate under the shadow of a tarpaulin in a sweat-provoking calm. Mrs. Jorham groaned and began to talk about iced root-beer, and frost on cranberry bogs. The captain said nothing. He was doing penance now. An hour later the cool breeze came from the sea. Then they would begin to tack out. For Captain Jorham had no desire to be boarded at night by human caymans from some boca, or Cayo del Coco. The number of "wrecks"

even in calm weather along these coasts was remarkable. It had already engaged the unfavourable attention of the British Admiralty
for many years.

"*Expulsis piratus, restitutio commercia,*" said Captain Elisha to
himself, taking out his lucky pocket-piece and surreptitiously spitting
on it. So by evening they would be ten miles out, and the coast a
long, undulating dream of blue. Then they would slowly drift in
again. Thus in long diagonal slants the *Wampanoag* lazed along.
One morning two breast-shaped hills hove in sight.

"Do ye see them there, Mr. Adverse?" said Collins twiddling the
wheel a quarter over and back to nurse every cupful of the fitful land
airs, "them's the Tits of Havana, and ye'll see the Morro before
night."

A tower with a banner on it rose out of the sea as they lay in the
noon calm. Then the wind came shoreward and by evening they were
near enough to see the sulphur puff of the sunset gun from El Morro.
An incredibly ragged pilot with a bouquet of flowers in hand for the
captain, and his mouth full of Spanish lies when he was not chewing
a fat, black cigar, rowed out and boarded them. He offered Anthony
a cigar for which he accepted one dollar.

"From the vuelta abojo, señor, the very darkest leaf. Now we have
exchanged gifts, bueno!"

Anthony lit the black torpedo expectantly. He had heard of Havana
tobacco. In a few minutes a light sweat burst out on his forehead
and the soles of his feet felt cold. He pressed adventure no further
then, but tossed the thing overboard. After a little he felt calm and
soothed; in rather an enviable state of mind. It was equivalent to
strong wine but unique.

In the calmest of all lights, between a setting sun and a rising moon,
they slipped into the great sack-shaped bay between the frowning
batteries of La Punta and El Morro. He had never seen so many
fortifications. The walled city lay to starboard, and the little Gibraltar of San Carlos, tier above tier of batteries with a vicious-looking
bristling parapet, along the water front to port. Soon they were gliding along the bay front of the flat-roofed city that thrust out its long
peninsula between them and the sunset. He could hear the horses now
trotting along the Paseo Alameda de Paula and the noise of wheels.

What a welcome familiar sound was that, the striking of horseshoes on good solid earth! All these land noises were welcome. How
he had missed them without knowing it! How silent the open sea
really was! Its tones were variations of only one voice. The bay
seemed to be full of different voices all calling to him; cries, laughter,
carriages passing and repassing, the rumble of a town! The tremendous sour-sweet stench of a tropical city and a festering harbour over-

whelmed him as the pilot dropped anchor in the Bay of Antares and demanded one hundred and twenty-five Mexican dollars for the astounding feat.

The twang of Captain Elisha's "God A'mighties," and other Biblical remarks to the pilot rolled up from the cabin to mix with curious hails from passing boats and the thudding of hard fists on canvas as the crew furled the sails and gossiped on the yards. Tomorrow, tomorrow they would be ashore, "Muchacha, muchacha" . . . An hour later the pilot left with ten dollars and buenas noches.

Mrs. Jorham came on deck to rock in the marvellous moonlight. She might have knitted, but the mosquitoes would not agree. Anthony climbed into the maintop above the pests and gazed inland at a circle of unearthly hills.

A few hundred yards across the water at Regla, a thriving little suburb with crowded docks and low, whitewashed houses, a lot of banjos and guitars were going strong. Some of the men started to clog on the deck till Mrs. Jorham snorted. They ceased. She gave a few vicious slaps at her wrists and went below. He was left alone with the banjos, guitars, and the moonlight.

And such mad, soft moonlight! God, what a rhythm was that on shore! The feet in the dance hall at Regla stamped it through an entire vacant interval of the *rumba* . . . now, *now* the frog-voiced guitars chimed in again. He waved his heels in the empty air and his throat swelled. "Habana, Llare del Nuevo Mundo y Ante Mural de los Indios Occidentales," *tunky, tunk tunk, plunk plunk-plunk,* the music went on.

The dew began to soak through his clothes. He jumped to a stay and slid down.

"Wall, ye wouldn't have come da-own that air way when ye come aboard at Leghorn," said Collins with a hint of pride in his voice as if he were responsible. He lowered his voice. "And na-ow she has her hook safe in the mud at Havaner. And I'll tell ye what, Mr. Adverse, we kna-ow who brought her acrost ta pond, eh?" He finally succeeded in closing only one eye and held the wink at last attained for some time. His eye opened. "Wall, ye'll be leavin' us na-ow I expect."

They were silent for a minute. A wave of homesickness at leaving the ship swept over Anthony. Collins looked grave. "I know," he said, "but barrin' the yellow jack and the stinks it's a fa-ine ta-own *tew-w-w.*" The last syllable twanged and twinged like a taut preventer stay in a gale. It lingered musically, a sad nasal farewell. Anthony went into the cabin and began to pack. Captain Jorham, who was just drawing off his socks, watched him thoughtfully. So far he had never alluded to any of the events of the voyage. Anthony took his sextant, oiled it, and put it away.

"Ye done right well with that, mister," said the captain picking his toes. He cleared his throat. "We're all obleeged to ye." He went over to "Elisha" and taking out a bag counted out audibly seventy silver dollars. At the clink of coin Mrs. Jorham's night-cap appeared through the slide. She watched attentively. The captain arranged the coins in seven piles and stopped.

"There's five more comin'," said his wife.

He made another half pile a little regretfully.

"Them's yer wages, mister," he said. "No argument, ye've arned 'em . . . from all I hear tell. Na-ow there's only one thing more I'm askin'. Even if ye're paid off, I'd like ye to try and help dispose o' these holy figures and figurines ra-ound to some o' the churches. Ye've got the hang o' the priestly lingo. You tell 'em for me, will yer?"

"Indeed, I will, sir," said Anthony. "You can count on me for anything as long as you lie in port. And I'll remember the marble, too."

"Na-ow that's right pert of ye," replied the captain. Mrs. Jorham nodded.

It was on the tip of Anthony's tongue to warn the captain about the hidden bottle. He wondered if the Virgin on the sideboard still had it. He strolled over that way. It was still there. But he did not want to bring up any embarrassing memories and refrained from mentioning it.

The captain leaned back in his bunk and lit a pipe. The mosquitoes hummed. He put the light out. The captain dozed and slapped automatically. A patch of moonlight flooded the floor. Presently Mrs. Jorham emerged in her night-cap and a long gown with a small vial in her hand. A strong aromatic odour filled the cabin. She came over and spilled some drops on Anthony's pillow.

"It's penny-riyal," she said. "Keeps the critters away." Then half hesitatingly she rubbed some on his forehead.

He was surprised to feel how soft and smooth her old fingers were. They lingered. She put some on his hair.

"Land sakes!" she sighed, "I ain't rubbed penny-riyal on sence Jane died." Her eyes glistened. He took her old fingers and kissed them.

"Good-bye," he said.

"We'll both hate to see ye go," she whispered. "Take yer pay. It's the old man's conscience money. He's turrible ashamed. Not that ye didn't arn it."

"Mrs. Jorham, how would you like to have me take you around

to some of the churches and cemeteries here and translate the inscriptions for you some day?" he said impulsively.

"Na-ow that ud jes' be *lovely*," she sighed. "And we'll have a keeriage." She giggled. Then she spilled some of the penner oil on the captain's covers and went to bed.

Anthony got up and put the silver dollars into his chest. When he turned he saw the captain was looking on with satisfaction. He waved his hand generously in the moonlight.

"Sonny," said he, "let me tell ye suthin' about this ta-own. Don't ye patronize none of them places with stone benches they call latrinas here. Ye'll catch suthin' ul make ye think ye've been spanked with a curry comb. The muchachas air worse. Na-ow in 'ninety-three . . ." He lay back embarrassed.

Anthony waved his hand appreciatively and climbed back into his bunk. The penner oil was still cool on his forehead and the homely odour of it permeated his dreams. He felt very safe in the new world. Captain Jorham snored; Mrs. Jorham coughed softly. It was like having parents.

Very early next morning Collins came with a couple of sailors and loaded Anthony's dunnage in the whaleboat. Collins was taking the first liberty party ashore. The men were to be paid a quarter of their wages and lined up eagerly.

Mrs. Jorham came to the rail with her knitting to say good-bye. She and the captain looked down into the boat as it was lading, talking with Anthony.

"You'll find me through Carlo Cibo, the factor at Regla, sir," said Anthony. "He's Mr. Bonnyfeather's agent here—just across the bay. That pink house behind the stone dock, they say. You see?"

"Aye, aye," said Captain Jorham. "I've got my cabin supplies and groceries from him many's the time. Look out! He's a bit of a shark if he's not yer friend. Keeps a fa-ine house for officers boardin' on shore, or used to. Ye won't forget the stat-oo-airy, mister. I'll be seein' ye soon I calalate."

"I won't forget, sir," Anthony replied looking up and smiling, "and I have an appointment to keep with your wife, too. All the churches and graveyards."

"Oh-*ho*," chuckled the captain, "so ye *have*, have yer?" Both he and Mrs. Jorham looked pleased. "Wall, git along then."

"Shove off," roared Collins, "let fall! Give way together."

The boat slid over the oily water of the bay that still seemed to retain in its depths at that early hour the deep purple stain of night. A school of silver minnows rose and fell back like a shower of raindrops before it. Philadelphia stood in the shrouds waving his apron, his face shining with a warmth superinduced by the glow of five dollars in his pocket. "Bes' luck, suh, bes' luck in de world!"

Anthony stood up in the stern sheets and looked back at the *Wampanoag,* a delicate tracery of spars and rigging against the rosy city beyond. The jolt and rumble of huge, solid-wheeled carts drawn by oxen began to come to them from the alleys of Regla. The boat nosed into the stone jetty by the pink house and Anthony jumped out onto terra firma with a little cold shiver up his spine as his heels ground into the pebbles of the new world.

"I am going to collect what is owed to John Bonnyfeather," he said to himself, standing still for a minute. "Whatever comes, I am going to get that money." That he felt would constitute his success. His own eventual interest in the matter did not enter in, he told himself. It would all be for Mr. Bonnyfeather.

It pleased him to see that the men who piled his chests on the dock were merely casually respectful as they would be to any other mate going ashore. Sorry that he was leaving the ship? He wondered. The young Spaniard who had released the swallow offered to stay and watch his stuff on the dock. Collins raised his eyebrows but Anthony nodded. Collins touched his hat and the boat made off for Havana smartly. Suddenly it stopped. "Toss!" The oars all flashed into the air and stood upright. Collins was standing up waving his hat. It was a nice compliment. Anthony could have asked nothing more. The man on the chests grinned.

"You know Havana?" asked Anthony, turning to him as the boat sped away again.

"Sí, sí, señor, like a Rodriguez," the man replied grinning. "Like you I leave the cursèd ship of the heretics here. Sí, sí, it is a fine town. I am your servant, señor. I kiss your hands and feet."

Anthony laughed. There was something about the man that he liked. A lean, thin-faced young fellow, smooth-olive, and black-eyed, with an orange neckcloth running down his chest like a flame.

"Very well then," said he. "I will try you for a week at ship's wages. After that we shall see."

"Bueno!" cried the youth, "I am your hombre. By the swallow I swear it!" He cast an invisible bird loose with his hands, kicked his heels in the air, and lay back laughing. To be on land again!

Leaving him with the chests, Anthony turned and began to walk toward the rambling, shell-pink edifice before him. Mr. Bonnyfeather's letter crinkled in his pocket. He swung his cane and beat a lively tattoo on the wide double doors. A stark naked, young negro boy,

not at all embarrassed by a hearty morning erection, opened the gate.
Beyond was a wide patio full of other naked children, mules, yellow
curs, and a number of negro women moving about in bright-coloured
turbans. An astonishing number of pouter pigeons ran cooing about
their feet, fluttered, and lit on the shafts and spokes of several empty
carts. He beckoned to one of the women and held up his letter with
a small coin.

"For Il Signore Carlo Cibo," he said.

"The señor speaks Italian! The master will see him then. Wait."
She rolled up a barrel for him to sit on.

"Go long, you dirty devil!" she cried, catching the young porter
across the buttocks with a switch. "Madre de Dios!" and she was
gone.

Anthony waited for half an hour. Several shameless cherubs of
both sexes surrounded his barrel, looking at him with wide, brown
eyes while gnawing sugar cane. He was finally offered some. A little
girl swiftly swallowed the tiny coin he gave her in return. She was
followed by the others regretfully.

"Doubtless," he reflected, "she will find it later on in safety."

A bull-like voice could now be heard bellowing from time to time
in some distant part of the buildings. The women hustled and the
pigeons fluttered at each throaty note. But they always settled down
again. A last his messenger returned.

"This way, señor," she said, and led him out to the street again and
around the corner of an alley to a small yellow door with a grille in
it. She unlocked this and took him upstairs onto a veranda that overlooked another patio full of banana trees and palms. A huge man
sat there in a hammock trying to comb out a mass of tightly curled
black hair. A long, sweating, red clay jar swung from the rafters
beside him. The woman drew up a cane chair and vanished. Presently the man in the hammock completed his toilet and came forward
holding out two fat, white hands.

"I am Carlo Cibo, Signore Adverse. It is a pleasure indeed," said
he in excellent Tuscan, "to be able to speak to a compatriot."

"I have written you letters several times, signore, about Brazilian
coffee. So our acquaintance is already one of old standing, I believe,"
Anthony replied in his best professional manner.

"And will ripen into friendship I am sure," added Cibo.

They both laughed at the preciseness of it.

"Come, come," said the factor, "we are getting positively Castilian.
'I kiss your hands and feet.' But, aside from that, have you had
breakfast yet? No?"

He did not wait for an answer but gave a roar that somehow included the word "almorzar." A parrot with a cloth thrown over it

on a stand near by took its head out from under its wing and began to caw and cackle. Eventually it clawed off the cloth and began to cock its eye at Anthony. It was the most gorgeous thing he had ever seen.

"Almorzar solo, maestro?" said a soft feminine voice from the patio below.

"Por dos," roared the man.

"Dos, dos, dos," cawed the parrot, preening itself.

Some children, evidently half-castes, peeped out of a room across the veranda. A little boy stepped out.

"Put your clothes on for the gentleman, you bastard," said Cibo affectionately. The boy returned, but a baby girl also in a state of nature dashed out of the door and climbed onto the man's knees.

"Kiss my dolly, papa," she cried thrusting a costly doll dressed like a lady of the French court into her father's teeth. "Kiss her."

"Ah, ha, Chiquilla!" he chuckled, tossing her up and making a loud smack at the face of the doll. He danced off with the doll on one arm and the naked child on the other. She shrieked with joy, pulling his black curls awry and crooning over his shoulder at every fat skip.

"Daddy Carlo," she cried looking at Anthony. "Nice, bad daddy!" The little boy ran out now in a shirt.

Suddenly Anthony remembered where he had seen Carlo Cibo before. It was on an oval plaque over what had once been the door to the old wine cellar at the Casa da Bonnyfeather. Plump urchins were capering after a good-natured, fat god. A procession of them staggered after him bearing a huge bunch of grapes. And Carlo Cibo was the man. A naked child was laughing in his arm, too. And that fringed sash swishing over Cibo's fat buttocks cased in tight nankeen, the gross calibre of the white linen socks ending in small, black, varnished shoes that clicked on the veranda like hoofs—yes, he had seen him before.

"Ha, ha," screamed the parrot, "ha, ha, wheee-ooooo." It dragged itself up the cane chair by its beak and perching on the back of the settee looked into Anthony's face with a most knowing eye, making conversational noises and clicking its beak.

Cibo came back and sat down breathless. A purple cast slowly faded from his face. "Ah," he wheezed. "I am getting a little older, avejentado, avejentado! It is very sad." He fanned himself with one hand. The little girl still clung to him looking at Anthony. Finally he was rewarded by her with a glittering smile.

"Ah," said Cibo kissing her. "I like them this age. I have many. When they grow up I have more. Always I have my babies to dance with me on the veranda. In the grocery business I can afford it." He put the little girl down and told her to run along.

"Cuba, it is a good place. I have done well here." He leaned forward and clapped Anthony on the knee. "You should set up here and try it, signore. Do you know?" He squirmed in his chair and managed to point with his entire body to a tall mulatto girl who was coming down the veranda with the breakfast. "See I am already giving you good advice."

Anthony looked up at the girl. Under his gaze her gait altered slightly. A ghost of a smile was born on the lips of both of them. He looked away telling himself it was nothing. But Carlo Cibo's "advice" had thrilled him. The nights on the *Wampanoag* had been lonely, he remembered. Those dreams—about "Miss Udney." That was strange. Florence, and not Angela had come to him. Yet he had made up his mind to be true to Angela, to remember her always. His eyes grew misty looking into green shadows of the banana leaves. Cibo smiled to himself.

Breakfast had come on a little mahogany wagon. There were two identical trays. On each was a brown jug of clear, black coffee, the heart of a ripe pineapple, white loaf-sugar, which Anthony had never seen before, and the saddle meat of some flaky, boneless fish fried in olive oil with green peppers. They took the trays upon their laps and ate comfortably, Cibo with a delicacy which Anthony could not help but notice. His fingers played with the bright, steel knife and the long, oval spoons skilfully. His hands were immaculate and white; ringless. They would have been dainty if the fingers had not been a little too stubby and luxurious. The pineapple was a dream of sunny flavour. They lay back in their chairs and lit mild, panetela cigars.

The sense of enjoying a delicious delusion overpowered Anthony. He seemed a thousand miles away from the *Wampanoag* and the blinding, blistering bay. Where was he? How had he come here? Cibo began to talk in a far-off, reminiscent voice while the wreaths of blue smoke drifted up to the ceiling from their cigars. He fingered Mr. Bonnyfeather's letter on the table beside him.

"You will pardon me, Signore Adverse, if I seem to have assumed too much intimacy in what I have just said. Your patron in this and other letters has been very explicit and full. He has explained to me that you are, as it were, the junior member of his firm. And I—for fifteen years now, I have been the honoured agent en Habana for the Casa da Bonnyfeather. In vain I have tried to collect this debt from the House of Gallego, for which I am responsible—in a way." He drummed on the table and faltered a little. "Perhaps I should begin at the beginning.

"We are both, as I understand it, under a peculiar debt to John Bonnyfeather. Of yours I have been told a little," he touched the letter, "and I can guess more. Many years ago I came here from

Livorno a ruined man. I had been dismissed from the House of
Franchetti there in disgrace. The chief clerk of that ancient establishment had engaged in peculations to a great sum. To cover his
tracks he involved some of the minor employees under him, of whom
I was but one. I was innocent, but I could not be convincing. With
five others I was let go. I sold a little house that had come to me from
my mother at Rosignano. I came to Havana where in a rash venture I soon involved what little I had. In desperation I wrote to Mr.
Bonnyfeather, who had known me, and at whose memorable table I
had sometimes sat. I told him my situation exactly, and that unless
I could prevail on someone to consign me a cargo on commission I
should soon perish of yellow fever in a Spanish prison. Signore, it
was like a scene in a play. The corchete in his cocked hat had come
for me when the news was brought that a ship consigned to me by
Mr. Bonnyfeather was lying in the bay. I do not believe in miracles,
but that one occurred. I disposed of the cargo to the House of Gallego
at great profit. From that day to this I have greatly prospered." He
knocked the long ash off his cigar and continued even more earnestly.

"As the agent for the Casa da Bonnyfeather my reputation was
made. Other merchants from various places were also soon dealing
with me. I was cautious, and careful to remember the authorities in
other things than prayers. After some years I became a Spanish subject and went into the slave trade with old Señor Gallego. Five years
of that made me richer than I have allowed anyone in Havana to
suspect. But slaving is at best a risky business, and I have gradually
ceased to have anything to do with it. I have cut down all merchandising also and have gone in for nothing but the importation of wines,
table luxuries, and cabin groceries. It gives me a little something to
do. For some years captains and ships' officers used to come and stay
in this house, but even that grew to be a nuisance, and I have had none
here now for a long time. In fact, except for the luxury trade in fine
groceries and rare comestibles, the details of which a few trusted
clerks manage, I have, as you see, practically retired. The only exception to this has been when our good patron in Livorno consigned
me a cargo. That I have, of course, always disposed of as much to
his advantage as possible, mostly to my former partners the Gallegos.
The profit, as you know, on merchandise for the slave trade is large,
although payment is sometimes delayed. For various reasons, which
I shall explain to you later, the account with Gallego has become involved. But do not let us talk about that now. I would say something else.

"From what I have already said you will understand why it is that
you will have every assistance that I can offer in collecting the sums
due Mr. Bonnyfeather. Also," he added smiling, "why it is that *you*

will stay here in my house in Regla as an honoured guest even if you remain in Cuba a lifetime. I should consider it as an implication that I am destitute of gratitude should you go any place else. A slur on my honour! Signore, we should have to meet! My benefactor, I see from his letter, regards you with affection. That is enough for me. Besides, do not mistake me—but I believe in first impressions—and I am disposed to be candid with you. I like you. Come, come, Signore Toni," he laughed. "Where are your things? Have you a servant? Have them sent up. Old Carlo does not often beg."

Anthony would have replied sooner, but he was somewhat overwhelmed. But no one could refuse to melt under the enthusiastic candour of Cibo. "It would be ungracious of me, signore—" "Carlo," insisted the man. Anthony gulped a little. "Carlo," said he, "to pretend to refuse. I am sure I am more lucky than I know. I understand you. I also have a debt to Mr. Bonnyfeather—not only to collect but to repay. I am sure he would smile in his kindly way to know what you have just said. I shall write him that in Regla near Havana is to be found what he once told me was very rare, gratitude. Carlo, I accept your hospitality with the same rarity."

"Bravo," cried Cibo leaning back in his chair. "You are an orator, friend Toni. And a heartfelt one! You should get along well. I prophesy it this lucky morning which brought you."

"Cheecha," he roared, throwing his cigar into the patio. A quarrel over the stump began below.

"Come, do you want to see my establishment?" He rose suddenly from his chair with a grunt. "I have only one complaint with life you see. I am getting too fat. It is a little difficult for me to move one leg past the other. I chafe. Cheecha!" He took off his sash and hung it over the railing.

The girl made her appearance.

"Get me a dry sash and take these breakfast things away. You know they draw flies. Tell 'Fonso to send for the gentleman's things. From now on he lives here. By the way, Signore Toni, where are your chests?"

"On the dock where I landed them."

"Not unwatched, I hope. Caramba, they will be rifled by this time!"

"I have a man with them, a Spaniard off the ship whom I took on for a week, perhaps rashly."

"No, no, you did well. He can sleep below and look after you. I will have a look at him though. Hurry, girl, *my sash!*"

When it came he draped it once or twice around his waist, and then tucking a smooth fold of it between his legs he tied the end into his belt. "Now I can walk in comfort," said he, "the silk is smooth and lets one fat chop pass the other." He swished slightly at every step as they walked down the long veranda. "Yes, it is a sweaty climate. One perspires. Come, come, after all it is much too hot already to go over the establishment. See, we have been talking longer than I thought. The sun is coming into the patio." He leaned over the rail and began to unroll a split-cane awning that fell like a curtain leaving them in a kind of cool, green gloom.

"Cheecha!"

"Sí, sí, señor," replied the woman from below now a little breathlessly.

"Take the cigar-end away from little Juan, and bring me limes and sugar, and . . ." he collapsed into his chair again. A roar from the child below followed the woman's departure. Presently the two babies came up and began to play with the parrot. The boy had taken off his shirt again.

"Ah, it is best so," said his father peering down at him. "August in Havana, my friend! Do you know what that means? But, Dios, take off your own coat! You must forget that you have one. You must get linens. A dozen suits. You shall be measured immediately, mañana. No, you will not need a sash as I do—yet."

"I hope the debt will not take that long to collect, Carlo." Already the name came easily to Anthony.—"Before I wear out twelve linen suits . . ."

"Por Dios, you will use three suits a day or more. Today—today in that costume you will do nothing! I shall do nothing. We shall sit here and talk, and drink, and smoke. We shall eat and sleep. What will be accomplished? Much! We shall have lived another day comfortably. No one can do more. Have you ever spent a day like that? I bet you, not. Try it."

"I remember doing so when I was very little," said Anthony.

"Do not remember, it requires an effort," cried Cibo, "do not remember anything except that it is now. Here is my recipe for preserving the present."

By this time the girl had returned with the ingredients. He mixed some clear rum, sugar, and lime juice, and removing a small peg from the hanging jar drew water. "Here in the veranda the water keeps always cold," he said, and dropped into the pitcher a bowl of crushed fruit giving it a peculiar spiral shaking. A delicate barm appeared on the top, half effervescent. Pomegranate juice had tinged it red. In each waiting glass was a coil of orange peel. He covered this, and handing a glass to Anthony, poured a gobletful down his own throat.

He poured it. His throat responded rippling. It was a drinker's throat pliable clear down to the chest and with a good bulge to it. Silenus, indeed, lacked only a few leaves in his hair.

Anthony sat turning over in his mouth small lumps of pineapple reminiscent of rum. When the breeze breathed through the veranda now even from the street beyond it felt cool. Safe behind the green blinds in the cool enclave of the porch, the fierce light and heat surrounded them, as the hours wore on, with a distinct menace. Action of any kind became more and more impossible. They dozed a little, awoke, talked quietly but eagerly, and dozed again. They were both at home.

For Cibo had about him a gift, a physical and mental quality of being that put you at your ease. It was not exercised, it existed. When it was exercised you grew merry, even hilarious. In his house it was impossible to be nervous or to worry about anything. All about you everything was quite obviously going well. The springs of abundance and fecundity seemed to have been tapped at some mysterious source. Nor did his abundance, or even a certain careless prodigality that accompanied Carlo like a rich music played with gusto, worry you. It was natural and instinctive. It was right and spontaneous.

Cibo was not only interested in himself but in what others had to say. He was the prince of listeners, and therefore bore the reputation of being a wit. When you related an anecdote to him a new quality was lent to memory. The events of the past seemed to have taken place in a halcyon glow of which, certainly up until the time you had met Cibo, you had not been aware. But now, as you were talking with him, you became fully conscious of their extraordinary significance and fine flavour. You felt that you had at last found the reflector of your own charming personality that you had long been in search of; one who enhanced your experiences without forcing you to exaggerate; one who could sympathize with you in your own delightful and hitherto unappreciated ironies. Yet, when you thought about it afterward, as you did when you stepped into the now banal and garish street, you wondered.

For if you looked at Cibo casually there was only a pleasant, curly-headed, middle-aged man with a sizable paunch seated in a comfortable chair, a man who wore a bright silk scarf like an alguacil. Was it in the smooth eccentricity of the brilliant sash that the charm was concealed? Hardly. Yet every person from the Captain-General of Cuba to Cibo's latest slave just in from the Rio Pongo and having his horny feet fitted with sandals to keep them from blistering on the griddle stones of the patio, felt it and expanded under it.

Despite Carlo's toast to "the present," it was the past, Italy, Livorno, and Genoa, that they talked about after all. With the long pent-up eagerness of an exile there were a million things, a thousand people, and a hundred places that Cibo wanted to know about. Anthony found himself, under the keen and amusing probe of Cibo's questions, reconstructing the life of the community that he had lived in.

Indeed, it was under such a searching that Anthony talked best. He had lately become aware of a certain reticence in himself that frequently evoked confidences which he was not inclined to reciprocate. Perhaps it was the essential mystery of his own origin which impressed him with the fact that in the final analysis he could not convey who he was in any usual terms. So, for the most part, he listened and thought. Yet he loved to talk, too. And with Cibo he felt to the full the melody of his own favourite keys. It was—it was amusing.

Before the morning had passed he had found time to tell in full the curious story of Captain Elisha's purchase of holy statuary at Genoa and the queer events of the voyage out. Cibo's belly moved up and down at the thought of the big Madonna in the cabin clasping to her heart a bottle of red wine. The eery expression of a faun laughing lengthened his jaws. He sat up.

"Do you know," said he, "I shall have to help that skipper of yours in disposing of his holy wares. Between you and me, Toni, I am a sad skeptic. It is fortunate for me that since the occupation of Havana by the English the Palace of the Inquisition is closed. There are books on my shelves which even now I would not desire to have advertised. Did you know I was a great reader, a student even in a desultory way, and *of course* a philosopher? From what you say of him, I agree with your friend Toussaint, though we should differ sadly on politics.

"There is a Spanish priest in Regla who is a great friend of mine. We have many an argument. You must meet him. Tonight! It is only upon food that we agree. Like all Spaniards he is a provincial heretic himself when it comes to wine—but on food, oh, on food"— he smacked his lips—"we are both exquisitely orthodox. So we meet often in sweet agreement at the table. During the past five years we have buried our minor differences about the nature of the spiritual world under mountains of dishes. We understand each other, Father Juan and I. I call him Father Trajan. Do you happen to remember the busts of the Caesars, Toni? When you see Father Trajan you will understand. It is that gallant old rascal of a Spaniard come to life again. A case of metempsychosis I insist. It has even worried— Father Trajan. Do you know the Catholic doctrine of the soul? No? Well, it is too hot to go into it now," he took a long pull at the pitcher, "but it is essential. And Father Trajan comes from Segovia. It is a very ancient, an old Roman town. Take one good look at his head when he comes. But don't let him see you do it. And now where am I?—oh, yes—I will tell you. I shall buy that statue of the Madonna del Vino and present it to Father Trajan's chapel, bottle and all. It would be an excellent jest a few years from now to ask him to look behind her robe. Did you say it was port? All that time then he would have been incensing a wine which he particularly dislikes. Ha, by the shade of Voltaire, I shall do it! Let us ask your Yankee captain to dinner tonight with Father Trajan. All parties to the deal will then be present. What! Ask the captain's lady, too? Not so, my boy. Why not? A cause de la scandale, mon ami. No, I do not care if her face is hopeless. In Havana gossip deals with more basic considerations." With the prospect of some excitement ahead he burned up a full half inch on his fourth cigar. After that they slept.

Lunch came on the little wagon and was rolled away. They did not move much after eating it. Carlo mixed some more planter's punch. Outside the fierce heat threatened to sap its way into their shady retreat. Lime-white splotches of sunlight percolated through the blinds.

Anthony looked down once into the patio and saw his sailor asleep in a hammock under the dense shade of a palm. A pickaninny was fanning off the flies. The only sound in the patio was the hum of insects in the sun. His chests had been brought up, he saw.

It was curious to think of his madonna being in this house. In the light of Carlo Cibo's proposed gift, for the first time in his life he thought of her humorously. How Cibo would laugh. The parrot gave him a wink and went on cracking seeds regularly. Like too long separated ticks of a clock they seemed to mark the passing of a more ample kind of time; to accentuate the somnolent leisure of the place. His eyes lost themselves in the cool green of the date and cocoa palms in the patio. The lizards streaked and flicked across the veranda. Carlo's two little bastards got up and went into a far corner and urinated. They came back again, curled up and went to sleep, the little girl with her head on her brother's stomach. Anthony lay back in his chair overpowered. Somewhere far away the huge carts were still jolting . . . somewhere . . .

At half past five the shadow of the patio wall suddenly seemed to engulf it. Almost instantly it was cool. They got up; bathed.

In a high-ceilinged room furnished with bamboo furniture and a mosquito net hanging ghostly from a suspended ring, Anthony dressed himself in a spotless linen suit that some former guest of Cibo's had left behind him. The very touch of it was refreshing, exhilarating. After the long sleep and floods of orange juice he felt light, very clear and cool, with a certain devil-may-care air and a penchant for the macabre in his mood. Downstairs the voice of Captain Elisha could be heard rumbling true to form. A sonorous, clean Spanish that he took to be Father Trajan's rang through the halls. He heard Cibo laugh and hurried down.

They were already gathering about the table. In this place you seemed to do nothing but eat and sleep, and yet he was hungry. He

found himself talking to, and at the same time half enthralled by
Father Trajan. It was about fish. Father Trajan would take him
fishing, mañana. Mañana the Virgin was to be installed in Father
Trajan's chapel at Regla, the Chapel of St. Paul. Most of Father
Trajan's parishioners were the wives of fishermen. "Quite early
Christian in atmosphere," said Carlo, and sniffed. Captain Elisha did
not see the point. But it was a question whether he or the priest was
the more pleased over the affair of the Madonna.

"A good bargain for a heretic and a pious gift to the church by a
pagan—was there ever such a combination of circumstances before!"
laughed Cibo as his guests left late with everything arranged.

"Tomorrow you must certainly go fishing with the father," said
Cibo yawning. "It will be an experience—for you. And we can take
up that matter of the debt again. Mañana, mañana," he stretched
himself and smiled.

"Good heavens," thought Anthony, "is the man going to sleep
again?" They both were!

"Well, how did you like your first day in Cuba?" queried Cibo.
"A fine life, eh?"

"J'en suis ravi, monsieur," said Anthony, and meant it.

He climbed into bed and looked through his mosquito netting that
caught the broad moonlight in a silver gauze. Outside, the guitars
and banjos were still going here and there. A strange, sickly, sweet
odour of some blossom opening in the moonlight outside his window
in the patio drifted in to him. He wished that Florence . . . that
Angela were with him now. How it *would* be—both of them!

What had done this? Was it Havana? Or was it Carlo Cibo's
wine? Mañana, mañana! Oh, rare new world!

CHAPTER THIRTY

THE MIRACLE IN THE CHAPEL OF ST. PAUL, REGLA

WRAPPED in one of Mrs. Jorham's patchwork quilts the Madonna del Vino, as Carlo persisted in calling her when Father Trajan was not around, was delivered early in the morning at the side door of the bare Chapel of St. Paul in the suburb of Regla.

Collins and some of his crew brought her and took the crazy quilt away again. Carlo, Father Trajan, and Anthony were on hand, each with a very different thought in his heart, as the Virgin was set on the stone floor and unveiled by the rough sailors.

A mason had already slung his scaffold and was preparing to install the statue in the niche behind the altar, where a poor little plaster figure without either beauty or prestige had long been the despair of Father Trajan.

Carlo was surprised by the serene beauty of the figure. In the shadows of the chapel the bright blue of her cloak was toned down until it fell in folds about her like memories of evening. He kept taking Father Trajan back a little distance "to give perspective"—and to prevent any chance of the priest's peering accidentally into the deep folds of the mantle.

The truth was, Cibo would have been ashamed to have had the wine bottle discovered now. It would look as if he had put it there.

Father Trajan was much touched by the gift; secretly mollified for many a remark of his table companion and sly dig at "the superstitions of the age." Now he would be able to obtain a grand indulgence from the bishop for Cibo. His friend's sins should be forgiven him. And there would be great joy amid the simple parishioners when their new Virgin was consecrated.

Perhaps it was a little irregular to have the mason put her in the niche this morning without notifying his superiors. But after all this was his parish. What possible objection could there be? And he would be able to beg a new cassock now for his acolyte. The present one was almost scandalous. Hey-ho! there would not be a more beautiful Madonna in Havana. He knelt down before her on the pavement and made a little prayer silently.

> "Mother of God, we are very simple and poor people who come
> to the Chapel of the blessed apostle. We must serve thee with

our hearts rather than with our gifts. Forgive, and be merciful,
gracious Mary. The candles are not of the best. But thou livest
in the light of the Father. Reflect his radiance upon us. Fill the
nets of those who kneel before thee here with fish. And remember thy servant who is a fisher of men, and Brother François,
who is digging roots now in my garden. Reward him for his
merciful heart, as thou art merciful, santa Madre de Dios."

He crossed himself and rose.

"Come, come, Carlo," whispered Anthony. "You must never say
a word about that wine. Did you see the father's face as he prayed?
You must promise me. It would be cruel. I should feel I had compounded at a sacrilege."

"Perhaps you are right," said Cibo.

"Perhaps!" said Anthony.

"Well, well, rest easy," retorted Cibo. "I shall not try to be funny
by being cruel. The priest is my friend, you know. We are really
fond of each other. My gift was kindly meant, too. We shall just
forget that the bottle is there. After all that is nothing but a silly accident. *We* are not responsible for it. I might get the mason to remove it."

They were standing outside the little door by now talking in low
voices.

"Let it go," said Anthony. "There would be awkward questions.
Let well enough alone." Cibo nodded but a little whimsically.

"A hundred years from now some curious verger will find some
remarkable port. I would like to come back and be that man." He
smacked his lips.

Inside the chapel Father Trajan and the workman lifted the Madonna into her niche reverently.

"And mind you," said the priest, "I want the new stucco, where
you have had to remove the old, smooth, and coloured like the rest
of the walls. You can decorate the panel below, can't you—a little?
I should like that."

"Sí, sí, padre, for two years now I have been working at the decorations in the cathedral." With the point of his heavy trowel he began to indent rapidly a deft little intaglio design of vines and flowers
along the base. He leaned back, looking down from the scaffold for
approval.

"You may go on," said the priest. "But *stop*—the cost!"

"I have been well paid by the generous señor grocer," the man admitted a little reluctantly. "A few more adobe flowers—" he shrugged
his shoulders. "For a few prayers for my mother I will add the whole
vine."

"One for each leaf," said the padre. "An acanthus. You know?"

"Sì," muttered the man. He began to mix.

"Do not forget to drop something in the box for the poor, my friend," said the father as he left to rejoin Carlo and Anthony.

"Ah! It is difficult to bargain with the clergy," muttered the mason to himself. "But I shall have the best of this bargain yet. Grow, vine! Burgeon my mother out of purgatory!" The point of his trowel and one finger flew. A delicate acanthus tendril with a thousand leaves began to unroll itself across the smooth face of the panel at the Virgin's feet. Outside, the voices of Father Trajan and his companions died away. The chapel was very close and still.

The mason worked diligently and fast. From time to time he laid down his trowel and wiped the sweat out of his eyes. At ten o'clock he got down from the scaffold and quenched his thirst at a cantina near by. He returned a little unsteady and went on. The tendril of leaves was almost done now.

He modelled the last fine spray of closed buds with his thumbnail and fingers. The scaffold shook slightly. The trowel which he had laid aside crept nearer the edge. Now—all but the last bud! He indented it in the stucco. Suddenly there was a clink, a tinkle, and the sound of gurgling fluid. The man looked about him uneasily, but he could see nothing amiss. Well, he would scrape up now and go. Caramba! His trowel was gone!

He hunted for it for some time. It was not on the floor. It was not on the altar, under it or beside it. It was not on the scaffold. He took that down. It had not fallen into the mortar bucket. He removed his dripping hand and sloshed it off in disgust.

"Madre de Dios!" And a nice, new, little trowel well balanced with lead he had let into the handle himself! One would think those little sneak-thieves and naked gamins would stay out of a church. He had had a pious mother, thank God! A fine generation it was getting to be with the Inquisition suppressed!

He left, staggering away under a pile of buckets and scaffolding on his back.

In the meanwhile Father Trajan's little party had threaded their way through the fishing quarter of Regla to his house on the water front. A small coral point projected into the bay, and there amid feathery trees at all angles, for the place was swept by winds at certain seasons, lay the priest's house bowered in green and surrounded by flowers and shrubs. Over the wall across the neck of land Anthony could see another priest hoeing vegetables in the garden, a spare, distinguished looking man in the robes and sandals of a Franciscan who evidently belonged to the Pauvres.

They walked into an alley of hibiscus mad with morning bloom, where the scarlet flowers seemed to hiss at them with their protruding, yellow-tipped tongues. They tramped through the gloom of the house and out of a blue square of doorway on the other side of it into Father Trajan's dooryard. Few who visited the priest were prepared for the pure loveliness of that little spot. It occupied the last few hundred yards, the very tip of the point of land. The house which lay directly across the narrow promontory screened it effectively from the town.

Here through the long years of undisturbed administration of his little parish Father Trajan had gradually brought back from his inland rambles every species of palm, fern, flowering bush, and vine that had pleased his vernal fancy as his eye had ranged over the estates and jungles of the Pearl of the Antilles. The gift of a rare flowering plant was to him more welcome than alms. Then too, his fishermen had brought him living shells for his beach and curious sponges and sea ferns for his coral caves. He had the gift of planting. Nearly everything he put down in either earth or water was soon at home.

Viewed from his bayside doorway, the result was what seemed to be a natural garden. The eye flattered itself and fell back tired with delight from the purple mass of a royal piñon to rest in a cool bed of ferns. Satiny lilies of plain and mottled colours looked at one from unexpected spots. There were smouldering clumps of anemones sprouting from cavities in the coral rock. Hanging from palms of unexpected shapes were orchids no one could have imagined, and against the faded coral-pink of the house itself bloomed four lusty trees of yellow, Moorish roses.

Yet, although every one of these things, except a few giant trees, had been planted by the padre, the place was still enchantingly wild. The glow of colour gradually ceased as the glance swept out to the point. Here was nothing but shadowy-green open spaces under wide-stretching date palms, waving ferns, and finally, grass; grass cut off clean and suddenly by the white circle of a tiny, moon-shaped cove.

"El paradiso del padre," said Cibo waving his hand.

"Ah, friend Carlo, you must let me praise this myself," cried Father Trajan, nevertheless colouring a little with pleasure at the compliment. "It is my one vanity.

"Come, señor," he continued, turning to Anthony, "I can see by your face that you will listen to me while I talk of my flowers. You have eyes to see, and you see! And there are some other things I must show you. We have an agreement to go fishing this morning, too. Carlo, will you join us?"

"What, broil myself for a basket of stupid fish I can buy for a peso!" exclaimed Cibo with genuine horror. "You know me better. I am for the veranda and my patio. But go along, my boy, do not let me prevent you. You had best take my palm leaf hat. Adiós then," he cried, doffing his hat with a wry face and exchanging it for Anthony's Leghorn which was too small for him. "And good luck. There will be turtle for luncheon," he called back. "Plenty for both of you. Never mind bringing the fish!"

"A heart of gold goes there," said the padre looking wistfully after Cibo. "What a pity that he injures his soul by the poor thoughts of his head. One should leave such matters to the church. But pardon, señor, you are of the true faith, I trust."

"I was raised in a convent, padre," said Anthony, secretly dodging the issue. What faith had he now? He wondered. He felt the key to his chest in his pocket—locked away there—safely?

"Oh, well then," said Father Trajan, as if there were a logical connection, "come, let me show you my fish ponds."

They walked down a narrow, wandering path toward the point.

"But look," cried the padre stopping suddenly at the top of a small knoll, "look! You can just see it from here."

A low cloud seemed to be spreading itself along and below the tidal bench that hid the beach from their eyes on the far side of the point. It looked as if a purple-tinged wisp of dawn mist had been blown loose from its cloud-bank and had caught on the tip of the little promontory that morning.

"I cannot imagine what it is," confessed Anthony. Father Trajan looked pleased.

"Hurry. It is really worth seeing," he said. "The most wonderful thing in the island, I believe."

Their path led through a reach of tropical bracken and suddenly emerged on the beach where a fishing boat was drawn up. Here along a low cliff for a surprising distance either way flaunted and burned a giant Bougainvillea vine. Where it had not climbed over the wind-carved pillars of coral rock and pre-empted the neighbouring trees and bushes, it was supported by the deck beams and ribs of an old hulk. This, stripped of its planks and half buried in the sand, had become a gorgeous pergola. There were seats here and there beneath it; even a low cairn on which nets were spread to be dried and mended. From the smooth, bleached sand of the natural floor below, the tremendous organ note of the vine's resounding mass of colour was reverberated back again in a deep imperial glow that harmonized ethereally with the body of bloom above.

Farther under the pergola were stained glooms of purple and magenta that shaded off near the front, where the glare of the beach penetrated, into dim violet shimmers to be seen only when you looked into the place directly. Sidewise they lost themselves beyond the range of vision into the colourless substance of the air. Yet even there Anthony felt them to be still going on. They might be faintly electric and account for something having raised his goose-flesh. Or they might have been transmuted into a rolling sound. For it was impossible to stand before this Bougainvillea and think of it as a purely silent experience. It had about it the quality of a muffled kettle drum; of continuous, distant, tropical thunder.

It was some moments before Anthony became aware of the fact that Father Trajan seemed to be looking at the vine through his own eyes. For the priest was gazing at Anthony as if lost in the expression of the young man who had gone a little pale under his tan. He stood wrapped in the vision.

"But who wouldn't be?" he thought. "It is all I have felt and dreamed about Cuba spoken in one word," he cried aloud.

"There are many ineffable thoughts like that in the forest, señor," said the padre quietly, "but none more beautiful. To think of it! I have been permitted to plant and tend this one with my own hands!" He held them up as if they did not belong to him but were mere tools that had been lent him. "Come under the leafy roof and look up. It makes even heaven more wonderful. Indeed, I cannot begin to say what I think about it. You will understand that."

They went under the pergola and immediately transfigured themselves. Anthony began to look about him half unbelieving. It was then, and in that place, that for the first time he saw Brother François face to face.

Seated, leaning back against a pile of old fish nets in a far corner of the place, where he had at first escaped their notice, was a barefooted monk in the brown garb of a Franciscan. The robe was brown in the sunlight, but in the light that filtered through the pergola it had about it the tinge of old blood. The man rose as soon as he saw himself discovered and came forward courteously. There was something distinguished and a little aloof about his carriage and walk, even an austerity. But no one could imagine being repulsed by him after a single glance at his face. On it was stamped hauntingly the rare expression of one whose strong sweetness of character had turned the indubitable marks of great sorrow into a kind of holy joy. Sympathy with him was evidently both a wise and a strong passion.

"I would like to know how one can look like that," thought Anthony. "He is not happy like a fool."

"Ah, Brother François, we have disturbed you I fear," said the priest. "We have found you out."

"Neither, I assure you, padre," said Brother François smiling. "When I saw you were having visitors I slipped back here to my favourite retreat. It was my hour of contemplation, but that is over now. It is time again to commune with human friends. May I introduce myself?"

He stepped forward and did so with a charm that put even the padre, who was somewhat awkward about such things, at his ease. It was the "monsieur" instead of the "señor" which gave Anthony his cue, and he replied in French.

At the sound of that tongue a sombre delight smouldered in the monk's eyes . . . "and so it will be pleasant to chat a little in French, if you will," said Anthony. "The Spanish comes as yet only practically. The other world must be left out for me in that language as yet."

"This one?" asked the monk half seriously, touching his forehead.

Anthony nodded. "I am afraid so." He noticed Brother François continued to look at him keenly. It was a little embarrassing, for his eyes seemed full of a banked fire that might break into flame.

"You learned your French at Blois, didn't you? It is an excellent kind they speak there. At Blois, I am sure. Perhaps I have seen you before? Just now I felt certain of it."

"I have never been to France," said Anthony greatly pleased. "My master was, I believe, from some place on the Loire. I am from Livorno. At least I was born there."

"Then I could never have known you. Ah! I remember now what it is. Yes, that *is* curious! But, your pardon, monsieur, it is nothing but a remembrance I will not trouble you with. And so you are going fishing with the padre, I see. I envy you. He and I are both fishers."

The padre was indeed already beginning to gather together his tackle but several articles seemed missing. With some annoyance visible on his face he excused himself to return to the house for the missing things.

Anthony and Brother François sat down under the arbour.

Evidently the opportunity to converse in French was a precious one to the monk. In the familiar accents of his own tongue he became ardent and even confidential. They exchanged news. Anthony was soon comparing notes with Brother François while mentally composing a long pondered letter to Toussaint on the subject of the French Revolution. And here he found to his fascination was a man who had been in the thick of it, one who had actually seen Robespierre.

There was something almost occult about this monk. He stirred you strangely. He removed your reticences for he seemed to have none himself. It would be possible, very easy—there seemed to be a spiritual compulsion upon one to succumb to his spell. . . .

"So you see, monsieur, I am after all not an émigré in the usual meaning of the word. To preach the gospel and really to live like Christ—it was not more dangerous in Paris during the Terror than it is here and now. All of us who do that are exiles. We are merely passing through the strange countries of the world going home to our Father. In our souls is all of his kingdom that will ever be here. Yet just for that reason it might be everywhere and now.

"I am not making you a homily, monsieur, or talking about myself. You will pardon my excitement. It is the remembrance of the past few years in Paris that comes across my view. One cannot, if one knows, speak of them merely with the kitchen voice, 'Thérèse, a little more gumbo in the soup!'—no, no,—that will not do. That is worse than being exquisite or gay about it. Also I do not speak to crowds or in them, whether in the plaza or dans l'église. Always it is to the man, or to the woman or the child that I come, and not always with words. Man, mankind, the state, virtue, the people, justice, fraternity —what are they? Words that do not correspond to anything but philosophers' dreams. They are the worn out table-talk of Greece and Rome. Liberty?

"Monsieur Antoine, for two years I followed the tumbrils and I stood on the scaffold. I saw the keen knife of liberty fall and rise to fall again, and each time on an individual's neck. That is the way of the state. And those hundreds of eyes! They looked down into the basket at the eyes there that looked back. It was unthinkable that what lay in the basket was the end. Those who thought so died there, indeed. For those who turned to me for some confirmation of hope, I then shared what I had given me, the Comforter. Robespierre himself could not prevent it.

"Do you know I went to see that man. Mais oui! At the little house of the cabinet-maker in the Rue St. Honoré—in April only two years ago. It seems a century ago. It was the day after Danton, Camille Desmoulins, and the others had passed under his window in the carts.

"The two ruffians who guarded the tyrant came to the door when I knocked. I asked for Duplay, the furniture-maker, and got him to carry my name to the little man upstairs. Robespierre knew me. We both came from Arras. My family was a very great one. Monsieur would know its name. Robespierre knew that I might have been a bishop but that I went into the country instead as a parish priest. You see we had both read Rousseau together. I remembered when de Robespierre was a provincial dandy who read bad verses before the 'Rosati' at Arras. He had a sweet voice then, and he had resigned a criminal judgeship to avoid pronouncing a death sentence. Think of it! It was the same voice that I afterwards heard raised in the Convention, 'It is with regret that I pronounce the fatal truth, Louis must die that the country may live!' Ah, he was full of regrets like that. But anyway I was shown upstairs.

"He and Fleuriot-Lescaut were seated together. Robespierre looked very white. The great voice of Camille Desmoulins shouting the prophecy of his death under his window the day before had shaken him. I saw that he was afraid. He was still the little dandy in knee-breeches, silk socks, and powdered hair. He turned down a paper with a list of names on it that he and Lescaut were talking over and looked up.

" 'Well, citizen?' he said, 'what is it? Ah! I remember you now.' He tried to smile. That was terrible.

" 'I have a very simple proposition to make to you,' I replied. 'You must be very sick of all this blood-letting and of being the god of Catherine Théot. Is it not so? See where your philosophic virtue has led you! You will have to kill us all. You alone will remain, for soon you will be the only one who knows how to practise virtue. Another plan is needed. I speak to you, *for* you, not for France or any other dream, but for your own soul. You believe that is immortal?'

" 'What do you propose, citizen?' Robespierre said. He leaned forward and looked at me with hungry eyes and a thin smile.

" 'Simply that you leave this room now and come with me into the country. You can change your name and disappear. Then we can go about the world just as Christ would have done, doing good. We need nothing. We need make no speeches or sermons. Let us just go out and let things happen to us as they will, and try to help and comfort any man, woman or child who needs it. Let us be kind, a brother to this man and that. Let us persuade no one, but pass on taking whatever road lies before us and leaving a good deed done in Christ's name wherever and whenever we can. That is all. It is an old and simple plan, to do good to men with the spirit of God upon one. Do you not see by this time that it is the only plan that will work? *Leave everything and follow me.* You remember that?'

" 'Why do you come here to me, and *today,* with a suggestion like this?' he asked. 'Do you not know that France is pressed down upon my shoulders, the hope of saving France, of the world!' He got up and moved about with Fleuriot-Lescaut gaping at him.

" 'But you are mad,' he flung at me. 'You have lost relatives. You are an aristocrat, a ci-devant count.'

" 'That is not so, citizen. You know that even before the Revolution I became a parish priest. No, no, it is not I that am mad. I come to you because you are an idealist of sincerity. I can see that.

And you are wrong, you have chosen the wrong way to help the world.
You are working through the state and through institutions. You
have made reason your divinity. See what it is doing to make men
divine. You know. Still within you, *you know!'*

"He made a furious gesture but I kept on.

"'You can disembarrass yourself of all this, citizen. There is a
way to do good and to save yourself by forgetting yourself. I have
found it. I am living it, and it is in me. Come! Let the Republic
flourish as it may. The Kingdom of God is just beyond the door.
Leave Robespierre here, my brother, and come with me.'

"Many that I have spoken to thus, monsieur, have been greatly
surprised. Under all that they pretend to be and through all their
bafflements I talk to *them.* They see the way opening before them.
In truth most men have thought of it. But the world is too much for
them. They keep their loss. Prudence insists on just a few chains
to hold them fast to something tangible. So they remain anchored
on their reef to be pounded to pieces on it when the tide of life ebbs.
It was so with Robespierre. For a minute he saw, he remembered,
he dared hope again. Then his face worked, and I thought he would
spring at me.

"Monsieur, if Fleuriot-Lescaut had not given a great laugh just
then I should have been guillotined. I believe in my heart he was a
merciful man. His laugh saved me.

"'Come, citizen,' he said, 'have this simple fool thrown out. *Disembarrass yourself,* as he says. We have not time here to argue with
a mad parish saint. A cabbage head,' he roared, 'a green cabbage!'
He pretended to kick me downstairs. I saw the tyrant standing at the
top with the list still in his hand. It was the first time he had laughed
in weeks, I suppose. I did make an unfortunate noise falling down
the stairs. But do you know I still think—almost I won. 'Almost
thou persuadest me,' his eyes seemed to say, and his hands shook. But
God had another way. I only offered myself as an instrument. Did
you see the padre when he held up his hands and said they had been
permitted to tend this glorious vine? I heard that, too. Ah! the padre
is a poet. A thought of God he called his vine. Well, it is best to
think of all of yourself as the padre thinks of his hands. You will
see then how thoughts of God flourish."

He looked up so that the violet tinge of the light filtering through
the vine fell full on his face.

It would be impossible to exaggerate the impression which this
narrative had made on Anthony. It seemed as if Brother François
had been pleading with him. It was not so much what the monk had
said as how he said it. Here was a man with an obviously complicated
knowledge and experience who was living by and pleading for a great

simplicity. The manner of an aristocrat and a courtier had been transmuted in him into a noble directness, a wise humility that was without fear. There was an ease about him that sprang from an assurance which did not annoy you. You simply understood that he was at one with himself and the world. Here was passion at rest and yet potential.

"Follow me!" Yes, follow along the way that child which the madonna held in her arms had followed into manhood, into something beyond, into the glory like the violet light on Brother François's face. Ah! what a way! That was what the madonna was holding out to you always in her arms—the child and his way. The most simple and direct one after all. Why had he never realized that before? What the monk had said had brought it home to him as a possible experience. Father Xavier had told him to think of the child. He saw what he meant now, he thought. To take up your cross and . . . *That* was not clear. Anthony had no cross. Life was delightful. Like the light under this arbour, beautiful, and colourful, and clear. Was not his private communion with the madonna enough for him? And yet she was holding forth something else to him, something that was very precious to her. Yet she would share it. It was a gift she seemed to hope you would take.

Yes, it meant that. Religion was not merely to refrain, and to worship, "to talk at night," as he used to call it. He smiled and he sighed too. No, it was a way. Had he really been travelling that way? Brother François had. By his overtones he seemed to make the music of that road clear. The road was life along which he went doing good. Had he been pleading for a companion? Why not join him, Anthony? It would all be simple and all very clear. The responsibility would be God's.

Simple things appeal sometimes even to complicated young men. Anthony sat with his head on his hand looking at Brother François.

"Thou knowest," said the priest very quietly, "to whom I have been talking. Hast thou heard me?"

"Yes, I have understood," said Anthony. But he could go no further.

Brother François waited a while. "Well, then—you have understood," he said. "That is the beginning. You must wait until you also feel. It is experience I mean. Then you will know, and then . . . then the answer will be yours to make and the road yours to take. But I see that it is not now. Only remember what I have said, if you can, when the time comes.

"Ma foi!" he looked up suddenly breaking the tension between them, "the sun is already overhead. You will not be going fishing *this* morning. This morning is no more. What can have detained the padre?

He is—well, he is a fisherman, and there must have been a reason.
Let us go and see."

They rose and sauntered down the path toward the house. It was
very hot now. Even under Cibo's palm leaf hat Anthony could feel
the exact spot of the sun. The little suburb of Regla that lay before
them seemed extraordinarily quiet. It was already absorbed in its
siesta. Not even a cart jolted. Suddenly with a startling clangour
the bell in the chapel began to ring.

"What can it be?" said Brother François wonderingly, as the excited clangour continued. "It is like an alarm." They quickened
their pace and entered the house. Father Trajan was leaning against
the jamb of his street door listening in a puzzled way. He looked up
when they came in.

"Pardon, señor, for my not returning. I will explain it shortly. I
was detained. Mañana! What I cannot explain now is the ringing
of my chapel bell. Possibly someone has been drowned."

Already they could hear the sound of running feet in the alleys
beyond the hedge. "Ah, I am afraid that is what it is. See, here they
come now to fetch me." A look of sadness overspread his features.
"I had best get the oil, I suppose. Who can it be this time?" He
sighed.

Two women made their appearance at the gate breathless, and
calling, "Padre, padre!"

"Ah, what is it, Juana, my poor soul?" said the padre from the next
room with apprehensive sadness.

"Padre, padre," clamoured the two fisherwomen now at the door, "a
miracle has occurred!"

"A what?" said the padre.

"A miracle," clamoured the woman.

"Yes, yes, by the blood of God it is true!" bawled the other.

"What is all this silly excitement about?" said the priest coming out
of the room indignantly with the viaticum still in his hand. "What
are they ringing the bell of my chapel for?"

"A miracle," shouted both of the women. "There is a new Madonna
in the chapel and . . ."

"Foolish women, I know it," countered the priest. "Did I not see
her brought there this morning myself? It is the pious gift of . . ."

"But she is bleeding! Her merciful heart is bleeding red blood
drop by drop on the altar! We have seen it! A great crowd is already
there watching. It is a blessed miracle from God!"

"Sí, sí, padre! Sí, sí, it is true! Come and see for yourself. Juana
and I, we alone have remembered to come and tell you." They stood
crossing themselves and trembling.

"Come, padre, let us see what this is all about," said Brother François. "I thank you, my friends." But the women had gone.

They hurried after them as fast as they could. The town was already alarmed by the bell. People dashed past them toward the chapel. A good deal of confused shouting could be heard here and there as the winds of rumour blew.

When they arrived at the door of the building it was already full and a crowd was seething about the entrance. With great difficulty a way was made for the padre and his friends. Inside the place was silent. Only the heavy breathing of the crowd and the clamour of the bell above was audible. Anthony could see that those near the altar were on their knees while those further back were craning their heads and staring as if fascinated. All were looking in one direction.

He became separated from the others and finally found himself pressed back against the side wall. Only after some difficulty could he manage to get a glimpse of the front of the church. Father Trajan was already before the altar kneeling. Anthony saw there was a red stain upon it. The bell had stopped now. You could have heard a pin drop. Suddenly there was a *plop,* a distinct drip like falling water. The stain on the altar ran over and dripped onto the floor. A universal sigh went up from the whole place. He raised his eyes to the statue in the niche above. Some time passed. Then he saw it himself. Something trickled out of the cloak of the virgin and splashed onto the altar. In the candlelight it was red, and it did look like blood. The bell began to clamour again madly.

Father Trajan turned to face his chapel, now jammed from wall to wall. Here everybody who could was kneeling. He burst into the "Magnificat."

A great thrill of joy ran through the crowd. The simple faces of fishermen, labourers, and negroes looked up at the miraculous statue, filled with ecstasy and awe. The face of Father Trajan was glorified. It shone with a proud benignity and utter conviction.

"In his own chapel!" Anthony thought. "Poor man! I should have let Carlo take it away. I did not think *this* would happen."

He assured himself he was innocent, but his heart smote him sorely. There was not one unbelieving face present. "Now," he told himself, "no one must ever know. I will see to that. What a seed Captain Jorham planted that night! A miracle!"

Then, terrible as it was, he wanted to laugh. Struggling with himself in the intense excitement and the stifling atmosphere, for the first and last time in his life he felt hysterical. He wanted to laugh and cry as the women were already doing.

The bell burst forth again into a mad peal. Outside there was a renewed shouting. The whole town would soon be there. How could he get out? The side door! He looked across the chapel. Standing wedged helplessly against a pillar so that he seemed to tower above those who knelt around him was the tall frame of Brother François. He was looking with an expression of intense pity and sympathy at the hundreds of faces staring ecstatically at the magical clay breast of the Madonna del Vino.

An hour later Anthony finally gained the door. The "miracle" was still going on.

Wine seeps slowly through terra cotta.

CHAPTER THIRTY-ONE

A DECENT MAMMALIAN PHILOSOPHY

IT WAS about three o'clock when Anthony finally succeeded in returning to Carlo Cibo's. He had won his way out of the chapel literally inch by inch, and he was tired and exhausted. Whether the heat or the excitement were the more intense would be hard to say. Already the news had spread far and wide. Boats, carriages, and caballeros were coming in from Havana. The cantinas of Regla, he observed, were doing a roaring business. But in the patio all was shade and quiet. Carlo was asleep on the veranda in his chair, his short legs dangling.

"Wake up, Carlo," said Anthony. "A miracle has occurred. Aren't you ashamed, you old heathen, to be asleep while such things are going on?" It was some time before Carlo could be made to comprehend. When he did his belly moved up and down so fast as finally to stop his laughing from sheer physical discomfort. He lay back in his chair and continued to snort with his hands on his sash.

"Miracles should not be permitted to occur in the summer," he said at last. "They are dangerous to people like myself. It is hard on the heart. I shall take it up with the ecclesiastical authorities. Unfortunately the archbishop, who is a friend of mine, lives at Santiago.

"But," continued he sitting up and laying his hand on his lips, "seriously, let me tell you, my boy, you and I must keep a close mouth about this. If we are questioned we must know nothing. *Nothing*— do you understand?

"There will be a tremendous to-do over the affair. The bishop in Havana may even be annoyed with Father Trajan for being a little too up and coming. Or he may suspect me when he hears I am the donor of the miraculous image. He is no fool I can tell you, that old man. So mum's the word. There will undoubtedly be an official inquiry, depositions before notaries, and all that kind of thing. The whole town is a witness. But they won't press it too far I feel sure. It falls too pat into their hands. With the population on both sides of the bay stirred up it will be impossible, silly to deny it. There would be riots. No, no, it will be confirmed. As you say—'A miracle has occurred!'" He lay back again breathless.

"Cheecha!"

"Sí, sí."

441

"More limes and rum, mucha, mucha! Turtle soup for the señor. Hurry, delay not, haste! The soup hot, with much fat, and sliced limes. Go!

"Ah, Madre de Dios, what a day! Did I not say you were lucky, Señor Toni? See—you reek with luck!" He spread out his fat hands over the pitcher with utter conviction. Even the lime peel dangled from his fingers convincingly.

"And the curious thing about it is that this time all the depositions and witnesses will be honest. The poor bishop will really be confused by that. The miracle should have taken place at the cathedral in Havana which they are just now redecorating. The bones of Columbus were brought there only last January. But the Madonna bleeds at Regla, in 'the suburb across the bay'! All the rules for miracles are disregarded."

A leer came into his eye. "The future of Regla is made. Peons from Moron to Guanes will be making pilgrimages. My house is already twice as valuable as when you arrived . . . Signore, I thank you! You are a public benefactor. Por Dios, the rest of the holy cargo of El Capitán Jor-*ham* will now sell for ransoms! Even the black robes who are now lying low at Belén will scramble for it. A plain padre will have beaten them. It is—it is simply magnificent! I drink your illustrious health." He tilted an entire pitcher of drink down his throat. His voice came out of the deep receptacle like an echo from a cave.

"Are you sure," said he, "your friend the captain does not remember about his bottle?"

"I am certain," Anthony assured him.

The pitcher gurgled with a satisfied note. Its angle became more acute. "How do you suppose," continued its sepulchral tones, "that the bottle was broken?"

"A jar when the statue was put in place, perhaps," mused Anthony, "or possibly some carelessness on the part of the mason. But I really don't know. Do *you?*" cried he, suddenly suspicious.

"No, no," replied Carlo coming out of his eclipse with genuine solicitude—and the mark of the pitcher on his face. "I tell you I had nothing to do with it. I suspect it *was* the mason. I had already thought of that. But it must have been an accident as you say. He would not tell. I'll tell you what. To make this miracle beyond cavil you must again make sure of Captain Jorham. Leave the fragments of the bottle and the mason to me. Tonight, late, I will make sure of both. I know a way. They will examine the statue, of course, and within a day or two. Father Trajan—we are both thinking of him, I know—dear man, he shall have his miracle without a cloud. When the confirmation comes from the archbishop I shall give the finest dinner that Cuba has ever seen. It too will be a miracle. You are the first invited."

"An invitation is the best way to make a witness remember. I noticed that at Mr. Bonnyfeather's table. Invited guests never forget," said Anthony. He wondered if all events for Cibo inevitably resulted in more and better food.

"I have known even *un*invited guests to remember my dinners," smiled Cibo. "But that is really one of the greatest compliments a host can receive. I'll tell you what! We shall have you, and Captain Jorham, and Father Trajan—and myself . . . ."

"And Brother François?" added Anthony impulsively.

"Ah, yes, the Frenchman! He *is* interesting. Did you know he is already in hot water with the authorities here for being a little too literal in his ideas of what Christ would have one do for slaves? He goes about nursing poor people with yellow fever and soothing the dying whether they are white or black. It is over the black that the trouble comes in, of course. It scarcely does, you know, after what has just happened in Santo Domingo, to have a man like that loose. The niggers might get the idea that God is sorry for them. Not in Cuba with a Spanish governor and garrison! Did you know the captain-general sent his aide to ask me to look the man up? Well, I did. He has an interesting story I can tell you! A little too interesting, and not regular enough. I don't think he'll be here long," said Cibo drawling a little. He began to mix more punch.

"Carlo, he is harmlessly extraordinary, isn't he? Brother François is a holy man if there ever was one," exclaimed Anthony. "What harm has he done?"

"Oh, he has been talking with you, I see," said Cibo. His face suddenly became quite serious.

"Yes, I agree with you, Toni. Brother François *is* a holy man. That is the trouble. He is not merely content to perform in the ritual of the church. He is one of your complicated primitives, a man who has penetrated behind the scenery of religion, one who intends to live the story which the ritual is supposed to illustrate. You see, he does not attack or interfere with the drama. That makes it a little difficult for his superiors. He does not provide them with an excuse to abolish him or thrust him out. On the contrary, as far as I can find out, he merely proposes to carry out their own precepts. That is, of course, profoundly embarrassing—to them."

Anthony tried to say something but Cibo went on.

"Brother François and his kind are the men who have always made Christianity a dangerous religion. Just when the church is about to be taken for a decorative and snugly-woven cocoon on a dead branch of the sacred tree, a place for a few fat slugs to hibernate where they have softly spun themselves in, *pouf!*—that cocoon bursts and the beautiful, living psyche of Christianity emerges. There is always a great running around then and waving of fine-meshed theological and political nets. The state is particularly anxious about such lepidoptera getting loose. Property! When the state can't kill a specimen quietly in a corner before its wings are dry, the church captures it and pins it on a card marked 'Saint Somebody.' Then the faithful come and see the body in a glass case, usually the glass is coloured. But there it is, catalogued, and belonging to its proper order. Now and then it may be permitted to work a few harmless miracles. A pile of crutches accumulates, or the story of the poor butterfly edifies the piously sentimental. They imitate its flutterings. Meanwhile the hard-working caterpillars keep making more Gothic or Romanesque cocoons for the slugs, always on the same closed pattern. They, of course, do not know yet what a Christian cocoon is really for." Cibo took another draw on the pitcher and ran on even a little more incoherently. "Now look at Jeanne d'Arc!

"The state is so frightfully careless and stupid about its executions. Executions, particularly the expunging of patriots or moral reformers, should be conducted in profound secrecy. To dramatize, or to allow news about such takings-off to circulate, whether the man is a criminal or a saint, is the best way for sovereigns to commit suicide. Yes, I often wonder at the politicos. They never seem to learn anything. Just about the time the world is getting bored by being asked by an enthusiast to adopt some kind of a life that no mammals could survive—Ha! the police descend! A great trial with all the implications of a Greek tragedy is staged. Soldiers parade, judges pontificate, women weep, priests snivel. After which the hero is then boiled in oil, or has his bowels let out, or is permitted to caper naked in the flames, or is hanged—or what you will. How can anybody forget him then?

"For saints I myself favour a dangerous foreign mission, transportation provided free. I have already suggested that to the captain-general. For people are already beginning to follow this Brother François about. His dramatic disappearance into the Morro would be embarrassing. He has friends. Whispers about him have already passed over the hills from plantation to plantation."

"How can you talk so, Carlo? It seemed to me just now that you spoke of him with affection. Don't you care? You are asking him to eat with you, too!" Anthony was now much in earnest and sitting up very straight.

"You do not understand me, Toni. I view all these matters from the outside, calmly. I am an unromantic Italian, a real Roman. I am purely practical. I am really the best friend Brother François has.

Ah, you smile, but listen. If he stays here his end is certain. He is,
I must tell you, of a great French noble family. He might have been
a bishop under the old régime. He left all that and went into the
country to be a parish priest. Then during the Revolution he drifted
to Paris. He took a minor part as a peasant deputy in the beginning
of the troubles there. I think he believed for a while that the state
might help the people. Then he saw through all that and was horrified
by the Terror. The last pink tinge of St. Jean-Jacques faded from
his mind. He then became a literal follower of Christ. How? By
joining the Franciscans, a Pauvre. He wandered begging into Spain.
A troop ship brought him here. The men were dying on board of the
plague, they say, and he swam out to nurse them at Cadiz. So you see
even the garrison knows him. That worries the authorities. It is all
frightfully irregular, of course, and could only happen in times like
these. Now he is helping the slaves. No, he doesn't preach. He says
nothing. But very shortly it will end in a tragedy for Brother
François.

"Now I know all this. For years I have dealt among the natives
and foreigners here and I have played carefully with the authorities,
too. Always I play to avoid great trouble. The authorities have come
to trust me. Yes, it has been profitable, but that is not all. You see,
I like brave men. I don't want to see them die. I prevent it when I
can. With Brother François it has gone like this: He has been ill.
I prevailed on the good padre to take him in and nurse him in his
garden. During that time his dangerous ministrations have ceased.
In the meanwhile the captain-general has spoken to the bishop. Our
good brother will soon be recognized for his work among the poor,
and it will be arranged with the proper local authorities of his order
that he shall go to Africa, to the field for which he has shown such
aptitude! Even now they only await certain papers from Santiago.
I have by just a few hints brought this about. If I had not, my friend,
your holy man would have died before this of the yellow jack in a cell
in the Morro waiting for instructions from Spain. They never come
for people like him. Tell me now, *am* I so cruel? Or would you
rather I should let him compose his own epitaph in some more romantic and heroic way?"

It was difficult for Anthony to reply. He found a large part of his
emotions ready to applaud Brother François and yet he could not protest entirely what Cibo had said. He saw, too, that behind Carlo's
somewhat cynical outline of policy there lay a well-meant human
kindness.

"You do not intend to consult Brother François himself, I suppose?" he said at last.

"By no means," replied Cibo emphatically. "Your enthusiast who

has a complete solution for everything on tap is always the last man
to know what is good for himself. Indeed, with the millennium
always just around the corner it is seldom that they take the trouble
either to support or to protect themselves. They hook their chins on
a cloud and then walk bare foot over all the broken bottles and old
nails which those with a less lofty gaze easily avoid. A suggestion
of shoes is hotly resented. In this case I am merely guiding the cloud-
hooked gentleman out of a path, where a pit with a sharp stake is just
around the next turn, into a road with perhaps a longer vista. Eventually, no doubt, he will find his own painful way to heaven. Several
people will doubtless be impressed. Yes, speaking even as a disinter-
ested pagan who wants all calvaries at a distance, I think I can see
the stigmata on Brother François's hands."

Anthony's heart leaped strangely. Against all the assurances of
Carlo there looked up at him as if out of a vision the face of Brother
François as he had seen it under the violet light of the vine. "I think
you are right about the stigmata, Carlo," he said after a while. "Perhaps I *am* romantic, but it did seem to me this morning that there was
something about the man that was—well—shall I call it divine? I
mean that the quality which saves men from being just animals has a
greater share in him than in me. It seemed to dominate his body
entirely. I am not sure they can kill that. Are you?"

Cibo passed his hand over his eyes. "No, I am not sure. But I do
not want to watch anyone trying. Well, you touch me there, Toni, I
will confess. In speaking of executions I should have added that ordinarily they get little attention, and for the most part do not deserve it.
Men seem to have an instinct about them. There is seldom any vigorous protest over the mere slaying of so much meat. It is only when
someone gets into the toils who possesses notably the quality of which
you speak that the wrench is felt."

"It seems to me then you are not so pagan after all, Carlo."

The man stretched himself and laughed. "We are talking a great
deal and it is getting late. Also I have now had my third pitcher today
and that makes me voluble and illogical. But what does it matter what
makes men talk if they convey their essential feeling? Brother François seems to have succeeded in doing that this morning to you. Confess—you are disturbed by him more than you would like to admit."

"Yes," said Anthony. "He stirred something in me of which I had
not been aware."

"Exactly," said Cibo. "You have grown quite heated about him
while we talked. You really care, and you are even ready to accuse
me of being callous. But I repeat it is *not* so. Let me try to unfold
my own philosophy a little. I think I see the basis of your feeling
under all this. It is not merely a French priest we are discussing, is it?

His unique personality, even briefly glimpsed this morning, touched you mysteriously. Didn't he?"

"I have already told you so. Why do you . . ." But Carlo was not to be interrupted.

"You should ask yourself, Toni mio—'*is* he really so unique?' You are young!" Cibo pointed his finger at him scornfully.

"When we are still young we think a great many people whom we meet are extraordinary. There is no one else in the world like them, we feel sure. Also our own precious selves are without parallel. We tell ourselves and each other, 'Neither we nor our friends, who are so unusual, are understood.' The world, we think, is not subtle enough to understand us. But we are wrong.

"The adult world is far too subtle to waste much time on us. It understands us instinctively by just remembering itself. It has thought through all our thoughts and is tired of our violent emotions. It does not need to care about youth because it knows youth will get older. Besides, it is too busy about the essentials of existence to go in for theories and feelings about them. Good old world! It is the young who do not understand it or themselves.

"From fifteen to twenty-five youth is busy talking about itself and trying to hatch doorknobs by brooding over them in a fever. Eggs— I mean events. They hatch themselves. Fate laid them pregnant on a warm beach. Everything that survives the process grows up according to the plan of its own egg. You can't do much about it. Not nearly as much as you think. No, really you can't!

"Fate is a wise old turtle. Imitate and accept her. Otherwise you will become feverish over the eggs you think you have hatched and go clucking and scratching about in the dust for chickens only to find that ducks must swim, and like it. When you learn that you are beginning to grow up. Grow up as soon as you can. It pays. The only time you really live fully is from thirty to sixty, provided of course you are healthy and don't die. No, the young are slaves to dreams; the old servants of regrets. Only the middle-aged have all their five senses in the keeping of their wits. I," said he, helping himself again to the pitcher, "am middle-aged; absolutely in my prime."

Anthony felt momentarily overpowered, almost an infant again. Then he saw how much Cibo was enjoying himself.

"My God!" continued Cibo lustily, taking another sustaining swig, "did you ever think what a terrible mess a young man really is? I mean a youth. That is—a kind of portable apparatus or attachment to three troublesome globes, one who has just stopped being a mad boy and has not yet been scared into being a decent man. One feels profoundly sorry for him. The only peace he can get is for a few hours after a girl has nearly killed him. The rest of the time he goes drifting about making a lot of noise like a ship upon which a perpetual mutiny is going on. He is always steered in the direction which his bowsprit indicates.

"Young men think life is a game, you know, an adventure. You hear them say so. Life is a mystery, not a game or an adventure. Birth and death are the only certain events in it. Eggs, eggs both of them! Maybe life is an egg? You can't tell what you're hatching. I'm getting drunk but never mind. (It's a wise man that knows how foolish he is when he's sober.) I'll tell you what wisdom is." He sat up earnestly and ponderously now.

"You now hear the most profound of all human oracles speaking. It alone holds the past and the future. Hearken to it, Toni."

Anthony had winced. It took him a few minutes to think of any reply to this unexpected and outrageous attack upon him.

"Your tongue and your oracle both sound alike to me," he said at last in desperation.

He was surprised and delighted to see that he had got home. "I always did think life was a mystery but not to be explained by a blast from the bowels," he continued making the most of his brief moment of victory.

"You underrate the guts," said Cibo at last. "What is even a wise book but a blast from the lungs made visible to the eyes? Man only makes foolish noises and smells in the face of mystery. No, Toni, do not get angry," he went on. "Forgive me for being a man . . ."

"Forgive me for being a young man then," said Anthony.

"I do, I do! Believe me, I like you for it in spite of all I have said," cried Carlo. "I shall even pretend now to be sober.

"Toni, I have been watching you. You interest me. You see and feel things so vividly it is a pleasure. Why then don't you let it go at that? Enjoy the fascination life has for you. What more do you want? Why ask 'why'? Why let your mind always be demanding of you, 'Give me an understandable and valuable goal; explain to me why I am here'? That is dangerous. That will eventually spoil the fascination for you. That is why Brother François interested you this morning. You thought he could provide answers for those questions. Is not that so?"

"Yes," said Anthony, "I thought this morning when he was talking to me I saw a way open up to live by."

"The way to Calvary! Come, come, Toni mio, you are not going to try that way?" He laughed. "Nonsense, of course not! You are only dallying with a romantic idea. I know. You are going to live life, all of it, for the sake of living. It is worth while. Besides, you can't avoid it, being what you are. Listen, let us not devote more time to our Brother François. I want to talk to you about the most interesting thing in the world, with perhaps one exception. Yes, despite all I have said, a young man. One whom I know better than he supposes. For you see, as I was about to say some time ago, as one gets older with a much broader basis for judgment"—he patted his paunch—"every new person is no longer a surprise. Men and women fall into types.

"Now you are a type. You are very practical, and yet, you are always aware of the mystery of things. You have not yet made up your mind what the world is like or what you are. You are not quite sure what you would be, a mysterious or a practical man, and you therefore cannot foretell how you are going to act. Things happen to you, and then you are always surprised by your own possibilities and limitations. Now am I right so far?"

"Very much so," murmured Anthony. "I have sometimes thought so myself."

"Very well then, it will help you to have someone else say so who is not yourself. Here, have another drink. That is the least that a host who likes an audience can provide. I would like to hear you talk more. But, no, I know you will not. You would rather listen and think. Very well then. Now is your chance.

"What I meant to tell you is that unless you come to *some* conclusion about yourself and the world you will be a mere wanderer. Not finding any surety within, you will unconsciously go about the planet looking for yourself everywhere. You will get bored, or you will produce your own expelling explosions, and you will go on saying, 'In the next place, over there, I shall be happy. There I shall be myself. There I shall find the true Anthony.' But it will only be another small part of you in another small place, not the whole man. Or, worse than that, you will grow desperate and become extreme. You will try to pretend to yourself that you are all spirit and the world is only a dream, or that you are an animal only and the world is all real. Both are possible with you, for you will only believe things after you experience them. Ah! that is your trouble, a young man's trouble, the experiences of others do not persuade you. Nevertheless—take another drink, for I am going to give you some advice. If this talk were not all about you, you would be bored, wouldn't you?"

Anthony laughed and drank deep.

"For *so* much I can go on then," said Carlo, measuring the tumbler at the level of his eyes as he resumed.

"Practise then what I call a decent mammalian philosophy. Go in for the body, my boy, but remember you are a man. At one end of your spine is a brain and at the other end something that needs constant companionship. The two extremities are utterly dependent upon what is put into the vacancy. About one half of the time the brain is busy devising means to fill that hollow. The other half of the time is taken up with the matter of companionship—and the complications which result. The *remainder* of the time"—Cibo paused—"is given over to intellectual and spiritual affairs. Other minor manifestations of man I need scarcely mention. They are merely notorious.

"Now *my* ideal philosophy is one which admits what I have just briefly sketched to be the basis of human nature. I practise it constructively. For instance, my business is to distribute fine groceries and minor edible luxuries in and about Havana. But I do not regard this as an end. It simply provides me the means of filling my own cavity by filling others, with sufficient overplus to provide some amusement for my brain—and companionship for the other extreme—also the means of travelling a little, comfortably—but I don't want to. It is impossible to get more out of life. How can you? Add to this that I have the respect and fear of my fellow men in this vicinity, and you will see that my cup runs over. I do not interfere with them but I make trouble for them if they interfere with me. My code of honour consists of a few things that I will not do. There do not seem to be very many of them. Pagan you say? No! For you see I really love my neighbours as I love myself." He finished the last of the newly mixed tumbler, wiped his mouth with his hand, and went on.

"As for the peccadillo of the soul I leave that to the church; heroics to the military. I am fortunate, for I have no desire for fame. It appears to me to be a form of egoistic insanity. I prefer the mellow good-fellowship of the moment. It is much more real and infinitely more satisfactory. It exists when and where you are. What will anything matter fifty years from now to Carlo Cibo? I do not care to see through the bottom of my last pitcher," he chuckled, "and for those who would make the world over by using either religion or the state as an engine I have no use. No theories are sufficient to include life, and it is life and not theories that I want to see get on. It is difficult to live where any one idea has it all its own way. I don't want to see the priests, the politicos, the merchants, or the slaves completely on top. Any one of them would make it hard for a man—for me. I play them off one against the other and go my own way.

"Well, you can draw your own conclusions about me and some for yourself. My suggestion to you is that you drop all of these minor matters that have been troubling you and go in for being a decent, thinking mammal—a man. Thus you will avoid trying to live either as a pure spirit or a dirty, stupid animal. So you will get the most out of life. I do not know what your prospects are, but no matter! Take up some line of livelihood that will let you live, and settle down to it where you can live by it and not for it. Everything else you will find will eventually drop into its just place." Unconsciously he patted his paunch again.

There did not seem to be any ready reply to make to this. Anthony was surprised to find that while they were speaking both Brother François and Carlo sounded equally convincing.

"You seem very sure of yourself, Carlo," he said half aloud at last.

"I am," said Carlo, "you see I have tried it out."

On the basis of experience Anthony felt at a disadvantage.

"At least I am engaged in one very practical thing," he said finally. "I am determined whatever comes to collect that debt from Gallego. It is not only the money, but . . ."

"Good! And it may take you far," interrupted Cibo. "While you have been performing miracles today, I have found out the latest disposition of your own affairs. They might take you to Africa. How would you like that?"

"Carlo, are you trying to ship me off like Brother François?" asked Anthony half anxiously and half in fun. "I am no missionary."

"No, no," laughed Cibo, "but you may find it easier to convert your bills in Africa than in Havana. Most of Gallego's assets are now on the Rio Pongo. That is the only kind of conversion I had in mind. In any event we shall have to see the captain-general—tomorrow, perhaps. I will tell you about it then. It is, to be frank, a difficult mess. But no more of it now.

"It is late. Have your supper in your own room tonight. I have drunk enough to continue to talk you to death. But," said he, reaching up anxiously and laying hold of Anthony's arm, "do not think I did not mean what I have said. Think it over.

"Wait! Is there anything you want? Are you lonely? Sometimes the best way is to bury your trouble deep. It leaves you then—pleasantly." He smiled reminiscently still holding Anthony's arm. "There is for example—Cheecha."

"Not tonight I think, Carlo," said Anthony. He had hesitated a little.

"Ha, not tonight, *not tonight!* Adiós then, señor, at least I may wish you pleasant dreams." It was hard to tell whether Carlo's tone was mocking or really as regretful as it seemed.

Anthony went to his room, bathed, and lay down. Cheecha brought the supper. After he had eaten she rolled the little wagon into the corridor. Then she came back again.

"Is there anything else I can do for you, señor?" she asked.

He looked at her. She stood huddled back against the wall a little, but her intonation had been both submissive and hopeful. He looked at her for a long while. She giggled. Finally he shook his head.

"Adiós, Cheecha."

"Adiós, señor," she replied, her shoulders drooping disconsolately as she wheeled the empty dishes down the hall.

It was very hot. The mosquitoes droned outside the net. The day had excited him more than he thought. Although he was tired it was hard to relax. In what seemed to be a state of wakefulness rather than sleep he had a silly dream.

Captain Jorham's bottle of wine had fallen on his own madonna and smashed it. He felt unreasonably sorrowful. It seemed irreparable. He thought he got up and went to his chest to make sure. It was very hard to get the covers off the statue. Faith had put them on. They were tied up in intricate knots. Finally he came to the madonna herself. Yes, there she was. She was holding the child out to him, extending it through the folds of the cloth.

The child emerged alive and came toward him out of the chest. There was a violet light about it. But suddenly it was not the child. It was just Brother François with the light of the vine on his face. He was trying to say something and was pointing out a road they were both to travel together. Just then Father Trajan rushed in and bawled out, "A miracle, a miracle has occurred!" Father Trajan thrust his hands into the chest and pulled out the madonna proudly. It was broken and streaming with wine. The statue could never be put together again. It was full of pieces of Captain Jorham's wine bottle.

"It is your miracle that has done this," shouted Anthony. He was furious at Father Trajan.

Brother François was standing by looking very sad at all this. His face was full of pity. Then Anthony saw that Carlo Cibo was sitting on the chest laughing. "What difference does it make?" he asked. He was smoking a cigar.

"Brother François will mend it," Anthony heard himself exclaim, and started up to give him the madonna.

"I cannot help you," said the monk and pointed to Cibo. "He is sending me away."

Nevertheless, Cibo and the monk began to struggle for the madonna. She began to come apart in fragments. An overwhelming sorrow seized Anthony and he began to weep like a child.

Then, as is the way with dreams, the whole nature of the affair changed without apparent cause while remaining to itself perfectly rational.

The fragments of the madonna now scattered on the floor coalesced and became Mrs. Jorham's doll. Cibo and Brother François now seemed to be fighting over nothing important at all. A feeling of great relief swept over Anthony. The room appeared to be flooded suddenly with sunshine. Cibo and he and the monk were now on the deck of the *Wampanoag*. It was dawn and he could hear the noise of cock-crow, a joyous sound. "It is only a doll," he shouted. "Give it to Philadelphia and let him burn it." Brother François disappeared and left Cibo standing there whiffing his cigar.

"Only a doll?" said Cibo. "You are mistaken!"

Instantly darkness returned. The cock-crow was nearer now but frightfully ominous. Anthony was plunged into the full terror of a nightmare.

He struggled to his feet to get away. But he was back in the room again. Cibo and the terrible doll were there, too. "Look," said Cibo pointing with the glowing end of his cigar. He could not help but look.

The doll had become much larger. She was towering against the wall, growing. In the deep gloom of the place she became gigantic. Only the end of Cibo's cigar showed now. It was going out. Complete darkness descended except where the doll stood in a kind of foul light. The doll was turning into Cheecha, huge, naked, with legs spread apart and rolling her stomach. "Bury your trouble," shouted Cibo, "bury it deep!" He pushed Anthony by the arm toward the black emanation in the corner. His grasp hurt. Anthony could smell her sweat now. He gave a stifled cry and struggled. It was too much to stand. It was loathing and terror unmitigated. He writhed, and awoke suddenly to find himself kneeling on his own sea-chest and leaning half-way out of the barred window into the patio.

All the roosters of Regla were crowing. It was the hour of false dawn. Under the window some shrub in the patio emitted a sickeningly sweet, musky scent. His arm was caught in the iron grille work. If it had not been for that he would have plunged out in his sleep into the garden below. Even that fall he thought would have been a relief from the dream. But he drew back at last cold and shuddering.

He cursed himself, and all the rest of them. The dream had been so vivid that he felt sure he had seen the actors in it as they really were. It was some time before he could shake it off. He lit a candle, drank a whole pitcher of water, and walked about.

Finally the mosquitoes drove him back to bed again, this time to an exhausted and dreamless slumber.

CHAPTER THIRTY-TWO

HONOUR AMONG THIEVES

WITH any important business in view the man Cibo shook off his lethargy completely and exhibited a native energy against which no climate could prevail. While it took several bowls of black coffee to clear Anthony's head of the wraiths of the night before, Carlo rattled on gayly at breakfast and exhibited triumphantly a mason's trowel and some pieces of a broken bottle.

"How did you get them?" exclaimed Anthony. The shards of broken glass seemed to have been retrieved from his dream.

"A few piastres in the right place also work miracles," replied Cibo, "as you will soon find, my boy, when you come to do business in Havana. But in your case it may take more than a few. By the way, we go to the intendant's this morning and perhaps to the Gallegos' later. You should call first for the clothes for which you were measured. You look hot and worn already. Let's be off while it's still early and cool. No business is done here after eleven o'clock."

They crossed the harbour swiftly. Cibo kept a smart cutter rowed by four blacks dressed in bright, cotton drawers. There was a polished copper strake around the boat under its brass gunwale. They both lolled back in cane seats in the stern in considerable style.

"This kind of thing pays here," explained Cibo. "Appearances count as much with Spaniards as with the Chinese. Even when I board a foreign man-o'-war I get attention. Mere bumboats are always told to sheer off by the officer of the deck. But all this, and my sash, look official. I have even been piped up the side. Why not have your man outfitted as an officer's servant? I see you have brought him along. Juan," said Cibo sharply, "sit up! Stop dragging your hands over the side. Your master is a rich man and we call upon exalted persons today. You must do him credit. It is the face we want."

The man dropped his handful of trailing gulf weed, squared his shoulders and looked pleased. "Sí, señor, I have noble blood. My mother . . ."

"Was a clever woman," said Cibo. "Act like her son." At the dock Juan leaped out and made fast with a flourish.

"You see," said Cibo quietly, as they mounted the broad steps to the Paseo. "Now keep him coming along that way."

The old city wall rose before them. Along it swept a broad, paved

454

avenue skirting the palm-fringed contours of the bay. A number of
pony-drawn hacks driven by black Jehus dashed up avid for fares.
But Carlo would have none of them. He dispatched one of his own
men on the run through the water gate near by. While they were
waiting one of the disappointed ponies reached over and ripped Anthony's sleeve from elbow to shoulder.

"They are carnivorous," said Cibo and laughed heartily. "Do not
laugh, Juan, it is not permitted."

In a few minutes an upholstered carriage with a fair-looking team
rolled up.

"What do you mean, you rascal, by coming for me with rope
traces?" said Cibo scowling at the black driver. "Go and return on
your master's time. Pompons, buckles, and straw hats! Do you want
to carry home a note with 'Six' in the corner?"

The man wheeled off to return in no time with his steeds in another
set of harness and with sunbonnets. It gave them a smartly indecent
aspect as if the two mares were disguised streetwalkers. Cibo motioned Juan onto the box and they drove off.

"There is a habit here when you are annoyed by a slave of simply
writing his name on your card with the number of lashes in the corner
and sending him home with it," remarked Carlo complacently. "The
card is usually returned later with thanks. The custom imparts a certain tone and discipline to a tropical community. Remember it. You
do not have to know the master. It is simply a local form of noblesse
oblige." Cibo pointed to the now positively decorous coachman in a
clean, white jacket, and grinned. A red ribbon had been added to the
whip.

"Already we have assumed nobility," said Cibo and leaned back.
"Voyez-vous, monseigneur!"

They rattled on through a labyrinth of narrow streets with endless,
heavy, flat-roofed parapets, whitewashed fronts and heavily grilled
windows; the inevitable patio. Most of the gates were still closed.
Havana discovered the same monotonous expression everywhere. It
was a frown with a straight line over its eyebrows as if it had acquired
it from staring at the sun. Behind the closed shutters one sensed the
sombreness of high, toneless chambers nursing the shade. A few
slaves carrying baskets on their heads and balancing from the hips
passed each other miraculously on the narrow sidewalks. Women in
black lace mantillas were still coming home from mass. Here and
there a water carrier laid the dust before some more pretentious
mansion boasting a wrought-iron gate. Yet every languid activity was
merely a prophecy of the certain coming of the midday heat.

Suddenly they drew up before the tailor's. It was a kind of cavern
in the street wall of a house. Huge wooden shutters, now propped up

as awnings, closed it in at night. A small, brown man who had measured Anthony at Regla came out bowing.

"All is ready, señor, we have only delayed for your choice of buttons. That will take but a moment." He produced a case of wood and coral samples. "But the English cloth button, or plain silver, is now all the rage."

In this little spider-of-a-man Anthony thought he understood the word "obsequious" for the first time. He seemed to secrete thread from his mouth, and his shiny lapels flashed with needles as he bowed. Against the rear wall of the place on a long table six little men sat cross-legged, sewing valiantly. On every head was a black skull-cap. They were memorable. In all his stay in Havana they were the only men not slaves that Anthony saw doing any manual work. Almost alone these tailors clothed the fashionable Catholic town. Thus even in Havana Abraham flourished as usual on his natural monopoly of work.

The fitting took some time. Cibo was particular.

Anthony remembered afterwards that it was here he finally became a sans-culotte. The knee breeches and long silk stockings of the eighteenth century were done up in a bundle. Except upon a few formal and artificial occasions he never wore them again. He emerged from this hole in the wall in long, close-moulded, narrow-waisted trousers cut with a wide Spanish flare from the calves down. There was a V-shaped slit over each ankle through which peeped a crimson sock with a clock. There was a short round jacket with a high, rolled collar. In Cuba there were no tails. Your caballero there haunted the saddle. Underneath the coat was a tight, white shirt with an open breast and pleated ruffles. They must be starched and stand up. A wide, silk sash with fringed tassels hung just to the left knee. The tassels were a reminder of the sword. But even in Spanish America that was going out for street wear.

The sensation of new clothes, which eludes final analysis, metamorphosed Anthony. For him the nineteenth century really began four years ahead of the calendar in that hole in the wall in Havana where the six Jews sat sewing. He had literally shed his old skin. He stood up light, and trim, and airy in the new suit of white drill. His loins were girded with the grateful clasp of the slippery sash and his feet thrust into light pumps with silver buckles which his buttons matched. The sweaty and always bedraggled lace of the old cuff was gone. The new sleeve ended in a clean line. There were no garters at the knees. His calves felt protected. His trousers flapped a little when he walked and they pulled evenly. It gave him a physical feel of confidence in his lower extremities. They were no longer ornamental. This was a costume in which one could do things. No ribbons!

In all these details Cibo stood by taking a keen and sympathetic interest. It was pleasant to know someone who could understand how he felt, Anthony thought. It would take the profound simplicity of an Italian to do that. Here was an hour and a place where you adapted yourself and made visible a shift in time. Another mode and mood of things had fallen upon the world. You put it on and then you lived it, henceforth another man. He remembered a naked child in the vestibule of the Casa da Bonnyfeather. Clothes were, he felt, the most intimate and internal things in the world. How tall and keen he was now, how supple and light, how able in this armour to prevail!

"Ah! Carlo," he said turning himself about before a mirror—and Carlo knew it was not vanity—"I shall collect that debt!"

"Good, good, you understand why we came here. Flap your wings and crow, my fine cockerel!" cried Cibo.

The Jew clucked over the unexpected English gold out of Mr. Bonnyfeather's roll, and they all laughed. Anthony felt the talons of the little man touch him on the breast.

"White! white like a true caballero of the town," exclaimed the tailor bowing them out.

"He means you are not burnt black like a rider on the sugar plantations," said Cibo as they drove off. "There is a ring where your collar used to be. But that will soon correct itself in this glare." Cibo hummed a little and laughed as he chatted away. The tailor amused him. He kept talking about him.

"Your Jew sees everything and yet never draws a romantic inference. He only flatters you by telling you that he does. You are pleased in spite of yourself and yet you know that he understands. The Gentile is nakedly revealed in the fiction which he lives by and yet is truly flattered by the Jew. So your feeling toward Jews is one of soothed-irritation plus constant surprise. That is why many either pet or persecute them. Very simple people cannot deal with Abraham; they are either lured into his net or driven to seize the club. The complicated balance of emotions necessary to a prolonged traffic with Jews cannot persist in peasants. Peasants take one extreme or the other. So your Jew stays in towns. I have dealt with them a long time. Many came here some time ago from Portugal. Lisbon was too hot for them. Your friend the tailor was one. He and I have managed a number of little matters together. I trust him.

"In dealing with Jews you should find out what they laugh at. If it is only at matters that occur below the belt let them alone. Simply do not deal with them. Most of that type have a kind of rat's-eye view of life. They see nothing but legs and their appurtenances going by even when they look up. But there are some Hebrews who laugh at the way the world is made. They are humorous with God. Beware!

They are wise. Make friends with them. They become powers in the state. Such men are wisely cruel and unbelievably kind. That is all included in the joke. I once saw the little man who just measured you driving in a closed carriage with his wife along the Alameda de Paula. He had introduced a new style into Havana and was watching all the aristocrats preening themselves along the Paseo. Through the curtains I saw him, sitting next to his moon-faced wife, laughing. Ah, Toni, it was terrible. You see, he knew. Most of the land-poor rich in Havana and Pinar del Rio are in debt to him, not only for clothes, but for jewels. He makes loans. If you want gold go to Moses of Cintra. He and I laugh together and we get along."

They turned into the Calle Obispo. Here were business establishments and awnings over the sidewalks. A languid flow of traffic toward the Plaza de Armas was already under way. At one place they stopped and Cibo called the proprietor out to him, giving instructions as to the outfitting of Juan with great particularity.

"After you get yourself shaved," said Cibo to Juan, "wait for us here. Do not disappear in your new clothes, my friend. The convict quarries are always short-handed. Very well, we trust you then." They drove on to the *Caxa de Consolidación.*

Upstairs in the hall of the intendant, where that personage seldom if ever came, Cibo was at some pains to introduce Anthony to several of the clerks, managing to indicate that any papers which might pass through their hands with the señor's name upon them would be accompanied by double fees. "His business is my own," said Cibo and lifted his brows. Assurances of extreme solicitude over the señor's correspondence followed.

"They have annual cause to remember me," whispered Cibo crossing the room. "This is Herr Meyier, a Rhinelander, the only man not a complete rascal in the place. He is the chief clerk."

A pleasant conversation followed. Herr Meyier warmed to Anthony even over his bad German. Anthony supplied him with all the German news he could remember having overheard for some time past from Vincent Nolte while Cibo sat by greatly relieved at so promising a turn of affairs. Cibo even pretended to like the beer which Meyier sent out to have brought in from his own restaurant. It was the only beer in Havana, and it was warm.

The sympathy of Meyier having been aroused for the predicament of his countrymen in Livorno, it was not difficult for Anthony to enlist his interest in his own affairs. They dropped into Spanish so that Cibo could follow. . . .

"As I see it," said Meyier, "there are several people with whom you must deal. It would help greatly if you get an official admittance of the debt from Gallego. Without that it is a question, señor, if you can succeed. At least it would enormously hasten matters. Merchants here under the old laws of the Indies are supposed to import only from Spain. Of course, of late years that has been largely disregarded and winked at, and foreign bills must eventually be paid or commerce would cease. But there is no legal way here for a foreign merchant to press his claims. He must go through the form of transferring his claim to a Spanish firm when it is then presented as a domestic bill and payment allowed.

"Now it is a curious thing," said Herr Meyier smiling, "but there is only one firm here whose foreign claims are ever successful in court. It is the firm of *Cuesta and Santa María.* Señor Santa María is a great friend of the intendant. He has retired, but lives, I am told, quite magnificently in the suburb of the Salú. He is said to have remarked once to the bishop at a state dinner that he was not very anxious to go to paradise for awhile since only the pavements there are made of gold."

"We are not especially interested in improving the celestial landscape for the señor," murmured Cibo. "Is there no other way?"

Herr Meyier consumed very thoughtfully the last of his beer. It was very tepid. He looked down the long, cheerless stone room—where the sallow clerks sat in their shirt sleeves at heavily gilded desks—with a hint of nausea in his pale blue eyes.

"Ach Gott, Cuba!" he said suddenly, and spread out his palms in disgust. "I am sorry for you, Señor Adverse. What is the amount owed by *Gallego and Son* to the *Casa da Bonnyfeather?*"

"About forty-five thousand dollars in round numbers," replied Anthony.

Herr Meyier languidly calculated something and rang a small silver bell.

"Engross that for me," he said to one of the clerks.

"Old Señor Gallego has recently died, hasn't he?" continued Herr Meyier while waiting. Anthony nodded. "In that case there may be complications. You might have to levy on his estate." He shook his head. "I am afraid that will never be granted. Every merchant-planter in the island would protest. What is the son doing?"

"He is in Africa," answered Cibo. "Since the death of the father the transactions of the firm have been in slaves. Gallego's schooner, the *Ariostatica,* is now outfitting in the harbour for Africa."

"So," said Meyier, pursing his lips, "*so?*"

"Would it be possible to attach the ship?" asked Anthony. "In that case we might come to some agreement with them, possibly an assignment on the next cargo of slaves."

"Dunder!" exclaimed Meyier. "I begin to see light." He rang the bell sharply twice.

"Bring me the papers in the case of the ship *Black Angel*—and of the *Ariostatica,* Gallego, now fitting out." His heavy bureaucratic face grew suddenly animated.

"Now, señor," said he when all the papers had been brought, "come into the bureau of the intendant." He closed the door behind them, listened for a full minute, and then walked to the far end of the room.

They all sat down again about a magnificently furnished desk with dust upon it. Herr Meyier flicked it with his handkerchief and laughed. "It is not likely we shall be interrupted here," he said sardonically, and spread the papers out before him. "Now, gentlemen, your attention if you please. Let us see if we can't avoid drowning the cat in cream. El gato Santa María, you understand. Here is what my clerk has engrossed":

$45,000 @ 18 piastres local legal exchange is 810,000 piastres.
$45,000 @ 15 piastres current foreign exchange is 675,000 piastres.
Hence, the difference between the legal and foreign exchange is 135,000 piastres.

(½ of 135,000 piastres is 67,500 piastres)

"The import of this is extremely simple," continued Herr Meyier. "If you place your claim in the hands of Señor Santa María he will collect it at eighteen piastres on the dollar, the legal rate, and pay you only at fifteen. That will place in his hands the difference of one hundred thirty-five thousand piastres which he and the intendant will divide. I understand they split evenly. For them, you see, a charming arrangement. But that will not be all. In order to engage the noble interest of these gentlemen a 'retaining fee' of eighteen thousand piastres is customary. Otherwise their valuable time might be wasted in ignoble pursuits. In addition to this you will, of course, have to meet all the legal fees. A jingling argument is the only one really convincing to the court. And on that too the masters of ceremonies here will also collect their percentage. If you leave Havana in a year's time with thirty-five thousand dollars you will be doing well. You can now see why sugar planting, for those who understand it, is so profitable. Very rich canes are usually crushed and squeezed twice in case any juice remains."

Carlo whistled whimsically and looked at Herr Meyier, shaking his head.

"You may well whistle, Cibo," said the German. "There is the possibility I think, however, of another way. Would you care to have me advise you, Señor Adverse? As it would be entirely extra-legal, a mere matter of policy as it were, perhaps you would care to—er, ah, make use of my humble services under the circumstances. I believe, if you saw fit to do so, you might not only collect the amount due you without the embarrassing deductions required by Señor Santa María, but finally emerge perhaps with a comfortable margin of profit. Call it interest on your long overdue account. What do you think?"

"You would not, of course, be averse to participating in the profits of so equitable an arrangement, Herr Meyier?" asked Anthony.

Cibo beamed with approval.

"As a silent, a very silent partner," said the German. "A reasonable percentage to be agreed upon, say five per cent on your claim, and ten per cent on any possible profits."

"And in any event two per cent on the claim," said Anthony.

"Did you say three?" murmured the German.

"Of course, how could you misunderstand me, Herr Meyier? And payable half in advance."

"Himmel! mein junger Herr, thou hast been nursed in the lap of Reason."

"I will be surety," added Cibo.

"We go on then!" cried Meyier. "Adiós, Señor Santa María! Will you condescend to look at these?

"They are the papers of the ship *Black Angel,* a slaver, which cleared for Sierra Leone it so happens exactly seven years ago today. Now notice," said Meyier rearranging the file, "that up until within three days of the time she sailed her papers are all in the regular form. Then what happens? On August thirtieth, seventeen-eighty-nine, an order of temporary sequestration of the ship by the captain-general of Cuba issues. A purser, sworn in as agent of the *Caxa de Consolidación,* is put in charge to collect certain sums due the colonial government by the owners. That is, you see, our purser accompanies the ship which is navigated by its captain still employed by the owners. *But* the cargo of slaves waiting for it in Africa is seized by the crown agent. Here, seven months later are the bills of sale for the entire cargo at public auction at Havana. That is the point of it all. The government agent being on board has prevented the cargo from being taken to a foreign colony, say, Barbados or Jamaica, and quietly run on shore at night. The sale takes place here as of government property. The amount due the crown with all expenses is deducted, and the remainder returned to the owners along with the ship. Even at that, I see, the owners came off fairly well."

"Why didn't the government seize the ship to begin with and sell it?" asked Cibo.

"The answer is very simple, señor, for two reasons. The ship would not have satisfied the sum required, slavers are only worth a tithe of their cargo, and there is no ordinance for the captain-general to proceed upon an order to confiscate marine property. His maritime authority is limited. No, no, I remember the case well! It was when you spoke of the Gallegos being in the slave trade that it flashed into my mind. Old Señor Gallego has recently died and his son is in Africa. The estate is a huge one. Undoubtedly there will have been a lapse in inheritance fees and other dues and taxes with the heir absent. If not, trust me, I am a man of arithmetical imagination. Do you see my plan?"

"To use the case of the *Black Angel* as a precedent and seize the Gallegos' schooner *Ariostatica* now in the bay?" asked Cibo.

"Exactly!" cried Meyier. "An order will be issued of temporary sequestration for the *Ariostatica*. We shall swear in our young friend here as the government agent in charge. He will go to Africa as supercargo, receive for the crown the cargo which Gallego will have ready for his ship, and return to Havana where it will be sold. That sale, gentlemen, will be conducted by the *Caxa da Consolidación* of which I have the honour to be chief clerk. Señor Gallego will have nothing to say about it. After the sums due the, er—*government*—are deducted, any remainder will be scrupulously returned to him. I regret to say, however, that it looks to me as if the entire proceeds of this particular voyage will be swallowed up. After all, Gallego will only be having his hand forced a little to pay a just debt. If in that process a certain profit is realized, inadvertently as it were, only ourselves and the captain-general will ever know. I am sure, Señor Adverse, that if you received the sum due you together with reasonable interest, your curiosity at least would be satisfied. You, you see, will have done nothing but collect your debt plus, let us say, expenses. Your time is of course—valuable. Speaking frankly, I feel I am entitled under the peculiar circumstances of the case to the small premium we agreed upon."

"There can be no question about that, Herr Meyier. Set yourself at rest on that point. But speaking frankly myself, and not from mere curiosity, there are one or two points I do not quite understand yet," Anthony replied. Cibo leaned forward a little alarmed as Anthony continued.

"In the first place, how and why will the captain-general be interested enough to issue the order? And what is there to assure me, in case of your death, for instance, or your leaving here for any cause, that I shall not be sent on a wild goose chase to Africa? Suppose I am successful and return with the cargo. You are gone. It is sold, and the proceeds pocketed by—well, the 'government'—why not?

Indeed, speaking absolutely candidly, I should feel much relieved if I thoroughly understood the real cause of your interest in my case."

"Herr Meyier and I are old friends," interrupted Cibo, "we play, I may say, very much into each other's hands. The scheme is a little more subtle than you suppose, Señor Toni. Things in Havana have ramifications all of which do not appear. His word and mine that you will receive the sum due you should be sufficient. Don't you think so?"

Anthony sat thinking for a moment. He was aware that the atmosphere was beginning to be a little tense.

"Yes," he said, "I shall accept either of your words, *of course*. But I must insist at least on knowing the reasons why you will not answer my questions."

Both Cibo and Meyier broke into a laugh.

"You might have been educated by the Jesuits, young man," said the latter.

"I was," said Anthony.

"Ah!" said Cibo. "To think of it! And how I have talked!"

"For the same reason you can rely on my discretion where my own interests are involved," interjected Anthony smiling.

Carlo snorted. "Tell him, Herman," he said to Meyier, "or he will find out for himself."

The German drummed on the desk for a minute.

"Ach Himmel! You are both against me. Then I shall a prophet be. It is modesty, you see, señor, which has kept me from speaking out. Carlo, is it for thee to laugh? I will tell you, sir, why the captain-general will issue the order. It is because I shall ask him. Carlo, is it not so?" The man puffed himself out.

"It is like this, Señor Toni," Meyier continued leaning forward and becoming familiar and convincing at the same time. "Have you ever heard of the Prince of the Peace? Yes! Well, he is the real ruler of Spain. By many he is said to be only the queen's favourite. He is that, but also much more. It is his desire to put vigour again into the government, to destroy where he can the worm of corruption."

"And to enjoy the increased revenues himself," interrupted Cibo.

Meyier made a deprecating gesture.

"Our friend is too cynical," he said. "Nevertheless it is true that in every part of the government some appointees of the Prince of the Peace are now to be found. They are put there for a purpose and they are feared, for they enjoy the confidence of this great minister at Madrid. That is why I, a German, an accountant, and an honest man, am now the head of the *Caxa da Consolidación en Habana*. I," he repeated, scrawling his own initials dramatically on a piece of paper, "am an appointee of the Prince of the Peace! Without these initials, no important government financial operation in Cuba is undertaken. With them much may be done. Is it not so, Carlo?"

"You scarcely ever exaggerate," said Cibo.

"But that is not all, my young friend. In Havana there are two parties. There is that of the captain-general and that of the intendant-general. It is a very curious situation. Some years ago the office of intendant-general was created over great protest to bring about a fiscal reform here. Most of the financial power of the captain-general was placed in the intendant's hands. Pouf! what happens? The second intendant-general who is sent out is a blood brother of Barabbas. Compared with his the clutch of a Turkish bashaw is like that of a gentle milkmaid. The cow—Mein Gott! she go dry! The intendant is a dangerous man, a successful politician, and he forms a powerful local party. He and Señor Santa María and the like had all but succeeded in diverting the revenues when I arrived. The poor old captain-general, he is alarmed. In me he sees an unexpected ally. He sends for me and weeps on my shoulder. 'Permit me,' he says, 'to draw my own salary. The intendant and Señor Santa María have consolidated the *Caxa da Consolidación*. They are patriots. I am only a viceroy.'

"That was seven years ago, my boy. The old captain-general goes home still a poor man. It is terrible. But a new one arrives. He also is comparatively poor, but he is a great hidalgo and a very cunning man. Very quietly we collaborate on undermining the intendant. The soldiers are now paid out of the revenues. I became head of the *Caxa da Consolidación. Some* money goes home to Spain. We entrench ourselves in, *ahem,* a comparative honesty, for we have to fight thieves and we intend to win. Then the grand reforms can take place. But in the meanwhile there is the intendant—and Señor Santa María. They are still very popular with certain merchants, with slave importers particularly. They protect them from foreign creditors. Do you see now? For this is where you, my young friend, come in!

"As I listened to you this morning I had suddenly the great idea inspired. I see instantly what has long perplexed me. I see how to frighten the friends of the intendant, provide an independent revenue for the captain-general, and permit foreign merchants to collect their debts. The mere threat of this will be sufficient. Señor Gallego shall be merely an example. It needed just your particular case to enable me to put two and two together, the *Black Angel* and the *Ariostatica.*" He slapped the papers.

"Señor, I am grateful. The payment of your own debt is assured, for it is upon that pretext that we shall proceed. The authorities in Spain and my master can be made to understand the situation. Despite the old laws foreign merchants must be protected and rascals suppressed. Indeed, I shall regard the payment of your claims as a kind of premium for your going to Africa to collect them. In a case like this it is only someone whose own interests are vitally involved that we would care to trust. Do you see? Will you go? Much depends on it. Much!" Herr Meyier looked suddenly harassed.

"It may be a little dangerous, señor. Keep your own council—and ours. The knife is not unknown here as a method of cutting Gordian knots. I myself . . ." His mouth twitched a little—"Ja wohl! It is true that I may die at any moment!" He ended on a note of scorn.

"I will go," said Anthony.

Carlo patted him on the arm. "Men are not always such rascals as you think, my young Jesuit," he said.

"Oh, Carlo, you overdo that, believe me," said Anthony evidently annoyed. "I was right in asking Herr Meyier those questions!"

"What! what! Must the old dogs and young ones always be snapping at each other?" exclaimed Meyier. He tucked his papers under one arm and led them both toward the door with a certain air of triumph. "This is a lucky meeting, you know," he went on. "Now one thing more. Get that acknowledgment from Gallego's clerk if you have to garrot him. It is vital. If you have trouble let me know. Ach, my friend Carlo, I rely upon *you*. Let us work together in this as in old times. I myself will see the captain-general tonight and let you know his decision. I have small doubt about it. You must be prepared, Don Antonio, to visit the palace later on yourself. His Excellency insists upon knowing all his agents personally."

"Would it not be a good precaution to make sure the *Ariostatica* does not sail too soon, Herr Meyier?" asked Anthony.

"Ach, what a wise infant you have brought here today, Carlo!" exclaimed Meyier. "His words are dollars. Ja wohl, I shall see to it. An order to the port authorities, quietly! And now, auf wiedersehen." He opened the door and bowed them out past the clerks with a formal and distant courtesy as if some purely routine matter had been tritely disposed of.

Anthony walked down and climbed into the carriage with his heart on fire. "To Africa!" he said to the driver. Carlo exploded—and gave merely local directions.

On the way to the Gallegos' they picked up Juan. He was standing on the curb still in his sailor's garb but with a new, silver-mounted guitar under his arm. He looked foolish.

"What is the meaning of this?" inquired Cibo turning red. But the man addressed himself to Anthony.

"Pardon, Don Antonio, the money which you gave me to buy

clothes—I have spent for a guitar." He ran his hands over its strings caressingly. "I do not know how I do such things. It is terrible. But I have a beautiful tenor voice. I lack accompaniment. Forgive!" He was white at the lips.

"You rascal!" said Anthony. Then he laughed. "Jump up, Juan. Driver, go on."

With the troubadour on the box they drove to the Gallegos'.

"You had better leave this to me," said Cibo, and went in.

It was sweltering sitting in the carriage under the leather top.

"Señor," said Juan looking around at Anthony with a dog-like affection in his eye, "shall I sing to you while we wait? I am your hombre. I would pour out my heart which is full of a passionate gratitude."

"Later on, Juan," said Anthony. "This is a respectable neighbourhood."

"Sí, sí," said the man and sighed.

Carlo finally emerged with a scared, middle-aged clerk who rode with them silently to the notary. The man made a declaration there setting forth that the sum demanded by Mr. Bonnyfeather was a just debt contracted by *Gallego & Son* for value received. He signed it as chief clerk of the firm, and an attested copy of his power of attorney to transact business during the absence of young Señor Gallego was attached. They left him still white about the gills.

"This paper has cost you five hundred dollars, Don Toni," said Carlo as they drove on toward the water gate, "but it is worth it. Never hire a chief clerk with a sombre past," he added. "It makes them too compliant with well-informed strangers."

A blue glimpse of the bay came in sight through the old water gate.

"Oh, I shall be glad to meet Cheecha with her little wagon on the veranda," said Cibo. "There is pompano today. The one fish I . . ."

He was interrupted by a scream of agony that made them both wilt. The thud of a whip, and the answering cries and moans of a number of black women gathered about a gate the carriage was just passing made a horrid chorus that accompanied spasmodically the whistling of a lash.

"Jesús!" whispered Juan. The strings of his guitar jangled faintly. The carriage stopped as if accosted by death. They looked through the gateway into the space beyond.

In the centre of a wide patio floored with blinding, white sand a great, black grating seemed to erect its sinister gridiron malevolently from the top of a little platform. Lashed to this so that he was spread-eagled helplessly against the blue sky beyond was a black Hercules of a man. His muscles bulged in huge knots and his head hung back straining as if it would tear itself loose and be gone. Under each whistling blow he rippled from head to foot and screamed hoarsely. "O God!" said Anthony standing up.

It was just then that they saw Brother François. He had emerged suddenly from a little door and was crossing the white, sunlit space to the gridiron in his bare feet and faded gown. He cried out and the sound of his voice filled the place with pity. The man with the whip turned. His large, jowled countenance fell flat with amazement. Nothing but the moans of the man on the gridiron could be heard.

"In the name of Christ," said the clear, quiet voice of Brother François, "this man is your brother." He took the whip from the man's hand. A dead silence followed.

Suddenly the man seemed to take in the situation. He gave a roar of astonished rage, and picking up Brother François like a child, rushed with him to the gateway. He hurled him into the gutter and started to return.

"Do not interfere, my son!" cried the monk getting up calmly out of filth. He caught Anthony by the coat and dragged him back against the wheel of the carriage. He put his cool hands on his cheeks. "This is for *me*. Remember, you do not understand yet."

When a kind of red darkness cleared from his eyes Anthony found Cibo holding him down in the carriage. Rage had loosened the caps of his knees till he shook.

Brother François was half across the yard again. He was following the man and calling. The fellow turned sullenly. Brother François advanced smiling, holding out his hand. "My friend," he said. The man gave a confused bellow and rushed him. He threw him down on the sand and kicked him. Then he turned to go again.

"My friend," said Brother François rising. He advanced upon him again still holding out his hand. The performance repeated itself.

"Sit still, young ass," said Cibo holding Anthony. "Let God decide. Who are you?"

Brother François was getting up again, slowly now. He stood swaying a little but he still smiled. Suddenly he tottered forward to the man. He held up his little crucifix and pointed to the negro on the grating. Then he held out both his hands as if he would give shelter to the dew-lapped head of the tormentor on his own breast. The figure on the grating gave a great cry and went limp. The man in the court-yard looked about him as if appealing to the common sense of mankind and fled. The whip lay on the sand.

"Now," cried Cibo. *"Now!"* He laboured after Anthony and Juan had dashed into the court where Brother François had fallen limp. The three of them picked him up and carried him limp as he was to the carriage.

"Go!" shouted Cibo. "Whip your horses, you black fool!"

Juan caught hold of the carriage from behind as it whirled off down the street. A shriek of despair from the women at the gate followed it as it wheeled around the next corner.

On the way back to Regla Brother François opened his eyes. They were pouring cool water on his face and hands. He said nothing. A great sorrow seemed to engulf them all. Ashamed of himself, Anthony cried out at the sight of the battered lips which hurt themselves to smile back at him. A tumult as of great waters had rushed through his soul. He sat and wept. Even Cibo was silent.

But at Regla Brother François insisted upon going home himself. He forbade them to come along. They watched him go down the little alley toward Father Trajan's, and as he turned the corner they saw him lift a basket of fish from the head of a small negro child whose legs wobbled under it. He took her by the hand. The negro boatmen grunted.

"I am afraid that this is the end of Brother François," said Cibo as they walked down the dock. "I hope we got him away without being recognized. Do you know what the penalty is for interfering with slaves who have been sent to the city-yard to be whipped? A monopoly of Señor Santa María, by the way. No! You do not know? Well, then so much the better," he said as he swung the little door into the cool green patio, "so much the better for your appetite for lunch. Cheecha!"

CHAPTER THIRTY-THREE

A MANTILLA INTRUDES

HOT countries, Anthony discovered, had a curious effect upon
him. He had ebullitions of emotion; they passed, and left
him much the same as before, dreamfully contented, merely existing comfortably. The crests did not disturb the form which was,
after all, Cibo in his chair on the veranda with rum and lime juice.
Then there was tobacco. He had begun to soak up a good deal of
that into his system, the dark Cuban leaf. It made contentment easy
and keenness uncomfortable. It prevented in a northerner the constant foolish necessity of doing something.

Despite the tremendous impression which Brother François's interference with the whipping had made upon him only a week ago—
what was it now?—only an event of the extremely remote past, he
thought as he sat smoking on the veranda with Cibo, while a half-moon
filtered into the patio and Juan fooled below on the strings of his new
guitar. That lad *did* have a voice undoubtedly. A half-mocking song,
no doubt addressed to Cheecha, mixed its soft chords with the moonlight and caused the parrot to shift sleepily on its perch. Tonight it
was deliciously fragrant and cool. Pretty late though. Still you could
not expect to sleep all the afternoon and all the night as well. The
end of his cigar glowed revealing Anthony's face a little whiter than
when he arrived, wrapt in a dreamful satisfaction. Cibo smiled to
himself.

Yes, on the whole, as Cibo said, he had been lucky. His visit to
Havana might so far be called a promising success. Brother François
was doing very well. Getting about the garden again—that man!
And as for Father Trajan—Anthony laughed as he thought of his
crowded chapel. Carlo had certainly been most convincing with the
bishop. It would take a long time, of course, to get the final confirmation from Santiago. Meyier seemed slow, too. But you couldn't
hurry the captain-general. You couldn't hurry anybody here, not even
yourself. And the *Ariostatica* had been detained.

He began to wonder how his clothes that he was to wear at the
audience at the palace the next afternoon were coming on at the
tailor's. Moses had promised them. Why couldn't Meyier settle all
those details with the governor himself? Curious old dog that German! Able, and honest according to his own lights. Really trying

to do a difficult job here. No one could live on a government salary
in Havana. They weren't expected to. Ah, well, if Africa was like
this it wouldn't be so bad.

"Good night, Carlo." The cigar streaked into the patio, and he
went to bed.

Tomorrow morning he would have to take Mrs. Jorham to see the
tombs. He wished now he hadn't promised her. Promises made in
one mood could come back to haunt you in another. "Damn the
beetles!" How they battered about the candle. *"Puff!"* In the darkness you were yourself again. No one on the wall . . . no, of course
not . . . in the chest. And a good riddance . . . Yes? Mrs. Udney's
sheets, ah-a-a . . .

But once on the *Wampanoag* again next morning it was not so hard
to recapture the mood of only a few days before. It no longer seemed
so far off. And both Captain Elisha and Mrs. Jorham were so glad
to see him, and Collins dry as ever. That solemn face!

"So ye're harbourin' our desartar, Mr. Adverse."

Captain Jorham made small bones about Juan, however. The prices
which he had recived for his miracle-working statuary had been
miraculous.

"They're all gone but Jesus," he said. "St. Lawrence yesterday, fire
and all, on an oxcart for some inland town. I'm holdin' out on the
Saviour for eight hundred dollars with five hundred and thirty offered and a vacant niche in the cathedral biddin' against a new chapel
at Cienfuegos." He rubbed his hands. "Say how *dew* ye suppose
they fixed that Virgin at Regla? Pretty slick, eh! Got any idears,
mister?"

"Not a single one, captain," said Anthony gravely.

"Sa-ay!" said the captain beating him on the back till he coughed.
"But here comes the old lady all set for seein' the t-umes."

Mrs. Jorham was indeed dressed for the occasion. Long, fingerless,
black gloves projected from her India shawl which was caught with
a jet breast pin. A straw bonnet upon which rested a grey dove still
glistened with camphor dust. A small sunshade, and a palm-leaf fan,
as a slight concession to the climate, announced her upon pleasure bent.
There was something eternal and widow-like in the droop of her shawl.
But under her bonnet her face shone. A neatly bound copy of the
Testament and four silver dollars distended her reticule.

Anthony handed her into Cibo's boat with great formality. She
sat on the cane seats rather doubtfully and raised a doll-sized sunshade
against the Cuban glare. From a strictly female point of view Mrs.
Jorham was undoubtedly one of the most intriguing women who had
ever landed at the water gate at Havana. The negro washerwomen
gathered there to discuss her.

Anthony hailed one of the carnivorous ponies. In what appeared to Mrs. Jorham to be a recklessly extravagant mode of travel they set forth to do epitaphs. But the churches were a flat disappointment to the lady from Scituate. What few tombs they contained were to her sadly lacking in a sense of inevitable doom. The smooth pomp of marble and basalt conveyed a feeling of security in the hereafter, even an aristocratic contempt for it which outraged her. In the tone of the epitaphs she missed a single whine. *"Every hour wounded; the last slew me. I flinched not till I fell."* There were candles burning before that! She turned away, longing for some stone that recorded a snatch of thoroughly abject hymn that a Protestant woman could sing with fearful conviction. These churches seemed to have been built by superior beings for man. She longed for her white wooden chapels with a fanlight over the door and a cold, northern light inside. Chapels that man had built for God! One could make up one's own mind about religion there. Here, as she looked about from one church to the other, she saw that religion had long ago made up its mind about her. She snorted and waved her palm-leaf fan.

To Anthony, Mrs. Jorham was intensely interesting. He was curious to understand her sense of Protestant outrage. They went to Santa Catalina, San Agustín, and Santa Clara. They saw the curious oil paintings on the walls of La Merced. In the bare, grey limestone of old Santo Domingo they sat down on the floor and rested. Here for some reason or other Mrs. Jorham felt more at home.

"What was it made her so indignant?" he wondered, "and so grim?" He would like to take her to the cathedral. Poor soul, perhaps it was her idea of pleasure that made her so sad? He had a notion to try on a good time for her benefit. Havana with Mrs. Jorham!

He went out and hired a double carriage, only one of whose wheels was very oval. With her little mushroom sunshade projecting over the back like the small targe of a defiant warrior they left the churches and drove along the sea wall and the Alameda clear out to the Cortina de la Reina, and out the Paseo de Tacón to El Principe.

"My!" said Mrs. Jorham, semi-approvingly, as the incomparable gardens of Los Molinos burst on her view.

Good, she was thawing!

He himself felt like St. Lawrence and it was only ten o'clock. Under an awning in the old Parque de la India they had claret lemonade. He took her to a luxurious shop on San Rafael Street and bought her an expensive fan. He whirled her around the monastery of Belén at Luz and Compostela streets. Dashing as recklessly as he could prevail on the driver to dash, he finally wound up on O'Reilly where he bought her a black mantilla and made her put it on. Why he did all this he could not tell. Mrs. Jorham had touched off something of the devil in him. Mrs. Jorham in a mantilla was so gorgeous a sole-cism he almost began to make love to her. He finally bought her a chameleon on a chain.

"They live in cemeteries, Mrs. Jorham, and change colour," he explained. But she did not believe him. She put the chameleon in her bag with the Testament and the four silver dollars. He felt profoundly sorry for it. In the great heat he felt sorry for a chameleon in a reticule. O God! Here he was driving about in Havana with an old woman. He did not know any other woman in the whole place. Yes, Cheecha! He bought another chameleon for Cheecha.

"Mrs. Jorham, Mrs. Jorham," he hummed close by her ear as they drove off again.

"What is the matter with ye, young man?" said Mrs. Jorham through a mouthful of black lace. He looked at her. She was having a good time! He had a notion to let Cheecha's chameleon run up the back of the driver. The horses might run away then. No! Instead he would take Mrs. Jorham to the cathedral and show her the tomb of Columbus.

Mrs. Jorham sniffed disdainfully at the holy water from which the mosquitoes rose as Anthony dipped his fingers in it. The interior of the cathedral was still full of scaffolding. Some frescoers at work held her attention. She had never seen a painter at work before. She stood looking up till she was dizzy. They went over and sat down on un-used stone blocks that had not yet been removed before the Admiral's new tomb. Several parties of fashionably dressed people began to arrive while Mrs. Jorham sat fanning herself. It was certainly cool and restful here after the scalding glare of the street. A verger came and uncovered the font.

"I alers did think Columbus was the bravest of them all. Crossin' the ocean fer the first time! It's bad enough now 'specially if yer husband can't navigate. Columbus believed in what he knew, of course. But it must have ban hard to get folks to do somethin' so new."

The distant wail of a baby interrupted Mrs. Jorham. She laid her fan spasmodically on her chest as if she had caught her breath. The organ started to play. Anthony looked up.

He was surprised to see the number of people who had come in. And the sound of more carriages arriving at the door could still be heard.

"There is going to be a christening, Mrs. Jorham, rather a fashionable one I think. Look, the bishop is here to bless the child. If we move over there in that corner we can see it all without disturbing them. Here by the big pillar."

"My! This *is* going to be worth while. Look at the jewels and laces and uniforms!" she exclaimed half to herself.

They drew back in their corner and waited while the family arranged itself about the font. The service began, evidently as long and complete a one as wealth and influence could obtain. Mrs. Jorham watched the small howling bundle of lace being passed from hand to hand, held up and waved about, sprinkled, and sung about in Latin. So much to-do over a baby made her think better of the Catholic Church. But that was not what Anthony was looking at.

Between the responses he had fallen helplessly in love.

The girl was standing directly opposite him just across the nave. And of such a witches' bundle and mad faggot of chances is fate composed that if he had not happened to move a little to clear himself of the pillar he might never have laid eyes on her at all. Or, if he had seen her otherwhere he might not have fallen in love. He might only have admired or yearned over her a little. Or he might not have really seen her. Her image might only have fallen upon his eyes with no penetration. But he did move.

And as he stepped out from the pillar, at that instant, his pupils were opened upon the extremely delicate and mysterious living substance behind them. Looking inward he beheld a divine image within himself. He could not have imagined it in all its overpowering charm and living splendour. It was something which now drew upon reality and had its own independent vigour and validity although it was nourished within him. Looking into the outer world he saw a Spanish girl in a mantilla, with nearly black-blue eyes and pale gold-gleaming hair, regarding him over her fan. And the outward and inner images became one. The next instant their eyes met.

Exactly what happened then he could not tell. There was undoubtedly a current that passed between them. He had an irrefutable intuition that what was going on in his own eyes was also occurring in hers. The effect upon his body was a kind of relaxed and breathless suspense. Unconsciously he leaned back against the pillar for an instant and closed his lids. When he opened them again he saw that she was still studying his face. Then a wave of colour rushed up from her neck and shoulders and she disappeared behind her fan.

Heavens, would she never come out of that eclipse! At the font the sponsors were promising on behalf of the wailing baby impossible things. Several millenniums passed. The fan spread a little. It came down as far as her chin.

Splendour of Angels! Already he had forgotten how lovely she was. You could only remember it when you really saw her. He must always be able to see her. Always! Why, she was smiling at him! At *him!* Already there was a great secret between them. He straightened up and leaned forward a little. She shook her head. It was just the dream of a shake. Ah! She saw him now. Who was that

dignitary beside her? Her father or an uncle, no doubt! **Damn his
soul!** Surely that man could not be . . . But be careful. He would
just answer her smile. He did so. The fan seemed to touch her lips.
No? Well, he could not be sure. Now it made a graceful curve,
opened out a little, and rested on her breast. She might have been
fanning herself! He put his own hand under his coat and looked at
her . . . Then he hastily managed to turn that heartfelt gesture into
a trite continuation of removing his handkerchief from his left pocket.
"Uncle's" eyes were taking him in coldly.

Everything that could be done for the baby was now completed. As
an impeccable candidate for the communion of saints it and its family
and friends departed, leaving Anthony leaning against the pillar hopelessly. Suddenly he realized he was being left in darkness. He rushed
out just in time to see her driving ayay.

"Señorita Dolores de la Fuente," said the verger. He gave the man
a gold piece and never knew it. Then he remembered Mrs. Jorham.
He rushed back again. She was sitting again before the tomb of
Columbus.

"Mrs. Jorham, Mrs. Jorham," cried Anthony seizing her by both
hands and dragging her off a marble block. "Mrs. Jorham, I'm in
love!"

"Now look here, young man, now look here," she said, snatching
at her reticule. "Ye *behave* yerself. The idear! But air ye in
love?" she said, "air ye?" peering out of her bonnet into his face.
"Swan to man, I believe ye be!"

The verger, scandalized, looked at them and then went away. For
short of arson the donors of a gold piece were, so far as he was concerned, invisible.

"You won't say anything, will you, Mrs. Jorham?" said Anthony
as the sober light of day overwhelmed him at the door.

"We'll just cancel secrets, mister, and call it square," said she. "I
never was one to talk much, except about sewing," she added, laying
her black glove on his arm. "Na-ow," she gave a little sigh, "ye
might take me home. Listenin' to that baby squallin' kind of made
me anxious over 'Lisha. I guess ye know *our* secret."

They found the crew of the boat from the *Wampanoag* waiting with
their jackets spread out on oars against the glare of the noon sun.
Anthony was keeping Cibo's boat until later.

"I did have a good time," said Mrs. Jorham as she arranged herself
in the stern sheets. She gayly waved her hand with the black glove
on it. Collins grinned back at Anthony as they pulled away. Anthony
saw her shawl fall out of its rigid folds into something more natural.
At a little distance over the water she looked smaller, even frail. Suddenly he saw what Mrs. Jorham must have looked like as a young girl.

That must be what was caught in Captain Jorham's eyes. Yes, he understood now. Mrs. Jorham was going home. That was what the *Wampanaog* was! Home! Whenever on sea or land, whenever . . .

"Dolores, I must find you!"

He ran up the steps again and jumped into a carriage. It was terrible to have business to do when he did not even know where she lived.

"Where, señor?"

"Ah, where indeed? Perhaps the driver would know!" But he could not bring himself to mention her name to him. Her name! He felt tears gathering behind his eyes.

"Señor?"

What the devil then! To the tailor's? His suit would not be quite done yet. But a last fitting before going to the captain-general's . . .

"Moses of Cintra in the Calle Obispo."

"Sí, sí! El judio." The man whipped up and drove off.

CHAPTER THIRTY-FOUR

THROUGH A COPY OF VELASQUEZ

IF CARLO had not warned Anthony to pay strict attention to the advice of the little tailor he could scarcely have brought himself to wear the suit which he found waiting for him at the cubicle of Moses. It was dark, but gorgeous, and of the style Incroyable which the smart old Jew had just imported from Paris. Such a collar Anthony had never seen.

"I have made certain alterations," said Moses, "a concession to local taste. Those who go to an audience with His Excellency should bear in mind that he prides himself on being a very modern man. It is not only in clothes but in government, señor, that to a certain extent he admires the French taste. 'New times, new fashions, and new minds,' is a favourite saying of his. Permit me to pin the waist a little tighter. It is the Herculean bust, that which looks so well on the orator when he gestures from the rostrum with one hand in his breast, which has now come in. Ah! I am always breaking my chalk. More pins, Sabathio. But I would not advise you to orate to the governor. Let him do the talking.

"Great men always talk a great deal," continued Moses, despite his mouthful of pins. "They realize by a lifetime of conversational disappointments that others seldom have anything to say. Have you not found it so yourself, señor? Pardon, I slipped with that pin. And many are coming to believe here that Don Luis de las Casas is really a great man. In six years he has worked wonders. The Marqués de Someruelos who will shortly be sent out to succeed him is also of the modern cast of mind, they say. No, it would never do to go to the palace resembling an old hidalgo. They are out of date here. And the general will observe you keenly. He will question you without your knowing it. It has been his method here always to see personally those who are doing anything for him. All those who serve him must first be his friends. It is thus that he has made headway against the intendant. By his Junta as it is called, Señor Cibo, Herr Meyier, Mr. James Drake—even the bishop and the military are of his party. I myself have the honour of making his clothes! You can see you have been fortunate in Havana in having your ends shaped by powerful hands. There now! I think that will do. Some last stitching and the iron! Ah, the hot goose! What would tailors be without

476

it?" He grinned and spat out the remaining pins. "A dangerous conversation, you see, señor. It would not do to swallow my words."

While the last touches were going on they went over and sat down, Anthony on a chair and Moses crosslegged on a table.

"Do you happen to know anything of a certain Señorita Dolores de la Fuente?" asked Anthony. "I should be glad of a little information about her." He was relieved to be able to say her name so casually.

"... y *Someruelos!* Do not forget that! Señorita Dolores de la Fuente y Someruelos, a niece of the incoming captain-general! Ah, the señor is to be congratulated on his eyesight. Yes, all Havana knows. She has preceded her uncle here with certain relatives and domestics to set up his establishment at Los Molinos. A lady with the true gracia of old Castile.

"It is because the present governor has permitted her to move into the palace that it is plain to all the world how the political wind blows. If the present and the newly-appointed captain-general were not both liberals the señorita would have to wait. As it is, the palace will now be all ready for her uncle when he comes. Extensive alterations are under way. All of the domestics are to have new liveries." Moses rubbed his hands.

"At the palace! I shall be under the same roof with her in a few hours," Anthony said half aloud.

"Pardon me, señor; but I do not think you will see her at Los Molinos," said Moses. "Don Luis has taken her under his wing like an eagle. It is not the custom here, you know, for young ladies . . ."

Anthony held up his hand. "I understand," he said.

Nevertheless, as he put on his suit for the audience he felt fired with hope. "Dolores was at Los Molinos!"

Moses charged for advice as well as for his cloth, Anthony discovered when he paid the bill. But it was worth it, he felt, as he drove on to Herr Meyier's small establishment in a street just off the plaza. And he was enjoying himself. He wished Vincent were along. How he would gape at this raiment. What had become of Livorno, anyway? In the vividness of the present his old days seemed to belong to someone else. Old clothes—he would have to get into them again to remember what they felt like. Even one's contour changed. He kicked the bundle of the suit he had worn to the tailor's. Then he remembered he had left his watch in it! Well, he was already late for the appointment with Herr Meyier. He knew that.

Herr Meyier had a number of papers to go over carefully. The order for the temporary sequestration of the schooner was made out, Anthony's appointment as government agent, and an authorization to seize the slaves. All of these already bore the seal of the *Caxa de*

Consolidación and lacked only the signature of the captain-general. Annexed to these were the long records of the process of the government in the case of the *Black Angel,* the rescript of the Council of the Indies confirming it, and a decision of the alcalde-major dated the day before called "Processional Confirmation of Precedent in Camera."

"All of these papers," said Meyier, "you will please notice, Don Antonio, are in triplicate. One set for you, one for my bureau, and copies for the captain-general. The last paper with the high-sounding title is the most important of all. It means that the highest court in Cuba has certified that the case of the *Black Angel* is a precedent upon which the executive government here can act. A 'procession' of other acts can now legally proceed from this first one. Do you see? 'In Camera' simply shows that the decision has been made at the private request of the captain-general and is confidential. No public notice of it is required. It is simply certified back to him as valid. Perhaps you do not fully appreciate the beauties of Roman Civil Law from the standpoint of a government official. From now on all that the executive has to do to seize any slaver is to—well, seize it—and certify that it is precedental with the case of the *Black Angel.* The viceroy's signature makes it so. It is then a fact in law. To re-establish possession for themselves the owners of slaves who have been subjected to the process must prove conclusively that the government is in error, that is, that the case is *not* a precedent. That is very difficult to do, and in the meantime the slaves must remain in the government's possession and may be sold. It is simply beautiful!

"I may say," said Herr Meyier getting up and walking about excitedly, "that this puts a weapon in our hands for which we have long been searching. The slave interests are powerful and have been the most active element behind the intendant and Señor Santa María, 'the patriots,' as they call themselves. Now they *belong* to us. Only one example will be needed. Señor Gallego is unfortunate. But that first example we must have.

"You must therefore thoroughly understand all of this when you take the papers to the captain-general to be signed. He is a penetrating and exacting man. I have explained your mission here to him and I have also stretched a point by indicating that it was you to whom we should be grateful for suggesting this process. That in a sense is true." He waved his hand deprecatingly. "Naturally I worked out the details, but let that go. He will give you the credit. We shall all participate in the benefits."

"Are you sure the captain-general does want to see me?" asked Anthony.

"I am not exactly certain why he *insists* upon seeing you but I think I know. This case is a very important one. Out of it may proceed much revenue for the palace. Don Luis would assure himself that he is placing this matter in competent hands. It will be for you to convince him of that. If he feels you can carry this seizure through, your own reward, the matter of the Gallego debt, will be a trifle. But I am being frank. If he does *not* like you, he will find someone else and there will be nothing left for you to do but to make your suit to Señor Santa María. There is much risk in all this for you. I do not conceal that. You must, for instance, on the way to Africa avoid—well, avoid falling overboard. But I think I am right in feeling that you will not be prevented easily or cavil at small things. By God! señor, *make* the captain-general like you. Become a convincing young man! In that case it may be possible the governor will have a further proposition to make you. If he does I advise you to accept. If not—" he shrugged his shoulders—"there is one thing more. What is your nationality? Where were you born?"

"I do not know," said Anthony turning red.

"*So?*" said Meyier looking at him appraisingly. Then he laughed. "Don Antonio Adverso, citizen of the Western Hemisphere, white, a subject of God? No, no, that will not do. It is a legal fiction you need in order to exist."

"I suppose I am English," said Anthony.

"Why, señor?"

"I cannot answer you, Herr Meyier, a matter of honour."

"Teufel! Englishmen are seldom mysterious about being English-men. But, we cavil unnecessarily. Will you take an oath of allegiance to the King of Spain in order that the law may be able to see you favourably, and hence for your own protection?"

But Anthony hesitated visibly. He felt very much the same about this oath as he had felt about Father Xavier's wafer. As he looked at Herr Meyier he could see that he was both disgusted and surprised. He was losing ground with him—and there was the debt. Should he sell himself to collect that? But why put it that way? This was only an earthly affair, himself and the King of Spain. He could bargain there.

"I will take the oath if you do not register it," said Anthony.

"Good! I will only have it attested, to produce if necessary," grunted Meyier, and sent for a notary. So Anthony swore with his hand.

"It is," he told himself, "a compromise."

They packed the papers in one of Meyier's portfolios and put a lead seal on it. "Himmel!" Meyier had said at last, leaning into the carriage. "Do not let trivialities interfere with your success, Don Antonio, even a citizen of the Western Hemisphere must live. Yes! No?" Anthony had left Meyier grinning and waving good luck.

Incidents like these that threatened to uncover the merely vague grounds for the supposition of his own existence were terribly disconcerting. They left him melancholy. Herr Meyier's banter about the oath had gone deep. With Meyier the oath was a mere formality. Herr Meyier was a German. He was sure of himself. He had been born into and turned out of a mould. He was irrevocable to himself and to all men. He remained a German no matter what oaths he took. But Anthony—what of him? "Citizen of the Western Hemisphere, white!" How deep that cut! In all the inherited loyalties of men he had no part. At the table of the sun he drank to no king. He had no right to be there which was humanly visible. Perhaps Cibo was right and he should attach himself to something. But Mr. Bonnyfeather's legacy had made that difficult because it was unnecessary. He did not even need to go on playing at making a living. Life would be just a game with the means assured and no ends to play for except to win. Win what? Undoubtedly he must find something. Suppose—suppose a citizen of the Western Hemisphere proposed marriage to Señorita Dolores de la Fuente y Someruelos. What would he say, for instance, to the de la Fuentes and the Someruelos? He knew what he would say to Dolores. That would not be in the realm of logical argument—but to *them?* And he knew now that they would be there, too. The best he could now do would be to whisper something to Dolores in the moonlight—and go away. Someone like that baby this morning who had sponsors for himself must be the final accredited cavalier.

Well, he would go on. He would see. Perhaps the Western Hemisphere might be a mould. Feeling vaguely English because he looked it, and being sure himself that he was born, he would pour himself out into the mould. He would find out. Now that the madonna had gone she would also take his cradle of the pool in the convent with her. It was the only one he had had. That—and a certain face on a miniature which he must never speak of.

To hell with all that, then!

Here I am. I know that. I will try following up one practical thing, call my object all, and see where it leads to. Object, the debt. I *will* collect that. I make an oath to myself. The oath to the King of Spain is purely contributory. It is a means. Result so far: I have achieved nationality. Supposing the debt to be "x" I shall simply work out its value to me in the terms of what happens while I collect it thus:

$$y \ (\text{The } Wampanoag + \text{Havana} + \text{Africa}) = x$$

Now then, I make a note of that. *Memorandum for A. A.* He set it all down—and

$$y = the\ unknown\ factor\ of\ myself.$$

Let us see, are there any other factors? Luck? Oh, well, this is a non-human equation, not a logical one. To supply the value of luck would require a constant unknown factor operating throughout. To be able to know that would also imply being able to know "x" in advance.

He put his notebook into his pocket rather pleased with his fancy.

"Hence you see," he told himself, "it follows . . . what follows? That I am being drawn by two horses to see the Captain-General of Cuba at Los Molinos and Dolores is *there*. Very good, that!—Driver, a little faster please. I *must* be there by four o'clock. So this is what carriages are about. How reasonable!"

Yet what he really enjoyed, now that all the important business was set down in a "mathematical" memorandum, was the mysterious and easy pleasure of forward motion as he rolled along over the new military road toward Los Molinos. Having a constant series of impressions follow each other in rapid succession without doing anything to produce them gave him the sensation of having increased life. He was enjoying as a more powerful being might enjoy. The horses had accelerated fate and made the world change. In the collection of the debt, in solving "x," this would be one of the most enhancing experiences he felt.

"Driver, faster! Use your whip!" They flew along now. The gardens of Los Molinos with the summer palace of the captains-general came in sight, a gleam of old ivory in a tossing sea of palms. In those living depths the wind blew the treetops back into white, glistening spots that shivered in the sea of green like the Caribbean lashing over a hidden reef. A sentry emerged from a gold-and-scarlet striped box and took his pass. Ten minutes later Anthony was ushered into the Hall of the Governors of Cuba.

————————

At first he could not see anyone there. The rather low room with grey stone walls and a moulded stucco ceiling looked more like a corridor than an apartment. It ran clear across the front of the main building with deep, recessed windows stretching from ceiling to floor. Through these, like reflections from the surface of a lake, fell the shuffling lights and shades of the waving palm fronds without which mirrored themselves and rippled aquidly upon the gleaming, ebony floor. Shifting spots of sunlight and half-lights flowed along the grey walls and lent an almost liquid aspect to the atmosphere of the room.

Indeed, it was no wonder that the eye at first lost itself in this ancient apartment. Had Anthony seen tropical fish come swimming through the windows he would not have been surprised. High, narrow

teakwood chairs, set at stately intervals; chairs upholstered in faded
red brocade shot through with tarnished silver threads died away
into the watery perspective as if all those who had sat on them were
dead and this was the cabin of a foundered galleon. It was not until
his eyes adjusted themselves to the somnolent and stealthy shifting of
shadows that at last in the centre bay of the windows he discovered
the captain-general himself.

He was standing with his back turned looking out into the garden
and had evidently not heard the secretary announce him, for Anthony
could still see his card lying on a silver tray before the governor's
desk chair.

"Your Excellency," said Anthony.

General Las Casas turned with a slight twist of annoyance. Seeing
it was not a lackey he hastily picked up the card, read it, and immediately broke into a quiet smile. Anthony could scarcely restrain a
start of surprise. Here was the same gentleman who had been standing beside Dolores in the cathedral.

"Come over, Don Antonio, I am glad to see you. Have I kept you
waiting long? Ah, I see. Well, you are not the first who has not
been able to find me in this—aquarium."

He pointed Anthony to a chair by his escritoire, answering his bow
with an easy and winning courtesy.

"You must really co-operate with me in helping to set aside the
old formalities of a viceregal court," continued the general leaning
his head on one hand and looking at Anthony frankly and keenly.
"Personally I find it impossible to get anything done in Cuba by insisting that this is the Escurial. It has shocked some of the old Cas-
tilians even here. But formalities are not the end of life any more.
Things have been happening in Paris, you know. One must admit
they exist. 'New times, new fashions, and new minds,' I often say.
I see you believe at least in cutting your clothes to the year. You
will not be shocked, I trust, if I do not permit you to kiss my hand?"

"Thank you, for breaking the ice of etiquette so thoroughly, sir,"
said Anthony. "I confess to coming here with considerable trepidation,
despite the assurances of your many friends in Havana."

"I was not aware my friends in Havana were so numerous," said
the governor. "But it is pleasant to hear you say so. You yourself,
Don Antonio, seem to have fallen into excellent hands. Herr Meyier
and our good Carlo Cibo have both been talking to me about you. I
have been given to suppose that it will not be difficult for us to arrive
at a conclusion about certain matters, and to our mutual advantage.
You have already made a very happy suggestion, I am told." Anthony saw his eyes rest on him inquiringly.

"I shall be frank with Your Excellency. A very small part of the credit for that suggestion is due to me. It was only something I said inadvertently which enabled Herr Meyier to . . ."

"Tut, tut!" exclaimed the governor. "You dispraise yourself. But I see you are honest even in claiming credit and that is, to say the least, refreshing here. Your inadvertency was a very happy one. Go on, make some more. But Herr Meyier has entrusted you with some papers, I believe?"

"Here," said Anthony laying the sealed portfolio on his desk.

"You may gain some insight into the conditions of this business," remarked the general as he extracted the documents and spread them out, "when I tell you that it is only to a messenger whose own interests are inseparable with their safe delivery here that these papers would be entrusted. Do you realize, my young friend," continued he opening his eyes a little wider, "that if certain gentlemen here in Havana had known of the contents of this portfolio neither you nor it would have arrived here this afternoon? As it is I have no doubt whatever that you are already being watched."

"I am prepared to take the risks which will inevitably be involved if Your Excellency sees fit to trust me," said Anthony. "It is true my own interests are involved in this affair but that is not my main motive, sir. I want you to know that. No, there is something more." He hesitated.

"Go on," said the governor, "I am really curious now."

"It is the thing itself," Anthony burst out, "the difficulties that are in the way, what will happen, my own determination to go through with it. I would find out for myself how I shall cope with this affair. But I suppose that is not what I should have told *you*."

The governor answered with a quick flash of his white teeth. He drummed on the desk for a minute with the end of his pen. Then he started to sign the papers.

"On the contrary I am very glad you have said it, Don Antonio. It puts a new face on the matter. We shall not simply be using each other for so much cash. It encourages me, in fact, to propose to you something further since you are a caballero with whom gold is not all. What I shall say now is between us only, as men of honour. Is that agreeable?"

"You have my word, sir, but I reserve my decision as to your proposal."

"Naturally. Do not imagine I would inveigle you. Quite the contrary. In fact, as you shall see, to a certain extent I shall have to commit myself to your hands." He leaned forward and began to sand the papers for a minute. Then he looked up frankly and continued.

"Señor, in a few months I return to Spain. I return there a poorer

man than when I arrived here six years ago. It might have been
otherwise if I had cared to play the game here with the intendant and
Señor Santa María. Meyier has told you of them? So! You understand then. But perhaps you do not understand fully. The 'game'
is to separate Cuba from the crown of Spain. Troubled times are
now with us and more ahead. With universal war brewing in Europe
we shall soon be separated for months from Madrid. Insurrection
gathers here. My successor, the Marqués de Someruelos, my cousin,
will soon be left here alone to struggle with those who call themselves
patriots. Need I add that their conception of patriotism is the concentration of revenue in their own hands? The intendant is not without influence at home. It has been only with the greatest difficulty
that I have succeeded in having a loyal successor to myself appointed,
a man of honour and ability, a liberal, but loyal. To smooth the way
for himself he has sent his niece out in advance to set up his household here at Los Molinos. Social prestige is very important in Cuba
among the great landholders. I am a widower and have been handicapped. But with the arrival of the Señorita Dolores we have been
co-operating in building up the viceregal court. When my successor
arrives there will be a court for the royalists to rally about. It has
been very difficult for her. She has had to disregard many conservative customs. But—*as you seemed to observe this afternoon in the
cathedral*—she is a señorita of singular charm."

He leaned back and laughed, enjoying Anthony's obvious confusion.
"I see to a certain extent you have already joined our party," he
continued. "That is well. Much serenading now takes place on moonlit nights in the gardens of Molinos. All the voices are terrible so far,
it is true. But we have gained a number of the influential young
caballeros to our side, for the cult of Dolores must also, by her decree,
be the policy of the King of Spain. There have been dinners—and
duels. Several troublesome patriots have been removed—honourably.
It is now fashionable to come to court on certain afternoons to kiss the
hand of the captain-general and that of the señorita afterward. Her
uncle when he arrives will already be enormously popular. Patriotism, which has only an intendant and a mustachioed Señor Santa
María, will soon be left cold."

"Do you want me to come and join the choir in your park then,
general?" laughed Anthony. "If so, you can count on me for *that*."

"Do so by all means," laughed Las Casas. "I shall instruct my
sentries not to fire on the night when you arrive. Let your soul overflow. But we wander a little from the point.

"Under all of this, you know, I am really quite serious. Would
you be interested, Don Antonio, for instance in being the agent for
providing the somewhat embarrassed Captain-General of Cuba with

an independent revenue? You might, *ahem, er,* participate—to a certain extent. I should add that you would deserve to do so for you would be providing the means for preserving intact the interests of the crown here."

"You mean," said Anthony doing some fast thinking, "that once in Africa you would like me to continue there for a while as your confidential agent."

"Your surmise has hit the mark very closely, señor."

"I could never consider engaging in slaving as a permanent business, sir, there is no need for me to do so, and besides I do not . . ."

"Certainly, of course not, that is for any length of time or in the usual way. My thought was this: once arrived in Africa establish yourself at Gallego's base and remain there long enough to ship me and my successor sufficient cargoes to permit us to get the upper hand here financially.

"We will undertake to provide you ships. They will be temporarily sequestrated from the friends of Señor Santa María. Thus the thing will work both ways to our benefit. It will hamstring them and provide us funds to pay the garrison and equip loyal colonial forces. I should say it would require some years to bring this about, provided you can keep sending slaves. It will not matter then if we are cut off from Spain. The commercial details of the matter will be handled by Herr Meyier through our good friend the rich grocer of Regla. Any reasonable arrangement which you and Cibo might care to make with the *Caxa da Consolidación* would, I am sure, be approved of at the palace." He smiled.

"You see the merit of the scheme is that the intendant and his friends will not be able to lay their hands on the root of the trouble at first. It will all be done quietly. You are not known here and it will be some time before they guess Cibo's connection, if at all. We shall take care to have the cargoes landed at Santiago, say, and marched overland if necessary. And slaves now are at a premium. I should hope for six or eight cargoes a year at least."

He paused looking at Anthony earnestly, again drumming on the desk. In the great room the sunlight was already beginning to fade.

"Can you give me a few men I can depend upon when the *Ariostatica* sails? It may be difficult to make this first seizure, in Africa," said Anthony. "Suppose that Señor Gallego objects."

"Ah," said the governor shrugging his shoulders, "that I admit is the rub. Frankly I cannot help you there. To put a crew on the schooner and send them to Africa, I have no power. My authority ends three miles from these shores. If I carried it with a high hand and put men aboard, the cat would be out of the bag. The *first* move must be perfectly legal and unsuspected. I can arm you with papers and nothing more. Those papers give you authority to tell the captain what to do and to attach Señor Gallego's slaves. You must contrive to do that and to establish yourself in Africa if you can. If this first move is protested I can simply say I am carrying out the unofficial policy of the present ministry to permit the collection of a foreign merchant's debt. If you make use of your opportunity and establish yourself, ah, then—*then* I shall take some risks in seizing ships. Until then why should I? Apparently I should simply be compromising myself for you. No one would believe that.

"As it is now only four of us will know, and the marquis when he arrives. Indeed, I should not risk it with any Cuban. They all have local connections. I wished to see you myself before I broached the matter. I believe you can succeed in this, Don Antonio. If you do, in two or three years you will be a rich man. In any event you will be taking much the same risks just to collect your present debt."

"It will take several years out of my life," mused Anthony.

"True, and very interesting ones they may prove to be," continued the general. "But there—I would not press you. Either you will want to do this as you say for its own sake, or not at all. I can understand that. I see by these papers, however, we are both serving the same master now—your oath of allegiance. I have always served my king well. The profit has not always been great. One does the best one can—and goes home. You will forgive me for having pressed all this upon you. I am surrounded by rascals here or incompetents. It seemed our opportunity might be mutual in several ways. Well, let us seal these and go. The señorita receives informally in the garden this afternoon." He looked up a little sadly and gave the bell rope a pull.

At some distance the bell tinkled musically. The door opened.

"Lights, Pedro, for a sealing." Presently the lighted candles came.

"There is always something childishly fascinating about this," said the governor as he began to soften the wafers for the seals in a little pan. The pungent smell of lit wax made him cough.

Instantly before Anthony arose the library of Mr. Udney at Livorno. He saw himself moving about there a ragged, stammering orphan with a priest's hat under his arm. That was who he was! He remembered now. He must be making his own place in the world. And now—he was looking at the captain-general of Cuba sealing documents that concerned that same orphan. He had come for them half-way across the world from the library of Mr. Udney eleven years ago. Why not gather in all that the wax might seal? It was running now, as it were, through the general's hands. Soon they would be hardened, those seals, once and for all. Florence Udney . . . No pigtails now . . . Mrs. David Parish thank you! Dolores, how lovely you are. In three years I might . . . in three years, who knows?

"Your Excellency, I have joined your party," Anthony said quietly.

"Good!" said Las Casas, "all the better that you did not jump at the first glimmer of a golden hook. It is more than that, isn't it?"

"Much more," said Anthony. *"All* I think."

The governor smiled and pressed down on the last seal.

"Well," said he, "since you have joined *my* party, I suppose you will have no objection to joining the one going on downstairs. No!" He laughed and put Anthony's sealed copies back in the portfolio. "The rest of these papers remain here, and with Herr Meyier. I shall myself add a confidential memorandum for the marqués when he comes. Depend upon it he shall understand. Now we go down to the garden. Don Antonio—" he looked at Anthony fixedly.

"Your Excellency?"

"I congratulate you. Permit me to introduce you to the Friends of the King."

They walked across the room together, Anthony's heart beating fast. To his surprise, however, they did not turn toward the door.

"How do you think I do as a politician?" said the governor. "I have had to learn it here," he grimaced. "I am not the first captain-general who found himself alone in Cuba, however. Look here!" They had stopped before a full-length portrait of Don Philip IV just opposite the governor's desk across the hall.

"It might," said Las Casas, "be a portrait of the old days here. It is a copy of Velasquez. A predecessor of mine had it hung here almost a century ago."

From the deep shadows of a black velvet curtain behind him the pale and utterly weary countenance of Don Philip looked out at them as if they were not there. The gold ringlets over his narrow, austere brow shone with as cold a lustre as the fishy-blue of his eyes. Disdainfully, with a smile that had nothing human about it except a hint of cruelty, he was drawing on a pair of long, thin gloves.

"You see?" said Las Casas. "It is the same king who once had a soldier executed for catching him in his arms when he fell downstairs. High treason! He had impeded the sovereign." A look of keen enjoyment passed over the face of the governor not unmixed with regret. "The king did not have to be a politician," he went on. "But it has been otherwise with viceroys in Cuba. They have sometimes thought that even a way of falling downstairs without attracting attention might be convenient. Even a century ago . . . now . . ."

He put out his hand and pulled the picture toward him. It swung out like a door. A narrow flight of stairs dived into the wall behind it. They descended these in two turns in the darkness and came out suddenly into a tropical garden below.

The garden had been there so long that it had forgotten it was in a patio. The smooth, grey stems of giant palms sprang upwards to a green clerestory above, a luminous Gothic ceiling which swam rather than rested on the cleanly curved boles of its natural pillars below. The eye lost itself in the fronded arches of palm leaves or wandered away through a maze of living columns to be reluctantly halted at last by the time-darkened walls of the palace beyond. It was the old tilt-yard of Los Molinos which the genius of some unknown architect had turned into a formal paradise for the viceroys of Spain.

A series of low terraces bordered with stone banisters and lined with ferns and giant cacti in green stone jars descended by regular degrees till they finally enclosed the centre of the garden. There was a level stretch of intensely green grass and ferns from the centre of which a fountain under great pressure lifted a constantly waving plume of spray. Water, indeed, was the secret of the place. The deep runnels of subterranean channels murmured with a constant moaning undertone as if the stream that had been diverted to refresh the place still softly complained. It was hard to tell whether it was the voice of the wind in the palms above or the rush of hidden water below that never ceased. It was a monotone that seemed to belong there and to be as natural as the cool shade of the giant palms themselves.

"An ancient tribe of peacocks once inhabited here," said Las Casas as they stood looking down a flight of broad Spanish steps that led to the fountain below. "The women's dresses moving about among the trees there remind me of them. It is a pity that hoops and brocade are now going out. We shall scarcely know what to do with places like this soon I am afraid. As for the peacocks—they had to go. They made a noise in the morning like filing glass. But come, I see they are waiting for us."

They were met at the bottom of the stair by a very old man of extreme Castilian gravity in a costume that might have done duty at the Escurial some decades before. Don Alonso de Guzman had been master of ceremonies at Los Molinos during the administrations of four preceding captains-general, and although he was now nearly eighty, he still contrived to impress even on a garden party a certain haughty air of mouldy etiquette that was only a memory even in Spain. To this personage Anthony was now delivered by Las Casas and a round of formal introductions began.

There was old Doña Mercedes, the captain-general's mother, who sat in a wheel-chair wrapped in heavy flaps of lace. A marmoset with a face like a bearded penny peeped out over her withered breasts. Above the low hum of conversation, the sound of water and of sere leaves, the dry, hacking cough of the old woman and the shrill whimpering of the monkey rang out disturbingly from time to time. As yet few of the younger generation had arrived. Everybody seemed to be waiting for the affair to begin.

In the meantime old Don Alonso struck his high, beribboned cane into the ground before the bishop, a sardonic, olive-faced old gentleman with a tight, churchly wig and a massive episcopal ring; before the Comandante of Police, Colonel Jesús Blejo; before Señor Gomez Calderón a rich planter, and Mr. James Drake, an English merchant of much influence. The old courtier bowed with the exact degree of deference due to each while he introduced Anthony.

Several officers of the garrison now began to arrive dressed in wide-brimmed, straw hats with heavy, silver lace bands. These Anthony thought looked anything but military. Two or three of the foreign consuls came in with their wives. By the time Anthony had made his rounds with Don Alonso it was understood that another rich, young Englishman with letters was on his travels. This explanation of his presence seemed to have invented itself for him and he gladly acquiesced.

"I suffer greatly from the dreadful humidity of Cuba," said old Doña Mercedes, evidently touched that a young gentleman should have expressed sympathy for her cough. "How I shall survive the trip back to Spain with Don Luis only the blessed Virgin knows. His Lordship here has promised me a hair of the blessed St. Teresa in a bottle to take along. Ah, he is a comfort, that man. I am just saying what a comfort you are, Your Lordship," she called out. The bishop came strolling over looking both saturnine and bored. "You will not forget the blessed bottle, will you?" she reminded him.

"You shall have it tomorrow," he said, and made an elaborate note of it in a black notebook with a gold cross on it. The old woman looked at him dotingly while biting the pink ear of her marmoset with her gums.

"As an Englishman, Don Antonio will scarcely understand how much your kindness means to me," she said.

"Don Antonio is a good Catholic I hear," replied the bishop. "It was he who brought the miracle-working Madonna to Regla, I understand."

"Scarcely that, sir," said Anthony. "I merely arrived on the same ship."

The old woman looked at them both with a live interest now and began to chatter in an animated way about the happenings at Regla. Evidently it was the talk of the town. Through her pious exclamations of admiration, wonder, and surprise, the bishop kept trying to pump Anthony. He walked all around the subject of the miracle like a cat but he learned nothing beyond the facts that he already knew. He looked disappointed.

"You see, señor," said he after they had bowed and walked away from Doña Mercedes, "frankly, I am glad to meet you here. Let us sit down for a minute. Your name has been mentioned to me already—our friend Señor Cibo. Only this afternoon we have had a long talk. What you say about the remarkable event at Regla confirms in every way what he has just been telling me—" the bishop smiled blandly—"I am much gratified. I trust, however, that no more of the statues which were so thoughtfully imported will prove to be miraculous. It would be somewhat embarrassing if the age of miracles were to return by wholesale. The faith of this generation would scarcely be adequate to the occasion. I trust you appreciate my conservative attitude, señor. What do you think?" He leaned forward putting his long upper lip over the gold knob of his cane and stared out into the garden.

"I am sure Your Lordship has nothing more unusual to anticipate," said Anthony. "The rest of the statues which Captain Jorham is now disposing of are in no way remarkable except in price. Of course, I do not pretend to speak either with authority or inspiration, only a certain prophetic instinct as it were."

"Ah, you relieve me greatly," sighed the bishop taking his lip off the cane. "All the ecclesiastical authorities want to do with miracles is to be reasonable about them. As it is there has been a great deal of unauthorized religious enthusiasm in Havana now for some time. As the watchful shepherd of my flock I feel it should be allayed. By the way, señor, you were present at a recent occasion when a French monk, whom I believe you know, interfered with the punishment of a slave. A very serious business!"

"Your Lordship seems to be very well informed of everything that goes on in Havana!"

"*Very,*" said the bishop. "It was also intimated to me this afternoon, with great discretion I might add, that you were expecting to travel to Africa shortly under somewhat favourable circumstances."

"Carlo should scarcely have spoken of it," said Anthony somewhat annoyed.

"Ah, do not say that, Don Antonio. You see he knew to whom he was speaking! After all we are all of one party here." He swept his stick around. "Under the circumstances I can even understand your sympathy for Brother François. You are very young yet after all. But you will also, I trust, understand my own great forbearance and the difficulty in which I find myself. The civil authorities are demanding I take some action about Brother François. Such things cannot go on." He paused significantly.

"My son, it occurs to me that if you could make things comfortable for Brother François on your approaching voyage you would be doing him a great favour. In fact I might add that I have arranged to have him, *er,* transferred to the African province. The captain-general and I have just had a little talk. He quite understands and has suggested that I inform you myself as the matter may be somewhat of a surprise to the good monk. I understand you start soon. By the way, His Excellency would like to see you for a minute before you leave this afternoon." He rose. "This has been most gratifying, Don Antonio; you shall have my prayers for a smooth voyage, I assure you." Without waiting for any reply he walked away smiling.

"I shall warn Brother François tonight," thought Anthony and rose to greet Mr. Drake who passed just then with his wife on his arm. They talked for some time.

"You hail from about Dundee, do you not, Mr. Adverse?" said the Englishman. "I think I detect certain—ah—Dundeeisms in your accent."

But there was no time to reply. The company suddenly began to gather itself together on the lawn. Those who had been strolling about under the trees now suddenly appeared. Old Doña Mercedes broke into a violent fit of coughing to attract notice to herself. But no one paid any attention to her.

The brittle, snapping sound of the sudden opening of fans revealed several women advancing along a faint path through the ferns and palm trees. They seemed to appear suddenly out of the background of greenery and were now standing by the fountain fanning themselves, laughing and talking to those who crowded up to meet them eagerly.

From the remoter vistas of the garden, where they had evidently been concealing themselves and smoking to avoid the boring preliminaries with the bishop and Doña Mercedes, five or six young caballeros also hastened forward. Several little wisps of blue smoke amid the shrubbery discovered their former hiding places. But all this Anthony caught out of the side of his eye. For in the centre of the group of señoritas by the fountain was Dolores.

He lost no time in hurrying forward himself, and it seemed to him a particular act of grace on the part of Las Casas that he rescued him from the formal clutches of Don Alonso to present him to Dolores.

"Here, señorita," said he, "is a young gentleman whom I believe you have seen before." He seemed to be enjoying the slight evidence of confusion in both of them which marked his words. "Don Antonio has brought us letters from important friends." This was evidently for the benefit of the young Cubans who were standing near waiting their turn somewhat impatiently.

Anthony was aware of a sweetly modulated voice with a surprising depth of tone saying something to the effect that Cuba was honoured by the presence of so distinguished a traveller. She was dressed in shimmering green with something in bright scarlet that fell down from her shoulders into long fringes. On account of the light which seemed to him to emanate from her garments their exact outline remained vague. He looked up to see her dark eyes smiling at him gravely while she manipulated her fan. A faint perfume slept in the lazy breeze she evoked.

"It is I who am greatly and unexpectedly honoured," he managed to reply not very happily. Then they both smiled at the immense gravity of this formal exchange—as if their meeting in the cathedral had already put them far beyond that. He saw the corners of her lips twitch a little with amusement.

"Have you brought along with you the charming lady who accompanied you this afternoon at the christening, Don Antonio, la inglesa?" She looked at him half mockingly over her fan.

"I regret, señorita," he began.

"Ah, *that* is a great disappointment," she said, "frankly my curiosity was aroused. None of us had any idea that young English caballeros were accompanied by duennas. Come, enlighten us, señor, who was she? I hope you have not trusted yourself alone here!" A titter ran through the group of girls behind her, some of whom Anthony now remembered having seen in the church. They looked at him archly awaiting his explanation.

"You do my moral character no great compliment, señorita, but you underrate the strength of the temptation it finds here. Can you blame me for needing protection? And besides it was I who was protecting the lady from the ardent caballeros of Cuba.

"As a matter of fact," he hurried on making the most of having turned the tables slightly, "I was merely showing the wife of a Yankee captain the epitaphs and tombs of Havana. She is a great authority on cemeteries and visits them all over the world."

The explanation aroused a gratifying interest. It was plain Mrs. Jorham and her cavalier had caused a good deal of comment. They had even been seen taking lemonade together. Anthony was presented to the other señoritas. The Cubans and several young officers now crowded up. The talk became general and extremely animated.

Evidently these garden parties of the Señorita Dolores were affairs of the younger generation. There could be no doubt that they belonged to her. She moved about here and there, always faithfully followed; the object of much ingenious attention, and with a dignity, a charm, and a serene enjoyment of her position which at once dominated everybody and yet put them at their ease.

Even Don Alonso recognized this. He withdrew quietly, accompanying the chair of Doña Mercedes which was wheeled off somewhere, leaving the light chatter and laughter of the group by the fountain uninterrupted by her cough. She and Don Alonso took coffee alone and exchanged the court gossip of previous reigns for hours at a time.

In the garden coffee and light confections were served by orderlies of the Andalusian regiment in the garrison. Anthony secured some cakes representing a Jew in the flames. He perched them on the back of a stone bench with coffee and a napkin and managed to catch the eyes of Dolores. She nodded and he came forward bowing to her cavalier. He, however, still followed.

"May I not have the honour?" Anthony said to her, pointing to the bench. He smiled at her partner. "I hope, señor, you will permit me to intrude without offence. You have often the valued privilege of drinking coffee at Los Molinos, while I, I remain here for only a few days. I ask a great sacrifice I know, but imagine the memory you will be conferring."

"If the señorita permits," said the young cavalryman who was with her, half hopeful she would not.

"Tomorrow, Don Esteban, I promise you. Don Antonio departs so soon," she said. "You would not be cruel!" She tapped the young soldier with her fan.

The lieutenant bowed with more courtesy than enthusiasm and went off to light a cigarro philosophically. Dolores and Anthony sat down on the bench with only the Jewish martyr between them.

"I eat my cruel words, señor," she said. "You are decidedly *not* in need of a duenna. Don Esteban is not easy to put off. You see I know."

His hand shook as he poured out her coffee.

"Are you really so much moved, Don Antonio?" Her fan folded itself together softly on her lap. She sat back and watched him, studying his face.

"Thou seest, señorita," he said boldly, looking up. The blood rushed to his face as he looked at her. Her shoulders rose and fell deeply. At last she sipped her coffee taking her eyes from his. He picked up the cup and drank from it where she had put her lips.

"He burns," said Dolores picking up one of the little cakes laughingly.

"Would you have no mercy for a poor devil in the fire then?" asked Anthony. "It is true I must go in a few days. Tell me, tell me at least that you are not glad of that. I believe you were glad to see me, that we did truly *see* each other when we first met this afternoon. All my life I have been looking for you and when I looked up, standing

there by the pillar, I thought—I dared to think—that at last I was no
longer alone. Just to have found you, just to know you are alive . . ."

"Be careful," she whispered, "the intendant is coming this way."
They waited, sipping their coffee together while a dark, middle-aged
man with a jewelled court sword passed close to the bench where they
were sitting. He bowed deeply to Dolores and gave Anthony a keen
glance.

"He knows he is not welcome here," she said. "Go on, Don Antonio, you were saying something, I believe."

"Was I, does it really interest you?" he asked. He leaned forward
suddenly with his napkin drooped over the cake dish and took her hand
from her lap under cover of it.

"Do not crush it," she said at last. Her eyes opened widely upon
him. "Yes!—I shall keep this cake," she said. She took it from the
plate with her other hand. "Now you must let me fan myself, señor!
Remember where we are!"

He sat back reluctantly trying to clear his eyes of a dazzling golden
light. The muscles in his throat relaxed again.

"Could I not see you somewhere else than here? Only for five minutes, but alone?"

She shook her head doubtfully. "It would be all but impossible."

"All *but?*" he said.

She laughed at him now. His disappointment was so grim.

"You are serenaded, señorita, I am told. Is it only the Cubans, 'the
Friends of the King,' who are to be consoled? Ah! Sorrow of the
Flame, Dolores de la Fuente, por Dios, you are well named!"

He saw that she looked at him tenderly despite herself. She brought
the fan up so that only her wide forehead with the pale, golden ringlets curling over the delicate hollows in her temples, and her eyes dark
as violets at twilight looked at him like a vision. He remembered her
that way; he remembered her always. It was like the forehead of the
face in the miniature.

"Dolores," he said, "I do not burn. Do not think that. I love you
with my soul."

He heard her gasp.

They sat for almost a minute and both were thinking the same
thing. Across the garden they saw that General Las Casas and someone else were strolling toward them.

"It would be very difficult," she said suddenly. "There are many
who come to serenade in the outer park but my windows open into this
garden. No one could climb the patio wall . . ."

"But if they did," he said.

"Quién sabe!" she replied. "Here is the governor."

"Give me the rose in your hair, señorita, that at least to remember you by. I beg you . . ."

"Ah! your pardon, Don Antonio," said Las Casas. "It is really painful to interrupt under the circumstances," he bowed to Dolores, "but I must detain you a minute. How do you get on with Englishmen, señorita?" he said.

"Very well, Your Excellency. Indeed," said she, putting her hands behind her head, and looking up at him from the bench with her head thrown back in a charming defiance, while her fingers seemed to rearrange her high, silver comb—"indeed, I wish they did not have to leave Havana so soon."

"So!" said Las Casas, taking a pinch of snuff. "Iay, señorita, I am afraid we shall have to disappoint you."

"Adiós, then, Don Antonio," said Dolores with an exaggerated regret as she stood just finishing rearranging her hair. She gave him her hand to kiss. As he bent over it, in the folds of their fingers as they met, he felt the petals of a rose.

"But will I ever see her again?" he wondered.

CHAPTER THIRTY-FIVE

THE TEMPORARY SEQUESTRATION OF THE "ARIOSTATICA"

"UPON my word, señor, I am afraid I *have* some bad news for you," said Las Casas to Anthony as they watched Dolores walk away. She disappeared down a path which Anthony did not fail to mark. Now and then, before she vanished entirely, he could still catch sight of her black fan waving through the palms. He turned to find that he had kept the captain-general waiting.

"This is Don Jesús Blejo, el comandante de policia en Habana," continued Las Casas with a slight twist of amusement still visible in his smile. "The bad news, under the circumstances, is that you will be leaving Havana about sunrise tomorrow morning, Don Antonio."

Despite himself Anthony could not entirely conceal his surprise and disappointment. He stood crushing the rose in his fingers and biting his lips.

"Por Dios! It is high time you were on your way, I think," exclaimed the governor with a slight gesture of annoyance. "Still," said he softening, "I do not blame you. But we cannot even for so charming a reason delay. You may have noticed that the intendant was here this afternoon?"

Anthony nodded, trying to look as if he cared.

"He came to complain of the detention of the Gallegos' schooner by the port authorities. To preserve appearances I was forced to give poor Don Jesús here a thorough rating." He turned to the man who stood by rather uncomfortably with a look of surprised chagrin still on his face. "I trust you fully understand that now, colonel."

"Since Your Excellency has been pleased to explain," he said.

Las Casas looked extremely annoyed.

"You see what subterfuges I am put to," he said striking his sword. "So the *Ariostatica* has been released for tomorrow. I had to promise it, and even to pretend surprise that she had ever been held. We have only a few hours in which to act. It must be tonight or not at all. I have given orders to Don Jesús to have ten men and a boat in readiness at the Maestranza from midnight on. Fortunately, due to his loyalty and care, you can rely upon those he will pick for duty. As soon after midnight as possible you will row out and put yourself in possession of the schooner. Allow no one from her to return to shore.

After you have once served your papers on the captain prevent all communication. You should be out of the harbour by sunrise. Make out to sea as soon as possible. The police will leave you and row in somewhere near Jibacoa. After that, señor, it depends on you. I wish you luck." He twirled his moustache and looked at Anthony a little doubtfully.

"You have my word, Your Excellency, to do all I can," said Anthony.

"Bueno!" said Las Casas. "This is a little more hurried than we had expected but it may turn out for the best. The intendant when he inquires tomorrow will simply be informed that the *Ariostatica* has been released as he demanded. He will suppose that the captain has lost no time in getting under way. And in that supposition he will be correct." He twirled his moustache again with more assurance now.

"You will be wanting a few hours to make your personal arrangements for the voyage, Don Antonio. Arm yourself," he added significantly. "But you will also have to return to the palace tonight to receive the final papers for the sequestration; the release to the port authorities in due form. I shall have my personal secretary make them out this evening. Return about eleven o'clock if possible. They will be ready then and I shall sign them. You will find Don Esteban at work in the big hall, the 'aquarium,'" he laughed. "Is there anything further you can think of? Ah, sí! a pass for the palace tonight, of course! What! There *is* something? I thought I had covered it all."

"Not quite all, sir," said Anthony hesitating a little.

"Ah, excuse us for a moment, Don Jesús," said Las Casas. He and Anthony took a few turns up and down the path alone. The comandante stood waiting by the bench.

The governor at last gave a relieved laugh. "I thought you were going to withdraw at the last or make some final costly stipulation," said he. "I am used to that."

"No, no," replied Anthony, "I would not bargain with you for this. I appeal to you as a man of understanding and sentiment. I am going —who knows to what? A half hour only, Your Excellency. Perhaps never again—quién sabe?"

"Ah, quién sabe?" echoed Las Casas. "But what would the lady say? I am not in authority *there* you know, señor."

Anthony opened his hand and showed him the rose.

"Madre de Dios! you are a dangerous man. It is high time you were on your way. But it shall be your pass. A half hour then— fifteen minutes if you have a bad voice. My windows also look into this patio."

Anthony spoke earnestly again for a turn or two. The governor broke out laughing aloud and finally nodded. "But I shall give orders

to search the guitar for lethal weapons," he said. "That will at least
save the comandante's face—and perhaps a quarrel between you. He
is a man of literal duty you know, a Basque. By the way, you will
treat him with marked courtesy. He is important here in the scheme
of things."

"What is the least which will not insult him, sir?"

"Not less than a hundred dollars I hazard," smiled Las Casas, "but
that is not all that I meant. He is somewhat nettled at having been
transferred from his regiment to take over the police. Pride—you
see?"

"It is a great pleasure to be associated in this enterprise with so
gallant a soldier," said Anthony as they rejoined the comandante by
the bench. "His Excellency has been speaking of your invaluable
services here, Don Jesús, I am honoured."

The man's jacket bulged slightly about the breast as he bowed with
a sudden and very marked cordiality. "I am at your disposal, señor.
It is but for His Excellency—and you—to command."

Las Casas was secretly much pleased, too. The police were his chief
reliance next to the garrison.

"Have passes made out to the palace for Don Antonio and his servant tonight," said the governor—"and a guitar." He smiled whimsically. "If the holders of the pass should be found during the evening
in the patio . . . I trust you will not be alarmed, Don Jesús. The
conspiracy is not aimed at me. In fact I have nothing to do with it."

"Except to bind me to your service with tender bonds," said Anthony bowing deeply.

"Ah! that remains to be seen," said the governor. "As you say,
quién sabe? And now adiós, Don Antonio. I wish you well in several
ways. Do not let the moonlight delay you too long. That is all. Don
Jesús will accompany you now as far as Regla. Make what haste you
can. *Do not forget that other matter, colonel,*" he called after them.
The soldier turned and saluted again.

Looking back from the top of the steps as they left the garden
Anthony saw the Captain-General of Cuba standing by the fountain
smoking a cigar. An hour and a half later, after a breathless drive
and dash across the harbour, he broke in on Carlo on the veranda with
the news.

———————

But Carlo refused to be hurried. In the brief tropical twilight he
was comfortably having supper. A large tureen with charcoal under
it simmered audibly.

"Sit down and have some pompano," he said. "The most delicious
of fish. The only one I really care for. Some fried yams? Yes!

I insist! What is a mere voyage to Africa compared to a supper like this? Ah! What you will miss! Tomorrow is the dinner I have prepared for you and Father Trajan in celebration of the miracle. And now you will be at sea instead! Well, well, you must go well prepared. Now let me show you something, since you are going to Africa, that land of servants. Sit here and drink your wine. It is not necessary to move now merely because you are going on a journey. Cheecha, send Tambo, and Eunice, and three bright boys. Also rouse Señor Rodríguez. Fly now!"

In a few minutes the various persons white and black who had been sent for appeared. Leaning back in his chair with a glass of Malaga in his hand Cibo gave his orders.

He had Anthony's chests brought out on the veranda and repacked by the slave girls. He had several other receptacles, iron-bound and provided with heavy locks, carried up by the black boys. From a list which he wrote out by the light of a candle he began to fill these with such a variety of articles, clothing, food, private trading goods, luxuries and necessities, that Anthony was amazed.

"When you have boarded the schooner tonight and taken possession hang a green light in the shrouds and I shall see that all this is sent out to you immediately. The boys will be waiting with the boat laden at the wharf. Have these chests stowed where you can watch them. Remember you are going to be moving from now on in a world of thieves. You are going to steal men, and in return you can expect them to steal everything from you they can. Do not waste any time thinking about the morality or philosophy of it. Use locks. I shall send you everything you can need for a year's stay. It will be the first charge on our trading account. It is fortunate that Moses has delivered all your linen suits. You will need them. The Rio Pongo alternates between a Turkish bath and a furnace. Sometimes the nights are cool."

For an hour Cibo continued to talk of nothing but slaving and Africa. He gave off a world of particulars and sound practical advice. He settled the last details of how he would act as agent for dispatching further ships if Anthony was successful. He drank two bottles of wine and described the Gallego establishment on the Rio Pongo near Bangalang, the tribes surrounding it, and the half-caste Mohammedans who came down in caravans from the interior to trade. He even touched on the rising opposition to slavery in the British House of Commons and its possible effect on the trade in general. At the end of his discourse, for it could be called nothing less, he presented Anthony with two cases both of English make. The large one contained a pair of splendidly mounted pistols and the smaller a set of razors, one for each day of the week.

"Use these," said he. "When you begin to look and act like a native it is time to leave Africa. I give you two, at the most three years. That is longer than usual. The blue medicine chest there is mostly full of cinchona bark for the fever. I will nail directions inside. Follow them or you will die. Did it ever occur to you that *you* can die? No? Well, you can. In fact you will. Delay it. Immortality should be shunned with intelligent forethought whether it is inevitable or not. Quién sabe! Cheecha, another bottle of wine."

In the meantime the moon was flooding the patio with a deeper and deeper light. All the ropes were on the chests. For good luck Anthony took a last look at his own with the sextant in it. He settled the little madonna deeper into some soft things under his great-coat and wedged her in. How curious that she was going to Africa, too! If it had not been that Cibo was sitting near he would have taken a peep at her. But he was in no mood for quips and raillery now. It had been hard enough to listen to Cibo at all with his own head dancing with Dolores, moonlight, and the adventure of the night yet before him. Only the man's immense kindness and the inherent wisdom of what he had to say had held him. And now—now it was time to go.

He sent for Juan who appeared grinning in his new servant's clothes. "Sí, sí, señor, I am all ready. Sí, I have the guitar." Anthony wrapped his boat-cloak about him and turned to Cibo to say good-bye. Then he remembered something.

He undid the bundle of soiled clothes he had worn to the tailor's that morning and from it took his watch. He gave Cheecha the chameleon on the little gold chain. It kept coming up between her breasts when she hung it about her neck, which was probably the reason that made her both laugh and cry out while at the same time she clutched a few coins he had given her. Her stream of blessings and thanks made him ashamed. After all she was not the woman he had seen in the dream. That was something else. Cibo laughed at his serious face.

"Leaving a chameleon at a girl's breast is nothing to worry about. Ha, Toni, what a tender conscience we have! A glass now. Something I have saved to the last."

He brushed some cobwebs off a small, green bottle with a reverential gesture and carefully filled two tumblers. It was a very old and mellow Montrachet.

"May whatever gods there be go with you," he said. They clinked.

Cibo walked down to the dock with Anthony. He was to cross again in the fast little boat. The dark bodies of the rowers glistened in the moonlight. Someone was patting a tune drowsily.

"Do you understand that I am grateful, Carlo?" asked Anthony. It was hard to tell now whether it was water or the men's hands slapping below the dock. Cibo drew in his sash very tight. He suddenly looked younger with his faun-like face smooth under the moon.

"All that is nothing," he said. "We could not help being friends. Remember me, your philosopher in exile."

"Adiós, Carlo. Farewell, farewell!"

"You should have waited for the supper tomorrow night, a great supper! I will send along some of the wine. Drink to . . ." Carlo's voice called after them as the boat flashed out from the dock. The swift click of the oars and the rush of water drowned his tones in the distance. The black rowers grinned and pulled together for the tip that was so soon due. Anthony turned around and waved his white hat.

It was a miraculous night. Havana harbour was one blaze of silver and the moon straight overhead. The city lay before them twinkling with a thousand little lights. Juan unslung his guitar. They fairly flashed by a ship where the heads of the watch lined the rail. The rollicking voice of the young Spaniard made the six negroes pull as one man. At every stroke Anthony felt the light, soft air cool against his cheeks. "Dolores, Dolores!" He had forgotten all about the *Ariostatica* for the moment.

Before his eyes burned a vision of the pale face of the Spanish girl. It was not merely a vague pictorial thought of her. As he looked across the molten silver of the bay toward Los Molinos an actual reflected image of her face seemed to be cast upon the water just ahead of the boat. The rich, full tones of her voice sounded in his ears. For a while she possessed him. When his brain cleared again he found himself still swinging to the rhythm of the oars and Juan's barcarole while Havana suddenly sprang up before him much nearer than it had been before. The lights in the harbour seemed to have shifted.

He took a deep breath of the warm salt air. Tonight belonged to him and to her. He was living fully and all for now. He was, he felt, the captain of events for the first time in his life. Things had come his way in Havana remarkably well. It would be his part to continue to make them behave that way in the future. His last monitor had disappeared; had been left, talking, on the dock at Regla.

He was glad to have left Cibo. He liked him. He was grateful. Yes, but he was glad to be sitting in this boat bound on his own affairs with the tiller in his hand. The only one with him now was a servant. Bueno, that was as it should be.

And he would take and drive the *Ariostatica* to Africa. How he did not know. But he felt sure of it, sure of himself as he sat there. Cibo's wine gave just enough of a tinge of madness to turn the city ahead and the harbour into something a little better than even the moonlight could confer. It was a slightly mad, transfigured world of Dolores and untold adventure, all marvellous, all good, all tinglingly vivid, that lay before him. It had no end. In it one was immortal. It was impossible to fail. The pleasures of it were as infinite as one's capacity to enjoy. It was hard, and youthful and real. And yet—it was beautiful and dreamful; it was moonlight and mad music over the water.

He sat up with an intense sureness and took active charge. The boat, which had been driving a little out of its course, he set directly on the water-gate lights. He stopped Juan and slowed the rowers to a steadier but more time devouring speed. The *Wampanoag,* he noticed, had slipped her mooring and was riding far down the harbour. So Captain Jorham was on his way. He must have sold all his statuary. Well, he had learned much from the *Wampanoag* he could use now. Adiós to her! Adiós to everything!

They glided into the slip by the water gate and he gave a gold piece to the stroke oar for the crew. A babble of African approval and well-wishes seemed to waft him up the steps of the quay. Two minutes later he was being whirled through the dim, narrow streets of the old city toward Los Molinos again.

Once beyond the walls of the town they began to trot swiftly and more swiftly along the straight, white road awash with mad shadows where the palm trees flaunted and rustled their lofty double row of seething plumes down an infinite avenue. There was a thin, gauzy mist blowing by here in the valley; there was a hint of northern coolness, the smell of heavy dew on grass and leaves, and a blurred-glistening of green things in the foggy moonlight. The horses broke into a gallop thinking they were going home. They bolted. To the expectation of happiness ahead was now added the exhilaration of speed. A divine recklessness rode with them. The tenor voice of Juan lifted itself in staves of some Andalusian love song that rang out over the vacant plantations like the chorus of an unearthly, lyrical hunt. A few dogs barked and howled in the distance. At the open doorways of huts dark figures outlined in the orange glow from within watched them streak past. The driver at last brought up his team beside a roadside fountain.

"He will founder them if he lets them drink now," said Juan.

"Let him," replied Anthony. "As long as we get to the gardens I do not care."

They sat listening to the beasts gulping and breathing and to the fall of the spout. A streak of moonlight fell full on a little slide of water that came down a steep slope of fern and moss-covered rocks just above the trough. In the shady nook by the road everything but the clear space by this spring was in shadow. Their eyes naturally came to rest on the brilliant little waterfall as if it were a piece of miniature landscape illuminated.

It was only for a few seconds, but as Anthony watched this weird little Niagara that seemed to be leaping forever out of a tropical elfland through a haze of maidenhair ferns, a gorgeous coral snake glided down to the brink of a still pool and began to drink. Under the moon its brilliant scarlet was turned to dark amber. It was so delicate in all its motions, so graceful, and so utterly wild that there was not the slightest hint of anything sinister about it. Its tongue like black, forked-lightning flickered into the silver water making all but invisible ripples, and the moon glinted on its small eye. Suddenly, when one of the horses blew loudly on the surface of the font just below, it was gone.

He had watched it without complications as Adam might have seen the first serpent in Paradise before the fall. It had, he felt, given an expression and a meaning to the tropical night in a language that lies behind words.

Juan proved to be no Cassandra. The tough little horses did not founder. Ten minutes later they were at Los Molinos.

A glare of candles in the centre bay of the front windows of the palace showed that the secretary was still at work, although it was now past eleven o'clock. In spite of the pass the sentinel on duty was obstinate. It was late, and he looked at them, but especially at the guitar, with profound suspicion. He insisted on searching the instrument. A sergeant came but he could not read. It was finally necessary to send for the comandante himself. While they waited Juan retuned his strings and groaned. He was afraid he had lost key. Finally Don Jesús appeared and the gates were opened.

As they went up the broad stairs to the Hall of the Governors Anthony took the occasion to press into the hand of the comandante "the least sum which would not insult his honour." Evidently Don Jesús carried about him some receptacle for such contingencies, for the roll of gold pieces disappeared, internally, as it were. It neither clinked nor bulged upon his person. Except for a slightly more familiar and affable manner, he remained exactly as he had been before. One eyelid, one epaulette, and a shoulder, all on the left side, sagged. His moustache also drooped in that direction and he limped slightly. Anthony wondered if it was on that side that he carried gold. Don Jesús had evidently expected Juan to remain in the vestibule, but he made no protest at his not doing so.

"When you have finished, señor, you will find me waiting below," said he. "If possible we should be at the dockyard in two hours at least. Dawn is early still, and Don Esteban has already taken longer with those papers than we expected. I will, if necessary, arouse His Excellency to sign them, but I trust you will be through before he retires. All is ready at the water front. I made final arrangements

on returning from Regla some hours ago." He threw open the great
door for them, and excusing himself, went downstairs again.

The secretary in the alcove looked up and nodded as they came in.
He introduced himself a little nervously.

"It will take at least half an hour longer, Don Antonio," he said.
"It is the making of three copies which consumes so much time. They
must all be original to take the seal. I am sorry to delay you. Will
you be good enough to sit down for a while? The chairs are not very
comfortable, I know." He made a grimace and shifted himself uneasily looking somewhat surprised at Juan and the guitar. Then he
snuffed the candles and resumed hastily. Anthony thanked him and
seated himself and Juan on two chairs flanking the large portrait of
Don Philip IV.

The sound of the secretary's pen and the tread of the sentry below
were the only sounds in the great apartment. Except for the bright
lights on the desk, where Don Esteban bent over his papers intent on
rapid and accurate copying, and a dim sconce by the door, the rest of
the room was in a flux of moonlight and the black, moving shadows of
the palms outside.

> "To all officers, servants, and ships' commanders and to all
> loyal subjects whomsoever of the Crown of Spain: Know that,
> inasmuch as the good ship *Ariostatica* of our port of Havana in
> Cuba . . ."

scraped the secretary's quill for the third time that evening.

Quietly opening the door which the portrait concealed, Anthony and
Juan disappeared down the dark, little stairs behind it.

Under the moon the shaded patio seemed to have suffered an unearthly change from the garden of the afternoon before. Long pencils
of silver light stole down through its palm-fronded ceiling, turning
the court into a kind of dream-forest where pools of white mist gathered in the hollows of its paths. Indeed, the fountain in the centre
remained the only familiar landmark.

Anthony had hoped to find some windows with lights in them. But
beyond the thicket of palms, on every side the dark walls of the palace
loomed without a break of gleam. He thought he knew on which side
her apartments lay—in the direction of the path which she had taken
that afternoon. But he could not be sure. He and Juan went as far
as the fountain. Anthony looked about him again. Not a human
light. Only a few fireflies winking here and there. Well, he must
risk it.

"Sing, Juan—your best now!"

"The lady is beautiful, señor, you say?"

"Lovely as the night," said Anthony with a catch in his voice and trembling with eagerness.

"This then!" said Juan.

The strings began a low prelude. Then the pleading tenor of the young sailor suddenly filled the old tilt-yard of Los Molinos with an even more ancient ballad.

In the middle of the second chorus Juan suddenly stopped. They both waited. A light in a double window above a balcony flashed out in the wall. Outside the tread of the sentry had stopped. They could feel the whole place listening. Someone, Anthony felt sure, had come out on the balcony. He ran back up the steps to look and caught the gleam of moonlight on gold epaulettes. Las Casas was standing on the balcony. Ah, he had thought that was the wrong direction for her room! Juan was singing again.

Suppose after all she should give no sign! How the governor would laugh at him! There was another light now. But not here, not so near the roof. Juan had stopped again. Anthony stood listening. Nothing but his own blood throbbing. Not a sound or a sign from her.

Then at the other end of the patio he heard a faint clapping of hands.

He dashed down the steps and taking the guitar from Juan tried to pick his way as nearly as he could along the path over which Dolores had vanished that afternoon. Presently he saw a light as if from one candle in a room on the second floor. He came out of the palms against the eastern wall of the patio abruptly. There was a dark gate with a heavy, wrought-iron grille just before him. Above that shone the dim glow of the window. Someone was standing there. He could just see her. She was in white with something dark over her hair. He looked up and stirred the strings of the guitar softly. The light tapping of a fan on the windowsill answered him.

"Señorita," he whispered, "I came to say good-bye and to thank you for the rose."

"Is it really yourself, Don Antonio? Where did you find your voice? I have another rose in my hair. Sing again and I will make a little snowstorm of the petals for you."

He came close under the wall and looking up saw her bare arm holding out something over his head. A few white petals floated down like tired moths upon him. Like a beggar he held up his hat for more.

"You are already well paid," she whispered. "No more without another song." He heard her laugh again.

"Ah, Dolores, for the love of God, do not tease me now. Thou knowest I have left my singing voice by the fountain. Roses are not enough tonight."

"You despise my flowers then?" she said.

He came closer under the window and stretched up his arms to her. "Come down!" he whispered.

As if to mock him she let the flower fall onto his breast.

He caught it to him and began to plead with her. A hundred endearing names which he did not seem to have known before leapt from his lips. If she would only come down to him, come down, only for an instant!

"Dolores, Dolores! Do you not know the few minutes we might have with each other in this life are passing. I must go to the other side of the world tonight. Now! In only a few seconds I must go. Will you only stand there? Come down, Sorrow of the Flame, do not let my heart die when it is so young. Dolores, Dolores!" He kept whispering her name. Then his voice broke. In the silence that followed he heard her catch her breath sharply above him.

After all he would have to go then without . . . but she was speaking.

"Take the guitar back to your man and tell him to sing . . ."

God! was that all then? After all she . . . he leaned against the wall weakly.

". . . they will think you are still by the fountain then. That will give us a few moments . . ."

Reprieved then!

". . . when you come back I shall be at the little gate below. Hurry!"

The candle in the room above went out. He picked up the guitar and dashed back to Juan. As he stumbled back once more over the little path the voice by the fountain rang out again and went on. She was standing behind the grille in the gate. Her face was outlined in a frame of iron leaves. He put his hands through the tracery and clasped them behind her head, drawing her toward him softly. Only her weight resisted him. For a long minute he kissed her on the mouth. After a while she unclasped his hands. What moved him most was that he discovered she had tears on her cheeks.

His hands sought her through the grille again but she laughed a little and caught him by the wrists.

"Anthony!" she said, still holding him as if pleading for a respite—he could feel her trembling—"you are wearing the wrong kind of sleeve links. See they are pearls!" She held his wrists up in a ray of moonlight. "I should send you away."

"Is it so terrible then?" he asked anxiously. "Tell me, tell me what have I done?"

She came closer again as if she thought he might leave. Presently she was explaining to him with her cheek against his own.

"Don't you know that when a caballero's lady is away from him only carnelians are worn? It is a sign that his heart bleeds. Pearls mean that the innocent one is near." She giggled.

"Mine do not lie then."

"Were you so sure as that?" she exclaimed pretending to try to draw away from him.

"No, no, only my soul dared to hope. And now tell me, tell me for once and all. Was I wrong?"

"Thou knowest," she said and clung to him.

"Promise you will not forget me, Dolores. If I never see you again, even if you know that I am lost, if you are married and I can never even speak to you again, you will not forget that we love each other? If our lips can never say it again, still we shall know. Say it is so. Say, at least, that we can go on remembering. Tell me that if I ever can come to you, you will still be there." He kissed her passionately.

"If you *can*," she said, and looked up at him with the resignation of love in her face. She hid against his breast—"if you ever can."

They stood for a minute as close as they could, with the iron-work cold between them.

"Ah, I am afraid," she whispered, "I am afraid it will always be like this." She reached up and touched the grille that separated them. He cried out and caught her hands to him again, kissing them.

Just then they heard a warning whistle from the fountain.

"You must go!" She thrust his hands out.

"Dolores, I will never see you again!"

"No, no," she exclaimed, "my soul will come back to me!"

He heard a key grate in the lock. The grille swung open and she was on his breast. For a moment the world died to them conclusively. They had abandoned it and taken refuge in each other's arms.

The low, shrill whistle of Juan revived time again. They stood with it ringing in their ears—that keen doom! He cried out an incoherent protest. "Hush!" she said. She kissed him and broke away. He heard the gate clash softly behind her and found himself alone. When he rushed to the grille again she had gone.

"Señor," said the tense voice of Juan, "señor!"

Anthony groaned.

"The governor has sent for you twice. He is coming down the steps now himself. Hurry!"

They rushed back to the fountain. Someone was sitting on the bench smoking a cigar. But to Anthony's great relief it was not the governor but Don Jesús.

"His Excellency has signed the papers and has been waiting to see you," the man said a little grimly. "I trust you will be able to explain to him your presence here? I am responsible, you know, for seeing that no intrusion occurs even by favoured persons!" Don Jesús looked considerably chagrined and eyed Juan in particular with obvious doubt.

"I shall take the entire responsibility on myself," Anthony hastened to say. The man was obviously nettled. "On account of my immediate departure His Excellency has been particularly generous tonight. There were potent reasons. Surely, Don Jesús, as a gallant caballero you will not ask me to *explain!*"

Don Jesús bowed a little coldly but managed to smile. "Permit me to congratulate you on your remarkable voice," he said. He still looked puzzled about something. They mounted the stairs together with Juan behind them. Suddenly, from the direction in which they were going, it became evident that Don Jesús could know nothing of the private stairs.

"So that was why he was angry and perplexed," thought Anthony. Indeed, they went out by the big gate. The comandante glared at the sentry angrily.

"Your man had nothing to do with my entrance," said Anthony. "On my honour! Set your mind at rest." Don Jesús looked instantly much relieved and nodded.

"Very well then," said he. "Señor, I shall wait for you here. We should now be at the dockyard."

Anthony received the papers from Don Esteban who was waiting. He was somewhat more deferential than before.

"His Excellency requested me to wish you"—he looked at a paper methodically—"as good luck and as much favour elsewhere as you have found in Havana."

"Convey my profound gratitude and assurance of devotion to His Excellency," said Anthony. The formal little Spaniard wrote it down. Then he delivered the papers to Anthony, took a receipt and bowed.

"Buenas noches, señor."

"Buenas noches."

Now he was whirling back again along the road to the city beside Don Jesús with Juan on the box. The moon was far west now. It was after three o'clock when the hoofs of their horses echoed under the ancient stone arches of the Maestranza.

———————

Don Jesús was no romanticist. He had arrested Brother François in the garden at Regla some hours before with as little compunction as one removes a snail from a flower. He was a Basque, and could any other European have been introduced to what went on inside his head, he would have been amazed at how absolutely four-square and literal was the world which Don Jesús looked out upon. It was this which made him such a magnificent policeman. His arrangements were always *almost* perfect. They included and took into consideration everything "as is." Had he also been endowed with a little imagination he might possibly have become a dictator. But he was not so endowed. Hence, he was merely comandante of gendarmes for General Las Casas; hence, the unexpected was to him enormously puzzling. Why, for instance, had a peaceable parish priest like Father Trajan smitten four of his best bully boys full sore with the stump of an oar last evening when he had arrested Brother François in the garden? And why had Brother François taken the oar from Father Trajan and thrown it away? How silly! He had pondered upon this on the drive from Los Molinos sitting next to the young señor who had entered the patio at the palace apparently through the wall. Altogether it had been a confusing night. He would be glad when it was over. The governor, he thought, had laughed at him—quién sabe?—and even to Don Jesús the deserted dockyards of the Maestranza looked a bit weary under a sinking moon.

Indeed, no building in the New World is so heavy with the futility of the past as the Maestranza. With a wisp of harbour mist drifting through its squat belfry that had tolled the passing of the treasure flotas of Spain, it seemed now in the silence of the tropical night as if Fate were withdrawing her last skein of lucky thread from the eye of a broken needle. Only an occasional stray waif of the royal Spanish navy came here now to refit amid curses out of the doubtful pickings of the past.

The deserted dockyard sloped down to vacant quays piled high with pyramids of whitewashed cannonballs and verdigrised cannon cast long ago from moulds that no longer gave birth to anything. In these guns rats nested, squeaking in the sterile wombs of thunder. Silent rope walks, and towering erections for weaving cordage swung like tattered spider webs against the stars. The watchmen slumbered. Here and there the bow of some abandoned and despairing galleon thrust itself upward at a desperate angle. A reek of low tide, festering pitch, and rotting teak filled the nostrils of Anthony as they threaded the mazes of this nautical cemetery where the bones of a monarchy obtruded from the slime.

At the foot of a flight of broad, stone stairs glimmered a single lantern that marked the presence of their waiting boat. It proved to be a large one rowed by eight manacled negroes. Its passengers were six bare-footed gendarmes in broad, cocked hats, and Brother François, who lay bound in the stern sheets.

Anthony exclaimed when he saw him, an exclamation half of indignant pity and half of self-reproach, for in the excitement of his departure and the absorbing events of the hours which had followed the

garden party at Los Molinos he had forgotten all about Brother François. So the bishop had been as good as his word! And he, Anthony,
had forgotten to warn Brother François. He reproached himself
bitterly. If it had not been for Dolores . . .! Now it was too late.
The best he could do was to prevail on Don Jesús to loosen the monk's
bonds, and he would not even do that till they were well out from the
dockyard and rowing down the harbour. Cock-crow had already
begun. What a paean it was this morning! Brother François looked
at him and smiled. There were red welts on his wrists.

The *Ariostatica* lay across the harbour about a mile away. The
barge drifted down upon her easily, swept along by the fast ebbing tide.

"Señor," said Don Jesús, "from now on I am at your disposal.
Those are my orders."

Anthony stood up and looked at the beautiful schooner that now
loomed up before him like the vague outline of a great swan. His
regrets vanished in excitement. He took command jubilantly and with
assurance. They stopped rowing and drifted down upon the ship
silently.

It was one of those breathless few minutes where much depends
upon the simple negative of *not* being heard. The shadow of the
graceful slaver stretched out monstrously in the dawn as if the black
purpose of the ship with its vast consequences were mystically mirrored in the quiet harbour. Anthony looked down into the clear water
and drew back again with a start which he could not entirely control.

Lying perfectly motionless scarcely a fathom beneath the surface
with its sinister head pointed toward the stern of the *Ariostatica* was
an immense hammerhead shark. It rose slowly toward them as if to
see what of interest for it the drifting boat might contain. The sickle
curve of its dorsal fin broke rippling from the water. It nosed the
planks softly, sending a slight tremor through the barge so that all
within it trembled as if the water of the bay itself had transferred to
them the message of an earthquake. For a moment they could even
see its long, grey flanks disappearing into the belly-pallor beneath.
The brown, expressionless walnuts of its eyes on their protruding,
transverse sticks looked at the boat and were satisfied. Some promising picture of sharkful hope must have mirrored itself in those black
lozenges of pupils for the great fish sounded and turned with a slight
phosphorescent glimmer to resume its station. As it did so they had
one brief and sufficient glance into its utterly utilitarian mouth.

Don Jesús crossed himself automatically and nervously motioned to
the crew to give way. The sound of the oars brought someone to the
taffrail of the schooner. The man did not seem to realize at first that
they intended to board. Only when they glided up and made fast to

the small boat drifted against the schooner's stern did he suddenly straighten himself up.

"Hola, what do you want?" he said sleepily. Then for the first time he became aware of the armed men in the barge and half turned as if to give an alarm. Anthony rose in the stern sheets and covered him with a pistol. The man's jaw fell.

The fellow gaped stupefied at the little circle of the muzzle. The gendarmes swarmed in over the stern and secured the sleepy watch. Except for the pad of bare feet on the empty decks of the schooner there had been no sound. A few sparks were coming from the ship's galley. Brother François sat forgotten in the stern sheets of the barge with the shark just a few feet below and behind him. The slaves' manacles rattled a little as they passed about a single cigar. Anthony and Don Jesús stood on the quarter-deck with the scared individual who proved to be the mate. They looked about them laughing a little. It had been ridiculously easy. The growing dawn made the harbour metallic and the *Ariostatica* rosy. She was theirs—and without even a shout.

"Where's the captain?" asked Anthony of the now sullen mate.

"In the cabin."

"Have the kindness to introduce me, señor," said Anthony. "By the way, what is your own name?" He thrust the man before him down the ladder without ceremony.

"What's that to you?" snarled the mate shaking him off roughly.

"Nothing much to me," said Anthony, "but *this* to you." He gave him a resounding kick in the tail.

They were standing in a low passageway leading aft. A dirty lantern burned there dimly. As the man rubbed his posterior and whimpered, Anthony could hear the rats scuttling in the hold. The fellow was evidently a futile coward. His face was as yellow and undecided as an omelette. Anthony remembered how McNab had dealt with such cattle.

"I have not yet the honor of knowing your name, señor," he said, softly moving toward him again.

"María Magdalena Sóller," the fellow piped promptly enough now, clapping his hands over his derrière again.

"Listen, Mary Magdalen," said Anthony. "From now on I am in command of this ship. Do what I say instantly, and life will be easy for you; fail, and I will kick you loose from your stern. Do you, as it were, understand?" He smiled quietly.

"Sí, señor," whispered the man apathetically. There was nothing in him which even thought of resisting what lay behind the frosty look in his antagonist's blue-grey eyes. Besides, the tall frame and shoulders of his new commander he now noticed almost filled the passageway. On the deck he had looked slim and youthful, but not here. Por Dios, what a mule's foot! Under his trousers the mate felt sure he already resembled a pansy bed.

"El capitán está la," he muttered.

"Captain who?"

"Ramón Lull."

"Bueno! Now go and hang a green light in the starboard shroud," said Anthony. "Have you one?"

"Sí."

"Sí, señor!" prompted Anthony. "And the green light quickly before it gets too light!"

"Sí, señor," repeated the man submissively, and scrambled up the ladder glancing hastily behind him.

Anthony went aft to the end of the passage and thumped on the door. He was amused to see that it was painted a cream-white and had a wreath of roses on its panel; a silver lock.

He looked about him. All the fittings were equally sumptuous. Evidently the *Ariostatica* had been built for a pleasure yacht. There was even an inlaid ebony deck. Christ, how elegant!—and filthy! Someone hummed a snatch of opera in a sleepy falsetto in the cabin. He banged on the door again with a will. A volley of shrill, Majorcan curses oozed through the panels like foul dew from a dirty rose. He gave the door the boot, springing the lady-like, silver lock clear out of kelter, and entered.

A small man in a silk skull-cap, who evidently owned the falsetto voice, for he was exhausting its abusive possibilities, sat up and arranged his nightshirt with the fluttered air of a startled canary. Seeing Anthony was a stranger he stopped and rested two white, smooth hands on the dirty sheet as if they had been paralysed. Behind him on the pillow Anthony could see the face of a quadroon girl with a wave of kinky, dark curls spread behind her like a fan. Save for the dark rosy-tan of her cheeks and the too-heavy lips, it might have been a face from a Greek coin that looked out at him. But the eyes ruined it. They drooped and were heavy-lidded as though tired with looking at a nightmare from which there was no escape. It was the countenance of a ruined angel. For an instant it made him so curiously uneasy that he forgot even the errand he had come upon. Then he laid his pistol and his papers on the table.

"You are the captain of the *Ariostatica*, Don Ramón Lull?" he asked.

The man slipped two thin legs from the covers and thrust his feet into a pair of ridiculously embroidered mules.

"Thou sayest it," he said managing to convey an insult.

"Do not 'thou' me, thou little man," said Anthony. "Listen to this."

He quietly read him the authorization for taking over the *Ariostatica*.

The captain took it very calmly, too calmly in fact. At first his only reply was to hum a few staves of a popular air from time to time. Then he asked a few keen questions.

. . . "I see, I see. I am still captain but you are in command. And the police are now on deck you say?"

"Six of them and the comandante," said Anthony.

"What does Your Magnificence command then? You see this is the first time I have ever been, *ahem*, temporarily sequestrated. I am still a little confused. I am sure Señor Gallego will be as charmed as I am. You will be *royally* received in Africa, señor, as the representative of the crown." He shifted the skull-cap back on his head and grinned at Anthony in a way the latter did not like. Evidently Don Ramón would play a waiting game. Anthony determined to strike hard now.

"In the first place, my hospitable friend," said he, "I shall require your cabin for my own use. You will move out of it immediately. Also, even more immediately, you will go on deck and get your ship under way."

"Impossible," said the captain.

"It starts to happen now," said Anthony taking up the letter he had been reading and revealing his pistol under it. "Or—shall I call the comandante?"

The captain's face fell. He looked about him as if for some way out, shrugged his shoulders, and began to put on his clothes. With his shirt pulled half-way over his head he burst into another volley of shrill curses. An invisible little man swearing helplessly in falsetto through a starched frill made Anthony rock.

"Ah, for the love of Mary do not laugh at me, señor," said Don Ramón reappearing at last with tears of rage in his eyes. "It is bad enough to lose one's ship and one's cabin without being laughed at too!" He whined on a little. "But you will permit me to keep my own cabin boy in the second room. I hope you will, señor," he added plaintively while drawing on his shoes slowly. The girl on the bed stirred uneasily. "You see I am much attached to him and he is my property. I cannot spare him."

"I have my own servant," said Anthony.

"It is a bargain then?" cried the man.

"Certainly," laughed Anthony, glad of peace at so cheap a concession.

The captain began to move about more cheerfully now as if he were well enough satisfied and had made his own terms. He even showed some alacrity and became voluble.

"In a minute, señor, in a minute. Three of the crew are still ashore. But we shall not delay. No, I assure you. I shall be on deck in a minute." He began to put on a pair of preposterous, green, satin breeches. "In five minutes we shall be under way." He put powder in his shoes. "Polio, rouse yourself! My essence, the new scent bottle, where is it?"

The brown body of "Polio" now emerged from the berth somewhat sullenly and without a change of countenance, walked over to a chest and after some bending over and rummaging gave the captain a small perfume bottle with a silver top. Anthony sat in astonished silence. If it had not been for the evidence of nature before his eyes he would still have thought that Polio was a girl. Suddenly an overpowering odor of tuberoses filled the cabin. The captain had removed the stopper from the bottle and was anointing his hair. Anthony got up choking and drove the little man on deck with a hearty curse.

Don Jesús spat over the side and grinned at the apparition from a band box which now began to walk up and down the quarter-deck giving shrill orders and humming operatic airs. The order was repeated each time by a huge negro in a green turban. With much confusion the anchor was finally weighed. Polio came on deck. Don Jesús spat again.

Anthony stood by the wheel taking it all in. He thought he had never seen such a sorry crew. There were some truly villainous faces among them. The best were a few blacks who all wore turbans.

"I do not envy you, Don Antonio," said the comandante. Anthony agreed. But he was soon busy enough keeping one eye on the deck and getting his own boxes on board. Cibo's boat had arrived. How glad he was Juan was to be with him!

The sails went up by jerks one by one. There was no wind yet but the tide was taking the ship out. In a few minutes they would be passing the *Wampanoag* lower down. He climbed into the shrouds and waited till they were abreast of her.

"Collins," he roared.

A familiar figure lounging by the *Wampanoag's* galley suddenly snapped to and looked about him with amazement.

"Here, Collins! On the schooner!" he cried. Collins ran to the rail.

"Where be ye bound?" he shouted excitedly.

"Africa!"

"God help ye!"

Captain Elisha came up in his night-shirt. Anthony saw them talking and getting smaller as the water between the ships widened. The captain cupped his hands.

"Wisht ye was aboard here."

Anthony waved helplessly.

"The Missus sends her regards. She says Lord love ye." He tried to call something back to them but failed. The captain waved his old night-cap. "And so say I," he roared.

It was too far to reply now. He could see them still watching the schooner, and he knew what they were saying about her sloppy sails. Oh, if Collins were only aboard the *Ariostatica*. How it would go then!

He leaned over the taffrail and looked astern. Cibo's boat had cast loose and was making back for Regla. Breakfast on the veranda—how pleasant that was! He wondered if Dolores were awake yet, and stood gazing back at the hills about Los Molinos.

The swift ebb at the harbour entrance took the ship and drew her out to sea. The wind outside filled her sails as she turned eastward, rising and falling slowly to the ground swell. The two boats that had drifted against her stern paid out behind and were towed along. The shackled rowers in the police barge were already sprawled out on the thwarts, belly down. Brother François was still sitting alone in the stern where he had been left an hour before. He was motionless. Anthony wondered if he was praying. He himself, he remembered, could no longer do so. He was alone now. There was absolutely nothing beyond for him to lean on. Cibo had put the last touch on that. Nothing was left but the world and Anthony. He had his own will and his wits to cope with coming events, and a bargain to keep. He looked back again toward Havana before turning to the deck and its business.

Following the ship a few lengths behind Brother François's barge he saw the black fin of the giant shark which had attached itself to the *Ariostatica*.

END OF BOOK FIVE

to call something back to them but failed. The captain waxed his old night-cap. "And so say I," he roared.

It was too late to reply now. He could see them still watching the schooner, and he knew what they were saying about her sloppy sails. Oh, if Collins were only aboard the *Ariostatica*. How it would go then!

He leaned over the taffrail and looked astern. Cuba's boat had cast loose and was making back for Regla. Breakfast on the veranda—how pleasant that was! He wondered if Dolores were awake yet, and stood gazing back at the hills about Los Molinos.

The swift ebb at the harbour entrance took the ship and drew her out to sea. The wind outside filled her sails as she turned eastward, rising and falling slowly to the ground swell. The two boats that had drifted against her stern paid out behind and were towed along. The shadded rowers in the police barge were ahead, sprawled out on the thwarts, belly down. Brother François was still sitting alone in the stern where he had been left an hour before. He was motionless. Anthony wondered if he was praying. He himself, he remembered, could no longer do so. He was alone now. There was absolutely nothing beyond for him to lean on. Cuba had put the last touch on that. Nothing was left but the world and Anthony. He had his own will and his wits to cope with coming events, and a bargain to keep. He looked back again toward Havana before turning to the deck and its business.

Following the ship a few lengths behind Brother François's barge he saw the black fin of the giant shark which had attached itself to the *Ariostatica*.

END OF BOOK FIVE

BOOK SIX

In Which the Bronze Goes
Into the Fire

CHAPTER THIRTY-SIX

A GRADUAL APPROACH TO AFRICA

NINE weeks—and they were only a little south of the Cape Verdes. Much had happened in that time, although outwardly all was the same on the *Ariostatica*. She was a fast little topsail schooner with plenty of space below decks. It was only her dainty lines that made men apply a diminutive to her instinctively. But she had met light, baffling airs from the coast of Puerto Rico onward and had lazed across the broad belt of the world. Only constant showers had kept her crew from running short of water. Some of them were already showing the early symptoms of scurvy.

A thousand miles from land Brother François had come down with the yellow fever. That and the persistent presence of the shark which had dogged them day and night were for some weeks the chief topics of conversation for the crew. Even the tense conflict which all on board felt to be going on between Anthony and the captain paled into insignificance before the persistence of the indomitable hammerhead who had been dubbed "Old Faithful." Every morning found his black fin in precisely the same relative position as the evening before. At night it moved a little closer. One attempt to hook the monster had all but ended in a catastrophe. After that they let the big fish alone. He seemed to know what he wanted when he followed a slaver.

"When he gets his belly full he'll go," said one of the old hands, "and not until then. But it's white meat he wants eastward ho. He knows. He's an old 'un."

Considerable humorous, but nevertheless nervous and superstitious speculation as to who might provide the tidbit was rife. Several youngsters who were persistently nominated as scapegoats were ready to fight. The sickening of Brother François was to them at least merely a providential designation of Jonah. But to Anthony and Juan, for the young sailor stood by manfully, it meant long hours of perilous nursing and the contemplation of the monk's patient agony.

Brother François had doubtless picked up the infection before leaving Havana, where he had secretly nursed many among those who were always being laid low by what amounted in that port to a perpetual epidemic. So when the headache and lassitude and the muscular pains began the priest was the first to diagnose his own symptoms. The only remedy available was common table salt in water and a

519

purgative. He drank large quantities of the former, disregarding what effect it might have upon hastening the scurvy. Nevertheless, in a few days his condition was pitiable.

The news of the nature of the priest's illness, which could not be concealed, had a peculiar solvent effect upon the miniature world of the *Ariostatica*. Authority backed by a strong hand was the only thing that might have held it together. But in the noble captain, Don Ramón Lull, authority did not reside. He had neither the will nor the courage necessary to enforce it. On the same afternoon that Brother François took to his cabin with Yellow Jack as a bedmate, the realm *Ariostatica* divided into three distinct spheres of influence.

Don Ramón, El Polio, and the estimable María Magdalena Sóller betook themselves to the quarter-deck where two hammocks swung under a piece of old sail sufficed temporarily for all three. Luckily for them the weather was calm and balmy. Only the shark disturbed their large view of things occasionally. But they did not look his way often. The captain's domestic arrangements might even be described as "nice." He and El Polio had the double hammock. A small sea chest of the captain's provided with drawers was arranged near by with a silver mounted toilet set on the top. This contrived to confer on the little quarter-deck of the schooner a certain boudoir atmosphere unusual on the Atlantic to say the least. It wanted but one fresh breeze to ruin so fragile and dapper an aspect, but that brisk breeze was long lacking. Such was the first kingdom on the ship where in reality only a titular captain reigned.

The second kingdom was the fo'c'sle, the third was the cabin. The fo'c'sle quarantined both the cabin and the quarter-deck. The quarter-deck had already quarantined the cabin. Mortal fear of contagion, fear made physically visible by the genial presence of "Old Faithful" just astern, was the effective warden of the marches.

Anthony and Juan were left alone, strictly alone, with Brother François in the cabin. Indeed, they had now the entire suite of cabins to themselves and the hold beneath it, although that perhaps, together with the rest of the ship's lower regions, might have been described as the neutral empire of the rats.

In the fo'c'sle seventeen temporarily affable, man-stealing ruffians held forth and carried on in such manner as it pleased them best to do. Their reign of riot was aggravated rather than tempered by the over-shadowing influence of one Polyphème, a Gold Coast Frenchman, possessed of one eye and one knife with either of which he could fix his victims suddenly even at a distance. This man was constantly begetting the twins Trouble and Confusion by a process of parthenogenesis.

So it was that in a few hours after it became news the illness of Brother François had produced on the *Ariostatica* a condition of static

mutiny. As usual there was not lacking a logical reason. It was believed by all the Christians on the ship that the air, particularly the
night air, communicated the contagion. Hence the more air they could
place between themselves the better for their health. Thus far logic
and Christianity. With the Mohammedans in the vessel it was
different.

They, as good followers of the Prophet, believed that death would
overtake them when Allah willed. For that reason they did not care
into what portion of the ship they went, whether it was inhabited by
the sick or well. All places were alike to them equally exposed to the
unreasonable arrows of fate. Hence, as universal prisoners they remained free. The practical conduct of the ship soon fell almost
entirely into their hands by pure force of circumstance. Captained
by the giant Arab negro, Ali Bongo, they went where common sense
and the occasional frantic voice of Don Ramón demanded. That the
captain still delivered orders from the quarter-deck, some of which
were still obeyed, either through necessity or caprice was the chief
reminder of the formal order of nautical life. Señor Sóller, the mate,
made daily observations and marked his charts there. There the four
Mohammedans also did their tricks at the wheel in regular succession,
oblivious of everything but the double wages hastily promised them.

For this essential service they were despised by the free spirits of
the fo'c'sle and carefully shunned as possible carriers of contagion.
For in quarantining itself from the quarter-deck, the fo'c'sle had by
no means been oblivious to certain privileges and exemptions which
Polyphème had pointed out would ensue. These were now enjoyed
to the uttermost. Any semblance of regular watches was given up.
Cards, quarrelling, and boozy slumber were now the order of both day
and night. The only systematic labour actually indulged in was the
plundering of the ship's stores in the main hold. When the languid
breeze shifted, a few of the crew sometimes condescended to trim the
forward sails, but nothing more. The only exceptions to this delightful state of relaxation were the cook and his boy, who were recon-
secrated to continue their usual labour by general acclamation and the
violent laying on of hands.

Thus the drifting *Ariostatica* grew more and more a slattern day
by day. Her standing rigging soon hung slack. Rubbish accumulated
on her decks. Even primary sanitary suggestions from the quarter-
deck were met by jeers. Food in wooden kids was shoved at the
officers through the quarter-deck railing, and the cook retired. The
same mess-kids were afterwards towed overboard in a bucket. Unfortunately the weather continued to favour this lax state of existence.
Half the time it was dead calm or there were only fainthearted, little
breezes interspersed with warm rains. About a hundred yards behind

the ship "Old Faithful" battened on the unusually succulent garbage
which now came his way. A small folding chair which Don Ramón
hurled overboard in a rage went the same way and did not even produce a flurry.

Meanwhile, Brother François was tended by Anthony and Juan in
the cabin. In the general state of affairs which had so unexpectedly
developed Anthony felt himself temporarily helpless. The captain,
indeed, did not fail to blame him for having weakened his authority.
He frequently sat safely at the top of the hatch and expressed himself
on the subject of divided authority with a laxative fluency. That there
was some truth in Don Ramón's profane complaints Anthony recognized. But it was also evident to him that the captain was glad of
the excuse and loaded upon its back all the blame for the trouble which
the man's own weaknesses had brought about. And then there was
another curious thing about Don Ramón; having once relieved his
mind, he would return happily to the quarter-deck. There, despite his
ridiculous position, he managed, as Anthony could tell from the noises
that went on just over his head, to have a genuine good time.

For through the deck planks percolated into the cabin, where Brother
François lay, the mild strumming of a guitar at night, the soft pad
of the feet of El Polio in some heathenish dance, and the falsetto of
Don Ramón raised in song. Such lyric outbursts were often greeted
from the fo'c'sle with an applause in which sarcasm and genuine appreciation were inextricably mixed. In the sound of that mixture of
vivas, howls, and catcalls, Anthony recognized what was the real
strength of his rival. He understood from that bad noise that while
Don Ramón might be temporarily isolated, there was yet a certain
sense of brotherhood between him and the fo'c'sle, a bad admiration
for his open and unabashed enjoyment of an unmoral existence.

Don Ramón's, indeed, was a simplicity of evil which those who still
suffered from dregs of conscience might well envy and admire. Between men who were ambitious to be abandoned and to prosper by it,
it was a bond. In any crisis Anthony felt that the captain and the
fo'c'sle would be found united against him. And he began to understand, too, that Don Ramón was cunning.

Perhaps his indulgence of the crew while the *Ariostatica* drifted to
Africa through the doldrums was, under the circumstances, somewhat
calculated. Don Ramón expected to reap his own advantage from it
when the time came. It was a little plainer now why the owners had
confided a ship to a man like Don Ramón. Perhaps they knew their
own trade well enough to understand that the ideal captain of a slaver
was one who had no squeamishness at all. At any rate the captain
would find his advantage in confusion while Anthony could only prevail by bringing about an order in which legal authority would be

recognized. That was the problem. Whether the crisis would arise during the voyage or upon their arrival at Gallego's slave barracoon at Bangalang, he could not tell. He must use his wits. That was all he had to depend upon. He had already taken precautions against purely sneaking violence. He and Juan went well armed and Don Ramón and Sóller knew it. That was that. Neither of them, he felt, would risk his own precious skin. Meanwhile, the captain and Sóller played cards on the quarter-deck, hoping that "yellow jack" would solve their difficulties by removing all the unwelcome intruders in the cabin. That was another reason why the "quarantine" was so rigidly enforced.

"How do you like your temporary sequestration now?" grinned Señor María Magdalena Sóller down the hatchway. "It might be a permanent one, you know." He shrugged his shoulders. Ali Bongo was instructed to resist any possible émeute from the cabin.

It certainly seemed likely that Brother François at least would leave the ship. There were small means at hand for detaining him. As the fever ran its inevitable gamut, Anthony sat by the priest's bunk doing the best he could. Compared with this trial his experience on the *Wampanoag* had been nothing.

"Certainly," he thought, "I have no reason to be in love with ships. I have strange luck there. It goes better with me on land." And for a time it went badly enough. He and Juan settled themselves as best they could to live through the state of siege. After that? . . . . "But sufficient unto the day . . ." Anthony told himself. Certainly it was all weird enough. Temporarily shoving his own problem aside, which it was plain might wait while the good weather lasted, he and Juan devoted themselves day and night to Brother François.

They carried him out of the dark, little hole at the end of the passageway, where he had been contemptuously dumped by Don Ramón, into the big stern cabin from which the captain and his ami had been excluded. A large window of leaded bull's-eyes set in a kind of battened casement ran clear across the stern. After two o'clock the place was flooded with sunlight. There was still a vile, faded carpet with an obscure coat of arms on the floor. There was also a large stain in one corner, deeper than all the others, about which ugly stories were still told.

The *Ariostatica* was a woman with a past. She had been built at Marseilles for a rich and recently ennobled banker some years before the Revolution. She had been called *La Vénus du Midi* then. It was said that on a cruise to Naples her first owner had murdered his mistress—in proof of which there was the stain. The story had followed the ship persistently. She had soon ceased to be an instrument of luxury, and after several evil vicissitudes had fallen to the Spanish slave trade cheaply enough.

Hence there was something undoubtedly sinister about the now queasy luxury of her cabins in which those silver fittings which had not been wrenched loose or battered away still glimmered through a film of filth.

Anthony and Juan did their best to remedy this by such cleansing as they could contrive. But even in his misery when Brother François was first carried into the place he sensed its atmosphere.

The Gallic humour of a ci-devant man of the world glimmered in his eyes as he lay looking at the bourgeois cupids romping in sooty roses on the smudgy, blue ceiling. It amused him to think he was being brought to die in an apartment faintly reminiscent of Don Ramón's tuberose perfume, a cabin whose upholsterer must have had about him a touch of debased genius, for he had managed to relate in a series of damask panels the innocent story of *Paul and Virginia* in a highly interesting way. The story had even been given a happy ending.

Just over the ship's bed that Brother François now occupied, Paul and Virginia were to be seen in that full consummation of their love which the too-pure and tragic pencil of their author had originally denied them. That such art is universal, the smudges and prints of the dirty hands of the slaves who had been packed into the cabin on the *Ariostatica's* last voyage from Africa testified in a truly touching way.

The hand of one huge negro seemed to have striven to tear the body of Virginia from the panel. And through a hundred other wishful blotches wandered the traces of a pair of wistful and delicate finger tips which Anthony thought he recognized as those of the youthful El Polio, the chicken. Anthony imagined he could see that arch youth locked in the cabin during his master's absence trying to seize from the panel what Don Ramón had denied him.

All this amused Brother François, for even in his approaching agony he still continued to be French. When he was carried into the cabin he managed to smile gallantly and to remark to Anthony that a happy ending to every story was what the multitude always desired.

"See," said he, pointing to the panel above him. "They have tried to tear love out of the panel of imagination and to make it real enough to handle with their poor dirty hands. Yet it remains apart. Comedy, you see, is what this unhappy age demands. Once I wrote about such things as that. It was long before the Revolution, before I had entered into real life. *Paul and Virginia* then was still thought to be charming." He sighed and settled back with an air of finality into the blowzy pillows.

"Well, I shall *try* to live up to my own criticism by making a proper end of it here. If not, pardon me for the trouble I am about to give you, mes amis."

Even then the fever was already upon him. He was talking in the accents of some former self. It seemed to be a soldier rather than a monk who lay there. But that was only momentary. He looked out of the stern windows along the wake of the drifting ship and at the tilting blue line of the horizon beyond. Through the bubbles a little behind the ship nosed the apocalyptic countenance of the shark like an obscene emanation from the bottomless deep. To the priest's now disordered imagination it seemed that the shark's mouth was so framed as to be able to utter only the word "Golgotha." He closed his eyes. Then he opened them at sunset, seeming to be able to gaze with a wide-pupilled, feverish glance out of his shadowed sockets into the red orb itself. The last thing he saw in the brief twilight was the shark which had moved a little nearer. He shivered.

"Men would be like that, my son, if God had not given them mercy."

They were the last words he addressed consciously to Anthony before the fever clutched his mind awry. He then seemed to be using his remaining conscious minutes to pray. "If possible let this cup be taken from me . . . Nevertheless . . ." he muttered. He motioned to close the window and shut out the vision astern. They lit a dim lamp. "Let the Comforter be with us here, my Father. Where two or three are gathered together in Thy name . . . Thou rememberest . . ." After that he held converse only with unseen things.

Yet such was the vital and moving spirit of this man that even in the days of delirium which ensued his personality expanded and dominated by a kind of vibrant quality, not only Anthony and Juan, but the dowdy appurtenances of the cabin itself. Anthony found it impossible to explain this impression to himself by this and that or here and there. It was too subtle to isolate, but it was not too intangible to feel. The quality of the man's being, now strangely released, as if by the heat of the fever, evoked in those near him a continuous state of high emotion. In this condition they were able to glimpse and even to share to some extent in the exaltation in which it was now revealed to them Brother François must habitually dwell. Anthony, indeed, wondered now at the calm exterior of the man even when his health had endured.

For that which dwelt in Brother François seemed to be coloured like, and to move with the speed and force of the flame that jags from sky to earth. Yet there was nothing momentary about it. Like the vision of that flame seared upon the eyeballs it remained. It was not ephemeral. It was the natural state and condition of the man uncovered. Anthony could apprehend now why it was that the strong body of Brother François, despite its calm exterior, had seemed to be worn and emaciated from within. Recollecting him now as he had been at Regla, he found that his mental impression of him was that of something which emanated light. Perhaps he had been wrong in attributing all that quality to the vine alone.

How wonderful must be the strength of that gentleness which kept such vivid potentialities in control! Whence came the ability to poise and balance them? No wonder the world was afraid of such men! No wonder everyone from the captain-general to the philosophic Cibo had been disturbed! Had they felt a vesicle of lightning near? Suppose this force had been released to irradiate a community, what then? Anthony sat looking at him—where he lay apparently dying in the murdered harlot's bunk—lost in wonder, oblivious to all else.

For the drama of this spirit even in dissolution made all else seem trivial; ordinary life flaccid. Even though the light of this man was now dimmed by the dark heat of his dreadful fever, though the lightning motions of his thought were disordered by illness; while he lay thus revealed by the weakness of the body, stripped spiritually naked, no one near him could pay attention to anything else.

"I am thy lamp," he muttered once, "behold the flame consumes the oil of me. Let it be acceptable."

After that he no longer seemed to realize his own predicament. Through days of sustained delirium he tended only gradually toward a state of exhausted unconsciousness. Not until the third night was the crisis passed. Then the collapse came suddenly.

During this infernally and celestially illuminated period there were few niches of Brother François's past experience which a nursing listener was not forced to explore. From the total-recall which streamed incoherently from the monk's parching lips Anthony was eventually able to reconstruct for himself the order of time and place which the delirium ignored. To the parentless listener even the man's childish babble and talk with his mother was breathless with a mysterious sweetness.

At some château in Picardy the two walked through an orchard and spoke of the birds. In a field placed only in space he plucked flowers again with a shy little girl. "Laugh again, Adèle, laugh again," cried Brother François rising up to listen. "Here are daisies for your apron. I have never forgotten you. I knew you were not really dead. Here are the flowers. See, they are fresh still,"—and he plucked at the foul bedclothes. Then there was his gay but stern father, whose ridicule was smooth as polished adamant. "But it is here among our own people that I belong, mon père." In those days it seemed Brother François had besought God to assure him he was not mad. It had been revealed to him that he was more fully sane than those about him. This it seemed was the cross he found hardest to bear. He was always pleading with the "blind," always. Versailles had been horrible. They were all blind there.

On the second night in the midst of much vacant converse Brother François became almost lucid again. In a flood of semi-coherent eloquence he was once more accompanying the tumbrils on their way to the guillotine. Not a few of the blind eyes of which he had complained were then opened for a last look at life. The exhausting tension, the fierce ebullitions of frantic souls, the last tender confidences— words spoken to those who clung to him desperately for even a glint of hope—these were all fiercely renewed as the days of the Terror became incandescent again in the monk's fevered brain. Anthony semed to feel the lean shadows of the buildings in the Paris streets falling across him as he rode in the carts with Brother François and the doomed.

In the chill lamplight of the cabin, silent except for the metallic cadences of the dying man's voice and the faint wash of the waves below, these scenes took on for Anthony far more than the vague outlines of a conversation. He participated in them fully and yet mystically as if at a distance. The endless monodrama went on interminably with all of the amazing detail of the mind which never forgets released again into life.

Clenched hands, weapons, impassioned faces tossed up in the words of the priest. Out of the sea of the streets came things which had long forgotten themselves. With Brother François Anthony overlooked the plains, the heights, and the abysses revealed by impassioned men and women about to vanish. He faced with them the thunder of drums, the prayers, pleadings, weeping; the laughter, the snarls, and the screams of the final act. "Ascend to heaven; son of St. Louis"—drums, and a tempest of jibes. One needed to have had faith, a true exaltation, to believe after that.

For the first time the desperate human necessity for hope beyond; the impossibility of rejecting it entirely when the whole being is really faced with the final riddle was flung into Anthony's face.

From such scenes the soul of Brother François seemed to turn with paternal fondness—as if on a visit to a beloved daughter and her children—to the people and the sylvan neighbourhood of his first beloved parish. For a while his spirit had found itself at home there as a pastor of peasants. His assumed patois itself was touching. His homely dialogues were compounded of a wise pathos, laughter, and tears. In all this, and in physical and mental intimacies beyond trace, intimacies which resided in the tones of his voice and the lines of his face—in all of them now poured out for hours on end like the seem-

ingly rational talk of a madman, he seemed to be speaking only from
the depths of some impersonal self.

Himself he did not remember, although he was occasionally vaguely
aware of Anthony and of Juan. They bent over him giving him drink
now and then. They rearranged his pillows and covers a thousand
times. They plied him with a little food which he long refused. They
even held him down. Once he caught Anthony's face between his
burning palms and exclaimed:

"I have seen you before. Yes, I know who you are. It was in
the face of that girl at the coach window that night at the inn that I
first saw you. Do you know her? Her husband killed the young man
in the courtyard. You remember? Surely you will remember what
happened to yourself! That Spaniard with the virility of great evil
about him who drove away with her into the night—he is still driving
somewhere, I know. Driving! Such men go on and on. It is a great
circle they move upon. Be careful, he will return! Remember! Tell
him I buried the young man. He looked noble even in the pit. Only
his horse missed him. No one ever came. Ah, do you know there
is more in that than you can see! I am sure of it."

He rehearsed the scene again and again. A duel in some forgotten
inn courtyard sprang into life. Swords clashed in the twilight while a
woman looked on. Brother François bore witness to the saints against
murder. "And don't you remember?" he kept asking Anthony—"and
don't *you* remember?"

But Anthony did not remember. The tablets of the past were razed
for him. Even Brother François could not recall what the doors of
birth had closed upon. Death might reveal them again, perhaps.

Overhead the strings of Don Ramón's guitar sometimes purred
softly. The eternal sound of water gurgling about the rudder washed
in from astern. The long light of sunset after an interminable white
afternoon lit the little cabin redly. From it, all that was banal and
trivial now seemed to have been banished. Anthony saw nothing but
the blue leagues astern marching to the horizon and the burning eyes
of Brother François in his bed against the bulkhead.

The sick man had now slipped from all reminiscence and was conversing with someone whom he saw standing in the cabin. So strong
was his own delusion that those who were nursing him could scarcely
keep from sharing it. They no longer dared to cross where the last
patch of sunlight slowly lessened about the centre of the cabin floor.
From this presence the transported man derived an infinite comfort.
An actual physical change for the better crept into his face. He no
longer moaned as he talked in whispers but grew calmer. When Anthony brought him some water he drank it eagerly for the first time.

"Courage," he whispered, "courage! See! I can take the cup now.

Yes, I will go. I will drink it all." He fell back again and spoke no more in words. The collapse had come. It would be some hours, Juan said, before they would know whether he would live or die.

From then on it was only the sick man's body that spoke. It seemed to have been left to conduct the fight alone. Its rumours of internal and external wars and troubles were terrible. The black throat and tongue bleated. The contorting muscles exacted from the breath which passed them with difficulty a continuous toll of unseemly sound. The nose, which was now growing peaked, collapsed flabbily about the nostrils, threatening to act as a fatal flutter valve unless the mouth gasped to relieve it. The bowels and stomach banished with bestial rumblings and hellishly humorous whistles from mouth and fundament gusts which all but overcame the two unwilling and horrified auditors imprisoned in the same cabin. It was necessary to rush again and again to the stern window to escape from a stench which anticipated the grave. And all this was only air.

At midnight what was now only the frame or case of Brother François, who had long been unconscious, rallied itself for a last essay. The fever mounted and became intolerable. Then from every possible vent of the body poured the liquids which discharged its disease— a clear vomit that finally became black, floods of urine darkly clouded and in unbelievable quantities, an irruption of bloody stools, a viscid stream from the nose.

With all this the two faithful nurses could not cope fast enough. They laid the discharging object on a succession of bedclothes on the floor and from time to time flung the clothes overboard. It was not the least of the trials of this night-of-nights that the shark ranged nearer and engulfed all that they threw into the sea. Terrified and sick, Anthony saw the indifference of nature.

It came upon him that the life of the shark was the same as that in the body of Brother François on the floor. Certainly what he knew as Brother François was in abeyance. He could not look upon the animated corpse of matter that now lay on the dirty carpet and still call it the man he had known. Something was withdrawn, he thought. What remained had only the life of the fleshly machine that laboured on. In the body of the man that animal life was weak and sickly; in the body of the fish it was horribly vigorous. But it was the same. One fed upon the other. Both bodies profited by the unspeakable exchange.

Early in the morning the body of the man seemed to deflate itself and collapse. It was the *stadium* of the fever, which now died away. They forced some wine through its lips. They wrapped the thing on the floor in blankets, for it now threatened to turn cold, and put it back in the bed. Nothing more could be done. The skin was smooth and dry and yellow, the eyes closed. They themselves, revolted and exhausted to the verge of staggering weariness, sat down in chairs and slept. When they wakened in the damp heat of the little cabin, Brother François had returned.

"Water, my friends," he whispered. "I am still with you again for a while!"

Anthony looked at him and wept. What now contained Brother François seemed like a parchment lantern in which only a feeble candle burned. Yet as days went on the light there grew stronger.

It had not been easy for Anthony and Juan to subsist themselves during this time. Without the negro Ali Bongo, and the chests which Cibo had contributed, they must have perished. From Ali Bongo, who was now the only person on the ship who would even hand them objects through the cabin hatch, they received water and occasional warm slops prepared by the cook. From the chests of Cibo came certain dainties, wines, and a few preserved delicacies that had probably saved the monk's life. Cibo had not been a fancy grocer in vain. Anthony now looked through these chests, which had been deposited in the hold beneath the cabin, and was amazed at the variety of useful articles and comfortable comestibles that they contained.

In this dark hold, while the monk's convalescence progressed, Anthony began to meet Ali Bongo who enjoyed pickles so much he would even risk his life for them. Here in the close atmosphere raw with bilge, over a candle, in the darkness of the ship's midriff where the beams and timbers obtruded internally in ribbed shadows, he and the black Mohammedan discussed the predicament of the *Ariostatica* and arrived after a week's time at a certain understanding.

Ali Bongo was a primal but sensible character. In the plan which Anthony proposed he saw certain advantages to himself and his fellow Foulah tribesmen which would not accrue to them by their merely remaining loyal to the ostensible captain of the ship. A present of one of Cibo's silver mounted pistols sealed the bargain and carried a fierce delight to the savage self-importance of Ali Bongo's practical soul. Here was a señor who knew better than to treat one who had been to Mecca like a slave. "By Allah, he would soon be a chieftain again!" He concealed the pistol in the folds of his sash and returned smiling to the deck. The only eye which noted the bulge at his waist, and drew its own conclusions, was the single one of Polyphème. That worthy concluded that objects of value were to be obtained by visiting the cabin hold.

The quarter-deck was somewhat nonplussed not to say disgruntled at the new aspect of affairs. Not only was it evident that neither Anthony nor Juan was going to be obliging enough to die; Brother François was actually getting well. He and his two companions now came on deck together. Their first appearance there gave rise to a violent altercation with the captain and the mate. The crew looked on afar-off with considerable interest, and did not fail to note that over the captain's bluster Anthony quietly carried his point. An appeal by Don Ramón to Ali Bongo, who was then at the wheel, found that tall heathen neutral. Brother François was carried up every day thereafter to sit in a cushioned chair near the stern. Anthony and Juan moved about as they liked, although constantly warned to leeward by the captain and mate who kept up their sanitary bluster.

Whether this bluster was sincere or fictitious now Anthony could not for a time be certain. Certainly both captain and mate were afraid of the yellow fever. But it was not long before it became pretty plain to everybody that Brother François's illness was being used as a thin excuse for a policy of isolation which had in view another end than that of health. What the fo'c'sle wanted, of course, was license. Why the captain also persisted in treating the cabin as if it were still a pesthouse was revealed strangely enough by the stars.

Anthony was now able to come on deck and renew his own observations. It was instantly clear to him that the position of the ship as marked on the navigating chart by Sóller did not correspond with fact. According to Sóller the *Ariostatica* was about one hundred leagues off the coast of Sierra Leone opposite Freetown. Anthony found her, after taking a lunar to check his longitude, at about 20 North and 30 West. A day's run further convinced him they were making for the Cape Verde Islands.

No doubt at Praia it was Don Ramón's plan to make port, hoist a signal of distress, and land those whom he would certify as convalescent to the authorities. There would certainly be a Lazar house at Praia. Who the "convalescents" would be, Anthony had small doubt. The schooner might have to lie in the roads for some days to accomplish this. But it would be too neat a way for Don Ramón to rid himself legally of his unwelcome passengers to be neglected. The Portuguese would pay small attention to Anthony's Spanish letters. It would be a fine thing to have all his high hopes end in quarantine in some filthy jail or dismal convent. The situation must be met instantly.

First making sure of Ali Bongo and his followers, who saw an end to their own expectations should the ship leave Anthony at the Cape Verdes, he approached the captain next morning on the quarterdeck as near as that nervous gentleman would permit. Don Ramón and Sóller were as usual playing cards. After some bluster they were forced to stop and listen while he pointed out to them the lamentable discrepancy between the ship's true position and the chart.

Anthony had now some time to study the captain. He had come to the conclusion that under almost any circumstance Don Ramón would do the easiest thing. It was a natural conclusion drawn from his cowardice and indolence. If one ruse was uncovered he would simply go on to another. "Anything to avoid bringing things to an issue," would be the captain's motto. In this case he therefore supplied him with an easy way out of the predicament.

He simply assumed that the calculations of Sóller had been in error. Nor did he neglect to salve that individual by mentioning that even an expert navigator and calculator frequently went astray through some fault in the instruments. That so accurate a mathematical mind as Señor Sóller's, an expert card player too, could have made an error of more than seven degrees in latitude was unthinkable. It was the instrument that was at fault! Perhaps it would be just as well hereafter to make use only of his own? At any rate, he himself intended to do so!

The captain and the mate turned a bit green at thus hearing their little plan dusted out. The mate was even inclined to argue. Armed with his data, however, Anthony was firm. He pointed out the imminent danger of shipwreck on the island reefs if the present course were continued. He assumed that it would not be, and laid out the correct one.

"The captain," he said after a little pause, "will be pleased to give the proper directions to the man at the wheel."

An interval of tense silence ensued. Don Ramón's hand remained trembling slightly upon a card which he had been about to play after a quarter of an hour's consideration. Anthony continued to look at him and smile.

"Don Ramón will recollect that by the letters issued under the seal of the captain-general I am empowered to direct the course of this ship. Through the captain if *possible*. It would be a pity if I were forced to take matters into my own hands." He leaned forward touching the pistol in his belt. The captain looked up and saw Ali Bongo grinning; Juan sauntering by.

Don Ramón scattered the cards from the board with an oath and gave the orders to Ali Bongo at the wheel. Sweeping almost a quarter circle down the horizon, the bow of the *Ariostatica* turned south.

For the rest of the morning the skipper and his mate muttered together pretending to be trying to reconstruct their game. Perhaps they were. What conclusions they arrived at Anthony did not know, nor did he much care. In the first crucial test he had come off triumphant. This was the ninth week out. The Rio Pongo, if the breeze

held, could be only a few days away. In those few days he must get
the ship into his own hands. It was the breeze, and Polyphème the
single-eyed, that came unexpectedly to his aid.

A few hours after the interview with the captain, Polyphème was
caught red-handed plundering the chests stowed in the cabin hold.
Wine and fine biscuit being enjoyed by the fo'c'sle had aroused the
suspicions of Ali Bongo. Hasty investigation showed that about half
the wine and spirit from Cibo's precious little store in the hold had
already gone. Anthony and Juan took turns at sentry-go there. The
bulkheads in the schooner were only temporary and somewhat flimsy.
On return voyages the entire space was given up to packing in the
bodies of slaves. All barriers were then removed. The place was
hot and stank of bilge, negroes, sulphur and vinegar, the last two
having been used to cleanse it after a manner in Havana. Sitting
there for three hours at a time was no joke. How the slaves endured
it for weeks on end Anthony could not imagine. But he had his
reward.

During his second trick as sentry he heard the sound of bare feet
approaching the bulkhead on the far side. There were a few stealthy
shufflings and a loose plank in the bulkhead was removed. A man's
body came through the opening. Presently the fellow produced flint
and steel, lit a candle—and found himself looking down the pistol of
Señor Adverse. It was impossible not to admire Polyphème a little
then. The expression on his face did not even change.

Anthony made him crawl ahead of him through the hatch into the
cabin. That was a mistake, as he soon found. He should have called
for Juan. He kept the man covered. But as he himself emerged from
the drop which led into the little passage above, the fellow dodged like
a lizard, and threw a knife. It had been aimed for the heart and it
pinned the inner edge of Anthony's left sleeve to the combing. Seeing
he had failed, and that the pistol still looked at him, the prisoner fell
on his knees and began to plead. From the expression on his captor's
face he was afraid his time had come. And in this he was not far
wrong. If he had made one move to escape, the finger on the trigger
would have squeezed. His one eye rolled now and he squealed.

Anthony locked him in an empty cabin and stood by a few minutes
longer while Juan fitted him with irons from the ample supply provided for slaves. No one said anything. It had all been enormously
easy, Anthony thought. Those on the quarter-deck had not even been
disturbed in their siesta. Warning Polyphème that any noise on his
part would bring Ali Bongo with a whip, Anthony pocketed the key
and went on deck.

He was delighted with himself for several reasons. The capture
of Polyphème in so ignominious a manner was an enormous stroke

of luck. More important, however, was a discovery about himself. In situations of great danger he did not grow weak and tremble; he became strong from anger. Even better than that, he did not get confused. The nerves he had inherited were good ones. What an inestimable gift! He had actually been so much in command of himself even when the knife came as not to shoot.

How curious it was that things like this should be happening to *him!* A man had actually thrown a knife at him! He looked at Brother François sitting back weakly in his chair near the stern. He was lost in another world, poor man! But Anthony—Anthony was a part now of events. He felt he could not even afford to talk too much with Brother François. No, Anthony was doing things! Let them be done then. He felt suddenly sure of himself. He could bend those about him to his own ends. Don Ramón dozing, curled up in the shadow of a boat, filled him with contempt. Certainly he could outwit that man! He turned suddenly hearing Ali Bongo calling to him from the wheel. The man was pointing astern. Some miles away a white squall was tearing down upon them, lines of white caps racing before it.

Anthony began to shout warnings and orders to take in sail. Juan hustled Brother François below. Ali Bongo and his men stripped the mainmast while Anthony stood by at the wheel. He meant to bring the ship to, but the confusion in the fo'c'sle prevented him. Instead of lowering away there, an argument ensued and the foresail was reefed and set again. Ali Bongo danced with rage. A few confused people were fumbling on the topsail downhauls when Don Ramón sat up and confounded everything twice over by countermanding the orders already given. Missing Polyphème, the men forward were at hopeless odds among themselves. While she was in this state of provocative déshabillé the squall romped down uproariously upon the *Ariostatica.* Luckily Anthony did not try to throw her up into the wind now. He let her drive.

Even under the reefed foresail the schooner keeled over so far as to ship combers down the hatches. The jibs and loose square-topsail beat about for a few seconds like the wings of a frantic roc and then literally leapt clear of the bolts to disappear ahead in a smother of foam. The rigging shrieked. Anthony saw the eyeballs of the entire ship's company bent upon him at the wheel. "Let go the foresheet," he roared. It was fouled! Ali Bongo crawled forward and hacked it with a knife. The boom swept around like a whip lash against the lee shrouds, knocking four of the gaping men cold. Ali Bongo rolled into the scuppers. For a minute the *Ariostatica* shivered.

Then she slowly rose righting herself and slipping off the tons of green water that had nearly foundered her. Amidships there was a lake where the cook and a large pot floated about with ashes and fire-wood.   Then the bulwarks gave way there releasing the load.   The ship bolted ahead like a whipped horse.

By some miracle the reefed foresail held.   More surprising yet El Polio ran forward and lashed the boom to the shrouds.   Holding with all his might against the spokes Anthony was just able to keep the schooner from broaching to.   With the aft sails and the jib gone, the drag of the foresail against the helm was terrific.   Presently two of the Foulah tribesmen came and relieved him at the wheel which gave him a brief opportunity to look about.

He turned to find Don Ramón standing behind him with his legs spread apart and his hands behind his back.   It looked as if through the whole crisis the captain had been coolly giving him orders.   Thus it was that with most of the men on the fo'c'sle Don Ramón secured the credit for having saved the ship.

For an instant Anthony was overcome by rage.   He felt himself losing control of his feet and hands.   A mad impulse to kick the pre-posterous little hypocrite clear off the deck and down the hatchway all but mastered him.   Then he determined to make use of the cap-tain's cunning for his own ends.

Seeing the man was really at a loss what to do, he descended upon him and taking him unawares, half by threats in an undertone and by loud firm suggestions, forced him to continue in the false part which he had assumed.   Before two hours passed Captain Ramón Lull had, as it were, been rushed off his feet into the command of his own ship again.

Anthony was greatly aided in this process by the reappearance of Ali Bongo who arose from under a chicken coop in the scuppers as if from the dead, but with a large cut over one eye.   His countenance was rendered sufficiently ferocious by blood and swelling to work miracles by itself.   If any had been washed overboard it yet remained to be seen.   The crew at any rate thought that Polyphème had gone that way.   Without a leader they were temporarily reduced to the condition of somewhat stubborn but confused sheep.

Under the inspired, piping falsetto of the captain, who by some miracle they did not understand was now issuing sensible orders, a new jib was broken out and bent on.   The ship felt the relief sensibly and no longer threatened to lay to.   Axes were produced and some wreckage on the fo'c'sle cleared away.   Anthony took the risk of the tools being turned to weapons.   From the fo'c'sle the men were worked aft.   Even the mate joined in and exerted his authority.   "Under a decent captain he might have done well enough," thought Anthony. A small area of the mainsail was now shown to the wind and the crew assigned to the mainmast were put to work on the quarter-deck without further ado. The tempest, indeed, with its more pressing problems had banished the fear of plague from their minds.

The squall blew itself out rapidly. By twilight they were sweeping along under a fine following breeze. The regular watch was called and those who failed to answer were used roughly enough. With a few curses and some grumbling the crew found themselves somehow at their stations, and discipline was enforced through the remainder of the night. At dawn Don Ramón was roused too, to his vast disgust. It was a final test. Juan stood behind him with a pistol, hidden by the mast. The captain was forced to issue orders to clean decks. Some of the crew came forward at this unparalleled insult in an arrogant mood. The turbaned Foulahs descended upon them from the quarter-deck armed with the belaying pins and began to crack heads. It was enough.

When the sun rose it beheld the decks of the *Ariostatica* holystoned. The ropes were neatly coiled and the brass binnacle glittered. Anthony's ideal of the deck of the *Wampanoag* with Collins and a rope-end skipping about it was at least approached. If there had only been a little paint! The yachtishness of the *Ariostatica* emerged from years of grime. "Sacred blood of a sow," said a pimply-faced Frenchman spitting on the deck surreptitiously and looking at the stain with comfort, "and this is a slaver!"

Anthony sat in the cabin that morning immensely self-satisfied. In a few hours, through quick thinking and some luck he told himself, he had broken up the captain's little scheme of isolation and through him had assumed control of the ship. Don Ramón sat across the table too tired with rage to be angry any longer. The desertion of El Polio to the fo'c'sle had, indeed, reduced him to tears. His favourite was now bunking with the rest of the crew. The shattered state of the highly nervous little captain was scarcely understood by those about him. His falsetto broke and ran a gamut when he spoke. The terrible Señor Adverso had threatened to put him to bed in the fever bunk which Brother François had occupied. He collapsed at the thought. He would do anything to avoid that. But he would also do anything to regain the solace of El Polio. The boy was his slave in law but Don Ramón was the boy's slave in fact. So far had his passion now carried him that he really cared for little else. The command of the *Ariostatica* was to him merely the means of regaining Polio. No one else in the cabin could imagine that. No one but the monk.

By long acquaintance and sad experience the passions of men were no longer much of a secret to Brother François. No excess of either good or evil could surprise him. The situation on the *Ariostatica* was to him painfully plain. Between the stalwart young man who had evidently suspended his ideals in order "to do things," what things, of course, he did not know, and Don Ramón who was mad with the excess of a single unnatural affection, the ship, he felt, and all the souls on her, was in a parlous way.

It might have surprised certain people to have known that in his heart Brother François felt there was little to choose between the baneful effects of obstinate, wrong human desires. Anthony's in fact he felt might in the end overwhelm more people than Don Ramón's. But he himself could do nothing. He was too weak. Scarcely able to move even in the chair in which he sat without dangerous exhaustion, he could only sit and think. What lay ahead he did not dare to dwell upon as yet. It would have stopped his heart. He lay and looked up at the bright colours of Spain that flaunted themselves from the peak where they had been hoisted at Havana. The gold and blood of them, he remembered, had always been associated with the banner of the cross. In the inextricable tangle of contradictions which this implied to him, for he believed in Providence, he sat back inert and benumbed. Only his own way was clear. But there was such a terrible light upon it that he could only face it now by closing his eyes. The body of him must sleep yet.

During the day both Anthony and the captain came to him; Anthony to try to make the invalid more comfortable, Don Ramón to obtain comfort from the priest.

"My son," said Brother François to Anthony after thanking him for some wine. "Has it not occurred to you already that you have made a bad bargain?"

Anthony went away angry. He did not care to think of that. Brother François was very sorrowful.

Don Ramón after much beating about the bush finally decided to risk his body by approaching the convalescent in order to save his soul. The monk's reassurances of all danger being past finally brought him to his knees near the priest in the shadow of a boat that hid them both from view. There he confessed himself and begged absolution. Brother François would grant it provided he would give up the youth. Don Ramón could not do that. He said so and wept. Brother François was again sorrowful.

The *Ariostatica* sailed on toward Africa. In a few hours Anthony knew she would raise the coast. At midnight she ran into an oily calm.

That calm endured for fearful days. Neither the water, the wind, nor the ship shifted. Only the lights of heaven had motion and a few birds that flew about the *Ariostatica* and went away again. Only they and the shark moved. The shark was still there. It ranged alongside from time to time expectantly. It nudged the ship and scraped itself against her barnacles sending a light tremor through her. The men swore now that it was waiting for someone. Half humorously they began again to throw dice and to draw lots. There was little else to do. The heat was intense. The shark was always there, by far the most interesting thing in their lives now. His persistence fascinated them. The lot one day fell for five consecutive times on El Polio. That night he heard some of the men whispering about him. In the darkness he crept out of the fo'c'sle and fled back to Don Ramón.

The days of utter calm in which the company of the *Ariostatica* seemed to have been condemned to the hell of their own society for the rest of eternity remained always a nightmare to Anthony. It was plain to him that what had been gained during the squall and the short time afterward was rapidly slipping out of his hands. By the fourth day of calm, with the glass still low but no change, no one could make believe to be in charge of the ship. The men separated themselves to the fo'c'sle again and no longer even pretended to pay attention to a hail from the quarter-deck. Only a half-pint a day of water could be allowed per man. And even that would soon exhaust the now depleted supply. A hundred miles over the horizon was land. But the crew did not know this. If they had been told they might have taken to the boats. Exactly what happened to the minds of those marooned on the idle slaver Anthony could not be sure. The changeless colour of the sea, a kind of breathlessness in the atmosphere, a perpetual expectation of something about to occur which never happened, the utter silence and the shark—produced the explosion that came.

There were a number of half-castes among the crew, all of whom, white or brown, were deeply tinged with Africa. What superstitious and fearful whisperings went on forward night after night and day after day as the wind failed to come, only those who put their heads together in the fo'c'sle and listened desperately might know.

On the eighth day a surly deputation came aft demanding that Brother François pray again for a breeze. He did so but nothing happened. On the ninth the liquid ration was halved. That something had been resolved upon by the men was now patent to both Anthony and the mate Sóller as they served out the water and rum with Ali Bongo and his men standing by armed. On these Mohammedans Anthony now pinned his chief hope. They belonged to a tribe in the interior, the Foulahs, who frequently came to the coast in little groups under some leader and made a fortune sufficient for the rest of their lives by serving a few years at sea, usually on a slaver.

Anthony had, he thought, bound them to him by the present of two chests of scarlet cloth, the promise of much more when they arrived, and the cancelling of a year off their sea service. At the end of six months he had promised to dismiss them into the interior again with presents of powder and firearms. That was the understanding, and for the most part they had stood by him. But in the mystery which was now afoot they stood aloof, he felt. The most he could get out of Ali Bongo was that whatever was toward did not concern a good Mohammedan and he would not interfere. The outlook was by no means cheerful. The cabin retired on the tenth night thoroughly prepared, but not for sleep.

As the night wore on Anthony relieved Juan who was on watch on deck. He took his place in the shadow of the mast and leaned against it. No one was at the wheel. There was not a breath stirring. The helm which had been lashed a week before, had remained so. Some distance astern a slight phosphorescent glimmer proclaimed the presence of "Old Faithful." All in the fo'c'sle seemed asleep. For a while he thought he was alone on the quarter-deck. In the moonlight he could hear the idle sails dripping dew. Then he saw the head and shoulders of El Polio. He was lying back on some of Brother François' borrowed pillows in the stern sheets of the captain's boat where it rested in its cradle on the quarter-deck.

At first he thought the boy was asleep, but now he saw his eyes open. They closed slowly again. The expression on the lad's dark face held him spellbound. There could be no doubt what was happening. He lay looking up at the stars with a film of ecstasy on his lids. His delicately beautiful features were flat and strangely shrunken like some water-lily that had broken from its stem and decayed a little from its first early bloom while drifting helplessly downstream. This stupor persisted for a long time. Then the boy opened his mouth as if to bleat. But no sound came forth. The jaw merely relaxed and hung down. When a living expression finally returned it was one of extreme terror. He lay absolutely still for so long that it was evident he was afraid to move.

There was something Anthony could not understand about this. The boy lay with his hands behind his head. If it had not been for that Anthony would have put an end to the business. But the sight of so luxurious and self-hypnotized a dreamer had amazed and fascinated him. No other solution had occurred to him. The face alone had held him spellbound. Watching it, he had become aware of profound and hitherto unsuspected abysses in himself. He too had almost been hypnotized. When the captain suddenly appeared above the gunwale of the boat Anthony stood as if frozen. Indeed, his back grew cold.

Don Ramón looked about him and thinking the deck was clear stepped out of the boat and began to sneak forward. He was within a few feet of Anthony before he saw him. They stood looking at each other. Both of them knew instantly that the other was thinking of the shark. That was why the captain screamed.

Whether those who had planned what immediately followed that shrill cry thought they had been discovered and rushed the quarter-deck immediately, or whether the tone of it had merely shattered the ten-day tension of the unbearable calm, Anthony could never be sure. They must have been waiting, perhaps even creeping up during the minutes before the captain screamed. Scarcely was the sound past his lips when a half score of the crew were upon him. Anthony had just time to roll down the hatch. They had not seen him standing by the mast in the shadow. He caught himself on the ladder and drew his pistol aiming it at the moonlit square above. Whatever came he meant to hold the cabin. But no heads came into the bright square above. There was a hellish clamour on deck.

It was the falsetto voice of the captain. Doubtless they were going to murder him. At any rate he was begging them not to do something. Well, he would not interfere for *that* man! Not after what he had just seen. Certainly the agony was genuine now. Don Ramón could plead eloquently. Then Anthony went cold all over again. Don Ramón was screaming to them not to throw the boy overboard.

Anthony shouted to Juan desperately and started to climb up the ladder. A scream of terror beyond thought rang out above just as his head and shoulders came out of the hatch. The rest was over in two seconds.

Someone dragged the boy out of the boat to which he clung desperately, and clutching him about the waist raised him high in the air. The whole mad group precipitated itself toward the stern like an avalanche. For an instant he saw the still childish limbs thrash in the moonlight as the boy was tossed outward. There was a splash just as Anthony leaped aft. But he was met by a return rush toward the fo'c'sle. Rolling and milling about, his pistol went off.

Yet even in the mêlée while trying to clutch somebody he heard the voice from the water. No one could listen to that and not go mad. He started to club someone with his pistol but the man broke away.

When he rose to his feet again the grey decks of the sinister little yacht were empty. He stood there alone in the moonlight. He was clutching a bunch of black chicken feathers in one hand. That was all.

It must be a frightful dream. He would wake up soon. Yes, that was it. Chicken feathers! He knew it was a dream. Sailors do not wear feathers in their hair. He gave a weird laugh and found his chest and ribs hurt him horribly.

"*Ju-ju!*" said a wild falsetto voice in his ear. Don Ramón threw his hands up above his head. "No use," he cried. "All over." He staggered and was bleeding at the mouth.

Anthony went and leaned over the taffrail. Infinite miles of a pool of quicksilver seemed to lie astern. In all that glittering level not a thing moved. The shark had gone. He cried out into the night. Whether it was a prayer or a curse he did not know.

Next morning a faint breeze began to push the *Ariostatica* along toward Africa again. By noon she had gathered considerable way. They raised the low coast by evening and burned flares for a pilot all night. The red, funereal glare danced for miles over the black water. Finally a similar fire answered them from land.

CHAPTER THIRTY-SEVEN

THE CREW GO ASHORE

ALL night the *Ariostatica* gradually drew in toward the land. About dawn she was standing off-and-on just keeping under way. Nothing could be done until they picked up the pilot. Now and again the ship lifted sullenly to black hills of water that surged under and past her, marching in upon the coast. Half an hour after some unusual giant passed Anthony thought he could hear its cataclysmic roar as it staggered against the mysterious continent still hidden in darkness to leeward.

The sun rose suddenly out of a level, steaming jungle that stretched eastward as far as the eye could reach. While he watched, the straight clouds brooding over it wilted. Then, as the air grew hotter and clearer, a million foggy wisps exhaled into the morning as if the camp fires of night were going out. The sun licked the dampness up like a thirsty cat's tongue. In an hour the atmosphere was blue-white and quivering like the heart of a furnace.

This, he saw, was a flat, a sullen and silent land. No merry song streamed upward from that stagnant sea of treetops to eastward such as had risen from the gracious forests of Cuba to greet the sun. The only voice here was that of Ocean. Apparently quite calm, it advanced relentlessly upon the strips of islands stretching away over the long, flat horizon where endless miles of monotonous lagoons dazzled the eyes. As though balked of its prey by these thin barriers the sea continued to wrinkle its angry lips along their bone-white beaches, roaring with elemental appetite at the forest beyond.

Although the *Ariostatica* was still several miles out, the hungry crunch and smash of the breakers saluted her with a premonitory snarl.

Only at one point was there to be seen any break in the seemingly endless barrier reef that now lay directly before the ship. It was where the Rio Pongo, slipping silently out of the enormous forest, slid into the sea. Emerging from endless flats, the river was only a convenient funnel for the tides with scarcely any noticeable current of its own. A sharp dent in the façade of the forest beyond the lagoons and a surfless break in the barrier beaches indicated the river's whereabouts. This, and the blue dome of Cape Palmas which loomed up faintly to the south were the only distinct landmarks in the entire region. All else was a level sea either of green water or of even greener vegetation.

Sóller pointed out the river mouth to Anthony.

"A good landfall, señor!" He grinned a little sheepishly. "We ought to make Gallego's anchorage by noon. Well, you will certainly get a warm welcome *there!*" He strolled over to the rail and turned his back. Anthony felt sure the mate was laughing. He looked at the river gate ahead without enthusiasm. What awaited him there seemed as inscrutable as the dim arches from which the Rio Pongo emerged.

Some time after sunrise a black dot, which the restless ocean had been tilting into sight now and then for about an hour past, resolved itself into the expected pilot's canoe. It was paddled by two Kru boys stark except for breech-clouts. In the centre under a palm hat of Korean proportions sat the pilot in a ragged, military jacket, smoking a calabash pipe.

He knocked out this basin for tobacco as he came up the ship's side, and much to Anthony's surprise hailed the quarter-deck in English. Sóller seemed positively disgruntled by this. Evidently he had been expecting another man.

The trouserless emanation from the deep, dressed exclusively in a cast-off marine's jacket with four brass buttons over the tail, proved to be from the factory of one Thomas Ormond, better known up and down the slave coast and for many a mile inland as "Mongo Tom."

Sóller tried him persistently in both Spanish and Portuguese, but the pilot shook his head. For this he was heartily cursed at some length in both tongues, a warm welcome, which as a free man he resented.

"Me sabe go-go Bangalang alri'," he finally insisted, turning to Anthony who turned him over to the good offices of Ali Bongo. A bargain was soon struck for taking the ship up to Gallego's anchorage.

The mate grunted uneasily and went below, evidently to discuss this unexpected development with the captain who had not yet ventured to crawl on deck again.

The pilot took over the wheel without further ado and continued in active conversation with Ali Bongo in some unknown jargon. It appeared that they had known each other. After a while Anthony managed to join in. Ali Bongo did the honours. Berak-Jaumee, he assured Anthony, was one fine, fighting friend, honest man.

Jaumee proved to be very proud of his "English." He had once made a voyage on a British whaler, it appeared. For that reason Mongo Tom, the Englishman, had taken him on. Jaumee was now not only the best but the only pilot on the river, Anthony learned. There were only two slave factories on the Rio Pongo, Mongo Tom's and Gallego's. Both were near Bangalang, a Kru village. Gallego's lay a little upstream beyond the native huts; Mongo Tom's below. Both slavers had once kept pilots, but——

"Gallego pie-*lot* no work no more."

"How come that?"

"Gallego no pay. Gallego no pay numbody. Him dade two moons. Feber! Gallego bery dade. Him hareem go-go big woods." Jaumee grinned.

Here was news indeed, news which it might be just as well to keep from the crew and the captain. If Gallego was dead, Anthony realized his only hope of getting matters in his own hands was a tight hold on the ship, instantly. Consequently he walked the deck doing some fast thinking.

The crew would be with the captain, he felt, when it came to a final showdown. If he could only break that combination! He sent for Juan, and did some intense talking with him and Ali Bongo. He was delighted to see how at the mere prospect of a clash the lean, black Mohammedan brightened up. It promised well, he thought. Ali Bongo had peculiar eyes with golden pupils like those of an eagle. Expressionless for the most part except of a constant fierce animal pride, as he and Anthony stood by the taffrail discussing calmly enough ways and means of taking over the schooner, Ali Bongo's eyes smouldered in the sun. It flashed upon Anthony for the first time how absorbing the business of killing might be. Nothing else could be compared to it for interest. It was the supreme gamble. In a ten-minute conversation with the big Mohammedan both of them had forgotten themselves entirely in the tense business at hand. Even lack of language had been no barrier. Where Ali Bongo's Spanish failed his expressive gestures went on like a more eloquent though silent tongue. They parted having reached a complete understanding.

The ship was now passing through the narrow cleft in the barrier beach. The tide here ran like a mill race. Thousands of square miles of salt lagoons and an entire river basin were to be filled in a few hours, and all through one lean nostril. It appeared to Anthony that the slight rise in the forest beyond was where the earth was expanding its chest in order to inhale the tide. The water about the schooner boiled with white sand. All sail had been stripped from the ship, which now glided forward rapidly and silently on the swiftly rising water floor. They crossed the wide lagoon behind the island in a few minutes and entered the boiling, sucking mouth of the Rio Pongo.

Instantly on both sides the great forest closed in upon the little ship. The roar of the beaches was cut off as if the soft, oozy mouth of the river had closed its lips over her.

Anthony had never dreamed of a forest like this. Huge palms shot up to unbelievable heights overtopping the ship's masts, he could not guess how far. The *Ariostatica* seemed to be slipping down a throat lined with smooth, green vegetation into the mysterious maw of the continent. She swung around curves easily and majestically as if driven by some power within her, bubbling along on the advancing crest of the tide.

No one but an experienced pilot could have avoided the sandbars of the sluggish river's innumerable turns. Anthony glanced at Jaumee glad to see that Ali Bongo was getting on so well with him. Evidently they were about to reach an agreement. In a few minutes he witnessed a curious ceremony. Each man produced a knife and after repeating some formula each pricked his own thumb. When a drop of blood appeared they then thrust them each into the other's mouth. Then they exchanged knives. Both spat upon the blades and saluted each other.

The pilot then walked over and kicked the two naked Kru boys who were stretched out asleep in the blinding sun. He began to say something to them . . .

"Time to serve out arms now, I think, señor." It was Ali Bongo who was speaking. Anthony turned to him startled, the man had come upon him so silently. "I have just made a blood brother of the pilot. He and his two boys there are now with us. You will have to provide the three rolls of red cloth I have promised. It is a great gift but their help is worth it. If the señor will act quickly now I think he can secure the ship. I will bring my men aft. The rest of the crew are at morning mess." He gave a keen whistle which brought the four other Mohammedans, who lived mostly on rice, and who ate and cooked by themselves in the galley, running aft.

Anthony looked about him mentally mustering his forces. Besides himself he had Juan, Ali Bongo and his four other Foulahs, the pilot, and his two Kru boys. It was possible that the cook and his boy might be counted on to stay with the ship. Brother François was, of course, in event of any physical clash, neutral. This was twelve at best, probably only ten in fact, that could be counted on to act together against the rest of the ship's company including the captain and mate. The odds were thus about three to one. In Anthony's favour was the rather unusual height of the schooner's quarter-deck, which had only one narrow approach from the waist of the ship, and the fact that most of the ammunition, although not all of the arms, was stored in the cabin.

Anthony sent Juan and one of the Foulahs to bring up an arms chest. Without attracting the notice of the crew weapons were quietly served out to those on the quarter-deck. Several loaded muskets were concealed in the bunt of the half-furled mainsail. As luck would have it, just while this was going on the head and shoulders of the mate Sóller appeared above the hatch combing. He was about to come on deck. He took in the situation at a glance and bellowed something down the hatch to the captain. Just then Ali Bongo clapped a pistol to his ear and hauled him on deck. He bound him to the mast and gagged him. Anthony and Juan dived down the hatchway.

They were too late, however. A scuttling noise and the rattle of irons in the cabin-hold told what was happening. They were only in time to see the manacled leg of Polyphème disappear through the loose board in the bulkhead. Leaving Juan to nail up the loose plank, which he cursed himself for not having attended to before, Anthony returned to the deck by way of the cabin. The captain had gone, too. Evidently he had preceded Polyphème. The crisis was at hand then! He ran for the deck.

As he poked his head up out of the hatch there was a deafening smack, and a bullet, which shattered the top of the combing, filled his cheek with wood splinters. He saw the captain standing on the fo'c'sle with a smoking pistol in his hand. The little man dodged behind the foremast and started to reload.

Everyone on the quarter-deck, including Ali Bongo, was now flat as a card. The pilot had let the wheel go and the bow of the *Ariostatica* was pointing toward the bank. The tide luckily enough drifted her sidewise upstream.

Anthony seized the wheel and turned the ship's head up the river again. The captain was having great trouble reloading. His hands and arms waggled out from behind the mast, working feverishly. Grabbing one of the muskets from the sail Anthony sent a bullet in the captain's direction that tore a long piece out of the mast behind which he stood. The shot was too much for the captain. He let out a wailing whoop and dived for the fo'c'sle. His appearance there, which was greeted by an encouraging roar from the crew, had been enormously accelerated by Ali Bongo's firing a pistol at him as he fled. All this had happened in less than two minutes.

Ali Bongo now came to life. He even persuaded his "blood brother" to return to the wheel. Seeing they had leaders who meant business, the rest of the men on the quarter-deck now ventured to raise their heads above the bulwarks and to handle their arms again. It was hurriedly explained to them that any further faltering on their part would result in their being hanged by the captain, if, and as soon as, he regained the quarter-deck. It was now win or die. This profound thought served to accelerate their zeal considerably. Even the Kru boys could understand it.

Indeed, their new flood of courage and enthusiasm over the success of the first blow went too far. The mere appearance of a head at the entrance to the fo'c'sle was the signal for an unauthorized hail of shots from the quarter-deck. Some of these, fired from behind Anthony, passed close to his ear. The fo'c'sle howled like a den of hyenas for a minute or two and then was quiet again. Now was the time to rush the quarter-deck if they had only known it. Every weapon aft was empty.

It gave Anthony an attack of goose-flesh to think of that. He exerted himself strenuously to put some discipline in his mob. The muskets and pistols were reloaded hastily. Some packing cases and bales were brought up and disposed as a breastwork along the forward rail of the quarter-deck. The four Foulahs who were used to muskets, to judge by the way they handled them, were placed behind this hastily constructed but effective enough barrier with instructions to shoot at anyone who appeared in the fo'c'sle door. Spare muskets were provided. One of the Kru boys was sent down to reinforce Juan at watch below at the loose bulkhead.

That bulkhead caused Anthony a good deal of worry. He did not want to have to meet a sudden rush from behind up the cabin stairs. The danger was thoroughly impressed upon Juan who began to make certain preparations. His ingenuity, Anthony found later, was considerable.

In the meantime, the ship, as if nothing extraordinary were going on, continued calmly enough to sweep on up the river with the tide. A babble of voices occasionally burst from the fo'c'sle where a kind of nautical town meeting continued to go on for several hours that morning. Considerable difference of opinion as to what should be done under the circumstances must have developed between the captain and the now thoroughly reckless Polyphème. That was as much as Anthony could make out. An intermittent pounding and smashing of glass, upon which Juan for some reason was engaged in the cabin below, drifted up the hatch.

Anthony was glad now that Sóller and the captain had freed Polyphème. Doubtless that was why the mate had stayed below so long that morning. It must have taken some time to file the locks on the Frenchman's irons. He discovered later that the man's leg chain had been cut through. Sóller had evidently meant to come on deck to make talk while the captain and Polyphème went forward to bring back the crew. What had been done, then, was just in the nick of time. Anthony had counted on the captain's waiting to act till they reached Gallego's. That had almost been a fatal mistake. He drew a deep breath. Where would he have been now if he had waited? A glance at the monster-haunted river did not reassure him.

They were now passing rapidly enough up a long, straight stretch of the stream. Except for the muddy shallows along the banks the

Rio Pongo here resembled a broad canal rather than a river. This reach in particular was literally dragon-haunted. From time to time, disturbed by the passing of the ship, crocodiles launched themselves from the banks with a resounding splash that sent flocks of parrots screaming above the treetops. From a reedy shoal the pink, cavern mouth of a riverhorse opened suddenly and bellowed at them. A calf like a huge, fat grub appeared swimming at its mother's side. The smoke from the ship's galley had drifted into their nostrils. Monkeys let themselves down by the natural ropes of vines that dangled and looped for interminable miles along the vast living wall of trees. They dipped their hands in the muddy stream and drank, only to shrink back chattering as they saw the ship, or a pair of saurian eyes looking at them from what appeared to be a half-sunken log. There was not a breath or any movement in the leaves now. The damp heat vibrated above the stream with thousands of midges and living motes of things. Clouds of stinging flies made the men swear and stamp. Butterflies only to be matched by the cascades of bloom on the flowering vines that made the walls of the forest both magic and impenetrable, fluttered down on the deck and waved their wings slowly in the sun. The dark, festering swamp, from which this prototype of tropical forests drew gargantuan life, smoked under dim arches at midday with little wisps devoured by the sun.

Even in the midst of burning excitement Anthony looked at all this with amazement. To what place had he come? While the four Foulahs crouched ready behind their bales of cloth and packing cases he smiled to see that neither the battle which had gone on above his head nor the semi-infernal landscape through which the ship was passing had prevented the cook from preparing his usual meal. The galley smoked as peacefully as its imperturbable occupant. In the copper caldrons the salt pork bubbled and sang. At dinner time a pair of white trousers on a stick was waved from the fo'c'sle.

After some preliminary parley Polyphème's face and single eye appeared a little above the deck forward.

"You will not starve us, will you, señor?" he said taking off his red cap and bowing with elaborate irony. The four guns of the Foulahs were trained at his chest but he paid no attention to them. He stood there holding the ball and chain that was still attached to his leg, grinning, and looking at those on the quarter-deck with a malevolent eye. He succeeded in making them all uneasy.

"Send the captain up. I'll talk with him," said Anthony.

"*I* am the captain now," replied the man putting his hand on his heart and bobbing again while his chain clanked. "If you have any business to transact with the crew, monsieur, you must do it with me.

Mais oui, you see I have just been elected." He swaggered a little, allowing the news to sink in.

"Put the captain on deck. I talk only with him," snapped Anthony in French.

"Ah, zat ees endeed unfortu-nate, Meester Adverse, ze cape-tain hav chess now, what you call eet hexpire. His noble heart hav stop beat. I tell you zat in your own goddam langweedge. It ees ze verity. Let me talk wiz you. I have ze bon pro-posal." He started to come aft.

"Careful, señor," whispered Ali Bongo.

Anthony halted the man just by the carronade amidships and kept him covered.

"You and me, we get togezzer now ze captain ees dade . . ." the sailor began.

"You're lying, of course," interrupted Anthony.

The single eye narrowed to a slit. "No! I swear eet, on my heart, monsieur." He bowed again slightly. His hand shot out of his chest. Anthony threw himself backward. His pistol went off in the air. It was the handle instead of the blade of Polyphème's knife which took him full in the chest. A number of muskets went off together like one gun.

The four Foulahs had fired straight into the fo'c'sle door. It had stopped the rush effectively. Forward someone could be heard screaming dismally. Despite a fusillade of shots which followed him, in the tense excitement Polyphème had dodged back again.

Anthony rose both bruised and foolish. To have had the same trick played on him twice! He picked up the knife and threw it into the sea.

It was just then that the noise broke out below. Evidently a scrimmage was going on in the hold. Suddenly it stopped. Then there was one shot. As he started down the ladder Anthony met Juan coming up. He was laughing.

"It's all over," Juan said. "I don't think they'll come back." He began to laugh again. "It was glass, señor. Broken bottles! I spread them in the hold in front of the bulkhead and waited. Dios! You should have heard the noise they made when I fired through the bulkhead. They all rolled over each other in the most fertile spot. Bare feet, too, Madre!"

"Was it indeed 'all over'?" thought Anthony. Unconsciously he found himself thanking the madonna, his own madonna, that it was not all over with him. His wishbone creaked where the knife handle had bruised him. A fine place he had brought himself—and the madonna to! Then he found himself laughing with Juan from sheer relief. A few minutes later the voice of the captain was heard begging for water for the wounded.

"They bleed down here badly, señor—for the love of Christ!" Anthony allowed this request. The return of the expedition from the hold had evidently sickened the fo'c'sle pretty thoroughly. He let the cook take some food down to them. Silence settled down upon the *Ariostatica* now. Her progress up the Rio Pongo was no longer marked by volleys and the screaming millions of parrots that rose in cloudy flocks. The tide was nearing the flood. The ship moved upstream more and more sluggishly.

They drifted slowly past the establishment of Mongo Tom. The forest opened out suddenly and a vista of rice fields, sugar cane, and plantains swept up to a large palisaded place, the slave pens. On a knoll was a comfortable-looking thatched house with a far-flung veranda. Anthony sent Juan for his glass. He could see a large figure, apparently that of a white man dressed in a loose garment of some kind, standing on the porch. The man was also looking at the ship with a hand telescope. Anthony made a gesture to him but he got no reply. Strangely enough no one else could be seen about. The place seemed deserted.

"Mongo Tom no like him people come say how-do Gallego ship. Many man's there alri'," replied the pilot to Anthony's questions.

Evidently there had been no love lost between Mongo Tom and Gallego.

"Him no like me bring up Gallego ship," continued Jaumee. "Jaumee free man," he added proudly. "Me *do!* Me work Gallego ship!"

Anthony nodded approval of these independent sentiments. "Me free man, me do!" he thought and smiled.

A canoe appeared at a turn ahead, waved a paddle, and turned back upstream. A few minutes later the pulsing throb of distant drumming seemed to emanate from the forest from all directions at once.

"Bangalang," said Jaumee.

The drums went on. The crew in the fo'c'sle began to call out. What was going to happen to the garrison on the quarter-deck, and Anthony, in particular when the ship reached Gallego's barracoon was not only described graphically but with obscene originality.

It was Anthony's intention to nurse this delusion of the approaching revenge of the defunct Señor Gallego. It fitted in with his plans for getting both the captain and the crew ashore without further deck fighting when they reached the Gallego establishment. It was no part of his scheme, however, to permit the crew to regain the deck before the ship anchored. As they approached Bangalang and several heads began to appear at the fo'c'sle hatch from time to time, he had one of the Foulahs fire another warning shot.

As the fo'c'sle hatch, a sliding door, was exactly opposite the quarter-deck, which faced it at an elevation of about ten feet due to the build of the ship, the effect of musketry from the quarter-deck only half a ship's length away was to plunge bullets directly into the fo'c'sle. They spattered against the forward bulkhead there with a devastating smack and a hail of oak splinters.

There was even a certain humour in this situation, provided one was on the quarter-deck. In order to protect themselves the crew had to keep the vertical, sliding hatch to the fo'c'sle closed; in order to sally forth or shoot back they had to open it. The opening of the hatch always announced itself by a loud screech of its ungreased rollers. By the time it was fully open, after several squalling jerks from within, five or six muskets were trained at the gaping door. Anyone who wanted to come up the fo'c'sle ladder then, and die at the top, was at liberty to do so.

Anthony reflected with a good deal of amusement and a curious chagrin that upon the combination of these very simple physical facts both his present and his future existence were entirely dependent. In several languages he could think of only one phrase adequate to describe the situation. "On les a."

When the drums began announcing the nearness of Bangalang and the end of the voyage, the forward hatch had been slid back in order to allow the profane advice of the fo'c'sle to reach the quarter-deck. As the loudness of the drums increased, showing the *Ariostatica* was nearly opposite the native town, the disposition of the crew to sally forth became imminent. A few heads were even risked above the level of the deck. At the same time a fleet of canoes making for the schooner appeared around the bend of the river just ahead. It was at this juncture that Anthony had caused the Foulahs to fire again. The demonstration was effective. Silence from the fo'c'sle and an outbreak of firing in the town around the bend greeted the volley.

The firing from the town was merely by way of a happy greeting to the long-expected ship. Bangalang, according to Ali Bongo and the pilot, was a village of Krus, a tribe of coastal negroes, mostly fishermen, who were of great service to both the slave establishments on the Rio Pongo. They had consequently been let alone. Slaves came from the interior. So there was nothing hostile in the approaching canoes, quite the contrary. Nevertheless, Anthony did not intend to permit natives to board the ship at this time. If necessary he intended to skip a few shots over the water to make the canoes sheer off. A happier idea was supplied by Ali Bongo, however. Several small kegs of rum were tied to a spare spar and set adrift. The canoes when they approached were warned off and the kegs pointed out. A few minutes later as the *Ariostatica* drifted past them, ten canoes were engaged somewhat violently in trying to divide four kegs between them. Muffled shouts from the fo'c'sle did not attract their attention.

The river now widened out into a series of lake-like tidal marshes. As the ship came in sight of the village, situated on an island knoll about a mile away over the flats, the drums in the place changed from a monotonous *tum-tum, tum-tum,* to a swift

> *Bonk, bonkty-bonk-bonk,*
> *Bonk, bonkty-bonk-bonk.*

endlessly repeated. Horns and screams of welcome joined in.

It was just at this point that Anthony felt a final crisis with the crew might occur. Everything depended on reaching Gallego's anchorage about four miles beyond the town. At her present rate of drifting it would take the ship an hour to do that, two hours perhaps. The tide was fast failing. He now sent two of the Foulahs forward to cover the fo'c'sle hatch point-blank and managed to slip Juan up the forward ladder to set the jibs. Over the miles of open flats breezes now and then rippled the water, while in the narrow river all had been dead calm. The ship increased her way considerably.

The rattle of the jib blocks on the deck and the drums of the village caused Polyphème to make another attempt. He raised his head above the deck level and found the single eye of a musket looking directly into his own. It was sufficient to convince even him utterly.

Nevertheless, the tension of that last hour was extreme. It was not until the schooner rounded a long, wooded point, and Anthony could look across another bay in the forest to the long barracoons of the late Señor Gallego, that he began to feel he might yet win.

A few minutes more, and he would have had to anchor below the point and hold the crew below all night. In the darkness almost anything might happen. As it was, assisted by some puffs that filled the jibs for several blessed moments at a time, he just made it.

The *Ariostatica* was brought to anchor about seven hundred yards from shore by a small anchor from the stern. With several possibilities in view Anthony was particular about this distance.

The tidal basin here was about a mile across. Gallego's place stretched along the water front where the stockaded barracoons stood. Various thatched houses attached to the establishment extended up a low, steep hill just behind. Many blacks, both men and women, could be seen running about greatly excited. On the porch of one of the houses farther up the hill Anthony's heart sank to see what was apparently the figure of a white man. Could Gallego be alive after all? If so . . .

"Him Ferdinando, Gallego factor," said Jaumee. "Him halfbreed." He spat on the deck.

It was curious that no boats were putting out for the ship, Anthony thought. There was not even a canoe by the docks. Whatever the reason was, it made things much simpler. Without further ado he intended to act.

He had the two whaleboats slung in the schooner's waist lowered and towed up to the bow. Sóller, who since his appearance on deck that morning had been tied to the mast, was now unlashed. In the excitement of the past five hours he had been pretty well forgotten. He now staggered across the deck moaning for water. When he found Anthony intended to send him ashore with the crew he collapsed. His plight was pitiable. It was plain that he must know that Gallego was dead. He had heard Ali Bongo and the pilot talking, it seemed, and had put two and two together. He now pleaded earnestly to be allowed to remain on the schooner.

"You will not send me to die like a dog on shore, will you, señor? I see your game. To turn me and the captain loose on shore with those bastards below! Dios, we shall be murdered! I won't go! I will serve you now. I can be valuable to you. I will be your man . . ."

Anthony was forced to turn Sóller over to Brother François who tended him in the cabin below. The truth was the sun had nearly finished him. At any rate he was no good to negotiate with the crew. It must be either the captain or Polyphème. The captain would be easier to handle. After a hundred reassurances and seemingly helped by Polyphème from behind the little man was finally persuaded to come on deck.

He was nervously shaken by the events of the last forty-eight hours. All his swagger was gone. He stood blinking in the sun in a sweaty, silk suit in which the colours had run. Yet it was strange to see how soon the ghost of his naturally cocky attitude began to return when he found he was going to be sent ashore with his crew. Anthony could see that Don Ramón still thought him a fool and could scarcely believe his ears or refrain from boasting about what he was going to do when once ashore.

Anthony pretended to be driving a bargain.

"In return for letting you go I shall expect you to put my own situation before Señor Gallego as—well, *as pleasantly as possible*," said Anthony finally.

"Certainly, señor, of course, with absolute cordiality, depend upon it. Your generosity and tender treatment will be properly reported, have no doubt. I promise it on my honour."

"In this case I shall *have* to believe you. My situation, you see, makes me dependent upon you from now on, captain. I trust you understand my precarious position with Señor Gallego."

"Believe me I do," grinned the captain in spite of himself. "I wonder you did not think of it before. But I shall do my best," he added hastily, seeing Anthony scowl.

"Have your crew pile their arms on the deck then, as I said, and get into the boats one at a time. As a gentleman of honour you may keep your own sword." Since the captain had lost his scampering through the hold early that morning the last shot was between his wind and water. He winced, seemed about to reply, then thought better of it and went below.

Some time passed during which a few laughs hastily suppressed drifted up the hatch. In rather short order the crew then began to toss up on deck a heterogeneous collection of weapons. These were hastily gathered up and taken aft. There was some parley over a musket which had not yet appeared. Finally it was tossed up with a curse.

"One at a time now," said Anthony. "At the first move . . ."

A decidedly bedraggled departure now took place. As the men emerged one by one from the fo'c'sle they were sent alternately to one of the two boats and made to sit down on a thwart. Those who had bandaged and bloody feet from walking on Juan's broken bottles looked especially glum and foolish. Both the procession and the boats were kept well covered by pistols and muskets. As there were twenty-eight men in all it took nearly half an hour, thirty as tense minutes as Anthony ever lived through. Looking down in the boats, where the men were forced to sit with folded arms, he had no doubt that both of them were loaded with a cargo of pure hate. Polyphème and the captain came last. The former still carried his ball and chain, while the latter had found a cutlass far too long for him. He had taken Anthony at his word but tripped on the sword as he went over the side. Even his own men grinned at him.

The tide had turned during these proceedings and the bow of the ship was now downstream. The two boats, with the captain in charge of one and Polyphème of the other, were both at a signal suddenly cut loose. The ebb swept them clear of the schooner. They were carried fifty yards before the tired, dazed men realized what had happened. Then there was a great scramble for oars. A yell of derisive triumph went up from those on the schooner and a few wild shots which Anthony could not prevent spattered the water about the boats. Polyphème produced a pistol from somewhere and fired back. His bullet crashed through the stern windows. Yells, curses, and threats were hurled back from the boats, which, thrashing the water wildly, pulled out of range as fast as they could and made for the landing by the barracoons.

It was not likely they would attempt to return immediately, Anthony thought. He counted on the confusion which would follow when they learned that Gallego was no more. Above all he counted on trouble starting between the captain and Polyphème. There were gorgeous possibilities there. He himself would play a defensive game. He had the schooner now and could wait. He would consolidate his own gang and stand off the others. "Tomorrow," he thought, "—and almost anything may happen on shore tonight—perhaps the final move can be made."

How thankful he was the tide had served them to the last. Undoubtedly he owed much to Jaumee's skill. It would have been impossible to keep the situation in hand if he had had to anchor lower down and keep the crew below all night. Things had been too evenly balanced. As it was, they had just come through by the turn—of the tide.

But to wait was not necessarily to be apathetic. He must keep himself clear-minded and up to the mark, awake. And he must now be merciless, he felt. Above all he must supply the energy to drive things through. Already his little garrison was drowsing about the deck and dozing from heat and fatigue.

He stripped and poured several buckets of water over himself. He took a pull of brandy, and then lit a black cigar to quiet his nerves. He roused the men again by serving out some grub and a good tot of rum to each. Under Jaumee's supervision he set them to work getting up boarding nettings while he and Ali Bongo put the carronade amidships into working order. Powder, round shot, and grape were got up and placed handy. As the ebb increased the *Ariostatica* had dragged on her small stern anchor and increased her distance from shore. This was now brought up. The large starboard anchor was let go, and the ship's head brought upstream with only a short length of cable out. A few turns of the capstan would free her now, yet the heavier anchor held her fast.

By five o'clock all was shipshape again. The boarding nets were rigged, cutlasses, and loaded pistols and muskets ready at hand. A number of lanterns and flares were made ready, and a large kettle of boiling water kept steaming in the galley. Anthony and Ali Bongo had also spent some time training the carronade on various objects. It had very simple sights and one hand screw for elevation. They now recovered it, leaving the lashings off its tarpaulin and the gun loaded.

It was now time to think of his men again. He got up a ship's chest and served out new clothes. He gave the Kru boys their bolts of red cloth and the Foulahs the merchandise he had promised them. In addition he presented the Mohammedans with a small roll of lead and a bullet mould apiece. He gave Ali Bongo the captain's silver watch, which he had left behind, and from a chest of trinkets fished up a cuckoo clock for the pilot. Another round of rice and boiled meat followed.

While all now sat about on the deck with expressions for which "satisfaction" was too lean a word, the fortune to be made by sticking by the ship was made clear and the disasters of failure again pointed out in strong terms. A blatant dose of praise mixed with a few cold threats for those who might shirk, or go to sleep on watch, completed Anthony's first speech. A burst of cuckooing from the pilot's clock just at the end brought a roar of good-humoured laughter from all hands. The crew was divided into watches under Ali Bongo and Jaumee and went willingly to their stations.

So far nothing but distant shouts and the barking of a dog had come from the shore. The barking now reached a crescendo of excitement.

Leaving Juan in charge of the deck Anthony went below for his glass. He found Brother François attending Sóller who was now better but still with a rather bad touch of sun. Even the bullet through the cabin windows had not disturbed him. Brother François returned to the deck with Anthony. He showed no curiosity or surprise. He sat in his chair and looked out over the wide stretch of jungle-lined water which the sun was now flooding with level rays as it neared the western palm-tops. He offered no comment.

Anthony wondered what he was thinking about. How useless he seemed here! Perhaps the priest's seeming apathy was due to that; perhaps he sensed his helplessness here himself. The tremendous, brutal lushness of the tropical landscape all about seemed to oppose itself to Brother François. Against the scale of things here he seemed insignificant.

But when he had once focused the glass on the scene ashore Anthony soon forgot all about the man who sat beside him. The short distance between the ship and the shore was only sufficient to provide a dramatic perspective. Through the glass everything, even small objects, was very clear and apparently close at hand. But he could hear nothing except the dog barking. The animal was now frantic about something. He began to search for it, running his glass over the long barracoons along the water front and then up the hill. Now he was on it.

It was at the dwelling house half-way up. What was going on there was absorbing enough.

CHAPTER THIRTY-EIGHT

A WHIFF OF GRAPESHOT

THE dog, a small, lean animal whose capacity for clamour seemed out of all proportion to its size, was tied to a pillar of the veranda, straining at its leash. The cause of its indignation and fury was the approach of the main body of the crew. They had now left the barracoons and stockade below and were climbing the hill toward what was evidently the master's quarters half-way up the first slope.

It was a thatched building of generous proportions. A number of blacks, both men and women, could be seen leaving the place from the rear carrying various belongings. The exodus was a general and hasty one. The figure of the man Ferdinando appeared at the main door once and then withdrew hastily again. Then the captain came out and stood with folded arms. He still wore his cutlass. The foremost of the crew now tore a small gate off its hinges, and followed by the rest rushed up a short garden path. They stopped short at the porch. The hound was baying frantically.

Some argument now took place with the captain. The little man waved his arms wildly. His words seemed to be having effect. He drew his sword. Several of the men clinched and started to roll over and over. Whether fists or knives were being used Anthony could not tell. Suddenly Polyphème stepped out from the crowd and drew his pistol. The captain dropped his sabre and turned for the door. There was a puff of smoke and the captain crumpled. Then the crack of the pistol reached the *Ariostatica*. The men swarmed like hornets into the house. The hound had apparently gone insane. Outside two figures lay in the little garden path before the porch.

The crack of the pistol on shore had brought all hands to the starboard rail of the schooner. Some few seconds later two figures dashed out of the house followed by some of the crew and made for the barracoons below. Anthony could not fix the glass on them, but in one he thought he recognized Ferdinando. The other seemed to be a woman, a young and active one it appeared, for she outdistanced her pursuers rapidly and disappeared into a clump of palms near the river front.

The man was not so lucky. He was headed off and hunted amid whoops and a great clamour for some time about the sheds near the

slave pens. His hiding place was evidently discovered once, for the
shouting broke out anew. Then it quieted down. Some of the crew
kept looking about, but in about ten minutes they gave it up and
trooped back to the house on the hill.

The cause of further lack of interest in their quarry was now apparent. A shed had been burst open and some barrels rolled out. A
number of kegs loaded on the backs of slaves were soon seen ascending
the hill to what was now quite patently the headquarters of Polyphème
and his gang. That worthy soon appeared on the veranda and had the
captain rolled away and the kegs rolled in. He then, to judge by the
noise, devoted a full five minutes to kicking the hound to death.

It was curious, but the screams of the unfortunate animal did more
to weld the crew of the *Ariostatica* into a unit against Polyphème and
the men on shore than anything that had happened so far. None of
the incidents of the fight coming up the river nor the miserable sights
of wounds and blood which it had produced could be compared with it.
Anthony remembered the cries of the child which had been trampled
by the French cavalry at Livorno and their effect upon Toussaint.
Evidently it was the voice and not the sight of suffering which most
moved men. Ali Bongo who stood beside him at the rail listening,
clutched the shrouds till the veins on his wrist stood out. And he was
a Mohammedan who held dogs accursed. As the agonized voice finally
ceased it now seemed to Anthony himself that he was engaged in a
holy war, and that behind the taking of the schooner and the capture
of the barracoon, which he planned as a final object, there was now a
splendid moral urge. The cool murder of the captain seemed nothing
in comparison with the nerve-shattering death of the dog. The captain
had died silently so far as those on the schooner were concerned, and
he was a man. Polyphème, in short, had now given notice to all concerned that he no longer kept even a sensible contract with nature. All
were concerned.

"Señor," said Ali Bongo, "tomorrow we make One-eye go tell
Allah about that. Allah can listen." He drew his finger across his
throat significantly. They nodded to each other with complete understanding.

"Well, my son, how is your plan getting on with itself?" said
Brother François to Anthony a minute or two later.

"Very well!" snapped Anthony, who was still leaning over the side
looking shoreward. Something ironical in the priest's voice had
aroused a host of questions in himself which he had thought were
asleep. He was about to ask Brother François if he thought he could
do any better himself, under the circumstances, when three men
emerged from the shore sheds and started to make a bolt for it toward

the landing where the two whaleboats from the schooner now lay
without a guard.

A wild whoop from some of the crew on the hill gave notice that
they were seen.

The distance from the sheds, and from the house on the hill to the
dock was about the same. The three fugitives, whoever they were,
had the advantage of a considerable start. Unfortunately, however,
the two boats were not tied close together at the dock. They had only
time to hurl themselves into the first and shove off before the crew
was swarming out of the barracoon gate just behind them and making
for the remaining boat farther down the dock.

The men in the boat pulled as rapidly for the ship as their desperation could contrive. They had already put a good stretch of water
behind them when the craft manned by Polyphème and his gang shot
out behind them pulling strong.

In the meantime, Anthony and Ali Bongo had snatched the tarpaulin
off the carronade and were trying desperately to bring it to bear on
the pursuing boat.

This was not so easy to do. They had left the carronade at too high
an angle. The hand screw which controlled its elevation proved rusty
and stiff. Before the elevation could be shifted to water level and the
gun trained, the crew were gaining fast. The boat ahead, rowed
awkwardly by only three oars, seemed about to be overtaken and captured before the eyes of those on the schooner. It was just at the
moment when the gun finally came to bear full on Polyphème's boat
that Anthony remembered they had no lighted match. He turned with
a groan. Ali Bongo was gone.

Just then he emerged from the galley tossing a blazing coal from
hand to hand.

"Keep her on!" he shrieked.

Anthony peered over the sights again. His target in those few
seconds had rowed past. He slewed the gun desperately at a guess.
Ali Bongo dropped the coal on the touch hole.

There was a terrific report and the carronade leaped back into the
air against its tackles.

A million waterfowl rose screaming from the marshes. About ten
feet before Polyphème's boat a round shot struck the water a stunning blow, half drowning its crew with sheets of spray and caroming
off into the wall of the barracoon beyond with a tremendous crash of
splitting wood. For several minutes nothing could be heard but the
screams of myriads of birds and the wail of women from the shattered building on shore.

Anthony could hear nothing at all. He was deaf but he was laughing. All of Polyphème's men had "caught a crab" at the same instant.

Their oars seemed to stick in the water and fight with them. Then they had rowed all ways at once. Now they were making back for the shore thrashing frantically. If they could only get there before those on the ship could reload the terrible gun! They did so. Ali Bongo was dancing from the pain in his scorched fingers. Anthony was helpless. About the same time that Polyphème and his men raced back through the big gate of the barracoon the boat they had been pursuing made fast to the ship. Its three exhausted rowers proved to be the half-breed Ferdinando and two stout blacks.

Anthony welcomed them although he could just then hear nothing they had to say. Nevertheless, from the very first he liked Ferdinando. Gallego's chief clerk, or factor, as he was called, carried himself like a man. Despite his pale lemon complexion, small features, and dainty hands and feet, his main impression was one of intelligence and energy. His face was both refined and forceful and he evidently took great care of himself.

Somewhat bedraggled now, his first care when they descended to the cabin was to wash and put his dark curls in order. A clean white suit which Anthony lent him went far toward winning his heart. Anthony did not realize it then, but to have been received thus by the white man in charge of the ship with courtesy and solicitude had reached the half-breed factor where he lived. It had conquered his pride.

The sun had sunk. Darkness descended upon the forest-river lands as if a curtain had been lowered. A thousand mysterious noises arose of night birds, monkeys, and an occasional deep bellow from the river banks which drifted in through the cabin windows of the schooner where Anthony, Brother François, and Ferdinando now sat at their evening meal. Downstream over the low point Anthony could see the glow of the village fires waving in the sky and the monotonous but frantic drumming gradually became audible again as his ears cleared.

Juan kept a sharp lookout on deck and repeated that there was nothing to be seen ashore except a few lights and an occasional shout from the house on the hill.

Ferdinando joined genuinely in Brother François's brief grace. He regarded his own presence at that meal as little short of marvellous. A recital of events on shore that afternoon soon confirmed the others in this opinion.

The captain upon landing had left the crew in the sheds below while he had climbed the hill to Gallego's quarters. His disappointment, rage, and chagrin on learning that Gallego had been thoughtless enough to die two months before were indescribable. The factor said he had never seen anything quite like it.

"It was a curious thing to watch, señor. You can imagine my own state of mind, too, with that one-eyed dog and his sons-of-bitches hanging around about the sheds below—waiting. At any moment they might find out that Gallego was dead. Both of us knew what would happen without having to be told. I can tell you, you came in for some hearty cursing. We were caught like pigs in a pit by your little trick. I suggested arming some of the slaves and started some of the house servants hiding the valuables. There was Señor Gallego's big cash chest in which he kept the silver trade dollars. We started to smuggle it out the back.

"It was just then we heard them coming, señor. Either someone had told them about Gallego, or they saw the chest. I cannot understand Don Ramón. What kind of a man was he? When we heard them yell and the dog started to bark the captain was so frightened he turned green. 'It is death!' he said. Then he vomited all over the room. He had just had a bottle of red wine. He fell down. Then he got up again and took his sword. 'I have my honour,' he shouted. I laughed at him then, God forgive me! He went out on the porch and folded his arms. Señor, he made the crew a grand speech. Some of them fought for him. He died like a brave man. You know how." The factor crossed himself.

"As for me, I did not wait. No use. When I heard that pistol shot I called my sister from her room and we made for the little creek behind the palms. Since Señor Gallego died we have had great trouble here. A number of our people kept slipping away at night to the village. I had all the boats and canoes towed around to the creek and watched. That is the reason no boats came out to you. You see I have been much worried all along as to what would happen when the *Ariostatica* arrived. Well, it has been much worse than I thought!" He ran his slim fingers through his curls. "Much worse! Only the devil knows what that froth-of-hell will be up to tonight. It is trade rum they broke into, fourth proof—barrels of it. Madre!"

"Where is your sister now?"

"Well hidden, I trust, señor. Ah, she is a clever girl, do not worry! She will not be caught like a chicken in a coop. Besides there are plenty of women in the barracoons. It is fire that I am worried about. If it once gets started in the thatch!" He put down his glass, pausing at the thought. "But who are you, señor, and how did you come here?" He looked up now a little apprehensively.

With great care, for he saw how valuable an ally this man could be, Anthony explained his position and the events of the voyage. Ferdinando sat listening amazed. On the face of Brother François now and then Anthony thought he detected a faint flicker of amusement. It did take a great deal of explaining.

"So it is your plan then, señor, to assume charge of the factory here?" said Ferdinando at last.

"Since Señor Gallego is dead I can scarcely do anything else, can I? In fact I find myself in charge already, don't you think?" Anthony replied.

The factor laughed a little wryly. "Undoubtedly it is true," he said. Then he looked up turning a little white, but with determination enough.

"And what of me?" he said.

"You will remain on as you are now," replied Anthony. "I had already made up my mind to that sometime ago. I see that you are—a gentleman!"

"You are the first that has ever said so!" said the half-breed leaning forward over the table and looking Anthony in the face. "I shall never forget it!"

Anthony went on deck and left Ferdinando talking with Brother François. He was glad to see that Juan had bountifully fed the two black boys who had come aboard with the factor. They squatted by the galley scooping rice out of a bucket with their own horn spoons which they habitually wore in their hair. They grinned at him and he nodded back. It was no small reinforcement he had gained. The odds against him were now only about two to one.

The night wore on quietly enough. Ali Bongo and his watch relieved Juan's. Ferdinando came on deck and they talked for hours. An enormous amount of information was to be culled from the factor. He was certainly a valuable man. Yes, he had been born here—at Bangalang. His father had been the captain of one of old Señor Gallego's ships. "A gentleman, señor, a Castilian." Of his mother he said nothing, nor of his sister. Anthony wondered how Ferdinando could be so sure that all was going well with her on shore. If it had been Anthony's sister, for instance . . . or was the half-breed merely indifferent? The moon came up very late, only a remnant of herself red and inflamed, looking through the fog that settled over the treetops. An increased roaring and howling of tribes of monkeys inundated the night. At Bangalang the tireless tom-tomers and drummers changed their rhythms again. Those drums! Not a sign on shore yet. Only the lights up at the residence and a few drunken shouts now and then. The barracoons lay miserably dark and silent.

Anthony went below and got his boat cloak and a thin blanket for Ferdinando. There was a certain damp-coolness from the river equivalent to cold. One felt it in the lungs. Ferdinando spoke of the ague. "You will probably die of that, señor. They all do who come here, sooner or later. Do you smell the forest? I do only when I remember it. It is that miasma that gets in your bones. It is a very unusual season here, the rains have been delayed; intermittent. Usually it pours for weeks at a time."

"You seemed to have survived," murmured Anthony.

"Ah, that is different. A dash of . . ." Ferdinando bit off another cigar. He enjoyed the fresh Havana immensely.

Anthony also inhaled slowly. It kept him awake and soothed at the same time. He realized as he leaned back and began his fourth cigar that night how much tobacco had come to mean to him. Here he could see it might come to mean even more. One would need it. A little brandy was also helpful, he found—on a night like this—a very little of course. He passed the flask to his companion who agreed.

Brother François went forward with a light and disappeared into the fo'c'sle. He stayed there a long time. Finally he came aft again.

"Come," said he, flashing the lantern on the two leaning back in the chairs apparently asleep. "I want to show you something. No, *you*, my son." He motioned the half-breed back. Anthony followed Brother François into the fo'c'sle. The priest held up the lantern.

There was someone huddled up in the forward bunk. The blood on the blankets was of a peculiar, dark purple colour, almost black, and shiny. It seemed terrible that the man's hair was still dark and curly. It seemed to have a life of its own. The face was *so* dead—turned toward the wall and grey-ash coloured. It was one of the oldest of the crew. Yet he had somehow the expression of an infant now. It was also monkey-like. It needed life to make it bearable. Cold and only half awake as he was, Anthony felt the fear of it, a repulsion to the clay of it leapt up in him.

"Who has done this?" something asked. "This is really you—like you. It might happen to you. Run away! You will be overtaken by this fate. Beware"—and all the time he knew and tried to deny to himself that he had caused this. His mind to relieve him started to show him a map design in the bloodstains. There were the Cape Verdes and just east of it a large black-purple stain. A little *too* heart shaped for Africa, not perfect, nature scarcely ever did . . . The lantern moved and the shadow of the bunk swooped over the sleeper. Anthony saw Brother François was looking at him.

"One of the crew," he said mechanically. "I don't know. They must have left him here this afternoon. He may not have been dead then. They should have . . . Damn it! Do you think it is *my* fault?" he ripped out. The priest's gaze angered him. Brother François did not reply. . . .

"Well, what else *could* I do? You know the circumstances. Would you just have stood by and let them murder us? Would you?" He felt sorry and angry now at the same time.

"What is it you are trying to do?" said Brother François.

"Collect a debt," snapped Anthony. "Three shiploads of goods were . . ."

"Look at the ledger now," said the priest. He moved the lantern so that the light fell into the bunk again. Anthony looked. They stood silent for a moment. The lantern guttered.

"What is the use of talking about it?" said he, and stalked on deck again. He felt vastly annoyed at Brother François. Let him bury the dead. Now! Why keep on being reminded? He roused Ali Bongo and gave directions. "Put two shots in the shrouds . . . Before it gets light." He was glad to be back on deck again.

A great deal of shouting was going on on shore. He turned to watch that.

"They must all be very drunk now," said Ferdinando coming and leaning by him at the rail. They stood smoking for almost half an hour. The door at the high house on the hill finally opened and disgorged a yelling mob. Several torches flared up from one. Then a lot of them together started to come downhill. The shadows danced weirdly clear out over the water. A kind of Walpurgis procession accompanied by flaring pine knots born by staggering and capering figures was streaming downhill. The crew stopped now and then to shout hoarsely and argue with one another. Something was up. They seemed to be pushing a cart. The lights glinted on metal. About half-way down they all stopped short. A shed roof cut them off. By climbing the shrouds, half-way up you could still see them from the schooner over the top of one of the water-front sheds. It was hard to tell what they were up to at that distance and in the waving light.

Suddenly a streak of red fire dirked into the night. A round shot screamed through the rigging like a banshee. The loud slap of the report followed. On the hill a cloud of sulphur smoke drifted back redly through the frantic torches. A wild shout of glee went up.

"Madre de Dios," said Ferdinando, "it is the saluting cannon, a five-pounder. Gallego kept it dismounted in the warehouse."

They could hear a fierce clamour in the barracoons now. Above this the little gun spoke viciously again. A loud cracking started aloft followed by a dismal crash as the foretopmast tore loose and smashed along the deck. The hill clamoured with triumph. It was certainly the devil's luck of a shot.

"Get below," shouted Anthony. There was no use exposing the men now.

"The chances are in the darkness they won't hit us again," said he to Ferdinando as they came down from the shrouds.

"No, but on the other hand we can't reach them," replied the factor. "You see from the deck here they are hidden up the slope just behind the shed roof." Anthony, Ferdinando, and Ali Bongo gathered about the carronade. Nothing but the dim glow of torches showed over the shed on shore.

"Shoot through the roof, señor," suggested Ferdinando.

"No, that will carry clean over them I am afraid. You see they are down the hill a bit and dropping their shot on us over the shed roof. It would take a mortar to fetch them from here. This long gun will not give us the angle."

A shot plunged into the bay and ricocheted over the schooner.

"One mans on shore, him sober," said Jaumee, who just then came up to join the nonplussed group coolly enough.

They all laughed a little wryly.

"What do, Jaumee?"

"Wait morning-light," grunted the laconic pilot wrapping his blanket about him and sitting down in the lee of the bulwark.

The advice seemed good. They could drop the ship downstream at dawn if necessary. It was uncomfortable sitting still, but risking grounding on a flat in the darkness was worse.

The shooting continued for some time and then stopped.

"About an hour till dawn, I take it," said Anthony.

"A little longer I think, señor," replied Ferdinando.

Then he leaped to his feet. A waving orange light was irradiating the water front.

"They have fired the boat shed!" cried the factor. "The powder!"

A long yellow flame licked through the thatch illuminating the water and making the *Ariostatica* stand out darkly. On her deck the long shadows leaped to and fro. The shed suddenly began to burn fiercely as a tar barrel in it commenced to vomit flames. The whole bay danced with reflections now.

"Get the anchor up! Juan," shouted Anthony. The men began to tumble up. Strangely enough the shooting was not resumed yet from shore.

"They are waiting for more light," said Ferdinando. An explosion of the gun followed as if in answer.

A maddening delay occurred getting the bars in the capstan. Then the *clank-clank* of the schooner's anchor chain coming in sounded over the water. An answering roar of voices came from the hill. The flames from the burning shed at that instant leaped higher. A full half of it was on fire now. A roaring and crackling came over the bay. Showers of sparks fled up into the stars. A white light beat along the water front. The dock and the barracoons behind it projected themselves clear as midday in a frame of blue darkness.

Suddenly the big timber gate at the water front was flung open and some of the crew rushed out and started to shoot muskets at the schooner. They were gunning for the men about the capstan. The bullets splashed about. A beam in the shed fell sending up a fountain of sparks.

"Help, señor," shouted Ali Bongo. "See!"

Anthony left the capstan and rushed to aid Ali Bongo at the carronade. Racing aft he glanced over his shoulder. Through the gate of the barracoon the rest of the crew was emerging rolling the little five-pounder before them.

"Allah, Allah," shouted Ali Bongo. He was stuffing the contents of a trader's chest of notions into the carronade; copper bangles, brass beads, knives, a small music box. It began to play "Richard, O mon roi."

"Out of the way, man, bring fire!" Anthony laid the sight square on the gate. The crew were bunched there, swarming about the little gun, a black writhing mass of men in the fatal glare. This time the match was ready. He blew on it. "Richard, Richard, O mon . . ."

The two guns from ship and shore spoke at the same instant. Splinters ripped from the bulwark of the schooner. Anthony felt the wind of the ball. But he had eyes for nothing but the fiery scene ashore.

In the gateway of the barracoon a wave of chains, toys, and slugs had mowed the crew down like the blade of a whistling scythe.

Not a sound could be heard except the crackling of the flames. Everyone stood rooted gazing shoreward. A red arm leaped up out of the shed into the sky; a thunderclap; a long roar. The whole shed vaulted into heaven bellowing.

In the intense glare of the powder explosion Anthony saw the whole of Gallego's place stand out like a landscape in a thunderstorm; the long sheds with the solemn dark palms drooping over them, the residence with its wide porches, the black jungle-covered hills.

"Mine!" he cried.

Darkness swooped; sparks and hissing timbers rained into the bay. He took a long, deep breath. The air felt cool just before dawn. He filled his lungs again to their usual rhythm. That had been disturbed only temporarily. Life in this new place was going to go on again. What were swift events? Merely an interlude. As long as the lungs and heart went on one went on with them. That is, one resumed. And now at last he was master. Let the new day come quickly! He leaned over the rail looking shoreward.

From the forward deck of the *Ariostatica* came the voice of Brother François saying the office for the dead. Presently there was a splash. Anthony turned and went below. No matter what happened a man had to sleep. Tomorrow and tomorrow and tomorrow?

CHAPTER THIRTY-NINE

VIEWED FROM GALLEGOS

FROM the porch of the "Residence" at Gallegos there was a sweeping view. The establishment lay on the first rise of ground inland. It was quite high enough to overlook the tallest treetops of the coastal jungle on the plain below it. At evening the sun could be seen flashing on the distant silver of the Atlantic that bounded its horizon westward. Also, Gallegos was high enough to catch the sea breeze at night. That was what made Gallegos possible for white men.

Southward, you looked out over Gallegos Reach, a kind of tidal lake in the forest about a mile across, where the Rio Pongo widened out swirling slowly when the tide changed. You kept on looking—if it was not midday and the waters below turned into an intolerable blinding flash—over the mangroves on the long, low point where the hawks nested to the wider reaches of the tidal flats and swampy islands about Bangalang lower down.

The huts of the Kru settlement were built along a brief stretch of sandy beach on a low island. By day the long fisher canoes could be seen drawn up on the sand in regular rows, and by night the native fires wavered and twinkled through the river mists. Over the roofs of Bangalang, five or six miles away, the long slave pens of Mongo Tom's establishment and the whitewashed house just above them stood out boldly from the clearing on the river bank which it occupied. Indeed, with a small glass, from Gallegos the slaves working in the manioc rows of the Mongo's fields could be seen quite plainly.

All the rest of the world to be seen from Gallegos was forest.

A vast, flat sea of treetops marched northward hundreds of miles toward the doubtful boundary of Sierra Leone, and Freetown. The same boundless ocean swept without an undulation southward toward Cape Palmas far over the horizon. Over this the eye ranged monotonously, the only breaks in the flat roof of the forest below were a few loops of the river west of Mongo Tom's where it suddenly narrowed again and twisted tortuously to the sea. Known to traders as the "Rio Pongo" from early Portuguese times, the river was called the *Kavalli* or *Cavala* by the various Kru peoples who inhabited the coast.

Gallegos was in a great many ways a pleasant place at which to live. It was situated in a nest of low hills just where the river finally emerged from the plateau behind it and debouched into the lowlands.

The ground here rose in three distinct steps from the stream.

Along the river bank, on a flat a few hundred yards wide, were situated the dock with the various stores and sheds attached to it, and the long barracoons or slave pens, which occupied considerable space. From these the hill rose fairly steeply to a level horseshoe-shaped inset containing some fifty or sixty acres of rich, black soil. Behind that again the crest of the little range of hillocks was reached by a rather easy ascent.

There the upland jungle began and stretched away eastward towards the unknown—or the "Mountains of the Moon"—if one preferred to take on faith the first object besides elephants and lions marked on the maps. At any rate, it was at this point that the trail from the interior emerged from the forest over which every year came Arab caravans with their human and other merchandise, which supplied the reason for Gallegos' being a place at all.

Not long after taking over the establishment Anthony had built himself a new residence. The old one, which Ferdinando now occupied, lay near the top of the lower rise and was constructed with wattled clay walls and a palm-thatch roof. One rainy season spent beneath its dripping cover, and many harrowing experiences with both white and red ants, had convinced Anthony of the necessity of a better abode.

During the endless, dreary days when the rain fell for weeks at a time he had amused himself by drawing elaborate and careful plans, not only for his new "castle," as he called it, but for the rehabilitation of the whole establishment which the last Gallego, not much of a man he soon learned, had allowed to fall into considerable disarray.

Labour was no consideration on the Grain Coast. The slaves who would otherwise have been confined to the barracoons were set to work as soon as the dry season returned the first November after Anthony's arrival. In the meantime experience had taught him a good deal about the country, and, as he sat late one afternoon on the porch of the new residence overlooking his domain, he felt justified in feeling that on the whole, for a new arrival, he had then planned well.

Not that in the light of what he knew now, after longer familiarity, he would not do some things differently. The slave pens should have been further enlarged, for instance, and the dock extended. It would save a great deal of time and worry to have the ships tie up to the dock directly instead of anchoring in midstream as they still had to do. But who could have foreseen that things would go as well with him at Gallegos as they had?

Indeed, there had been that anxious four months the first year when he had not been sure that any ships would ever anchor at Gallegos at

all. Old Mongo Tom, too, had certainly made all the trouble he could.
Thank the stars that was over with, the old dog! Well, he was brought
to heel now, and probably for good and all. For all practical purposes
the entire landscape Anthony now looked over, from the new veranda
at Gallegos to the Mongo's fields six miles away across the bay, was a
very—well, a very Adverse one. Yes, on the whole, a great deal had
been accomplished since the *Ariostatica* had pulled in three years before—a great deal!

He leaned back in the ample cane chair and threw his palm hat on
the floor. It had been a hot day and he had been all over the plantation. It was two months till the autumn rains yet and things were
pretty dry. But that was to be expected. Also the irrigation helped.
Now for a bath and a drink!—or a drink. Why wait? The house
servants brought back from Cuba had it too easy anyway. They
needed a mistress.

"Cheecha."

"Sí, sí, señor."

"Rum, and limes!"

"Sí, sí."

It was like Cibo to have sent him that girl. Well, he could well
afford to as far as that went. Cibo had had his pick now out of many
a shipload. Fourteen ships in three years! And the fifteenth swinging at anchor below there now, *La Fortuna*, a new one to the trade.
He hoped Cibo had not forgotten to send the right kind of trade
goods. Another caravan was due soon, despite the nearness of the
rainy season, and the stock in the warehouse was low. Not a slave
in the pens and Mongo Tom had less than fifty, all old ones, too! The
neighbouring country was pretty well worked out.

He lit a fresh Havana that had just come on *La Fortuna*—and enjoyed it greatly. The mould here did play the mischief with tobacco.
The smoke drifted straight up to the ceiling. The sea-breeze would
not be in for an hour yet. Twenty minutes after the sun went down
the wind changed, by the clock. Gad, how well he knew the ways of
the place now; the seasons, the clouds, and the winds; their rhythm;
the very look and smell of things!

In a few weeks the cloudless sky would commence to become a little
hazy. Already the river mists were thicker at night. Then the clouds
would begin to pile themselves up higher day by day. Great cliffs
and mountains of them would finally tower up height beyond height
till it was dizzying to look up into them. The sunsets were beyond
thought then. Soon there would be lightning at night; far-off thunder
muttering. Then nights of a long battle-roll of it and on into the
day, and then—the clouds would approach each other and exchange
broadsides. They would dissolve into one grey pall, a few drops

would fall, a shower, and—as if spigots had been turned on above—
one long month by month downpour. It did not seem to rain by
drops. For three months it slanted past, and furiously down, as if
each slant were an individual and perpetual jet from a hole in the sky.

But it would be better this rainy season, the first in the new house
since it was finished. It might even be comfortable, and there would
be a let-up in the perpetual man-hunt. There would be time to put
things in order, to go over the accounts, and to make plans for next
year.

There would also be time to devote to Néleta! No more surreptitious meetings because of Ferdinando's pride. That half-breed! So
was his sister! What of it? No, they would live together now in the
same house! Brother François could look as sad as he wanted to.
Neleta would be housekeeper now. Housekeeper! He smiled, and
drifted away on a vision that relaxed him in the chair.

Ferdinando could not expect him to marry her. Marry her? He
laughed.

Ferdinando was making too good a thing of it as it was. He
was sorry now he had allowed him head-money on every cargo. It
was enough for Ferdinando to have the run of the place as factor—and
his sister was the mistress of the big house on the hill. What a fool
he had been to wait so long to bring her up from her brother's. It had
gotten to be like acting. Let her come and live with him. He was
master here. Master!—a rich one, too. To think that only three
years ago he had been trying to collect a debt for Mr. Bonnyfeather—
and now . . .

He let his eye wander over the ample plantation that lay just below
the house.

He had built the house well below the crest. The shadow of the hill
behind it gave two extra hours of coolness in the morning. All his
planting was doing well; the coffee, the rows of cassava; cocoa, maize,
yams, rice and eleusine; pumpkins, gourds, cabbages, sweet potatoes,
and okra. They flourished, and with only a little tending. Next year
he would increase the acreage and put in indigo, cotton, sugar cane,
and ginger; enough manioc to supply the whole establishment. It
would take a few more field hands but he was not going to ship every
last man, woman, and child that came down with the caravans to
Havana any more.

No, he was in a position to hold back now and dictate a little. He
would build up a permanent establishment here and he would make it
self-supporting. If anything happened to cut him off from Cuba he
would be able to go along then on his own account. About twenty
field hands, ten Foulahs for a garrison, and a few more house servants,
well-trained ones, would do. This year would see the whole place

stockaded. It had been a big job, ten-foot tree trunks from the croco-dile creek behind the hill to the river front. They swept clear around the place in a convincing horseshoe. With the next gang that came down he would stockade the creek bank, too. The thorn boma there was only good to keep out the chimpanzees.

It was a relief to get rid of those rascals and the monkeys. Watch-ing big Diana monkeys with the orange behinds ransack the new fruit orchards had been a trial. Shooting them from the front porch was all right by day—but in the morning! Well, he was pretty well en-closed now, and by next summer he would have quantities of oranges, limes, and lemons. The papayas were already prodigious and there were shiploads of bananas. The cocoanuts, avocado pears, and figs one had to wait for. But not long. Now that the little zebra-goats couldn't get in and girdle the trees any more! They *were* devils. He wondered if Cibo had sent him the pineapple cuttings. They ought to do well here.

Next spring, the wonderful spring after the rains, when the air grew clear and the sun seemed to pull things up out of the earth by their tips—spring would see Gallegos the little paradise he had planned. No place on the whole Grain Coast would be like it. And he would live here with Neleta and keep on accumulating. Neleta would look after the house as it should be looked after. Some day he would go back, rich. He would settle in London or Paris, and live! He would invite Mr. and Mrs. David Parish to dinner—to a very formal dinner under very fine chandeliers, a splendid place, butlers and lackeys, the Bonny-feather arms. Why not? Perhaps Dolores would be at the other end of the table. But to give all this up now; Neleta, the house; not to see the growth next spring; not to go up-country after being here three years! Unthinkable! Yes, it would be very lovely next spring, and it would pay, pay highly, to stay. After all, what would he be doing in Europe? Really he couldn't imagine that. One dinner with Flor-ence was not a life.

The wild fowl were going now, going south. As he watched a great flight of them lifted from the reach below and made off over Cape Palmas way. The handsome little sparrow-hawks that lived on the rocky point above the mangroves seemed excited about it, too. But they stayed. In the spring all the ducks would come back, and the great black swans. The rains certainly could not be far off.

He had forgotten the Christian calendar here. He told time only by the rhythms of the seasons. The swinging back and forth over the sky of the vast flocks of birds just before and after the rains, the slow ranging and rearrangement of the clouds, the shifting of the winds, and the gradual dying out of the intense green of the forest below him as the dry season advanced marked the passing of the year.

Even the stars failed him in these latitudes. They were all strange, and much inferior, he thought, to the northern constellations. Only the wandering planets and the moon came back like old friends. The sun was so fierce it seemed another sun. Gradually one learned things about the tropical sun; how friendly and how deadly it could be.

Yes, he acknowledged to himself, he loved it all. Gallegos had become home. This month—he knew it was February from the manifest of *La Fortuna*—this month it had all, rather suddenly, become "home." He knew he was going to be here a long time now. Perhaps Neleta's coming to the house had something to do with it, but he was not sure. Perhaps?

He finished his drink, the early evening drink, that he had to admit now he depended upon. It made him feel himself again after the day in the sun. His face lost something of a certain mask-like quality it had taken on. The yellow tinge that had grown under his tan faded. His eyes grew bright and the small red veins at the corners of them stood out a little.

He felt now, after the rum and lime juice and sugar had taken hold of him, he felt as he had when he first came from Havana three years ago. Why was it though, he could no longer get as much done in the day as he always planned to do the evening before—after the drink? By noon it did not seem to matter. Last year it had not been that way. But, pshaw! how could he feel better than he did now? All bronze, not an ounce of fat on him! He put down the glass to watch the sunset. A drowsiness overcame him. The darkening blue dome of the sky with the black lines of birds streaming across it down to the lower range of the horizon beyond the two lakes slowly faded. The birds seemed to be going downhill from the top of a bowl. He closed his eyes.

Half an hour later he wakened chilled by the sea-breeze and went in to change into dry clothes. He shivered slightly. Sitting in sweaty clothes in the cool wind was the one thing you should not do. It was almost dark now; stars. He looked out of the window at the dank river mists gathering below. Fever lurked there. He took his drench of cinchona bark. Horrible stuff, bitter! He killed the taste with a good swallow of brandy. Then he felt warm again. His feet lightened under him. He hustled into a heavy cotton evening suit and put on a cravat. The captain of *La Fortuna* was coming up to dinner tonight. Ferdinando would be up too to go over the ship's manifests with him. It would be the first dinner when Neleta would sit at the table. How would Ferdinando take it—and Brother François? Well, they could—*take it*.

He shrugged his shoulders and went into the eating room.

CHAPTER FORTY

THE MASTER OF GALLEGOS

DON RUIZ DE LA MATANZA, the captain of *La Fortuna*, which now lay anchored in Gallegos Reach, was a Toledan of ancient family who had seen better days. There was a decided but a native hauteur about him. Only in a way was he glad to find himself in the merchant service—via a naval court-martial which could only be said to have been lenient.

Even in the Spanish navy the practice of selling the cannon out of king's ships for old bronze had to be discouraged, and the wrinkles in the official forehead had frowned Don Ruiz into the streets without even his sword left to protect his outraged honour. The terrible dilemma of begging for work had made even a Matanza pliable, however, and after some years Don Ruiz wriggled himself onto a merchantman's quarter-deck.

A fine full-rigged ship was now his, *La Fortuna*. Originally built for the Manila run, she had splendid cabins and great hold space like the galleons on whose track she had followed. As a balm to his hurt pride Don Ruiz ran her like a king's ship in all ways—except selling her cannon for about half what they cost. He had only consented to enter the slave trade, on account of the very high profits, and by the clever solicitations of Carlo Cibo at Havana.

Anthony could see as soon as he entered the eating room that Captain Matanza was inclined to hold himself aloof. Mere slavers were evidently not his usual company. The very way he emphasized the "de la" in presenting himself showed that. And he was evidently nettled that only the factor Ferdinando had greeted his distinguished arrival.

Anthony, however, had taken a leaf from the excellent book of John Bonnyfeather in how to receive and entertain ship captains. He no longer met the ships as soon as they anchored but sent out Ferdinando. He then received a report as to the nature of the ship's commander, read personal mail which the vessel brought him, and with all necessary human and business details thus thoroughly in mind sent an invitation to dine to the captain.

All this had its effect. If it did nothing else, it induced the more surly rascals among ships' officers to recollect what decent manners their memories might still retain. And it impressed all newcomers with the fact that in dealing with the Master of Gallegos familiarity

573

was not in order, for as long as they lay at his anchorage, he held not only the whip hand, but the face cards in every little deal. To be invited to dinner at the new residence was therefore something to remember, and to talk about afterwards in Havana.

Indeed, the approach to the new house had been planned somewhat for its "diplomatic" effect. A flight of broad steps hewn out of the living rock of the hill led up from the sheds and barracoons on the flat to a loopholed palisade on the level of the plantations. From this a straight road of beaten clay lined with giant funtumas already twenty feet high, so rapid was their growth, gave a clear vista to the house itself situated about an eighth of a mile across the cultivated fields of the little plateau and half-way up the final rise beyond. Beyond that the pointed posts of the palisade could be seen against the sky, crossing the hill in a bristling arc.

The house itself was built of large, native brick made from the same clayey soil in which coffee flourished so well. It was absolutely four-square and surrounded on all sides by a veranda of noble proportions set on natural pillars of dracæna trees. These had been stripped of their bark, leaving the smooth, oily surface beneath to harden and glisten in the sun. The rafters of the roof and the porch were the same, making one sheer start from the peak of the roof to the eaves of the veranda. Anthony had covered them with red tiles which had been brought as ballast in an empty slaver from Cuba. Not only was this the only tile roof on the West coast, it was also the only rain and snake-proof house-cover in that part of Africa. The outer walls of the place were whitewashed.

Seen from the anchorage, this house had the appearance of a large white tent with a red roof, the flag pole projecting from the centre court and the shadows under the poles of the veranda completing the illusion. It was only when it was approached closely that its essential solidity and capabilities for defence became apparent. A small trench supplied with flowing water, that was really only a defence against ants and other pests, completely surrounded it and gave it somewhat the look of a moated grange. The heavy shutters of the few outside windows might be seen by an observing person to be loopholed, set at commanding angles in the wall, and few and far between. The door was small and would have taken a cannon to dislodge it. Indeed, the outer openings were scarcely more than holes for ventilation, and the house depended for both air and sunlight upon the large and beautifully planted central patio, where a spring bubbled up, and to which the house was open internally on all sides.

All these details had by no means been lost upon the ex-naval eye of Don Ruiz de la Matanza as he ascended the hill with Ferdinando. Nor did he fail to note the Foulah sentry protecting the stockade parapet with an elephant gun, nor two heavy culverins in concealed enclosures where a man kept watch night and day with a match burning. From their emplacement just a little below the house round shot could be plunged onto the deck on any vessel below. In fact the whole establishment and the river bays for several miles were subject to the muzzles of those guns. Whatever else he might be, Don Ruiz had already decided before he entered the house that its owner was no fool. His experience at supper that night continued to strengthen this opinion.

His impression of Anthony when he entered the room was that of a tall and powerfully slender young man, the quiet assurance of whose bearing was rendered attractive and rather remarkable by his extreme ease of movement. A certain polished aloofness of manner, which to anyone but a Spaniard would have seemed a trifle old-fashioned, gave him a dignity that scarcely coincided with his years. This precocious gravity was really a projection of John Bonnyfeather rather than Anthony's inward conviction of pride, but it had the effect of making others feel at first a little puzzled and uncomfortable and so constituted for Anthony at once a means of attack and a hidden but powerful reserve.

His voice, when he spoke, which was not often, had now greatly deepened. It ranged when he was angry or scornful into the bass. Ordinarily it remained quiet, mellow, and clear. But he enunciated his words now with a certain assurance and precision not altogether pleasant. In two years the master of Gallegos had acquired the easy habit of command, but he had also lost a certain natural persuasiveness which had once been a positive charm. This, to tell the truth, he was not at all aware of.

At first there seemed something hard-bitten about his face to a newcomer like Don Ruiz. It was very—almost too regular in feature. The finely chiselled nose would have been too sensitive and feminine if it had not been for the hard chin beneath it and for the nervous but firmly set mouth. No one could tell what his complexion had been, he was now burnt so black. His eyebrows were bleached white and his lids slightly puckered. The whites of his eyes were no longer boyishly clear but tinged slightly yellow. His large pupils seemed to veil themselves as if they had something to conceal. It was this quality of the eyes, always directed somewhere else even when looking at you, that lent Anthony a certain mystery which few who saw him failed to feel. In the final analysis it was hard to tell to whom you were talking. It even seemed as you came to know him better as though the gracefully directed precision of the young man before you was somehow controlled from otherwhere.

All the negroes noticed it. Even the wide and pleasant forehead,

the now closely cropped but still wavy and sunny hair could not overcome the impression. Ferdinando had once mentioned it jokingly.
"The niggers say a wizard has stolen your soul, señor."

Anthony's unexpected and electric outburst of fury had left the half-breed a paler and a wiser man.

To Anthony it seemed that he was at last finding himself; at least he told himself that. Or perhaps he was creating a new self out of the vivid incidents and the cruel, stark realities of the life about him. He was "doing things"; he was being a very practical and a successful man in a situation that had required courage, finesse, adaptability, and grim determination to carry through. In three years he had not only "collected" the debt due to Mr. Bonnyfeather but he had also put himself in the way of being a fairly rich man. What had happened to the firm of *Gallego & Son* in the process he did not know and he did not much care. That some payment as a sort of rental for the place on the Rio Pongo was made to the Gallego heirs he had finally elicited from Cibo after several inquiries. "Herr Meyier is taking care of that out of head-money, and the forced lease has been declared legal. I advise you to drop the matter forthwith as it annoys His Excellency. You have nothing to fear." That was all there was to that. He was master of what the blast from the *Ariostatica* had won, and he did not intend to go out by the same way he had come in.

Yet in growing into the kind of a mammal which Cibo had so strongly advised, there was a part of Anthony which seemed to be withering by the way. It was the part of him which lay locked up with the past in the fireproof storeroom he had built, where the chest which had come from Livorno reposed with Mr. Bonnyfeather's books, the sextant, some smaller, more youthful clothes, and his old madonna. Not since he had arrived at Gallegos and buried fourteen of the crew of the *Ariostatica* in Brother François's new graveyard, had he once opened it.

Yet it was upon this part of him that his eyes looked when they turned inward. And it was the refusal to listen to certain old promptings that turned his pupils stony and had given him a fixed mask-like cast of countenance. It was all that which turned him white with fury when it had been suggested to him by his half-breed factor that what lay locked up in the fireproof storeroom might be his soul.

He had jumped the doubts as to which was the better man of the two, the old self or the new Master of Gallegos. His will was now all on the side of the latter and it took less and less willing, he thought, to keep himself the Master of Gallegos from day to day. As that man he was devoid of visions. There was no doubt what was real and what was unreal to the newer man. The things of the body were now no longer merely on a par with dreams. They already mostly were, and might soon come to be altogether the whole world in themselves. It was difficult for him to have achieved this. Two things above all helped him to maintain it; intercourse with Neleta and what he poured into himself from a glass. With only a little stimulant, so far, he could attain for the time being what seemed at least to be a solid basis of personality. Indeed, it was more than that, it was the sensation of a complete unity, of being absolutely physical. Tobacco soothed and allayed; wine stimulated and completed. Neleta was beyond all this, Neleta was indescribable consummation of the flesh alone. He did not need to think about her. He consumed with her. Neleta was fire.

On the evening upon which the captain of *La Fortuna* had been bidden to dine Anthony had finally decided to bring this fire to burn openly as it were upon his own hearth. The girl had so far lived, ostensibly at least, with her brother Ferdinando in the factor's house below. She was now to be the mistress of the new residence, and of its master, to run the domestic side of the establishment, and to provide what Anthony had found only she could provide. It was not the nice moral code of the Grain Coast which had hitherto prevented this arrangement from being consummated openly. It was only the hope on the part of Ferdinando that his sister might marry a ship's captain and leave Africa, and a certain lingering reluctance in Anthony to take on any open obligations when there was no necessity for doing so. But Neleta had become necessary and he was now about to admit it. He shook off the recollection of Angela's "marriage breakfast" which occurred to him as they sat down to Neleta's supper. It had taken several glasses of Constantia to effect that.

"It is a 'wyn' which the Dutch raise on the Cape, captain, better I think than Malaga. Certainly it is stronger," he remarked as they sat down to supper. "I secured a whole legger of the Drakenstein of ninety-five for thirty pounds!" and he filled the captain's glass for the third time before the meal from a squat, marble-coloured magnum.

Under the urge of the sunny spirit imprisoned there, which was now released around the whole table, the captain's reservations vanished. The manner of the strange señor inglés became more cordial, he observed, as the meal advanced. His host, as it were, became more and more at home in his own house.

"You see, Don Ruiz, we manage to be fairly comfortable here on the Rio Pongo. We are not such terrible people as rumour, I hear, sometimes paints us."

"I have already discerned that," replied the captain. "Green turtles are not the only attraction on the Grain Coast. Other things also go

into making one's soup palatable here, I observe." He smiled, looking at Neleta at the table's end, with more admiration than respect.

"A great deal of sherry," murmured Anthony. "It gives a certain
dryness which I mightily like."

The captain somewhat hastily returned to the former subject.

"I am really better prepared to find things as they are than you
might suspect, señor. Our friend Carlo Cibo was quite glowing in
his accounts of your establishment here. Under ordinary circumstances I would not put *La Fortuna* into the slave trade. She is a very
fine ship . . ."

"So I am informed," Anthony interrupted. "Carlo was equally
glowing in his accounts of *La Fortuna*. I might add that we are both
grateful, captain, at having a ship like *La Fortuna,* and a responsible
and understanding man like yourself, come out to Gallegos. When
we began here we had to put up with what we could get. At that time,
about three years ago, the captain-general seized what ships he could
at Havana and sent them along. Some of the specimens of both
human and naval architecture which came to the Rio Pongo then would
make your eyes hang out on your shirt. As soon as I could I protested vigorously. Most of the losses in this business are through
stupidity. Brutality and dirt! There is no need for either. 'Send
me fast ships with intelligent officers and I will double your profits,'
I wrote home. 'Charter them if necessary. What is the use of throwing your cargoes into the sea?' It was a long time, however, before
they could understand my arithmetic. So I can honestly say, that it is
very gratifying to see a ship like *La Fortuna* riding at anchor here
and to be able to entertain her captain as a gentleman deserves. I
trust you will find your errand thoroughly worth while. *To your
return,* Captain Matanza."

Don Ruiz clicked glasses and with evident satisfaction.

"To you, señor, and—to the lady," he replied rising to the occasion.

They all drank to Neleta, standing, Brother François and Ferdinando, too. Anthony was thankful to them and Neleta radiant. Across
the table her sibilant monosyllables came bidding the captain welcome
to Gallegos graciously enough.

"Thou art a Catalan! . . . señorita?" he exclaimed.

Anthony overlooked his familiar address. It would not do to press
things too far—probably no harm was meant.

"My father was from Barcelona, señor."

"Ah, then you know the Rambla there, perhaps?"

"Very well, indeed, I have played along it often. When I was five
years old my father took me and my brother to live there. We *lived*
for five years."

"You are dark for a Catalan, señorita. There are many blondes in

Barcelona, but mostly the plump, sleepy kind," he laughed. "Perhaps your mother was from Sevilla? It is there the honey-coloured señoritas are found at their best. Pardon, but I admire them greatly. And you wear the shawl thrown over your arms, too. Ah, it is my admiration which has carried me away. Sí, the women of Valencia are beautiful. But let us talk of Barcelona sometime again, señorita. With the señor's permission, of course!" He added that hastily, having become aware of a sudden drop in the temperature. Ferdinando sat looking into his plate as if there were worms in it. He hated his negro blood.

Neleta murmured some politeness in reply and turned to Brother François. "How were his orphans coming on today?" . . .

"As I was saying, captain," continued Anthony, engaging that gentleman's somewhat reluctant attention again, "we shall look forward to your returning here often. Now if you will follow my method of storing your cargoes and taking care of them on the voyage home, you will find them in better health when you arrive than when you leave here. It will also keep your ship sweet and clean and I have persuaded Cibo to offer a higher bounty for a healthy shipment delivered in prime shape. He can well afford to do that out of the higher price they will bring. Due to the invention of a cotton-picking machine I hear there is now a great demand in North America for sturdy field hands."

The captain now began to prick up his ears.

"The hunters up-country have been instructed this time to bring down as many Gora warriors as they can round up. I should tell you that we gather our cargoes here in three or four ways. I depend still for the most part on the caravans of slaves which the Mohammedans bring down from the interior about the end of the dry season. You get all kinds from them, good and bad. But you can never be sure. So this year I have also organized some raids of my own under an Arab by the name of Ali Bongo, who is an excellent man. They are working now in virgin country north of the St. Pauls among the Gora forest people. They are a very fine race, totally unlike these ugly coast niggers, the Krus and Gubos, Putus, Sikons and whatnot. The Gora are lighter in colour, of pleasing, almost European features. The lips, of course! They make excellent servants and respond to good treatment. I hope to make up your cargo for the most part from them. My friend Mongo Tom across the bay there works all the local country about here and up and down the coast. By a special arrangement I take them off his hands. Between us we control all the trade on the river. There are also other ways of gathering slaves as you shall see before you go. You will probably have to lie here two or three weeks as the barracoons are practically empty now and you have arrived before the caravans. In that time, if you will, you can pick up a good deal of information about the best method of handling your people on the return voyage. It would be to our mutual advantage, certainly greatly to your own, if you will condescend to profit by our experience. A dirty ship and silly crowding, for instance, can cut profits in half."

"Your able factor has already been telling me things, señor," said the captain. "I can well believe there are tricks in this trade as in any other."

"Ferdinando *is* an excellent man," said Anthony in a low tone. "I back him to the limit. At the same time, captain, if you feel obliged to come to me about anything, please be at liberty to do so. You will find me reasonable, and close-mouthed. I run the place and no one else."

"Thank you for that, señor. You know the chief difficulty a ship master has is with agents and subordinates from whom there is no appeal except . . ." He made a coin-counting motion.

"You do not need to fear that here, Don Ruiz."

The captain raised his brows a little and smiled. "At least you can count on me to follow out your suggestions and learn what I can," he continued. "I am genuinely anxious to do so. My great pride, señor, is my ship. *La Fortuna,* ah, she is *beautiful!*" His face lit up as when he had been speaking of the women of Seville a few minutes before. "I would not have her filthy, have her smell, her beautiful feathers all smeared, fah!" He held his nose. "I have seen slavers that way. But cargoes are hard to come by now with this cursed war on. I come here only because I must. Ah, pardon me, I forget, but I do not criticize, señor. Not you! We all make our living as we must in this world, not as we should like. It is my ship! I . . ."

Anthony laid his hand on the man's arm. He had found out what the man honoured most. "A ship is not the worst God in the world," he thought, "especially when she is a goddess."

"Come," said he. "You are from Toledo I am told—of the family Matanza! Do you remember this? It is luck that we have it—the last ship in . . ." he drew the cork carefully and filled the captain's glass. The captain sipped.

"Peralta, señor, Dios de Dios! You will be offering me trout from the Tagus next. Ah, that tinge like a remembrance of muscat, the smell of it! It *is* Toledo." He closed his eyes. "I can see the Puerto del Sol! Did you ever see the women of Toledo? They walk in black satin slippers over the sharp, sharp little paving stones there. And their arches never touch them. Firm little bridges over a million sharp diamonds! Toledo!" He opened his eyes looking a little foolish. The wine was gone.

Anthony filled his glass again.

"Gracia, gracia."

"A La Fortuna, sí?" said Anthony.

"Ah, Madre de Dios, señor," murmured the captain draining the
second glass of Peralta. "Thou understandest!"

Anthony laughed and the captain hastened to explain.

"It is a relief to find things so." He spread out his hands in a
gesture of glad acceptance. "Of Africa and the trade I have heard
terrible things. True, your Cibo was persuasive, and *La Fortuna* was
lying idle. But I would scarcely have risked her, no, I am sure I
would not have come if I had not been asked by Cibo to see the last
cargo you sent landed. Madre! the ship, that little *San Pablo* was
clean and the niggers all well and dancing. It made me laugh to see
them. They were so glad to be in Cuba. You should have been there.
They were each given a red cap and a blanket. They forgot all about
their friends and country, dancing about like monkeys and putting on
new clothes wrong side before. Imagine it! When a cart came they
were overwhelmed by the horses. They did not know beasts could be
made to work. Then a black postilion in a silver laced hat, sky-blue
coat, and white breeches came riding up. They could never get
through feeling his polished jack-boots, and watching him leap on
and off his prancing horse while his spurs rang. He cracked his whip
and told them what a fine thing it was to be a slave of the white man.
And they believed him. It was better than anything they had ever
known. They all ran to snap fingers with their lucky brother. And
the prices they brought next day at the sale! Ah! but in some ways
that was *not* so good. The women will cry for their children." He
ended looking a little grave.

"I have no doubt what you say is true," said Anthony. "I have
never seen any of my cargoes landed in Havana but I know what kind
of a life they leave here, captain, and there is no doubt that they go
to a better place in Cuba. You see what most people forget is that
these people are already slaves in Africa. They have been captured in
war, or seized for debts, or condemned as criminals or for witchcraft.
Any excuse is enough to make a man or woman a slave here. The
powerful chiefs regard the weak or unfortunate as just so much walking capital and they draw their interest by putting them to work. It
is the way that this part of the world not only does business but exists
and it always has been that way. On the whole, the life they go to on
any plantation run by Europeans in America is better than what they
leave here. They are safer, more comfortable. Even their hardships
are comparative luxuries. The English, I believe, are the worst
masters. Jamaica, they say, is a bad place to go, even worse for a
slave than Africa."

Anthony looked up to catch a smile on Ferdinando's face.

"Señor Adverse is eloquent sometimes, captain," said the factor. "He should add that there would not be nearly so many slaves captured if it were not for the temptations the white man brings in the way of goods."

"Yes," said Anthony a little reluctantly, "that is true. It is curious to think that after all it is the desire of the European merchants to sell cloth, firearms, rum, and various manufactured articles that makes men slavers here. That, and the necessity for cheap labour in America and the West Indies. That is what makes the New World go."

"Go where?" interrupted Brother François who had been talking to Neleta.

"Ah, father, I will not argue with you tonight," laughed Anthony. "You are not a trader. The father is opposed to all this," he explained. "He spends his time here making it as easy as he can for those who are gathered in by the raiders. I will show you his good works tomorrow. They are, well—remarkable. I co-operate, you know. That is all I *can* do." He frowned a little. "Try some of this Arab stew, captain. It is curried lamb with rice balls seethed in milk. Do!" He heaped Don Ruiz's plate for him and refilled his glass.

The captain and Ferdinando now devoted themselves to their plates and sundry items of commercial news. Brother François had fallen silent, Anthony observed. Neleta ate quietly. Only in her eating did she betray her native origin, everything was managed with a spoon and two fingers. With apparently no effort she simply made her food disappear as if by sleight of hand.

Anthony sat looking at her at the other end of the table momentarily forgetful of everything but the coming night that they would spend together. It had been a long time now! Occasionally her eyes, that shone in the candles with a greenish flare, looked out at him from under her long black lashes. From time to time they lightened like a leopard's half concealed in moonlight. The spidery-silk fringes of a Manila shawl drooped from her tawny arms and its embroidered magenta roses seemed to clamber over her breast and shoulders as if a tropical vine had found a strong, lithe young tree to flaunt itself upon in some open glade of the jungle. Under the shadow of her yellow bodice her breast rose and fell slowly with a deep visible motion that timed with a slight widening of her keen nostrils or a flash of her large white teeth.

The colours that the girl wore would have overpowered most European women; they would have been bizarre. But there was something so vivid about Neleta, so brilliantly passionate and virile without a hint of nervousness, that the magenta roses in the gleaming white shawl and the golden yellow of her dress were reduced by her to the equivalent of more sombre tones. What she put on, she made a part of her. Yet she triumphed over what she wore, for through the folds of her shawl and the yellow silk of her dress her body shone with even more luminous curves and lines.

Neleta was the crown of all this new life Anthony had carved out of the forest and seized for himself. She was the walking answer— and how she could walk!—to the objections expressed and understood which Brother François—that the mere presence of Brother François—constantly posed.

It was still a puzzle to Anthony how Brother François could still disapprove of him and yet be affectionate and kindly. Indeed, it was the affection in his disapproval that was hardest to stand. But he would forget all that—tonight! After he had gone over the ship's mail and the invoices with Ferdinando—then—then he would give himself to Neleta. It was like that. He would give himself to her. She would be waiting.

He leaned his head on his hand looking at her with the strong, calm glow of wine thoroughly upon him. In the light of the candles and of the palm-oil lamps, where cotton wicks floated throwing a mellow glow through the calabash rinds, the room swam with a soft suffused pallor while Cheecha and her assistant girls came and went silently on bare feet like ministering shadows. One side of the place was screened from the court by long strips of white muslin sewn together and on this he could see the shadows of palm fronds moving in the moonlight. The spring gurgled in its stone basin beyond. The red-striped native pottery stood out above the table-cloth in startling patterns, and the faces and voices of his guests seemed hazy and distant as he lost himself inwardly in a dream of contented approval, wordless, and imageless except for what lay vaguely before him. It was a feeling of satisfaction and equilibrium that he would allow no thoughts to mar.

It was Neleta who finally motioned to him. The others had finished. She and Brother François left. Ferdinando dumped the mail pouch on the table. With a bundle of black cigars before them they spread out various papers and got down to the business of the evening.

Anthony set aside the bundles of newspapers in various languages which Cibo assiduously collected for him from ships' captains at Havana. They would serve to while away many a tedious afternoon during the rainy season, although some of them were nearly a year old.

The business of being a slaver, Don Ruiz could see, was an intricate one. Indeed, Anthony's long hours spent with accounts, correspondence, and invoices at the Casa da Bonnyfeather now stood him in good stead. Most of the slavers on the Coast, he discovered, had failed largely because they kept no books. They were always in debt when they closed out, or they got careless and turned over the warehouses to clerks who robbed them. Gallego had left his keys to the old woman in charge of his harem. Ferdinando had been helpless under her pilfering. Anthony had shipped her off to Cuba as he did not wish to be poisoned. She had gone aboard ship foaming. The rest of the seraglio had departed with her. It had been a memorable day. He grinned remembering it, while he ran his eye over the statement of the last voyage which Cibo had sent him.

Carlo Cibo, Agent, Regla, Havana, Cuba, to the Master of Gallegos on the Rio Pongo of the Grain Coast, Africa.

Voyage Statement of the Schooner *San Pablo,* 90 tons burthen, Miguel Gomez, Master

1. Out Costs

Fitting Out:

New sails and extras	956.43$
Carpenter's bill	1,005.00
Cooper's bill	684.22
Provisions:	
For crew	784.90
For slaves (on return trip)	560.21
Wages Advanced:	
18 men before the mast @ 50$	900.00
To captain, mate, boatswain, cook, and steward	440.00
Trade Goods:	
Muslins, muskets, powder, lead, cigars, copper wire, beads, trinkets, mirrors, rum and 500 Maria Teresa dollars, etc.	9,849.60
Gratifications:	
To Port Officials	150.00
Clergy for blessing the ship	25.00
Police	200.00
Governor's Secretary	50.00
To owners for use of ship during temporary sequestration	1,200.00
	16,805.36$
Commission to Señor Carlo Cibo @ 10%	1,680.54
Total for voyage out	18,485.90$

2. Costs Return Voyage

Wages:

Captain	225.00$
First Mates	175.00
Second Mates	125.00
Boatswains	90.00
Cooks' and Stewards'....................	257.00
17 men before the mast..................	1,872.00

Head-Money:

Captain's @ 3$ a head...................	681.00
Mate's @ 2$ a head.....................	454.00
Other ship's officers @ 1$ a head........	454.00
Water casks and medicines purchased from ship *Mercedes* at sea on return voyage.............	83.50
Total for voyage home..................	4,416.50$

3. Charges at Havana

Captain-General's honorarium	1,000.00$
Gratification Herr Herman Meyier.........	500.00
Gratification Clerks at Caxà da Consolidación..........	155.00
Havana pilot	10.00
Wharfage	25.00
Subsistence of slaves on shore before sale.........	136.00
227 slave dresses @ 2$...................	454.00
Mid-wife's fee at lazeretto (twins)........	2.00
Coffin for mother	5.00
Hire of wench for wet nurse..............	1.50
Sundries, purser's cash disbursements, and all extras.....	984.60
Sale announcements and barkers-up........	32.00
Auctioneer's fee at 2%..................	1,422.92
Total charges at Havana................	4,728.02$
Total all expenses......................	27,630.42$

4. Returns

Proceeds of 221 slaves at auction.............	71,146.00$
Proceeds of 5 female slaves by private view sales.........	2,730.00
Proceeds twin infants born Havana...............	20.00
Proceeds gold dust, ivory, and palm oil................	18,124.00
	92,020.00$

RÉSUMÉ

Total proceeds slaves and cargo............. 92,020.00$
Total all expenses........................... 27,630.42

                Net profit on voyage................... 64,389.58$
J. Garvin, Clerk.

. . . You will see by this [Cibo's letter ran on] that business is not half bad. There is a great dearth here of slaves due to the disturbed state of commerce since hostilities began, and healthy ones especially bring large prices. The Yankee brush with France has blown over and there has been an influx of Yankee bidders for the Carolina rice plantations and the Virginia cotton and tobacco fields. Bueno! What do you think—your Jew tailor bought the twins and is raising them in his back patio. All Havana is laughing at him. Like most Shylocks he has a soft spot in a hard heart. His Excellency is also in a seventh heaven over additions to his revenue. I have, mon vieux, arranged to split with the government on this cargo, their share three-quarters net proceeds on the slaves. In other words, you receive 11,566.40$ as all expenses are charged against the slaves, and the government gets the remainder. This does not, of course, touch the proceeds from the gold, ivory, etc., as that is disposed of quietly on the side and is no one's business but our own. You will therefore get a total of 29,690.40$, less my 10% consignment commission which you must admit, as a fellow mammalian, I deserve. I am forwarding by a sure carrier your share of these cargoes to *Messers Baring Bros. Co.,* as you requested a year ago, and I enclose the bills of exchange on London. I suggest that you write them to put part of your now snug little fortune at interest. Not all of it. The world sometimes turns upside down and only those with light, liquid assets float to the top again. Now as to "La Fortuna"—I have chartered her. She is not sequestrated.

An excellent large ship with a decent captain whom experience has educated. Trust him—distrustfully. I told you of him elsewhere but I am glad to have secured him. His ship is large and fast, which cuts costs in the end, and will make fewer voyages necessary. You can load twice as many niggers as on a small schooner. I have laid out heavily in the trade goods "La Fortuna" brings you, and followed your advice carefully. You should find everything you requested except the muskets which are now at premium in Europe. I send you instead brandy, rum, and blankets. You will have to do as best you can with the Mexican silver dollars; no Austrian are to be had. Blame Buonaparte. You will also find your pineapple cuttings. Let me know how they thrive. I prophesy that the chief monument of your existence will in a few years be pineapples in Africa. A sugary epitaph shall be thine—but who will remember even if it is in every mouth? The only lasting good we accomplish is when we play with nature. All else is vanity. I have another baby, the nineteenth. According to Father Trajan God never runs out of souls, and I am built like a bull. Happy, happy world!

By the way, do not neglect to look in the little satin box in the purser's pouch. A lady at the palace was *most particular* about it. She has asked me twice about you. Why don't you write her? You neglect your opportunities, I swear. Or are you comforted? How did you find Cheecha? You do not say. When do you come to Havana again? Never? Your chair on the veranda yawns for you. Send me some words of affection, my boy, I grow old—and lonely. It is the fate of old bulls. Adiós then till anon, thine.

CARLO.

Regla, the 7th of January, A. D. 1799.

As he leaned back reading this he could almost feel Carlo's warm, fat hand grasping his own. But the date chilled him. Two months ago now! How far away it all was! No, he had never written Dolores. Somehow he couldn't. He undid the little box Cibo had spoken of and sprung back the lid. A pair of carnelian cuff links, nothing else; no writing. He closed the box again and after a while put it aside. He would send her an ivory comb.

Ferdinando and the captain were busy checking invoices. A discrepancy had arisen over two kegs of biscuit. Bother! "Charge it to my account, Ferdinando." The factor did so, saying nothing. "A curious man," thought Anthony. His negro blood made no difference. He was an accountant. All he cared for was to balance his accounts. His sister was not that way, thank God! Neleta! It was too heavy a mail to finish tonight. He would only read a few more letters, some from Livorno. The rest could be finished—mañana.

He bade the captain and Ferdinando good night.

"Tomorrow we can go over the place together. It has been a pleasure, Don Ruiz. Let me know if there is anything you need. Call on me! The factor will see you aboard. Certainly, I shall be glad to convey your compliments to the señorita . . . Ah! thank you! I heartily agree." The ass, if he only knew! Would he never go?

The house seemed silent as their voices died away down the hill. From a beam overhead a little wood dust trickled down on the table.

White ants again! They must have been in the wood. He would
have to remove that. The devil! He shook the dust off a letter a little
savagely and opened it. McNab's writing.

> . . . the maister canna hold the pen the noo. His hands be
> sair twisted and he walks seldom. It gars him sair ye dinna come
> hame. He says to me—"write and say—'There is plenty for you
> here. Do not tarry too long. I would see you again, my son.
> That would be better than the monies you send. I commend you
> nevertheless for your care in that. Come home. The house is
> dark without you.'"
> I say amen to that, Maister Anthony. We (mysel', Mr. Tous-
> saint, and that *faithful* woman) are still here. I draw salary for
> nothing. Mr. B. is lying in the great bed as I write. He spends
> much time there. All of it soon. Do ye ken what I mean? Cap-
> tain Bittern of the "Unicorn" has taken many prizes. We keep
> that quiet. My accounts await your return. Young Mr. Vincent
> Nolte calls for news of you oftener than we have it. I trust your
> health continues as mine does, and will last you home.
>
> Your humble obd't servant,
> WILLIAM McNAB.

"Home, come home!" Would they never cease? Where is home?
Italy and the Casa da Bonnyfeather? All Europe was like the Casa
da Bonnyfeather, he thought, a building with frescoes of old, lovely
dreamful things fading and flaking off its walls, where forgotten gods
feasted on oblivion overhead, and little men crawled underneath keeping accounts and writing letters about things; where Toussaints sat
forever at desks and dreamed hopelessly of love, and mumbled of freedom and of golden savages, and ate their hearts out and were afraid
of themselves. Go back to that? Go back to the Villa Brignole and
Father Xavier; to the dead gardens under the moon and the music of
the crazy woman; that opera that would never be sung?

He did not belong to all that. He belonged to a different and better time, something that he remembered had brooded in the court of
the convent about the fountain; something that the bronze boy was
remembering as he looked at the water, that the leaves of the great tree
and the pigeons had spoken of before Father Xavier came and explained it away as only a reflection in the fountain, a dream.

It had been real once. In the villages of Italy on those morning
drives with Angela he had caught glimpses of it, a world that remained
in fragments; that let itself be seen by segments out of the corner of a
wise young eye. It was the world he had found once with Angela;
once, too late, a lost world. He could not "go back" to it. He would

have to find it, or make it here. Here in the forest where the germens of it remained.

He leaned forward a little over the table, seeing nothing but light, and resting his chin on his hands. It seemed to him that he understood at last what the bronze boy by the fountain had gone blind looking for in the ceaseless, monotonous changefulness of the water that flowed past him like time.

It was what he himself was going blind looking for in the waters of change that flowed past him forever and forever, the mysterious fluid of events that looked so clear as it dashed for a moment into the sunshine, streaming from some mysterious source and flowing ever in one direction on into the unknown. Yes, it was *like* that.

He himself might be the other bronze boy, the missing twin who had disappeared from his brother's side by the fountain ages ago. Perhaps he was? Perhaps, he had only come back again to watch the water for a while. Perhaps, that bright vision of the beautiful playmate, the boy whose face was in the fountain, the child who had lain amid the branches and talked with him was real. Perhaps, he had been talking with himself then after all. Who knows who I am? What knows? And who cares! . . .

The lovely madonna that had visited him that night with Angela, she might have cared, would have . . . but no more. In his being he knew he would never find her again. With Neleta all was dark as he lay—nothing there but his frame. But that remained! That *remained!* He would enjoy all he had left; prove to himself he was still alive . . . feel. Wine! He poured himself another glass.

The candles had long burned out now, even the palm-oil lamp was waning. He rose and swept aside the letters—from the world of cobwebs. Mañana! What did they matter? He blew out the light. The distant howling-boom from the forests seemed to fill the chamber. It was always stronger on moonlight nights. He breathed heavily in the darkness, listening. The little owls in the orchard below kept bubbling. Somewhere a mouse shrieked. But beyond these shrill, near noises constantly rose and fell, now in high chorus and now in shattered undertones, the voice of the fathomless jungles that surrounded Gallegos; the roaring of crocodiles in the valley below, the far-off trumpeting of herds of elephants, the howling of monkeys hurling themselves along their treetop avenues through the moonlight, going nowhere. At Bangalang someone was comforting himself with a tom-tom. The throb of it rather than the sound came, a dim pulsation in the wind. The stridulous cry of quadrillions of insects made

the night quiver. He stood and trembled with it. Like a dancer lend-
ing himself to irresistible music he gave himself to what seemed to be
a tune remembered by his bones and muscles rather than his mind.
The frame of him swayed to it. The warm air from the patio bathed
him luxuriously and wandered under his loose clothes. He let them
fall to the floor listlessly and enjoyed the stimulating, soft freshness
of it caressing him from head to foot where he stood. The rank, male
flowers of hundreds of papayas in the plantations below imparted a
tang to the breeze as if lemon blossoms were being crushed by his feet.

He kicked the clothes under the table, and enjoyed the silent tread
of his bare feet while gliding down the corridor to his room at the
end of it. There was not a sound in the house now. Cheecha and
her girls slept in the wing on the other side of the court. The main
door locked itself and closed by a weight. Surprises in this country
might be final and fatal. He had tried to eliminate surprises by insects, animals, and men. Only the terrible or ingenious succeeded in
finding privacy in Africa. There was a certain fascination in having
attained it against the entire scheme of things; in maintaining a successful defence against a perpetual siege. When he entered the room,
completely at ease about his understood isolation with the woman who
shared it with him, Neleta was asleep.

She lay on a light couch which she had pulled out from a corner and
placed for coolness close to the rush screen that formed the wall of the
apartment where it opened upon the court. Through this the moonlight penetrated covering part of the floor with a carpet of small parallels of light and shade and the walls with a dim pallor. She lay breast
down, coverless, with her head resting lightly on one arm flung easily
before her as if she had been swimming in the river of night and had
paused in her stroke to dream awhile and float down its tide. The
curious effect of parallel black stripes and silver fell obliquely across
her honey-coloured hips.

Although he was already tense with the certainty and anticipation
of finding her awaiting him, this peculiar pattern of light and shadow
with its background assumed for Anthony—as soon as it arranged
itself before his eyes where he stood naked in the dim centre of the
room—that supreme importance which the state of fire always has
everywhere in the universe. All that he was, all the world about him
seemed to be drawn on a hurrying wind into the living symbol before
him and to be sublimed there.

The meaning of that symbol was to be understood only in terms of
feeling. With it the individual mind of Anthony had little or nothing
to do. For him the gears of existence were shifted automatically by
the signal of Neleta's naked hips from the secondary and rational
order of existence into the primary and material. To it his own part

of the alphabet of the eternal word answered convincingly. Matter was about to get the necessary business of its preservation in a certain form accomplished, and the means to this end now violently emanated heat as a preliminary to the process. Anthony was aware of all this. He did not think of it in so many sentences as he stood for a minute looking upon Neleta asleep in the barred moonlight; he apprehended it all as though it were expressible in one deep-breathed word, the exquisite hieroglyphic of which was the form of the woman before him with all her secrets bare.

The meaning of it was action, the supreme action upon which all other acts depend. Perhaps the only thought he had as he moved through the moony twilight to consummation was a realization that only by the addition of his own body to hers could the letter of the word be made complete. But this realization could scarcely be termed a thought, for the primal knowledge of it was accompanied by so intense a glow of pleasure that it was completely resolved in feeling alone.

He shifted her head slightly and she awoke looking up at him half dreamfully, contentedly settling herself in her nest face down. He put his arms about her, locking his hands on her breasts and letting his weight come upon her. She sighed fondly, and locked her legs about his own.

The union of Anthony and Neleta was physically a complete one. It was that of a mature man and woman who were together often; who knew what was to be expected of each other, and how to act. Neither had any doubt of self and each was wholly absorbed for the time being in the other. In this way they were able for considerable intervals of time to escape completely from themselves and to become another which was both of them. Theirs was not that ghastly wraith of love summoned forth from the grave of the body by friction to die feebly with nervous gasps and hatred, nor was it the spasmodic wriggling of curious younglings interested in experimenting with themselves. They were not furtively surprised at last by a really intense, final throb of pleasure. Nor was one completed suddenly and the other left desperate. Once having given themselves to each other, everything else was taken care of for them by forces over which they had, and desired to have, no control. Indeed, the supreme contentment of it all was that once locked together all that followed was involuntary. They participated in and became one in another impersonal self. The reward of obedience to the will of that self beyond them was a long continued and increasing ecstasy that just upon the verge of becoming unbearable blessedly relieved itself and left them to rest in each other's arms.

In the morning they would wake to see that the sun was making a golden pattern through the screen where that of the moon had been silver the night before. They would hear Cheecha and her maids moving about in the courtyard beyond with that peculiar rippling quality of sunlight in the tones of their talk and laughter that only the morning voices of Africans can convey. They would get up quietly without saying much, and giving each other a kiss of peace and happiness, would put on some light clothes and go out to breakfast in the courtyard.

After that the housegate was unbarred, the bridge of steps let down over the little "ant-moat" before the veranda, and the work of the day began. Neleta busied herself with the house and its keeping, in all the generously supplied details of which she took an immense and efficient pleasure. Anthony found himself pleasantly overwhelmed by a thousand details that in the voluble persons of blacks, whites, and yellows clambered for immediate attention and decisions of considerable moment to many souls. He used the cool morning hours diligently.

On the morning after the supper with Captain Matanza of *La Fortuna* the "barkers" came in from the hill country, saying they had persuaded a large Arab caravan to come and trade at Gallegos. All was instantly in rapid preparation for its advent. To give certain direction to the guides, and to honour the approaching Arab mongo, or chieftain, one of the cannons began to fire at regular intervals.

CHAPTER FORTY-ONE

A GLIMPSE INTO THE FURNACE

"IT IS quite unusual for a caravan to be coming to us at this time of year," Anthony remarked to the captain as they sat smoking together on the dock, watching *La Fortuna's* cargo being whipped out of her hatches under the active superintendence of Juan. The squall of the winches and the shouts of the crew working block-and-tackle came over the water. Several large boats and rafts plied back and forth. The morning was sticky-hot and the river valley breathless. In the brown water the velvet shadows of the barracoons wavered sullenly as the boats passed. Anthony removed his wide palm hat from time to time to mop his face.

"Like bronze beginning to sweat in the fire," thought Don Ruiz, who had seen cannon melted, "just when the first drops begin to run. After a while the metal collapses—suddenly." He was feeling like a rag himself this morning; inclined to be weakly reminiscent. He found it hard to be interested in anything.

"Oh," said he, "I thought caravans just kept coming." He looked faint. Anthony laughed and passed him a flask . . . They both felt brighter now . . .

"No, usually they get here in November when the dry season begins. *La Fortuna* is the magnet now. You see some time ago I sent barkers with special inducements to one of the chief Foulah mongos back in the hill-country, the Ali Mami of Futa-Jaloon. He is an Arab ruler who lords it over a great reach of territory stretching, I do not know how far, north-and-east up toward Timbo. The boys who returned this morning tell me the old scoundrel has been raiding far-and-wide and has sent down his nephew, one Amah-de-bellah, in charge of a big caravan.

"Amah, by the way, is a very intelligent and pleasant young Mussulman; black, but a gentleman according to his lights. I have had some amicable and profitable dealings with him before. Indeed, he is anxious to convert me to his own faith and has even invited me to visit his uncle's capital. I may do it yet.

"But come, they will not be here for several hours yet—have another pull at this—helps, eh? . . . Well, we might as well see what is going on and get you familiar with Gallegos. I make it a habit to go over the place every morning." He shoved his hat back on his head. They rose, and chatting together, strolled down the dock into the big warehouse.

"We rebuilt this after a fire when I first came," Anthony explained. "The smaller buildings up the slope are for storage, too. It is a good idea not to have all of one's cocoanuts on one tree, you know. This shed is where the actual trading goes on, however."

In the grateful shadow of the place the captain now looked about him with considerable interest.

The building was a long barn-like structure with lofts. The ceiling was provided with trap doors. These were now hanging open, and various bulky packages of trade-goods were being lowered in preparation for the approaching caravan. A bolt of striped cloth suddenly escaped from someone's hands in the loft above and streamed down out of the darkness like a flapping serpent. Cries and shrieks of raucous laughter arose. Half the Kru boys on the floor stopped trundling bales to help rewind the cloth. They got tangled in it. It took Ferdinando with a cane to restore order.

Nevertheless, the shed continued to hum with excitement, loud talk, songs, whistling, and a rhythmic stamping as the luxuriant cargo of *La Fortuna* rolled in from the dock and was hoisted into the lofts or trundled to the opposite end of the building. There was an air of triumph about it; the sheer joy of the Ethiopian at being surrounded by plenty and largesse permeated the place. The Kru boys whooped. A trolley on a travelling pulley ran from one end of the shed to the other and was whisking back and forth, dangling a net full of bales and clinging black boys who screamed with delight at the spinal thrill of an aerial ride. Like large liver-coloured flies their bodies seemed struggling in a vast spider web as they passed through the grotesque shadows of the beams and windows that barred the place with transverse shadows and shafts of light. The air danced with dust in a thousand sun pencils, and the captain now saw rather than heard the sound that permeated the whole atmosphere, for the very motes in the air were leaping to the low but swift and nervous lilt of drums. Gay and humorous greetings met the two as they continued along the warehouse floor, the captain's brass buttons, fat legs and skin-tight trousers causing many an eye to roll back till it showed as white as the grin beneath it.

"Merry enough!" said Don Ruiz who was now feeling the effects of a half-pint of brandy.

"It is the only way to get things done in a hurry here," replied Anthony, "songs, and excitement. If you get the right beat going you can move mountains." He pointed to two youngsters at the door working away delightedly at small hand-drums. A blue-black Mandingo buck shuffled by doing a slide-and-slap under a mountainous bale.

Don Ruiz burst into a laugh. In the fellowship of humour the man roared back like a gorilla.

"These stevedores and boatmen are all Mohammedans hired from near-by coastal villages; mostly Krus," continued Anthony. "It pays. Their wages are less than what slaves would manage to steal."

They stopped for a moment at the extreme end of the shed in a railed-off space. Here under the eyes of Ferdinando chests were being opened; bale covers were being ripped off and the contents spread out for display or heaped in convenient piles while two armed Foulahs watched every move.

"Samples, here," said Anthony. "The chief traders, and petty chiefs make their choice out of this stuff. But we can't linger too long now. Come this way."

They stepped out of the factor's office, already brilliant with striped cloths, brass jewelry, and rolls of copper wire, into a long porch covered by half-transparent tarpaulins slushed with beeswax. The place basked in a kind of amber glow. There was a wide, beaten-clay floor under the awning, several stone blocks with rings in them, an X-shaped whipping post. A low bench provided with mats for squatting extended the whole length of the place.

"The slaves are stood up and examined here before the goods are paid over. I watch that myself."

"Do you use the post much?" asked Don Ruiz.

"Not often, but now and again," said Anthony. "The captured witch-doctors sometimes need a little nine-tailed magic to convince them. I leave that to Ferdinando. He knows." He passed the black post rather hurriedly. The tarpaulin-covered porch led directly into the first of the barracoons that lined the water front for some distance beyond it.

The barracoons were long sheds built of heavy, hardwood timbers flat on two sides and driven into the ground so closely together that not even a knife-blade could be inserted between them. A wide opening in the roof for air and sunlight extended down the centre. The space for each slave was marked off with whitewashed lines on the stone so that the floor in its semi-gloom looked like a board upon which some giant game might be played with pieces six feet by four. Each space was provided with shackles to keep a pawn from moving itself, however, and there was a wooden pillow, a stool, and two earthen pots in every "square." A more lavishly furnished corner screened by mats with small, round windows in them marked where the two overseers kept watch.

Four of these barracoons, each with its number given in red strokes on the door, lay separated by about a twenty-yard interval. But they were so disposed that each formed one side of a square. The intervals between were heavily barricaded. At Gallegos there were two of these inclosed squares or slave pens.

"For the most part we shackle the slaves only at night," said Anthony. "In the day they exercise in these yards if the weather permits. That keeps the barracoons from getting musty. We feed them up well, make them bathe often, and get them fattened up for the voyage."

"Why, you could house a regiment here!" exclaimed Don Ruiz.

"Yes? Well, as a matter of fact, in the last three or four years several regiments have passed through them. Did it ever strike you, captain, that a large part of the New World will inevitably be rather African? Hundreds of shiploads of these black people have been going west now for hundreds of years. And Africa is now being poured out into America and the islands faster than ever before. Yet they are still calling for more from Boston to Buenos Aires. This war between England and Spain has only put up the price."

"Niggers don't count in America," said the captain tossing away a cigar stump indifferently.

"Each counts one, and they might possibly have children," mused Anthony.

"What the devil do we care!" grunted Don Ruiz. "Isn't it profitable? You yourself seem to be making a pretty good thing out of them. What are you worrying about? And yet, pardon me, but it did seem strange to me, señor—last night I thought of it—that a man like you should be slaving. No offence, of course," he hastened to add. "It was merely a passing thought."

"It *is* strange," replied Anthony laconically, looking about him for a moment as if he found himself in a curiously unexpected place.

The captain grinned. "My mother intended *me* for the priesthood," he said.

"Perhaps mine did, too. Quién sabe? But after all it is what we do that makes us what we are, isn't it?" queried Anthony half to himself.

"Quién sabe?" re-echoed the captain. His eyes also for a moment had become bleak. Suddenly they both recognized each other's look and laughed.

"Exiled, eh," thought Don Ruiz. "Regretful," thought Anthony.

"Try one of these, amigo mio," said the captain producing his cigar case. "These long, black fellows from Havana make one forget. The real leaf! I smoke ten a day. By evening the ground under one's feet becomes velvety. It seems to give a little when you step out. Even the prodding fingers of destiny are made blunt by tobacco. It was discovered just in time. Think what we should be without it! This age is like a busy mother-in-law to a man of feeling. We can no longer marry the world and be happy with it. Madre!" He struck

fire like a craftsman, and they ascended the hill together in a cloud of
blue smoke.

The little gun near the residence was still faithfully banging away
at intervals. There was so little breeze even half-way up the slope
that the yellow powder-smoke drifted slowly in long ribbons through
the plantations. After each explosion the parrots settled back into the
trees again. Anthony paused suddenly beside a small foot-path leading down from the road into a wooded hollow.

"Turn aside here with me for a moment and I'll show you what
you have forgotten," he said. "It is more interesting than the barracoons, I think."

They threaded a small thicket of date palms and fig trees, and soon
disappeared from the road amid the dense shade of an ever-more luxuriant little oasis as the ground grew lower and damper. Already it
was getting cool. Suddenly they came out into an open, palm-lined,
grassy place about an acre in extent. A small stream rushed down it
babbling fondly.

The water gushed out from under a low cliff; raced for a few hundred yards as though frightened by the sunlight, and then disappeared
into the hill again with a surprised gurgle through a rock that parted
its sandy lips to drink it in. They both stooped and drank eagerly
of water so evidently pure from a manless world. Refreshed, they
rose and looked about them.

Before them half a dozen beehive huts were scattered about the oval,
green levels in a rough semi-circle, like straw dwellings of enormous
honey-gatherers. At the upper end of the glade was a Lilliputian
chapel built into the rocky outcrop from which the stream itself sprang.
There was a rude wooden cross before it, large, out of all proportion.
There was even a miniature belfry in which hung an old ship's bell
upon which the sun struck with a single brassy glint in the surrounding ocean of green.

Seated on a stool at the foot of his rood was Brother François in
his now much-faded gown, sandals, and a large planter's hat. There
were nearly a score of young darkies about him. They were repeating
in unison something he was teaching them and the high murmur of
their voices came to the two unobserved onlookers, where they stood
in the shadow of the palms at the edge of the clearing, faintly and
mixed with the responses of the stream—yet with the universal accent
of happy childhood. It instantly reminded Anthony of the fresh gales
of young voices which had sometimes come through the school windows at the convent while the pigeons and fountain talked together

in the court below. It was a sound like the leaves in that lost valley
of the Moselle stirred long ago by a cool morning breeze. He remembered it. For a while both he and the captain forgot their cigars which
accumulated a long ash while they stood watching and listening. Don
Ruiz felt he might wake up at any moment as a boy again in his room
at Toledo with the vocative Tagus gossiping a hundred feet below.

Both men, in fact, found something peculiarly affecting in the little
scene before them.

Yet the sheer reality of it, drenched as it was in the stark, equatorial
sunshine, the vividness of the black children dressed in white cast-off
rice bags lying about their master like so many animated handkerchiefs
on the glassy green of the grass conveyed its own meaning in a deep
and natural tone. It was a bass note in which there was not even the
suggestion of a sentimental tremolo.

On account of the noisy stream neither Anthony nor Don Ruiz
could hear what Brother François was saying nor the children's replies.
But from time to time the man's face shone out from under his hat
when he looked up to speak, and the effect of his words could be seen
by the ripples and wriggles of his small congregation. What he had
to say was evidently something they were glad to hear. But more
than that—it was because he was saying it that they listened.

No one—Anthony felt sure—no one who had not seen the tenderness, that strong and vivid look of affection upon Brother François's
face, could have imagined its gentle strength. When he looked up
and spoke, his features succeeded in their own particular way in giving
a personal and living meaning to the general abstraction called
"mercy."

"Do not disturb him, señor," muttered the captain in a changed
voice. "It is a saint we have seen." He turned as if to go and then
stopped to look back again. They both stood watching farther withdrawn now under the airy groins of some date palms, like cathedral
sightseers, who, blundering upon a service in a side-chapel, had shrunk
back at the thought of disturbing prayers.

It did not seem to Anthony now that Brother François appeared
impotent against the world which surrounded him. What the man
was doing there, what he was, looked permanent. Because his work
was so invincibly humble as to escape notice, it seemed likely that it
might prevail. It had, he thought, the delicate strength of flowers that
perish easily and are constantly being trampled upon, but which succeed nevertheless in transmitting their unchanging pattern of beauty
through aeons of seasons. Suddenly he thought of Father Xavier,
too—

And was instantly reminded of a fossil water-lily that he had once
seen in a cabinet somewhere; the cabinet was dark. Oh, yes—he had

seen it at Maddalena Strozzi's. But he always thought of Brother François and light . . .

What was it he had been thinking about light that day on the *Wampanoag* while Mrs. Jorham had been showing him her sewing? What was it, now? Oh! . . . *said let there be light and there was* . . . *The Word* . . . or something. Well, well—at least the captain too was touched by this scene today, and he was no softy, God knows . . . stole cannon, Cibo said . . .

Now in these dense forests all about Gallegos trees fell but the light beat down and the forest went on. The light healed wounds and scars and nourished seedlings to fill up the places of trees that fell in the forest . . . that fell there and rotted. And all the seedlings struggled up toward the light. Those that couldn't get out of the shade died. But strange things lived in that perpetual shade; their forms were nightmares, horrible . . . no light! "How is it, Anthony, you have been so long a lurker in darkness, a mighty bringer down of trees—and men? Brother François has hidden these children from you." Yes, he always begs for the very young and sickly—"And now look! Why are you crouching here in the shadows . . . afraid of the light?"

"O Mother of . . . !

"Stop! You must remember you cannot say it. Carlo said . . . And I know."

The *boom* of the little gun on the hill above shattered his reverie and the captain's simultaneously.

They turned without saying anything further and took a short-cut up the hill. Their path now led them directly to the foot of the low cliff that hid the small valley from both the road and the residence. Indeed, from the house veranda the valley might not have existed. It might have been merely a dip in the hill over which the eye shot directly to the barracoons below. But just from the top of the rocky outcrop, which otherwise hid it so well, all of it was visible at one glance. The cliff was not high but steep. They stood breathing a moment after the climb and looked down.

They saw the small chapel again and a graveyard with white crosses hidden in the trees, which they had not seen before. There was a surprising number of crosses—considering. Women were moving about the beehive huts with children hanging on their breasts. From rows of banana trees purple blossoms and ripe clusters also depended heavily. It was all intensely green, silent, fruitful. The place seemed to have dropped out of the world into a hollow. For an instant the spell of it clutched at them again. There were no shadows there. High noon . . .

Just then the little bell rang out softly and clearly.

They watched it turn on its wheel. Its clear notes fell out of the silence like quicksilver dropping out of darkness into sheer light. The captain crossed himself automatically. Anthony stopped his own hand just in time. He saw all the children and people below there kneel down. From the chapel came a distant voice. He knew what that man in there was saying—those words—

"God have mercy upon us . . ."

he thought . . .

Suddenly from the hill above came a great shout and the crackle of musketry.

A nasal singing and the mad beating of tom-toms could now be heard emerging from the forest beyond the stockade and getting louder. The little gun began to answer as rapidly as it could.

"Well, captain, your slave caravan has arrived," Anthony said.

"Mine?" laughed Don Ruiz looking a little startled. "You are *too* generous, señor!" They went up again without looking behind them. Anthony thought once that he could still hear the bell. Yet it must have stopped. And hell was to pay about the stockade gate. What a waste of powder!

————————

At the residence all was now in final frantic activity, although Neleta had been actively preparing for the advent of the caravan since early dawn. A portion of the veranda had been screened off with mats and a huge cocoanut rug spread on the floor. Chairs for Anthony and the captain of *La Fortuna,* a prayer rug and a sheepskin for the approaching mongo of the caravan completed the arrangements, except for a half dozen Foulahs armed with flintlocks and cutlasses who now disposed themselves as a guard of honour. Behind the door Neleta stood ready to receive her guests, with Cheecha and the other women slaves. As the honourable mistress of the house, she wore a long embroidered veil over her face and shoulders.

Anthony and the captain had scarcely had time to snatch a cooling drink and seat themselves on the veranda before the battery on the slope below began to fire smoky salvos and the caravan was seen filing through the stockade gate on the hill above. As the nephew of the Ali Mami of Futa-Jaloon, Amah-de-bellah was to be received as a prince of the blood. At the same time the ample defences of Gallegos were also made sufficiently plain.

The procession which now began to unroll itself through the gate and to advance down the slope toward the residence seemed to the unaccustomed eyes of the captain bizarre if not positively weird. So strange were the aspects of the men and beasts who walked and stalked in it that it might have been an embassy from another planet, he thought.

A crowd of painted Mandingo barkers preceded it. They were dressed only in breech-clouts, but armed with the deadliest weapons of noise; enormous oboes that shrieked and grunted like pigs in the flames, cymbals, tom-toms, jar-drums, bull whistles, and gourd rattles on long sticks. These, and fifty other hellish devices, produced an atmospheric disturbance that, added to the salvos from the cannon, raised the wild-fowl from the marshes for miles around. And out of this immense volume of sibilant, wheezy, roaring, and brassy noises combined throbbed a continuous syncopated undertone of drumming and rattling to which the mob of naked heralds advanced shuffling and stamping; meanwhile howling out like a pack of lyrical hyenas the surpassing power and generosity of their approaching chief. Those who could no longer howl, droned.

Amah-de-bellah himself now appeared mounted on a fly-bitten but stalwart grey barb reduced to its own skeleton by having dined for two weeks past on nothing but tropical moss. The chief was followed by a fat, black dervish on a vicious mule. The holy man held a whip in one hand and a huge Koran wrapped in a prayer rug in the other. Three of Amah-de-bellah's wives in long white veils in which there were only eye-holes appeared next like ghosts riding upon diminutive donkeys. These little asses, which continually brayed and sobbed, were driven forward by thorn whips in the hands of the harem attendants who took turns at beating them, although themselves loaded down with great-pots, mats, vast umbrellas, bundles of apparel, and hut furniture.

Commerce having thus at once advertised itself with its usual modesty and exhibited its veiled cause, its inevitable and necessary armed escort followed.

In this case it consisted of a guard of some fifty or more fanatical Foulahs dressed in the white robes of peace and their own skinny, black legs. They rushed through the gate in a body, firing matchlocks, whirling, shrieking, capering, and waving bright scimitars in the air. The hair of this jungle militia was in each case frizzed-up into a kind of cock's comb dyed purple-red by a delicate solution of iron, urine, and lime. As they streamed after their leader in a mimic mêlée they managed to confer on the word "ferocious" a new and more sinister meaning.

All of them, however, and the people who had just preceded them, were now brought together half-way down the slope, where Amah-de-bellah had halted to await the rest of his caravan before advancing in state to the veranda. An interval of unexpected and consequently dramatic silence ensued.

In the midst of this, without any prelude whatever, a long, dark, glistening body commenced to crawl through the gateway as though a legendary serpent were sliding into the stockade. It really seemed at some distance to be one body. As it came nearer, however, it was seen to be composed of hundreds of naked, human bodies rubbed shiny for their approaching sale with palm oil and rancid butter. In the sun they glittered like ebony scales. Bamboo withes stretched from one tight neck-fork to another bound them together into one interminable, twisting line. Soon the small forms of children could be made out darkening the intervals between the passing legs of this huge millepede as it wound down the slope. Hovering about it, and along its flanks, were white-robed Arabs with rhinoceros-hide whips. An occasional report like a pistol-shot from one of these instruments helped to keep the worm crawling fairly rapidly.

Although the best of all his merchandise had thus arrived on its own legs, Amah-de-bellah did not at once advance to the veranda. He delayed for nearly half an hour while various minor chiefs and forest traders, each accompanied by his own slaves, native wares, and pandemonium, came through the gate. The bulk of the caravan, indeed, consisted of these people.

In the meantime Anthony and Captain Matanza sat solemnly and quietly smoking cigars.

"It would, of course," remarked Anthony, lighting another, "be far beneath the dignity of such potentates as ourselves even to notice the fact that so small a thing as a caravan of a thousand souls has arrived in our back yard. It is like having a policy toward an earthquake. It is not even to be thought about till it announces itself."

"The best people at home treat a revolution in the same way," said Don Ruiz. "Until it sets fire to their houses, or cuts off their heads, it does not exist."

"Precisely. In the same way we should lose caste if we seemed to notice that Amah's people are here. As yet he is only 'about to arrive.' Nevertheless, there is no objection to my men distributing the gifts of welcome in advance—as I see you have noticed. These 'gifts' are carefully calculated. They are really part of the trading and will later on be returned in kind. I leave this part of the preliminaries to some of my own Arabs, who estimate carefully what each one of these small traders has to offer and welcome him accordingly. The liberality of the trader is judged by this earnest of his desire to trade. Amah and I have not exchanged gifts yet. We will do that at the big dantica, or trade-talk, that will shortly take place here. But here they come!"

A renewed outburst of mind-sickening noise now shattered the silence. Aided by men with bull-whips, Amah could be seen riding along the flank of his motley host licking it into what might pass in Africa for a semblance of order. A large cock-ostrich at the rear of the column gave the most trouble and dodged about with such gargantuan effeminacy and nervousness in his mincing strides that Anthony and the captain were hard put to it to remain solemn. At last having settled all to his liking, including the ostrich, Amah rode to the head of the procession and tossed his cloak in the air. At this signal the whole howling host precipitated itself toward the residence like a dark flood.

The space before the veranda on the far-side of the little moat was soon dense with a hustling, black mob. The numerous petty chiefs thrust and elbowed each other trying to press forward. Fights and jabbering ensued. But for a few minutes nothing could be heard on the porch except the thunderous chanting of Amah-de-bellah's barkers answered by Anthony's men; each side trying to outpraise their respective masters till wind was exhausted. Presently the armed Foulahs in the centre faced outward, and by beating on the bare ground with their musket butts succeeded finally in clearing a semi-circle at the expense of numerous sore toes. Silence, except for the braying of donkeys and the squalls of babies, was at length restored. Amah and his dervish now advanced into the centre of the cleared space, where a prayer rug was spread by the latter. On this the chief knelt facing Mecca and returned thanks for the safe arrival of his caravan. As he rose hundreds of voices insisted in bastard Arabic that there was only one God and Mohammed was his prophet.

The captain was now more than ever amazed by a scene which had become somewhat familiar to Anthony. Behind the thin line of red-combed, white-robed Foulahs clustered a forest of dark faces made monstrous by lip disks and rings in their noses and ears; rose a mountainous landscape, tier upon tier of grass-wrapped elephant tusks, roped boxes, bundles, and mat-covered bales. A shimmer of copper bracelets, torques, and arm bands together with spearheads and polished muskets caught the sun and tossed it from point to point. Long, cigar-shaped bundles of damp banana leaves smoked wispily upon the heads of the fire-bearers. On the hillside beyond, rows of yoked and shackled captives looked on apathetically. A fetid smell like that of a neglected monkey cage mixed with the pungent odour of burning leaves caused Don Ruiz to cough and puff hastily at his cigar. Weaving back and forth over the fuzzy heads of the multitude, the chinless face of the ostrich peered insanely, blinking with pink and inflamed lids.

Prayers finished, Amah-de-bellah took the Koran from its bearer and held it to his forehead in token that all he was about to say was true. Gifts were now exchanged between him and Anthony. The Mohammedan received a fine Mexican saddle with evident pleasure; Anthony a small goat's horn filled with gold dust. He was amused to note, as he hefted it, that what it contained was worth almost exactly what the saddle had cost.

The preliminaries having been settled Anthony came forward, and bidding Amah welcome with much ceremony, conducted him to his sheepskin on the veranda. Here the captain was introduced and cordially met, for with a happy impulse he took his watch out of his vest pocket and presented it to the mongo. A heavy, gold bracelet from the chief's arm left both parties extremely satisfied. Neleta now appeared with a small silver dish and from this before the whole assembly the three men on the veranda ate dried rice cakes dipped in salt.

One of Anthony's Foulahs now advanced to the edge of the porch and announced that the powerful Master of Gallegos and the mighty Mongo having eaten salt together—as all might see—Gallegos bade the servants of the Mongo welcome. Five bullocks and innumerable sheep had been slaughtered and were roasting at the fires below, where ample camping space for all was to be had. By the blessing of Allah, trade would begin this afternoon—at the firing of a gun. In the meantime let all depart, find quarters, and refresh themselves at the superb feast provided by the matchless generosity of the Master of Gallegos. The usual tribute to monotheism and its prophet proclaimed that the dantica was over.

The crowd broke and raced down the slope, every petty trader trying to outdistance the others to a choice camping place. These had been so arranged as to lie under the muzzles of the cannon on the hill and the guns of the ship. The armed Arabs, the bearers, and slaves followed at a more leisurely pace, leaving the three on the veranda alone. Neleta had already conducted the wives of Amah to a hut in the courtyard, nicely furnished, and erected that morning out of new mats. Neither Anthony nor the captain looked at the three veiled apparitions which passed them. Presumably they did not exist.

It was amusing to Don Ruiz to see—once all ceremonies were concluded—how easily Anthony and Amah conducted themselves. They fell into a long and friendly talk assisted by one of the Foulahs who acted interpreter. Anthony's "Arabic" was by no means satisfactory yet. The trade jargon of the Grain Coast, indeed, was a compound of Arabic, Portuguese, Spanish, and Mandingo in which the first predominated. Fingers, knuckles, and toes supplied arithmetic.

This was the third caravan which Amah had led to Gallegos. Anthony and he had entered into what amounted to a partnership based on a general admiration for each other's resourcefulness and the mutual advantages of co-operation. Amah watched the inland trails constantly and swept into his net all the small traders going to the coast, in the meanwhile carrying on a holy war against the heathen upon his uncle's borders. In this way he was able to gather together large caravans of both slaves and traders, offering to the latter his "protection," and incidentally watching that they did not skip off to trade at the establishments on the Grand Sestris, Timbo, or elsewhere. For this "protection" he levied a tax. But unlike other leaders of caravans he collected the tax and no more. On the whole everybody was satisfied.

Amah was very anxious to have Anthony come inland with trade goods to Futa-Jaloon in order to supply his uncle with arms, ammunition, and European merchandise directly. He had promised Anthony protection and an ample supply of slaves at home-prices, and he had been pressing in his invitation on his last visit a year before. On the present occasion he now renewed this request with the information that his uncle had promised to proclaim an annual market at his capital and not to invite any other European traders for a period of three years.

After an hour's talk, in which all the details for the journey were settled and an ample escort promised to Anthony whenever he should ask for it, Anthony in turn promised Amah to visit him at Futa-Jaloon when the next dry season should set in. Greatly pleased at having obtained consent to his cherished project and at the account of the fine cargo of *La Fortuna*, Amah retired to his mat hut in the courtyard. The separate shelter prevented him from living under the same roof with slaves and Christian dogs. Here he partook of his own rations and solaced himself in retirement with his wives. The little court was full of his furniture, animals, and servants, and Neleta was consternated for her flowers.

At half past two the boom of the gun announced that trade had begun. Anthony, Don Ruiz, and Amah-de-bellah betook themselves to the water front below.

The swiftness and orderliness of trade had been considerably accelerated at Gallegos by reaching an agreement beforehand with the leaders of caravans as to the prices to be paid for various kinds of goods. This did away with endless chaffering and making dantica with swarms of small traders over every ox hide and piece of ivory. Slaves were another matter.

As a caravan must be entertained at the expense of the establishment until trade was over, time was dollars.

The barkers now went about among the fires and camp huts announcing prices. Ferdinando threw open the small trade-window of his storeroom while Amah and Anthony sat just outside with a scales between them. Several Foulahs armed with whips kept back the halffrantic mob that now pressed forward. The province of Amah was, ostensibly, to see that none of his followers suffered short weight or measure, but at the same time he took care to deduct the caravan tax from each trader's return as it was paid out. The storeroom now began both to fill and to empty itself rapidly.

Hides, beeswax, palm oil; ivory in large tusks, lumps, and small teeth; gold dust, and baskets of rice were weighed or measured and disappeared into Ferdinando's window while barkers distributed in return cotton cloth, bars of tobacco, powder, salt, rum, trade dollars, and great quantities of copper wire which would later appear on the arms and legs of forest belles in massive coils and ornaments. Meanwhile the purchase of bullocks, sheep, goats, and poultry went on about the fires.

Profitable as this petty trade was, it was minor compared to the trade in man himself which was to follow. It was soon disposed of and the examination and barter for slaves began.

Under the porch-like structure covered by tarpaulins the small slave traders—who as men of some importance and property assumed a dignified mien—had squatted along the low bench provided for that purpose like so many dark, heavy-lidded Buddhas. A beverage concocted of goat's milk, eggs, sugar and rum was now served out in great quantities, to which, despite religion, the Mohammedans were partial, calling it "milk-sweet." A gong was struck, loiterers were cleared away, and Ferdinando threw open his sample-room where the best of his goods were now arranged in tempting display. The crowd of traders then filed through the room to see what was on hand and to receive a customary good-will gift. A large bale of London "beavers," which had been included in *La Fortuna's* cargo by error or chance, proved to be unexpectedly popular. The majority of the traders returned to their places under the tarpaulin in high hats. Even Brother François, who was always present at these sales of human bodies, went aside with Captain Matanza to laugh.

Amah-de-bellah designated the turn of each trader, and as he did so the man had his merchandise walked-in and lined-up before the block. Every slave as his turn came was cut loose from his fellows and stepped up onto the big square stone. The examination and appraisal was carried on by two expert Foulahs under the eyes of Anthony and Amah.

The inspections proceeded rapidly but meticulously. The slaves were stark naked, and from the crown of their head to their toe-nails they were thoroughly appraised. They were made to squat, to get up, to lean over; to dance and to walk about. They were asked a few swift questions and the tones and intelligence of their replies noted. Their mouths were pulled open and their teeth examined; the whites of their eyes; their pulses, and the colour and texture of their skins.

The two Foulahs had reduced the proceeding to a swift and efficient but varied ritual. They were alert for every possible symptom of disease. A swelling, an unsoundness or a malformation was spotted by them off-hand. In particular they were on the watch for slaves who had been doctored up for the occasion. And there were a hundred clever tricks in that black art.

The number of those rejected was small. By this time it was known that "painted horses" could not be sold at Gallegos. Both the unerring rejection of the unfit and the exposure of tricks by the examiners were now the occasions for derisive laughter. The traders enjoyed it particularly when some well-known old rascal of their number, or a newcomer, was nicely shown-up.

The plight of the rejected slave, however, was terrible. The rage and chagrin of his luckless owner was usually extreme, and, as the property had been officially pronounced worthless, it had been found necessary to take care of such cases after a special manner at Gallegos to prevent sickening tragedies. Unfortunately, this arrangement was peculiar to Gallegos.

Indeed, the very worst that could happen to a slave was to be rejected as unfit; the best, since he had already suffered the huge misfortune of being sold or captured, was to please both his old and new owners by being valuable. For that reason nearly all of those who had wit enough to appreciate their own predicament tried to appear attractive on the block.

To Brother François, who, seated on a stool, viewed these sales from the crack behind Ferdinando's door—since his presence in the sales-porch gave mortal offence to the pious Mohammedans—the barter of human bodies for the goods piled just behind him in the sample-room was an experience of inexpressible pathos and agony.

It was not only that he believed that his Master had given His body for these dark children of the forests and that they were truly the sheep of His fold, but having been born where and when he had been, Brother François understood the meaning of the word "liberty" in both its practical and abstract sense. It was, in fact, the favourite word of his age. Consequently, every one of these scenes was, for him at least, a Calvary. The perspiration ran down in his sleeves. Occasionally he wiped his palms on his now almost transparent robe. If it had not been that he also believed that violence was always both wrong and futile he would have rushed out as his ancestors had once done to die fighting in the midst of overwhelming numbers of paynims.

But this belief and the glimpse of a certain face before him kept him temporarily inactive. The face was Anthony's.

To most of the others present, including the slaves themselves, the occasion of their barter was merely one of more than usual emotional interest. But not much more. Passions of all kinds, especially the passion of greed, were unleashed, it is true, and everyone participated to some extent .even if unconsciously in the drama of the occasion. For even the fate of a slave is the fate of a man or woman, and therefore potentially dramatic. Hence, there was even among some of the traders themselves a dim, half-conscious sense of the tragedy of it all. A note of relief in their jovial and too-hearty laughter showed this when some trivial comic incident cropped up; when some fat man tripped ascending the block, or a black houri wriggled under an appraising slap on the buttocks. They proved to themselves how funny, how very humorous it was. "How they have to laugh together," thought Brother François, "the laughter of merchants—where everything is for sale in a sad, bad, merry world—and 'we' are getting our little profit out of the joke. 'We,' who know that men and women can be traded for things, we practical men. Laugh, brothers, laugh! For laughter shows we are such good-fellows after all. Who better than we when we get together? Who shall impugn 'Us?' Is it not custom, commerce, and therefore fate immutable?

"How shall I explain my plan to those who believe in trading men for things to call it profitable. Yet even these savage traders have some dim feeling that something is wrong somewhere. They laugh to balance the depressed inner scales. Is there no one here to whom I can appeal? That young man there with the rigid face—Anthony?"—thus Brother François sweating on his stool.

At first Anthony had also smiled; had tried to. But he could no longer do that. At this game of human barter his features registered what he wished he could feel about it, nothing at all. In the final analysis he did not really care for the goods which trade brought him. He told himself he only cared for the mode of living trade made possible. There was something in that. A great deal, he insisted—but not so much after all, he knew. Otherwise he would not have insisted upon it to himself. For even a mode of life was only living, doing. And it was action and not gain which was his profit. Perhaps, it was the sense of power, then? Yes, that was the masculine secret, deeper than love of women, or friendship—or God. That was what women were always curious about and would like to have—and lost it in getting it. Power is what a man keeps for its own sake and not for what it will do for him. Power he was determined he would trade for nothing at all, but he would trade all things even men for it. That was what he meant by "getting things done." Let them be done then! He would identify himself with the power that can act—anyhow in all directions. It was that kind of a man he would be. Having was only incidental to doing.

Therefore, his expression was much the same whether the slaves wept or the traders laughed—the same no matter what went on. As the cause of both tragedy and comedy he remained calm in the centre of both. His words were fewer than ever now; only necessary ones to get things done. Consequently he was respected as a strong, silent man by nearly everyone about him—who also feared him because they did not know what he wanted for himself or how he thought or felt. The nature instead of the amount of his price was unknown. How could they alter his will—what bribe? None apparently. Hence, he made the rules for, and directed the game of life on the Rio Pongo as the one who was mysteriously best fitted to do so, and would and could.

Not that he stated all this to himself as so much philosophy. It was rather more largely a program of instinctive action into which he had drifted after being launched in that direction as a "citizen of the Western Hemisphere," where so many of the world currents and the tides in the affairs of men between Europe, Africa, and America were carrying him along. His association with Brother François had so far tended to confirm him in the opinion that even the "subjects of God" could do nothing about it. And one had to live as—to be a man. That was what Cibo had insisted upon. Be practical. And Anthony had felt that Cibo was right. There was only one thing which kept Anthony from feeling entirely successful, practical,—he could not entirely stifle his feelings. During a slave-barter he always became peculiarly aware of that. Somehow this trading in men in the sales-porch seemed to be the whole crux of the matter.

"If what I be depends upon what I do—and this is what is being done! Then?"

His feelings rose up against him. It was all he could do even to conceal them outwardly on the days of slave-barter. He therefore looked more than usually self-possessed and grim, calm and determined. Yet what a dry, fiery oven was heating within him.

For as the afternoon advanced, adding incident after incident, as one purchased body after another stepped from the stone block to the barracoons—Anthony's state of feeling became all but unbearable. He was now beholding, he knew very well, the inmost core, the essence of doing things in order to get them done. The process was as naked to him as the slaves who stepped onto the block. Each one of them in fact personified it, and the effect of the afternoon's procession was cumulative. He was at once fascinated and tortured. What if his state of feeling should prevail over his will and become his whole state of being? What would he *do* then? What would become of Gallegos?

The slow friction of his determination and his emotions turning in different directions, turning, as it were, on the pivot of his personality, twisted it, threatened to tear it apart; generated a slowly mounting heat. That heat was of necessity kept smothered within from the time the trade-gun fired till the porch was emptied. The irritation of it crept slowly along his nerves out to the ends of his toes and fingers. His hands and feet felt dry, and his mouth parched. He would sometimes send for a drink. Nevertheless, he would feel a mounting impulse to discharge this nervous pressure in outbursts of anger at trivial mishaps; to wreak vengeance on something or somebody outside him for his own miserable state within. But policy forbade that. He must remain calm and sober, the Master of Gallegos, beginning with himself. By evening he would have dark circles under his eyes where the lower lids had set up a minute twitching. Then suddenly something would collapse within him; give way. Even tobacco was no help now. It rather sickened him. Going home up the hill he would suddenly feel small, and cold. A slight shaking as of a weak ague made his steps a little uncertain. And how tired he was! The climate would get him yet, damn it! Neleta would be waiting too, damn her!

While a caravan was at Gallegos, on those nights, even Neleta was no solace. After a day of burning he was left cold with her at night. Last time Amah had been here it was worse than ever. He had dreamed his old madonna was smothering in that chest where she was locked up. Somehow he was in there too and struggling desperately with her to get out. The bed covers had slipped over his head and Neleta had wakened him, still struggling. It infuriated him to be going back to dreams like that again. Great God!

To Brother François, watching from the crack behind Ferdinando's door, the expression on Anthony's face and the scenes on the block were complementary to each other. He understood the cause of that expression. He had seen the will and the emotions at war before, turning men either into jovial pigs or iron masks. It was, he felt, one of the commonest symptoms of the moral disease of the world he knew. How to make both the will and the feelings of a man work together so they shall both feel at ease at what he is doing—how to be a whole man? "What to do, and what not to do, in order to be?" That was his question. "Or it might be—it might also be, what not to have in order to be," he told himself. There was only one to whom he could look for perfect direction in how to be a whole man, he had found. And because he had found abundant life in that direction, despite what might happen to the carcass of him, he desired to share it and re-explain it by living it. Seemingly the most passive person at Gallegos, Brother François was in reality one of the few people in the Western World who had positively identified himself with the power to be.

The truth was that this extraordinary man did not feel that through the crack of the door in Africa he was looking on at anything unusual. The slice of life he saw there seemed to him, although presented in primitive and uncomplicated terms, to be quite an ordinary one. It was merely another case of where sympathy between men had become inoperative because greed for the possession of things and profit at the expense of others had reduced part of the population to slavery. In a place where things were valued more than men it was inevitable, he saw, that men should be reduced to the state of being less valuable than things. In that case, what more natural than that some men, those who could not help themselves, should actually be traded for things? "Sambo for three kegs of rum and an ell of cloth," he thought, imagining himself to be a trader. "My helpless brother for my own happiness! And certainly with three kegs of rum—and an ell of cloth, certainly I shall be happy. Shall I not be rich and envied? . . .

"But how does this differ from the universal commerce of the world for personal profit? Is it not all a trading of my brother for an ell of cloth or some more intoxicating substance? Did not my own father trade the bodies of his serfs for his ease, for his fine clothes and court career, his library and his château?"

And how many merchants and bankers and statesmen were doing the same thing. Because their system was more complex was it essentially different? No. What he saw here, if it differed at all, differed in degree and not in kind, he told himself.

Perhaps, this door slit in Africa gave a really more penetrating and genuine view of the system than if the door had been slightly ajar and he seated on a stool behind it somewhere else. For here the slaves were called "slaves" and the things for which they were expended were piled up in Ferdinando's sample-room all about him. It was naked men for naked things, and the traders out there bidding openly.

The cure for all this Brother François believed was only to be brought about by awakening sympathy in the hearts of men, man by man. And there was only one way of doing that, he thought—by presenting them with the opposite example of the way of his Master and letting them see it work. Words would not do; a billion sermons had been preached since St. Paul began. Theories and philosophic concepts died because men could not or did not embody them. Only the example itself, the way of his Master embodied in a man's life might avail.

In his humble and often faltering way, by the help of prayer and by a hard-won sense of communion in which he sometimes seemed to touch the fingers of Christ himself, Brother François stumbled blindly, sometimes mistakenly, but always sincerely and constantly, along the ineffably difficult way of being an exemplar.

If he sweated and sometimes wept as he looked through the crack of the door at the world working for its own undoing, while at the same time he felt the cold and faintly puzzled, but hostile eyes of Ferdinando fixed upon the middle of his back, it was nothing new and surprising to him. Nothing was here which by the unexpected shock of it could cause him to deliver himself over to his emotion and nerves and break out in a desperate but futile demonstration. The body-changers he knew could not be driven from the temple with their own whips—if at all. He had simply come to regard Gallegos, and his own little garden-valley in particular, as a kind of Gethsemane. It was a place where after much agony he prayed and waited, sure of the glory of failure—meanwhile doing what good he might according to his plan.

At Gallegos this plan consisted in buying up, for whatever he could get together or beg, the slaves rejected on the block; nursing the sick ones till they died; or keeping the crippled and maimed in his garden where their light labours sufficed in that climate to support the little community. A few of these unfortunates he had even been able to rehabilitate completely, but not many. Most of them soon came to rest in the ever-growing graveyard. In particular, however, Brother François concerned himself with children.

Many an exhausted black child, unable to follow the caravan any longer, who had seen the long file in which its mother was yoked disappear into the shades of the forest, now owed its existence to him. Lying in the forest waiting for darkness and the inevitable end, dumb with exhaustion and fear, it had heard the leaves rustle, screamed— and found itself in the arms of the good shepherd of Gallegos.

"For I also," said Brother François, "hunt like a lion, and do seek my meat from God."

He was followed upon these not infrequent man-hunts along the trails of caravans by an old Susu warrior wise in forest ways whom he had cared for till he could wield a spear again, and by a woman he had once come across in a raided village with her breasts cut off. Yet because of that she was now the best of several nurses in the cluster of beehive huts in the little valley; fierce and fearless in her work of mercy. On her expeditions into the forest with Brother François and his guide she bore a basket on her back to carry back the living meat which the leopards had not yet found.

What extra goods and help he needed to carry out his plans in the valley, Brother François had always asked from Anthony. It was given to him without question, usually by a written order on Ferdinando.

The little settlement attracted small notice and few visitors of any kind. There was nothing to be had by going there. There were orders against anyone disturbing it, and it remained a kind of enclave of peace, an *imperium in inferno*, for the rescued unfortunates and children who dwelt there. In a few years by a kind of natural evolution it had developed a self-sufficient economy which was at once primitive, native, early Christian and communistic. Beyond a few iron tools, some wine for himself and his sacrament, a little cloth, flour, and medicines, Brother François asked nothing more than the privilege of being let alone. The only opposition he met with was from Ferdinando, and this was latent rather than active.

The truth is, that small as was the charity the priest required, the method of charging it on the books puzzled Ferdinando. The half-breed, although he had acquired most of the outward manners of civilization as a youth in Spain, had in reality only one vital touch with it. It was the very primitive and unemotional one of commercial book-keeping. Except for his clothes, his European manners, and his always perfectly kept books, Ferdinando was a savage. He did not know to what account to charge the small sundries issued from time to time to Brother François. It worried him greatly. He was enormously chagrined at finally having to ask Anthony about it. The latter's ironical suggestion that he should start a new page headed "Losses by Acts of God and the Public Enemy" only confused him the more. When he came to balance his books he had no idea how to handle a comparatively small but ever-growing account which seemed to be a debit with no possible credit to balance it. How could one liquidate something which was perpetually suspensory and ever increasing? An element of confusion was thus introduced into the fatuous order of Ferdinando's confused mental world. It finally became a rough pebble in his mental shoe. Shift it as he might, he could not get rid of it. By the spring of 1799 it had grown to the lump size of 126 pounds three shillings and sixpence. The factor determined that he would some time balance his books and show profit. He had a scheme. As yet he had not said anything about it to Anthony. It could wait. The charge went into "Accounts Temporarily Suspended." It was impossible for even Brother François to guess that in so simple a fact as that lay the Nemesis of his quiet valley. He continued to receive from time to time certain small benefits.

Small as this help was it had, nevertheless, enabled the monk to accomplish much more than would otherwise have been possible. And it was a constant indication to him that Anthony had not altogether succeeded in suppressing a part of himself which Brother François still had hopes of resurrecting as the whole man. During the three years he had spent with Anthony at Gallegos he had become intensely aware of the bitter struggle going on in the soul of a young friend over whom from their first meeting his own spirit had yearned. In that time their intimacy, for the most part a rather silent one, had, despite the frequent pain of it, deepened. Nor could Brother François forget the cabin of the *Ariostatica*.

There were a thousand little things that showed that this was so. The priest could not make up his mind to abandon Anthony. If he left Gallegos, as he had often considered doing, it seemed to him that he would be writing over its gate the hopeless inscription. And within those gates dwelt a beloved friend. "Not lost, not lost," he whispered, watching him.

Alone among the many Europeans who now came and went on the Rio Pongo, the monk was the only one cultivated and sensitive enough to understand the tragic irony in Anthony's fate—that tendency in affairs to enrich with things men who do not care for them. Anthony, he saw, might well become one of those characters abandoned by God and insulated from man who must find in the mere conduct of business at once their rich material reward and their utter spiritual poverty.

The face of Anthony reminded him now, while he stood by watching the proceedings on the slave-block, of the features of several other hopeful young men he had once known. Men whom he had seen in later manhood metamorphosed, or disguised to be great merchants, financiers, subtle priests, or ministers of state. What was once living and mobile in their expressions had become firm and fixed; what was formerly the strength of sweetness had become the power of sternness. Even now he felt that an appeal for mercy might be answered from Anthony's lips by a negative good reason or put off for expediency's dear sake. The unconscious smile that had once lurked on his mouth like sunlight striking through an open door had vanished. The door was tightly shut. Such faces Brother François knew could only be relaxed by a stroke of God—or the guillotine. He prayed for the stroke, and yet, because he loved the man for whom he prayed, he would avert it. He closed his eyes.

But despite many memories and the thoughts which thronged upon him out of the past, there was in this present scene before him a purely incidental and very human fascination to which the monk was thoroughly alive. He would open his eyes again and lean forward peering through the crack of the door.

Just over the block a section of the tarpaulin had been removed and the light streamed down in a brilliant slant of white radiance on the black bodies of the slaves as they stepped up one after another while the afternoon wore on. It was curious to see how under the necessity of selling themselves for as high a price as possible basic types of character emerged and all else vanished. The coquettish woman was now all smiles, even her muscles flinched under the prodding fingers of the indifferent appraisers in an alluring and half-playful way. The frightened young girl seemed to know now that virginity was her chief asset and trembled for her modesty as touchingly as she could. Youths and boys danced and shouted to show how gay and active they were. The notoriously fecund Gbandi women stood huge and cow-like, as if ready to receive whatever burdens were about to be laid within or upon them. Mandingos, who made the most prized house servants in Havana, were already compliant, a little furtive and too obsequious; ready to answer even a painful whack with a laugh. Mothers clung to their babies apprehensively. It was found easier to let them hold them while they mounted the block where they were indifferent to all but the child on the breast. Even the Foulahs hesitated to waken the tiger in them by handling the baby. The very young trembled, scared by something new. The naked, sullen warrior looked about him still using his last weapon, silent contempt. In Africa, as elsewhere, maternity and martial honour were the only things which would not sell themselves, which rose supreme to all personal misfortune. Warriors Anthony occasionally secured for his personal force on the plantation. He bound them to him by giving them weapons and their freedom. When he spoke with them he felt at ease again.

As the sun neared the edge of the western jungle and its level rays struck with sudden revelation along the line of squatting traders still waiting for their turns under the tarpaulin, Brother François rose, and gathering up two unfortunates who were his for a little tobacco and powder, led them uphill to his valley. One of them was an oldish man who had proved to be nearly blind and the other an emaciated girl tottering with weakness. The mercy which had overtaken them they could not as yet comprehend. The sounds of twilight happiness in the little valley only bewildered them, for they had forgotten the kind of sound that accompanies peace and contentment. What the bell meant they had yet to learn.

In the sales-porch the last batches for the day were being rapidly worked off. The amount due a trader was written on a chit by Anthony and given to him. A duplicate went to Ferdinando. His storeroom was kept open till late at night paying off in goods. Already the lanterns were lit there and the bales coming down from the lofts. A sunset gun put an end to the day's proceedings. The last slaves were led off to the barracoons and the merchants returned to their tents and huts. Anthony and Amah-de-bellah climbed to the house on the hill as twilight was falling.

While he stood alone on the veranda that night after supper, Anthony told himself he had no cause to be dissatisfied. The trade had gone well. He had also struck a good bargain with Amah for the bulk of the slaves in the caravan. *La Fortuna* could sail soon now, loaded down. From the courtyard came the weird wailing of some outlandish wind instrument in Amah's huts. It irritated him greatly. He could also hear the wild rejoicings about the camp fires below. They were just over the edge of the hill but the red light of them beat up into the sky. The fog-wraith over the river reflected it back in a pulsing glow. If the drumming could only be stopped for tonight! Tonight he was tired.

He was always tired after a day like this; depressed. He hated himself. His face which had been so stern and fixed all day worked in the darkness. He was glad there was no one there to see him. He shivered. He felt as if he had been listening to a perfect babble of reproachful voices for hours, and that they were right. Perhaps after all he could not become what he had set out to be. He leaned on the railing gazing at the lights on the ship in the harbour. The red light in the fog flickered as the fires waned and leaped. The hill fell away so steeply at night! It seemed suddenly as if he stood close to an abyss, the edge of the world. Pandemonium was at the bottom. The drums drummed and drummed and drummed. He was going to fall and he was right on the edge now. "God . . . I *am* falling. Ah—eeee . . ."

"Neleta!"

Twice before she had heard him cry out that way. She was with him in an instant, soothing him and reassuring him. She felt sure someone had bewitched him and was trying to steal his soul. The witch-doctors often did that. She had seen the blacks dying when their souls were stolen. They looked strong but they just went out and died in a few days for no reason at all. She would see her old aunt at Bangalang about this although Ferdinando had long forbidden her to go there.

Perhaps it was only a touch of the fever!

But he looked so different tonight as she mixed him a strong drink that she felt uneasy. She put her arms around him and held him closely to her in bed. Yet she did not seem to possess him. When the moon rose she raised the net a little to look at him. His face was

much younger now.   It was not like the face of the Master of Gallegos.
It was not the face of the man she knew at all!

"Madre!"   Ferdinando or not, she would certainly see Aunt Ungah
about this.   After all her mother's people did know a thing or two!

Outside in the courtyard the wailing oboe still went on as if someone
had charmed a snake out of its basket and was afraid to leave-off
playing.

CHAPTER FORTY-TWO

THE VISION OF LIGHT

FERDINANDO'S books promised to show a startling profit in the exchange of *La Fortuna's* cargo for the merchandise of Amah's caravan. There were three hundred and twenty-eight slaves in the barracoons at Gallegos, and down-river Mongo Tom had unexpectedly kicked in with forty more. The ship was to pick them up on her way out. But she could not carry all of these people at once without undue risk from plague and British privateers. Anthony therefore determined to split her cargo, leaving about a third of the number to wait for the *Ariostatica,* which was expected back again in a month or so. Don Ruiz grumbled a good deal at seeing his profits cut but was too well satisfied on the whole to be angry.

Still, all this was embarrassment of riches at worst, and the entirely unsentimental Ferdinando could not understand why the Master of Gallegos continued to look disgruntled while he studied his factor's statement showing the flourishing state of their tangible affairs. The half-breed took a profound satisfaction in it. He had, in fact, done not a little toward bringing it about. Besides, his own profit on head-money was considerable.

"Three hundred twenty-eight plus forty equals three hundred sixty-eight dollars," he told himself. He wished Anthony would ship the whole batch on *La Fortuna.*

"When this cargo is turned into gold and bills of exchange at Havana, señor . . ." he pointed out. But he received only a lacklustre look.

"You have done very well, Ferdinando—I suppose," Anthony said finally—and closed the big ledger with a bang.

"As Amah is always saying, 'It is written,'" he thought. "Mohammedans seem to get both justification and comfort in that. 'It is written!'" He glanced at the columns of Ferdinando's meticulous figures again, and stalked out of the warehouse office in a cloudy mood.

For Anthony found no comfort in the statement of his "profit." This time, even after the departure of the caravan, his fit of glumness had lasted.

The various small traders had departed early, disappearing into the fathomless forest on the far-side of the stockade, silently, and with no farewells. In the morning their fires would be ashes and they were

618

gone. Now they had all left but it made little difference. By day the heat and the silence that lay on the place seemed intolerable. Yet the wailing of the flute in Amah's hut at night was even worse.

Amah and his three wives had lingered on in the courtyard. At last he left with a final "feu de joie" from all fifty of his Foulahs' muskets; with gifts, and an urgent reminder to Anthony of his promise to visit Futa-Jaloon. At least it was a relief to get rid of the flute, Anthony felt. Neleta had the courtyard replanted. She invited Don Ruiz up to dinner every night now in order to cheer up Anthony about whom she was much worried. He had somehow slipped away from her. Finally, she suggested a fishing expedition to the barrier reefs.

He caught at the idea eagerly. He was tired of Gallegos, he told himself. Neleta was right. What he wanted was a change. He would arrange to go down-river on *La Fortuna* and stay at the out-islands till the rains began—a week or two at most. Some of the Krus could come with him. The clean sand and open sea were just what he needed. And it would soon be clouding up now. A good drench of fresh air untainted by the forest—sunlight! Bueno!

Now that it seemed as if he too were going with the ship Anthony began to press *La Fortuna's* departure with something of his old zeal. Ten days in barracoons had already done wonders for the slaves in resting them up after their long march to the coast. Most of them had begun to look sleek and even contented. There was not only lots of food but Ferdinando saw to it that there was also drumming and dancing. He held a dantica and told them about the happy lot ahead of them in Cuba. There was a great snapping of fingers over that. No sickness had developed. So far so good.

On the day before the ship's departure, which was always one of great feasting, the head of every man, woman, and child was shaved smooth. Finger-nails were pared down to the quick to prevent scratching when the inevitable fights for sleeping room should take place aboard ship. *La Fortuna* took in her last water cask. Lights were doused early in the barracoons and silence rigidly enforced. At the first grey of dawn the transfer to the ship began.

The slaves were taken out by batches of ten in boats and canoes. As they stepped on the deck they were stripped of every rag; of even the smallest article they might still possess. Every bead and the tiniest fetish and charm went overboard. Buckets of water were then dashed over them and they were mercilessly scrubbed by a gang of Mandingo boys who enjoyed their job immensely and who were more vigorous than gentle. The gangs were now marched forward and their shackles struck from them while they dried off and shivered. Cries and lamentations whether from children or adults were ruthlessly suppressed. The work proceeded with the greatest order and dispatch.

Every slave was made to wash his mouth out with vinegar. As each approached the hatchway he was seized by a gang of tattooers, thrown over a spare spar and had three white dots tattooed on his back. This was the Gallegos mark which had been substituted for branding with a hot iron. It was also, as a matter of fact, indelible, and the ancient way of marking slaves on the Grain Coast. But there was more trouble over this proceeding than anything else. Many of the people as they were stretched over the spar thought the end had come. It required the attention of a stripling armed with a large paddle both to stimulate and to quiet them. At this task the boy was an artist.

The slaves were next separated and led below. Whip in hand the mates and boatswains superintended the stowing of the cargo. The women were stowed on the starboard side of the ship facing forward; the men on the port side facing aft. All lay with their heads in each other's laps and on their right sides as this was supposed to favour the action of the heart. A clear space along the centre of the deck was kept open for the guards and for other necessary passing to and fro.

Between-decks the ship had been scrupulously cleared of every loose article from stem to stern. Wherever possible even the bulkheads had been removed. Short of pulling up a plank or ripping out one of the ship's timbers from its bolts, there was literally not a single article in the hold of *La Fortuna* that could serve the slaves as a weapon of any kind. Small reed canes were served out to certain chosen trusties, each one of whom was put in charge of a gang of ten and held responsible for their discipline. The reward for this service was a little tobacco and an old, white shirt that served to distinguish these "mess-leaders," as they were called, from the black, naked mass of their fellows; a mass that now rapidly filled the long decks of the ship from end to end.

Into the dark cavern of the ship's hold fell here and there streams of pale daylight down the open hatches, each barred with a heavy iron grating against which a lion might have hurled himself in vain.

About these apertures, that served for both egress and ventilation, black faces and forms stood out in startling silhouette and ranged back, growing dimmer row after row until ebony blent with the darkness. In the remoter parts of this floating cave only the flash of eyeballs and white teeth could be seen or it was flecked here and there by the light shirts of the mess-leaders. Between-decks the slaves squatted by day or lay by night during the entire voyage until they wore the planks smooth and greasy. When the weather permitted, and if they seemed docile, meals and certain periods of exercise on deck were allowed.

Outbursts, or infractions of sanitary rules, quarrels or lamentations were promptly visited either by the canes of the mess-leaders or by the whips of the overseers. For the furiously recalcitrant or rebelliously sullen there were irons, and the deep, solitary darkness of the regions of rats and bilge-water below. It was an absolute rule that no fire whether for lantern or tobacco could ever be taken below. So their nights were spent in pitch darkness when not even the overseers ventured amongst them, and their days in deep gloom.

Thus even before she left the anchorage at Bangalang the 'tween-decks of *La Fortuna,* like every other slaver, had taken on for her unwilling passengers all the aspects of a troubled, grotesque dream in the darkness from which there is no escape even by waking.

The first effect upon coming aboard was to reduce even the African temperament to silence. A few women sat rocking on their hunkers and crooning. Here and there a deep guttural in some forest dialect disturbed the gloom among the men.

Presently the ship cast off from her buoy and began to slip downstream with the ebb tide. The angles of light streaming down the hatches shifted slightly. The helm creaked. The shock of the saluting cannon jarred the ship and made everybody start. One at a time dark shadows began to slip forward to the latrines at the bow and to return. This traffic of nature was an incessant one. It was both enforced and restrained by the negro overseers with a cat-o'-nine-tails lashed to their wrists, men who were known as the "masters-of-the-hold." Two of these were always on watch and were regularly relieved.

Anthony stood on the quarter-deck with the captain while the transfer was taking place, explaining and hastening the process. Matters had gone very smoothly. It was just after sunrise when the ship cast loose and began to drift down the river, slowly at first, but gathering way as the drag of the ebb became heavier. Juan was acting as pilot. He knew every trick of the Rio Pongo now. As they doubled the long point that jutted out between Gallegos and Bangalang, and *La Fortuna* was swept along by the full force of the midstream current, Anthony could no longer conceal his elation that seemed to grow in proportion as Gallegos was left behind.

When at last the palms on the point finally shut out the barracoons and the residence a load seemed to have dropped from a basket that had been pressing his head down between his shoulders. He was amazed at his own cheerfulness. Don Ruiz also looked at him with surprise. He had not up until then met the free-and-easy young man to whom he now found himself talking.

They went into the stern cabin of the ship and discussed an excellent breakfast. The stern windows of this high, Spanish-built vessel were thrown wide open. It was like floating along in a wide, glass house well above the water. They could look for miles over the low islands and flat brown-coiling reaches of the river. The morning sun touched the brass cabin lamps and the captain's silver table-plate till it glittered. Don Ruiz had a good steward and drank a mixture of Java and Mocha that was heartening. The cabin was cool and airy. Anthony looked about him at the neat panelling and ship's furniture. It was pleasant to be in touch with civilization again. In the forms of things in the cabin all of Europe seemed to be concentrated. Suddenly he was at home again.

Don Ruiz enjoyed being host. He talked engagingly of the dangers and fascination of travelling in Spain. With Anthony he forgot *La Fortuna*—and her cargo. Caramba! This señor inglés was a caballero! One could afford to know him. "More coffee, Pedro." Anthony wished he too were going on to Havana and said so. In the grand Castilian manner he found himself presented with the ship and entreated to remain on board as a perpetual passenger and owner. It was hard not to accept.

They were passing Bangalang now. From the beach below the little fisher huts on stilts half a dozen canoes put off and raced past the ship making for Mongo Tom's. They were going to bring the rest of the slaves aboard there. Half an hour later the ship was lying-to off the Mongo's establishment while the canoes plied back and forth rapidly. A noise like a porpoise breathing announced that Mongo Tom was ascending the ship's side. Loud, complaining rumbles in a husky voice went on for some time on deck.

"He wants a salute fired," said Anthony listening. The voice was curiously exasperating.

"Come down," shouted Don Ruiz at last impatiently.

He was answered by an elephantine grunt. Something not entirely human appeared at the cabin door. The presence which there heaved itself into view was, in every sense of the word, overpowering.

Two large, negroid feet with projecting heels and long yellow toenails, only one of which extremities was wrapped in a frayed rice-straw sandal, provided a seemingly insufficient support for the majestic belly that projected above and beyond them in a cosmic periphery. From this hung down in indescribably greasy and yellow folds what had once (*circa* 1780) been a pair of white canvas trousers. But the action of time had long ago reduced these *bracæ* to a state of filthy fluidity that Lazarus himself might have been shy to own. Furthermore, they were suspended from a startlingly clean and brand-new piece of shiny Manila hemp tied in the middle with a bud-like knot.

There was something shocking about this sartorial item. It seemed to mark the too cute, imaginary equatorial belt of a Jovian planet that might laugh and discard it at any moment. It was artificial and unnatural. To those who had to talk with its owner for any length of time it was an irritation rather than a comfort that the implied catastrophe which was always imminent never finally occurred.

Indeed, it was difficult for the eye to pass much above the central boundary of this human mass, for immediately above the small belt-knot, as if put there to remind the onlooker of what it had once been like in infancy, was the navel of Mongo Tom now expanded by the general distortion of his girth into the exact semblance of a large, alert-looking ear.

It was to this, much to Anthony's amusement and his own dismay, that Captain Matanza found himself addressing his remarks in too-loud a voice while the Mongo lowered himself into a well-stayed chair. A wrinkling of the man's paunch in the vicinity of its ear seemed to reply.

"Dios," said Captain Matanza looking at Anthony as if to ask, "Can this be possible?"—"Have a cigar?"

"Carried *nem con,*" said the presence whose portliness seemed already to have made him the chairman of the little meeting in the cabin. He banged his fist on the table so that all the dishes jumped . . .

"That is to say in Spanish, señor captain, 'there is no dissent from your not unexpected proposal.' "

Don Ruiz bowed—to the ear apparently—and Anthony burst into a roar of laughter. Both of the others looked at him in surprise. The captain's face flushed. What might have been meant either for a scowl or a smile wrinkled the fat, moonlike countenance of the slaver as if a gelatin pastry had registered an earth-tremor that had passed on leaving the pie intact.

He stuck the cigar in his mouth and lit it, exhaling smoke in a series of whirling rings. Out of this half-invisible megaphone the voice of an habitual drunkard issued as though at a considerable distance.

"Now he looks like a ham with a single clove driven into it," thought Anthony. The voice continued in curiously correct English as if it were wound up and running down.

"My father, sir, had two ambitions: the first was to circulate the scriptures amongst the natives of these coasts, and the second to introduce them to the noble amenities of parliamentary procedure. It was he who once described their internecine bickerings as both unreasonable and unnecessary. In order to further his laudable ambitions he allied himself with a princess of the Susus. I am the offspring of that union. My father, sir, was an English doctor of divinity."

"So I have heard some thirty times before," interrupted Anthony. The Mongo emitted a number of rings. Having re-created his speaking trumpet he paid no attention to Anthony but went on.

"I have devoted myself to more concrete and practicable things," the voice did not seem now to belong to anyone at all. It was both debauched and cultivated—"With the exception of four years spent in England in clerical company, as the pet of bishops in fact, during which time I translated the Gospel according to St. Luke into Susu, I have busied myself here with transferring the benighted denizens of these forests to Christian lands where the light of the gospel could shine with unadulterated fervour upon 'em. This, in my very humble estimation, is preferable to sowing seed among the tares *in partibus infidelum.*"

Anthony had had to listen to this talk a number of times before. Even the cadences he knew had been inherited from the Mongo's father, a renegade missionary. It was now only a fine formula, a kind of dantica by which the Mongo felt he established himself with white men as a respectable character. One corner of the mouth now lapsed and a succession of smoke rings emerged travelling at great speed.

"The Society for the Propagation of the Gospel in Foreign Parts and His Grace of Canterbury have honoured me . . ."

"The captain does not understand English, Tommy," shouted Anthony.

The face with the cigar suddenly smoothed out and collapsed into a kind of indeterminate human landscape down which the sweat poured in copious streams.

"For Christ's sake, then, give me a glass of grog," it said.

The request having been complied with, and the bottle left on the table, the rest of the interview went on in Spanish for the benefit of the captain.

Don Ruiz thought he had never seen such a man as the Mongo. His coat, evidently donned for the occasion, stretched only half-way across his shirtless chest. But in the middle area between, nature had supplied a frill in the form of a hirsute ridge that stretched from just above the umbilical ear to the region below the neck. Here the hair became exceedingly luxuriant and very red. It was also hard to tell whether the man suffered from elephantiasis or was just enormously fat. Even the top of his head was fat. The hair there had retreated into a number of puffy places like small, wooded islands, and the inhabitants of this curious archipelago could occasionally be glimpsed passing in a leisurely manner from one island covert to another. Mongo Tom stunk like a dead fish in August, and no one on the Rio Pongo could recall what his colour had been in early youth. It was now a sort of yellow-mahogany darkened by tobacco smoke.

His mind, however, when not totally obscured by drink, was exceedingly clear about all his personal affairs. This obscene mountain could both boast and bargain. It took as keen a half-hour of dickering as Don Ruiz, who was a sharp man himself, had ever listened to, before

Anthony could complete the bargain for the forty slaves which the Mongo had brought aboard. In the process of this they went on deck again and looked over the new arrivals.

"Sink me if they ain't as likely a flock of bucks and lasses as you're likely to find," insisted the Mongo. " 'Ary a one over twenty-five. The pick of three villages up the Sestris. Fine gels! I'd like to try 'em out myself." He gave a throaty chuckle. "Now what do you give for the lot? What d-ye offer, Mr. Adverse? What!"

He was finally lowered over the side clutching the price in his huge, fat paw. Anthony and the captain watched him being ferried ashore as the ship again cast loose and began drifting toward the sea.

"How long do you suppose you have to be in Africa to get like that?" said Anthony.

Don Ruiz laughed. "Don't worry, señor. Several thousand generations on your mother's side at least, it seems."

Anthony shook his head. He had already thought of *that*.

"I must get out of this soon," he muttered. He looked forward to a glimpse of the open sea eagerly. He hoped Neleta would not have any children. It was curious that she didn't. He wondered about it. For three hours they twisted and drifted around the curves through the jungle where the *Ariostatica* had once battled her way going up. It was all sadly familiar now.

This was his fourth trip to the coast. The crocodiles did not seem to have moved. He shot at one from the deck and missed. The women with babies who were kept on deck in the bows cried out. Suddenly it began to get cooler; suddenly he could hear the whisper of the sea. *La Fortuna* slid down the last, straight, canal-like reach of the Rio Pongo in the grip of the strong ebb and flung herself free of the forest.

Across the beautiful, blue lagoons between the islands gulls were flying. Green and white glints with fiery opal hearts gleamed far and near in the water as the clouds shifted. There was a low mist on the other side of the islands where the surf pounded, a stiff salt breeze, white caps far out. Look at the huge roller coming in over the bar! Oh, what a glorious clean-washed world! Life again, life!

He gave a glad cry that brought Juan running from the wheel. He raced back again before the ship could yaw, having caught the infection of joy himself from Anthony. He set his hat on his head jauntily like the Juan of old times and gayly gave orders to set the jibs. The sound of the surf grew louder and louder as they drew slowly across the broad lagoon.

The first batches of slaves came on deck and sat down about a kettle to eat. It was just ten o'clock then. They were made to say a brief Latin grace. They would learn it soon. A bucket of salt water was passed into which they dipped their hands. A kid of farina and beans was placed before each gang. At a motion from a leader they dipped their hands into the food together; at another signal they swallowed. Attempts to snatch or to avoid eating brought the canes into use. All appetites were assumed to be the same. Both men and women were now given a whiff or two on a pipe passed about rapidly. They clapped hands, shouted "Viva la Habana," and having received a pint of water apiece were sent back into the hold again.

"Do not let too many at a time come on deck, captain," advised Anthony. "Wait till you find out their temper."

Don Ruiz nodded. He was anxious now as the ship was rapidly approaching the narrow inlet. Anthony turned to hasten the preparations of the Kru boys who were going to take him and Juan ashore. His light boat which could be paddled was slung out ready to lower. As usual a great moiling and bubbling of sand and muddy water was going on in the cut through the barrier reef. The pace of the ship increased. Suddenly *La Fortuna* was seized by the violent current whirling through the tidal gulf and spewed out into the open sea beyond. She stood shivering a moment. Then her jibs filled again.

"You have her, captain," shouted Anthony. "Adiós. Come on, Juan!"

The boat was lowered with a rush and cast loose. For a moment the black bulk of the ship with her blind ports loomed hugely above them. Then came a great whispering mound of green water. As the boat rose the ship seemed to sink. Through her wooden walls Anthony heard a long muffled groan, the crack of whips . . . then he was swept landward, boiling in on the crest of the mile-long roller with the backs of the Kru boys before him bending frantically to the paddles. Juan lay back on the stern looking up at the sky ecstatically. The pace was terrific now. Suddenly they were hurled forward into a smother of foam. The boys leaped out and raced the boat up the shelving beach. They all leapt out onto the firm, clean sand. He watched them carry the boat into the sand dunes as if they were still impelled by the last wave. And out there——

La Fortuna hurried westward a glimmering mountain of sail with a daylight moon looking at her wanly.

There is the fellowship and aid of human companionship, the consolation and sustenance of religion, the healing and health-giving power of certain land and seascapes. All of these have balms with which to poultice the slowly bleeding bruises and contusions of life. But they can rarely be invoked or singled out like some chemical drug in the *materia medica.* They occur like wild, healing herbs sown accidentally and reaped by chance. It is a mistake to suppose them to be panaceas. They are at best palliatives or restoratives, but often excellent ones for the time being, particularly if they are imbibed without the patient's being fully aware that they are being administered. His trip to the coastal reefs long remained in Anthony's memory as one of those curative experiences, an episode which, without being able to explain, he regarded as having both prolonged and enhanced his existence.

And there *was* something enormously clean and invigorating about these islands washed by the tides and scoured by the sea winds; there was nothing mysterious or shadowy. They lay drenched and soaked, quivering in eternal, tropical light. He felt this as soon as he stepped ashore.

For unknown miles before him the virgin beach of the narrow, barren strip streamed northward. It finally hid itself in the white surf-mist that at some distance ahead glowed with rainbow patches now and then when a league-long roller crackled and smashed. Gulls darted along under the curl of these translucent green combers and miraculously escaped to go lilting off over the surface again. The wind blew keen and fresh, warm, but robbed of its dank forest languor and the odour of rotting vegetation. The salty tang of it cleared the head.

Above all there was an overpowering sensation of the downpouring of white light on the sand and water; of the upbeating of blue rays again; of immense wastes and spaces of cobalt sea and robin's-egg sky. Beyond and beyond stretched the taut, black thread of the horizon. Here was boundary. Otherwise it might have been eternity.

Seaward, soapy flounces of green water wavered along the beach in ever shifting patterns of melting curves. Landward, marched a mimic mountain range of dazzling white sand dunes crowned by a miniature tropical table-land. There was not even the memory of man here. Nothing living accompanied Anthony but flocks of sandpipers that always flew a little ahead, alighted, and waited for him to catch up with them again. Then they would take wing with a whirr and faint, shrill cries that only accentuated the solitude. They left dainty tracks fading into the wet marge. And there was a species of beach crab to be discerned only by its shadow flitting across the sand. In the glare their bodies were invisible. Thus to the sound of wings and waves, and in the midst of a perpetually dissolving net of milky shadows that flowed away before him he walked all that afternoon.

The hollower boom of the surf as it broke against the more abrupt prism of the beach uncovered by the ebb at last warned him that it was time to return. He faced south and began to retrace his footsteps. He had covered two leagues or more. Yet his elation on landing was not yet expended. He swung his arms and legs joyfully. One could walk forever on the smooth silver of these firm sands.

The sun sank. The brief, tropical afterglow faded leaving a bitten remnant of the waning moon to pour grey glory along the strand where castles of foam bubbled and flecked away like piles of melting opals. The white surf-mist became suddenly ghostly and magical. The returning tide began to sound a slowly ascending scale. Soft voices seemed to cry to him from the surf from time to time. His eyes widened and felt comfortable again. Suddenly it seemed as if his whole scalp had loosened. In the first cool of the evening he bathed in the beach pools and trotted along the edge of the sea with the stinging salt water racing around his calves.

What a relief it was not to have the roaring and the howling of the forests suddenly begin at twilight! Here there was no sound except the rhythmic boom of the breakers and the whisper and lisp of the waves as they swished up the beach. They seemed to wash his mind as clean of memories and forebodings as they did sand and seaweed from the interstices of protruding lumps of brain-coral that rose here and there above the sand.

Yes, it was a timeless place.

Here he could live again for a while the untroubled life of a healthy body using its mind for nothing but the needs of the instant. He was trotting along over the sand in the present only. Even the thud of his feet no longer bothered him. He seemed to skim lightly, without an effort, shoved along as if he were on vanes by the light, tingling thrust of his bare toes.

A mile ahead of him a yellow glow sprang up a little way inland among the dunes where Juan and the four Kru boys had made camp. Supper would be ready! He was suddenly very hungry. He took a final plunge in the surf opposite the bivouac and came in hand-over-hand in a glorious smother of foam. He followed the men's tracks up into the dunes.

There it was pleasantly warm again where the sand still gave off the stored heat of the day. From a little sand ridge he looked down upon the camp. A forked, orange flame kept the shadows dancing in the hollow amid the scrub-palm thickets where they had pitched for the night. The five men lay sprawled about the fire, their assegais thrust into the sand with the broad blades twinkling in the firelight. The sound of their murmuring voices and a low laugh drifted up to him with the odour of roasting meat. Thank heaven there were no women here! What need of them? Here for a while, here it would be like the garden before Eve and her daughters came. But it would not be lonely. There would be the strong, friendly, passionless existence of males with all the million details that women were always bothering about left out, dropped and forgotten. Here they would kill and eat, sleep and swim, talk when they listed or remain silent. Here they would live alone and clean in a brief, happy brotherhood of fishers and hunters till the rains came.

Good then were these long, barren islands with the ocean on one side and the wide, blue lagoon on the other; good the golden net of unknown stars above and the peerings of the sun and moon in their majestic transits. Here the eternal sweep of the salt winds had reduced the scrub thickets to something tame and manageable. The mischievous monkeys and the huge, hungry swallowers were absent. Only beach rabbits and a tiny species of deer; only the sea-birds haunted these coral rocks and pleasant groves. On the landward side the cocoanuts grew down to the border of mangroves. Little arms of the sea penetrated this ancient reef of time and ended in coves bordered by silver, sickle-shaped beaches; strands untrodden, unknown, strewn with glorious shells, secret and beautiful. And it would all be understood, it would not have to be put into words and explained. Down there by the firelight where his fellow Adams awaited him—they knew already. They waited for him with their spears thrust into the sand.

He threw his useless clothes in the bushes and stepping out into the moonlight gave them a hail. Loud shouts of greeting came up to him and the figures about the fire leaped into sudden, vigorous life.

From a barrel sunk in the sand that afternoon Juan gave him a clear, tasteless drink. It was a freely-flowing fisherman's well he now looked into. They dined on beach-birds, and the roasted carcass of one of the small deer speared that afternoon. They roasted some yams in the fire and ate them with a little salt. Pipes were passed around. One of the Kru boys told of adventures spearing sharks. They wrapped their blankets about them and dropped off to sleep.

In the morning the place seemed to be washed and scoured by light. It grew brighter, fiercer. The blue sea through a dip in the dunes became opalescent and luminous. The shadows of hawks passed over them. The palm leaves clicked together in the breeze.

But they no longer heard the incessant voice of the ocean or the clack of the little forest. They had blent themselves with that tune and had become a part of it. It was eternal. It was always now. They existed in warmth, health, infinite leisure and a universal bath of light. The mind of Anthony which had become a place of gloomy shadows signalled to his body that all was well again. Suddenly he had become young and at peace with himself.

Juan looked up at him that morning while he plied the fire with dry palm leaves. The flame, which was invisible in the white light that engulfed it, could be seen only by its orange tips and the heat shadows streaming over the sand. It was merely a part of the burning day itself. Light going back to light. The dry leaves returned to light in the process. They returned to that from which they had come. There were no ashes. It was quite an obvious process. You saw it without having to think about it, just as you saw the water from tidal pools running back into the ocean again, leaving perhaps a little sediment.

Juan had grown into a powerful man. There was something a little Gipsy-like about him. He was intensely sensitive to the moods of others, yet he himself was perennially gay. He lay back now, as he had lain that day on the dock at Regla, and kicked his naked heels in the air. A gay challenge to heaven it was, a kind of triumph in the light over the silly shadows of things.

"What is gloom, my master?" he seemed to say. "Do I not also live in the eternal light in which I know, and knew from that morning when you watched me send the swallow back, that your own being is also bathed." Pretending to strum a guitar he sang in his clear tenor,

> "Wild, wild is the child
> In the vale of Bembibre
> As he leads his white flock
> Where the low willows grow.
> Where the steep river calls
> I have heard him at noonday
> Go down by the pools
> Of dark waters below.

> "And I heard him again
> When the glory of evening
> Beat red on the heights
> Where the wolf is his foe.
> Mad, mad are the songs
> Of the vale of Bembibre;
> Wild, wild is the voice
> Of the child of Minho."

That day they fished a little, swam, slept,—and when evening came they slept again. Anthony wakened once to watch the meteors falling like tears of light down the dark cheeks of the sky. The moon had set. That most mysterious of the constellations, the Southern Cross, smouldered and winked. Over the dunes the chant of the surf sounded like deep basses intoning an elegy for a world beautiful but forgotten ages ago.

At first Juan had kept a calendar by nicking a log every day with an axe, but he forgot to do so after a while and the log was used for firewood. They knew, if they cared to know, what time of day it was by the height of the source of glory, by the length of the shadows of the dunes. Yet night constantly surprised them as morning always did. To Anthony the nights and days had already flowed into one thing that was a mere sense of continuance. Something refreshed but not interrupted by sleep.

They took the boat out and chased great fish in the lagoons. The shadows of them could be seen through the colourless water, stealing along against the white sand banks. They would drift down quietly and dart the harpoons into the blue mottled shade that had suddenly resolved itself into a shark basking in the warmth. A terrific battle would begin. They would play these great fish for hours. The boat would be towed along by them, with the water being dyed behind by the dark banner of the monster's blood. Sometimes they would have to cut loose to avoid shipwreck. Or, at long last, the terrific face of the thing would be brought to the gunwale and heaved up. Then the assegais would plunge and hack. It was sheer, mad butchery. Great and little fish would rush in from all sides as the trail of blood seeped along the reefs. From a hundred holes in the coral, blunt, and parrot-nosed beings rushed forth to eat and be eaten. The snapping and tearing and the whirling would rapidly become universal. Then they would cut the still twisting mass loose and watch it turning over and over, sinking in a great whorl of feasting things, flashing, tearing, stabbing and writhing.

Once they pursued an apparition like a giant water-bird that waved its way with wide, black wings through the liquid atmosphere. It was a large whipray and nearly proved their undoing. They lanced it and it started. After one tremendous burst of speed that nearly swamped them it turned and attacked the boat. Its great liver-coloured flukes came rushing up out of the water lifting the boat half-way out of the element when it struck. Then it sounded and turned on them again. But they did not wait. They made at top speed for the beach and watched the dark cloud dart into the shallows after them. There it floundered about for some time and finally made off. Juan spent the next day caulking the boat.

But all this was incidental, a sort of punctuation of the long, date-less flow of days in the white dream of light. Anthony liked best to spend hours angling off a rock with sand fleas for a little rainbow-coloured fish that would seldom strike, or to wait patiently with one of the Kru boys in a small sandy valley among the dunes where the tiny deer, not much larger than great rabbits, would finally approach the lure of a scarlet rag waving on a stick. It would take them hours sometimes, but they would always come at last. Then the bow would twang, and supper transfixed by an arrow would be kicking in the sand. One of the boys could kill these little fawn-coloured animals with his assegai. It was the last test of skill with the spear, for they ran like lightning in zigzags. Yet the spear guessed right nearly every time.

With four such Nimrods there was no use for firearms. The single musket they had brought was never used. Food was no worry. They would drain a beach pool and fill a basket with mullet. The rest they left for the gulls and fish hawks which became absurdly tame. And there were cocoanuts, groves of them, meat and drink. And no ants! Only a few exhausted butterflies blown over from the mainland reached the barren reefs across the protecting moat of the far-flung, wind-swept lagoons.

There was one cove in particular which Anthony regarded as peculiarly his own. It was understood when he went there he was not to be disturbed. It was closed from the sea by a reef through which nothing but small fish and water could penetrate. It was a clean, white basin with a few cocoa palms hanging over it from a bank that curved inward overlooking a narrow beach just above the reach of the ordinary tide. Here he swam for hours and slept in the shade of the bank. Here he indulged an endless glowing day-dream, peopling the beach with bright god-like figures that seemed to come to him like visions of a forgotten world of light and song. He was filled with an infinite, happy regret for this lost world, the world which the antiphonal voices of the surf lamented at night, singing together in sad, liquid basses as if they would have it back again with the morning.

Even in the daytime the strange, far-off echoes of those watery voices sounded incessantly in the hollow of the shell-like cove. At last he thought about nothing. He listened. He saw the light striking down through the limpid water, where, on the bottom, the shadows of the waves moved in faint, grey etchings of the movement of motion itself. A few shells lay down there, twisted whorls of things. At first he thought they were dead and empty. But as the days passed and the utmost minutiae of his surroundings burnt into his brain by the incessant stream of light he saw that they also moved. Their triangular relations to one another changed.

And it was light, light, light!—the perpetual tropical beat and shimmer of it, the overpowering glare and the living, burning glory of it in all its colours and angles and shades and airy and watery prisms and essences that now at last saturated him until his very blood ran with it; and the farthest, darkest chamber of his mind admitted the effect of it. The light was in him now. He understood one day, as he lay on the beach timelessly gazing into the water of the cove where the light seemed to concentrate, that he was like and one with the rocks and the trees and plants about; one with the creatures that moved only a little down there on the sand-floor under the water. He saw that the whorls of their shells, which now glimmered up to him greatly magni-

fied, and the whorls on the trunks of palm trees that marked the ascending helix of their seasons were of the same signature, nature's
tellurian, the writing of the name of light.

And all that he had been thinking about light for years past, all that
had been going on in his mind about it when he did not know it,
coalesced. As on that day on the *Wampanoag* when Mrs. Jorham had
interrupted his vision, he ceased again to think in progressions. He
apprehended. He thought all at once. He saw. He closed his eyes
to see better. . . .

He was floating now in a boundless place without direction. It was
absolutely dark. He could no longer open his eyes. Only his mind
existed in the gloom. In his thought was stored the quality of light.
"Let there be light!" Instantly a flower of light bloomed furiously in
the void. It was a day stream beautiful beyond expression that spread
outward in all ways at once, a sphere that instantaneously pre-empted
all of space and yet was forever spreading. Where it was not was
nothing. Where it reached was light. All things with bodies were
part of and existed only in this flower of light. To watch the shifting
of its endless petals of things from stars to seashells was to peep at
time. To see the whole flower itself ever expanding through the nothing of darkness was to see all of time and to see it as one flash. For
though the flower existed for eternity, that which looked at it as from
a great distance and apart from it saw it as one outgoing flash. Instantaneously everything from the beginning to the end had happened.

He opened his eyes and realized that he had closed them only an
instant before. He was in his body again. He moved his arms and
legs. He felt painlessly exhausted; happy. It was some time before
he could tell the difference between the voices of the surf and the blood
whispering in his own ears. He began to play aimlessly with a small
palm-nut smooth to his fingers. He started tucking it into the sand.
"A tree will spring from it," he thought. "It is alive. . . ."

The thing came out of the ground like a snake. It put out a leaf,
another. Its leaves whirled around with the sun in a great ascending
spiral. For an instant it waved its green hands fully-grown against
the light. Then it dropped seeds. The tree withered to its base again.
It was gone. He was still holding the seed in his hand. He finished
tucking it into the ground. "So that is the way trees grow! They
and the seed are one. To the master of the flower-of-light they too are
a flash. I am. All things are. 'A thousand years in his sight are but
a day.' Aye, a billion aeons of ages—one swift flash."

He thought no longer now. He lay on the sand utterly quiet in
spirit and still in mind. The feeling in his body was equivalent to a
long wordless prayer. Without an image or mediator he worshipped

his maker, the creator of light.   Finally the tide came up and lapped over his hands.   He left then and went home to the fire.

That night a brief spatter of rain fell on them.   But Anthony did not feel it.   He slept as if he had exhausted himself by a ten-mile run.

Juan was worried.   The rainy season with its first storms must be close at hand.   But he would say nothing about it, he decided.   What if they did get wet—mañana.   He pulled the blanket closer while looking up at the hazy stars and hummed a soft, lilting tune.   Life was very pleasant here on these barrier beaches.   After a while they would go back again.   The tune died away in his throat.   The voices in the surf sang on.

CHAPTER FORTY-THREE

THE IMAGE BEGINS TO MELT

TO AN epicure in odours the village of Bangalang just before the rainy season closed down would have been an adventure without illusions. At that time even the native canoes plying between Mongo Tom's and Gallegos passed it to windward. There were great piles of drying and putrefying fish on the beach, the kettles were busy trying-out palm oil,—and the combination of fish-guts, greasewood, and rancid vegetable-butter was something that only the inured inhabitants and the delighted buzzards of the vicinage could stand. Great clouds of these birds continued to arrive daily, attracted by a place which advertised itself so well to Buzzardom. As a consequence, the palm thatch of the fishers' huts showed, even at a distance, as if covered with melting patches of snow.

The hut of Ungah-gola, Neleta's maternal aunt, occupied the most salubrious site in the redolent town. That is not to insist that its environs suggested the jasmine in full bloom. But the house was built over the water, and what was thrown through the floor-door, its only entrance, was regularly removed by the diurnal besom of the tide instead of decomposing leisurely in a more normal manner. To a woman of eighty,—by far the oldest woman on the Grain Coast, where the female life-span was usually brief—the absence of flies was something, as was also the exclusion of both rain and sunlight which the rather superior construction of the hut afforded.

Ungah-gola, indeed, according to the standards of her neighbourhood, was well-off. In one corner of the hut she had an old ship's chest full of cowrie shells. Her battery of earthen pottery was luxurious. She had several large mirrors, one of which was suspended from her neck, and the amount of copper wire wound about her fat arms and legs was prodigious. All this, and the ample furnishings of her hut, she had accumulated slowly by the simple process of outliving three husbands and telling fortunes. For many miles up and down the coast there were few Kru fishermen, whether Mohammedan or pagan, who ventured upon any important undertaking without first consulting the wise widow of Bangalang.

On a stifling afternoon toward the end of the dry season—which was now so unusually protracted as to have caused the old woman to mistake the droppings of buzzard dung on her roof for the first spatter of the long-expected rains—Ungah-gola was awakened from her half-comatose siesta by the sound of paddles rattling in a canoe, which was evidently being moored to the piles beneath her hut.

Some young fisherman in trouble, she supposed.

She sat up, and glancing in her mirror renewed the circles of white paint about her eyes. Presently the shaft of light in which she was working was obscured, and the head of her niece Neleta appeared coming through the trap in the floor.

A series of excited greetings and inquiries passed between the two women, who had not seen each other for over two years. Neleta was made welcome with an unusually prolonged finger-snapping, which the loose joints of old Ungah contrived to accentuate as if a skeleton was acting host. Neleta deposited her presents of food, cloth, and brass jewelry at the old woman's feet, and while Ungah discussed a soft pork pie with succulent sounds in the darkness, the young mistress of Gallegos unfolded the secrets of her troubled bosom to her invisible but highly audible aunt.

"Art thou not with child yet?" croaked the crone at last, choking on a pig's knuckle.

"No," said Neleta, "that is one of the things I have come to talk with thee about."

Her aunt grunted and sucked the marrow out of a bone with a loud *plop*. Neleta could see nothing but the white rings about her eyes.

"Is the white man without seed, then?" the crone queried disdainfully.

"Nay," said Neleta. "He is copious, and I am replenished often. But he does not burgeon within me."

"Thou art like thy mother," said Ungah. "Though her strong husband strove with her nightly, she brought him only two children in ten years. We come of a rather barren race, you know. I myself with three husbands had only four children—but we live long," she added. "We live long! *Um-m-m.*"

She grunted, and threw the wooden base of the demolished pork pie through the door. They heard it splash in the water below.

"I have thought," said Neleta after a long silence, "that it is because someone steals my husband's soul at night that we have no children. His body is perfect but his seed gives no life."

"And thou?" said Ungah, holding up a brand which she blew upon while peering at her niece.

"I?—*I* am a woman!" said Neleta proudly, standing up and dropping her robe. Her aunt peered at her and grunted.

"Come here," she said.

Under the fingers of the old woman the girl trembled.

"Tell me of all this," said Ungah, who appeared to be satisfied with her niece and began a rice pastry soothing to her gums.

A long talk followed. Neleta elaborated her theory: In his sleep, it seemed, Anthony became another person. Brother François would pay no attention to her fears. And Neleta was alarmed. Before Anthony returned from the islands she was resolved to do something about him. Her mother's people, she felt, would understand. Aunty Ungah would give her a charm—or a drench. Would she not? Everyone knew witchcraft could only be fought with witchcraft.

Ungah grunted sympathetically and spat at the name of the Christian priest.

It had been hard enough to slip away from Ferdinando, Neleta went on. He would have no further dealing with his mother's people. Aunt Ungah softly cursed him. "He would beat me," insisted Neleta, "if he knew I was here now." She appealed again to her aunt. "Thou knowest from whom the rice and presents come. Not from Ferdinando," she said. "And I am now mistress in the great house. If I had a child. Only just one!" She started to moan like a savage woman bereaved. Her aunt determined to call in help.

She blew several toots on a conch shell and a few minutes later the form of Mnombibi, the local wizard, her collaborator in many a mysterious mischief, thrust through the floor-door. The shells on his ankles, filled with dried peas, rattled as he drew his feet into the hut and he squatted peering into the darkness. There were now two pairs of white-rimmed eyes staring at Neleta. They seemed to be floating in the dark like ghostly spectacles. After some palaver the trouble was explained. Would Mnombibi provide a charm to keep Anthony's soul in him while he slept?

He would—for a consideration—and on his own conditions. He must have something belonging to Anthony, a nail-paring or hair, for instance. Also he must be allowed to visit Gallegos surreptitiously and see for himself how the land lay there. Especially, he must see the artificial cave of the white wizard with the dead tree before it. He had heard much about it. He questioned Neleta closely about Brother François.

The half-breed girl felt herself between two fires here. As a nominal Christian she feared the priest; a savage at heart she feared Mnombibi more. Her answers conveyed nothing to the wizard but further aroused his jealous suspicions of the white man's magic. It was said that those in the white wizard's charge, the children, wore charms about their necks which prevailed over all native spells. They were freed, he had heard, from the spells of the forest and river. How was it done? Who was the white man's *Duppee?* Mnombibi would find out.

Late afternoon saw Neleta and Mnombibi gliding back to Gallegos in a swift canoe. In the bottom of the boat was the wizard's kit. It consisted of two small bags tied at the neck, an ebony box, and a shaggy cocoanut painted with a devil's face. This occasionally rocked itself from side to side as if alive, while from within came clicking noises from time to time. Neleta sat saying nothing, both pleased and terrified. Two scared, young fishermen shovelled the canoe along rapidly.

They arrived at Gallegos an hour before sunset and considerably ahead of Ferdinando, who had gone to visit Mongo Tom. Neleta sighed with relief. It was easy enough to smuggle Mnombibi into the big house. She left the gate open at the man's bidding. From one of the bags he took out a dried baby's head and placed it on the threshold with the wizened face looking inward. It was a charm which nothing African could pass.

Once in the house he tied on a hyena's tail behind and began running about on all fours, sniffing in every room and corner. He nearly scared the maids to death, including Cheecha. They cowered grey-faced against the wall. Over Cheecha he lingered for some time. Finally he thrust his hands into her breast and pulled out something on a chain. It was the chameleon Anthony had given her in Havana, now large and fat. He broke it from its link and went on. Cheecha collapsed.

Arrived in the room where Anthony and Neleta slept, Mnombibi was doubly particular. So far he had not been able to smell out anything or anybody himself. He intended to make doubly sure now. The chameleon he suspected, but he knew how to dispose of it. He now opened his second bag, and bidding Neleta stand on a stool, waited.

Presently the large, flat head of a blind snake rose from the sack. There was a white fungous growth over its eyes. It looked like Mnombibi. He addressed it as "my dear nose," and bade it smell well for him.

The snake began to glide about the room. With its black, forked tongue it seemed to taste its way through space. Finally, after about fifteen minutes of apparent searching, it calmly returned to its bag and subsided there in oily coils.

Mnombibi snorted.

It was as he thought. The evil influence was not in the house. He would have to look outside. As a precaution, however, he fed Cheecha's chameleon to the snake. For some minutes a double-headed animal seemed to be peering from the bag. The small arms and head of the chameleon with rapidly blinking golden eyes protruded from the snake's mouth. Neleta still stood on the stool fascinated.

Mnombibi now spoke to her while he secured the snake. She left the stool and going over to a chest took out Anthony's hair brushes. She plucked several brown strands from the bristles. These she delivered to Mnombibi. He now opened his ebony box and rapidly began to fashion from beeswax and ashes the rough semblance of a pronouncedly male figure. In the wax he carefully incorporated Anthony's hair.

He now demanded double his fee and received it. He was sophisticated enough to know the value of gold coins. Until they were paid into his right hand he continued to hold the wax image in his left. Neleta had no doubt whatever that it was her man which Mnombibi had in his clutches. She was therefore glad to ransom him at twice what she had at first promised.

Mnombibi next gave her some further directions, and the horn of a black goat to hang under her bed. He told her that if he could prevail over the white wizard she should have a child. Her husband's soul, he said, would stay even at night as long as she kept the figure safely. He asked some further questions about Brother François and warned her against going to him. Any mention of the afternoon's doings would break the spell, he said.

He finally left after removing the dried head from the threshold. It had worked. The maids, who had made a bolt for the gate as soon as his back had been turned, had been stopped by it in the courtyard. He rattled the shells on his feet at them and promised them baboons for husbands if they ever mentioned his visit. He showed them the painted cocoanut shell and they shrieked. The last they saw of him was his broad, evil grin disappearing through the gate under the glare of his white spectacle-like eyes.

Neleta locked the wax figure of Anthony in her chest of drawers. A small spider that seemed to be spying on her she killed with her slipper. She was pleased to find that from that day forward her slightest wish was law with the maids.

Ferdinando, who was returning from a day's visit with Mongo Tom, stopped to light his pipe on the way up the hill just where the path turned out to Brother François's little settlement. He stooped low behind a rock to keep the tinder in his box from blowing away, and got out his flint and steel. It was at that moment that Mnombibi coming downhill passed him like a shadow and disappeared in the thicket. Ferdinando paused with his steel in the air. Then he realized he had not been seen by the witch-doctor, whom he had recognized.

Full of curiosity, he slipped his feet out of his pumps and followed noiselessly.

From time to time he caught sight of the black figure gliding through the plantation. Presently they both came to the edge of it near the little chapel. Mnombibi concealed himself in the long grass. Ferdinando crouched and watched Mnombibi. Some minutes passed. The chapel seemed to be empty and no one was about. A low hum of conversation could be heard coming from the huts, and the voice of the stream. Ferdinando at last became impatient. Why had the witch-doctor come here?—he wondered.

Just then Mnombibi wriggled out of the tall grass like a snake. He passed over the short space of lawn on his belly and made for the door of the chapel. He was careful to avoid the shadow of the cross that near sunset stretched long and black across the sward. At the door he paused for an instant, pressed close to the wall and peering in.

What Mnombibi saw was a perfectly smooth stone hut with one window, the cross bars of which threw the same kind of a magic shadow on the floor that rested on the lawn. At the far end was a stone table with candlesticks on it. "Seven-headed snakes," thought Mnombibi. This was evidently the table upon which the Christians ate their god. He had heard of that. The place was quite patently an artificial cave in which the god was kept locked up. There was even one small light hanging from a chain so that the god could see. The lamp had a red eye. Mnombibi was afraid of it. It seemed to watch him. But he must have a look at the god, nevertheless. The place was half dark, too. What was that against the far wall over the table?

Braving the guardian eye, he wriggled in half-way to the stone table and looked up. On the wall was the god of the white magician stretched out and fastened by nails on a tree.

"So—that was the way they kept their god prisoner! Perhaps, if the white witch-doctor could be caught and nailed up that way . . . eh! Then one would have both the god and the man who kept him, too. Both safely nailed on a tree! That would be a fine end to the white man's rival magic. And all the powers of the god on the tree would be in the keeping of Mnombibi. An idea—an idea to be considered carefully!" As a first trial of strength the witch-doctor made a face at the crucifix. That was carrying matters a little too far, perhaps—considering that watchful eye. He thought he saw the figure squirm in the shadows. It might get loose! He turned and crawled for the door. Suddenly he heard men walking and talking just outside. He rose to make a bolt for it.

Just at the door he met Brother François and the old Susu hunter, who acted as a sort of sacristan and was coming to ring the evening bell. For an instant the three stood as if petrified. The red-rimmed eyes of Mnombibi in their white circles glared devilishly at Brother François.

Ferdinando stood up in sheer excitement to see better. In his confused mind, where the stiff Latin ritual of the cathedral at Barcelona, seen in his boyhood, mixed with the earlier savage memories of his mother's hut at Bangalang, he instantly saw implicit in the group before him a trial of supernatural skill. It was the witch-doctor *versus* the priest.

Greatly startled by the sudden apparition at his chapel door the priest made the sign of the cross. Mnombibi instantly hurled the painted cocoanut at him, dived into the grass, and wriggled away like a snake, the grass rippling behind him. Brother François was so surprised at this curious procedure that he actually caught the strange missile that had been hurled at him and stood holding it, half-bewildered, turning it over in his hands. The bestial face painted on it glared up at him. An extraordinary series of events now took place.

The old Susu took one glance at the devil's head in Brother François's hands, and giving vent to an angry and frightened howl struck it from his grasp. He kept shouting something in his dialect, evidently a warning to the priest. The nut rolled some distance away. Meanwhile, the old warrior kept dashing about frantically looking for something. Finally he darted to the bank of the stream and returned with a heavy boulder. He poised this over the nut and brought it down with great force. The thing cracked open and a colossal tawny spider darted out. It crouched back in the grass fiddling with its mouth. It emitted an indescribable, locust-like sound. The blood of all those looking at it ran thick and cold. Suddenly the Susu attempted to spring on it and stamp it flat. It ran up his leg. The man flung himself into the air, twisting and spinning. A shrill, whistling scream tore from his lips. Brother François and Ferdinando saw the spider leap from his extended arm while he was still in the air. It made for the ledge of rocks.

"Kill it, father," shouted Ferdinando, now darting forward. "Kill it! Kill it!"

The priest was terribly startled. He had not known Ferdinando was there.

They seized sticks and made after the thing. But it was too late. Once they caught sight of it again, but it made off into a rift in the rock strata.

"It has stolen the man's soul," shouted Ferdinando who gave some signs of being hysterical and was twitching all over.

"Come, my son, you are too good a Christian to believe *that*. Mon

Dieu!" said Brother François. He laid his hand reassuringly on the half-breed's shoulder. Ferdinando shook it off.

"You will see, father. Por Dios, you will see!" he snarled. "You cannot help him now."

They returned and found the old man lying on the grass face downward. He had blanched a slate-grey all over. When they turned him over there was foam on his lips.

"He will die," said Ferdinando, "in a few days. That devil has gone off with him. This is only a breathing corpse."

Brother François, who had been horribly shaken, could not find a mark on the man's body. From sheer nervousness and pity he began to shed a few tears. Ferdinando looked at him with contempt. They carried the old warrior to a hut together.

"You will not say anything about this, will you?" said the priest humbly. "The people here would not understand."

"They would understand well enough," said Ferdinando, He stood watching Brother François working over the man. "No use," he added. He stood a little longer. Finally he shrugged his shoulders.

"Good night, father." He said it contemptuously, and left.

On the way up the hill a spatter of rain hit him in the face. What a tale he would have to tell Neleta at supper tonight! There could be no doubt that Mnombibi had won. He felt a greater contempt than ever for Brother François. In this country a priest was no good. What was he doing at Gallegos anyway? He wished Anthony would come back. Caramba! he had better hurry himself! It was coming on to rain with a vengeance. He started to run.

Over the steaming forest and plantation the roar of the oncoming rains set in, modulated by growls of distant thunder. Ferdinando was soaked. He drenched himself inside with rum and hot water that night. Neleta had to help him to bed. She was greatly worried. Anthony should have returned before this. She took the little image out of the drawer to look at it. She had forgotten that her chest of drawers stood all afternoon in the sunlight. To her horror the figure had partly melted. She ran out on the porch in her night-gown. There was no sign of Anthony's canoe having returned.

Westward toward the Atlantic the lightning snaked through the clouds that now hung low over the coastal forests, vomiting rain. Neleta shivered and went in. The bed was cold.

CHAPTER FORTY-FOUR

THE HARD METAL RUNS

THE rain that had soaked Ferdinando overtook Anthony on the river half-way to Gallegos. He had delayed at the barrier beaches far too long.

Nevertheless, the last morning there had dawned as clear and golden as any that had preceded it—and the rains usually announced themselves by several days of scud and showers driving before.

But not this time. The vast, low-hanging cloud of the main deluge had simply lifted itself over the horizon about noon and driven down on them with lightning zigzagging along its inky front. Thunder rumbled and stumbled along the coast for hundreds of miles. The low, continuous mutter of it had been their first warning. Then the cloud came with high, billowing thunderheads and cut off the amber light like a sliding shutter. Men wandered about under it as if in an eclipse. The world had instantly slumped from clear, cheerful sunlight into grey gloom. A steaming rain, which grew colder hour by hour, slid down upon them in slanting cascades that dashed off their shoulders faster and faster.

They had hastily packed their few belongings in the rowing canoe and fled up-river before the cloud. But not fast enough. The first full deluge and the violent squalls that always accompanied it caught them toward evening ten miles below Gallegos on the Rio Pongo.

It was dark as the inside of a tar barrel. The forest moaned, washed and crashed. The gusts seemed to be trying to lift their light boat out of the water and spattered the river around them with torn branches and leaves. They could steer only by flashes of lightning as night came on, and the tide failed them long before they could make Mongo Tom's. To force the boat upstream against both the ebb and the rapidly swelling current was soon impossible. There was nothing for it but to try to land and wait for the turn of the tide. To tie up, or to drift and bail, would be to court disaster from the lose débris of the forest that now began to hurtle at them suddenly out of the darkness.

Landing was not to be so easily accomplished as thought of, however.

The mild drainage ditch of the dry-season, Rio Pongo could now scarcely be recognized in the boiling, swirling current full of dead trees and forest garbage which flashes of lightning revealed streaming down upon them like a broad brown ribbon hurling itself out of the darkness. Already the river had overflowed its low banks. To be battered over the fallen trunks and root-knees in the shallows was sure destruction. They paddled anxiously along the edge of the rapidly submerging forest looking for some slight rise of ground but found none. It was scarcely possible to make headway now. Then an eddy sucked them upstream, and a jagged bolt, that seemed to strike the river itself just ahead, revealed a grotesquely shaped sandbar with a few trees on top still rising above the flood.

They paddled under the lee of it and flashed their one dim lantern along its pitted banks. A large hole under the great roots, and a sickening smell of carrion caused one of the Kru boys to call out a warning. He was too late. Anthony caught the gleam of the lantern on two yellow eyes under the roots, and then the beast was on them.

A crocodile disturbed guarding its festering nest acts impulsively. This one tried to climb into the boat. One of the Krus thrust his assegai into its mouth. It swerved. But the boat was half full of water and the lantern out. Then the tail of the monster came around and struck the craft a shattering blow.

"Pull," roared Anthony.

Luckily the Krus stuck to the paddles. Their last stroke shoved them into the bank. Everybody swarmed out and up over the roots and stood on something flat and solid in the downpour. Anthony began to shout their names. They were all near him—and all there— somewhere in the darkness.

A great scrambling and thrashing broke out on the bank below.

"Madre!" screamed Juan. "He's coming up after us!"

Another flash revealed the determined saurian coming across the low plateau of the sandbank straight for them. In the intense dazzling glare the fanged, lizard smile, the flaring curve of the upper lip and the swift preposterous waddle of the squat legs of the thing seemed to be rushing upon them for an eternity. Beyond was the brown, bubbling slide of the river, and against it the bare branches of dead trees thrashing despairing arms into the air.

Darkness swooped again.

Anthony found himself with that vision still seared on his eyeballs while he sat high up in the limbs of one of the trees. His action had been absolutely automatic. The tail of the beast went battering about down below. It jarred the thick tree perceptibly. He felt it through his tightly gripping hands. By God, that fellow meant business!

Anthony and Juan were sharing the same tree with a young Diana monkey. It whooped and swore at them till the steadily descending downpour, which varied from a drizzle to drowning cloudbursts that drummed on the river, silenced it. In lulls they heard its teeth chattering and their own were soon joining in chorus. In the infrequent lulls of wind and thunder the miserable men in the trees called to each other. The voices of the Kru boys already sounded weak and thin. The hopeless twittering of these drenched and shivering human birds first suggested to Anthony that they would probably perish here miserably. Hours passed while the mad rain beat upon them.

A boat came down-river beating a gong. They set up a noise like the wailing of souls in purgatory but a squall drowned them out. When it was over the boat had passed them and gone downstream. Those on board would be looking for a light.

Morning it seemed would never come. It was impossible, Anthony felt, that only a few hours ago he had been warm and dreamfully happy on the beaches shining with sunlight. This was a different world he was in now. Its signs were darkness, furious rain, cold, and the vision of the crocodile charging in the lightning glare. How could one night leave him so weak? He fastened himself to the limb with a belt.

The wind died toward morning and the rain let up. The light finally filtered through a dark, bulging canopy softly flowing over the tree-tops close above. A new misery now developed. In the calm unnumbered swarms of gnats and mosquitoes fell on them. A Hindu god with fifty hands could not have defended himself. They were bitten till they felt they were going mad. The mosquitoes lit in grey patches and drew blood.

It was possible to see where they were now. It was a flat sandbar about a hundred yards long and twenty wide. Its sharp nose pointed upstream and its top was only a few feet above the flood. It was the cherished abode of scorpions and a caravanserai for crocodiles. How they had ever landed safely in the dark and got as far as the trees was a mystery. As the water kept rising the number of saurians large and small that came out from under the roots where the sand was rapidly being washed away was astounding. Five or six of them started to roam around under the trees snapping at each other. All of the Krus had lost their spears. Their boat was no more. The monkey looked about him and moaned scratching his orange-coloured thighs. Juan looked up from a lower limb with a face so swollen and red that it looked like the ape's behind. But no one laughed.

"What next, master?" said Juan with swollen lips.

"Breakfast," said Anthony trying to grin.

"Sí, for the crocodile," said Juan. He leaned against the tree a symbol of swollen despair. The Krus dripped from their branches like so many black scarecrows on a grotesque gallows, silent.

Quite obviously there was nothing to do. They did so. They sat. Anthony felt on fire all over, dull and feverish. He moved into a more comfortable crotch and tried to think. He dozed instead. The wind had driven off the gnats. But he was thoroughly poisoned. His eyes were swelling shut. Suddenly everybody began to shout at once. A constant dismal screeching went up from the treetops punctuated by the howls of the monkey. Down-river they had heard a shot.

Suppose the boat should pass them again? It might. He could no longer see. Only a glimmer through his puffed cheeks. He pulled off his shirt and began to wave it and roar till he was hoarse.

The sound of the frantically beaten boat gong came to him as a reprieve. Then there were shouts and a great many guns went off. The crocodiles hated to leave home. It all seemed far away. He was too ill to care now. His arms and legs were too swollen to move. He was afire from head to foot. At last he felt himself being lowered dizzily out of the tree. Someone was pouring something heavenly cool and soothing over him. He choked on some good Holland spirits.

"A man could lie down and sleep now. No more lightning in the dark forest or mosquitoes. A man could lie down and sleep. A man could . . ."

Three hours later they were back at Bangalang and he was being carried up the hill. Neleta put him to bed weeping over him but he couldn't see her. It was she who had sent the boat. He didn't care.

"Let me sleep, I tell you, let me sleep." He dozed off in a kind of poisoned coma.

Two days later the swelling suddenly subsided and he was shortly able to get about a little. But he felt weak and had great white circles under his eyes in a face that was otherwise like a mask of bronze. The sun, indeed, had burnt him bronze all over but most of the good of the trip to the barriers had been undone by the night on the sandbar. And he would take no advice. Ferdinando kept on insisting that he take double potions of the cinchona drench to ward off the fever. But he was sick of the bitter stuff and began to smoke cigars constantly and take large quantities of rum, sugar, and hot water instead. He used up most of the Cape wine and was stupid after dinner. In that way he would get some sleep. Otherwise he would want to prowl at night with a cigar in his face.

Neleta was avid for him after his absence. She used him now. He tried to get some passive solace out of her desire. That only seemed to madden her the more. In the morning he would lie with marks of her teeth all over his breast, too indifferent to get up. Outside the rain streamed down for hours at a time. The forests steamed. Once in a while the sun would come out for a few minutes and turn the little courtyard and the room into a Turkish bath. There was blue mould in his shoes in the morning. His clothes were clammy.

A week of unexpected and exceptional clear weather brought him a little reaction of will power. He went down to the docks to watch the loading of the remainder of the slaves still in the pens onto *El Argonautico,* a ship direct from Havana. This cleaned the last of the people out of the barracoons. He felt relieved. There would not be any more for some months. Caravans did not come in what was usually the beginning of continuous rains. There was a heavy mail to go over, some of it from Livorno.

Mr. Bonnyfeather was dying—the letter was five months old. Probably the old man was gone by this time. He paused, surprised to find that the news caused him almost no emotion of any kind. He couldn't feel anything any more. He had some wine opened at the warehouse and drank in Ferdinando's office which he had never done before. Two bottles of Malaga brought a faint sensation of sorrow. Ferdinando kept worrying him about what to do in his books with the material furnished to Brother François. He cursed Brother François and Ferdinando and opened letters listlessly.

. . . Mr. Bonnyfeather has directed me to write Captain Bittern at Gibraltar to call at Gallegos for you and bring you back to Livorno. He is most desirous of seeing you before it is too late. The "Unicorn" is expected at Gibraltar almost any time now. Address Captain Bittern there, giving the latitude and longitude of the Rio Pongo. Be sure to communicate that data to him. He does not know the Grain Coast. The "Unicorn" has been making many prizes of late. The war with Spain is profitable to British privateers, etc. . . . How do you find life with the golden savages? McNab and our mutual Faith are both well. . . .

It was Toussaint writing. The rest of the letter was about European politics.

"How did he find life with the golden savages?" My God! He spat on the floor. He was too tired to write Captain Bittern. Let him find the Rio Pongo if he could. It was on the maps.

He turned over some letters from Havana. Cibo was sending the *Ariostatica* again in two months' time. "His Excellency is most desirous of slipping as many ships through the net of British harriers as possible."

Humph! Suppose the *Unicorn* should pick up a few of His Excellency's ships and sell them for prizes? He grinned at the thought. Would he go back with Captain Bittern if he appeared now? He didn't know. Probably not. He couldn't make decisions any more off-hand. He felt like—like a fish left on a hot beach.

He swept the mail into the drawer and went back up the hill. Perhaps it might help if he unburdened his soul to Brother François. He turned in at the little gate and found the priest sitting disconsolate after having buried the old Susu some days before. Anthony had to listen to the whole story of the spider. It horrified him strangely.

Brother François had not been able to do anything for the man. After a while he had just stopped breathing. A terror rested over the little settlement since the event. The priest felt helpless in the face of superstition like this. He looked it. He kept on protesting. Anthony felt for the first time there was no help in him any more. He said nothing about his own troubles. His soul had been stolen too, he told himself half whimsically. He stumbled on up the hill.

In the sun the wine came on him strong. He felt dizzy and there were spots before his eyes. Brother François was no good any more, he told himself. He went in to his bed, fell asleep, and wakened with the shakes and fever. That night on the sandbar! Fever was in his bones, he felt his joints grind. The rains came on for good that night. Three days later he was nearly stricken to death again. The chills, the fever, and the rains went on. Malaria began to burn and freeze him.

For the rest of his life that long rainy season at Gallegos remained in his mind as a vague but horrible nightmare. He got steadily worse. It was always dark outside. But within him it was darker still. In a few weeks the world appeared as if he were sitting far back in a cave. At a great distance, and in a curiously blurred way, things went on happening at the entrance to the cavern. He himself was chained in there. He began to wish he were dead.

Every three days something invisible crept upon him in the darkness and shook him like a rat. His teeth chattered and clicked. Then he burned and sweated. Liquor brought a temporary relief. He drank steadily, constantly, and increasingly. He drank a great deal at night. He was soon utterly confused. Neleta kept annoying him by trying to keep him in bed. He would fight with her, drive her off. Yet he knew he should not. She meant well. He hated her now because she loved him. She would not go away. Ferdinando he would not have in the room for a moment.

The factor, however, took this philosophically enough. He was glad to find himself to all intents and purposes the master of Gallegos. Joseph soon introduced certain minor practices about the place which Pharaoh would never have countenanced.

Brother François for one fared ill. Neither Ferdinando nor Neleta welcomed him at dinner. Indeed, he would have ceased coming to the house on the hill altogether if it had not been that he longed to do all he could for Anthony. He was not able to break the clutch of the fever. As he sat by Anthony's bed he was always conscious of Neleta's eyes resting on him. They were baleful. She managed on one pretext or another to exclude him as much as she could. He had no knowledge of what Mnombibi had told her, of course. Nor did he know that Neleta threw all of his medicines away.

Anthony for most of the time appeared to be in a stupor. At any rate he would say very little to Brother François. He refused all offers of spiritual help and a suggestion that he should receive the wafer. In a dim but deep way Anthony was conscious of the struggle that was going on over him between Neleta and the priest. The atmosphere of the sick room when Brother François was present was very tense. Anthony begged to be let alone.

When he could think at all clearly he felt sure he was going to die. As he grew weaker and could no longer get drink for himself even at night the conviction grew upon him. Neleta, in fact, had gradually cut down altogether on the rum. Although she had undoubtedly saved him from killing himself more rapidly, and he looked better, his sensation of suffering was now more conscious and therefore more intense.

It was getting along toward the end of the rainy season. His chills and burning fever had continued for weeks on end. He was now frequently delirious. Of those days of burning and weakness in which external and internal events were hopelessly confused a few things afterward remained in his memory with the startling clarity of a prolonged, drugged dream. What was illusion and what was fact he could never entirely separate. Both the possible and the impossible seemed equally true. The real and the unreal presented themselves in a succession of ever-flowing images that merged one into the other. In them his moody thoughts were mirrored as if they were taking place in space subject to the dissolving effect of time. They became the equivalent of events for many weeks.

Space seemed to have prolonged itself. It was longer than it was wide, and the length of it frequently varied. Sometimes the ebony foot-posts of his bed were very close to his face. He could see the strange Ethiopian gargoyles carved upon them grimacing at him, now so close that the darting tongues of the grotesque beasts were about to lick his face, now a hundred feet distant with his bed stretching all the way between like a path to a gate.

Perhaps this triumph of length over breadth was aided by the fact that Neleta's looking glass stood on her chest of drawers exactly opposite him across the room. In it he could see himself and everything that went on in the room. Neleta had once covered it with a cloth, but the blankness before him he found intolerable and begged her to take it off. When she did so the world seemed to be re-created again. The concentration of light in the mirror seemed to reflect itself back into the gloomy cavern behind his eyes where he was now afraid to be left alone with himself in the darkness.

The glass was a large French mirror, the envy of all the maids. He had given it to Neleta when she had become mistress of the house. By stepping back a little she could see all of herself in it. The drawers on her chest were built to recede like steps and so she seemed to be standing before the glass at the foot of a low flight of stairs. Indeed, everything in the room led up to and found itself re-created in the glass in a kind of golden atmosphere which the glow coming through the lattice-blind from the courtyard accentuated, or the candles by night. All the life of the room went on in the glass in a sort of dreamful penumbra.

It was there that Anthony saw himself lying on the bed with the bronze colour gradually fading from his face as if the fever were melting it away while his features became thinner, his skin sallow, and his eyes large, staring, and haggard. Now, indeed, he could look into his own eyes for hours at a time, face to face with himself. In the mirror also sat Brother François who seemed to gather about him the light that filtered in from the screen. With this the ethereal kindliness and bright unfaltering affection of his smile blent as if of the same quality. Years afterwards it was the head of Brother François surrounded by light that came back to comfort memory as the enduring image of the man.

He must frequently have sat by the bed of the sick man for hours, for with this memory alone was there afterward any voice. What it had said Anthony could not remember. But to it he had replied. They had talked together. Never a sentence of those surely ghostly conversations afterwards came back to recollection. But what was Anthony stripped of all habiliments, stripped, indeed, almost of the flesh itself, talked with Brother François. The import of it vanished but the comfort and refreshment remained. It was always Anthony's impression that it was this spiritual medicine which had permitted him to survive.

When Brother François had gone he would then see Neleta again moving panther-like about the room. He would see her bending over him, bringing him water, of which he now consumed enormous quantities, tidying up the chamber, putting flowers by his bed, smoothing his pillow and weeping sometimes when she turned away. Yet there was always a certain fierceness about her, an air of possession in her every movement. She would often lie stretched out on the bed beside him fanning him, dressed in a long spotted silk gown. She would raise the screen behind him whenever she could and he could see the waving green leaves of the plants reflected from the courtyard behind him. In the mirror it seemed as if there was a leopard lying in the forest by something stretched out helplessly. He would go to sleep with the cool breath of the fan and the warm breath of her mouth alternately felt upon his cheeks. He had come now to accept her utterly. Neleta was in the mirror, too.

There also came and went other things and people. The bearded face of a stranger who came to bleed him. He learned afterwards that this was the new mate of the *Ariostatica* who was by way of being an amateur surgeon. At any rate the bearded man with the basin and lancet came several times. He felt quieter and weaker now. In fact after the third blood-letting he reached the nadir of existence. Luckily the *Ariostatica* and her "surgeon" sailed soon. But he knew nothing about that at the time.

It was while he lay in what was all but a fatal lethargy after the third bleeding that Brother François came for the last time. Just that day it was too much trouble to move his eyes to one side or the other. Besides, the world receded into a dizzy darkness everywhere except straight ahead of him. Brother François in the mirror was greatly excited, animated, protesting. He seemed to be trying to get the man on the bed to do something. Anthony saw it all as happening to somebody else in the mirror. Why did they trouble *him* this way? They might let *him* die in peace at least. He heard a sound of voices arguing.

"Oh, if he could only leave all this!"

Ferdinando and Neleta were in the picture now. Brother François was holding on to the bed in the mirror pleading. Suddenly he saw him rise and turn away. His face went out. It was quiet again. Blessedly quiet. Everything went out of the mirror shortly. It grew grey, the light faded. Darkness was filling his eyes. He lay very still, on the balance, just breathing. Something terrible had happened, something for which he could not be forgiven. Brother François had gone. Well, he would go, too. "I will leave them." He gave up. The world suddenly ceased.

The poignant atmosphere of tragedy which had conveyed its emotional contagion to the sick man so near the brink as to be numb and insensate—lost, indeed, to all understanding of its cause and only dimly aware of its emotional effect—had been the doing of Ferdinando.

When the *Ariostatica* had arrived at Gallegos she found the slave pens empty, the last of those brought by Amah's caravan having been shipped on *El Argonautico* some months before. Sóller who was in charge of the schooner was impatient to return. It was the middle of the rainy season and no new supplies of captives could be expected for some time. Yet both Sóller and Ferdinando were peculiarly anxious to make an excellent showing on the books for Anthony when he should recover. No ship had ever been known to lie idle for long at Gallegos without receiving a cargo. Ferdinando was determined that the only case of one doing so should not occur while he was in charge. Sóller, who had been put in charge of the *Ariostatica* after the death of the captain some years before, still felt himself to be a doubtful case in the opinion of Anthony. He was now anxious to make good. He and Ferdinando now put their precious heads together.

Mongo Tom, it was found, had a number of young slaves in his pens. They were scarcely more than children, left overs from the last shipment, and he was anxious to get rid of them. The youth of the batch put an idea in Ferdinando's head as he and Sóller looked them over. Why not seize the children under Brother François's charge and so make up a full cargo for the *Ariostatica?* It would also immediately provide a way to balance that irritating open account on Ferdinando's books and show a nice profit on the goods supplied to Brother François for some years past, goods the half-breed considered to have been wasted. Sóller was enthusiastic. He even saw an element of humour in carrying off the priest's flock. Healthy children brought from $25 to $50 apiece since the trade had been curtailed by the English war. Bueno!

The longer Ferdinando thought of the scheme the better he liked it. If Anthony recovered he felt his business acumen would be praised; if not—if Anthony died, he, Ferdinando, would be temporarily at least the Master of Gallegos. Well, he would show his authority while he had it anyway. Brother François should be put in his place as an impractical beggar and hanger-on.

Whereupon the practical Ferdinando put the Gallegos blacksmith to work shrinking leg-irons to fit snugly about young shins. Taking a goodly supply of these in several buckets he and Sóller, accompanied by four or five Foulahs, sneaked down the path toward Brother François's little establishment on the evening before the *Ariostatica* was to sail.

The peaceful sound of the bell came to them through the trees as they neared the place and they found the entire population of the beehive village gathered before the small chapel engaged in the simple service which always marked the end of their day.

Even such entirely forthright and up-and-coming fellows as Sóller and Ferdinando were given pause by the sight of the priest at his own forest altar and engaged in prayer. They waited till he had finished and blessed his flock. Sóller, indeed, now began to hold back a little. He had once been a choir-boy in Spain. Ferdinando, however, with the triumph of Mnombibi thoroughly in mind, gave no signs of wilting. He called out to his men, who, without mincing matters, laid hold of those nearest and began fitting them with leg-irons. Startled by the appearance of so many strangers, some of the youngest gathered about Brother François and began whimpering. The rest stood in scared silence. Seeing the irons one of the women groaned.

"What are you about?" said Brother François coming forward swiftly, the colour mounting to his face.

Ferdinando drew back a little. The priest kicked the irons out of one of the Foulah's hands. The rest stopped work and looked up at Ferdinando who snarled at them to go ahead. The sound of chains and locking resumed. One of the youngsters screamed.

"Do not interfere, padre," sneered Ferdinando. "I am master here now."

"You?" said the priest.

"I!" said the half-breed. "*I* am master now."

"He is dead then!" said Brother François. "Why didn't you call me? You heathen!" His voice rose with a sudden scream.

Ferdinando shook his head. "Not dead!" he said, and looked defiantly at the priest.

"What does this mean, then?" said the priest.

"Cuba!" grinned Ferdinando.

"No! no! In the name of God—*no!*" shouted Brother François. The next instant Ferdinando went down under the solid impact of a blow on the mouth that half stunned him. The priest had apparently gone mad. He was beating the half-breed over the head with a bucket. The little lawn before the chapel resounded with horrible cries and childish screams of terror. A worrying sound came from the throat of the priest who was shaking Ferdinando like a great dog dealing with a stoat. The children rushed into the chapel. Someone tangled with the bell rope and a brazen clamour as of fire bells broke out.

But the Foulahs, all lusty Mohammedans, now threw themselves on Brother François and pulled him off Ferdinando. The half-breed got up spitting curses and teeth. He ordered the priest bound. Sóller interfered.

"He is a white man, you know."

"Hold him, then," screamed Ferdinando stamping about crazy with rage and pain, and wiping the blood off his lips. "You might do something yourself to get these brats down to the ship," he gasped at Sóller.

"Never mind the irons, drive them down," cried the Spaniard. "Use canes!" He broke off a section of bamboo and began to round up the flock. Some of them broke away and ran to the priest. He cried out without words and struggled.   Presently he grew calm and stood weeping.   Ferdinando cursed him.

Unfortunately most of the children had taken refuge in the little chapel.   These were now driven forth in charge of several big Arabs with long sticks.   One or two others were rounded up after a chase and scramble.   The entire flock was then herded pell-mell downhill. Only a few old women and one or two sick men remained.

"Let them alone," said Sóller.   "They're no good."

"The curse of the Almighty God on you, Sóller," cried Brother François.

"What!" said Sóller swaggering up.   "What's that!"

The two stood close together for a moment.   Gripped in the arms of the two Foulahs, who were taking no chances, Brother François, who had been leaning forward as if he would throw himself at Sóller too, suddenly straightened up.   He stood looking directly into the face of Sóller which was now poked close to his own, with a defiant expression on it.

"You do not know what you are doing, do you, Sóller?" he said almost gently.   A puzzled, clownish look spread half belligerently over Sóller's coarse features.

"Well, I guess I know my business," he blurted out.   "I guess I do."

"May Christ forgive you," said Brother François and let his clenched hands fall by his side.

"Now that's what I call being a Christian," laughed Sóller, and set off down the hill whistling.   He was secretly relieved at having the curse removed.   Feeling quite sure that he had frightened the priest into forgiving him, he swaggered somewhat in his walk.   Ferdinando had rushed off to bathe his face.

The two Foulahs, lacking further orders, and somewhat abashed at holding a white man prisoner, now let go of Brother François and walked away.   He sank down at the foot of his cross and lay there. Presently he was joined by the woman with her breasts cut off.   She began to make soft, hopeless sounds in the growing darkness.   In the cluster of beehive huts there were no lights any more.   Only the little stream continued to rush on through the valley filling it with a sound of watery voices like those of children far-off and at play.

Towards midnight Brother François rose and went into his chapel to be alone.   He lit the candles and celebrated mass.

It was the following morning that he had gone to make his final plea to Anthony.   The *Ariostatica* had not sailed yet.   She was still swinging at anchor waiting for the down-tide.   Brother François had small hope of finding Anthony in a condition to interfere, or even understand, but he could not let even the slim last chance of retrieving his flock go by. It was then that Anthony had seen him in the mirror for the last time.

But Anthony had been too ill to respond. He had in fact lapsed into unconsciousness while the priest, almost beside himself, had pleaded with him to interfere. Neleta much frightened, convinced that Mnombibi was certainly correct and that Brother François was a hostile influence, had called Ferdinando. The two had literally carried him from the room and thrust him from the door. From the hill he could see the *Ariostatica* getting under way. He watched her till her masts were veiled by the long point as she drifted past Bangalang. It was a half hour of sheer despair.

He went downhill to his deserted little hamlet. He knelt for a while in the chapel and was finally able to say, "Thy will, not mine be done," with a sincere heart. Then he called to the two old men and the three women who still remained to him and told them to pack up hastily. Two small donkeys that grazed near by were caught and loaded with a few pots, kettles, nondescript bundles, and the meagre furniture of the little chapel. The bell he threw into the stream. The wooden cross from before the chapel door he strapped over the back of the largest ass. He would not leave that at Gallegos.

The small procession headed by Brother François, with the only musket of the party over his shoulder, started uphill through the trees and passed through the stockade gate. The large cross on the small donkey waggled with the beast's ears. The Foulahs on guard had often seen Brother François go and come. They made no effort to stop him. They watched the priest, the donkeys, the two crippled men armed with spears, and the three women with bundles on their heads cross the rough clearing on the other side of the stockade and descend toward the wall of the forest. Half-way down Brother François took off his sandals and shook the dust off them.

He put them on again, and disappeared into the jungle that stretched toward the rising sun and had no end.

CHAPTER FORTY-FIVE

THE BRONZE IS SUBLIMED

T HAT peculiar quality of sunlight, at once soothing and cheerful, which strikes through broad and lush green leaves, filled the eyes and the room of the sick man when at last he became aware of his surroundings again.

How long he had lain helpless he had no idea. So deep was the oblivion of weakness after the fever finally left him that he had lost all sense of time. Time did not seem to have been going on as he had always felt it to be going on during the night while he slept. This time existence had paused, and he had awakened after a distinct lapse.

But he was now fully conscious and rational again, he told himself, conscious of the difference between what went on within him and what occurred without. Although, over neither the outer nor the inner world did he as yet attempt to exert deliberate control. He was too weak. Yet he was aware from the very first opening of his eyes that afternoon, with the blind rolled up behind him and the pleasant sunlight streaming in through the leaves, that what went on in the mirror did not occur of itself but really took place in the room. And what he saw in the mirror was curious enough.

There was that night, for instance, when he had wakened and seen the black witch-doctor from Bangalang talking with Neleta. Both were plainly in the room, although but one candle by the mirror was dimly burning. He could even hear the husky, bass voice of the bearded negro whispering. What was going on? Why should he feel afraid of this man?

After a while he remembered why. This was the witch-doctor from Bangalang that Brother François had told him about, the man who had brought a spider to steal the old Susu's soul. Brother François had not believed that, nor had he when he first heard of it. But now—in his extreme weakness he was very much the child again. He was simply and unreasoningly afraid. He lay still that night with all the instinct to escape notice of a hunted thing.

Neleta took something out of a drawer under the mirror and showed it to the man with the white spectacles painted about his eyes. When you could not see him in the shadows you could still see his eyes floating in the glass. They came and went. You lay still. The man was much excited by what Neleta was showing him. When he moved

656

about there was a sound as if a baby were playing with a rattle some-where; *shuck-shucka-shuck, shuck-shucka-shuck.*

He was squatted in front of the mirror now doing some kind of monkey-business. He waved his arms about and burned feathers. There was a little fetish placed on Neleta's chest of drawers just before him. Mnombibi was making dantica to it.

How the burning feathers did smoke! It was an outrage—making a stench like that in a sick man's room. An outrage!

"Neleta!"

He began to make protesting noises in his throat and coughed. Then he saw Mnombibi on his hands and knees crawl past the bed and scuttle through the door. He saw that, and it was not in the mirror. And yet here was Neleta soothing him and assuring him it was nothing at all but a bad dream.

Well, well, perhaps? But what was the stench of burning feathers then? And that damned little manikin before the mirror, where did it come from?

It stayed there nearly all night. He saw it again and again. Yet next morning it was gone. It was all very confusing to a head still swimming dizzily.

And he had thought he was getting so much better!

He pondered all this till he grew tired and gave it up. Neleta still swore that he must have been dreaming. He lost confidence in him-self. It gave him a decided set-back in recovery. Thinking the mat-ter over, he decided he was not wholly rational yet after all.

He grew a little stronger day by day. Nevertheless, it was a long, tedious process. Trying to sit up, the whole room had reeled. He lay back and decided not to force matters. The man he saw looking back at him from the glass was more like the youth of four years ago than the bronzed Master of Gallegos who had greeted him there only a few months back. He was very thin again. The hard lines in his face had relaxed. It was not nearly so mask-like and determined. Yes, he was more like—"like Anthony,"—he thought. It reminded him of old times.

Neleta was silent. She acted at times as if she were frightened or was holding something back. His mind dwelt meanwhile a good deal on the past, the Casa da Bonnyfeather, and even the convent came back vividly again.

In this moody vein it comforted his reminiscent fancy to insist on having his madonna brought out and set up before the glass on the chest of drawers. Something so familiar would give him a comfort-ing sense of reality again. There could be no doubt what was before the mirror now. If any fetish was to appear there before his eyes, let it be one he knew—his own.

It was extraordinary how difficult it was to prevail on Neleta to get the shrine and to have her put it just where he could see it when he went to sleep as he had as a little boy. Surely he was entitled to so harmless a comfort, a souvenir of old times, he told himself. Yet he had to insist; to send for Ferdinando at last and bid him open the chest in the fireproofed shed; *to go and get it,* and no more nonsense about it.

It was Cheecha who finally took off the cover in which Faith had wrapped the shrine at Livorno. Neleta would have nothing to do with the madonna. She even appeared angry and worried. He had had to caution her that he valued it highly and would not have it touched.

So there she stood again. He had forgotten how beautiful she was. The blue of the heavenly little canopy, the gorgeous robe of the Virgin, and the mother-of-pearl at her feet glowed in the bare room. He almost felt like talking to her again as to an old friend; or that Father Xavier might come into the room at any moment. Would that he could, good man! But where——

"Where was Brother François?"

Suddenly it struck him that he had not seen Brother François lately. Why didn't *he* come to visit him? How strange!

He had gone on a journey, said Neleta. Doubtless he would be back shortly. She put Anthony off as best she could. Brother François, he remembered, had often been away for as much as a week or two at a time.

"Very well then, ask him to see me as soon as he returns."

Neleta promised. Both she and Ferdinando were now worried. What would Anthony do when he learned why Brother François had fled into the forest? Ferdinando said the returns from the sale for the *Ariostatica's* cargo would come back on *La Fortuna,* which was expected in soon. Then he would be able to make a fine showing with his books. That would be an acceptable excuse, he felt sure. At most there would be some grumbling, perhaps a perfunctory reprimand. He was complacently certain of it.

"You fool!" sneered Neleta.

Ferdinando felt uncomfortable again. Neleta knew Anthony better than he did. He had learned that much. Perhaps he had better conceal the matter as long as he could.

Neleta was glad enough to have Brother François removed, even if it should cost Ferdinando his place when Anthony found what had happened. But she felt that it was Mnombibi who had been the real cause of Brother François's departure. For a while the conjuring and her plan had seemed to be working well. Not only had the Christian priest been driven out and his supposed influence over Anthony removed, but Mnombibi on his last visit to the house had reconstructed the melted man-fetish. In this Neleta believed lay her influence over

Anthony and her hope to have a child by him. It was the Christian priest, of course, who had caused the wax to melt. But that set-back had now been overcome. It *had* been rather awkward to have Anthony wake up that night and find Mnombibi in his room. But she had been able to reassure him about that, she thought. All was going smoothly when Anthony had insisted on having the madonna placed before her mirror. She feared it. In that virgin image she instinctively beheld a threat to all Mnombibi's conjuring of fecundity. She determined to get more advice at Bangalang.

As soon as she could she made another surreptitious visit to the Kru town. She and Aunt Ungah and Mnombibi had a long discussion upon the new turn of affairs. Neleta was for destroying the madonna, but Mnombibi laid his interdict on that.

The witch-doctor was really greatly puzzled and somewhat afraid of the white man's fetish that Neleta assured him was an important one in Spain. But although he saw in it the possibility of unknown trouble, he also thought it would provide him another opportunity to visit Gallegos with the usual reward in view. However, it seemed best to wait until he should hear what Brother François was doing. For the Christian witch-doctor was the power who might make the new fetish dangerous. Mnombibi had already set inquiries afoot about the whereabouts of Brother François, whom he considered to be his one dangerous rival and an interloper in the neighbourhood. Yes, on the whole it would be best to delay.

He retired to his hut and kept Neleta waiting in Ungah's until it was almost dawn. He thumped his drum and made dantica with his spirits.

Neleta was much bored. She sometimes suspected both priests and wizards. The smell of fish was very strong for one who had become used to a civilized house. And there was nothing but a hard wooden pillow to put her head on. When Mnombibi finally emerged he announced that if Neleta so much as touched the Virgin her own fetish would fail. She returned with a wry neck and gave Mnombibi nothing for his trouble, at which he took to his drum again.

Mnombibi's was not the only drum along the coast by any means. That spring there was a good deal of thumping and "wizard-talk" from village to village, especially on dark nights. Ferdinando noticed it, and so did Anthony as he lay awake through the long night hours. That drum at Bangalang was interminable! To Mnombibi, however, came the news, tapped out and relayed over miles of jungles from inland villages, that the white witch-doctor had settled down in a new refuge established in the hills. Runaway slaves were welcomed and protected there. The dead, black tree was planted again before his door. That was what Mnombibi wanted to know. So the tree *was* the main fetish after all! The drums suddenly ceased. Mnombibi began to lay his plans.

At the house Neleta was mortally careful not to touch the madonna, which she now disliked the more for being afraid of it. The dry season had set in again. Anthony began to recover more rapidly. The caravan from Futa-Jaloon came down from the hills.

Anthony had forgotten his promise to Amah-de-bellah to visit Futa-Jaloon. But the escort to take him back to the Ali Mami's capital had been punctually provided. He was confidently expected to return with it. Both the messages and gifts which had been sent him were flattering. If he accepted the welcoming-gifts he could only do so as the approaching guest of the forest potentate. If he refused them it would be a deadly affront—and he was largely dependent on these hill-people for his trade. Indeed, Gallegos might not be tenable without their friendship. Certainly it would be uncomfortable and dangerous.

Despite that, Anthony hesitated. He was still weak and comparatively helpless. The journey up-country might finish him, he felt. Neleta was unalterably opposed to his going. She clung to him. It was old Mehemet Ali, the leader of the caravan, who finally persuaded him to leave.

He was a gay old fellow with a large paunch, a ribald sense of humour, and an ingratiating smile. A huge pair of horned spectacles under a snow-white turban lent him, when occasion required, an air of gravity and wisdom. The combination of these qualities was hard to resist.

He promised to provide a horse-litter for the trip up-country. He extolled the healthy air of the hills as the best way to recover from fever. He gave such an enticing account of the hospitality in store at Futa-Jaloon that the difficulties of the hundred-league trek through the jungle and hill-country rapidly took on the aspect of a happy adventure. Finally, with tears in his eyes, the old rascal pleaded with Anthony not to be the death of him. If he returned without the expected guest, he said his head would no longer remain in that happy conjunction with the lower parts of his body which he claimed to have found highly satisfactory and hoped to continue to enjoy.

"Do not, my son," said he, "be the cause of such a sad parting—and remember, I cherish the only solace of twenty-one wives."

"My father, prepare the litter," said Anthony laughing, and despite Neleta's vehement protests he gave orders to pack.

He sent for Ferdinando and gave him off-hand but minute instructions as to the conduct of affairs at Gallegos during his absence. Ferdinando listened carefully, and decided to say nothing then about Brother François's leaving. He regarded Anthony's departure as a happy solution of that difficulty. Why bring it up now? He had already sent Juan on a trip up the river for ivory. He now cautioned Neleta to behave herself and keep her mouth shut.

It was the middle of June when Anthony finally set out, and the long, hot days had already turned the lowlands about Gallegos into a vapour bath through which the stars glimmered only as blurred lights when evening came. It was high time to be breathing the free air of the hills again, he thought as they wound day after day along the narrow caravan trails through the steaming forests. He realized that in his debilitated condition he could never have survived another miasmic summer on the coast. An unconquerable weakness and lethargy seized upon him. He swung from side to side helplessly in the cradle-like litter that had been contrived for him. Most of the time overcome by lassitude and the sleepy motion, he slept.

They moved perforce very slowly. Only after five days did they begin to ascend. On the sixth they camped at evening amid the hills.

Their camp fires twinkled along a dry, rocky height under clear, keen stars. Anthony had not seen the constellations wink and glitter that way for nearly four years. A heavy stone seemed to have been lifted off his chest. His lungs no longer laboured. They expanded eagerly and easily, drawing in the cool, dry air faintly perfumed with sunburnt grasses.

All the sensations of his body responded and became a joy to him again. He lay in his tent experiencing a sensation of lightness akin to intoxication. He was still giddy when he moved about. But it was heavenly to lie quiet, feeling as if gravity itself had relented. Only a little more and it would release him entirely. He remembered how a stranded boat seemed to become lighter as the tide rose, till it floated away.

"I have escaped all that fever in the furnace below," he thought,— "come up under the clean, clear stars again. Perhaps I was not melted and cast into hard bronze down there after all. Anyway, I shall live and go on now. I shall keep going on. My other, my real self is not going to die. Tonight I feel something alive and stirring within me as if it knew it will soon be set free to go on with the tide."

For the first time in months he was able to merge into sleep happily. Like a healing spring he felt the waters of rest begin to permeate him.

Presently he seemed to have made an unalterable decision—or it had been made for him. He could not state to himself exactly what it was. But he was utterly content with it. In the space between wakefulness and slumber he felt abundant joy flow through him, a feeling of having come to a conclusion eternally right. Energy flowed into him from beyond himself. It gradually flooded and refreshed his being with a great sense of peace and well-being. Why had he cut himself off from this refreshing river that flowed from the same eternal source and was the spiritual counterpart of light? How long he had been using only a stagnant little part of it! His own will had shut the valves of his soul against it! He was tired, worn-out holding them closed. Now he had given up and life-giving waters swept through him.

Now he could let his body stretch out at peace with the life within it; at one with its contained self. He knew he would awaken from sleep refreshed. He would not have been holding himself against the tide all night long, swept this way and that by evil dreams, almost torn apart. He would awaken one with himself. And through the day?—

No longer would he pass the daylight hours as at Gallegos—like an actor in an endless play with a futile meaning and a logical little plot; a play where every motion must be the result of consciously exerted will. Acting! How tired, how exhausted that had left him! What a vile stage was Gallegos, and how hollow was the animated metallic figure that had moved upon it, worn out, burned out by fever of mind and body, empty of itself. That figure had melted down at last and now lay almost sublimed. Was it about to float off leaving nothing but a few burnt-out ashes behind?

For he *had* succeeded in becoming that impervious, expressionless bronze boy that stood watching the river of existence flow through the fountain; not caring whence it came or where it went; interested only in the interplay of shadows and pictures on the little pool at his feet where for an instant the eternal water flashed into the light for him alone. And he had become tired of it at last, because finally he could see nothing but his own shadow falling there. That shadow had blotted out all else. Yes, he had succeeded in becoming the Bronze Boy who had lost his living twin; who stood looking at his own shadow on the water till his eyes had gone blind. He had succeeded in damning himself! Yet tonight?

Surely tonight some mercy had been vouchsafed him! He was being swept on with the waters again; being bathed in their strength. No longer would he stand and only look across their surface. They were running deep now, down, down . . .

Very deep in him, just at the verge of sleep, lay the images which expressed life to him. They were the primary semblances of things upon which his blank eyes had first feasted in infancy when he played about the fountain in the convent courtyard under the plane tree. There the dream within the dream had first begun.

For him those images were always there. In the daytime they might be sunk beyond sight and crowded down, but still there; the unseen ones who at the direction of the unknown master of the drama

pulled the moving strings of his emotions behind the scenes.   Yet they
could always be seen again when the depths of his being were stirred.
And then they moved in a drama of their own, his drama, having
taken on the meanings of meaning for him through the accumulated
experience of years.

These subliminal dreams of his soul in which he saw his own life
mirrored and dramatized were not childish to him no matter what the
nature and appearance of the dreamful actors might be; no matter how
beautiful, grotesque, outrageous, or obscene the mimes became.   This
play moved beyond the petty censorship of common sense, wrapt forever from the carping of logic, under the rules of socialized morality,
safe from the wakeful world which it triumphantly caricatured or
glorified with the free imagery of a primal poetry that transcended
reality.   It was his glass of truth, like a mirror provided by God.
The reflections upon this glass of sleep made him laugh, weep, love,
hate, burn with lust till the seed spouted of itself from his loins.   They
comforted him with visions of the dead-alive again; they fascinated
him with strangely glorious landscapes, and forgotten things; they sent
him reeling through caverns pursued by dripping monsters of his own
begetting, shrieking with fear.   Any play is *the* thing, the presentation of life in the terms of life itself.   But there is also the play within
the play.

Anthony had always known this instinctively.   It was his faith *in*
himself.   For the greater part of his existence he had lived by it.   The
last three years at Gallegos he had tried to deny it utterly.

Tonight in the little tent under the stars, where he breathed the light
mountain air again after weeks of fever, the sudden release, the sudden
relief of having been rescued had almost cut him loose from his physical moorings.   He was, in fact, at the crisis of his inner and outer
sickness, and what sustained him from within, that which he had so
long denied as true now threatened to withdraw.

His first impression of returning strength and renewed determination as he went to sleep that night had been due to the sensation of
comfort experienced from a complete relaxation upon being carried up
into the cool hills.   It was due to weakness as much as anything else,
and that weakness now released him too far.   What had for a few
minutes been a feeling of delicious ease soon let him down into an
utter lassitude, an increasing numbness that began to verge upon
nothing at all.   Almost asleep, as if something had whispered a warning to him he began to realize the necessity of a last desperate effort
of the will to escape from approaching oblivion.

He was gliding down a steep slope in the dark with sickening speed.
There was a tremendous cliff at the end.   Somewhere in the billowing
mists that filled the empty abyss at the end of the world was a far-off

glow, a smudged, cloudy glory in which the madonna had wrapped herself.

If he could only speak to her she would save him. But he had refused to do so for so long that he was unable to cry out now. He filled his lungs to try. A hand came down out of the darkness and clamped itself over his mouth. He struggled. He was nearing the verge . . .

"Madre . . ." he choked.

Then he fell. He kept on falling——

Down . . .

Down . . .

Down . . . ice-cold waters closed over his head. He had finally become the bronze boy and he sank like heavy metal.

He touched bottom and lay there . . .

Air! He was drowning. Give him one more breath! One!

With a *tremendous* impulse he shot himself upward again through the dark, cold water.

He came out!

He seemed to burst through and fill his lungs again.

The heavy dew had by now stretched tight as a drum the fabric of the tent in which Anthony lay. A late, cloud-troubled moon had gradually climbed above the tops of the surrounding trees. In the shifting black-and-silver shadows in the tent, where the filtered moonlight seemed to concentrate and congeal like a semi-gaseous fluid, the man who had just hurled himself up from oblivion by a last desperate effort now opened his eyes still filled with the horror of his dream.

There had been an overpowering sensation of speed to his return. As he opened his eyes the impulse of it seemed to be carried forward into something else beyond him, and to leave him. Something rose up from his body and was carried by the momentum of his return into the misty light beyond as if he had projected it out of himself.

It stood naked in the shifting moonlight.

He had seen it before—when it was younger. It had had the face then of the child who had laughed back at him from the fountain before Father Xavier came and told him it was only a dream. It was "Anthony." It was the dear first playmate, the lovely child who had laughed down at him from the branches of the plane tree while the filtered sunlight danced over him . . . that face in the miniature . . .

But now it was older. It stood naked in the mist, now wrapping itself in shadow and now burning clearly in a figure of light again. The face of it, noble with a man's strength, was also sad with unfulfilled desires and hopes; with dreamful eyes like wide, undiscovered seas. Flowing out dimly and more dimly into the darkness, flickered its brush of burning hair. In that nest a phoenix might be reborn; might rise suddenly and soar away.

So for an instant it stood as if bewildered at having been cast forth into the cold outer moonlight. It shivered and turned to look sadly at him, its eyes wide with a strange wonder like those of a child looking upon a dead playmate; wild with a grief-stricken and lonely surmise. The lonely twin stood looking for a while at its birth-fellow. Then it turned to go . . .

He threw himself upon it.

He wrestled in the moonlight over the floor of the empty tent. It was more powerful than anything he had known. He was in love with what was choking him and struggling to be gone. The breath of his throat rattled as he struggled with it. He wound his arms around this strong impalpable thing more precious to him than a dying child. He clasped it close and felt it burning into him again. The chest of it seemed to collapse into his own and to fill his lungs with fire. Every breath was a fiery agony . . . His veins glowed . . .

He cried out with a terrible voice, "Water! Water!"

The hoarse, throaty cries from Anthony's tent filled all the sleeping camp with alarm. The sentries who had been on watch against a possible lion came running. They stood listening now to the silence. Old Mehemet Ali tore open the flap and found the guest of his master lying exhausted on the floor of his tent with the contents strewn about in intolerable disorder.

Finally they brought him a drink. He *could* breathe now. He was going to live!

Old Mehemet stood by uneasily peering through his foolish, wise-looking glasses. "Now, my son," said he, "you will get better. Those who come up into the mountain air to recover from swamp fever are sometimes given to fits. Your cries were terrible. I thought you were fighting with a lion."

"I was," said Anthony feebly.

"There, there," said the old man soothingly. "We shall not leave you alone again until you get much stronger."

It was near morning. The camp did not go to sleep again. The men built up the fires and waited for dawn, getting what comfort they could after such an eery alarm from the tones of their own voices in casual conversation. Here and there a few laughed at the white man's nightmare.

All the rest of the way into the foothills Anthony slept. Some days later they heard the distant thunder of the snake-drums at Futa-Jaloon throbbing their greeting. It would be a long visit for him, he knew. He must really get well this time. He steeled himself for the indescribable tumult of an African welcome to an Arab town. Already the war-horns, the neighing of horses, the drums and musketry sounded as if a battle were in progress.

* * * * * *

Six months of the barbaric but bountiful life in the hill-country about Futa-Jaloon had more than put Anthony on his feet again. Indeed, it had put him on four feet, for he had been made free of the splendid Arab stud kept by the Ali Mami. For the first time he had tasted to the full the joys and benefits of noble horsemanship. Over the wide plateaus, the opulent valleys, and through the open forests of the foothills surrounding the town he and Amah had chased the deer, coursed antelope, and hunted leopards. They had camped under clear stars in thorn bomas about the leaping fires in lion country. They had returned to the little capital to experience a literally royal welcome. For while at Futa-Jaloon Anthony had seen a palace revolution take place. The old Ali Mami had died and Amah-de-bellah had succeeded him, not without a little street fighting marked by the timely demise of several nephews. Now Amah sat on the ivory stool tasselled with ostrich plumes, which passed for a throne.

But this unnoted ripple in an otherwise blank page of history had caused little change in Anthony's status as a guest. If anything, it was for the better. He and Amah-de-bellah had become, despite the barriers of blood and language, very genuine and fast friends. Language, indeed, had not stood between them long. During his convalescence Anthony had taken pains to master the bastard Arabic of the Foulah hill-country, if one can be said to "master" a dialect in which the vocabulary is strictly limited and most of the grammar forgot. As for blood—any strain that produced so splendid a figure of a man as Amah deserved admiration. In spite of the fact that he really was one, Amah-de-bellah looked and acted like a king. That is, he was a free man, sovereign enough to impose his will on his fellows and himself at the same time. His was a good will.

The bond between him and Anthony was one which, though nowadays rare, once developed in more heroic states of society perhaps the chief moral virtues in man. It was friendship based upon an essential compatibility in manful attitudes and pursuits; in war, hunting, barter, and the frank relaxations and conversations of the camp fire, the tent, and the town.

The Arab hill-town, to be sure, was neither heroic nor Utopian. Outwardly it was merely a collection of a thousand or more white, flat-roofed houses clustered about a large rambling building of sun-burnt bricks known as the "palace." Through the centre of the town ran a loud mountain stream, and there were pleasant enough open squares shaded by palms. The place was surrounded by a double stockade with a packed earth parapet. There were wooden watch-towers over the gates and several miles of date trees, palm-nut groves, and market gardens around about. These were by far the most pleasing feature of the Foulah capital.

Six or seven thousand Arabs of a very mixed strain, ruled over by a few families of purer blood, lived here and dominated a surprising extent of territory by continuous and ruthless raiding of their darker, heathen neighbours. Slaves for both domestic use and for barter were a drug on the market. They were, in fact, the debased, sweated currency of a constantly fluctuating realm.

From Futa-Jaloon to the coast stretched about three hundred miles of low, hot forest region largely unknown. This was a no-man's-land of obscure forest tribes who raided each other and in turn were raided by the Foulahs whenever their own territory to the east amid the high hills had been hunted out.

The climate of the place was salubrious; the soil ridiculously fertile with the mixed abundance of a temperate hill region near the equator, where crops succeed each other in an endless round. In addition there were flocks of black native sheep, herds of cattle, and immense droves of half-wild goats and swine. Game of all kinds abounded.

It was not altogether surprising, therefore, that Anthony had remained at Futa-Jaloon month after month.

His hitherto retarded convalescence had here been rapid. At the end of half a year he was stronger than he had ever been before. The six months at Futa-Jaloon marked a sort of mental pause in existence for him. The atmosphere of the place was timeless. He lived only for the day and had cast off for the first time in his life cogitations about the past; plans and worries about the future. After his nearly fatal collapse and the struggle that night in the tent on the way up from Gallegos he had realized that he must devote himself to regaining his strength and becoming thoroughly reintegrated, no matter what happened to his affairs. Existence, and not the ways and means of it, was now the end in view.

In this, Amah-de-bellah had proved himself an understanding and solicitous friend. There was no limit to the hospitality and courtesies of the princely Mohammedan. To the stranger who had come ostensibly for purposes of trade, the house of his host soon proved to be the most comfortable and hospitable roof under which he had ever been. Anthony was nursed back to health by Amah's mother and sisters, who, though they never dropped their veils, were none the less skilful and solicitous nurses. Nor was it the first case of complicated swamp fever they had dealt with. They purged him, fed him, and cheered him back to strength as if he had been one of their own blood.

As he grew able and anxious to converse again Amah had come and talked with him for hours, squatting on a low clay bench covered with the skins of various beasts. Dressed in the long white robes of his tribe and rank, with the water-pipe bubbling musically at his feet and the sweet smoke curling from his fine, clean-cut lips half-parted in a pleasant open smile, Amah emanated a high-bred courtesy and an engaging charm with every word and gesture. This was all the more striking due to the somewhat hawklike cast of his features and his glittering black eyes that Anthony felt might just as easily and naturally take on the pitiless stare of the falcon who has been shown a swan.

Strong friendship begins with respect, traverses admiration, and ends in a trust and affection which continues to combine the first two. The process is greatly accentuated if the friends in the making are both willing to confer and receive favours without conceiving them as obligations or weights on the scales of influence which must ever be kept nicely readjusted and precisely balanced. A true friendship transcends this mere tit-for-tat game of influence played between urbane self-seeking acquaintances. It finds its equipoise in the discovery that both parties have a trust and belief in some eternal relationship beyond themselves. Then, no matter how differently they may approach that common centre, they understand their actions and attitudes to be upon a mutually permanent ground.

It was so with Anthony and Amah. They had begun by respecting, even by fearing each other a little. They had opened their minds to each other during the long hours of conversation and had each been agreeably surprised and moved to admiration by the qualities of the other. And they had, as their reserve vanished by mutual degrees, discovered that each had at some time in his life given himself up for lost and knew that he still continued to exist as if by an extended act of mercy and not by his own transcendent strength and cleverness. In this profound compromise of their egos, differences of race, creed, and custom seemed trivial.

As became a Mohammedan, Amah's outlook upon things was somewhat fatalistic. He might strive and will; Allah would decide. His mortal dangers had been met and had passed him by in foray and battle, for he had been a warrior since boyhood. Arrows and spears had been loosed at him and had been turned aside to quiver in the hearts of others stronger and wiser than he. Thus, said he, "God has tempered my pride."

Anthony had won the same sense of his place as a servant of a superior will by internal rather than external strife. It was the vision of light upon the barrier beaches which had finally brought him to a mental acknowledgment and conviction of himself as a living atom of the whole, but as an atom nevertheless possessed of an atomic will of its own. It was the struggle with himself in the tent that night on the way up from Gallegos that had shown him how to use that will. That it had also been a struggle with death he had no doubt.

But he had been permitted to return. He had been permitted more than that. He had been permitted to see and to understand what kind of a being he was; to recapture and retain himself. That curious entity that lies in so many of us forever unknown, an entity that when outraged sometimes strikes back at us like a mysterious enemy, or becomes weary to be gone—had been revealed to him naked. It was the quality of his mind so to see things—to see them rather than to hear them and to make words about them. The emotional meanings of that vision of his outraged and departing self were plain. Plain also was the departing glow in the mist which he had called upon but which had answered him no more. The temptation to become a mere ruthless doer for the sake of doing had been passed. Gallegos had passed him by like one of the arrows of which Amah had spoken. True, it had also like them fleshed itself in the hearts of others and he was partly responsible for that. He had helped aim the arrow.

But the nearly vital wound which he had given himself was going to heal. Had, indeed, already closed. His triumph in that was so great as to preclude much thought of the wounds of others. How he could liquidate this experience, how close-out at Gallegos he did not yet know. The method, the impulse for that must be disclosed by events.

For a while he was too weak and exhausted by his long fever and the fever of the spirit that had accompanied it to make any practical decisions. Something must help him to that. He prayed while he still lay ill for something to strengthen his will to enable him to make the break. His will was weak and tired now after years of forcing himself against himself. In his heart he acknowledged this weakness. He was no longer the strong, self-sufficient Master of Gallegos. Knowing more now, seeing much more clearly—he felt he might still fail. But there seemed no immediate answer to this impasse. He left it, waiting. For the time being he wiped the slate of dreams and cogitations blank.

Thus it was that Futa-Jaloon became for him a kind of dateless experience. As he looked back at it afterwards, it remained forever like a halt in time. It had about it a bit of the calmness of eternity, a place where he had slipped out of the swift troubled rhythms of the West into the changelessness of the East. Futa-Jaloon, indeed, was a small outpost of the Orient. And it was all the more marked with that feeling because, for Anthony, it lay between two distinct epochs of his life.

Early impulsive manhood had gone. It had died, had been burnt out in the fever; passed with the era of the Bronze Boy in the fierce furnace of tropical heat and mad desire. Henceforth he knew himself not as merely becoming but as to a great extent become.

This inward conviction undoubtedly reacted upon him physically. He not only grew well again, but the process went further. Once having conquered a constant internal doubt and conflict, he now gave outward signs of inward rest, of greater strength and assurance. He became heavier and stronger, less brittle and metallic in his body. Yet more sinewy and tougher. He became less liable to be broken and shattered; more resilient and flexible. By day he was tireless, and at night he lay down and slept like a child.

He thanked God for this. He told himself that he had won through onto the untroubled table-land of mature middle life. It now seemed to stretch before him to an unbroken horizon. At least he could not see beyond that imaginary line. Meanwhile, he lingered on the plateaus about Futa-Jaloon and in the house of Amah-de-bellah, comforted at the world's end by unexpected and generous hospitality; by trust, and as time wore on, by affection. He seemed suddenly to have found not only himself but a brother and a family in that house. He even had a horse and a dog. He had never known the dependence and devotion of animals before; how deeply it tried and tested a man. And here too he had not been found wanting. All the gold of the Indies could bring him no more. All that was wanting was a wife and children. Amah on more than one occasion had said so laughingly. Soon he had grown more serious.

All this, however, was suddenly put an end to by the unexpected appearance of Juan with disconcerting news from Gallegos. Anthony had heard only twice from Gallegos since he had come up into the hills. All had been "as usual" and "going well," according to the quite literal Ferdinando. But now his writing was different.

La Fortuna was lying in the reach again waiting for cargo. Petty trouble had developed between Don Ruiz and the factor, which, to judge by both their letters, promised to become serious. In the midst of this an English ship called the *Unicorn* had suddenly appeared in the Rio Pongo and now lay covering the channel below Gallegos with her guns. The English ship was commanded by a horrid, determined gentleman by the name of Bittern who claimed to have come to take Señor Adverse to Italy. And he would not depart, nor let anyone else depart, until he had seen the said Señor Adverse to whom he insisted the *Unicorn* belonged.

Here Ferdinando's letter broke into a wail. Was it possible that this was true? If so what was to become of them all at Gallegos, with England and Spain at war, and an English armed ship owned by their master in the river? Wasn't this rather hard to explain? Also what did Anthony think Neleta was doing all this time? etc., etc. The factor permitted himself a few perplexed but rather tart liberties.

At all this Anthony felt somewhat inclined to laugh. Don Ruiz and Ferdinando faced by the implacable Captain Bittern was not without its humorous aspects. But his smile faded as he read on. Ferdinando had now seen fit, at a safe distance, to illuminate his employer about the departure of Brother François. Furthermore, the cargo of children had been sold at a considerable profit. This point the factor took some pains to drive home. Anthony was some two hundred pounds better off by the transaction, he discovered—when he was able to look at the paper and see the neat copper-plate writing of his clerk again.

And [said Ferdinando, evidently sure of himself] it is on the whole, señor, much better that we are rid of that padre once and for all here at Gallegos. He has attempted to set up again at some place about the headwaters of the Rio Pongo, I hear. This has caused a great stir amongst the coast tribes whose slaves have been slipping off to his crazy settlement.

So far has this matter gone since you left that our own trade is being interfered with, too. A great gathering of the coast tribes recently took place at Bangalang and after a deal of drumming and witch-finding set off yesterday inland. I think this bodes no good to the padre. We wish him no harm, of course, but I did not think it *necessary to interfere.* Mnombibi, of whom you have heard, is his enemy, and I did not desire to antagonize the natives so near at hand upon whom we must depend. What we now fear is that on the way back they will be crazed with the war-fever and attack the settlement from the land side. We shall then be between these devils and the deep sea, with the Englishman waiting down river. Come home, Señor Adverse. We are short handed . . .

The letter ended in a thoroughly scared whine, a half-breed left alone to his own resources!

Anthony flung the letter on the ground with a round curse and looked up to see Juan's eyes resting upon him.

"Juan," said he, "it is my fault. I have stayed away too long. I know . . ."

"Sí," answered Juan looking at him reproachfully. "I have come myself this time to be sure you hear the truth. It is much worse than you think. That man Ferdinando is a half-breed wolf. He would sell his own children. Everything! He and his sister—caramba! She is a bitch without brats. Someone should give her some. It is 'Cheecha, Cheecha,' all day long now—and the sound of the whip at the

house on the hill. Ah, pardon, señor, but it is true. Sí! I have come
to tell you, and to bring you the letters of Captain Matanza. Without
Don Ruiz we would be in a bad way. I have been living on *La Fortuna* myself for a month past. Your factor when he is drunk is the
kind of a man that makes the knife itch to go home, ugh! If you are
a man, señor, you will come back now. Brother François gave me
this on the way up. I found him! From his hands I received the holy
food. He is well but . . ."

"You *saw* him!" cried Anthony. "Give it to me!"

He tore open the small scroll of native matting. Inside, written
across the torn page of a missal in some dim vegetable fluid that had
run he made out very faintly:

> A moi, mon ami, for the love of Christ—and the peace of your
> own soul. I appeal to the last . . .

The rest was a hopeless blur. But the import of it was like an explosion in Anthony's brain. "Mnombibi—Brother François."

Juan had reached him where he and Amah had come out to hunt
some leopards that had been causing the villagers trouble in the level
tract of country just below Futa-Jaloon. It was a wide, park-like
plateau that stretched out from the foothills to plunge down suddenly
into the coastal jungles some leagues to the westward. The hunt was
to begin on the morrow. It was a full-moon night. Hyenas were
laughing somewhere in the distance and the pack of eager hounds they
had brought with them was baying with melancholy harmonies at the
cloudless, copper disk just beginning to rise redly through the trees
and the smoke of the evening fires.

Anthony tossed Ferdinando's letter into the flames.

"Can you still ride, Juan—after your long journey?"

"If it is with you—homeward."

Anthony nodded and led the way to Amah's fire. Something in his
gait and demeanor made Amah look up and grow tense.

"What has happened?" he asked.

"My brother," said Anthony, "the hand of God has been laid upon
me. I must go."

"Bismillah!" exclaimed Amah, "but you will not go alone!"

"No, lend me men and horses, my friend, I too will go hunting
tomorrow, but in the forest below for those who trouble a holy man."

"Allah be with you then," said Amah, and gave a shrill whistle.
In five minutes twenty men were armed, mounted, and waiting ex-

pectantly just below the chief's fire. They were used to forays by night. Anthony's horse was led up.

Amah rose suddenly and facing Anthony laid his hands on his shoulders.

"My brother," he said, "for seven moons now we have eaten salt together and we have deeply tasted the same savour. Is it not so?"

"Allah reward you for it, Amah my friend," said Anthony much moved. "The savour of your bread and salt has been sweet to the tongue."

"Ah! It comes upon me suddenly I shall not see you again," said Amah. "May the glory of the face of Allah light your path forever." He raised his hands high above his head in a mantic gesture seeming to release a sudden force as he opened his palms to speed his blessing upon them. The men waiting below shouted.

"Wait," said Amah, "there is something I would send with you." Then he hesitated as if he had changed his mind. "My friendship will follow you," he said.

"Farewell," they both said it together and laughed. Anthony mounted.

"Go!" cried Amah.

They swept out over the level grass land with the fresh night-wind in their faces, the little troop galloping hard, and close together.

Amah saw them pass over the grey face of the rolling grass country like a small, white cloud scudding under the moon.

"Kismet," he murmured.

Presently he made a sign to one of his men. "Loose Simba," he said.

At the first halt, as they drew up to breathe the horses, Anthony was overtaken by the powerful hound that he had been hunting with for some time past. It ran up and lay down at his feet. He knew it was a parting gift from Amah, who valued his brave dogs more than his gold. Amah's friendship would follow, as he had said.

They were in the saddle again in a few minutes, speeding over the gentle, mile-long waves of the hill pastures with only the next horizon and clumps of trees here and there, like ships anchored on a sea of moonlight, to guide them. Shadows of antelopes and jackals fled before them. They galloped long and hard, they rested—and galloped on again.

By morning they had come to the great escarpment where the plateau fell away sheerly and then tumbled down through several miles of eroded foothills to the low, coastal forest two thousand feet below. A grey cloud through which here and there, on a few isolated high places, the tops of tall palms wrapped in mist thrust themselves upward with a funereal effect, stretched as far as they could see. Three days westward through those orchid-hung, steaming depths lay Gallegos.

Juan pointed out a range of low hills toward the far horizon which was already beginning to shine in the dawn while all else still lay drab and level as far as the eye could reach in that direction. It was there he said Brother François had made his refuge. Those hills lay a good ten hours' journey along the caravan trail to Gallegos. Anthony's heart smote him to think that he must have passed them close-by on his journey up. "If he could only have known—have seen Brother François then! Now, perhaps, it was too late."

Reproachful voices seemed to rise up to him out of the forest below. He turned away sad and sick at heart; full of foreboding. Those hills seemed far-off, dark as Calvary. Yet he must not permit himself the disconcerting luxury of remorseful reverie. He must save himself to press on. If he could only arrive before Mnombibi and his tribesmen! *If* he could only do *that!*—all might still be well.

They settled themselves on the edge of the plateau for a brief halt. It was essential to let the horses rest and get their last bellyful of the good grass before plunging into the leafy gulf below. Between them and the coast there was nothing but dark forest. It was the country where he had lost himself, Anthony thought. He longed for a glimpse of the sea beyond, for the free path across which, under the clear stars, ships came and went. In one of them he could sail away.

But would he?

Would he, when he got home with Brother François safe again, have the courage to make the final break from Gallegos? Neleta, the much cherished plantations, the whole order of the existence he had built up for four years would be there—reaching out for him. At the top of the cliff, before he plunged back into the forest again, he tossed in his blankets and wondered. What would mere dreams in the hills be when once more he lay in Neleta's arms in the castle he had built for himself? He was strong now, stronger than ever before, and the fire of life beat in his veins.

As the first heat of the morning poured over the plateau and turned the forest below into a thousand smokes, they rose, saddled their beasts, and plunged downward through the bare, clay foothills. An hour later and the roof of the jungle had closed over them.

The narrow caravan trail, forever lost in glimmering half-lights, led hither and yon. It looped and twisted through swamps and made detours to strike the muddy fords of black, sleepy streams. Not a ripple of breeze stirred the palm-tops a hundred feet above them. Eternal silence, and the immemorial twilight of the primeval forest bathed in stupefying heat closed them in. Now and then they halted while vines that had grown across the trail were being cut through. It was evident that the trail followed the tops of slight ridges through trackless reaches of swamp. Bad as it was, it was one of the best roads

in Africa from the hill-country to the coast.   Horses could follow it
if they could survive the flies and insects.   They halted at noon in a
forest clearing, an inane paradise of orchids and vines covering the
fire-scarred sites of native huts.   It was here they heard drums.   They
were very distant.   It was a shaking of leaves rather than a sound.
It shook Anthony like the leaves.

He now pressed his men and horses to the limit.   They began to
rise out of the swamp again.   About three o'clock Juan pointed out
a fork in the trail they might otherwise have passed.   They took this
and rose rapidly.   Evidently they were now among the nest of low
hills they had seen that morning.   Presently they could trot again.
They did so, stopping frequently to listen, and with scouts out ahead.

Suddenly they emerged into a series of open glades.   Great springs
broke out clearly from under masses of black, volcanic rock.   Here
was the source of one of the main forks of the Rio Pongo, the Foulahs
said.   They turned sharply to the right still following Juan's lead and
entered an open, bowl-shaped valley.   At the upper end the embers of
what had been a cluster of huts only a few hours before still shimmered with heat and smoked hazily into the afternoon sunlight.

They were too late.

Anthony sat his horse drearily.   He cursed himself and his luck
darkly.   Here and there in the grass he saw the glimmer of dark
bodies.   Several vultures flapped away.   There was the busy noise
of flies.   Mnombibi's people must have raided the place some time that
morning.   It was the drums going down-river that they had heard—
after the raid!   Most of the people they would carry off.

"And that devil Mnombibi had been in his room that night with
Neleta!"   He ground his teeth.

But Brother François, Brother François, where was he?

Someone gave a dismal shout and pointed.

Against a black outcrop of cliff several hundred yards away Anthony
saw a white body apparently suspended in the air.   It did not move.
His spine crept.

He slid down the neck of his horse, which was cropping the grass,
and stumbled forward in a tumult of agonized horror.   He looked
for the rope.   The arms were held out stiffly.   At first he did not see
the dark beams of the cross against the black rock in the cliff's shadow.
Now they suddenly seared themselves on his mind forever—and the
man hanging there.

The cross stood before a little cave which Brother François had
evidently made his chapel.   He ran and fell down by it.   He cried out
so that the hound which had followed him cowered and whimpered
and was afraid to come near.

After a while the man on the ground grew silent and lay still . . .

"Why did this have to happen to him? It was more than he could bear. Now he was lost. He was in hell *now*. If time would only pass. Let it be a year from now, instantly!" He tried to pray.

"Father," he cried, and looked up.

There were none of the comforting conventions of the carved crucifix there. The naked body, welted from the shoulders down, was bound to the beams with thongs of rawhide. These had drawn tight in the morning sun, which had passed slowly, blistering the tonsured head. The dark, clotted locks hung down before the face like a scorched curtain. Through the hands and feet were thrust long mimosa thorns that dripped slowly into black clots on the stones below. But the shadow of the cliff had now advanced beyond the little cairn of rocks where the cross had been planted. Already it was enveloped in advancing shade. It grew cooler.

The man on the cross shivered and opened his eyes.

"I."

"*Tonight thou shalt be with me in paradise. . . .*"

"I?"

Not yet! This was the terrible earth yet. Hands, feet, fire!

"A moi," he cried raising his face. His head sunk again and he looked down through his hair, hanging.

He heard a voice below him. He saw dimly. After a while he remembered.

"Anthony," he whispered, "my son . . ."

The sound fell into the ears of the man below like dry burning leaves.

"Alive yet!" cried Anthony. He stood up. He could do something. He looked.

Not too late . . . ? Yes—yes, too late—and forever too late. . . . Oh! "You are dying."

The leaves of sound began to fall again. The cross shook. The man on it was trying to speak to him. He looked up again at that agony. It was for him. *His*. The wind blew the hair back from the face. It was only the body fighting there he saw—fighting. Suddenly Brother François's face, the beloved face Anthony had known, peered through it. The lips moved not of themselves but to the music of the mind.

"It is you who are dying. Not I."

Anthony stood fixed, turned to stone. He saw that face lift to the sky.

"Remember me . . . Jesu . . . I still live . . ."

"I LIVE," he cried with a triumphant voice.

"GO!"

The body of him leaped upward against the thongs and thorns. The cross rocked against the sky. Then it was still.

Silence again.

A column of ants approached and began to ascend the cross.

The man below stood looking up but seeing nothing. After a while a cloud seemed to be passing across the top of his mind. He seemed to be looking up from the bottom of a well. Presently he knew it *was* the sky he was looking at. He fell backward out of eternity into time, and caught himself. He fled up the hill.

When he came to himself he was lying in the grass with a circle of dark faces peering down at him and the hound Simba licking his hands.

"Not worthy of that," he thought. He caught them away.

Then he threw his arms about the animal and burst into an agony of weeping.

It saved him from going mad.

They stayed in the valley all night and built great fires to keep the beasts off. It was necessary to appeal to the Foulahs for help. Luckily the only one of them who could read his Koran remembered that Mohammed had said Christ was one of the prophets who had come before him. It might therefore be permitted to help bury Christ's servants who had been slain by the heathen. After some urging, and the promise of gifts at Gallegos, they were persuaded to set about gathering large stones for a tomb. But they would not touch the body on the cross.

Anthony and Juan were left alone to that. In the flickering light of the leaping fires they unbound the now shrunken form from the tree where it had suffered. They wrapped it in a rich cloak Amah had given Anthony. They laid it on the rough stone altar at the end of the cave. It was a naturally cloistered cavern. They stood the long cross lengthwise against the low wall of the place. Juan left and returned with some white rock-flowers he found near by. He spread these about softly and wept. Anthony saw that he had left his shoes at the entrance.

"Look, señor," he whispered. "They have stolen the silver crucifix that the good padre kept over his altar. There must have been Christians among them."

Anthony shook his head. He could neither weep nor speak.

The torches began to go out. The night deepened. Anthony thought of Brother François's face under the light of the vine that day at Regla.

"The light has taken him back to itself. I saw him go," he thought. "It is well with him now. I cannot bear it here any more. I am only a man."

"He will pray for us," said Juan when they stood outside under the stars again. "Our sins will be forgiven." Anthony pressed the simple fellow's hand. He waited while Juan went for the Arabs. They blocked the narrow entrance of the little cave, piling one great rock on another. They brought the earth down over the front.

The sound of the stones falling one on another was the language that night of Anthony's thoughts as he sat alone with Simba by the fire. The others might sleep. Yesterday had altered him beyond the language of the tongues of men. In an indescribable way he felt himself to be a totally different man. Like the blade of a sword taken hot from the fire he had been suddenly plunged into cold eternity for a moment and permanently tempered. When he had reeled back from the foot of the cross he had stumbled into time again. But his metal had been changed.

How this new man would act, who he was in fact, he must now find out for himself. Nor did he feel that the tempering of himself had been the end intended for what had happened to Brother François. "No, no, a thousand times no!" He was beyond any egotistic superstitions about this martyrdom which to his own inner world had been like a cosmic catastrophe, a spiritual earthquake which for a few moments had left him standing alone like the only man left on earth, face to face with God. It could have been intended for him alone no more than an earthquake could have been aimed at him or a storm at sea.

Yet he had been involved in it. He had even been instrumental in both a wilful and involuntary way in bringing it about. Looking into the embers of the dying fire in that valley of the shadow that night, he faced all the implications. And his own part in this happening and the meaning of it to him, accidental as that might be,—or providential if accidents were part of providence,—was part of them. The meaning of it remained with him alone.

Alone among those present he had had eyes and ears to understand. The Foulahs could only gather stones to make a tomb. The others slept while he watched and in his own manner communed.

Even Juan slept. Poor fellow, the marks of tears were still there on his simple, peasant face. In his handkerchief, wrapped up in sweet-smelling leaves and hidden in his breast, were the three thorns that had pierced Brother François's hands and feet. He had asked for them. Anthony knew they would eventually go to the little chapel overlooking the sea in Juan's native village in Spain. There the pious tale of the returned sailor would go round. There would be pilgrimages from the local countryside, perhaps. It would be like the "miracle" at Regla. Surely, surely *that* could not be the end of Brother François —three thorns in a gold box on a country altar? No! no! Someway, somehow, he must yet learn how, he should carry that light farther. When the time came he would light it again. He would take up the torch he had left burning out in the cavern. Perhaps Juan would take up the one he had left there in his own way. Perhaps, the thorns on the altar and pilgrimage were one way of remembering, of keeping the torch lit. But he must find his own way of shedding that light. Now he knew what the madonna had been holding out to him. The child in her arms had leaped into the man on the cross.

He wrapped his cloak about him closer in the darkness and gazed into the dying embers, not asleep, but lost at last in a wordless reverie. The night passed. The titanic fingers of the sun thrust fanwise through the eastern clouds. The tropical dawn came with a single stride. Suddenly the intolerable sun smote him on the eyes.

"Let there be light!"

"Go!"

"Go. May the glory of the face of Allah light your way," Amah had said.

"Go!" It was the last utterance of Brother François, whether addressed to his own spirit or to Anthony's, Anthony did not know. It would have been like him to have thought of another even at the last. Now the entire universe seemed to be filled and to be thundering that word accompanied by speeding bolts of light that struck the hills themselves into day.

The beams sped on into the west where that word of action was the way to salvation or damnation. In Futa-Jaloon, in the east where the dawn came from, men might sit and let the fate of Allah overtake them. They might wait for it there. But he, Anthony, was going back home. He must go now. He must *go!*

He called to the sleepers and they rode out of the shadows of the valley as if they could leave them behind forever.

CHAPTER FORTY-SIX

THE "UNICORN" CHARGES HOME

ON THE same morning that Anthony was slashing his way through the forests toward Gallegos, Captain Bittern of the good ship *Unicorn* was walking the quarter-deck with a faster tread and shorter turn than usual. He had been lying—and stewing— in the Rio Pongo for over six weeks, and he was thoroughly fed-up with the landscape just below Gallegos and immediately opposite Bangalang. With this view of things, a thoroughly monotonous one, the entire ship's company was for once in exact agreement with their captain.

Only once since they had arrived in the Rio Pongo to fetch home their new owner—about whom rumours were rife in the foc's'le—had the prospect from the deck been changed, and then only enough to shift the angles of things in the view very slightly. Yet this change, to the eyes of the captain at least, had been quite important.

He had warped his ship about a half mile across the bay from her first anchorage to take advantage of what is known to admirers of the art of artillery as "defilade space." In this case it simply meant that the guns from the hill-battery at Gallegos would be forced to overshoot the *Unicorn* in her new berth, due to the prominence of a small rise of ground on the long point of land between them and the ship.

Captain Bittern had picked out the one safe spot in the broad reach between Gallegos and Mongo Tom's with the canny eye of a privateersman who had cut-out many a tall ship and felucca from under the noses of barking Spanish shore batteries. Although he had now come on a peaceful private mission to an out-of-the-way spot, he bore an English letter of marque, the Spanish flag waved at Gallegos—and he was taking no chances. He still regarded minute protuberances in the landscape, such as now shielded him, as small but important works of God in favour of British enterprise. In a world where the majority of mankind persisted in disagreeing with him and his countrymen about the superior nature of British institutions, he had trained himself to see eye-to-eye with the deity in regard to defilade space and other small matters—and, oh, the difference to Captain Bittern!

Hence, from the quarter-deck of the *Unicorn* the view was not quite so devoid of interest as it was from the fo'c'sle, where the beauties of defilade space were not fully understood. As the captain paced back and forth he noted with some satisfaction that the *Unicorn* was not only safe in the precise spot where he had moored her bow-and-stern with springs on her cables, but that a few turns on the capstan would bring her broadside to bear on the river channel just where ships rounded the long point coming down from Gallegos. For a full half-mile or more he could simply "lack them through and through" before he got a gun in reply. And the same would also be true for any hostile craft coming up the river to the south of him. Besides, both Mongo Tom's and Bangalang lay directly across the flats within easy range of his guns. Both places, therefore, continued to furnish him with fish, green provisions, fresh water, and other small comforts, with alacrity—but at prices which were only less ruinous to them than finding themselves all blown to hell, which was the alternative named.

Don Ruiz had taken all this in through a glass from the main top of *La Fortuna* where she lay by the new quay at Gallegos. If the English-man intended to blockade Gallegos until Señor Adverse came back, he, Don Ruiz, could do nothing about it. He would simply wait until Señor Adverse returned to solve the difficulty. In the meantime, he would continue to take dinner every night at the big house with Ferdinando and Neletá. Perhaps, after all, it was Neleta who kept the blockade from being broken. *La Fortuna* was more heavily armed than the *Unicorn,* and Don Ruiz was a brave man.

But this particular morning Captain Bittern was by no means satis-fied with the view. He kept man-o'-war discipline on the *Unicorn,* but the crew had just come aft in a body to inform him respectfully that tomorrow would be New Year's Day, 1801, and the articles under which they had shipped would "hexpire." The question was: should he try to wait any longer for the new owner of the *Unicorn,* who seemed to have disappeared into the interior and might be dead of fever, or should he up-anchor and make sail for London, where con-siderable sums in prize-money as well as pay and discharges awaited him and his crew?

"After all—what was he doing here? And why should Captain Bittern boil himself and his men any longer for what had been the whim of an old man—and a dead man at that? He had served John Bonnyfeather faithfully for thirty-seven years, but now that he was gone, and his affairs were being administered by *Baring Bros. & Co.,* why was he bound any longer to serve them or this young Mr. Adverse, who was only the heir by law and no relation to his old employer? No! Perhaps he had been a bit too grateful to the past in undertaking to bring the *Unicorn* to the Rio Pongo. And a devil of a time he had had finding that muddy ditch. The charts were crazy.

"What luck some people had! Mr. Adverse—who was *he?* A

pleasant young dog who had been smart enough at learning his ships accounting at Livorno, he remembered. But, good Lord, the old man must have left him a cool hundred thousand at least! And Mr. Adverse seemed to have been doing remarkably well here, too. Maybe there was more to it than appeared on the surface? McNab had hinted at something once over a demijohn or two. Sandy McNab, that grand old crab, and Toussaint—what would become of them all at Livorno now? Where would that woman Faith go? She could take care of herself, he'd warrant. A very smooth piece, she was! Perhaps he should have spoken to the old man about her being in the house—and all that. A woman that would kneel down over a chair and let a man . . . pshaw! Whose business was that? It had been a wonderful night in the cabin. And now they would be selling the ship at auction soon. The chair, that leather-padded monument of romance, would have to go. He might buy it in for about £2. For £2?

"£2—£2—£2 . . . going. £2 and 1. Do I hear the sea-faring gentleman with the rings in his ears say £2 and 1? Good! Ah, £2 and 2 now. Thanks, father in Israel. £2 and 2, £2 and 2 . . . going . . . going. Do I hear sixpence more? The captain with the rings in his ears again, do I hear 2½? Yes! Going, going, going, gaw— £2.3 . . . Gone!—sold to the father in Israel for two pounds and three shillings. Take it away!

"Farewell chair, farewell.

"Captain Bittern has no more use for chairs—had only once, only once. He was raised up a pious man. He has had his own reward. Now he is going to live in a cottage in Chelsea with his niece and her two yellow-haired 'orphans.' She trusted in man. Served her right, served her right! But they are nice little girls, little girls. No more chairs for Captain Bittern. Of what use now are chairs except to sit upon?

"On Sundays—on some Sundays—he would take them all in a hack to the Muggletonian chapel at Spitalfields, where he had sat as a wide-eared, wooden-faced youth and listened to the Prophetess Johanna Heathcote expound the scriptures. How mouse-like his mother had been with a little brown tippet wrapped about her, sitting meekly on the cold chapel benches. A silk-weaver's daughter, she was. A mouse —he wondered now how his father had ever got her with him. It must have been a surprise to her, a distinct nervous shock. She wouldn't have believed there could be a woman like that Paleologus girl. She enjoyed it. It wasn't even sin with her. Maybe the prophetess would have understood. She had worn a deep, respectable bonnet too. Prim you might call her. But now, now that he came to think of it, she was a fire-ship, a fire-ship in disguise, by God, sir! She would have drifted down on you with the church pennant flying, and then—grappled with you—and spouted flames in the dark. *Ha, ha . . ."*

Mr. Spencer, the young gentleman purser, who had been taken aboard at the request of Sir Francis Baring to represent the executors, nearly stepped on his wrist as he heard the grim captain suddenly burst out into a loon-like laugh. He took the news forward. It might mean they were going home. He opined hopefully.

Jenkers, the sailmaker, shook his head.

"You don't know 'im like hi do," he said. " 'E's jes thort o' suthin' narsty. 'E's figurin'! An' if we gets hall our prize-money wen we gets t' Lunnon, we'll be bloody lucky, we will."

"I shall speak to the new owner about it when he comes aboard," said the purser loftily.

"Aye?" sniffed Jenkers, *"wen* 'e comes aboard. Wen will that be? That's wot we hall warnts ter know. You might himpart your hinformation to the marines. Tell 'em the ole man larfed."

"Now look here, Willum Jenkers . . ."

But it was just then that both Mr. Spencer and Jenkers heard the sound of drums and tom-toms. They were apparently away up-river yet—but coming down. They both leaned out of the port to listen.

"Belike it's them Bangalang 'eathens comin' 'ome again," said Jenkers. "You might tell that to the ole man. 'E's a bit deef, 'e is." Mr. Spencer returned aft.

Meanwhile Captain Bittern had come to a decision about going home. He would wait the last day of the old year out and sail on the morrow. He could legally hold his crew to the end of the voyage. But it would have to be a bona-fide voyage, under sail. He couldn't dawdle any longer in the Rio Pongo and pretend he was cruising. He might but he wouldn't. It was time to go. It would take him some time to square things with the Barings when he got to London, anyway. The *Unicorn* had been out since '96 off and on, and had made a lot of captures. And now he would get his own share and let the Barings settle with Mr. Adverse if they could find him. He couldn't— and he had done his best.

It was the Barings who had given him instructions when he had last put in to Gib to sail for the Rio Pongo to get Mr. Adverse. Sir Francis Baring himself had written. He was a schoolmate of John Bonnyfeather and very anxious to find Mr. Adverse to do the right thing by him, it appeared. Spencer had also let slip that the affairs of Mr. Adverse very much needed his return to Europe. It would pay him to give them personal attention, he said. There was Mr. Bonnyfeather's estate, there were the dozen or more prizes the *Unicorn* had taken, and there were large sums of money which Mr. Adverse had been smuggling through from Cuba by foreign bills of exchange.

Well, whatever came, he would see that his crew got their pay and
their prize-money out of it. Even if Mr. Adverse never showed up it
would be an admiralty and not a chancery case, thank God! Four
years of privateering at the end of a long career, and the last of the
Bonnyfeather fleet! He had kept the old house-flag flying to a profitable tune on the *Unicorn*, long after it had been hauled down at
Livorno. Well, it was all over now for him. Mr. Adverse would have
to look after his own, and if he was dead . . .

"*Well*, Mr. Spencer, what is it?"

"*Drud—druda*—drums, sir," shouted the purser. "Coming down-
river fast, sir," he bellowed.

"Damn you, do you think I'm deaf?" said the captain.

He went to the taffrail to listen. The *Unicorn* was swinging free
with her stern pointed up-river toward Gallegos. It was a clear, hot
day and the long point stretched over the water a mile away upstream
like a sharp pencil laid on glass.

Captain Bittern heard the drums.

They were certainly loud and insistent enough. There was a certain
triumphant slam in their rhythm that grumbled over the water inso-
lently. A large fleet of war canoes was emerging from the forest just
where the river first swung east into the jungle above Gallegos. More
and more kept coming around the bend.

On account of the point Captain Bittern could not see them yet.
But from the docks and hill at Gallegos they were soon in full view.
From the decks of *La Fortuna* Don Ruiz counted three score and four.
It was the combined armada of the Kru coastal villages which Mnom-
bibi had assembled for the crusade inland. A number of allies from
Mandingo villages farther upstream could be picked out by their longer
spears and leaf-shaped paddles. All were now returning to celebrate
at Bangalang the success of the expedition.

A formidable gathering which it would be best not to meddle with,
thought Ferdinando watching from the porch of the residence. In his
time, even as a youngster at Bangalang, Ferdinando could not remember seeing so many war canoes. He was glad they were not coming
home by the land side. He hoped devoutly they would pass and go
down-river without making trouble or asking for rum. This fellow
Mnombibi had raised himself into the position of a war prophet for
the whole region. He might be hard to deal with in the future. Yes,
he certainly hoped that this fleet of war-maddened, grotesquely-masked
warriors, with blue light flashing from hundreds of spears, with the

thump of tom-toms and the roar of drums and conch shells rolling over the water would go by.

Don Ruiz beat to quarters on *La Fortuna*—and Captain Bittern heard that.

The canoes passed Gallegos with obscene gestures shoreward and loud shouts of triumph. Something had broken their fear of the white man. His prestige about Gallegos had vanished. Ferdinando could guess why. On the bow of the long, black war canoe from Bangalang, which had not been taken from its shed for a generation, capered a man with a white-spectacled face, waving a silver crucifix in one hand derisively. The fleet bunched lower down where the current swept them together in a slowly swirling eddy just before it streamed around the point. Here they gathered about Mnombibi's canoe, with much *boo-booing* on conch shells and the roaring of bull-whistles, to hold a palaver.

The success of Mnombibi's raid on Brother François, although trivial from the standpoint of loot, had been immense in morale. Some lack of plunder had been made good at the expense of several unfortunate villages on the way back. The witch-doctor's influence was now paramount. Not only had he nailed the white man's wizard to his own tree, but he had carried off the white man's fetish and now held it in his hand. There it was, nailed down too. It could never get away. All its strength was his now. The secret power of the white god had passed to Mnombibi. It was Mnombibi and his followers who were henceforth in possession of the white man's magic superiority. It was they who were now invincible.

Mnombibi believed this thoroughly, although with him the raid had been a mere matter of professional etiquette and business. Brother François had set up a rival shop, and had paid the penalty. But some glimmerings of reasonable doubt had caused Mnombibi to pass by Gallegos and the big ship there which had so many guns. These qualms he knew had disappointed his enthusiastic followers. But he had other plans. There was the smaller ship in the reach below just off Bangalang. His suggestion that they should take the *Unicorn* to the beach, burn her, and share her copper rivets as the dividends of certain victory met with pandemoniac approval.

This decision, though popular at the time, must have been regarded later by the small minority who survived it as mysteriously unfortunate. On Mnombibi's part the error was a theological rather than a tactical one. His acquaintance with the complex nature of Christendom, with the doctrines of certain obscure Protestant sects in particular, was sadly limited. His plan was to drift down easily upon the *Unicorn* and engulf her. In much the same manner he had quietly walked in upon Brother François—and there had been no trouble at all.

But Captain Bittern was a Muggletonian. There were only two hundred and eighty-three of those Saints left alive in the entire world on December 31, 1800. Being in the minority, however, had never troubled them. Even in England not one of them had ever been known to resort to compromise. Nowhere in the inspired book of Lodowicke Muggleton, *The Divine Looking-Glass,* which the captain read every night, was the doctrine of non-resistance pressed upon the Saints; quite the contrary. It was not even mentioned. Captain Bittern would no more have thought of submitting to crucifixion, for instance, than it would have occurred to him to preach a sermon to sea-gulls.

Curious as it may be—all this, when taken in conjunction with the invention of the late Friar Bacon, held a bellyful of surprises for Mnombibi and his sixty-four canoes. As they rounded the point and began to drift down upon the *Unicorn,* a voice resembling an annoyed sea-lion's barked on her quarter-deck.

A sound like a large clock being wound up drifted across the still water as the ship walked around to her anchor and faced the flotilla. The twelve eyes in her side opened all at once with a small round pupil in each. Like a beast of the Apocalypse she gazed across the glassy sea at the approach of black Apollyon.

Mnombibi on the bow platform of the leading war canoe moved a little uneasily. But it was too late to turn back now. His prestige was hopelessly involved. He began to take a few chaste dance steps, mindful of his attendant spirits and the balance of the canoe; and to chant softly to his twenty-four rowers, "*Goling, golah, ssh . . . goling, golah, ssh . . .*" The sharp overhanging prow shoved across the flat water that whispered beneath his feet at every stroke. "*Goling, golah*"—five hundred yards . . .

A yellow cloud rolled out from the side of the *Unicorn.* It billowed higher and higher shot through with incandescent flashes of red lightning accompanied by terrestrial thunder. The intolerable tattoo was both regular and incessant. When the gun at the stern was through firing the bow gun was ready to resume, and the red flashes passed through the sulphur cloud exactly five times.

Don Ruiz, who with the rest of his crew had scrambled into *La Fortuna's* rigging, wild with excitement, now sat there green with envy at the Englishman's gunnery. Under the concentrated hail of grapeshot that beat the river into foam and bloody spray the black flotilla dissolved. Only five or six canoes could now be seen landing frantically at Bangalang.

In an interval of eery silence the smoke curtain slowly rose from the *Unicorn* upon what proved to be the next act.

Her capstan began to clank again as she brought her unused broad-

side to bear on the town. Her twelve starboard guns let loose as one.
The volley of chain-shot cut through the piles of the huts at Bangalang
as if a man had taken one long swing at that village with a giant
scythe.

Aunt Ungah-gola's shebang slipped slowly sidewise into the river
and then hung precariously on only one stake. It was too well-built
to collapse. So, she still sat in the high corner where she had been
cleaning fish just a moment before. One of them flopped gasping
down the tilted floor and swam away. The frame of the house shook
again. This time Aunt Ungah screamed. Through the hole in the
floor the genial, young crocodile which had flourished for some years
past upon her superior garbage was now coming home with a fixed
smile.

In the morning calm the smoke drifted slowly away from the now
silent *Unicorn* across the bay toward Mongo Tom's. There was not
enough wind to scatter it. The Mongo sat with a jug on the veranda
somewhat dazed by the rapidity of events taking place before his
rheumy eyes. He scarcely knew what to make of them. Trade would
certainly be ruined! From time to time he scratched selected islands
on his head. Suddenly out of the sulphur murk to windward three
canoes came tearing for his beach. He called his overseer and gave
orders to lead the survivors to the nearest barracoon. "It's an ill
wind—" said the Mongo, "even on a calm day."

As Captain Bittern sat in his cabin that evening over a mess of salt
pork and palm cabbage, he quietly remarked to Mr. Spencer that fresh
fish from the river could not be considered a delicacy any longer.
"Otherwise," said the captain, "they would go well with these greens."

"Yes, sir," replied Mr. Spencer, turning a little green himself.

"Most of the mess that still floated went down with the tide, but
you never can tell."

"No, sir, you certainly can't," agreed the purser.

"Not that it will make much difference," mused the captain, "now
that we're leaving. It's too bad we can't wait any longer for Mr.
Adverse. But at least our visit here will be remembered. I think——"

He bolted the centre of the cabbage.

"Quite!" exclaimed the clerk.

"Tell Mr. Sharp when he calls the larboard watch to ask Mr. Aiken
to step down to see me."

"Yes, sir."

"Good night to you," grunted the captain abruptly.

Mr. Spencer lingered a while over his errand. He was much bored
at going to bed every night at eight o'clock. He would rather have
messed in the steerage. But as a gentleman representing the great
house of *Baring Bros. & Co.*, Captain Bittern had done him the honour

of the cabin table and he could not help himself. He knew only too well that whatever the captain said was fate. Mr. Spencer after speaking to Mr. Sharp went to bed.

The captain snuffed the wicks on a pair of fat ship's candles and sat down to read as usual. He opened *The Divine Looking-Glass* at the last page and took out a fringed canvas book mark. On it his mother had embroidered when he first went to sea:

A 1757 D
Thou art responsible to God alone

The book had been printed in 1656, and the captain had divided the unbroken, solidly-printed, square pages into 365 paragraphs by ruling them across with red ink. He read one paragraph every night of the year, and either the first or the last paragraphs, which were identical, he skipped on leap years. Thus his spiritual as well as his earthly navigation proceeded by regular observations, and his exact position in both spheres could be precisely entered in his brass-bound diary. That book reposed, together with a King James version of the Bible, in a rack with a strap across it. Beside the Bible and the diary, there was room in the rack for *The Divine Looking-Glass*, a table of logarithms, and a treatise on the use of "Napier's Bones."

On this particular night the captain carefully printed, in a minute script on the back of the canvas marker, *"Finished reading for the 43rd time, 31st Dec. 1800"*—and this time read the last paragraph of the book of Lodowicke Muggleton, which now lay open before him:

And lo, and behold, the spirit within me was quickened and spake, saying, "Thou art immortal from both before and after, and the Kingdom of God on this earth is within. Arise, recollect it, and make thy share in it plain, lest thou be like unto a beast of the field that remembereth not; neither is he remembered. Behold the grass springeth and the mark of the beast is washed away. Enter thou into the kingdom as becomes a man and remember what man is like." And I cried out, saying, "Lo I remember." And the spirit said unto me, "Take thy pen then and write." And I saw two small angels of God like unto manikins that did ride upon little saddles upon my pen. And one was a dark angel, an evil servant of the Lord, and the other did glister like the bright waters of the rivers of Heaven. And the angels talked one with the other. And what they said I wrote, understanding not all of it but setting it down, for those that sat upon the saddle rode hard, and faster than I could follow. And they did open up the heavens and the earth unto me like unto a box of mirrors wherein the reflection of one thing is cast upon the glass of another so that the origin of the image is reflected back upon itself. And therein I saw not my own face but all things else. And there was nothing about which the angels spake together and pointed out to me that I could not remember as though it were yesterday becoming his own tomorrow. And this is the memory of the sons of God, and of men, and of the heavens, and the earth and the oceans and the beasts thereof that I have set down and sealed with my name that bare witness to it in the divine looking-glass.

Not understanding these things, but being much moved thereby, Captain Bittern, after a short entry in his diary covering an eventful day, prepared to turn in. He heard the watch called as he did so. The first mate stepped in.

"You have orders, sir?"

"High tide's about dawn tomorrow, Mr. Aiken. Stand by to take the ship down with the ebb. Have your people get the stern anchor up now. You might outen the candles there. Good night."

Mr. Aiken seemed to hesitate.

"Well?" said the captain looking through his night-shirt with which he was having a terrible time.

"The new owner has just come aboard, sir."

"The devil you say!" snapped the captain. "He must have been damned quiet about it then."

"Yes, sir. He and one man came up by the stern in a small boat. And you're to send your gig up to Gallegos tomorrow to fetch a dog aboard," said the mate with a ghost of a chuckle.

The beak of the captain suddenly rose triumphantly out of the night-shirt.

"Did you leave him rotting on deck like an old sail?" he roared.

"Yes, sir," gulped the mate.

"Be damned to you, Aiken, *that's* no way to treat your owner. Pshaw! Mr. Adverse, Mr. Adverse, where are you?" the captain shouted going on deck in his night-gown.

"Standing on my own deck at last. And thank God I am," said Anthony. "Is that your ghost, Captain Bittern? You look like the captain of the *Flying Dutchman*."

———

Anthony had heard the rumble of cannon early that morning while he and his troop of Foulahs were slashing their way as best they could through the jungle toward Gallegos. He listened, filled with misgivings, at the distant mutter of what to him was a mysterious fusillade. He wondered if Mnombibi's people were attacking the establishment, or whether the *Unicorn* and *La Fortuna* had at last fallen foul of each other. He pressed on now even more rapidly than before. But the path which he had ordered Ferdinando to keep clear for some miles inland was half overgrown through neglect, a mass of vines and creepers piled with ants' nests. The bridge at the five-mile creek had been riddled by termites and they had to make an exasperating detour through a swamp where the leeches clung to the horses' legs. Hurry as fast as they could, it was several hours after dark when the well-known stockade finally loomed dimly across the clearing and they rode through the open gate without being challenged. All this did not speak well for Ferdinando's care and discipline. Anthony's wrists beat anxiously at first at the silence. Then he saw all was well. But it was plain from a hundred signs of neglect that the Master of Gallegos had indeed been away.

Yet how familiar it all was. One glance from the hillcrest, and he could tell even by the few lights burning here and there through the trees and over the harbour that the place only awaited his return, and in peace. The moon began to rise. Beyond the long point he saw the *Unicorn* riding at anchor and his heart leaped. They were taking in her stern anchor. He was just in time then. In time to go? How beautifully the moonlight lay through the black stems of his palm groves; how mellow were the golden squares of *La Fortuna's* ports glowing by the quay. The night breeze brought him the heavenly perfume of orange trees in blossom.

Under the moon Gallegos lay like some Arabian Avalon asleep in its palm groves, redolent of spices, twinkling with the green lanterns of a million incredible fireflies carrying the intermittent lamps of their dim loves through the silver blur of the nocturnal atmosphere. And all this enchanted garden he had made; planted the trees, nursed the blossoms—and stolen the men. How many bits of paradise amid the forests had perished that his might be patched-out here? In the dark house there Neleta would be asleep now. And in the bay below lay the *Unicorn*. And he was going to go? He was going to leave— Circe! Yes, he had found the holy sprig of moly hanging on the tree. He would go now. But, oh, he had forgotten how lovely was the song of the Sirens in the moonlight. And he had not bound himself to the mast yet. Quickly! Let him do so, or even now, even now it might be too late.

He told Juan to lead the Foulahs quietly to the little valley that would be deserted now, and to see that they were well looked after there. The huts would be empty—very empty now! He warned him not to rouse Ferdinando nor to let it become known that he had come back. The tired men led their horses to the brook eagerly while he turned in at the path to the house.

He had considerable trouble in getting anyone to unbar the court-yard gate. It was Cheecha who finally came. She would have cried out if he had not stopped her. He told her to stay at the gate and to waken no one. He left her there weeping large Ethiopian tears of joy at his return. For the first time it came upon him fully how faithful Cheecha had been. Poor Cheecha, poor soul!

And Neleta?

He turned down the hall quietly and entered the room.

Instantly the sheer familiarity of the place defied his resolution to leave it. Everything was exactly as it always had been. The same bars of moonlight fell across the same woman on the bed, asleep, waiting. Surely nothing could have happened to him since he had seen her last. No, he was only coming home at the end of the day to go to bed as he had the night before—and the night before that. Tomorrow they would get up and have breakfast and he would go on as usual. Why, what had he been thinking about? All that had happened for months past, the entire experience in the hills, seemed to have been suddenly cancelled. He would simply go to bed with her and take her in his arms.

How silent it was. Only the forests far-off, roaring and grunting to the moon. They would go on forever. Here in the room—

Her regular breathing coming and going deeply through the dark-ness was the unbroken connecting thread of life and passion upon which all these familiar things, and all the emotions and meanings that surrounded them from one end of Gallegos to the other, were hung. Neleta was the life and centre of Gallegos. He felt suddenly that she was the mysterious cause of it. Without her it would never have been. He could not have made it. It was Neleta who had made him master of Gallegos, and Neleta was mistress of it all.

So he stood there haunted by her. It was not desire alone. The magnet that drew him to her was more immense than that. She was simply the pole of it, of all the life of the Grain Coast. In her the lines of all its attractions met and centred. And he felt them now like pal-pable things pulling him toward her where she lay asleep on the bed. How could he be the negative to that? He just managed to look away —whether to begin from old habit throwing his clothes across the well-known chair there or not, he never knew. He sat down and began to take off his shoes—and he happened to look up.

On Neleta's dresser across the room the moonlight gathered in the mirror with a concentrated silver glow. And in this dim effulgence, dripping with a white, watery light, stood the madonna just where he had left her months before.

She too was familiar.

But with the familiarity of other things, of past days and places, that rushed into his mind now so that the room and all within it, except the little statue with the dim glow about it, was driven outside and lay plainly and objectively beyond him again. He was no longer merely a part of it. He slipped his feet back into his shoes and went over to the chest-of-drawers where the figure stood.

He remembered now. He was going to take her away with him—along with a hundred other little, personal things he could no longer bear to be without—comforts, and remembrances which a man cannot replace, things he had missed sorely time and again lately. That comfortable set of razors Cibo had given him. Lord, how he had missed *that!* Certain favourite clothes—and the cuff links Dolores had sent him. Dolores!—where was she tonight?

Lost! He had lost all of them. Angela his lover, and sweet cool Florence Udney—the feeling of northern spring and violets, the cool strong burgeoning of innocence and youth. What fire had melted all those snows away that should have melted kindly to the moon? It was the hot tropical sun—and Neleta.

Why, he had staggered into her by chance like a drunken bee that falls suddenly into a flesh-coloured orchid hanging on a hot wall! And the flower-trap had closed over him; the little hairs of it covered with honey dew and the great smooth inflamed petals with tawny speckles on them. God! How he had lain there dying of ecstasy with his wings folded and gummed. Caught! With the light far-away, and the green forest beyond. It was still roaring tonight. It would roar like that forever. It was imitating the sea . . .

"But the sea is my home," he said. "And I will go."

He took a grip on himself and began looking for the tinder-box. It was not in the usual place. He stumbled over Neleta's shoes. Damn! Cheecha had always put things away. It was Cheecha who had really run the house and made life physically tolerable. Not Neleta. Neleta was legs in the spasm, eyes rolled back, confusion, things in heaps, perfume—and a sudden witch-radiance at dinner when the orchid hung over the wall. My God! where *had* she put the tinder-box now? On her best shawl, of course,—and a great hole burned in it—he lit the candles—the shawl from China. Don Ruiz had given her that. Let him. Anthony would make use of it now.

He spread the madly figured shawl on the floor and began to throw things into it helter-skelter. After it was "packed" he would waken Neleta and tell her . . . would he? Yes. But defer it now. Pack. Wait and see. He began to ransack his chests like a burglar working speedily—but not quietly. The things were his—weren't they? The bundle grew. So did the racket. A lid fell with a vicious smack. He laughed.

Neleta opened her eyes. She understood instantly what was happening and without saying a word got up and threw herself on him.

"No! You are not going. No! No!"

Her passionate negative was as resolute as his positive intention of leaving—more vehement. It was much harder to go than he had supposed. It rapidly began to become doubtful as she clung to him, pleading, commanding, suggesting, enticing with a thousand variations and tones of "no." This was not an argument. It was Neleta. How to resist her in the flesh? No, it was impossible that he should do this thing.

At any rate he found himself dragged onto his knees and kneeling by the bed; leaning over her with her arms around his neck. She begged now, whispering to him. Pity for her began to overwhelm him. He put his head on her breast. She began to smooth his hair and draw him closer. He felt tears on her cheeks. Some of them were his own. His arms stole about her. His hands went under the pillow to bring her head closer to put his lips on hers again.

Then his fingers clutched something hidden under the pillow.

It seemed to be shaped like a forked radish, smooth, softer as he held it—wax! Suddenly he remembered Mnombibi rocking himself before the mirror that night. Could it be . . . he would see.

He rose with it in his hand, powerfully, tearing himself loose from her. Her coiled hair whipped smoothly across his neck as he drew back. He took the thing over to the candles where the madonna stood. Yes! It was the witch-doctor's horrible little manikin, a fetish with an enormous thing cocked up at him, a blind, silly face. He saw his own hairs running through the half-transparent wax.

So it had been no dream that night. Neleta *had* brought that devil Mnombibi into his room. She had procured this. Somehow, somehow Neleta had been the cause of horrible things. Brother François! And Anthony had been sold to the devil, too—for what? As he looked at the grinning fetish he turned sick. A noise behind him caused him to whirl about.

She was crawling over toward him through the moonlight. She had left the bed stealthily. Some of the covers dragged behind her. They came off. She was naked, crouched, ready to spring. It was the fetish she wanted! "To hell with it!" He smashed it on the floor and trod on it. The next instant he was trying desperately to prevent her doing the same to the madonna.

She carried him back for a minute. She swarmed up him biting like a great cat. She wrapped her arms and legs about him. She gave the hated virgin figure on the bureau a kick. It rolled over and smashed. She screamed with delight. He held her off, wrestling with her as he had wrestled that night in the tent. A complete horror and hate of her, a burst of fury gave him full strength.

What had he been born a man for?

He bore her back to the bed and bound her there hard and fast with a twisted sheet. It was degrading, even funny for an instant—and painful. Then it was fearful and horrible beyond usual experience. The abysmal face of the dark woman looked up at him, thrown back, the long white teeth longing for his throat. Her eyes smouldered with yellow and green glints. The incomplete, man-eating soul of her lay revealed twisting on the bed like an unformed thing half torn out of its cocoon. But dangerous, strong, hungry, furious. Like Faith— witchcraft!

This was what he had been trying to mate with—a body alive. Madre! He might have had children by it.

She had forgotten her Spanish now and raved at him in some mad gibberish. His spine crept. One of the candles burnt out. God! He would be left alone with her in the dark again.

He swept the madonna, and everything else on the floor and the dresser, into the shawl. The big mirror fell with a hard smash on the remaining candle. Pieces of it rained about his head as if someone were hurling them at him. He dashed out of the dark room dragging the bundle after him like a thief. Her voice followed him down the hall.

Cheecha stopped him at the gate. He stood there half-mad with rage and the pain of his bitten arms. He felt like wrecking the house. For some time he did not know that Cheecha was clasping him about the knees. Then he shook her off. He was looking for something to kick . . . he stepped over her.

"Master, take me with you," she cried after him. "Master . . ."

He turned around, touched by something desperate in the tones of the woman's voice. She had sunk back on her haunches in despair.

"Neleta will kill me now," she said looking up at him in a last appeal. "Tomorrow . . ." horror convulsed her features. "She will think you care."

Poor Cheecha, poor soul!—he knew it was true.

"Go down to the docks, I will look after you. Go now." She fled before him into the darkness.

A few minutes later he found her waiting dumbly. He whistled for Juan who came out of the shadows. The three of them got into a small boat and rowed out to *La Fortuna* while Cheecha held the bundle, wrapped up in Neleta's shawl, like a child in her lap. It was all that Anthony was taking from Gallegos. He made her leave it in the boat, and whispering something to Juan, sent them forward.

Don Ruiz was engaged in a game of solitaire. For the sixth time he had had an extraordinary run of luck with himself that night. He was amazed but genuinely glad and relieved to see Anthony.

"What had the cannonading that morning been about?"

"Oh, you should have been here, señor." He explained at great length and graphically while Anthony sat looking grim enough. So Captain Bittern had swallowed Mnombibi and his people at one gulp—just as he remembered he used to drink soup. That plate was clean.

Don Ruiz went on to say that things had been going from bad to worse at Gallegos since Anthony had left.

While Anthony was putting himself into decent shape again after Neleta's mauling, by the help of the captain's wardrobe, Don Ruiz kept pouring complaints into his ears about Ferdinando. Cibo, it appeared, had been greatly put out over various transactions in which the factor had overreached himself. "Make a dog a king, señor, and the whole court will soon be snarling." Anthony gathered that Don Ruiz and Cibo had become bosom friends in Havana. He was glad of it. It suited his plans. He led up to the point he had in mind by relating some recent events.

Don Ruiz, Anthony was glad to see, could still be shocked. He was all for hanging Ferdinando for murdering a saint. Anthony shook his head.

"I have thought of that," he said. "But there must be no further vengeance. Brother François would not have it so. The slaughter this morning must have been horrible. Under the circumstances I cannot blame Captain Bittern—but no more. Besides, such men as Ferdinando are really savages. I know that now. According to his light he tried at first to serve me. The rest was my fault. I was deceived as to the man's real nature by his delicate manners. But he is a half-breed, you know, captain. His mother came from a hut in Bangalang. As for his sister——"

Anthony paused. Whether this was news to the captain he could not tell. Don Ruiz's expression did not change. Anthony hurried on while hastily donning a new shirt, his own having been ripped to tatters.

"It is my intention, captain, to leave Gallegos tonight, to go aboard the *Unicorn* and never to come ashore here again. For many reasons I am finished with Africa forever. When I am gone there will be nothing to prevent your taking over the establishment. Ferdinando's blunders, as far as the ledgers go, are small ones. In the main you will find a going concern in excellent shape. You and Carlo Cibo will have to handle the Havana end of the game between you. I shall write Carlo, of course, the first opportunity. I shall from now on devote myself to my own affairs in Europe. You can count me out here as having left six months ago. That is fair enough. Now what do you think?"

"One minute, señor. Let me consider." Don Ruiz who had been walking up and down rapidly sat down and played out his uncompleted game of solitaire. Anthony went on dressing.

"That is extraordinary," said Don Ruiz after a little, "for the seventh time tonight I have played out on the same card." He held up the queen of spades. Then he reshuffled the cards slowly, laid one out on the table and laughed.

"Yes," he said. "I will do it. Have you no stipulations, señor?"

"One or two personal ones," began Anthony, pausing now and then while he carefully tied back his hair in European style again. "The woman Cheecha who is now aboard, is to be taken to Havana on this ship and turned over to Carlo Cibo to be given her freedom. I shall see that she is taken care of through him. Also see that the Foulahs who came down with me are properly entertained and sent back with gifts to their hearts' content. Later, from Europe, I shall send you certain cases which I wish you to forward faithfully by the first caravan to Futa-Jaloon. They are for Amah-de-bellah. By the way, cultivate his good-will."

"And the señorita?" said the captain drumming a little on the table.

"Let her stay in the big house as long as she wants to. I expect to arrange for certain sums to be paid her quarterly through Spanish bankers. She can claim them at Havana if she has a mind to. They will come to her regularly, but it will take me some months to arrange for them. In the meantime——"

"Perhaps, she had best remain at Gallegos till *La Fortuna* sails—after this next trip," suggested Don Ruiz. Anthony agreed.

"That is all," he said.

They shook hands on it.

The captain's eyes took on a far-away look.

"It is not true, then, señor, that you married the lady just before the padre left—when you were so ill? Ferdinando gave me to suppose . . . ah, pardon me. I understand now. Pardon."

"So that was the reason Ferdinando had been so anxious to get rid of Brother François! If I had died Neleta would still have been mistress here. No one could have contradicted them. Ferdinando again! What shall I do with him?" he thought.

Nothing! He would do nothing. He would let that remain like his own account, to be settled with Providence. He was guilty himself. He would not judge and punish Ferdinando. No, he was done with Gallegos and all its affairs. He put on his coat and sent for Juan.

"Don Ruiz," he said as they walked together to the ship's side, "I am leaving you at the edge of the world here. You can easily fall off."

There is no law here except what men can find in themselves. I tried to make my own and could not live by it—others died. But you are in charge now. You can settle certain matters to suit yourself. I go for my reasons; you stay for yours—the cards, for instance—but I warn you." He paused by the binnacle and bared an arm bitten from wrist to shoulder. "And that is only one thing. There are other marks, deeper. These that you see are only on my arm."

The captain of *La Fortuna* bowed and smiled. "You are fair enough, señor. I thank you for the warning. But I am not afraid. In my country there is a proverb, 'When you go among the women take your whip along.' But," he added hastily, "I am a man of honour, a caballero."

"So I have been told," said Anthony a little bitterly.

Don Ruiz replied vehemently. "Believe, believe me, I also have learned by sorrowful experiences. I know, for instance, that it is not just the woman who is driving you away. No, you go on account of many things; because of yourself, to be a free man. Is it not so?— And you do not wholly credit me with knowing that. I am a man of feeling, too. And there are many ways to feel. My way may be right for me."

"That is true," said Anthony. "I beg your pardon."

They shook hands again. "Good luck—good luck."

"Farewell, amigo," cried Don Ruiz looking over the side now. "I shall do the best I can. It is my fortune here. Yours there. But we shall not forget the good man we saw in the little valley that day. Never. You know. Adiós, adiós, but I won't say good-bye forever. Ah—quién sabe?"

They shoved off.

In the small boat with the bundle sitting alone in the middle of it Anthony and Juan slid rapidly downstream and rounded the point. A few minutes later Anthony was standing on the well-remembered deck of the *Unicorn* shaking hands with Captain Bittern.

There was only one thing he had forgotten. It was the hound Simba. He sent a boat back to Gallegos for him a little after dawn. Don Ruiz returned him a note.

I have everything in hand this morning and am holding hard. Fire a gun when you leave and you shall have from *La Fortuna* an honourable farewell in reply. Here is your Havana mail, which I forgot last night. Adiós.

But they weighed anchor quietly and slipped down with the gathering ebb while the river was still misty. Juan piloted them out. The *Unicorn* seemed to greet the open sea with delight.

"Look, señor," cried Juan, pointing happily to the long barriers where they had spent the days of light together, "that was the best of Gallegos. Let us remember that—and the padre." He crossed himself. "Now we are out in the open sea again, I turn the ship over to you. Ah! We shall see Europe again, Spain! You will let me go home for a while, won't you?"

"If you will promise to come back to me," smiled Anthony.

"Sí, wherever you are I will come to you."

A few minutes later Anthony heard Juan's guitar on the deck below. Beginning mournfully, it continued some time in a melancholy strain. Then suddenly the strings released themselves into a mad tumble of lyric joy. The voice of the hound Simba joined in, whining with excitement. Anthony held on at the wheel himself. He did not look back. By noon the low coast lay behind the eastern horizon. He heard the ship's bell again marking the relentless march of time—and went below for the midday meal with Captain Bittern in the cabin.

Other things besides the dinging into his ears of time and tide reminded him he was back in the midst of his own world again. One was the way Captain Bittern drank his soup. He raised it on an even keel to his exactly horizontal mouth; he looked across the level surface of it as if he were taking an observation and saw ice on the horizon. The slit in his face opened. The plate tilted and the soup vanished. It was gone! Eating to Captain Bittern was part of the grim business of life. If he ever tasted anything, no one, probably not even Captain Bittern, knew it. There was no time for it. Anthony was swept back again to the remarkable gastronomic legerdemain of the captain at Mr. Bonnyfeather's table. The Casa da Bonnyfeather rose up before him and all those who had sat about the board there. And the great pile of correspondence that awaited his attention completed the sensation of having come back to the world with a vengeance.

Baring Bros. & Co., Mr. Bonnyfeather's executors, were clamorous in ink to have him come home. Their agent awaited him at Livorno. It was now essential to close-out the affairs of the House of Bonnyfeather in Italy and on the spot. Anthony grinned at their assurances as to the trustworthiness of their agent at Leghorn.

> . . . Herr Vincent Nolte, a young man with a rising reputation for able banking in difficult times, the heir of an ancient concern with which we have long dealt. You may have every confidence in him, and he is authorized to advance you . . .

A long accounting followed.

He looked at the totals in amazement. It was thrust upon him now and at last with a full and keen realization that he was rather, yes, decidedly, a rich young man. He could go where he liked. He could do what he wanted to. So the "lonely twin" was going to be free. Why had this favour been shown him? he wondered. Through what inexplicable channels the water of events took their way. Where would they next break into the light again and spread out before him? Oh, let them run deep and quietly for a while underground. It had been a terrible pool into which that other Bronze Boy had been plunged. He at least was gone forever—only the lonely twin remained. He, by the grace of God, had somehow been set free.

He leaned forward putting his head down on his arms amid the clutter of his papers on Captain Bittern's table. He shoved aside *The Divine Looking-Glass* which the captain in his hurry had left lying open the night before. The canvas book mark with its broad, black letters fell out under his eyes. He read what was written there with profound astonishment and considerable awe.

After all—what was an accident?

At any rate, he would not forget this one—either. He felt the ship quietly sweeping on. Into another world again! The bell on deck began to strike musically. . . .

END OF VOLUME TWO

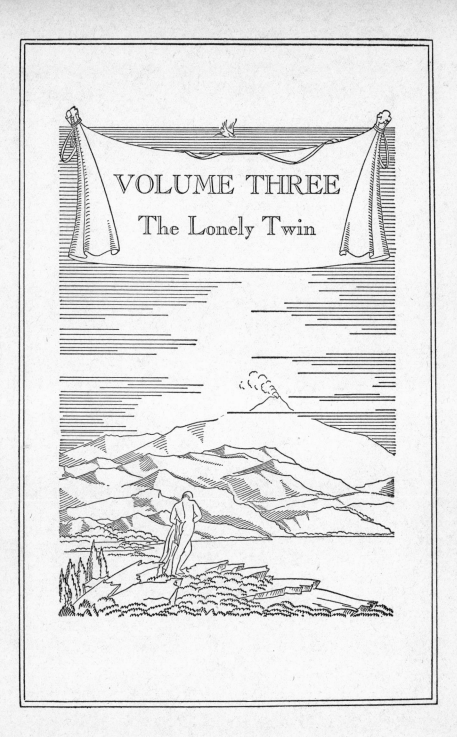

VOLUME THREE
The Lonely Twin

BOOK SEVEN

*In Which a Worldly
Brother Is Acquired*

CHAPTER FORTY-SEVEN

REVERBERATIONS

DON LUIS leaned back in the coach, which had been comfortably repaired at Dijon only a month before, and inhaled the scent of the vineyards about Livorno with considerable satisfaction.

He was nearing the end of a year's journey from Madrid by way of Paris, and the certainty of resting his bones in a good bed that night lent an additional charm to the admirable vistas along the ancient highway between Pisa and Leghorn.

These, however, he was fully prepared to admire for themselves alone.

After an absence of nearly twenty-five years upon his estates in Spain, the Marquis da Vincitata was returning to visit Tuscany, the land of his predilection. And he was thinking, as he leaned back in the luxurious, albeit somewhat faded upholstery that still lined his old-fashioned coach, that a return to Italy must ever be to every civilized European a home-coming.

He had even composed an epigram about it.

At the particular moment when he swept with a clatter of sixteen hoofs through the hamlet of San Marco he was attempting to write the epigram upon a small slate which he kept handy for the purpose. It was not often possible to write when travelling, although the coach was now slung upon the best steel springs. But so level and straight was the Roman highway, which had lately been repaired by Bonaparte—so smooth was the stone pavement upon which the coach was now rapidly and invincibly rolling, that in this instance Don Luis had no difficulty whatever in writing upon the slate without breaking the delicate point of his stone pencil.

At this triumph of modern engineering he looked up with an amused and faintly-pleased expression about the eyes. The crow's-feet on the pouches under his heavy lids contracted a little ironically and he started to drum with his thick, powerful fingers on the surface of the slate which rested on his knee. The scent of the vineyards had caused him to remember something that interfered with his epigrammatic style. Finally, with an angry motion of his club-like thumb, he obliterated what he had just written upon the slate. He looked at the smudge and laughed, for he had not really intended to wipe out the epigram but to destroy only the uncomfortable memory which had just been forced upon him.

During the course of his frequent journeys—and upon diplomatic business he still travelled a great deal—the marquis had composed several thousand epigrams. He first set them down upon the slate and later transferred them to an elegant, morocco-bound notebook that reposed together with a pack of cards, the latest French novel, some goat cheese, and a bottle of white wine in a small locker on the side of the coach. This alcove had once, long ago, held a figure of the Madonna belonging to his girl-wife.

It was a bright memory of the dead woman, vividly but unconsciously forced upon him by the odour of grape blossoms, that had interfered with his writing. He looked annoyed. He brushed his hand over his eyes, and went on again.

The peculiarly sardonic and sententious style in which Don Luis composed his epigrams was a balm to his injured ego which had never ceased to suffer from the wound inflicted upon it by the unfaithful conduct of his wife. It was for that reason that there were thousands and not merely hundreds of epigrams now safely copied into the morocco notebook. Don Luis had thus taken his revenge on fate by secretly continuing to drip vitriol upon everybody and everything under the sun. His sarcasm was a kind of spiritual pus that he wiped away privately with page after page of the notebook.

Outwardly Don Luis had scarcely changed at all. He even looked a little better preserved. Indeed, there was something about the marquis that reminded some close observers of a living mummy. One almost crippling attack of the gout had brought a Spartan diet into his regimen. He lived principally upon sour wine, cheese, and goat's milk. And he knew exactly how to physic himself after those banquets for which even a Spanish grandee and an old diplomat semi-occasionally had to unbutton.

For a man well up in his sixties the conde de Azuaga, as he was known in Spain, was really remarkable. But the most remarkable thing about him was that the world went on taking his spry, youthful vigour and unimpaired energy as a matter of course. It did not, except in a few cases of old men who enviously failed before him, remark his vigour at all.

In Estremadura, where Don Luis had spent a great deal of his time, the life was both healthy and hardy. Those who survived it in infancy usually lived to a vigorous old age. There were priests there who had been known to have had children at the age of ninety. And it was for that reason that the nobility in the neighbourhood of Don Luis' estates frequently sent to Valencia, or other provinces, for family confessors whose ripe old age was less likely to break forth into ridiculous blossoms. In Estremadura there was,—yes, undoubtedly,—there was something in the air. Don Luis had breathed it in calmly, and preserved its fire.

After a decade of retirement in Estremadura the marquis had gradually begun to resume his position of natural influence and inevitable emolument at the then much disordered court of Spain. For this he was excellently fitted by both inheritance and long practice. At the supine court of Charles IV he possessed an enormous advantage over even the most selfish of timeservers; he was no longer troubled by any social conscience whatever. Over those who matched him in this respect he was still superior, for his own selfishness was complex and conservative while theirs was simple and immediately voracious. Those dull glimmerings of virtue, which even the most lupine of statesmen occasionally employ as beacons of direction in an otherwise purely opportunist piloting, did not in the midnight oceans of Don Luis' soul mark even a distant headland. He steered only by the fixed star of self-interest with a Machiavellian craft. It was in this sense that the conde de Azuaga was in a very real way a "prince" among men.

The Marquis da Vincitata and conde de Azuaga had in fact been endowed by an all-wise Providence, that accomplishes its mysterious ends with the deadly foil of evil as well as the sword of justice, with an awful and profound mind. That the colour of his soul was Stygian was only natural, for it is in the darkness of night that mental lightning without thunder makes its finest display when it strikes. The marquis' self-interest consisted in what he was interested in, and that can be described most laconically as a passionate desire to hold back the hands on the clock of time. With that end in view he had gradually thrown himself back into the ways and places of influence, body and soul.

Don Luis had within him a strong sense of the trend of the age; of the becoming of men and peoples in the stream of time. And as this, when combined with the practical ability to influence events, is undoubtedly a trait of genius, the advent of the conde in his gloomy coach at the Escurial just before the French Revolution broke out had marked a distinct epoch of pause in the history of his own peninsula.

He proposed to preserve it as a perfect Christian Tibet, and for a time he succeeded.

He left no record of his strange and stilling influence. He wrote nothing, except the epigrams in his notebook. His method was the ancient, and often most effective one in human affairs, of a devious personal influence. He attached himself to the right men and left them at exactly the right time. He drove hither and yon in his gloomy coach, which for many years had remained slung upon the chains with which he had furnished it for his wife's martyrdom. A call paid by the suave, and inevitably correct, conde in this vehicle driven by a cat-like coachman was like receiving the ambassador of smouldering subterranean powers whose force is known but whose depth has never been plumbed. Virtue and sanctimony were forced to listen to his wisdom with respect, while the superficially sinful were left both envious and scared. A few ardent young spirits who opposed him had been questioned as to the basis of their curious opposition during the last ample days of the Holy Office. Thus, opposition to Don Luis was always dangerous; co-operation inevitably paid. Consequently, the ends he fostered throve, and the web, which the constantly widening circle of the peregrinations of the coach left upon the map of Spain, found an ever more and more powerful and alert spider sitting upon the faded rose-coloured upholstery at its shifting centre.

Don Luis was not "popular," of course. It had never occurred to any mob to shout, "Long live Don Luis," or to any assembly of notables to drink his health. It would have seemed preposterous, unnecessary. He somehow carried with him everywhere, and under every conceivable circumstance, the suggestion that he would inevitably outlive and prevail over those with whom he dealt. All this was largely due to an unquenchable desire for revenge upon life which now directed the movements of the marquis' soul. He would have liked to stop all other life than his own. And in that event he would have valued his own existence only because it would have enabled him to watch over a universal calm. The marquis was therefore known as a "conservative."

Indeed, there was only one positive desire left in his still active but negative nature. It was an harassing sensuality that still hoped for long-protracted and callous intercourse. It constituted, as it were, the secret, youthful vigour of his senility, and, when actively exerted, held a certain kind of mysterious and unexpected charm for older women. It was for this reason that the marquis as he made his rounds always kept at least one of his drooping eyelids half open, and he was no longer at all particular as to where he could slake a passion that was both dull and violent at the same time.

His reactionary hopes, however, had not prevented him from making those necessary outward concessions to change without which even a "conservative" cannot conserve. These were for the most part exhibited in his astute political manœuvres, his meticulous dress, and in the constant, almost affectionate, rehabilitation of the coach.

He liked to recall that he had won the coach from the Duc d'Orléans at a lucky run of cards in what he looked back upon as better days. For various reasons he had cherished it and rejuvenated it from time to time. The vehicle had almost become a part of him. In the course of time it received new tires, new wheels, new axle-trees and new shafts. It had been dragged over Spain, Portugal, and France by horses and mules that had died in its service and left the body of the coach behind them. Only that had remained the same. In its lines were expressed the luxurious amplitude and the heavy ruthlessness of the ancien régime. Its cat-like coachman had been promoted. He still rode upon the box in a coat-of-many-capes like a tom cat dressed in frills. But Sancho was now Don Luis' valet and general factotum, and the coach was driven by his son, a young man with grey hair, a round, ocelot-shaped head, and wide, greenish eyes. This personage, known as the "Kitten" in Madrid, flourished a whip and said nothing except to his horses or mules. These he occasionally addressed in a tempest of lewd squalls, while he drove with an uncanny skill that seemed to be reckless.

Towards the end of 1799 Don Luis had gone to Paris to try to arrange the little matter of transferring the southern part of Portugal to the prime minister of Spain. He and the First Consul Bonaparte had found that they understood one another. Pourparlers had rapidly changed into conversations during the course of which the character of the Prince of the Peace, the queen's favourite, and the general sorry mess of affairs at the court of Spain were amply discussed. These conversations were carried on with a masterful directness on the part of the first consul and a faultless, self-serving innuendo on the part of Don Luis that rapidly brought about an understanding between these two men as their admiration for each other increased. Napoleon saw in the marquis one whom it would be wise to favour in order to use; Don Luis beheld in Bonaparte a man whom it was imperative to serve well in order to profit amply. They got on.

"What sort of a man is the Prince of the Peace?" asked Bonaparte whirling about upon Don Luis, as he walked up and down looking out upon the gardens of the Luxembourg which he was just about to leave for the Tuileries.

"A man of large parts, citizen-general, necessary and assiduous in the service of Her Majesty both day and night."

Bonaparte smiled wanly.

"I have heard that he is also the friend of the king," he said. "Is there no one to whose interest it would be to enlighten His Catholic Majesty as to the state of his own domestic affairs?"

"Several, now in exile, have made the attempt," replied Don Luis. "But His Majesty's family party at the Escurial has been carefully arranged to insure the royal peace of mind. I might add that the unique relation the Prince of the Peace holds to the king has thrown a new and romantic light upon the power and privileges of a viceroy."

Napoleon smiled again, this time not so wanly. He began rapidly to discuss the basis of a new treaty with Spain in which the payment of a larger annual subsidy to France was the most important item. It was at this interview that Don Luis first mentioned to Napoleon the possibility of the cession of Louisiana to France. He merely suggested it, as it were. It was difficult to transfer bullion from Mexico to Spain on account of the British fleet but a continent could be transferred at Paris, by a stroke of the pen. Napoleon shook his head. It was ready money he wanted. But he remembered the suggestion and turned it over in his planetary mind.

The upshot of several such conversations was surprising to several persons. The Prince of the Peace failed to get his Portuguese principality but was assured of French support at the court of Spain. For this he could grind his teeth—and be thankful—to both Don Luis and Bonaparte. The precise way in which the gratitude was to be shown was carefully provided for and understood beforehand.

The Duke and Duchess of Parma were also surprised. It was agreed that they should pack up and move their thrones to Florence, as Napoleon had new arrangements for Italy in view and was graciously willing to endow their Etrurian Majesties-to-be generously, at the expense of a helpless ally. Don Luis was commissioned to inform them tactfully of the little surprise in store for them, after arranging certain details beforehand through the Spanish ambassador at Paris.

The mission to prepare the authorities at Florence was one which for several reasons filled Don Luis with a peculiar satisfaction. He liked moving royalties, who had to pretend to be thankful to him, like figures in chess. He liked returning to Italy, where the Renaissance had been taken seriously, he said. There was a decidedly Roman pagan side to Don Luis. He had finally reduced his Christianity to nothing but ritual with no moral implications. And a trip to Tuscany in particular coincided exactly with certain private business of his own in that region.

Thus, as usual, Don Luis was able to conduct his own and the public business as one. Before leaving Paris he had obtained certain letters from the first consul which insured the return of his confiscated estates in Tuscany. The dilapidated castle and small hill-town of Vincitata was nothing to Napoleon, who was therefore glad to return it to Don

Luis upon whom he counted for further confidential advices when he should return to Spain.

In all of this Don Luis had been acting as the confidential agent of the Prince of the Peace. But he had seen fit to see eye to eye with the first consul, because perforce he must, and because as a matter of fact, it was in that way that he could make the best terms for Spain. At least he had obtained the promise of French support for the policies of Godoy, the queen's favourite, who was already anathema at home. Don Luis was also casting an eye into the future as every good diplomat should. A vague but stupendous outline of the plans of the young Corsican general with the Roman head had begun to dawn upon Don Luis. On one occasion the general in the coat with green facings had honoured the marquis with one of those metaphysical discourses on European affairs which so many people had made the mistake of not taking seriously. Don Luis did not indulge in that error. He had experienced a curious sensation while he listened to Napoleon, one of having participated in a similar interview somewhere else, very long ago. It had, he told himself, a kind of Trajanic ring about it. Just why, Don Luis could not be sure. But the experience of recall had been a powerful one. He dismissed that, but he retained in his head the vision of a great European empire with Paris as the new Rome. This suited the spiritual politics of Don Luis, and for the first time in many years there stirred within him an emotion akin to enthusiasm. For a minute or so the two men, who were conversing across a desk with the map of Italy laid out upon it, had been bound together in a profoundly deep and naturally flowing conversation as to the destinies of European civilization. It was above religion, national politics, and folk morals. For a minute or two what the Roman Empire had accomplished centuries before was reconstituted in a room over the portico of the Tuileries in Paris in 1800. Two free and ruthlessly candid intellects had dropped the petty conventions and prejudices of feudal provinces and looked upon Europe as a whole. Don Luis remembered afterward that Napoleon had lapsed into Italian in the excitement of finding himself understood, and he considered that to be the most majestic compliment which could have been offered him. Indeed, he looked back upon that interview as the crowning moment of his career. It had had about it the flavour of a meeting of Roman augurs, but of augurs who took themselves seriously and had eagles to unleash. Don Luis was able to add a few quotations and observations from some of the Sibylline books of the West. Then, as it were, the curtain had been withdrawn again. The sense of immediate communication in a mutual dream lapsed. Napoleon went on in French.

It was this that had caused Don Luis to smile ironically as he swept

over the Roman highway, recently improved by Napoleon. It was
only a small spur of the great system that had once linked Europe into
one Latin whole. It was possible, however, that the whole system
might now be repaved. He hoped so. It would give to life in the
West a principle of direction in which every individual might participate with a sense not only of becoming, but of being with a sense of
having been. At the present time society in Europe was composed of
innumerable tangents from a curve that had dropped into a burst of
shooting stars in the Renaissance and Reformation. Every person
who was possessed of anything more than a purely conventional consciousness was now aware that he must steer by himself alone. Those
remnants of the curve which still remained in Italy and Spain were
hanging in limbo. It might be possible that a French segment would
complete the old; no, a new and more magnificent Roman arch. Britain
could go to hell her own way. What could be done with a people who
had subordinated everything to a desire to trade? No, no, they were
out of the arch forever. Barbarous! Don Luis reached for his slate
again. The horses seemed to be galloping in hexameter.

It was at this point that the odour of grape blossoms had interrupted
him. As an odour will, it recalled with extreme vividness certain
scenes of his own secret life. The gears of his mind were suddenly
shifted from impersonal politics to purely private considerations, as
though a hand from without had been laid upon them. It was curious
how those two seemingly disparate worlds were bound into one and
made inseparable by the rapid and unceasing motion of the coach. As
the vehicle rounded the curve at the southern end of the village of San
Marco, Don Luis felt himself pressed back into the upholstery by the
invisible hand that laid upon him the feeling of motion. He leaned
against the momentum and stuck his head out of the window, bawling
at Sancho not to go so fast. For some reason while the coach had
swung him he felt angry. But the mood soon passed and, as he
looked out over the landscape covered with vineyards in blossom, he
was immediately presented gratis with a view of a somewhat similar
countryside on a spring evening a quarter of a century before.

The coach he remembered was ascending a hill on a road through
the midst of vineyards, approaching the Château of Besance. On the
very seat where he was now riding sat his wife Maria. He remembered how the sunset had dazzled in her golden hair.

He turned, almost expecting to find her sitting beside him, and
shivered a little at finding nothing there. The now faded rose of the
old upholstery was merely touched into a sort of mockery of its ancient
splendour by the approaching sunset. Here and there, over the back
of the carriage, moved a few spots of shifting pentecostal fires.

The marquis felt suddenly as if he would like to get out of the coach.

Where, after all,—where was it taking him? He felt for a minute that another hand than his own had really directed its motion. He had only collaborated with it. Perhaps he had not done so well in being sure he was always the master of its direction. A rare emotion crept upon him. He felt a little fearful of being all alone where only the lights and shadows of the outside world flickered over the inside of the old carriage—exactly as his thoughts flickered through his mind. He stuck his head out of the window again . . . "what, for instance, had become of Maria's child?" It might be a wise precaution to inform himself. The convent where he had left him was in the immediate neighbourhood—the "Convent of Jesus the Child." Don Luis smiled ironically again and decided to pay a visit to the mother superior. He could very easily concoct an excuse. Should he?

Just then they topped the rise of a small hill. In the valley beyond the marquis saw a large, rambling building with red roofs. An immense plane tree rose out of its midst about whose top a flock of pigeons was circling preparing to return for the night. It was this glimpse of the place which decided Don Luis to take advantage of its vicinity.

He called to Sancho and pointed. The man raised his eyes slightly and nodded. "So they *were* going to stop there again after all!" Sancho had wondered if they would. With the same grinding reverberations that the tires of the coach had aroused from the same stones twenty-five years before he caused the vehicle to pull up before the lane leading to the convent.

This time the marquis was somewhat longer in transacting his business at the convent than he had been on his previous visit. He had a long interview with the mother superior, whom he found to be an able and evidently painfully discreet woman. She was now directing the most exclusive convent-school for aristocratic young ladies in Tuscany. Mistaking Don Luis for a wise parent with a daughter to educate, she insisted upon showing him over the entire establishment. Don Luis was forced to be politely patient, and to look at kitchens, laundry, and schoolrooms. He reflected as he went through the kitchens, as a revenge for being bored, that everything that woman used even for cooking had been invented and was made by man. He afterwards entered this in his morocco book. In the courtyard, however, he lingered with genuine admiration. Never, he thought, had he seen so antiquely somnolent, so pagan and classic a fountain. The statue of the bronze boy, who stood staring at the water with those peculiarly blind eyes that Phidias had perfected in Western sculpture, caused the cold springs of the marquis' internal aesthetic tears to melt discreetly. He even murmured a few words of admiration to Mother Marie José, who, thinking them to be an ironical compliment, tried to hurry him through what was now a long-deserted portion of the establishment; one of which she was thoroughly ashamed.

As a matter of fact, Don Luis, as a connoisseur, would have liked to own the statue. He inquired as to the missing twin. The mother superior did not even know what he meant. She looked at the statue of the lusty young boy somewhat askance. It was unnecessarily exuberant, she believed. Rather an unfortunate representation of the Christ Child for a girls' school, she thought. She could not discuss that, however. "Probably the twin was carried off and lost during the Renaissance," reflected Don Luis; "lonely enough in some modern garden even now, perhaps. Ah, well, he could never hope to find the twin." They went on into the refectory where upwards of thirty young ladies, dressed in elegant, but unbelievably prim costumes stayed with whalebone, sat bolt upright saying nothing. A sad-faced sister read to them of the blessed poverty of St. Francis, while they ate an iced sherbet.

"The niece of the unfortunate Duchess of Parma," said Mother Marie José indicating a gypsy-like girl near by . . . "The young Countess of Monteficuelli," she whispered.

That young gypsy managed to look discreetly down her nose at Don Luis. Don Luis allowed the lace from his sleeves to droop a little more elegantly, and bowed. He might have been acknowledging the presence of the Empress of Austria. The compliment was at once discreet, impeccable, and tremendous. To a young girl overwhelming. The breath of the world he brought in with him caused the envious bosoms of the other young ladies to stretch tight against their whalebones even in the Convent of Jesus the Child. Mademoiselle Monteficuelli blushed. Don Luis felt suddenly much younger again.

" . . . And we have many other noble names represented here," the mother superior was saying. It was her principal argument. "Permit me to show you the rolls for some years past." She had often won her bid by laying her face cards upon the table.

It was exactly what Don Luis had hoped for but had been at a loss to bring about. Once having begun on the records, he pretended great interest; he kept going back. It was not difficult at first. Every teacher will talk about her school, for since that is all of life that she knows, she thinks that is all there is in life to know how to talk about. But finally Mother Marie José became anxious. There were certain entries in the 1770's which she was *not* anxious for any prospective patron to see. The curiosity of the stranger, however, was insatiable.

"What is this?" said Don Luis, scowling, and looking somewhat scandalized. "An orphan boy, Anthony, apprenticed to the English merchant John Bonnyfeather, what! what!" Here his face darkened like a thundercloud. There could be no doubt he *was* shocked now.

"Dios!" thought Don Luis. "Who would ever have thought *that?* To his own grandfather! Impossible! No, true! Yes, it *must* have been Maria's child. Here was the receipt by the old merchant for the little madonna and his own ten gold pieces. Even the black bag and the cloak. Hers!" He felt her cold hands in his own again as on that night in the mountains. A sudden chill went to his heart. Life was not so simple as he had thought. He wished now he had left his wife's bastard in a basket in the mountains. Nature has a way with her. This unlooked-for eventuality actually gave him a headache as if he had received a blow between the eyes.

Mother Marie José felt much the same. She had always feared that entry would be misunderstood. She hastened to explain the presence of an orphan boy with the greatest detail. Don Luis now saw all the records. She forced them upon him. There could be no doubt about it. For a few moments he sat with an expression that almost reduced the protesting mother superior to tears. At last seeing the effect he was producing on the good woman, he rapidly recovered himself and reassured her.

"Believe me, I understand the matter *fully,*" he said.

He determined to remove any unpleasant impression from her mind by an act of generosity. "After all the woman's worst failing is a little profitable snobbery," he thought. He would have to be careful, therefore, how he offered to confer a gift. The convent was no longer the home of charity. A way out of the difficulty came aptly to his mind.

"You have evidently mistaken my motives in visiting here, madame," he explained. "I myself am childless, but in former times my family were among the many noble patrons of this holy place. I have not been in Italy for many years, but, as I was travelling this way, I could not refrain out of a sentimental, yet I trust pious, prompting of the heart from paying you a visit. You will understand, therefore, that my curiosity about your records was a natural one, *ahem* . . . I might say an inherited one. Permit me to congratulate you upon your superbly judicious management; your highly distinguished clientele."

Mother Marie José blushed. The scar under her headdress burned with pride.

"It was my hope," continued Don Luis, "to confer some passing benefit upon you. Charity, of course, is now out of the question. Your excellent management! But I feel sure, or rather I make bold to hope, that you will not refuse a mere memento of my regard. That old statue by the fountain now—" Don Luis could look embarrassed when he liked—"it is . . . well, it is scarcely what one would choose as an item of ecclesiastical decoration under your present circumstances. The ancients were of course naïve even in their piety. We

have become more chaste.   More may now be left safely even to the
imagination of religious young ladies.   Do you not agree with me?"

Mother Marie José lowered her head.

"Of course!   Well, it was my hope that you would permit me to
have an elegant, modern bambino in the best Florentine style installed,
and the—er—somewhat outmoded, not to say dilapidated statue now
in the courtyard removed.   I should make only one condition.   The
gift must be anonymous.   I am going on to Livorno tonight.   I will
send the workmen some time this week.   Do not give them anything,
the rascals.   They will be well paid."

He looked at her keenly.

The mother superior was making self-satisfied and pious noises in
her throat.   Not only had she swallowed the bait, she now seemed
to be chortling over the sinker.

As she parted from Don Luis at the door, she gave him her blessing
with such a genuine warmth and humility for having misjudged him
that he was forced to bend low to hide his natural emotions under
the touching circumstances.

In the coach it was not necessary to conceal them.   He sat there,
as evening fell and he began to approach Livorno, with a look of
mingled grimness, curiosity, and amusement.

In settling his connection with the Bonnyfeather estate and closing
up the old building which he had rented to his erstwhile father-in-law,
there might be more to settle than he had supposed.   Well, he was
ready for it.   In a very short time he would know.

Just as darkness came he drove into the courtyard of the old Casa
da Bonnyfeather and got out of the coach.   The place seemed to be
deserted.   He felt annoyed.   He had sent word of his arrival.   But,
no.   There was a light coming through the chink of a shutter.   Somebody, a female, was coming out.

"Good evening, my good woman," said Don Luis.

Faith Paleologus looked at him and smiled.

CHAPTER FORTY-EIGHT

OLD FRIENDS GROWN OLDER

THE *Unicorn* had been battered about the Bight of Benim and generally bedevilled by gales and head winds for many weeks after leaving the Rio Pongo. Captain Bittern finally fetched a tremendous leg away across the Atlantic before he put-about and beat back for Gibraltar, gradually edging north. In early April he at last made port at the Rock, where with two topmasts and most of the rest of his top-hamper blown away, he had to refit and revictual.

Anthony was at a loss what to do with the ship. His own nationality was so vague that he was afraid of serious legal complications over her prizes when he finally came to settle his affairs in London with *Baring Brothers & Co.* It might be difficult to explain to an English court how a gentleman who had taken an oath of allegiance to the King of Spain, and had for long run an establishment under the Spanish flag, also owned an English ship that had been preying on French and Spanish commerce in the meantime.

He finally decided to get rid of the *Unicorn* by sending her under Captain Bittern to London and having the Barings sell her while they were still acting as Mr. Bonnyfeather's executors.

This plan suited Captain Bittern to a "t." He asked only for the padded chair as a keepsake. He received the entire cabin furniture, plate and all.

"Very handsome, very handsome, indeed, Mr. Adverse," he said, turning a little red in the face. He had asked for the chair only to save £2.3, he told himself. He could never admit his one romantic slip. Somehow the wind had been taken out of his sails with getting the chair, and so much else, gratis. He almost wished he had waited for the auction. He was sure the chair would have gone for,—well, just about £2.3. Now it would only make a good elder's seat at the chapel in Spitalfields. Certainly not at the cottage. Certainly *not!*— after what had occurred on that chair. He wound the chronometer— his now—thoughtfully. It was a nice chronometer—but it was too late now. It would always be too late. All the time left to him was bound now to be highly respectable. Well, he had seen a good deal in his time—in the time that was past.

While Captain Bittern refitted, Anthony began to find his way about Gibraltar. With a good-sized draft awaiting him from the Barings and a fat letter of credit on London, there was not much trouble in doing so.

It was amusing to see, as a sort of foretaste of what might come later, that he easily and rapidly became a person whose importance was taken for granted; whose antecedents were honourably involved in property. Already a door-opening rumour of his being a young man of great wealth had gone the rounds. The *Unicorn* was thought to be his "armed yacht" which he had contributed to the cause of king and country—and, if his patriotism had proved profitable, who was there to cavil at that? Before a week went by he was "commanded" to dine with the governor.

Indeed, he found he might linger on at Gibraltar indefinitely, passing the clear, spring days, that slipped over from Africa so early with a breath of summer in them,—days that set the flowers in the quarry gardens on the Rock to blooming madly,—seeing people, eating dinners, riding, being introduced by and to hopeful mothers, who tactfully withdrew leaving him "alone" in the moonlight—while they watched.

He might go to tea every afternoon in neat, bare, little military houses with green jalousies outside and pretty women within pouring Bohea out of china more sinolesque than the Chinese. Would he have Scotch marmalade or ginger out of neat, blue jars covered with rattan? To tea or not to tea—that was the question. People like the Udneys, and cool, tall girls like Florence were everywhere. And it was all very pleasant, very pleasant indeed to be back again in this world of his own kind; a world of uniforms, bonnets, long white gloves that wrinkled at the elbows; of white bread, yellow butter; skirts with white, mousy slippers twinkling under them, and always tea, jam, cards, whisky; the boom of artillery from the heights, the ships' bells below, and the shouts of the stevedores. Then there were Sundays when all the sailors marched to church. And the purple-blue of the middle, mother-sea made a moat around it all.

What with the ships of the fleet coming and going and a big war-time garrison on the mysterious Rock, there were endless dances, receptions, and affairs. Innumerable boats were always going and coming with dapper little "snotties" in charge, who sprang out on the quay and drew their ridiculous dirks while they landed in charge of a boat's crew of great bearded fellows in glazed hats with a yard of ribbon falling over their left eye; men who could pull, and pull all together.

Here was all the assurance of British official society, naval and military, with its well-ordered social classes, the stratified atmosphere in which it lived and breathed. But with the dullness of peace times worn off. For these were stirring times. Security was given a fillip by the constant hazard of war surrounding it. Respectability was hurried while lovers and husbands made love as men who might never come back again to women who would be left behind. Everywhere was that unarguable moral fervour about "us and ours" that it is the peculiar genius of the English to manufacture and to store up in vast, static quantities before, during, and after a national fight. Like the sparks from a cat's fur, most potent in bracing weather, it snaps at the least stroke the wrong way in war time. Then the lion is feeling his best with his mane full of great and petty lightnings.

At first Anthony was almost taken-in by this inherent righteousness and moral potentiality generated by the necessity to win. It was overpowering, especially in the wardrooms of the fleet, or at an officers' mess ashore; over the port with the candles lit and gold epaulettes drooping down the shoulders of scarlet tunics. Then it was especially convincing from its calm self-assurance and quiet understood boasting and humour; in its ignorance of what it was really opposed to.

It was especially convincing to Anthony, since it was carried on in what he felt to be—more than any other—his native tongue. Of course, he was assumed to be of them, and therefore with them and for them. What other side could there be than "ours"? And besides it was not possible for them to understand one whose fate had turned him into a mere European, a wanderer of the West which no longer had even the ghost of an imperial political body in which to contain its oversoul. The age for that had gone by, or had not yet come. By accident he had fallen into that vanished age. Its ideal had been reinforced in him in Africa, where he had unconsciously looked back upon Europe as one. Now suddenly, suddenly as if into a steaming hot bath, he had stumbled back into Europe at Gibraltar to find it divided against itself and vapouring and seething in a kind of prolonged explosion.

Even in a few days' time at this English outpost Anthony had found himself both attracted and repulsed in an infinitely complex way by his brothers of blood and tongue. They were a delightful people, but they seemed to have forgotten something which he remembered and to be content not to look for something which he must find. If he had ever had any false spiritual pride he had left it in the valley with Brother François, yet he could not help but feel that he belonged to a larger unit than to any that all the stir of affairs and the social order at Gibraltar had now to do with. That society was self-sufficient. It was even too self-contained. It was insular, cut-off. He must look for a larger, perhaps a more empty country, he felt.

This was the essence he distilled from the total experience of plunging back into the world of the West at a British post. At Gibraltar the light of the days he was living in was concentrated into a narrow

circle and made more intense by the broad sun-glass of the nation
focused behind the fortress.   Here England was projected in all its
various colours in the living prisms of its garrison, men, women, and
children.   He thought of this one bright Sunday as he watched the
garrison and the citizens of the English town being paraded, and
parading to church, the Church of England.

He went in and listened to the service.   He could do little more.
Here were many of the forms he knew, strangely preserved but somehow having suffered a clammy sea-change.   The many things which
they were now about and still sought to embody were not the *one* thing
which they were once devised to show.   That supreme unity had
somehow vanished.   There was no doubt about it, only the god of
England dwelt there.   He was perhaps a captain, even an admiral in
the British service.   The Spirit of the World had gone.   God was
no longer Our Father, but the god of our fathers—and of "us"—our
fathers' precious children.   How had that happened?   He did not
know, but he felt it.   Then he remembered something else like it
otherwhere.

What was it Mrs. Jorham had felt uneasy about in the churches in
Havana?   Was that still another thing, too?

After the service he climbed with a party of officers up to the pinnacle of the Rock—that is forever England's—and looked out over
Spain, and across the straits back and down into Africa.   And he let
his eyes wander freely over the blue sea and the arms of it betwixt
and between.   And again it all seemed equally good to him, part of
the great indivisible world, of which, despite an already large dose
of it, he knew he could never see and hear, taste and smell—and feel
and think about enough.   The range of cannon was surely not the
criterion of the boundaries of it for those who were invisible spirits
of another time; those who, even while the guns muttered, could slip
between.

They descended the Rock again to Sunday evening tea and potted-
ham, while a salute rang out in the harbour below.   For Anthony it
was a parting salute.   He still might have gone on to London in the
Unicorn.   Next day he let her sail for "home" under Captain Bittern.
He sent Juan "on leave" to Tarifa, his native town, nearby and regretfully sent Simba with him.

Taking the able little purser, Mr. Spencer, along with him, Anthony
found passage for Malta in a naval supply ship.   At Malta he hired
a fast felucca and its crew to slip him into Livorno.   They glided
into the harbour one dark night only a few hours after Don Luis had
dismounted from the coach in the court of the Casa da Bonnyfeather.

Anthony, Mr. Spencer, and a few chests and belongings, among which was the bundle taken from his room at Gallegos that had not yet been untied, were all quietly set ashore on the deserted quay of the Darsena.

Anthony was standing again at the same corner where he and Father Xavier had shared the orange between them over fifteen years ago. He was sure now that he had received the larger half. Along the familiar water front the dark water lapped in the starlight. But the Darsena was well-nigh deserted. Since the French and English had been quarrelling, commerce had languished, especially by larger craft.

It seemed curious not to be going home. Surely, surely John Bonnyfeather would come down the old steps at the casa to greet him. The fire would be blazing under the portrait of King James and the misty room aglow. But he was gone and the casa was only a pile of stones now, one of a series of house fronts along the quays. Impossible! He could not resist going to see. It was only a few hundred paces away. He left Mr. Spencer sitting rather disconsolately on the piled luggage. Under the arches his heels echoed. This was the gate.

It was open, swinging a little in the night wind and creaking. There was not a light in the court. Overhead the stars burned like lights on a sable pall. The fountain was still. It had been turned off. A mysterious air of fear seemed to rest over the whole place. It was like looking at a tomb. What was that vast vague outline against the stars, a vehicle of some kind, a hearse?

He tiptoed in, reluctantly, aware of a kind of hostility that emanated from the great coach. Perhaps it was due to its strangeness, its great bulk, the dead windows agape in the night, the funereal droop of the trappings from the driver's seat. What was this catafalque doing here? In the vague starlight it took on for him the outlines of the hieroglyph of warning. It simply meant "beware." In the stables beyond a horse stamped three times hollowly. It seemed as if a curtain somewhere in the night was about to go up. He was vaguely aware of a stage lying behind it. All the stir and expectancy of a play was there, waiting. A cloud passed and the stars shone through. He turned away disappointed. For a minute it seemed as if he had been about to see through. The feeling of something grisly and oppressive returned. The Casa da Bonnyfeather was positively hostile. He had not expected that. He poked his head into the coach just to prove himself. It smelled of Malacca snuff. He tiptoed out. The gate creaked in the wind behind him. The arch boomed hollowly.

Mr. Spencer was still sitting on the luggage when he returned.

"Wait just a few minutes longer," Anthony said, "and I will get you help."

Anthony took the familiar short cut to the square of the Mayoralty and a few minutes later found himself knocking at the door of the old Casa da Franco. There was now nothing but a neat brass plate on the door with the legend "Herr Vincent Nolte, Banking and Foreign Exchange." But a light streamed out over the threshold as if there was someone living here and awake to welcome him. Nevertheless, he had to knock several times. He heard voices calling in German upstairs. Feeble steps approached and someone fumbled at the door chain. "Franko," the Swiss porter, stood there. "Why, he has grown old!" The man recognized him. "Mr. Adverse!" It was a glad cry, a welcome given unconsciously. The old fellow made quite a clamour over him. Someone looked over the banisters and giggled. A tall woman with corn-coloured hair and wide, blue eyes was coming down the stairs in a dressing gown and slippers. Anthony looked up at her rather startled. She was like a Valkyrie.

"Don't you know me?" she cried.

"Das kleine fräulein," whispered old Franko.

So it was. It was his little mädchen who used to sit knitting by the window.

"Du lieber!"

She came and kissed him laughingly on both cheeks.

She led him upstairs holding onto his arm, stopping to tell him the family gossip on every step. By the time they got to the landing with the brass rail about it and the statue of Frederick the Great in its niche, they were both in gales of laughter.

"His Majesty Vincent is still asleep," she called out.

"The devil I am," sang out Vincent, his voice now grown richer and deeper. He had only waited to dress. He came down holding out both his hands. "We've been expecting you for weeks!" They stood grasping each other by the elbows. "My God!" said Anthony.

The tears sprang into their eyes as they looked at each other. "Come up," said Vincent, "and see how you like the bedroom with the new chintz curtains. Anna has been getting it ready for you every day for a month."

"I have not," she said. "It's *been* ready."

A faint reminiscence of beer and sauerkraut brought the room they were about to enter to Anthony's view before the door opened. And there it was; the long table and carved chairs, the pewter, the geraniums in the window and the bird cages with cloths over them. Franko was hurrying about lighting candles. One of the maids was setting a corner of the table evidently for a midnight supper. Old Frau Frank hurried in out of the kitchen whence savoury odours exuded. The lines on the side of her nose were much deeper. She peered more under her moony glasses. But the arms that came out of her short-sleeved wrapper were still rosy and strong. Her grey hair and cap belied her.

"Ach—ach!" Anyone would think Anthony had been her son.

"Do not kill the fatted calf, Frau Frank," he laughed.

"Nein, nein, shust a leetle snack. Kaffee und . . ." She disappeared into the kitchen again. The door banged on a clatter of dishes. A tray with Münchner and pretzels came. Excuses, more food would follow.

"Prosit."

Anthony, Vincent, and Anna.

They sat down and started to talk to one another all at the same time.

Anna was going to be married soon—"think of it, little Anna—ja wohl"—to a rich Düsseldorfer. A look of bland happiness overspread Anna's features suddenly making her look like a young mother with milk in her breasts. This approaching marriage was somehow the most important news. Anthony seemed to have come back just to hear about it. The girl described the home of her betrothed at Düsseldorf. Anthony sat watching and listening, all at once feeling a touch of melancholy. It was for this that his little mädchen had been knitting and sewing even years ago; even when she didn't know it. How naturally and inevitably some women fulfilled themselves! And yet the quality of life was rich for Anna. Yes, he knew that. There were tones in her voice, the way her hands moved, and her feet—to music—to *the* music. Not guitars in the moonlight. No, no, heavily-strung viols auf dem grünewald, deep, unhurried, low-toned instruments invisible where the sunlight filtered through the oak branches and the Kobolds could be heard clinking briskly in their smithies under the huge, dark roots. Sweet forest, strong and ancient and blithe. Her bracelets clinked like hammers on elf-gold. He sat dreaming about her, and the music welled up in his heart in a splendid chorus. A new experience. More than a tune, full-throated, manifold. She tossed her head in the lamplight. The suite ended at last with the sound of birds in the branches, and a flute somewhere away off in the cool, quiet glades. Dear Anna! He would give her something beautiful for her wedding, and there would be gifts for all her babies when they came. She looked at him, and seeing he understood the current of her life, suffused her eyes with his own. Vincent looked on in the current, too, and smiled. The flute ceased.

Frau Frank had come in with a pot of steaming coffee. She sat down wiping her hands on her apron while two tears ran down the runnels in her cheeks as she described Anna's trousseau. Schön, sehr schön. They began to eat pigs' feet and sausage. The wedding dress just basted together was shown him in a ribboned box. An immense cake powdered with nuts and cinnamon was brought in; more coffee, very black; more beer—wine. The world became softly rosy; the room delightfully bright and warm. Every shining pewter and silver thing duplicated it.

Vincent opened a new box of cigars with a small, gold knife on a chain. He rattled his seals. He was as much of a dandy as ever. But he dressed now with a careful solidity and a lambent good taste about him that just managed to be impressive and colourful without being crass. He dressed as if someone were just about to strike a beautifully polished brass gong—but had sounded a full rich tone on a harp instead. His was the latest French mode now. He felt the Continent was going that way—Bonaparte's. The English were in the offing for a while. He lived by Paris and not by London. While the armies and ships were deciding it between them—he lived on the Continent and made loans. He looked, and he was, prosperous.

Yes, he was going to Paris—had been waiting for Anthony to join him. They must talk it over, tomorrow. There was a great scheme under way amongst the bankers for floating the next French loan. Certainly he was in on it! And he had a proposition to make' to Anthony. He had the very best connections now in Paris—the very best. There were *some* people he wanted Anthony to meet in Paris on his way to London. He took it for granted Anthony was going to London. But they could go as far as Paris together. "Think of it, my boy, Paris!—travelling together—old times again! Ach!"

"Herr Gott, Toni, I do luf you," he said suddenly overcome. "What a grand gentleman you have become. And now you are rich, too! Ooo—ooo—it is all coming true, everything we dreamed and more." He started to cry into the beer from sheer happiness and the tremendous, alcoholic sentimental implications of the divine past. Everything in which he himself had taken part was romantic to Vincent. Consequently the future was magnificent by implication, for some time in the future he would be looking back upon it as his past. The tears actually dropped into the foam on his dark beer. And yet Vincent Nolte was in all details of business the most practical of men. He was a sheerly German combination of moonlight playing across the hard marble of a banker's façade behind which the owner counted his marks with a nosegay of forget-me-nots on his counter. He kept his accounts of interest due in an iron safe with a knight painted on its oiled door, ate sausages—and cried or laughed over his beer. And in addition Vincent had spent most of his youth in Italy.

"Ach, Toni, I have great plans. You shall know them tomorrow."

They sat looking at each other very happy, pleased, agreeably surprised with the changes of time.

Anthony saw that from Vincent the last of the pink, rabbit-like impression was gone. His hair prematurely verged toward grey and stood up in a mane in which the ears were lost. His mouth had hardened. The eyes could be cold as they were blue. His high, white stock made him positively impressive with the expanse of splendid waistcoat beneath with a solid splurge of gold seals and a heavy chain across it. There was a round chin that might have been voluptuous if business had not hardened it sufficiently to make it look merely abundant and successful. He emanated an optimistic but convincing warmth. An able man on the make.

To Vincent there was still something decidedly mysterious and strongly reserved about Anthony. But the suggestion that this something might be vague and weak, in the final analysis not sure of itself and incapable of action, had vanished. As a banker Vincent had already acquired a considerable knowledge of people. Some men he knew intended to do what they promised but could by no means do it. The signatures to the well-meaning promises of incapable men were the hardest and most necessary things to watch against. He had, at the first, accumulated a number of small signatures like that. They had cost him dear. "Bad paper." Really one was safer in dealing with a rogue than with people who under other circumstances become other men. The world was too much for them. Anthony was not one of those.

One did not know exactly who or what he was—that was the aloofness of him—but one was quite sure that Anthony himself knew what and who he was now; that he was secure within himself and that "there was good security there." And Vincent felt instinctively as he looked at him that evening with all the keenness and illumination of a fresh view, while he was still a stranger, that Anthony had seen much more of the world than he himself had. Vincent was a little jealous of that, and yet, he was proud of it, too. One could not place Anthony exactly as belonging to this class or to that profession—or to just one nation. He was fair and blue-eyed, northern, but browned now; bitten deeply by some land of constant sun. How tall and strong he was. And yet when he had first come in Vincent had not noticed it. It was the way he moved and dressed that concealed it. Obviously one could not think of Anthony's clothes as being put on. They seemed a part of him. Vincent had never quite been able to achieve that. No, there were always clothes on Vincent Nolte. And he knew it. He saw them himself. Yes, "there is a difference between being a mere man of the world and a gentleman at home in the universe," Vincent remembered. He had not read much lately—the new French loan, but it had been said in a good German book.

But that smooth grey suit, almost silken in texture, the easy roll of the collar, and the neat flamboyance of the cravat—how did it all manage to sit so quietly upon Anthony from his varnished boots to the grey pearl pin at the throat? How the head rose up from the wide shoulders that supported it! Yet he had thought of him as being slim. He must have found a tailor at Gibraltar. The English were good at that. "It will be interesting to see what he does with all the money," thought Vincent. "I wonder if he knows how much he has? Tomorrow," he began. . . .

The door at the end of the room opened and old Uncle Otto shuffled in. He was in slippers and a dirty dressing gown. Anthony jumped up to greet him. It was a shock to find that the old man's mind was nearly gone. He remembered Anthony, but he did not know that he had been away or that he had come back. Only his general kindliness remained as a vague sort of friendship for all that moved. He responded to the warmth of the greeting. Here was an occasion, a general-warmth. He sensed that. He even brightened a little. He clutched Anthony by the arms looking up at him, trying to remember something. "Thou," he said. He smiled immensely pleased at under-standing so much. His teeth were gone. Then for a minute a queer look of instinctive, childlike understanding came into his face. "Thou hast found the light," he cried. "Thou hast it! Warm," he said. He tried to lay his withered old head on Anthony's shoulder. They led him away. Frau Frank was greatly embarrassed. She treated him like a child. "Be polite," she said and almost shook him. Uncle Otto objected.

He sat in a chair and gesticulated and made noises. It was impossible not to look at him. "Go to church," said he suddenly. "It is there. I found it. My wife hung bedclothes over it, sheets. But it is there. It shines through. God has given it to his little boy again. And I am so small, so small."

"Uncle, uncle," said Anna. "Here is a footstool. Do sit up now."

"Ja, give it to me. I will pray on it," he cried. "Anna, my little one, thou knowest, too. Let me."

She held him up soothing him. Vincent shook his head.

"We have had a hard time with him," he said.

"Die deutsche, evangelisch-lutherische, protestantische Kirche," exploded Uncle Otto.

"Ah, the poor little papa," said Frau Frank, wiping her eyes. "Do you know he seems to hate me now. He says I am lost." She could not keep from weeping. "It is terrible. And I am the mother of his children. You would think he might remember that. But no. He sits brooding. You would think he saw something away off. It is nothing that he looks at. Eyes like the sky, wide. Ever since Buonaparte came that day and he was arrested and locked up he has withered. Now he is just a moon-baby."

Anthony tried to comfort her.

"Buonaparte?" shouted the old man. He shuddered and seemed to wilt. "Brigand," he muttered. He looked around apprehensively and collapsed into a sort of breathing heap.

Vincent was much annoyed at having the evening impinged upon this way. He bundled the old man back to his room. But Frau Frank, who went along with him, came back afterwards to listen and sit with her hands folded in her lap, watching the young folks. Anna insisted on hearing from Anthony where he had been. He began to tell her something about it. He had to go on, and the hours slipped away rapidly. Vincent and Anna sat spellbound. Frau Frank finally tiptoed to bed unseen. They would not let him stop. At last the light began to come through the window. The birds in the cages began to stir.

"Good Lord," said Anthony, breaking away suddenly out of the midst of Africa, "it's morning, and that poor fellow Spencer is still sitting on my luggage at the quay!"

They roused Franko and sent him out with two boys, who returned in a few minutes with the boxes and the young Englishman. He drank some warm coffee and staggered off to bed with a pale, reproachful look. Anna giggled. They snuffed the candles and went to bed themselves.

Outside the dawn began to break in the square of the Mayoralty at Livorno. Anthony could see two tall poplar trees, one on each side of his window. "The best thing about Europe," he thought, "is the beds. No, it is friends! I am home." He slept till noon.

CHAPTER FORTY-NINE

WHAT BANKING IS ABOUT

VINCENT NOLTE was now doing most of the banking and financing for the port of Leghorn and the surrounding territory. He had been among the first to see that the struggle between England and France was going to be a long one, and to arrange his business accordingly. Regular trading had almost ceased, but there was considerable intermittent running of cargoes as the fortunes of war varied in and about the Mediterranean. Livorno had become the centre of this activity. Most of the travellers who came to Italy or crossed it still landed there. The profits on what cargoes did come into the port were enormous, and there was a large fleet of small craft, sloops and feluccas, that slipped from port to port, from Italy to France to Spain, and back again.

Vincent had promptly closed up the old merchant firm of *Otto Frank and Co.* about five years before and devoted himself to taking risks on cargoes. He made innumerable small loans to small shipowners at high rates. He took care of letters of credit, and slipped bills of exchange through the blockade whether it was the British or the French who were in the offing. In a short time he had concentrated in his hands a surprising volume of business. People in Rome, Florence, Genoa, and Venice depended upon him. The ruling families and bankers of the whole northern part of the peninsula now corresponded with him to transact innumerable affairs, from delivering letters to buying French wines or English manufactures for them or selling their oil. "Nolte can do it" rapidly became a byword.

From this kind of petty business it had been only a natural step to making larger loans of all kinds for short terms and at high rates. In the high financing of the various petty states of Italy Vincent was soon heavily involved. Into his schemes he had drawn bankers at Paris. In short, he was now embarked upon the troubled but interesting sea of European finance during the Napoleonic wars.

The whole lower part of what had been the old Frank warehouse was now taken up by Vincent's clerks, and the ground floor of the dwelling on the piazza was given over to his private bank, its agents and secretaries.

On the morning after Anthony's arrival he had spent the time as usual in his bureau, but at noon he informed his chief clerk he would be "absent from the city" for a day or so, and went upstairs to Anthony's room where they had luncheon together. He brought with him sheaves of papers. Seated together, looking out on the wide piazza, Vincent began to discuss with Anthony the state of his own and his friend's affairs. For the first time Anthony now had the opportunity of reading John Bonnyfeather's will.

The old man's business acumen and foresight were abundantly plain. For some years, prior to 1796, he had been busy rapidly converting his assets into cash, both his ships and merchandise. He had deposited these sums with northern bankers at Hamburg, Rotterdam, and London. In doing all this he had sustained some inevitable losses. But at the time of his death toward the end of 1799, his whole estate, which amounted as nearly as Vincent could then figure it to about £93,000 sterling, was in liquid cash assets concentrated in the hands of *Baring Bros. & Co.*, of London, his executors.

The only items yet to be liquidated were the *Unicorn,* some merchandise which still remained in the vaults of the Casa da Bonnyfeather, and a lease on that building, which still had five years to run at rather a heavy rental. The fourteen prizes which the *Unicorn* had "accumulated" rather complicated matters, since nothing could be done with the funds which their sale had brought until the estate was finally settled. To do that "It will be absolutely essential for Mr. Adverse to hasten to London, after he settles his affairs at Leghorn, with as little delay as possible," wrote the Barings.

"Your affairs here," said Vincent, "consist in being identified and accepted as the legal heir under the will according to the forms of the local law. There will be little trouble over that, I feel sure, for I have retained your old friend Baldasseroni to look after the matter. But until you personally probate the will at Livorno the Barings write that they can do nothing in London but invest. You must arrive there with all papers in due form for proving your title as John Bonnyfeather's heir. Here is a list of the documents that will be necessary, sent on by their lawyers."

Anthony laughed to see that the Barings' solicitors were Messrs. *McSnivens, Williams, Hickey & McSnivens.* He now sent for Spencer and had him bring up the accounts and correspondence which the purser had brought with him from London. Most of this consisted of the accounts and disposition of the sums deposited from Havana for Anthony's share of the Gallegos trading. They amounted with interest to £16,834. Vincent whistled.

"You have lined your nest well, my boy," said he, not without a touch of envy. "I myself never know just where I stand as most of what I have is constantly being loaned out, and the best security is now liable to be swept out as the map changes. However, I guess I can take a risk on this."

He tossed the latest letter from the Barings across the table.

> . . . we are greatly relieved to learn by your last advices that you have heard from Mr. Adverse from Gibraltar and that he will soon be in Leghorn. It is also exceedingly satisfactory to learn that you know him personally and are familiar with his antecedents as he is, of course, a complete stranger to us. Kindly advise him to make all haste with his affairs in Italy and impress upon him the convenient necessity of his repairing to London without delay. It will greatly oblige us if you will explain to the gentleman our desire to close-out our connection with the Bonnyfeather interests, as we are primarily merchants and traders, and have consented to act as executors of this estate only at the instance of the senior member of the firm, Sir Thomas Baring, Bart. He for personal reasons of ancient friendship consented. Our situation, however, is somewhat anomalous. Your good offices, Mr. Nolte, will be greatly appreciated in making our position clear. You may advance Mr. Adverse any sum up to £1,000 on our security, should he desire it, at the usual commission.
>
> Latest advices from Paris indicate that a peace will probably be negotiated shortly, etc., etc., etc.

"Well, how much do you want?" asked Vincent, rattling his seals. "Shall we spend an hour or two haggling over the rate?" They both laughed.

"Wait for a while till I see," said Anthony. "I brought a little gold with me from Africa. Now what else is there to do here besides probate the will? The merchandise still at the casa, of course . . ."

"And the lease. I advise you to buy out of that for a lump sum. The property, as you know, belongs to the Marquis da Vincitata, who, by the way, is now in town. He has made it convenient to come here to talk over with me certain details as to the forwarding and refunding of the Spanish subsidy to France, through Leghorn. You see the British watch the French ports like hawks, and sending bullion over the Pyrenees is a ticklish matter even when they can get it from Mexico. I have arranged a rather clever method of exchange through a neutral state." Vincent puffed himself a little and they both laughed. "Evidently the marquis wants to close out his own affairs here too and you will have to see him. He will want to sell you the old casa, but don't buy. Watch yourself, for he is brilliantly canny. Oh— there are also the legacies to some of the old servants, under the will.

I see McNab comes off well. Well, now, I should say you could close-out all these matters in a week, get the will probated, and start with me for Paris, say, next Sunday."

"Why Paris?"

"I will tell you. Believe me, you are not the only one who has been doing things since you left here. I have a proposition to make to you, Toni. Now *do* listen to me." He ran his hand through his hair in considerable excitement.

"You see, it is like this. The expenses of a general European war have surpassed the most spendthrift imaginations. The royal mistresses of the ancien régime with all their intrigues; our formal old dynastic wars were positively impecunious adventures in bankruptcy compared to what has been going on now more or less continuously for over a decade. People who based their calculations of government expenditure on the experiences of other times cannot even imagine the demands of the present. To cope with modern conditions it has taken men of a new cast of mind, men whose mental and financial speculations leap across old national boundaries to embrace the affairs of the whole world in a planetary economy. Naturally, there have been only a few people capable of this scope of thought and management among either bankers or politicians. Certain Jews, of course, who have always understood the world to be one market, have profited. Then there is Pitt, and a few British merchants and bankers like the Barings who have understood. But above all others in his capacity to keep the wheels of finance moving under the brakes of war is G. J. Ouvrard, the great Parisian banker. That man is a genius.

"For some years now he has been finding the cash for both peaceful and war-time operations of the French government. I would also mention a certain Monsieur P. C. Labouchère connected with the important house of *Hope & Co.,* at Amsterdam. He is a son-in-law, by the way, of Sir Francis Baring. I want you to keep M. Labouchère in mind—and—and there is also in the south of Europe," said Vincent with mock humility, "my humble self. Ja wohl, there is also Herr Vincent Nolte!"

In his excitement at this pleasant thought he offered Anthony a pinch of snuff in his best professional manner employed after the consummation of a successful deal. He began to walk up and down feeling his watch chain, while the tones of his voice became heightened and more metallic.

Indeed, as he went on explaining the intricacies of the majestic scheme he was engaged upon, the new and the old Vincent Nolte—the happy-go-lucky youth who liked to bet and take a chance on everything uncertain, and the new, staid young banker with a wise, knowing gleam in the corner of his eyes—twinkled in and out and played hide-

and-go-seek with each other between the sentences as they fell from his plump mouth.

At one instant he was the incorrigible, gambling boy sticking out his tongue and licking his lips over some spicy anecdote of golden profit reaped by your lucky great-ones, and at the next the persuasive, solid, financial adviser and investor playing hypnotically upon the open vowels and deep gutturals of sonorous words as if a variation on his theme had emerged suddenly from a nest of wood instruments. Vincent was talking now in German and now in Italian. And frequently when he broke into the latter, there would be a sudden little bubbling run on a piccolo, a kind of plunging laughter. Then he would be brought up short, stopped suddenly by a feeling of boyish inferiority from the past as he looked at Anthony. He would be embarrassed, standing there laughing at himself, with his heavy watch seal in his smooth, rosy hand.

Anthony admired Vincent; was glad of his success and proud of his friendship—and yet, as he sat watching and listening, he could not help but wonder in the back of his head how it was that the affairs of a continent tended to drift into the smooth, rosy hands of men like Vincent. To what was that manual gravitation due? But another thing he saw at the same time quite plainly. It would not do to laugh *with* Vincent when he laughed at himself. He must permit him to bury the ridiculous contrast between his past and the so-important present which his own presence inadvertently evoked. "Yes," thought Anthony, "I must be careful how I recall old times to him. He is not sure of himself yet. The plaster of the professional manner is only beginning to set. It must not be jarred loose or the lathing will show through. I shall always, with Vincent—until a good many years have passed—always take the present enormously seriously." So he sat grave and silent, looking like a staid young merchant himself. On this basis the two young men continued to get along famously.

"And so," said Vincent all over again, but very much the banker now, and determined to remain so, "you see it is like this:

"What all the governments must have is bullion in immense quantities. And at the present time that is exactly what they haven't got. England must have it to pay her sailors and her subsidies to her allies to fight France: the French need it to pay their soldiers and buy colonial produce from neutrals while they fight England. At home both governments make their paper money go somehow. The Bank of England suspended specie payment five years ago, and French assignats also went clear out of business. Now it is francs. But try to get metal for them—try it! Yet both the English and the French have to have hard money when it comes to making their settle-ments abroad. Only victory or peace will make their paper money generally valuable, and no one knows who will win. No, they have to have cash—gold, silver. And who has it? Why, that placid old milch cow, Spain."

He nodded at Anthony wisely.

"But the money is not *in* Spain. Oh, no—that is the joke. Bonaparte would have had it long ago if it had been there. The bullion—immense supplies of it—is locked up in Mexico. For years now the veins of Potosi have been bleeding into the Mexican treasury and the great pool of silver lies dammed up there. Spain has not been able to tap it, for the British fleet sails between. It was M. Ouvrard who was the first to get around the difficulty, and more or less by accident. Bonaparte had played a joke upon him.

"Ouvrard had advanced great sums to the French treasury and had through influence received the contracts to furnish both French and Spanish fleets with supplies. In payment for that he was given by Bonaparte six useless Spanish royal drafts on the Mexican treasury for the accumulated sum of four millions of piastres. Finally Ouvrard, who was nearly ruined by this, sent his brother of the firm of *Ouvrard De Chailles & Co.*, of Philadelphia, to Mexico. He reported that he had seen there the marked chests set apart as a separate deposit for the liquidation of the six royal drafts in Ouvrard's hands, and that besides that seventy-one millions of coined silver dollars were lying idle in the Mexican fiscus waiting to be shipped to Spain. It was in the next stroke that Ouvrard showed himself to be a financial genius.

"He knew that Pitt with his endless demands on the Bank of England had put the governors at their wits' end to furnish coin even for foreign subsides, and he also knew that just at that time the East India Company was under the necessity of obtaining great sums of silver for Eastern trade. He, therefore, approached Pitt, through the neutral firm of *Hope & Co.*, at Amsterdam—you remember I told you that Labouchère there was the son-in-law of Sir Francis Baring—and he was consequently able, through the pressure of the Barings on the prime minister, to agitate the matter of permitting at least some of the Mexican hoard to be released.

"Pitt was at first obdurate and blustered a good deal about trading with the enemy. But as hoarding continued and the stringency increased, Pitt became more and more inclined to listen to the representations of Sir Francis Baring. At last the matter was arranged, and although England was at war with Spain, four British frigates were dispatched by secret arrangement to Vera Cruz with orders on the Mexican treasury, supplied by Ouvrard through *Hope & Co.*, at Amsterdam, for many millions of silver dollars. Just how much no one here knows. For these drafts on Mexico Ouvrard received drafts to a like amount on British merchants for colonial produce and merchandise, which was imported by way of Holland and the Hopes into France.

"It was said that the six chests marked for him were also brought over as 'tobacco.' I am not sure of that, but I do know that he sold the foreign merchandise all over Europe at enormous profit. The British, of course, received the silver dollars in England and some of them were restamped and put into circulation by the bank. The rest were poured into Europe and India. Those loosed in Europe soon gravitated, due to the exactions of Bonaparte, to France. Both the fiscal and commercial situations were relieved all round—and the war could go on."

"How did Ouvrard get his Spanish drafts for such large amounts?" asked Anthony.

"Oh, I thought I had made that plain," said Vincent. "Spain has by treaty been paying France an annual subsidy and Ouvrard took Spanish drafts on the Mexican treasury, which had been sent to France, in payment for his loans to Bonaparte. Bonaparte was glad to palm them off on him as they seemed uncollectable." Vincent laughed.

"Now bear with me," he continued, "and I will show you how *we* come in." He looked significantly at Anthony.

"The relief already experienced by this welcome supply of Mexican silver has been so considerable and profitable that the combination of Ouvrard, *Hope & Co.*, and the *Baring Bros.* contemplates further action along similar lines. They have now under way a plan to get the bulk of the Mexican bullion to the United States and to reship it, or the goods which it purchases, from that neutral territory to England and Europe, chiefly, of course, through the Barings at London or the Hopes at Amsterdam. I may receive the southern consignments here at Leghorn, and, if even a few cargoes reach me, at the present price of colonial produce my fortune will be made. Ouvrard, of course, will continue to furnish the capital in the form of his drafts on Mexico, and the rest of the affair would be carried on by either English or American ships sailing from one neutral port to another. Ships consigned to the Barings or to *Hope & Co.*, or their correspondents, and insured by Lloyds would run an excellent chance of being allowed to proceed even if searched by British cruisers. It is really a remarkable plan, don't you see? For those in the charméd circle the blockade is to be broken and both England and France will profit by the silver. That, of course, is a dead loss to Spain, but somebody must pay for war.

"Now here is what I want to interest you in, Toni, my boy. At several places in the United States it will be necessary for the Hopes, who are the go-between in this affair, to have confidential agents-resident for the purpose of receiving the Mexican bullion, shipping it, turning it into neutral goods, and investing it for the time being until it can be safely and profitably transmitted to Europe in the most advantageous way. These agents will set up business as regular merchant firms, correspondents of the Barings and the Hopes, and the bullion will be turned over to them ostensibly as their operating capital. Naturally, as great sums will be involved and the whole success of the operations will depend upon the discretion, honesty, and ability of the agents-resident in America, the posts would be filled with carefully selected and marked young men. I need not add that it will be profitable—but above all it would be interesting.

"Your old friend David Parish, by the way, has been asked to go. I have also been asked to take-over at New Orleans, which is in Spanish territory, but a convenient place for receiving the dollars. I cannot go, however. My operations here are already too large and important to think of giving them up. In short, I have other plans. But you, my dear fellow, would be ideal for the post. You are footloose, well-off. You can speak English, French and Spanish. You have already engaged in deals with Spanish colonial officials and you are now on your way to see Sir Francis Baring himself in London.

"You see it all seems to point to you as the ideal man for the New Orleans post, and I believe you would like it. You always used to say you wanted to see the world. Well, here is a marvellous chance to go on seeing it and to engage in its affairs honourably, and I have no doubt with great profit. Why not, why not? Don't just shake your head. Herr Gott! Do you know, I have written about you already to Ouvrard, and to Labouchère at Amsterdam. I want you to meet them, the French bankers particularly, and that is the reason that I especially want you to go with me to Paris. Now *do!* It is only tentative as yet. At least come along and talk it over with them. That can do you no harm. That will be seeing—meeting the world, Toni. And what else would you be doing anyway?"

"Ah, yes, that is true," thought Anthony, who was not over-persuaded. "What else shall I be doing?" At last he promised Vincent to think it over with more enthusiasm than he felt.

"So David Parish was still alive. Curious he should put it *that* way. And he might be seeing him again—see *him?* How many children did Florence have now?" he wondered, and sighed.

"Oh, it won't be as bad as that, *really*," said Vincent a little nettled.

"Dear Vincent," said Anthony, "I was thinking about something else. I appreciate all your thought of me. I—I was thinking of little Florence Udney." They both laughed together now. And this laughter was always a bond between them.

"Aha. I always suspected something there," said Vincent. "Well,

Parish has not done so badly. Entertains Talleyrand at Hamburg, I
hear. Mrs. Udney has been living with them. I'll bet she never
plays 'Malbrouk' to Florence any more."

He whistled a snatch of the old tune that unexpectedly trickled like
moonlight into Anthony's thoughts. Vincent smiled at his friend's
expression. A clerk opened the door.

"His Excellency the Marquis da Vincitata is in the *case* asking to
see Herr Nolte. We thought we had best tell you, sir," said the
boy still looking a little pale about something.

"That's right," said Vincent. "Come on, Anthony. Let's go
down. We both have business with him. Let's tackle this old fox
together."

Don Luis was sitting leaning forward on his gold-knobbed stick
in the rather handsome room Vincent had fitted up for himself as his
office. He managed to convey the impression to the two young men
as they came in that they and not he were being received. Anthony
was at first rather fascinated by the older man, whose manners were
so suave, formal and polished as to carry even into the little *case*
looking out into the square at Leghorn the atmosphere of the court
of Spain. He treated Vincent with a consideration that was evidently
flattering, though not without an ironical twinkle at times. And in
his sardonic gravity Anthony was somewhat surprised to find himself
included.

Vincent introduced Anthony by name, which conveyed nothing to
Don Luis, and mentioned that Mr. Adverse was the young "Englishman" about whom—"you may remember, Your Excellency, we had
some correspondence at Paris relative to his taking over the post as
resident at New Orleans."

The marquis bowed a little more condescendingly than before.

"His Excellency, of course, is fully familiar with the Mexican matter I have just been explaining," added Vincent to Anthony, and then
turned to Don Luis again. "I thought it might be well to invite Mr.
Adverse to sit in with us on our discussion today before you and he
take up the little matter of the Bonnyfeather lease. He is the heir,
you know. I am anxious," smiled Vincent, "to enlist Mr. Adverse
in the Mexican matter. You can rely on his . . ."

The marquis had started slightly. He turned half about in his
chair to look at Anthony who was now sitting in the window with
the afternoon sunlight streaming in from the square beyond. Anthony
looked up. He was suddenly aware of a vital interest in the old man's
stare. The old eyes licked over him from head to foot, half-veiled
under their heavy lids. Anthony felt himself turning a little cold.

There was an instant's silence, extremely tense and awkward for some reason.

"You have no objection I hope, sir," added Vincent quite anxiously.

Don Luis recovered himself.

"Certainly, certainly *not*," he muttered. "No, proceed!" he added with sudden fervour.

"One would think he was giving directions to his coachman," thought Vincent, angered at the tone.

A curious uneasiness had now gripped everybody in the little room. Vincent's caution was awakened by it. He wrote something on a card, and calling one of the clerks, sent him out hot-foot for the advocate Baldasseroni. "The old fox! One can't be too careful," he thought, and began to discuss with Don Luis some of the Spanish ramifications of the plan to import bullion from Mexico.

In this scheme Don Luis was strongly interested. He had recently had long interviews with Ouvrard at Paris and he began to recount at some length the turn that affairs had taken there.

". . . As for the arrangements for the cargoes and the minted money which are to be landed here at Leghorn, you must make your own terms with M. Ouvrard in Paris yourself. He and I have come to a very satisfactory understanding, I might add, as to the honorarium to myself and the Prince of the Peace. We shall deduct that at Madrid," smiled the marquis. "All that arrives here you can figure on as net for yourself in computing your own percentage. I trust a *fair* part of the original value finally gets to Paris, Herr Nolte. We leave that to your discretion. Remember there will be more than one cargo." He grinned a little wanly, and continued.

"It has also occurred to me that the matter of shipping produce from the Spanish West Indies direct could be arranged—possibly— by securing from the Spanish authorities themselves certain licenses to trade made out in blank, you know. I forgot to mention that to M. Ouvrard in Paris. Will you do me the honour of suggesting it to him when you see him as a proposition coming from me? Neither of us need suffer if M. Ouvrard cares to perfect such an arrangement. Assure him, please, that I can bring it about. Someone who speaks Spanish well should come on to Madrid sooner or later to negotiate the matter. In the meantime . . ."

For nearly half an hour Vincent and Don Luis continued to discuss the details of trade, finance, and politics involved in the combination of M. Ouvrard, the Hopes, the Barings, and Herr Nolte.

Anthony listened surprised at the ramifications of the scheme; at Vincent's grasp of details and quick suggestions, which evidently kept Don Luis on the qui vive.

As time went on, however, he began to become more and more

aware of Don Luis, and in an unpleasant way. The man filled him with an unaccountable dis-ease and an unreasonable hostility. Here was someone who, without the slightest reasonable cause for doing so, he felt was an enemy; a being to beware of.

As he sat in the window listening to the discussion the feeling became stronger and stronger. It was absurd, he told himself. The old man had hardly said two words to him as yet; had only favoured him with a few sidelong glances. Yet he was sure, was perfectly sure, there was a hostile appraisal in those eyes. He felt toward him very much as he had felt toward Mnombibi that night when he had seen him in the glass. But why? There was something a bit toad-like, something of the sardonic Punchinello countenance in the older man. But why should that make him loathe the very way he wore the buckles at his knees?

His spine crept a little coldly as he looked again. He was glad of the sunlight striking warmly through the window onto his own coat. Well, he would *not* look at him then. He would look away. Where was it he had felt that way recently; eerily repulsed—warned off? Ah, yes, in the courtyard at the casa the night before—and with Mnombibi.

Now that he came to think of it, now that he was looking away, he still seemed to be seeing Don Luis in a glass somewhere, some-where—an ugly little fellow. The noise of the talk grew far away and buzzing—an ugly fellow, spider-like—"pshaw!"

He turned to the window and began to look over some bound maga-zines. Why did Vincent keep old things like that lying about? Some old consignment probably that had miscarried. The *European Maga-zine*—April—nine years ago! Good Lord! He turned it over and began to read with one part of his mind:

> This extraordinary young man's taste for fame was so early displayed, that a female relation of his persists to say, that at the age of five years, when a relation of theirs had made him a present of a Delf bason with a lion upon it, he said, he had rather it had been an angel with a trumpet to blow his name about.
>
> On quitting this female relation to go to London, he said, "I wish I knew Greek and Latin." "Why," replied she, "Tom, I think you know enough."
>
> "Aye, but," said he, "if I knew Greek and Latin, I could do anything; but as it is, my name *will live two hundred years at least.*"—Chatterton used to say, that . . .

A sound in his ears like a distant pistol shot made Anthony sud-denly look up. The marquis had sprung back the lid of his patent snuff box. The conversation with Vincent was evidently over. Don Luis took a pinch and brushed some loose grains off his vest. He snapped the lid to again. A faint odour of Malacca snuff drifted through the room. Instantly the coach in the courtyard and the clouded, starry sky of the night before came into the part of Anthony's mind which was not reading.

Don Luis was speaking to him.

At the other side of his mind, as if in a glass pressed close to the corner of his eye, a vision of the coach with light flashing from its windows streamed off into starry space against a rack of wild-looking clouds . . . "the . . ." he turned the page

. . . *the* greatest oath by which a man could swear was, by the honour of his ancestors.

The type on page 286 of the old *European Magazine* slipped uphill into oblivion as he closed it quickly, suddenly aware that the conversation which he was about to begin with the marquis was a dangerous one and concerned him vitally. At the very first tones of Don Luis' voice he had been instinctively on his guard. He had almost flinched as he heard them.

It had been no small test of Don Luis' now nearly automatic finesse that in the conversation with Vincent he had never fumbled once, although a great many ideas had been kept going. His mind too, had, as it were, divided into two parts. That facet directed toward Vincent was compact of politics, finance, and calm caution; that turned toward Anthony was in a rage and a secret turmoil. For when Vincent had introduced Anthony as Mr. Bonnyfeather's heir it had instantly occurred to the marquis that this was also the apprentice from the convent—Maria's child. It would be just like fate to play a grim trick like that on him. He went hot and cold at the thought. "Just like the humour of Beelzebub!"

During the talk with the young banker Don Luis had occasionally stolen glances from under his heavy lids at the other young man who sat in the window where the sunlight fell across his hair. And it had given the marquis a sick feeling about the heart to notice that the ends of that young man's curls, where they were thin and the light came through them, twinkled with red and golden glints as he bent over his book there—"damn him." For an instant Don Luis saw the face of Maria sitting in the coach bathed in the light of sunset as they rode along; as they rode along and along toward the Château of Besance twenty-five years ago. O God, how he had loved her— and hated her! And here was the son of the young Irishman seized of his grandfather's estate by an act of God—or the devil, who knew

which,—reading a book. Oh, splendour of the white Corpse of God!
It was true.

At that instant Don Luis felt that the Controller of Fate hated him
—and he returned that sensation cordially. He hated the world, and
he determined, as he had never determined before, to throw himself
against it. In a way which only a Latin European could understand
he took the course of events as a personal insult. Fate had outwitted
him. He would be even with it yet. He writhed a little in his chair.
Then he steadied himself, took a pinch of snuff—and turned to Anthony who had just closed his magazine.

"I understand you are to be congratulated as a *very* fortunate young
man, señor," he began in a silken tone. "It is not every orphan who
finds a benefactor and manages to inherit his estate. No doubt, if
your parents were alive, they too would be charmed by your felicity."
He smiled a little. Somehow he had managed to be insulting. The
blood rushed to Anthony's face.

"I have been fortunate in some respects, sir. But I had no idea
until shortly before the death of John Bonnyfeather that I was to be
his heir. And I have no relatives I know of, no one to share with
me in what you have been good enough to style my 'felicity.'"

"Of course, I did not intend to insinuate that you were a designing
young person," resumed Don Luis. "My interest in you is, after
all, a natural one. Perhaps you may recall that I had at one time
the peculiar honour of being your benefactor's son-in-law?"

"And might have been his heir," thought Vincent pricking up his
ears.

"I had never heard *that*," said Anthony obviously astonished.

"Do you mean to say," said Don Luis icily, getting out his pocket
spectacles and looking Anthony over as if he were a curiosity, "that
your—a—guardian never mentioned to you that the Marquis da
Vincitata was his son-in-law?"

"*Never*," said Anthony, looking that nobleman over so calmly that
Don Luis could scarcely sit still.

"The cool young liar," thought he.

"I heard your name mentioned once or twice casually as the owner
of the premises upon which Mr. Bonnyfeather conducted his business.
But nothing more."

"I will ruin you for that remark," thought Don Luis—and in the
intense struggle of his inner feelings permitted himself an instinctive
question which he would ordinarily have carefully suppressed. He
seldom laid himself open to rebuff.

"Did the old Scotchman never mention his daughter to you at all?"

A thousand speculations were rushing through Anthony's head.
He felt himself on the edge of a gulf into which if he could only look

he might know his own mystery, but . . . "the greatest oath by which a man could swear . . ." and he seemed to hear the grave tones of the old man's voice in the courtyard that day exacting his promise. "Why was it? Why had Mr. Bonnyfeather made him promise? Who am I?" he thought. For an instant he looked with a peculiar speculation at Don Luis, with an expression of self-struggle that the marquis noted instantly as he leaned forward a little and gripped the arms of his chair.

"That is a point which it is a matter of honour with me never to discuss," said Anthony. "I am sure that Your Excellency will understand me if I put it *that* way."

"He knows," thought Don Luis. "I 'will understand,' eh—I *do!*" The implacable look with which he favoured Anthony was not lost upon Vincent, either, who saw at the bottom of everything a financial trap. Doubtless Don Luis had in mind the possibility of contesting the will.

"I might add," said Vincent suavely in what was meant to be a soothing voice, "that the matter of probating the will has, of course, been carefully attended to."

" '*You* might add,' " repeated Don Luis witheringly, while preparing to go. "Well, adding is quite in your line, isn't it, Herr Nolte?" He turned swiftly.

"Good day, Don Antonio Adverso, perhaps we shall have the honour of meeting again." He bowed mockingly but with a grave face.

"Ah, who knows?" said Anthony in Spanish. The lines about Don Luis' mouth contracted a little. He took his stick and went out.

"Now what the devil?" said Vincent after he had left.

Anthony was striding up and down. "How those noblemen of the old school do despise us bankers! Well, I shall show him a thing or two." He called into the office to send up Signore Baldasseroni, the advocate. "Now as soon as this lawyer fellow shows up go out and get the matter of proving the will attended to instantly, my dear fellow. I hope that you do not mind my having lied a little for you. The old one is evidently on your trail."

"Do you think so, too?"

"I am quite sure of it," said Vincent. "If ever I saw one man hate another——"

"My God, what have I *done?*" said Anthony with a half-humorous, half-serious quirk.

"What is the use of moral speculations?" asked Vincent. "The thing to do now is to register the will. Will that lawyer *never* get here?"

The door opened and a fat, little man with a limp, carrying his hat in one hand and mopping his brow with a flaming orange bandanna, entered quite out of breath.

"Why, Signore Adverse," he panted, "this *is* a pleasure, an unexpected pleasure. I haven't seen you for years. La la, how you've thickened up!"

He went limping about, very effusive, clapping his hand to his tail every now and then. "Of course, I remember you." He made a wry face. "You were there when that M. Toussaint put a bullet in my behind. A sad, a memorable occasion, very sad." He launched out into a description of his acute sufferings as a cripple, meanwhile laughing and hopping about like a wren. The whole atmosphere of the room cheered up. The sulphur reek which Don Luis seemed to have left behind him was blown away by the breeze that had puffed in through the door with gay Signore Baldasseroni.

Vincent soon cut him short and explained the situation. Signore Baldasseroni produced a huge watch and noted that the office of registry would close in twenty-two minutes. He and Anthony gathered their papers together hastily and tore out. Down the sunlit street they went and across the piazza to the Mayoralty, with the little advocate hopping along with his hand on his hip and chattering.

They registered the will. For an increased fee the clerks kept the office open beyond the usual sacred closing hour. Every paper was stamped. Signore Baldasseroni produced the most grave and respectable witnesses, whom he seemed to keep on tap. "They will swear to anything," he whispered. "I hold them for a small monthly retainer. I trust, Mr. Adverse, you will see fit to repose your legal business at Livorno in my hands. My retainer is reasonable, my refreshers modest, my reputation unblemished. This I admit, signore, rests upon the questionable evidence of my own applause, but you may verify it if you will. Permit me to call one of my witnesses, *Beppo*."

Anthony laughed and clapped the little man on the back. "I feel quite safe in your hands," he said. "I shall instruct Herr Nolte to remember you from time to time on my account. What I want is someone who will keep an eye to my interests and not turn up as the counsel for the other side, witnesses and all. You know that *sometimes* happens here. But we, you know, have been through an affair of honour together and I am the star witness to your constancy during trials."

Tears sprang into the eyes of Signore Baldasseroni. "Ah, thou alone knowest to the full my bravery," he cried. "Toussaint and McNab they always laugh when we meet. If you would only tell the clerks here, signore, it would enhance my reputation."

"Some time when it will not embarrass your modesty as it would now, I shall do so," whispered Anthony.

They crossed the street together—friends for life—while the clerks looked over their gold coins and locked the big bronze door. In Vincent's *case* Anthony paid the spry little advocate a great many compliments and an astonishing retainer. They all had a bottle of wine together.

"You have done well," said Vincent after Baldasseroni had left. "You can depend on him now in the matter of the lease and everything else. And that is important. For Don Luis might otherwise persuade him to change clients. It is the curse of law practice here. Baldasseroni keeps a whole boarding-house full of witnesses, with costumes. He always wins my cases. Our old friend Signora Bovino, by the way, makes a wonderful witness in cases involving domestic disputes." Vincent grinned and put his feet over the arm of his chair. "Well, let's go up and see what the women are sewing on now. Anna's preparations are a triumph."

For the rest of the afternoon Anthony sat in the window under the bird cages while Anna, Frau Frank, and Vincent chattered; while the women and two sempstresses sat stitching at Anna's trousseau. There was something so bright and airy in the room, so domestic and homelike with the constant flashing of white thread and needles, with gold thimbles on white fingers twinkling in and out through soft folds of delicate cloth, that the two young men from time to time looked at each other in mutual enjoyment of peace, happiness, and home.

"After all, this is what banking is about, isn't it?" laughed Anthony as Vincent passed him to light his pipe in the kitchen.

"Ja wohl!" said Vincent.

Anna smiled quietly over her embroidery and held it up to the light.

"See," said she, "it is a white dove with a red rose in its mouth. Now what colour must I make its eyes?"

On the perch just above her, where the warm rays of the afternoon poured through the open window and the curtains waved in the breeze, a canary began to blow golden bubbles of sound from its throat. It sang as if its heart would burst.

"Ach," said Anna, "Ach, mein Gott! I am so happy."

Anthony looked out into the empty piazza. In the breast of his coat the proven will of John Bonnyfeather, merchant, of sound mind and sound body, crackled drily. A lump came into his throat.

In a few days all this would be gone forever. For some reason or other, just why he could not remember now, he was going to London.

The canary sang again and again.

CHAPTER FIFTY

DON LUIS REFLECTS BY CANDLELIGHT

THE inn of the "Blue Frog" had for several generations been one of the best kept caravansaries of the Mediterranean littoral. Perhaps more than any other institution in Livorno—and it was an institution—it had realized the original dreams of the Medicean founders of the free port by attaining a complete cosmopolitanism.

Like all really great inns, it had not depended for support nor derived its atmosphere from a purely genteel clientele, which is so dully alike everywhere. It had catered to everybody, from travelling cardinals to sailors getting rid of their pay. And it had done so by sprawling out along the piazza into various pavilions where each kind of man could find others like himself gathered together eating and drinking, playing and talking according to his nationality and class. In that respect the "Blue Frog" was unique.

But its reputation depended upon, and had been spread abroad chiefly by distinguished travellers; by prosperous ship captains and merchants who had tarried under its roof memorably. And the common item in their universal praise of the "Blue Frog" was always its abundant and tempting fare.

It was the boast of its proprietor, one Lanzonetti, that any guest at his inn could obtain there, not only the best in Italy, but that no matter from what remote portion of the globe the traveller hailed the inn kitchen could also supply him with his favourite, native dish. Lanzonetti had been able to do this by gradually assembling a bevy of remarkable cooks from sundry regions and by collecting from every traveller—who either condescended to take an interest in his "universal menu" or to order a strange dish—a recipe, which the innkeeper immediately proceeded to enter in a carefully cherished book, to experiment with and to improve upon.

A cellar of inspiring proportions and catholic selection contained everything from the rice wine of China to Canary vintages. It was especially rich in importations from England and Germany of brewed beverages of all kinds. In the next cave was a museum of choice sausages. Lanzonetti's main success as a host, however, had been due to two cardinal principles of cookery; he never permitted a woman to enter his kitchens, and he had a whole battalion of saucepans always bubbling over innumerable small fires.

In the late 1770's the "Blue Frog" had been at the height of its prosperity and glory. The art of eating and drinking had during that decade attained among the privileged classes in Europe a high crest of perfection from which it afterward for many confused decades declined. The traveller of the day was usually a landed, frequently a titled gentleman, with leisure and elegant discretion; possessed of taste as well as appetite. The nice craft of purveying to him might be rewarded by reputation as well as gold. Lanzonetti had won both. His recipes were much sought after and went out to all the world like tracts of a society for the propagation of the gastronomic gospel in foreign parts. As far away as "Strawberry Hill" Horace Walpole had learned how to coddle eggs in mulled wine.

Don Luis had stopped at Lanzonetti's at that, to him, regrettable period of his life when he had been making the arrangements for his marriage. On account of his present abstentious diet he remembered the place with more than the usual pleasure of an old epicure. It was only natural upon his return to Livorno even after a quarter of a century that he should again put up there. But alack and alas—the good "Blue Frog" had meanwhile suffered a sorrowful transformation.

To be sure, the main building of the inn still looked across the piazza at the establishment of Herr Nolte directly opposite, but it was no longer known as the "Blue Frog." It existed, or rather it languished, under the now fatal name of the Osteria del Inglese. A recent hasty attempt had obviously been made to obliterate the unlucky designation by painting out the last word of it with the device "Français." But the older letters were again showing through, and the now nearly ruined proprietor, a tall, thin Tuscan by the name of Fratelli Rabazzonie, could not even afford a little new gold-leaf to repair what amounted to a serious political error on the part of his sign. Indeed, in his own spare body the proprietor seemed to personify the lean and sickly times he had fallen upon.

Upon the night of his arrival Don Luis had looked Rabazzonie over doubtfully. He did not believe in thin innkeepers, and there was dirt on the man's apron. Nevertheless, since it was late he risked taking the front chamber on the second floor overlooking the piazza. He was quite tired, and although the room smelled mouldy and the bed was a distinct disappointment, he slept tolerably well. The marquis had left the coach at the Casa da Bonnyfeather, after having refused to stay there despite the preparations and the rather pointed welcome of Faith. For it had suddenly occurred to Don Luis as he descended from the coach in the courtyard that the matter of terminating the old lease had not yet been negotiated and he *might* be laying himself open to a technical charge of trespass by staying in the house. The horses, however, he had risked leaving in the deserted stables under the care of the Kitten. He brought Sancho along to the inn.

Don Luis was awakened shortly after dawn the next morning by the arrival of luggage under the charge of some noisy porters at Herr Nolte's just across the square. Breakfast was poor, luncheon terrible, and the unexpected encounter with Anthony that afternoon unnerving. On the evening of his second night in Livorno Don Luis sat in his dingy chamber at the Osteria del Inglese confronted with what for a man in his condition was a "ferocious" supper. The blue veins on his forehead stood out even farther than usual as he rang violently and demanded the proprietor.

"Landlord," said he, when that individual had entered and sat down without permission,—"another evidence of degenerate times," thought Don Luis,—"landlord, this food and this room," he swept his arm around overturning a decanter, *"might* be considered hospitality by shipwrecked sailors with desperate appetites and sea-sore bodies, but by no one else. Do you call this supper? The oil is rancid, the wine sour"—he went on for two minutes—"the servants decrepit and the beds Procrustean."

"No one has ever complained of being bitten by anything but fleas before," said the surprised host. "I tell you, citizen . . ."

"Citizen?" roared Don Luis. "Citizen of what? Don't you know they don't talk that way any more—not even at Paris?" (Twenty years ago, he reflected, he would have caned the man for a similar ignorant impertinence.) "But what the devil *has* happened to this inn? One used to be received here as a Christian gentleman instead of like a relapsed heretic at a country branch of the Holy Office. The bed! Do you expect to charge patrons for the privilege of being put to the question? Holy Zacharias—and Bellerophon . . ."

In the course of a quarter of an hour the landlord, who had at first sought to defend himself, was reduced to a few stealthy tears for his own misery and a lurid description of his misfortunes in order to stem the tide of steady abuse that flowed into his ears as if they had been manholes in a flooded street.

The man's misfortunes it so happened interested Don Luis, who now felt a little relieved at having successfully vented his spleen upon him. And he also saw in his story a certain confirmation of his own opinions as to the recent decline of civilization. Any inn, he felt, was a social barometer; this one in particular had been so for all Europe. And its glass was now low, *ergo*. Condescending to indulge himself in a bottle of fine, old Greek wine fetched by the landlord's suggestion from the last rack in the cellar, he finally put the tips of his stubby fingers together, leaned back, and listened to his host's recital with a philosophical air of "God help us all."

"It is the times, signore," said the man, coughing a little and spitting into his handkerchief,—"the terrible times that are responsible for your pitiable supper in what was once the abode of cooking. You remember it otherwise, you say. But consider, how can I help it? My wife, when I married her, was a woman well-off. It was her *all* that went to purchase this inn for me from the retiring owner, Lanzonetti. He agreed to help me supervise the business for a year. But he was a smooth one, that fellow, and he hated to see another going about in his place. He died only three months after I came—and would you believe it, sir,—but the jealous dog took his famous book of recipes into the grave with him. He had it buried in his coffin, clasped to his breast. It is with him now—in hell. My trade fell off—naturally! Distinguished Englishmen, for example, who ordered turtle soup and received frogs' legs instead, became violent. With my wife always in the kitchen, the old cooks soon left. To retrench my losses I gradually closed up one after the other the various extra pavilions along the square. The inn—he shrinks inward towards his great warm heart in the kitchen, year by year. In seventeen-ninety nothing but the main house is left. The frog has lost his legs! I change his name and hire me all new servants who remember not the times before. Seventeen-ninety-four—most of the men go with the army. No one remains to serve here but old women. The English have stopped coming. Seventeen-ninety-six—the *great* General Bonaparte, he arrives. Ah!—*all* business ceases then. I am forced by decree to keep open. To live I must sell the fine, old wines to soldiers. I change the name again. But no good. All Frenchmen are in the army. No one travels. My wife goes off with an Austrian hussar to Vienna. Only two crones are left who stay on for bed and board. Eighteen-hundred-one—*the very distinguished gentleman from Spain* arrives and complains of his 'despicable' supper." He shrugged his cadaverous shoulders hollowly—"What would you, signore? What can I do?"

"There will be a peace shortly, I think," said Don Luis, sympathetic in spite of himself. "Your trade may pick up again."

"It will be too late," cried the innkeeper, letting his long hands fall loosely on his sharp knees. "I have the terrible sickness of the lungs. Long before peace comes I shall be hunting that swindler Lanzonetti with his book of recipes through hell."

"You will find him frying in his own grease in the most comfortable spot there," said Don Luis. "But tut-tut, man, it's not so bad as you think. (It's a great deal worse.) Cheer up. At least you are rid of your wife."

"Si?" said the man.

"Si!" said Don Luis.

He had been moved by certain items in this tale of woe and now wished to offer a certain modicum of sympathy. He dismissed him with more kindness than the man expected after paying him on the spot and right nobly for the wine, which had been offered as a present. The innkeeper could not resist gold, however. Wishing Don Luis good night in a mournful voice, he left him alone with the cobwebbed bottle and one candle.

"At least the fellow had enough sense to understand the delicacy of a disguised gratuity," thought the marquis. "He might have been a democrat and *so* insulted. Well, good luck to him—in hell.

"Yes," thought Don Luis, "he and I have lived through some strange times the last two decades or so. It was a better world when we were born. Nowadays the wives of innkeepers—and others—go off—*ahem*—with hussars. 'Eighteen-hundred-one,' as that fellow says, June twenty-third my own dear wife's bastard so unexpectedly turns up." He clenched his hands.

" 'Anthony,' eh,—takes after his sainted mother. Has his father's reach. Leave him to Providence? Shall I? I suppose the sins of the fathers may still . . . I might try to help that idea along a little, circumspectly, of course. No more errors, no more going too much out of my way. Let opportunity serve." He sipped his wine slowly.

He did not mind so much finding that Anthony had inherited his grandfather's estate. He regarded that as merely a gratuitous insult, a quizzical prank of fate—a—a long deferred slap on the jowl after he had carefully and patiently wiped away the spittle of outrage from a too-trustful eye. Probably he might expect that in the nature of things. No, it was meeting again with the young gentleman at all that had upset him. He had done his best to prevent that. It had, in spite of him—occurred. And how much did the "young gentleman" know? Everything?

He gulped another glass of wine and wiped his lips, which were still red and a little too full like over-ripe cherries with a worm at the heart.

A number of frantic moths were circling rapidly about the big glass candle-shade on the table before him. To Don Luis they seemed to be making visible rings in the air as his eyes grew heavier and a little bleary. Behind them his mind was strangely active. Indignation and old Greek wine are peculiar stimulants. When he felt as he did tonight he often found relief in venting his thoughts on the morocco notebook. It was better than sheep over a stile at any rate.

Futile anger is the base counterfeiter of epigrams, he wrote. His hand trembled a little—and then: *Three things never elicit any enthusiasm: a pregnant bride, a reasonable religion, soup without seasoning.* "Perhaps I am drawing too much on my own past experience," he thought, "but the soup tonight was saltless. Why must everything be personal?" He dipped his pen again.

Men say they can discuss their affairs dispassionately in the terms of general propositions. But let a man make a remark about the enormous amount of quackery in medicine, for instance, and a woman will immediately wonder how much he owes his physician. In nine cases out of ten the woman is right. It is the tenth man, a genuine philosopher, however, whom she will set down as a fool. She understands the others. Why is it, then, that women seldom or never write poetry, which is the art of talking about one thing in the terms of another? There is a reason: In poetry women are talked about in the terms of something else. That appears to them to be a waste of time.

"Prolix," thought Don Luis. "I am tired, and ordinary in thought tonight. I *have* had better nights. Let me see." He fluttered the pages of the book backward scanning it listlessly . . .

"Education of the Young"

Boys should be kept in a monastery until they are old enough to be condemned to the galleys for life. Girls . . . "damn them!" He flipped a solid inch of pages and nearly broke the back of the book. The writing he was looking at now was firmer than usual. His hand had not trembled when he wrote this: *Once tangle the threads of two lives firmly together, and no matter how apparently remote and disparate their future courses may become, it is quite likely that it will require the good offices of the blind lady with the shears to cut the final tangle.*

Certainly the meeting this afternoon tended to confirm him there, he thought.

He dropped his quill and lay back pondering. He was in a state where, with his body too sleepy to write, his mind nevertheless galloped on; speculating; throwing off grand, shadowy visions; coining figures of speech and tags of phrases; watching itself and talking to itself about what was always going on in the old house just under the thatch.

"—which is now getting rather thin in spots under your wig," said a disgruntled voice with a note of suppressed terror in it.

"What is the use of thinking about *that?*" demanded another.

"In fact what is the use of thinking at all?" a whole crowd seemed to shout. A single-toned voice went on like the blood in the listener's ears:

"What you *think* is a candle there with the moths going around it —and around and around it—is really the planet Saturn."

"Yes, and wouldn't it just be a good idea to blow out Saturn and go to bed—be in a dark room, tired eyes."

"A dark room? Yes! With the Dutch countess whom you met travelling once, at Besançon—the dark room there, ah—here it would

smooth out that inner palsy that you are still shaking with after being
so angry this afternoon."

"*He* was there this afternoon."

"Well, we have not decided what to do about him yet. What—to
do?"

"Let by—the countess was five years ago. And how are you now?"

"*Can* I still?"

"I?"

"Not a doubt—never!"

"Let's all get in the old coach then and drive around to the Casa
da—Palazzo Gobo tomorrow where *she* is. Let's try."

"It's rather shameful at your age, though."

"Never think of it. No one need know. Who cares now if . . ."

"Get the lease arranged. Never mind *him*. Stay at your own
house. She is still there. Do you remember you asked her when you
were first seeing Maria what she was doing there—and she smiled just
the same way? Why not? It will not be long now until no more
beds—no beds at all—but one."

"Stop that. Think—what?"

"Why, how uncomfortable the bed here is. How the old house has
tumbled down."

"Yes, it is like Europe. All the nice arts of living are being forgotten—and in a mad effort to make everybody comfortable and
happy."

"But why *not* spread things out?"

"There never was enough to go round for everybody to have enough.
No, it will all end in everybody, even those that have something now,
having nothing—or getting things they don't want. What is life
without land, rank, honour? Bonaparte, I tell you, has the right recipe
for such philosophy—you stop it with soldiers. How to make them
obey?—he knows."

"Aye, can't you see the inn 'shrinking,' as that fellow said? He
didn't know why it was happening to him. Only a phrase, a name,
'Bad times, Bonaparte.' But it was that explosion in Paris that started
to do away with the 'Blue Frog'—and other things—things I regret.
Oh, what an ass was the sixteenth Louis! To let them come to Versailles. Even that day at the Tuileries the Swiss could still have
stopped it. It was inevitable? Versailles had changed them into cere-
monial kings. They couldn't act—only act. Versailles was a crest.
Versailles was getting like something Hindu, Eastern, something completely conventional in art and life. It was a way, and something that
could go on that way by itself. The West will never see anything like
it again. Already they are forgetting what it was in itself. Bonaparte should have been—be king."

"I dedicate myself to making him so!"

"Don't be pompous."

"For unto us a child is born, unto us a son is given: and the government shall be upon his shoulders . . ."

"Rejoice, rejoice, the prince of war is born, eh?"

"Now you are being silly and impious."

"Not to myself. *I* know what I mean."

"Not to myself—umph!"

"None of this is meant for the book. No, no, don't rouse me—the me that writes. I know what I think. I pin my old hopes on this new man from the past. I talked with him in Paris. I remember. He is inevitable."

"It is all inevitable. The past is always inevitable. How could it have happened any other way than it did?"

"Is the future inevitable? Can't it happen any way?"

"No, it only seems to be open for anything. In reality it is already as inevitable as the past."

Here a wizened old man with very white hair and beard, who looked a good deal as Don Luis might at ninety, suddenly thrust up a wide, flat stone under which Don Luis *knew* he was always hiding. He stuck out his tongue and shouted, "You are a fatalist!" whereupon the stone fell down on him like a lid again. Some of the white hairs of his beard were caught under it. They kept on twitching in a horrible way, especially one pointed tuft.

Don Luis stirred uneasily in his chair. He had been expecting this to happen—he remembered now. The old party under the stone usually presaged trouble. He could orate the marquis into a nightmare when once aroused. Don Luis therefore hurriedly began an argument that he pretended was meant for himself alone. But out of respect for the head, which he knew was still listening under the flat stone, he addressed himself to himself in his suavest and most diplomatic manner.

"Let us, then, take an example," said he. "*Was* it inevitable that King Louis should stop the Swiss firing on the people that day at the Tuileries?"

The beard caught under the stone twitched violently. (Don Luis' face twitched in the candlelight.) He gasped. The old man was looking at him again.

"How can you ever know enough to argue *that?*" said the greybeard, and began raising the stone farther back like a lid. Don Luis suddenly slumped lower down in his chair.

"Well," said Don Luis defiantly, "let us take something I *am* thoroughly familiar with, then,—something from my book, for instance."

"Our book," corrected the head, his white throat beating like that of a snake or a frog when breathing.

"Ours," repeated Don Luis hastily, afraid the lizard body of the old man would appear, too. It was nevertheless some satisfaction to be corrected by someone who looked like himself.

"Ours—I will repeat the passage for you, *Once tangle the threads of two lives together, and no matter how remote and disparate the course . . .*

"I remember it," hissed the head testily, and threw the stone back with a bump. Don Luis felt a distinct ground-shock as if a distant powder magazine had exploded somewhere. It annoyed him. (He had just slipped off the chair onto the floor.) He shouted indignantly.

"I was merely going to apply the passage specifically to test the truth of it. I was merely going to ask myself how it is that after I, as a reasonable man, take all precautions to prevent it, this bastard turns up again. Don't you see that the truth of the passage *we* have written *and* the idea of inevitability, past and future, are bound up in that?"

"Certainly I see *that,*" said the old man emerging triumphantly now and snatching the argument out of Don Luis' mouth—"since you ask me—" he added softly.

Don Luis groaned. He *must* get this terrible old man out of his head. He tried to brush him away like a fly. It was almost impossible to move his hands. He just managed to touch his forehead—and knocked off his wig.

"Certainly I can see that," continued the old man not at all disturbed. "It is all perfectly simple. Any event will do in a case like this, either King Louis's Swiss or your own meeting with the young gentleman this afternoon. All events in history are equally mysterious. They simply happen. We, as it were, merely stumble across them. One thread crosses another. But let us take your meeting this afternoon. *Why* did it happen? But you admit it is futile to ask *why. How* then? Well, I am not so sure you could show me how it happened. Let me see:

"By following your separate threads of existence backward and forward across the pattern of events it might be barely possible to see how the encounter this afternoon happened. But only partially. You do not know all the facts. It is quite true that your lives were once looped together long before when the child was born. For a short time they even ran in parallel lines, which, I might point out to you, became visible in the ruts made by your coach between the mountain inn where Maria died and the hole in the convent wall through which you, sir, so trustfully thrust the black bag, and the stuff that was in it, back onto the loom of God.

"You thought the parallel lines might safely be allowed to diverge and become lost in the general pattern of Europe after that. You were willing to chance that they might come together at infinity. You could settle the account then, you thought. Perhaps you forgot how deep and how far the heavy wheels of your coach have cut those lines-parallel into the roads of the past.

"With a little larger view of the nature of things, at the time, Don Luis, you might even have allowed for the tendency of threads which have once been brought so closely together by the teeth of the weaver's shuttle to run across each other again at some other point in the pattern. After all it is by an infinite number of such crossings that the dots in the pattern are made, and it is an infinite number of those dots, where one individual thread crosses another in the warp and woof of events, out of which whole scenes in the tapestry of history are woven.

"That web, a tapestry, or pattern—whatever one may conveniently call it, when considering it as a cross-section of a sliding future passing across a flat page,—is constantly being created and interwoven out of the stuff of human lives. It is now, at this instant, as it always has been before, made up of an incalculable number of separate threads marking the course of lives. These have in themselves each a certain amount of free will that resides in the essential tensile strength and the calibre to which they have originally been spun; in the colours of character in which they are dyed. And between the compulsion of the weaving shuttles and the free will of the threads there is always a certain amount of interplay in order that this piece of weaving with living matter upon the loom of history may proceed. For as every weaver knows, there must always be due allowance for unexpected give and take. It is only where the threads cross one another that they are firmly interlocked and loop-stitched together; tied up in a knot.

"But that living web must also proceed out of the past by some living compulsion dictated by a tendency in the general scheme of things akin to the particular compulsion in an egg or seed to change only along certain peculiar lines into what is always becoming something else, but always within certain bounds; never the maple into the oak tree. Thus as in the particular thing, so in the great general Thing of history—the huge exuding, creeping, weaving proceeding eternally and mysteriously goes on.

"This living web, which slides mysteriously out of the past from beyond the vaguest, fabled memory of things remembered, extends into the future complexly, strangely; utterly transcending the mightiest powers of even immediate anticipation. It grows, that is; it changes. And on either side invisible binding filaments of it extend beyond our human senses like the cords on the side of a piece of weaver's work that are afterwards cut off. These are what hold it on the frame of things and they are not even known to us. So now you have the loom backward and forward and from side to side.

"From above and underneath it is forever being worked upon by the moving shuttles that go and come and never pause, and by the wheels of direction that rack and shove the fabric on, always in one irrevocable direction. And now, you see, you have the loom from all sides.

"Thus any particular crossing of the threads, or knot in the fabric, any event, is merely a point at the centre of a sphere which has been tied or has come to pass because of forces working upon it from all sides at once. How then say that one thing is a cause and another an effect, when each is alternatively the other according to how we call it? Above all, on a flat page, how show conclusively how one knot in two threads got tied, much less project a general pattern?

"How, for instance, convince yourself, my dear sir, because you once carried a child in a coach from the hole in his mother's side to a hole in a convent wall that you must inevitably meet that child again when he has grown to be a man—and on a particular day in a certain banker's office in Leghorn, Italy? Or, to put it the other way, how could you be sure when you abandoned him to God that you would or would not meet him again? In fact, how can you be sure you will not keep on meeting him again, or never see him at all? Is it fate, or is it chance, is it cause and effect? Well, that depends finally upon the nature of the Eternal Weaver and his method of procedure. By the way, what *do* you think of Him, Don Luis? For it is upon your conception of his nature that you will act and conceive all other men to be acting. Not upon what he is, but upon what you conceive him to be. That is where your interplay as a thread in the fabric comes in, isn't that true? Well, what *do* you think of Him after all?"

To this demand of the voice there was in the soul of Don Luis no answer at all, only the sound of chanting in a cathedral.

The little man upon his stone now became visible again. He laughed and jumped up and down upon it till Don Luis struggled in his sleep.

"So, you prefer to stick to your own particular little question and let the major premises alone. That makes action easy, of course. Even if it ends in disaster. Those who trouble the gods have little time for men. Now *there* is something for Your Excellency's morocco book." The shrill laughter of the little man with the beard caused the man slumped down beside his chair to groan in his sleep.

"Go back to hell," he said aloud. The chill echoes of his mumble boomed through the mouldy chamber of the old inn.

The little man suddenly flipped the stone upside down and disappeared into the earth. On what had been the bottom of the stone Don Luis now began to see a dull phosphorescent glow that slowly took on, while he watched it as if hypnotized, the changing, shifting character of the web he had been dreaming of.

On the table the candle which was now nearly burnt out began to jump and flicker. The wick fell flat and burst momentarily into a broader flame. The moths began circling more rapidly about it.

On the now glowing map before him Don Luis began to follow among a thousand other visions the future track of the coach. It led straight toward an immense range of mountains whose snowy pinnacles glittered distantly in an unearthly moonlight. The coach drove on across the plain. He and someone else were in it. Suddenly the face of the housekeeper at the Casa da Bonnyfeather looked out of it much painted and bedizened and with a supercilious, satisfied expression of vulgar pride that caused him to laugh. A look at the range of saw-toothed mountains ahead served to silence him.

His dream now gathered up into an overpowering sensation of speed. There was a chasm just ahead. The speed became unbearable. Don Luis felt himself in the coach, falling. He braced himself for the crash. It came as a nervous shock that half opened his eyes. The coach had hurtled off into space and burst against the opposite wall of the gorge amid a shower of sparks and little lights that twinkled out from and all over the map on the stone before him. This had now suddenly grown gigantic as if he were looking at a whole hemisphere at once. Its shifting outlines were so huge and so writhing with life as to be terrifying beyond thought. On it the gigantic mountains into which the coach had recently fled were now only tiny, glittering lines like a clump of glow-worms seen by their own light. All about them rolled and tossed the twinkling camp fires of armies. The red glare of burning cities coloured the night. Here and there puffs of white powder smoke shot through with vivid red lightnings broke out. Into the midst of these Don Luis was suddenly plunged. The smoke reek was intolerable. Men were killing each other in the darkness on all sides. A tremendous salvo of artillery burst out just above him. He tried to scream but could not.

Clear over the face of the map, usurping it and taking its place, sprang out the Roman features of the little Corsican general to whom he had been talking in Paris across the desk only a short time before. It was like looking at a Caesar's head on an Augustan cameo ten miles high. The laurel wreath on the brows glowed intolerably as with the concentrated blue light of millions of diamonds. The mouth opened to speak. Another terrific crash of artillery which lit the head with lambent flames woke Don Luis from his sleep.

He had slumped down onto the floor and was leaning in an agonizing position against the slipping chair behind him. A thunder-storm accompanied by violent bursts of wind and sheet lightning was passing over Livorno. The rain spattered through the shutters. On the table the draught had thrown the wick onto the candle drippings.

Inside the big glass shade the table-cloth had taken fire and was smoking and rapidly running holes with sparks.

Don Luis dashed the lees of the wine over it. Muttering a few sleep-drugged imprecations upon everything in general, he staggered stiffly to his bed, stepping on his wig as he did so.

He was awakened next morning by the glare from the piazza beyond striking through a broken lattice of the decrepit shutters directly into his eyes. It was still quite early.

He rose, dashed a little cold water on his face, and going to the window with the towel still in hand threw the offending shutter open and looked out.

As fair and clear a June day as ever dawned on Italy after a thunderstorm filled the square at Livorno with sparkling light. The sky overhead was a faultless blue bowl. Against the wall of Herr Nolte's establishment opposite, someone in dressing gown and slippers was seated leaning over a cane in the sunlight and drinking in the first warmth of the morning with all the hunched-placidity of a crouching and withered old man. Don Luis looked at him while wisps of the dream of the night before gradually cleared from his head. To see someone so much older than he freezing in the sunlight while he still felt as strong and vigorous as he did that morning, unconsciously filled him with sudden joy.

"It is going to be a good day," he said and flipped the towel. "There is one old fellow over there whose thread in the general pattern has nearly ravelled out. What an idea the web was. I wish I could catch it up in a sentence or two for the book. Por Dios! what tricks the brain plays on us when it is going to sleep. Does it?—or do you *see* your ideas then? I shall have to tell Bonaparte about Europe and his head." He laughed, and then turned a little pale. "Madre! I must be getting senile myself. I shall soon be relating my dreams. Can't you see them muttering, 'Here he comes!' Old? Not yet, by Lazarus! There are a good many surprises left in this old carcass."

He began to rub his arm vigorously with the towel. A number of gamins gathered below looked up and pointed in his direction. In the sardonic features of the figure moving in the square of the window above, one of them had suddenly seen a likeness to Punchinello. A burst of laughter followed to which Don Luis paid no attention.

Carts laden with vegetables and flowers, with their wheels muddy from country roads and the storm of the night before, began to call upon their customers and to cross and recross the piazza, leaving a pattern of wheel marks on the washed flagstones of the square. The interlaced designs rapidly grew more intricate. A flock of milch goats making its morning round left here and there the seal of a small cloven hoof.

A convoy of convalescent soldiers going home rolled rapidly across the square, the wounded riding on caissons, wagons, and nondescript vehicles requisitioned from the countryside. Some sat silent, holding bandaged arms clasped to them painfully, others smoked. A small group on one wagon broke into a snatch of song. A peculiarly brazen trumpet rang out the notes of "Column right." Don Luis started. He had been looking at the growing pattern on the flagstones fixedly for some minutes now. It was hopelessly intricate; beginning to fade in the sun. He turned, rang for Sancho, and gave him orders to prepare his breakfast himself. "The food here," said he, "gives me the vapours. Or perhaps, it was that Greek wine last night."

"Your Excellency should drink only what we have brought along," said Sancho picking up the wig and removing the burnt table-cloth without comment. He tied a large napkin around Don Luis as if he had been a child. "Foreign wines give you indigestion now. You must remember, sir."

Don Luis leaned back and looked up at his whiskered servant, laughing a little.

"The bottle last night was in memory of my honeymoon here—some time ago. You remember, Sancho?"

"No, señor," replied the man looking at him solemnly.

"Thou art a comfortable servant, Sancho," said Don Luis.

"What would you think if I asked someone to travel with me in the coach back to Madrid, Sancho?"

"A duenna for your nieces? One is greatly needed. Certainly— an excellent idea."

Only Don Luis smiled now. "Have the coach around at nine this morning. I have some legal business to transact—about that lease."

"Sí," said Sancho and blew out a small spirit-lamp under the breakfast bowl.

"And tell that señorita at the casa to prepare for me after all. I can't stand it here any longer. The beds at the casa are at least comfortable."

"Sí," whispered Sancho.

"Now then—" said Don Luis.

Sancho raised the bowl of chocolate to his master's lips and held it there. His master's gnarled hands, like the paws of a monumental lion, lay heavily on the table as he leaned forward. The chocolate was exactly the right temperature.

Don Luis sighed.

CHAPTER FIFTY-ONE

THE COACH AND THE BERLIN

IN THE cobbled area behind what had once been the ample stables of the "Blue Frog," Anthony and Vincent suddenly emerged from the door of the old coach-house, tugging together at the long shaft of a four-wheeled carriage.

The vehicle followed reluctantly out of the gloomy arch as though indignant at being forced into the light of day again.

"Come forth, Lazarus," shouted Vincent, heaving mightily.

Answering, ghostly squeaks from the rusty axles caused Anthony to explode. Just then the front wheels came upon the incline, and to a sound like that of a cat running across an organ keyboard an old berlin galloped its two frantic steeds in shirt-sleeves into the alley below. They swung the pole just in time to avoid being crashed into the wall opposite. The old carriage, its windows hung with cobwebs, came to a halt with a despairing screech.

Even the dying Rabazzonie—who for once had made a fortunate deal and sold something for more than it was worth—laughed until he coughed violently. He looked at the scarlet spray on his handkerchief—and put the coach-house keys back in his pocket, still surprised at finding them jingling on something else metallic there.

Having brushed off the straw and dust amid a good deal of back-slapping and mutual banter, the new owners of the old berlin resumed coats and began to examine their purchase with rueful faces and an occasional chuckle.

"I warned you not to buy it in the dark," said Vincent.

"*You* warned *me!*" replied Anthony hotly. "Why, you were so anxious to get it yourself that you kept bidding against me in there. No wonder Rabazzonie wouldn't take it into the light, though."

"Toni, it was mad of you to give hard coin for it. Look at it!"

"Not so bad after all," sniffed Anthony. "Wait till I'm through with it."

Yet he was forced to grin with Vincent, too.

For the relic of antiquity which stood resurrected before them was like all dilapidated old carriages in having about it an air of insufferable complacency. "In me," it seemed to say, "you behold the *ne plus ultra* of something that has *so* unfortunately passed. In me you behold the fate of all particular styles. Some day your own wheels will stand still in time."

Meanwhile, the spiders and cockroaches abandoned it to run back into darkness, as if they too knew where the past had gone, while the carriage remained to stick out its tongue at the present.

The green paint clung to it in scales and its mouldy leather curtains hung limply like folded bats' wings. Its roof was sadly buckled and swaybacked. Two large, dusty lanterns glared like a stage-dragon's eyes, one on each side of the box whose moth-eaten hangings hung down in elf-lock fringes. Behind, a high, hooded seat cocked itself up like an extravagant pump-handle tail, while the shaft in front burrowed into the ground. Standing there in the bright sunlight of the silent alley, the old berlin resembled a cross between a griffin and a snipe that had been disturbed hibernating but had now comfortably gone to sleep again in the very act of digging up a worm.

Anthony and Vincent kept on joking about it despairingly with the full, flat irony of young men while they continued to scramble in and out of it as if trying to wake it up; slamming its chattering doors, examining its wheels and axles, poking its cushions from which the mice leaped. Then with as much gravity as if they were driving to Schönbrunn for an audience they sat down in it together and burst into peals of laughter at their own expense.

"At least the wheels are all right," insisted Anthony.

"Yes, but we just *can't* go to France in it," groaned Vincent. "They will arrest us for *émigrés* trying to return disguised as ghosts in the family coach."

"It was you who suggested it," replied Anthony, poking him in the ribs. "'Member? You said that after the battle a year ago the Austrians requisitioned everything on wheels to retreat in and the French came and took everything that was left—or something logical like that—and that you can't sit a horse—and that this old berlin was a great idea—and that you were the only one that remembered its existence—and we should certainly be captured if we went by sea—and——"

Vincent groaned again. "That's right, rub it in."

"Of course," continued Anthony, now enjoying himself greatly, "it *will* look strange for that prosperous young banker, Herr Nolte, to drive into Paris in what looks like Richelieu's désobligeante exhumed." He bit off the end of one of his much prized Havana cigars philosophically and gave another to Vincent as a consolation.

Vincent sat back puffing it, gloomy enough. All that he had said about getting a carriage this side of the Alps was true. And he had set his heart on making the trip to Paris with Anthony not only in comfort but in privacy and luxury. The old berlin, which he knew had been accidentally overlooked by frantic quartermasters, was a last hope. The Tuscan posts were not only impossible, they were improbable.

And a saddle did give him piles.   No doubt Anthony thought that was funny.   It wasn't.

Having now reached an impasse on the subject of the berlin, they continued to sit in it quietly for some minutes, smoking their cigars in the warmth of the brick alleyway which was pleasant enough at that hour in the morning.   Vincent was trying to rearrange his plans for getting to Paris.   He was greatly disappointed at finding the old carriage hopeless.

It was all very well, he thought, for Anthony to sit there blowing smoke out of the windows as if they were already on the way.   But he, Vincent Nolte, had important international business to transact at Paris.   He had an appointment to keep with M. Talleyrand, and several bankers.   And, as usual, he was being left to make all the practical plans.   Undoubtedly friend Anthony was still somewhat of a dreamer.   From the expression on his face now you would think he was a boy again playing coach—looking out of the window that way!   Well, that would never get them to Paris—never!

"As a practical man of affairs, Vincent, did you ever consider the philosophy of modern travel?" asked Anthony suddenly.   Vincent stirred uneasily.

"No."

"Well, it goes something like this: None of us are content any longer to live in the present and to enjoy things just as they are.   We are always thinking about the past or the future; trying to readjust what has already happened to us or making plans ahead.   The present under those circumstances hardly ever exists for us.   It is always, in our days at least, just a time-between.   In other words, we never *are*, we are always just about to be.

"Travel is the one exception to this perpetual uneasiness of always becoming.   It is only when we are travelling that we exist as we were meant to exist; in the present.   Everything then becomes quite vivid and real.   We have left the past behind us and the future must wait.   There is nothing to be done about it.   So just for a little, in transit, we give up our dear rôle of being our own tin fates and live.   Suddenly it is now—for a while.   And we are happy; surprised how pleasant it is to live, to be ourselves.   I have noticed that a great many people can find each other and be friends when they are travelling, but let them once arrive and they lose themselves and each other again.   They wonder, 'How could I have ever found *that* fellow interesting on the ship or in the coach?'

"Do you know, when I first set out to see the world I thought it existed only in the places I was going to.   I was in danger of becoming a series of deferred destinations.   Now I know that travel, that 'in-between' is the time when one lives.   I am going to try to turn all destinations into part of one journey, the long journey from the beginning to the end, you know."

"What a philosopher you are getting to be, Toni," laughed Vincent. "And just like all the rest of them.   Here you are philosophizing about travel, and all that, while sitting still in a funny, old-fashioned, useless coach that won't go.   No, I haven't thought about 'travel.'   But I notice that I shall have to make the practical plans for this journey. It's lucky you know one or two men of affairs, my boy. · But I have a little business to transact at the bank this morning."   He started to go.

"Now, *my son*," said Anthony making him sit down, and returning his paternal manner with interest.   "You're quite mistaken.   The trouble is you are just like all the rest of the bankers, you can't even apply philosophy at second-hand."

"*Fo!*" said Vincent.

"No?   Well, I'm going to prove it to you!   'As a matter of fact'— as you always say in your letters—I have a little surprise in store for you this morning.   I am going to show you what money *can* do.   You know you laughed at my making a strict, eight o'clock appointment with Rabazzonie, who, you say, has more time than anybody in Livorno. He hasn't; he has very little time left in Livorno.   Didn't you see the red spots on his handkerchief?   I took no chances and bought the berlin last night—cheap.   I just let you bid it up this morning in your excitement and gave him the difference.   After all, what are a few measly scudi more or less to a rising young banker?   Now wait a minute.   That isn't all.   The play really begins at nine o'clock.   I have arranged for a little meeting here, a kind of post-mortem over our deceased friend the berlin.   They ought to be here soon."

"Who are *they*?" demanded Vincent a little sulkily.

"Our old friend McNab for one.   I put this little matter into his hands."

"Oh, you know how to pick your agents well enough," yawned Vincent, pretending to be greatly bored and stretching his feet out on the opposite seat resignedly.   "McNab can make a Spanish dollar weigh an English pound.   Toni, you're an old fox to make me give Rabazzonie twelve scudi extra.   I'll charge it on your account as expenses. · I certainly will."

"He needs it," replied Anthony.   "Call it charity."

They both grinned now.   Since Anthony had come back he and Vincent had been matching wits in several directions.   This was a rather unexpected score.   They were now about even.   They sat waiting for McNab and his work-gang to appear, smoking contentedly.

"Almost nine, now," said Anthony, taking out Mr. Bonnyfeather's watch.

"What a turnip it is," remarked Vincent.   "And all that spread of heavy seals on the chain. I don't envy you that part of your legacy. A little old-fashioned, eh?"

"Tut, tut," said Anthony.

A rat scuttled along the ancient brick pavement of the alley and stopped to look them over. It was very quiet in the old berlin with the leather flaps hanging down. Vincent jogged Anthony's elbow. Through a slit in the front they could see that someone had entered the end of the alley from the square. He was standing relieving himself against the brick wall. It was Don Luis. They laughed. He was so furtive and yet hearty about it.

"The old goat," whispered Vincent. "Look how he stamps around. It's still a positive pleasure to him. If you want to know what a man's like, watch him against a wall, when he isn't looking. There's philosophy for you."

But just then Don Luis looked up suddenly becoming the marquis again. He had smelled cigar smoke. Glancing down the alley, he saw the grotesque old berlin with wisps of smoke curling up from it. Its lamps positively stared at him. He had a good mind to rout out the boys who must be in it, apprentices smoking their masters' cigars. "And the best Habana at that. The young thieves!" He gripped his cane.

In the berlin Vincent and Anthony held their breaths.

"Pshaw!" said Don Luis, and strode out of the alley. He was busy that morning getting the antique statue from the convent safely shipped off to Spain. They heard the door of a coach slam and the heavy wheels rolling away.

"Would you have run if he'd come after us?" laughed Vincent.

"Yes," said Anthony. "Do you know, I hate that man, Vincent."

"Why?"

"It's unreasonable, I know, but I hate him just the same. He makes me feel desperately uncomfortable and insecure. I can't help it. Damn him! I want to fight him—if he only wasn't too old."

"It's just as well then you let Baldasseroni close that matter of the lease with him instead of having a personal interview—even if you didn't come off so well."

"Oh, well, let him keep the stuff in the cellar, and the old furniture! The last time I went to the Casa da Bonnyfeather, the evening I landed, I walked up to the old place and looked around. And there was that great coach of his standing like a hearse in the court. Do you know, I felt warned-off. The coach smelled of snuff, and when I got the first sniff of it next day when I met the man in your *case* . . ."

"Oh, you're getting to be an old woman," said Vincent. "But here comes McNab. Now what is all this about? Here's the great Signore Terrini, too."

Not only were McNab and Terrini coming down the alley but half the master workmen in Livorno as well. There was Beppo Tulsi the blacksmith, Garnarlfie the cabinet-maker, and the little upholsterer with his apprentices. Their shoes clattered like a squad of soldiers. McNab spoke up rather proudly.

"It was na sae easy as you maun think, t' gather a' the great-hearts ye now see before ye togither for a tryst the morn, Mr. Anthony. They're a' sae bashfu' an' min at trustin' a body the noo. Sin' the French came every ass maun hae his hock in guid siller laid doon in his ain fist. Min' yoursel' or they'll be playin' nieve-nieve-nich-nack wie ye.

"Mon!" he cried, giving a start as his eyes for the first time took in the complete decrepitude of the berlin. "You'll no' be bamboozled into throwin' away guid, bright siller on yon negleckit, auld-warld trumbler, will ye? I wouldna ride a leaguer-lady o'er the plainstanes in it."

"Now, now, Sandy, hold your horses," laughed Anthony, "the money's not spent yet, and——"

"Na, na, but it's *aboot* to be," cried McNab, "and I'll hae na more to do wi' it." He continued to stay, however, out of curiosity.

"Terrini," said Anthony leaning out of the window and tapping that now shabby artist on the shoulder, "do you remember that sketch of me you did in Mr. Udney's library years ago, when I was a boy?" Terrini nodded uncomfortably. "Well, you have been using it ever since, haven't you, for the body and hands in the portrait of every merchant's brat you have daubed in Leghorn. I know how your best talents lie. Well, take the body of the old berlin and work it up into a fine modern portrait. Something fit to carry a prince of the blood travelling incognito through foreign dominions, something that will convey—without attracting undue notice—a sense of wealth, stability, and the utmost modern good taste. That's all I want you to do with the old lady, Terrini."

Vincent lay back beating a little dust out of the seat before him with his cane, whistling softly.

"I give you carte blanche, Terrini, as to materials, wages, and your own designs."

"Mon!" exclaimed Sandy as a last protest.

"The only stipulation is that you submit all your accounts to McNab for approval after the work is done."

Sandy grinned. "There, there," he said to the artist whose face had fallen. "I won't be cutting your own profit more than half and the costs two-thirds, rely upon it."

They all had to laugh, for McNab knew them and they knew McNab.

He had not lived in Leghorn for half a century without learning the fiscal peculiarities of his neighbours.

Leaving the smith looking about under the carriage and the rest gathered about Terrini in earnest consultation, Anthony, Vincent and McNab strolled over toward Vincent's *case* across the square.

"Well, are you satisfied, Vincent?" asked Anthony. "Sandy here will, I hope, be able to find us some horses somewhere." They were all talking in Italian now.

"Aye," said Sandy with a rueful shake of the head. "But I hate to see you leaving Livorno again, Master Anthony."

"I'd take you along if you knew where you wanted to go, Sandy."

"Thank you, sir," replied the Scot, his face becoming sad and perplexed, "but there's the rub. Since you've distributed the old master's legacy, Faith is the only one of all the old crew left at the casa that knows what she wants. It's curious, but none of us seemed to realize that the old life there was really over until Baldasseroni settled that lease for you and the old landlord took over the place again. It was too bad about the furniture. I've slept in that bed of mine for two and forty years."

"I'm sorry about that," said Anthony. "I should have thought of it."

"No, no, there's nothing to reproach yourself about, sir. The old master left us all enough to buy—mony a guid bed and a wee house to put them into." He broke into Scotch for a phrase or two, apparently a little excited about something. "But there'll be nobody to lie in them but ourselves and it *will* be a bit lonely—for me at least," he added significantly.

"You don't mean to say that Faith and Toussaint—" said Anthony.

"Aye," said Sandy.

"Was he happy?" asked Anthony.

"Like a boy with his first girl—for a while."

Anthony suddenly felt cold.

"Mon!" cried Sandy forcibly, "yon's a terrible woman. It must be inside the skull of her. Past middle-age and every new moon she's like a goat on the hills again. Did you ever see her eyes then, peerin' oot o' that great bonnet o' hers when she goes out? Do you know, Mr. Anthony?" They had come to a stop now. Vincent gave them a look and walked on. He was not in this, he saw.

"Yes, I know," said Anthony. McNab was still looking at him. His gaze became more searching.

"You don't mean to tell me that she bothered you when you were a boy, sir?" Anthony did not reply. He had grown silent again.

"Puir laddie!" exclaimed McNab. "Why didna ye come to me?"

"You know why," said Anthony looking at McNab. He had just guessed why himself.

"Aye," said the old man lowering his eyes. "We all paid there. And she's my ain cousin, too. But when she gave me the go-by and took up with Captain Bittern that time——"

"Oh, *did* she?" said Anthony. Suddenly they both laughed.

"By gad, she must have been sent into the world for educational purposes!" Anthony exclaimed. Somehow he suddenly felt relieved at what McNab had let slip. Since so many had shared in Faith she became a cosmic experience. He and McNab, and Toussaint, and Captain Bittern—and—and—were brothers. He linked his arm in McNab's and they went across the square. For the first time in their lives they were really talking to each other.

"Yes, sent into the world," replied McNab, "but not by God, by auld hornie. It's not her Scotch blood, of course."

Anthony grinned.

"Well, well," continued Sandy, "I suppose it's the mixture then. She's a kind of she mule, you know. Some mule mares are always in heat but Percheron, stallion or jackass makes no difference, they never gender. I suppose," speculated Sandy, "they want something they haven't got and keep trying for it. Yon woman's verra parseestant. It's the cradle and the grave with her." They had come to the steps of the office now and stopped.

"Will you come and have a talk; stay for dinner?" asked Anthony. "The Noltes, you know them from old times, they'd want you."

"No, no, thank you, sir, I'm moving to my new lodgings this afternoon. But I wish you'd send for Toussaint and talk with him, Mr. Anthony. You see the landlord, the marquis, is coming to stay at his own house. Toussaint and I have to get out but Faith is staying on, sir."

"What!"

"Yes, sir, there's no doubt of it. There's something up. Long before you came to the casa, in the old days, I think there was something between them. She was Maria Bonnyfeather's maid, and when the marquis came a-courting the old man's daughter, well, Faith was around, too. And——"

"I see," said Anthony. "Well, I shall send for Toussaint to come round for supper tonight. I wondered why I had been seeing so little of him. Good luck to you, Sandy, you know any time you . . . that is if you ever——"

"I know, sir, I know. And I'll keep in touch. It's the old blood that calls to us all. Good luck to *you*, Mr. Anthony—Adverse."

He shook hands and left Anthony standing on the steps pondering.

The closed door again!   He shook his head as if to clear it of cobwebs.

Anna called down the stairs to him. "Come up, Toni, I want you to meet somebody." They were all talking German and laughing up there excitedly.

"So her prince from Düsseldorf had come, had he?"

Why was it as he ascended the stairs he began to think of Angela? Something in Anna's voice, he supposed.

Pearls!

Why hadn't he thought of it before?   That was exactly the wedding gift for—Anna.

In the courtyard of the Casa da Bonnyfeather, where the foul remains of stagnant water in the fountain were fast being licked up by the sun, leaving a film of green slime behind it, Toussaint Clairveaux was loading two small chests onto a cart.   One contained his clothes and the other his library of second-hand books.

These, a few clothes, and the small legacy left him by Mr. Bonnyfeather were all that he had accumulated during about half a century of labour and existence.   The legacy he had invested in a small cottage on the outskirts of Leghorn.

Faith stood on the steps watching the chests being carried out in the same mood that she had watched the departure of Mr. William McNab some hours before; that is, with considerable satisfaction.   She had quietly completed her arrangements with Don Luis for remaining on as his housekeeper, and she was now seeing the last of the old régime depart with a complacency that bordered on enthusiasm.

The fact that for some time past she had allowed Toussaint, faute de mieux, an easy access to her bed made no difference to her feelings of relief at his departure.   They had merely been left alone together with the establishment practically closed up, and it had amused and soothed her to allow Toussaint to think that his lifetime of devotion was being rewarded.   McNab had merely laughed and let them alone.

Toussaint as usual had built up a romantic and blissful future on the basis of what he considered to be Faith's surrender to his long siege. "Her heart's citadel has at last capitulated," he assured McNab.

"Just temporarily starved-out," replied Sandy, and went his own way, waving off the demands of Toussaint for an apology as one would placate a child or a madman.

Toussaint on his part had bought the little cottage with vines about it some time before and furnished it charmingly.   Since the great revolution had somehow failed, he and Faith would now live apart in a dream of happiness close to the heart of nature in the hills. He had even tried to read *Emile* to Faith.   The embrace which followed after one paragraph he could never forget, never!

He now wiped the sweat from his forehead after lugging out the chest of books and arranged a sack on the seat.

"Tiens," said he.   "All is ready, mademoiselle.   Have you packed your bag?   We can return for the trunks later."   He stood waiting for her in a dramatic stance.

Twenty years before there had been something hawk-like and gallant about the little Frenchman, a kind of ardour which only the young intellectual fanatics who had brought on the revolution for the rights of man had possessed.   It was their mode, the peculiar sign of their class and generation.   It had not been funny then, because it was dangerous, genuine, and new.   In his own mind Toussaint was still one of those, who, if you would only listen to him, could bring the golden-age out of a cocked hat.   He extended his own, now frayed and worn-out, toward Faith, and stood waiting with his brown cloak at just the right droop from shoulder to ankle although it was a hot day.   The "consummation of his love" had given him all his old confidence.   The hat was even arrogant.

"Come, mademoiselle," said he.

To Faith the little man standing in the courtyard had nothing hawk-like about him.   He looked to her like an old bantam cock crowing defiantly upon a deserted dunghill.   She smiled, and deliberately began to close the big double doors.   She took out a great key from the ring on her belt.

"You may leave it in the keyhole," called Toussaint, climbing into the cart himself.

"*May* I!" she said and burst into a peal of mocking laughter.

He looked up startled—just in time to see the door close her in and him out, and to hear the lock shoot home.

The man on the cart burst into a roar of laughter.   "Pretty neat that!"   He hated the French anyway.   They had taken his other horse.

Toussaint ran up the steps and beat at the big doors frantically.   No answer.   He poured through the keyhole the kind of eloquence that was out of date.   That it came from his heart made no difference to the closed doors.   Only the echoes in the courtyard replied to him.   He heard them now.   He heard his own voice.   For the first time he recognized it for something frantic and ridiculous; something which even the stones hurled back.   It struck him down.   He lay on the steps and writhed while his ego withered.   Then he lay still.

The man on the cart got down after a while, picked him up and dumped him like a sack into the back of the cart beside his chests. Toussaint, the works of Rousseau, and sundry out-of-date garments were drawn out into the country and deposited at the vine-covered cottage. The carter gave no change for the gold piece which the small man, with his head sunk on his breast, proffered mechanically while he sat on his library by the roadside. It was a hot day.

About twilight Toussaint got up and went into the silent, little house.

He sat there for some hours with his head in his hands. A full moon began to peer at him through the window. "Clair de lune," said he, and spat.

He went out now to one of the chests and opened it. From a compartment on one side of his books he took out one of a pair of duelling pistols. It had not been fired since his affair of honour with Signore Baldasseroni.

"I shall do even better this time," he said.

He removed the charge carefully and cocked the piece.

"Meldrun!" said Toussaint Clairveaux to the moonlight, and put a bullet through his brain.

About the same time at the Casa da Bonnyfeather Don Luis was climbing into the bed of his late father-in-law with almost pious grunts of satisfaction. Outside, the shadow of the coach stretched half-way across the court in the moonlight. The bed was undoubtedly a good one and the sheets smelt of lavender. Indeed, the marquis had every confidence in his new housekeeper.

He had even left the door of his room open.

––––––––

For Anthony, the news of Toussaint's mad little tragedy served to give a dark poignance to rejoicings at the Casa da Nolte over the marriage of Anna to her Düsseldorfer and to the brightly concealed agony of Frau Frank at her only daughter's departure with her husband. Anthony said nothing about it until Anna had gone. But he could less than ever abide the thought of the strange new order at the Casa da Bonnyfeather. There was now something distinctly gruesome about it. With Anna away, the life of the Franks' house seemed to have vanished, too.

The whole past at Livorno lay heavily upon him. He wished to be rid of it forever now and to settle his affairs in England. With a growing impatience he awaited the revamping of the old berlin by Signore Terrini. Some days went by. Uncle Otto continued to sit in the sun and mumble. Then late one afternoon Terrini himself drove around in the rejuvenated berlin and even McNab had to admit that the "siller" had been well spent. The carriage was a little masterpiece, much too smart, indeed, for the sturdy but rather plebeian nags harnessed to it.

The ridiculous high seat behind was gone.   The vehicle had been slung evenly on new "C" springs so that it no longer seemed to be always about to bury its nose in the earth.   The wheels were lacquered jet-black with bronze lions' heads worked on the hubs.   The remodelled body was decorated with oval panels and the glass of the windows and the door was set in the same graceful shape.   The top was no longer sway-backed but hip-roofed.   And the whole carriage was enclosed with the fine, grained leather, enamelled in blue, for which Leghorn was famous.   Furthermore, the top was so contrived that the rear half of it would let down as a hood, otherwise kept in place by two polished metal rods.   All the seams of the leather were held together by a bronze filigree that traced itself over the entire upper half of the carriage as a metal vine.   The box was covered with grey felt ending in dark blue tassels, and there were two bronze side-lamps held in the beaks of eagles, which Terrini himself had designed and cast.

The little artist, who for a long time had found no work in Leghorn except the designing and decorating of coaches, had surpassed himself, and he was obviously proud of his chef-d'œuvre.

· "Of course, signore, with cost no consideration!—" He waved his hands as if the berlin could take wing and might be shooed away.

And indeed he had managed to express in its lines a lightness and grace that were astonishing.   The long sweeping curve of the back with the platform for the trunks had bronze handles for the footman to cling to.   It gave the final effect of a piece of flying light-artillery with metal gleaming in the sun.

"There will be nothing like it in Paris, Toni, not even the aimables who drive out in their 'Anglo-cavalcados' to Chantilly can rival you," said Vincent, who was a little envious.

"That is what I thought," replied Anthony and smiled a little.   "I told Terrini here to give me the latest mode, and he has done so."

"Yes, I have done so.   The Greek mode is going out.   It is the Roman effect I have striven for," gratulated Terrini.   "Look at the bronze chains on the poles and the harness fittings, classic.   You must get better horses in France."

"We shall.   But we might as well begin now on the present team here and the postilion and try to smarten them up."

Next day little Beppo, the Florentine vetturino, who had been engaged as one familiar with the passes over the Alps, was lifted out of his large jack-boots and leather coat and provided instead with a smart livery of bottle-green and a half-moon cocked hat with a tricolour cockade.   He was also induced to drive from the box, although he preferred to ride one of the horses.   That, however, was too old-fashioned to be tolerated.

Beppo drew double wages, for they had decided to go light and not to take on a footman until the other side of the mountains. Consequently he was effervescent with his unbelievable good luck in a slack time. In a few days he could manage his team like a charioteer even from the box. He cracked his bronze-handled whip while he rolled through the now comparatively deserted streets of the town on practice drives in the early morning. The blinds would be opened a little and excited voices behind them would comment upon the dashing appearance of the little berlin as it whisked by. Some oil meal, a clipping, a tail docking, and the removal of what had at first appearance looked like mops over the horses' feet, vastly improved them. At least they looked as if they might show a clean pair of heels.

Vincent attended to the passports. He had official friends. Otherwise there might have been difficulty for Anthony, who could not prove that he had been born. Described as a Tuscan gentleman on pleasure bent, he and Vincent set forth early one August morning in high spirits. There was an ample hamper of delicacies cooked by old Frau Frank, who kissed them both and saw them off with her blessing and tears.

As they trotted down the ancient street the last thing Anthony saw was the Swiss porter Franko bowing his affectionate thanks at the open door, and the already corpse-like face of Uncle Otto with his mouth open, asleep in the sun.

In the cool of the morning the horses whirled the little berlin on its slickly greased axles across the worn flagstones of the Mayoralty and flashed into the Strada Ferdinanda.

The team had just settled into a good spanking trot when a coach-and-four going at breakneck speed dashed out of a side alley and recklessly bore down on the berlin. The driver of the coach had evidently lost control of his horses and for some minutes the two vehicles galloped side by side, racing together down the Strada Ferdinanda toward the north gate. Poultry, and unfortunate fruit and flower vendors scattered before them like leaves in a gale.

Beppo had swerved only just in time. He was now doing all he could to rein in his own team, badly frightened, excited, and all for making a bolt of it. In this resolve they were much encouraged by the four splendid, coal-black horses racing beside them neck and neck. Ears laid back, eyes straining, and foam flying from their bits, the four galloped as one in their black collars, drawing after them easily and with a steady pull a huge, black coach piled high with luggage. It rolled along evenly upon its heavy iron tires that sang as they struck the paving like a dull bell.

There was something both ominous and thrilling in those iron tones. Anthony and Vincent had at first braced themselves for the crash that it seemed must inevitably follow. Then, as nothing happened, they sat back again tight-lipped, watching the familiar houses flash past and listening to the alarming, staccato tattoo of the galloping horses' hoofs. They were both thinking of the same thing. The arch of the Porta Pisa a short mile ahead was wide enough to admit only one vehicle at a time. Presently Anthony leaned back and laughed. Vincent looked at him as if he had just discovered he was riding with a madman.

The coach and the berlin, as though attracted by some invisible force, now gradually began to draw nearer to each other as they rushed down the middle of the broad avenue; dust rolling behind; spokes glimmering in a mist of speed.

The madness of the horses had spread its nervous contagion to both drivers, who were now exalted by excitement above all ordinary cares about life, limb, or happiness. They had now but one fatal end in view—to get to the narrow city gate first. Meanwhile, they began to abuse each other in the most provocative Spanish and Italian filth,— grandly pianissimo and fortissimo—and to pray profanely to the horses to burst their wheezing guts, but to get first to the gate. A mile of heartbreak had already made the sobbing nostrils of the poor beasts look like the bells of inflamed trumpets—then breed and skilful driving began to tell and the light berlin, which had a small lead, slowly but inevitably began to lose ground while the heavy coach gained.

A wail of all but feminine despair from Beppo, a tempest of chuckling squalls like the triumphant cries of a victorious tom cat from the box of the coach led the mere owners of the two racing carriages to suppose that they might now *possibly* be able to register an opinion with the drivers as to the immediate necessity of their deaths.

It was for that reason that both Anthony and Don Luis thrust their heads out of the precisely opposite windows of the coach and the berlin at the same moment—and found themselves looking searchingly into each other's faces. At the same instant the wheels of both carriages struck the smooth granite ramp that led to the narrow arch of the Porta Pisa.

"Good morning," called Anthony, leaning nearer. "We seem to be bound to meet."

Don Luis looked at Vincent, who was lying back in the berlin with a pale face; glanced at the black tunnel of the gate, where the guard was now beginning to run about frantically, and peered at Anthony again. In the three seconds which had thus passed the horses had taken as many strides nearer the inevitable crash.

The face of the young man only a few inches from the marquis was nevertheless quite calm and smiling. He seemed to be enjoying the situation. A reluctant gleam of approval widened the fixed smile on Don Luis' lips. The tires continued to sing brazenly. It was quite

plain the coach could not gain enough in the short distance that remained to avoid collision.

"Well?" said Anthony.

"*You* pull up," shouted Don Luis. "I can't. My horses—" The
rest was lost as the coach again forged ahead slightly.

"Beppo!" roared Anthony, "pull up."

The little Florentine, who was letting his horses rush toward the
archway with the bits in their teeth, while he sat staring at death
hypnotically, was suddenly awakened from his trance and stood up,
jerking the heads of his team violently.

The coach passed the berlin in a flash.

It made straight for the archway. A sentry who was just running
across the roadway with a chain suddenly thought better of it and
darted back.

The whip licked out like a snake over the backs of the four coal-
black horses. It burst like a series of pistol shots under the echoing
vault of the arch through which the coach, now rocking frantically,
disappeared with a sullen roar.

A tremendous running about of the military, in the same kind of a
flurry that follows the disappearance of a fox from a raided hen yard,
marked its transit.

The tardy fury of the guard was now vented upon the berlin which
dashed up just in time to be halted by the chain. Vincent's well-meant
and really profound thanks for the obstacle which had finally stopped
them was taken for sarcasm. Both he and Anthony were arrested and
rearrested as one sleepy officer after another was aroused to come down,
rubbing his eyes and cursing at being awakened at dawn. The captain,
who came down last, was chagrined at finding no one but the well-
known banker Herr Nolte and his friend, both with passports in order,
being detained apparently for nothing. He in turn cursed the guard
and returned to bed. The runaway having been explained, drink
money distributed, and the horses rested, the berlin was now permitted
to proceed while a disappointed crowd dispersed.

The last familiar object which Anthony saw as they topped the first
rise on the way to Pisa was the tree above the convent with the pigeons
circling about it. "Contessina—where was she?" he wondered. He
might stop—but it was only a passing thought. Vincent was in no
mood for whims just now. Still pale, Vincent applied himself from
time to time to a sumptuous array of silver flasks in a leather chest on
the seat before him. His colour and eventually his high spirits began
to return. Long before they reached Pisa his own remarkable calmness in the face of danger was thoroughly re-established in his own
mind. As he looked at the place from a distance, not only the tower
but the Baptistry seemed to be leaning.

They were approaching the walls and jumbled roofs of the town after sunset.   It seemed fitting that they should drive through its grass-grown streets in the twilight.   For Pisa appeared to Anthony to be a town glimmering upon the confines of sleep; the few cloaked citizens they passed, to be wandering somewhere in a detached dream.

Vincent had to be helped into the inn, *Grande Albergo Accademia,* a deserted, rambling place about whose doors a throng of whining beggars instantly gathered.   They started up from holes and byways; they came gliding out of the dusk, exhibiting their sores, withered arms, crippled babies and filthy rags in the rays of the dim lanterns of the berlin, till their numbers became alarming.   Vincent's ill-timed, drunken generosity brought more.   The innkeeper at last fell on them with Beppo's whip and cleared a passage to his own door, shouting a warning to Beppo to keep a sharp eye on the luggage.

Supper, such as it was, being over, and Vincent asleep on a table, Anthony took a short turn in the starlight of the old square where the tower leaned and the dimly striped front of the Duomo and Baptistry, from which the town seemed to have receded in order to leave them alone to their own peculiar beauty as things memorable and apart from the ordinary affairs of mankind, served only in some sort to compose his mind.   He felt curiously disgruntled tonight.

The first day of the trip by which he had set such great store had been disappointing.   He had listened to Vincent talking, trying to reinstate himself after the fright of the runaway.   He had listened mile after mile.   He hoped by tomorrow that Vincent would be able to live with himself without talking about it.   He decided if necessary to give him a day to sleep it off.   He had something to do at Pisa that he did not wish to be disturbed in.

Perhaps, though, it was Italy that was disappointing.   He had never realized how poor and how barren Italy was.   Could it be he would find all of Europe like that?   Africa and the West Indies had given him new eyes.

These old lands where people had lived for untold ages seemed worked-out.   Or was it the climate?   The soil itself seemed tired. Plants and animals were scarce.   Travellers always talked about "the luxuriance of Italy."   Where was it?   People existed here on a round of the comparatively few things they could grow, grapes, wheat, poultry, and some reluctantly slaughtered domestic animals.   They were ingenious in making many combinations of a few things.   But underneath was poverty, the poverty of nature.   He remembered the genuine luxuriance, the abundance of the plantations at Gallegos.   And there were no taxes there either.   Here the cost of being oppressed and thwarted was frightful.   The supper tonight!—sour wine and macaroni—the crowd of beggars at the inn door—ancient, festering misery. He had never in the worst slave gangs seen anything like that.

These beggars could, of course, feast their eyes every day on del Sarto's St. Agnes in the Duomo—where Angela had sat on the steps starving, and had found Debrülle.

"Why had John Bonnyfeather asked to be buried in Pisa?" he wondered.

A wave of homesickness for the hill at Gallegos, with the moon on his palm trees and *La Fortuna's* lights twinkling in the river below, swept over him. Or—he would like to be going home to a good rum drink in Cibo's patio at Regla. And tobacco—Europe knew nothing about tobacco. What was snuff? A mere whiff. He lit one of his precious, black cigars and felt better. Havana—there was a town that knew what plenty meant! He sauntered back to the inn followed by a shadow that near the window, seeing he was a stranger, began to whine and hold out a hand. He turned about to curse it, man or woman. And then remembering Brother François, gave the hand a piastre he found in his pockets from old times.

Very tired, he slept soundly and cleanly on the rear seat of the berlin and was awakened by the loud crowing of the poultry in the stable yard. Vincent was not up yet. Except for a poisonous old woman who brewed him some coffee, there was no one about. He went into the square and looked about again. Surely this was another place, not the town of the night before.

On that magnificent early August morning Pisa was magical. Light with a red-purple tinge streamed from its stones. He thought he had never seen anything so fantastically beautiful as the Duomo and Baptistry alone there across the square. And the reason for the leaning tower was now self-evident. It gave the last, perfect, wizard touch. No, there was nothing like this anywhere. He took a deep breath of the cool morning air and plunged his head in the fountain where two young girls, one with her jar on her head, stood watching him with smouldering brown eyes. They went away laughing.

"Si può far 'un piccolo gíro della città, signore," said a mild-voiced old man, peering up at him from under the wreck of an incredible felt hat. Anthony finished drying his face.

"No," he said, and then relented. There was something curiously prepossessing about the figure of the old man before him, who was dressed exclusively in patches and had only one stocking.

"The other went yesterday," explained the old gentleman, for such he was by his accent. "It was silk, and you know, signore, even the aged *must* eat occasionally. True, I have not yet been able to stain my other leg. But I scarcely hoped to find custom this morning.

Heaven has sent you. Accept me as I am. For a soldo I will——"

"Done," cried Anthony. "Do you know the Campo Santo?"

The old man raised his head and smiled. "Si," he whispered. "It is where the rich are sometimes buried even yet."

They slowly walked across the square talking; old harlequin in patches proving by every careful intonation and nice usage—as genteel poverty having worn out its good clothes must do—that he was the product of better days. His face looked drawn and transparent and he tottered a little. They sat down on the cathedral steps for a moment.

"Perhaps you will breakfast with me?" said Anthony after an erudite little talk about the beauties of the Duomo died away faintly.

The old man could not deny his Adam's-apple a twinge of antici-pation.

"A glass of wine now?"

"Thank you, signore, I shall accept your first invitation with pleas-ure, but only after we return from the Campo Santo. To tell the truth, I have not eaten—at least not this morning," he added hastily. "Let us go while it is still cool."

Anthony accepted this compromise with the old man's pride. He rose and walked less hastily.

"Perhaps," said he after a little, "a host might be permitted to offer his guest an arm."

It was gratefully accepted. And with age leaning thus on youth they entered the frescoed cloisters of the Campo Santo with its low green mounds, where long shadows and the bright glints of morning mingled together along the grass and under the peaceful arcades like memories of grief and joy resolved.

And Anthony knew at once why John Bonnyfeather had asked to be buried at Pisa. Here the past could never be disturbed. Here he was deeply lapped in it forever. He had retired into the still green walls.

"Don't bury me at Leghorn near to that fellow Smollett," he had once said, as usual veiling his gentle humour in a half-serious joke. "I do not like his vibrant, Protestant twang. It would disturb me. Give me consecrated and silent earth." Anthony remembered now.

He stopped the old man from telling him how the earth in the place had been brought from Mount Calvary.

"Yes, I know," he said. "I am looking for a grave."

"If it is a new one I shall know where it is," said his companion. "There are not many who can afford to be buried here now," he added with a strange touch of pride.

"About a year ago," explained Anthony.

"Ah, the old merchant from Leghorn! Yes, he was the last. A very quiet funeral. It is over here, signore, close by the way out."

The grass had already covered the mound that they now stood looking down upon. In the crumbling remains of a low brick wall that crossed the place, probably the ancient foundations of some forgotten tomb, was set a new white stone. The inscription was in Latin, not of the best:

Near Here Rests in Peace
A Caledonian of Noble Blood,
The Last of his Name,
A Faithful and Loyal Subject
of
James III
King of England, Ireland, Scotland
and France

———— : ————

He lost his titles but conserved his honour.
God prospered him and he remembered
In turn the poor and the fatherless.
Pray for him

In trying to carry out the last request on the stone, Anthony found himself at last addressing his verbal thoughts to John Bonnyfeather. He could not think of him as dead. He seemed merely to have withdrawn himself into this quiet place as if he had gone down the hall at home and shut the doors of his room behind him. In the back of Anthony's mind arose a half-conscious impulse to knock at the stone and enter. He would find Mr. Bonnyfeather seated at his desk writing with a plume pen, or with his slippers on reading a book. Something in Latin. It would be cool and quiet there. And he would ask a question.

What was the strange tie that bound him to John Bonnyfeather? Was it blood?—"noble blood?" "The last of his name"—said the stone. Perhaps his race still went on. That smiling girl's face in the miniature—who was she? Something deeper than he could understand, something essentially mysterious but real linked him with this dust asleep in the Campo Santo at Pisa. He was sure of it now. What was it that he had promised never to try to know? Faith knew. That sardonic old marquis knew—something. *He* had been John Bonnyfeather's son-in-law. Great God! Could that man be his father . . . ? No, no, impossible! He knew his own body well enough to know he was not of that flesh. "To . . . the fatherless," said the speaking stone. Blessed comfort in that line of script.

It was curious, it was not grief he was feeling as he stood thus whirling a thousand things from the past through his mind, it was transcendental respect, an abysmal regret that he would never be able to make the old man know that his boy had grown up and come back again wise and feeling enough to understand and to be grateful. That was what he would have liked to try to whisper to him down through the short grass on his new grave; and to say: "Yes, I know *now* that honour is the best of all things and the hardest to keep, and that you were the most honourable of men. No dross could buy your sacred dreams and no vicissitudes purloin your self-respect,—and so I more than love you for it."

Then came grief. For he suddenly saw that such complete things can be said only to the dead when the caricature of the body has gone, leaving the portrait of the spirit clear and luminous; when we cannot even catch at their hands again to ask to be forgiven or to cry out that in all charity now—with the sorrow of life upon us and with the love of Christ, and of man, and of woman, and little children in our hearts —we too understand, forever, and too late.

A sigh from the old guide, whom he had utterly forgotten, roused Anthony. With a look of complete weariness and exhaustion the old gentleman had just sat down on one of the grass mounds to wipe a bead of sweat from his forehead.

"I am sure," said he after a little, fanning himself weakly with his faded hat while looking up and smiling, "that whoever is beneath this mound will not grudge me just a moment's rest out of his easeful eternity. I *am* a little tired this morning." His mouth trembled faintly as he put on his hat again.

Anthony's heart troubled him that he had kept so pleasant an old man standing so long in the sun. There was a touch of half-ghastly, old-world grace about him and his patches. It was, he thought, a little like talking to the ghost of John Bonnyfeather disguised as a respectable Lazarus. A little like him—out of the corner of one's eye— a sort of ragged-glimmering of lost, coffined gallantries.

"Come," said Anthony, "did you think I had forgotten my breakfast invitation?"

"By no means," replied the old gentleman, again frankly grateful for the support of a young arm. "But you must not suppose I was thinking *only* of that, signore. I was truly,"—and he looked up ingenuously—"I was truly thinking of you. I, you see, have my own dead here in the Campo Santo. And I so much desire to speak of them this morning," he hurried on, "that I thought, as I looked at you—I thought you would understand how the hunger of the heart is sometimes greater than that of the belly, and that you would let me tell you their names just so they might be on the lips of the living again, in the morning light. Will you?"

"Why, yes,—of course," said Anthony.

"Well, then," said the old man, "lean down . . ." He whispered two names.

"My little girls, you know." He straightened up proudly as if the syllables had renewed his strength. "Here they are—only a few steps—this way. And we can go out that gate there. Here they are!"

It was quite evident that the old man was looking beyond the carpet of tenderly cared-for flowers that covered two small mounds side by side—that—to judge by the light in his face—he saw angels sitting in the tomb. His parchment-like skin shone with a reflected glow.

They stood there quietly for a minute or two.

"Thank you," said the old gentleman, as they went on out the gate and across the square. "To me you are no longer a stranger here," he continued still holding on to Anthony's arm. "The dust of both our families mingles in Pisa, signore. For me that gives you the freedom of my city. If I still had my own house, you should be my guest. It was that one over there." He pointed to what had once been a fine dwelling, now much dilapidated. "I come of an ancient family here, the Raspanti," he muttered. "And, I also am the last of my name."

For a moment before going into the inn they stood at the door and looked at the old house, where a collapsing balcony once beautifully carved staggered across a blind, shuttered front of flaking pink plaster. "None of us have ever been beggars, signore—may I ask your name?"

"Adverso," said Anthony. "But come, Signore Raspanti, it is only fortune that makes you my guest this morning. *My* good fortune," and he made the old man that stiff, old-fashioned bow that Father Xavier had taught him at the convent years before. He thought he had forgotten it.

The old man removed his hat with the true, antique flourish and put it under his left arm. He placed his right hand over his heart.

"You are very hospitable, a man of honest feeling, Signore Adverso," said he, and entered the inn with a sigh.

Vincent was already up and about with his high spirits renewed. Beppo was shaving him in a chair while he urged on the old woman who sat in the corner to hasten her plucking of several newly killed fowls. Vincent gave a shout as Anthony came in, and with the soap still on his face rose to meet Signore Raspanti with a gay formality. He shouted through the lather.

"Toni, we are going to begin our journey all over again today. That damned runaway shall not count as part of it. It was just bad luck."

"No, no," said Beppo. "They meant to drive us down. They flashed out on us from the alley on purpose like—*that*."

"Look out," roared Vincent, "you will cut my throat. Jesus!"

"But I am *right,* signore," insisted Beppo.

"Perhaps he is!" mused Anthony. "Here, landlord, a glass of wine for Signore Raspanti, my guest,—and some biscuits. Until breakfast comes, you know," he said to the old man, who looked grateful.

"Nonsense," roared Vincent. "It was just the horses. Anyway we are going to start all over again from Pisa this morning on top of a worthy and a proper, soul-sustaining breakfast. Ah, we are good at breakfast, aren't we, Toni? Do you remember? Some Asti, landlord. Look alive, man, get your spit going."

He sat up now looking fresh and pink after Beppo's scraping, rubbing his fat, full chin half comically and laughing from sheer inward good-nature just as he had when a boy. His spirits were catching to all.

A slight tinge of colour like rouge on a wax rose began to show even on the yellow parchment face of old Signore Raspanti. He sopped his biscuits in his wine and let them rest against his gums while he sucked without making a noise, noblesse oblige. He instinctively disliked disturbing noises. He hoped that the ticking of Signore Adverso's watch, for instance, which he had stolen from him in the cemetery, and which was now making an alarmingly vulgar noise in his own tattered waistcoat, would not disturb any ear but his own. One *must* think of others. He instinctively put his hand back over his heart in that gallant, old-fashioned way.

The landlord came in from the court dragging one of his half-naked brats by the hair, who whimpered as he was set to work at the spit.

"Four chickens! One apiece," bawled Vincent. "One for the guest and Beppo!" He waved toward Signore Raspanti, who rose and bowed, with his hand still on his heart in grateful but careful acknowledgment.

The landlord smiled. He began to lay the table for four. If the gentleman wished to eat with his servant, he had drunk enough wine that morning to have his eccentricities catered to. Before Signore Raspanti, however, he left only wooden spoons, and smiled again. Three law students from the university dropped in for coffee before lecture and sat looking on.

The old woman who had just split open the fourth chicken broke into a lament. It was a laying-hen full of ripe eggs. Everybody laughed at her dismay and profane lamentations.

"Put them in the gravy, mother," said a fat priest from the Duomo who just then wandered in. He gave everybody his blessing, including the law students who laughed at him, too.

"The father watches the inn chimney, signore," said one of them to Vincent. "When he sees smoke he comes over to extend the blessing of the church to those who are able to make the spit turn." The priest grinned sheepishly but with great good-nature.

"Even the light haze of an omelette will bring me running now," he admitted. "Since the French burned my little farm I grow lean." He took in slack on the immense rope about his waist. "That will do, I think, Pietro," said he to the urchin at the spit. "Let me see." He rose and going over to the fire twisted a wing from one of the chickens without even stopping the wheel. "Yes, it is quite done. Just at the turn, signore," he cried, turning to Vincent. "I like mine not too dry. Do you?" Everybody laughed at his cool impudence.

It was impossible not to include everybody. Indeed, nearly everybody was just waiting to be included.

"Draw the tables together—here," said Anthony.

"Gentlemen, will you join us?" shouted Vincent to the three law students. They looked at one another as the younger generation will when bidden too heartily by their elders, even to a feast.

"Do," said Anthony, "join us in our little celebration. It will have the blessing of the church, I am sure." He winked at the young men. Hesitation vanished. There was a great scraping of chairs being dragged over the tiles.

"What are your favourite wines, my friends?" asked Anthony. A babble of local vintages drove the old woman to the cellars with her hands over her ears.

"Two bottles apiece," roared Vincent after her. The students now looked impressed.

"Father," said Anthony, grinning.

The priest gabbled something in Latin while the steam from the fowls curled up from the table under his nose. It was a laconic grace.

The meal began with a clash. In a corner by the spit the young urchin looked on gnawing dreamfully on a drumstick.

The discovery of the morning proved to be the students and the new wine to which they introduced the company. It was the first of the local harvest and only lately pressed.

"In a few days, sir, it will be acid and ordinary," said the oldest of the trio, a tall lad with flashing eyes, a restless air, and an immense mane of jet-black hair that he continually tossed back out of his eyes. "But just at this stage of working it is full of bubbles and creams as you drink it." His gay talk in a strong French accent ran off the surface of things very much as the bubbles effervesced from the wine. The priest stuck to Canary and smiled. He had a good reason. The new wine was light to the taste but proved heady. In a short time the table was seething with talk and beggars were gathering about the inn, attracted by the noise and rumour of plenty.

"Open the door and let in the sunlight," bawled Vincent.

"And the rabble, too?" inquired the innkeeper. "Father, can't *you* do something?" the man asked, seeing the crowd outside.

The priest went out and closed the door behind him. They heard his voice for some time but could not hear what he said. When he came back he left the door open and no one was there.

The innkeeper nodded his acknowledgment and admiration of the father's powers of speech.

There was a sudden lull of talk as the sunlight streamed over the table.

"Saints and angels! What time is it?" queried the youngest and palest student anxiously. "Remember, you Jacopo, there is a lecture in the porch at nine."

"On the Code Justinian," mumbled the dark-headed boy into his mug. "Dry, oh dry!" He poured the remainder of the priest's wine into his own glass and drank to the company, giving the two "illustrious signori from Livorno" a neatly turned toast of thanks.

"Have you ever rolled in the dust of the civil law, signori? You would know then how I hate to leave this—and you," said he, putting down his glass. "But it must be almost nine, isn't it?"

Anthony fumbled for his watch.

The bell of the campanile began to toll the hour. Shouting to one another and calling their hasty farewells, the three students dashed out and raced down the street. They took the life of the party with them.

Silence fell on the little common-room of the inn. Anthony sat looking across the table at Signore Raspanti, who was apparently watching a spider on the opposite wall.

"You look ill, Toni," said Vincent. "Has the new wine been . . . ?"

Anthony waved him off and continued to stare at the old man.

"What time is it, Signore Raspanti?" he asked.

"The bell has just struck nine, I believe," answered the old gentleman with a little quaver. "Shall I go out and see?" he added, rising hopefully.

They were all looking at him now. The seconds ticked out by the stolen watch against the ribs of the old man measured his heart beats. His mouth fell open and he shook.

"Have you by any chance lost your watch, my friend?" said the priest to Anthony.

Anthony nodded. A rush of blood clouded his face.

"Give it to him, Raspanti," said the priest harshly.

The old man brought the watch with its dangling seals out of his breast and slowly pushed it across the table toward Anthony. Then he collapsed, weeping hopelessly with his head in the gravy plate.

"Pig!" shouted Beppo, jumping up and starting to shake him.

Vincent pulled him off. "Leave him to the police," he growled. "Go and get the horses harnessed and wait. We leave shortly."

"A word with you, signori," said the priest. He took them both over to a corner.

"Do not call the police, I beg you. Let me tell you something about this old man. He is a pitiable case. He married unhappily. His wife left him with two baby daughters. They both died on the same day, and as he had no means left but his house, he sold that to bury them both together in the Campo Santo. Otherwise it would have meant the common pit. He did not turn beggar as he might, but for years has acted as cicerone in Pisa. When travellers came here in the days before the war he made just enough to exist—and to get one of his daughters out of purgatory. Now only a few travellers come. He starves. Maria is in heaven and Euphemia in the fires. He says they both suffer at being parted, and it is his fault. Can you imagine that? It is only lately he has begun to take things. When a traveller comes now he gets what he can. The tick of your watch, you see, would have been heard in eternity."

"Hum!" said Vincent.

"Forgive him, signori, for the love of Christ." The fat priest's face worked painfully. "I am not his confessor, you know, or—" he put his hand over his mouth. "He goes to one of the canons at the cathedral. I saw the seals dangling from your waistcoat this morning, signore, when you went across the square with old Raspanti, and I thought—yes, when you came out of the Campo Santo with *no* seals dangling from your waistcoat, I thought—'Euphemia will soon be in paradise, provided I do not inform the canon. And if I inform the kindly looking young signore, Euphemia will not go to paradise and old Raspanti will go to jail.' I really came over here to see you both. The old man was hungry, too, no doubt of it. Well, you know what has happened. But I do not think the police are going to help. Anyway, you have your watch back, and—Well, he will be hanged, you know."

They all looked again at the old man lying with his head in the plate of gravy. He did not move.

"How long have his children been dead?" asked Vincent.

"Over ten years," replied the priest reluctantly.

"Gott im himmel! and all that time this canon what's-his-name has been sharing the poor old devil's tips. What do you make of that, Toni?" shouted Vincent. "The lousy swine!"

The priest put his fat hands over his ears now. Anthony pulled them down again.

"How much?" said he, "to get Euphemia out of *the canon's* hands?"

"About twenty soldi will see her through—now, I think."

"You think? Perhaps I had best go to your metropolitan here."

"No, no, I am sure of it."

"You will tell him so before I leave?"

A reluctant nod gave assent.

Anthony went over to Raspanti and raised him up on his chair. He wiped the tears and giblets off his twitching old face. Then he took his watch and put it back into the old scarecrow's waistcoat. Then he threw his cloak around his shoulders.

"You make a mock of me, signore?" gasped the old man. "I did not *lie* to you in the cemetery. They *are* my children there."

"I love you," said Anthony and kissed his dirty, smeared old face.

"Great God!" said Vincent in complete disgust.

"Now, father, you *tell him!*" insisted Anthony.

"Landlord, landlord," shouted Vincent, "the bill!"

"Come on, Vincent. He'll find us soon enough," cried Anthony, and rushed out still sick at heart.

"You're drunk," laughed Vincent as he stumbled down the corridor after him.

They climbed into the berlin just as the anxious landlord dashed out after them waving both his apron and the bill frantically. He was paid.

Anthony detained him, talking to him for some minutes in rapid Tuscan. Money changed hands. "Si, si, si, si, si. A place at my own table from now on. A bed. The Scotchman from Leghorn will see to it, you say. Have no fear . . . Yes, certainly it was the priest. The canon! that *is* a good one. The French hanged him a year ago. The wrong man, you say. No, they were right there, too. But here comes the one they missed."

The priest rushed out of the door, his face a fiery red. "Gone?" he shouted to the landlord. "You let them go when . . ." Then seeing the berlin he stopped short and tried to grin.

Some beggars began to close in about the coach whining.

"Here are your twenty-*five* soldi," said Anthony, pouring them into the priest's hands.

"Five extra for possible accidents in limbo," he growled.

"Signore, signore, stop, let me thank you," screamed old Raspanti, coming down the corridor. "My children are in paradise. I thought . . ."

"Get on, Beppo, drive off," Anthony shouted.

"Alms, alms, for the love of Christ, alms . . ."

The berlin dashed out of the beggars circling about the fat father, who held up his hands in terror.

"Would you rob the church, you swine? You black . . ."

They heard no more. Looking back, Vincent saw the old man with a smeared face, with Anthony's cloak flopping behind him, trying to run after the berlin while he waved his tattered hat wildly.

He looked at Anthony who said nothing.

"Did you give him Mr. Bonnyfeather's seals, too?" asked Vincent.

"No, I kept those," replied Anthony, taking them out of his pocket and looking at the old crest on the middle one.

"You weren't as drunk as I thought then," grumbled Vincent. "But that is the last time, my boy, that I buy *you* any new wine, anywhere."

CHAPTER FIFTY-TWO

OVER THE CREST

IN THE marble porch of the Via Emilia Professor Monofuelli was droning away in Latin to about a dozen sleepy students upon the inexhaustible subject of the Civil Law.

During the recent French and Austrian struggles over Italy the University of Pisa had almost closed its doors. The restless times had drawn away many of its students, contracted its revenues, and even scattered the faculty. Professor Monofuelli had come over from Padua to lend a helping hand.

He felt, however, that he was not being fully appreciated. Five students had slept through his entire—and celebrated—lecture on the Pandects only the afternoon before. And it was not much better this morning.

To be sure it was both sultry and shady under the old, marble porch, open on one side to the empty and grass-grown street. The benches in the hall near by had gone to make Austrian soldiers warm only the winter before. But certainly it was hot enough now. The professor wiped his forehead with his handkerchief and brushed the snuff that fell out of it off his faded peach-coloured, velvet coat.

Perhaps he was just the least bit sleepy himself. He had given only an hour to the distinction between *fas* and *jus,* but without his usual enthusiasm. And three students had been late. They had missed *fas* entirely. Well, it was a distinction that those who merely expected to practise law could ignore. But historically—historically *fas* was important. It was all very well for Dontelli at Bologna to ignore *fas,* but there could be no doubt about it that *jus* had developed out of *fas.* He would give it to his students. He would repeat it for that fellow Aristide Pujol, one of the late ones. He had come in late with two others, at a quarter after nine at least. They had been drinking somewhere (he knew)—new wine! That was all very well, but then—then there was *fas.* He rapped on the desk and reversed the hour-glass. The red sand in it began to run the other way.

"Signore Pujol—*signore!*"

That young gentleman sat up.

"Aha! signore, attention! I am about to repeat something for you. It is not my custom to repeat myself."

"Only your lectures," thought Pujol.

"You are from beyond the Alps, my young friend, aren't you?"

"A Frenchman, Excellence," grumbled Pujol proudly.

"*Ahem,* all the more reason then that you should not waste your time in Italy in sleep. How many times does the distinction of *fas* appear on the twelve tables, my friend from Gaul?"

"Once, I think," grumbled Pujol.

"You think? Well, you are correct. Repeat the passage—the law itself."

The young fellow did so.

"Not so bad for a barbarian, I must admit, Pujol. But the accent, your Latin accent is terrific. It is worse than that of the barbarians from the schools in Britain. Now listen, that denunciation goes like this." The professor filled his lungs.

"*Patronus, si clienti fraudem faysit, sacer esto.*"

But the professor was startled by the flat effect of his own voice. He was used to lecturing in a room with a dome in it at Padua. There he could tell the difference between the Latin of Ulpian and the Latin of Gaius by the sound in the dome. His own genuine accent came back to him. But here—here there was nothing; no return; no sonorous, encouraging effect. Only sleepy students gaping up at him. And that young Frenchman laughing at him, laughing! In his indignant disappointment he absent-mindedly reversed the hour-glass again. In a few seconds the sands ran out. A gust of applause swept the porch, the first he had received since arriving at Pisa. He cleared his throat for a philippic *contra* Aristide. It should be remembered and remembered, but——

At that moment the sound of rapidly approaching wheels turned every head away from him.

A smart, an extraordinarily handsome, little carriage was coming down the street. Just then the back hood was let down by an arm reaching around out of the window. It revealed two quite young but evidently very prosperous gentlemen sitting side by side on the rear seat. One was tall and spare with a peculiarly ardent expression, golden-brown hair, and a pair of eyes that looked searchingly out of a sun-browned face. It was a face so regular and yet so alive and mobile that you remembered it. The other young man was astonishingly blond, white and pink. And you felt that some day he would be fat and contented. Just now he was laughing, with his arm thrown back over the open hood, displaying inadvertently a handsome ring and a positively gorgeous expanse of waistcoat. Both young men were wearing high, English hats of remarkable mould under the wide brims of which their hair curled and flopped. The bronze, and blue leather upholstery of the carriage glittered; the horses approached at a spanking trot; the driver flourished his whip in a decidedly intoxicated manner.

There was something so gay about the whole equipage, such a debonair assurance seemed to accompany it, that Professor Monofuelli instinctively consigned it to hell in one erudite malediction while he rapped for order and a return to *fas*.

The sound of his well-worn gavel was the signal for the Frenchman Aristide Pujol to rise, throw his books down the steps, and rush out of the porch just as the little berlin was passing.

He ran along beside it for a few yards—"just like a beggar," exclaimed the professor later on in disgust—and then leaping on the step began to talk to Anthony, who leaned forward to catch what he was saying.

"You are going to Paris, aren't you, signore? I heard you say so this morning." His eyes shone with excitement.

"Yes, can we take a letter for you?"

"No, signore, but——"

"But what?"

"Will you take *me?*"

"Why!—well, there is hardly room."

"I could go on the box, sir. I can drive. I will do anything you ask on the way. Serve you and the signore. Take me. I am rotting here at Pisa. I must go—*go!*"

"Go?" said Anthony.

The young fellow nodded, tears in his eyes.

"We can't delay for you, you know."

"No, no, just as I am, now."

"Well, Vincent?"

"Why not?" said Vincent.

"Climb up," said Anthony. "Stop a moment, Beppo."

By this time all the students in the porch had rushed out onto the steps and were craning their necks after the carriage. They broke out into a clamorous shout when Aristide climbed onto the box. But he did not look back. He went on. His former classmates returned to the lecture and threw themselves down on the hard stone benches rather desperately.

"Great things are doing in France, Excellence," said one of them as the little man began to rearrange his much-fluttered notes.

"So I have heard," said the professor opening his book again. He sighed audibly. "But, that our conversation may return to the point from which our Gaulish friend has just digressed—let us ourselves return to the law. As Cicero has so aptly said for us: 'Though all the world exclaim against me, I will say what I think: that simple little book of the Twelve Tables, if anyone look to the fountain and sources of laws, seems to me, assuredly, to surpass the libraries of all the philosophers . . .' "

The berlin trotted out of Pisa into the green, rolling country beyond and took the road for Florence at a more rapid pace. Beppo began to sing as the hills about his native place began to become familiar.

At Florence they stayed only long enough to rest the horses, to arrange for some travelling papers for Aristide, and get him a few clothes. He had left in his vest and shirt-sleeves.

Both Anthony and Vincent were glad they had given way to impulse and taken Aristide along. A merrier, a keener, and more willing helper they could scarcely have found. And he was painfully grateful. His constant, half-impudent but always good-natured comments from the box amused and sometimes convulsed them. He had also, Anthony soon discovered, the faculty of causing things to get done. "My mother was from Gascony," he said, "and my father from Auvergne. I therefore understand how gullible, how selfish, and how kindly in little things most men and women are. You make them laugh, and then—omelette." He could drive well, and he understood not only the civil law but horseflesh. "At Milan, signore, if possible, we should get other and more horses. These were not good enough even for Austrians to retreat on."

Soon they were heading north again and leaving Tuscany behind. The first certain notice of it was the change in the type of roadside shrines and the shorter horns of the cattle.

That Tuscan type of shrine, where every article used at the Crucifixion from hammer and nails to spear and sponge is displayed with terrible, literal exactitude, while the figure of Christ himself is omitted or made conventional as a mosaic in St. Sophia, began to give way to more naturalistic representations of the Passion. At these, no matter what their mode, Anthony tried not to look. For his own reasons the sight of any cross was a peculiarly painful reminder. Indeed, it is doubtful if any traveller for centuries had passed casual, wayside crosses with such a living knowledge of the reality of the scene they attempted to represent. Yet he could not ignore them. And they constantly gave rise to certain trains of thought which for his own mental health he desired for a while to let lie dormant.

He had come to the conclusion that he must for a year or two at least try to obscure in normal human companionship, at not too highly emotional a level, the incandescent light of the visions of his African experience, which still dazzled him, especially at night.

He had not opened the bundle from Gallegos with the madonna in it. That was to wait for a while, although it was along with him even now, travelling in the dark boot of the berlin, just as the knowledge and the harvest of all the memories in the bundle travelled in the closed box of his mind, waiting. When he looked at that little figure again he must be able to do so with a whole and healed soul; with tender but level eyes.

Yet reminders of Brother François were constantly leaping out upon him in Italy. They staggered him at times; almost forced him into hysterical, dramatic—and hence he was sure—eventually foolish action. He had kissed the genteel old thief at Pisa and given him his cloak in return for stealing his watch. And Vincent had said he was drunk on new wine. Well, he *had* been drunk, but not on new wine. "Wine of the vintage of A.D. thirty-three," he thought as he looked up to catch the shadow of a cross arm falling across the carriage. Yes, that was the trouble. He must not be "drunk," not even upon old wine. Wine should be sustaining: "Give us this day our daily bread."

He was glad that Vincent understood. How much he needed a practical, happy, able friend like Vincent, who loved him and yet loved the world, too.

He had told him all. Vincent had wept, and yet he could laugh at you when you were "drunk"—and get you along over the particular roads of the world which you had to travel, towards Paris—or London, or whatever was the immediate rational goal. Yes, thank God for Vincent!—and let the horses trot now,—where was it they were going?—oh, yes, towards Milan, with that good-natured, keen, human, young Pujol on the box next to the ridiculous Beppo.

He gave himself up to being a traveller and nothing else.

He enjoyed the halts; the women about the town fountains; the inns, half stables, half human dwellings with something of the antique world left over that he had glimpsed and shared once with Angela. Certainly in the inns of Italy the fragments of it were scattered over her hills and along her still half-Roman by-ways. *Antiquia*—that was a good world, refreshing, real, and primitive. He enjoyed waking up mornings to its sounds; the loud peasant dialects, children playing, and the comfortable noises of cattle, lambs, doves, and chickens. In Africa he had missed the sparrows, he found.

But he was not to see much of Lombardy. As they emerged onto the level and often swampy plains a cool wind had come down from the snowy mountains to contend with the summer heat. The whole country was veiled in mist. Long rows of poplars loomed through it. It lifted only occasionally for bright, plangent gleams of level, green meadows and white towns. They heard the muffled bells of

unseen chapels ringing through it. Or carts loomed up suddenly and
were swallowed like wraiths, as they trotted on into denser fog and
cooler weather.

And it was now that they first began to hear the voice of bugles
and to meet frequently with French troops. An occasional column
of them forced them to draw up and pull aside. Their trumpets
shouted afar off, echoing.

"It is the voice of France," cried Pujol. "Soon, soon I shall be
chez moi." He began to shout and sing.

They could see nothing of Milan as they approached it. It was
late one evening and the moon over the city was only a bright, fleecy
blur in a world of silver fog that veiled the houses and the cathedral
spires from sight. Milan was nothing but glimpses of the legs of
passers-by from the knees down in the light of blurred lanterns; moonlight along the bases of walls, and link boys making a red smudge
drifting through the mist. But the inn near the Scala was a good
one. No fog could veil that. They stayed for several days.

They sold the old team and bought four new horses. None too
many to pull even the light berlin over the Simplon, which pass they
had decided to take instead of the Great St. Bernard, followed by
Napoleon only the year before, but since then cut to pieces by supply
trains and artillery.

From being little better than a dangerous wagon track only sometimes passable, the Simplon, over which Bonaparte had chosen to
maintain his communications with Italy in the future, had already
been made practicable for troops and carriages in all but the worst
winter weather. The French idea was to make the Simplon available
for artillery and wagon trains at all times, and to that end they had
already pierced tunnels and galleries on the Lombard side and were
at work in great force on the Swiss slope grading and constructing
avalanche shelters.

"If you can get the permission of the French commandant here to
take the route, signore, I would do so," said the innkeeper. "By far
the better you will find." Vincent had little difficulty in having their
papers stamped "par la nouvelle route militaire."

Aristide had also proved himself such an able diplomat in negotiating the deal in horses that Vincent told him he had already earned
his way to Paris and supplied him with suitable clothes. In fact, the
whole party was now provided with rugs, gloves, and heavy coats
that seemed incredible to Anthony after years in the tropics and in
the present Turkish bath atmosphere of August in Milan.

It finally cleared up a little on the last day of their stay and they
drove out on the Corso to try out the new horses with Aristide handling the reins. Beppo, with his troubles doubled, was now only too

willing to ride behind, his new, braided coat-tails flapping in the wind quite à la mode.

On the Corso, despite a decided wispiness that still draped itself along that magnificent drive, the Milanese fashionables and nobility were already out, driving in the handsome turnouts for which the city had been famous for two centuries at least. The berlin was accompanied through the gate by a tumult of other carriages.

Indeed, driving on the Corso, rain or shine, peace or war, was the chief test of social position in Milan. One either drove and lived or did not drive and vaguely existed. Noble families impoverished by the troubled times, often reduced to an abject poverty indoors, nevertheless frequently managed to maintain, at the expense of appetite and clothes, a vehicle of some kind with two beasts to draw it. One would not do. One old marchesa who was known to be nearly starved, anaemic from nothing but cabbage soup and crusts, was much admired and pointed out when she drove daily in the still tolerable family coach with crest and running footmen. When one of her horses died the local assembly of nobles had provided her another by subscription. All this was current gossip even at the inn.

There was certainly something very Spanish about the Milanese, Anthony thought as they drove along the Corso with the sun glittering on the spokes of varnished wheels and the jewels of heavily veiled women. Spain was to be seen not only in this inevitable custom of the evening drive after the siesta but in Milanese manners and talk. The stately salutations, the simultaneous removal of hats by gentlemen, and the fluttering of black lace and painted ivory fans as the carriages passed and repassed reminded him of the Alameda de Paula at Havana. And the town was full of Spanish architecture.

He long remembered this drive with peculiar pleasure; the sun falling in trembling pencils and half-mystical gleams through the melting mist about the ghostly scarved poplars, with the dark prickly mass of the great cathedral dominating the town behind; the river of carriages streaming along to the sound of subdued feminine laughter and the sharp snap of fans; to the gleam of jewels in the sunset. What a splendid river it was, the most civilized he had ever seen.

And not a little of the pleasure came from being an acceptable, even a notable part of it. For the little berlin with its blue leather traced with bronze leaves, its four fine horses now in spick and span military harness with scarlet blinkers, caused many a head to crane on its neck. Whether the young men who sat looking out over the lowered hood, smoking black Cuban cheroots,—which, they had accidentally discovered, created almost a furor wherever they went,—were found as acceptable as the berlin, they had not time enough in Milan to discover. But a number of eyes that examined them over the tops of fans seemed more friendly than critical. And the fans reminded Anthony of Dolores. In fact, for some reason or other, Milan, as he explained it to Vincent, made him homesick for Dolores.

"There is no use going through the world thinking of cities in the terms of women one has loved and lost," said Vincent, a little jealous as he was forced to listen for the second time to a tale of Dolores and dolour. "If you do, when you once get to Paris, you will never be able to admire another town."

"How do you know, Vincent?" said Anthony, who really had some doubts of Vincent as a cavalier.

"My boy," said Vincent, "when we do get to Paris I am going to take you around to a little house on the Rue de Vielle du Temple. It was formerly the hôtel of an ancient and respectable, a noble family. But it now belongs to a certain young banker from Livorno. I want you to look it over and consider its—well, modern advantages. In fact, I have hopes you will like the place so much that you might decide to acquire another near by. Several kinds of business, mundane and even semi-domestic, can be transacted most satisfactorily in one of these refurnished, family hôtels. Since the Terror they are all the rage. You might send for Neleta—or Dolores—or——"

"Dolores is not the kind one sends for," interrupted Anthony considerably irritated, "and as for Neleta, I am done with all that kind of thing I told you."

"Tut, tut, mon vieux, you speak as if you were feeble and travelling from one source of hot restorative waters to another, and in vain. You will presently recollect yourself. Why, if you don't look out, you will be talking of marriage like an impotent young man or a debauched ancient. Remember you are not a *poor* bachelor."

"I *have* been thinking of marriage."

"But not of getting married, I hope," groaned Vincent. "That is quite another thing."

The argument, for it developed rapidly into that, continued until they had made the turn on the Corso several times and were returning for supper.

It was now late twilight, and the mist was beginning to settle again. Aristide lit the lamps. A number of belated carriages, as though seen through a curtain of thin, silver gauze behind which a procession of lights was taking place, likewise hurried rapidly home toward the city gates. The effect of a carnival in Brociliande was soon heightened by multitudes of fireflies and the rising of a harvest moon.

Aristide drove rapidly. They began to overtake one carriage after another and to pass them swiftly. Vincent and Anthony both leaned over the sides of the open hood, letting the cool evening rush into their faces while feasting their eyes on what was a truly marvellous scene. A glow of torches moved on the distant battlements where the night guard was being posted, and wisps of mist caressed their cheeks from time to time with smooth, cool fingers. As they drove into and out of these fog pockets, suddenly the whole scene as if by art-magic would be cut off and then renewed before their eyes. They exclaimed to each other with astonishment and delight. It was like watching a feast of lights in elfland through a magician's milky crystal where the vision was now clear and now clouded by less tangible dreams.

Then, suddenly, as they flashed out of a streak of fog, a familiar shape loomed up before them. To Anthony it seemed in a curious way to be the centre of all those other dreams driving through the mist. And although he had come across it suddenly and recognized it instantly, he felt that he had been looking at it for a long time before; that it had been waiting for him behind the curtain of mist; that it was inevitable that on this particular drive he should overtake the coach of Don Luis.

This time he would pass him or know the reason why.

He touched Vincent on the arm and felt immediately that he had electrified him with his own unreasonable excitement.

"Get on, Pujol, get on, *pass that coach,* and don't let it overtake you. Hold tight, Beppo," he cried.

The whip cracked. The startled horses leaped ahead, going at headlong speed while Aristide stood up.

Don Luis, also going at a fast clip, heard a carriage coming up behind him at such a pace that he turned to look back. He was in no mood to race on the Corso, but he hated to be passed. Like *that!*

For just as he leaned out the berlin flashed by. The coach lamp glared into the berlin; the lights of the berlin shone for a moment into the faintly rosy interior of the coach. Sitting upon the faded upholstery in the moonlight with her arm in Don Luis', Anthony saw Faith Paleologus dressed in the extremity of fashion with a necklace of emeralds smouldering about her neck. She gave a faint scream as she looked into the berlin and Don Luis burst out with an oath. Both of them were as startled as Anthony. Then the berlin passed the coach.

They heard the coach picking up speed behind them, the whip snapping, and the lumbering of wheels. The two vehicles streamed down the Corso with the fireflies swirling behind them, regardless of protesting cries from other drivers.

But this time it was the berlin that flashed through the city gate and left Don Luis to the indignant welcome of the guard.

To have a lot of smoky lanterns poked into the coach and flashed over himself and his mistress until the whole carriage stank of tallow, of garlic and sour wine from the candid mouths of French conscripts

caused him positively to flow with profanity. He considered the incident to be a deadly insult. He began to recollect who he was and
"what" had caused it. He sent Sancho out to find where Anthony
and Vincent were staying. From midnight on, a smug little man
with grey whiskers watched the inn.

The berlin set out for the mountains about daybreak. It was followed a few hours later by the coach with four horses and two lead
mules that ate out of the Kitten's hand like tame rabbits. As usual
Don Luis had a plan, and, as usual, the plan was not entirely impractical.

Don Luis leaned back well pleased with it. Before they were over
the mountains he hoped in several directions to have solved for all
time his long standing and harassing domestic problems. It was still
foggy and he occasionally poked his head from the window to make
Sancho stop and listen for a carriage ahead. Behind him the wheel
tracks of the coach and berlin stretched out in lengthening parallel
lines.

Meanwhile the berlin, about ten miles ahead, had ascended out of
the fog and was rocking along at a steady trot with the jagged, snow-
glittering pinnacles of the confused, cloud-haunted Alps ahead and
the golden statue on the tip of the cathedral spire behind losing itself
rapidly in the blue sky with an occasional parting flash. The plains
of Lombardy far below were nothing but a smooth lake of mist, with
poplars on hilltops sticking up as if fishermen had staked out their
nets here and there in the placid sea. Just before nightfall the hearts
of all the travellers in the berlin were at once rested and uplifted by
the fantastically beautiful islands of Lake Maggiore springing from
water turquoise in the sunset and in the midst of archangelic scenery.

"Nothing in the world is so unbelievable as Isola Bella by moonlight," said Vincent as they left it behind after supper to push on to
Duomo d'Ossola at the foot of the pass. They arrived there with
tired horses towards midnight. Aristide insisted that there must be
ample rest for the animals before they began the ascent. "They will
be able to start tomorrow evening," he said. "That will give us full
daylight towards the summit. And the ascent par la clair de lune,
messieurs," he said—for he had soon discovered with joy that he
might just as well speak French as Italian to his friends and employ-
ers—"c'est merveilleux. I have seen it that way before, superbe,
ravissant, incomparable, virginal." Having paid the Alps the greatest
compliment possible in French, he went off to examine the shoes of
his horses, whistling in the half-frosty air.

Already the breath of the mountains had brought back to Anthony a feeling of light, boyish vigour that he had forgotten since some cold winters in Livorno years before. He began to enter fully now into Vincent's high spirits and Pujol's gayety, even to surpass them. He was in fact entering upon the long, sustaining vigour of ripened manhood verging toward its crest.

He stood out in the roadway that night at Duomo d'Ossola under the stars and the now preternaturally clear moon just beginning to wane but with its black markings clear as an etched plate, and listened to the rush and whisper of the snow-fed Ticino that filled the air with a continuous, low melody that came from no direction at all. The others had already gone indoors to find what cheer they might at that late hour. And as he stood there listening to the lonely voice of the mountains implicit in the snow water that forever fled away somewhere into the night, the mood of a great and yet a calm and serene exaltation fell upon him, lifting him out of himself and comforting him.

And it too had its own music that also came from nowhere.

Without effort, as if he were only a listener, began a magnificent concord of the abstractions of innumerable sounds. The voices of the great heights and ramping crevasses, of the snowy pinnacles glittering in moonlight uttered themselves through him, plucking from his heart-strings an inconceivably majestic and complicated harmony addressed to the stars and the black mountain sky beyond. The hymn died away at last with a soft, satisfactory, almost human melancholy, somehow exquisitely pleasurable as if the heights murmured regretfully now of their memories of past ages to the plains below.

It was a purely personal, an automatic, an incommunicable experience. It did not occur to him that some men attempted to set such things down. He knew nothing of staff and clef. "Music," he said, "go on." But the thing was not to be summoned. It occurred. All that he knew was that in that moment the meaning of the night enriched with all his past experiences of solitude, passion, grief, love, and joy had suddenly been transmuted for him and made understandable in the terms of sound.

There was no motif or prelude in this experience as there had been in that concord of wood sounds that he had heard as he looked at Anna that night, now ages past in Livorno, it seemed. His music tonight had been full, complete; devoid of weak longings and little regrets. It was the cry of his being at the full.

"Well, so let it be then for a while." He turned and followed the others into the inn.

"Tomorrow," he thought, just as he swung the door open, "we shall be going over the crest and on, down into France."

The osteria, or "hôtel" as it was now called, at Duomo d'Ossola was immemorial. Apparently the only change that had afflicted it since the elder Pliny had come that way gathering magical, Alpine plants was in the numbers and generations of its fleas. The hams and flitches of bacon hanging amid its rafters were contemporaneous with its ancient oaken beams, and as tough. But there was no doubt about their being well smoked. For the fireplace consisted of a great pile of stones large enough to roast a whole ox, over which a cave-like cupola of baked, red clay led upwards, presumably in the direction of several flues.

It was true that some smoke, on the principle that accidents will occasionally happen, escaped by this Gargantuan yet ridiculous chimney. But for the most part it lingered infernally and habitually about the shoulders and knuckles of hams, the leeks, the garlic, and the sooty bottles and crocks in basketry containers that perpetually threatened the guests who moved beneath them with a fatal rain of preserved-plenty should the roof ever collapse—a contingency not so remote as the landlady was disposed to think.

At night the sole light in this hell's-kitchen was from a small flame lost in the huge fireplace. About this, as Anthony entered, Vincent, Pujol, and Beppo were seated on three-legged stools. They were impatiently waiting while several sleepy and well-smoked girls and an old woman with complexions like the hams were attempting, with all of the usual clamour, lament, and confusion of primitive females trying to perform a simple domestic action—to scramble some eggs. All that was lacking was the eggs. Beppo had kindled the fire.

A long consultation in mountain dialect, an argument, an outburst of fury on the part of the oldest woman, a loud slap in the face for the youngest granddaughter—finally began to produce results. The older women climbed into a loft leaving the girl who had been slapped to do the honours. A hen under, or rather over, the delusion of raising a family was loudly disturbed in one corner by the slapped maiden and relieved of six of her prospective cares. These mixed with some herbs in a pan were put over the fire. But the hen proved to have been right after all.

It was Aristide who confirmed her. He had volunteered to take what he called les haruspices. He sputtered, holding his nose, and dumped the sacrifice out into the fire.

Frau Frank's hamper was now drawn upon and still proved itself triumphantly adequate. The girl, who had attempted the omelette, and who still sat wretchedly upon her stool, was invited to share in the cold sausage, bread and wine. She was soon not only comforted but by far the most amiable of the party. Rugs were spread upon some benches, Beppo flung himself upon the floor, and the party entered upon a gallant attempt to rest.

From his bench in a far corner Anthony watched the grotesque shadows leaping amid the rafters. The place was like a witches' brothel. In the centre on the stone "altar" by which the girl still sat with her unbraided elf-locks snaking about her face, the fire leaped fitfully, now flickering out into the darkness of the room with a smoky-yellow tongue and now licking the inflamed, sooty sides of its terra-cotta cavern when the draught veered up the chimney. From the benches where Vincent and Pujol were stretched out, and from the lean curs on the floor, arose occasional lightning movements denoting fleas stabbing home. Presently the daughter of the house got up and looked about her.

After considering the several benches deliberately, she walked quietly over to that upon which young Pujol was resting and began to climb in under his blankets.

A foot placed firmly on her stomach, and propelled forward by a vigorous straightening of the young man's knee, hurled her back toward the hearth, where she gracefully collapsed upon a stool and passed a few interesting moments trying to inhale. She then resumed her expression of rapt contemplation, finally arriving at the conclusion that apparently she had been repulsed.

Everyone in the room except the snoring Beppo was now watching her, secretly convulsed. After a while she got up again, rubbed her stomach, and obviously began to consider once more the now rather nice question of—"with what man shall this young woman sleep?"

"Love is a wonderful thing, Toni," whispered Vincent. "Did you keep your boots on? You may need them."

"Monsieur is jealous," hissed Pujol.

"*You* interfered with nature, Aristide," muttered Anthony.

These mutterings and groans not sounding inviting, the girl decided that the united opinion of the bench was against her. She made no appeal. She walked over and quietly inserted herself under the horse-blanket on the floor with Beppo. A few sleepy grunts of surprise, ending in a dying fall, and sighs of settling satisfaction showed that a delicate situation had been gratefully accepted by Beppo.

Nevertheless, the benches proved to be by no means lonely couches. Each traveller soon shared them with cohorts of fleas. In a short while a spirit seemed to move all three at the same time toward the inn yard. Here they met amid oaths and laughter to engage in a mutual hunt by lantern light. Beppo was either immune or was solaced beyond mere flea bites.

The berlin they found soaked with dew. They dragged some straw from the stables and spreading their rugs upon it again attempted to rest.   Looking up at the familiar northern stars, fresher and clearer against the black mountain sky than he had ever seen them before, in spite of the moon, Anthony finally counted himself to sleep by trying to number the infinite.

Perhaps it was unfortunate that he did so, for some time between midnight and morning Don Luis quietly passed through the village in the coach.

A few hours' rest farther down at Arona had apparently sufficed for Don Luis' horses.   He had guessed that the berlin would stop over at Duomo d'Ossola, most travellers did so, and he made sure of it by sending Sancho to have a quiet look at the inn yard.   There Sancho had not only seen the berlin empty, but its crew all laid out on straw in the moonlight like so many corpses.   He reported as much to his master, who nodded contentedly and drove on.   By daybreak the coach was miles ahead and making good time up the Val di Ticino toward the pass.

As he looked down onto the plains a little later, Don Luis was delighted to see a violent thunder-shower moving down the valley far below him and sweeping out toward Ossola with blowing arcs of rain.   He could have asked nothing more than that the tracks of the coach should be erased.   It had not occurred to him that they might be.   He had had to chance that, and now— This time, at least, the gods seemed to be with him.

He remarked to the Paleologus, who was sitting beside him, that it was raining in the valley.   It was the only general remark he had made to her since leaving Milan.   She acquiesced to the weather— and his opinions about it.   Otherwise their conversation was nil. Faith understood her position exactly.   Her rôle was not that of a talkative companion.

At Milan, in a renaissance of almost youthful bravado during this unexpected Indian-summer honeymoon it had been the noble marquis' whim to flaunt Faith before the world on the Corso as his mistress. For that he had bought her some astonishing costumes and jewels. She had carried them well.   She had carried it off with just the requisite amount of subdued impudence toward respectability and enough triumphant vulgarity to proclaim that she was his mistress and not a female relative.

In short, she had allowed herself with a cunning blatancy to be seen for exactly what she was, a handsome middle-aged harpy with something genuinely mysterious about her inherent in a look of suffering about her deep eyes and wide brows as if her daemon had led her through fiery landscapes looking for a rare incandescent blossom that she had never found.

Such was the mistress with whom, at the age of sixty-eight, Don Luis found solace, comfort, and an unexpected release for fires that still smouldered warmly under the hard, cool lava of his own exterior; fires that were still capable of darting forth in a subterranean pit flashes of yellow flame as if a deposit of sulphur had suddenly sublimed after having nearly boiled away.

Over the meeting of two such volcanic natures there was bound to be a certain amount of stench released which might possibly arouse the hostility of nose-holding neighbours ploughing in greener and more domestically-fertile, in less scoriac fields. Perhaps, that is one reason why such women as Faith invariably reek of perfume. She had chosen for hers a combination of musk and sweet-poppy that was slowly but surely overcoming the odour of stale Malacca snuff with which the coach had long stunk.

For stenches, moral or otherwise, Don Luis now cared very little, however. Indeed, he rather enjoyed their piquancy. He had found what he wanted, and, without any undue commotion, he intended to enjoy it before he died. An event, by the way, which still seemed remote to him.

In Italy, where he was now known in a few official quarters only, it had pleased him to be perfectly open about his affair after leaving Livorno. Going through France, and upon his return to Spain, he intended to be a little more circumspect; to let his new star dawn slowly upon his more intimate friends and relatives rather than to have it burst suddenly out of a cloud which might throw some of its shadow on him.

Sancho's suggestion had therefore been followed out and Faith was now dressed with a taste and restraint that might indicate a duenna being brought from Italy for the instruction of certain young grandnieces in Madrid. She had accepted this temporarily less glamorous rôle with alacrity and understanding.

It still permitted her to make Don Luis thoroughly comfortable wherever they went in a hundred small ways that he had never known or had long forgotten. He realized, now, that with great means he had long been living a kind of Spartan camp-life under the rather stern care of Sancho. In short, he had much needed a woman to look after him. Now he had found one who, without disturbing his thoughts or threatening any legal or social complications whatsoever, comforted the man. In personal service Faith was solicitous by day and ingenious at night. And it so happened that she was the only person in the world who could sympathize over Don Luis' past without at the same time wounding the proud marquis' honour.

The Paleologus on her part knew all this. She wanted security. In finding it in Don Luis she felt her cup ran over and she did not intend to drop it or spill it lightly. This was her last chance, and she played for it consummately. As they drove over the Simplon they were supremely well-pleased with each other.

Don Luis did not intend to have his plans interfered with a second time, particularly by the son of the man who had wrecked them before. He intended to put a final stop to trouble from that quarter. The trivial incident of the race on the Corso at Milan had outraged him beyond all ordinary imagining. He planned to act this time so that, whether he succeeded or not, no blame could attach to him. But he was now a little superstitious about Maria's son. He might fail. Experience had taught him that. If so, he determined to be still in a position to bide his time.

It was with these thoughts in his mind that he continued to ascend the pass as rapidly as his four horses and two mules could be persuaded to drag the coach toward the clouds.

The violent thunder-storm accompanied by pelting globes of hail had struck Duomo d'Ossola shortly after dawn and driven in the tired sleepers in the courtyard. They found an even more elemental disturbance going on inside. The old grandmother had descended early to get breakfast for the party and had stumbled over Beppo and her granddaughter as one object. When Anthony and the others rushed in shaking the hailstones and rain off their hats and clothes, she was beating her granddaughter with a convenient piece of firewood till the girl's ribs resounded. She had also just finished-off Beppo who was dazedly looking on from a far corner by the single light of his one, as yet, unclosed eye. The girl was now screaming more with terror than with pain, for it looked as if her grandmother meant to kill her. The dogs barked and howled, and the imprecations of the old woman rushed out of her mouth like the sound of the hail against the tiles.

Seeing that the gentlemen were not for murder before breakfast, she finally left-off to sink down exhausted, weeping by the ashes of her hearth fire. The girl, feeling her bruises and sobbing, attempted to rearrange the tattered remnants of her bodice which had been nearly clawed off. In this she was gallantly assisted by Pujol, who felt a genuine remorse for having brought this trouble upon her by his repulse of the night before.

"I should have sacrificed myself. As a Frenchman I should have managed it sans scandale," he assured Anthony. "Now look!" He pointed to the girl, the old woman, and Beppo all in misery.

Beppo it was plain would be of little use going over the pass. Both his eyes were now closed. For him the old woman had nothing but curses. She spat at him like a lynx when he blundered near.

"Now it is the fourth generation. *His* brat! I shall soon be having travellers driven away from the roof by its squalls. May the evil-eye wither your womb like a dried tripe, harlot, little bitch," she screamed, seizing her club again. The girl shivered. "Pig, stunted boar," she screeched at Beppo, waving her stick.

"Why don't you keep him on here, mother?" suggested Vincent.

"I have kept too many men in my time," said the woman. "What they want is a fire, a bed, and something to eat. The less they have to move on their feet after a while, the better they like it. Soon they are flabby and nothing but a mouth. The breasts of my mercy for them are dry."

"But this fellow is a vetturino and you need one about an inn like this. We already owe him a hundred soldi and we will leave him as much more for the girl's dot. That is something, isn't it?"

The old woman still muttered but sat considering.

Beppo groaned.

"Make it two hundred, Vincent," added Anthony. "I will go half."

"Two hundred soldi," said Vincent reluctantly.

"That is something," admitted the old woman. "I need a horse, too . . ."

"Otherwise we shall just take him and drive on," said Vincent.

"Three hundred soldi, altogether?" asked the crone looking up.

"Si," murmured Beppo, "my wages, too."

The old woman clucked with her gums. "Come here, girl," she said at last. "Get down the dog-grease and set your betrothed to work on your back. He might as well learn now how to salve a morning's beating so you can get breakfast."

The swollen-eyed Beppo without further comment began to rub the dog-grease into his future wife's back. Secretly he was well satisfied, but he did not intend to admit it. His had been, he thought, an excellent night's work. The woman in Florence could shift for herself now. Well, he wasn't married to her. What did she expect?

Pujol was delighted. There would be one less man to haul over the mountains. Vincent had been quick at getting off for less than it would have cost to keep the useless Beppo in France. Anthony felt he had assisted at making peace. Breakfast such as it was passed off well enough.

Pujol was ready to start earlier with a lightened load. As soon as the roads ceased to be torrents he gave notice of harnessing up. The storm rumbled on into the plains behind. The old woman sat counting over her three hundred soldi by the rekindled fire.

No one would have recognized her as Lucia, the kindly, pleasant maid of Maria Bonnyfeather less than thirty years before. In that time she had had three husbands and thirteen children. The inn at Ossola she had bought with the last of Don Luis' gold pieces after much wandering about amid Swiss villages in the Italian cantons. She had no more idea who Anthony was than why the French had eaten her out of house and home the year before and given her only paper money. As she attempted to bite some of the more doubtful looking soldi she regretted her teeth. She put aside one soldo. It was to send to her first husband's cousin to put edelweiss on Maria's sunken grave. No soldo, no edelweiss; she knew the Swiss. Now that her little slut of a granddaughter had a man she would take these soldi and go back to Tuscany. She would like to be buried where the sun was warm. Holy mother, the snow in these mountains! It gave her bones the shivers. And that little fool would have given herself away just for the fun of it. But what was to be expected, with soldiers about the place the whole year before? She would leave the happy couple—her blessing. She wrapped a few yellow-grey locks about a peg of a comb that seemed to be fixed in her skull, scoured her sooty face off with the under-side of her second petticoat and went to the door to watch the berlin start.

"How do you suppose people ever come to be as horrible as these?" asked Anthony, looking about for the last time at Duomo d'Ossola and its inn.

"It's their own fault," grumbled Vincent comfortably. "They don't have to be here. Just bad human nature, I suppose."

"Perhaps," replied Anthony, unaware that the reason he was sitting in the luxurious little berlin was because Don Luis had decided not to let him stay on the knees of the filthy old woman peering out of the door and trying to curtsy to him as well as her lumbago would permit. "But I suppose fate does have something to do with it."

"Not much, Toni. It's what a man does for himself that makes him what he is. What can you expect of these people though? Look at those two brats there, for instance."

Two half-naked boys were peering at the varnished doors of the berlin which reflected their delighted grimaces.

The view which included a number of lean, rooting sows was certainly not encouraging. From every crazy balcony with a tottering stairway rotting up to it, from every eccentric hovel along the street,—terrific scarecrows male and female, gaunt and starved faces, rheumy-eyed and goitred carlines and fearfully-peaked children could be glimpsed gathered to see the rich travellers leave. The bolder or more desperate beggars were also gathering.

"I am starving, signore. The soldiers have left nothing." . . . "Signore, I want something to eat. I tell you I am hungry, my belly grinds." . . . "I fought for the Austrians—and now look," said an old soldier revealing a seethed stump. "Dear and very charitable milords of England, I have a dislocated hip," drooled an old woman. And she had. "Dear and very charitable milords, rich and gracious signori, my hip has kept me in hell for twenty years. My hip, sweet and kindly signori, for the love of God and his saints, signori, my poor old hip. I can neither lie, stand, nor sit, signori. I am hungry and in great pain. It is true." Her palsied hand slid into the window, shaking, and gnarled as a griffin's paw—"My hip, milords of England, rich and high-born gentlemen of God, my poor old hip, my hip . . ."

"Get on, Pujol, you rascal," roared Vincent. "Never mind that little buckle."

The babble for alms grew threatening and clamorous. They were forced to throw out some small coins to get the horses through the mewing mob.

"God bless you," screamed old Lucia, secure in her soldi. The beggars scrambled and cursed. The berlin strained forward through the mud. Children ran up the street after it holding out their hands and screaming. One persistent little urchin who raced with them half a mile finally got a coin the size of his little toe nail.

"Farewell!" he shouted with his last breath, and collapsed by the roadside clutching the picaillon.

"That is the last of Italy," said Vincent. "Why, Toni, what's the matter? You look pale."

"It's the high air I guess," replied Anthony, and looked out of the window at the incredible mountains just ahead.

The last of the Italian hamlets was left behind as they started upward more noticeably. Soon they could look back at miles of little villages apparently asleep in the warm sunlight below. The sound of cow bells ceased. The roar of the snow rivers became louder. They climbed up a slanting plateau through an inferno of wind-tortured trees which were already shedding their leaves. Already it was noticeably colder. Remnants of the morning hail-storm glittered along the roads and in tree boles like fresh-broken glass. The wink from these beds of scattered diamonds answered the blink from the snow-fields above. The breath of the horses became faintly visible.

Now the way pitched upward violently. All roads travelled before seemed to have been level. They were dragged through a region of bare rocks, pebbles, and boulder-débris where the horses panted and struggled. The angry tumult of a river suddenly leapt myriad-voiced out of the earth. The road became a skidding track along the edge of a gorge filled with mad, rushing froth and uptossed arms of spray hundreds of feet below. They crossed the torrent on a new bridge over its raving water and struck into the living stone of the mountain between two walls of rock.

It was a mere cleft with the daylight leaking down greyly as if through a crack in a vault overhead. Even the gloom failed them as they headed for a cavern where their voices and the sound of the struggling hoofs were lost completely in the subterranean thunder of a cataract that hurled itself close by into an invisible cleft. Only the weight of the water could be felt making the earth shudder. The mist rose before the mouth of this newly-pierced tunnel in spectral veils. It coated the leather of the cushions and their clothes with pearls of moisture as they entered its darkness lit only by the foggy rays of the lanterns. Here the road took its upward way along a cliff with the river bellowing a sheer quarter of a mile below.

They spun out of this cave into full day to cross over another dizzy bridge. The road contorted up and up through the fierce barbaric gorge of Gondo overshadowed by black-fronted terraces and the smooth lowering foreheads of precipices that put their heads close together a thousand feet above as if plotting some overwhelming mischief while throwing cyclopean gloom and staggering shadows along perpendicular miles.

"You should have seen this by moonlight," shouted Aristide, while he breathed the horses. "That is a real test of driving. The pass is not what it used to be. The work of the French engineers has already made a great difference."

But Anthony was glad they had come by day after all. There was still plenty of opportunity for Aristide to prove his skill in tooling along the horses. And the grandeur of full light on the infinite view was beyond all expression and experience.

They were ascending the last rugged ravines of the pass, now overlooking planetary wastes of black rock; peering down valleys floored with clouds that opened suddenly to reveal further eagle-haunted wells of space full of clear, slippery air with toy villages in a lake of sunlight at the bottom. Yet they were still looking up at Gargantuan heights over smooth, rosy snow-fields lying in the wrinkled patterns of hollows and crevasses. And from these half-frozen beds of moisture torrents slipped away to foam down the faces of cliffs. They leaped sheerly into nothing, hanging in tremendous sliding beards of water that smoked into pointed, swaying clouds of vapour still unsupported a mile below.

Here and there the arcs of more distant waterfalls glittered like the bow of promise, and directly above and beyond them, filling the whole moon-like landscape with a reduplicated bellowing roar, the main stream of the Gondo took at one leap the abyss out of which for many hours they had now been climbing.

It was frequently necessary to breathe the horses now. It was piercingly cold. They walked often beside the berlin both to ease the beasts and to keep warm. Their red mufflers floated out behind them in a keen, icy blast that howled and shuddered. The bronze vine against the blue leather of the carriage was now etched in white frost. Despite the great altitude and the difficulty of breathing which they stopped often to overcome, they were exhilarated, intoxicated by infinity below and around them and by the crisp, clean lightness of the frosty air. They shouted with pigmy voices and sang. The impalpable glaze of some infinitely thin but slightly opaque substance seemed to have been lifted from their eyes and brains, permitting sight and feeling to become utterly clear. A hitherto unnoticed weight was gone from their shoulders.

Towards the middle of the afternoon they emerged upon the smooth snow-field at the summit of the pass, scurrying with wreaths and wraiths of snow. Here the wheels sank into the drifts and the horses floundered.

The French were building a hospice a short distance beyond. Black figures gathered like numbed bees in the snow about the already frozen foundations.

"Winter has set in a month early up here," said a young corporal who approached them and examined their papers before one of several timbered huts whose chimneys smoked invitingly. "We will give you a lift over the crest. The first shelter for the night is about five miles below. The engineers for the new road are staying there. You will find good company and wine. The first consul is impatient—'le canon quand passera-t-il le Simplon?' he keeps asking, they say. Now there is a man who makes things go. All marches when he but speaks."

They went into one of the shelters for some brandy and warmth while a team of oxen with old army blankets on them was being driven up and hooked to the pole of the berlin. Then they set out for the last haul through the drifts up to the crest marked by a rude, wooden cross.

Neither Vincent nor Anthony spoke as they trudged up the final slope in the track broken by the carriage. Already the western lights were beginning to redden. Over the plains of Lombardy the thunderstorm of the morning had grown into a vast, rolling cloud-pall washing against the domed fronts of the Apennines. It was a sea of ink clouded with silver. From it, at a seemingly infinite distance, the rays of the sun were dashed back onto the snows of the summits with infernal tinges of red that turned them violet. Here and there long pencils of light searched down into red, lighted patches of the valley floor streaked with silver rivers, infinitely, unutterably far, and sheerly below.

Towards the arc of the crest the titanic skyline of the Alpine ranges with snowy domes, with the sheer, wind-fretted needles of superior peaks, began to dawn upon them as they raised the view into Switzerland beyond.

They stood for some time on the ridge of one of the world's high gables, just where the track passed the rude cross of the ridge itself, and looked about them.

"That," said Vincent, "is France down there." He pointed westward as though towards the plains of another planet that appeared in a dim golden haze beyond a riot of peaks where the earth dipped away into nothing.

Anthony looked eagerly. He was seeing the world at last. This was the top of the tree of life again. Below in the golden haze was the great courtyard.

It was their whim to ride over the crest. They went back a little and climbed into the berlin from which the oxen were now unyoked and standing with their breath blowing out beyond them like patient, fiery monsters stalled in the snow. The nostrils of the horses smoked too while their coats steamed faintly.

"You will find it not such bad going from here down," said the sous-officier. "The snow is less on the other side just now, and then— it *is* going down. Merci, merci bien, messieurs." He threw up his hand in farewell.

"Allons," shouted Pujol.

The horses plunged forward through the snow, seeming to know that relief was just ahead. The berlin came to the crest, slanted, and began to slide downward on the other side of the pass.

CHAPTER FIFTY-THREE

THE FORCE OF GRAVITY

TRAVELLERS who have been ascending a mountain in a carriage and have long felt the force of gravity pulling against them are invariably surprised and relieved when they finally top the crest and begin to roll down the other slope, aided instead of hindered. They now have the impression of being personally favoured by a new and friendly power after having overcome the unreasonable opposition of the old. That this impression is unconsciously taken for granted by them is only to say that it is the more profound. Then, to this fundamental feeling of release and relief is immediately added speed; speed, which confers an added illusion of freedom and power.

It was certainly so with the passengers of the berlin. Their sudden access of good spirits upon topping the pass lasted them half-way down the first descent. The night spent in the company of the French engineers near the crest did nothing to take the edge off their exhilaration; quite the contrary. But they were no longer so impressed by the tremendous height. It had become external. Their passage next morning through the new, arched ways under the glaciers, where icicles hung like dripping stalactites, became merely a novelty, an adventure in the realm of ice. The galleries of shelter for voiding avalanches were only a clever convenience whose pillars threw amusing effects of swiftly alternating light and shade into the berlin. The brakes seemed to be answering the nasal twang of the detachments of General Turreau's sapeurs doing their best to make the way smooth for cannon before winter came. With these ragged soldiers lately detached from the Army of the Rhine Pujol exchanged a hundred carnal remarks about their scarecrow appearance. Remarks which, as it proved later, were to be remembered against him. But nothing could now dampen the high spirits of the young Aristide, a Frenchman returning to France.

Below the regions of snow the road had been temporarily completed, and they no longer met any troops. They met with no one at all. Perhaps it was for that reason that they gradually became more silent as the day wore on and they began to realize the berlin as nothing but a small fly-like object crawling over precarious bridges, down the sheer faces of granite cliffs, and through the twilight of horrible ravines toward the gorge of the Saltine, which roared louder and ever more ominously below.

They could only hear the river. The gorge was covered by a stagnant, grey cloud that seemed to have taken refuge there from the wind which continually ravelled away one end of it, where it extended out into the clear area of the lower valley. As they descended into the cloud's upper mists the day gradually became darker, and in the gorge itself the white river whirled and swayed downward over its riven blocks and boulders to disappear in the twilight beyond as if it would lure those who followed the road along its banks to inevitable destruction.

The cloud, which had been a grey floor from above, was, seen from below, a dark, glimmering ceiling leaking and dripping a kind of pearly rain into the canyon. And this misty-drift was also flowing downward toward the mouth of the gorge, draping the bold escarpments and Gothic rock pinnacles with funereal scarves of strangely glowing mist. A more gloomy and purgatorial vista could scarcely be imagined. And it was all the more impressive and depressing to those in the berlin, who were suddenly plunged into it as though they had been flung into a limbo where darkness was hiding, because they knew that above and below them the snowy mountains and the green valleys were still bathed in cheerful light.

The adventure which overtook the berlin in the gloomy gorge of the Saltine always seemed to Anthony to have happened in a dream. That it came suddenly, was fatal, and occurred apparently for no reason at all, only enhanced its nightmare quality. There were even certain grotesqueries about it.

Anthony left the berlin to answer a call of nature. It was just where the new road made a sharp turn around a shoulder with another sheer face of rock some little distance ahead. He was forced to climb a small hillock for the sake of privacy, and as he sat in that semi-contemplative frame of mind peculiar to certain occasions he happened to notice that the old road had formerly swung inward behind the hillock just ahead of where the berlin was waiting. Presently he started to return to the carriage that way.

The short stretch of abandoned road had only one set of wheel ruts on it. They were made by broad, firm tires like those of an artillery caisson. A number of horses, at least four, he casually noted, perhaps more . . .

He happened to glance away from the river and up the old road. He saw the wheel tracks led straight into the face of a small rise in that direction. His curiosity was aroused. Since Africa a trail meant something to him—and here was a manifest impossibility.

Sheerly on the impulse of the moment he followed the old road for a few yards and came to a face of shaly rubble where, whatever-it-was, and six horses, had driven into the hill.

There could be no doubt about it. There was no room here to turn and the thing had not backed out. The hoof marks all led one way. They, and the broad, heavy wheel lines went directly up to a twenty-foot embankment—and continued into it. It looked as if something infernal had concluded just at this point to go home. In the Plutonian scenery of the dark gorge that conclusion did not seem so unreasonable. For a minute he stood nonplussed. He kicked some of the shale aside and saw that the wheel tracks did continue into it. A small slide followed the motion of his foot. It grew. A miniature avalanche of stone and earth followed He leaped aside to avoid it

Doubtless *that* was why the engineers had driven the new road into the solid cliff face around the turn just ahead of where the berlin was waiting. The old route was a short-cut, but through precarious ground.

He wondered if "whatever-it-was" had pulled through that slide of shale . . . if Faith and Don Luis were sitting inside the hill there, covered up, coach and all, with tons of rock. He had not thought of the coach since leaving Milan but he now knew that he was looking at its trail, a trail that led fearsomely into the heart of a hill.

Lord, how unreasonable his imagination was! It gave him the creeps to think of those two sitting in there in the darkness, forever—and yet he hoped they were. He hoped they were, with everything that was in him; walled-in; thoroughly checked for good and all. No more driving about. That coach, he knew it now, had been bound upon some vast mischief. "Let loose," was the phrase, "let loose." And now it was walled-in. Hurrah!

But was it?

Instantly he was made cautious by that thought. "It might have gone through." He laughed at himself. The problem became a practical one. *"Got* through," he meant. "Let's see——"

With considerable caution in order to avoid starting any more slides, he climbed from rock to rock over the mass of débris across the old road. The wheel marks continued on the other side of it. "Too bad!"—but they did go on——

For about a hundred yards along a kind of deep rut that went down just ahead through a "V"-shaped opening between rocks. That slide must have just missed them as they passed. He felt sure of it—had *just* missed them. Why had they turned in this way? Why?

He ran along the sunken road, crouching, and suddenly found himself looking out into an empty, misty space just ahead.

The old road now dipped down violently. The wheel marks here were deep, fresh! He climbed up behind a big boulder and looked down.

The coach-and-six—so he was right about that—the coach-and-six was standing on a good-sized mound about a hundred feet below him and only a giant's stone-throw away. All the horses and mules were harnessed. Someone wrapped in a cloak was dozing on the box. The horses' heads were hanging, but all pointing down toward the new road along the edge of the gorge. The thing was waiting there in the twilight, every line of it—waiting.

Anthony looked about him carefully. Someone must be on watch, he thought. He had no doubt now that little Beppo was right. Don Luis *had* dashed out on the berlin purposely at Livorno. They must have been waiting there in that alley. It was to have been an "accident." And now they were waiting here in a titanic alley, nature's own; and they had the berlin in a magnificent trap. He could see it all at a glance. The whole scheme lay below him laid out on a chessboard. "Coach to move and check berlin"—for good and all. He wiped his forehead. For the first time he understood fully what the hatred of Don Luis meant. That man and Faith were sitting down there in the infernal, cloudy twilight of the gorge, waiting.

A skein of mist detached itself from a sharp rock-needle and lengthened out, slowly stretching downward. It drifted quietly through the dark, open windows of the coach. While it did so he stood spell-bound.

The mound on which the coach stood was the height of ground in a boulder-strewn amphitheatre several acres in area indenting one side of the gorge. The new road swung into it suddenly, coming downstream around a bald shoulder of granite. It then continued directly along the edge of the gorge. There was no wall along the edge yet. Not even a rail. It went off sheer. From the depth below small clouds and mist were rising. The river, by its distant roar, must be a quarter of a mile away—down.

Anthony smiled grimly. All that the coach had to do was to dash down from the mound onto the berlin when it came around the bend. The "angle of incidence," he told himself, had been nicely calculated. The vehicle on the inner track was bound to win. The berlin would certainly be forced into the gorge.

Just then he heard Vincent and Pujol calling him.

A whistle immediately came from the granite shoulder just above the road. "So that was where they were watching!" The man on the box of the coach came-to with a start and gathered up the reins. Even the horses were listening.

Anthony turned and dodged back along the old road, keeping low. He had been gone about ten minutes. He slithered down over the débris and came out upon the berlin. Pujol and Vincent were now bawling for him lustily. His expression was enough to silence them instantly.

"Have you seen a wolf?" began Vincent.

"Worse," said Anthony, and rapidly outlined the trap ahead. He drew the scheme of it in the road for Pujol, who looked at it calmly. Anthony hoped for a suggestion from Vincent. But the practical man of affairs had now nothing to say.

"You have pistols, monsieur?" asked Pujol.

Anthony nodded.

"We might go up and get that fellow on watch. M. Vincent can guard the carriage here." Pujol smiled at Anthony.

"*I* am ready to go, too," said Vincent, getting out firmly but very pale.

"It won't do, Pujol. That fellow up there on the rock will see us coming and bring the others down on us. I had thought of that," replied Anthony.

Vincent got in the berlin again—rather hastily.

"I know!" said Pujol. His face beamed. "Look here!"

He dragged Anthony over and showed him a cotter-pin through the end of the shaft-pole. It had a ring in it. "There is a little catch underneath," said Pujol, "that holds it in. We can remove that and tie a spare rein through the ring. Pull it, and the horses go forward harness and all leaving the carriage behind. You pull the pin and put on the brakes. I will ride the lead horse. Do you see? It is the coach that will go over—in between. Right *through* us." Pujol waved his hands.

"Good for you, Aristide," said Anthony.

They set to work frantically. The little catch was pulled out; the rein fastened through the ring.

"What are you doing?" said Vincent. They paid no attention to him. Anthony was talking swiftly to Pujol.

"They only heard you calling," he said, climbing onto the box while Pujol prepared to mount the left lead horse. "They can't see us for about fifty yards yet; not till we get clear of this hill. Then it is about two hundred more around the turn, a very sharp one, mind. I suppose the signal for bringing the coach down on us will be a shot—to make us look the wrong way. *Don't look back.* I'll shout when I pull out the pin. Gallop on. Don't let the horses stumble when they jerk loose, mind that. Ready?"

"If you fellows . . ." said Vincent sticking his head out.

"Go," shouted Anthony.

Vincent was thrown against the back seat violently. The berlin tore down the road. "I might have left Vincent out of this," thought Anthony, "but—" He heard a pistol shot overhead. They began to take the curve.

"Much, much too fast, Pujol," muttered Anthony. He was pale

enough himself now. The berlin began to slide toward the edge.
The horses ahead swung around the curve. He checked the little
carriage with the brakes. It swung; it almost pivoted. The right
rear wheel glittered in space. For a fractional instant it spun free.
There was a bump, and the berlin hurtled on.

Inside, Vincent swallowed his lights. A pistol which he had taken
out dropped from his hand. The berlin was tearing along the edge
of the gorge out of which the mist rose. Into this home of clouds
Vincent vomited.

With one hand on the brakes and the other on the rein to the cotter-
pin, Anthony looked back and saw the coach coming down from the
mound. The Kitten was driving standing up. He had not expected the berlin to come around the curve at a mad gallop, and he
was lashing his horses. He expected to strike the berlin a glancing
blow while moving on an inner circle, and then to sheer off and in.
It looked easy—and it would have been. But now in order to catch
the berlin at just the right point the coach must itself come headlong
down the little hill. Much faster than Don Luis had intended.

It was doing that. The Kitten seemed to have gone mad.

The clatter of twenty-four hoofs, and the heavy wheels rushing
over the stony ground to his left burst upon Anthony's ears above
the roar of the cataract below on the right. He looked—shouted—
and pulled the pin. He clamped down the brakes. He was nearly
thrown off.

A space had instantly appeared between the berlin and its four
horses that were now galloping frantically down the road ahead, dragging the thrashing pole and tangled traces after them.

Through the clear interval just ahead of where the berlin had come
to a violent stop the huge, black coach and its six beasts rocketed off
into the cloudy gorge.

It made an almost complete circle in empty air.

The Kitten had tried to swerve. He had pulled the lead mules
around violently. But the coach had gone on; swung its three teams
like a whip lash, and snapped them off the road.

Those brief instants had seemed long. The Kitten was still standing up when he went down. The last thing Anthony saw was the
two mules trying to gallop in. They fell scrambling. Their faces,
their long, writhing lips, white teeth and eyes went over the brink.
The worst thing was the faces of the two mules. They had understood. . . .

From the gorge not a sound came back. It was some seconds
before Anthony realized that he was sitting listening intently, waiting
for a crash that would never be heard.

At last he stood up on the top of the berlin and looked about him.

It was only now that he fully realized what the stratagem had implied —death. He took it for granted that Don Luis and Faith were both down there in the gorge of the Saltine. He was not glad of it now, and yet he could not be sorry. It did not seem to him that he had done wrong.

Down the road Pujol put in an appearance coming back with the horses, which had galloped far before he could check them. He knew what Pujol would say, "Voilà, monsieur; allons nous en."—And they would go on. He started to climb down.

"Vincent . . ."

Just then he heard someone laughing.

It was Faith Paleologus.

She and Don Luis were standing up there on the mound looking down at the berlin. They were only a short distance away. Sancho was sitting at Don Luis' feet and rocking himself to and fro. His master had put his hand on his head. Echoed from the rock faces of the cloudy amphitheatre, the cool feminine laughter was reduplicated unbearably as if the gloomy, sardonic spirit of the gorge were holding its sides over this chef-d'œuvre of a jest.

And to Faith, there *was* something enormously humorous about the disappearance of the coach. Don Luis' plans had been *so* well laid. The Kitten was *so* sure of himself—and suddenly gravity had taken charge, flicked the coach off the earth and left them all standing there with Pujol racing on down the road like a madman. The horseless berlin with Anthony standing up on it looked exquisitely helpless and silly. How surprised the Kitten must have been —that sure little fool-of-a-man. *Flick*—and he was gone, mules and all. She had had to lean up against a rock to contain herself. She was sorry Don Luis had lost; and she was glad Anthony had won. So contradictory a rush of emotion demanded laughter or tears even from her. It was overwhelming. She must make a noise. She began to choke——

"My morocco notebook is gone," said Don Luis childishly, in a tone of voice that might have announced the fall of Rome.

Faith had instantly become a machine for laughter.

"Taissez vous," growled Don Luis after a while. Her curious half-hysteria was a little catching even to him. "Sancho here has lost his son. They are a family which has served mine for generations."

"The last, señor," whispered Sancho. "Gone?"—he waved toward the river as though he could not believe it.

"I'll take the whip to you, madame," said Don Luis fiercely.

"Gone!" said Faith, and went off again.

It was true. There was no whip. The coach which carried it had gone—the coach had gone! He realized it now, fully.

"Fetch me a club, Sancho," roared Don Luis.

"There are nothing but rocks here. Little ones," whined Sancho. The tears that streamed down his face were for his son. He sobbed and picked up a handful of pebbles.

"Hell's-devils!" rapped out Don Luis—and burst out laughing, too. The coach had gone; he and Faith remained. In that laughter they were married.

"You didn't think I would be such a fool as to sit in it, too?" he asked, taking her by the hand almost sympathetically.

"No, no," she replied. "I never thought that! I wasn't laughing at *you*."

"No, at the other thing," he said satisfied. "Well, it does interfere sometimes."

She nodded.

They watched Pujol fastening the pole onto the berlin again.

"Not so bad," admitted Don Luis grudgingly.

"*Very* good," said Faith.

He nodded.

Anthony picked his hat off the ground. He hesitated a moment before clapping it on again. Then he made a flourish toward the mound, and pointed toward the berlin with it.

"Do you want to go down in *that?*" said Don Luis, turning to Faith. "We might, you know."

"No," she said.

Don Luis took off his hat and bowed his refusal.

The young man below replied. He put on his hat and climbed into the berlin.

"That particular incident is closed," said Don Luis. "Now how the devil are we going to get down the mountain?"

In the distance the berlin trotted around the next rock shoulder, going down.

Vincent was really in a bad way, Anthony discovered as soon as he climbed into the carriage. He simply could not forgive himself for having shown the white-feather. He insisted that he had. It was painful. Besides that he was really physically ill. They stopped frequently while he got out.

He felt better when they emerged into the sunlight of the valley below but Anthony could see that the shadow of the gorge still lay between them.

"I want to talk to you, tonight, Vincent," he said.

"Oh, do you still want to?" asked Vincent.

"Why, of course. Do you suppose I have no sympathy for any other way of feeling but my own? Now it won't do to have you suspecting me of despising you. Don't be ridiculous. Buck up."

It was better after that. They hurried on through several villages in the upper reaches of the valley. Anthony was determined to out-distance Don Luis completely now. Doubtless one of the army wagons would pick them up. A work detachment came down every evening. It would never do to find himself in the same inn with him. But, my word, it would be cold up there this evening. He wondered what they *would* do.

They came to the last part of the descent, a series of zigzag roads down a succession of terraces that towered above and slipped away into nothing below. And beyond that—soft, warm weather; a valley glittering gold and green with pastures and wheat-fields; the bronze, yellow, and copper-covered domes and spires of a Swiss town.

Here they put the tired, strained horses in a comfortable post stable, Pujol, tired as he was, saw them all rubbed down before he came in to join Anthony in the hospitality of a genuinely civilized little resort.

There was a party of Protestant merchants from Geneva who had driven over to spend the last of the summer. Anthony thought he had never seen such extremely decent people. They were more im-peccable than the most respectable English and seemed to belong to no class. "Freemen," he thought. The place was spotless, supper delicious, everybody spoke French and there were no beggars. For the first time in his life he ate fresh, unsalted butter and saw thick cream. Vincent, poor devil, had gone to bed. "My, what he is missing!" he thought. There were some pretty good things in Europe after all—de la crême, par exemple,—and——

He went out whistling, and looked up at the Gargantuan barrier over which by some miracle he had come to this clean, fresh, civilized, warmly-human little hotel. His whistle died away. The contrast seemed a little ridiculous—but good. Perhaps he was revelling a little too much in it. Faith and Don Luis up there nearer the glaciers might be spared this sense of ant-like smallness tonight. They might be finding themselves in a place more fitting to their souls than their bodies. There was something tremendous about them, he felt. "Equals of mine, of a different kind. My opposites, but equals. We have met, and passed. What next? No, I am not flattering myself. There is no one to hear. And I know myself now. I too might have gone down standing up. I am grateful. Do *You* hear? *I* am grateful."

And he ran his eye up the vaulting terraces only a few miles away. He threw back his head to look up the smooth, snowy slopes. He bent his neck back to see the huge, glittering peaks and pinnacles up there glistening amid the glittering stars. Such things as these also were in Europe.

Somewhere along a mountain road half-way up the barrier, like a spark crawling imperceptibly down a wall of sheer darkness, descended a tiny, winking light.

He watched it for some moments, thinking. Then he turned out of the chill, clear night to go in. A light was also shining in Vincent's window. He was waiting for him then.

Anthony meant to have a good talk with his friend tonight. To unburden his heart. He meant to tell him how he had set out over the mountains with a certain ideal in his heart, an ideal that had been reinforced by that experience at Pisa. How he meant to try to grow in the grace that had been Brother François's until he could return good for evil—and how he had carried out that resolution by causing the death of a man and six helpless beasts. And his friend had thought that he would despise him because he, Vincent, was not capable of great physical courage. Why was it that Vincent had always looked up to him; had in most things been Anthony's follower even when they were boys? It was true. Now, if their friendship was to endure, Vincent must know how and where Anthony had failed— and failed time after time. He would tell him that. He would tell him how he had failed in Africa. Vincent was not the only one who faltered and grew ill on high and dizzy roads—not by a long shot!

He opened the door of the room and saw that his friend had been waiting for him anxiously. The room was bright with candles. Vincent looked up from the bed, where he lay still rather pale, to give him a delighted and relieved smile.

"I heard you whistling in the garden and I thought you might have forgotten," he said.

"No, no!" He felt a little awkward and was at a loss how to begin.

An old charwoman in a spotless, frilled cap and glistening wooden shoes came in and made the fire. She gave them both a cheery good night. It was easier now. They seemed at home when she had gone.

And so they talked well into the night. They talked about everything with all the windows and doors of their spirits open. They passed in and out and saw each other's dwelling houses with no locked rooms.

"—And I think," said Vincent, "that under certain kinds of trials I too could be courageous. In fact, I know I could. And I am sorry that I was annoyed over the berlin, because you were smarter than I was about it and made a lovely, swift thing when I could see nothing but old bones. Do you know that I have been taking it out on you all the way from Livorno in a hundred little ways? I felt it necessary to be superior—Mein Gott! I was—jealous!"

"Why, do you know I must have been insufferable about the berlin myself, Vincent. And the funny part about it is I meant all the time to give it to you. I was going to wait till Paris. You remember I laughed when you said, 'There is something in the latest mode,' that day at Livorno when Terrini brought it around. Well, I thought then of your calling on M. Ouvrard in it; how surprised you would be when you knew it was yours. Then I began to like it *so* well. Oh, well, you see how it was. But there—the berlin belongs now to Herr Vincent Nolte."

"Ach, mein lieber freund," said Vincent, his eyes shining. "Es ist für ewigkeit."

"Ja wohl," said Anthony and laughed happily as he went out.

"Toni," Vincent called after him in a stage-whisper as he went down the hall to his own room, "I did forget to tell you something." The plump German face of Herr Nolte peering through the half-opened door looked very red under the flannel night-cap. But it was very serious.

"What?"

"I was thinking of getting married myself." The door closed almost violently.

And so the Alps were crossed.

CHAPTER FIFTY-FOUR

THE PLAINS OF FRANCE

OUT of Switzerland, through a canton where all the women wore round fur caps even in September, as if the country were garrisoned by shakoed regiments of females, they trotted down to Vevey along the metallically smooth reaches of Lake Leman. Then, leaving the miniature villages of chalets clustered behind them at the feet of mountains, they pushed on to Fribourg.

St. Peter, standing there in the public square with a key so large—"that the lock which it fits has to be opened by gunpowder," said Vincent, did not detain them long.

The disconcertingly rickety bridges over mountain torrents, the steep downward slope of the snow-thatched roof of the world were now left behind.

Toward Bâle the road meandered playfully and without much reason from one village to another. The women here, even the little girls, wore broad white stomachers with small aprons, fan-shaped hats prinked out of white gauze. The old men stood smoking large white pipes before very small inns. Every house had its thatch descending in low overhanging eaves over pointed windows set with round panes like bottle-ends, and each seemed to be the cottage in the wood to which the ogre lured children with candy. Only the ogres were gone while the fair-haired children remained. "Plainly, this is the toyland of my German nursery books," mused Vincent. "The forest has been cut away and left the villages exposed. Any person can see that." And he was much pleased by the fancy.

Everything pleased them mightily now. They moved in an amber haze of enjoyment somewhat heightened by a conscientious sampling of the various brews and vintages of the several neighbourhoods through which they successively passed.

"I think the horses are thirsty again, Aristide," Anthony would say.

"Oui, monsieur, ils souffrent. Ils s'en mordront les pouces."

So they would all get out, to let the horses drink, until the surfeited beasts dipping their soft noses in sparkling pails would only wrinkle their lips a little in the water and stamp with surprise at so much damp solicitude.

As they went down the valley both the brews and vintages grew better. "Wine rises to its peak in Burgundy and beer foams to its crest in Bavaria," quoted Vincent. "The spirits of the right and left bank thus rival each other in a balance of excellence. Along this route one can enjoy both sides at the same time." But for all that Anthony noticed that Vincent stuck to beer rather closely and he to wine. And this was now the most serious difference between them. "Toyland" seemed by a natural transition to extend itself into an elfin country that they passed through by night going on into the early morning hours. It was the tumbled landscape of the Jura Mountains, or rather hills, for they seemed nothing more than that after what lay behind. But they were musical with waterfalls under the late remnant of the moon, pines and crags faëry with September mists. And so on to the famous hostelry of the "Three Kings" at Bâle, where the Rhine ran green and clear under its windows; as yet unmuddied by the long expected autumn rains.

At Mulhouse they were both moved to get on faster. Leaving their own horses behind them to be brought up by easy stages, they hired post and galloped down through Colmar to Strasbourg with fresh relays every few miles. Aristide sat in the berlin now enjoying himself beyond measure.

If he was not the soul he was at least the wit of the party, and he knew how to argue them past the columns of French troops along the Rhine roads till even the wagoners let them go by with a grin. Here began a second foretaste of that song of bugles that grew into a swelling chorus as they continued down into France until the very spirit of the land seemed to be giving tongue and to be loosing its silver élan, and bright, brazen "Ça ira" into the golden atmosphere. If the church bells had been the subdued hymn of Italy, the bugle, when the church bells were now silenced as often as not, was the voice of sovereign France. Only in the walled cities the old iron clangour from the steeples still went on. But it was answered now by the trumpets of recruits drilling for the armies of the first consul that shouted back from the fields and from the walls and citadels over the roll of revolutionary drums.

Strasbourg, however, seemed quiet enough. There was something undisturbable about it, Anthony thought, with its towering cathedral spire and the crooked streets full of peak-roofed houses.

Before one of these the berlin stopped.

It was the house of one of Vincent's new relatives by the marriage of Anna, a relation for which there was no word in any European language to express at once the remoteness of its degree and the heartiness of its recognition. Just as the cross on the Simplon had marked the height-of-land of their journey, the hospitable house of the glover Herr Johann Bucer at Strasbourg marked the summit of wassail, good-humour, and gusto of the trip.

Life in Livorno had not altered the fundamental Teutonic tastes of Vincent. Amid a host of new, blue-eyed, burgher "cousins" and straw-haired river-maidens from the Ill and Breusch, he advanced to the complacent sound of city rebecs in the chambers of the Aubette where, despite the Revolution, the gavotte and minuet still survived. He drove to the Temple Neuf on Sunday with the berlin packed full as a case of sausages with juvenile Lutheran relations. He went to sleep with the rest of the Bucers, Von Stürmecks, Brants, and Toulers while the pastor passed the sand twice through his hour-glass in Alsatian Deutsch. He sat at the place of honour, at a succession of boards too firm to groan under the hams, würste, fat geese, pâtés de foie gras, and Hochheimer which they had been built to bear up under, while he and Anthony ate, danced, dozed, smoked, and talked themselves into the heart of the family to the vast delight and relief of Anna at Düsseldorf, who received in due course of post an account of these rejoicings in the refined hand of a female cousin.

. . . And there has been *a good deal* of talk, too, my dear Anna, for no one could have been more gallant than our cousin and his friend, and some modest hopes and speculations on the part of certain prospective hausfrauen whose cheeks are too firm to tremble but not too red to blush in spite of all the cooking. I hope you will be coming here next spring for your first lying-in which I hear is . . .

Anna's eyes overflowed with mixed feelings as she put on the pearls which Anthony had given her, for dinner that night. Ach, if he would only marry into the Von Stürmecks it would be schön, sehr schön. Everything with Anna was schön.

But Anthony had no intention of doing that. It was evident that Vincent had, however. And it became necessary for his friend to remind him that the berlin was at least expected to carry them to Paris and was not meant solely for the delectations of Fräulein Katharina Geiler, charming and incapable of walking as she might be.

"For my part I have now seen the collection of watches made by Uncle André, the collection of ritters' swords assembled by Uncle Franz, and tomorrow I am to *hear* the collection of musical spheres and scaled glasses in the camera of der alte Uncle Fritz. Vincent, I just can't listen to it. Not to another glass, or sigh over the sorrows of Werther while the taps drip in the cellar. My capacity has been reached. And you know I have stood by you loyally, too."

Vincent admitted it with gratitude; admitted even his now somewhat vague engagements with M. Ouvrard and other bankers—in Paris. After a formal call upon the fräulein and her mother and a supper at Herr Bucer's that promised to ruin their digestions permanently, they found Aristide with some difficulty in a house on the Bröglieplatz and prevailed upon him to harness up their own horses which had also been eating their heads off. And so westward now till the peaked roofs, the star-like citadel of Vauban, and the high spire of Strasbourg vanished from view as they left the valley of the Rhine behind and headed across the pleasant land of France.

If he had been alone Anthony would have continued on down the Rhine and crossed the channel from Holland, but he wanted to complete the trip with Vincent and to meet some of the bankers in Paris, particularly Ouvrard, which Vincent was so anxious to have him do.

Vincent had by no means permitted the subject of the Spanish-Mexican silver he had discussed with him at Leghorn to drop out of sight; in fact, they had discussed it frequently as they drove along. It now began to appeal to Anthony as "something to do" for reasons of which Vincent had no idea.

It was doubtful, Anthony felt, if he could bring himself to settle down in Europe anywhere. He would not feel any violent national enthusiasms. If anything, by sympathy he was inclined to feel himself English, but the sojourn at Gibraltar had done something to jar that. The idea of going to America where he might put his roots down in new soil appealed to him. If he remained in Europe he would have to give allegiance to some sovereign or society for which in reality he would probably never feel more than an assumed loyalty. That this was in many ways unfortunate, he acknowledged. But that due to his upbringing and later experiences in Cuba and Africa it was also true, there was no use denying. How become a Spaniard, a Frenchman, or an Englishman overnight? No, it would be like his oath to the King of Spain in Havana, taken but not registered. But once in America he might become part of a growing community, not the master of it as at Gallegos, which was a personally cultivated mushroom, but part of a living, growing organization in which he might find a wide scope for his ideals, his abilities, and his natural desires. Then too, the adventure of the thing appealed to him. "New Orleans," "Louisiana,"—the names called. He would still see the world and he was already aware of something that most Europeans, even intelligent and travelled ones that he had met, did not seem to have an inkling of—that Europe was not the world, Europe was only a small, at present he could see, a very disturbed and disturbing part of it. "Yes," he thought——

"The subjects which men think about and to which they attach the significant verbs of action should always maintain some connection with objects—out of which after all the subjects develop. The trouble with the verb *to be* is that it is intransitive. And there has been a lot of intransitive thinking done in Europe in the past. I suppose devoting your life just to being yourself, and you nearly always follow someone else's pattern, is rather selfish. If a great many people should all start out just 'to be themselves,' following no set pattern, things would get pretty rotten and static. The French seem to have gotten tired of that plan and broken it up. They are probably trying to find a new one. That may be what all the excitement is about. A little hysterical to judge by the bugles and drums. I wonder what that man Bonaparte thinks? What are his subject and his object? Evidently he is a kind of human verb between them. I tried being just that at Gallegos—to do, to do, to do—it is not enough. Besides my object was wrong there. It nearly ruined the subject," he chuckled. "What else was there I learned?

"When I was a child Father Xavier said in effect, 'Be (a certain kind of man) in order to please God—the church will tell you what pleases God. You can become in that pattern by doing what you are told to do. Take the wafer and seal the bargain.'

"John Bonnyfeather said, 'Be honourable (my code) and devote your life to transferring goods from one place to another. You can live on the tolls *like* a gentleman.'

"Cibo said, 'You can't become anything but a healthy, pleasure-loving human animal—act in such a way as to be wise within those limits. Happiness will follow.'

"I said to myself, 'Do in order to keep on doing. Life is action—' and in four years I nearly went mad. I can see now I much mistook Cibo.

"Brother François said, 'Lose all sense of your own being in doing good to others—in that way you will be reborn in God. In Christ is the pattern which the church preserves. Imitate Him.'

"And now where am I? Physically, somewhere between Strasbourg and Nancy going west. Politically, nowhere. Financially, lucky. Spiritually, waiting in a limbo to make contact again with the world. For that is the first step in carrying out my own vision of the plan. I must in some way put down roots in a place, associate myself in primary human ways, somewhere, somehow, and soon. And the first step is to know and to find people. And why not men of great affairs as well as little ones? My wealth and my training make it possible. I have cemented my boyhood friendship on this trip with Vincent, who loves me. Why not let that be the entering point and this Spanish-Mexican business the wedge to follow after? It will provide a thousand vital associations. I might drive it in deep—to a wife. I might drive it *home*. And besides what else—I can't become a mere spending dilettante. Well, I shall talk with these bankers at Paris, and with Sir Francis Baring in London, and Mr. Labouchère at Amsterdam on the way back from England—if I come back. I might live there, of course. Poor Florence!—Yes, I shall at least find out, and then——"

"We ought to get to Metz sometime tomorrow," said Vincent sleepily. "Make up your mind, my boy, I'm going to sleep for the first stages of this journey to Paris. I can't help it. Strasbourg has worn me out. And I really must, I really *must* you know, be able to think when I come to talk to Ouvrard—and Talleyrand!" Vincent whistled and sat up uneasily. "Yes, you were right, we delayed too long. You should have made me leave before. For that Katharina now I really do not give a damn. What did you think of her?"

"Sehr schön," replied Anthony noncommittally.

Vincent nodded after a while and sank back to sleep as well as the road would permit. At least the cushions were soft and the springs strong. A smile gradually gained over his anxious expression. "You are right, Toni, sehr schön. It was worth it. We shall see these fellows in Paris just the same. I wonder if, after what has happened, I should still deliver Don Luis' message to Ouvrard—those blank permits for Spanish produce from the colonies, you remember."

"Yes, I don't think the marquis is one to let his hates interfere with his income," replied Anthony. "Besides his little plan was directed against me."

"*I* was in the carriage, too, don't forget," muttered Vincent.

"That was merely accidental from Don Luis' standpoint, I suppose."

"I think you are right—again," said Vincent after a while, and dozed off along a good stretch of road.

"Why was it so many people took his advice or depended upon him when it came to acting?" Anthony wondered. Here was Vincent. Their association had been and continued to be almost boyish. Yet Vincent, he knew, was an astute and able man. Important men had entrusted him with important affairs; believed in and counted upon him. Yet he was turning to Anthony for advice and the signal to act just as he had always done. Of course, Vincent's professional manner was different. The natural and domestic lining of his professional front was exposed to Anthony—and yet? And there was Pujol out on the box, ambitious and keen. He had left Pisa to get into the main current. Young Aristide was no fool. He said he did not intend to forget what he knew about the law—and he knew a great deal. He couldn't stand hearing it talked about any more. He wanted to practice it in Paris. And somehow, somehow, Anthony knew it, Aristide had picked him as the means to put himself upon his way. He would expect Anthony to help him—and he would. Perhaps that was it, he not only would—he did. The quality of one's personality was a curious thing. It reached out and drew others along with it. It had drawn an ex-slaver, a German-Italian banker, and a law student all into the little berlin and the horses were drawing all of them together to Paris.

The swift drumming of hoofs fell like music on his ears. "Go"— the command still seemed authentic. Its fulfilment contented him. He looked out with satisfaction upon the shifting landscape; lost himself in it.

They rolled into Nancy about midnight, after considerable trouble at the gate, and slept like logs. Pujol had made a fast trip.

From now on they settled down to travelling in earnest. The autumn of the year 1801 was dry and crisp. The rains delayed interminably. The roads smoked with dust under the horses' feet while they overtook the lumbering diligences that looked like travelling houses; while the important military posts rushed by them. An occasional detachment of Moreau's ragged cavalry ambled along with a disgruntled air, recalled from the Rhine. They were discontented. Their victories had not been won under the eye of the first consul. Their battles did not count. It was whispered their general was in disgrace. To Aristide's quips they replied with curses.

At Varennes an old sergeant descended from his horse and kicked Aristide all around the stable yard. The sport was like to become popular. Other troopers prepared to join in. Anthony and Vincent were forced to interfere and provide enough pourboire to last the troopers to the Marne in order to get Pujol off. From an upper window a hard-bitten major looked on approvingly in a uniform which still affected a Jacobin slovenliness. Vincent thought of protesting to him.

"I would not do so, monsieur," whispered a neat-looking young corporal. "They say the major was with Carrier at Nantes, one of the old terrorist enthusiasts. Ma foi!" The young fellow started violently and froze to attention. The major was roaring at him.

"Sartain, cochon, what are you saying to those aristocrats, you rascal?"

"Rien, mon major!"

"Throw them out," roared the officer, evidently full of wine.

"We will go," shouted Vincent. "I shall complain of this at the Tuileries, monsieur le major."

The major's face clouded. "Les Tuileries!" and then, "This is Varennes, *citizens*. You remember—Varennes?"

"We are going," Vincent assured him.

"Oui? A l'enfer," muttered the major and went back to his bottle. The older soldiers looked at them sullenly and jibed at the berlin.

Pujol said nothing now. His bottom throbbed as they drove hastily out of Varennes, and there were indignant tears in his eyes. "I will get that major some time," he said. "Wait!"

"Nice customer, that," said Anthony.

Vincent was purple with rage. "Wait!" he also said. He looked out over the wide waste of the Argonne where the clouds were drifting serenely along the wooded ranges. He was thinking how times were changed since the Prussians had been driven back here—and bankers were not without their influence again. "We and the serene, indifferent landscape remain," he thought. "The farms and trees push over the graves while interest goes on. Idealism is very expensive and the voice of the people dies away into the chest of the first consul —which is now empty and needs Mexican dollars, I understand."

"What are you grinning at, you old miser?" asked Anthony.

"Did it ever strike you what a wonderful thing geometrical progression is in peace times?" replied Vincent. "I mean applied to government consols, you know."

Anthony shook his head. Vincent had his moods too, sometimes. They galloped through Les Islettes and slept at Sainte-Menehould.

The vineyards and small hill farms began to change into the wide wheat-fields and the towered granges of level farms as they pushed on towards Paris. Here and there a gaunt fire-scarred skeleton of a château rose amid fire-blasted park trees.

"Not many aristocrats have seen fit to return yet," muttered Pujol. "I hope my father will be able to keep his new lands in Auvergne. We don't want the émigrés back. What an ass that major was. Vive Bonaparte! He knows the solid people who are behind him. No mobs and no seigneurs. Just let us keep the land."

They stopped at Mourmelon to let the horses rest, and looked out over the broad plateau on the other side of the river.

They crossed the rolling Champagne slowly. The beasts were tired now and they could get no relays. All the horses had been taken for the artillery or were being kept for the military couriers. It was lucky they had their own. At Rheims they had to fight to keep both teams. Vincent had to produce all his credentials. As it was they were regretfully allowed to proceed.

"A great requisition and impressement is under way," explained an old officer in what had once been a royal regiment of the line, one of the maison du roi. "Times *have* changed I can tell you. Now everybody must serve under the Revolutionary law. The newest arrangements for enforcing it have just been perfected at Paris and they are trying them out first in the valley of the Marne under the eye of the first consul. He is driving about from one arrondissement to another, I hear. Watch you don't meet him—with four horses. War with England, they say."

"I thought it was to be peace," said Anthony. "The negotiations are under way I was told."

The captain leaned into the window of the berlin confidentially, where it stood before the prefecture on the square at Rheims. He shrugged his shoulders till his epaulettes flapped. "Peace? Yes, for a little perhaps. But what is it, la paix? Only a little time to let the old world wheeze and breathe easy after a good blood-letting. In a few years its veins are swelled out dangerously again. In the forehead they begin to throb. And then—it has another stroke. It calls loudly for the basin and knife to save it. Le roi, le peuple, le consul premier, what is the difference who the surgeon is it calls upon? The operation is the same. I have in my time seen them all operating. The people are the worst. They like guts all over the place covered with symbolic olive branches and doves. Beautiful!—les fêtes de la paix, little white doves with red feet and those cheesecloth arches, quelle magnificence! I have trained my horse to rumble behind when he passes under them. He is an old war horse and understands. And what after all are all those young men doing in this classe which Bonaparte is calling to the colours—to preserve peace, of course— ah—one must hasten to add that. Why, I will tell you, trying to keep the girls quiet and placid and endeavouring to drink up each harvest as it occurs.

"Venus, le vin, it is not sufficient. Men must live even if only for a few weeks. War is vivid, a thing of flame and thunder. It takes one out of the house under the stars. It exchanges the bubbling of babies for the mewing of eagles and the cough of cannon. What is the difference if one dies? One dies anyhow. I am sorry, of course, for those who lose their superior colons for Schömberg-Lippe—quelle dommage! But for France—what are a few bones, a leg? if France asks it? Is it not then a leg of honour, a limb beyond compliment, a foot shrivelled in the divine fire? Voilà!" He roared suddenly caught in the flames himself.

A tremendous fanfare of trumpets came beating back from the façade of the cathedral at Rheims. The square vibrated with it. A squadron of glittering, spick-and-span cuirassiers trotted across the

place, its musicians ahead on grey horses. People drinking under
the little awnings about the place rose, and turning white in the face,
screamed. The scarfed staff at the prefecture ran to the doors and
windows and shouted. The regiment had come to aid in numbering
the people. The patient Jewish-looking saints and the long angels
carved on the front of the church, where Jeanne d'Arc had crowned
her rascal sovereign, looked out as they had for eleven centuries, and
trembled. The bells above burst out, the gargoyles grinned. "Vive
Bonaparte, vive Napoléon," roared the streets of Rheims, "vive la
France."

Pujol sat and gaped. Something had happened to France while
he had been toying with *fas* and *jus* at Pisa. The old captain rushed
away.

"Get on," cried Anthony. The berlin started. "That captain was
drunk," he said.

"They are all drunk here," replied Vincent. "Don't let it catch
you."

"It's got Aristide, listen to him shouting up there. Vive everything." They were galloping recklessly through the main street.

"Don't kill the horses, Pujol,"—Anthony looked out of the window
grinning. Pujol suddenly looked ashamed. "Vive la loi," he muttered—"I live by that." They went more slowly and carefully now.
Rheims with its roaring steeple was left behind.

They descended upon the Marne at Dormans just above Château-
Thierry. They asked the way of the curé, "Tout droit." The first
consul was just across the river at Crezansay yesterday, mustering.
"Look out," he said, eyeing the horses. They laughed and went bowling along, the river on their left.

"We are lucky to see the Marne valley so beautiful and sunny this
time of year," said Vincent. "Did you ever see anything so golden
and peaceful? The spirit of the harvest seems to be resting here just
now. Usually by October it is soggy and full of driving rain. One
might imagine that little valley of the Verdon across there to be undisturbable with its overhanging forest-clad heights looking down on
the spires of old villages. Look how the meadows and the stubble
of the wheat-fields reflect the light. It is as clear and white as the
wine they grow hereabouts. That deserves a better reputation than
it has, by the way. It's a little like the Rhine along here, but chalky
soil, you know." He leaned out, gazing across the river with a genuine enthusiasm for the landscape rare for him.

"Would you like to live in France, Vincent?"

"It depends upon how rich I get, and how safe property is going
to be here. Yes, sometimes I have thought of it—Paris? I have
been living there for about half my time the last two years, you know.

But I was thinking of the country rather; a place to settle down in. And right along here is one of my favourite spots. It reminds me of Germany, a miniature Rhine. I would like to be able to take that old castle of Martel there on the hill and rebuild it."

"And bring Katharina from Strasbourg for its princess," hinted Anthony.

"Ja," said Vincent.

"Living in France because it reminds you of Germany is a very curious German reason to live in France, isn't it?" teased Anthony. "And of course it *must* be a castle on a river."

"Ach," replied Vincent a little irritated. "You mistake me. It is because it is so beautiful just here. Everyone has favourite spots. Call it my castle in Spain then. A castle in Spain might suit you better, nicht wahr?"

"It might," admitted Anthony, "provided——"

"Dolores," grunted Vincent. "But *do* look at my view now. Around the curve here we begin to see Château-Thierry. Am I not right?"

And Anthony had to admit he was. There was an unexpected, delicate charm about Château-Thierry dreaming in the sunlight, set in the midst of flat, emerald meadows along a steel-blue river with enormous, bold, green hills behind it. They came upon it around the curve suddenly and there it was lightly poised by the river-bank like a white bird about to take flight; the arches of its white bridge leaping easily; its inexpressibly graceful belfry soaring against a background of verdure; the flying buttresses of St. Crépin's church rising in splendid uplifting curves; the golden clock tower and copper spires glittering above ivory houses,—lacelike, wonderful, a village that had become a little city and kept the charm of both.

"La Fontaine had his house somewhere hereabouts," mused Anthony. "I remember Toussaint talking about it. He came here once to see the poet's library. Great rows of books all bound in sumptuous leather by the Sun King, he said. Poor Toussaint! I wish he were here now. This place reminds me of some of his dreams."

"I can't imagine shooting myself. Can you, Toni?"

"No—not exactly. Not now anyhow."

They turned into the main street and found themselves unexpectedly in the midst of old acquaintances. It was the troop of cavalry that had treated them so roughly at Varennes. As they drove past the prefecture someone gave a shout. A couple of troopers ran out and seized the heads of the horses. Their old friend the major was standing on the steps smiling significantly.

"Bonjour, messieurs les aristocrates," said he. "So you haven't got to the Tuileries yet—not even with *four* horses?"

They were forced to alight.

Major Luçay—for they were soon only too familiar with his name —was, they also discovered, in charge of the requisitions and enrolment of recruits in the arrondissement. The local civil officers were evidently afraid of him. He and his sullen veterans of Hohenlinden had been temporarily detached on their way home to perform what they considered to be local police duty and were cursing their mal chance in meeting the general who had given them orders. The induction of recruits and the requisitions had been merciless. It was noticed that Luçay was especially severe on young men from the better class families. He would listen to no pleas for exemption however reasonable. The atmosphere at headquarters was turgid.

Without even waiting to inquire who the travellers in the berlin were, the two best horses were led off. "We take them in any event," coolly remarked the major, and then proceeded to examine their papers and passports with an eye microscopically critical.

He was evidently disappointed to find Vincent and Anthony were foreigners, and their papers in order. With Pujol it did not go so well. His certification by the French commandant at Florence as a French student permitted to return home caused Luçay to smile under his dirty, red moustache.

"He is simply a vagrant of military age," he said. "Enrol him, sergeant." And Pujol was enrolled. "Since he knows horses, put him down for a cavalry dépôt." That was all the reply made to their continued protests.

Poor Aristide was in tears. "I am ruined, M. Toni, I shall lose precious years. I am a student of law. I go to practice in Paris, monsieur le majeur," he shouted at Luçay desperately.

"The law is that you be enrolled," said the major. "It is finished. Take him away."

"M. Toni," cried Aristide aghast as he was led out, "M. Toni!"

"I shall see you through, Aristide," said Anthony.

"Wait!" said Vincent.

"No doubt, Herr Nolte," said the major leaning forward and looking Vincent in the eye, "no doubt you will have me cashiered for this."

"Well, since you suggest it, major," replied Vincent, "I shall."

Luçay digested this with difficulty, and it was made no easier for him by the scarcely repressed cheers of the civil staff. The mayor, a scared, thin little man, wrapped almost to extinction in the folds of a tricolour sash, followed the two foreigners through the door. He would have liked to kiss Vincent on both cheeks for his temerity.

"I am helpless, monsieur, I want you to know that," he cried, standing on the steps. "I apologize that this outrage has overtaken you in my arrondissement. This major is a Jacobin—one out of the Terror who still persists."

"We know about him," said Vincent. "I shall go to my friends in the right places at Paris."

"Bon! But I wished to tell you that the first consul is even now at Nogent, only an hour's drive down the river. If monsieur *has* influence?"

"Come on," said Anthony. "Let's see him. I'll drive. Merci, monsieur le maire."

They climbed up on Aristide's box together and started. "That way, that way," cried the mayor, pointing. Just then the major came to the door. Vincent looked back at him and took off his hat. The man looked uncomfortable.

"I'm proud of you, Vincent," said Anthony.

The two gentlemen on the box of their own berlin drove leisurely out of the town of Château-Thierry. The least appearance of nervousness or flight would, they felt, bring the redoubtable Major Luçay after them. As it was from the steps of the prefecture he watched them go, regretfully they thought.

Once across the bridge over the Marne and around the first short curve in the valley, Anthony touched-up the horses to a good fast pace. The remaining team missed its leaders and was inclined to shy at every opportunity.

"We shall certainly have to pick up another driver between here and Meaux," said Vincent nervously. "Anyway it would never do to drive into Paris on the box ourselves."

"We won't have to do that," replied Anthony firmly. "Who that you know is likely to be with Bonaparte at headquarters?"

"Are you really going there now, Toni? It might be better to go on to Paris. I know Fouché there. He and Ouvrard understand one another. I thought . . ."

"Now look here, Vincent, let's see this thing through now. You want your horses and driver back. Are you really going to let that rat of a cavalryman make you forget who you are? Of course not. We are going to the first consul himself if necessary. And we are going to get Aristide released, too. Make no doubt of it. He is going to drive us to Paris, and once there I want him started on the way to be an avocat, and by your influence."

"If you really believe I can do it, I will," said Vincent. "Coming to think of it, I do know de Bourrienne."

"Who's he?"

"Bonaparte's secretary. And he goes with him everywhere."

"There you are," said Anthony. "And here we are, too. That must be Nogent ahead there down the valley."

He began to fan along the horses and Vincent's indignation at the same time.

CHAPTER FIFTY-FIVE

THE LITTLE MAN AT GREAT HEADQUARTERS

FOR some hours on the afternoon of October the fourth, 1801, the hamlet of Nogent l'Artaud on the left bank of the Marne a few miles above Paris had temporarily become the nervous-centre of Europe and the focus of its most intense energy.

Napoleon had been moving about through the villages of the lower Marne valley watching certain provisions of his new law for the enrolment of recruits being put into operation there. He was carefully taking note of the temper of the population under the workings of an altered system of conscription, and watching its faults and merits before applying it universally. He had driven down from Epernay that morning, intending to return to Paris by way of Meaux next day. He had settled suddenly and unexpectedly upon Nogent as temporary headquarters, as it was his custom to do, by stopping his carriage in full career, getting out, taking over the principal house for himself and quartering his staff on the village. It seemed unlikely that he would choose such a place as Nogent, and that was precisely why he had done so. For it was in small places where no one expected him that he could best see for himself what was really going on.

France had been at peace with the rest of Europe for almost a year. On the very day that Napoleon stopped at Nogent he was expecting to hear at any moment that the preliminaries of a peace had also been signed with England. The news would be semaphored down from the Channel to Paris in a few minutes and a courier would soon find him on the Marne. At last reports the parleys at London had reached their final and critical stage.

These negotiations, and a thousand other things, were in his mind while he talked to the thunder-stricken officials of the little town, looked at the military rolls for the arrondissement, complimented the lieutenant in charge of the muster for his zeal, entered ten houses in fifteen minutes to see that entries on the rolls were men and not mere names, asked for the tax returns and remarked some lax, local favouritism in regard to personal property returns, noted that a bridge at Nogent would relieve congestion at Château-Thierry in case of military operations in the Marne valley, that the heights just above provided excellent artillery emplacements to command that town,—and then walked back to headquarters with his tired young adjutant, wondering meanwhile whether Cambacérès or brother Joseph Bonaparte would be the first to bring him the final details of the English news.

"Probably Joseph. He will rush to point out how valuable his advice has been, while the amiable Second Consul Cambacérès will certainly get lost on the way and stop somewhere to dine. Still his dinners do have more influence than speeches. I wish my family would drop the democratic rôle now. Joseph and Lucien—how tiresome they are with their everlasting talk about 'public opinion, public opinion.' I am public opinion now. People believe what they are told to believe, and I intend to tell them. Only one's family, of course, will never believe that.

"'It is not going to last,' mother says. Pauline tells me mother keeps putting louis d'or into that coffer-clock with the sphinx on it that Kléber sent her from Cairo. Kléber, he hated me. Now he is gone. Well, one should not have empty cisterns in a garden in Egypt where Arabs with knives can hide. Mother will soon be hiding gold napoleons with *my* head on them. She *might* believe it then. Perhaps? But what does last? Institutions—a dynasty? Mon Dieu, if Josephine would only conceive! 'Climb into the bed of your royal master, little Creole.' Is it not soft enough? I will embroider it with imperial bees. Be the queen of the hive. Princes—I must have princes for the house of Bonaparte! Give me two years' peace with England —and then." He looked grimly at the eagles on the stands of colours before the door of the humble house he had chosen to honour with his presence. As long as it should be a house no one who ever passed its threshold could be able to forget that his shadow had once brushed it in passing. Already that shadow lay across the world.

Within, his secretary had cleared out the front room and set up the bronze-clamped camp furniture that now accompanied him everywhere he went. In the room down the hall his narrow, military bed with a soft mattress and a hard pillow was laid out. His valet had drawn the blinds.

"In half an hour, Bourrienne," said he. "There are today's letters to dispatch and last morning's post; the sack from Italy first. Sort it! No more widows' petitions! I want the Piedmont reports, too."

De Bourrienne replied patiently and sighed as his master and former schoolmate went down the hall. He missed his comfortable rooms and the smooth routine at the Tuileries. These country inspections were the devil. Napoleon lay down and composed himself for sleep.

Outside the guard was posted. A sergeant went through the house. He found a boy hiding in a cupboard. "I wanted to see General Bonaparte, only to see him," he kept bawling.

The man shook him. "Taissez vous. The general sleeps. Little swine! Well, look then, idiot." He kept a firm grip on the boy's collar.

Looking into what was ordinarily his father's bedroom, young Pierre Mortier saw a man in a green uniform with white facings lying stretched out on a cot. He was lying on his back with his hands folded on his breast. The eyes were closed. The pale olive face was like a wax death-mask; like the profile on a coin. The slightly damp locks clustered about his brows and over one ivory ear. The nostrils were faintly transparent. The only sign of life about him was a faint wrinkling of his thin lips when he breathed, and the crease in one boot which also occasionally wrinkled uneasily as if the left foot twitched. Young Pierre did not know that England had hold of that leg. But he never forgot the room.

Usually it was as confused as his bibulous father who slept there. Now it was another room, preternaturally neat. It had been swept clean and everything familiar in it removed. Only the sunlight kept coming through the same crack in the blind just over the figure of the sleeper. On the peg where his father's dusty hat usually hung was a small-sword with its hilt wrought in gold eagles set with diamond eyes. On this the sunlight lit and spattered.

It played in little metallic shivers over the walls. It lighted the face of the sleeping general on the bronze-knotted cot; gilded the uniform of young Beauharnais, the adjutant, who sat on watch with folded arms over against the wall. Suddenly the beam brightened, the hilt gleamed, intense the glory streamed. It lay silent across the faded carpet of the room of the father of Pierre Mortier, aged ten.

"The lightning—it sleeps," said the child breathlessly. "Dans la chambre de mon père!"

Bonaparte opened his eyes and looked at the boy out of his sleep.

Pierre saw the brown pupils widen, light like amber and darken again. The waxy lids closed.

"Voilà, Joséphine, c'est lui," muttered the sleeper inaudibly. On his brain the sunlit image of a boy's face transfigured with wonder and pride burned out slowly into nothing. He breathed once heavily and slept on.

The adjutant and the sergeant smiled at each other. Young Eugène de Beauharnais put his finger on his lips and motioned for them to go. He stuffed his handkerchief in the broken shutter. The grip on Pierre's collar tightened and he was marched off down the hall to the back door, but not in an unkindly way.

"Here," said the sergeant gruffly. "Here is a sou for some little cakes. Remember you saw General Bonaparte. *Thou,* thou little cabbage. Think of it! Now be off and keep quiet, or—" The sentry who passed just then with walrus mustachios and a gold tassel on his busby touched his musket fiercely and grinned. The boy dashed off happily. They were not so terrible after all. He had a sou and had seen the general.

"Il est colossal, colossal," he boasted as he shared the cakes with some other urchins up the street. But he said nothing about the sunlight. He was going to go back to his father's room to examine that later on. Something wonderful had come into that room, something that had certainly never been there before. Just then he and the other boys started to shout and run after a berlin, with two gentlemen on the box, that drove rapidly into Nogent with the autumn dust rolling up behind it in golden clouds.

It drew up before the house of Pierre's father where the new silk flags with the eagles stood by the door. The sergeant ran out. The boys stopped to watch curiously. One of the gentlemen was evidently very angry about something,

"General Bonaparte is sleeping and cannot be disturbed," said the sergeant firmly, twirling his moustache and looking the angry German gentleman up and down. One of the horses gave a loud whinny.

"Hein!" said the sergeant.

"It would seem that he may be disturbed unless you detail one of your men to take the berlin to the stables over there," said Anthony. "We have lost our driver. Here is something for the fellow who will look after the horses." He gave the sergeant a heavy coin and climbed down. The man's expression changed.

"If you have a real reason, messieurs . . ."

"We are not merely selling eggs, I assure you," said Vincent nodding towards several peasant women with baskets lined up across the street, waiting for the headquarters commissary to appear. "It is a matter of genuine importance. Is M. de Bourrienne here or in Paris?"

"Ici, monsieur. You know him? Here, Frampton, take care of these gentlemen. They have business with the general." The sergeant pocketed the coin. "For God's sake get that mare's nose in a bag before she whinnies again," he said to the orderly. "If the general has been wakened—" he pulled his beard anxiously. "What name shall I give to the adjutant?"

"Tell M. de Bourrienne that M. Nolte, the banker, and a friend wish to see him immediately. Important!"

The sergeant went.

In a minute or so de Bourrienne himself came to the door. He looked none too pleased.

"Ah, good day to you, Herr Nolte." He bowed in a perfunctory way at his introduction to Anthony.

"General Bonaparte is asleep now," he said. "And if you have come up from Paris to worry him about the rate on the funding of that next advance on rentes I advise you to return to Paris before he wakes. He gave Ouvrard himself a bad half hour over that only Monday last. Surely you must know it. He will certainly recollect you, and——"

Vincent interrupted him.

"It is something entirely personal, a military matter, not financial at all. And I have no doubt, monsieur, you can yourself aid us, if you only will, without annoying General Bonaparte. In short, we have been outraged and I come to you for redress."

"Tiens," said the secretary looking much relieved. "That is different. Come in. Orderly, chairs. Will you excuse me for a while, messieurs? You see I am vitally engaged for the moment. The first consul wakes"—he drew out his watch—"in fifteen minutes." He sighed a little and wiped his brow. Vincent and Anthony sat watching the scene before them with great interest.

In an adjoining room some staff orderlies were rapidly setting up field-desks and chairs and arranging pens and stationery. They were so precise about it that it was evidently a matter of long-standing and perfected routine. An adjutant looked in and checked every pen, ink-pot, sand-box and quire of paper. He rearranged the large chair in a better light. Two civilian clerks entered and sat down on camp stools. They sat waiting, alert, uneasy. On a large table in the main room, where Anthony and Vincent were sitting, three assistants were sorting dispatches under the watchful eye of de Bourrienne. Orderlies brought in large leather bags. The secretary broke the seals. The contents were dumped out and rapidly sorted.

"Milan and Piedmont," said de Bourrienne. "Let the others alone." His eyes and his hands flew over the contents of the spilled bags. A small pile of documents rapidly accumulated in a little green basket. The rest were seized upon by the clerks who began to endorse upon them and throw them into other leather bags hung before them.

On the small pile in the basket before him de Bourrienne began to operate. He put the letters from the Bonaparte family into a small box marked with a "B." There were several of them. Those from Lucien Bonaparte, then at Madrid, he put with the Spanish dispatches. He looked through the rest of the documents with marvellous rapidity and wrote out a description upon each. He arranged them in a certain order and put them back in the green basket.

Two couriers, who had just found the whereabouts of the first consul's headquarters, dashed up. Their dispatches were also brought in. De Bourrienne put his hand to his head and smiled at Vincent. Just then Beauharnais came down the hall and looked in. "All ready?" he asked, and returned.

A minute later they heard the sound of a crisp, rapid step and the sharp click of a scabbard against a boot.   Everyone in the room rose and felt as if they were runners in a race waiting for the word "go."

A short man with a head a little too large for his body entered the room. He stopped, looked. Energy radiated from him like heat from the sun. Everybody present was positively electrified by it; swept out of their own orbit into his. The force came from the head, from the eyes, and under the brows. To be suddenly faced with it in the ordinary course of life was equivalent to opening a cupboard to take down your hat and finding a cobra looking at you with its hood spread. The next move would be with the terrible head. And you knew, you felt eternally certain, that the head knew what that move would be. All action except that which it initiated was paralysed; what it once began must be followed out.

"At ease," said a high, clear voice. Someone else seemed to have spoken. The work went on; seemed only to have begun. The dispatches seemed to be sorting themselves. Bonaparte held out his hand blindly. De Bourrienne put the green basket into it. "Et, monsieur le banquier-là?" he said, looking keenly at Vincent. He did not appear to see Anthony. Nevertheless, both of them rose again and bowed. De Bourrienne murmured something they could not hear.

"Eh bien!" replied Bonaparte, and slipped into the room where the two civil clerks sat waiting. They dipped their pens. He began instantly to dictate letters.

From where he sat against the wall Anthony could see diagonally into the room opposite where Napoleon was working. He could even hear part of what he was saying and catch glimpses of him as he passed walking up and down. An intense quiet and absorption had gripped the house. All noises now came from outside except the scratching of pens, the flop of papers into bags, an occasional low-spoken direction from de Bourrienne.

Outside the sentries paced alertly, very erect, conscious that the general was awake again. Horses stamped at pickets between the trees down the village street. Orderlies came and departed. Now and then a dusty courier dashed up with a clatter. Others left and the sound of their hoofs died away in the distance toward Paris. The long afternoon sunlight began to verge toward the close of day. The high, clear voice in the other room went on. Bonaparte also paced back and forth there like a sentry. He was dictating to the two clerks alternately.

They sat at opposite ends of the room. He passed between them, leaving a terse paragraph with each as he turned. He was dictating a letter to the newly appointed superintendent at the Ecole Militaire, prescribing certain changes in the courses of mathematics for artillery officers: " . . . those who show themselves incapable of feeling and tracing the abstractions of geometry from the models of cones and cylinders in cages which have just been supplied should be slated for the infantry. It is essential that every artillery officer in the French armies should from now on be capable of seeing the parabolas in various trajectories as physical facts. His mathematics and physics must coalesce . . ." and then his sword would gleam as he passed the door again, and Anthony heard him say to the other clerk: ". . . it is too early yet to assume openly that the newly acquired districts in Piedmont are French soil. They should still be treated merely as garrisoned districts and the local laws respected in so far as it may be convenient. In a year or so from now these districts may be incorporated in a department. In that event this matter should then be referred to . . ." and so it went on.

His head sank a little forward on his chest. His arms went behind him as he walked. Presently he went over to the green basket and began to read its contents letter by letter, but at the same time from some other portion of his mind he kept both the clerks busy. He threw the letters on the floor as he read them. He read, talked and walked on; ordering, reorganizing, building bridges, establishing schools, directing the kind of cloth to be used in women's dresses, urging on the codification of the law, repairing prisons, and confirming court-martials, arranging for the exchange of the officers captured by the British in Egypt, altering the procedure of the new tribunals to try brigands and the form of the oath to be taken by returning émigrés, refusing Mme. de Staël permission to return to Paris, dictating the movements of the returning columns of troops from the Rhine. New clerks stepped in and took the places of those worn out. The voice continued rapidly, smoothly, tersely, inevitably, bringing order out of chaos, hope and energy out of despair, changing the history of the world.

Trying in vain to keep up with him, the indefatigable de Bourrienne and the secretariat about the table toiled on and said nothing. They were engulfed. Napoleon had slept for half an hour previously. He went to sleep instantly and he woke as if he had just been re-immersed in the source of energy. He awoke with a mind as clear as spring water but as incisive as acid. But it was deep and wide as well as limpid. In it an entire epoch as it was on any particular day was poised just upon the verge of becoming something else; was held in suspension; every part of it generally and particularly from armies to individual corporals, from cities to houses and roads seen clearly, understood and in process of being manipulated by a will that had not yet become merely the habit of ego, by a body not yet the host for cancer. For the next four years the first consul and emperor continued to wear out relays of ministers and staffs of generals without a sign of fatigue. He first charged France with his energy and then exhausted it. Nothing on earth had been seen like it since the days of Julius Caesar.

The scene before them was so charged with the vital atmosphere of time in the making that Anthony and Vincent felt themselves to be participating in it directly and waited for de Bourrienne without remarking that he was keeping them doing so. In Anthony's mind the constant appearance and reappearance of Napoleon pacing across the space of the half-open door of the opposite room became synchronized until Bonaparte appeared to be nothing but the pendulum and governing instrument of the machine in motion all about him. Although the impression was only a half-conscious one at the time, it was nevertheless the deepest and the most lasting that Anthony carried away with him. It was with a start of surprise that they saw de Bourrienne break off and begin to cross the room toward them with the evident intention of hearing Vincent's complaint. The secretary drew up a chair and sat on the arm of it swinging one leg over the other.

"Believe me, messieurs, I am delighted to have the excuse for an interruption. For five days and two nights now in half a dozen villages"—he wiped his face with his handkerchief—"this has gone on. But I hope you have not had a serious misfortune." He looked at Vincent, who rapidly related his troubles with considerable eloquence and heat.

"Most exasperating and a piece of unwarranted, petty spite," said de Bourrienne. "But it will be somewhat difficult for me to do anything about it directly. I can issue no military orders, you know. I am only the general's secretary. But I tell you what I will do. I can send in a memorandum about this occurrence among the papers that go in to be signed in a few minutes. In that case he may ask to see you personally, Herr Nolte, and he is not very fond of you bankers as you know. Do you care to risk it?"

Vincent nodded. "Decidedly," he said.

"Very well then." Taking a pad on his knee, de Bourrienne wrote rapidly. "Will that cover the facts?" He read the note.

"Quite. Only the major's name is Luçay, not Lacey," said Vincent.

"Thanks for that correction. Names that go in there must be right. Luçay? Luçay?—where have I heard that name before?"

"With Carrier at Nantes, they say."

"That may help you." He scribbled something more on the memorandum. "Confidentially, we are weeding out the 'friends of the people,' you know. Well, wait. It will not be long. I wish you luck."

He went back to his work but then looked up suddenly and said, "Do me the honour of remaining for dinner this evening, messieurs. Pardon my preoccupation. I should have asked you before. It will not be much to boast of, a military mess. But there may be amusing talk."

They accepted with delight.

"Your papers go in shortly now," said de Bourrienne, and went on again.

"Will Bonaparte be at our table, do you suppose, Vincent?" asked Anthony.

"Hardly, de Bourrienne and his civil assistants probably mess alone on these inspection tours. He is much liked, you know. Very friendly. You may be surprised to hear that he has dined with me at my hôtel twice. Ah, wait till you see that place, Toni! But there go our papers."

The voice in the room had ceased. De Bourrienne had immediately sent in the bundle of papers to be signed. He knew better than to lose an instant. Napoleon sat at his desk now. His pen flew in that indecipherable scrawl which was already his signature. He stopped. He was reading a brief memorandum in the clear hand of his secretary.

"General: The notorious Jacobin Luçay is at Château-Thierry. 'Major.' Army of the Rhine . . . fomenting discontent . . . merciless requisitions . . . M. Nolte and friend robbed of horses and driver . . . requests immediate return. Proceeding to Paris on business of rentes with Ouvrard and M. Talleyrand."

"Luçay? Luçay? Ah—that red-moustached scoundrel of the Noyades, who tried to interfere with my emplacements at Toulon. What is he doing at Château-Thierry? That *is* curious. He used to be in the artillery."

He scrawled an order and gave it to an orderly. He gathered up the signed papers and came out. He stopped to say something to de Bourrienne when his eyes fell again on Vincent and Anthony. He came over to them and they both rose. He was looking at Vincent.

"Well, monsieur le banquier, I have sent for your man and beasts. Also for the person who detained them. When he arrives we shall see. You *are* M. Nolte, aren't you?"

Vincent bowed.

"Ah, yes, I thought I remembered you and M. Ouvrard together one day about the Mexican bullion and treasury drafts. So! You see I seldom forget. That was a year ago, wasn't it?" He seemed to take great satisfaction in this.

"Your remarkable memory for names and faces is famous, mon général," said Vincent. Napoleon looked pleased.

"It is inconvenient to some people. Well, have you succeeded in getting any more Mexican dollars? No? About to—bien! I must talk to you after dinner about it. Bourrienne—" He looked at his secretary. "Good, you have already been asked. My Bourrienne often anticipates me. A rare quality. He does not abuse it." He glared at them suddenly. "I have found, M. Nolte, that you bankers frequently do. You are a sad lot, you buzzards that follow my eagles. Do you suppose I do not know what a fine thing your friend Ouvrard has made out of his army contracts? And now it is supplies for the Spanish fleet. Mon Dieu! I am going to dust some of the crumbs off him. Tell him so." Bonaparte folded his hands behind his back and looked up at Vincent and Anthony who towered above him like a couple of ostriches over a bantam eagle. He suddenly became aware that the room must be secretly amused by this, and hopped up on the table where he sat cross-legged with his sword over his knees. He felt his short stature keenly at times. It was one of the things that forever drove him to lengthen his shadow.

"I should regret being made the messenger of ill-will between two of the ablest spirits of the age," replied Vincent.

"I am not sure I can accept your compliment on the basis of that comparison, M. Nolte," said Bonaparte, taking up an ivory ruler and beginning to tap one boot sharply. "It implies at once too much and too little. What do you think?"

"Both General Bonaparte and M. Ouvrard are masters in their own fields. That your own genius embraces and includes that of M. Ouvrard he would be the first to admit. It is for that reason I feel your message might carry a too devastating criticism. M. Ouvrard, as well as M. Bourrienne here, has faithfully anticipated your desires upon occasions. I am sure he looks forward to being able to continue doing so." Vincent smiled engagingly.

Napoleon was not displeased. He distinguished instantly between respect and servility. "Well, we meet upon common ground at least, M. Nolte," he said. "No, you do not give way. It would seem that your interest in your friends is not entirely expressed by percentage. That does you credit. Let us admit then, I do not know M. Ouvrard in the same way that you do. Quelle dommage! *Like* my good Bourrienne, you say, M. Ouvrard anticipates my desires. I reply—not without his *own* 'anticipations,' and I understand they are always negotiable. Come, you must admit there is a difference in their motives."

By now the entire room was listening with ill-concealed curiosity. Napoleon's love of baiting bankers was notorious and well appreciated. He was now merely relaxing himself after a strenuous day's work, and it was all the more amusing to him that with a certain mischievous maliciousness he had been able to entangle in an invidious and damaging comparison the names of the greatest financier in France and that of his sensitive secretary who was present. Hearing his own name mentioned several times, de Bourrienne could not help but follow the argument, and he was now only pretending to write with his face burning. Napoleon looked at him and chuckled inwardly.

The little man seated on the table bending the ivory ruler across his knee was intensely pleased in his own curious way. He never laughed heartily. He seldom smiled. His sense of wit and humour was caustic and brazen. Even his lighter moments such as the present one resembled a rapidly spreading patch of verdigris on polished bronze. He had now succeeded in making everyone in the room thoroughly uncomfortable. He had placed one Herr Nolte, banquier, in the uncomfortable dilemma of denying an influential friend or of traducing M. de Bourrienne in his own presence. Meanwhile, he, Napoleon Bonaparte, remained the centre of all this uncomfortable attention and was perfectly at ease. He now smiled and bent the ruler on his knee till it appeared ready to snap.

"Come, M. Nolte, what have you got to reply to that?"

"The motives of both gentlemen in serving, Your Excellency, must be correct," replied Vincent, who was tired of being sport at another's game and wished to have done with it.

"Oh, you merely evade me? I shall ask your very tall friend here, then? Or is he too a banquier? Do not be embarrassed, my Bourrienne," he cried, turning half-way about. "What is there to blush about? Je suis sur que ce large monsieur la vous fera la grande justice!"—he let one end of his ruler flip pointing straight at Anthony and looked at him. "Well, monsieur?"

"M. de Bourrienne, I am sure, mon général, does not feel any embarrassment at having his motives for serving you discussed openly. It is only your great confidence in him which so affects him."

"Present this gentleman to me, Bourrienne. Upon my word he deserves it of you," said Napoleon.

There was a general relief at this end to so uncomfortable a verbal skirmish. De Bourrienne and Vincent now withdrew a little and talked in low tones. The clerks, at a nod from the secretary, departed, leaving only the orderlies on a bench in the corner. It was only a short time till the mess would be served and work was suspended.

"This is the only hour when the general permits himself a little leisure," whispered de Bourrienne to Vincent. "I can tell you it is a boon to his staff. But I am afraid your friend is in for a good quizzing, by the signs. The general's method is to squeeze the last drop of information out of anyone who looks interesting and then leave him like a dry sponge. But you have doubtless experienced being cross-questioned by him yourself. Let's go over and sit down a while. I am still waiting for a courier. I hope your horses do come tonight. With the staff quartered in the village, there will not be even a garret room." They sat down, Vincent congratulating himself that he was not in Anthony's shoes.

For Bonaparte was now standing immediately opposite Anthony looking up at him quizzically, his legs apart and clasping the ruler behind his back. It was so much like a big boy being called up by a little schoolmaster that de Bourrienne and Vincent were both forced to stifle a smile that neither wished the other to see.

"Disembarrass me of your height, monsieur," said Bonaparte pointing to a chair. He sat down himself with his boots stretched out before him, looking at the toes. "I have seen you before, I think," he continued without lifting his eyes. "You are very tall. Are you an Englishman?" He looked up now.

"From Livorno," replied Anthony.

"Yes! You were standing there once in a window looking down at me. Beside you was a man with the face of a fanatic."

"That is so, mon général," said Anthony, obviously amazed.

"Fanatical faces in upper windows within easy pistol shot of my carriage are always impressive to me, monsieur. Like M. Fouché, I have the habit of spotting and remembering them."

"I am not a fanatic, mon général. And neither Your Excellency nor your minister of police has any cause to remember me," said Anthony, making no effort to cover his anger.

"You mistake me, M. Adverse. I did not say *you* had the face of a fanatic. What has become of the man who did?"

"He shot himself—recently."

"Bien, such fellows are bound to shoot somebody. In this case both wisdom and determination seem to have pulled the trigger together. So you are from Livorno?"

"Si."

"Did the clothes you are wearing now originate there, too?" asked the little soldier quietly and in Italian. He continued to study the toes of his boot.

"No."

"Where?"

"In Gibraltar. Nevertheless, General Bonaparte, I am *not* an Englishman," insisted Anthony in undoubted "Livornese."

They continued for some time in Italian. Bonaparte was soon satisfied on that point. It was not a conversation but a series of interminable questions from the little general in whom Anthony now recognized the typical insatiable curiosity of an Italian islander displayed on a cosmic scale. Certainly the grilling was as severe a one as he ever underwent. Now that Napoleon's Anglophobia was laid aside, there was no longer apparent any point or direction in his curiosity. It simply spread out over the map. It demanded to know what was going on everywhere Anthony had been—and how. There was obviously no malice in it, Anthony recognized. He soon saw that Bonaparte felt he was conferring an honour in using him as a human textbook, manifestly to be thrown aside when the information should be exhausted or prove dull. Indeed, he now found some amusement himself in what took on the form of a game of knowledge, and on that basis, a ghost of a smile passed between them. Nor could he help but appreciate the keenness of the questions as he felt the quality of his personality as well as endless facts being brought out by his replies. Perhaps that was what Bonaparte was after. He was always interested in and looking for men. Or perhaps he was only curious as usual, or amused. Anthony could never be sure. All that he knew was that the quiet, incisive questioning went on till he felt wrung dry.

Napoleon was insatiable about conditions at Gibraltar, but not more so than about Havana. The predicament of the Spanish governors-general of Cuba amused him. "Go on," he said, "tell me—" and he propounded a string of questions. "I thought so," he replied. "And so you found yourself in Africa. On the Rio Pongo? Where is that?" "For ten minutes one would have thought he intended establishing his capital there," said Anthony to Vincent afterward. "I found that I knew more about Africa than I thought. It is a curious thing, Vincent, to have another man's will reach out and force you to remember things you did not know you knew."

"Eh bien," said the insatiable little man finally, after at last permitting Anthony to talk himself for some time about trade in Africa. "Good—I see you are a man of affairs and business. Neither of us is entirely the fool of circumstance then. That is much. Yes, it is something to achieve anything; to make a thought become tangible. With most men it dies in 'I think' or 'I say.' How difficult to combine *I think* and *I do*. Thought in action—that is to be like God." He tapped his boot with the ruler, seeming rather to have spoken to himself. Then he leaned forward almost violently.

"That is why I do not like bankers," he exploded in Anthony's face. "And in another hundred years if I do not stop them they will own Europe—the world. Financiers cannot act. They never *do* anything. They are passive, they spin webs and every wind, blow peace blow war, brings them flies. They are not the fit repositories for power. What is the use of a power that forever keeps still? A powerful oyster, hard outside and jelly within. An oyster cannot act, move— GO!"

He leapt to his feet and swung about with the same motion. He stood listening with his back turned, while the last word he had uttered still rang in Anthony's ears with the force of gunpowder.

Anthony sat looking up at him. He felt as if he had been given a ride on the outer ring of Saturn and flung off into space.

Napoleon was listening to the sound of a horse at full gallop coming down the Paris road.

"From London, Bourrienne," he said. "Yes, I am sure." He folded his arms and waited.

And it was thus that Anthony always remembered him, standing there, alive, the bronze forehead touched by a pencil of sunlight. The motes in it seemed to be streaming out of him into the room.

"You will excuse me, I am sure," said de Bourrienne, glancing at them significantly. "Here, Jancey," he called down the corridor. "Look after the general's friends." A grey-haired clerk in staid, black clothes led them through the house and out onto the lawn behind it. The Paris road ran along one side of the space and on the other the turf slipped down easily to the river. Under a number of horse-chestnut trees, towers of molten gold in the late October afternoon, the orderlies and mess attendants were laying several long tables with white cloths.

A fat young officer hurried over to meet them.

"Your names and ranks, messieurs, if you please," said he. "I am the adjutant of the mess and must seat you. Have you servants? I could use them."

"Unfortunately, no," laughed Anthony.

"Detained for the cavalry by a major at Château-Thierry," grumbled Vincent.

"Oui? That is too bad." He reeled a little. "But it is gay here, isn't it?" he cried. "I have had them set the tables under the trees. A remarkable autumn to be able to do that. Warm and dry. But —nom d'un chien!—what should we care about the weather? One of the carriages of M. Cambacérès has just arrived here, a little too far ahead of him. It was loaded with good burgundy. What could a good mess officer do?" He steadied himself. "Come, confirm me in my opinion—about the weather." He led them to a small rear room of the house piled with baskets of wine.

"You see I *am* a mess officer. I like it. I would rather be that than a general of division." With his tongue in his cheek, he poured out of one of the second consul's cherished bottles a dark purple wine that filled the little room with an inspiring bouquet. "*Um-m-m, yes, it is gay here,*" he insisted, looking out the window at the scene beyond. "An incomparable lawn, little birds singing their hearts out in the sunlight"—he gulped the glass—"oh, how ravishing the country is; nom du petit Jésus! for nearly a week now I have not seen a woman without sabots, but courage, tomorrow we shall be in Paris. I contain myself therefore, and—I contain a good deal. Just now I contain four bottles of the excellent wine provided by M. Cambacérès, the second consul of the Republic.

"Encore? Oui! I insist. I am, I tell you, the mess officer. The wine of the second consul. Le gros, le beau, the innocent and sensible M. Cambacérès who understands what government is about. To the second consul—and your good health. The first consul, he drives about inspecting, winning battles. Making people do things. All are uncomfortable wherever he passes—everywhere. Suddenly this afternoon at the third bottle I see it. I, the mess officer, have my vision enlarged to proportions co-co-colossal. I see,—what do I see? In the front of this house the first consul of the Republic conducting what he thinks is the government. Is it? What is behind it? Why, this!" he cried, running up and down now keeping his hands on the table. "This!" he kicked, and one of his boots came off. "*This!*" and this time he finally kicked open the door which he had been aiming at. "Voilà," he shouted. "Voilà la vrai France que persiste toujours." Caldrons of soup, long loaves, piles of roasted fowls, and salads, greeted their eyes and a general reek of savoury steam and odours drifted out to them from the little kitchen where all was a scene of confusion, the several headquarters chefs stumbling over each other in their haste in a kitchen meant for a small civil family. The little officer leaned in and laughed.

"Is it that progress advances itself in here, mes enfants?" said he to the cooks.

He stood for a while in the entrance with one boot in his hand, hopping about like a fat duck. The cooks roared at him and shut the door. He had been drunk ever since M. Cambacérès' carriage of wine had arrived.

"Come, messieurs, come. I still want to show you my view of things. My view of politics. Messieurs, I insist upon it. No, it will not be necessary for you to take one boot off. Not at all. One merely returns to the lawn. One *throws* one's boot and follows it." It went smashing through the window. "Voilà! Maintenant!" He led them outdoors, and placing his feet wide apart, suddenly ducked his head down and looked through his legs at the men setting the mess tables under the trees.

"That is what the government is really about. All governments." He was holding onto his own fat legs now patting them with satisfac-

tion while he continued to gaze upside down and purple in the face at
the scene behind him.

"Take my view of it, but for an instant. It is revealing. *I insist.*
From here the yellow leaves on the ground under the white tables . . .
beautiful . . . someone has been tossing gold about there. I will roar
if you do not look—my way."

There was no getting out of it. Either they had to take the mess
officer's view of things or he would undoubtedly "roar." And then—
they would be found there. It would be ridiculous—and they would
be able to explain it only by laughing; by laughing as they were now.

So they bent down and looked. Three of them in a line. Their
hats dropped to the grass and their hair hung into them. The mess
officer made appreciative noises.

And it was in that position that Aristide found them, coming suddenly around the corner with the chief clerk of M. de Bourrienne in
his sober black suit.

"Voilà!" said the old man. "But what is it that it is?"

They rose scarlet-faced. "Here is your servant, messieurs," said
the grey-haired clerk sadly, backing off a little with his eyes large and
round.

Aristide sat down on the step and began to hold his ribs while they
shook him. The old clerk looked on scandalized.

"I shall report this. I shall report you, M. Latour, you the adjutant
of the general's mess, to M. de Bourrienne. You have seduced the
guests of the first consul."

"Pas de tout, pas de tout," insisted Latour. "Come, Jancey, you
sad old Huguenot. Take my view of things." He started for the
old man, who fled.

Latour, Vincent, Anthony, and Aristide remained beating one
another on the back.

"Encore une autre," cried Latour, staggering a little. He led the
way back to the little room beside the kitchen.

In another room at the front of the house Napoleon and de Bourrienne were reading the London dispatches which the courier had just
brought. The news was incredibly good. The preliminaries of peace
had been signed, and the British ministry had agreed to concessions
which had been advanced only as diplomatic demands. France was to
regain her lost colonies.

"This is the greatest victory of all, mon Bourrienne," said Napoleon.
"The empire which the Bourbons lost I shall regain—these colonies
from England, and Louisiana from Spain—all in a year. It is in-

credible. Dealing with this ministry is not like dealing with Pitt. Let them keep Malta. I will quarrel with them over that later. Give me a five years' peace to raise armies—and then—" He began to stride up and down the room his feet winged with triumph. Nothing could stand before him now. He felt exalted above all that had gone before. The lowly steps that descended into the past—incredible that he should have ever had to traverse them. A vast imperial staircase led into the future. At the top, still distant, exalted, stood a figure of himself crowned with laurel. Up and down the stairs crawled a host of ants that had once been men. He wiped his feet on the carpet and laughed.

"The major Luçay reports himself," announced an orderly.

Bonaparte looked at the man but did not see him. He was planning the next step on the staircase. "These fools on the Tribunate shall be silenced. One law—and one will to enforce that law. A broom for the ants in opposition. Cambacérès must force on the code. La code Napoléon." A fat, lazy fellow the second consul. Pliable—but slow. They were all so slow. Some would not move at all. For the immovables—a hypodermic injection of lead. He smiled, more arrogantly than a few hours before. . . . This peace with England—who would have thought it possible on such terms? They must be in a bad way across the Channel. The continental system was ruining them. No more imports from England. People would have to do without tea—and sugar. Surely patriotism should be able to do without tea. Besides, those who had their feet on imperial stairways were not likely to trip over teapots. No, no, Austria was the next hazardous step. Next time he would crush her. . . . He clenched his fist and looked out the window.

Brother Joseph, a little fatter than he used to be, had just driven up and was climbing out of his chaise. A bourgeois Italian. It reminded Napoleon of Ajaccio. The biggest merchant in the town—eating an orange under an awning—or the most prosperous country gentleman near by. My God—he wanted to put a crown on that head. If he could only get the family to live up to him. Joseph couldn't even be taught to look stiff-necked under a fashionable hat. He looked a little uncomfortable now—from the neck up. An umbrella, eh! And it was the driest autumn in years. He wasn't going to give it to young Beauharnais—was he? La parapluie du frère de l'empereur se presente à l'adjutant du staff. He could see it in the *Moniteur* for a few years ahead. That kind of thing could undo the crossing of the Alps. Bon Dieu! He *was* giving it to Beauharnais! Josephine was right. This kind of thing must be stopped. He rushed out.

"Joseph!"

"Napoleon, mon frère, congratulations. Didn't I tell you if you would write to M. Fox it would turn the trick? And now he is coming to see you, you the friend of liberty. Now we can all settle down in France safely." He kissed Napoleon on both cheeks. Beauharnais stood by at attention holding the umbrella over his arm.

The greatest man since Julius Caesar stood at the door of the little house in Nogent perspiring. He had just been defeated. In the presence of his invincible elder brother a curious lethargy came over him—always. Joseph had only to appear and Napoleon was little brother again.

"Come in," he said. "I am glad to see you. Give your hat to Beauharnais, too." There was some comfort in making Josephine's relatives realize who the Bonapartes were anyway.

"Damn them," said Beauharnais as he hung Joseph's dusty hat and umbrella on a peg in the little hall. He shoved the hat sidewise and went out to drink with Latour. He found the party in the little room was very merry.

Napoleon, Joseph, and Bourrienne did not even notice Luçay although he had stood up as they passed through.

He sat down again fuming as the door closed behind them. The aristocrats were coming back. But who was this little Corsican general to keep a patriot waiting? "Luçay, friend of the people of France," Marat had called him that once. He remembered it. He sat cursing the work of time.

The mess bugles shattered his bloody reverie. Bonaparte came through the door.

"Oui, il faut manger," Joseph was saying with an air of great wisdom.

"Good evening, citizen-general," said Luçay rising in his disheveled uniform and scraggly moustache like an apparition of the past before Napoleon. The old official title, now tacitly disregarded by all who were wise enough to do so, grated dreadfully on Napoleon's ears. "Citizen-general—" and he had probably just signed a peace with England. Who was this fool? His eyes took in the sans-culotte major hastily.

"Luçay—M. Nolte's horses," whispered Bourrienne.

"What are you doing at Château-Thierry, Luçay?"

"I and my veterans were ordered there to round up recruits by one of the aristocrats on your staff, citizen-general. Otherwise we should now be being paid off in Paris, I suppose. That is if the citizen-general is really going to pay the Army of the Rhine." He smiled slowly.

"And so you enforce the law by taking a pair of good horses from a fat German banker, citizen-major."

"Yes, for the Republic, citizen-general."

"No, for the republican Luçay. For his farm to which he returns like Cincinnatus to plough after the wars—on land also furnished by the aristocrats. Is it not so, *citizen-major?*" They stood looking at each other. Luçay's eyes were glaring.

"Well," said Napoleon at last, "you may keep the land. *I* have guaranteed that."

"Tyrant, to think I have lived to serve you!"

"Do not let that trouble you, *citizen*," said Napoleon. "Give me your sword. Take it, Joseph."

On the way through the hall Joseph Bonaparte hung the sword of the friend of the people on the same peg with his own hat and umbrella. Napoleon smiled. He felt a sudden appetite for supper as a burst of talk floated in from the lawn. The staff, both military and civil, were already waiting for him about the tables. They all stood silent as he took his place.

"Begin," said he, and sat down abruptly.

Anthony and Vincent were sitting at de Bourrienne's table. The meal began dully enough. After the time they had spent drinking with Latour and Beauharnais in the little room, sitting out in the twilight with the rather silent company assembled under the trees seemed flat by contrast. Napoleon and Joseph Bonaparte were some little distance away at another table and confined their remarks to each other. De Bourrienne was tired and said little. Most of the others at the table were under-secretaries and clerks. The sound of faint conversation, an occasional laugh, the sunset jargon of birds and the voice of the evening wind through the branches above gave a certain low-toned solemnity to the occasion. A row of heads along the street wall, where the population of Nogent had gathered to watch the first consul eat, began to drift away.

All this was changed, however, before the second course was laid.

A great coach accompanied by a small escort of cavalry came rumbling up the Paris road. A trumpet burst out. Everyone started laughing. A cheer went up from the street.

"Voilà," said Latour, stooping down as he hurried past toward the gate. "The real government has arrived. Now you will see."

The coach came in and drove ruthlessly across the lawn. It stopped not far from where they were sitting. In it sat a man of great amplitude in all his proportions. A wide, cocked hat nodding with red, white, and blue plumes perched a little awry on his forehead. The plumes nodded and curved over his large, beaming face like flames.

The coach shook and leaned as he got down out of the door with some difficulty, disclosing as he did so lacquered half-boots with gold tassels, a wide expanse of white breeches, smooth and tight as a sail in a gale. Then his tremendous tricolour sash appeared and above it a blue coat embroidered with golden laurel leaves that climbed up into the points of a monstrous high collar—as he finally disentangled his broad shoulders from the coach and stood upright. He was not fat. He was well proportioned. He was simply vast. And he stood there in the sunset with his plumes waving above him like a Gargantuan specimen of the Gallic cock about to crow. The crowd along the wall cheered. Some of them thought that Bonaparte had just arrived.

"Cambacérès, the second consul—" said one of the clerks in reply to Anthony's glance of inquiry.

"It may be an amusing evening after all," de Bourrienne confided to Vincent.

Everybody, even Napoleon, was already looking pleased. Cambacérès hurried across the lawn to Bonaparte's table where room was hastily made for him and a young man who accompanied him. Two chairs were brought. But only one of them, that for Cambacérès himself, was set at the first consul's table. They saw Cambacérès presenting his young friend to Napoleon, who was apparently none too pleased to see him, for he called out to Latour and coolly directed him to seat the newcomer at another table.

The rejected guest was brought across to de Bourrienne who received him with some embarrassment but kindly enough. A place was found for him next to Vincent and directly across from Anthony.

"Permit me to introduce myself, monsieur," said he, his voice trembling slightly. "I am M. de Staël. I trust none of your clerks, M. de Bourrienne, will be troubled by my presence." He added this bitterly. The colour raged into his cheeks again. Napoleon's affront had evidently been a bitter one. De Bourrienne hastened to introduce Vincent and Anthony and to engage young de Staël in conversation. He responded gratefully and with evident relief, but a cloud passed over his face from time to time as he glanced at the consular table.

Anthony thought he had never seen so completely civilized-looking a person as the youth who now sat opposite him. Young de Staël's easy gestures, and the gentle tones of his voice, his exquisite costume, and his animated but powerful expression all conveyed a peculiarly memorable effect. His features were not regular or handsome according to any usual standard. He was simply and quietly distinguished, charming and satisfactory without exerting himself. Of all those at the headquarters mess that evening, not excluding Bonaparte himself, de Staël was the only person whom Anthony truly envied. Indeed, he already felt indignant with Napoleon for having rebuffed him; in sympathy with his cause—whatever it might be.

Vincent, de Bourrienne, and de Staël were soon engaged in talk. Jancey, the grey-haired clerk, next to whom Anthony was seated, had little to say. He still looked upon Anthony with disgust and made no bones about it. His expression resembled that of Mrs. Jorham when she was looking at the cathedral in Havana, Anthony thought; sour and not a little suspicious. Nevertheless, although he was forced to sit silent, he was soon aware of a subtle change in the whole atmosphere of the occasion.

It emanated from Cambacérès. At the first consul's table a great deal of laughter and loud talk was now going on. Cambacérès had come to congratulate Napoleon on the peace and to bring him the details of the negotiations. The news of the occasion spread from table to table and magnified by rumour was soon all over the place, among the guards, and out in the village.

Napoleon sat in the centre of all this flattered into good humour by the incense offered him by his good-humoured colleague; content to sit, as he liked best to do, the apparently indifferent cause that radiated success. Even in the garden of the simple house of the horse-leech at Nogent, where he had chosen to quarter himself, he was the centre of glory. And it was the second consul's intention to heighten that effect. It was not mere flattery that led Cambacérès to do this. True, it might pay. But the future arch-chancellor of the empire took a peculiar pleasure in being a sort of horn of plenty for the government; in extolling the first consul by distributing good cheer in the form of diplomatic dinners, official feasts to functionaries, and popular carousals. It was all there was left under the Constitution for the second consul to do. It suited his nature, and he did it well. There was an unexpressed understanding between himself and the first consul about it. Tonight if the first consul of the Republic was bestowing peace, Cambacérès as his colleague had come up from Paris to see that plenty should accompany it.

Four apparently empty post-chaises that had followed him now began to be unloaded. They contained innumerable packages prepared by Beauvilliers, the Parisian restaurateur. Cambacérès sent for Latour and amid much raillery forced him to discover the whereabouts of the wine which had arrived "dangerously early." Bottles of the excellent vintage which Vincent and Anthony had already sampled were now distributed to all. The simple fare already prepared by Latour's cooks for the headquarters was sent to the guards, who at some little distance away gathered about the camp fires along the river and began to sing and cheer. Cressets were lit. The scene became brilliant.

The scarlet-and-blue uniforms of the mess attendants moved about in the red glare of torches. They were bringing dishes from the deceptively empty-looking post-chaises to the long staff tables under the horse-chestnut trees. The yellow leaves drifted down and lay upon the white cloths about which the gilded and booted staff of the first consul of the French Republic jangled spurs, flashed epaulettes, and held up glasses of the excellent burgundy of the popular M. Cambacérès like so many rows of rubies in the torchlight.

"To the health of the first consul." Napoleon had replied with "Glory and prosperity to France." It was his only active part in the proceedings of the evening which was now obviously handed over to Cambacérès. Napoleon even sat a little apart under the largest tree with his chin on his hand, looking on. In his simple uniform and plain sword over his knees he stood out with startling contrast to the all but weird variety of the brilliant uniforms of his staff. The expression on his face did not change at all. Only his eyes moved.

He did not laugh over the English Goose, "cooked for the occasion," which was produced as the grand finale from the now genuinely empty chaises, nor applaud a really apt reply to Cambacérès made by brother Joseph. He merely sent for his cloak as it grew cool.

Anthony sat watching him from the "civil table" of M. de Bourrienne, where the secretaries sat, which was somewhat withdrawn from the others amid the shadows. All there felt themselves to be spectators and had now for some time said nothing to one another. De Bourrienne had accepted a cigar that glowed in the gathering darkness. Along the wall most of the town was gathered to watch the first consul eating, as only a generation before it had once gathered in the same place to see the king of France and Navarre dine hastily under the same trees on his way to Rheims. Hearing the news of the peace, the little mayor of Nogent came to offer his congratulations. He was received by Bonaparte and sent to one of the tables, where he and his sashed assistant fared well. Undoubtedly peace was a good thing and the first consul the saviour of France, if one took a mess officer's view of the situation.

"Didn't I tell you?" whispered Latour as he passed Anthony once. "M. Cambacérès knows what it is all about." He tripped happily on. This was the only "after dinner conversation" that came Anthony's way that evening. Vincent, de Staël, and de Bourrienne were now silent. Jancey had turned his glass down and gone in to write. The whole affair was suddenly terminated unexpectedly. Cambacérès held a surprise, however, to the last. He had brought some fireworks from Paris.

A burst of rockets soared over the river to the delight of all those watching along the wall, and as a finale a large "N" framed in burning laurel contrived to float for some time in the air and reflect itself in the water. This brought an acclamation from the soldiers encamped along the Marne and from everybody else—except young de Staël—and the ex-major Luçay, who with the citizens of Nogent had been watching the rejoicings from the street. He now turned away, his heart full of dark imaginings, to ride off with a burning "N" in his brain.

Napoleon had been visibly pleased by the "N." He now left his chair to go in, and the groups around the tables scattered.

"Come in," said de Bourrienne. "There will probably be a brief conversation this evening in the house. And the first consul, M. Adverse, wants you to talk with M. Cambacérès about Africa. Please recollect to do so. Cambacérès, you see, is responsible for the African Company which has just been renewed."

"I shall consider myself included as the second consul's guest," said young de Staël.

"As you will, monsieur," replied de Bourrienne, and they went in.

Anthony found himself left alone with de Staël as they crossed the lawn towards the door of the now brilliantly lighted, little house.

"You and Herr Nolte have had a rather strenuous crossing of the Alps, I hear," he said. "He has been telling me about it. Would you recommend the Simplon route?"

The others had hastened to separate themselves from de Staël in so marked a way that he could not but notice it.

"In another year the new road will be . . ." began Anthony.

"Do not let me embarrass you, M. Adverse," said the young man suddenly. "It will perhaps be better if you do not permit Bonaparte to see us together." He stopped by the threshold looking proudly miserable. The others had already entered.

"I do not know what differences you and General Bonaparte may have, monsieur," said Anthony, "but I shall be glad of your company now or upon any other occasion."

De Staël looked at him gratefully.

"I have come to request General Bonaparte to grant my mother permission to return to Paris. I am afraid it is useless. She is a woman whom he hates. But I shall persist," he said simply.

Anthony had never heard of Mme. de Staël, but he wished her son's mission might be successful and said so. They walked down the little hall and entered together the front room of the house from which a hum of voices proceeded.

The dispatch tables had been pushed back against the wall. Napoleon sat in a chair by the fireplace with his boots resting on the empty grate and his cloak still wrapped about him. He looked sallow and cold beside the ruddy Cambacérès standing with his plumes almost brushing the ceiling.

Bourrienne, Vincent, Beauharnais, and a number of staff officers were seated about talking in low tones. The gathering had about it the feeling of being only temporary; about to break up and go to bed. Everyone except Cambacérès looked tired. From the look of headquarters that evening anyone might have supposed a dull, minor campaign to have been finished and the staff to be returning home. A lackey in plain livery who passed about some coffee and rum was the only mark of state.

"These inspection tours are not without their compensation," Anthony heard de Bourrienne remarking to Vincent as he came in. "It is a relief from the formalities of the Tuileries"—but his attention was instantly transferred to the two consuls.

"*But,*" Cambacérès was protesting to Bonaparte, "if you expect me to give state dinners and to entertain for the government, you must permit me to import civilized delicacies. One must have sugar, and it does not grow in France. Where do you suppose the nougat came from tonight? It's no scandal. Smuggling is now universal. I must have those fellows released. The prefect at Boulogne must be instructed. Every ambassador has this privilege . . ."

"Manage it then," said Napoleon. "In your case I acquiesce, but reluctantly. British trade must be struck down. I am afraid you as my colleague set a sorry example. But there is a gentleman I want you to talk to." He motioned toward Anthony. "He can really tell you something about the African project. I have questioned him myself. Does the company advance?" Cambacérès shook his head. "Like the codification of the law, I suppose. You must get on, mon Cambacérès, get on," he cried impatiently. "Monsieur, you—" he said pointing to Anthony. "Present him, Bourrienne, present him. Come here, M. de Staël, I wish to speak with you now."

The weary de Bourrienne presented Anthony to Cambacérès. But it was impossible for them to start a conversation just then. The room had suddenly grown quiet. Everybody was listening to the high, clear tones of the first consul. He had now turned about in his chair and was leaning back addressing young de Staël, who stood before him with a natural ease and quiet carriage that seemed in some sort to have recommended him. For Napoleon's voice was less harsh than at first.

"—far from annoying me, monsieur, your frankness has pleased me. I like to see a son plead the cause of his mother. You are young; if you had my experience you would judge of things better. I shall even explain myself. Nevertheless, I do not wish to rouse in you any false hopes. It is impossible that I should permit Mme. de Staël to return to Paris. I do not want women about who make themselves men, any more than I want men who render themselves effeminate. What use is unusual intellectual attainment in women? What has it always been? Vagabondism of the imagination. To what does it lead?—nothing. It is but the metaphysics of sentiment. I do not say your mother is deliberately a mischievous woman; I say she has that effect. She has a mind; she has too much, perhaps. But it is a mind insubordinate and without curb. She was brought up in the chaos of a crumbling order and a revolution. She amalgamates all that disorder and she might become dangerous. If she were repatriated she would make proselytes. I as head of the state must see to that. It would be weak of me to permit it. The greatest curse of nations is the weakness of will in the great-magistrate. The next is for him to be funny. The last and most fatal is for him to be serious and to permit others to make him seem funny. That is governmental suicide, madness. Sarcasm is the seed of anarchy. Hence, I shall not let your good mother return to Paris to become the standard of the Faubourg Saint-Germain. She would make little jokes. She would attach no importance to them, but *I do*. My government, M. de Staël, is not a joke; I take all matters seriously. I wish this to be known, and you can tell it to the world."

"But my mother wishes to see only a list of acquaintances and old friends which she will submit to the minister of police," interposed de Staël.

"Fouché, bah! He can arrest pickpockets and assassins but not ideas. No, no, my young friend, the trouble with you intellectuals is that you do not yourself understand the importance of ideas. They are like new mechanical inventions. Some are clever; most should be suppressed. Their social implications are dangerous. Their cleverness and convenience are generally seductive and illusory. Your mother lays ideas as a hen-ostrich lays eggs. She has no responsibility. I am to be left to deal with whatever hybrid hatches out—while she makes jokes in the Faubourg Saint-Germain. You underrate me, you even despise me as a man of action. Yet the philosophy of action, I say, is the greatest idea in the world. It is natural that you, the grandson of Necker, should not understand me. I am that idea, action; in me it is personified and exists in the flesh." He leaned forward now much excited and with imperial gestures.

"You have not read the last work of my grandfather," protested the young man, greatly perturbed; "in that he does you full justice. Perhaps it is the reports of his book . . ."

"I have read it from beginning to end—in two hours. Yes, he renders me pretty justice. He calls me 'the necessary man'! And according to him the first thing to do was to cut the throat of this necessary man. Why?—because he interfered with the ideas of M. Necker. Your grandfather was an idealist, a fool, an old nuisance. He was one of those theorists who judged the world by book and chart, who thinks man is an 'economic animal.' Economists are blockheads who make financial plasters to stop the running sores of the body politic. They do not even know that a nation may have a sick soul. Bankruptcy is an effect—a sign of dissolving organs. The money provided by the great M. Necker ran off like pus from the cankerous sores of France. Yes, I was necessary—indispensable, to repair all the fooleries of your grandfather; to efface the injury he has done to France. It was he who caused the Revolution.

"Now I wish you to remember this, M. de Staël. I do not address you alone but all those to whom you will return. You are still young and sensitive enough to feel when a man is sincere—even a great man. I speak for your own good as well. Remember, authority comes from God. Respect it. The reign of terror is at an end. I wish for subordination. The chaos of ideas is over. I am applying to them the solvent of action. It is only when ideas are embodied in force that they attain energy, work. Listen. When I was your age, monsieur, I thought of rivalling the fame of Newton. It was the world of details which then attracted me, the action of force on atoms. Newton has very little to say about that. It is important. I could not follow out my thought. The profession of arms was forced upon me by circumstances, but I made certain analogies from the world of nature, the rôle of chance, of what happens when one thing collides with another. And I did not forget that they *were* analogies and that there is also the world of men. You have a good head. I suggest that you follow out my train of thought—there is the institute. *There* is a career for you. But no, you will go on making epigrams in the salons. I foresee it. At the age of sixty—a book of amusing little recollections and bon mots, par M. Auguste de Staël—Bah, monsieur, that is death. That is what your mother, whose cause you plead without understanding her, will do to you. Let her go to Vienna, she will learn German there—encore une autre accomplissement pour la femme. How old are you now, sir?"

"Eighteen," said de Staël, with tears in his eyes.

"And only the son of your mother," Bonaparte smiled quietly at him. "Awake, M. Auguste de Staël, or it will be too late." He rose dramatically.

"Does your mother need funds?" he asked as an afterthought.

"She does not ask for them, mon général."

"Then she shall not receive them," said Bonaparte.

A trumpeter outside began to sound tattoo.

The first consul got up to leave. "Bourrienne, we return to Paris tomorrow. Joseph, I wish to see you. M. Nolte, you and M. Ouvrard I shall expect shortly on the Mexican business . . . I am glad to return your horses. You will not be troubled further. It was an excellent thought of yours tonight, mon Cambacérès. We are all in your debt." He returned the salutations of the company and disappeared with Joseph Bonaparte down the hall. All now looked at Cambacérès.

"Bon soir, mes amis, I know you are tired," he said. "My poor boy, I am sorry to have brought you from Paris for such a wigging," he continued, taking young de Staël by the arm. "I should have known better. Auguste, you have met this gentleman?—M. Adverse?"

"I shall not soon forget his courtesy," replied de Staël and took leave of Anthony with great warmth.

"Bon," exclaimed Cambacérès obviously pleased. "You will come and talk to me in Paris about Africa then."

"I should not presume to advise you, monsieur," replied Anthony.

"Nonsense, of course not." He lowered his voice. "We understand the enthusiasm of Bonaparte. I shall be glad to see you. Doubtless you can tell me much."

Anthony thanked him and joined Vincent who was taking leave of de Bourrienne with many expressions of gratitude. The little secretary saw them to the door and they hurried out to find Aristide.

"I'll bet you he will be with Latour," laughed Vincent—and he was. They insisted that he should come with them. After three "last" glasses with the adjutant of the mess they accomplished their cruel desire.

"How did you manage to get in there, Aristide?" asked Anthony.

"By flattery, monsieur. Must we go now? Burgundy like that is scarce. We have been lucky, I think."

"There is no place to sleep in the village."

"We might stay up all night—in there."

"Get the horses, Pujol," said Anthony. "We must be in Paris tomorrow. You will end in the army yet, you rascal."

"Ah, I am truly grateful for that," he cried. "Wait for me at the gate. In two minutes!"

Their last glimpse of headquarters was a curious one.

As the berlin drove off down the Paris road they saw M. Cambacérès, the second consul of the French Republic, leaning over the wall in conversation with an old peasant woman with a basket. A sentry near by stood at present arms.

"He was pinching the breast of a duck," shouted Aristide from the box as they rattled out of Nogent. "I saw him."

"Your driver is zigzag, Vincent," said Anthony. "A little less noise, Aristide," he called, looking out the window. "You will bring down the patrols."

"But it is true, M. Antoine," said Aristide, bending down very confidentially, and dangerously, "they tell me that the second consul buys *all* his own poultry."

They both leaned back in the berlin and laughed. "My God, what a day!" cried Vincent. "Do you know, up until this moment it has all seemed to be perfectly inevitable. But we might not have gone to headquarters at all."

"But we did, and it was worth while, wasn't it?" said Anthony, and smiled to himself in the dark.

"Decidedly," agreed Vincent.

"Get up, all my four horses," cried Aristide triumphantly from the box. They sped on through the night and found beds at a late hour in the little village of Rebais.

But it was not to be their last glimpse on that trip of Bonaparte. On the road between Esbly and Lagny he overtook them, descending upon Paris.

It was a long section of new highway lined with young poplars lately planted. They heard the bugles coming up behind them. An outrider with a trumpet appeared suddenly on the crest of a hill and galloped past at a furious rate with his horse in a lather of foam. He motioned the berlin to one side violently. They drew up. Nor did they have to wait long.

Four splendid Arab horses with grey coats and white feet suddenly flashed into view and came down the hill with their hoofs in perfect time. Their bodies grew out of the perspective inspiringly and leapt past with a tension against the beautiful, light carriage like that of tireless, steel springs unwinding in oil. Napoleon was reading a book. De Bourrienne sat facing him. They came out of the perspective and they dwindled into it. The drumming of hoofs thundered; diminished rapidly. The four horses leaned all together as they took a distant curve. The varnished back of the carriage, with the cocked hat above it, flashed in the sun once—vanished. The trumpet ahead had already died away incredibly into the distance. It floated back now as if echoed from the distant past. The carriage had seemed to be going faster than time.

There was something inexplicably impressive about the vision which had just passed. For to all who sat in the berlin it was not the mere sight itself that lingered in memory. It was the curious, complex feeling of the meaning of it. A meaning for which there was no word, and which seemed to be embodied only in the man with the cocked hat who sat reading in the carriage and yet was going so fast that he was overtaking events.

"It is not the same as when we saw him in Leghorn, is it?" said Vincent.

"No," replied Anthony. "Somehow that was just an amateur, a preliminary affair."

The other carriages and escort were evidently miles behind. They did not wait for them.

They whipped up and followed in the wheel tracks of Bonaparte.

It was late in the afternoon when they finally displayed their papers at the old gate of Picpus and found themselves at last rolling through the narrow and crooked streets of the Faubourg Saint-Antoine.

It had been necessary to hire a driver at the gate, for even Pujol admitted his inability to cope with the apparently crazy ruthlessness of Parisian traffic.

Anthony was thoroughly confused by his first glimpse of the whirl and maze of a great city. All sense of direction was lost in him. The short streets twisted and turned and ran into one another in a seemingly hopeless maze. Most of the roofs were peaked and the fronts of the houses leaned back, which served to give some light to the narrow streets. There were no overhanging balconies as in southern towns. A wilderness of chimneys and dingy swinging signs, the latter fast falling into decay in favour of the new street numbers painted on every door, was the principal mark of the changing era. Now and again a glimpse could be caught over the roofs of the frowning battlements and turrets of some medieval building.

"The Temple," said Vincent. "They are tearing its tower down. The Bastille has gone, you know. This is the Rue des Francs Bourgeois and we are driving into the Marais. It is still as it always was. Look, that is the Hôtel de Sévigné. I feel at home in this part of Paris. It is not fashionable certainly, but rents are cheap. These cochers always pretend not to understand.

"No, no," he shouted, "*not* by Saint-Merri, *not* Rue Saint-Martin. You tell him, Toni. He knows I'm a German." The little cocher in a glazed cocked hat and a coat of many capes grinned at Anthony as he repeated for Vincent, "Au coin des Blancs-Manteaux et des Archives."

He swerved suddenly to the right, drove through a labyrinth of dark alleys where sullen-looking workmen hurrying home shouted after the neat carriage. He managed to splash the horses and the body of the berlin in a vile smelling pool and then drew up suddenly before an old tavern with a soldier standing by a cannon for a sign.

"*L'homme Armé,*" said he contemptuously getting down.

"You pay him, Aristide," said Vincent, "and remember he splashed the horses for you. We shall leave them here. Now then, do you see that little turret on the house at the corner just ahead? Well, that is the Hôtel de Baule. You walk up there and turn to the left on the Rue de Vielle du Temple. I live at number forty-seven. When you have seen to the horses and locked the berlin in the shed, give the key to the innkeeper. He knows me. Come around then. I shall tell the concierge to expect you and the luggage. But mind you, I don't want to find all the bronze stripped off the berlin."

"I have been to Paris before, monsieur," said Pujol, and turned to settle with the cocher.

A crowd of gamins gathered. Aristide turned on the cocher with a torrent of invective.

"You have abandoned me to a Gascoigne," shouted the surprised cocher after Vincent and Anthony. He actually looked shocked. They looked back from the corner of the Rue de Vielle du Temple. The berlin was going into the inn yard.

"Wait a minute, Vincent. There is something I want to bring along myself," said Anthony. He ran back to the little inn.

Aristide and the cocher, who was now laughing, were preparing to sluice down the horses in the stable yard together. They were friends for life, it seemed.

"I forgot something, Aristide," explained Anthony. Out of the boot he extracted the bundle he had not opened since Gallegos and swinging it over his arm went to rejoin Vincent.

"Now, Toni, I am going to show you something," said Vincent again, and led the way down the narrow, old street. He stopped before a seventeenth century house with a wide gate boarded across. Its beautiful spandrils projected above the tops of the planks with dimly gilded spearpoints of wrought iron.

"It is quite safe to take down these boards now," said Vincent while they waited, "but I want the privacy they give. Before you leave for London you will be in love with the old place. A snug retreat for a young banker. We shall call on Ouvrard tomorrow, mon vieux. Toni, I want you to consider that Mexican business!" He rang again impatiently.

"I am going to," said Anthony.

"Splendid," cried Vincent. "But what have you in that bundle wrapped up in a woman's shawl?"

"My luck," said Anthony.

"Paul," shouted Vincent, beginning to hammer on the door. "Are you dead?" A little square in the boards opened and an old man who still wore his hair in a queue looked out.

"Nom d'un nom, c'est vous, M. Nolte! Quelle impossibilité!" He swung the gate back. A small courtyard full of Renaissance carvings disclosed itself. A little stairs led up with a sweep like those of a graceful woman's skirts to a raised green garden with a sundial. On the wall directly before them was a bas-relief of Romulus, Remus and the obliging wolf. Someone was hastily opening shutters upstairs.

A flustered-looking, flaxen-haired little bonne suddenly plumped out of the passageway beside them and began to curtsy with a dust pan in one hand.

"Where is Mlle. Hélène?" demanded Vincent.

"Alas," said the girl in Alsatian patois, "she has gone for a visit with her brother, the hussar."

Vincent coloured to the eyes.

"Never mind," said Anthony.

"But he *is* her brother, by the cross I swear it. You shall see," insisted the maid.

"Set covers for four then tonight," chuckled Vincent. "Tell them, Paul."

"Yes, yes. He really is her brother, monsieur, and a nice fellow. All has been quite in order since you left. Très comme il faut!"

"Well, well, so he *is* then. Send for our baggage to *L'homme Armé* and for the young man there prepare a room. The guest chamber for M. Adverse, here. He remains until he goes to London. And, Paul, the gate is always to be opened for M. Adverse night or day whether I am here or not. My brother! He really *is*, you know."

"Aren't you, Toni?" said Vincent, taking him by the arm with considerable emotion.

"Oui, oui, monsieur," said everybody all at once and laughed.

The little bonne sped before them up the stairs opening doors. They began to ascend spiral steps in an old tower. They turned down a hall with beautifully carved doors. Just ahead one was half-open that gave a glimpse of a polished floor with white reflections. Somewhere a small clock chimed seven times.

END OF BOOK SEVEN

BOOK EIGHT

In Which Prosperity Enforces Loneliness

BOOK EIGHT

In Which Prosperity Enforces Loneliness

CHAPTER FIFTY-SIX

A METALLIC STANDARD IS RESUMED

BEFORE he left Paris for London Anthony was so thoroughly engaged in the great scheme to pry open the rusty flood gate of the Mexican treasury and turn its stagnant pool of bullion into the thirsty channels of European finance that he had all but forgotten his determination to order life from within rather than to have it overwhelmed from without, a determination which he had brought with him and cherished out of Africa.

It was true that the inanimate form of that ideal still lay vague and dormant in the twilight depths of his being, but it was like the neglected image of his little madonna that he had brought back with him from Gallegos wrapped up in Neleta's shawl along with other memorabilia of the past—and toilet articles. It was seldom remembered, and never brought out for contemplation. It simply reposed, probably safely enough, in a closed cupboard at numéro 47, Rue de Vielle du Temple, where he and Vincent Nolte for several months in the late autumn and early winter of 1801 conducted life in a gilded-bachelor style of existence that made them at once enviable, convenient, and valuable to a widening circle of influential friends.

Through the wrought-iron gates at numéro 47 came and went, not a constant stream, but a lively trickle of numerous petty bankers and a few great financiers. There were also merchants and agents of all kinds; politicians, and certain government officials and personages.

"The House of the Wolf," as numéro 47 had long been called from the Roman plaque on the wall, had in fact entered upon a new era and busy days. Those who now met there acted, talked, and thought in ways that were new and all their own.

To be sure, Vincent Nolte did not gather friends about him to hold them and arrange them like so many iron-filings in the lines of the force he radiated. But he did have a certain influence. He was one of many magnetized, though not highly magnetic personalities, possessed of a certain modicum of attraction and force that kept the various motes in the current of the times in motion. His local segment of influence was Leghorn and Southern Europe. But in Paris he fitted into the general sphere of European finance, and on the whole acceptably and ably. This was recognized by several and sundry, and the post of Paul, his concierge, was by no means a sinecure.

Paul, indeed, was an ideal concierge for the House of the Wolf—or, for that matter, for any other house. He had seen the de Vaudreuils, its original owners, depart as ruined émigrés and he had remained loyally at his post while royalists, republicans, terrorists, directors, and consuls passed. It was he who had boarded up the gates in the secret hope that their beautiful griffins might sometime display themselves again, for he believed in the permanency of fabulous things. Certainly not even the griffins themselves could have been more fabulous than the styles of human character and costume which had passed through his portals during the incredible decade. In the course of ten furious years Paul had been forced to become either an amused observer of mankind or a cynic. He chose the former.

"Eighteen-hundred-one, Year Nine, as the newspapers must still say, encore une autre mode. Hein, let us answer the little bell and see what it is like then," he would mutter, shrugging his shoulders. He had long ago learned not to be surprised by anything, and never under any circumstances to laugh aloud. "That is why," he said to Vincent, when the latter had retained him, "I am an ideal concierge."

On the whole, Paul felt, the world was once more becoming more credible. Those who now rang his bell were suave rather than grotesque and madly enthusiastic.

For in Paris in 1801 one was no longer a cultured-natural longing exquisitely for the refined simplicities of a pastoral Utopia or a carefully-unkempt ruffian provided with convenient anarchical rages and a pike to help usher certain philosophic ideas into the world and those who opposed them out of it. One was no longer even a trousered Grecian devoted to naked simplicities and frantic fornication. Outwardly one was a somewhat puzzled kind of a Roman, hesitating whether to admire more the busts of Brutus and other republican regicides that the first consul had installed as a precautionary measure in the Tuileries along with himself, or, the now carnivorous-looking eagles on flags and standards that were undoubtedly beginning to preen themselves imperially and to look one way only as if prematurely afflicted with a touch of neck-stiffening, heraldic pip.

Inwardly, of course, much of all this was still unreal and confusing. One knew, if one had any flair for permanence, that it would pass; that one would secretly remain what one always had been—a good medieval European with perhaps just a saving-dash of the classic sciences and enough Semitic mystery and habitual morality to make life supportable. If one were none of these things, if one were perchance madly oneself, or merely some hard-working French artisan or peasant; one was not one. One was not even a minus quantity. One did not count.

But the ones who frequently, and in some cases habitually, now passed through the boarded gates of the House of the Wolf were again among those who counted. Counting, indeed, was their all-absorbing interest. Nor did they reckon any longer by ancestors and family. Their houses were counting houses and their great names illustrious by firms. But none of them intended to count just one. One in their society, which was, if anything, Carthaginian rather than Roman—one was not anyone until one had become at least one-hundred-thousand something else; francs, guilders, pounds, dollars, or whatnot.

Nothing, perhaps, could have made this notable change in the ways of counting more apparent than a comparison of the little door-books kept by Paul, the first literate concierge of the House of the Wolf, and those of Paul the second, his son and proud successor. Under Paul the first the entries had been, even as late as 8th Janvier, 1785,

Ce Soir

La Princesse de la Tour d'Auvergne
M. le Duc d'Ayen, Madame la Duchesse de ditto
Le Curé de Saint-Eustache
Comte de Ségur, Madame la Comtesse de ditto
M. de Miromandre de Saint-Marie, Madame ditto
Docteur Franklin, philosophe, et sa dame (sans titre)

Under Paul the second, the prestige of the House of the Wolf continued to be made manifest, at least to Paul himself, by such entries as these: 3rd Fructidor, An IX,

Ce Soir

Collot, de la mint
Barbé-Marbois, de la fisc
J. G. Ouvrard, banquier
Herr Nootnagel, de Schwartz & Roques, Hambourg
Perregaux, banquier
Fulcheron, ditto
Cinot, de Cinot, Charlemagne & Cie.
deux autres—

and after each one of these entries was a faint estimate in pencil of the number of francs which Paul thought, or had heard, these guests of the house to be worth. The "deux autres" were merely Talma, the actor, and Nicolas Isouard, a young musician, both tolerated because M. Ouvrard patronized them and brought them along. But of course they didn't count. How could they?—they had nothing to drop through their fingers.

There were others that Paul merely jotted in his book; various bank messengers, brokers, and runners for commercial houses who had business with Vincent. These received no names. Only their business was noted. But no matter how the various comers-and-goers at numéro 47 were now entered in Paul's book their interest if not their business was always the same.

Most of them were to be described by the then rather new word "financier"; that is, the handling of the symbols of value, the game of it, and only incidentally the gain of it was their chief interest in life. In their various business schemes all social, political, religious, and racial differences were tacitly disregarded between them in order that commercial and banking operations might prevail and go on.

For the simultaneous disappearance in France of so many of the kind of people who had once lent distinction to the door-books of Paul's father, and the weakening of their hold on society everywhere else, had opened a new era for the kind of gentlemen who counted and figured in ledgers and on door-books in the year 1801.

Quite distinctly the possessors and manipulators of capital were coming into their heyday. The Revolution which had ideally devoted itself to the "rights of man" had in reality cleared the way for the unrestricted power of the capitalist. The feudal aristocracy had vanished, and with it the social stigma upon "usury" and trade. There were now only two ways of really counting: either by bayonets or by money. The ballot box by which the new order had hoped to be able to ascertain the voice of God, also by counting, was already discerned by some astute men to be a human oracle that could be either bought or coerced.

Here and there international plutocrats, who were eventually to absorb the powers of autocrats, aristocrats, and democrats, had begun to appear. There were even a few isolated individuals who had already evolved the machinery by which the state was to be manipulated. But there were only a few of them, for as yet the theory of financial control was scarcely understood.

But it was already a social feeling, an attitude capable of being shared with others, accompanied by a genuine sense of growing importance even among the lesser lights and small-fry engaged in banking and mercantile operations.

They felt themselves able to say to one another with truth, "We are coming men." Their class feeling was that of sharing an increase er which was being daily conferred upon them by fate. That is one of the most potent feelings that unites men and forces them to act together. They felt it strongly; they felt a growing air of triumph and mastery when they met together even informally. It shone in their faces and confirmed them in their manners. It overflowed in their correspondence—and in that era commercial correspondence first began to overflow the world.

Merchants and bankers everywhere in Europe and America, as if by mutual agreement, now abandoned the old separatist formulas by which they had so long operated. The mercantile and colonial era was already over; national restrictions were beginning to waver so far as they were concerned. In an age of constant warfare they began to collaborate, unconsciously for the most part and always "patriotically" —but nevertheless effectively and consistently to overreach, undermine, and checkmate the arbitrary regulations of hostile governments in restraint of trade.

Hitherto money alone had not been thought quite enough to entitle one to great consideration. In the end riches might procure but they did not immediately confer power and prestige. Certain human graces, certain inherited manners that included a not entirely material code of honour, above all, well-understood and definite responsibilities to both church and state had for ages been demanded and expected from those who possessed property. But now all was changed. The financiers in reality had no superiors in power, not even titular ones. They were accountable only to themselves and their peers. In that sense, but in that sense alone, they had become aristocrats.

Bonaparte understood this. He felt some element of aristocracy to be inevitable and even attempted to re-create it. But he desired an aristocracy accountable to the state. "Aristocracy always exists," he insisted. "Destroy it in the nobility, it removes itself immediately to the rich and powerful houses of the middle class. Destroy it in these, it survives and takes refuge with the leaders of the workshops and people." Napoleon's hostility to financiers, his outbursts of rage and his sarcasms directed against such men as Ouvrard, were due to his comprehension of the fact that the financiers were not interested in anything but finance; that the unrestricted power of money in their hands tended to become a kind of ritualistic game, a thing-in-itself without any regard to its function as a political and social fact, just as the monarchy had become a ritual without meaning at Versailles only a generation before. In the European empire Napoleon hoped to create, the financiers were merely to play a necessary part. To the unrestrained power of plutocrats the little man at the Tuileries was consistently hostile.

"What is a merchant?" he once demanded of a crowd of Hamburg bankers and traders. "I will tell you: A merchant is a man who will sell his country for a small-écu." This was hyperbole in miniature. Nevertheless, truth was present. M. Ouvrard, for instance, and the other guests of the House of the Wolf did not intend to sell their country for a small-écu. No, no! The accusation was unjust; they sweated under it. They were men of larger interests. They would not sell their country for anything less than several milliards of grand-écus. But they knew that they could do it. And some of them, those with the greatest financial acumen, had already set out not only to sell their own country but all the others in the world "into the bargain."

The smaller-fry still acted on more traditional principles. The thrill of power also attended them, but it was not their sole motive. Vincent, for instance, loved to be domestically important, to be able to provide the means for and to engage in a kind of medieval merchant-class life such as that still carried on at Strasbourg. That life was gross perhaps, but at least it was ample and generous. It still supposed that the profits of trade were to be spent in a whole-souled way for human relations and family life. It could still value a friend for himself and not solely for his influence. Vincent's struggle was carried on between a desire to retain some of these "Hanseatic values" and the fascination for purely abstract financial power which the period of war-time finance opened up to him. Was he to remain a merchant living in a whole-souled way or to become a manipulator of government securities and loans devoting himself to the game? He was not generally conscious of the situation. It became visible to him only as the necessity for decisions arose upon various separate occasions.

To Anthony the game of finance was never in itself overpoweringly fascinating. By training and experience he understood its methods of procedure and it was only natural that he should enter into it rather than take up politics, or go into the army, or merely amuse himself going about spending. A man without a country speaking several languages, he found himself peculiarly adapted to take part in international schemes. He could even lose himself in them to a certain "successful" extent as a mere actor in a rôle which fate seemed to have thrust upon him, because there was no other to play. Like a great many other young men, then and since, he felt forced to go on doing something "real" even if his ideals remained locked up. He was not the only one whose madonna was in a bundle in the cupboard.

Yet with Anthony there remained in a peculiarly vivid manner the memory of another rôle, of another way of acting which implied a choice of his own instead of a mere assignment by fate. It would turn the world from a place in which to write letters and speak lines and play financial and other games into a reality, and yet into a mystical city where one could be a whole man and act like one.

Anthony still hoped to work through one rôle into the other. In a curious way, which only his own personality could envisage and contain, he entered upon this attempt by taking part in one of the greatest international financial intrigues of the time.   It was a great plot. Through it he hoped to take his place in the world, and then . . .

In the meantime the mode of existence at the House of the Wolf offered every facility for becoming involved in the financial currents of the time.

The two young men felt themselves to be quite in the main stream of events.   For a while this was a highly satisfactory sensation.   If Anthony had his reservations he was not inclined just then to state them even to himself.   He felt drawn by the tide and swam in it, although not so heartily perhaps as Vincent who swam with it and felt glorified.   Neither was fully aware where the tide was taking them. They felt themselves to be going—and that was enough for the time being.   Certainly it was better than stagnating, which seemed to be the only alternative.

They arranged life accordingly and the House of the Wolf by consequence became entirely masculine.   "Love" even in its more ephemeral and lighter manifestations seemed out of place in what had become essentially an abode of finance.   Masculine associations were bound to predominate there.   The only human affection which could flourish in such an atmosphere was friendship.   Perhaps it was even more to their credit than they knew that they were able to cherish so well the bond between them.   The strains put upon it served only to bind them tighter.   Not until years later did they understand that in this loyal association lay the principal element of their success.   It enabled them both to act with a confidence which neither could have experienced without the assurance imparted by a completely trusting partner.   In the warmth of this understanding and loyalty the natural petty jealousies upon which young men's partnerships so often founder were transmuted into so many friendly rivalries.   They became merely the urging of the spur toward a success to be mutually shared.   And because of this friendship between them they seemed for a while to be living in halcyon days.

The final "divorce" of Vincent from la belle Hélène, who had for some time previous to Anthony's arrival shared Vincent's loneliness, was indicative of a new era.   The parting of Vincent and Hélène was not painful.   It was amusing.   It was even characteristic of belles Hélènes everywhere.

She had never returned from her visit with her "brother, the hussar."   She had simply continued on in his fraternal care.   He, however, had called one afternoon, politely, suggesting that, *as he was the best fencer in his regiment,* his "sister" was entitled to compensation for having been suddenly surprised out of her boudoir.   "Her chagrin, monsieur, was of a terrible completeness at not being asked to return. Her modesty has been shattered by your suspicions. Elle souffres."

"I shall be liberal," said Vincent—and he was, "but there is no reason, monsieur le frère de mademoiselle, why mine should be the only private house in Paris where liberté, égalité, and fraternité are still practised with a complete sans-culotte abandonnement. That legend reads well only on *public* buildings now. I hope you agree?"

"Are you also a good shot with the pistol?" inquired Anthony apparently from mere curiosity and over his newspaper.

"The profound sentiments of monsieur le banquier are acceptable, I am sure," said the military gentleman, departing hastily with some francs.

"I don't want to interfere with your domestic arrangements, Vincent, even temporary ones," continued Anthony, feeling in honour bound to lay at least one posy on the cenotaph of the vanished mademoiselle. "I can make myself comfortable chez *L'homme Armé,* you know."

"Ach—that you should think so!" cried Vincent. "What was that little bud-of-love to me? It is a relief that she has departed. It is terrible for two people to try to read the same newspaper from one knee. I know *now* I was tired of it. Anyway, Paris is a young man's paradise. There are two Eves here under every forbidden tree. Besides, you know, I left my heart with that great rosy-one at Strasbourg. Du lieber, it is for *her* that I suffer now!" And he looked so comical and so sincerely and sentimentally miserable at the same time that they both enjoyed it immensely.

Anthony was wise enough, nevertheless, to take the hint, if it was one, about the newspaper. He had both *Le Moniteur* and *La Liberté* brought up every morning. And this feeling of each to his own newspaper and an open exchange of views afterwards became the spirit of the house and pervaded the entire establishment, affecting to some extent all those who came there.

The shutters on the rez-de-chaussée looking out on the little court and the green garden with the sundial were now thrown open, and they breakfasted in what had once been the drawing-room of the ancient hôtel, eagerly discussing the news, planning a thousand projects and the day's adventure—for all serious business was still that to both of them when they were together—with a flow of understanding and a facility for sound invention and prevision that astonished them both; which, indeed, occurs only when two minds are thoroughly at one and working profoundly at ease together. A shared responsibility made decisions doubly easy. And, as is so often the case when two friends ollaborate for the sole purpose of collaborating, the practical results of their work were accompanied by astonishing good luck. For a month or so during the late autumn of 1801 in Paris this was true with Anthony and Vincent to an unusual degree. All that they undertook prospered. The more off-hand they seemed to be about it the better it went.

————————————

They began by calling on Ouvrard, a vigorous and florid man who received them, as he did everyone who would engage with him in his schemes, eagerly. No one at that time, not even he himself, knew how rich he was. It was only his schemes that were complex and subtle. He himself was in his address and manner simple, direct, and kindly enough. On that particular day he and Vincent discussed eagerly a speculation in government stocks in which they were both vitally interested. It was only toward the last of the interview that apparently as a side issue the Spanish-Mexican scheme came up.

Ouvrard showed immediate interest, however, when he learned that Anthony was shortly to visit the Barings in London, and why.

"It was my thought," said Vincent, "that here is an opportunity to urge upon that important firm, and possibly to present to Sir Francis Baring himself, the full details of the scheme at the instance of a gentleman of independent fortune who is already favourably known to them as a client; one whom they cannot suspect of any political motive. That, as I understand it, has been what has so far delayed our progress. We advance slowly by correspondence. Letters are cold."

"It is very difficult to be candid and explicit in this matter and entrust it to the posts," said Ouvrard. "I can see your point. Well, would you be willing to convey certain proposals to Sir Francis Baring in person, M. Adverse?"

"Provided I was fully acquainted with the contents, M. Ouvrard. I should at least want to know the nature of the risks I might be taking."

"Practically none, I assure you."

"I think it is also important," added Vincent, "that if M. Adverse is eventually to take over the agency at New Orleans he should be fully acquainted with the whole plan, for it is at New Orleans that the initial supplies of bullion, the whole capital for the enterprise, will first be received into neutral territory. In a sense, if the thing goes over, all operations will begin from there."

"Ah, pardon me," cried Ouvrard. "I had not identified your friend here with the person you had written me about for the post at New Orleans. The name slipped me." He turned to Anthony with much greater interest. "I recollect you now. You have had considerable experience with Spanish colonials, haven't you? I thought the suggestion of your going to New Orleans excellent. But how will the Barings feel about it?"

"I cannot be sure," replied Anthony, "but it has occurred to me that since my entire fortune is now, and I trust will remain long, in their hands, they could not find anyone who would be better bonded from their standpoint for handling the large sums which would have to pass through my hands at New Orleans."

"An excellent point," agreed Ouvrard. "Well thought of. It seems in a way to slate you for the post. For to tell the truth, you touch upon the crux of the matter there. It has been impossible so far to agree about the method of investing the capital in the United States, once it has been released; that is, we disagreed about *who* was to do the investing there. As there will be in the aggregate millions of dollars released from Mexico by my drafts over a period of time, its deposit and temporary investment in America before its eventual transfer to Europe, whether in the form of merchandise or specie, is a vast problem."

"I should not care to be involved in that," said Anthony. "I should prefer to have my duties at New Orleans, provided I go there, confined solely to the receipt and transfer of the specie. I should then deliver it to whatever agents in the United States may have been designated."

"The profits for the agent will largely be in the 'temporary investments' he may make, I should think," smiled Ouvrard.

"I should prefer merely a reasonable percentage for handling."

A card was brought at which Ouvrard looked. He got up and put his fat hand on Anthony's arm.

"*And* expenses, M. Adverse, do not forget expenses." He smiled. "But the details must be settled later. You must excuse me now. It is the secretary, de Bourrienne," he whispered to Vincent, "the new advance on the rentes, I suppose. Now when shall I see you next? Supper tomorrow chez vous? Non! I dine with M. Talleyrand. The next day? Bon! Wednesday evening, then."

He followed them to the door. "*What* a charming equipage you have, Nolte," said he as he glanced out of the window. "Where can I have it copied?"

"A present to me from M. Adverse."

"Ah," sighed Ouvrard his brown eyes watering, "the latest London mode."

"Let me send it around to fetch you Wednesday," said Vincent. Ouvrard looked childishly pleased.

They bowed to de Bourrienne as they passed him going out.

"You have not met any more patriots who like horses, I hope," said he laughing. "Did I tell you that fellow, what's-his-name, was dismissed?"

"No, but we rather suspect M. Ouvrard here," said Anthony. "He has taken a fancy to the berlin, too."

Ouvrard roared and clapped him on the back. The door closed. It opened again. "If I were you I would take up those consols, Nolte. Mais oui!"

"Well, I said I would have that major cashiered," said Vincent with tremendous satisfaction as they drove home after the interview, "and I *did.*" Anthony said nothing.

"Ouvrard is a genius but the most vulgar one in the world. Did you notice how he said 'Talleyrand'? But anyone who has anything to lose can take dinner with Talleyrand. Gott! that old fox, he can smell the cheese in the beak of any corbeau a mile away—and make him drop it. I should tell you, mon vieux, that Ouvrard is said to be partial to young men. I think you can go to New Orleans if you want to."

"Damn," said Anthony. "But why do they always take me for an Englishman—the latest London mode, you know. Pshaw!"

"Because you look and act like one, Toni," said Vincent with a shrug.

"But I don't *talk* like one."

"When you are not speaking English, no. But what's the difference? Well, I am going to take Ouvrard's tip and invest in this last issue of the government stock. You had better come in with me, too. It will go up, you know. Let's go to the Bourse now."

Anthony was surprised at the amount Vincent put into French consols. So was Vincent when he got home. "But government securities are bound to go up with peace coming on," he insisted. Yet he looked anxious and read his newspapers Tuesday morning avidly.

The consols had gone down a little.

The dinner with Ouvrard Wednesday evening, however, was a cheering affair. After several hours' talk over the wine he finally spread his hands out on the table, leaning down on his fingers as if he had cards under them, and said, "Attention, messieurs," like a little drum-major.

"I am about to make you a proposition.

"You must be aware, M. Adverse, that in talking with you this evening I have, to be frank, been acquainting myself with you along several lines. The business is an important one and I wished to be satisfied first about a number of matters. Suffice it to say I am. Also, Nolte, I am inclined to think that your suggestion of leaving all the details of the handling of the capital in America to the Barings, if they will undertake it, is the only solution. The matter sums up this way then: I supply the drafts on Mexico; the Barings undertake to get the specie or its equivalent in goods to Europe, making as much as they are entitled to in the process. I will see to the disposal here of whatever comes through their agents." He rubbed his hands. "In that way I can at last recoup myself.

"Messieurs, at the present time I have at my *case* bills on the Mexican treasury for seven millions of dollars. Think of it! They are sight-drafts made over by the Spanish royal treasurer to France as part of Spain's annual subsidy by treaty. The first consul has given them to me to pay me for feeding and clothing his soldiers. He has laughed and thought to ruin me. 'The silver is there,' he said. 'Go and get it.' Well, now we shall do as he suggests. This is my plan.

"You, M. Adverse, will take with you to London my Mexican drafts to the extent of one million dollars. You will suggest to Sir Francis Baring that this is only a first earnest of my desire to further this enterprise and that the money when realized is to be used as working capital for the firms or agents which he may see fit to set up in America. You will also tell him, that as soon as he has his arrangements perfected in America and in Holland, for I imagine that is where most of the goods will be finally received for European distribution, I shall supply him with further drafts for as large amounts as he can handle at one time, and without question. And I am prepared at this time to guarantee that within the next two years I can furnish him drafts to the extent of thirty-five millions of Mexican dollars if he can arrange his forwarding operations on a large enough scale. Urge him to do so. One affair of three millions has already been pulled off. Why stop? I *must* realize on this Mexican paper or it will ruin me. And what is it to the Barings if I make my own arrangements with our government officials here to admit goods on the side?"

"There is also the British blockade," said Vincent.

"That is their affair," cried Ouvrard. "This is a matter of international finance; each side will have to fool its own government. All sides will profit. It is a good thing. A tremendous amount of idle capital will be put to work. And peace will shortly be signed anyway. We must catch fish while the tide serves. I am afraid the peace which is still negotiating will not last long. When do you start for London?"

"In a few days."

"Bien, you will want certain credentials to pass you over the Channel. See Talleyrand, also Fouché. I shall, as it were, smooth the path." He stroked the table-cloth gently. "When you are ready call at my *case* for the drafts. You must not let anyone see them or permit even a rumour that you have them to leak out, for if Bonaparte learns of this he will immediately smell a mouse.

"And now then, good night. It is a great mission you go upon. You will not suffer by it, be sure. Be careful how and what you write ꝏve all things. The best letters are those that are never written."

He swung his luxurious cloak, lined with Russian furs, about him, gathered up his purple gloves, his huge beaver hat, and the stick with a carnelian handle and left with a rich suavity of manner that his walk denied. He ground his boots into the floor as if they were sabots.

They went downstairs and saw him into the berlin which he had now offered to buy.

"You still think it advisable to hold onto this last government issue?" asked Vincent, leaning into the carriage. Ouvrard looked at him calmly. He gave an almost imperceptible nod.

"Talleyrand has borrowed money to take it up," he said, and raised his eyebrows.

The berlin started down the narrow street, its candles burning dimly. Behind its oval window the large, white face and huge hat of the banker looked out like a florid picture set in too-refined a frame.

"I wonder if he was lying?" muttered Vincent.

The next forty-eight hours were some of the most troubled ones that Anthony had ever spent. For two days he thought Vincent was going mad.

From somewhere came a rumour that the peace negotiations were being broken off. A young German banker who had also bought the last government issue heavily ran in to tell them about it next morning about ten o'clock. He was green and shaking. He consumed half a decanter of brandy. Vincent could take nothing. His pink complexion was now a dull, smooth white. They drove headlong to the Bourse. The square was a pandemonium of coming and departing carriages with the gamins employed as messengers rushing about. The police had already resigned and were standing in the slow drizzle with their long capes wrapped about them, taking what shelter they could and merely looking on.

"That is a bad sign," said Vincent gloomily. "Fouché has been known to act promptly when there is no truth in depressing rumours."

It was impossible to force their way into the old buildings from which a constant yelling, as if a thousand poisoned dogs were all dying there, proceeded.

They finally worked across the square and took shelter from the rain in a small shop, where a number of other investors were sitting around. Chairs were being let-out there for a franc an hour. In them those who were being ruined sat as long as they could keep from rushing out to sell. Others immediately took their places. Quotations were brought in every few minutes by boys, who yelled out what was written on the small wooden blocks they carried showing the stock, the hour, and the price. In the shop these were passed about dismally from hand to hand and then stuck in a wooden frame, each stock on its own line.

As the day wore on it was curious to note that the successive waves of men who came to sit in the chairs were more and more handsomely dressed. All the small speculators had been sold out. Only those who thought they could still afford to hold on, or who held such large blocks of consols that they could not sell now without being ruined, would still pay a franc for a chair.

Limonades and sour wines were no longer brought in. Nothing was ordered but the best cognac and coffee for the gentlemen in ruffled stocks, deep, brown coats with many-capes, silk waistcoats, and elegant boots, who nervously compared notes in acceptable accents and exchanged snuff as the market continued to fall.

Vincent said nothing and sat perfectly still. A downward swoop of ten points at one fell blow after a brief rally about two o'clock seemed to have left him frozen.

"Is it so bad?" said Anthony. "Hadn't you better get away from it for a while?"

"I must stay," croaked Vincent hoarsely. "It is all. And Anna's, too. I borrowed." He put his hand on his friend's arm and drew him down to whisper, "I know how a man could shoot himself now. I'm not going to." He smiled through clenched teeth.

"Don't think I would let you be washed out, mon vieux," said Anthony.

"I shall see this through myself, Toni. God bless you," said he, and continued to sit.

A young man dressed in silk and broadcloth, with his dapper boots resting on a chair for which he had paid an extra franc, began after a while to talk to Anthony. He had a dark, Jewish cast of features and wore large rings.

"Are you hit very badly?" he said.

"If it stays down, yes," said Anthony, not caring to explain that his only interest was his friend.

"That is exactly the way I feel," said his new acquaintance. "I don't believe in the rumour of the negotiations with England being off. And I'll tell you what it is, I believe Ouvrard and old Reynard Talleyrand between them are responsible for starting war rumours. When things go to where they want them, then they will buy in. I tell you I have been expecting it. Yesterday this issue started to go up, and I learned then that it was Talleyrand's agent who was buying in large quantities. He stopped at eighty-seven. Then Ouvrard went to see Talleyrand. I'll bet what happened was this: Said the old fox to the fat pig, 'Why not put it down, buy it in cheap, and then put it back again?' Joseph Gallatin, the Swiss banker, was at Talleyrand's last night too, and this morning when the Bourse opened *he* got of a large block of governments. That started things. 'No peace with England. Old Gallatin must know,' said everybody, 'He was at Talleyrand's only last night!' And now look! Even the peasants are beginning to come in with one or two bonds. I tell you, if there was anything to it, if the market was in any real danger, Fouché would have closed the Bourse at noon."

They went over and looked through the shop windows, where a stuffed baboon stood displaying on both arms gentlemen's canes and knick-knacks, which were the usual stock in trade of the place whose chairs were now at a premium. The rain had turned to snow. The steps of the Bourse and the square were packed with a sea of backs, hats, and hunched shoulders watching the blackboards upon which a clerk leaning out of a window wrote hieroglyphics from time to time. A groan went up from the mob.

"Five off, at a clip!" said the young Hebrew to whom the hieroglyphics seemed to be familiar.

Vincent came over and joined them, shaking. "I believe Ouvrard *was* lying the other night," he said. "They are down to thirty-four, and I bought at— Mein Gott!" He moaned. A gamin with a set of discouraging blocks rushed in. An old aristocrat who looked as if he might have been a courtier at Versailles in his youth dropped a snuff-box on the floor and wilted as if he were going to have heart failure. Anthony picked up the box for him. It had a portrait of Marie-Antoinette on it. The old man extended it with a trembling hand but with the grand manner.

"It is a curse, monsieur, for having bought republican securities. 'Securities!'—it must be M. Voltaire there in the window who called them that."

He rose, took his cane and lunged at the baboon which collapsed into a corner of the show-case, grinning diabolically at all those in the room.

"I am going to sell, *sell!*" shrieked a staid-looking man apparently addressing the monkey. He rushed out. Two others began to shuffle their feet uneasily.

"Ouvrard has just jettisoned two thousand shares," yelled someone, sticking his head in the door. "Do you hear, Henri? Oh, he is gone!"

As if at a signal everyone in the place but Vincent, Anthony, the old aristocrat and the young Hebrew rushed out. They rolled over each other getting down the steps. A handsome, middle-aged banker picked himself up out of the gutter after his colleagues had stamped him flat, and wrung the mire out of his beard. The young Jew broke into an ecstasy of laughter, looking up at the face of the baboon. Vincent began to move toward the door, shaking. Anthony laid hold of him.

"Wait, Vincent," said Anthony. "I don't think he was lying. I feel sure of it."

"I *sell*," said Vincent. "Enough to get home on!" Anthony looked appealingly at the young Jew who was regarding the little drama before him quizzically.

"Stay and get rich, monsieur," said the Hebrew with sudden sympathy, his smile vanishing. "Why not?"

Vincent hesitated; collapsed in a vacant chair. Anthony gave him a drink from a glass of brandy someone had abandoned.

The old man in the corner snickered behind his hand.

Suddenly a roar went up from the mob. A carriage escorted by police was trying to make its way to the Bourse. It lodged half-way across the square. Someone, they could not see who, got up in it and shouted something.

"It's a messenger from the Tuileries," said the young Jew going out on the steps. "I can see his scarf."

The mob about the carriage began to swirl. In five minutes everyone in as many blocks knew that the rumour of renewed war with England had been officially denied.

A boy dashed up and thrust a note into the hand of the young man on the steps. He walked in smiling triumphantly.

"Ouvrard is beginning to buy," he said. "Now you will see. That lot he threw on the market was only to save his face."

"Up we go," he shouted, snatching a block from a passing gamin.

The confusion outside was now indescribable. A great crowd of hatless men rushed out of the Bourse and down the steps, waving their hands frantically. The mob outside broke up into eddying groups buying and selling. The old man in the corner got up and going over to the window put the stuffed monkey back into place almost affectionately. He then went over to the young Jew and extended him his snuff-box.

"For the first time in the history of my family to one of your race, monsieur. *Do me the honour.* I have been watching your face during the last hour and it is the most beautiful one I have ever seen. It has been worth forty-five thousand francs to me."

He bowed and went out.

Vincent joined in the laugh. He seemed to have been healed by a miracle. They waited till the Bourse closed, shook hands with the young Jew, who declined to be driven home by them, and wound their way through the groups in the streets who were still eagerly buying and selling while shaking the snow off coat collars. Everyone understood what had happened now. Everyone was trying to recoup himself. Consols soared.

"I shall sell tomorrow morning before the big ones begin to cash in and the crest falls off," said Vincent. And he did.

He came home enormously complacent.

"How much did you make?" asked Anthony grinning.

"Toni, I shall never tell you," said Vincent. "I have learned my lesson. I shall never risk my reason again. I am ashamed."

Anthony laughed at him. "So our friend the Israelite proved a *profit* after all," he said after a little.

"Yes," cried Vincent leaping up. "But it was you who kept me in that chair. You! And now I am rich. Du lieber Gott, I am rich!"

"If I were you," said Anthony, "I would turn those paper francs you have made your profit in, into coin of some kind and make a cache of it in England. I begin to see now how wise was old John Bonnyfeather in several ways."

"I'll think it over," replied Vincent. "But first I will recoup Anna, and I am going to transfer her investments to *Hope and Co.*, at Amsterdam. How *could* I ever have borrowed from her? Think of it!"

"Yes," said Anthony, "when I was sitting by you in one of those damned, hired chairs that day I saw Anna sitting in her window at Düsseldorf, under her canaries. There must be flowers in that window, too. I guess she will be big with her baby by now. You remember that day at Livorno when we both agreed what banking was about?"

"Ja," said Vincent, and sat silent for a while. Neither of them ever referred to the matter again.

An urgent letter from the Barings, this time addressed to Anthony, served to hasten his departure from Paris. Old Sir Francis Baring himself had written briefly, enclosing his few lines like something alive encased in the documents which surrounded them.

> My dear Sir:
>
> Only a lifelong esteem and boyhood friendship for your benefactor persuaded me to undertake the administration of his affairs. It is that alone which now prompts me to tender you my advice.
>
> Delay no longer. I am in receipt of your letter of recent date and I shall be pleased to see you personally when you arrive here. But no matter how alluring the prospects of future gain may appear to be in the Spanish-Mexican scheme, to which you allude

so enthusiastically, your further tarrying in Paris at this time is like to endanger what you have already inherited. Between a comfortable certainty and a gilded possibility no reasonable man should ever hesitate. Suffer me at least to remind you of that. I assume that you are reasonable.

The accompanying letters will inform you of my particular reasons for writing you this. As you have not been brought up in England, you may not perhaps fully appreciate the evils of falling into the hands of those who at a staggering charge turn the hearty, human curses of their clients into feeble legal-prayers to the Court of Chancery.

The enclosed advice from Messers McSnivens, Williams, Hickey, and McSnivens is therefore, be advised, sufficiently alarming. I trust we shall be able to stave the matter off until you arrive.

Your humble obd't servant,
Francis Baring, Bart.

"Well, that settles it. Doesn't it? If Ouvrard isn't ready to have me go yet I shall leave anyway. Go!"

"Let's drive round and see him now," said Vincent seeing that Anthony was so determined. For some days they had not heard from the banker.

The rest of the day was a busy one. They found Ouvrard at the Tuileries with some difficulty but as it proved later fortunately with Talleyrand.

"Come in, come in," said Ouvrard, after the servant whom they both bribed and threatened to announce them at the ministry of foreign affairs had finally done so, "I have just been going over our scheme as it now stands with the bishop upstairs," he whispered, grinning. "He can see no reason why with peace coming on we should not begin operations promptly." He filled his chest for a long talk but Anthony took his opportunity.

"That is exactly what we all feel, M. Ouvrard, and as I am leaving tonight for London I have come to you for the drafts you spoke of desiring me to carry to Sir Francis Baring."

"Tut, tut," said Ouvrard, still puffed up like a fat peacock with the wind he had inhaled for a long period. "Tut, tut, I don't want you to leave right away." The plump hand had come out and rested on his arm as if it would detain him.

"I am sorry, monsieur, that I am unable to make my own convenience entirely yours," replied Anthony; "perhaps in any event you will aid me with having my passports properly endorsed. I understand that despite the suspension of hostilities there are still difficulties."

"Tiens!" exclaimed Ouvrard, stepping back. "It is someone like you that we need to put action into this affair. I myself, I talk. Yet much is accomplished by talk, you will observe, much is done by words . . ."

"The passports are the first step now, aren't they?"

Vincent looked shocked that so important a man should be interrupted in the midst of his words.

"You are right," said Ouvrard. "Come up and we will see Talleyrand now."

They found the former bishop of Autun looking out the window with his back towards them when they entered. Anthony caught a glimpse of his face in the full light as he looked out across the Tuileries gardens and before he seemed to be aware that they had been announced. He did not turn instantly. He seemed to complete his thought, whatever it was, and then turned. Anthony felt it to be a curious thing that the expression on the face of the minister of foreign affairs had not altered in the slightest as he came forward a few steps with a slight limp to acknowledge their presence. He seemed to accept them simply as facts with the self-same completely quiet smile, a very slight one, with which he had been looking out at the grass and trees a few seconds before.

There was something vaguely familiar to Anthony in that smile, something just a little sinister in the shell-like curve of the lips which the smile overcame but did not cancel. Theirs was a moulded self-possession. The eyes, rather small but steady and keen, confirmed the self-possession of the mouth without adding anything to whatever faint warmth the smile might have been useful enough to convey.

And yet the man was not cold. He was animated, alive, no doubt of it. But imperturbable. By always compelling all who approached him forever temporarily to suspend their judgment as to his motives he perpetually kept their attention—and then he would vanish, usually with a portion of Europe in his portfolio.

"Permit me, citizen-minister," Ouvrard was saying—"mes amis, Herr Nolte, whom you will remember, and M. Adverse."

The citizen-minister bowed, limped once and sat down, at the same time indicating that there were other chairs with a courtesy that seemed to make standing up only a little less futile than sitting down. For a moment they hesitated.

"In America, where I lived for some time," said Talleyrand impersonally, "they have a marvellous contrivance called a rocking chair. I have long thought of furnishing the suite of the minister for foreign affairs here with them. They give one the impression of always being just about to attain equilibrium without ever permitting anybody to do so. Do be seated, gentlemen."

They did so while he continued, "I hear you are to be congratulated in holding on to your government stock through the recent flurry, Herr Nolte. There were only a few who were wise enough to do that. They say a certain young Frankfort Jew also made a great fortune."

"I did not make a great fortune, monsieur," began Vincent.

"He became only moderately rich," put in Ouvrard laughing.

"Well, what more do you want me to do for you, gentlemen? I do not suppose, of course, that you came here to express your gratitude. The rumour about the negotiations being broken off was absurd. M. Ouvrard will confirm me, I am sure."

"Ridiculous," said the banker. "The first consul could not have chosen a more fitting person than his brother Joseph to negotiate the treaty. Look how well he did at Campo Formio. I trust you will say so, M. Adverse, in the proper quarters when you arrive in London."

"I shall be delighted to do so provided the citizen-minister can see fit to smooth my way across the Channel."

Talleyrand opened a cahier before him and began to finger its leaves. "Your purpose in going to—London—monsieur?"

"Is to transact some private affairs with *Baring Bros. and Co.*—and—" he looked at Ouvrard, who smiled encouragingly, "to convey to Sir Francis Baring several Spanish compliments from M. Ouvrard."

Talleyrand smiled. "Your formula is apt enough, M. Adverse. I also hear you have the habit of making friends. M. Auguste de Staël expressed himself warmly about you yesterday at Cambacérès'. I admire Mme. de Staël enormously. I am under great obligations to her."

"It was nothing, I merely acted on impulse, I assure you."

"I have no doubt of it," replied Talleyrand. "When do you leave for London?"

"Tonight, if possible."

"And you are living now at?"

"Forty-seven, Rue de Vielle du Temple—with Herr Nolte."

"The House of the Wolf," said Talleyrand amused. "Now when I was at Saint-Sulpice I remember . . ." he smiled and waved his hand —"and you are gay there?"

"Very," said Anthony and was echoed by Vincent.

"That is well. You sustain a certain tradition. I will tell you that much." He looked at them both with a reminiscent satisfaction. "The twins of the wolf, eh! But come, that is my affair.

"What I was going to say to you, M. Adverse, is, that since you are going to London, I wish you to deliver certain letters for me person-ally. They will be sent around to you with the rest of your papers 's afternoon. Now when you deliver these letters merely say this;

I am *personally* sincerely desirous of a lasting peace between Eng-

land and France. Convey that impression from me as a *personal*
expression of my opinion to those to whom the letters will be addressed.
Ah,—two things more—assure Sir Francis Baring that no difficulties
will be thrown in M. Ouvrard's way by me—quite the contrary. The
first consul's attitude on British goods you understand is unalterable.
But colonial produce, that, of course, is a different thing.

"And now, monsieur, this is really important. From a certain shop
in Bond Street—I will write the name on this slip—I wish you to have
sent to me twelve dozen pairs of ladies' gloves, grey with pearl buttons,
and this size." He put the piece of paper about his own hand, marked
it, and handed it to Anthony. "Mme. Grand will wear no others," he
said to Ouvrard.

"In spite of your doubts as to gratitude we are all grateful, citizen-
minister," said Vincent as they rose.

"Véritablement," cried Ouvrard.

"La gratitude n'existe pas," said Talleyrand. "But do not neglect
to get the gloves at least, M. Adverse. I shall reimburse you for
them," his eyes lit up a little.

He did them the honour of limping to the door before bowing them
out.

"Who is Mme. Grand?" demanded Anthony, going down the
stairway.

"Sh," said Ouvrard. "La bishop—ess. And now let me drive
round to the *case* with you. Ah, the little berlin! I wish you would
do something for me in London, M. Adverse," said he, lying back and
taking up most of the room on the rear seat. "Have your dealer
reproduce the little vehicle for me, but upholstered in red morocco. An
improvement, I think."

"I shall see what I can do with my dealer," replied Anthony. The
man looked pleased.

At the bank Ouvrard delivered to Anthony ten drafts on the Mexican treasury, each for one hundred thousand silver dollars.

"They are sight-drafts," said Ouvrard, "signed, you will notice, by
Godoy, the Spanish prime minister, and by the royal treasurer of Spain.
Anyone who presents them is entitled to receive the specie."

"There is nothing to prevent me from cashing them for myself
then?" said Anthony.

"Nothing but yourself," replied Ouvrard, sealing the package.
"Well, it would not be *quite* as simple as that. One does not call with
a wagon for a million silver dollars, you know, and just drive off.
When the time comes certain letters of identification and confirmation
will be provided for me by M. Talleyrand to the Mexican government.
But you know the procedure in such cases. Do not lose them,

though," he said, raising his finger half humorously. "It would ruin Herr Nolte."

Anthony looked from Ouvrard to Vincent.

"Why," laughed the banker, "didn't you know Nolte has gone bond for you?"

He delayed them for another hour going over endless details.

"My God, Vincent, why didn't you tell me you were going bond for me?" said Anthony fingering the package with the drafts gingerly as they drove back to the House of the Wolf. "Suppose something *does* happen to me!" he exclaimed again as they got out of the berlin.

Vincent did not reply but in the courtyard he stopped and putting a hand on Anthony's shoulder pointed with the other to the plaque of the twins sharing the milk of the wolf. "From now on, as always before already," he said in German, "between us it is still going to be like that?"

"Yes," said Anthony, "and a fine picture of two young bankers sucking the guts out of the state . . ."

"Ach, go on with you," said Vincent. "It is a good sign, a lucky one, Gemini—this is a gay house. Even Talleyrand said so. I wonder what he . . ."

"A government messenger has been waiting for you for an hour, monsieur," said old Paul just then appearing from within breathlessly. "I have been watching him while he waited. That was why Jean opened the gate."

They rushed upstairs like two boys. Anthony signed for the packet from the Tuileries and scarcely waited till the messenger was gone to break its seal.

"Look," he cried, "an order for government posts as far as Havre. The prefect there is to 'expedite my waftage,'—what a curious expression."

"Give me the first post billet," said Vincent, "and I will send Paul out with it now to the government stables. How will it do to have them call for you about nine? A last dinner here, you know. And your luggage will take time."

"That reminds me of something, Vincent. I want you to take care of this bundle for me." He brought it from his room.

"A woman's shawl, eh," said Vincent grinning.

"No, no, that is not it at all. There is something in it which—oh, do not ask me to explain. Keep it safely here till I return. I leave it with you—in the House of the Wolf," he added solemnly.

"Very well, Romulus, Remus hears you," smiled Vincent, and then ked solemn enough himself as he took the bundle and locked it up.

' the hour of nine exactly a light post-chaise with two horses and a government postilion drew up at numéro 47. A sergeant of gendarmes emerged from it.

"May I see your papers, monsieur?" He examined them carefully while two leather trunks and a valise were being strapped on.

Vincent stood holding a lantern lugubriously over the signs of departure.

"I wish you would do something for me when you get to London," he laughed, imitating Ouvrard, and leaning into the carriage at the last. "Have your dealer line this with red-morocco-and-pink-and-green satin—and bird-lime—" he flashed his lantern over the battered interior of the old post-chaise ruefully. "And keep yourself warm, Toni, mein Gott, England is not Africa! Wait, wait a minute, you have forgotten something." He stormed back into the house.

For a minute the grim, grotesque shadow of the postilion and his horses, the post-chaise and its vacant windows stood waiting, leaning forward a little, projected on a blank wall across the narrow street by the lantern Vincent had left on the curb. The ancient bell at Saint-Merri near by tolled a quarter. The sergeant looked impatient. A little snow was beginning to fall.

"All in the house wish to thank you for your extreme generosity, monsieur," said old Paul. Anthony shook the old man by the hand. A horse stamped. The gate flew open and Vincent rushed into the street and began to stuff something through the window of the carriage.

"For winter," he cried, "to keep you warm, Herr Gott, to keep you warm."

"Allez," snorted the sergeant.

Anthony wrung Vincent's hand as old Paul dragged him back, and the post-chaise clattered up the crazy old street. It turned left and rattled along the cobbles of the Rue Saint-Antoine. It turned right, and passing the dark front of old Saint-Merri, headed north along the Rue Saint-Martin, a straight Roman road.

The post-chaise was not going any faster, however, than had the chariots along that same road seventeen centuries before. Nor was it, perhaps, going quite as safely.

"Monsieur goes armed?" asked the sergeant.

"Yes."

"Bon! It is well. I go as far as the Porte Saint-Denis with you. I do not leave the city. You will receive your first galloping relay and an armed guard at the gate. It is better since the first consul has sent around his tribunals. But the post of the Republic is not the post of the days of the kings. Few travel, everything has fallen off. In my boyhood for a few écus one could send a package or even a money order on a banker from any city in France to another. They say if Bonaparte is made king things will go better. Perhaps? He makes good roads for soldiers. But one can no longer send money and letters safely. The Revolution has made men less honest than they were when God was in heaven, the king on his throne, and the devil in hell."

"Are you a legitimist, sergeant?"

"No, monsieur, but in these days I would simply advise you to go armed. Such moral sentiments as still exist do not help deliver the mails. I know that. I myself have secured you a carriage with sturdy wheels. That Committee of Safety was so busy removing heads that they had no time to put on wheels. You had best buy your grease too or the pigs will answer when you drive past. They sell it at the barriers. And now I leave you, citizen—bon chance." He would not be paid. "My opinions cost me a great deal," he said and went into the guard-room laughing.

Anthony felt for his precious papers. They were still there.

At the Porte Saint-Denis before the barrier a fire was leaping like a wild beast in an iron cage. The horses were changed rapidly. Four, instead of three, were now attached. A glowing brick was taken from the fire and put in an iron box. This on a bed of sand was put in to heat the carriage. It was now beginning to snow still harder. A north wind rumbled against the old battlements, the red fire leaped fiercely in the black night. Would they never get through comparing his papers? The sergeant on guard came out with them at last. "All right," he muttered. The armed guard climbed up on the seat behind. "If the citizen would be kind enough to provide cognac?" said the sergeant. "I can get it at the gate canteen for him. It will be cold for those outside." "Three flasks," said Anthony. A rumble of approval and the slapping of the guard's hands on the roof followed. The brandy came. All took a swig. The barrier was suddenly opened letting the wind sweep in bitterly. The postilion broke into a torrent of abuse, and leaning low along the back of the beast he was riding, lashed his teams forward into the storm.

It was the first great winter storm Anthony had ever seen. A gale of a distinctly arctic character was sweeping down from the Pas du Nord accompanied by flurries of fine snow. The roads were frozen as hard and as smooth as iron. The horses which knew every foot of their own familiar stage with a stable at either end galloped steadily by the light of a waning November moon. The guard on the open seat behind crouched low behind the trunk on the roof and beat his arms about him to keep his hands from freezing. Occasionally the horn blared and a dog barked. Then the devouring sound of the hoofs and wheels continued.

Inside the heat of the brick gradually died away. The windows ˜med over by the breath of the solitary traveller in the post-chaise ˜e more opaque as they froze until he sat insulated in a little world of frosty moonshine.   He wrapped about him the heavy bear-skin rug that Vincent had stuffed through the window at the last.   He drew his feet up on the seat under him and sank back gratefully into its comforting folds.   The world outside seemed to have fallen away. He could not sleep, but as the swinging and rocking, the long forward slide of the carriage continued and the cold became more bitter and penetrating, his process of retreating into the rug continued and he withdrew farther and farther into himself.

He heard them change horses at Villiers la belle Gonesse but after that no more.

Sitting half-awake and numb in the amazing cold, he now retained only what seemed to be the fundamental residue of realization.   He was being taken somewhere swiftly and he felt now that he was travelling absolutely alone.   Within him was an utter stillness and calm.   If he could only retain that.   Was it possible?   He wondered.

CHAPTER FIFTY-SEVEN

YOUR HUMBLE OBEDIENT SERVANT

London, 28 December, 1801

DEAR VINCENT,

I arrived here on Weds., the 27th inst., coming up by coach from Plymouth through as bitter a snap of weather as anyone remembers having seen. The trip across the Channel was like to be my last.

You know we both wondered why my departure was arranged by way of Amiens. It was plain enough when I got there. The conference to make the treaty of peace is getting under way there and there is considerable coming and going of envoys, secretaries, and personages by way of Havre de Grace. Otherwhere the blockade is still strict. I received every courtesy as a "messenger." At the prefecture I ran into M. Joseph Bonaparte who was just coming out from seeing the prefect. He remembered me although not my name. I think he thought I was you, but he soon caught himself up very pretty. He told me how Luçay was dismissed. We really did not have so much to do with that as we thought.

It did me no harm, I think, to be seen talking with the first consul's brother. The prefect gave me an order for a special dispatch lugger at Havre when I should arrive there, which I did two days later.

I shared the ridiculously crowded little cabin with a young English diplomat by the name of Spencer, with de Lanark, another messenger of Talleyrand's who looked at me somewhat askance because I would tell him nothing, and young Lord Francis Russell, son of the Duke of Bedford, who was accompanied by his tutor, the Reverend Hinwick Orlebars. The last two were returning from a tour of the lower Germanys and had been blown into Havre by the gale which scattered the blockade it is said from the Scheldt to Finistère. By some influence here the Englishmen were permitted to depart and were glad even of the crowded cabin. As I was in a merry mood at getting off in such style I had the innkeeper send down a large hamper of wines and eatables, which proved in the event a mighty comfort to us all in extremity.

Young Russell was especially desirous of spending Christmas with family in Bedfordshire and he and I combined with the persuasive l to prevail on the skipper to put to sea, rather against his own judgment I think, and the protests of the tutor, a clerical gentleman with small stomach for gambolling with Neptune. There was a lull in the gale the morning of the 19th inst. We put forth, got half-way over, and had raised the cliffs when a brawling norther cold as the hinges of doom swept us down channel like so much fluff. The seas were mountainous and all we could do was drive straight away. The crew, four sea-rats in red knitted-caps, and their pock-marked captain were all but worn out. The water-butt went by the board, and no fire could be lit. My basket with two fat geese, some pastries, and several bottles of wine served to keep us alive. The cold was unexpressible. Your bear rug saved the life of the clerical person, if that is anything to you. He sat wrapped in it eating goose's drum-sticks occasionally and praying continually. The other gentlemen, Spencer and de Lanark, rolled about puking on the cabin floor. Their plight was truly miserable, especially so since young Russell, who still has the merciless humour of a boy that can see but not yet feel the miseries of his fellows, plagued them unmercifully by offering them bits of goose liver with emetic results. The sight of his tutor praying in a bear skin sent him into gales of mirth. As I was afraid some in the cabin might gather enough strength to do him bodily harm, I took the young bear up on deck, where, despite the spray and the cold, we managed to be gay and shared our wine with the crew, who were grateful.

Taking it altogether, the experience in the Channel is one of the worst I have ever had. On the third day we got a glimpse of the coast that the skipper recognized as a bit of Cornwall, and as the wind blessedly relented and veered, we were enabled to beat back up the coast into Plymouth late on the afternoon of the 23rd.

I went to the "Swan," as nothing could have induced me to take the night coach for London which all the others did, except Mr. Spencer who came down with a bad attack of pleurisy. I went out and got him a leech who bled him. He seemed very weak, poor fellow. Young Russell and his tutor hired post and were both pressing I should come along. In this I am flattered to believe they were sincere enough but the invitations of sons and tutors do not necessarily imply the welcome of fathers, especially if they be great ones, so I saw them off in a flurry of snow with a merry toot of the horn and young Francis waving his hat and shouting back "Happy Christmas."

A sinking sensation of being left alone followed (Christmas is made much of here). I went back to the "Swan" and a good sea-coal fire and excellent dinner in my own room, where, for the first time in a week, I was both full and warm—and thankful to God for still being able to be so. The lugger is shipping a new mast, I hear.

I strolled about the town next day. This is the cleanest country I have ever been in. It is strange to hear English spoken everywhere

and by everybody.   My talk is a little curious, I fancy, but passes well
enough.   They take me for Scotch if for anything.   I shall devote
considerable attention to polishing the roughness off my tongue and
write you in nothing else.   This is the language in which I find I do
most of my thinking.   Little else was spoken, you may remember,
behind doors at the old Casa da B (what a polyglot world Livorno
was).   I also took occasion to provide myself with innumerable warm
clothes.   I shall gradually become hardened to the northern winter, I
suppose, and it will do me good, but at present I do suffer greatly.
Almost as good as your bear skin are my Havana cigars for comfort.
My stock is running low and I grow alarmed.   They smoke the Virginia leaf in pipes here.   Only the best is tolerable.

The pleasantest thing that has yet happened to me in England overtook me in Plymouth.   I found Mr. Udney in the public room just
as I was about to leave for London.   He gave a rumble and a shout
when he saw me and would not hear of my going up.   All my things
were carried back upstairs again by his order.   Saving your own welcome, I have never had a man so glad to see me.   I was quite overcome, and I believe he was, too, for he did swear dreadfully.   Had
just driven down from his place near Totnes in Devon to transact
some business in Plymouth.   Really an excuse to get away from a
lonely old house, I take it.   Mrs. Udney is in Amsterdam on a visit
to Florence, the Parishes having recently removed there from Rotterdam since David has now joined interests with *Hope and Co.* in
Amsterdam.   If I return that way I shall see them.   Mr. U. much
cut-up over Florence's having no son or "any other children," as he
puts it.   He claims it must be David's fault, who I gather is rather
a cold fish.   The old man is a breeder of horses and I shall not set
down his speculations about dear David which were not only frank
but downright technical.   He was greatly interested to learn that I
was going up to London to claim my inheritance.   It seems he knew
of it through the registering of the will all along.   When I told him
I hadn't, he cursed J.B. for a sentimental old Jacobite.   He is quite
sure I was no relation to J.B. and told me how he and Father Xavier
arranged to have me apprenticed.   All quite accidental, which in a
way relieves my mind.   After all, when you come right down to it,
a great many people do not know their parents any better than I do,
even if they do know their names.   What do you know about your
own father, for instance?   (I don't expect you to reply.)   The upshot
~f it was we had Christmas dinner together, and a right merry one,
   I got off for London next day leaving the old gentleman, whose
      ` quite white now, standing with a very red face in the door of
         ·an," thumping his stick and swearing and insisting that I must

come down to Devon for a visit, which I think I shall do, if conditions permit.

I got here the 27th, awful weather as above mentioned, and am staying at the Adelphi. This morning I called at *Baring Bros. & Co.* to notify them of my arrival and was most courteously received by Mr. John Baring. If not glad, they were certainly relieved at seeing me, as also to discover, I think, that I was not a Sicilian or a Red Indian. I have an appointment for tomorrow, when I may be able to mention that I have an important matter to convey from M. O. to Sir Francis. I requested Mr. John Baring to convey my profound appreciation, gratitude and respect to his father, at which he looked genuinely pleased. I think the slaving business gave them the idea I was a rough and ready customer. I was—but I am not.

You shall hear from me directly as to further developments. This letter is sent by way of Helgoland and Amsterdam by a special messenger maintained between the Barings here and Messers *Hope & Co.* there. The blockade is unrelaxed. I have not yet bought M. T.'s gloves for him. If you want to know what London is like breathe heavily on your shaving glass and then try to look in it. That is as much as I have seen of it so far, so I will not give you any "reflections."

This rather in haste as the Baring's messenger calls for it shortly and sails tonight. With luck you should have this in two weeks. There is some talk of re-establishing the Calais packet and mails. I think of the House of the Wolf fondly—heaven fend for you and good luck follow.

Your humble obd't servant.

A. A.

P. S. Send by way of Messers Hope at Amsterdam when you answer and address me care of *Sir Francis Baring, Bart & Co.*, Bishopsgate Street, London. They operate abroad as *Baring Bros. & Co.*

To Herr Vincent Nolte, at the House of the Wolf, 47 Rue de Vielle du Temple, Paris.

London, 29th January, 1802

Dear Vinc,

Almost a month has gone by since I wrote you and I suppose that by this date you must have my first letter. A great deal has happened in that interval which I shall attempt to relate rather in the order of its occurrence than that of its relative importance.

First, my own affairs financial are satisfactorily in order; secondly, the great Spanish-Mexican business, if not launched, is at least set up on the ways and lacks only about £100,000 to knock the blocks from under it and start it moving. That is a large "only" I admit—but to the events themselves:

My own humble affairs were settled with greater dispatch than at first seemed likely.

On the 29th of last month I called according to appointment at the counting house of the Barings in Bishopsgate Street and was received by Mr. Charles Wall, who oversees most of the routine correspondence of the firm. I was taken to the second floor office, a splendid, panelled room furnished with teak furniture and various Indian rarities assembled by Sir Francis, who for many years has been a director of the Honourable East India Company. He now, I find, seldom appears in the city and has turned over the practical conduct of his affairs to his older sons Thomas and Alexander.

In this ample but arctic room I found assembled about an immense teak table in which the candles, for there was a rayless fog outside, reflected themselves funereally, Mr. Thomas Baring, John Hickey, Esq., of the firm of McSnivens, Williams, Hickey, and McSnivens, barristers; a gentleman by the name of Flood from the Bank of England, and several accountants and clerks with various piles of papers. Mr. Thomas Baring seated me beside himself and Mr. Hickey, of whom more later, accepted one of my precious Habana segars after smelling of it like a posy as if it had been an unexpectedly large refresher, which indeed it was. We then, together with Mr. Wall, who took notes, settled down to business.

The first matter taken up was the sum due me from my remittances to the Barings from Africa. These I found to my great satisfaction had been turned into ready money deposited in the Bank of England, and despite the heavy discount on the acceptances of the original foreign bills of exchange, amount with accumulated interest from the Bank to 17,034 pounds sterling, ten shillings, and four ½ pence. The transfer of this goodly sum from the account of the Barings to myself was effected with due formalities by Mr. Flood. I then paid Mr. Thomas Baring 2½% net for his firm's handling of the transaction and gave and received receipts. All this was properly witnessed, stamped, recorded by notaries and I know not what else. The whole transaction was overlooked by the genial Mr. Hickey, who with an apparently casual manner combined the eye of a hawk, and at one point shook the precise little Mr. Flood into an ague by pointing out that by the omission of a comma in the transfer the whole sum was made liable to be claimed by the crown. Mr. Flood protested his good intentions. "Pooh, pooh," said Mr. Hickey, "don't dribble self-ng testimony, Mr. Flood, punctuate. Nearly all the tragedies in es of my clients come from little *commac* effects. I have a live luxuriously on the fees arising from this one for the rest of my life by not putting a *period* to it. What will you compound with me for?" Mr. Flood's hand shook as he inserted the comma and Mr. Baring laughed. Hickey is an Irishman, or his father was, and he is said to have made the original pun before the woolsack about litigants being the lambs that furnished the fleece to stuff it with. I tell you all this because I thought you would like to know how the Barings conduct business, since you transact a good deal with them yourself.

The firm is purely a family affair. Sir Francis is responsible for and still directs its policies. As an old member of Parliament and one of the most powerful of the Whigs he has great political influence. Thomas looks after the London house with Wall who is his brother-in-law. Alexander is now in Amsterdam with the Hopes, and, as you know, M. Labouchère of that firm married a Miss Baring. The Barings and Hopes act as one apparently, the latter looking after continental affairs. They are to all intents and purposes a family unit. There is also a Mr. Henry Baring, who I understand is very brilliant but addicted to high play. He and David Parish are very close. They are brothers in whist.

As soon as Flood left, after requesting me to call around and identify myself with certain officials at the bank, we went into the matter of the Bonnyfeather estate. I produced my copy of the will probated at Leghorn and other papers, which Hickey found in order and expressed his satisfaction over. He would, he said, in a short while if all went well, be able to put me in possession of the estate, which had been invested by the Barings in ways too numerous to mention here. I asked Hickey what he meant by "if all went well," and he replied that a very ridiculous but none the less serious situation threatened the inheritance. Without going into the legal phraseology and technicalities of it, for which I naturally take my attorney's word, let me explain—because it is—or rather, thank God, it *was* funny.

You will recall old Captain Bittern of the *Unicorn,* no doubt. Well, when I left Gibraltar I gave him the cabin silver and furnishings, among them a chair which he particularly affected for some reason; a chronometer, etc. This was just a small token of appreciation for years of faithful service, and he was not a man upon whom one could press banknotes. "Independence" is his watchword.

When he returned home he quite properly removed these effects to his own lodgings. The ship was then sold at auction by the Barings. The young cub of an attorney in charge of the proceedings dug up an old ship's inventory, and finding that Bittern had removed the cabin furniture, etc., he had the good old skipper taken up for larceny and the goods seized. This was bad enough, the Lord knows, but worse followed.

Captain Bittern had presented the chair to a chapel at Spitalfields, the shrine of an obscure and fanatical Protestant sect known as the "Muggletonians." Furthermore, that chair had been consecrated as the seat of the prophetess, an ancient and fiery old party by the name of Johanna Heathecote. When the bailiffs arrived to claim "her chair," as near as Hickey and I can find out, a riot of no inconsiderable proportions unrolled itself.

Spitalfields is a hungry weaving neighbourhood with a lot of people thrown out of employment by the war. Before the rolling around in the chapel was over the friends of the saints had assembled outside, attracted by what seemed to be more than just the ordinary scufflings of schism.

When the bailiffs, battered and bleeding, emerged with the chair, the crowd, recognizing in them the enemies of mankind, made common cause with the saints and forced the poor fellows to take refuge in a stone stable near by, where some rascals set fire to the straw. The mob, for it had rapidly grown to those proportions, then turned its attention to the bakeshops in the neighbourhood and was proceeding to I know not what further mischiefs when a detachment of the guards and a number of special constables fell upon them, arrested a number of poor souls, put out the fire and rescued the bailiffs who were all but smothered but still had the chair.

Thus the throne of Great Britain triumphed over the chair of the Pythoness of Spitalfields, the latter being sold next day at auction to a Jew for something under £4. God save the King.

I give you Hickey's account of the affair more or less. Several murky fellows found with bakers' loaves under their arms, who are no doubt honest workmen when there is any work, were locked up by the authorities along with the fighting prophetess and the Muggletonian saints and elders. Of course, nobody at the Barings' knew anything about this until it had all happened and the saints were keeping the rest of the prisoners at the Old Bailey awake by singing nasal hymns.

This all happened about three months ago. All of those taken up have now been discharged except two louts with bad records who it seems did set fire to the stables. Hickey did his best to smooth matters over,—enjoyed it in a way, I gather—says that old Johanna Heathecote almost ruined her chances by preaching to the judge and insisting that his lordship was damned now and for all eternity for meddling with God's people. An excited young attorney objected that her evidence was irrelevant and immaterial and his lordship was 'eased that he chuckled the saints out of the dock. It must really 'een rather grand, I gather, but it nearly cost me my inheritance. ̣ people and Captain Bittern were outraged. They might have proceeded against the Barings in several ways. I don't understand the exact legal situation. Suffice it to say, that if they *had* entered suit for the return of that chair the ownership of the *Unicorn* would have had to be adjudicated. As the ship and her dozen prizes were part of the Bonnyfeather estate, and as some of the prizes were made after Mr. Bonnyfeather's death, the status of the whole estate would undoubtedly have been involved. The Barings were only executors, and for an alien heir who had not yet appeared to make good his claim. The whole thing hung on nobody's questioning who owned the property before I established my rights under the will. If a suit was started many a poor barrister would scent big pickings, Hickey says, and the whole thing would have galloped into Chancery. I might then have spent all I made in Africa (and the rest of my life in London) trying to get something for my children, if I ever have any. When I tell you, Vinc, that the whole estate with the sums realized for the *Unicorn* and her prizes comes to £137,000 odd you can imagine that I looked across that table at the Barings with considerable interest while Mr. Hickey explained. It wasn't so funny then.

Mr. Thomas Baring had been the first to realize the grave state of affairs when a deputation from the Spitalfields conventicle headed by Captain Bittern called upon him. They wanted their consecrated chair given back. Luckily they had retained no counsel and Mr. Baring sent for his, Hickey, whom they listened to as he had aided in getting them released. I am vastly indebted to that man. He suggested to them that they should be legally represented. Luckily for me the poor souls actually asked Hickey to recommend them counsel. He had counted on that. They even wanted him to act. He explained why he could not, without making them feel he was "on the other side," and secured a young cousin of his who consented to advise them.

It was arranged to refurnish the Muggletonian chapel at Spitalfields, to contribute to their charitable fund and to settle the Heathecote woman in rather snug lodgings for life. Thank God she is old, as all this comes out of my pocket. I am afraid Hickey is a sad old fox as he went for six consecutive Sundays to service à la Muggleton at Spitalfields. I believe he would have been converted to keep them out of court. The red carpet and cushions for the benches certainly helped, and the chosen people were at last got off the subject of the chair—all but Captain Bittern. He insisted on the identical chair and threatened to undo all the good work by bringing suit. Hickey had the good sense not to offer him money and of course started a frantic search for the chair. He had, he thought, traced it a day or two before I arrived and he went to reassure Captain Bittern. The old fellow was sullen, however, and would say little. When Hickey told him I was in England he brightened up, however, and admitted he would see me. This was the situation on the morning of my first interview with the Barings.

So we went out to try to get the chair worth £137,000.

It is past midnight now and I shall put off till tomorrow the account of what happened. I had a good dinner tonight at Wattiers and—my eyes are heavy. You shall hear, too, of the Mexican affair in due course. It marches.

22nd January

(I meant to finish this ten days ago but have moved my lodgings since. Will tell you about that later, but have missed this week's messenger to Amsterdam. No mails yet. Anyway, I shouldn't care to trust what I have to tell you to the French posts.)

Out of a conceit for convenience I shall entitle what I am writing you tonight—

Your Humble Obedient Servant and Captain Bittern's Chair

As soon as we left the Barings we took coach and hurried over to Threadneedle Street, where I identified myself and my signature with certain of the bank's officials as Mr. Flood had suggested, and from whence I departed with a goodly sum in banknotes but could get no gold. I also settled with Mr. Hickey for a well-deserved but nevertheless startling fee. I must confess to you that when I drew this money which was partly the proceeds from selling my fellow men I had a superstitious qualm that perhaps Captain Bittern's chair was to be the instrument of my being scourged by Providence. If so, it seemed curious that I alone should be singled out.

We now took coach again and called at various places, with which I am not familiar, where Mr. Hickey expedited in so far as he could the acceptance and recognition of myself as the lawful heir under the will. The fees were again in each instance—large. We then proceeded in the general direction of a place called Hammersmith where we arrived about two o'clock in the afternoon, and had a most vile luncheon of heavy lumps of soggy dough and boiled mutton with small beer. We then set out through various highways and byways— wiping away the beads of perspiration caused by the difficulties of digestion—in search of the house of the Jew who was thought to have bought the chair at the auction and to reside in this vicinity.

I must for the moment, however, return to the subject of the lunch-The English speak of being "fortified" by such food—and the 's a just one. For two hours that afternoon I felt as if one tadels of Vauban in a characteristic star-fish outline had been built of solid masonry in my bowels. The assaults of digestion were successful only after a prolonged rumbling of nature's artillery.

I should also have mentioned that the carriage we were riding in was the property of Mr. Hickey and was provided with a wheel-and-notch contrivance registering distance on a dial, the like of which I had never seen before. It is certainly ingenious although not very necessary. There was also in the carriage with us a nigger servant who had been left with Mr. Hickey by his cousin William that is now in Bengal. Although he was wrapped in a suit of quilts, the poor black devil's teeth chattered with the cold. He is much persecuted by the other servants when left at home alone and prefers to accompany his master and freeze rather than remain alone at the house. I tried some Arabic on him but he only continued to click his teeth. A large beefy Yorkshireman drove us. In this style we got as far as Starch Green, inquiring for an hypothetical Hebrew. At last we learned from an estate-agent that a German by the name of Mayer had taken a house in the neighbourhood of Shepherd's Bush and that we must return that way by Goldhawk Road. As this nomenclature sounded promising we did so.

By now it was half past four, foggy and beginning to get dark. As we drew up before a gloomy, dilapidated mansion of pretension to former affluence my heart sank.

Mr. Hickey remarked that the place must have been built by someone on the outside of the South Sea Bubble just before it burst—and, indeed, it had that sullen look of having been surprised at birth by the sudden withdrawal of the silver spoon from its too-expectant mouth by the false fairy Finance. Hickey looked at it and laughed.

I could obtain entrance only to the rear garden and that with some difficulty along a porch of collapsing pillars. Eventually I found myself in the rear close, where much to my surprise I found a very neat and semi-Corinthian dovecote devoted to what appeared to be the scientific raising of carrier pigeons.

There was no one about, not even a dog, but as I stood there in the yard there suddenly came out of the foggy sunset a whirr of wings and a pigeon like a bolt from somewhere else. It alighted and entered daintily by a small door in the cote. I was somewhat startled at the same instant to hear from somewhere in the house the distant tinkle of a small bell. How the device was arranged I do not know, but I am sure the bird and the bell were no coincidence.

I was just about to knock when the back door opened and a young woman, obviously a Jewess, came out. After some little difficulty she secured the bird which had just arrived. She did not observe me, for I stood back under the shadow of an old wagon shed, but I saw her remove something from the tail-feathers of the pigeon and return to the house. "From father at Frankfort," I heard a man's voice exclaim in German. "He should start them earlier in winter. The night confuses the birds sometimes." Just then the door closed.

Certain now that someone was within, I went round to the front door and beckoning to Hickey to join me—knocked loudly. The same young woman who had secured the pigeon opened the door.

"Is Herr Mayer at home?" I asked in German.

"Ja," she said, noting the carriage over our shoulders. "He has just returned from Manchester," and ushered us in.

"Rachel, you should not say I am just from Manchester. Let no one be unnecessarily informed," I heard the same man's voice admonish the girl in the back of the house.

"*Ssh,* they speak German," she replied.

"What!" cried he. "Are they here already, impossible!"—and then raising his voice—"I shall be with you directly, Jacob, I am only in my gown now."

We both looked at each other and laughed. We also looked about us with considerable curiosity.

The house had evidently been furnished from a number of auctions. Every piece in it was second-hand. But the interior had been made as spotless as the outside was dilapidated, and I am bound to say that a great deal of nice taste and discrimination must have been evinced by the person attending the sales. For all of the furnishings, rugs, carpets, clocks, sofas, desks, and secretaries; everything from the andirons to some warm oil landscapes on the walls, must have been bought-in with as careful thought as no doubt it was bid for. And most of the pieces, if one did not look too closely, matched. But there was a strange air about it all. No one could have possibly mistaken it for an Englishman's house. Here and there was an oriental or bizarre bit, something of unknown use, which gave the effect of suddenly coming across in a book written in a European language a page printed in Hebrew. I shall say no more, save that drawn up before an unlit fire was the chair of Captain Bittern, reupholstered, and I am bound to admit, a handsome, ample piece.

I had scarcely had time to gather these impressions when we heard steps coming down the hall and Herr Mayer entered. He was considerably startled to find that we were not "Jacob"—and so was I—startled I mean—for the gentleman before me was none other than the young Hebrew who had sat next to us in a hired chair through ⁱurry in rentes in Paris.

ᵃᵛᵉ a whistle of surprise, and then begging my pardon bade welcome with grave courtesy.

harmed to see you," said he in German. "Our last meeting

was such a profitable occasion that I cannot help but remember you pleasantly, although I do not know your name."

I told him.

"I hope that does not belie my remarks about your luck," he replied.

"I hope not," I said, and sat down firmly in Captain Bittern's chair.

Herr Mayer looked at me and raised his eyebrows. "Then——?" said he.

"I am in peculiar difficulties, Herr Mayer," I said as frankly as I could, "and, through a strange train of circumstances, you may be able to relieve my anxiety without any risk to yourself."

"I shall be happy to lend you any reasonable amount, even a very large one on such excellent security as the Barings represent. Their word is as good as their bond. It was unnecessary for them to send their attorney along with you," said he glancing knowingly at Hickey. "To what extent am I asked to oblige you? Money is tight you know . . ."

As all this was in German Hickey was none the wiser.

"You mistake me," said I, "although naturally enough. I have not come to borrow. I have come to buy. And I have brought Mr. Hickey along just to assure you that I am completely . . ."

"I have no doubt of it," said he smiling.

"—sane," I continued, "and that I would be more than considerably obliged if you would consent to part with the very comfortable chair in which I am just now sitting."

"To *what?*" he asked amazed. We looked at each other. I saw an expression of pain and amazement flash from his eyes. He appeared extremely hurt as only a proud and sensitive Jew can be.

"I buy second-hand furniture," he said at last, "but I do not sell it, Mr. Adverse. You are unfortunately mistaken as to the nature of my business"—he was indignant now—"I am afraid I cannot part with the chair. As you say, it is a very comfortable one." An expression of scorn and contempt caused his eyelids to droop.

"Now you have mistaken me," I cried. "I certainly did not suppose what you think, nor have I come into your house out of curiosity. It seemed better to be quite frank about the reason for my coming here than to try by some subterfuge to purchase the chair and to fail, perhaps, by puzzling you and arousing your suspicions. I have simply come for the chair and nothing else."

"Why do you want it?" he asked, looking mollified by what I had said. "I am equally frank, you see, about my own curiosity."

"I am afraid I cannot tell you. My reasons are purely private. All that I can say is that the chair has nothing valuable whatever concealed in it, that your retaining it will vastly embarrass me, and that you will gain nothing by keeping it except a possible perverse satisfaction in doing so. That, I hope, you are incapable of feeling."

"Upon my word," said he, "I begin to see great merit in the lines of that chair." He smiled a little.

"Come," I said, "you have something that I greatly desire. That is valuable to me. I admit that. But that value exists only for me. You cannot realize on it from anyone else for the value does not exist for them. And I do not intend to make this chair valuable for you. In short I do not intend to permit you to realize on my predicament. I can simply go away, and I shall do so. I shall then regard your not giving me the chair in my extremity as a judgment of God. I shall go away without it."

At that he looked at me queerly, Vincent. I realized that now for the first time he believed that I was making an appeal to him man to man and not just trying to drive a good bargain.

"Surely," he said, "you did not expect me to make you a gift of the chair."

"Under the circumstances," I replied. "I felt that I was dealing with a man who might be generous enough to do so. I thought perhaps you would not permit the mere accident of your ownership of this article to ruin me."

"How much will you give me for the chair?" he asked after hesitating a moment.

"Not a penny, beyond the cost to you at the sale and your repairs. I thought, Herr Mayer, that you did not sell second-hand furniture."

"I don't," he said, "and so I am not going to sell this chair."

At least a half-minute's silence ensued. I saw him studying me intently. I decided to play my last card.

"May I take the chair with me now then, or shall I send around for it tomorrow?"

"So you *did* believe I might give it to you, after all!" he exclaimed. "You are the first Gentile I ever met who did not imagine that because I am a Jew I am also Shylock. That play I am sure has cost Christendom infinite millions. Everyone who approaches us thinks he is an Antonio and acts accordingly. I thought you had brought Portia with you," said he grinning at Hickey. "How much do you think your client has given me for the nice chair he is sitting in, Mr. Hickey?" he asked in English.

"God knows," groaned Hickey. "I do not understand German." ˺ooked at me apprehensively.

Mayer has just made me a gift of it," I said.

t! what!" grumbled the lawyer. "Why! I thought he was

ːaid Mayer with a fiery pride.

"Jesus Christ!" bumbled Mr. Hickey.

"Me too," put in Mayer. And at that it was impossible for any of us to restrain ourselves.

"Bring a light, Rachel," he called. The girl came in and lit the candles. We had been so intent on the chair that it was only now that we realized we had been sitting in almost total gloom. Mayer looked at a very large and handsome Swiss watch with enormous seals attached. Outside we could hear Hickey's Bengali coughing dismally in the coach.

"It is now nearly six o'clock," said Mayer, "and I wish you would both do me the honour of remaining for supper. We shall have to stretch it a little," he smiled. "I and my sister live alone here very simply, as you see. We have only come to live in England recently. I shall hope some time to have the pleasure of entertaining you both more magnificently. Who knows?"

He was so inexpressibly sincere and simple in his desire to have us remain that I accepted. Hickey, however, would not do so. "I must return tonight," he insisted. "How will you get home, Adverse?" he asked somewhat brusquely. "This is Hammersmith, you know."

"I shall be happy to send Mr. Adverse home in my own phaeton later on, Mr. Hickey," replied Mayer. "You will not wait and return with him?" he asked a little wistfully. I am glad to say Hickey responded nobly.

"Believe me, it is not prejudice which keeps me from dining with you, Mr. Mayer. I really do have to return at once. Permit me to say that through your accommodation of Mr. Adverse I consider you have also put me under a great obligation to you. I can assure you he does not exaggerate the importance of——"

"The chair," laughed Mayer.

"Exactly," said Hickey.

"Perhaps you had best take it with you in the coach, Mr. Hickey. My carriage is small and it will look strange driving through the city late at night with a large chair slung behind."

So Hickey drove off with the chair.

"It is too late to reach Bittern tonight," he said just before leaving. "Let us hope he has not made any move this afternoon. We must catch him first thing in the morning. I shall call early for you at Bishopsgate Street."

My evening with Mayer proved intensely interesting. A great weight was off my mind. I felt boundlessly grateful to him. I was particularly touched by his sending the chair home by Hickey as if to remove all doubt of his intentions. He himself did not refer to it again. I thought the least I could do, however, was to satisfy his curiosity, which I did. He was vastly amused, and did not for a instant show any trace of regret, even when he learned how great an apparent opportunity to profit at my expense had lain in his hands. I am sure he realized that I meant what I said about not intending to bargain for the chair. But by telling him how great was my obligation I was also enabled to convey to him some sense of my gratitude. Our conversation flowed with a rare ease, nor was our compatibility due to wine. He was soon unfolding to me the state of his own affairs as I had already done with mine. As a genuine confidence had been established between us by the chair, the usual diffidences seemed to have been broken down as if by an acquaintanceship of long standing.

You would scarcely guess, Vinc, from my description of the style this Hebrew lives in that he and his family are already a power in European finance. His father, who lives at Frankfort, is a great collector of coins and medals and has just been made financial agent for the elector of Hesse-Cassel. He is also negotiating a loan of ten million thalers for the King of Denmark, in which I believe Ouvrard is interested. There are four brothers, Anselm, Solomon, Nathan, and Jacob. Anselm has great influence in northern Germany and is heavily interested in Prussian and Bavarian loans, Solomon has a branch of the house at Vienna also doing well, and Nathan, who is my friend here, was sent over to England about a year ago to arrange for the shipping of English manufactures. He has his own house at Manchester. The house here at Shepherd's Bush near London is only a temporary affair, rather a secret one I gather. Eventually he intends coming to London when he has established himself well enough to set up properly.

I call your notice at some length to this remarkable family as in my opinion you will soon have to reckon with them. They do business for some reason under the name of "Rothschild." Nathan will not tell me why.

Their system is a most interesting and vital one. From what I can gather they have a strict family compact by which the house is eventually to cover Europe. Each brother is to become a financial power in the particular capital in which he has been sent to reside. The children of the various brothers are to marry their cousins and the strictest loyalty is to be maintained, each aiding the other and all each other. The head of the house is to remain at Frankfort. They have ʾady gone far toward building up this system. Jacob, who is still ʾs eventually to take over at Paris. In the meantime Nathan ʾhing the English branch and goes over to Paris frequently, the reason we saw him there that day.

ʾthers already maintain a network of agents in influential ʾr news both financial and political and a complete system of pigeon posts from one capital city to another. By this scheme they are enabled constantly to anticipate the market everywhere both in buying and selling operations, but especially in government loans and stocks. They have also a number of fast sailing-craft in their hire.

The house at Hammersmith is, I take it, the pigeon post establishment for England. Seeing the pigeon arrive that day I first called on Mayer opened my eyes and I have since seen hampers of pigeons arrive, doubtless those to be dispatched from here. He has never said anything about this himself and gives out that he is a fancier which passes well enough. His sister keeps the house at Hammersmith without even a servant for reasons of secrecy, I suppose. That is typical. Nothing out of the family.

I have come to know Nathan rather well, however. Have seen him a number of times since our first meeting and the growing intimacy is evidently welcome to us both. He began operations here on very small capital but has increased it remarkably. The seeming rashness and boldness of his operations repulses some people, who do not know, of course, that he is trading on advance information. They think him merely lucky so far. I hope to succeed in interesting him in the Mexican scheme, but of that in its place. And now to bring my own affairs to their conclusion, as well as this long section of my letter which is really a sort of running diary for your benefit——

Hickey and I drove out early next morning to Captain Bittern's cottage at Chelsea where he is living with his niece, a widow with two little girls. Yes, we took the chair. Hickey did not alight from the coach, however.

I went in alone to see the captain, who I believe likes me, although no one would ever suspect it who does not know him. He seemed to regard me as a kind of providence, because I suppose I inherit, for him at least, the prestige of the head of the house which he served for over forty years. In relating his experiences in prison he broke down. I can only say it was for me a terrible experience. He has become a sort of minor prophet of his sect and was rabid about the chair. When he brought the subject up I simply said I had brought it with me of course; that I regretted his sufferings enormously and wished not only to restore the property that had been taken from him so unjustly but also to testify further my esteem for the works of the Lord at the Spitalfields Chapel and to provide for the proper education of his two grandnieces, who, as he kept saying, are "nice little girls—little girls"—and indeed they are.

To my great relief he acquiesced in this and actually smiled when the chair was brought in. He is to have the satisfaction of returning it to the chapel himself. At any rate all hostile threats of actions at law completely subsided and Mrs. Quaire as I went out followed down the little door-yard and whispered that she would see that "uncle didn't make no more fuss," with tears in her eyes. So I left Captain Bittern sitting at ease in the chair. Counting Hickey's "honorarium" for what he calls "purely diplomatic services," that chair cost me well-nigh £700. Yet because it introduced me to Mayer I think it was worth it. I am greatly impressed by that man.

The light is beginning to steal through the windows of my new lodgings, yet my pen is still sliding on. There are no birds in London except sparrows, as yet, and I miss them. Lord, how dreary is the fog and snow! I long for the sun—where is it? I *must* stop now. The Barings effected the transfer of the Bonnyfeather estate to me two days ago and I have now nothing to fear except the well-known slings and arrows (do you know them in German?), and my own unknown capacity in the presence of a great sum of money. I need your advice. Tomorrow, by the gods, you shall have the Mexican business set down, and then the whole book can go off to you by the next messenger. I am lonely, or I would not write you so much. But to have a single confidant anywhere is balm to the soul. And so I talk to you with my pen.

God bless me it's seven o'clock a.m., unless Protestant steeples all lie.

                                                   27th January, 1802

So much for good resolutions about finishing my letter "tomorrow." I have missed the messenger again. Mr. Henry Hope returns to Amsterdam day after tomorrow, however, and has himself kindly offered to carry this across and see it forwarded to you at Paris.

I will give you a résumé here of the present status of the Mexican business rather than a narrative of how it has developed, with such comments on the personalities I have been dealing with as I trust will prove helpful both to you and M. Ouvrard.

As soon as the crisis in my own affairs was allayed I intimated to Mr. Thomas Baring that I should appreciate the opportunity of thanking Sir Francis in person. Anxious not to seem to be taking advantage of a personal interview, I also hinted that I had a confidential matter from Ouvrard to deliver to the head of the firm. I can tell ⸱ Thomas pricked up his ears, and an interview with Sir Francis, ⸱ visiting Mr. Henry Hope at Richmond, where the latter is ⸱ ⸱ew house, was promptly arranged. The conjunction of ⸱ ⸱h houses seemed auspicious.

⸱ ⸱hased a fine little turnout and provided myself in ⸱ ⸱h the proper clothes, sparing no expense and taking ⸱ ⸱ is by way of being a conservative dandy and understands good form, the best tailors, dealers, and shops. I derive, I confess, an immense satisfaction in seeing a certain orphan arrayed impeccably. My armour! At any rate I drove to Richmond in that style of perfection which stops just short of foppery. My reception there by Sir Francis Baring and later by Mr. Henry Hope, to whom the former presented me, will always remain one of the warmest recollections of this frigid isle.

We retired to the library, where there was actually a fire. Sir Francis was, if I do not flatter myself, almost affectionate in his manner. He was obviously gratified by my expressions of gratitude, in which, however, he cut me short to reminisce of his schoolmates John Bonnyfeather and your father Johann Nolte. He inquired eagerly about you, and repeated several times his sense of satisfaction that the "sons" of his schoolmates, for so he phrased it, should be doing so well in the world. "The best things in this world," he said, "flow from noble friendships. It is an immense satisfaction to me to find you young men continuing ours into the second generation. I hope you will both marry and have children." He was quite insistent on that point and also inquired about your operations in Paris. I was thus enabled to introduce naturally enough my bringing over of Ouvrard's treasury drafts.

Please tell M. Ouvrard that Sir Francis was greatly impressed by this evidence of his, Ouvrard's, confidence and serious desire to forward the scheme. He discussed the whole matter from his own standpoint most candidly and later called in Mr. Henry Hope to join us. In short we spent the whole morning on it. I stayed to luncheon and we resumed in the afternoon.

I shall not give you those conversations in detail till I return. The upshot of the matter is, after several such consultations, in which Mr. Thomas Baring and Mr. Wall have also been called in, about as follows:

Both the Barings and Hopes are convinced that Ouvrard means business. The initial drafts for a million dollars they consider ample to set up the machinery in America. They will, however, demand complete control of these operations without any interference as to the temporary investment of the funds in the United States and elsewhere; also the designation of the personnel of the firms to be set up in America and the merchants to be utilized there as correspondents in forwarding the neutral goods into which the capital will be turned.

The entire relation between the Barings in London, the Hopes in Amsterdam, and Ouvrard at Paris is to remain without exception confidential. All correspondence with England is to be avoided and M. Ouvrard himself is to come to Amsterdam to guarantee the Hope of his ability to continue to provide drafts on the Mexican treasr to the extent he mentioned. Also they would prefer that he should, once the agents are established in America, place in their hands at Amsterdam further drafts to the extent of seven millions if possible, and five at least. The last I think will be a condition of their beginning operations, the drafts to be cashed by their agent.

If the above arrangements are agreed and adhered to by M. Ouvrard, both Sir Francis and Mr. Henry Hope pledge their good names to exert themselves to the utmost to replace in Ouvrard's hands, as soon as commercial operations will permit, the equivalent in value of his drafts either in specie or in goods. Their own method of profit and its extent must be left in their hands, and should losses occur they must be borne by M. Ouvrard out of the capital provided. Also there are to be no written agreements and the whole transaction is to rest, as it must and should, on the mutual confidence of all parties in one another's integrity.

Under no condition is the source of the capital involved to be revealed by anyone. It is also suggested that in this stage of the affair the necessary preliminary correspondence should be carried on between you and me; you to negotiate with Ouvrard, and I with the Barings and Hopes, thus leaving no direct trace.

Let me know as to M. Ouvrard's attitude toward these proposals without delay—for the Barings are extremely anxious if the thing goes forward to take advantage of the peace now being made at Amiens, the duration of which they do not anticipate will be long. Therefore, haste.

I enclose Sir F. B.'s personal receipt for the Mexican drafts which he made for me in duplicate and one of which I retain. I am also arranging to have Montgomery and Ticknor build a coach for Ouvrard which will cost in French money about 14,000 francs. Does he desire it? It will be a magnificent one. I enclose the drawings which cost me £6, 8s, and I should like to be reimbursed whether O. takes the coach or not. Kindly convey my respects to him, and tell him so.

Now one thing more. Before the drafts for one million now in Sir F. B.'s hands can be cashed, an estimated expense of establishing agents in America of £100,000 will be involved. That must be forthcoming. Mr. Henry Hope at first insisted that Ouvrard should provide it all. I have, however, represented to him that the good faith of all parties should be made manifest in this, and Francis have arranged between them to guarantee £50,000 rest that Ouvrard should be asked by you to contribute you, I, and Nathan Mayer take up the remaining us. (Take Mayer's participation in this on and say nothing about it.) We understand cis is satisfied I should go to New Orleans.

That seems fated. Get me some maps and books about Louisiana. All hail to the House of the Wolf. I shall continue to write whether I hear from you or not. Things are looking up here with the peace coming on. I have bought considerable English stocks on Mayer's advice.

Your humble obedient Servant,

A. A.

P. S. This should reach Amsterdam by February 2nd at longest— kindness of Mr. Henry Hope.

Paris, 10th February, 1802

Dear Toni:

Your letter from London of December 28th last reached me somewhat sooner than you had opined, being brought down from Hamburg by P. T. Lestapsis, who has come here on business for Messers Hope. He is staying at the House of the Wolf.

I thank God you arrived safely and have had a cordial reception at the Barings. I shall await further advices as to the progress of your own affair and of the Mexican project, on tiptoe. Pray proceed as rapidly as possible in the latter. There can be no doubt Ouvrard is anxious to finish that. I shall tell you why.

He came storming in here two nights ago having had a terrible interview with the first consul in which the latter forced him to loan to the state most of his gains to date on government contracts, taking gov't bills on next year's revenue as security. Bonaparte is angry over the recent flurry on the Bourse, no doubt suspecting the cause, and has commanded Ouvrard to retire for a while to Castle Raincey— O.'s magnificent estate.

O. is therefore in a perilous position with most of his liquid assets in the hands of the government and is wildly desirous of cashing in on the Mexican drafts which the first consul cynically contrives to pay him for supplies furnished to Spain. My own idea is that Bonaparte intends to force O. to cash these drafts and knows that with his many associations he will in some manner be able to do so, in which case Bonaparte will be able to hold O. accountable for trading with the enemy and at the same time have the Mexican silver put into circulation here. I would explain this to the Barings and Hopes. To protect himself O. is anxious to put things into their hands—*and will make any terms not absolutely ruinous.* Anything is better than nothing. Now no more business till I hear from you further as to devel opments in London.

The news here is that the treaty making at Amiens proceeds favourably to France, your friend Joseph Bonaparte and Talleyrand doing well for themselves. Rumour has it that the peace with the supine British ministry of Mr. Addington will be used by Bonaparte, who is soon to be known only as "Napoleon" by the way, as a breathing space in which to prepare for the invasion of England. There is no let-up here in military activity. "Napoleon" is more popular than Bonaparte. Rentes soar.

Here is some personal news for you—*important*. Don Luis is in Paris. He is arranging the matter of selling blank permits from the Spanish crown to trade with its colonies. These are to be put in the hands of Ouvrard for certain loans and concessions. O. has already approached me about fitting out ships at Leghorn to trade with Cuba. This may have important personal developments for you. Ouvrard also says, "If M. Adverse can successfully arrange matters in London with the Barings and Hopes *I shall accompany him on his way to New Orleans as far as Madrid* in order to perfect arrangements there by means of these permits for the shipment of specie from Mexico to Louisiana." So be ready. You and Don Luis may be doing business together yet! I met him at Raincey and he bowed most courteously without even the change of a wrinkle over our last meeting. Faith was at the Comédie with him the other night, looking handsome. Neither of them seem to have suffered by their experience. I wonder how they got down off the mountain. They go to Madrid shortly I have ascertained.

Now one thing more. *Angela is here.* I saw her at the Opéra Comique in *Jeannet et Colin* in the leading rôle. She is no less a person than Mlle. Georges, who created such a furor at Vienna, and Milan as the cantatrice in the operas at the Teatro della Scala. They say that at Milan a year or so ago the first consul was very partial to her and that he had scenes there about her with Josephine. He is also said to be calling upon her here, secretly; that she is his mistress! What there is in these rumours, of course, no one knows. Probably it is idle talk. No doubt simply because he applauds and admires her at the opera along with the rest of the world tongues wag. The only thing I can say for certain is that he is always present when she is on ᵗʰe bill and Josephine is usually absent. C'est ça.

ᵂ I'll tell you what I have done. I have sent her an exquisite ᵉʳy large pearl necklace made-up by Fossin with that little ᵗ names you used to keep muttering and laughing about ᵗ sure I got them *all* right, but nearly so. I simply ᵗ House of the Wolf on it. Now tell me I have arls went yesterday and I have heard nothing me, Toni, is a real romance and I could not refrain from getting you into it just to see what happens. You can pay me for the pearls, mon vieux, a pretty sum, if you are angry. Yes, the lady is beautiful—and Herr Gott, her voice! Do not suspect me or be jealous even before breakfast.

Fräulein Geiler and her mother arrive tomorrow, "pour une petite visite." I shall hire a double coach, the berlin will never do, and we shall see the town. I am on fire. Thank God, Hélène has· gone. Her "brother" has been arrested for killing a Russian prince in a duel over the cards. Six aces turned up in one pack which each claimed the other had furnished. "Cinq et un" they call it here. The prince was sent back to St. Petersburg pickled in brandy. I hope they will not guillotine poor La Force for plunging a Russian into paradise.

Your talk with Mr. Udney sounds interesting and throws a curious light on the past. P. T. Lestapsis tells me Parish is cold steel, able, terribly lucky at cards, and regards his domestic establishment as merely one means of advancing his one interest in life; to wit, D. Parish. Be careful there. David is on the inside with the Hopes and has made a great deal of money for both himself and M. Talleyrand, whom he entertained beautifully. Mrs. Udney I have no doubt revels in all this. As to Florence—who knows? I shall be amused to hear when you get to Amsterdam. I am sorry for the old man. If you go to see him be your usual silent self.

I shall await your next with mixed anxiety and expectation. I regard you as lucky and Ouvrard concurs.

"Certain people," he says, "have the habit of being fortunate in their collision with events. This has little to do with their ability or character. It is a product of personality plus a fated life rhythm. Their cogs fit into events when others find no slots. Hence, they turn with the wheels of the times and help turn them. My success in life is largely due to my being able to pick such people out by instinct."

I thought that might cheer you. I believe it, too. But that is not why I believe *in* you—you know—through everything. You return to this house when you return to Paris, remember that.

Your humble obedient servant,
Vincent Nolte.

P. S. Your mysterious bundle is safe.
N. B. I contemplate a long engagement.

London, 10th February, 1802

Dear Vinc,

No word from you yet, which is to be expected. This is purely personal. I jot things down from time to time and will send them on in a bundle after hearing from you.

Mr. Udney has written. I am to come down to see him in the
spring if I am still here. Deep snow here now, a horrible form of
the element that gets down your boots. My new apartments are in
Farringdon Street close by the bookseller Routledge. I live alone
with a valet and houseman. A woman comes in to cook and clean.
I thought of taking up with a Covent Garden actress, one Mrs. Arnold,
a young widow. My tropical lassitude has notably vanished. But
the widow has a baby daughter and Hickey suggested other complications, so I shall remain in the paths of virtue. Hickey and I go about
town a good deal. This is at my expense but he is quite frank about
that and desires me to understand that he is not using me or selling
his acquaintance as he can live as well as he wants to on his own
income. And in this I believe him sincere for he has never failed to
advise me correctly. He says as long as my Havana cigars last he
will stick to me through thick and thin. I have also visited some clubs
with Henry Baring and lost and won considerable amounts. This I
ceased to do at the request of Sir Francis who is alarmed that anyone
connected with the firm should be seen at the tables as constantly as
is Henry. The young gentleman promptly dropped me when he
found my estate was not to be the means of an evening's amusement.
He goes to Amsterdam shortly.

I have called at M. Talleyrand's "glove shop." He enclosed in his
package an English bank note with directions to purchase the gloves
for Madame G. with that particular note. It must have been marked,
for when I received the gloves I found there was something in each
pair. It proved to be a large sum of money in bank notes and the
following communication.

Monsieur: the letters you have been asked to deliver to certain
persons have nothing in them but an authenticating signature. You
will act accordingly.

I was at first greatly puzzled by this until it occurred to me that
M. T. desired me to deliver only his *personal message.* Thus the
letters with his signature would serve to authenticate me as coming
from him and without any possible complications if they were stolen
or lost or not delivered. The "glove shop" is, of course, French agent
headquarters here. I shall avoid it in future meticulously as I do not
wish to become involved in something I have no interest in furthering.
It might totally ruin me. I returned the "gloves" by my man with
an oral message to the "proprietor," saying I would deliver certain
letters out of personal esteem for M. T. but that I must positively *not*
be counted on in the future. My man George returned with the reply,
"Monsieur is wise." I related the whole circumstance to Sir Francis,
who congratulated me on my good sense and arranged to have me see
Messers Pitt, Fox, and the Prime Minister Addington.

Vincent, please call on M. Talleyrand, convey him my profound respects, and tell him I have "delivered the letters." That I found Mr. Pitt in a flowered dressing gown drinking port in the afternoon and that he said, after listening to my message, "Tell Talleyrand that even a sick hound knows the difference between an anise seed bag and the trail of an old fox trying to get the weather gauge by sneaking up wind. I greatly regret that due to the late hour the figure is a mixed one." For another three hours we discussed only port and the orations of Cicero. I had to be carried out and I assured him with tears in my eyes I was not a French agent. "By Gad, I never thought so," said he. "None of them they send to me can drink above four decanters. Tell that to Talleyrand, too. He employs nothing but white-wine merchants to peddle his lies. Your Latin is better than your English, young man. It has been an afternoon. *Vale.*"

Mr. Fox, whom I found at a pub, said, "The noble spirit of freedom, which is professed in France and practised in England, will light the mutual path to peace which both nations should tread. Tell M. Talleyrand that I am myself coming to France shortly and that I should be surprised but rejoiced to discover in him an ardent colleague."

Mr. Addington asked me what I wanted, after fingering the letter gingerly. When I replied, "Nothing,"—he laughed, and after some consideration said that he hoped M. Talleyrand would continue to enjoy good health. He asked me what I did in England and I was, I think, able to satisfy him on that score. He acted like a dull confused man. I was surprised to find him so.

Explain to M. T. why I cannot take his "gloves." I do not intend to be worn out and thrown away. The peace they say here will be ready soon. Now no more for a little.

19th February

Dear Vinc:

Your letter of the 10th instant arrived here today brought on by Mr. John Williams Hope from Amsterdam. By this time you must have my second and I shall anxiously await your reply to my specific questions as to Ouvrard's guarantees.

In the meantime, the information you gave me as to O.'s situation I have passed on to the Barings and Hopes, and on the strength of it they are this week making full plans for the setting-up of the agents and correspondents in America. The heads of both firms are now in London and their conferences, which I have frequently been asked to attend, go on apace. Sir Francis is particularly impressed with the possibilities opened up by Ouvrard's being able to furnish blank permits to trade with Spanish possessions. He feels that they can be combined with our present plans to enormous advantage.

Angela! I dare not set down what passes through my mind and heart as I write that name. You did right nobly to send the pearls. Tell me swiftly what is her reply and where she lives. I do not believe the stories about her, but they trouble me. I find I care much. It will be hard to wait for your letters. I would like to hurry back to Paris. But it would be running away from the battle here. Good luck to your own sweet and ample fräulein and you. Write—*send by special messenger*. All these expenses I will take up promptly when I return. Do not save money now. Its best use is to stop anxiety.

Vinc, please send by one of your feluccas out of Leghorn for my man Juan and my great dog Simba who are both near Algeciras in Spain. I wish them to meet me in Paris when I return. Juan would be invaluable about the House of the Wolf and Simba could be the night watch for Paul. I suggest you get skipper Manchori in his swift little *Stella Maris* to call in direct at Tarifa for them and land Juan at Marseilles. I enclose a letter to Juan. Also, on second thought, a good fat draft on Amsterdam to sweeten my accounts with you, pearls and all.

Instead of keeping this letter for further jottings I send it off tonight with a bundle of London newspapers via Helgoland. Only diplomatic mails as yet to France.

Get me Juan. It comes across me I shall need him.

Your humble obedient Servant,

A. A.

Paris, 3rd March, 1802

Dear Toni:

This in vast haste. All your letters, including that of February 19th last, had arrived by three days ago, some grossly delayed, also the newspapers which have been eagerly read and are already called for by borrowing friends.

I devoted a night to studying your correspondence in order to be able to act carefully, and snatching some sleep early in the morning, called the berlin after breakfast and started out to see Ouvrard at Raincey. We spent the day over the Baring-Hope proposals. Now then to speed all things to a conclusion:

Ouvrard accepts the conditions as laid down by Sir Francis Baring and desires both the Barings and Hopes to hasten perfecting the American forwarding arrangements without delay. He says should any doubt arise in their minds about any *particular* to proceed on the assumption that he has *already* approved it. He must realize on the immense sums locked up in these Mexican drafts and all means which lead to that end are proper means.

Let me add that you cannot overestimate the necessity for dispatch. Ouvrard is in a precarious way and if he fails it will precipitate a panic of major proportions on the continent. I myself have loaned him 500,000 francs.

As soon as the agents are ready to proceed to America Ouvrard will repair to Amsterdam and place in the hands of the Hopes any amount of drafts on the Mexican treasury which they may be able to handle. "Bonaparte is choking me to death with them," he says.

Now then—I enclose you a draft on the Bank of England for £30,000, mine and Ouvrard's share of the advance working capital which you and Mayer are to bring up to the agreed £50,000; the Barings and Hopes to contribute the balance of the total of £100,000. Also a letter from Ouvrard to Sir Francis Baring in confirmation of your negotiations, which is to be the only correspondence, and which he requests shall be destroyed.

Now, mon vieux, a thousand congratulations on your able handling of this matter which has roused Ouvrard to an embarrassing style of encomium. Insist upon the post at New Orleans. The first pickings will be there, and millions of specie will pass through your hands. You are to return with Ouvrard from Amsterdam to Paris and he takes it for granted you will go on with him to Madrid. No details now, but prepare yourself. I know you can be as persuasive in Spanish as you are in English. As for your own inheritance being placed in your hands—thank God for it, and don't give away any more chairs. I read your account of that with all the thrill of a Gothic romance.

I have heard from Angela. I devote my next letter to her. Also I have sent for Juan by post to Leghorn today. Johann Frank, my cousin, carries on there well. The *Stella Maris* shall go.

Send me no more drafts, you ridiculous fellow, or I will charge you a ruinous discount, storage on your precious bundle, and board and lodging for Juan and the hound Simba when they arrive. We are both rich, my boy! You remember too well the philosophy of McNab in estimating your friends.

Anna has a young Düsseldorfer, ein knabe.

Ever your humble obedient servant,

Vincent Nolte

I have not seen Talleyrand yet. This must go *now* by P. T. Lestapsis. Angela must even wait.

London, 13th March 1802

Dear Vinc:

Your letter with Ouvrard's confirmation and the draft arrived here yesterday by Lestapsis—I love the man's moniker—who arrived ory-eyed from lack of sleep bringing it.

I immediately hunted up Mayer, procured his £10,000. Drew an order for my own and driving around to Bishopsgate Street took up Mr. Thomas Baring, whence we all proceeded to Richmond where we found Sir Francis and the two Hopes at "East Sheen" and went into conference.

The great scheme is under way. Inform O. that it is being pressed night and day.

The Hopes return to Amsterdam shortly to perfect final arrangements there and will wish O. to come to them there in May.

This without further comment but vast relief. Doubt not both our shares in this matter are appreciated here. Lestapsis, the somewhat battered Mercury, goes back with this and is waiting below as I write. Consider that without further advice all goes well.

Yr. H. O. S.

A. A.

For God's sake tell me about Angela, you devil.

———————

Paris, 15th March 1802

Dear Toni:

I know you will curse me for my delay about Angela. Business, my boy, before romance. I have seen Talleyrand and he actually laughed heartily at your message, "Tell monsieur he has a gay spirit and has done well." Now Angela——

I have not seen her. She lives at Meudon. Debrülle, now old, toothless, and fatherly, called. He asked for you and would say little to me. He said he had written to you once in desperate circumstances years ago and heard nothing. I assured him you could not have received his letter in Africa. He seemed pleased to hear that you would be in Paris shortly and said that "Mademoiselle" thanked you for the pearls and would communicate when you arrived. He seemed to be concealing something and was embarrassed. I asked him if he needed funds. He said *not from me,* and departed.

I am sorry I cannot tell you more. Evidently I am not expected to call on Mademoiselle, and I shall not. It is rather curious. That is all.

Your friend,

V. N.

P.S. Instruct the builders to proceed with Ouvrard's coach, a draft will follow.
N.B. Take out your £6.8 for the plans.

London, 30th March 1802

Dear Vinc:

Peace was proclaimed here today. Mayer knew it the morning of the 28th. A little bird told him before breakfast, which he took with me at Farringdon Street. We drove around to the Exchange and I put all I could muster into government stocks. A rumour as to a hitch in the negotiations at Amiens had sent government stocks down the evening before. They soared this afternoon after the heralds with silver trumpets went about. Very picturesque, to me a golden sound. I sold out this evening and made a cool £13,000 odd. Mayer's takings are enormous. He immediately came and borrowed £10,000 from me which I gave him on his own note without security at current interest. Our association is a curious one. He is very silent; so am I. I know, for instance, he is not now recouping himself for the lost opportunity of the chair. He knows that I know it. His winnings on Change make no change whatever in him. That puzzles most Englishmen, I think. Nine-tenths of them pay no attention to any person who does not possess property. Poor men with ideas here are merely ridiculous. A Jew who is rich and does not care fills them with secret awe. The expression "A man of sterling character" exhausts all compliment here. There must be now, or there must once have been, Englishmen who were "beings" instead of "havings," but I do not meet them. My misfortune, perhaps, but a sore one. If I lived in England I should simply become property.

One of the most curious things about this country is everyone's horror of expressing any emotion. All the upper classes seem to have stolen their faces out of a wax works. The complexions are impeccable and the expressions moulded. I am frequently suspected and despised, I find, because my expression sometimes changes.

Mayer says that only the complexions of the English are due to the climate. The fixed expressions are due to the necessity of all respectable persons, i.e., all people with property, maintaining an emotional status quo as the custodians of things. They cling like clams to the rocks of property and they look like them, closed, shell-fast. Pry them open, and a faint muscular withdrawal takes place as the bivalve slowly shifts uneasily and gets a grip on itself in order to close tighter. Occasionally an impious foreigner, usually a Frenchman, inserts an uncomfortable fact or even an idea into one of these clams that has

been taken off its guard while breathing. The shell then closes, and
after a due period of expressionless effort at digestion, the idea is
exuded in the form of a smooth pearl of wisdom in English literature.
Respectable writings here are now confined solely to scientific and
economic treatises. Everything else is purely romantic. Poets, novel-
ists and musicians, it is thought, appeal merely to the emotions. Emotions are not real when no one has any fervent feelings except a fixed
fervour about property. I argued with Mayer about this, and he is,
of course, not being entirely serious.

Yet there is much truth in his way of putting it. Only the lower
classes here, he points out, can still laugh, dance, sing, swear, drink and
fornicate without being embarrassed about it. They have no property.
But that will not last long, he says. "You ought to live for a while
like I do in Manchester. They are tiring out the whole population
on the weaving machines there. Those people no longer laugh. They
drink to be able to forget. If the English win out against Bonaparte
half the world is going to get to look like Manchester, because the
English themselves must keep running away from it in order to live,
and they have nothing but ideas out of Manchester to take along with
them. The Greeks took Athens, the Romans took Rome, we take
Jerusalem, and the English will take Manchester along wherever
they go."

"Why do you come to live here?" I asked him.

"I will tell you why," said he. "On the continent the old quarrel
between Athens and Rome on one side and Jerusalem, no, let us say
Carthage on the other, is still instinctively understood. It is known,
for instance, in France, Italy, and Spain that Jews are still oriental;
that they dislike Greek symmetry and perspective and despise Roman
order and logic. They are, in short, hereditary enemies of the classical state which insists on conceiving of itself as something eternal and
divine no matter what its form. The Jews believe something else is
eternal and divine and have no state. Their philosophy is not political.
It is racial and individual. Their only organization is the synagogue
and the family or firm. They therefore exist in, but apart from,
Western society and are suspects. Now in Latin countries this is
clearly recognized and precautions are taken by the Gentiles accordingly. There it is still an idea against an idea. But in England the
state is merely a 'commonwealth,' a means of controlling interests,
for there are no ideas of state above property. Anything, even religion, can be compromised, bought, and sold. It is the greatest auction of the ages. I find myself at home in Tyre and Sidon, London
and Manchester, with Jerusalem destroyed; and I find myself still a
stranger in Paris, with Rome—not destroyed. I am devoting my life

here to removing those memories of Rome which still make it uncomfortable in England for Hebrews. It is like this: In Paris M. d'Ayen offered me a pinch of snuff for helping him keep forty-five thousand francs and his pride. In England I shall some day be elected to Parliament, out of respect for my property, and sell snuff to the local d'Ayens so that it will cost them dear every time they sneeze in my face. But they will not do so. Snuff is going out. It makes the English change their expression, and no man of property can afford to be seen doing that."

After that he borrowed £10,000 from me and sent me a snuff-box with Bonaparte's head on it. "I have no use for this one here," he said.

I think this snuff-box with the first consul's head, for which Mayer has no use, throws some light on why he borrowed the ten thousand as soon as I made it. He is investing heavily in the "commonwealth." From what I can gather a great portion of the family takings on the continent are also being concentrated in his hands and put into English rentes. He believes, I know, that in the coming struggle, in which this peace is only to be a brief breathing space, the English will win. I feel that my money he borrowed is as safely invested as it can be. Also I have arranged with the Barings to keep the bulk of it invested here, in which the example of Mayer encourages me. After all *England is an island* and the conflagrations of Europe are stopped by the Channel. That is the most important historical and geographical fact in the world.

10th April, 1802

This is a jotted letter again, you see. Your news of Angela, and Debrülle's strange visit fill me with both anticipations and forebodings. Of course, I never got his (or her) letter, which? I shall write you no more about Angela, because the subject tends to fill my mind. I loved her and I think I still do, though God knows what she may be like now. Still the past holds. I send you a brief note enclosed to be sent to her. Read it so that you will understand my attitude. It is possible Debrülle is merely after money from me, but I doubt it. Now no more about that till further developments.

Spring came here with a bound. The season is strangely advanced. I go down to Brighton frequently, where the crown prince has repaired very early this year. He is building an outrageous Aladdin's palace there called the "Pavilion," at a disgraceful cost. The bubble domes of it already begin to rise. I have a room on James Street near the sea and yesterday saw H.R.H. in a striped chariot, that seemed to have been dragged through the rainbow, driving along under my windows with a whole boatload of trollops—titled ones I suppose. He is a handsome dog but looked flushed and sleepy. These Hanoverians get no shouts from me. All the dukes, sons of the mad king, are wastrels, too.

There are over seventy coaches a day now they say to and from Brighton. The roads are wonderful and the way they change horses a marvel. I drive my own curricle and keep two horses on the route. Rather expensive. I have nothing else to do and find casual company at Brighton. I have found a pretty face at Cuckfield in the Weald of Sussex on the way down—or up—the most charming village I have ever seen. Hickey took me to White's where I dropped £56. At Brook's with Henry Baring I won £28 about two months ago. I shall call it even and let the clubs alone. There has been so much lucky chance in my life that I do not wish to tempt Fortune at her own game.

Brighton, 24th April

Have installed the pretty face from Cuckfield in my rooms at James Street here. We drive about a good deal. Dolly is a simple and true little soul, a cobbler's daughter. Parents dead. We orphans have joined forces. "Divided we stand, united we fall." This is a quiet, uncomplicated affair. We are just like a boy and a girl who are in no danger of being caught. The time passes without our knowing it. I stay out of London much now. I am merely waiting for the heads of the two houses to perfect matters here when I go with Mr. Henry Hope back to Amsterdam. A letter from Udney. I am to go to see him at "Spichwich" in Devon near Widdecombe-on-the-Moor. *We* go by way of Bath. Good-bye.

A.A.

P.S. Ouvrard's coach is a-building. I shall ship it to Amsterdam and drive down to Paris in it with him, since that is *his* plan. Madrid has some attractions, you know. I do not fear Don Luis any more with his coach gone.

London, 28th May 1802

Dear Vinc:

This is my last letter from England as I leave for Holland before the next French mail.

I returned to Farringdon Street yesterday morning after as ethereal a journey as any fallen angel can enjoy in this sphere. I drove with Dolly in the curricle as far as Bath, which I much desired to see. The trip down the New Forest with "the darling buds of May" breaking forth into a green haze and the birds coming in from the south along with the sun, the stopping off at little inns overnight with the noise of streams coming through the windows and my dear little Hebe in a dream of pleasure in my arms—is beyond the powers of expression to describe. And yet I am sure I can convey it to you, you sentimental old German compound of Rhinegold and moonlight. Only this was English moonlight in the month of May, and the magnificent road leading to Bath clicking under our wheels by day, a pair of fine little mares in neighing fettle to the curricle and the shining mail coaches sweeping by with the sound of their horns dying away and overtaking us as if a universal hunt were up and away. The guards *did* blow the horns at us, as might be expected when one does not remove one's arm from a girl's shoulders even for the Royal Mail. And I have no doubt we both shone under the hood with the same colour as Dolly's curls against my shoulder; with the kind of light that only lovers give off (or sunlight on willows) for we were really mightily happy.

Strangely enough I was all the more happy because this experience was made poignant by a conviction I cannot shake off that this is the last really youthful, love-in-springtime full of May buds and golden sunlight I shall have. It is true I grow older, but in England this spring I seem to have grown younger. The trip to Bath was like some of those morning drives with Angela about Livorno as a boy. Indeed, I think I have to some extent thought of Dolly as Angela.

We had a glorious week in Bath, very gay, bathing in the morning and taking the triple glasses in the pump-room, riding about in chairs, and scaling the romantic cliffs that look down upon the town. Everyone goes to evening service in the Abbey after dinner, then the pump-room again, and then rushes out to the gaming tables and ballrooms and routs. This is the only town in England where I have continually heard happy music. I spared nothing for Dolly's gowns and she was in seven heavens at once. Her voice is so pleasant the bad grammar doesn't need to be noticed. Sussex talk. We stayed at a house in Great Poultney Street, number 36, where was a gentleman M.P., a Mr. Wilbur Farce, who finding I had been in Africa kept me up three nights running asking questions about the slave trade, till I excused myself for a more congenial occupation.

I left Dolly with a Mrs. Razzini, wife to a former musician, highly respectable, and with an Italian understanding. Dolly cried only a little (as the house is in Gay Street) and promised to wait for me— well provided, I might add.

I drove down to Exeter and thence over to Totnes, where Mr. Udney met me at the "George" and we had a *rouse* and a *bouse,* which is two names for the same thing. "Spichwich" is not far from Prince-

ton and Widdecombe. It is a pleasant house at the top of a combe
filled with ancient, mossy beeches and looks out over the moor from a
space of lawn and terrace. Mr. U. alluded to Florence scarcely at all.
Mrs. U. still at Amsterdam with the Parishes. The house very quiet,
and I am glad of it, as I needed a rest and felt inclined to drowse with
Mr. U. and the dogs before the empty fireplace. Much good ale, local
hunting talk, riding over the moors that are haunted by something
that speaks in the winds from over the heather; something sad and
infinitely remote and of the far past and yet whispering always in
one's ears. I am sure of it. You know I can hear voices. Mr. U.
was like a father. I think we both agreed to play our respective parts.
I enjoy finding "parents" here and there as well as other forms of
casual affection. The greatest event at "Spichwich" was having the
two churchwardens from Widdecombe, Messers Peter and Sylvester
Mann, in to dine at which much broad Devon with brewed beverages
to wash it down. I stayed on eight days and Mr. U. said, "Good-bye,
my boy, I shan't see you again in this world damme!" and rode off
with a very red face up a lane blowing his nose like a horn.

I returned to Bath to take Dolly back to Sussex and found her already engaged to marry one A. Taylor, the son of a baker, who peddles
hot buns to the chairs and has made a good thing of it. I own this
was a surprise, but soon saw its advantages and took Mrs. Razzini's
advice to leave them both my blessing and depart. Dolly will have a
decent dot. The widow, of course, must have helped them. *The
banns were up when I returned.* This is best for the girl, too. I
drove back to London, lonely again, but relieved of the anticipations
of certain tearful farewells.

But farewell now to London and England. I leave with Mr. Henry
Hope by Harwich. My man is packing me now. I find your letters
about various matters awaiting me and have read them carefully. But
no answer to business matters now. All is well for the Mexican
project. It will be launched from Amsterdam, from whence in a few
days' time I shall be able to send you the final particulars, probably
before I myself arrive at Paris. Ouvrard's coach (set up in neat
cases) has gone on to Holland. I hope I shall find Juan and Simba
at numéro 47 when I return. I long to see you again. My letters
have only shaved the surface of events here. Thanks, my dear fellow, for your affectionate and unfailing thought of me—for the welcome that I know awaits me at the House of the Wolf and that lends
such genial warmth to the offing. No trouble about passports now.
From the Low Countries next D.V.

Your h.o'b.s.

A.A.

t'Huys ten Bosch,
Wood of Haarlem,
9th June, 1802

Dear Vinc:

I arrived at Amsterdam five days ago but have delayed writing in order to be able to give you more important news. Discussions have been going on here ever since we arrived toward perfecting final arrangements to set up the apparatus in N. America for forwarding the Mexican bullion. M. Ouvrard's not arriving until yesterday caused me considerable anxiety, as I could see that P. C. Labouchère, the active head of *Messers Hope & Co.*, at Amsterdam, was not inclined to move in the matter until he was assured that the further drafts on Mexico were forthcoming. O.'s arrival, however, settled all that. Not only did he bring the drafts but ten blank licenses to trade with Spanish colonies, which require only the names and destinations of the ships to be filled in and carry permits for cargoes both ways. There is now no drawing back and I give you below a schedule of the projected organization.

America

David Parish (of Parish & Cie, Antwerp) to be Resident Agent-in-Chief of all funding, forwarding, insuring, and investing in North America—to reside at Philadelphia, Pennsylvania, in the United States.

A. P. Lestapsis (of the Amsterdam counting house of Messers Hope & Co.) to be at Vera Cruz, Mexico, but under the Spanish name of "José Gabriel de Villanova," supposed to be acting for the House of Plante of Santander, confidential agents there for the Spanish crown. Lestapsis will cash the drafts at Mexico, forward the specie and look after all cargoes arriving under the licenses.

Anthony Adverse, General Receiving Agent (accountable to both M. Ouvrard and Messers Hope & Co.) resident at New Orleans, Louisiana, to receive all specie shipped by Lestapsis from Vera Cruz and to transmit it to Parish at Philadelphia.

Carlo Cibo, agent at Havana, Cuba (my suggestion).

Commercial agents at the ports of Boston, New York, Baltimore, and Charleston in the Carolinas to be designated by Parish upon his arrival in America.

Great Britain

Baring Bros. & Co., London. They, or the firms designated by them, to receive all specie or cargoes shipped to the British Isles and exchanged thence to Europe.

Europe

Messers Hope & Co., Amsterdam, to receive, and to assign to and designate all correspondents for cargoes shipped to the continent.

The Hopes have arranged through Mayer to have the "Rothschilds" at Frankfort look after the disposal of goods in the interior of northern Europe. Ouvrard will himself look after French and Spanish assignments, and you, of course, *it is understood* will be allotted the cargoes for Leghorn as correspondent for Italy.

Parish and Lestapsis sail shortly for America where they will, with the present capital subscribed, make all arrangements for setting up what will undoubtedly become, once the specie starts to flow, one of the major, if not the largest commercial operation of modern times. It is now expected that with the signing of the peace only comparatively small amounts of the bullion brought from Mexico to the United States will be shipped as specie to Europe. Not much in coined silver at any rate will be shipped at any one time, owing to the risk and the enormous insurance. It will be beyond count more profitable first to invest the capital in the United States and transfer it in neutral goods, cargo by cargo, taking advantage of the most favourable prices for colonial produce in the British Isles and Europe, by shipping it to the correspondents of the Hopes and Barings who offer the most favourable terms. They, of course, do not intend to cover or receive all *if any* of these cargoes themselves. They will simply designate the firms to do so. Thus neither the House of Hope nor Baring need appear on ships' papers at all. In case war breaks out again the whole transaction will be between neutral firms in America and neutral firms in Europe. Only the profits will accrue to the Hopes and Barings since their correspondents will, of course, handle such cargoes for the usual commercial agent's fee. But those profits will be immense, for with the English blockade and the French attempt to shut out all English goods, colonial produce is now at a premium all over Europe and the expectation is *to double the value of the original capital received in America by the time it reaches here.* Nor is that all, cargoes from the Spanish colonies will themselves first be sold in the United States at great profit.

David Parish will, therefore, have on his hands a commercial business, both the buying and selling of goods of all kinds in the United States. He will also have the rapid investing of colossal sums of money to look after (at least seven millions in the next two years), to say nothing of the amount of credit which the mere possession of the original capital in cold specie will generate. No one can calculate that, especially in a new country with a raw banking system. And all this, in order to facilitate its transfer to Europe at every opportunity, must be kept in liquid assets.

The meeting yesterday afternoon, in the cabin of one of Messers Hopes' ships, for the greater privacy, was a momentous one. Present: Messers John and Alexander Baring, Messers Henry and John Williams Hope, P. C. Labouchère, M. Ouvrard, David Parish, and your humble obedient servant. On account of the signing of the peace it seemed possible at the last moment Ouvrard might withdraw and attempt to cash his bills direct. I persuaded him, walking up and down the deck beforehand, not to do so. I represented that the peace would probably be of short duration, as most people think, and that *in any event* it was to his interest to have these vast sums concentrated in the hands of honest and neutral people like the Barings and Hopes, where the first consul could not lay his hands on them. This last argument went home, and we then proceeded to the cabin where the final arrangements were made.

Ouvrard particularly cautioned Parish of his responsibility for not creating either furors or panics in the United States owing to the sudden influx and withdrawals of huge sums in bullion; above all not to invest in lands in a new country where the temptation would be great. Parish, I think, did not much like being advised even by so able a man.

David has been chosen for the American post because of his brilliant management of certain colonial deals for the Hopes, successful owing to a consummate intrigue with Talleyrand whom he entertained, as you mentioned, so brilliantly some time ago. He is also great friends with Alexander Baring who married a Philadelphia heiress, Anna, daughter of a Mr. William Bingham, banker of that city, the richest man in the United States, it is said. Hence Parish's path in Philadelphia is smoothed. My own feeling about Parish is that he will organize brilliantly and administer—not so well. This will not affect me at New Orleans, however.

My work there will be confined to arranging the means of carrying the specie safely from Vera Cruz to Louisiana and to shipping it north. I am to receive 2% on all sums *received,* deducting my share in silver dollars, and charging all expenses to Ouvrard. It would be enormously risky to ship direct from Vera Cruz to Philadelphia, owing to British cruisers, pirates, loss by sea on a long voyage, and the staggering insurance. The run from Vera Cruz to New Orleans is a short one and the facilities for dribbling the specie north to Parish in small amounts on swift, little ships from Louisiana, without attracting notice or running the chance of losing several chests in a single disaster, dictate the choice of New Orleans. Equally important is the fact that both the Hopes and Ouvrard desire to have me as a neutral receiving agent accountable to them both, thus preventing all argument as to the amounts of capital actually shipped and received from Mexico. Parish is not more than content. And so I go to New Orleans—but not instantly.

It will take Parish and Lestapsis some months at least to proceed to the United States, organize their affairs there, and acquire agents. In the meanwhile, I am to go to Louisiana by way of Madrid with Ouvrard. By the time I arrive in New Orleans Lestapsis should be in Mexico, Parish ready in Philadelphia, and we shall begin operations. I look forward to *finally establishing myself for life* in a new country with profound satisfaction, and, I confess it, with enormous curiosity as to the outcome. Quién sabe?

The rest of my letter will be a short account of some of my more casual doings here.

After the meeting we all came out to this place, t'Huys ten Bosch, Mr. Henry Hope's magnificent (I use the word carefully) country estate near Amsterdam in the Wood of Haarlem. It is quite literally a palace. The Hopes first made an enormous fortune by putting the empire of Russia into European finance, hence a striking presentation portrait of the Empress Catherine II hangs in the grand salon. There is also an extraordinary gallery of old masters, and a park and garden in the Dutch style beyond compare.

Mr. Henry Hope was sensible of my having influenced Ouvrard to continue in the enterprise, and after dinner one night called me out on a balcony overlooking a world of tulip beds and expressed himself unreservedly for that and my other diplomacies. I take pleasure in being praised by a man like him. We talked for an hour while Ouvrard held the others within about the pianoforte, his fat hands and great rings flashing over the keys in a masterful way—he is passionately addicted to music. Before we returned to the room the old man was telling me with tears in his eyes that he was being disgraced by his niece here, who is carrying on with a Dutch officer of dragoons, one Captain Dupff. I was both touched and surprised by this confidence and tell you it so that you may see in what personal estimation I am held by the head of this great house.

I spent the next morning with Ouvrard having his coach, shipped here in sections, set up. He is childishly pleased with it. I shall almost be afraid to ride to Paris in it as it looks like the one the prince came around in to carry off Cinderella after the glass slipper fitted. There is a portrait of Fortune and her wheel on the ceiling, cornucopias spilling largess from each corner, red morocco upholstery, silver gilt hardware, mirrors! For *God's sake* come out to Raincey in the berlin and pick me up there.

I also dined with Labouchère, the Hopes' partner, with whom a rather curious incident. He insisted upon my meeting his "young sister," and on the way out to his place explained to me what an excellent match she would make and that "a young man with great interests to conserve" could do worse than to ally himself with Messers Hope & Co., Labouchère et al. I admitted the premises but nothing more.

On arriving at the gentleman's house I was introduced to his sister, who, although twenty-five in body, was I am sure not over ten years old in mind. She looked at me over an endless Dutch dinner with the blue, uncomprehending stare of a Dutch doll. Her proceedings were at last so ludicrous that Labouchère himself was forced to smile, and I departed early, leaving him smoking a pipe gloomily and shaking his head. I have said nothing and he appreciates *that*. "Py Gott it ees no gee-hoke," he said to me only yesterday. "Fifty thousand florins joost go to hell van she tie." He looked at me still a little hopefully I think. "Eef you *haf* friends," said he. So here you are, Vinc—florins and a silent wife, commercial affiliations, and a respectable brother-in-law. Come and grow fat—and tulip bulbs.

The big event was yesterday with a dinner at the Parishes'. Four of us, a very formal affair, with David at one end of the table with his eye on Florence at the other. Mrs. Udney, who did all the talking, just across from me. Mrs. Udney seemed labouring under some repressed excitement. She took such a pride in the style in which her daughter was being kept that it caused me to catch from Florence the only smile that I received.

Florence is a beautiful woman, pale, rather suppressed, and devoted to doing everything for David in the best possible form. He himself was most hospitable, talked entertainingly after supper, and made me welcome without a trace of doubt, for which I admire him. I said nothing about my long visit to Mr. Udney because I suddenly understood while talking to Mrs. Udney that *he* will never say anything about it to *her*. We ended with a rubber or two at whist in which David carried off the honours, apparently without effort. And so I kissed hands good night and promised to pay my respects before leaving.

I am glad Philadelphia is a long way from New Orleans.

The only feeling touch I had that evening was when I told Mrs. Udney I regarded my visit to their house at Livorno as the foundation of all my good fortune and wished to send her a small token of gratitude. She looked both pleased and touched and said she and Mr. Udney took a pride in me and would like me to write them from

America. I sent her a beautifully jewelled watch with her monogram. And so *vale* to a house without children—and that indescribable air of futile perfection in a barren woman's housekeeping at the Parishes'.

I forgot to say that the sea treated me elegantly this time when we came over—a swift sloop from Harwich to Helgoland, the great smuggling centre, where we picked up Nicholas, the English consul at Hamburg, a strange person with a squint, who keeps walking over everybody's toes and perpetually apologizing. Hence known as " 'Scuse-me Nick." The voyage to Vlissingen was picturesque but uneventful. From there hither by coach. I am well. The Dutch dine one as if the trolls were making the ogres merry—Gargantuan and endless and frequent are the meals. I long for France again. We shall have some months in Paris, I take it. Ouvrard will be leaving here shortly and I shall be seeing you, and I hope Juan and Simba too, soon after you will be looking on this.

With merry anticipations and profound gratitude,
                    Your humble obedient servant,
                                    Anthony Adverse.

CHAPTER FIFTY-EIGHT

GLORIA MUNDI

OUVRARD remained day after day in Amsterdam negotiating a
loan to tide him over his embarrassments. His own financing
was so intimately bound up with the French government's that
it was impossible to extricate himself without also supplying the needs
of the French treasury at the same time. It was characteristic of him
that he undertook to do this indirectly; that the discussion, which went
on for nearly three weeks at t'Huys ten Bosch, laid the basis for an
immense loan to Spain to enable her to meet her obligations to France.

So far had the control of Europe already fallen into the hands of
financiers that as yet neither the French nor the Spanish governments
were informed of the many good things in store for them. Ouvrard
simply made his arrangements to have the money available. After he
had completed certain transactions with those in power at Paris and
Madrid the loan was to be "offered."

Anthony was both impatient and fascinated by these proceedings.
He was anxious to get to Paris, and every day spent in Amsterdam cut
down his prospective stay there, for he knew it was Ouvrard's intention to hasten on from Paris to Madrid as soon as he could. Yet
linger he must, for since he was to accompany Ouvrard to Madrid it
was essential for him to be familiar with all the implications of the
bankers' schemes.

"I rely upon your knowledge of Spanish, of course," Ouvrard said
to him, "but you will not find yourself, when we get to Spain, a mere
interpreter by any means. There will be, I foresee, many occasions
when it will be much better for me to appear by proxy than in person.
And from your handling of the Mexican affair in England I am convinced that you can do equally well in Spain."

There was, therefore, no way out but to listen carefully to the conversations about Mr. Hope's great table at t'Huys ten Bosch in the
evening and to visit various financial personages in Amsterdam with
Ouvrard in the forenoon. This Anthony found was interesting
enough; the amazing web of European finance began to become more
generally visible to him as they called on the sundry Dutch spiders
engaged in spinning it. In this intricate tangle he soon discovered
that the Mexican affair was only one supporting strand.

Also it was impossible not to admire Ouvrard more and more as his

927

resourcefulness, his wide, clear knowledge of men and contemporary affairs, and the strange persuasiveness of his personality exhibited themselves in infinite variety. While they drove about from one establishment to another he explained, speculated profoundly about the future, or reminisced about his startling rise through all the changes of the Revolution from his clever beginning as a young paper-merchant at Nantes.

So far as Anthony could discover the man seemed to have no personal life whatever. His whole existence appeared to be a series of brief but vivid contacts with merchants and financiers. Each one of those interviews actually was, or had in it the elements of becoming, a minor or a major crisis, as the case might be, due to the fact that the ownership of property always tended to shift whenever Ouvrard appeared. Thus the man moved in a perpetual state of importance amid the tense atmosphere of an excitement which he alone appeared to be able to control. His was the reputation of a legendary alchemist and a Midas combined. For it was whispered and believed that wherever he appeared he might turn to gold whatever he touched; and that he might also, in an equally mysterious way, transmute the best of bullion into lead. All this was accomplished by the magic manipulation of paper. Even the bankers he dealt with believed that. And there was some truth in it, for Ouvrard, who was the first great modern financier, had discovered that a gold coin was merely the concrete focal point for an enormous aura of credit. He was always careful to keep at least a faintly auriferous tinge in even the pinkest glows of credit which he evoked. So he remained a not altogether fictitious Midas. Both the empire and the restoration were enabled to exist largely because of him.

There was only one person before whom his prestidigitations were performed under a completely understanding and always watchful eye; one who always demanded the rabbit, and who did not care whether it came out of a sleeve or a hat so long as it could be used for soup. At the very name of Napoleon Bonaparte the fat tail of the famous financier resembled that of a plucked goose; one upon which not even the pin feathers remained, for he had been plucked bare several times.

"What have you been doing, Ouvrard, since I have been away?" the first consul had asked upon his return from his last Austrian campaign. "So you thought to control me by supplying my wife at Malmaison with paper francs." He tore up Josephine's notes and stood with an amused expression staring up into Ouvrard's astounded and blanching face. "Voilà, you are repaid. The obligation, which never existed, has now no record. In the future, monsieur le banquier, you will remember that if I am not the fountain of credit I control its conduits." He took a turn up and down the room and laughed. "I am going to punish and educate you by forcing you to undergo a spiritual experience." Whereupon he had sent Ouvrard to four months' solitary confinement.

Of this, his only subjective experience, Ouvrard was never tired of talking. He returned to it while he and Anthony drove about Amsterdam or while he chatted in the rooms of t'Huys ten Bosch again and again.

He told how, to escape from his despair at finding himself alone, he had scattered a box of pins on the floor of his cell and picked them up one by one counting them each time to be sure that none were lost. Of this experience in prison he always spoke in the present tense while all the rest of his verbs invariably dealt either with the future or with the past.

"It is the hunt for the always one missing pin that keeps me sane," he said, half closing his eyes. "There are a thousand and one of them. One has been missing for a week. I find it at last in a crack in the stones of the floor. There is not, I am sure, a happier man in France now than I. I am successful once more." He opened his eyes as if to be sure he was not still in the cell, which was the only room that had ever genuinely contained him, and exclaimed, "What is the difference what one is busy at so long as the mind is completely occupied?"

"But suppose you cannot find the missing pin?" hazarded Anthony.

"Oh, I keep on looking for it. I am sure it is there and it's bound to turn up," laughed the banker. "I wait till I guess right as to its whereabouts or I keep on recounting them to be sure my mistake is not in numbers. I might have found them all, of course. It is best to be sure before looking again. But what is the difference? The day passes and pretty soon it is night anyway."

"Don't you get to counting in your sleep?"

"No, no, you mustn't do that," insisted Ouvrard seriously alarmed as if he were giving advice to a fellow prisoner. "That's dangerous. You take exercise by chinning yourself on the window bars of your cell till you're tired-out and can sleep."

"Didn't you worry about the cracks some, too?"

"Well, I do, you know, a little. But then I find the pin. And you will have to admit there is a point to that. And furthermore let me tell you I borrowed the pins to begin with from the turnkey's wife who trusted me because I was in jail, young fellow."

He held up a warning finger and laughed as he climbed out of the coach before the doors of *Vandevar & Van Group* to arrange some details of his loan.

"In that crack," said he as they drove off again, "I found fifty thousand pins."

M. Ouvrard was in need of a great many pins, and he was not

through looking for them in all the various cracks in Amsterdam until the end of July.   Consequently it was the beginning of August, when after a five-day drive down from the Low Countries he and Anthony finally arrived at Raincey.   Vincent came out to meet them.

Nothing would do but that they must stay the night, for the great banker felt in a peculiarly affable frame of mind after returning from a trip in which he had not only rehabilitated his affairs but had laid immensely promising lines for the future.   Château Raincey was his pride.   Here only, in its superabundant luxury, he felt that his success became visible.   Could he have had the title of baron his cup would have run over.   So they rode about the park that afternoon, where every vista of the ancient coverts had been formalized and an army of marble statues and unnecessary fountains introduced.   All of the latter were squirting.

Surrounded by new Calypsos, Bellerophons, Venuses, tritons, and Andromedas the deer moved about uncomfortably under the colossal oaks, annoyed by exotic shrubs and intrusive fenced plantations which supplied an excuse for an army of gardeners at a loss what to do.   The statues looked smooth and smug and the whole domain gave the impression of trying to be formal without having arrived at a satisfactory reason for being so.

Ouvrard, of course, admired most his greenhouses and the endlessly trained wall-trees which supplied fruits out of season for his table. They were taken through a mile of glass houses and finally brought around to the model village where agriculture was being encouraged by the proceeds from rentes; where every picturesqueness was both old and new.

And then there was the house, miles of it.   An old château at the front, it staggered behind into a "Roman bath" supplied with hundreds of windows and chimney-pots.   Here one enormous room led on into another, streaked with afternoon sunlight as they toiled through it; silent except for the ticking of endless ormolu clocks; filled with vast, lion-clawed sofas, chaises-longues, and tête-à-têtes where no one sat talking to nobody about nothing amid classical braziers, Chinese jars, chairs apparently waiting for Cleopatra, and the hanged ghosts of swathed chandeliers waiting, waiting for some event so important that it could never occur on a mere planet like the earth.

"You see I live on a large scale but very simply," said Ouvrard, waving his chubby hands at two befrogged lackeys to open the leaves of a cavernous portal for them at the end of a hall paved with mosaic. "These are my own little quarters where we can all be quite cozily comfortable."   And the man was right, for he lived in what had once been the châtelaine's quarters in the old château, where the rooms were small, the ceilings low, and the furniture old, comfortable, and domestic.

In these quarters Ouvrard seemed to be an entirely different person; a simple and amiable man. Here he became amazingly personal again in all his anecdotes; grew plaintive about his painful corns and advised both his young guests as to the best place to get boots in Paris—and other really vital matters—while he sat paring apples and stroking his fat cat. He showed Anthony the famous box with the thousand and one pins still in it, and was desirous that he should count them. But supper intervened and splendour was resumed once more.

The three ate at one end of a series of long tables where a hundred guests might have sat down. Candles blazed upon silver pyramids that rose toward the ceiling and wax tapers glistened in the pendent masses of crystal that drooped toward the floor. A great sideboard ascended by a series of steps provided the high altar from which dishes, in an endless stream of opulent courses, were brought by sleek, middle-aged acolytes loaded down with looped aiguillettes. The wine flowed fragrantly out of the extremely distant past.

Although this dining-room was monstrous, it was too overpowering to be funny. Even the most sophisticated and cynical were secretly impressed and bowled over by it. For it was in fact the crystal cavern or cathedral of the deity of endless possessions, the nave and altar of immaterial finance transmuted into things. It expressed all that perfectly in its outlines and bodily services with the chief manipulator and possessor sitting at the head of the great table in the glare of a thousand candles and long mirrors. Lush dinners here, when anybody came, were the climactic experiences of Ouvrard's abstractly-conjuring soul.

Yet as he sat there that evening, no amount of wine could evoke in Anthony the feeling that he was sitting again at the table of the sun. He was somewhere in a subterranean cavern being served by jinn. Perhaps, if the cup were rubbed the wrong way, the whole table might vanish and leave them sitting in the dark.

They talked that evening of the decree of the senate and plebiscite which had made Bonaparte first consul for life.

"From now on 'Napoleon,'" murmured Ouvrard, "in the style of other kings. Well, well, we bankers will at last know how to proceed now. It is delicious to feel that for a while at least the world is not just going to dissolve again." He looked about the huge room, dark at the other end, with some satisfaction. "I remember," said he, "when Napoleon needed cloth for his ragged uniform coat. I arranged that for him through Mme. Tallien. And—I suppose—I shall keep on doing so till the end. Let us drink to the new era."

They did so silently, and were then led off to the picture gallery

where a succession of classical scenes by David and other moderns of
the same school depicted the Homeric adventures of statuary in paint.
At the end of the gallery was a portrait of Ouvrard by one of David's
pupils. They stood before it trying to imitate the self-respect and
reverence of Ouvrard for himself as he called for a light and looked
up at it. Upon a dock, apparently at ancient Ostia, Ouvrard in the
toga of a Roman senator stood superintending the unloading of a
preciously-freighted ship.

"If there are secret stairs behind this picture," thought Anthony,
"I wonder where they lead to?" But there was no time for explora-
tion, for once having penetrated to the inmost shrine of Château
Raincey it was now time for bed.

"I shall not see you young fellows tomorrow morning when you
depart," said Ouvrard. "I need some hours of rest, and shall sleep
late. But hold yourself in readiness to leave for Madrid at any time,
M. Adverse. And if I were you, I would take what time you will
have here in Paris for preparing your affairs and your outfit for New
Orleans. There are many things one can purchase in Paris which I
understand are not on sale in Louisiana," he smiled. "But if you do
as well in Louisiana as I expect there will not be many things you cannot purchase in Paris when you return from New Orleans."

Three lackeys with flambeaus led them off through dark corridors
to widely separated rooms. Vincent and Anthony had scarcely had
time to say anything to each other.

As he composed himself for sleep that night, for the first time since
his landing at Gibraltar over a year before, a devastating doubt and a
feeling of the futility of the course he was pursuing overtook Anthony.
Perhaps it was the somehow exhausting tour of the park and château
of Raincey that had done it. Was he devoting himself with Ouvrard
to picking up a great many pins? Into what new crack in the cell of
existence had he himself rolled? This afternoon especially he had
been enormously bored. And when one is bored one is either being
sinned against by others or sinning against oneself. So far the elation of returning to civilization had borne him along with it. He had
crossed the Alps on the very wings of it, he saw. Tonight it suddenly seemed to have ebbed. Tonight at Château Raincey, as he hid
himself in an immense and ornate bed in a vast chamber, where the
only sound was a clock ticking dismally, the antithesis of that mood
from which music occasionally welled up within him lay dull and heavy
upon his soul. Upon the beach of time where he was walking suddenly the waves had ceased to say anything that he cared to hear.

A sudden impulse to abandon it all, to cut loose from the strings
that bound him to property brought him up out of the bed again and
took him to the window, where into a kind of dull, opaque moonlight

he looked out into the night and beheld the statues standing about in the cemetery-like park.

The immense window stretched from floor to ceiling. It would be perfectly easy to step out of it—into what?

He slipped into a dressing gown, and leaving a candle beside his door to mark his room in the huge corridor, he walked downstairs toward a distant noise of human voices at the other end of the house in the servants' wing. Presently a light and the sound of dishes being stacked amid whistling and laughter stopped him before a closed door. He hesitated a moment and then pushed it in. It was the scullery. Four or five servants, men and maids, were finishing washing up the plates from the feast of two hours before. Silence suddenly ensued when they saw him.

"What is there monsieur desires?" said a young man coming forward respectfully. "Is the bell pull broken?"

Anthony shook his head.

"I wish to sit with you here a while and talk. Will you let me? I am very lonely in the big room."

Some of the girls laughed. The man drew up chairs to a small table and sat down with Anthony. For some time they were a little embarrassed. Then the young servant began to speak of the farm where he lived. He was interested in that. He was about to be married, and he was interested in that. They talked for over an hour. The others finished their work and went, one of the servants placing a cold fowl and a pitcher of milk before them.

At midnight Anthony returned to his room. The candle by his door had almost burnt out. He blew it out before the window and watched the faint ghost of smoke trail into nothing in the moonlight. Then he climbed into the huge bed and slept soundly. "Life is nothing but moods from somewhere else," he thought. Something of the peace of Jacques Claire, the chief scullion, remained with him.

He had forgotten to draw the curtains. A few hours later a magnificent August morning poured intensely through the shining eastern windows of Château Raincey and awakened him as with an embrace from the angel of light.

The new day brought a mood he never forgot. It was an exalted one, the mood of trumpets and bugles. As he looked out on the park that morning he saw two stags bounding and fighting amid the trees where the early, level fingers of the sun streamed through the aisles of the ancient oak forest. Even the statues looked alive and rosy now.

He dressed hastily without calling the valet and ran downstairs to find Vincent had done the same and was already at breakfast. They

beat each other on the back as if they were meeting for the first time.
Indeed, yesterday they had not met at all.   They both talked at the
same time until they laughed at each other.

"Thank God, Ouvrard's not up," whispered Vincent.   "Let's not
take any chances."   He gave orders for the berlin to be brought
around without delay.   "I have an idea this is going to be one of our
rare days," he laughed as they heard the wheels grating in the drive.

"I have trunks from England," said Anthony.

"Have the butler send them on later by cart, then.   Let us go
swiftly and freely this morning."

That was easily arranged.   No one at Raincey had any cause to
complain of their tips.   Something like a uniformed guard of honour
of about twenty servants managed to get two or three hand bags to
the berlin, with the maids bowing in a bank of short petticoats and
bodices behind.   The news that Jacques Claire had received a comfortable gift for his fiancée just after breakfast had electrified the
usually tomb-like château.

"It was to be understood now why monsieur's coachman had embraced him, that tall young man who only looked like an Englishman,
and besides, monsieur's coachman was a fellow of great élan and pride,
unespagnol.   Ah, the esprit of their meeting on the steps was beautiful.   Monsieur had been so surprised, even overwhelmed—and no
wonder.   For the great dog had darted out from under the berlin like
a lion and sprung upon him.   Was it not drôle to see him seize monsieur's hand in his great fangs and mouth it?"   Those who could not
say "oh" and "ah" many times had lumps in their throats because of
the sounds which the dog made.   Such sorrowful and happy cries.
And is it not well known that such animals are sagacious?

In fact Anthony had been nearly pulled apart by Juan and Simba as
he came down the steps.   The berlin had driven off with the dog
leaping along beneath it giving tongue so that the stags on the other
side of the wrought-iron pickets scrambled to their feet while M.
Ouvrard stumbled out of his bed and peered through the curtains, to
see what the devil all the confounded clamour was about.   The sound
of it died away joyfully down the Paris road.

It was three hours' rapid posting from Raincey to Paris along the
fine, new river road that flowed like a satin ribbon along the bank of
the Seine.   Vincent was happy with the success of his surprise.

"Juan has done very well with the horses," he said.   "In fact he
can do almost anything from laying a new floor to pressing my clothes.
It is almost like having Aristide on the box again.   By the way, I have
Aristide well started on his career as a clerk for Cambacérès.   He
writes dossiers for the new law commission.   Simba I admit is something of a problem, perhaps you can manage him."   He looked out

happily at the smoke of Paris rising like a thin haze some miles away over the low hills. "Ah, it is good, Toni, to have you back again. Did you know Katharina has accepted me? Ja wohl!" They whooped together, causing Simba to bark again under the berlin. "I will tell you one thing more and then no more of anything either business or life but let us just live in today which is so bright and golden. One would almost think the Seine was the Rhine here today, nicht wahr? Well, Anna's little Düsseldorfer died. I thought you would want to know—even today. Don't cry," said he, wiping his own eyes. "It is all over now." A few minutes later they were both smiling again. "One must drive on, you know," cried Vincent, waving his arms.

They stopped to change horses where a canal boat was waiting deeply in a stretch of locks where water-lilies grew. A child brought them a small bunch of these, roots and all, for a sou. They laid them dripping on the floor and drove on with their fragrance filling the berlin.

"Here we are driving on through the harvest again like old times," said Anthony after a while.

"Ja," smiled Vincent, "it looks as if peace had come to France at last. The first consul is a great man."

It was not until nearly half an hour later that they began to hear a distant song of trumpets, fifes, and drums. On Montmartre the cannon began to boom.

"I had forgotten," said Vincent. "Napoleon is holding a great review today in the Champ de Mars. It is to celebrate his election for life, I suppose. There will be a presentation of eagles and standards and the swearing in of recruits.—Juan," he cried, "try to get us in, in time for the march past. Drive to the Spanish ambassador's first and we will try to pick up Señor Montijo there."

Their pace quickened. The distant trumpets, the clashing of church bells and the boom of cannon brought a wave of the far-off excitement of the city rolling over the fields.

It was like approaching an African village, thought Anthony. Only there was no hysteria in this excitement of sound. It seemed to be controlled, regulated; to flow from a deeper and more lasting impulse than had the fusillades and tom-tom beating that greeted him upon approaching Futa-Jaloon. That was mere savage child-play compared to the mighty thunder rolling out over the peaceful harvest from Paris in this August forenoon while the peasants toiled in the fields.

As they drove through the city streets deafening peals of bells broke out over their heads from the steeples, while from every side the bands of the regiments in garrison sang marching troops to their rendezvous.

All Paris was streaming toward the Champ de Mars. Cavalry

wheeled at the end of street vistas, and artillery rumbled. Citizens
walked, rode, and ran. The guns on Mont Valérien and at the
Invalides marked the minutes alternately. Here and there above the
heads of the multitudes flags passed, swept along by a river of bright
troopers that flowed like streams of blood or grey and blue and silver
through the more drably-clad Parisiens. At the Pont-Neuf they
waited while a whole brigade of artillery trundled past trotting
swiftly relentlessly, all at the same pace, with little gamins riding on
the axes and caissons, beside the cannons, waving their hats and
shouting. It was tremendous and yet it was gay. It was Paris, the
new Paris which had suddenly found itself and was rising stronger
and clearer and more magnificent out of the ashes, the blood, and the
grime of the old. The endless front of the Tuileries from one pavilion
to another was draped with colours and standards. It shone. Today the new-born phoenix who lived there was going to soar.

They hurried quickly through some tortuous by-streets and picked
up Señor Montijo at the Spanish embassy. He could provide them
with a permit for the ambassadors' carriage-stand, which was why
Vincent had remembered him. And with the dapper young under-
secretary, glad enough to be able to chatter Spanish unreservedly, they
soon found themselves admitted to the "aire des ambassadeurs" and
pressing forward to the ropes with the families of the legations seated
amid flapping foreign ensigns behind. A little crowding among the
hangers-on, and they were looking out across the wide, level sweep of
the Champ de Mars.

Perhaps it was not an accident that the stand for the ambassadors
of foreign powers, and for what remained of the legislative bodies of
France, had been placed directly opposite the reviewing tribunal before
which the armies of the victorious Republic were to pass under the
eye of the first consul. Certainly it was not an accident that his
tribune reposed on the exact spot occupied by the Altar of the Nation
only a few years before. The fierce heat engendered by internal and
external wars had fused the two objects. To the vast majority of the
spectators Napoleon and France; the Altar of the Nation and the
tribune were now one and the same thing. A political poet and a
dramatic military genius who understood the use of symbols had
chosen this day of his elevation to the consulship for life to make them
actually and visibly so.

Napoleon had been brought forth on a bit of tapestry covered by the
legendary deeds of the heroes of Homer just after his mother had
hurried home from mass. He liked to remember that. The birth of
the first consul, who consciously intended to grow into the emperor,
was now to recapitulate the original event. But it was France which
was now laid out upon a classically decorated background about to be

safely delivered of a demigod. He moved with great precision. The presentation of standards was to take place at high noon and to be followed by a great banquet and civic feast tendered by the municipality of Paris.

At 10.30 exactly the sudden cessation of cannon, church bells, and all military music announced that Napoleon was hearing mass at Nôtre Dame. This impressive silence, in which the whole city seemed to participate as in a prelude of worship, lasted for nearly half an hour during which time nothing was to be heard except the earth-shaking tread of troops marching down from the Barrière de l'Etoile and massing along the embankments of the Seine. At 10.45 a sudden peal of bells proclaimed that mass was over and the first consul leaving the cathedral.

At 11.00 the guns at the Invalides boomed the warning of his approach. A few minutes later his coach drawn by the six white horses presented by the Emperor of Austria after Campo Formio emerged from the gate of the Ecole Militaire and moved slowly down the Champ de Mars. At the same instant from the opposite end of the field a battalion of the guards began to advance to meet it. No commands were heard. In the huge vacant area of the fields of manœuvre there was nothing but the glittering carriage with the six superlative white horses; the advancing oblong of the guards. These two things must inevitably meet in the centre of the field opposite the tribunal.

Napoleon sat erect in the carriage. He no longer had colleagues. He was enormously alone. So great was the spell of that lonely figure in the transverse cocked hat and the green coat with white facings that the fascinated multitude looked at him, looked at the carriage advancing toward the guards, and the guards advancing toward the carriage, in electric silence. Its number was sandy. Everybody in Paris who was not blind or paralysed, an ancient or an infant was there. The people swarmed both barriers of the long fields from the Military School to the river; they climbed trees; they ascended backward in waves onto the adjacent housetops. No one uttered a sound. The carriage and the troops met. The guards wheeled with that magic of mathematical motion in life which only soldiers possess, advanced obliquely to each side of the tribune, countermarched, halted, and came to present arms with fixed bayonets. On each side of the tribune there now extended a living wall of steel.

The man in the carriage got out with his hat on. He walked alone across the ample space that separated him from the tribune, the focus of countless eyes. He began to ascend the stairs through a forest of eagles. They tipped the flags, still tightly wrapped about their standards. These, when he descended the stairs a few minutes later, he would present rapidly to the troops. On each side of the stairs a

colossal bronze tripod smoked. At the top of the stairs was a curule
chair, and the sky.

A horse neighed and a woman screamed. The multitude broke out
into a brassy roar. The sound grew in volume, died down, rose in
ever ascending waves of delirious enthusiasm and lifted Napoleon to
the top of the steps. He turned, stood there with his hat extended in
his hand for five minutes and sat down. The regular acclamations
from the troops on the river banks still proclaimed his name.

Something of a surprise now developed. A procession of young
girls dressed in white and green, the youngest of whom bore a laurel
crown on a satin cushion, approached the tribune. At this unexpected
intrusion of the feminine into what had promised to be a purely military occasion the crowd shouted again. Napoleon came down the steps
and held up his hand. A childish voice was heard reciting a brief ode
in which "Paris" conferred the wreath of victory on her hero. Napoleon lifted the child in his arms while she placed it on his head, amid
appreciative roars from the mob and soldiers.

Apparently by a happy thought of the moment he beckoned to the
children to seat themselves amid the flags thus charming untold legions
of Parisiens into pandemonium. The human noise eventually subsided. He reascended the tribune and lifted one hand.

From the lower end of the Champ de Mars a thousand trumpets
smote the summer morning flat with one stunning fanfare of clear,
brazen sound.

The bugle is the essential voice of France. Other nations employ
the instrument to give military signals, but they merely blow upon
hoarse war-horns by comparison. Through bugles the French soldier
releases his sublimest emotion in a wordless song. In it are mingled
the tones of the Roman buccina, the far-calling of the mighty horn of
Roland, the shouts and shrieks of Joan of Arc. The song is irresistible. The trumpets are torches. From the mouth of French
bugles flames the fiery, golden soul of France.

A front of trumpeters a quarter of a mile wide and four files deep
started to march up the Field of Mars. Before them twinkled the
batons of the drum-majors, behind them thundered twelve files of
drums, snare, tenor, and bass. It was the massed field-music of the
veteran armies of Italy and the Rhine. The trumpets ceased and the
drums began; the drums stopped, a thousand scarlet tassels tossed,
there was a brazen flash, and the trumpets spoke again. So to alternate thunder and lightning the long lines advanced like rigid rulers,
scarlet and blue, scarlet and blue, legs passing; every elbow of every
drummer thrown upward at the same time, rolling sound before them.

As the lines swept steadily forward the spectators began to go mad.
The flanks of the marching lines aroused on either side along the

barriers as they passed whirlpools among the people; dashed a spray of hats into the air. All those who were still seated rose as one man. It became necessary to shout, or stifle with excitement. Those who remained silent did so at the cost of tears. Here and there women began to faint and to be trampled upon. The drums and bugles passed on. Before the tribune the long lines wheeled, advanced, countermarched, and at one signal—stopped.

In the midst of this sudden, stupefying silence every eye turned once more to the little man in the curule chair. But he no longer seemed little. He stood now at the top of twenty-four steps exalted against the sky; above the eagles with laurel on his head. To the multitude, exhausted, but still beside themselves with emotion, still looking up at him, he had become a god.

In the blinding August noon a hot whirlwind swept down the field and vanished.

"It is the ghost of the Republic," croaked a voice in Anthony's ear. He turned astounded to see a venerable, clerical-looking man with a fine, wide forehead standing just behind him. He was clasping a green umbrella close to one side of his chest and muttering to himself. He had been weeping, too.

Just then the drums began again.

They were now tapping a cavalry trot. The god had not remained doing nothing long enough to become ridiculous. At precisely the expected moment the manifestation of his powers began.

All the landscape from the Barrière de l'Etoile to the Pont-d'Iena, from that bridge to the Tuileries, began to move upon the Champ de Mars in a sliding avalanche of men. The trumpets gave tongue, ceased.

A column of cavalry poured across the bridge, emerged on the level parade of the field like a bright sword thrusting itself into a brown body, and trotted along the west barrier. A bugle screamed. The leading squadron wheeled on a right pivot, drew sabres and charged. As each squadron reached the same mark it executed the same manœuvre.

The irresistible might of the god on the tribune was now visibly apparent. In a moment, by a majestic magic, the Champ de Mars was a square mass of armed centaurs, the earth shuddering as if with subterranean thunder, the sun playing with dazzling lightnings along the descending lines. So overpowering was the solid reality, the threat of weight in this mass of cavalry, that the spectators at the end of the field directly before it milled about in panic and tried to scatter. But at a point some hundred yards ahead of them the line drew off by the centre into column, rushed at an even more furious gallop through the central arch of the Ecole Militaire; hurtled head-long down the Avenue Saxe.

From the stand of the ambassadors, where Anthony and Vincent were looking directly across the middle of the field toward the tribune, the effect was a curious and memorable one. The horses seemed to be galloping furiously upon a treadmill. As each line passed it was immediately followed by another precisely the same. The motion thus compensated became static. The square of charging cavalry, renewed by its feeding column at the rear and drawn off in a similar flume of men at the front, continued to move at tremendous speed and yet to occupy precisely the same space of ground by the force of a calculated discipline in space and numbers. At the exact centre there was always an officer rising in his stirrups to salute the first consul. This continued for the space of nearly half an hour while the dust rolled until the field smoked; while the hoofs thundered.

It was some moments before the multitude became fully aware of this curious vision of irresistible force in furious motion maintained in statu quo. All the recklessness, the threat, the enthusiasm, and the élan of the Revolution were still contained in the terrific square of charging figures upon which a perfection of order had now been conferred. All, without thinking, beheld this. They saw it—and the man who had brought it about was standing upon the tribune before which the colossal tripods smoked.

It was suddenly borne in upon Anthony that the silence of a few minutes before while the first consul had been attending mass was a mere salute to the past, the brief acknowledgment of a faded sacred memory. *Now, in* this overpowering and thundering present, he was participating with the French nation and all Paris in the living worship of Mars whose emanation stood opposite upon his altar, crowned with victorious laurel, playing with pure force.

The thunder muttered into a new and more continuous rumble. The lines of cavalry had suddenly changed into artillery. The square of men sitting upon horses melted without losing outline or substance into lines of men sitting with folded arms upon caissons with golden cannons flashing behind. A noise as of ten thousand chariots quivered in the air. The crowd broke into an ecstasy of cries echoed and re-echoed by the signalling bugles. Where had been the haunches of galloping horses were now lines of glimmering wheels with the smoke of battle drifting through the spokes. The cannons passed and the endless lines of infantry, blue, grey and scarlet, furnished and twinkling to the last accoutrement, strode after them, saluted the first consul, and passed. Their meaning was perfectly expressed by the sound of the enormous march music to which they advanced.

There were not many present who understood the full significance

pectators were
iting for the
ambassador,
ove as precisely
They were, he
idly but of indi-
lines that rippled
ed steel. The old
bune and at once
had forged. He
etermined to make
more flattering than
se who do not temper
uttered gloomily—and
tion.

s distributing eagles to
chosen to receive them.
to receive their colours
ards had come forward.
rled flag from its socket
re placed it in the hands
words. As each soldier

behind him, he moved to
the last step, he presented
eterans in a brief and fiery
he turned, pointed to the
waiting regiments heard.
are the honour of the nation
ur hands. I shall send them
ctory follows. Swear that it
your lives."

uthentic sound of the military
ledged. Paris had heard noth-
as Augustus and raised on the
palace just across the river from

d at the head of a brilliant staff
he multitude swarmed over the
Coaches, citizens, and soldiers
the thronged bridges going home.
swam glowing warmly in the azure

mist of Paris
loons rising b
gaping crowds
The distant st
barracks follows
drunkenly on the
with the next ge
tantly home.

The huge crowd
to get the berlin out
fierce dispute over the
and Portuguese ambass
envoy, Mr. Livingston,
ing out and hiring a f
drove off, leaving the n
The British left next b
good management of h
upholders of the House
come to blows when the
drove off in all directions

"The young man with I
tor who is trying to sell to
fine Yankee notion that no
interest me and Ouvrard.
amusing talker though—" b
Juan drove up with the ber
during the review, had torn

"I *had* to lock him in," s
went wild. In his country, S
horns mean the beginning of
different here, but how was I

"Well, we shall just have to
cent, climbing in gloomily and s
which the stuffing bulged. An
big hound which still whined a
mood.

"You can't start so much excite
at least with an animal," remark
good deal put out over the appea
right, you know. It's too bad."
had to laugh.

of these advancing lines. By far the majority of the s
now overpowered and satiated. They were merely wa
final scene of the occasion to go home. The Prussia
however, leaned forward a little. The lines did not m
as did those of the guards of his master at Potsdam.
saw, not composed of human automatons moving rig
vidual and enthusiastic men. Yet they were lines,
with life and with the resiliency of beautifully temper
general of Frederick looked up to the man on the tri
admired and cursed him for the perfect sword he
knew that the world could be altered by it. He d
his speech to follow at the Hôtel de Ville ever
that which his secretary had prepared. "Tho
their metal must temper their words," he m
looked at Napoleon again with reluctant admira

The first consul was now descending the step
the various standard bearers who had been
The newly recruited regiments which were
were massed before him and their colour gu
On each step as he descended he plucked a fu
and leaning forward with an imperial gestu
of a soldier with appropriate and inspiring
received his flag he unfurled it.

Thus, as the brilliant standards unfurled
the bottom of the tribune. There, on
swords of honour to a couple of chosen
speech that all the recruits heard. The
flags, and lifted his voice so that all the

"Soldiers, these eagles and these flags
which I deliver for safe-keeping into yo
in her defence where glory leads and vi
shall be so, swear to defend them with

He raised his own hand.

A tremendous roar followed, the a
tumult by which conquerors are acknow
ing like it since Julian had been hailed
shields of his veterans at the Roman
Nôtre Dame fifteen centuries before.

The review was over.

Napoleon mounted his charger an
rode off to the Hôtel de Ville.
Champ de Mars in every direction
struggled with one another across
The golden dome of the Invalides

on a hot afternoon. From the Jardin des Plantes bal-
y virtue of hot-air floated over the devoted city and the
. The device was still a novelty. They were magical.
ains of military music where the troops returned to
d by groups of marching and capering gamins slept
molten August air. Trees drooped, and nursemaids
eration of conscripts in perambulators turned reluc-

---

had pretty well scattered by the time they were able
f the enclosure roped-off for the diplomats. A
precedence of departure between the Austrian
adors delayed everybody else. The American
aroused considerable laughter by at last walk-
acre in which he and a fellow citizen quietly
onarchists involved in metaphysical questions.
force of several red-faced grooms and the
rses, and the Dutch followed behind. The
of Braganza and Hapsburg were about to
police removed the barrier and everybody
at once.
Mr. Livingston," said Vincent, "is an inven-
Napoleon a boat that is to go by steam. A
one here takes seriously. He has tried to
He also has torpedoes on the brain. An
ut further conversation was checked when
lin. Simba, who had been shut inside it
ff most of the upholstery with his teeth.
id Juan. "When the music started he
eñor Nolte, such sounds on drums and
a lion hunt or a war. Of course, it is
to tell a dumb beast that?"
have it all done over again," said Vin-
howing Señor Montijo to a seat from
thony was some time in quieting the
d trembled and appeared in an ugly

ment and not have something happen,
d Anthony to Vincent, who was a
rance of the berlin. "I'll make it
Simba growled in reply and they

They dropped Montijo at the embassy and continued on across the old turning bridge by the Tuileries.

"Look!" said Vincent at a carriage that forged by them. Anthony had just time to catch a glimpse before the rather smart phaeton ahead turned a corner. A grey-haired man in a beaver and a young woman in a bonnet with curled plumes upon it were its passengers. Both were handsomely dressed. He could not see the woman's face. She sat with her grey-gloved hands lying in her lap almost resignedly. Anthony looked at Vincent inquiringly.

"Angela and Debrülle," said Vincent. "Shall we try to follow them?"

"No," he replied after a moment. "She might not want us to."

Vincent nodded. "Debrülle left a note for you some days ago when he learned you would soon be home. I have said nothing about it so far."

"Good, let us not think of it now," replied Anthony. "I shall wa to see her, but just now I want to do nothing but go home to the House of the Wolf. Here we are in the faubourg now."

Vincent was pleased and showed it. They turned the corner by *L'homme Armé* and drew up at "47" with a warm welcome from old Paul. Simba bounded out and darted up the circular steps before them barking. Once upstairs they began to rush about like a couple of boys home for a holiday. The trunks had come in from Raincey and Vincent was soon exclaiming with tears in his eyes over his gifts from England. Generous himself, it was a curious quirk in his make-up that always made him astonished and delighted when anybody gave him something. Anthony had taken full advantage of this.

"I am looking at the little plaque of the wolf and the twins with greater ease of heart than I have known since I left here," said Anthony, strolling over to the window and looking out with quiet satisfaction in his eyes.

"Ja!" said Vincent. He put away his gifts and had the water-lilies they had obtained that morning brought up and arranged in a bowl.

"For Anna, you know," he sighed. "Ach—that little Düsseldorfer. For two years she has been making things for him already," he muttered, rearranging the flowers that were now wilted. "With these roots though they will even bloom again perhaps. Sehr schöne blumen."

"They *are* lovely," said Anthony. "Let us keep them here on this table while I stay. They are better than words. And we shall both know what they mean—*who* they are."

The flowers remained, expanding slowly in the water, reviving and slowly filling the room with a subtle fresh fragrance.

"And for only a sou!" said Vincent, smiling and brushing a fly off his forehead with his cuff.

A pile of mail Anthony disregarded, and they spent the rest of the afternoon talking in the deep chairs, coats off, a big meerschaum pipe and many Havana cigars accompanying their talk of all that had transpired, until it began to grow dusk. Simba stretched out on a rug beside Anthony and slept, the hair occasionally lifting along his spine while he growled in dreams at the sound of the distant drums still rolling here and there far away over the city roofs.

"It is complete now," thought Anthony, "even the wolf is here. If this afternoon could only last forever! Why not? Why did he always have to go? And this time it would be forever."

"Vincent, you will have to come to see us at New Orleans some time. You must."

"Ja," said Vincent taking the "us" for granted, "if Katharina will go so far. Himmel, you will not be here when I am married! Ah, who knows?" His eyes grew large and blue looking into the future, a little frightened.

"What do you see?" laughed Anthony.

"Nothing," replied his friend, "nothing. Do you remember that Bovino woman said I was to die poor and that you . . ."

"Oh, nonsense, Vinc. I have met some real witches since then. How you do remember things! I had forgotten that. It's getting dark. Let's go out to dinner tonight. Paris will be en fête after the review. Call a fiacre and let's dress."

"Ach, my new English clothes," exclaimed Vincent. "We'll go!"

Simba followed Anthony down the hall, nudging him. Juan was in the room laying out his things. Juan gabbled in Spanish unmercifully while Anthony was being shaved. Shouts of delight from Vincent's room over his own splendid appearance when arrayed in what came out of the London bandboxes announced his satisfaction with perfection. Juan, who considered his master's property to be his own, had calmly opened the bundle from Gallegos and extracted from it the set of razors Cibo had given to Anthony in Havana. These he had put in excellent shape and he was now running one of them rapidly over Anthony's chin.

"Does it go as smoothly as it used to at Gallegos?" asked Juan. Lying back in a big chair with his eyes closed, Anthony waved his hand in satisfaction.

"It is much better than when one is alone and compelled to do everything for oneself, isn't it, señor?"

"Much, much better, Juan," said Anthony so emphatically that Juan almost cut him.

"Sí," replied Juan, stropping the blade and looking down at his

master whose eyes remained closed. "But you are not alone any
more. Simba and I, we have come to stay with you. Wherever you
go we follow."

"Even to the other world? I go to Louisiana, you know, Juan."

"Sí, señor, even to the other world," said Juan eagerly. "I am a
little tired of this one," he added in a far-away voice. "That swallow
I sent back to my town from the *Wampano-ag*—you remember, señor?
Well, he must have fallen into the water or gone to the wrong chimney. When I got back home from Gallegos I find my girl is married
to a fisherman and has two fat boys. She milks goats and fries the
sardine for another."

"The world is full of girls, Juan."

"Sí, but is there comfort in numbers, señor? One should also consider that."

A few minutes later Anthony and Vincent were rattling over the
cobbles of the old faubourg to supper at Frascati's. The gardens
were brilliantly illuminated and there was to be a display of fireworks
later in honour of the review. They picked up a young banker by
the name of Joly from Antwerp. He had in tow a Count von Haxen-
thausen of the Royal Danish Life-Guards who aroused some amusement by comparing everything he saw in bad French with something
else in Copenhagen, and there was also his friend, a Major Holstein
of the Queen's Jäger from the Island of Amager, who said nothing at
all but grunted with appreciation of the supper. They managed to
leave the Danes watching large "N's" in fireworks coming out of a
fountain surrounded by fiery pinwheels, and started walking through
the salons furnished to the last extremity of gilding in the new Roman
style.

It was the thing to do, to stroll at Frascati's, where everybody agreed
that English politics were perfidious and men's clothes from London
perfection. The women had been forbidden by the first consul to
dress in English cloth. They managed to look quite acceptably
Roman, some were still even quite Greek, in sandals, high waists and
puffed sleeves half-way to the elbows in the silk of Lyons. The most
striking thing about Frascati's, however, was its brilliant lighting. A
thousand pounds of wax candles a night were consumed in the lines
of chandeliers, inverted pyramids of crystal that ran the entire length
of the salons. Lackeys in oiled canvas coats with a movable ladder
went about snuffing them. The salon was the place to be seen; to stand
by a pedestal and be admired.

They saw Garat the singer with a book of music in his hand talking
to the dancer Frémis. The place was full of people from the em-
bassies. Lord Whiteworth, the newly arrived English ambassador,
hurried through to a private garden party with his own wife, which

caused considerable surprise. Murat, the Governor of Paris, passed
through after dinner with a brilliant suite.

"That is Mme. Récamier, the banker's wife, over there," said Vincent. "She comes here every Wednesday night to be seen and to
play cards. It is said that he insists upon it as there are stories she is
unhappy with him. There is the Prince of Nassau, the fat little fellow
in the brown pelisse, coming up to talk with her. Most of those uncomfortable looking people are émigrés who have returned since April.
You can tell them by the old-fashioned bow. Come over here and
meet these Italians. Look, that is Miot de Melita with your friend
Joseph Bonaparte. Come over; I know him. We should not lose
this opportunity. Melita is an ardent Bonapartist and would turn all
of Italy over to Napoleon—remember that."

They found themselves received casually but cordially enough. The
consul's brother questioned Anthony eagerly as to conditions in England. Most of the talk turned on the recent suppressions and changes
that had gone on in the Tribunate since it had offered opposition to the
formation of the Legion of Honour, which Joseph maintained was a
democratic institution. "It is something that is likely to last," said
he and then looked suddenly embarrassed.

"The only formidable opposition left," said Melita to Vincent, "is
not from orators but from a certain general, Moreau," he whispered.
"Have you heard the bon mot? Il n'y a que deux partis en France
maintenant, les moreaux et les immoraux. Ah, I am afraid we are
all among les immoraux here," he laughed. "Come and see me,
Herr Nolte, about that municipal loan for Milan—tomorrow. Good!"
They bade one another good evening and passed on.

"That *was* a stroke of luck," said Vincent. "Well, it pays to be
seen here, you see. Look, there goes Mme. Grand, the lady for whom
you got the gloves. Napoleon wants Talleyrand to marry her. There
is certainly a good deal of the lady. Well, it is time to leave when
the older dames begin to arrive. You would scarcely think there had
ever been a revolution here, would you? Now I'll show you the other
side of the medal."

They hired a fiacre and went to a dingy little place with a few
candles in bottles, the Hôtel de Saint-Pierre in the littered alley of
Saint-Pierre-de-Montmartre, near the Messageries. Here the girls
still wore the red caps of liberty and nothing else, if one insisted.
They did not, however. An hour of sweaty atmosphere and a bad
imitation of the carmagnol purchased by a drunken Russian nobleman who had heard of "Liberty," and wanted to see her dance, sent
them home sleepy and laughing.

"Poor Toussaint," said Anthony. "What would he have thought
of Liberty in red drawers?"

umped over the
by the smooth
apoleon. They
ey looked out at
n sedately pacing
ace du Carrousel.
always been there
xcellent little mid-
flooded by placid
e a lion. And it
the Carrousel to the
ow over langouste en
led them for the dis-
e little Hôtel de Saint-

of the window tonight.
world of Paris and the
he had entered into it

a out of the bundle that
ashed the mother-of-pearl
icked it onto the floor at
pped. Probably travelling
harmed.
r and have it repaired. He
light and went to sleep like

W ATER-L
alone in th
lated mail.
drooping on its ste
beginning to open.
ginning to show. He
roots completely, and

Most of them were
mittances and statem
e from Dolly at Bath
nks—she was evident
not write you any more
He lit his cigar with th
into nothing.

Women, he reflected,
a good deal. There was
comfortable for life, Capt
ing something nice every q
back with her mark were t
new cottage with her bun-b
interest on capital and refle
least the results of some yea
John Bonnyfeather—decease
All that he could say was tha
future . . .

He sat fingering a note with
in bold, precise German script

Dear Mr. Adverse: I
Weds. morning next. Pr
the suburbs by request, but
be under the necessity of e
think you will agree, whei
All under this roof look for
expectation of long deferred
nothing ominous or mercenai
been an ever constant friend

"And even those were insecure," said Vincent.

Anthony began to spout pages of *Emile* as they
Paris cobblestones already replaced here and there
pavement of the new boulevards being laid by N
laughed at the sound of the prose of Rousseau. Th
the horses ravished from Venice, the old Roman tear
against the sky on the new triumphal arch in the Pl
They loomed high against the stars as if they had
and would remain permanently. They enjoyed an e
night supper looking out on the court at numéro 4
moonlight, where the shadow of Simba passed li
was all vastly satisfactory, from the horses at
shaded candles on the little table by the wind
casserol, and other small platters, which cons
appointment of Montmartre and the despicabl
Pierre.

Anthony did not feel at all like stepping out
The mood of the enthusiastically contented
new era was on him. He felt tonight that
at last.

Before he went to bed he took the madon
Juan had untied. Neleta, he saw, had sm
inlay at the Virgin's feet when she had k
Gallegos. The shrine was also badly chi
had done that. But the statue itself was u

Tomorrow he would take it to a jewelle
left it standing on the bureau in the moor
a child.

And then tomorrow there was Angela.

CHAPTER FIFTY-NINE

"LIES are fragrant," thought Anthony, as he sat
e big room next morning going over his accumu-
One bud he noticed in particular that had hung
m only the day before had now revived and was
The flesh-like pink-and-white of its petals was be-
e renewed the water in the bowl, covering the
urned to his letters again.

current bills or tradesmen's announcements,
ents from London.   There was an ill-spelled
, stumbling over a few sentences of awkward
ly quite happy—and, "He thinks I had better
."   Again he was glad it could end this way.
e note and watched the childish writing crisp

on a purely banking basis were costing him
he prophetess at Spitalfields—not *his* fault—
ain Bittern's nieces, Cheecha, Neleta draw-
uarter in Havana, if the receipts that came
o be believed, and Dolly at Bath in a nice
aker.   He reckoned up these payments as
cted that they would have represented at
rs' labour in earlier times on the part of
d.   And now there were Angela's pearls.
at it all seemed unavoidable.   But in the

a large monogram seal on it addressed
At last he opened it.

shall do myself the honour of calling
epare yourself for a little journey to
under certain conditions which I shall
xplaining to you.   The precautions I
you understand, are sensible ones.
ward to your visit with the profound
hope.   Do me the credit of reading
y in these lines.   From one who has
and supporter.

"Papa" von Brülle

day—and it was
e excitement and
a.   "Damn that
over.   It was de-
ed at any moment.
his mad world.   He
dove-coloured morn-
ts "Herr von Brülle"
oom again, where the
rning breeze and sun-

ere could be no doubt
th but with the dignity
l himself well.
stwhile somewhat stagy
m.   His lion-like mane
reaked with grey-silver.
turning white contrived
e deep tones of his voice
nthony observed, dressed
only an actor could attain
t.   He moved a little too
sincere.   Only a hint of
ntable, the half-mysterious
ble that seemed to emanate
ront and his high, silk cravat
t alcohol and Debrülle were
iends.
xcellent and sonorous French,
n is likely to bring pleasure to
great deal of liquid has gone
he sighed.   "Let me see, it is
nce our little breakfast together
nd shakes many things out of
s."   He looked at Anthony be-
ust a trace of amusement there,
ttle uncomfortable.
His voice shook quite unex-
nself.
or her," smiled Debrülle.   "It is
from the heart.   And you are not
hesitated a little—"my son?"
ever been *that*.   Ah, I did not mean

to convey any sl
mistake me, mon

They both laugl

"I should never
I have reason to be
you suspect. No, v
stances that might ha
we were never that.
well, you will recolle
certain promise that I
was it made," he cried
he continued, recoverin
So I must tell you that
I have long looked forw
I look after your little s
a great woman out of
agitation stooped to pick

"I want you to remem
call you that—I want yo
morning at her charming
Cinderella sitting in the as
from which she rose—ah,
princes. No, it will not b
shepherdess, but Mlle. Geor
he checked himself and wav

"I—I have a right to say
why; she is grateful. Whe
greatly. I was betrayed, che
timental, I suppose. I have
since. That is why I was me
had her way. In everything
acting. There only I have been
singer, have taught her all she
when we starved, and held out
triumphs. Pardon, might I
monsieur?"

He took the fiery cognac grate

"I am grateful, too," he said a
curiously and drinking. "I owe
ever known."

"Yes?" said Debrülle, "I am gla
come back. It is she who has insis
have not opposed it. She has al
looked a little miserable. "What I

The note was dated Saint-Germain-en-Laye, Mon
Wednesday morning now. He rose in considerabl
perplexity. Vincent had gone out to see Meli
Milanese loan"—he would have liked to talk this
cidedly strange. And Debrülle might be expect
"*Von* Brülle," eh! Well, such things counted in t
called Juan and had himself arrayed in his best
ing suit. During the struggle with the new boo
was announced. Anthony descended to the big
green window draperies waved lazily in the mo
light.

Debrülle was genuinely glad to see him—th
about that. He came forward with great warn
of a man well past middle-age who still carrie

Age had done a great deal for him. His e
heartiness had softened into a dramatic cha
was still impressive but less luxuriant and s
A carefully trained moustache and a vandyke
to be at once distinguished and benign. Th
were fatherly and reassuring. He was, A
with a perfection of taste and detail which
without merely seeming to be playing a pa
impressively—and yet his gestures were
something ever-present and yet unaccou
glamour of a hidden weakness and trou
palely from the starched frill of his shirt-f
might convey to a careful observer tha
inseparable, long-suffering, and secret fr

"Well, monsieur," said Debrülle in e
"your long-expected return from Londo
more people than you might think. A
under the bridge since I saw you last,"
now at least seven years ago, isn't it, si
at Livorno? And time has wings a
them. Some unexpected ones perhap
nignly and smiled. Yet there was j
Anthony thought. It made him a li

"And Angela?" Anthony asked.
pectedly. He could have kicked hin

"Ah, I see that you still—care
only actors who can assume tones
a very good actor, are you,"—he
"No," said Anthony. "I have n

ur on your profession," he added hastily. "Do not
père."
ied heartily.

have thought so," said Debrülle gayly. "In fact
lieve that you have been more partial to us than
ve began by being good friends under circum-
ve caused trouble between unfeeling people. But
We *understood* each other somewhat unusually
t. And I wish to tell you that I have kept a
made to you that morning at Livorno. *Thus*
l dramatically, raising his right hand. "Yes,"
g himself, "I *am* an actor, and you are not.
this is one of the great moments of my career.
ard to it. I wish to tell you that not only did
nepherdess, par le bon Dieu, monsieur, I made
her." He dropped his cane and with great
it up.

iber, my son, for I have a right in a way to
i to remember when you go to visit her this
little house at Saint-Germain, that she is not
shes in that kitchen at Livorno. The ashes
truly now to have the slipper tried on by
e Cinderella that you will see or your little
ges, who is now the idol of Paris, the—"
ed his hands emphatically.

this to you. Angela may even tell you
n I was a very young man I suffered
ated out of life. Sorrow made me sen-
always been merciful to the young ever
rciful to you. In all things Angela has
but in the training of the voice and in
her tyrant. But I, Debrülle, the poor
knows. I have sung for her myself
the hat. Now the princes arrive—she
have a little something to drink,

fully. Anthony remained quiet.
t last as the man sat looking at him
you the greatest happiness I have

d to hear that. And now *you* have
ted upon seeing you again. No, I
ways had what she wants." He
am asking now is that you should

omance, not even
sider her situation
o not wish to in-
For years I swear
ülle,"—he mumbled
alf tenderly—"but I
w now what that is.
l sometimes. If you
e decanter filled again.
I noticed that when I
he poured out.

"Promises only com-
e at Saint-Germain you

nk? And yet after all it
ed the old actor, looking
Mlle. Georges is now of
reat interest," he insisted,
ise on his head, his hands
with an important frown
e little man at headquarters

cried Debrülle, carried away
lle, plucking flowers. Thus.
marble bench. A sword is
ebrülle's walking stick caused

feet with that act, Debrülle."
d the old actor, pleased never-
iated. "No, no, my dear boy,
imagine him when he forgets
himself cannot believe it. He
tely afterwards."
and how much he was imagi-

been plunged into a comic night-
absurd and dangerous, laughable
as happening to Angela. And it
complicated for him even to try to

house is watched," continued De-
nsul or Josephine that is having it

done I don't k[...]
shrugged his sho[...]
will be ruin to b[...]
doubt of it. You [...]
take this risk. I ha[...]
it will work. It wil[...]

"What am I to d[...]
Anthony.

"No, no," smiled I[...]
disguises listed genera[...]
darmes. There is als[...]
once knew the list by h[...]
de Bingen' to 'Zingari[...]
there should be only fo[...]
to attract the notice of g[...]
Now there are none liste[...]
'Querulous old papa retu[...]
ful. What chance has F[...]
Well, M. Antoine, this i[...]

A few hours later An[...]
Debrülle's double cabriole[...]
had been no difficulty. A[...]
Debrülle tipped heavily at [...]
coach. About a mile shor[...]
lane and took along behin[...]
Debrülle. "Let me explain [...]

"Until the last opera seaso[...]
that time a certain person ha[...]
had merely received consider[...]
from a former and more intim[...]
past. Some weeks ago we w[...]
would retire to the country for[...]
in absolute seclusion for the su[...]
command. On our arrival at [...]
we were conducted to a little vill[...]
appointed in every way. It is [...]
terrace of Lenôtre with a garden[...]
Forêt des Lôges. There our fir[...]
the old convent a school for the [...]
Mme. Campan, a former femme d[...]
maintains a school for young chi[...]
and Emilie de Beauharnais, Josephi[...]
Now both Napoleon and Josephi[...]
Campan's school and she advises h[...]

not simply regard this second meeting as a beautiful r
if she regards it that way. I would ask you to cons
truly; perhaps, even to remember others. No, I d
trude. Who knows what is in a woman's heart?
I have been only a father to her; old Papa Debr
the phrase over several times half ironically, ha
have loved her, loved her—and I think I kno
It is something a little hard to bear to the end
wouldn't mind it would help, I think, to have the
Ah—yes. Herr Nolte's cognac is excellent.
came here before." His hand shook a little as

"I . . ." began Anthony.

"Do not promise anything," said Debrülle.
plicate life. And I am afraid when you arriv
might misjudge my motives."

"Then we do go this morning?"

"Why, yes, of course. What did you thi
will not be so simple as *she* thinks," exclaim
paler and worried, "and for a good reason.
great interest to the government. Ah, of g
getting up suddenly, clapping his hat crossw
behind his back and walking up and down
and a subtle bit of mimicry that brought th
at Nogent instantly to life.

"Ah, you should see him in the garden,"
by his own art, "walking with mademoise
And becoming romantically pensive on a
always in the way." The shifting of D
Anthony to choke.

"You might have the Comédie at your

"And the police on my neck," laughe
theless at finding his divinest bit apprec
it will never be known. But can you
himself? No, it is incredible. He
runs away from the memory immedia

What Debrülle had actually seen
natively acting it was hard to say.

Anthony sat feeling as if he had
mare, something that was at once
and terrible. So this was what w
was true! His emotions were too
name them.

"But the trouble is now that the
brülle. "Whether it is the first c

1ow. Perhaps, both of them—or Fouché?" He
ulders. "It makes no difference. In any event it
th of you if you are seen going there. Have no
an see that Angela is really anxious to see you to
ve thought of a way. It is so simple that I believe
l depend on your doing exactly what I tell you."
o, disguise myself as a blanchisseuse?" laughed

Debrülle, "That is merely one of the forty-seven
lly as suspect under 'B' in the primer for gen-
the nun with boots on who calls for alms. I
eart from 'Almagne commercial avec bijouterie
avec les perruches sages.' It is curious that
rty-seven ways of being just plausible enough
endarmes. It is an odd number, undoubtedly.
d under 'Q.' So I am inventing a safe one.
rning home alone.' This brandy is wonder-
ouché himself against Debrülle thus inspired?
the plan . . . "

hony found himself seated on the floor of
approaching Saint-Germain-en-Laye. There
parently they were not even being followed.
he toll gates so that no one looked into the
t of the village a farmer trotted out of a
d them. "That is a new scheme," said
our situation.

n was over we lived at Meudon. Up until
l not visited mademoiselle in Paris. She
able evidences of his regard, continued
ate acquaintance at Milan of three years
ere told to give out that mademoiselle
a complete rest and would remain there
mmer. This was not a proposal but a
Saint-Germain very early one morning
a exquisitely furnished and beautifully
just at the end of the great lime-tree
that has a private entrance from the
st consul has recently established in
children of his Legion of Honour.
e chambre of Marie-Antoinette, also
ldren at Saint-Germain. Hortense
ne's daughters, were educated there.
ne take a great interest in Mme.
im on all his educational schemes.

There is therefore every excuse for him to come frequently to Saint-Germain. He often brings Josephine with him for long conferences with Mme. Campan and then makes inspections at Lôges.

"Now, Mlle. Georges' little villa is strategically situated just half-way between the new school in the forest of Lôges and Mme. Campan's in the village of Saint-Germain.

"Occasional and unsuspected opportunities for a little relaxation between inspections and conferences are now possible with Mlle. Georges. He comes by the gate that leads into the forest. For instance, Mme. Campan's pupils recently gave Racine's *Esther*. Pressing reasons of state unfortunately required the first consul to depart early during the performance while Josephine graciously remained. No doubt they met happily next morning. I was invited to see *Esther!*

"We at the little villa are very quietly watched to prevent anyone disturbing us—and for other reasons. I have long been supposed to be mademoiselle's papa and I can therefore go out. But when I do, I am always followed. Bonaparte himself thinks I am 'papa' and that Angela is a young widow. He found us thus in Milan. You see, my boy, I am playing a most difficult part, whether in a comedy or a tragedy I do not know yet. The gods have not yet written the last act. I wonder how you will collaborate with them. I have done the best I can." He looked out at the landscape with a tired and troubled expression. "I should like when this is over to return to Düsseldorf."

"Düsseldorf?" cried Anthony, looking up at him from the floor.

"Yes, I was born there," said Debrülle. "I love that town. But we are entering Saint-Germain now. Keep low." He himself shrank back farther in the carriage.

"Now," he continued in a low voice, "as we turn up the drive I shall open the carriage door a little just before we arrive at the house. When I say 'go' it will be almost opposite a flight of steps that goes down into the garden directly off the road. You must jump down them and be below the level of the bank before the carriage passes on. You will find a little gate immediately before you. Here is the key. Go in without delay and see whom you will find there.

"You will not be seen," Debrülle reassured him. "The watch is kept from the road that looks down the drive. Once you are below the bank level you are safe. They will see no one get out of the carriage except myself. When it drives on I shall simply be standing on the steps with this bundle under my arm. See what I have brought her—" he cried—"but, no, we are too close now. Wait till we are at home. We shall not be disturbed at all, unless he comes. Then—in that case I would ask you both to remember poor papa who has always brought home the bundles and would like to die quietly in Düsseldorf.

If necessary, hide. S'il vous plait, monsieur." He moved down and shook Anthony by the hand.

They drove on a little and turned in. Anthony gathered himself for a spring. To the right of the road a grassy bank sloped precipitously. "Allez!" said Debrülle.

Anthony jumped, tripped, and rolled down the slope, cursing and laughing, to rise dusting off leaves and grass. Before him was a small lyre-shaped gate in a high walll. He ran forward stooping, unlocked it hastily, and stepped through into the silence and green shade of the walled garden beyond.

The place was much larger than he had expected. The wall enclosed at least a half-acre of tangled, neglected shrubbery and ancient oak trees. He could scarcely see where the paths had been. They must have been neglected for twenty years. A squirrel with its cheeks full of acorns made him an elaborate and ironical bow and departed. A gust of anger swept over him. His knees and elbows smarted. The sense of anticlimax at this lonely reception was unbearable. There was no one in the garden at all.

He pushed on through what had become a thicket, where only a few cultivated shrubs still lingered, putting forth unnoted blossoms. Presently he stumbled upon what had once been the main walk of the place, densely shaded by venerable oaks. He sat down on a neglected stone bench and began to pick the burrs from his clothes. At one end of the walk he could see a door half overgrown with ivy, and at the other sunlight reflected from a pool with leaves floating in it.

He was not going to go up and knock at the door as if he were begging to be let in. He would sit here till somebody came to find him. Debrülle was a dramatic old ass—telling him to jump that way—into a weedy wilderness full of squirrels. Well, he would sit on this bench if necessary for an hour or two. And if nothing happened he would go away. He had come to find Angela, not Mlle. Georges. Let her wait. Let Angela come to meet him at least half-way. At any rate it was cool here. He had burst through the briars overheated, almost panting. He was not really as anxious as all that, he told himself.

People did use this walk. There was a fresh print of a small foot in the moss near by, a child's apparently. Certainly not Pan's— although it was so quiet and so near the forest here.

He settled himself to cool off and wait. A long while passed. A bird came, alighted on the arm of the bench and looked at him. He did not move. The feeling of summer-in-the-woods came over him. Angela would come out presently—and they would go and sail leaf boats in the pool together, "Maea, my delightful one, little earth-mother." He began to mutter over the names of the lost children who had once stood by the fountain at the casa. There was comfort in the old spell. He closed his eyes to shut out the world. Nothing but the green oak shade, the very colour of the strong, quiet dream that lay deepest within him, remained. He sat there as though he were sitting alone at the bottom of a cool, deep well where the light struck down greenly, or as if he were playing under the tree at the convent again lying on his back and looking up through the leaves. It was something to be at home again. He sat drawing strength from it. On a few minutes of this he could exist for years to come.

The mood passed. Perhaps it was what he had been brought here for? Probably the best thing he could do now would be to go away. He and Angela had shared that mood together once. It was too much to expect to find it twice. Why should they? He opened his eyes. Things took shape slowly again out of the dim light. "What are tears for?" he wondered. "They always spoil the forms of things. How damnably silly of me." And yet—these were not tears of self-pity. He was amazed as he realized that they were just drops of pure happiness that had overflowed from the superabundant waters of natural contentment which he had once more discovered within. Good water that! Life intoxicating in a world without end . . . clear now.

Standing before him leaning over the rim of a hoop he saw a boy of seven or eight years regarding him with a fascinated curiosity. They looked at each other with similar eyes for some time.

"What are you crying for?" whispered the child at last. "Aren't you glad to see me?" he added a little louder.

"Yes," said Anthony, surprised into a purely instinctive utterance.

The boy smiled. "Mamma said you would be," he ventured. A sudden embarrassment overcame him that leapt into excitement. "Can you roll a hoop?" he cried. "Can you? Look. I can."

He set off down the long walk striking the speeding circle, running, leaping. Anthony rose, looking after him. No one except himself had ever run just exactly like that. A pressure of triumph and emotion surged up into his temples. "Alive, alive!" The boy was living. He ran. The circle glittered before him. Suddenly the man standing by the bench bared his arm and put his mouth on it.

"Firm, living flesh, you are going on."

The waters *had* overflowed into the world.

"Angela, Angela!" he shouted. "Angela, where are you?"

He started for the door of the house. But the child, who had run to the far end of the walk, was returning now faster than ever.

"Wait," he shrieked, "wait! I want you to see *me*."

He found himself overtaken and surrounded as if by a crowd of little boys. He *had* to stop.

"Look," the youngster kept calling—"look how I can make it go!" and he began to drive his hoop, with which he was certainly most nimble, in skilful narrowing circles about the man who stood in the path. Suddenly he stopped it, and striking an exact imitation of the attitude of the larger man before him stood looking up into his face. "Aren't you going to play with me?" he asked.

He took the hoop and they began to run down the path with it together—faster—faster.

"Look out, mother," shouted the child. "Don't! You'll stop it."

Anthony stopped and looked up covered with confusion. A soft, mellow laugh rang in his ears. She was standing in the path just ahead of him with the child clinging to her skirts and demanding his hoop indignantly.

"So I am in the way, am I?" she said a little wistfully, at the same time clutching her young and looking at Anthony half defiantly. The boy caught her mood and stamped his foot. "Go away, man," said he. "Let my mother alone!"

At that she laughed again and came forward and kissed him, while for a moment they forgot the child entirely. It was the same with them as before he had begun to exist.

Papa Debrülle let them in the door with a strange mixture of pride, satisfaction, and disappointment. The sight of them with the boy between them coming up the steps together caused him to gulp his Adam's apple ludicrously and dash the tears from his eyes. Hovering over them, he was overpowered by pride, a happy and sentimental old German.

"Ach!" he cried, blowing his nose loudly, "it is old Papa Debrülle who has always foreseen this. And now at last—the day—it comes. But you, Angela, you with whom I have laboured to make you great in expression, you and Anthony say nothing. You stand there each holding the boy by one hand. And it is the great dramatic moment of your life that passes! Have you not a single gesture?"

He sat down on the steps disconsolately and took the boy on his knees.

"You at least, little Tony, will not forget old Papa Brülla, will you?" And the child solemnly promised he would not, which moved them all greatly.

Debrülle in fact had not meant to watch. He had pictured himself as stepping aside. It was to be his crowning and perfect sacrifice. But when the time came he could not live up to his own plot. He had been forced as by a superior power to peep through the door at the scene in the garden, which he had planned. And not a gesture, not a single attitude, nothing of the training he had bestowed on Angela had rewarded his hungry eyes that fed upon the emotions of others. Debrülle, indeed, lived entirely vicariously. It was the secret of his constant interest, his love and sacrifice for others. And now those for whom he had slaved had refused to act. Yet hope ever springs anew.

"It is little Tony," he cried at last in more misery than he meant to show, "that I will make a great actor."

Somewhat comforted by at least having become the centre of things, they at last persuaded him with pathetic protestations of gratitude to come into the house. He sat at the head of the table and said grace. Angela and Anthony looked at each other. The child had shut his eyes tight sitting in a high chair. For a moment they both gave themselves over to the illusion of domestic simplicity and peace.

Angela smiled inwardly. "What would Bonaparte think if he could know he had furnished the villa of Mlle. Georges at Saint-Germain for this?" She longed to be able to tell him, "that preposterous, sudden, little man." Yet—"let no one here be harmed by him. Let *me* win against the king of the world," she prayed in her simple heart, "since my lover has come back too late. Let me win alone."

Overcome, she took Anthony's hand and pressed it close to her just to be sure that Angela Guessippi was not living in a dream. It was her fear that his return would persuade her to try to do so.

If he had not believed by other testimony than his eyes Anthony would not have known at first that Angela was Angela. To be sure, he did finally rediscover in her, hidden somewhere, in certain tones of her voice and in what is permanent in the cast of anyone's features, his sweetheart of the pagan mornings about Livorno and the slim shepherdess who had sat beside him at the "wedding breakfast" at Signora Bovino's. But that was only Angela, the girl out of whom had grown and burgeoned Angela the woman. The woman had been unpredictable from her slim and modest beginnings. She came to meet him in the present, a Juno of splendid proportions with a golden voice, imperturbable, and yet majestically magnetic. She came as an incredible and an overwhelming surprise. Her self-contained vitality, the large but symmetrical and gracefully-moving bulk of her swept his sweeter but more fragile and younger memories of her irrevocably aside.

Anthony had not changed so much to Angela. She saw in him what she had both hoped and expected, her youthful lover grown into a virile and yet elusively charming man., Angela had become. Anthony was still becoming.

She was now in her first full flower.   She knew what she wanted, and she intended to have her ambition, for which she had toiled conscientiously and unremittingly from girlhood on with Debrülle, fulfilled. The child meant much to her but her great moments at the opera, and they were great ones, meant more.   It might have been different. Under other circumstances she might have cared more for Anthony and the child she had borne him than for the place she had won in the world by her talents and work.   But she was now just about to realize her ambition to the full and she saw no adequate reason for turning aside to try to colour the bold and unconventional, but nevertheless courageous and noble lines which she and Debrülle had sketched into their picture of life with the soft pastels of lost dreams.

Except for the lines of the plays and librettos which Debrülle had taught her, except for the notes of her songs, which she followed more easily than the printed words beneath them, Angela was still illiterate. But she had a prodigious memory and a calm, clear mind.

Seven years behind the footlights of northern Italy, Vienna, the lower Rhinelands, and Paris; the constant necessity of imagining herself into innumerable rôles had rapidly conferred upon her a sophistication that was both apparent and real.   She understood other people and she understood herself.   And all this was made apparent by the way she moved and by the sound of her voice.

She had learned, what so few women ever learn: how to get up and sit down.   She knew where to stand and where not to stand in a room. In short, she occupied space as if she had inherited an ancestral right to do so instead of having had an awkward, a boring, or even an animated nervous task thrust upon her by a puzzling plebeian necessity. In that, at least, she was still pagan.

Nothing is more difficult than to recall to life the peculiarly personal charm of a great actress or singer.   Memories, letters, diaries, portraits—even the burning testimony of poets is in vain.   Mrs. Siddons, Rachel, Jenny Lind—like the lamp that Hero lit, like the bells of Babylon, only a legend of their alluring glow and molten music now remains.   But how different to have seen and heard.   Only that way and in no other did men know *who,* and not merely what they were.

Who was Angela?   Debrülle knew; Anthony.   But all that anyone can know now is that Angela was Mlle. Georges; that all Paris on certain evenings waited for her impatiently, sat rapt in silence while she sang or walked and talked, and roared afterward with tremendous applause.   Even that human meteor Napoleon felt an attraction which had produced at least a temporary eccentricity in his orbit.   No one could do more than that to him. And if that seems inexplicable, as indeed it was to Josephine, then there is only one other explanation possible. And that is that Mlle. Georges was Angela.

To sit with her in the little music-room of the villa that had been so exquisitely decorated in Pompeian style while she sang and practised with Debrülle accompanying her, his grey, lion-like head nodding or shaking itself in approval or disapproval while the clear notes ran the gamuts of music and the emotions at the same time—that was actually to experience her charm.

She dressed in a white, high-waisted gown with plain gold bands on her bare arms, with open-work sandals caught with silver, the saffron edging of her thin cambric dress-stuff outlining its classic folds. To look from Angela to the portrayal of some Roman matron or an ample yet air-born goddess in the frescoes was to find a resemblance that seemed more than accidental. In that Angela was fortunate. Both the style of dress and the type of her features realized the conscious ideal of beauty of the time. She was not unaware of this and had made the most of it.

Debrülle worked her hard and yet in that both he and Angela found a zest and a pleasure. The room with the harp in one corner and the grey pianoforte with the mother-of-pearl inlay and the candelabra on each side with trim wax candles was the centre of the house. As for Anthony, he could have sat there listening and watching indefinitely.

"Ah, your tones are richer since he has come," said Debrülle. "Now, once more, that cradle song of Tantiani's. It is one of your best encores. It seems to quiet them. There is nothing, you know, like dismissing an audience in tears. Lean a little lower as you rock the cradle, Angela, and softer, softer as you leave the little one going to sleep. You must count ten steps to the door; one for each bar— and the last—smooth—ah, one hardly hears it. It is far, far away when the curtain comes down. Now then——"

And his strong hands would run over the keys smoothly, and standing there in the afternoon shadows of the music-room with the pianoforte chiming its quaint bell-like chords in quiet harmony the voice of Angela would liquidly begin.

She sang to him. In the weeks that he came and went at Saint-Germain she filled his heart with gracious music. In the evenings, after the boy had been put to bed, she would sit down by the harp and they would lose themselves together in the other world of sound. He sat silent. The words of her songs, when there were words, meant nothing. Yet at these times they found each other so deeply that to return to the device of sentences and converse casually seemed by comparison to be only touching finger tips in a grey mist.

At these times Debrülle also came and went in the same way that he had sustained his constant part in both their lives, but especially in that of Angela. In the later summer evenings when a cool wind was already beginning to fill the house and garden from the forest beyond as though with a premonitory chill, he would come into the music-room and lighting the candles on the pianoforte stretch out on its lyre-shaped, ivory rack some well-chosen sheet of music. This, as if by premonition, he always suited exactly to their mood. Then a duet of harp and pianoforte would begin, accompanying the voices of the man and the woman, who in all but bodily heredity had become father and daughter. Then Debrülle would be gone to keep watch on the terrace to see that all was clear when Anthony left the house and went home.

But it was not necessary to return every time to Paris. Anthony had taken lodgings about a mile down the lime terrace from the villa in a quiet little place that overlooked the town and the Seine. Saint-Germain was as always full of summer visitors, especially before and after the fête of Saint-Lôge, which was the crest of the season. His presence could be no cause for remark unless he chose to make it so.

And of course he did not. He and Debrülle between them took infinite precautions. They were able to manage his comings and go-ings through the forest gate behind, which at certain hours they dis-covered was not under observation. Indeed, the watch on the house was rather a desultory one, confined rather to shadowing Debrülle and Angela when they drove out and to occasional questioning of the servants. These were loyal to Angela. The two women who served her in the house and a nursemaid for the child were attached to her and had long been with her about the theatre. Nevertheless, their interest as well as their sympathy was enlisted. As the summer wore on Debrülle became convinced that the surveillance they were subjected to was not one of jealousy but for the protection of Napoleon himself from having his visits noted. He came seldom. When he did so it was not without warning, usually when they had notice of his being in the neighbourhood of Saint-Germain.

Thus for nearly six weeks through August and September Anthony was able to divide his time about equally between Saint-Germain-en-Laye and Paris. He was happy beyond all expectation.

Ouvrard was delayed and delayed. He was negotiating an enor-mous deal in wheat which was to be exported to Spain where the dearth was extreme. This had the secret approval of Napoleon who was gradually extending his net about the Spanish royal family. It was vital, however, to keep the price of bread reasonable in Paris, for it was known the harvest was a good one. Of this Napoleon had particularly warned Ouvrard. But in spite of his precautions his wholesale buying of grain became known. Speculators rushed in.

The price of wheat in a year of plenty soared; approached famine prices. Unrest began to be evident in Paris about the bakeshops. The garrison found its cavalry suddenly increased.

Napoleon sent for Ouvrard and forced him to work out a new system of loans both to feed Paris and to supply the Spanish wheat. The genius displayed by Ouvrard in doing this moved Napoleon to reluctant admiration. In private he even admitted this to Ouvrard but he intended nevertheless to use him for the scapegoat. He was quite frank about it.

"You do not need to mind," said he. "You will soon be off to Spain, where you can appear just in time to save the government there by stopping the famine. That will put them finally in our hands. They blame the bad harvests in Spain on Godoy. Save him and use him. But here in Paris I intend to be the only saviour of the people. Let the price of bread go up two more sous. One sou this week and one the next. But no more. Do you understand? Then I shall step in. Already they are beginning to call upon me. But mind you if I have to bring in the artillery you will never get to Spain. You were inept, Ouvrard, in letting your wheat operations become known. I warned you. I shall simply use this as another occasion to demonstrate that France cannot do without me. But do not present me with any further opportunities, my friend, or I shall have to ask you to retire to Caen. I shall take occasion to whip you in public soon. Do not forget to wince properly. Now make your arrangements to relieve the market here instantly. Let us be exact, let us say that on September thirtieth the price of bread falls four sous. I will supply the edict and arrest recalcitrant bakers—you will supply the wheat. You can make up the loss in Spain. Do we understand each other?"

"As always," said Ouvrard. "But I would like you to remember," he added, "that no matter at what cost I have always seen that the troop rations are ample and honestly provided."

"I led them to victory when they were hungry, monsieur le banquier," said Napoleon, tapping his snuff-box. "You are like all merchants, Ouvrard. You are incapable of understanding me because you cannot understand my motives. Do you think men die for rations? Ouvrard, you are a great mathematical hog. If you ever threaten me again I shall give you a hypodermic injection of lead. Look, you stand there fascinated. Do you know why? You are afraid? No—you are hearing the truth. It convicts you to yourself." He waved him out.

With such speculations in the air the House of the Wolf was not without its interesting evenings. It was Vincent who was to convey the French wheat to Spain. Anthony spent about half his time in Paris and the rest at Saint-Germain-en-Laye. Yet, despite the intricate financial web that went on slowly weaving itself with wheat, Mexican silver, Madrid, and New Orleans in the offing, for him it was a peculiarly calm and serene autumn.   Until Ouvrard should leave for Spain Anthony was merely standing-by waiting.

Paris, he discovered, was an excellent place for a wealthy young man to tarry in.   He provided himself extensively, not only for New Orleans, but for the permanent life in America from fire-arms to a well-selected library.   He read all the books he could about Louisiana, and he interviewed several people who had lived there at various times. In some sort his future there began to become vaguely visible.   He pored over many old, confused maps.   On the advice of a young Yankee who had floated down the Mississippi on a flat-boat and been arrested by the Spaniards for his pains, he took up pistol practice at Fantan's gallery, where a number of old duellists explained the finer principles of the art.

He and Vincent went about together endlessly.   They were even invited once to the Hôtel Salm.   They danced at a ball at the Tuileries. They dined—and then Anthony would go out to Saint-Germain again.

He spent long mornings there playing with the boy in the garden. They became complete friends.   He brought the child endless gifts till Angela put a stop to it.   They sailed boats in the fountain and they played bear in the thickets and leaves.   They told each other long stories and conducted campaigns with armies of lead soldiers.   And all the time Anthony filled his eyes with the sturdiness of the youngster who was a combination of his own body and the brown health and quiet serenity of Angela.   All the time he kept filling his eyes and heart with the surprise and wonder of his living son.

He would take the boy to New Orleans with him.   He began to dream of their life there with this child growing to manhood in the new country.   He began to speak to Angela about it.

It was the child who forced them at last after weeks had gone by to come to some conclusion about their own relations.   These—with a curious instinct on both their parts to let the delightful well-enough of the present alone—they had avoided coming to any conclusion about.

They had not renewed their intimacy on a passionate basis.   With both of them that seemed already to have been fulfilled.   They remembered it; it coloured all their association that summer, but as something which had been completed, which did not have to be repeated.   There would have been something fumbling, something blundering and unnecessary about returning to physical beginnings.   They had begun there, fulfilled themselves, and gone on.   The days in the garden together with the child, the evenings in the music-room, a deep and quiet companionship which they experienced together as a kind of bright and tranquil happiness for hours at a time did not seem to point them inevitably to bed.

And yet they were in love with each other. They cared for each other more than for anybody else. And they were happier together than when apart. Perhaps the crux of the affair was a certain sense of fatality that lay deeper than all else, an instinctive understanding and acceptance of the fact that do what they might, each had a separate life to live. And so no matter how they met, they met ultimately to pass on and live apart.

Yet it was this feeling that also lent a poignancy to their hours. If it was not the same as passion, it brought with it a similar degree in intensity of emotion; a yearning and pity, a desire to love and comfort each other beyond the easy warmth of the flesh.

So fragile was all this, and yet so real and complex, that both of them shrank from laying rude hands upon the walls of dreams to tear them apart. They were content by a mutual understanding to live for weeks, snatching what hours they could together, in the present only; thankful for it, tacitly disregarding both the past and the future. To begin to plan anything was to begin to plan the end. And then suddenly one day they found themselves engaged, as they knew they inevitably would be, in doing just that.

They were sitting together watching the boy sail his boats in the pool at the end of the sunken garden during the afternoon hours which seemed to pass without beginning or end. An occasional low rumble of wheels from the high road beyond the wall and the distant notes of Debrülle composing a song at the pianoforte drifted through the thicket. He had been ardently telling her about his plans for New Orleans, hoping she might say something that would show she felt she might have a part in them, building carefully, erecting his air castles in the other world with open doors. But she had said nothing and he fell silent.

The boy by the pool had curled up and gone to sleep while he talked. It was for him more than for her that Anthony had been pleading, Angela thought. It had frightened her and *he* felt it. He faltered how to begin again. They both looked at the child each seeing the other in his face, and for an instant the awareness of the unity of feeling which had bound them together so completely that night at Livorno brushed them with its wings again. She crept into his arms.

He kissed her. And an agony of regret for all they had lost in each other welled up in both of them unbearably so that all that had been their happiness and peace and pleasure in each other was quite suddenly and unexpectedly transmuted into pain, into an exquisite and impossible yearning for themselves to be as they had once been. Angela, who had thought that it would be so, lay still in his arms. As he bent over her it was suddenly revealed to him what the sorrow of embracing the beloved dead was like.

Instantly he was all defiance, determined to overcome the unreasonable and inevitable, driven to reasserting his own will and reconstructing life.

"This time you will come with me, Angela. What is the difference what either of us has done? We have found each other again. And this time there is the child—out of our dream."

She crept close to him, alive again.

"That much of it came true," she cried. "Do you care?"

"Care!" he exclaimed. "Am I not trying to tell you so? Why won't you come with me and bring the child? I will go anywhere, do anything for you. I can now, you know. Where shall it be—Italy, Germany, France? England!" He suddenly flamed up at the thought. "Marry me. I will give you and the boy a home there. You do not know how we could live in England. Away from this little man of battles that troubles your peace. All the best of the past is in England, the future safe, free. We could have our dream there again and watch the boy grow up, right, a gentleman. Or will you come with me to America—anywhere? Only it must be *our* life. Not music only. Not precious moments snatched from something else. Why not? We should be happy. What more is there we can find anywhere than each other? Marry me this time. Didn't I beg you before when I was poor and a boy and knew nothing—only that I had found you and that that was all? Why do you always go away from me, Angela? Why? Something died in me that morning at Livorno. You killed it. Yes, I know now I started to die then."

"But you lived once with me, too," she whispered. He did not answer her but did not let her go either.

"You cannot get more," she cried. "We were used as we were meant to be. There is no reward except in remembering what we were to each other. Forgive me. I know now that I should have married you then. But how could I know it then? What could you have done? How could you have married me that morning, Anthony? There was too much against it. We did not know enough to act in spite of everything, to live and let the world die. I was a woman and I turned to Debrülle who was a man. Time had not made you a man yet. But what was I to do? I could not help that. I did the best I could and I am grateful to Debrülle."

"I will take him along with us," said Anthony. "We will not leave him alone."

For a moment she lay looking up at him. Her hand went up to his hair. "Oh, my lover, my only lover," she murmured. "You are very good to me."

"And so you will come with me then, Angela, Angela Maea," he cried.

An indescribable sense of hope and relief, of life become a livable certainty overwhelmed him. He got up in triumph and went over to lift up the sleeping boy to put him in her arms. Then—then they would all be together at last and they would get up and go into the house and tell Debrülle. And hereafter it would all be well. Why, he felt like a boy again confident of eternal happiness. He could have thanked his own little virgin with a childish prayer. He must, he felt, thank something. She should stand by the hearth with the child in her arms. He picked up his little son and caught him to him pressing his smooth face to his own. What had died in him was alive still in the child. Thank God, thank God for that. He turned toward her and came over the grass slowly, carrying the boy so he would not awake. He felt the relaxed childish form settle against his shoulder, the weight of himself and Angela and the boy. "Anthony" he was called! All this he was carrying at one time, knowing by sensation, by weight and warmth and by the sight of the unconscious, sleeping face that so moved his hope and pity—above all his pity—what it was to be the father of that child.

Angela had meanwhile been leaning back against the trunk of one of the old forest oaks that still lived on in the garden like the giant survivals of a sturdier time. She sat in a pile of dead leaves amid the roots. Through the thickets and garden tangles that were no longer formal came the notes of Debrülle's song for which he had now constructed his accompaniment.

It was a simple melody, his own words in German, sentimental and vague in meaning. Yet when joined to his music it meant something; something that was new and strong then in the world, the swan-song of romance. The music and the vague little lyric of Debrülle's, when the two were combined and the words and notes became one, was compact of a curious sorrow for itself that was already sweeping all northern Europe. It rose out of a conviction that the world was growing old, that the best of love, and high living, and adventure could be found only in the past. At best only a few moments of life at the full could be tasted in these days. One was no longer young enough, even when one was very young, really to live them, to be of them. Ecstasy was vanishing. Reality was old and hopeless or new and ugly. "We have parted," thought the thinker in the blind chamber, "the light is growing dim. Let us sit here and be sorrowful and do the best we can in the daytime. Psyche has left us. We are only bodies again. Oh! how beautiful she was. Make us a song, write us a book, give us riches that we may lure her back and be at one with her again. Oh 'magic casements opening on the foam of fairylands forlorn'—*that* window was perfect!" Already the generations had begun to crowd to that window, the last out of which the departing sunset glow of the living day was still visible. "Soon we shall be sitting in complete darkness," whispered the feeling of time, "look, even look backwards while you can."

Soon it was to be forgotten what those who crowded to the window were weeping about. The foam on the magic seas turned to madness, to froth. Tears were to become so terrible that they became funny. Men could no longer bear them.

But in Debrülle's time they were just beginning to wet the eyelids a little. Out of his own life and his own generation he had made a song about them. It was to be a new encore for Angela when the next season began. After the mock-classical play was over she would come out and sing this song. That was what the audience was waiting for; for this strange new yearning and sadness that brought them up standing, trembling and weeping, while the first consul sat in his box with Josephine under the wax candles, bored. What were they all weeping about? He would give them another Roman empire for which to die; order, glory, and stability again. Let emotions be saved for patriotism. Come back to the Tuileries, Josephine. Mlle. Georges was, of course, charming and after all he was a man. Yes, he understood the emotion of the people when she sang to them. He understood better than they did. He would possess the cause of it, Mlle. Georges herself.

She had been his prisoner all summer at Saint-Germain. He had not come often. He did not stay long when he did come. He came like a flame blazing, was quenched instantly and was gone. And then Anthony had come again. What was she to do? Debrülle had made her a new song with which to speak to the people. What it was she said to them she did not know. The sadness of what Debrülle had lost himself he had re-created in her. The sorrow of her own loss of Anthony, her personal feeling in Debrülle's tune and words, she made them all one. The woman as always conveyed herself personally. But the world heard its time-feeling speak. She did not know that or care. She sang to it everywhere and it laughed and wept. Those were great moments. Something uttered itself through her. Something that Debrülle knew about and put into his little songs. She felt herself being used then completely. She was the voice of it, possessed. Anthony could never possess and use her again fully. The child had been their song. She had fulfilled herself there.

How could she tell him?

He was coming over to her now bringing the child. They were to live together again. He was demanding real life of her. He was strong and could live. Life was still the same as song to him. How could she face that again? The strength and the belief to do so had died in her. It had been transferred to the boy.

"Let Anthony keep him in his arms," she thought. "They can sing life together. Nothing is left me but music. It is too late."

She pressed her head against the rough bark of the tree closing her eyes and listening to the completed portions of Debrülle's song which he was trying over and over. His baritone in the distance and the rich chords of his accompaniment blent smoothly and came warmly through the leaves.

> "Oh, there's never a dove in last year's nest,
> Or a swan to come back to me."

He stopped, fumbling musically for a better harmony for the next line.

"Debrülle, I will stay with thee," she whispered, and looked up to see Anthony standing there with the child, waiting.

She shook her head at him.

"What has happened?" he cried, clasping the boy close. He woke and cried out, demanding to be set down. Anthony let him go. But he stayed beside his father holding onto his coat. She stood looking at the two men before her for a while. Then she put her hands behind her head and hummed the stave of Debrülle's song.

"Oh," said he miserably. "Is that the answer?"

"Yes," she whispered.

"And that means 'no,' " he said.

Neither of them moved for a minute. They were both white with emotion. He looked down at the boy who was dragging at his coat-tails.

"Keep him," she cried. She came forward and clutched at his breast a moment. He could not answer her embrace.

"We will tear you apart between us, won't we?" said she laughing distractedly, and kissed him. Then she burst into tears and fled into the house leaving them alone together.

He spent the bright agony of the rest of that afternoon in the garden with little Anthony. The pool with the dead leaves on it, the oak tree where she had sat, the green where for a moment with happiness found he had taken the child up from the grass to carry him back to his mother were engraved on his memory permanently. It was etched without colour by the sharp acid of the emotions he had undergone there as if his brain had been bled white.

All his comfort remained in the child. His sorrow was not for himself now, it was not the dizzy sickness of his first parting with Angela at Livorno. It transferred itself into calmness and resignation, into an overwhelming access of pity and determination as he looked at the child. As he played with him gently there, as if he were playing with some emanation of himself again in the convent garden, he determined to do well by him and not to use him unmercifully as a comfort for himself.

He sat down by the pool and began to help him sail his boats again, losing himself with the boy on the miniature dream-ships that the wind blew back and forth. There was one water-lily growing there that they caught upon. In all the world which had gone pale white for him that afternoon it seemed to be the only thing that still retained its delicate warm flesh colour. Then he saw the boy's face close beside it puffing his cheeks out at a small sail. How the boat flew! The perfume of the flower came reminding him of the bowl on the table in Vincent's room.

He began to think of Anna in the empty house at Düsseldorf, of the pearls he had given her that had once made him think of Angela. And there was Anthony with his cool cheek in the water looking at the water-lily with wide-open eyes.

"Water-lilies are fragrant," he said.

"I love a big, cool flower like that," said the little boy. And then dashed cold water on his father in pure male embarrassment.

"Come on, my son," said Anthony. "I understand. I will send you home to one. Would you like that?"

The boy looked puzzled but the man was evidently in earnest.

"If I can take my ships along, too," he said.

"Bless you, all of them," cried his father. "And I shall give you more."

The child gathered up his little fleet contentedly and they went into the house together.

The music-room was going full blast. Debrülle was playing over his new song with tremendous enthusiasm. The pedals on the pianoforte thumped and squeaked. As if she would shatter the ordinary air and make an impossible but more ecstatic and passionate atmosphere in which to palpitate perpetually, Angela was hurling herself through the brief chords of passion and the weak longing and yearning of Debrülle's swan-song. The house, silent and subdued, with all the life in it halted in order to provide an intimate audience for the woman's loud, melodious cry for more feeling than existence could possibly sustain—waited—waited with the serene patience of inanimation, the sunlight basking upon its terraces, the wind tossing playfully in the tops of the ancient oaks in the garden. And with them on a bench in the shadowed hallway also waited the man and the child.

Anthony took the boy in his arms, and this time he offered no resistance. He sat contentedly enough upon his father's knee as if he had gladly taken refuge there from the furious and clanging bursts of sound for which everything else had been temporarily thrust aside—but was still waiting with sure prescience to resume.   To all that, song and silent waiting, Debrülle had composed a perfect accompaniment. The pianoforte seemed to spill over with music, trying to interrupt life, trying to create something apart from it, yearning futilely over its inadequacy to exist, emotion without a cause or an end even in thought.

"Mother is singing again," said little Anthony.

At the sound of the child's voice someone in the music-room got up and closed the door.   Whoever it was that did it managed to convey a hint of impatience at a universe that interrupted a song.

The man and the boy looked at each other and understood what each was thinking.   They and the house and the things about them suddenly seemed to have ceased to be listening to the song in the closed room.

Anthony determined to take his son with him to Paris that night.

He went upstairs to the nursery with him to see about getting his things together.   The nurse made no opposition, although she informed her mistress.   With the swift understanding of a woman, and without any questions, she began to beg Anthony to be taken along.   She seemed to regard the boy's departure as a fait accompli.   A will in fixed determination can indeed make itself felt to be such.

It was now about six o'clock in the evening and the little boy sat quietly eating his last supper in his mother's house.

Behind the closed doors of the music-room Angela and Debrülle, with the scratched score of the new song scattered on the floor, sat in an excited, and on Debrülle's part, a reproachful and tearful debate. He did not wish to give up the child.

"You do not understand me," insisted Angela again and again. "You blame me and yet it was you who took me away from him and made me Mlle. Georges.   You, Debrülle!"

"You . . ." he cried, rising up and tossing his grey mane back with his hand in a tragic gesture that was for once both dramatic and real. "You . . ." a conflict of emotion overcame him.   But no one, not even he himself, ever knew what he was going to say.

"Listen!" she cried.   "Ah, now—you see, you hear?"

Down the walk from the wicket that led into the garden from the forest came the crisp, swift tread of a pair of military boots and the click of a sword.

Debrülle fled.

Angela turned to meet the conqueror alone.

CHAPTER SIXTY

PANEM ET CIRCENSES

NAPOLEON had little or no curiosity about the domestic establishment of Mlle. Georges. At Milan some years before, when he had been attracted by Angela in the first full bloom of her success and womanhood, he had become acquainted with the fact that Debrülle existed and that there was a child in the actress's house. Debrülle had long been accepted about the theatre as Angela's father and mentor. He was always addressed by Angela, and everyone else, as "Papa." He looked and he played the part. As for the boy—Angela was an actress and her great lover had neither the curiosity nor the inclination to be jealous of her past. She was a young widow, they said. Possibly—why not? At least there were no present difficulties; which was admirable. Also she had herself proved discreet about their relations. It was Josephine who had deliberately hunted up this obscure affair in Milan herself. He had carefully ascertained that. He had never forgiven her for it. Neither Angela nor Debrülle had ever asked for anything. Naturally he saw that they were comfortable. The villa at Saint-Germain was even luxurious. He thought so as he strode into the little music-room and found Mlle. Georges standing there with her music strewn over the floor. But he intended to reward her, to be greatly generous as he could afford to be now. And he had thought of a way to be princely to Angela and to be even with Josephine for her unnecessary trouble. It would attract just enough attention thoroughly to annoy and rebuke her without really compromising himself. Paris would merely be amused. No one could prove anything. Editors, if necessary, could be prosecuted. But best of all Josephine had that very morning unwittingly suggested it to him herself.

It was the thought of it that gave him a more than usually self-satisfied smile as he strode up the path that afternoon. His coming was quite a surprise at that hour. He had just ridden over from Saint-Loque. He was delighted to find the evidences of the genuine consternation and pretty surprise which his arrival must naturally have produced in her strewn about the floor of the music-room.

"Mademoiselle!" said he, pausing a moment on the threshold to look about, "do not, I beg you, permit me to interrupt so lovely a thing as a new song. Let me be the first to hear it." He assisted her gallantly

970

in retrieving Debrülle's composition and rearranged it for her on the little ivory rack. He stood by the pianoforte with his hand on his sword waiting for her to begin. She began her own accompaniment gayly. She began to sing. She got as far as

> "Yet creatures of wing that fly and sing
> Must fly if they would go free"

when the words choked her. Even an actress could go no further in her own tragedy. "Poor Angela, poor helpless me," she thought. She struck a discord and broke down weeping for herself.

Much touched by this display of great and genuine emotion, by the cries and tears which his arrival had evoked, he led her to a couch with eagles on it and sat down. Every eagle had an "N" in its mouth. He observed them with satisfaction. "Napoleon—Napoleon—Napoleon." The universe from armies to couches shrieked it back at him. He could hear and see nothing else. Doubtless, Mlle. Georges had been lonely without him. He had not visited her for a long time. Poor woman! He began to comfort her.

After it was over he would tell her about the surprise. The diamonds must certainly be magnificent ones or Josephine would not have asked for them.

Debrülle had fled directly to the nursery both to be out of the way and to warn Anthony. He found him sitting having a bowl of bread and milk with the boy. Anthony refused to be moved by Debrülle or the fact that Napoleon was in the house. A certain hardness of mood in regard to Angela and her affairs left him cold. "As a matter of fact," he said to Debrülle, "the nursery is the last place where the great little man will come, and if he does he will find us all eating bread and milk. Have a bowl, my dear Debrülle. Marianne, a bowl of pap for the little papa."

The nurse, who was "ravished" by excitement, amusement, and the danger of the situation, as only a Frenchwoman could be and contain herself, departed wide-eyed for the kitchen, where she enlarged on the sang-froid of monsieur eating milk with the innocent while cet homme de l'enfer conduisait encore une autre victoire en bas.

"There is no more milk," said the cook showing signs of hysteria.

Anthony and Debrülle sat silent. They heard the pianoforte begin and Angela break off in the middle of her song.

"My words and music!" exclaimed Debrülle, "to think that he has heard them."

Anthony felt his mouth harden with contempt. Little Tony demanded his cabinet before going to bed. Anthony found it for him. The silence continued downstairs. Both the child and Debrülle sat looking grave for different reasons. Overcome by the situation, Anthony leaned back and laughed. He felt greatly relieved by that.

"How romantic it all is, my dear Debrülle!" he cried.

"It is life," whispered the older man dejectedly looking about him. "My God, how terrible that is!" He wiped his brow, which had broken out into a cold sweat at the sound of Anthony's laughter. "He hardly ever stays more than an hour," he added deprecatingly.

"Good night, little papa," said the boy, coming over to Debrülle. "I am going to bed now. Go away. I want to sleep. Where is mamma?"

Debrülle covered him up and kissed him.

"When do I go to town? You promised, you know, big man," said the boy, sitting up again.

"Tonight," replied Anthony, soothing him. "Go to sleep now and when you wake up I will take you along."

The boy looked at him with delight and wonder.

"I will go to sleep quick then," he said and shut his eyes determinedly.

Debrülle took Anthony by the arm and led him out of the room. He was weeping. They went down a long dark hall at the top of the house. There was a deep window at the end of it. They sat down there and looked out into the garden. It was twilight now. The house was still quiet downstairs.

"I think I shall go down," said Anthony, "and . . ."

"Don't be crazy," whispered Debrülle. "That would only ruin us all. None of us could avoid this, you know. It was fate. Do you think she could help it? Think!"

"No," said Anthony after a while, looking out into the garden, "I suppose not." He had suddenly seen Angela in a new light. Perhaps it was for the good of the boy after all that she had given him up. Perhaps as Debrülle said, "she could not help herself." Debrülle's grasp on his arm relaxed. He heard him sigh with relief. Silence engulfed them and it grew darker in the long hall. He could no longer see Debrülle's face.

"When we left you," his voice began after a while whispering out of nothing, "we went on to Naples. It was there that Angela found that she was with child. I was doing well then. The company finally got to Vienna and the boy was born there. We knew he was yours. We called him Anthony. It was Angela who would not let me write. Ah, we were both proud. I had done well by her. She was also succeeding and working hard. Mon Dieu, how I worked her. It was a happy family. Mine, I called it. Can you blame me?

"Then very hard times came with the wars. The theatres at Vienna closed. We starved, everything for the baby. It was then that I wrote you and I heard nothing except, long afterwards, that you had gone to Cuba. I sang in the streets for them and held out the hat. I never let her do that. Angela would never let me write to old Bonny-feather."

"Thank you for that," said Anthony. "Your letters never came."

"I know," said Debrülle. "At last we heard the theatres were open again in Milan and we followed the armies there. We both sang our way to Milan with the child. I knew Lotti at the Scala. It was there that Angela emerged. A lucky chance at a fine part and she triumphed. It went on night after night. She became great. It was at Milan that Bonaparte saw her. He came to our house. What could we do? You must know how it would be. At last we came to Paris. It was not because of him. No, it was not that. She came here to shine brightly and she has done so. It was only this summer we came into his grasp again. She suffers him, I tell you. She has done the best she can. The boy has had every care. I myself have begun his education. And now, you will take him from us?"

"Yes," said Anthony, "he goes with me."

"Ah," said Debrülle—"he goes!" He said it with so much relief that for an instant Anthony was furious with him. Then he understood what he meant.

From the gravel path below came the rapidly diminishing tread of boots. They were almost—almost running. The muffled beat of hoofs from the bridle path that led from the little gate directly into the forest was heard and was gone. It was already quite dark. Apparently he had been completely alone. They had not even caught a glimpse of him. The stars were beginning to come out over the black mass of the forest.

In the darkness Anthony reached out and sought the old actor's hand. "I understand you both, now," he whispered. "You are a hero, Debrülle. I will do everything for the boy, not only because he is mine but for you and Angela. Believe me, I will not think of myself but of him. I have a plan. At Düsseldorf . . ."

"At Düsseldorf!" exclaimed Debrülle. "I have friends, relations there. I could be near him. Angela could sometimes come. It is home. But you were saying, yes, at Düsseldorf you were saying?"

"I can tell you later," said Anthony. "What can I do for you, my dear friend?"

Debrülle choked.

"Ach, mein Gott," said he in German, "you can get me a drink. It is wine that I want." He got up and stumbled down the hall.

"I will go down now," he said, pausing at the head of the stairs. "Wait. I will tell you if she wants to see you again." His feet dragged down into the darkness and silence below. Anthony heard him striking a light somewhere, the clink of glass, and the man coughing over a decanter.

"What an end to it all," he thought. "Debrülle's only refuge is a chemical reaction. Something to give the lie to fate." He sat waiting. "Well, it has been fate. What else could the man do? How otherwise could he escape from the responsibility for four lives that he had romantically assumed?"

"Angela," called Debrülle.

"Here, mon père."

Her voice came up to him rich even in the note of despair that he recognized, thrilling him as always. He heard them whispering, a door closed . . .

—but whatever they decided he meant to take the boy with him to Paris that night.

Presently Debrülle called him. "Come down now," he said.

He found the door from the music-room open, a fan of lamplight lying across the hall. Angela was sitting alone on the couch. A part of her dress which had been torn was wrapped about her. She was very pale and still trembling. But he had never seen her so magnificent before. Her dark eyes shone wide and strangely. She looked up at him with a courageous tenderness and a feminine patience and endurance that overwhelmed him.

He loved her now. Loved her completely with no romance or mists of dreaming, but clearly and wholly in the grinning face of fact. She let him take her in his arms.

"I needed your comfort just once in a time like this," she said. "It is cruel of me, but I wanted you to see me now, I wanted you to understand. Do you see why we could never live together again?"

And he knew that what she said was true. He tried only to give her what comfort he could by holding her close to him. For a few moments their hearts beat together.

"Now take him and go," she said. "Do not ask me to say good-bye to him, too. Tomorrow morning I shall just say, 'He is gone,' but he is not dead for he is with you." She kissed him for the last time.

"How can you, Angela?" he cried.

"Just as you can, Anthony," she said, rising and standing triumphantly before him. He saw her supreme now in her greatest part. "We can both finish our song."

"Yes," he said, "I know. Yes, we can do that. And so I will go again."

She caught her breath.

"No, no, do not touch me, do not touch me again. I couldn't bear that. It is enough."

"You are right," he said. "But, my God, I won't see you again. It is over." He turned to look back. She was standing there firmly, yet her hands involuntarily reached out toward him.

"Come and hear how bravely I shall finish this song which has been scattered tonight," she said and dropped her arms. "At the first night, the opening of the season, you know. I can sing it if I know you are there, Anthony."

"I will come, Angela."

"Good," she cried, with a miraculous gayety. "It is like you to promise that. Why, we are not going to be stopped, are we? The performance as billed is going on." She waved a sheet of notes at him. "I think, though, while I am picking up this scattered music from the floor you had better go. No, don't try to help me." They looked at each other and smiled. She stooped and started to pick up her score again. She rearranged it and put it back on the pianoforte. The wind had scattered it badly when Napoleon had gone out—the winds of the world.

Mlle. Georges went over to a mirror and looked at herself critically. Her dress was torn, she noticed.

"That sudden, little man. He had done that—mon Dieu!" She laughed.

And then she listened to her own laughter as critically as she was looking at herself in the glass.

"Debrülle was wrong," she said. *"This* is my great moment and I am perfectly cast for a tragic part."

"Come down here, mon père," she cried, for she could no longer bear being left alone. "I want to show you something. This moment is yours, too."

The audience she had summoned arrived with a bottle in its hand.

"Look," she cried, pointing to the glass, and she went through her gesture and laughter again and again. He sat watching the reflection, fascinated. She could repeat it indefinitely now.

"You taught me that, without you I could never have done it. I wanted you to see it now that it is completed."

"It is perfect," cried Debrülle. "Magnificent! My God, Angela, but you are a great woman."

She went through with the gesture and laughed again.

Debrülle emptied the bottle, watching her till he nodded.

Four hours later, at half past three in the morning, Anthony got home to the House of the Wolf with his son asleep in his arms.

The last few weeks in Paris assumed a character which Anthony could never have imagined. The House of the Wolf was turned at one stroke from a bachelor's establishment run on strictly male lines to a domestic "child-garden" swarming with women.

Marianne, the nurse, and the wife of old Paul established young Tony in a nursery the day after his arrival. The two maids who came in by the day were always hovering near. Juan and Simba followed him about with a similar expression in their eyes. Anna came from Düsseldorf answering in person the letters which Anthony and Vincent had written. Katharina Geiler and her mother arrived shortly afterward, having heard the news from Anna on her way through Strasbourg. At the end of the month Frau Frank appeared, having made a record trip via Marseilles. She was positively jealous to find even Anna there before her and immediately assumed control of the house. Nothing could be done about it. Uncle Otto had been buried only a few weeks before, and the active old woman who had felt her life ended in the empty house at Livorno suddenly found it renewed and flowing vitally at Paris. She seemed to grow young again. Debrülle kept coming in from Saint-Germain and spent hours in the house. He regarded all the plans made for the boy as his own.

Anthony and Vincent, of course, had had no idea what a call upon maternity with a romantic plea in it would evoke. Life in its fullness had simply and unavoidably descended upon them from all points of the compass at once. They undertook to cope with it as well as they could in a sort of mutual defence, which was of course only partly successful. That is to say that nothing turned out any longer as they had expected.

Anthony would have been horrified at bringing all this down upon Vincent if he had not discovered from the very first that Vincent liked it. Vincent's surprise at finding that Anthony had a son seven years old—"at three o'clock in the morning and the father doing well," as he put it—was only matched by his pride and delight. He kept thumping Anthony on the back until his shoulder was sore. And Vincent was now "Uncle Vincent." When the women arrived he became, so far as the household was concerned, paterfamilias, and he liked it. He had written a few days later to Fräulein Geiler suggesting that they be married at Christmas. "Ja, you watch and see," said he to Anthony. "You are not the only one that can have boys. Wait,"—and when Katharina and her mother arrived to purchase the trousseau he went strolling about with a knowing air. The empty wing of the house across the court was now fitted up for the women. It was Juan who called it the harem. And in a curious way little Tony, who played with Simba in the court and liked him better than anyone, even his new papa, was the cause and centre of it all.

He was a quiet and self-contained little fellow, brown like Angela but with his father's eyes and hair. He had been used to constant changes of abode and living everywhere. Mother, he knew, had gone away somewhere. She had often done that before. He saw Debrülle often. Everybody at this place made much of him. His new papa took him about Paris in a carriage and the tall cool lady, Mamma Anna, as he had soon learned to call her, put him to bed at night. Already he liked her better than Marianne. Next to going to sleep with his head resting on Simba he liked going to sleep in her lap. All this he took for granted. How long was it going to last? he wondered. Nothing had ever lasted very long before, he remembered. They always went on to some place else. But he could not bear to think of leaving Simba. At the very thought of that he would get up and shout.

Anthony found himself in an abysmal difficulty about what to do with the boy. He wanted to take him with him to America. Yet everybody was against that.

"Yes," said Vincent, "when you have established yourself there and have a home. But to drag him with you to Madrid and then half-way across the world to New Orleans before you know what your life will be like there. Suppose he gets ill on the ship." He shrugged his shoulders. "Nice for you," he said.

He talked it over with Anna. Perhaps he had sent for her too hurriedly, he sometimes thought. He knew she would come. And she had. She said little, but it was plain she longed to keep the child.

"Let me have him if only for a few years. I will do well by him; love him like the baby I lost. When he is big and strong I will send him to you." But even now she wept at the very thought. It was Anna who said the least. She did not, like the rest, oppose him. But her every attitude seemed to plead with him. "Let me take this child home and to my heart." And, in a way, Anthony loved Anna. They were at peace together—water-lilies—it was to her that he instinctively and perhaps too impulsively turned.

As for Debrülle, he could see nothing but Düsseldorf, and education was his theme. There was truth in it. He also could not bear to lose the child. He too would retire to Düsseldorf shortly, he said.

Poor Anthony—they were all against him. "Delay—wait—after a while. When you are settled—when he is older—consider him instead of yourself." And it was that argument that finally turned him, for he had promised Angela to think of the boy first.

Anthony did not have enough experience with women in the full domestic round to know that not one of them who advised him so well and so earnestly upon this vital occasion could imagine his own joy and consequently his affection and yearning over the child. Like most people they were disposed to take paternity lightly. "Love" is supposed to have feminine connotations in human affairs. There is really no word to express the emotions and attitudes of fatherhood. The relation of women towards children is so physically necessary; so obvious and overpowering in its double necessity that the father can be easily lost. It is not until social chaos begins to ensue that the loss begins to be felt. Long before that, however, myriads of individuals deprived of the male element in everything but their bare conception begin to drift through life the victims of unchecked emotion. Historically the increasing dominance of woman is marked by emotionalism and revolution, romanticism, feminism triumphant, hysteria. The end is either a return to a balance, a reaction where the man reasserts his authority in the family, or anarchy. The paternal state, which tries to be Our-father-which-art-on-earth, is always accompanied by the loss of the subtle qualities of fatherhood in individual men. When patriotism becomes matriotism, nature and force reassert themselves in human affairs. Sympathy has been mistaken for the truth.

All the women, young and old, who united to persuade Anthony not to take his son with him did so for the reason that in each case they wanted to keep the baby. As his own feelings in regard to the matter had no name, he was at a loss how to persuade either himself or them that his desire to keep his son with him was right. Indeed, this was hardly discussed. There was a great deal of head-shaking and tongue-wagging over Angela. The boy had lost his mother. That he had found his father was scarcely important. What was needed, all agreed, was a woman to take Angela's place. And there was Anna, whose baby had just been buried.

So Anthony laid Isaac on the altar. It was agreed that little Tony was to go to Anna at Düsseldorf. For a while, of course, only for a while.

Surrounded by the approving faces of all at the House of the Wolf, he felt supported and fairly happy in his decision. Alone with the boy his feelings persisted in reasserting themselves. Once as they rode through the Paris streets on some errand or other with the boy leaning against him and talking gayly of the magic sights beyond, the thought of parting with him became unbearable. "This is part of your being," said his voices, "and you are leaving it behind?"

"Yes," he answered himself determinedly. And something in him hearing its sentence pronounced died. At a toy shop he overwhelmed little Tony with too many gifts. He asked to go back to Simba.

"My God," thought Anthony. "They will ask to have Simba stay with him, too." He began to make much of the dog, which loved him blindly. When he stroked his head he growled and closed his eyes.

A message from Ouvrard made Anthony realize that at length the end of his days in Paris was at hand.　They would be leaving Paris for Madrid about the end of September.　Ouvrard himself began to come around again in the evenings.　Vincent had kept evenings sacred to the continuing of his affairs.　In spite of his engagement, the boy, and the women in the household, banking, as he explained, had to go on.　It did so now in the evenings in the sense that Vincent meant of keeping up his acquaintance among men of affairs in Paris.　Paul was busy at the gate every night.　Among the many who arrived and departed, Ouvrard sat usually till after midnight, looking tired.　He had taken lately to drinking a good deal.　His enormous speculations in wheat worried him.　The price of bread was going up in Paris and interviews with Napoleon, which had now become frequent and harassing, put him under a strain that was visible in his face and motions.

At length one evening he came in looking much relieved and related what had happened that day at the Tuileries.　An incipient bread riot had precipitated the interview in which the final arrangements for a little drama had been laid.

"All is now ready," said Ouvrard.　"I am to be released at last.　I have satisfied him that I can supply the wheat to the Paris bakers.　On the first of October the price is to come down to normal when the shops open in the morning.　But I am to appear at the Comédie, a comedy indeed," he grunted, "the evening before.　It is the opening night of Mlle. Georges in *The Templars*.　Bonaparte and Josephine and all Paris that counts will be there.　After the play there is to be a 'riot,' a carefully staged one, outside the theatre.　Thus the good shepherd of the people will learn with amazement that they are hungry.　He will turn to me on the steps before everybody and give me a tremendous wigging.　I will drive off in disgrace—to Spain.　He will then announce that the price of bread is to come down and plenty restored.　Next morning the edicts will be up all over Paris and the bakeshops open, full of good brown loaves.　All I have to be is the villain.　Hein, that is not so good.　I am going to be miles from Paris by morning.　You can never tell how a little joke like this might end for the goat.　And you, my boy," said he to Anthony, "must be prepared to leave with me in the coach.　How will you like that?　By God, I'll need somebody."

"I will leave from the theatre with you that evening," said Anthony.　"I shall be at the play, too.　I shall be waiting for you outside."

"Good," cried Ouvrard, looking much pleased.　"There will be two villains then.　Well, you still have a day or two to send your things on ahead.　We shall travel light and fast ourselves."

Anthony nodded and looked worried.

"Don't let it trouble you," said Ouvrard.   "The hostile mob will be hired, you know.   It will not go too far—I hope."

But that was not what had worried Anthony.   He had just realized that he had forgotten his promise to Angela to hear her sing Debrülle's song.   Now he would be there.

The next two days he dashed about doing last things frantically.

On his final day in Paris at about three o'clock in the afternoon Anthony found himself strolling down the Rue de Rivoli at a more leisurely pace than he had employed for some time past.   A thin, bright autumn mist lent to the vistas and distances of the superb city of the West a nostalgic aspect which sorted well with his own mood within.   Paris, which is so prone to colourful mists, especially in the autumnal season, seemed to be moving before him now, but at a distance; bright, gay, and absorbed as ever in its own vital interests, yet mysteriously tinged as if with a faint, transcendental purple like the memory of the funereal scarves of the remote past.   They had vanished, but they had left behind them in the atmosphere through which the cheerful pageant of the present moved so gracefully and swiftly a trace and a tinge of mystery and sorrow as if the haunting presence of mutability were not altogether, not quite invisible.

He had just finished his last errand.   At the House of the Wolf he knew Juan had everything ready for him to depart.   That evening when the boy went to bed he would kiss him good night.   He would not tell him he was leaving.   Of course, there was to be no scene.   It would just be "going to bed."   And then, afterwards, he would go to the theatre to meet Ouvrard.   Angela would sing her last song— the last for him—and they would drive away into Spain.   He looked about him.   God, how he loved it all, Europe, France, the civilized world into which he had been born, but where it was so hard, impossible almost to find a soul-satisfying part.   What was it all about; why was he always hurried on through it at great speed toward an invisible and mysterious goal?   Why was it that from the lips of everyone from Brother François to Angela, always under different circumstances, but still as if with the repetition of a ritual, fell the fatal word "go"?   What was the meaning of it, what was the sense of it?   Out of what general underlying consciousness and necessity in everybody did this command and injunction inevitably arise?   No one had ever said "stay," "tarry," except Neleta—and she was not really a European at all.   Tonight once again he would "go."   Go to Madrid and beyond that?—suddenly the vast and senseless abyss of the ocean rolled before him—he stopped, leaning up against the bars of a shop window—

beyond Madrid he would fall through that abyss into the unknown, the new and other world.

"What is it all about?" he wondered. He would be utterly alone again. He stood there stopped, hesitating, even dizzy for an instant, groping for an inner necessity to keep on going. He closed his eyes to shut out the irrational moving world, demanding some answer. He must have stood some minutes apparently looking into the shop window. Nothing came to him but a faint image of the little madonna he had loved so much as a child. He had not seen her thus for a long time. This time he did not impatiently destroy her. Her return in some unexplicable way brought him a dim comfort. He was aware that she represented to him a source of inward strength upon which it was possible to draw. It was as though someone in a parching land, where he had long been wandering, had suddenly given him a sparkling drink of cool water. "So—that did not go, then! No, he could take that along."

"Would monsieur kindly step aside?" said someone. The world flooded back. An elderly gentleman with an elegantly trimmed beard and a gold-topped cane was standing beside him asking to be allowed to look into the shop window.

"Certainly, certainly"—he apologized for his reverie.

The old man smiled.

"They are wonderful diamonds," he said. "I don't blame you."

On the 30th of September, 1802, the window of Fossin Frères, the smartest jewellers in Paris, was attracting a good deal of passing attention. There were only three things exhibited there but they were all well-worth remarking. There was an exquisite ebony case lined with black velvet in which reposed a necklace of giant blue diamonds sparkling like cold crystals of pure ice in a winter sun. Beneath them was a small placard inscribed by a master penman with inimitable flourishes:

Much Admired
by the illustrious, the Citizeness,
Josephine Beauharnais Bonaparte,
Consort of the First Consul

250,000 francs

The old gentleman whistled, and continued to feast his eyes upon the stones.

They and the case in which they reposed were set upon a kind of extemporized monumental hillock of black velvet drapery the front of which was a large, black stone polished until its surface was a perfectly reflecting mirror. It was placed so as to catch the street scene before the window in full, even to a small and melancholy image of the sun that seemed to flood the mirror from within its remarkably dream-like perspective with the light of another planet.

Miroir des Artistes

said a card at the foot of this melancholy and yet magic glass—and behind it, behind everything in the window, diamonds and all, forming a delightfully romantic background and set in a thin gold frame, was a landscape, which could only have been painted from a scene reflected in the glass. For it was not of this earth, it was a pastoral vista through the horned-gate of dreams.

"They say," said the old gentleman, "that Josephine has been making life uncomfortable for Bonaparte because he will not buy her these diamonds. Her privy purse is as always exhausted and he has refused to advance her the sum. At any rate she has been here to see them three times. I know that, the younger Fossin told me. Well," he shrugged his shoulders, "it *is* a large sum. But they are glorious . . ." He continued to expatiate on them but his voice had become only a drone in Anthony's ears. He had lost himself in the reflection of the street scene before him.

When he first glanced into the black glass purely by chance and just as he was about to turn away, he had had a startling experience.

He felt as though not the scene itself, but the real scene as he saw it bathed in the colour of his own imagination was exposed in the window. Not only was the semblance of things as he saw them reproduced but the mood and philosophy of them, too. There it was with all the unity of reality, and yet set apart in the stone just as the world must be reproduced in every individual, as it was in himself, with both the images and his feelings about them contained in one another.

He watched pondering. It was another moment of wordless understanding like that of the vision of light. The small sun within the stone—for the scene did not at all appear to be on the surface; the illusion of three dimensions and a perfect perspective was even accentuated—illuminated the scene as if it were the very source of light. Far up the avenue a small carriage moved away into the darkness within; another drove rapidly out of it, passed by, and was gone. The faces and gestures of passers-by came and went in a perpetually perfect little pageant; went into the dark past at the back of the mirror, where they dwindled slowly as if into a failing melancholic memory, or came from and vanished suddenly beyond the boundaries of the picture and were gone.

There was something both amusing and irrevocable about this.

You could not possibly tell whence they came and whither they went. They existed in the "now" of the mirror—and then no more. He did not connect anything that went on outside the boundaries with the activities in the mirror. It was all mysterious there, unreasonable, a perpetual coming and going apparently without order and cause. It was like his own days in the world; lovely, full of colour and feeling, dark and melancholy in the depths and yet a brilliant dream going on; going on without any cause. His own face remained the only fixture, as long as he was there to watch. Only as long as he remained there could he be in the picture at all.

How it had changed since he had first looked on it that day with Father Xavier on the water front at Livorno, without seeing his own face. Then it had all been outside, very clearly outside, beyond, and so clear and bright. How eager to identify himself with it he had been. How good the orange that the priest had stood sharing with him had tasted—and now— Why, one could be a polytheist in a world like this where everything was its own mysterious reason moving in a general atmosphere of illuminated melancholy. What if the colours *had* become more mysteriously perfect and romantic. They were only illusions. He could not help seeing the block and the scientifically polished stone in which they were all contained.

He must remember, in order to cast off the lost feeling that the picture transmitted, to look up, to recall that beyond its borders was . . .

A young man with a portfolio the same as that carried by M. Talleyrand's diplomatic messengers suddenly emerged from a cabriolet that had driven up to the curb hastily, and dashed into the shop. Anthony turned to go, his reverie for the time completely forgotten. He would never have given the carriage another thought, but just then a hand came into the shop window from behind the curtains and removed the diamonds in their case. Two or three loiterers gathered almost instantly looking at the now useless card. A gendarme was sitting in the carriage. The young man with the portfolio emerged as hastily as he had entered, gave those before the window a keen glance, and drove off.

"To the Tuileries," said a frowsily dressed woman who had been watching. "The price of bread goes up more every day. Certainly, but the Creole must have her diamonds. Two hundred and fifty thousand francs." A murmur of agreement arose. Quite a little crowd had now collected about the empty window. The woman spat on her hands and picking up her heavy basket walked off. Anthony lingered for a little out of curiosity. When he left a good-sized crowd was elbowing up to the window to read the card and to look at the place where the diamonds had been. He wondered if Josephine would wear them that night to the play. Before evening most of Paris was wondering with him—and going to find out that night at the Théâtre Français.

———————

Anthony said "Good night" to his little son in the nursery at numéro 47 and turned away quietly. He had a devastating premonition that it was a final farewell, one which he could not shake off.

At the last minute he had a wild impulse to pick the boy up in his arms and walk out with him.

"Oh," said Anna, who caught a glimpse of his face. "Why, my dear, we hardly thought of you at all! Be sure, though, it is for the best."

She kissed him.

With Anna there to pity him he turned and walked out. She thought he was not quite as grateful as he should be and tucked in the child overcome with tenderness for him.

They had a brilliant supper. Everybody dressed gala for the great opening evening. Ouvrard came for them early. There were to be two parties in the best boxes that evening. Juan climbed onto the carriage as it had been arranged he was to take the place on the trip of Ouvrard's footman. Simba trotted under the body of the great coach engulfed in its shadow. Vincent and Katharina Geiler and her mother had kept them waiting and they arrived at the theatre late. The first act had already begun. There were some indignant murmurs as the lackeys lighted them to their boxes. "Ouvrard!" The whisper ran over the place. Talma, who was in the leading rôle as Ignaz de Molay, was indignant at the distraction and came forward spouting the lines

"Why interrupt my meditations when
I had withdrawn from money-grubbing men . . ."

to the vast delight of the whole audience and Napoleon, who could not have managed it better himself. Not having heard the lines, Ouvrard bowed to the applause which seemed to be directed toward him and the parquet shrieked with laughter. He wiped his forehead and sat down.

Renouard's *Les Templiers* was a melodrama in which the melody had already begun to encroach on the drama. Talma's "Grand Master" was a good, fat, ranting part. Lafond and Mlle. Georges were King and Queen. The latter was especially lyrical and was of course in love with the "Grand Master," while the King as the villain of the piece kept insisting in bass that the Templars must be suppressed. At the end of five thundering acts he was given his own way. Angela

parted with her doomed lover in a duet which was encored twice. The
curtain fell but the audience still sat waiting for the great event of the
evening. Mlle. Georges was to appear as herself in a solo which had
been written especially for the occasion.

Anthony had sat watching the curtain go up and down and looking
out over the first-night audience. Certainly it was the most brilliant
in the world. Coiffures and white shoulders, jewels, uniforms; the
endless decorations of the diplomatic corps and the presence of innumerable generals with their staffs male and female blazed in colourful glory under the new patent chandeliers. These alone that evening
had seemed to be real. For Anthony the play had passed without
illusion. It seemed to be taking place like a meaningless scene in the
glass in the shop window that afternoon. At the end, as had been
prearranged with Ouvrard, he got up and left the box to be near the
doors. The banker soon followed him rather nervous now over his
own part in the little drama from real life that was shortly to take
place on the steps; anxious above all else to be sure of making his
get-away. There had only been time to give Vincent a hand-clasp as
Anthony left the box where Anna, the Geilers, old Frau Frank, and
several guests were sitting. He went out and made sure that Ouvrard's big coach was waiting at the bottom of the steps. Usually the
first consul's was the first called, of course. But the superintendent of
gendarmes gave him a knowing glance and a wink. He was evidently
in charge of the scene. An unusually large crowd of rather ragged
persons had already gathered to watch the first consul depart. The
usual groups of police stood about the portico and on the steps. Having assured himself that the way for Ouvrard's coach was open,
Anthony returned and stood waiting at the back of the theatre.

Napoleon usually left the play before the end of the last act. But
tonight he had lingered and kept Josephine. Everybody sat looking
at them. It was Mlle. Georges for whom he was keeping Josephine
waiting, said the knowing ones. "Now we shall see."

Suddenly Debrülle, looking enormously distinguished in a faultless
black suit and with his iron-grey hair waving back, appeared in the
orchestra and took charge of it. It was to be his triumph, too.
Josephine sat fanning herself languidly. Debrülle raised his arms.
Napoleon and the entire audience with him leaned forward. The soft
prelude to the song began and the curtain rose.

Angela was standing dressed just as he had seen her a hundred
times at Saint-Germain. But around her neck and flashing down over
her breast rippled the diamonds Anthony had been looking at in the
window only a few hours before. He knew them instantly by the
peculiar spread and the set of the necklace. But he would have known

them anyhow. He looked at Josephine. She was just resuming again with her fan which had paused slightly.

The harp rippled and somewhere in the run of notes Angela's began.

With the door into the street already open behind him, Anthony stood at the opposite end of the theatre looking down a little at the stage. And as she raised her head to begin singing she looked directly up at him and he knew she had seen him. He stood waiting with his hat in his hand. As she had promised she sang her song bravely, overwhelmingly. She swept the whole theatre along with her into a mood of impossibly delightful sorrow for something unknown but lost, a mellow and golden yearning, a veritable swan-song.

> Oh, there's never a dove in last year's nest,
> Or a swan that comes back to me.
> And my swallow that flew to the darkling west
> Was lured by a magic sea.
>
> Yet creatures of wing that fly and sing
> Must fly if they would go free,
> So my heart will follow the questing swallow—
> Though he fall in the sunset sea.

That was all. It was over.

He raised his hand, holding up his hat to her as the applause broke out; jammed it on his head, and walked down the steps.

A wave of anger and hot resentment swept over him. Why couldn't she have come and lived with him? They were still clamouring about her song in there. Her triumph—and Debrülle's—suddenly seemed to him worthless; silly, sentimental. They all, Angela and the hundreds who were applauding her so madly, wanted emotion without being bothered by connecting it to anything in life. Great emotion and no cause for it! He had been sold-out, he felt. Even the boy had been snatched from him. He hated Anna, too. Nothing was left for him now but to begin life over again. There was that vast ornate coach he had had built for Ouvrard in London waiting for him at the bottom of the steps.

Well, he would go down and get into it. It was as convenient as any other vehicle in which to be carried away from all this.

He stood on the steps and lighted a cigar. The good, strong tobacco steadied him and he did not hate everything about him so intensely any more. He only calmly loathed it. He decided *not* to hit the gendarme who was standing near, after all.

Ouvrard, however, could take care of himself. He was in no mood to be baited by Bonaparte along with Ouvrard. There was no use in getting himself shot tonight—for a few diamonds. Anna had the boy——

He got into the coach and found Simba on the seat.

"I closed him in," said Juan. "Underneath he growled at the crowd."

"Good old boy," said Anthony. The hound rumbled and the hair along his neck bristled. The audience was beginning to come out now. Ouvrard appeared on the steps.

A roar broke out from the crowd watching from the far side of the street.

"Bread! We starve. To hell with profiteers."

The police scarcely appeared to be able to restrain them from rushing up the steps. Ouvrard stopped and hesitated.

"Down with the bankers," screamed a shrill-voiced group of women.

"Bread, bread. We want loaves," chanted a deep undercurrent of male voices.

Napoleon and Josephine appeared. Pandemonium broke loose, in which cheers for the first consul, threats against Ouvrard, and demands for bread struggled to predominate. In the coach Anthony sat restraining the growling hound with difficulty.

By this time those who had emerged from the theatre, realizing that the anger of the mob was concentrated against Ouvrard, whose name was constantly being uttered menacingly, had withdrawn from him and surged back under the porticoes. He now stood half-way down the steps and alone. He had not meant to become thus entirely isolated. Things had just worked out that way.

Napoleon folded his arms and looked down at him frowning from the upper step.

A tremendous roar of approval went up from the street,

"Vive Bonaparte, à bas les banquiers."

The fashionably dressed crowd from the theatre stood silent and awed. They had not expected to emerge into a street full of the terror. They shivered. Here was the terrible people loose again. Only the little man on the upper step could save them. They waited. Napoleon raised his hand. The street grew quiet.

A group of women fishmongers waving petitions was permitted to come up and present them. Josephine clung palely to his arm.

"What! Bread is now ten sous!" he exclaimed indignantly.

"And no bread," screamed one of the women. "We starve in a year of plenty."

"Horrible," said the first consul. "The speculators have conspired against us. It is true what you say, my friends," he cried, tapping the petition which he had not read. "I shall see to it."

One of the women who had not long before sat knitting by the guillotine could not neglect her opportunity even if she had been hired.

"It is you fellows in epaulettes and the bankers who grow fat now while the people grind their teeth on nothing, citizen," she stormed, putting her hands on her hips. Unfortunately she was of an enormous bulk herself.

Napoleon grinned craftily. He was still quite thin.

"Which of us is the fatter?" he asked slyly.

They loved him for it.

He took her paper and went half-way down the steps toward Ouvrard reading it. Then he stopped.

"Citizens," he cried. "I have heard your complaints. They are just ones. I thank you. You have but to cry and I hear. Tomorrow the bakeshops will all be open. There will be bread. The price of the loaf is fixed at two sous. I make it so. I will punish those who interfere, those who speculate with the peace of our domestic lives."

He turned and stretched forth a hand to Josephine who came down the steps regally to stand beside him.

A stupendous roar of approval and enthusiasm leapt toward the stars. Again he raised his hand. Even to him it had become real now.

"And I shall begin to punish now," he cried. He turned to Ouvrard. "It is you and your confrères, monsieur le banquier, who have caused this silly dearth in Paris. Did I not warn you?"—Ouvrard bowed his head—"but you would not listen to me. I banish you to Spain. There is a famine there. Do not return until I send for you. It is just. Go"—and he pointed to the coach waiting.

In the midst of silence Ouvrard descended like a broken man and climbed in. Then the mad crowd, delirious with enthusiasm and approval, broke loose again.

They had started instantly but they could scarcely get through. The gendarmes were not pretending now. They were having a genuinely difficult time of it. Simba began to bay. At this unexpected note of fierce defiance from within the carriage a rain of filth began to descend upon it. Anything would do. As it turned a corner and broke away down an empty street a stone smashed through the rear window and struck Ouvrard on the head. He groaned, and wept from mortification. Small gilded pieces from a shattered horn of plenty in one corner descended upon his hair. They raced for the barriers while Anthony held onto Simba.

Behind them the silver trumpets of the first consul's escort let loose. He was leaving the theatre now. "Vive Napoléon! Vive le Consul Premier!"—and on that night, for the first time, here and there arose a voice calling "Vive l'Empereur!" Napoleon smiled.

In her dressing-room Angela put the diamonds back into the case and bent over them. Her tears fell onto the black velvet where they sparkled like small, loose stones. She wished now she had not given him up. Josephine had not cared, after all. What a triumph!

Rolling southward that evening beyond the barriers, Anthony looked at Ouvrard stanching the cut in his head with a handkerchief dipped in cologne. Simba was quiet now.

He lay back and looked up at the figure of Fortune and her wheel in the ceiling. It was very dim in the reflected moonlight. Only the mirrors in the luxurious coach flashed as it rolled cumbersomely toward the Pyrenees. Some of the spokes seemed to have fallen out of Fortune's wheel.

"Jésus!" said Ouvrard, and shifted the handkerchief.

CHAPTER SIXTY-ONE

SHOES AND STOCKINGS

THE management of the Fonda of San Esteban at Bayonne devoted itself not only to the entertainment of travellers about to enter Spain but also to alarming them thoroughly over what they were going to encounter there. One would have thought that its suave, garlic-fed proprietor, Jean Pellicier, received a government subsidy from Paris for persuading his guests not to leave France. If he did not actually turn them back by his tales of robbery and bitter hardship to be encountered beyond the Pyrenees, he at least succeeded in detaining a great many, particularly the well-heeled ones, for several days longer than they might otherwise have lingered.

Much to Anthony's annoyance Pellicier was thus able by his undoubted gift for lurid narrative to delay the departure of M. Ouvrard and his little party from day to day. The great banker was in no mood to encounter further afflictions just then, particularly physical ones.

His chagrin over the last scenes at Paris, the stone which had bounded off his skull, the sounds and sights of popular contempt and hatred which had so signally marked his departure had completely unnerved him.

Loud indignation—even assumed indignation—had been a totally new experience to a man who had always been used to quiet triumph or at worst to private disgrace. It had seemed easy enough to agree to assume the rôle of scapegoat. Ouvrard had by no means anticipated the emotional effect which had followed: he now felt and acted as though he were really guilty, as if he had actually had the sins of others laid upon him.

As he lay back in the coach on his way down from Paris, with his bandaged head still throbbing from the bump on it, the vision of Napoleon descending the steps of the theatre so menacingly appeared between the flashes of light that troubled his eyes when the coach jolted into a rut. The clear denunciations of the first consul rang more and more accusingly in his ears. Then he would hear the answering roar of the mob, and with a perceptible nervous jerk he would re-experience in imagination the smashing impact of the stone.

There could be no doubt that the man was suffering. One glance at his face was sufficient to attest it. Anthony remembered how old Uncle

Otto's ego had wilted after his encounter with Napoleon and he suspected that something similar but on a more important scale had happened to Ouvrard. In that surmise he was only partly right. The explanation lay deeper, for the events at Paris had jarred a deeply hidden but delicately poised balance in the banker's nervous system.

There were in his life certain primary emotional experiences which it was essential for him to conceal from others in order not to have to admit them to himself. While he had never been threatened with public scandal (he had even been meticulously discreet in obtaining his somewhat curious necessities), the finer and more sensitive side of his nature was greatly troubled over his vagaries and had often impelled him to imagine what it would be like to be exposed to contempt.

In reality Ouvrard's secrets were not so shameful. Had they been known he would have been laughed at and pitied rather than despised. But he had long ago convinced himself that he differed deeply from his fellow men; that his sins as well as his successes were great. His desire for financial power was therefore to justify himself in the eyes of others. Even his sometimes overwhelming generosity was a kind of blackmail paid to fate to induce her to remain discreet and kind; or to thank her for having always remained so. In his attempting to act the scapegoat for Napoleon at Paris a curious thing had happened; the pre-arranged farce had suddenly become an unexpected tragedy.

For the first time in his life Ouvrard had been exposed to popular contempt and he had wilted under it. That night on the steps of the theatre his feeling of guilt, which he had so long concealed even from himself with an almost complete hypocrisy, had suddenly triumphantly asserted itself. It substituted what he knew he actually had done for the imaginary transgressions against which the mob had roared. The effect was instantaneous and automatic. Reason was no aid against this mental self-conviction. It had seemed right to him that he should be pelted with stones. He had even enjoyed the contusion as a kind of penance; as a substitute for what might have been worse. He had driven out of Paris like a sensitive and quivering criminal, a temporarily broken man.

Like so many others of his type, Ouvrard had never given a thought to the nervous results of his own morals. To find himself suddenly altered by a sublety within him astonished him. He was afraid. All his overpowering optimism and genial self-confidence had suddenly vanished.

The trip through the sombre regions of the landes from Bordeaux, with the autumnal fogs from the ocean drifting through the drooping pines, with the contorted branches of cork trees mirrored in dismal, leaden ponds, had only served to accentuate a mysterious melancholy which he could not shake off. As they neared the frontier towards the end of a depressing October afternoon, the unearthly blue of the Pyrenees fading into vague, titanic outlines against a pale sky—at sight of which Juan had burst into joyful shouts—contrived to depress him even further. He thought of the unknown difficulties and dangers in the mysterious and "hostile" regions beyond them.

Only the firm, huddled mass of the roofs of Bayonne with its squat, canary-coloured church tower served to reassure him.

For to Ouvrard all the landscape of the misty country about him seemed to partake of his own inexplicable morbidity; to be haunted by vague but unpleasant and threatening titans. He sensed them moving secretly along the almost invisible blue and empty horizon of the distant ocean, amid the vanishing wraiths of the ever more mystical mountains marching down into Spain.

But upon Anthony, who had for some time already given over the hopeless task of trying to cheer up his unexpectedly gloomy companion, the effect of approaching the Spanish marches was quite the opposite.

He already knew enough of Spain and Spaniards to hope that in the country beyond the Pyrenees he might be able to find certain mystical aspects of existence still conserved in space as they had once, in days past, been present in time. At least the monuments and evidences of such beliefs would still be visible, he thought, not only in buildings and fashions but in customs and speech and attitudes; perhaps in the minds and spirits of the people themselves.

Everyone who had been to Spain assured him that Spain was "behind the times." It was for that reason more than any other that he desired to go there.

"Few moderns," he thought, "can resist the exquisite compliment they pay themselves in patronizing the past. It permits them to assume that they themselves are superior and yet sensitive enough to feel and understand the merits of their own age above all others; it permits them to assume tacitly that as time passes men grow better; that they increasingly triumph as the heirs of the ages as if nothing were ever lost in the process of inheriting."

And everybody in France and England had seemed so sure that the days they were living in were ineffably superior; that it was a great age, reasonable, liberal, cultivated, humanitarian, comfortable. "Yet it is curious," he thought, as he sat looking out of the coach window at the country about Bayonne, "that no one seems to miss something that I expected to find in Europe, but which is no longer there.

"No, it has curiously vanished, only a few vestiges of it remain. But I have heard that in Spain much modern detail and many small comforts have been sacrificed and even suppressed to retain eternal relations in time. I have heard that people still live there as though their own days were contained in a great brooding stillness.

"And perhaps, too, I myself have not learned yet to get the most out of travelling about the world and living in the present, living in the now only, as I tried once to explain it to Vincent. It may be that now is only complete when it is time felt in something that is not time.

"I can feel now-in-eternity in wild countries and on the ocean, for eternity remains in the landscape and the sea. That was the best of Africa. In America I may find it again. I do not find it these days among men in France and England. Yet I was born into it. It was in my courtyard at the convent. For a while as a child I awoke and I lived in an eternal now. I am looking for what I have lost.

"Now it is said that Spain is like a monastery where the lost faculty of living in an eternal present has been miraculously preserved. Well, we shall see!"

He looked at Ouvrard asleep against the cushions. His face was twitching. How could he possibly have told Ouvrard what he had been thinking? Ouvrard was going to bring about great changes in Spain. He was the advance emissary of Napoleon. Anthony looked away, and out across the Basque country and the darkening western ocean toward the mountains again. The Pyrenees, he knew, cut Spain off from the rest of Europe as a tremendous physical barrier, a wall against change, a grim, difficult reality. But at the distance of a few leagues they did not look to be merely mountains. They seemed to be vast curtains hanging down out of heaven as if they would preserve inviolate the secret of what lay behind them.

Ouvrard had looked upon them with foreboding in his present state of mind. But to Anthony, as the great coach rolled on through the greying twilight of the Basque country toward Bayonne, the thought of the strange far-country stretching before him made his heart leap up with the anticipation of penetrating beyond. Surely the land that lay there in the midst of smouldering amethyst could not be in the same world from which rose the squat, uncompromising church tower of Bayonne only a few level miles away.

And suddenly he recaptured the feeling of adventure, the hope that lay in the lure of the unknown. Even the necessity of helping Ouvrard out of the coach before the matter-of-fact hotel in the town and of seeing him safely to bed, for by now the banker had come to the conclusion that he really was a sick man, could not destroy it.

That night he and Juan went out after supper and loitered along the quays where fisher boats with dim lanterns burning under their half-decked cabins cast shadows into the mist drifting in over the landes from the Bay of Biscay as if here were a whole fleet of which Charon was the admiral.

"Yes, they are waiting to ferry souls into the west," laughed Anthony to himself, and told Juan the legend. Juan looked rather serious about it. The husky tones of Basques speaking their mysterious language occasionally rose with an astonishing effect out of these dark hulls. Spars, ghostly, half-furled sails and spidery rigging, the earthless smell of loot from the great waters seemed to call to both of them to step aboard, hoist sail, and be gone.

"There must be a country somewhere where the woman who loved you did not always go away, where sons were not always torn from their fathers' arms. Was there? Was there no place on earth where even a glimmer of eternity penetrated the present?"

He returned to the inn, pondering.

Charon's fleet proved to be by far the best of Bayonne. In a week Anthony and Juan were both tired to death of this limbo between two worlds where French and Spanish were spoken indifferently as if they were one language. They were bored by the flat narrow streets and uncompromising canary-coloured cathedral; by fish, rags, and stinks. All the life and colour. of the place seemed to be concentrated about the Spanish diligences which they were forced to watch depart for Madrid daily while Ouvrard sulked and hesitated.

The banker's condition, Anthony was already aware, might change the whole tenor of the trip to Spain. He had become curiously timid and helpless. Even the smallest decisions were now too difficult for him to make. All the details of arrangements were left to Anthony and Juan. Anthony had expected to take a certain amount of responsibility during the trip, but he had not expected to have to make up the banker's mind for him. If things went on like this he would not only be "interpreting" but actually initiating and conducting the negotiations at Madrid.

To persuade Ouvrard to leave he had the drivers of the diligences brought up to reassure the banker. He gave out his presence under an assumed name to avoid rumours of tempting pickings going on before. He began with great care, and after careful inquiry, to hire an escort at Irún just over the frontier.

But despite the constant assurances of the jaunty mayorals who drove the diligences that the camino real between Irún and Madrid was the best and safest of roads, Ouvrard was not to be easily moved. In their leather gaiters, brown embroidered jackets, and peaked hats covered with velvet pompons he saw only the garb of such prosperous bandits as he had been warned he might expect to find. The suggestion that he should leave his comfortable, cherished coach at Bayonne and confide himself to their care in a diligence appeared little sort of mad to him. He was taking a considerable sum along with him, and the first words in the noble tongue of Don Quixote that he learned to mispronounce lay embedded in the proverb, which his host assured him all travellers to Spain should get by heart, "La ocasión hac el ladrone."

So while Simba strained at his chain and barked at the departing diligences in the courtyard, Ouvrard sat in the common room listening to rumours and buying warm, woollen sashes to wrap about his middle, green phials of insecticide, sheets, soft pillows, blunderbusses for the guards, biscuits, mattresses and stew pots. In short, he strove to buy security for everything in a country where he was assured nothing was to be had, not even security.

He pored over a guide-book written by Pellicier which the innkeeper sold to his guests for ten francs. Page eleven daunted him:

> "I would like to have something. I am tired."
> "Have a chair," replies the Spanish innkeeper.
> "Good, but it is nourishment I want."
> "Well, what have you brought?"
> "Nothing."
> "What—nothing! Why, how can I cook it then? You are in Spain. The butcher's is there; the banker's yonder. Go and buy what you can. If there is any coal perhaps my wife will feel like cooking."

"Think of it," cried Ouvrard. "And we go *there!*" He purchased the carcass of a sheep, sausages, and some pickled fish of which he was very fond. There was no room for a cask of wine. "But chocolate," he said, "makes me bilious." He groaned. Already his room looked like a ship chandler's store.

Seeing how things were, Anthony at last resorted to stratagem and suggested that Napoleon might change his mind and send for Ouvrard to return to Paris.

The next morning early they were on the way to Madrid.

They crossed the Bidassoa with the Spanish guards sleeping on the grass at the far side of the bridge. One of them rose and grunted over their passports until money changed hands. And then in the streets of Irún, lined with oriental-looking houses and overhanging balconies, they were suddenly plunged at one stride into Spain.

Here they left the horses behind them. Ten mules were harnessed to the coach. They were shaved. They were thin. They looked indecent. Every detail of their skeletons, their muscles, and their veins like the model of a river system stood out. It was as if ten rats with pointed ears and hairless tails had been furnished forth by an evil and sardonic magician. And each one of these mules was vicious in his own little way. Only the Spanish could understand them.

The escort was also picked up here. It consisted of six miqueletes, or guards, mounted on mules and armed with muskets. A professional mayoral drove the coach. A zagal, or footman, sat by him who was to do nothing but put on the brakes. Two grim ruffians known as trabucos armed with brass-mouthed blunderbusses sat on the top and smoked cheroots. All of these gentry wore rope sandals; sported breeches trimmed with buttons of filigreed coins. They shone in chestnut jackets with broad blue cuffs, scarlet sashes; choked in flamboyant cravats that thrust their heads up into peaked hats waving with ribbons and silk tassels. Only the knights of the road could afford such finery. They were a proud and distinct class.

"Voya usted con Dios," shouted postmaster Ramón, from his little coach office at the Posada de las Diligencias near the gate at Irún, as, with all luggage strapped on outside and piled knee-deep within, the coach prepared to start. A small crowd had gathered attracted particularly by the carcass of the large sheep which hung down over the rear of the vehicle staring backward with glassy eyes through links of sausages.

Ramón along with others was somewhat amused by the nervousness and solicitude of Ouvrard, who, now about to take the final plunge into the unknown, kept looking out of the window at the preparations, fidgeting, and rolling his eyes homeward over the landscape toward Bayonne as if he were leaving the earth instead of his own country. He could see the horses being led back over the bridge into France. "Where they belong," said the mayoral, walking along his teams of rearing, biting mules. "Mon Dieu!" whispered the banker huskily. To him the whole scene looked like the preparations for a journey to the moon. It was in truth grotesque enough.

The great London coach glistening in the bright, dry sunshine appeared to have been captured by a crew of bronzed bandits that had swarmed upon it out of the caverns of a bad romantic dream. It seemed to Ouvrard that he was the victim being abducted in some picaresque incident enacted out of the *Arabian Nights*. He sat back trying to live through the nightmare. To Anthony the spirit of adventure had suddenly embodied itself costumed and with an appropriate background. He sat puffing a cigar, the bouquet of which set the beggars to whining. He refused to have his enjoyment curtailed by Ouvrard. Juan, seated on the top of the coach, was touching his guitar and premeditating a song for home-coming. It was all familiar to him. To the escort and guards the occasion was nothing but itself— the usual, and after all, the best way of getting from Irún to Madrid.

And it soon proved to be the most rapid, too. Contrary to all foreign opinions, travelling in Spain, so long as one did not leave the great royal highways that had been constructed during the reign of Charles III, was swifter and smoother than in any other country of Europe. There was not in all France a road that could compare with the camino real that led from Irún to the capital.

They were off—violently.

The ten liver-coloured devils hitched to the coach rushed up and down the alarming descents and inclines that mark the steep rolling country between Irún and Orayzún as if they were so many incarnations of the speed demon. The narrow road could be traced for miles ahead running like a taut, stretched tape until it lost itself among blue mountains. It zigzagged the hillsides and leapt deep, dry torrents upon bridges that seemed to be pierced rather then supported by slim, pointed arches. Always situated at the bottom of slopes these bridges were negotiated at a frantic gallop with brakes-off just as the level stretch of the approach was reached. The thin stone boomed like a drum under the heavy wheels and the cavalcade. Passing the lumbering oxcarts in the narrow highway was accomplished by volleys of whip cracks and miracles of skidding that left Ouvrard puffing. From the roof above, cheroot stumps tossed away by the zagals and mayoral fell fuming and sparking into the body of the coach. They burned holes in the upholstery and rugs of the helpless passengers and added the last diabolic touch. At a brief stop to breathe the mules and tighten the harness Anthony emerged and begged those seated aloft in the name of Spanish gentlemen to desist. A raising of hats and profuse apologies followed. There were even bows, but after a few miles the rain of fusees was resumed.

Progress, however, was now slower as the mountains were approached.

They were passing through a country a little reminiscent of Switzerland. The houses were of wood and resembled chalets, but with their beams painted a deep blood-red. In the distance amid patches of green oaks and pines these villages looked like little flocks of brown chickens gathered about the old hen of a church.

At Orayzún the relay was changed. It was like a battle of drunken centaurs. Amid biting and kicking mules, tangle of ropes and harness, squalls and brazen braying, the torsos of men suddenly reared up triumphantly above the dust and confusion as they passed the coach windows dragging the new relay into place by their noses, mounting them and beating back the menace of white teeth and rolling eyes with their heavy felt hats. All was ready when the escort, which had lagged behind, rode into town and the battle began all over again.

Standing oblivious to the clouds of yellow dust that rose about the coach as if it were the prize of conflict, morose figures in immense ragged cloaks and hats pulled down over their eyes watched the proceedings without further comment than a glitter of brown eyes above their muffled mouths and sharp noses. They looked like bedraggled brown hawks, whether caballeros or beggars it was impossible to say. In them were concentrated the poverty and pride, the indifference and the suspicion, the fatalistic spectatorship of the male population of Spain. It was impossible to tell what they were thinking. Perhaps they were not thinking at all. They remained standing, impassive. There was something Arab-like about them. They were the first touch of eternity in time that Anthony had found in Spain, and he continued to see them everywhere as long as he remained in the peninsula.

They were whirled indecently out of Orayzún and at nightfall dined at Astigarraga where even to Ouvrard his own fears of starving became ridiculous.

Beds, curtains, and towels were dazzling white, the inn painfully clean. Great mountain girls, set-up like dragoons and with thick chestnut braids falling to their waists, brought supper: meat soup powdered saffron colour with paprika, loose, white bread with a soft, golden crust. The puchero followed. Brought in separate dishes, it was finally combined into one on the diner's plate. Chicken, mutton, slices of roast beef, bacon and ham, spiced sausages stuffed with chorizo and pimento formed the foundation of this solid edifice which was then topped with a verdura of vegetables, greens, and the everpresent garbanzo or chick-pea—and over this was poured a highly spiced sauce. Juan showed them how to mix it.

They had just laid down their comb-like forks and narrow pointed spoons and prepared to retire when—the other courses appeared. Chicken fried in oil, haddock fried in oil; and then roast lamb, asparagus, and salad. By this time Ouvrard was laughing, for the door still continued to open bringing other girls with other trays. For dessert macaroons and almonds smoking from the roasting pan, then goat's-milk cheese, queso de Burgos, justly celebrated, and at last a little tray with a bowl of glowing coals for lighting cigarettes; finally Malaga, sherry and brandy.

"Juan," cried Ouvrard, "cut up the dead sheep on the coach and give it away."

"I will keep it for Simba," replied Juan. "In Spain it is not thought necessary to feed a dog. A sheep will last him to Madrid." Gorged to repletion, Simba slept on the top of the coach, his nostrils twitching at the cigarro smoke the rest of the way to Burgos.

They were wakened at two o'clock at night to set out again. The country became wilder and hillier, the inns more primitive, the vil-

lages "pueblos." In the province of Alava at the foot of the mountains of Salinas amid an uproar beyond description a "procession" of
oxen was added to the five teams of mules. With goads, whips, and
the help of men on the wheels, men moving up and down the long
line of animals that disappeared around curves far ahead of the coach,
they accomplished the ascent.

It was now day and cold; the Pyrenees behind them could be seen
lying like great piles of draped velvet caught up into sharp ridges as if
the gods had abandoned the planet just here and let their rich draperies
fall behind them along an endless floor. Before them the silver filigree
of snows on the black forehead of the Sierra Nevadas tumbled along
a cold emerald sky. Azure and lilac shadows tinted their precipices
below the long rolling snow barrier of their continuous crests. They
were not like the Alps, tumbled, inchoate, and incomprehensible.
These Spanish mountains were remote, regular barriers that seemed
to have been raised with a purpose. In the dry clear air, but at a tremendous distance, they seemed to be walling-in a grim country inhabited by giants who might sit upon them, resting in Cyclopean blue-shad-
owed seats with their thin, white hair in the clouds and their mighty
feet set like sphinxes on the red plains below.

At a distance, looking over the plateaus and escarpments, the tangled
veins of dusty watercourses, the interior of Spain, treeless and without
verdure, looked as if it could nurse such a race.

The moisture-healed slopes of Biscay were now far behind them.
They were moving toward the plateaus of León. Something African
had already crept into the landscape despite patches of beautiful culti-
vation, as if the Sahara from over the rim of the world had cast a
stony mirage of itself upon these parts and barrenness were creeping
north. They had first encountered it at Vittoria which they had entered by torchlight, the crescent horns of the oxen going on before
them through the deserted and shadowy streets until the parador viejo
was reached. Here there was much trouble with the authorities over
baggage, hard mattresses at the posada, and nothing but a bitter jicara
de chocolate when they left in the dark just before dawn.

As they pushed forward next day through Miranda the prophetic
hints of barrenness they had already encountered began to be fully
realized. The path to its full realization was a fitting one, the rocky
pass of Pancorbo, which is the entrance to old Castile and León.
Here they climbed through long, rocky, narrow valleys like gloomy corridors and passed between the two granite monoliths that lean toward
each other like an arch left unfinished by a race of giants. It is the
gateway to old Spain.

All that was usual and familiar was now left behind over the heights

of Pancorbo. Briviesca at the foot of the pass seemed to be a city in
another world. Inns and stables were now one and inseparable. The
road led on through a succession of evil villages grey as dusty lava.
Pradanos, Castil de Peones, Quintana Dueñas, Quintanapalla—these
were the towns of a country of bearded old women, withered, moled
and wizened; witches who gathered about the fires at night to ladle
guisado out of their giant pots to scare foreign travellers; hags who
looked as if they might ride off on their thick brush brooms.

All the women went barefoot here, and for some reason Ouvrard
kept complaining of this. He was plaintive about it. While they
stirred the stew with long ladles he would complain of their lack of
shoes.

Nothing was said in these wretched ventas that were usually placed
just outside the walls of towns to avoid paying gate-taxes. They were
the worst inns they met on the route. In the red firelight under the
beams, muleteers and caballeros, children, and the great greyhounds of
the country all alike sat silent awaiting the distribution of bread, salt,
and meat.

"This is not like the south, not Seville, señor. See those fellows
wrap themselves in their cloaks after supper, pull their hats down
closer and take six puffs from a cigar. There is not even a song.
The nostrils of the girls are like black caverns with snuff. It is so dry
here even their stomachs must be puckered. I would be afraid to sleep
under the same cloak with them. I have not even been asked. Shall
I get out my guitar?"

"No," said Anthony, "this is no place for music, Juan."

Only once did they hear music. It was far away and late at night,
a low, sinister singing accompanied by an eternal rattle as of hard
dried peas shaken in a box in three-time. An eternal dry rasping that
returned upon itself to a slow stamping of feet.

Time here in these huge, dry valleys was like time at Futa-Jaloon.
It did not seem to pass. Day and night might shift the colours of the
landscape but time seemed to remain the same. The coach went on
through it. It hastened but it seemed never to arrive anywhere. As
they turned west toward Burgos, by the last hovel in the pueblo of
Quintanapalla, Anthony saw a figure that remained with him in memory as the spirit of the place. It was that of a youth leaning against
a pumice-coloured wall.

From the waist down his cloak had rotted away. But his straight
legs, firm and brown as those of an Arab, braced him solidly against
the wall. There, with his arms folded, and the remains of his upper
garment thrown across his lean shoulders in magnificent tattered folds,
he stood proudly; triumphantly existing; looking down across the
sun-baked plains of León with black-diamond eyes. When the time

came he would beget a son to take his place by the wall. With inexpressible contempt and immobility he watched the coach go by. Not even a silver onza cast at his feet could wring from his thin, incurious lips the customary "Voya usted con Dios."

At Burgos once more they lingered.

Godoy must have received notice of their approach through the French embassy at Madrid, for the authorities were positively obsequious and the party found themselves lodged and entertained by the alcalde but with more ceremony than comfort. A letter from the Prince of the Peace was waiting for Ouvrard and was delivered resting on a brocaded pillow. It bade him welcome to Spain with a hundred abject and stately phrases. But the cunning favourite of the queen, who now ruled Spain with all the authority of both his royal mistress and her husband, rather than as a mere prime minister, was careful not to commit himself to anything in advance. He offered to send an armed escort of honour but at the same time he advised the banker to keep his arrival strictly private at Madrid for fear of arousing premature opposition to his schemes.

Pondering this, Ouvrard moved himself incognito to El Parador del Dorado, the best fonda in the city, and gave himself up to the luxury of physical comfort and mental misery, showering gratificacioncitas upon the mozos and muchachas until Juan interfered through sheer disgust.

"All these things, dos almohadas limpias con sus fondas, and such trifles I can obtain for you with a smile, a cigar, or a proverb, señor. Have you never heard the saying 'the generous pay more for a grape than the careful do for a bunch'? They will think you are mad if you go on showering double-duros about."

"I *am* going insane," said the banker. "Send for M. Adverse when you go, for I am afraid to be left alone."

When Anthony came into the room Ouvrard complained to him that ever since Paris he had felt himself "dividing within."

"Do not laugh at me," he begged. "I assure you it is so. I can explain it to you in no other way. I am at the present time not one but two men. That is, I know I could become either one of two persons. I cannot make up my mind yet which I want to be. I might remain, let us say, myself, the man you know, J. G. Ouvrard financier—or I might become, oh, *that fellow who is so interested in shoes!*" His eyes gleamed and he sat up. "Yes, I shall have to do something for him. Ever since Paris he has been becoming me. All these new scenes make it easier for him to be. Mon Dieu, do something for Ouvrard! He is being pulled apart."

So Burgos was a somewhat curious interim for Anthony.

The first "cure" that occurred to him for Ouvrard was wine. With this Ouvrard was inclined to agree. He would not see a priest or a leech nor would he try tobacco. For some days he stupefied himself and lay quiet under the influence of mountain Malaga fortified by brandy. It was necessary for someone to be on watch during his return to consciousness when his misery was extreme. Anthony and Juan took turns. In his leisure intervals Anthony managed to see a good deal of Burgos. It was the first Spanish town he had really had time to examine.

And he could have done no better. Here he found at least the relics and legends of what he had been looking for. Burgos the palladium of Spain, the home and tomb of the Cid, Burgos the shrine of Mary. He remembered it forever—the domineering castle and the mighty cathedral rising on the hill out of the clustering roofs of a rough half-circle of houses, the montañas behind them, the old walls and the green plantations along the sparkling river of Arlanzón at its feet.

While the great banker lay deep in the fumes of wine trying to decide in a troubled sleep who he might be, Anthony found who he himself had been or might have been in ages past. He explored this precious enclave in time where the living age of Europe was still preserved, and still to some extent dreamed alive and even walked in its streets. He explored it from the plaza with its naïve bronze fountain of Flora to the Gate of Santa María, where the image of the Virgin rose above the battlements along the river front, reminding all who entered that this was her town.

Indeed, in every conceivable place in Burgos, and in every attitude and episode of her story and legend, the goddess Mary was to be found. Here she was still a living reality. He thought of her and dreamed of her again as he walked the pleasantly planted little paths in the river valley toward the Isla and the nunnery of Santa María la Real, where Ferdinand and Isabella have left the story of the Conception carved over the gate.

In one of the cloisters open to strangers near the hospital for pilgrims he sat for hours surrounded by silence and the round-headed arches, and found before he left he could pray again.

He asked for help and guidance in bringing up his son. He sat hoping in a wordless petition for the return of his child. At least he recovered peace again.

As he threaded his way back to the fonda through the narrow streets, which the small river El Pico cleans and freshens by being led dashing along them in a stone watercourse, the swirling waters bore away with them the tumult of feeling and perplexity that had come with him from Paris. He was aware of the feeling of being at one with himself once more. Out of a renewed integrity of being he felt able to act. He was sure this was not due to any subtle change in his body; on the contrary, this feeling of health that brought with it a capability for happiness in all the incidents of life seemed to proceed from a conviction of wellness and peace within. It was an outgoing instead of an income.

"Yet how strange and unexpected are the accidents of life. How they vary between man and man," he thought. "While I find peace, Ouvrard lies there at war with himself, fighting for his very entity for some dim cause unknown. Perhaps I can help him now. How, I do not know"—and he returned to the fonda to find Ouvrard awake, anxious to talk with him. For hour after hour the man with a twitching face poured forth to him in a brilliant exposition his entire plan for the shipping of immense quantities of wheat to Spain with all its political and financial ramifications. He was high-strung, brilliant as though lit by a consuming fire from within, entirely the banker again.

"If I can only stay this way," he sighed. "What was the matter with me?"

"Do not try to remember," said Anthony and hastily expressed his admiration for Ouvrard's brilliant scheme, which had about it the elements of inspiration in its daring and originality. "And it was so lucidly and compactly explained," he insisted. He was being quite ingenuous, too. For it had startled him to come in and find a man whom he had left only a few hours before in a confused stupor, suddenly speaking with the clear accents of genius. His genuine astonishment and admiration showed in his face.

It was amazing how Ouvrard responded to that.

"So, then, you do find me myself again," he whispered. "Yes, I can see that you do. You do not know how much that means to me." A look of childish gratitude suffused his features.

"You will not leave me?" he said. "I am this way sometimes. Twice before! You will stay even if I become that other fellow for a while? Will you? There is no one to care, you see. No one!" He looked pathetically pale and anxious again.

"I will stay," Anthony promised. "I will see you through this time, my friend. And you are going to be well again soon, I know it. You must rest and forget everything."

"Mon Dieu, I can go to sleep then," whispered Ouvrard, and sank back with the look of fear and perplexity fading from his face.

Nothing could have been more curious than those days spent at

Burgos. There were other talks with the banker, who was slowly coming back to himself.

Thus between excursions into the town, replete with a thousand emotional and intellectual adventures, sounded the voice of Ouvrard discussing with nervous avidity the great deal in wheat; the means of obtaining influence in Madrid; shaping as he lay back in his alcove with a bloated, nervous countenance pale against the pillows the scheme that for the next five years dictated the economic and political history of Spain—while occasionally, only occasionally now, and far less frequently than at first, he would have to babble something about shoes.

"Keep the barefooted girls out of the room, Juan," said Anthony, "or we shall be here the rest of our lives"—and then he would go out to walk up to the Calle Alta along the wall of the castle, where in the old parish of St. Martin were ancient houses that fascinated him; La Casa del Cordón of the Velascos, where the Constable of León had lived, with the rope carved over the door, and the Casa de Mirando with a patio snatched out of a poet's dream. Or he would loiter through the Plaza Mayor with its new shops ranging under noble arcades, where proud, penniless loafers in threadbare capas lingered wistfully and the children sold bright yellow flowers and incense.

Everywhere, in walls and at corners, on houses and in little churches, were the shrines of Mary, usually with a woman standing before them praying. The town breathed of this female worship. Apparently it existed because of it. And all these little shrines were only reminders and approaches to the great one, the cathedral in the centre of the town.

Its twin towers crowned with delicate spires of open stonework seemed to be fluttering with lace. Its clustering, filigreed pinnacles rose triumphantly and lavishly above the sombre roofs of the quiet city like a burst of rich music out of silence, suggesting the wealth and enduring sensitivity, the miraculous passion of the spirit aspiring to write its eternal thought of beauty above the flat and drear arrangements of physical life. There were three portals, and above the middle one with her motto worked into its magic balustrade, veritable memories of the Virgin's Conception, Assumption, and Coronation dreamed alive in the pliant stone.

Then he would pass through the portal into the interior.

What manner of men were those who had wrought this? Out of what rich daily experiences shot through with wisdom and vivid emotion had this flamboyant and yet austere testimony to the communion of the soul of man with the Eternal overflowed? What was the secret of the life-giving quality of that story that had inspired and contained it? Why was it being forgotten? Had the spirit of man tired in its attempt to commune with God?

Here in this cathedral at Burgos was the record of an incredible spiritual energy. Something not at all preoccupied with building things of use to enhance the ease of physical existence. It was beyond that. It was the expression of the attitudes and experiences of pure being that had builded here. How could the age out of which this had risen be called "poverty-stricken"? Those who had built and carved and painted here had been more than happy. They had left the record of their ecstasy in a divine orgasm of stone.

The very skeleton of the place leaped and vaulted upward. The lines of it suggested an energy terrible because illimitable in its proportions; a force greater than the body of any plant or animal could express. The most majestic avenues of palms with their interlacing fronds in the sunny sky overhead were only natural in their stresses and strains compared with these cathedral vaults and groined arches and buttresses that had caught the underlying mathematics of boundless space and expressed the terrible abstraction of The Thinker whose thought is the universe. That was the necessary element of terror and mystery in which the shrines of Mary and the altars of her Son, in which the stations of the cross were all contained. "That is why," he thought, "it is not comfortable to live in a Gothic building. The curves of it frighten one, they express the *super* natural; thought which transcends the necessities of matter and the world of the senses." No, those who had built here had not gone to nature for their forms as had the builders of pagan temples who made stone groves. When these men wrought, the spirit of man had already gone beyond that. Burgos had congealed out of abstract thought that was still the wholesome servant of emotion.

It had been necessary to cover the unbearable implications of its soaring arches with a wealth of natural forms; to fill its interior, floors, walls, and ceiling with a wealth of works of art that imitated the prodigality of nature. To dwell upon the labour expended, the patience, the excess of energy lavished upon them caused thought to stagger and lie down.

In its illimitable profusion Burgos was like the natural world itself. Even the dead gods were here. In a half abandoned favissa or storeroom, once the old sacristy, lay the damaged images and the abandoned figures of saints used in processions, with the time-darkened portraits of a hundred bishops of Burgos glaring at them from the walls.

Anthony was in a mood for all this. After his loss of Angela and the boy he lost himself eagerly in the emotions and thoughts of art and architecture, in experiences which were safe from any intrusion by man. Burgos for him was like healing music.

Especially, he loved to linger along the choir stalls in which the ancient wood with its yellow high-lights and mellow shadows seemed to be less a medium for handicraft than the dreamful substance of thought itself that the carver had suddenly arrested in motion. And what dreams were there, fantastic, prodigal in invention and as ruthless in imagination as those of God; another world swarming with foliage whose delicate tendrils sprouted into hands or legs. Here amid the fretted and contorted branches of a fabulous, submarine forest dolphins spouted wide-flaring sea-fans from dilate nostrils, sirens rode upon undulating dragons, while overhead claw-winged chimeras like the souls of misers emigrating to paradise flew above charming little islets situated upon the confines of sleep and sanity where cupids tried on capricious masks, gladiators wrestled, bears played upon harps while peasants harvested the fruits of elysian champagnes, wanton girls teased a monster to the point of ecstasy, and little boys squirted into shell-carved fountains with infantile, Rabelaisian glee. And yet—step back but a few paces—and all this became grave, solemn, part of the architectural unity of the whole building, a fitting frame for the pallid, austere faces of the canons themselves.

There was a stairway here, one mass of twisting monsters that ascended like a flame to a mysterious door that any man might be afraid to enter. And there was also the retable before the high altar adorned with cascades of silver and crystal suns, where from the fruitful breast of a recumbent Abraham spouted and soared upward the genealogical tree of Jesus Christ. Above it the Virgin sat throned in the clouds lit by a glory as of far-off morning, while through the marble leaves and blossoms below her glinted the gold and silver of the moon and stars.

Down the enormous nave of the cathedral this inconceivable tree seemed to bear the fruit of glory at its radiant top and to shout Hosannah! It was impossible to turn one's back upon it. Even the long figures of the dead with stony hounds and bat-winged griffins at their feet, sleeping behind gratings and withdrawn amid the gloomy side chapels, seemed to hear it.

Afterward—after he had left Burgos—and only the dreamful symbols of it remained, it seemed impossible to Anthony that he had spent only a few days there. Concentrated into that experience were the merged messages of innumerable lifetimes hurled at him in the sublimated language of art. Chiefly he bore away with him an enormously enriched and nobler realization of the meaning of his dreams of the Madonna. He had added nothing to his personal philosophy about her. But in looking upon her life-endowing dream as it had also existed in the hearts of others and was depicted at Burgos on every side he had extended and clarified her emotional meaning in his own soul. In her, he felt, was the image of the way in which the Eternal Spirit was conceived by man.

On a door-post that was for the most part passed by unnoticed was a small image of her, exquisite but daring in its conception. She was not meek and contrite. She stood there with her head thrown back, breathing in with an expression in which sensuous pleasure had been transmuted into spiritual ecstasy an invisible influence from the flame-wrapped symbol of love. It was humanity in the transports of conceiving God.

And Anthony turned away from this, to remember it forever, but thinking at the time how he had wasted and debased himself and sought life only in the body—and found it denied to him. "Next time . . ." but perhaps this realization had come to him too late. The premonition troubled him—and there were other things . . .

He was afraid, as Ouvrard continued to recover rather slowly, that a plethora of seeing and sights at Burgos might stifle his appreciation. There was, he was aware, a ridiculous side to it, as there always is to everything. He had only, for instance, to permit himself to be shown the renowned figure of Christ made of a stuffed human hide, painted, and crowned with real brambles to have taken once more to reading and snickering with Voltaire. But he did not wish to take the one step from the sublime. It was too easy. The threshold of the ridiculous is always a slippery one. He preferred to conserve what he had experienced in order to ponder upon it afterward like the memory of divine music uninterrupted by a fatuous and comical noise.

Yet he might have failed. High moods are not long in passing. But he was saved from loss of untarnished treasure by being plunged from the divine, not into the entirely ridiculous, merely into the human. For it was while he was standing one afternoon before the retable that on the other side of the high altar he discovered and overheard talking in common-sense English the Honourable William Eden and the honest and always whimsical Mr. Richard Ford.

His attention was first attracted to them by the sound of a prolonged chuckling wheeze. That he afterwards discovered was Mr. Ford's version of laughter.

"So," said the cultivated voice of the Honourable Mr. Eden, "you still solemnly maintain that trout fishing is a more dangerous sport than bullfighting."

"Not solemnly," replied Mr. Ford, "there is nothing funnier than being right."

It was at this point that Anthony had overheard the wheeze.

"But, my dear Dick," rejoined his companion, interrupting his survey of the genealogy of Christ through a pair of German-silver pince-nez—which he folded up and put back in his pocket authoritatively,

"I do not see upon what grounds you can possibly make such a silly assertion."

"As usual, you are looking at the matter from your own standpoint only," insisted the other; "suppose you consider it just for a moment from the standpoint of the trouts."

"Ow-ah," said William, making the English noise for surprise, "but first count your fish, count your fish before you catch them," he added hurriedly and looked at Mr. Ford in triumph as if he had found exactly the right proverb to quote him off the map.

"Eggs, Billy, eggs! You are thinking of eggs. I say!" wheezed the amiable Mr. Ford.

Mr. Eden turned very red in the face.

"By God, so I was," he muttered. "So I was."

They joined each other in a hearty laugh. It was quite evident, however, as they walked away that Mr. Eden was rallying for another attack. He was making noises in his throat and merely trying to readjust his fish and eggs.

It was impossible for Anthony to restrain himself. So far as he was concerned the cathedral had vanished. He wished above all things to learn the outcome of this argument. "Why, after all—why *was* trout fishing more dangerous than bullfighting?" In hurrying to overtake the pair disappearing through the door ahead he nearly trod on the toes of an old canon who looked up with the expression of a Torquemada as he brushed past.

But he had missed most of the reply of Mr. Eden when he drew near them at last. He could just hear him saying a little indignantly:

"I am perfectly willing to take the standpoint of either the trout *or* the bull in the matter, but I still can't see how that alters the argument. Men, and for that matter horses—*men,* I say, are frequently killed in the bullfight. Did you ever hear of anyone's ever being pulled in and devoured by a trout?"

"Such fishes, when hooked, invariably escape," countered Mr. Ford. "But you will admit that if fishermen are to be believed the brooks must be full of them."

Mr. Eden snorted.

"You have reminded me of a danger in fishing which I had over-looked, Willum," cried Mr. Ford. "You have proved my argument. No, no! No, sir," he continued without permitting his companion, who was now waving his walking-stick incoherently, to reply, "believe me, you much overrate bullfighting. It is only a favourite subject for foreign authors who visit Spain to enlarge upon. As a matter of fact it is less dangerous than the most sedentary occupation I know of in England."

"How can you—?" Mr. Eden managed to say.

"Why, as the Scotch clergyman once said to God, I can prove it to thee by statistics. There are more aldermen killed every year in London by turtles than matadors in the whole kingdom of Spain by bulls. Now isn't that a fact?"

They both stopped short in their tracks to laugh again. Mr. Ford because he had just thought of the argument, and Mr. Eden because he had been vanquished in so jolly a way. And they halted so unexpectedly that Anthony almost blundered into them.

"By George," said Mr. Ford scowling suddenly, "*we're* being followed! Well, sir?"

"I couldn't help overhearing what you were saying in the cathedral just now, and I admit following you just to see how the argument turned out," said Anthony in English, turning red as a beet. "I hope I haven't . . ."

"Certainly not," said Mr. Eden.

"Quite," said Mr. Ford.

"By George!" exclaimed Mr. Ford, seizing Anthony by the waistcoat. For a moment he thought Mr. Ford must have serious intentions—"if it isn't made by Rowland!" At the same time he exhibited the tag of the same London tailor on the top of his own vest. "'Straordinary, precisely the same . . . Well, good taste and curiosity meet then. It is time we introduce ourselves—by George!"

They did so.

They discovered they were all staying at the same fonda.

"*Dies mirabilis!*" exclaimed Ford. "We only arrived there this morning—by diligence."

"You must pay no attention to him, Mr. Adverse," said Eden as they walked up the street to the fonda. "He is full of inconsequential facts. How would you suppose we arrived—in a sheet let down from heaven?"

Mr. Ford snorted but Mr. Eden went on.

"Dick is taking notes for a guide-book to Spain. Everything goes in it from *Abades* to *Zzonsa*—"

"It is sadly needed. Every intelligent traveller feels the lack," Mr. Ford wedged in.

"—And when it is finished, two volumes of it," continued Mr. Eden, who was not to be put off, "it will be . . ."

"An excellent guide-book to Spain," thundered Mr. Ford, "full of that admirable redundancy of impertinent information with which every good guide-book should reek."

"Not at all," continued the even tones of his companion. "It will be like everything else you have to say. It will only prove your own theses. In this case it will merely show how superior everything in England is to everything in Spain."

Mr. Ford stopped and appeared to be threatened with apoplexy.

"Now take the argument that you just overheard, sir," continued Eden, taking Ford along by the arm. "All that was merely to persuade me to put off seeing the bullfight at Madrid in order to go trout fishing with Dick here in the mountains."

"Do you fish, Adverse?" exclaimed Ford hopefully. Anthony could see it was a crucial question.

"Indeed I do," he cried enthusiastically. "I love gaffin' sharks—"

"Sharks?" bellowed Mr. Ford. "Sharks! No, no, trout, salmon; trout, salmon!"

Mr. Eden leaned up against the wall of the fonda of El Dorado where they were now arrived and laughed immoderately.

"Another fact for your book, Dick," he shouted. "The snow-fed brooks *of the Sierras are not frequented by sharks*—make a note of it."

"Go to the devil, Willy Eden," grinned Ford as they entered the inn together.

Anthony stopped by the door astonished. In one corner of the room by a window Ouvrard was quietly eating a hearty luncheon.

He looked like a man who had just received overwhelming good news after a prolonged and exhausting anxiety. Anthony was at first afraid that he would resent the presence of strangers. But Ouvrard proved pathetically desirous of companionship and from the first got on with the newcomers uncommonly well. He exerted himself to be likable with all of his old charm to which was now added a certain dignity, as though he had passed through a great sorrow from which a sympathetic wisdom had been acquired. Most of his vulgar assurance and fat vanities had vanished. He no longer appeared to strut even when he sat down. What he lacked now was a certain faith in himself which still made it difficult for him to make decisions.

The irrepressible Mr. Ford by dint of unceasing badgering of Mr. Eden at last obtained his desire, and it was decided that the whole party should pause on their way to Madrid for a fishing expedition. They had now tacitly joined forces. Ford and Eden were delighted to have found a fellow countryman in Spain, for so they considered Anthony, and Ouvrard's apparent gayety under misfortune had recommended him to them as well as his boundless generosity. For his own reasons Anthony had hopes that with good luck a little fishing might serve to restore Ouvrard's self-confidence. So it was decided to send the great coach on to Madrid with Juan, Simba, and the luggage and to pursue the rest of their way by diligence. Most of the escort, which was consuming the banker's substance in gorgeous idleness at Burgos, now found themselves suddenly dismissed. They departed grumbling, and not without threats.

With Ford, Eden, and himself all well-armed and tolerably good shots, Anthony felt safe enough for any ordinary contingency. Indeed, he took very little stock in rumours of the perils of the road.

The departure was still somewhat delayed by the banker who had been bled too profusely by the leech he had at last employed. He finally, however, recovered from his weakness and they set out. Mr. Eden and Mr. Ford were provided with professional paraphernalia for fishing that they both carried with them as a matter of course. There were creels, reels, rods, and boxes of artificial bait by which Mr. Eden especially set exaggerated store.

The ancient diligence provided by the Compañia Catalines was of a seventeenth century vintage. It resembled an omnibus and was pierced along its preposterous length by doors and windows of contorted shapes as if its architect had had the Alhambra vaguely in mind. In the days of Isabella the Catholic, Mr. Ford thought that it had been painted in chrome and vermilion. Its behind, which was fatter than its before, was entered by a collapsible ladder that seldom failed to collapse. It was slung from spindle-spoked, concave wheels of gigantic circumference by cords of esparto-grass. The long benches of its interior, provided with red satin cushions adorned with chenille trimmings, did not in the end prevent bruising the bottoms of passengers, for this cabaña on wheels whizzed through space in a delirium of motion imparted to it by the united effort of ten vicious mules.

"And in this," said Mr. Eden, as he collapsed resignedly on the stern ladder, "we are going to fish for trout."

A peasant woman of superb and plastic proportions, under the impression that this was the public diligence departing for Madrid, was sitting in one corner of it when they entered. And it proved impossible to convey to her in any known dialect that she was in error.

"Try some of your damned arguments on her, Dick," said Mr. Eden at length beside himself with her obstinacy.

While the rest of them sat convulsed, Mr. Ford, who was an erudite gentleman, lavished Catalonian, Castilian and Aragonese upon her. Not even her expression changed. Her sloe eyes like those of a basilisk looked at him with contempt. He was at last reduced to gasps, a little bastard Basque, and maledictions in Latin.

"Nothing will move her but a derrick and a papal bull," he cried.

In the meanwhile the coach departed with Juan and Simba at the top. The great dog set up a dismal howling as he saw Anthony lean out of the window of the diligence to wave to Juan. They exchanged a gay farewell. The ribbons of the guitar fluttered from Juan's neck as the coach turned the corner. The baying of Simba diminished in the distance. For a moment a sinister feeling clutched Anthony. He turned to find the woman still sitting.

As a last resort the mayoral in an astrakhan jacket and sheepskin trousers was called in to remonstrate with her. But he might have been as Russian as he looked for all the effect his words had. At last she crossed herself. They all sighed. But she merely removed from her bodice a breast like a bean sack and applied its gathered nipple to the mouth of a small, pink pig.

"She is a wet nurse, señores. Doubtless she is employed at Madrid by a noble family and does not wish to go dry," said the mayoral, shifting his sheepskin trousers.

"Doubtless," said Mr. Eden, listening to soapy noises.

The woman returned the pig to a small basket.

"Do you realize, Willy, that this maternal succubus is going with us to Madrid?" shrieked Mr. Ford.

"Quite," replied Mr. Eden imperturbably.

"Voya usted con Dios," roared Richard Ford at the mayoral. The man bowed.

They started.

Mr. Eden was forced to lend assistance to M. Ouvrard, who had been hooked in the deepest vein of his biological French humour. He took the banker's head on his knees.

Between paroxysms of laughter Anthony sat in the corner remembering at the same time with a sense of indescribable loss the fluttering ribbons of Juan. Mr. Ford and Mr. Eden began to get out little cards with artificial flies and feathered hooks upon them.

Anthony looked at them. How serious they were about it. To him life had lately become too ludicrous even to bear thinking about. Soon they would be fishing. Nom d'un petit nom! Think of that!

It seemed fitting that just about this point Mr. Ford should point out the town of Vibar and remark that the Cid had been born there. "What did it matter? Suppose he hadn't been born," mused Anthony, just then unwilling even to think that.

Mr. Ford proved to be correct about other things. The headwaters of the river Urbel were found to be swarming with fish. The decayed town of La Pinza where they alighted was situated on a trout stream. The lazy trout on the higher reaches of the stream could actually be seen basking in pools, big fellows. Once they caught the glint of salmon leaping a falls. But none of these fish would bite. No matter how carefully they cast and whipped the pools there was not a single strike. They changed flies; they rotated flies. They let their bait drift downstream; they drew it slowly up. Nothing, not a nibble.

It was irritating to return to La Pinza and find the pig being nursed.

"Caramba!" said Mr. Ford.

"Perhaps it is because zey are English flies and very artificial," suggested Ouvrard towards the end of a second fishless day.

"Not at all," asserted Mr. Eden. "It is due to the phlegmatic temperament of Spanish trout."

"Try ze vurrum," suggested Ouvrard.

Mr. Ford looked horrified—and there were no worms.

"I vill show you zen how as a leetle garçon I take feesh in ze Vosges montaine." He began to take down one of his stockings.

They all gathered about the banker, whose preparations were mysterious.

He unravelled some brown yarn from one of his woollen stockings. He prepared a line with a small, clear pebble tied on just above the hook. He then broke off a short length of yarn and threaded it carefully on the hook with an end floating free.

"Ha," said the great financier, "ze vurrum artificial. Now you see !"

They tiptoed over to a near-by pool, where lying on his belly Ouvrard lowered his contrivance directly before the face of a large gasping trout sunning itself under a great root with its head upstream.

The tame animal swallowed hook and all. Ouvrard jerked it out onto the bank. His triumph was extreme. He went about repeating the performance. He caught salmon as well as trout. He rose rubbing his hands. He was a successful man again. Respected, envied.

They filled their creels and returned to the village to be received as only successful sportsmen can be. The fish were delicious and the dinner hilarious. Even the wet nurse appeared to enjoy it. They lingered for some days in these high, clear valleys amid the towers of ruined castles and dashing waterfalls. Anthony enjoyed himself hugely. Ouvrard was shouting like a boy. Half of one stocking was ravelled away. Ford and Eden were deep in the bliss of endless argument.

When they decided to leave at last, the woman took her place in the corner of the diligence, without comment. She rode with them to Madrid. She alighted at the Puerta de Hierro and gave the mayoral fifteen reales ten maravedís. She disappeared around the corner into the sunrise with her pig in the basket.

The diligence moved on through the streets of Madrid now slightly acrid with wood-smoke. It was December and the washerwomen in the dry rut of the Manzanares were forced to break the ice on the few remaining pools. They left the diligence in the Calle de la Montera. Mr. Ford and Mr. Eden parted from Mr. Adverse and M. Ouvrard with mutual admiration and regret. They also went their several ways; Anthony and Ouvrard to the Fontana de Oro where they refreshed themselves on agraz mixed with manzanilla wine.

Neither Juan nor the coach had been heard of. "Mañana," said Anthony to Ouvrard who looked worried. "Mañana. Remember we are in Spain." Yet Juan should certainly have arrived by this time. "What," he wondered, "could have become of him?"

At three o'clock in the morning he was awakened by the deep baying of Simba.

CHAPTER SIXTY-TWO

THE PRINCE OF THE PEACE BEYOND THE PYRENEES

THE baying of Simba did not awaken Anthony immediately. Yet even in his sleep—for the sound started him dreaming—he knew that something was terribly the matter. At one time he thought he heard Juan calling him, too—far-off. But he forgot that when he awoke. Only a strong impression of the eery and sinister had been added to the bell-tolling voice of the great hound that echoed through the caverns of his nightmare. He struggled up in bed. It was real.

Simba was in the courtyard below.

The scene in the patio while he stood by the window, instinctively drawing on his clothes, was so vivid as to tinge with its wild, emotional colouring his entire sojourn in Madrid. The great court of the posada of the Fontana de Oro was awash with red torchlight and fleering shadows. And in this atmosphere of funereal-macabre all hell was let loose.

At first he could make out nothing but glare, smoke, and pandemonium. Then—

Simba was baying at the open gate. He was being kept-off by a crowd of half-dressed mozos and link-boys with clubs, sputtering flambeaus, and a raving pack of curs at their heels. Under the black arches of the stables, amid skeletons of coaches, more torches were making red rings and ovals in the darkness as they were whirled into flame while grooms armed with pitchforks and shovels rushed out.

Just then Simba charged.

The scared waiters and yard attendants scattered before him. A pistol went off, followed by a shrill howl of agony from one of the coach dogs. Simba tossed another over his shoulder, a big, black-spotted fellow with its throat torn out. Just around the corner from the window a door banged. Before it the fierce clamour as of a wolf-pack in at the kill, followed by worrying sounds, began. The curs scattered. One of them was being eaten alive. Then there was another shot.

All this had taken about ten seconds. With his trousers on backward, and the exaltation of battle in his heart, Anthony rushed out. At the bottom of the stairs, which he descended headlong in the dark-

1015

ness, and at the end of a long corridor, several whey-faced waiters in shirts and drawers were standing in the dim rays of a smoky lamp peering out into the darkness through a grating. A man nursing a sprained wrist and groaning sat on the floor with a pistol still smoking beside him on the tiles.

"Body of Jesus!" cried another as the sound of sniffing and claws traversed the threshold, "it's the devil himself." Several crossed themselves. They clutched at Anthony's arm as he approached to unbar the door.

"Santiago, señor, there is a great mad dog out there! Would you let him in at us? Caramba, crazy Englishman, what can your little stick do? For four days now he has terrorized the whole quarter and stood-off the guards at the Puerta de Hierro. No one can hit him even with a bullet."

"My dog!" said Anthony. "Open the door."

At the sound of his voice an indescribably fierce and pathetic whining came flowing in over the sill.

"You see—he knows me."

He whistled. The hound began to throw himself against the door till it quivered. His voice filled the entire inn.

Anthony picked up the empty pistol from the floor and pointed it at the group of scared but obstinate servants. They broke away from him, racing up the passage. He pulled the door open and stood behind it. Luckily it opened inward or he would have been devoured by frantic love. It was fully five minutes before he could venture out and throw his arms about Simba. When he did so the dog put a grizzly head over his shoulder and moaned with affection and relief. He twitched and trembled all over.

In his room upstairs—no one had offered to stop him—he examined the dog carefully. One of his ears had been shot or half bitten off. It was hard to tell which. A great peeling scar as if from a knife wound raked half-way over his shoulders and along his back. It looked as though a gigantic cat had clawed him. And he was starved and stone-bruised and filthy.

Anthony talked to him in Arabic. "What is it, Simba, what happened?" he cried as he sat on the floor with angry tears in his eyes trying to bathe the wounds. The hound whimpered.

But his powerful tail continued to flog the floor in a mad tattoo of joy at having found his master, while at the same time he rested his muzzle on Anthony's knee and in his own language poured forth a story of outrage and tragedy. There could be no doubt of the emotional meaning. That was clear. Only the incidents were lacking.

"I won't leave you again, my friend," cried Anthony. "That's a promise. Give me your paw."

He swore, washing out the deep cut on Simba's back. It was evidently some days old and badly caked. The noise in the patio outside had subsided. Simba rumbled on in his chest.

Ouvrard came in in gown and pantoufles. He was much perturbed. "Hein, when I was a little boy I used to wish animals could talk— and now this one does. Mon Dieu, if he only had words! How did he ever find us here?"

"Picked up my trail in the streets, I suppose. We walked here from the Calle de la Montera, you remember. Pure chance. He may have been wandering about the streets hunting for me. He would do that."

"Juan must have arrived in Madrid then. Where do you suppose he is?"

"Juan?" said Anthony.

They looked at each other significantly. At Juan's name Simba had begun to bark.

They spent the next day inquiring for Juan and the coach but no one had heard of it or seen it. On the following morning they went to the authorities but they had no better luck there. Simba was well known. Sí! everybody knew Simba. He had appeared suddenly from nowhere and had terrorized the streets. The señor would do well to purchase a stout chain and to look carefully to the staple. It was fortunate that only beggars had been bitten. Gold would heal them. The alcalde bowed them out.

"Mais, c'est impossible," complained Ouvrard. "That a coach, that that coach, ten mules and a man should vanish. I will wait till I can bring pressure to bear in high quarters. It will not be long. I shall soon have their bread here at my mercy." He ground his teeth. "We shall see then, par le bon Dieu! We shall see."

In some respects Ouvrard proved to be an able prophet, but it was many and many a long day before they heard of the coach. And Juan——

"Poor Juan!" thought Anthony. He had not given up looking for him yet. But his heart was filled with foreboding at Simba's crying at the name of "Juan."

And so—the great deal in wheat got under way, unluckily enough, while Anthony did his own hair with the ghost of Juan leaning over his shoulder; while Simba slept in the bleak winter sun in the patio, keeping his secret, growling and licking his wounds.

———————

They did not stay long at the Fontana de Oro. Richard Ford called one morning to see how they were getting on and casually confirmed them in their opinion that it was the worst hostelry in Europe.

"Not only are the beds populous but the muchachos play guitars in the patio while you are being eaten. That is carrying cannibalism too far." Messrs. Ford and Eden departed for Toledo behind the usual number of mules, and they saw them in this world no more.

They took the hint of the departed, however, and moved to the Casa de los Baños, kept by one David Purkiss on the Calle Caballero de Gracia near the Puerta de Hierro. It was much frequented by government couriers, who came there to remove the mud of Mercia, Aragon, and Valencia from their anatomies. But as M. Ouvrard never bathed, having once caught a cold at Arles in doing so—he merely wiped his face and sometimes his neck in the morning with a powerful gillyflower cologne—the adobe in the baths was to him immaterial.

These moves on the part of Ouvrard were not unimportant. His rise to influence and the course of his negotiations with the crown ministers during the government's speculations and peculations in wheat could have been marked by them. The humble taking-off place was the establishment of Señor Purkiss. From thence M. Ouvrard rose and eventually soared into more congenial, luxuriant, official, and exalted surroundings, all in the course of about six months. His way-stations towards the golden sunshine of royal favour after taking-off from the Casa de los Baños were in rapid succession La Fonda de Genies in the Calle de Peregrinos, the French embassy, the Palace of La Buena Vista in the Calle de Alcalá, belonging to the Prince of the Peace, and the apartments of Philip V at San Ildefonso.

Anthony did not follow the banker. He remained with Señor Purkiss and kept comfortable vigils in a suite of rooms with a large fireplace. He hired one Pedro Manuelos, a polite and silent edition of Sancho Panza with some sartorial technique, to look after him. In the absence of Juan it was a consolation to be shaved without conversation. In fact during his stay in Madrid he began to grow a little morose. His complete loneliness began to pall upon him. He missed Vincent. He thought despairingly of Angela. He read a deal of Spanish literature good and bad. He fondled Simba, of whom, as his one remaining friend and fireside companion, he became unduly fond. So much for blustering evenings spent indoors.

The world outside was a different matter. He was busy there, a cog in a great intrigue, and he was still fascinated by it. He took immense pains with his Spanish, trying to banish from it not only the mannerisms of a foreigner but all traces of the colonial accent he had acquired in Cuba. His pleasure in high Castilian became an all but sensual thing. In the language, he felt, resided all that was living of the genuine magnificence and the true greatness of Spain.

A large part of his time was taken up in going about with Ouvrard whose Spanish was at first infantile. He got on rapidly but in the beginning of his negotiations he was dependent on Anthony. As Ouvrard did not wish to disclose fully the nature of his mission nor the policies of Bonaparte toward Spain, which he was initiating, he took some care for a while to whom he revealed his presence in Madrid. He desired to make his first approaches without arousing unnecessary opposition.

There was a streak of genuine diplomacy in the banker. He took due note of Spanish pride, punctilio, and prejudice. He wished to work through them rather than against them. Avarice, flattery, and persuasion were always his face cards in a pack where fear was a carefully played ace of clubs. It would have been well perhaps if Napoleon had not finally insisted upon making clubs trumps in Spain. Ouvrard did not think it was necessary to take all the tricks in order to win. "No," said he, "Godoy is the knave, which in this game takes the king and queen." He began therefore by sending Anthony to the Prince of the Peace to make known his arrival at Madrid.

"You might sound him out a little and learn all you can. Keep your eyes about you. Get him to talk. Here are a few leading questions—and a letter from Bonaparte. You will obtain audience as a confidential messenger from the Tuileries. The initial impression you make will count for much. I would arrive in an ordinary cab. We want no attention now. Meanwhile I shall myself go quietly to the embassy and arrange for some credits. All my gold and luggage was in the coach, you know. No papers, thank God! It is ridiculous, but I haven't even a change of linen left. Must we start the conquest of Spain in dirty shirts then? Bon chance, mon garçon. I see your ruffles are still fresh."

They each took an antediluvian hackney. "Mine makes a noise like a pig whining," thought Anthony.

Coaches, however, were not the only things giving vent to hungry sounds. The bad harvests had filled the streets of Madrid with beggars. As the government was bankrupt, and the king did not take even enough interest in the queen to prevent his being a cuckold, there was no hope that he would suddenly become a father to his people.

There was only one fountain of bounty left in the country, one turgid source of honour that remained. It was the man who slept with the Queen of Spain, the Caliph of Ali Babas since the world began, a noble beggar on horseback who had stretched forth his unashamed hands to fate murmuring, "Por el amor de Dios," and received the golden fleece and the usufruct of the Indies. Whatever was left he alone might still give away. If the beggars licked their lips when he passed it was from envy as well as hunger.

It was upon this remarkable individual that with not a little well-concealed curiosity and natural contempt Anthony was about to call. His introduction, delivered in the name of Ouvrard, was a brief note in the lightning-like script of the little man in the Tuileries.

Thus Mercury jolted on in his squeaky chariot down the Calle de Alcalá with the paper thunderbolt of Jove in his pocket.

Don Manuel de Godoy Alvarez de Faría Ríos Sanchez y Zarzoa, Prince of the Peace, Duke of Alcudia, Count of Evora Monte, Grandee of the First Class in Spain, Commander of the Knights of Malta, Knight of the Golden Fleece, Grand Cross of the Order of Charles III, President of the Council of Castile, Generalissimo of the Spanish Armies, Colonel of the Household Troops, High Admiral of Spain, etc., etc.,—sat in an upper room of the palace of La Buena Vista and looked out through the high windows at the dank light of a Madrid morning in April. The room was cold, but Don Manuel was notoriously a warm-blooded man.

Nevertheless, he gave a slight shiver. He was listening to the wheezing drone of a blind man hawking handbills just under his windows on the Calle de Alcalá. God alone knew what they were saying about him now. And that fellow with the saw-like voice was especially persistent. He went to the window. Yes, it was the same man led by that half-starved, black bitch like a hound come from hell to guide blind Rumour about the streets. He sighed, picked up a pen, threw it down again and subsided into his chair by his desk. He would sign the papers—mañana.

It was a gorgeous desk, almost effeminate with its small medallions of heathen goddesses and its miniatures of court ladies set in wreaths and scroll work. It had been sent by Louis XV to Philip V on the latter's birthday. Now it belonged to Don Manuel. Under the desk was a handsome pair of legs—also the property of Don Manuel. They were well shaped, a little gross and too vigorous. Yet they went perfectly with the desk; that is, they were of the same era; obviously idle, sensual, over-decorated, and effeminate, because no longer meant merely to support a man. They were for something more than that, as their costume showed: shoes with high, red heels, plump calves in puce-coloured stockings, a diamond garter with a cameo miniature of the Queen of Spain on it, and above that a Dionysian development thrust rearward into a soft green silk cushion and clothed smoothly in canary-coloured knee-breeches. A complicated arrangement on his breasts of looped ribbons and cordons of the various orders to which he belonged, or that now belonged to him—it was hard to tell which— had only one disadvantage. They made it difficult for Don Manuel himself to see the blazing diamond star pinned over his left nipple. But the sweep of his shoulders clad in rich, blue watered-silk and hung with gracefully drooping epaulettes with tassels of spun gold was manly.   Above their straight line rose a flamboyant countenance with red, sensual lips, a flat aquiline nose, and a high Gothic forehead so narrow as to convey the impression that there was not much in it. That impression, however, was instantly relieved by a wealth of dark-brown ringlets that swept luxuriantly away from it in long romantic waves upon which the white ribbon that confined them slept like the sail of a becalmed treasure galleon seen from afar.

Such was the grandee of the first class in Spain who was now annoyed by the wheezing of the blind beggar selling handbills in the street below.

There were no newspapers left in Madrid.   With a diligence that might otherwise have been commendable Don Manuel had seen to that. But there were still handbills.   Despite the greatest care, they continued to appear from time to time.   And they were always hawked by the blind.   News in Spain was invariably sold by blind men.   It was a Castilian trick.   Even in Madrid it was impossible to convict a blind man no matter how complacent the alcalde might be before whom he was haled for selling libellous printed matter.   "I have not seen the great infamy attributed to the King's Minister," they would swear by the heart of Jesus.   And the joke was always appreciated. "Go then, and God go with you, innocent one.   You have broken no law."

It was true.   Even "Yo—El Rey" could do nothing about it.

Godoy had often thought of complaining to Don Carlos about the lax state of the press law.   But invariably the king would ask to see the handbills.   And that was distinctly *not* to be thought of.

It was becoming painfully apparent to Don Manuel that there were some things that even El Rey could not do.   Fixing the price of bread, for instance, or paying the troops out of an empty treasury. It was not Don Manuel's fault that the harvests had been bad for two years.   Yet people blamed him for it.   How unreasonable—in fact, "Caramba!"   And to have the people hungry and the soldiers penniless at the same time was a foul conjunction for a royal favourite.

"Hunger has no punctilio."

He could remember copying that for old Dr. Guzman, his tutor, only a few years ago.   It was just after he had first . . . first fully convinced Her Majesty that he was a man of large parts—and natural understanding—fully equal to lightening the most burdensome duties of the king.   Her Majesty had been most gracious.   In preparation for his becoming the choricero not only should he be able to play the guitar, she would also have him taught to read and write.   It would

be convenient.   So he had learned to sign his name, beautifully.   And
he was fond of quoting all the proverbs he had copied for Dr. Guzman.
*"After lightning there is thunder."—"Another Tuesday will follow
Monday."*

When he presided over the Council such profound saws gave him a
certain air of wisdom.

It was only Don Luis da Vincitata who dared to laugh.   Dios, how
he hated that man!   He would never forgive him for having given
him the title of "Your Peculiar Magnificence."   Don Luis had moved
it in full council and it had been passed with acclaim.   To think that
for a year he had been charmed by it—"Your Peculiar Magnificence."
It was not until Don Diego, his secretary, had whispered into his ear
that . . . shocking, it was quite shocking.

But he saw the point.   He was not one to dismiss a secretary for
frankness.   He did not wish to be flattered.   The great should have
the truth told them.   Yet; it must have taken a good deal of courage
to tell a man of his peculiar magnificence what Don Luis had said.

Still, he had not let them laugh at him for long.   He had married
the infanta, Doña Tuda, and that had made him a nephew of the king,
a "serene highness."   It was Don Luis who had suggested that Doña
Tuda should be made "lady-in-waiting."   She had not had to wait long.

He started.   He had never thought of it before.   Could Don Luis
have been making fun of him with his wife's title, too?

He was very suspicious of that old man now.   Don Luis had tricked
him nicely enough on the transfer of that province in America to
France.   *Lou—Lou*—what was its name?   Oh, yes, Louisiana!
Monstrous!   He had never meant to part with it.   He had been ca-
joled out of it.   Don Luis had assured him when the secret treaty
was made that it was only "put in pawn," his very words, only a security for the payment of the French indemnity.   And then—Bonaparte had sold it to the Yankees for fifteen millions of dollars.   He
licked his lips.   That money would have been welcome in Spain.   And
now they were blaming him for that, too.

Perhaps it would be a good thing to get rid of Don Luis da Vincitata?   Somehow or other he always seemed to play into the hands
of Bonaparte in the end.   It seemed to him now, as he sat thinking
over the past, that ever since he had been at court it was Don Luis
who had really directed the course of events.   Yet he was only a
councillor, a mere confidential agent of the crown.

Yet since he owed his introduction to court to Don Luis he had
naturally been willing to take his advice—to be grateful.

He remembered how Don Luis had driven down to Badajaz in that
great gloomy coach of his one July morning in '84, he was only seven-

teen then, and found him swimming and strumming a guitar by the banks of a stream.

"Put your shirt on," Don Luis had said, "I am going to take you to court and make a royal body-guard out of you. You play the guitar well, don't you, my boy? Take it along—to accompany your other instrument. You may be able to play some notable duets. Her Majesty is much given to stringed instruments."

And so this old friend of the family had driven off with him just as he had taken his older brother to Madrid before him. "But I am much disappointed in your brother," Don Luis had told him. "He forgets his friends. Now I think you will go further. You are much more of a man." And Don Luis had been right. He was always right. That was the trouble with him. But he ought not to keep him waiting this way. He was no longer a boy with a guitar. He was the Prince of the Peace and, as Don Luis must know (damn him!), the father of the queen's youngest son. Don Luis knew a good deal, didn't he?

He reached forward on the desk and began to play with the sander. It was a silver figure of a peasant sowing. When you pressed the spring the peasant swung his arm and sanded your letter nicely. He amused himself and scattered sand all over the top of the desk. In the anteroom he could hear Don Diego skylarking with the pages. When he was a boy he had loved to be tickled, too. *But now it was different.* Few people had any idea what the Prince of the Peace had to put up with. Her Majesty was still *so* playful—and then there was Doña Tuda—the infanta. As his wife of course she had her moments. There were two of them to look after and he was thirty-five now. He was coming to appreciate how a man might devote himself to experimenting with nothing but water-clocks, as the king did.

He never got any credit for his good ideas, and lately they were blaming him for everything. Few people suffered as much for Spain night by night as he did. Did they think he could be a father to the royal family and a father to the people, too?

He walked over to the window and stepped out on the balcony. Would Don Luis never arrive? It was eleven o'clock now. Well, there he was getting out of that new coach of his. The latest London make. It had been a joy to ride in it yesterday. Marvellous springs. Don Luis' remarks about the wheel of Fortune painted on the ceiling had gone a little too far though. After all, who was he to dig the Prince of the Peace in the ribs—and grin?

"Bread, and the beggar on horseback," cried the blind man, waving his handbill. "A new ballad, señores. For a maravedí, read.

Famine, and a warming pan for the queen's bed. Read, señores. For a maravedi. Bread and the beggar on . . ."

Don Manuel closed the window behind him angrily and stepped back into the room.

"Good morning, Manuel," said Don Luis. "How is it with you—by the Grace of God?"

Don Manuel resented that. He resented all that the intimacy implied and the tone in which it was conveyed. But there was such a sturdy and vigorous air about the hale old man who stood before him, whose outline seemed to occupy a square in space rather than an oblong; above all there was such a complete unity and calm self-assurance conveyed by the massive mahogany features and the grizzled temples of the old lion, that Don Manuel quailed. Instinctively he started to whine a little.

"Do you hear what they are saying about me out there?" he asked plaintively.

"Well, can you blame them? They are very hungry and there is nothing like the lack of a few meals to make poets write. Under your beneficent administration we are like to have a renaissance of satire. The acid muse never sings clearly with pie in her mouth. She needs mouldy crusts to thrive on."

Don Manuel felt the edge rather than the point of these remarks.

"The dearth *is* extreme," he admitted. "And I have not been able to do anything about it. It now amounts to famine—"

"Pooh!" said Don Luis. "Spain has been hungry ever since we drove out the Moors."

"—and the soldiers near the city are unpaid," continued the Prince of the Peace with a note of genuine concern for the military. "Even the household cavalry is six months in arrears. I have a remonstrance here." He lifted a scroll of paper that rustled ominously.

"Eh!" said Don Luis. "You should have let me know before this. I will do what I can. But it will take at least a month to drive swine in from Estremadura." They both remained silent for a few minutes.

"Can't you do something with the new French ambassador?" asked Don Manuel.

"You mean toward withholding the payment due on the subsidy?" Don Luis looked doubtful. "I might," he said at last.

"It would save us," cried Don Manuel. "We could import wheat and pay the garrison for the winter."

"And then what?" asked Don Luis.

"There may be a better harvest next year—and the Mexican flota will soon be in, shiploads of silver bars, seventy million dollars by the viceroy's account."

"I have a little bad news for your Serene Highness," replied Don Luis. "An advice has just come through by way of Paris that the British have annihilated the Mexican treasure fleet."

"What? Why, we are not even at war with them!" shouted Don Manuel.

"We are now," said Don Luis. "When a nation captures and sinks your ships at sea, then it *is* at war with you. Need I enlarge on that?"

"But what excuse have they? It is national piracy!"

"They consider the cession of Louisiana to France a hostile act," replied Don Luis. "Now that it has been sold to the Yankees the Mississippi is forever closed to England and Bonaparte has received fifteen million dollars. It will enable him to go on with his English war again."

"That is *your* fault," bellowed Don Manuel. "You assured me that the province would eventually be returned. It was only to be held as security. You brought M. Lucien Bonaparte here to confirm that while he was still ambassador. You have permitted Napoleon to embroil us with England. We are ruined." For some minutes Don Manuel in an unusual but sincere access of passionate anger and alarmed patriotism, not unmixed with personal forebodings, bellowed on.

"Calm yourself," said Don Luis after he had listened as long as he cared to. "If you go on this way your voice will be ruined for accompanying the guitar. That would compromise your position with the queen even more than you say I have." He grinned a little. Don Manuel sat panting.

"As usual you are only partly right," Don Luis continued a little languidly. "That has always been your weakness as a statesman from the time you first went to bed with the queen. It is true that I desire to see France and Spain aligned against England and I worked for it. But I also hoped to build up a great Latin empire in America, and, as we were weak in Louisiana, I thought to preserve it by transferring it for a while to the more powerful protection of France. That was arranged for in the secret treaty after my discussions in Paris with Napoleon. Both Lucien Bonaparte and I were sincere—I believe the first consul was, too. M. Lucien writes me that he opposed the sale of the province to the Yankees to the very last, even to the verge of the bath."

"To the what?" croaked Don Manuel.

"To the *bath,* I said. The final papers were signed by Napoleon in the bathtub."

"Did he offer any excuse?"

" 'I need the money.' "

"Oh!" said Don Manuel inanely. "Does he bathe often?"

"No. We shall be able to keep Mexico, I think."

Don Manuel grunted. "At any rate we are done for here," he said despondently. "They are already rioting in Barcelona. They call themselves anti-clericals."

"Take advantage of that," cried Don Luis. "Organize a similar party here. You can sack a few monasteries, seize the loot, and then garrote the ring-leaders. There are enough silver crucifixes and pyxes in some of these monasteries to pay the army for a year."

"Or—I might seize the funds for the hospitals and give them government securities instead," cried Don Manuel looking brighter.

"You have your moments, Manuel," admitted Don Luis.

"But then what? That is only a temporary expedient at best."

"I have a plan for you," said the older man seizing his opening. "I want you to send me to Mexico to look after the safe forwarding of treasure there. You can give me special letters of instruction to the viceroy."

"But the British," objected Don Manuel.

Don Luis raised his hand. He began to explain to the Prince of the Peace the plan of M. Ouvrard to forward Mexican bullion to Europe. It took him a long time to explain it to Don Manuel.

"Well, I suppose so," the favourite finally admitted suspiciously, remembering Louisiana. "It seems the only way out." Then he looked more cheerful. A way to rid himself of Don Luis had suddenly occurred to him. "Shall I have the necessary credentials to Mexico made out and signed by the king?"

"Yes. And there is one thing more," said Don Luis.

"There always is," muttered Don Manuel. He looked up inquiringly, however.

"Before I leave I want my wife made lady-in-waiting to Her Majesty."

Don Manuel raised his brows in surprise.

"Yes," said Don Luis, "I have allied myself with the descendant of an imperial house, a lady with a noble past, a Paleologus. A quiet wedding in the country."

"I congratulate you," said Don Manuel. "I shall speak to Her Majesty about making a place for her among her camaristas tonight."

"Do so," said Don Luis. "It always pains me when I have to go over your head to ask the king for a minor favour. His Majesty is always willing to gossip, though."

Don Manuel winced.

"And this fellow Ouvrard?"

"I advise you to listen to him. He is the mouth of Bonaparte."

They bowed to each other more coldly than usual as Don Luis withdrew.

On the mantelpiece in the gorgeously furnished anteroom where Anthony had been kicking his heels for half an hour an ormolu clock began to strike noon. The two pages stopped skylarking and stood by the portières ready to bow stiffly as the latch on the cabinet door clicked.

"Now, monsieur, if you will give me your letter for His Highness," said Don Diego, extending his hand.

Don Luis emerged. He and Anthony stood looking at each other. The pages unbent and looked up at Don Luis in surprise. His hand remained behind him on the door-knob.

The clock suddenly became audible clicking away in its glass case.

While the clock ticked for twenty seconds or more both Don Luis and Anthony were thinking at a speed which no timepiece could record.

Don Luis was not merely made uncomfortable by being confronted by Anthony again. It was true that at the mere sight of him a lifetime of emotion never failed to shake even his iron-clad equanimity. But there was now something more than that. He had thought Anthony was dead. It was like being confronted by a determined ghost. For a moment his hand did not leave the door-knob.

So Sancho had lied then. Or the ruffians he had hired to waylay the coach had sold-out. It was only the servants that had been murdered. The details could be ascertained later. The result was clear. Anthony was standing there, and Ouvrard must be in Madrid, too. Probably both of them had escaped. He had failed again.

His hand did not leave the door-knob yet.

There was fate in this. A sudden resolution formed itself in his mind. He had tried three times now and lost. All that was connected with Maria was unlucky for him. Had been so from the first.

The game was about even so far. Why not call it off, forever? Tempt fate no further. Wisdom consists in not paying too high for anything. He would not be surrendering. He would merely be calling a draw.

The door-knob clicked.

Meanwhile an extraneous fact had forced itself upon him, just as in times of great pain the sufferer will notice the presence of a fly on his hand. The face of one of the pages looking up at him was that of a sardonic young imp. "I wish I had a son like that," said the old man's mind. "He is like me."

"Of what blood are you, my boy?" said he breaking the tension that all felt.

"Pedro to serve God and Your Honour and of the family Sidonia, Your Apostolic Reverence," said the boy who traced in Don Luis a certain humorous resemblance to the papal nuncio who had called only the day before.

Don Luis was delighted with this impudent tact.

"Here is something to get you into trouble," he said, and spun him a gold piece that never touched ground.

"After all, Maria's son was like her. A good type, too. The extreme opposite of his own. But a mould that he had once admired. Fate evidently needed both of them in the world. Goth and Latin." The dark man turned to the fair one.

"Welcome to Madrid, Don Antonio. It is somewhat of a surprise to find you here."

Anthony was vastly astonished. He had seen Ouvrard's coach at the door with Sancho dozing on top of it as he came in. A hundred speculations as to what Don Luis would do when he confronted him had run through his head as he sat waiting. But he had not expected this move. There was absolutely no hostility in it. Intensely on the alert, he suddenly felt disarmed. It was not only the words of Don Luis' greeting. The fire and brimstone were absent. As usual he said what he thought.

"Nothing could surprise me more than to be welcomed by Your Excellency. I should have thought it impossible."

The older man looked at him quite frankly. "You are mistaken, Antonio," he said. "I would like to talk to thee for a moment alone."

If anything could have astonished him more than the use of his first name familiarly it was the note of appeal in the old man's voice. He looked at him keenly for a moment.

"I can see no objection," he said.

Don Luis looked relieved. "Don Diego, if you and the young gentlemen will do us the favour of withdrawing for a moment?"

Don Luis motioned toward a long table and they sat down on opposite sides of it.

"I trust you will not misunderstand my motives in what I am about to say, Don Antonio," began Don Luis showing signs of conflicting emotions—which he gained the better of as he went on; "nor that you will expect me to explain. It would be impossible for me to do so. Nevertheless, I hope we may arrive at an understanding." He paused ponderously.

"I have never desired to trouble you, Don Luis. Recollect, you have been the aggressor. Before we discuss anything I therefore feel entitled to make clear to you how I feel. Since I am certain that there is nothing petty in your nature, it has been forced upon me that your motives for wishing to be rid of me must be profound ones. That they inhere in the past is so obvious as to be inescapable. Perhaps you suspect me of either possessing knowledge which I do not have or of a determination to investigate. In either case you would be mistaken. I do not wish to pry into the motives for your hostility. *Why* I do not is my own affair, and, to set your mind at rest, known to me alone. But I must also say this: if you persist, sir, in harassing me I shall feel forced out of pure self-defence to investigate what otherwise I should feel in honour bound not even to speculate upon. I shall say no more."

"Believe me, you put your case even more strongly than you suppose," said Don Luis. "I can now fully credit what at first I am bound to say seemed to be impossible; that is, that you had neither a knowledge of nor a desire to pry into certain matters of the past. But recent events in my domestic affairs have already confirmed me in that opinion. I allude, sir, to my nuptials with the lady who had your youth in charge. She is a better friend of yours than you may be disposed to credit."

Anthony could not conceal a look of astonishment.

"I am seventy," said Don Luis, "but I am still young enough to desire happiness. As we get older loneliness does not become more attractive. My pride in my wife is that of Pluto for Proserpine." A menace seemed to have crept into his tone. "You may shortly have the honour of meeting her at court."

"Is the old man getting garrulous," wondered Anthony, "or does he wish to seal my mouth about Faith? All this is only just as impossible as——life." Don Luis was looking at him but there was now no hostility in his glare. On the contrary . . .!

"I wish you both peace," Anthony said quietly. "What is it you desire of me?"

"Just that," replied Don Luis, "peace. From now on let us agree not to annoy each other in any way. Let the account be closed; paid in full. I admit that I opened that account with you. But you also admit you are not in a position to judge of my motives for doing so; that you do not even desire to know why. I leave it to you to close it, if you will, for both of us and with honour."

"Where is my servant?" asked Anthony.

"Where is *my* servant?" replied Don Luis. "As for the coach . . ."

"It is before the door waiting for you now," exclaimed Anthony. "Let us waive that in our account. It is M. Ouvrard's. You can settle it with him. But my man?"

"Upon my word I know nothing about him," insisted the marquis. They looked at each other for a moment steadily.

"For my own reasons then," said Anthony, "and not for yours, I accept."

They rose simultaneously and bowed. Anthony with a little stiffness that he was at no pains to conceal; Don Luis with a stately courtesy and grandeur which implied that in the young man before him he at last acknowledged fate as an equal. Anthony could not know why, but he felt the great resignation and equality of that gesture to be the genuine sign-language of the old man's heart.

A minute later he stood by the window watching Don Luis drive off. The hair that rose into points on each side of Sancho's cocked hat was now a peculiar grizzled grey; his smooth mouth sinister. "Beware. He is always driving . . . with the great vigour of evil" . . . where had he? . . . he remembered now. Brother François. In the cabin of the *Ariostatica* that night . . . a feverish vision. It must have been that. Why should it occur to him now? What connection? Unfathomable. He could not trace it down into the dark depths of intuition.

What mysterious vendetta had he and Don Luis been engaged in? Their hostility was psychic, instinctive. He had felt that from the first. Its roots went down into the darkness beyond reason or memory whence bitter juices are drawn. And where was Juan? He choked. Had he been right in meeting the old man half-way, after all? Now that he and Faith had joined forces, perhaps something was completed. Loose ends had met. The dark ring could be left hanging in space. He saw it, like a spinning noose in a cloud. Why? What? He longed to know, bitterly.

How curious! It was as hard to give up this hate as it would have been to deny a love. "John Bonnyfeather—if you can hear me—I have kept my promise in splendid difficulty." A sound from the land of the living recalled him. He turned to find that the secretary had returned to the room. He seemed more respectful than he had been before, almost obsequious. He must have delivered the letter from the Tuileries then.

"His Highness is waiting for you impatiently, señor. This way if you please."

He had not entirely shaken off the mood of his reverie as he stepped into the room. Out of the corner of his eye he caught the grin on the face of that imp-like page as he announced him.

"Don Antonio Ada—*vairs*," shrilled the urchin as if a bowstring had twanged.

Don Manuel Godoy, Prince of the Peace, stood against the light before the high window. He shimmered in silks and diamonds. His soul glittered with success. There was nothing dim or chaste or virtuous about him. He was like Ganymede in the strong arms of Jove, rosy—and only a little troubled. Proud that he had been snatched up to dwell upon Olympus, he had the easy expression of one who might still discern clouds but only by looking down upon them.

And instantly—without having any volition in the matter—even as he stepped through the door, Anthony knew that he had been sped like an arrow to strike this glorious creature down.

Against so inhuman an intuition he recoiled with horror and denial. He felt a great pity for the man before him. Sympathy begets sympathy. Don Manuel responded nobly. And in this seemingly auspicious atmosphere of fellow-feeling they met.

"You come to provide us with the staff of life, I am told," said Godoy graciously, letting Bonaparte's open letter flutter to the floor. "Need I say that in that case you are welcome to this hungry Madrid and to Spain? When will M. Ouvrard do us the honour of calling himself? I am impatient to see him. Let us waste no time on polite preliminaries. People starve."

"I am prepared to lay the general scheme before you now," replied Anthony. "M. Ouvrard will discuss it in detail if you are favourably impressed with the plan."

"Let no one disturb us, Don Diego," said Don Manuel. "You may close the door. I shall be closeted with this gentleman for some time."

Thus the great deal in wheat, Mexican silver, the Spanish royal family, and the peninsula of Spain got under way.

The grim archer, if he had any lips, might have laughed. Certainly he would have grinned as he watched the first arrow he had loosed flash to its mark.

Don Luis had not lied to Anthony when he said he did not know anything about Juan. He had left Sancho in Paris some months before to keep track of Ouvrard. He frequently employed Sancho in private espionage and had found his old servant both clever and faithful. Sancho never appeared himself in these affairs of his master, which were so closely connected with government intrigues that it was hard to tell just where the public business ended and began. He was only the agent. He supplied the means and directed others whom he took into his hire or bribed.

In Paris he had been harboured at the Spanish embassy as a butler, and it was not long before he was receiving a stipend from M. Talleyrand for supplying enough tidbits of gossip to gain him some credence at the ministry of foreign affairs. In this way he had been able to mislead the French on one or two minor matters and at the same time to devote himself to ferreting out the business of M. Ouvrard while under excellent cover.

Knowing what he already did know of Ouvrard's affairs, Don Luis was enabled to piece out the information which Sancho forwarded him into a clear picture which frequently permitted him to act or to give advice that seemed to have about it the quality of a mysterious prevision.

He was particularly anxious to know exactly when Ouvrard set out for Madrid in order to warn the Prince of the Peace, over whom he must retain his influence in order to advise him how to act. Sancho had therefore been instructed to follow Ouvrard as soon as he set out and to keep a close tab on him as he travelled through Spain.

Don Luis' policy was a complicated one. He was convinced that the only hope for Spain was to entangle it firmly in the Napoleonic net. His patriotism was genuine, but of a far-seeing, almost metaphysical variety.

He saw his country in the not-too-remote future as the thriving province of a great Latin empire with its people secure in a code of well-administered law; with the arts reviving and commerce flourishing in the midst of a federated European peace. The bright and rising star of the new and fortunate Caesar at Paris was to bring this about. Thus in a curious way characteristic of his time Don Luis was able to reconcile an intense conservatism and an all but radical idealism. Spain was to progress but by going backward. The Middle Ages were to be swept aside and *Hispania* was to rise out of order political and ecclesiastical; out of flourishing cities, bursting oil presses and flowing aqueducts. Individuals and institutions which stood in the way of this were to be swept aside. Even religion to Don Luis was political. Indeed, it might be said that Don Luis' religion was politics.

As time went on, and it seemed more and more probable that old as he was he might actually live to see his dreams and hopes realized, Don Luis had changed from a purely static reactionary to one who desired to accelerate the trend of events. His growing enthusiasm re-endowed his hale, old body with an all but youthful energy. He enjoyed an iron-clad health. The solution of his domestic difficulties and the companionship and comfort which he found in his new wife, who was not only looking after her husband but engaged as well in pious works, seemed to have turned the clock back for Don Luis even as he would have liked to turn it back for Spain.

Some marvelled that one who had sat on the council of the old king should still retain his influence upon the reigning monarch. Only a few realized that Don Luis dominated him. Yet it was so. He was the conscience of the dull Charles IV. He held the whip-hand over Godoy by his knowledge of that guilty secret of which he alone could have convinced the king. The queen was afraid of him. His influence had provided Crown Prince Ferdinand with the tutor who afterwards persuaded him to play into Napoleon's hands. The old man held no official position except his place on the Council of Castile. There most of the government business went on before his eyes. He said little. He looked down his nose while the ministers squabbled. Floridablanca, Count Aranda, and Urguijo had all had their day and joined one another in impotent retirement. Don Luis da Vincitata, Conde de Azuaga, at the age of seventy remained to advise the king whose advice to take and Don Manuel Godoy, the queen's favourite, what advice to give to the king.

The first faint rift in this admirable arrangement, admirable at least for Don Luis, coincided with the journey of Ouvrard to Spain and was due to the fact that he was accompanied by Anthony.

Sancho had not expected that. It was a complete surprise to him. He saw in Anthony not only an enemy of his master, the bastard son of the wife who had betrayed her husband, but also the destroyer of his own offspring, the late lamented "Kitten." The hard-bitten old tom cat's hair rose at the sight of Anthony riding towards Madrid in the luxuriant coach of Ouvrard, while his own son and his master's long-cherished vehicle kept each other dizzy company in some whirlpool at the bottom of an Alpine gorge.

At a discreet distance behind he had trailed Anthony from Paris. The delay at Bayonne had served to wear out what little patience and restraint he may have had. He sat brooding for days in a dark hole nourishing his implacability. The second delay at Burgos had done the trick.

Sancho there persuaded himself that he would be doing both his master and himself an excellent turn by knocking the passengers of the coach on the head before they reached Madrid to make further trouble. He felt that his arrival with so fine an empty vehicle to take the place of the one he knew Don Luis still grieved for might go far towards explaining the mysterious disappearance of its former owner. As for Anthony, he expected his own reward there, and no questions at all from Don Luis, perhaps even a pat on the head.

So he departed from Burgos a day before the coach, knowing that it would soon follow, to arrange a royal welcome for it with some cloaked gentlemen of leisure not averse to being paid in advance to plunder. They lay in wait not far from a convenient spot where the camino real entered a defile in the desolate hills north of Madrid. Sancho himself, out of a delicate hesitation to involve his master, remained at a convenient hamlet near by.

All did not go as smoothly as might have been expected. It was true that the coach was handed over to Sancho about dawn one morning without his asking any questions and with no one but the mules as witnesses of what had taken place. But a great deal had evidently taken place. The noble caballeros who had engaged in the adventure of the night before seemed to have been overtaken by a pack of wolves. One of their gallant company was missing, and the rest could only be described as "all chewed up." Only the large sum in gold which they had found in Ouvrard's strong box could begin to console them for the united loss of an ear, a kneecap, several fingers, and various convenient if not essential muscles amongst them. Sancho's failure to mention the presence of Simba was commented upon with a wealth of simile that exhausted the animal kingdom and the calendar of the saints.

"Go, and the devil go with you," they said, and slunk home still grey in the face.

Alone in the box, save for Juan's guitar which had been overlooked and was still strapped to the iron railing, Sancho drove down the road toward Madrid in the greying darkness. It was no help as the light grew brighter to see that the guitar and its ribbons were splashed with blood. He wiped this off with his head-kerchief and throwing it on the road drove on at a headlong pace.

But he was still some miles out of the city when the dog overtook him. He came out of the darkness behind and followed silently for some miles. Then he began to give tongue.

The little cat-man on the box shivered. He lost his hat. The dog picked it up and trotted along beside him looking up at him. He was evidently judging the distance for a leap. Sancho lost his head. He lashed at Simba with the whip. The hound dropped the hat and began with a devilish cunning to stampede the mules.

He took an unholy joy in it. He nipped them when they lagged. The sound of his furious baying, the rumble of the black coach, dim in rolling clouds of dust, roused successive hamlets that morning and died away down the road toward the city. The rumour spread that Satan had been caught out after cock-crow and was fleeing back to hell carrying a shrieking soul along with him.

Be that as it may, at half past six in the morning ten foundered mules staggered through the Puerta de Hierro with an hysterical little coachman on the box who begged for an armed escort to take him to his master.

Nor did this appear such a joke to the guard a few minutes later when a lion-like apparition with a voice like a cathedral bell stripped the leather breeches off a horrified sergeant and rushed past the paralysed sentries with nothing but a bayonet scratch to show for it.

Sancho got his escort but they rode in the coach. The reign of terror in the streets had already started.

"You fool," bellowed Don Luis beside himself with rage when he at last understood Sancho's story. "And you bring ten mules and a bloody coach into my courtyard so the crime will come home to me! Christ deliver me from thee. Get out of my sight."

But a few days' cogitation and a talk with Faith put another aspect on the matter. Don Luis decided the best way to do was to brazen it out. He would treat the coach as his own, and drive about in it. No questions as to whose it was would then arise. He was considerably amazed to discover that Faith had tears in her eyes. "For the boy she had nursed," she said. Well, it was a natural explanation. He called Sancho and punished him by making him drive about while the dog was still loose in the streets. Nothing happened. The regiment on guard was changed, and the incident forgotten.

Don Luis was not superstitious, far from it. But under the circumstances it was only natural that he should have felt his heart flutter for the first time in his life as he came out of the door that morning and met Anthony. He was getting to be an old man.

That was one reason he had decided to compromise with fate in the form of Anthony.

But there was still the coach and M. Ouvrard. Don Luis now felt badly in need of a magnificent lie. Something that would out-Spanish a French banker.

At last a splendid idea occurred to him. He chuckled over it. He felt relieved at having the vendetta of a lifetime settled at last, and arrived home in high spirits. He called Sancho an amateur murderer, and cackled with Faith over the dinner table about her going to court. There was only one fly in the ointment.

Since M. Ouvrard was still in the flesh, perhaps he himself would not find it necessary to go to Mexico. The Frenchman could be trusted to see that the bullion was actually shipped. Everything depended on that. Well, let Don Manuel make out his credentials to the viceroy at Mexico. He could simply stick them in his pocket and stay in Madrid. At his age that would probably be the wisest thing to do. He drank his Canary a little thoughtfully, however.

Anthony had no idea that he would remain seven months in Madrid. Yet until the last few weeks before his departure for New Orleans the time passed rapidly enough. At first there was a large number of people to be interviewed with Ouvrard who, as soon as his plan had been officially accepted, set up shop.

The banker's scheme was vast but in its main outlines a simple one. The Spanish government was bankrupt, due to the failure of the treasure fleet to arrive from the colonies and an archaic system of farming the domestic revenues. And there was also a condition of famine with all of the usual attendant unrest.

Ouvrard offered a loan, which he had arranged for at Amsterdam the year before, sufficient to tide the government over its immediate crisis. He offered to ship into Spain, from the huge reserves that Napoleon had permitted him to accumulate in France, wheat in abundance and at a reasonable price. All that he asked for security was a blanket assignment on the then purely hypothetical revenues of the kingdom in the form of sight drafts dated six months in advance on the royal treasury for the principal and interest due him. He had only two modest stipulations to make; that he was to be permitted to have an adequate supervisory control over the collection and disbursement of government revenue as long as the crown was indebted to him, and that all loans for a period of some years should be negotiated through him alone.

All this seemed too good to be true—and in the end it was. But to the Prince of the Peace and the harassed crown ministers in the early winter of 1802, J. G. Ouvrard, and his obliging assistant Señor Adverso, seemed to have stepped out of the diligence in Madrid like gods from the machine.

Within a month after their arrival the treasury found itself bursting with cash. Wheat was flowing in from Marseilles by the shipload and the price of bread lower than it had ever been. Surprised garrisons guzzling their back pay and wolfing their rations had nothing to grumble about but new shoes. His Majesty was enabled to slaughter three hundred seventy deer with the help of two field pieces and seven hundred horsemen. Her Majesty and her ladies appeared again in new gowns and real jewels. The voice of Don Manuel Godoy's guitar was once more golden—for it was through the Prince of the Peace that Ouvrard made most of his "arrangements." To make happiness happier, when the first loan showed signs of exhaustion it was given a new lease of life by another advance.

Who now so popular as M. Ouvrard? He was received at court and by the nobility. He was blessed in the streets by the populace and followed about. And all those connected with him shared in his popularity. He was always a very busy man and so was his secretary. They set up shop for a while at the French embassy. And then, in order to salve national sensitivity and suspicion, Ouvrard moved to the ground floor of the Palace of the Prince of the Peace.

The staff of this modest little bureau, called the "Office for the Consolidation of Foreign Loans," in reality controlled the government and destinies of Spain.

Ouvrard seldom appeared there. He left the direction of its affairs to Anthony who had for his assistants several discreet French and Spanish clerks whose mouths were closed by magnificent salaries always paid. Most of the work consisted in reorganizing the machinery for collecting and disbursing taxes by gradually appointing foreigners to various key posts; Frenchmen whenever possible, or those known to be reliable and favourable to Ouvrard's policy. Careful accounts in double entry were kept with a rough trial balance struck at the end of each day. For the first time in history it was possible to say just how much Spain, and M. Ouvrard, were worth. There was a constantly growing volume of correspondence between Ouvrard and Paris; with bankers in Holland; with French grain dealers and merchants all over the world; with the Spanish authorities at home and in the colonies.

Every effort was now made to ship all the bullion and colonial produce possible through the British blockade by the employment of neutrals. In particular every pressure was put on the Barings in London and the Hopes at Amsterdam to hasten the organization of the mercantile machinery being organized in America by Parish. The whole success of the scheme in Spain was dependent upon the success of Parish in the United States. If the funds lying dormant in Mexico could not be transferred to Europe either in the form of bullion or negotiable goods to establish credits, Ouvrard was done, the bubble would burst.

He had about two years to go. Then the loans which had been made by the bankers in Holland to the Spanish government would be called. With this money he had started the boom in Spain, financed the government, and purchased French wheat. All that must be repaid out of Mexican silver, since the domestic revenues of Spain were not sufficient to meet this charge and the demands of the French treasury for the stipulated subsidy at the same time.

It was a great gamble with the American ramifications becoming more and more important as time went on.

Ouvrard, however, was not satisfied with merely making a great profit on wheat and government contracts; with his commissions on loans; with having the operations of the Spanish treasury concentrated in his hands as a monopoly. He went on expanding and obtained licenses in unlimited numbers for trade with the Spanish colonies. These permits he peddled about Europe to various merchants, stipulating in each case for a percentage of the profit for himself and the Spanish government. These operations combined in 1805 in the firm of *His Catholic Majesty Chas. IV, J. G. Ouvrard, and Company.*

The banker finally moved to the Escurial and directed his affairs from the palace of the kings of Spain.

Then Napoleon sent for him to Paris. He disgraced him and mulcted him. M. Ouvrard's trading operations and the emperor's European system had come into hopeless conflict. But Napoleon retained the grasp on the Spanish treasury and fiscal administration which Ouvrard had built up. It was the entering wedge. The entire royal family and Godoy were next taken over and imprisoned in France. Then followed the French columns, the occupation of the country, and King Joseph Bonaparte at Madrid.

But all that was in the future. Success and inflation were now in the air. Ouvrard was in his element. Life was so interesting and real for the banker, he had again become the financier so successfully, that the other fellow under his hat who was so interested in shoes could only roll his eyes occasionally. He grew fatter and dressed more gorgeously. He kept driving about from Madrid to San Ildefonso when the king was there; from San Ildefonso to the Escurial, where the queen for the most part stayed; from the French embassy to the palace of Buena Vista, where Godoy held court on an equally royal and more prodigal scale. There were innumerable people of position to be seen and interviewed in order to secure their influence.

"It is true," said Ouvrard, "that we shall consolidate our position in Spain"—and without warning he would pick up Anthony at the Bureau of Consolidation and drive anywhere.

Thus amid accounts, letters, interviews, calls, court functions, and long secret conferences at the French embassy, where Beurnonville, the new French ambassador, Don Luis, Ouvrard, and sometimes Godoy, and Cabarrus, the agent for the Spanish treasury, frequently met—Anthony's winter in Madrid was a hectic one.

Afterwards he could recall very little of the intricate negotiations, the conflict of personalities and interests, the infinitely complex web which Ouvrard spun until he was enclosed in it himself along with the flies he lured. And he doubted whether anyone else could follow it, or understand it, or remember it for long.

To take his own mind off it for a few hours in order to enjoy life was to feel all of its gossamers slipping out of his brain and to look back upon the whole scheme as a dusty cobweb hanging in some dark garret of the mind.

Those who got anything out of the negotiations, he observed, kept their minds fixed on a few primitive factors—and withdrew in safety with several chests of a positive material-something, a profitable concession, or a definite bribe.   He pondered this and began to turn over the routine at the bureau to the clerks and to the chief agent sent on from Paris, one Maurice Dreyfus, who was deep in the confidence of M. Beurnonville and interested in nothing but finance.

Anthony did not intend to permit Ouvrard to prevent his going to America.   He kept that thoroughly in mind.   He was not going to be a fly in the web left buzzing over papers.   Still he made the most out of going about with Ouvrard into high and curious places while he waited impatiently for news from Parish that he had perfected his arrangements and that it was time to take up work at New Orleans.

Once relieved of the technical nonsense of accounts and secret correspondence at the bureau, of the immense flubdubbery of finance and merchandising-politics attempting to deal with life on the basis of the mathematics of things, Anthony's senses began to become vivid again, since he began to give play to his emotions once more.   The streets of Madrid no longer looked white and unreal to him when he went out.

He began to feel the life in them.   He experienced it in its own terms of feeling.   His brain was no longer bled white as it had been when he emerged from the Bureau of Consolidation after having maintained a fixed state of mind from morning till night.

"No wonder those who live that way eventually become interested— well, in shoes, let us say.   One cannot always be nothing but your esteemed correspondent, or the causer of additions in books, without having an immense wealth of feeling left over to lavish upon something."   He laughed as spring began to return, as the dry winter winds that swept the streets of the capital began to grow mild and a little humid, when the smell of wood smoke began to be replaced by that of early flowers hawked through the streets and piled in great bunches about the approaches to the Puerta del Sol.   Who could pass them by, or their girl vendors in short skirts and brilliant bodices, looking back over their shoulder—a high comb, a short, impudent puff of a cigarette, a gleaming smile?   Not Anthony.   One must at least buy an early rose.   "There are tides in the affairs of man as well as in those of finance," thought Anthony and purchased a few early roses. One could rise even from the ashes of dead fires, he discovered, surrounded by pleasant little flames that warmed but did not burn.

"So!" said Ouvrard, "you are *not* going to stay here in Spain as my agent and conduct the bureau for me?   After all this you are going to New Orleans?   And so you make the most of it here, eh?   Ah, I can see that."

He tried to look disappointed and angry but he only succeeded in looking envious.   He even had to laugh when he was punched in the ribs in a familiar way.   He liked to be with Anthony.   In his company it seemed to the older man that it was really worth while being rich, that life was worth trying to buy.

The Manzanares had its brief flood and poured roaring under the great bridge. The days grew warmer, hot. M. Dreyfus at the Bureau of Consolidation settled his square-rimmed spectacles on his more than Roman nose and complained of the antiquated formula which M. Adverse had used for figuring interest on national debts.

Anthony and M. Ouvrard drove out through gales of spring flowers to the court at San Ildefonso.

Out of a welter of recollections of Spain and Madrid a few memories always remained clearly with Anthony. There were of course innumerable bullfights. To be precise, seventeen in all. For the return of prosperity brought with it a consequent lavish outlay on the part of the authorities, and the populace craved not only bread but bulls. From a state of thrilled-fascination his progress to satiety at these spectacles was a rapid one.

The slaughter that season was unusually comprehensive. Maddened animals, wreathed in smoke and a necklace of firecracker banderillas exploding in the flesh of their necks, charged and galloped, bellowed and died tamely or magnificently, while los aficionados went through a succession of splendid frenzies. But whether the bull expired buen estoque or by the media luna, the end was always the same.

Ouvrard sickened a little on these occasions. The spectacle of wornout and blinded horses treading in their own bowels or dragging their glistening, liver-coloured guts behind them for yards was always to him overpowering. He complained of the stench. Yet it was necessary to go if one was to be thought of as "the friend of Spain." The seething colour and frenzy of the multitude in the great ring remained with Anthony. He took to watching the faces about him as being even more enthralling than the spectacle in the arena. His composite memory of them was that of the expression of Spain.

He came to the conclusion that it was difficult, if not impossible, for a foreigner to understand what the bullfight was about. That it satisfied a deep craving of the Spanish nervous system there could be no doubt. Mere enjoyment of suffering as an explanation; the usual complaints of cruelty indulged in by aliens were, he was sure, superficial and beside the mark. They were too easy. For there was some deep expression of the meaning of life in this ritualistic spectacle. It was drama, a tragedy in which the heroism, danger, and chance were real even if the setting was artificial. It was the nearest approach to reality that a theatre could make. It seemed to him to be an expression of the triumph of the spirit of the people over the land, over the climate, over the aridity and barrenness of the landscape and the rigid social and class conventions in which the Spanish nature dwelt.

Spain was ancient. It impressed him as being antique. The hand of the past lay heavily upon it. There was a certain overpowering monotony in its landscapes and sunlight. Its life moved slowly and languidly with a dolce far niente. It was true that a curious hint of northern Africa, like the promise of a far distant and yet inevitable doom, was reflected from its skies, as though they remirrored the brazen Saharan lights into the north with a prophetic glance. And such things are what colour a people's soul as they live out their planetary destiny. One could not imagine too much, however. There was also diversity, there was brilliance, a flaunting of colour in buildings and costume, a hint of passion and intensity in the swish of skirts, in the swagger of caballeros, in the little boys playing el toro, always playing el toro, violently. But all these passionate things were seen by contrast. They had about them the aspect of a protest against something grim and Baal-like, something implacable in the land itself that even in the cities was never far withdrawn. And then——

Suddenly, out of all this welled up in a reassertion of unexhausted and undaunted energy the seething and frenzied spectacle of the bullfight.

In the bullring the Spanish people became united. All classes and distinctions fused into one passionate entity. On the sullen forehead of the bull was laid all that was Baal-like and implacable. He stood there staring at Spaniards, black, horned, bovine, the obstinate and ferocious emanation of the land. And the Spanish people in the persons of their gaudy and brave matadors, the beribboned cavaleres of Spain, played with him; ever holding him in fear and admiration, but having their revenge and torturing him amid the flapping of cloaks, the glitter of swords and the galloping of horses. And then they finished him off, they triumphed over that old bellowing el toro with punctilio and ritual. The short sword of Spain went down between his horns and into his heart.

Yes, one could scarcely doubt this feeling. El toro was a sacrificial victim, he was dragged off in triumph. And when he was driven down from the hills in droves, before he went into the arena, those who could not even afford tickets for the ring to see him die waited with knobbed sticks along the streets to whack him as he went past in clouds of dust.

It was religion, this merry hatred of bulls. It welled up from something deep in the feelings of Spain. Spaniards who felt it did not need to understand it or to have it explained. It was in their blood.

In the patio below his window at the Casa de los Baños Anthony

watched the gamins playing el toro. One afternoon the game became
unusually boisterous and realistic. A number of lounging, adult figures wrapped in capas condescended to stop and watch so well-acted
a mock spectacle. The boy who was being baited made an excellent
bull. The sport became fast and furious. At a given instant the
children's imaginations fused and the game became real. Hysterical
urchins closed in from all sides and began to kill the "bull." The
clamour was shrill and fearful. Simba rose on his chain and bayed
at the other end of the court.

By the time he reached the patio Anthony found that some of the
men standing about had already interfered. And apparently none too
soon. Young señor Toro stood bleeding and battered, his clothes in
fragments; swollen and trembling with the lust of battle and excitement. He had a deep gash in his scalp and the blood trickled into his
eyes. But he was not surprised nor frightened. He stood there
bullet-headed and proud with the men who had dragged him from
sacrifice laughing at him.

"So they were going to kill thee, little bullkin," said one.

"Sí, señor," replied the lad, draping the remnant of his rags about
him grandly. "I was the bull." And he limped out as if it were the
most natural thing in the world that he should be butchered.

Whoever the god that lived in Spain before Christ and Mohammed
came, he had almost received a human sacrifice that day.

Anthony decided that this game of el toro was a Spanish religion
he could not participate in to the full. And he was glad of that.
Still one did not go to the bullfight just to be sorry for the horses, like
Arabella Hookham Frere, the sister of the British envoy. Decidedly
there was more to it than that.

In April the entire court moved to Madrid to celebrate the Infanta
Maria Isabel's first communion. Afterward there was a great state
dinner at the palace. Anthony had reasons for always remembering
it, although it was an accident that he went and sat where he did.

Beurnonville and Ouvrard had indulged themselves beyond measure
at the opening the night before of a new French pâtisserie in the Car-
rera de S. Jerónimo where the tarts were full of invention, genius,
and apricot jam. On the way home they had stopped to drink bottled
beer and lemon juice, much admired in Madrid.

The ambassador of France and the envoy of Mammon were soon
laid prostrate in adjacent beds at the French embassy. A sudden use
was found for large Sèvres vases that had hitherto merely adorned
the hall. A state banquet was now unthinkable. So they were rep-

resented respectively by the chargé d'affaires, de Calincourt, and Anthony, both scandalously gay at the misfortune of their superiors and their own good luck.

"Let us arrive in the state coach," said young de Calincourt. And they did so, with the precedence of the ambassador, while the Flemish company of the Garde de Corps in their facings of yellow-and-silver on duty in the courtyard came to "present" to the arms of France.

"The madrileños call those soldiers chocolateros," remarked the young Frenchman in rather too loud a voice as they emerged between a wall of lackeys.

Don Tomás de Iraqui, colonel of the regiment of Pavia, immediately came forward twirling his blue-black moustache and scowling. "Permit me, my dear colonel, to congratulate you on the martial appearance of your men," added the young chargé d'affaires hastily. The colonel broke into a blue-black smile under his brass helmet as they passed on.

"Phew!" said de Calincourt, "a close call. That fellow is the devil with pistols."

They crossed the court in the red glare of torches escorted by liveried link-boys. Behind them the heavy coaches of the ambassadors continued to arrive to a continual clash of arms. The rumble of wheels, the voices of men and the low laughter of women were lost in the vague echoes of the vast court. Before them the great palace glowed from one wing to the other with soft, yellow lights and the glitter of crystal chandeliers behind lace curtains in the still unfinished square windows. Above the glazed balcony and between the arches heavy statues of the Iberian Roman emperors looked down from dark niches, while overhead on the balustrade of the flat roof a company of the kings of Spain advanced with stony faces glittering in the moonlight. It was the quality of this façade to make one pause to look up and then hurry past it into the portals.

They ascended the famous state staircase between the marble lions. Lackeys in the livery of Castile, like so many coloured statues, held flaming flambeaus on every fourth step with halberdiers between them who struck the butts of their halberds in salutation on the stone.

As it was half past six, and the guests were arriving rapidly, a continual thumping swept them upward through the whirling flames of the flambeaus to where the bewigged statue of Charles III grinned at them with his baboon-like face at the top. Here they were met by the Duque del Parque, commander of the Royal Guard, glittering in a gold-inlay cuirass and a helmet bursting into a gigantic white plumed crest. He inquired their names and rank and passed them on to the ushers.

" 'All this will end in a clap of thunder,' says the first consul," whispered the irrepressible de Calincourt as they were led through an endless range of enormous state apartments with ceilings a riot of Tiepolo's tepid frescoes; with velvet, glasses, tapestry, gold-tasselled furniture, and lace. Hundreds of grim portraits glared at them and seemed to march with them down walls lined by stiff guards in jack-boots and scarlet-and-blue.

"Here is nothing amusing, all is truly royal," the Frenchman continued as they walked suddenly out of comparative gloom into the glare of the Salón de los Embajadores with two empty and lonely thrones under a canopy at the far end.

The number of guests invited was upwards of three hundred; dignitaries, the diplomatic corps, nobility, and distinguished persons. They assembled rapidly but they seemed to make no impression on the vast room. There was not a single note of gayety or happiness. Conversation went on here and there in low tones if not in whispers. Underneath the oppressive ceiling, where the majesty of Spain, the virtues of dead kings, and the costumes of the provinces flaunted heavily, sublimes rasgos de sublimes ingenios, the company sat weighed down, lost amidst colossal pier glasses and gigantic marble tables; pale under mountainous portières of crimson and purple velvets.

"Apollo himself would be a mere glow-worm here," acknowledged de Calincourt, impressed at last.

It was no small test of the amazing virility and physical brilliance of Don Manuel Godoy that he appeared to shine and glitter even in these overpowering surroundings. His arrival, indeed, served to inject positive signs of life into what had promised to be a decidedly leaden occasion. Despite the almost frantic efforts of several Bourbon sovereigns, who had imported from France the traditions of gayety, the Spanish court had never ceased to retain a certain funereal air. Godoy could by some personal magic dispel this.

Into the dark, straight tunnel of the lives of the royal family, which had as its most gorgeous vista the candles of requiem mass in the mortuary chapel at the Escurial, Godoy came like a ray of sunshine dancing with all the colours of the rainbow along their cavern path. This sunny quality of his nature and a certain dog-like fidelity, a warm, human tenderness and affection had endeared him to both king and queen. They could both afford to overlook his amatory irregularities, they felt, at the price of retaining through life, in the case of the king an unswerving personal friend, and on the part of the queen a lover, who, if he sometimes wandered, always returned. It was a curious and a complicated relationship but it stood the test of tragic circumstances and the long lapse of time.

It was this man, who at the height of his success and favour now entered the room where the subdued guests of the court were apathetically waiting for the sovereigns to appear. Contrary to all etiquette, he was leading the youngest son of the queen, the Infante Don Francisco de Paula, by the hand. A veritable rush now took place in his direction, for no matter how much he was envied and hated he was also fawned upon by all those who had anything to obtain by his favour. And nearly everyone from ambassadors to country grandees had something to obtain.

Some crowded about the little prince, by far the most jovial of the royal family, and listened to his childish wit and gayety, which had already endeared him to the court. This they knew would recommend them to Godoy even more than direct flattery, for he was passionately attached to the brown-eyed little prince whose father he was said to be. In the meanwhile Godoy conversed gayly with all who approached him, from time to time making an anxious survey of the apartment as if he were looking for someone who was expected but had not yet arrived.

Young Don Francisco, skipping across the room through the wilderness of gigantic chairs and tables, jauntily commanded the musicians to strike up. This they hesitated to do before the sovereigns had appeared, but they were also embarrassed to refuse "His Highness," who, just tall enough to peer over the top of a balustrade, menaced the first-violin with his royal wrath. They compromised, and a much subdued pianissimo of wood instruments began to breathe through the vast apartment the "Woodland Moments" of Beccherini.

The atmosphere immediately cleared. A great many people were soon on their feet moving about. The giant chairs seemed to disgorge the company from their maws. The sound of light chatter, an occasional laugh with an undertone of reserved masculine voices, and ringing sallies in the high, clear voice of young Don Francisco marked the turning point of the evening.

While Don Juan Antonio Melón, the king's chamberlain, moved about distributing the cards of precedence with names of the ladies that gentlemen were to take in to dinner and the precise order of the procession and seats at table written upon them, the empty thrones at the far end of the room seemed to have withdrawn even farther into solitude and aloof disdain.

Anthony found himself pledged for the evening to the dowager Countess of Montarco, a raw-boned widow, whom he thought Don Juan took a certain malicious punctilio in pointing out seated under a Gargantuan purple curtain on a green chair. This combination not even her liberal rouge, diamonds, rice powder, and the stiff brocaded dress and whalebones of the previous reign could entirely overcome.

"Jésus!" whispered de Calincourt, who had drawn Mlle. Zinoviev, the ravishing young daughter of the Russian ambassador, and was looking over Anthony's shoulder at his companion's fate, "my hearty commiseration. But she is very pious, they say."

An hysterical yodel on a flute, representing an Italian composer's idea of a nightingale luring his mate by moonlight, made the moment none the easier to bear. It looked like a terrible evening. This was the court of Spain and etiquette had spoken. Yet Anthony could not bring himself to bow before the old harpy under the portière. He looked about him in despair.

There were plenty of young and beautiful women in the room. That one, for instance, talking to John Hookham Frere. Her back was so perfect in that long white gown and her golden hair in a little Grecian knot was reflected so delightfully in the pier glass that one did not even need to wait to see her face hidden just then by the ample shoulders of Albion's statesman. She tapped Frere on the shoulder with a fan and he moved away laughing. Anthony drew in his breath —and held it.

It was Dolores who had been in eclipse.

The lights in the room seemed to eddy . . . he saw clearly again.

Since his arrival in Madrid he had scarcely thought of Dolores. He had not even inquired. After Angela the world had seemed denuded of possible mates. Rose girls—they sold flowers for the buttonhole—no more. And now—now he was about to conduct the horse-faced relict of Don Quixote in to dinner. Intolerable.

"Never! Something *must* be done about it."

A lackey approached him. "Señor, His Highness has been trying to get your attention for some time."

He looked up startled. Godoy was undoubtedly looking his way anxiously and nodding. Anthony crossed the room rapidly to where he was standing somewhat apart from the crowd talking to Don Luis. A Milanese suit of mail with its visor down on a stand just behind them gaped open-mouthed over their heads.

"Where is M. Ouvrard, Don Antonio?" inquired Godoy anxiously. "Several matters have arisen which I hope to discuss with him tonight."

Anthony explained the banker's condition so vividly as to cause even Don Luis to smile.

"Most unfortunate," said Godoy, "but you can probably tell me! Have the pay chests for the dockyards at Cadiz left yet?"

"His Highness as Grand Admiral of Spain is naturally solicitous for the payment of our loyal mariners," said Don Luis with a grimace. "His zeal does him great credit," he remarked as he bowed and withdrew. An angry flush rose in Godoy's cheeks.

"They leave Wednesday. Do you wish them delayed?"

"Ah, you anticipate me, Don Antonio. It would be most kind of you to request M. Ouvrard to do so. Another, a more pressing need for the money has arisen here at Madrid. The queen—" he stopped for a moment—"Her Majesty has decided to refurnish her equipages —new horses. *Devil take that old man!*" His resentment against Don Luis suddenly flamed out. "To tell you the truth he is most exasperating. Er—no, you will not say anything, I know. You have been most discreet since you have been here. I observe you do not even ask for anything. Others are not so. I have done much for Don Luis." He drew Anthony into a window-niche and continued rapidly.

"I want you to do something for me, Señor Adverse, a personal favour. You will not regret it! Some time ago Don Luis had me obtain for him special letters to the viceroy in Mexico, commissioning him to expedite the silver shipments from there. Tonight he coolly informs me that *he* has decided it is unnecessary for him to go." Godoy grew livid as he said this and paused.

"I am sure we should not want his interference at Mexico," replied Anthony instantly on his guard. "We have already our own agent at Vera Cruz, you may recall."

"True, I realize that. Our arrangements have altered since the commission was granted. But, I shall be frank with you. *I* wish to have Don Luis go to Mexico."

Anthony started. "It might ruin us," he began.

Godoy laid his hand on his arm. "Don't you see the old man has built his own trap? If M. Ouvrard will only suggest to His Majesty that the services of Don Luis will be *required* in Mexico—"

"But—" objected Anthony.

"Why, then," continued Godoy, "I will simply have the instructions to the viceroy in regard to his mission slightly altered. He can be sent into the northern provinces of New Spain to expedite the flow of silver from the mines. Oh, I shall do his rank and ability full justice! He shall go as governor of the most distant desert province in the north. Of course, I forget its name. Santa Fé, isn't it?"

"I am sure I can't enlighten Your Highness," replied Anthony pondering.

"Well, there are maps, fortunately," sighed Godoy, "large ones with very small towns on them. Now you will speak to M. Ouvrard about both these matters, won't you?"

"I shall speak to him tomorrow," said Anthony, "It is most necessary he should know."

"Bueno!" exclaimed the Prince of the Peace. "Recollect we are dealing with a dangerous old man."

"I am well aware of that," said Anthony with conviction; "but there is a little matter in which I wish Your Highness would aid *me* tonight."

"So?" said Godoy.

"I have been placed at table with the lovely countess yonder—" cried Anthony, pointing out the old woman across the room.

"Ah, she should have a parrot perched upon her shoulder," grunted Godoy.

"—and I wish," he continued, "above all things to sit next to that lady over there."

The sleek, black eyebrows of the Prince of the Peace, which lay across his brows like two smooth, fat leeches, crinkled slightly and then lay still again as if they had resettled to their congenial task.

"Doña Dolores de Almanara, eh! Well, your taste does you credit, señor. But I warn you. Her husband is a rich old Mexican hidalgo whose jealousy is as deep and dark as his mines. And the lady is rumoured to be cold."

"I had the honour of her acquaintance some years ago in Cuba. The rumour is not well founded."

Godoy laughed. "I will do what I can for you," he said. "Let me see. Go and fetch the roll of precedence for me from the chamberlain," he said to a servant to whom he beckoned. "Peste!" he cried a few minutes later. "Don Melón is bringing it himself."

"I merely wished to remind myself of some of the names from the Russian embassy, Don Juan," roared Godoy, running his eye down the lists.

"Most difficult," squawked the old man who was quite deaf and thought everyone else was, too. He pulled Godoy down to him confidentially. "Barbarous!" he cackled into his ear, "but all spelled correctly, every one correctly." He went off tapping the paper with a knowing air.

Godoy and the Russian ambassador exchanged a wink. He then turned to Anthony.

"It is impossible to change the rolls, señor. Once the order of precedence is settled only a revolution can alter it. But the gentleman who is to sit with Doña Dolores is standing over there." He pointed out a tall, cadaverous young man. "He is the Count Lancaster of Portugal. There is royal blood in his veins, so ancient that even the English have forgotten it. His tastes are expensive and his barren estates covered by thin sheep. He might be willing to exchange cards. Well, I shall do all I can for you. I will introduce you myself." He sent for the man.

"Everything at the court of Spain can be bought except the crown jewels," murmured Godoy as the count approached, "and they are at present in pawn. It would be most embarrassing if Their Majesties should have to conduct the next audience in dull pastes. I trust you will endeavour to delay those pay chests, Don Antonio."

"I shall speak to M. Ouvrard," repeated Anthony.

"This gentleman has a gallant request to make of you," said Godoy to the count as he presented him to Anthony, "which I shall esteem it a favour to have you consider." With a brief inclination he left them alone. . . . .

"Your proposal is to say the least rather unusual," said the Portuguese, his dark face showing no signs of relaxing in hauteur. "The privileges of birth are valuable, especially if one does not happen to possess them," he added condescendingly.

"And even if one does they may be valuable," countered Anthony. The man shrugged his shoulders.

"I am prepared, señor, to bet a thousand dollars on the turn of our dinner cards that you think they are worth no less."

"I *have* gambled," confessed the count smiling, "but always for high stakes. May I ask you to point out the lady whom you wish to bet I will sit with?"

With great misgivings Anthony pointed her out.

"Corpo de Bacco," cried the count. "It is the angel of constipation herself!"

"Two thousand!" murmured Anthony, prepared to bid his entire fortune by millenary units. "Paid tomorrow in new-minted coins."

A gleam as if from bright reflecting metal appeared upon the countly forehead. "Señor," said he, "your princely offer does adequate homage to my rank."

They laughed and exchanged their seating cards.

With a feeling akin to the anticipation of a crisis Anthony left the empty suit of armour gaping by the wall and went to find Dolores.

She saw him coming toward her half-way across the room. Her eyes widened and her hands for an instant fell into her lap and lay there. Then, with that familiar gesture that he remembered so well, she reached up as if to arrange flowers in her hair. It was the ivory comb that he had sent her from Africa which she was wearing. She settled it a little more firmly. And then, moving her fan slowly, waited calmly enough.

And so he knew that she had not forgotten him.

Whether Dolores' husband was of as jealous a nature as Godoy had indicated, Anthony never discovered. He had only time to present himself with the usual compliments and to watch the white-haired Don Guillermo limping off to find his own table-companion as hastily as his old legs would let him. Then the doors at the far end of the room were suddenly thrown open and a master of ceremonies carrying a black wand announced, "His Majesty, the King of Spain." A white wand next announced the queen from the opposite doorway, and the entire company rose to their feet and crowded forward to be able to see and make their bow when the sovereigns should appear.

First there came walking backward out of the king's corridor the Duque de Bejar, an emaciated grandee with spidery legs. He was clad in bright yellow silk and held aloft with a trembling arm a heavy, silver candelabrum whose candles guttered in the draught. He heeled outward and hindward as if making geometrical leeway, covering a remarkable stretch at each backward step.

Immediately afterward there appeared in the arch against the glow of flambeaus behind him a tall, thin man with fine silver hair and a curved nose that projected over his chin. He had remarkable, childishly-blue eyes that matched the colour of his faded coat pulled down from one shoulder by the weight of the mighty gold and diamond star flashing and sparkling on his left breast. A tight, white vest laced with gold, crossed by a blue ribbon and buttoned with emeralds, seemed indispensable to prevent his chest, which had already slipped, from collapsing about his knees toward which it pendulously tended. He wore leather hunting breeches splashed with deer blood, which he was said never to have changed except for his coronation and marriage, white hose gartered with scarlet ribbons, and Cordovan shoes with red heels and gilt buckles. The most remarkable thing about him was his circular profile and the bland futility of his florid countenance frozen between affability and surprise. Charles IV of Spain walked eagerly. All in the room bowed low and the ladies swept him curtsies, to which he replied by a slight inclination from what had once been his waist.

The king took his place standing before the empty thrones and was followed across the floor by a detachment of halberdiers clad in yellow-and-scarlet silk who trod noiselessly and whose steel weapons glinted with bloody lights. They seemed a fitting prelude for the sinister figure which followed them.

Gloomy, pale with ennui, and with his hands blotched by futile chemical experiments, Ferdinand, Prince of the Asturias, followed his sire apathetically, dressed in dull green and indifference, haunted by his grinning tutor the Canon Escoiquiz and by Matias his valet and the slinking Moreno, an assistant barber, who had been given court rank and followed him like a cat. He bowed to the court unseeingly and stared at it with a fixed snapping-turtle expression to which his curled side-whiskers, his low beetling brow, his parrot-like nose and Austrian jaw protruding far beyond his upper lip combined in a startling effect of senseless ferocity. All the vices of the Bourbons and the wrong obstinacy of the Hapsburgs were stamped upon his features and lay dormant in his soul. He had the flushed cheeks of a tyrant when excited. He looked like Caracalla come back to trouble the world in knee-breeches and a mulberry-coloured stock.

The Prince of the Peace, the ministers Cabellos, Cabarrus, and Don Gaspar Melchior Jovellanos; the knights of the Golden Fleece, and the Order of Christ, having ranged themselves about the sovereign in an open circle glittering with orders—the queen at a given signal advanced.

To Anthony, unused to the bizarre whims of royalty, the guard of Her Majesty provided a shock.

She was announced by a pack of Spaniels whose long, shaggy, brown bodies with almost invisible feet dragged their lengths slowly out of the door before her and undulated over the green carpet like so many silky caterpillars crawling across a leaf. A dozen or more of these pop-eyed harbingers, which all seemed to be suffering from Graves' disease, always preceded her.

Queen Maria Luisa, slightly double-chinned with a fine dark down on her upper lip, dressed in the new Greek style but with diamond pendants in her tall wig, paused in the doorway with superb bare arms clasped with pearl bracelets locked with rubies, her ivory shoulders shining under the candles, and curtsied to her spouse.

A gasp of flattering but sincere admiration arose from the court. The eyes of Godoy sparkled. The queen was leading by the hand the Infanta Maria Isabel still in her communion costume of Mirandella lace so ancient that a golden-ivory glow tinted her wintry veils crowned with lilies and sparkling with frosty diamonds. Alone among the royal family she was wholly beautiful, arch, gracious, with exuberant colouring, a princess with a certain poetry in her glance, and a deer-like walk. At sight of her, in whose honour they had assembled, the ancient Catholic loyalty of Spain burst into a discreet enthusiasm of welcome and the rapid clicking and breezy opening of painted fans.

"The rest of the royal children are being put to sleep, I suppose," whispered Dolores, which were the first words he had heard from her. She was smiling a little sadly. "I envy the queen her beautiful daughter."

"Yes, but not I when I am looking at you—ma doña," he said, putting her gloved hand over his arm.

"Don't," she said. "We are only going in to dinner, you know. You must promise me not to forget that. Do you hear me?"

"Yes," he replied, "I think so." And to himself, "Do I hear you?

Am I really standing here with your arm, Dolores, on mine? 'What will I do in Europe?' "—he remembered asking himself that at Gallegos long ago. The thought of a naked orphan scuttling through a big iron gate at Livorno flitted before his eyes. And now—how that boy enjoyed dreaming he was in the palace of the King of Spain. In a moment it would all vanish. . . .

She looked up at him laughing, understanding his mood, and pressed his arm. "They will be going in in a moment now," she said. "I am glad . . ."

His Majesty, who always argued with his chief musician Olivieri, at last had done. The brassy "Royal March" of Jarnowick boomed out. Marshalled in perfect precedence, the procession set out led by the royal family and the halberdiers.

To Anthony, who now looked down at Dolores, with flushed cheeks and a mounting excitement and delight, the evening had already taken on that aspect of a gloriously-coloured opium dream, mad with light and splendour, which it never lost. He accepted it and doubted it at the same time as one of the supreme surprises of life that seemed too vivid to be true.

They moved through a succession of colossal corridors with groups of guards and domestics standing about lost in the perspective; with the gleam of steel and the intense scarlet of the robes of the papal nuncio Casoni burning on ahead of them; with the music growing fainter behind.

Past an endless succession of cabinet treasures and objects swept from the wealth of Europe and the Indies the glittering serpent of the procession dragged its length slowly.

"C"-shaped tables with the guests seated on the inner side surrounded the banquet hall facing the long, straight board of royalty and the ambassadors at the far end. Mersquitz, the queen's confessor, said grace assisted by two acolytes and an almoner. From the royal chapel farther down the corridor the scent of stale incense mingled with the fading sweetness of the pastoral lilies with which the tables were trimmed.

Into these unexpectedly complete and perfect hours which had been vouchsafed him, Anthony merged himself, forgetful of the past and the future, wholly content to be sitting next to Dolores and listening to her voice. And she also. Yet the intense and quiet joy of the man and woman who were meant for each other, who revelled alone together in an island of mutual consciousness amid the other feasters, was all the more poignant for their awareness of what was passing in the river of time.

All the dying order of the Old World surrounded them in its deathly-complete and uniformed ranks. Constellations of heavenly-named honours winked from the breasts of the exalted gentlemen to the crescents and jewelled comets caught in the cumulous clouds of ladies' hair.

Liveried servants were pouring vintages of the early years of the eighteenth century; years long vanished. The last cask would soon be broached, the last toast flung. Versailles the beautiful and perfect epitome of all this was dark and silent. The world had swept around it and gone on. "All this will end in a thunderclap." Only the calm before the storm surrounded the palace of the King of Spain, where the great company feasted while the mellow, saffron lights glowed from its windows like the dwindling radiance of a pharos that is being left behind. Without giving a thought to it, every feaster felt that he was rapidly floating away from it down the river of time. That feeling gave the zest and spirit of the occasion. It lent it its *carpe diem* and its hectic glitter; the "high" taste to meats that had been kept too long; its hysteria of loyalty for the feeble crown.

In the midst of this it was surprising for Anthony and Dolores to find without an effort an island of refuge in each other, a still and quiet section of eternity in time. Yet within it they lived more vividly than those without. It was quiet and still there only because it was nearer the whirling centre of things. No wonder that for a few moments they played, and played successfully, that they had always been together and would never part. "If it were only so," was the overtone in both their minds.

So it mattered very little what they said to each other.

Anthony found himself telling her of his wanderings and his hopes. He even spoke to her of Angela and the child he had left behind. And in a few words she understood.

"Do not doubt," she said, "go on. You have done well. I fail greatly, too." He long drew comfort from that.

They did not allude much to Cuba. All but the fact of their meeting there now seemed childish—the moonlight and the garden. They knew they had grown now into man and woman moving in strong sunlight and deep shadows; moving on into the afternoon of life with night ahead.

Her marriage had served to link enormous haciendas in Mexico. There were no children. Don Guillermo was old. A faint flush stole into her cheeks. After tonight Anthony must never try to see her again. Pastures must be kept welded to silver mines. Her life was lived for the peons on those estates. Much could be done for them and she was devoted to that. They would return to Mexico soon. She travelled great distances there, rode hundreds of leagues on horseback. Beyond El Paso del Norte was a great wind-swept country she loved.

They had a great house in the capital, a serene city, where Popocatapetl and the "Sleeping Woman" dreamed under blankets of snow in the soft sunsets and dawns. Names, places, a whole life and world he had never heard of flashed into hazy being mixed with strange glows and exotic colours while she spoke. Her husband was rich and powerful. His wife could be very useful to many. God had bound her to him. Yes—she was content.

A blast on a silver trumpet brought their world to an end. They plunged back into time. The company rose. The last toasts were drunk standing amid a wild enthusiasm of drawn swords. Castile and Aragon hailed their king.

"Viva el Rey . . . viva . . . viva . . . viva."

He saw her elderly husband come and lead her off. They bowed politely, distantly.

"Farewell, ma doña."

"Adiós, Don Antonio." She smiled over her shoulder.

Royalty left by a private passage and the guests streamed out to lose themselves in the vast, deserted apartments beyond.

He stood for a moment looking at the chair where she had sat.

"Has the señor lost anything?" said an officious lackey coming up.

"Sí."

The man began to look under the table. Anthony laughed and walked out. Under his feet he felt faint earthquake shocks. The organ in the chapel was rumbling. The king insisted upon requiem mass every night after midnight before he slept. Don Carlos himself frequently impersonated the corpse. The stones of the palace were trembling.

In the courtyard he met Don Luis. The old man was waiting for him excited about something.

Don Luis wished to make sure that Ouvrard would *not* suggest to the king the advisability of his going to Mexico. He would make good the matter of the coach with M. Ouvrard. It was not his fault that he had it. It was equally embarrassing to return it or to explain. Would Anthony smooth the way to an interview with Ouvrard? If so, Don Luis would be glad to tell Anthony certain matters of great interest concerning the past. That would explain everything. Don Luis wiped his brow.

"I shall speak to M. Ouvrard in any event," said Anthony.

"But not until you have seen me first, Don Antonio!" cried Don Luis. "It is something that concerns you vitally. You must hear it now. Come to me at the hour of the siesta, tomorrow. There will be none to disturb us then."

"Very well, I shall do so," said Anthony, after a little pause.

At that Don Luis took him by the arm and led him across the court. "Your promise brings a great calm to me," he said. "Old ghosts

must be laid. I wish to be haunted no longer. I am old. I shall
soon be joining them." He laughed languidly.

"Let us begin now," he added. *"Señor, I wish you to meet my
wife."*

Anthony turned, startled. They were standing by the coach under
the arches. From the window a white hand was extended to him.

"All that was a long time ago," said the voice of Faith Paleologus
out of the darkness. She spoke in English with her odd Scotch accent.

"Eh?" said Don Luis.

Her hand moved searching blindly. Anthony bent over it and
kissed it.

The great coach drove off into the night leaving him alone under
the stars.

_____

But the meeting between Anthony and Don Luis, in which Anthony
was to have learned "certain matters of great interest concerning the
past," never took place. The accounts of the good and evil of a lifetime cannot be balanced by explanations, and the books closed. The
balance is carried forward into other lives; into actions and reactions
until equilibrium results. Only time can liquidate in full. Don Luis'
offer had been made too late.

Madrid can be lonely, sultry and hot at the hour of the siesta. Its
vistas, especially in those quarters occupied by the houses of the
wealthy and powerful, are frequently silent and deserted. The inhabitants are only slumbering. Yet, except for the rumble of a distant
carriage or the sleepy whine of a beggar in some comfortable alcove,
the streets are as dead as those at Pompeii. The feet which traversed
them only a few hours before seem to have vanished and to be no more.

On the afternoon following the state dinner Anthony stood before
the gate of the Casa de Azuaga ready to keep his appointment with
Don Luis. He peered through the grille into the patio. There was
no one in sight.

The house was a little sinister. One of the oldest in Madrid, it
had been constructed at a time when defence could not entirely be
overlooked even in domestic architecture. There were heavy, iron
gratings, a frowning, blind façade, and a decidedly narrow gateway
calculated rather to prevent than to welcome ingress. In fact, the old
building vaguely reminded one of Don Luis himself. Although the
patio had been planted with trees and a formal garden laid out in it,
only a dim glimpse of greenery could be caught from the street through
the grim shadow of a tunnelled arch.

Anthony knocked. An echo answered. He tried again. There
was still no sign. He became impatient, for he had an appointment

with Ouvrard later and he had no doubt but that Don Luis would take his own time. At last he reached in, unlatched the gate with some difficulty, and walked into the patio.

After long thought the night before, he had arrived at the conclusion that he was no longer called upon to refuse to hear what Don Luis might have to say. He had kept his promise to John Bonnyfeather. The mystery of his birth, whatever it was, now concerned him and Don Luis alone. Don Luis would soon be dead, in the natural order of events, and he alone would be left to know—whatever there was to know. He could not even be sure that Don Luis could reveal the mystery of his origin. But he thought so. For a hundred reasons he felt sure of it. If Faith knew—he could not help that. So far as he was concerned he would continue to keep the secret safe from the world, if there was anything dishonourable in it. And—he seemed to see Faith's hand coming out of the darkness and to hear her saying, "All that was a long time ago."

There was nobody in the court. He started across the central path of the garden toward the door. Perhaps Don Luis himself was waiting for him there. A hedge momentarily cut off the view of the house. The path led to a central oval.

There was a new arbour here that had recently been planted about a formal fountain. A statue stood above a pool. He looked at it casually—and could scarcely prevent a loud cry of surprise. It must be the Other Bronze Boy, the missing twin. At least it must have been cast from the selfsame mould. This was not a mere resemblance.

And then—as he examined it more carefully—it was borne in upon him with irresistible conviction that it was actually his old companion of the convent pool, the Bronze Boy! If he knew anything in the world, he knew *him*. He knew his own brother!

There was the dimple in the left cheek, the mark of a stone he had once thrown at the Bronze Boy—a thousand years ago, it seemed now. It was the only thing Father Xavier had ever whipped him for. For a moment he felt himself wriggling on the knees of the priest again and shouting with pain. One did not forget things like that. Sacrilege!

If Don Luis had committed a personal assault upon him he could not have been more outraged than he was now. Indeed, that would have been only physical. But to have ravished this statue away from the fountain and the tree—that was to commit a spiritual nuisance in the holy place of his soul, to dissolve its bonds of permanence with the past. The refuge to which he had returned in dreams and reverie had been invaded and spoiled beyond repair.

It seemed horrible to him that the Bronze Boy was in the possession of the Old Man. He did not care to know how it had gotten here.

The fact, with all its overpowering emotional significance, its mysterious and sinister overtones, was more than he could bear.

He understood by the nervous shock with which he had blundered upon that part of himself held prisoner here what the nature of the influence of Don Luis and of Faith had been upon him. He apprehended it figuratively; with a mental nausea; with a blind fear of fate, and of the power over him which it implied.

No, he would never see Don Luis now. He could not even bear to think of it. There was something here which impelled him to flight; to go on forever thrusting off that influence; denying it, balking it. If the Bronze Boy were a prisoner, Anthony at least could still walk out of this garden free. He had better do so while he could.

"Go?"

Yes! go now. Go to the new world beyond the ocean, torn loose like the Bronze Boy from the roots of the past—perhaps even from the roots of the great tree. Be it so. What did it matter who his parents had been; their names? They were dead to him. He had come out of darkness. But in the courtyard he had been born into the light. And the light remained in him. It was part of him. He could take that along—forever.

He stooped down and washed his hands in the fountain. He held them up like a cup before the statue and let the stream run out through his fingers like the years that had gone. And then he held them up to the light, cool, empty, and clean.

"Farewell forever, old playmate," he said, looking up for the last time into the antique-youth of the bronze face with its blind eyes watching the water with that mysterious archaic smile.

He felt as though that stare followed him as he walked out. Then he discovered as he neared the gate that after all he had not been alone.

Sancho lay asleep on a bench by the wall. His back had been turned that way as he came in. At least he felt sure Sancho must have been there then. Sancho evidently took his siesta seriously. His sleep was audible; a kind of faint purr. On the ground beside him was Juan's guitar.

It was the same one Juan had bought that day with Cibo in Havana. The one with the Indian's face carved below the bridge. He picked it up very quietly and holding his hand across the strings walked out with it. It would be missed.

Don Luis, at least, would know he had made his call.

Half an hour later, like a troubadour in a cab, he arrived at the embassy to keep his appointment with Ouvrard.

Anthony was determined to leave now without further delay. Even Ouvrard had to agree that it was foolish to wait any longer for letters from Parish. If the Mexican scheme was ever to go forward, it was time to be preparing for the reception of the bullion at New Orleans.

They spent the balance of the afternoon winding up several matters. Ouvrard talked a great deal. He was still recovering from the dire effects of beer and lemon juice and lay abed looking out wistfully over the covers as though he would like to plead with Anthony to remain, but did not know just what inducements to offer him or exactly how to go about it. Anthony had always been a puzzle to the banker. There were several awkward pauses now in their talk. It seemed as if Ouvrard was always on the verge of a sentimental appeal which he just managed to avoid. At any moment—Anthony winced.

"I have sent a draft in your favour to Herr Nolte. The size of it may surprise you—pleasantly," said Ouvrard at last, glad to find himself talking business. "At any rate it will obviate any foolish argument on the value of your services for many months past. Knowing you as I do, I was bound to anticipate that. Now no protests. It is too late. You underrate the importance of money, Anthony. I am sure you do. I tell you you cannot have too much of it."

"Let us not argue that now, monsieur," replied Anthony. "I suppose it all depends upon what you think you can buy."

Ouvrard shifted his hands uneasily and changed the subject. "As for Don Luis and the coach—my boy, *leave that to me*. I think Godoy's suggestion of bundling Don Luis off to Mexico rather a good one. Don't you?"

Anthony said nothing. He sat looking grim.

"Ah, yes, poor Juan," cried Ouvrard. He reached out for the guitar and examined it. "Undoubtedly his." He shook his head and began fumbling with the strings. "Poor Juan!"

"I shall speak to the king," said Ouvrard, picking out a little tune with his thumb. The guitar jangled as he put it down.

"Wild, wild is the child," its ghost of music seemed to say.

The vision of the barrier beach at Gallegos suddenly obsessed Anthony. He rose and stole out of the room for a moment.

He had meant to go back. But once in the hall—where the Sèvres vases had all been replaced—he decided not to do so. He simply went down and got into the carriage.

"To the Prince of the Peace—and be smart about it," he said to the driver. He would get what letters he needed to the authorities at New Orleans and his passport from Godoy—now.

"Hey," cried Ouvrard looking out of the window, suddenly aware of what was up. "What am I going to do with this guitar?"

"Keep it. It belongs in Spain."

A look of pained surprise sat on the face of the banker.

"Just throw me down my hat that I left on the table. It's all I want," cried Anthony.

Ouvrard's pale face disappeared from the window.

The carriage drove off.

"Hein," said the banker, looking out again, "that clever young fool has gone! And without . . ."

He sat on the edge of the bed holding the empty hat in his hand. His eyelashes were suddenly wet. He gave the hat a kick.

"If he had only left me his shoes!—those beautiful boots he had on the first time I saw him—why, the history of Spain might be different."

Suddenly he cringed. He was alone now, absolutely alone again. He gave a great French gesture of resignation, climbed back into bed, and pulled up the clothes.

A few days later Anthony and Simba sailed from Lisbon in the good ship *Lothair,* Captain Edgecombe, bound for New Orleans.

END OF BOOK EIGHT

"Just throw me down my hat that I left on the table. It's all I want," cried Anthony.

Odravak's pale face disappeared from the window.

The carriage drove off.

"Ha!" said the banker, looking out again, "that clever young fool has gone. And without..."

He sat on the edge of the bed, holding the empty hat in his hand. His eyelashes were suddenly wet. He gave the hat a kick.

"If he had only left me his shoes—those beautiful boots he had on the first time I saw him—why, the history of Spain might be different."

Suddenly he cringed. He was alone now, absolutely alone again. He gave a great French gesture of resignation, climbed back into bed, and pulled up the clothes.

A few days after Anthony and Simba sailed from Lisbon in the good ship Ariadne, Captain Edgecombe, bound for New Orleans.

End of Book Eight.

BOOK NINE

In Which the Tree Is Cut Down

BOOK NINE

In Which the Tree Is Cut
Down

CHAPTER SIXTY-THREE

BY THE RIVER OF BABYLON

"LAND HO!"

Out of the blue bowl of the Gulf—a distant black line like the rim of the cup brimming over. The tone of daylight shifts. The free rhythm of the ripples alters. The sun no longer splinters daz-zling upon a glaze of pure blue. Over a vague waste of tan-coloured miles, where the water still retains an implacable urge southward, the Mississippi languidly pumps the yellow blood of a fat continent into the slowly contracting and expanding heart of the sea.

It is astonishing to pass over the frothy line of a tide-rip from the dominant, cobalt sparkle of the Mexican ocean into the yellow domain of the river. Objectively it is like watching a cloud-shadow loom suddenly over a wide, bright landscape; subjectively it resembles the alteration of the underlying mood of the soul from one of calm cheer-fulness and hopeful anticipation to another of vast and vague mel-ancholy, sustaining itself bravely only by an assumed outward gayety from the onslaught of some subliminal fear.

All the low coasts of this region of the world are dominated by the mighty vein of the planet for which there is no sufficient name. The tongue of man is not adequate to compass the idea of the feeling which the river engenders in him. His favourite names for it are like the names of ancient gods, attempts not to name it at all.

"Mississippi," he whispers, hoping the river will not hear him. "Father of Waters," said the Indian, paying it rhetorical honour, as though it were the ghost of the old man of the tribe to be appeased. And "Ol' Man Ribah, Ol' Man Ribah," sings the black man with a nice, deprecatory humour while he teases the banjo, artfully absolving himself by laughter and melody from a thought that is too great to bear.

How ritualistic is the negro's whimsy by the waters of his river of Babylon! He is not the only exile there.

Here in this low-country of moss-swathed swamps and forests, where the oldest continent bleeds to death slowly through a million bayous and half-stagnant, tidal estuaries, all men build along the banks like muskrats, hoping that the river will let them stay. Man gambles with this river as he gambles with much the same kind of thing on the slopes of sleeping volcanoes. He gambles successfully for a while—and then he loses. And his character partakes of that. He says little about it, for like other gamblers he is silent about the main chance and very gay about the little ones; melancholy and mercurial; that is your Creole.

For him the feeling of the river is always present. Like no other river it hangs like a sword above the head. The memory of it is like a ghost walled-in and murmuring. Through the generations, under the flat, horizonless sky, its secret tongue speaks menacingly. *"Mississippi, Mississippi, Mississippi,"* lisp the ripples, nibbling along a thousand miles of levees. The bells of passing ships reach land faintly here. For on its lower reaches men do not speak of the "banks" of this vast river but of its "coasts."

Forty-two days out from Lisbon, with the weeds hanging in submarine beards from her copper, the good ship *Lothair* picked up its Cajan pilot off Breton Island and headed for Octave pass.

"We're sho' gettin' somewhar and *to* somethin'," chortled the cook's boy as he whacked open a huge watermelon the pilot had brought.

"First fruits," thought Anthony, "of a land running over with sugar and water, if rumours and the present view of things mean anything at all."

He and the other three passengers, two Scotch clerks and a Portugal wine merchant, looked at the endless expanse of swamp on all sides of them; at the muddy eddies fuming past the side, secretly disappointed at this newest part of the world, a land literally in the making, an abode as yet fit only for mud-turtles and alligators.

Glistening bones of trees lined the low, muddy beaches, shoals, and islets. Like the skeletons of defeated monsters, at a little distance they seemed to strew the legendary battlefields of time. Now and then the hand of a bleached and fallen giant drifted past the ship, writhing slowly in the current.

Here was decidedly no note of welcome. Here was indifference. There was even a hint of warning.

Through the days to come in America Anthony was often to be reminded of that. An indefinable hint in the ragged forests, an indefinite high-light like a gleam from outer space in the sunshine—and he would remember. He would become homesick for something missing; nervous about some gigantic-nothing that cast no shadow but was there. To him, at least, there was something in this continent that waited and was inimical to man.

In the south he found it only brooded. Yet even there, because of it, no one could ever keep still. To escape it men inveterately sought the company of one another. It did not matter whom. Anything or anybody, not to be left alone in America. The mouth of the Mississippi spoke the truth.

"Whist, Mr. Adverse," said Mr. M'Quiston, the representative of Scotch drapers who clothed the Creoles extensively, "'tis no prattling mountain bur-rn we've blundered upon." Swinging at anchor in the mouth of the river, alone in the limitless glow of a yellow, summer twilight, even the ship seemed inclined to agree with him.

Out of deference to certain piratically-inclined gentlemen farther up the coast at Barataria, the captain had omitted a riding light. But nothing hove in sight. Only a half-submerged log nosed the ship disconsolately all night. *Bump*—all the watch sat waiting. Surely the thing must have gone by now. They would continue their yarns and then—*bump* very stealthily, and then *bump* again.

Nothing is so disturbing as to have something underneath trying to get into a ship.

Yet the next morning was bright and cheerful enough. A steady southwind swept them along bravely against the current. The low country ahead, as the "coasts" closed in, sparkled with lakes and glowed with dark, green forests of shining leaves. From the bayous and creeks ragged, long-haired habitans in dugouts came out from time to time to trade with them. After exchanging muskrat skins and snowy heron-plumes for calico and knives on the deck, they departed again into the cavernous mouths of their muddy streams.

Low, weathered houses behind veils of live-oaks and grey mosses began to look out across the water higher up. A few plantation boats were occasionally glimpsed, like moths adrift. Once a line of carts drove along a levee as though on the surface of the water and disappeared into a wall of distant canes. A Spanish warship flaunting her gorgeous colours and under bare poles drifted down, and much to their relief, drifted past.

"A guardacosta," said the captain, "bound for Havana or for Vera Cruz."

It was the only ship they passed on their hundred-mile voyage inland. Against the current they now moved sluggishly. On the afternoon of the second day they close-hauled to round a great bend in the river and came in sight of New Orleans.

Anthony climbed to the masthead. He had come half-way across the world to make this place his home, and he cast his eyes upon it with a peculiarly quickened though unconscious insight. It was the first general impression that forever coloured the infinite particulars which were to follow. To an eye used to nothing but the loneliness of waters during a long voyage, New Orleans conveyed instantly the impression of a small but rapidly growing port.

The wide, yellow road of the river, golden in the afternoon sunshine of a hot July day, swept with a magnificent curve bulging eastward and swinging west again. In the curve of the crescent the little city and its plantation suburbs stretched for a distance of about two miles from horn to horn.

It was long but it was not wide. It was only a new moon as yet.

Immediately before him, in the very centre of it, lay a cluster of three or four thousand roofs. Red-tile and slabs covered low Mediterranean-looking buildings in a bank of dusty trees. The eye ranged rapidly over this settlement—from which the blank face of a stuccoed barracks or convent stared out boldly here and there—to take in the shingled roofs of wooden houses amid gardens just behind. Then the fields and the swamps began again. There was a canal and a basin. A few straight roads and snatches of bayous led to the eastward. And beyond them, making itself visible by a mirage-like blink, lay the levels of Lake Pontchartrain.

The nucleus of the town was still enclosed in ruinous palisades and swampy ditches. These ended in two bulldog forts upon the levee from which floated the gold and scarlet of Spain. There was a small battery in the centre. But the city had already burst out of this military chrysalis and extended along the levees north and south.

Two guns fired from Fort San Carlos near the canal now certified to the town the arrival of a foreign ship.

A few carts kicking up the dust behind them, and slaves in bright turbans, that could be glimpsed here and there making their way somnolently along the levees, were rapidly replaced by a crowd of brightly-clad people who swarmed out of the streets of the town onto the water front. For the most part they stood waiting about a market house near the battery.

A boatload of officers, in gold braid and bright blue uniforms, put off for the ship. Somewhere under the trees in the park-like square before the cathedral a military band began to play. Over the quarter-mile of water between the ship and the levee came the "March of Fontarabia" and the smell of the town.

Ships did not anchor here. They tied up to the levee. North of the market a fleet of them stretched away, their spars at all angles.

Altogether Anthony counted fifteen; about ten of them Yankees, he judged. The rest were Spanish and there was one Frenchman brightly defiant with a tricolour. But that was by no means all the commerce of the port. Anchored three or four deep farther up the river along a sandy flat below the levee was the strangest assortment of craft he had even seen.

Arks, and keel-boats, rafts with log-huts upon them, canoes, and flat-boats formed in that direction a kind of slatternly water-city that served to extend the town. Naked children bathing, the distant barking of curs, cattle and horses grazing along the swampy banks completed its rather unkempt and miserable scene. Even a mile away it was obviously the most raucous part of the water front. It clamoured shrilly. It whooped. It relieved itself with bare backs pointed toward the Creole town. Its savage citizens wrapped in midnight, coonskins, and delirium tremens terrorized the few sedate residents of the Faubourg Ste. Marie as they ruthlessly rolled homeward through its vegetable gardens. Such was the "Batture," or the American landing.

The old French and Spanish town was in fact already besieged on all sides by the Americans. Those who descended upon it out of the illimitable northern forests congregated upon the Batture. Those who sailed to it from Georgia and the Carolinas and Floridas anchored their schooners in the Basin Carondelet and the canal. There was always a small fleet of the latter. Every year there were more of them.

As Anthony descended he paused in the maintop to look down upon one of the curious craft from up-river which came drifting within a few yards of the ship.

It was an American edition of Noah's ark built of logs with the bark on. From its square windows looked forth eagerly the bright, hungry faces of children, houn' dogs, and calves. It glided majestically by to the sweet sound of lowing. Somewhere within its bowels an egg was being laid.

Noah himself in an iron-grey beard, coonskin cap, and ragged deerskin fringes leaned against the immense, oar-like rudder over its stern and ruminated upon the wad in his cheek with the selfsame motion as the cow in the window below him. Occasionally with a superb aim and insouciance he spat into the cow's eye. A rattling of horns followed.

"Seth, you kep' that po' critter rattlin' the hull way down from La'ville," complained his wife, who was seated on the flat roof in a rocking chair, cuddling her youngest wolverine. "For *gawd's sake* shift that wad t' tother cheek!"

Those lining the bulwarks were close enough to see the requested transfer of ammunition successfully accomplished.

Surveying the ship somewhat contemptuously from his own slab quarter-deck, the hero in deerskins looked up at the gentleman in the maintop with a smart twinkle in his eye.

"Wall, stranger, be ye lookin' over the real estate?" he asked.

"Real estate" was Greek to Anthony, who contented himself with a friendly nod.

"There'll soon be a pa'cel o' fine lots in the city. It's boun' to grow."

"I hope I shall find mine a pleasant one," replied Anthony, moved to take the man seriously by something simple and earnest in his expression.

"Eh?" said he a little confused. "Oh—sartin! Thar's lots o' corner lots left. Me, I'm low-katin' lower down." He gave the oar an impatient shove.

"Now jes' let the river take you, Seth," put in the woman, beginning to rock. He looked at her gloomily. "Easy for her," he said and spat over the new side.

As Anthony came down the ratlines, the Spanish port-officers boarded the ship. They were accompanied by a lanky man in a black suit much too tight and short for him. His bony wrists extended far below his cuffs and he wore a huge beaver hat with a black scarf about it.

The passengers' luggage had been piled on deck since early morning and an iniquitous inquisition by the self-important colonial officials began.

Never in any place in Europe had Anthony experienced anything like it. It was quite evidently the intention of the "authorities" to confiscate the major portion of his extensive outfit for themselves. Everything he had brought with him was against the law to import. Yet their most strenuous objections were instantly quieted by the exhibition of his passport signed by Godoy—which set the chief officer to bowing and scraping—and a bribe so pitiful that he was ashamed to offer it.

"Ah, if the illustrious had only said he bore letters to the governor! Ah, ah,—and—ah! And where would his nobility reside ashore?"

"Where, indeed?" Anthony had scarcely thought of that. Yet now that he had "come home" at last, what roof was there to shelter him?

With a knowing look the customs officer in a string of Spanish civilities that made Anthony laugh presented the lugubrious gentleman in the beaver hat as one likely to solve all difficulties—"both in life and death," said he with a grin, leaving them together.

From his vest pocket, where he also kept a mossy comb, the man in black, who began to address Anthony in vile Spanish, now drew forth a large tortoise-shell card. On it was written in Spanish, French, and English:

Doctor Melancthon Conant, LL.D.
Purveyor, Victualler, Jobber, and Undertaker
at the port of New Orleans
in the Province of Louisiana.

"Speak English," said Anthony impatiently. "You're an American, aren't you?"

The man straightened up with evident relief and shoved his hat back to an impudent angle. The scarf of official mourning floated out gayly from it in the breeze.

"I calalate I am," said he. "I'm from Bosting."

Anthony looked at him doubtfully. There was something confusing to him in the man's whole make-up. He was patently pious and yet whitely-obscene at the same time.

"—and an official in a Spanish port?" he asked.

"Wall, stranger, we from our vicinity dew rize most anywhar we're put."

"Putnam?" said Anthony reminiscently.

"No, no, Conant!" cried Melancthon, again extending the tortoise-shell card.

"I made myself handy here, ye see. I drawed the teeth of Don Andres Almonaster y Roxas in his own front parlour when I came here nigh seven year ago, and I drawed the wisdom teeth of the governor settin' in the Cabildo—painlessly. And he remembered me. I larned Spanish and I made myself ginerally useful." A sudden gleam came into his eye. "Ye don't happen to have a gum-boil or two that needs lancin' right na-ow, do ye?"

"Not one," said Anthony almost regretfully.

"No, I can see yer ivories shine like a two-year-old hoss's. But jes' keep me in mind when they dew begin ter ache. It takes 'em a long time ter rot out. But I don't believe sufferin' helps the character. I give relief. Keep that in mind—*Melancthon Conant gives relief.*"

There was no getting away from him. They were preparing to make fast to the levee now. But the man had him fairly buttonholed.

"It's a boardin'-house I want to talk to ye about. Na-ow I kin fix ye up fine." He rolled his eyes over Anthony's luggage, calculating. "A gen'leman like yourself with sound teeth, money, and warm blood ul want to live free and easy. I have a little arrangement with a free lady of colour in the Faubourg Ste. Marie. Mother Marie can cook elegant gumbo. It's lonesome. Ye can make all the noise ye want. And yet—it's right convenient. Comfortable beds and lots of company for 'em."

"I know that kind," said Anthony reminiscently.

"Ye mistake me, 'deed ye dew. Few of these gals bite, an' if they dew ye don't care. *Y'seewhatamean?*" He whisked off his hat and drew out of it, as though he were producing a rabbit, an extraordinary leather-folder which he began to unroll with a sacerdotal calm.

"Gin-u-ine portraits," he whispered, "drawed from life by a imigree artist, late of Versailles. Cost me a dollar apiece." He stood waiting for his fish to bite.

On the leather sheet now dangled before Anthony's eyes, each in its own little pocket and painted on thin ovals of ivory, were a baker's dozen of miniature masterpieces of pornography. It was impossible not to look at them. St. Anthony himself would have succumbed. The artist had been genuinely inspired. The girls, who ranged from the colour of the ivory itself to warm chocolate, reclined upon hotbeds of the imagination dimpling with hospitality. The chef-d'œuvre was reserved for the centre. It was round instead of oval, and a stepchild of the Renaissance. It represented Apollo begetting a demigod upon the body of a ravished octoroon.

"That 'air one," said Mr. Conant, "is painted on alabaster and cost me five dollars. Hold it up to the sun. Ain' it life-like? It's transparent."

"It certainly is," admitted Anthony; "but I don't think I'll be stopping at Mother Marie's."

"No?" said Melancthon, shocked into a dream of disappointment.

"No!" said Anthony. And then suddenly inspired by the devil, "But you might show these to Mr. M'Quiston, the Scotch gentleman yonder. He looks lonely."

"He does!" said Mr. Conant and hurried over to him.

Leaning against the bulwark, oblivious to the confusion of the preparations for landing going on all about him, Anthony watched the pantomime.

Mr. Conant approached Mr. M'Quiston with so pious an air that the Scotchman's face, which at first registered its usual suspicion at the approach of any stranger, suddenly shifted into the right Sabbath expression appropriate and habitual at the approach of the cloth. His hands, however, remained firmly in his trousers pockets, where he always thrust them at the too-near approach of anybody.

Mr. M'Quiston had a small purse in each pocket.   He kept his eggs in two baskets.

Mr. Conant's introduction of himself was so lugubriously proper, however, that it was obvious Mr. M'Quiston felt he was being welcomed home.   His face relaxed.   Still he extended no hand.   Mr. Conant's hat came off.   Mr. M'Quiston looked a little contemptuous. And then—the leather rabbit came out of the hat.

It fell before the face of Mr. M'Quiston like a theatre curtain. There was a long pause while Scotland met Art and Lust wrestled with Avarice.   Virtue triumphed.

Suddenly Mr. M'Quiston was heard trumpeting through his nose. "Mon! Awa wi' it, awa wi' it!   Dinna ye ken I canna e'en afoord to ogle sic a maisterpiece?   Dinna ye ken ma breeks air auld sax years sine?"

Mr. Conant became the personification of sorrow again as the rabbit folded up.

Mr. M'Quiston was then left fully revealed, flushed and pop-eyed, paralysed from the waist down.

"Thank God," said he, "thank God my pockets are still like new." Mr. Conant's threatened appraisal of Mr. M'Quiston's teeth was completely ruined by the long continued and disturbing merriment of Mr. Adverse.

There was undoubtedly a silvery contagion in the sound of Anthony's laughter.   There was nothing cynical about it.   It was merely exuberance tickled beyond restraint at the vagaries of the human scene.   Because the laugher seemed somehow to include himself in his own laughter, people were seldom made angry by it.   Even the canny Mr. M'Quiston did not feel it was exclusively at his expense.   As the power of motion was slowly reconferred upon the Scot, he was forced to grin with something like the expression of a pumpkin redly illuminated from within.

But in so flat a neighbourhood as New Orleans Anthony was himself startled to find his laughter being echoed back to him in the tones of his own voice.   He turned toward the levee to find the source of the phenomenon.

And it was thus for the first time, but by no means for the last, that Anthony saw the ever-memorable Dr. Terry Mitchell holding his sides over certain spiritual implications in the fleshly scene.

He was not more than ten paces away, leaning against an old pile on the levee.   He had evidently been enjoying thoroughly the events on the deck just below him while the ship was being made fast.   His three-cornered, cocked hat drooped just a little over one eye that narrowed and twinkled as he took a pinch of snuff and remarked:

"So you are not going to be staying at Mother Marie's?"

With a flourish of a fine cambric handkerchief he removed at once all traces of tobacco from his nostrils and laughter from his lips. But his smile would break out again.

"I rather thought not," he added.

They both laughed again. It was curious, but a genuine fellow-feeling had already sprung up between them.

"Have you any ideas about a comfortable and decent place to stay?" asked Anthony.

"Very decided ones," replied the gentleman on the levee. "The combination you mention is rather rare in this our raw little Babylon. Unless you have friends here——"

"None in America," said Anthony.

"Neither have I," said he. "But I do happen to know of a well-kept little place. No ravishing ladies. Will that? . . . No? Well then, suppose you leave your baggage on board for a while and come along and see for yourself. I'm not a hotel runner, understand!"

"Of course not," said Anthony, and crossed over to the levee. "I'm much obliged to you."

"I'm thinkin' I'll be coomin' along wi' ye mysel' the noo," said M'Quiston, who had followed him.

"Who the devil are you, sir?" snapped Mitchell, bridling. "I'm damned particular about my company."

"I'm frae the fur-rum o' McTavish, McTavish, and McTavish o' Glasga," said M'Quiston.

"Tell them all three to go to hell," blazed Mitchell.

"I'm thinkin'," began M'Quiston—but what he thought remained known to his Maker only. Three Kentuckians standing near by in coonskin caps and long knives broke out into a loud laugh in his face.

"Come on," said Mitchell grinning.

"Howdy, cap'n, howdy," said the three with great respect to Mitchell as he passed them.

"Good day to you-all," said Mitchell curtly enough, and followed by Anthony, led the way up the levee.

What appeared to be snow scattered here and there Anthony now discovered was cotton. There were a few bales of it to be seen along the levee, but they were outnumbered a hundred to one by casks of sugar and barrels of rum with which most of the ships were loading. Despite the great heat that shimmered along the water front, the scene was an animated one.

Black stevedores dressed in a mad variety of rag-fair costumes pushed, hauled, and carried for the most part on their heads, unbelievable loads of all kinds. There were only a few drays rumbling along dustily now and then. Wheeled transport of any sort still seemed scarce. French and Spanish sailors, an occasional officer or soldier in faded and ragged uniforms made up the bulk of the whites. In the shade of a long building on low white pillars, as they neared the crest of the embankment, negresses with bright turbans sat before piles of fruit and vegetables, chattering and shrieking with excitement over the arrival of a new ship. Some Indian squaws remained in one corner impassively weaving baskets and smoking, watched over by a tall brave with a single feather in his hair, who stood wrapped in a tattered blanket and imperturbability. Pickaninnies fat and gangly sprawled and raced everywhere, getting into everyone's way and out of it miraculously. Already Anthony was familiar with the begging phrase of the place, "Lagniappe, misu, lagniappe, masa, una picayune."

"Me Mericain," insisted one little nigger racing up the levee after them out of the yellow waters of the river itself. "Me savvy God-dam." He broke into a stream of hair-curling profanity, and then, dodging Mitchell's boot, pranced on ahead of them to overtake Mr. Conant, whose long, black scarf floating back from his beaver hat had gone on before without a single prospect to follow it. No lagniappe being forthcoming, the boy put his hand to his nose and began to sing to Mr. Conant at a safe distance:

> "Si to te 'tit zozo
> Et moi-memo mo te fusil,
> Mo sre tchove toi-Boum!"

"*Boum, boum, boum,*" cried the boy for every step. Several other booming urchins joined the first, and Mr. Conant, amidst general laughter, was boomed off the levee.

"He is the only white man in New Orleans they would dare to do that to," remarked Mitchell. "We both follow the medical profession, by the way. I as a surgeon; he as an undertaker. I like to introduce him as my 'distinguished colleague.' The story goes that he steals girls' corpses for Madam Marie's house and brings them to life for the night only. They go back to the tomb at cockcrow. Saves payin' 'em wages, y' see. Well, I wouldn't doubt it. Wait till you see the girls."

They now reached the top of the levee, a grassy street stretching along the stockaded walls. There was a gallows, with a number of children of the better class watched by their black nurses while at play about it. They found themselves looking across the Place d'Armes and down the Rue Ste. Anne.

It was the very heart of the little city. Hitherto Anthony had been repulsed rather than attracted by what he had seen.   But the view before him was now so novel and interesting that his heart began to go out to the place instinctively.

Behind the doubtful shade of a line of dusty willow trees were the graceful arches of the Cabildo, or Hôtel de Ville, and the still towerless cathedral.   These buildings stretched clear across the bottom of the square.   Except that the place was unpaved and had patches of withered grass on it here and there and the charred remnants of an old picket fence, it already looked ancient and might have been mistaken at first glance for the square of almost any minor Latin town. The sides were lined with various small boutiques and restaurants and by the Halles, a large open building serving as a general market for vegetables and gayly fluttering merchandise from embroidered muslins to gaudy handkerchiefs.   But if the architecture was familiar, the crowd was novel and unique.   It could have been assembled only in Louisiana.

The guard mount of the garrison was over.   The band had marched off to barracks, and the crowd, which had gathered to watch it, was breaking up.   Fiery Creoles carrying rapiers and dressed in the extremity of Paris fashion rubbed elbows with voyageurs, habitans, and coureurs de bois.   Cajans and breeders from the Attakapas prairies, their blue homespun cottons redolent of cattle, bawled at each other and trod on the toes of émigré nobles accompanied by yellow sirens from San Domingo speaking a honey-smooth, island French.   Flaxenhaired Saxons from the "German Coast" a few miles up the river gathered about the coffin-shaped carts of Catalan and Provençal marchandes selling callas.   Milk and coffee women walked about on the outskirts of the crowd like giants, balancing immense cans on their turbaned heads.   At this hour they did a roaring business as did the hawkers of piratically come-by trinkets shouting "Barataria, Barataria."   Dirty Houma and Natchez Indians stalked grimly about in silent contrast to the constant chatter of blacks of all types, hues, and outlines, dressed in braguet, shapeless woollen shirts or an old bag.

And surrounding all these, apart from them, seeming to be waiting for something to happen, or to be about to close in upon the noisy and happy Creole crowd, stood the Américains, the *Kaintucks* from the unknown northern forests, the Long-knives who had borrowed the sullenness if not the stoical expression of the savages with whom they had fought.   They lounged in doorways or leaned against walls in small groups or strode with quick, long, nervous strides, brushing people aside.   But whether they stood, sat, or walked, they all chewed tobacco and sprayed the landscape so copiously as to guarantee them the right of way in all directions as though they were the messengers of kings.

> "American rogue,
> Dressed in nankeen,
> Stealer of Bread,
> From Mr. D'Aquin."

quoted Mitchell under his breath, as a flat-boatman in homespun jeans reeled past them out of a barrel-room shouting, "I'm a bahr-eatin' cattawampus. I'm a child o' the snappin-tartle."

"Lord, *must* they come here, too?" he muttered.

"This gets in your blood," he added, waving his hands about the square. "I hate to see it turned into a hog-pen. It's a nice little country. Hope you'll like it."

"I think I shall," said Anthony.

"You mean you reckon you will," he laughed. "It's some time since I've heard English spoken.

"This is the Rue Ste. Anne. The Hotel Orleans, where I see our Scotch friend is going, is up Chartres there to your left. If you don't like my little hang-out you can go there, too. Mind you don't step off the banquette. The dust is knee-deep now. When it rains the mud comes to your hips."

They continued thus for four or five blocks, walking on the keels of old flat-boats which in some places still bridged swampy holes, until the brick and stucco houses ceased. Then they passed through a break in the old stockade into a square surrounded by gardens and unpainted cypress houses standing on piles. There was a marine basin here with a canal leading out into a tangled swamp beyond. A number of schooners lay at anchor here as though moored in the square itself, with men in great straw hats loafing on their decks.

"This is the corner of the Place Publique and the Rue Claude. You may want to remember it if you desire to send your luggage here," said Mitchell. He swung open a wicket gate and led the way toward a neat, frame house whose ship-like balconies overflowed with flourishing potted plants.

"Ba'tiste," he roared.

A completely bald man, round and with duck-like feet, appeared at the door, flourishing a spotless cloth and wiping a long-stemmed glass.

"Ha! Miche le docteur, vat?"

"Here is another guest for you, and he's a gentleman, by God! Show him that corner room overlooking the basin. I want some human company. What's for supper?"

"Ha! hit his not so mooch, no, de stuff, has hit his dose cook, and hi ham dose cook."

Ba'tiste patted himself on the chest as he said this, and Dr. Mitchell patted him on the back.

And so it was that Anthony came to stay at that curious combination of club, hostelry, and rendezvous of gourmands known as "Ba'tiste's," and to the inner initiates of the octagon room off the kitchen as the "Bald Duck."

———————

The long voyage, conveying the impression that Europe was infinitely remote and all its experiences left behind him forever, the novel scenes and interests into which he was suddenly plunged, but above all, a determination to make the life of the new country into which he had come *his* life—and to look to the future rather than the past for guidance—all these things had their full effect upon Anthony.

He phrased it to himself by saying that the "weather of my soul has cleared." He was released into action again without having the springs of it stagnated by such a complexity of moral, social, and practical considerations that they could scarcely flow at all. The "guilt" of the past had been liquidated—he could go on. But in a new way. For there is a profound difference between proceeding on the basis of cautious experience accumulated out of the past and on hope based on one's predictions of an untrammelled future.

Freedom was not merely a political theory in the new continent, he found; that was the least part of it. One could disregard politics and government altogether, if one wished to, by simply following the track of the sun for another few degrees westward. Freedom existed in the ease of untrammelled actions. One was accountable to one's self alone. At least Anthony did not forget his accountability to himself. A good many others did, he found. His experience was like that of many other immigrants. Perhaps he differed from the majority of his fellows only by being a little more conscious of the moral nature of the change.

One immediate result of his cogitations on the subject of the new country was that his own affairs and his desire to find himself settled in Louisiana with a genuine stake and interest in the community rapidly thrust the machinations of Ouvrard and his Mexican silver not into the background, but into a purely secondary place in his regard. That is, within a few weeks after his arrival he found himself pushing forward the plans to transfer the bullion to Parish not as the end for which he had come, but merely as the means of weaving himself more deeply into the interests of the place. Yet for that very reason he worked more feverishly and circumspectly than if he had felt himself to be a mere agent acting for Ouvrard, the Barings, and the Hopes.

He found a large pile of mail awaiting him from Parish, who

had kept writing to Anthony, at New Orleans instead of through
Ouvrard's bank at Paris.   David's letters, Anthony was amused to
see, began anxiously about four months previous, became plaintive,
then indignant, and were now, if not actually menacing, furious, to say
the least.

Where was Anthony?   What in God's name was he doing?   Did
he not know that Parish had perfected his arrangements at Philadelphia, Baltimore, New York, and Charleston, and that Lestapsis was
now in Vera Cruz and had drawn the first instalment of $750,000
from the Mexican treasury?   Then woe on woe.   Lestapsis had
chartered a ship himself.   It had arrived safely at Philadelphia but
the insurance was 60 per cent.   Out of 200,000 silver dollars only
$80,000 remained.

> It is plain [wrote Parish] that New Orleans is the only prac-
> ticable port of entry.   I beg of you in the name of old friend-
> ship, if for no other consideration, to perfect your forwarding
> operations with Lestapsis at Vera Cruz, and act.   Otherwise, the
> capital advanced by the Hopes and Barings for my mercantile
> operations here will be exhausted.   My bills are already accepted
> only at a mischievous discount . . .
>
> P. S.   Mrs. Parish and Mrs. Udney add their solicitations to
> mine.

"That is going a long way for David," thought Anthony, smiling a
little to think how cool Parish had once been about the necessity of
any agency at New Orleans.   "So Mrs. Udney is with Florence in
Philadelphia."   He tossed down the letter, laughing.   "Well, it looks
as though I shall have to act.   Ouvrard did delay me too long.   No
wonder David is anxious."

So he went down to the levee and without further ado chartered
the schooner *Ariel*, Captain Clemm of Baltimore, to carry letters to
Parish at Philadelphia, announcing his arrival and the reasons for his
delay.

> Within two months I hope to have the produce of Mexico
> under way to you [he wrote].   We had better arrange a con-
> venient cipher, by the way.   My regards and assurances to both
> the ladies.   The "postage" on this letter comes to $750 gold—
> I have paid it.

Captain Clemm sailed, not without having spread a rumour that
there was a madman in town who paid in gold instead of depreciated

colonial livranzas. As a consequence Anthony found that anybody would do anything for him, short of committing suicide.

Standing in the shade of the old Boucheries, Anthony watched the *Ariel* drop down the river until she disappeared around the bend beyond Makarty's plantation. He wished he had thought of sending Florence some of the Indian bead-work which a squaw was just then displaying at his feet. But on the whole it was better not to irritate David.

Dismissing so casual a thought easily, he purchased some black Havana cigars at another stand, and enjoying his first genuine smoke in some months, for he had run out of the weed on the voyage, he strolled on down the levee in an enviable frame of mind to deliver his letters and the dispatches from Godoy to the governor.

He had no idea, as he crossed the little parterre at the corner of the Rue de la Levée and Toulouse Street, that he was making history. It was all most casual. The governor's "palace" was a plain one-storey building along the river front. It looked like a tavern. There was not even a military aide on duty. He wrote his name on a card and scribbled under it—"bearing dispatches for His Excellency from the Prince of the Peace"—and gave it to an old negro servant. Presently he was led through the hall to the back piazza screened with lattice-work through which some grooms could be seen rubbing down horses in the stable-yard at the end of the garden. Two gentlemen in shirt-sleeves, with their coats hung upon the backs of chairs, were seated on the porch discussing a bottle of wine.

It was hard to tell which one was the governor. In fact, neither of the gentlemen was himself at all sure about it. One was the French prefect Laussat sent by Napoleon to receive the transfer of Louisiana from Spain according to the terms of treaty; the other was Don Manuel de Salcedo, Spanish governor-general, who had arrived from Havana in June to turn the province over to France.

The transfer had never occurred.

Since March Laussat had been waiting at New Orleans for General Victor to arrive with final instructions and the French troops necessary to garrison Louisiana. The English prevented. Neither troops nor further instructions had arrived. In March Napoleon sold Louisiana to the United States. No rumour of that event had as yet percolated to New Orleans, although it was now almost the end of July.

The interregnum, for it amounted to that, had been one of good-natured anarchy. The Spanish authority had officially continued, but the loyalty of the Creoles had always been for France, and Laussat had been cheered and fêted wherever he appeared. He and Salcedo had spent most of the time on the piazza in their shirt-sleeves, waiting for orders, drinking endless quantities of rum lemonades as the days grew hotter, and questioning Fortune.

Instead of Louisiana's being transferred to France, 2,190 livranzas had been transferred to Spain in the person of Don Manuel by the means of a dice box.

"Perdu!" said Laussat just as Anthony entered the porch—and the dice settled. "Peste," he whispered. "What can this fellow want? He looks like an American."

"In that case he will want everything," said Salcedo. "He says he bears dispatches from Madrid."

Anthony was received civilly but rather coolly, he thought. He delivered Godoy's letters to Salcedo.

While the governor withdrew a little to read them, he and Laussat sat conversing. The Frenchman was starving for news, and Anthony's Parisian gossip, less than a year old, came to him as though a breath of fresh air from the boulevards had swept through the porch lattices. He wanted Anthony to stay and talk all day. He called for a bottle of champagne.

Suddenly they saw that Salcedo was laughing. The paper with a long seal like a watchfob on it shook in his hands. He peered over the top of it and looked at the French prefect and laughed again.

Silence—a sense of something impending fell on both Laussat and Anthony.

"Do you know what has happened, Laussat?" grinned the Spaniard. "Your master has sold Louisiana to the United States."

"What!" cried the Frenchman, sweeping the dice up from the table in a gesture of agitation. The new-brought bottle of champagne tottered and rolled to the floor where its contents gurgled away unnoticed. "Impossible! What do you mean?"

"Listen to this," said Don Manuel—and read a passage of his letter from the Prince of the Peace, which even included the bathtub incident. That had rankled in Godoy's mind. He had not been able to keep it out of his dispatches, which in some respects were always childish.

Salcedo was not given to reading his confidential dispatches before strangers. The dramatic opportunity of surprising Laussat had simply been too much for his Latin temperament to withstand. He now turned to Anthony a little apprehensively.

"If you please, Señor Adverse, you will say nothing about what you have just heard in confidence here. It might be awkward to have such a rumour spread about."

"The news is already general property in Europe, Your Excellency. For that reason I have said nothing about it here. I supposed it was generally known."

"Quelle difference?" said Laussat. "I shall return to that beautiful Paris, now—and shortly."

Then they fell to questioning Anthony about European news. He spent the rest of the morning with them, and parted on excellent terms.

"I shall do what I can to speed the Mexican affair as the letters requested. But it will not be much now, I am afraid," said the Spaniard. "I shall soon be going, I suppose," he added a bit sorrowfully.

"Yes," thought Anthony, "and leaving behind you the first chance for a really good squeeze. Too bad!" He did not neglect, however, to thank Salcedo and whetted his interested hopes by suggesting that an early shipment of bullion from Vera Cruz might be arranged if one of the guardacostas could be employed to bring it over.

The governor shook his head with evident regret. "Impossible," he said. "We should then have to divide our little percentage with the navy at Havana." Then his face brightened. "I tell you what you do, señor. See the Lafittes!"

"A good idea!" cried Anthony, who had no idea in the world who the Lafittes were. "I thank you."

They bowed most affably.

Two days later a ship from Bordeaux, which had managed to give the English the slip, brought the news of the sale of the colony to the United States. The province was first to be turned over to France and then delivered to the Americans. The town seethed with excitement. The Creoles were wild with disappointment, the Americans with joy. The Kaintucks swaggered uproariously and built a great bonfire down by the Batture. While the serenos went about announcing in French and Spanish that it was "a clear, dark night and all well," the glare of the leaping flames cast a portentous red glow along the levee and the Kentucky rifles cracked in triumph as Mr. Jefferson's health was drunk in raw, white whisky, and rum.

But there was one American who did not toast Mr. Jefferson and the United States. He was Dr. Terry Mitchell.

The doctor belonged to that small but rather influential group of Americans from the eastern seaboard cities both north and south, who already some years before the purchase of Louisiana had begun to invade New Orleans. They were a curious conglomeration of far-seeing merchants, many from Philadelphia, downeasters looking for cargoes, adventurers, and gentlemen whose brilliant operations at home had conflicted with the restraints of criminal statutes or the common law.

All these, to distinguish them from their western fellow citizens, the Kaintucks, were known to the Creoles generally as "Yanquis." It

was not until a great many mortgages, maturing in Boston, and the
fiery protests of Virginians and South Carolinians annoyed to the
point of pistols-in-the-morning taught the Creoles better, that it was
realized in New Orleans that Yankees came only from the sacred, interest-drawing soil of New England.

"Dr. Terry M.," for so he loved to refer to himself, was among the
first to have shot a Creole gentleman for making this geographical
error. The community had not at first understood so nice a distinction. Even the unfortunate M. La Chaise, who had died in great
agony with Dr. Mitchell's bullet in his liver, was perplexed to the last
as to just why he had been challenged and polished-off. Only three
things were evident to everybody in regard to Dr. Mitchell: first, he
was a gentleman of enormous punctilio and the courage of his convic-
tions; secondly, he was a miraculous pistol shot; thirdly, he was the
best surgeon and doctor of general medicine that anybody had ever
heard of—never mind what his colleagues might say.

Everything else about Dr. Mitchell was to everybody else, save a
few friends and admiring cronies, obscure. In the entire city during
his life there, there were only two people who ever fully understood
what he laughed at. One of them was Anthony Adverse and the other
Edward Livingston. It was only when he was with Dr. Mitchell that
Livingston could fully find the way to laugh at himself.

The three dined together, if not invariably, at least so frequently in
the octagon room at the Bald Duck that *Mitchell, Livingston, & Adverse* before long began to take on some of the aspects of a firm name.

Shortly before Anthony's arrival, Livingston had left Ba'tiste's,
where he had long been living, for quarters more convenient from a
business standpoint uptown. The doctor had felt Livingston's absence
keenly and had for that reason seized upon Anthony as a likely companion. He had not been mistaken in his impulse, he soon ascertained,
and the acquaintance in the course of a short time had rapidly become
an enduring one. Ba'tiste took no other lodgers. Livingston's room
remained vacant, and the roly-poly little proprietor devoted himself to
cooking those suppers for which he was famous.

The establishment certainly was an unusual one. The permanent
residents consisted of the fanatical little cook himself, his two gentlemen boarders, and three old female slaves. These all lived in the
house. At the other end of the garden, facing the square convenient
to the Basin Carondelet, was an old stable that had been converted into
a bar and barrel-room. It was known as "The Little Jesus" and
catered exclusively to the crews of the schooners, Floridians and
Georgians for the most part. These were served and kept in bounds
by one William Wilson from Maryland and his powerful, wrestling
Welsh assistant David Ap Poer.

Ba'tiste thus managed to serve all classes in the city with the exception of the Kaintucks. His house in the evenings was a rendezvous for Creoles who knew how to appreciate his art. They had their own salle à manger. A steadily growing clientele of the Yanquis was accommodated for the most part in the octagon room, while in the converted stable on the square Minorcans from Florida and Crackers from Georgia looked Messrs. Wilson and Ap Poer in the eye, not always calmly.

Mitchell, Anthony soon discovered, lived upstairs in a suite of rooms with a fiddle, several cases of duelling pistols, a medical library and a chemist's outfit that gave his apartments somewhat the appearance of an alchemist's den. The doctor was greatly given to experiments. He made up his own prescriptions, and rose regularly every morning at seven o'clock for pistol practice in the garden.

The house had been built by the French military engineer Piuger and the octagon room was evidently a domestic by-product of his art. Mitchell's quips on it were endless. Anthony had the bedroom above, which partook of the same octagon shape. He became greatly attached to this high, sunny coign with its many windows looking in several directions: west by the roofs of the town; northward over plantations to the broad, yellow expanse of the river; eastward down the long canal through the swamp to the levels of Lake Pontchartrain. The basin and its shipping lay directly before him, almost at his feet.

With the doctor's fiddle crooning away down the corridor and some of his own things laid out, it was not long before he began to feel at home. To be sure, it was far, far away from—everything. And the sunsets with the high clouds like plumes blown back upon themselves towered vastly above the rude, flat lowlands. The swamp pools amid the cypresses glared with dull red eyes. It was lonely at that hour for Anthony Adverse—but then there was supper. The crowd began to drop in from the town. There were wine and cards and billiards if one wanted them. And there was always Dr. Terry M.

"I never meant to come here," said Mitchell, who had at last grown a little confidential one rainy evening, sitting over some mulled wine. "But the country itself gets in your blood if you stay—along with the fever and other things. I like it. And I know I'm going to die here. I mean of old age." He smiled a little. "If the smart Americans could only be kept out, lower Louisiana under the dons or the French might grow slowly, the only way anything worth while can grow, into a fine, mellow little country. Now we are going to have floods of democrats, oratory, humbug, Protestant anarchy, and the world and man for sale at the river mouth. I hate to see it. I do! Damn Mr. Jefferson, and damn Bonaparte for selling out, I say." He held up his glass and looked through it reflectively.

"Well, don't join me unless you feel like it. But since you're soon going to be a citizen of the great republic by force of the treaty you might as well know something about it." He drained his glass and set it down.

"About forty years ago I was born in Philadelphia. I remember the place with some amusement now. My mother was a Quaker girl who was thrown out of meeting for going on a pic-nic with my father on Seventh day. The result of their crime was a nice little house on the Wissahickon—and myself. Nevertheless, I was brought up in an atmosphere of disgrace. My father was the rake-hell of his family, because he decided to live on what he had, like a gentleman, instead of working like a navvy. And he would never have me baptized. I inherit his temperament, which he once described as a cross between Lucifer and a mule. That means he didn't believe things just because people told him. He wouldn't take orders. He liked to kick people when they tried to drive him. And he had a pride that lasted longer than any Christian conscience. Naturally great trouble for me has ensued. But I like it, and I can shoot crows with a pistol." He looked up at the ceiling.

"I remember once sneaking into a Quaker meeting with my outcast mother. We sat for two hours in a cold little room. At the end of that time an old rogue by the name of Fox had a revelation from God Almighty that the taxes in the third ward were too high. The God of Pennsylvania was speaking. He is the personification of political economy and Ben Franklin is his high priest. Morality consisted in making correct small change, never mind what you did with the rest, and doing your necessary reliefs away from home. The German farmers used to bundle.

"You don't know it?

"You go to bed with a girl to save firewood, but you have bags on to prevent accidents. It's a sort of venereal blind-man's-buff that saves fuel and virginity at the same time. I saved the fuel.

"So father sent me to Edinburgh to keep me from being married to a field of cabbages in Lancaster County, and to learn how to have my revenge on humanity by practising what is called medicine.

"I came back to Philadelphia after the late glorious Revolution and found things had gone from bad to worse. Everybody was now just as good as everybody else, even a little better. I met a young fellow by the name of Wistar who had interesting theories about medicine. They were lucid theories, and they started me thinking. My family, I found, except father, had all been patriots. That means they fought for their pockets against the king's and tried to pay for the war in paper money. It didn't work, of course, and they had to invent a government to take the place of the Parliament and the King they had driven out. They wrote down their profoundest thoughts on the subject in Philadelphia and called it macaroni. A West Indian adventurer by the name of Hamilton has reinvented collectable taxes and solvency for 'em. An uncle of mine, by the way, drew the map on which the United States was laid out during the treaty. The map is only partly accurate.

"Well, I went through a yellow fever plague at Philadelphia and then sailed for Nassau, where I heard a great many decent Tories from Virginia and the Carolinas had gone. I spent a year on a barren island called Eleuthra, living on turtle eggs and memories of Edinburgh, and then took ship on impulse and came here. So now you have me.

"My own case is only a particular in the general mess, of course. But there were a great many people who felt just as I did about the glorious Revolution. They moved away from it; some to Canada, and some to the West Indies. I came here. And now I am going to be made a citizen of the Republic by treaty again.

"You can remember this about Americans, since you're going to be one too. There are two main kinds: those who come from east of the Alleghanies and those who are born west of them. 'North' and 'South' is what they talk about among themselves, but that difference goes only as far as the mountains. West of the mountains they are all what they call 'Kaintucks' here. The Kaintucks aren't Europeans any longer. Here is a rule for dealing with them that I ought to charge you money for: Treat every Westerner as if the world had just been created Tuesday; it is now Wednesday and you are a passive thunderbolt delighted to meet the first and only man."

"What about the Easterners?" asked Anthony.

"Three general kinds—" began the doctor, "but here comes our friend Ed Livingston. You've often heard him talk. He's one kind. Fine old New York family—caveat emptor. A little careless about municipal book-keeping at home. Finds the climate of Louisiana permanently congenial; not nearly so hot as New York when he left it. A little worried about extradition and the text of the new treaty . . ."

"What's that?" said Livingston, who had caught the last phrase and turned scarlet.

"Sit down, sit down," cried the doctor. "I was just talking politics with Toni, the ex-blackbirder here."

It was now Anthony's turn to burn under the collar.

"Look here, Terry—" began Livingston.

"Nonsense, nonsense!" shouted the doctor. "What is the past, the

Constitution, or a treaty between friends? Ba'tiste, three bottles of burgundy, some of that white Spanish soup, bisque of crayfish, and poulet and rice à la Creole. What do you say, gentlemen? Or would you rather have it pistols-in-the-morning?"

"By God, you're a card, Terry," said Livingston as they laughed and fell to. "Now I have a little proposition I want to make to you gentlemen."

A roar followed. Livingston always forgot that he always began supper that way. But this time he succeeded in interesting them. Like so many other propositions, all that this one needed was someone else's capital to demonstrate it. . . .

"How would a hundred thousand silver dollars as a first deposit do?" asked Anthony.

Livingston reached forward searching his face. "Do you mean that?" he cried.

"I certainly do."

"Told you he was lined with it," insisted the doctor. "Ba'tiste!" He rattled the empty bottles.

"Now you fellows listen to me," said Anthony, his eyes beginning to sparkle.

Anthony had waited for some time before he had seen fit to reveal to anyone the nature of his business in New Orleans. But the opportunity offered by the rainy night and the two whom he had now come to know well enough to have confidence in had not been lost.

Livingston's "proposition" had been to start a "Merchants' and Planters' Bank." It was, of course, to be a bank of issue. When the American régime was installed, he hoped to be able to bring enough political influence to bear to have his bank designated as the depository for federal funds. Upon these an unlimited issue of wildcat money in bank-notes could be issued.

"And then," said he, "there will be the Indian funds. The Natchez will eventually have to be paid off for their land. The specie will come from Washington. We can pay the Indians in bank-notes and hold the coin as deposit. No one needs to tell the Indians how to cash the notes. Probably not many bills will come back from so great a distance. It will be clear, clean profit. All that we need is Toni's Mexican silver here to start the ball rolling. The knowledge that large shipments of bullion are being deposited with us is all that we should want to establish our credit. Do you really think you could arrange to leave a hundred thousand on deposit with us between shipments, Toni?"

"Provided we can count on setting up regular and fairly safe for-

warding operations between here and Vera Cruz. Once we get the
dollars here I have no doubt we can arrange to get them on to Philadelphia. While the stuff is in New Orleans it will have to be kept
somewhere. Why not in our bank? I can't see myself burying it in
the garden and sitting up over it with a pistol all night."

"You don't bury anything here," remarked the doctor, "not even
the dead. You strike water six inches down."

"It isn't the water that worries me," said Livingston. "It's Lafitte
and the Baratarians. How is Adverse ever going to get shiploads of
dollars past those pirates? The river mouth is a regular nest of them
around Barataria. For the past five years they have been bribed to
let ships for New Orleans alone only by giving them complete control
of the slave trade. Even at that . . ."

"Lafitte?" said Anthony. "Why, it was Lafitte that the governor
spoke of!"

"I see what he meant!" exclaimed Mitchell. "Now leave it to me,
Livingston. Go ahead and organize your bank uptown, I'll take Adverse to see Jean Lafitte at the blacksmith shop tomorrow. He owes
me a life or two. If we don't have silver coming here by shiploads
by the time you are ready to open your doors, I'll eat my hat. Now
what's your plan, Toni, to get the stuff to Philadelphia?"

"I shall open up business as a general merchandising concern, dealing principally in sugar and cotton, and as a correspondent of *David
Parish and Company,* in Philadelphia. I shall buy or charter a number of fast sailing craft and ship specie, unknown to anybody but ourselves, to Parish as fast as it comes in."

"Good," said Mitchell. "It looks to me as if we had both ends and
the middle of this proposition in order. Now let's get on with it before the Americans take over the government and start to make laws
about everything."

"Amen to that," said Anthony.

Next day he and Dr. Mitchell went to see the proprietor of a blacksmith shop on St. Philip Street between Bourbon and Dauphine. The
heavy rain of the night before had made the distinction between the
river and the town purely academic.

Outwardly the blacksmith shop of the Brothers Lafitte resembled—
a blacksmith shop. The usual number of sorry nags were standing
about on three feet with the fourth held in the leather apron of a
negro smith stripped to the waist, while the hot-iron sizzled against
the hoof and the nails went home. The usual number of curs stole
and fought over that choice tidbit of dogdom, a hoof-paring. The

usual number of children with black-beady eyes peeped in through the wide doors, attracted by the glow of red-hot metal, the whale-like puffing of leather bellows, and the musical clink and ring of iron, anvil, and hammers. But that was all that was usual about the black-smith shop of the Brothers Lafitte.

On the unusual side of the ledger it might have been entered that the negro smiths all seemed to have been chosen from a race of giants. A good many of them were scarred with both sword and whip, and one of them, the tallest, had lost an eye. The muscles of these huge fellows rippled like snakes in the mud under the black, glistening films of their sweaty hides, and they could fit iron clod-hoppers on a vicious she-mule as if Cinderella herself were bashfully extending one foot to be fitted with a glass slipper.

Add that these slaves of the lamp were bossed by a white jinnee from Georgia seven feet tall by the name of Humble, the pride of Catahoula Parish, where gouging was a fine art, and that M. Jean Lafitte was in the custom of calling upon these who owed him moneys or had trade favours to dispense, accompanied by a bodyguard of very black blacksmiths—and one need add no more.

Gentlemen who insisted upon challenging M. Jean Lafitte to duels with colchemards, the Creole short sword, or with pistols were waited upon by Mr. Humble in the rôle of M. Lafitte's second. He would greatly regret the unfortunate illness, or absence, of his principal and suggest that the matter could be settled immediately with hammers in six feet of water in the nearest swamp. Otherwise, a thousand dollars would heal M. Lafitte's asperged honour, which was sensitive about gossip. Thus horseshoeing tended to prosper.

The close family feeling between the brothers Pierre and Jean Lafitte was touching. They were not only hand in glove but hand in purse. If they had been Siamese twins it could scarcely have been more diffi-cult to tell which one robbed you; whether it was Pierre with his gang of able ruffians at Grande Terre near the mouth of the river or Jean at the blacksmith shop in New Orleans. Those who had anything to import or export, whether merchandise or members of the family, made a point of seeing Jean in New Orleans in order to avoid seeing Pierre at Grande Terre.

Hence, the giant Humble was by no means surprised when Dr. Mitchell appeared at the smithy entrance with Anthony in tow and pointed inquiringly to a barred passage leading to the rear of the shop.

"He's thar," said Humble, "but he ain't done riz yet. How 'bout the gen'leman, doc?"

"A bobcat," said the doctor. "Take a good look at him so you don't mistake him for a muskrat when you're out skinnin' some night." He added something in a low tone to Humble.

"Yo don't say so!" exclaimed the man. "Stranger, I'm powerful glad to meet yo-all." For some days afterwards Anthony's right hand was out of business.

The yard and sheds behind the smithy were piled with an assortment of merchandise and valuables that spoke well for the enterprise of the "Privateers" at Barataria. There was the smell of spilled spices, and in one corner of the compound a couple of unshaven ruffians in red caps and greasy canvas drawers were pawing over a chest of cashmere shawls.

"It's not often they stop an Indiaman," said the doctor. "Look at that smashed teakwood screen there. But come on; they don't like you nebbin' in just after a haul."

A mulatto woman opened the door of a small, brick house at the far end of the yard, and muttering something incomprehensible in Gombo, led them into a kitchen with a dirt floor.

Seated before a table, upon which stood a large, smoking tureen of boiled shrimps, was a dapper little man dressed in an exquisite, bottle-green suit, buckled pumps, and a frilled shirt. This, with his eyes, which were very large and had curious yellow pupils that seldom shifted, gave him the air of a frog. The resemblance was still further increased by his habit of pitching pink shrimps into his mouth and gulping them as if they were so many insects. He greeted the doctor with a smile and nodded to Anthony, who did not for some time realize that here was the celebrated Jean Lafitte.

The doctor began to explain the object of their call. At first Lafitte seemed to pay no attention to him and the shrimps continued to vanish accompanied by copious streams of fragrant Java coffee. As the doctor talked on, however, the dark little man at the table shoved aside his plate, and resting his head in his hands and his elbows on the board, gazed piercingly at the two visitors before him.

At the end of half an hour, during which Mitchell had made an ardent plea for his co-operation, Lafitte began to question Anthony keenly.

Anthony replied frankly and with few reservations, for he had come to the conclusion that he would have to deal with this powerful river-baron either on the basis of a complete understanding or an open defiance. Defiance would entail obtaining and manning ships powerful enough to defy the flotilla of Pierre Lafitte at the entrance to the Mississippi. That might be impossible. It would certainly be enormously expensive, and it would surely imply an insufferable delay. It would be better to pay; pay, if one had to, through the nose. . . .

"As I understand it then," said Lafitte, "the doctor's suggestion is that on each of these shipments of bullion a moderate toll should be levied by us to permit them to pass. I should say about half would be a fair division—under the circumstances."

"That would never do," replied Anthony. "You do not quite see the realities of the situation. You must remember, monsieur the blacksmith, that you are not dealing with some helpless merchant. My principals have supplied me with unlimited resources to carry out this project, and if you do not care to participate reasonably, I shall go to Havana, outfit my own fleet, and ferry the bullion over from Vera Cruz in your teeth."

"And pay seventy-five per cent in squeeze to the Spanish authorities," grunted Lafitte.

"No, you are mistaken. I have dealt in Havana. I know the ropes there. Carlo Cibo is my agent. And besides, my principal would not permit of the squeeze."

"He must be a powerful principal," sneered Lafitte.

"He is," replied Anthony. "His name is Napoleon Bonaparte."

Lafitte wiped his lips thoughtfully. "I begin to see," he said.

"Certainly," cried Anthony. "I knew you would. You are a man of imagination. There is nothing to prevent your taking our first cargo, for instance, and keeping all of it. But that would be the end, wouldn't it? And, if you levy a terrific toll we go elsewhere—and that also will be the end without even a beginning."

"What is your proposal then, M. Adverse? Allons!"

"It is simply this: I propose to employ you and your brother to bring the bullion from Vera Cruz to New Orleans in your own ships and to pay you damn well for doing it."

"So you would trust us, eh?"

"Certainly. I am dealing with men of honour. I understood that from the first."

Lafitte could not entirely conceal his pleasure at this. "Go on," he said.

"Well, the point is that since these operations must continue for some years, you will in the end profit much more by protecting them and making delivery safe so that we can afford to load large sums every voyage instead of driblets. And there must also be no interference with the trans-shipments to Philadelphia."

"Oh, zat ees annozair sing," said Lafitte. "You pay half ven you go up and you pay half ven you come down. Vy not?"

"Come on, Adverse, we'll go to Havana," said Dr. Mitchell, rising. "They don't strangle the golden goose there as soon as it peeps. . . .

"You're one big Cajan fool, Jean Lafitte," continued the doctor, pounding on the table till the shrimps jumped out of the pan. "This is the biggest chance that will ever come your way. Think of it! The whole province will boom with this cash going through it and you will be the dog in the manger. Don't ask me to tend any gun-shot wounds again. You're not worth the time I spend on you."

"Now, doc-tair, asseyez-vous," said Lafitte, gulping a little. "You are always like ze hurricane." He sat for a minute. "I tell you vot ve do. Ve go talk zees ovair wiz my brozair Pierre chez Grande Terre. Dimanche prochain."

"Good!" said Mitchell. "I thought you'd see light."

"And you tell Mr. Edaward Leevings-ton go ahead wid ze bank," said Jean laughing. "Zat ees good idea, I sink. Ha! Ve all make vera mooch monay! N'est-ce pas?"

"That last remark was very encouraging," insisted the doctor as they strolled down the swampy little street together, being careful to stick to the raised banquette, although potted plants dripped on them from the little balconies overhead. "If we have many more rains like last night's there will be fever again. It never fails."

"I think Lafitte was only putting me off," replied Anthony, who regarded himself as immune to all fever since African days.

"No, no, he only wants time to communicate with his brother Pierre at Barataria first. That is why he put you off till next Sunday. You will see, Pierre will consent. It is now only a matter of terms. I will go along with you when you go to bargain at Grande Terre, if you like."

"For Lord's sake, do. How is it you stand-in so well with them?"

"There are often a good many gunshot wounds and cutlass slashes to bind up among them. I never ask questions and I keep my mouth shut. The presents I receive from these pirates permit me to live well here and to practice medicine instead of ancient magic on honest men."

"How do we get to Barataria?" persisted Anthony, who was not so interested in medicine as the doctor was.

"Wait till Sunday, and you will see," said Mitchell. "That will leave you a few days to attend to other matters. I want you to meet people here. That is always useful. Everybody, anybody. Just get around."

"Why?"

"I want to use you later on," said the doctor, "so I want you to be successful. You see, I am completely selfish about it. Now let's step in and pass the good news along to Ed Livingston."

That able promoter needed very little to encourage him. He was soon to be found hustling about the city in a large planter's hat, an alpaca coat, and long, baggy cotton trousers, enlisting his clerical help, renting a building, installing counters and a brick safe, and informing prospective depositors of the credit facilities which "our sound and enterprising financial institution will shortly be enabled to extend to those of known enterprise and integrity. The subscribed capital is already one hundred thousand dollars Mexican. Those who wish to subscribe to the capital stock of this bank of deposit and issue, in a community with illimitable prospects, are invited to do so at ten dollars a share. The offices are at the corner of Royal and Conti streets."

"Rumour, credulity, and hope form the basis of credit," said Livingston as they took dinner one day at the Orleans Hotel shortly after the interview with Jean Lafitte. Dinner was at 2.30 in the afternoon. The rest of the day until supper was devoted to digestion and liquid accelerators.

As if to confirm Livingston's remarks, who should walk up to the bar and subscribe for ten shares of stock but Mr. M'Quiston. He was doing well, he said. McTavish, McTavish, and McTavish would be "vera pleased." He himself was settling in New Orleans.

"Our friend Melancthon Conant has put down the cash for a hundred shares, and there are others in small amounts," continued Livingston, who looked surprised in spite of himself. "Who would have believed it? All that I need is another thousand dollars cash to open the doors."

"I will provide that," said Anthony, who had brought $10,000 in Spanish gold pieces. "Open up tomorrow but don't make any loans till the first shipment of bullion comes in. Oh, you might discount a thousand dollars' worth of the best paper secured by merchandise just to start the ball rolling. Say, thirty days at ten per cent and three names. Keep enough coin in the tills to make change."

Dr. Mitchell roared. "With an ex-slaver, a fugitive from justice, a Scotch clerk, and an undertaking-tout as the backers of this 'great fiduciary operation,' it ought to be a pronounced success in this world."

"And why not an M.D. too?" suggested Anthony.

"Well, why not?" replied Mitchell. "It needs a touch of respectability."

That evening the "board of directors" seated about the table over turtle steak at Ba'tiste's voted the doctor one hundred shares of stock for his "valuable services in encouraging the promotion of said fiduciary institution."

Dr. Terry M. laughed. He had no idea that his collateral heirs would be made comfortable for two generations.

The next day the *Merchants' and Planters' Bank of Deposit* opened its single door. In two weeks it received $3,000 in paid up capital

stock. It made loans of $2,500 and had on file applications for $180,-
000 more.

But the curious thing about it was that everybody believed in it.
Even Anthony believed in it. An idea tossed about in conversation
had actually become an interest-drawing fact. He slipped around to
the Creole who owned the lot where the bank stood and bought it one
morning for $450. Thus what later on was to become the famous
Citizens' Bank of New Orleans got under way.

The years 1803 and 1804 witnessed rapid and far-reaching changes.
In New Orleans the long somnolence of the colonial era and the dependence upon Europe passed away. Down the current of the mighty
river and across the tides of the Gulf the Americans swarmed in upon
Louisiana in argosies of arks and rafts, in flotillas of ships and schooners. They began to approach it overland from Kentucky and Tennessee as well.

The ceremonies of the passing of the old and of the beginning of
the new order took place before Anthony's eyes.

On the last day of November 1803, he saw Salcedo on the balcony
of the Cabildo deliver the keys of the city to Laussat and heard Casa
Calvo, the Spanish commissioner, absolve the provincials, and incidentally himself, from all allegiance to the crown of Spain. The
tricolour was raised over the Place d'Armes amidst the wild rejoicing
of the Creoles, and for about three weeks Anthony found himself by
legal fiction at least a citizen of the French Republic. It was during
this brief interval, while the American troops were arriving and Governor Claiborne and his modest staff were preparing to take over the
province, that he visited Barataria.

Very early on the appointed Sunday morning the giant blacksmith
Humble knocked on the door at Ba'tiste's and informed Anthony and
Dr. Mitchell that all was ready for the journey.

"M. Jean is already at Grande Terre with his brother Pierre," said
the man. "They are waiting for you."

Dr. Mitchell nudged Anthony at this as if to say, "I told you so."

They crossed the Mississippi to the right bank in a ferry worked
by an old horse which forever ascended a treadmill with an expression
of perpetual surprise. To the Kaintucks who lined the levee this
paddle-wheel boat appeared to be a miracle of ingenuity.

They scrambled up the levee at McDonald's plantation and, striking westward through the swamp along the banks of a drainage canal,
came after several hours' terrible, muddy going on horseback to a
deep, narrow, and tortuous bayou. Here a long pirogue hollowed out

of a single huge cypress awaited them.   It was manned by ten negroes with paddles.   They were chained together at the waist and watched over by an old Canary Islander, or "isleño," who had lost both ears but still had the active use of his eyes, two pistols, a cutlass, and a whip upon which he was engaged in fitting a new lash when they entered the boat.

At a grunt from this genial coxswain they set out.   Now for the first time the nature of the country about New Orleans became apparent to Anthony.

The bayou, which was forty miles long, twisted and squirmed through the impenetrable swamp.   Currentless, it led through a perpetual half-gloom under a tunnel of cypress and water-oaks draped, hooded, bearded, and garlanded with masses of Spanish moss.   As the banks grew lower, on either side could be seen the exotic green of the southern forest, its knees and shrubs bathed in water with an occasional hummock rising out of the perpetual grey-green gloom. Turtles and cotton-mouths abounded, and innumerable herons standing on one leg in the gloomy shallows.

All was silent.   Except for the rhythmical dip of the paddles and a song with endless verses in Gombo, that the paddlers took up stanza by stanza, while the swamp listened, they might have been moving through a green limbo where creation was not yet complete.

> "Mouché Préval
> Li donné grand bal.
> Li fait nègue payé
> Pou sauté ain pé.
> Dansé Calinda, dansé."

And they would round a turn to see the inevitable heron flapping off with its long legs tucked under it, into the shadows.

> "Li donné soupé
> Pou nègue régalé;
> So vié la musique
> Té baye la collique.
> Dansé Calinda, dansé."

And they would round another curve. . . .

About twilight they emerged suddenly upon Lake Cataouatche, just as the long lines of waterfowl came to hide in the rushes for the night. It was an infernal mere, red as a demon's eye in the sunset, surrounded by cypress swamps and a dismal hearse-draped forest resonant as darkness fell with the eery whistling of ducks' wings.   As the light dwindled, the bellowing of alligators and the harsh screams of nocturnal waterfowl resounded from all sides. *"Nox, nox, nox,"* croaked the frogs. And the endless sorrows of the whippoorwills began.

They built fires here on a bit of beach, ate supper and rested. The vastness and loneliness of the place descended upon all of them. The dim lake reflected the misty sky. It was impossible to tell where space ended and the earth began. Both whites and blacks felt it. They seemed to be lost together in a place without limits.

"What lies to the west of these swamps?" Anthony asked the Canary Islander.

"The prairies of the Opelousas," he replied.

"And beyond that?"

"Llano estocado, señor."

"And then?"

"Los Indios, perhaps. Who knows? Wide, wide!" He gestured out into the darkness. He raked the fire together as if to lighten the threatening space about him.

By the other fire, in a subdued voice breathing insufferable regret, Anthony heard one of the slaves crooning in his half-African dialect.

> "Ninette, do you remember the cool brook
> Through the palm grove,
> Do you remember the green banana trees,
> And the pool there in the sunlight
> Where we lay at ease?
> Ah, what fun we had there together,
> You and I, little pet!
> But now the brook has stopped.
> It died of regret.
> The palms droop by its shore—
> Even the water could not embrace you forever—
> Do you remember the brook, Ninette,
> Do you remember anything anymore?"

Crude as were the words, the tone, the intonation, and the primal music with which they were uttered did the trick. In the brain of the white man his own complicated and magnificent music began.

Anthony lay back in his blanket in the firelight and listened to a symphony played on the invisible and muted strings of thought. It poured out over the threshold of his spirit as if the dark and bright angels of his nature had suddenly seized viols and sat within the prison house of the body blending in harmony the magic pain of the past and the golden hope for the future. It was the song of the exile turned pioneer. It began by moving him to tears and it left him buoyed up and sustained by hope.

These mental reverberations of abstract sound, a harmony that expressed completely the emotional meaning of experience, as though he and the world had been blent into one in order to hear, this music seemed to be presented to him; to be a benign gift that brought with it a catharsis for existence itself.

How long he lay listening that evening he never knew. Dr. Mitchell poked him with the butt of his pistol and "awoke" him at last. Pine torches were flaring in the darkness and they were once more on their way.

Fatigued now beyond thought of melody, the crew sang no more. The grey trees drooped like deserted tents in the late moonlight as they passed them.

"By the rivers of Babylon . . . we hanged our harps upon the willows—"

The words suddenly flashed into his memory from somewhere as he saw himself reading in his room at the Casa da Bonnyfeather as a young boy. The light burned steadily and the madonna stood in her niche. For a moment an insufferable feeling of homesickness swept over him. Would he never get home again? Home—where was it? Here?

He lit a cigar and distributed the remainder, one to every man in the boat. A sigh of satisfaction went up as the men inhaled. They looked at him gratefully.

At least the land provided an herb to dull the ache in the hearts of the exiles it sheltered.

Great is tobacco, a leaf from the foliage of paradise, a shrub rooted in contentment, manna of the west!

The men resumed the paddles again and they sped on southward into the dawn across Lake Salvador. They threaded another endless bayou, slept, crossed Lake Villiers, plunged into the Bayou St. Denis, and finally emerged from the gloomy forest into the sparkling reaches of Barataria Sound. It was on the morning of the third day that they came in sight of Grande Terre.

A fleet of six schooners and three ships lay at anchor before a settlement of about a dozen houses at the bottom of the cove. There was a battery commanding the landing, several small warehouses, and a primitive shipyard. The place wore a bright and pleasing aspect. There was a blinding white beach. Behind it rose the vivid green of the everlasting oaks and shrubbery of the coastal island where a few cattle were pastured. The chenière of Grande Terre had been inhabited from ancient times, as the large shell heaps forming mounds and banks here and there along the beach showed. The pirate town was in fact indebted to the vanished Indians for its convenient water front and raised banks. It had not yet grown into that metropolis of buccaneers and thriving mart of illicit trade to which it afterward attained. Already, however, there were long rows of slave pens hidden behind the dunes. Two of the ships in port were blackbirders, and the third, to judge by her shattered bulwarks and pockmarked hull, was a recent prize.

As they landed, Anthony could not help noting the signs of discipline and order on every hand. The town was neat and clean. The houses of brick and cypress frame, long, low and of a pleasing contour, had flowers in the windows. A white-washed residence with green shutters at the head of the street would have done credit to a colonial official. He had no doubt it was Lafitte's. Except for the frowning battery, there was little sign of means of defence. The tortuous channels, shoals, and sandbars were, indeed, the pirates' main reliance. There were gardens and flowered dooryards behind picket fences and lines of fluttering wash—all of which domestic rather than martial appearance was explained by the number of well-dressed women and children playing about. All labour was performed by slaves, of whom the most humble seaman could have his share.

They were met by a young fellow dressed like a merchant officer, neat but weaponless, who led them to Lafitte's house. They found the two brothers together opening the letters of a ship's mail. These lay scattered about the floor of a large room furnished exquisitely but to the point of exuberance. A hundred ships' cabins had contributed to it.

"Here's your man!" said Jean to his brother, as Anthony and the doctor entered. He motioned to a woman with a baby to leave the room. "Bonjour, mon grand petit docteur."

"Pierre, this is Meester Ad-vairse. He talks Spanish."

"Welcome, señor," said Pierre Lafitte. "How was Bayonne when you last saw it? I hear you were there recently. It is my father's town."

"It still smells of fish and garlic," said Anthony, laughing.

"Ha! Tell me about it," said Pierre. "I would give a hundred dollars for a plate of fresh sardines." They sat down to talk.

Both the brothers affected green. But Pierre was over six feet tall and even in the house wore an otterskin cap and a huge cutlass with a gold-inlayed ivory handle. There were rings in his ears, and his fine white teeth and piercing black eyes flashed simultaneously into a frown or a smile. He concealed nothing. It was plain that thought, feeling, and action with Pierre Lafitte were one and the same thing.

As Anthony took his measure, he knew that the interview about to take place would be the crisis of his own commercial career—that he would have to think faster and talk more clearly and persuasively than he had ever done before.

"I am told by little Jean," said Lafitte, "that you have something important to talk about, señor."

"Gold, Señor Lafitte; Mexican silver, millions of it."

"Ah, ha," cried Lafitte, shaking the rings in his ears. "In that case, I reply like the skittish señora with the boy husband when the big matador whispered something into her shell-like ear.

"'Let us get together, my bully one! Why not?'"

CHAPTER SIXTY-FOUR

THE SNAKE CHANGES ITS SKIN

IT WAS weeks later, and past the middle of December, when Anthony stood once more upon the levee at New Orleans. The "interview" at Grande Terre had drawn out into a long negotiation.

"Well, what news?" cried Livingston, who had been haunting the water front for days. "I thought Lafitte must have swallowed you and the doctor, pills and all."

"He did," said Mitchell, who liked to speak first. "He took our medicine."

"With a large amount of orange juice to make it go down," added Anthony a little ruefully. "But the upshot of the whole matter is that a shipment of bullion will be in from Vera Cruz shortly and more will follow. Jean Lafitte is bringing the first shipment himself. After that, one of his fast brigs returns for it regularly."

"Thank God, the bank's saved!" said Livingston so piously that Mitchell smiled.

"Otherwise it would have been the same as heart failure with you, wouldn't it, Ed?" he remarked. "Well, you can thank Toni here. He handled the piratical brothers like a young Ulysses. Upon my word, I say hats off to him."

To Anthony this remark of the doctor came as his chief reward for two long years' work. When the first shipment of bullion arrived and was safely on its way to Parish at Philadelphia he intended to get incontinently drunk. "But there's many a slip," he thought uneasily as they walked down the little street toward Ba'tiste's, chattering gayly.

It was evening and the serenos were going about the Place d'Armes lighting the dim oil lamps that swung here and there from brackets. "A fine clear night and all's well," one of them sang out from sheer habit, despite the fact that a few drops were beginning to fall and it was a dank, misty evening with a fog blowing in from the river. They laughed.

"The old watch will soon be gone, I suppose," said Mitchell. "The Americans take over on Monday, you know. Wonder what the place will be like in a few years?

"Well, these old lamps won't throw much light into the future anyway. You can't even see the present by 'em. Let's go, it's beginning to rain," cried the doctor a little impatiently.

"They're better than nothing though," insisted Livingston as he avoided the next pitfall and picked his way along gingerly. "Many an old rip's got home by 'em and—"

"A fine night and all's well," shouted the sereno they had left behind. As if to rebuke this insistent official optimism, from somewhere up the Rue de Conti came a burst of funereal singing and the glow of torches. A few melancholy shouts and the screams and wailing of a mob of women could be heard like a chorus accompanying a dirge-like chanting that grew momentarily louder.

"Some big bow-wow among the Creoles is wagging his tail for the last time, I suppose," said Livingston. "Come on, let's see the obsequies."

They turned the corner on impulse, and walking down a block, took shelter in the doorway of the old Spanish tavern at the corner of Demaine Street.

"Can't be a funeral," asserted the doctor. "There's no hearse, and look at the people swarming out of the houses as they come along. Looks like a riot."

"There's the hearse," said Anthony as a high, draped object lighted by rows of torches came around the corner of the street below. It was surrounded by nuns led by the archbishop and some clergy.

The chant grew louder. Through the river mist and fine, pearly rain the procession approached slowly. The effect of the torches and the voices in the fog was indescribably solemn.

Redemisti virgam hæreditatis tuæ . . .

"Lord! I remember now," suddenly exclaimed Mitchell. "Of course! It's the Ursulines. They're leaving tonight on the last Spanish transport for Havana and taking the statue from their chapel along with them. That's what the row's about."

Leva manus tuas in superbias eorum in finem . . .

"Only some of the old girls are staying on. A good many are French émigrées and the word 'republic' has them scared stiff. They say that fine atheist Jefferson wrote them a reassuring letter that would do a Christian gentleman credit. But only a few believed him. It's carrying the Mary off that makes the crowd yowl. Listen to that, would you!"

Et gloriati sunt qui oderunt te, in medio solemnitatis tuæ.

"She's been here since the French came, they say—and now she's going."

Posuerunt signa sua, signa: et non cognoverunt . . .

"And a damned good riddance," added the doctor.

"That's right, doc! Jim Cyarter and all the Cyarters and their kin up-river ul say it with ye." It was a tall American speaking; along with several others dressed in fringed shirts, he had left the bar and crowded to the door of the tavern to see the procession go by.

Quasi in silva lingnorum securibus exciderunt januas ejus in idipsum: in securi et ascia dejecerunt eam.

Two acolytes swinging censers passed leading the procession.

"What are you going to give the Cyarters and their kin when she's gone, doc?" said Anthony in a low tone just by Mitchell's ear.

The doctor started a little but rallied. "What do you give a sick man when the fever leaves him?" he said.

"Pills?"

"No. Rest, reason, and fresh air."

"I was thinking of the soul."

"The soul is a priestly lie," exclaimed the doctor hardily.

"Right again, doc," cried the irrepressible Mr. Carter, who had no idea he was horning-in. "In our neck o' the woods thar's far too many trees to cut down yit to worry about yer soul." He sniffed the incense suspiciously. "I tell ye . . ."

The clergy passed. The smell of pine torches and a whirl of smoke and sparks swirled up into their faces.

Incenderunt igni sanctuarium tuum:
in terra polluerunt tabernaculum nominis tui.
Dixerunt in corde suo cognatio eorum simul:
Quiescere faciamus omnes dies festos Dei a terra

—thundered the Creole mob taking up the chant.

Twenty-five or thirty Ursuline nuns with their heads on their breasts, many with tears running down their cheeks, were now passing directly before them. The sound of their chanting had about it that singular touch of hysterical woe, which only the voices of women can convey. Their pale faces looked out of their hoods like so many variations upon the mask of tragedy. In the centre of this black-robed group of women was a kind of ark which had been contrived for the occasion and heaped with the last late blossoms of the year. Over it was erected a miniature pavilion of cloth of gold. The sides of this little tent were of some sort of transparent gauze, sufficient to permit a number of wax tapers sheltered behind it to burn steadily with a clear, saffron light. Bathed in this quiet radiance, as though she had gathered the aura of the past about her and was departing in its golden mist, sat a remarkably gracious and life-like statue of the Virgin holding the Holy Child on her knees. In her flower-filled ark carried on the shoulders of four huge porters she seemed to be float-ing above the heads of the wildly seething mob amid the red glare of funeral torches in a divinely self-poised calm. For an instant even the Americans standing in the door of the Spanish tavern were re-duced to silence. But not for long.

"Hell!" exclaimed Carter, suddenly wrapping a wolfskin jacket closer about him and striding off in the direction of the Batture. His hatchet-face seemed to cleave its way through the crowd.

Disengaging himself from his two companions, Anthony slipped away to follow the procession.

It halted before the steps of the cathedral where the archbishop blessed it and scattered holy water on the crowd. A few drops fell on his cheeks. Led by a tall, fanatical monk, Father Antoine, who lived in a cell, half-hut and half-bower, in the bosk behind the cathe-dral, the procession now proceeded to the water front. The levee was black with the assembled inhabitants of the Vieux Carré. Like float-ing globes in the river mist the lights of the Spanish transport could be seen where she lay anchored in the stream farther out.

The crowd was silent now. Only the dirge-like voices of the nuns continued. The torches and the glowing ark were carried to the marge where the boats from the transport waited.

"Ah, monsieur," exclaimed an old Creole mother to Anthony while she wept under her shawl. "C'est le dernier moment que nous aurons notre belle vierge en Louisiane."

The nuns had ceased now. They were getting into the boats. The ark was lifted reverently by the Spanish soldiers and deposited in the stern-sheets of a barge. There was a sharp command and the sound of rowing.

The glowing tent of the Virgin, seemingly floating of itself a few feet above the water, disappeared gradually and dimly into the heavy mists of the midstream. As if the river were swallowing it and blot-ting it out, her form was seen no more. Only the giant crucifix of the monk remained elevated in silhouette in the glare of the torches.

For a while the crowd stood hypnotized. Then a cry of mingled rage, chagrin, and despair went up from it into the night.

Now that it was too late, Father Antoine and some of the more indignant gathered to protest—against what they scarcely knew—in front of the cathedral. But sheets of rain began to fall and the ardour of the crowd dissolved.

"For God's sake, Toni, what are you doing here?" Dr. Mitchell's voice came suddenly out of the darkness. "I've been looking for you everywhere. You'll get an ague staying out in this. Here put this on—" and he threw about Anthony's shoulders a dry cloak that he had brought from Ba'tiste's. "We thought you'd given us the slip and gone home."

Under the warm cloak Anthony still shivered a little, but not from cold. The effect of the scene he had just witnessed was too deep and complicated for mere phraseology. He said little to the doctor as they hurried home, knowing that Mitchell, who had not an iota of religion about him, regarded even an interest or sympathy for it in others as a weakness.

Indeed, from time to time at supper that evening both the doctor and Livingston glanced with a slightly puzzled expression at their friend.

Anthony went to sleep that night with snatches of the song he had dreamed by the banks of Lake Cataouatche, the chanson of the slave, and the dirge of the nuns in his ears. The next morning he was awakened by the thunder of cannon in the Place d'Armes. It was Monday, the 20th of December 1803.

The entire city crowded to the square before the Cabildo to see Laussat, the French prefect, deliver the province into the hands of Governor Claiborne and the government at Washington. The new American regulars and some of the Creole militia lined the square. The tricolour came to half mast as the stars and stripes rose on the same staff. For some reason the halliards slipped, and the two flags remained for a few moments tangled together, half-way up. The crowd roared, cursed, and wept. Laussat made a gesture of farewell. Then the stars and stripes rose to the thunder of cannon, the cheers of the Americans, and the strains of "Hail! Columbia, Happy Land!" A body of French volunteers laid the tricolour reverently away. Governor Claiborne made a neat speech promising justice, religious toleration, and prosperity—provided no one gave any trouble. And it was over. Louisiana was part of the United States.

"Well, how does it feel to be a citizen of the great, new republic!" said Mitchell, slapping Anthony on the back. "Come on," he laughed, "let's go to the Café des Exilés and have a drink."

Days of change, of swift and accelerating change. Time seemed to be moving in a crescendo upon an infinite scale. Life sped with a new and more profound momentum. The new pace could be measured by contrast, for the old French and Spanish City, the Vieux Carré, as it soon came to be called, positively refused to be hustled; to change its ways. It obstinately remained "foreign," a thing unto itself, cherishing the old Creole ways and hoping to the last that some·· thing, that anything, would happen to save it. That Napoleon would win, that . . . that—

Like a beautiful woman who in her girlhood had found the styles, the attitudes and manners that suited her best, and had determined to go on wearing them, Creole New Orleans continued gazing at herself in the mirror of the past until the glass cracked.

The Americans came swarming down upon and inundating the little city from the same direction and with something of the same energy as the current of the mighty river that brought them. In a short time the city council was petitioning the governor to tear down the old walls and fill up the moats. One could walk for two miles on the roofs of the flat-boats at the American landing. In the Faubourg Ste. Marie a shanty-town of bars, boarding-houses, and gambling dens awaited the flat-boats. The levee began to awaken every morning to the rumble of drays.

From the "tower" room at Ba'tiste's, where he lived for three years, Anthony saw the boom town begin to surround and besiege the old one, even to level and breach its walls. But it was as no idle spectator that he sat there. No man in the city had a more active part in its affairs than he. In many ways his past training and experience had fitted him eminently for life in Louisiana. Above all, his command of many languages now stood him in good stead, for New Orleans was a polyglot port if ever there was one.

The forwarding of the bullion, once the active co-operation of the Lafittes was secured, had been reduced to the status of a commercial routine. Their powerful protection had not been secured without paying royally for it. The brig *Felicia*, under the command of a talented desperado by the name of Dominic You, made the voyage between Vera Cruz and New Orleans for the mere trifle of $10,000 a trip—and in addition there had been an initial squeeze of $100,000 to come out of the first delivery. Besides that, 10 per cent was to be deducted and paid to Jean Lafitte out of the gross total of each voyage. But even with Anthony's own commission added to these charges plus the purchase and maintenance of swift schooners to convey the bullion to Philadelphia, he found that the cost of delivering the silver to Parish was a trifle over 12 per cent of the value of the moneys furnished by Lestapsis at Vera Cruz. As the insurance between Philadelphia and Vera Cruz was 60 per cent on minted money, he felt inclined to congratulate himself.

Indeed, it was doubtful if the Lafittes would have assented to act on such terms if it had not been for the promise of large credit facilities at Livingston's bank. If Pierre was a corsair pure and simple, Jean was a business man of no mean abilities. He had his thumb in many a pie in the development of the country and understood that being able to discount notes was often a more convenient and available method of obtaining the use of capital than rushing a quarter-deck. Besides, quarter-decks were not always rushable. The British and Yankees, it seemed, were peculiarly obstinate about their marine property. On the first of April 1804, a helpless-looking West Indian trader had turned out to be H.M.S. or U.S. something in disguise. There was no time to find out which. Five broadsides of grape and canister had sickened curiosity, and Dr. Mitchell had been summoned to Barataria to saw off legs and arms, set bones, sear stumps with boiling oil, and probe for bullets, while strong men made whimpering noises like nestsful of kittens. He returned looking pale, and with the entry in his notebook that wounds infected by bluebottle flies healed mysteriously well, if you just let them alone.

Under the circumstances Jean Lafitte's enthusiasm for banks was not entirely mysterious. Let Pierre roar and be the devil of a fellow at Grande Terre if he wanted to. He, Jean, could walk around to Mr. Livingston's bank at the northeast corner of Royal and Conti streets and return with what he needed, on both legs, and without having been met by a blast of grapeshot. That had its advantages.

It had been a great day, of course, when the first shipment of bullion came in. You had come stamping in one morning at Ba'tiste's and summoned Anthony to the water front. The *Felicia* lay at the levee ostensibly unloading hides. Under them and along the keel were seven hundred and fifty kegs with a thousand newly minted Mexican silver dollars in each. Jean Lafitte took a hundred and ten kegs of them home to his blacksmith shop, and the rest were conveyed to the new brick vault at Livingston's bank. All this after nightfall.

But no one can keep sailors from talking. The next day the rumour was all over town. It was gold that the *Felicia* had brought. Five millions of it was in Livingston's vaults. Only three millions, insisted others. A gentleman from Wheeling, Virginia, had an eye gouged out by a gentleman from Chartiers Creek, Pennsylvania, over this minor difference.

Even the old Creole city turned over a little in its sleep, and the rest of the place hummed. It felt the life blood of capital coursing in its veins. The sensation was intoxicating.

"Ah reckon thar's more caboodle in that scamp Livingston's vaults than the rest o' the hul goddamned territory's wuth," announced a Georgia planter leaning against the bar at the Orleans so that the handle of a pistol stuck out between his coat tails. No one came forward on the negative side. The slight exaggeration was felt to be too close to the mark to be arguable.

As the shipments to Philadelphia were managed with great secrecy and dispatch no one at the end of six months' time had any idea how much money was at "Livingston's." It was possible to manage the reshipment of coin without talk. The ship that sailed with it left no one behind to do any talking. Mr. Livingston was, therefore, in a delectable state. His "fiduciary institution" continued to enjoy a fabulous credit that he was not averse to exploiting.

Anthony's first adventures in the business methods of the community were with the bank and in organizing a fleet of fast schooners to keep in touch with Parish.

The latter he accomplished through the good offices of Captain Clemm, who had returned in record time from Philadelphia with a letter from David breathing relief at finding Anthony at New Orleans.

Captain Clemm was immediately sent back to Philadelphia with the $250,000 and instructions to round up five more vessels like his own with dependable skippers and crews. He was able to accomplish this gradually, and towards the end of the year found himself the commodore of a flotilla of six schooners and three lateen rigged dispatch boats that sailed like witches. The last being the idea of Mr. Adverse.

A shipyard to take care of these boats and to keep some hold on their crews while they lay in port was established on the right bank of the river opposite the city. There was a crude dry-dock, sheds, and a frame barracks for the men and log cabins for slaves. Visitors were forcibly discouraged.

Anthony had several reasons for establishing this place, which rapidly became known as "Algeciras" or "Little Algiers." From the right bank by way of the bayous he had communication with Barataria, and it became evident early in the game that the best way to bring in the silver was to land it at Grande Terré and ferry it up the bayous. The frequent presence of so many of Lafitte's men at the yard soon gave the place its uncertain reputation and the piratical name that long stuck to the locality.

There were other advantages. Several days were eliminated between beating up against the river current, and once at Algiers, the bullion could be loaded directly and dispatched without either causing rumours or having to be deposited at the bank. The latter became more and more important as time went on, for the influx of so much cash, in fact its mere presence, tended toward a disturbing inflation of credit. Anthony in Louisiana and Parish at Philadelphia both dealt

with this problem as best they could. They were not altogether successful. It was a very real problem, an inevitable concomitant of
Ouvrard's scheme.

Livingston, for instance, had not been content to use the 100,000
silver dollars which had been left with him on deposit out of the first
shipment of bullion as basis for establishing the bank's credit. Anthony had used a rather wide discretion in thus detaining so large an
account. But he felt the necessity of providing at New Orleans, in
order to facilitate his own operations, a bank with all the financial
and trade ramifications which a bank implied. In this decision Parish
had heartily concurred. But to Livingston it had been an opportunity
to start the printing press.

The notes of the new bank were quite admirable pieces of design.
There was an American eagle with a slightly buzzard-like expression
on every bill. The gallant bird trailed a cloudy ribbon in his beak
over the helpless town of New Orleans. On this appendage was curtly
inscribed

"Under My Wings Every Thing Prospers"

and then—"The Merchants' and Planters' Bank of New Orleans will
pay to the bearer on demand one silver dollar." It was soon a dead
heat as to which was more nebulous, the motto on the cloudy banner
born by the eagle or the promise of the bank. Mr. Livingston printed
two hundred thousand one dollar bills and rapidly put them into circulation by means of loans.

The usual number of skeptics were paid off in real dollars but the
new Mississippi Bubble continued to float. It was necessary, however, for Mr. Adverse to step in and stop the printing press, which
he did only after an unhappy scene with Mr. Livingston. As an upshot of this several new gentlemen were asked to sit on the board.
Alexander Milne, John McDonough, Bernard Marigny, Shepherd
Brown, and Judah Touro served to no little effect as a balance wheel
to Mr. Livingston's printing press.

Nevertheless, in three years, a half million dollars from nowhere
was pumped into the city and became real enough to draw interest for
the bank. With some of the profits Mr. Livingston began to buy up
the land around the American landing. A great many "gentlemen"
of all kinds were "much obleeged" for loans. Businesses, shops,
speculators, and plantations all felt the tonic effect of the small injection of silver that had sufficed to start the heart of credit beating.

Anthony himself now began to launch out. He speculated a little
in real estate, not always successfully. He began to look around for
land for a suitable plantation and house. In a short while he would

settle down and send for the boy. That was always in the back of his mind. It would never do, of course, to have him living at Ba'tiste's or in the city. He must first set himself up at home. He wrote his plans to Anna and to Vincent—and heard nothing. But that was not surprising. It might take a year or so to bring their replies. In the meanwhile he established himself as a general merchant by the means of a floating warehouse anchored at the American landing.

He bought-up a number of flat-boats, had them caulked at the shipyard, and using them for floats, built a platform on them with stores, sheds, a house for the clerks, and a long display counter in a room rigged up as a general store. This "flotage," as it was called, was moored to the levee and had boat landings and a narrow bridge to the bank. It was a surprising affair about a quarter of an acre in area. It cost little, it paid no taxes, and it rose and fell on the bosom of the floods. Ships moored alongside, discharged and loaded.

Mr. M'Quiston was prevailed upon to become the "captain" of this floating emporium with "sax clarks" for a crew. They were all his countrymen. The business proved unexpectedly large in volume and in the end profitable to a degree. All kinds of European merchandise was exchanged for the raw produce of the country brought down the river. Among other things, a brisk trade in furs sprang up, and coureurs de bois who ascended the Red River and the Missouri to points far beyond the ken of the map makers tied their canoes and arks up at "M'Quiston's Store," along with Scotch-Irish traders from Pittsburgh, Long-knives from the "Dark and Bloody Ground," and thrifty settlers from the Western Reserve. The scenes at the counter, where the tobacco and sugar scales were kept busy all day long, where woollens from Manchester were exchanged for beaver skins from the upper Alleghany and Monongahela, held a certain fascination for Anthony. The tales of the country of the unknown West stirred a vague longing in his soul to see some day these primeval forests and to pass beyond them to the fabulous, teeming prairies of the buffalo and the horse Indians.

Consequently, he spent considerable time at the flotage. He struck up a friendship with some of the coureurs de bois who had been farthest into the unknown. He staked them generously and trusted them. And in the end he had his reward. He fitted up a bunk and room for himself, took Simba with him and lived there for weeks at a time. The Kaintucks were always offering to trade the proceeds of their voyages for Simba.

"Man, you could sic that ar' houn' dog on painters."

About the American landing Simba and his master became well known. And because they went their own way quietly, looked able to give trouble, but never worried little dogs even when they barked at them, they were liked well enough. In the city Mr. Adverse, not only on account of his possessions, although these were rumoured to be even greater than they were, was popular. Even among the Creole planters his excellent French and other qualities had gained him a peculiar standing. After all, he was not just one of the Yanquis. His occasional presence at the cathedral, although it was observed he never attended mass, was, to the Latins at least, reassuring.

With the shipyard at Algiers, the floating store at the Batture, the bank, various properties, and the constant attention and adjustments incident to the shipment of the bullion, Anthony's worldly affairs engrossed a great part of his time, besides affording him hundreds of contacts and acquaintances.

The book-keeping for his own private affairs threatened to become inextricably mixed with the accounts of others. It frequently kept the light shining from the "tower-room" windows till nearly dawn. Yet he could entrust it to no one else. And that sense of order in all things that old John Bonnyfeather had instilled into him still insisted upon having its way. If others in the city did not know how their affairs stood, Mr. Adverse was always able to strike an accurate trial balance. The genial doctor, however, began to complain of his aloofness, and Anthony could see that when his correspondence with Europe should be added to his correspondence with Parish he would be overwhelmed.

He remembered old Sandy McNab living on his pension at Livorno. He made a long report to Ouvrard his excuse for dispatching a schooner to Italy by way of Spain about the end of the year 1804. Seven months later it returned with McNab, white-haired but hearty, and still wearing the identical Leghorn hat which he had bought with Anthony's shillings twenty years before. Their meeting was humorously affectionate. Sandy was installed in the room at Ba'tiste's, formerly occupied by Livingston, as the most confidential secretary that man ever had. In an atmosphere redolent of tobacco, newly-bound leather ledgers, and a tang of whisky, to say nothing of a renewed interest in life, Sandy ripened slowly like a winter apple. And there was many a heart-easing talk over old days at the Casa, while Simba beat the rug with his tail.

"It's a shame ye canna rent yon tike out for a duster," said Sandy. "There's naught in the scripture agin beasts workin' o' Sabbaths. But for a' sic minor losses, yer doin' weel, Maister Toni."

Sandy's laughter at hearing that Faith had married Don Luis was Homeric. "A fine precious pair o' toortle doves. Mark it, mon. No good ul coom o' their cooin'."

But there were some aspects of the past that Sandy never touched upon, for he also had his promises to keep. And, "Wha—" said he to himself in his own quaint way, "wha would be thankfu' for haen their ain' mither proved a whoor?"

Besides, it was not the past that engrossed Anthony. The future continued to unfold itself engrossingly:

Arch Street, Philadelphia,
Pennsylvania,
June the seventh, 1806.

Anthony Adverse, Esq.,
My very Dear Sir:

Your undersigned correspondent is in a curious quandary, one which, I venture to say, is not common among the ordinary run of men of affairs. My own situation is this: I am now at a loss how to bestow the monies which you are constantly forwarding me, at once to the best advantage and in a manner consonant with my instructions from Messrs Hope & Company.

Since February 1803 I have received from you on the bills drawn by Ouvrard on the Mexican treasury, and cashed by Lestapsis, a total of 11,329,000.32$ Mex (please check). With the utmost exertion it has been possible to forward to Europe only a little over 6,800,000$, thus leaving a vast sum to be invested here in a new country where the mere presence of so much cash is instantly magnified incalculably in terms of credit and leads to a dangerous inflation.

For instance, my last purchase of Government securities has driven them up beyond all reason. Deposit in banks leads to wild loans and the emission of floods of "wildcat" notes. The withdrawal of a deposit for sudden shipment thus becomes difficult or impossible without leaving the bank insolvent. Nor will any explanations or warnings prevent this. Loans to individuals are little better.

I have loaned a large sum to a Swiss by the name of Cazanov who came recommended to me as a sound man. He has invested heavily in the lands of Northern New York State, and, to preserve my own interests, I have had to advance him further sums and to take over many thousands of undeveloped acres in that howling wilderness as security. Ouvrard warned me against this, you will recall, but I have been helpless.

I shall soon be forced, even though winter is coming on, to make the arduous journey over the Alleghanies in order to obtain from one Blennerhassett, a mad Irishman, who has built a magnificent lodge in the wilderness near the forks of the Ohio, an adequate mortgage security on his properties for sums lent him on my account by a Mr. Chevis of the Philadelphia Bank. Since my health has been precarious, Mrs. Parish has heroically decided to accompany me—and *you may be sure* that her mother will go with her.

I mention this both to give you some idea of my many difficulties and to set your mind at rest in regard to a certain fact.

You seem to have inferred from my last letter that we were expecting a domestic accretion. I know not how you could have so misread my phraseology. Alas, your felicitations are without justification in the event. I should be more willing to gratify the natural longing of a woman to hold a child in her arms did I not feel that the duties of my wife require her to grace the board of her husband's establishment rather than to languish over the cradle of his heir. But to more important matters:

Most of the money sent to Europe so far has been in the form of neutral cargoes. The profits on these have been immense. But it becomes more and more difficult to ship anything from here, either produce or bullion, as the restrictions of the British blockade against the Emperor Napoleon are tightened from month to month. Hence, although both the Hopes and Barings are satisfied, my own difficulties increase as to how to invest safely the sums held over here, and I doubt if those at home with only a European outlook can envisage them. I have asked for assistance, and recent letters from Messers Hope advise me that Herr Vincent Nolte of Paris and Leghorn has been retained by them to collaborate in our American operations. I can assure you he will be welcome, for I am frankly unable to give adequate attention to the multitudinous demands made upon me. I am informed that you are acquainted with this gentleman. Should he arrive by way of New Orleans, pray provide him with proper entertainment and careful information in advance of his arrival in Philadelphia.

I inclose you, for forwarding to Lestapsis at Vera Cruz, further drafts on the Mexican treasury, signed, in this instance, by the King of Spain himself, for the sum of four millions of dollars. I am told that we may soon expect more! The prospect of further enormous sums to place here on doubtful security, with shipments to Europe more difficult every day, alarms me. In this dilemma I am frankly asking for your further co-operation.

Kindly invest locally as much as possible from the further shipments of bullion you receive at New Orleans. I suggest that you try to forward it to Europe in the form of cargoes of cotton, rum, sugar and such other colonial produce as may come to hand. Bill these shipments to the Barings at London, as they will then be permitted to pass the British cruisers. Let the Barings make their own arrangements for the transfer of the value of these cargoes to Holland. Our responsibility will be at an end with the arrival of the cargoes in England.

Now this is throwing more on your shoulders than you guaranted to assume. Yet I feel justified, under the circumstances, in calling upon you, and you can name your own remuneration in reason. This is your authority for making all necessary outlays for the furtherance of the prime object we both have in view. With every assurance of continued esteem and personal regards from me and my family, who are always very particular about you, believe me always, and in any event—

Yr. humble obedient servant,
DAVID PARISH

To Mr. Anthony Adverse,
Cor. of Rue St. Claude
    and the Public Place at
    New Orleans, Territory of Orleans, U. S.

This letter completely changed the tenor of Anthony's life in New Orleans. He was impelled by it to become the chief purchaser of cotton, sugar, and rum in Louisiana, and to extend himself in every direction that promised a profitable opening for shipments abroad. He took up land himself and planted a great acreage in cotton.

Parish's letter had alarmed him. The man seemed to be losing his grip. Never before had David become so personal—and so complaining. He wrote to Vincent at the first opportunity, urging him to come quickly, painting the life in the new country in glowing colours. "Bring Katrina and set up here. And, Vinc, if you love me, bring my boy, no matter what Anna may say." He wrote this and threw away the pen in excitement. To think of meeting Vincent and young Tony at the levee! "My God, life will be worth living then!" He called to Simba and rushed out to send the letter down river by a dispatch boat in order to catch a Spanish brig that had left that morning. The letter went.

On the same day Vincent Nolte was taking leave of Mr. Hope at Amsterdam in order to sail for New York. Katharine was dead. The House of the Wolf was desolate.

On the first rising ground to the west of the city, in what was then the Parish of St. Charles, Anthony built and laid out the lovely plantation of "Silver Ho" upon which he lavished the fondest dreams of his soul and a wealth of hope. The outlay was in proportion. For the first time he opened the strings of his own purse indulgently and to his heart's content. For it was here that he intended to live and die and to bring up his son. His longing to see the boy and to welcome him into his inheritance had already caused him to look upon his arrival in the near future as an indisputable fact. It was one of those "facts" which the brain dares not dispute with the heart. "Yes, at any moment young Tony and Vincent might arrive."

It was for that reason that he hastened the construction of the house beyond the precedents of the neighbourhood and built it of frame instead of brick, as he would otherwise have liked to do. But, as it was, he built well; of cedar and cypress and yellow-pine hewn out of his own swamps to the north near Lake Pontchartrain. For he had bought for his own and leased on account of "David Parish" a domain that ran clear across the "neck" from the lake to the river.

The house stood on what in the low-country passed for a knoll, a kind of low ridge covered with live-oaks, ashes, great-flowering magnolias, and clumps of pine. He cleared it carefully, accentuating its park-like aspects, leaving a patch of primeval woods at a distance of about a quarter of a mile surrounding the house.

You came upon Silver Ho suddenly. You emerged from these grey woods into the green of wide, embowered lawns dotted with live-oaks, each a pavilion of tattered moss shot through with a shimmering splendour. For it is the peculiar quality of these great trees to catch the light and hold it in the masses of their mossy nets. "That is why it is called Spanish moss," thought Anthony: "No gold slips through its fingers." There was a sharp curve in a clump of these giants and then you saw the house.

From a grove of magnolias its pillared face, chequered with white and gold shadows, looked calmly at the broad reaches of the Mississippi rolling along below it a full half-mile away. Its copper roof flashing in the sun—for he had drawn upon the shipyard extensively in his building—was for some time a mark for pilots before they rounded the great curve of the river above New Orleans. At last the roof weathered with patches of green, and the house seemed to sink back into the trees surrounding it until it became part of the magnolia grove itself.

It was not in any sense an extraordinary mansion. It belonged to the time and place. Ample, well-suited to the climate and hospitable, it had wide-flung verandas, high ceilings and generous lights. Both the house itself and its surroundings breathed abundance, leisure, and a capacity and love of living which in more northern climates would have been regarded as extravagant or unmoral. Upon the interior the skilful hands of ship carpenters left that mark of neat convenience, grace, and symmetry, the secret of which perished with them and can only be imitated.

Silver Ho was peculiar, however, in one respect. It was a whim of its owner. The young architect James Gallier protested, but Anthony insisted upon having his own way. Every stairway and hall, every entrance to the interior of the house led off from the large central room whose main embellishment was a great chimney. There was, to be sure, a rear entrance to the "L." But the "L" itself led into the big hall.

This provision was perhaps not so whimsical after all. By closing one door you closed all of them; that is, you closed the house. And on Silver Ho there were to be only a half dozen white men and eight hundred slaves. Insomnia in Louisiana was not due to the climate alone. One door to a house was a positive sedative.

Simba was to sleep in the living-hall. Anthony had his desk, his library, and his papers there. In that place the master of Silver Ho was to be at home—and his son and his son's sons after him. At that date one still peered into the future with some promise of permanence. Into the chimney-place to the right of the fireplace Anthony built a niche. And into this, when the first fire should be kindled upon the hearth, he intended to put his madonna, which had been so carefully refurbished by the jewellers in Paris. Here her wandering was to have an end at last. Here about the hearth, lares and penates visible and invisible were to shed the lustre of their calm and benign presences in the firelight. And there was to be peace.

Such dreams have been dreamed before and since. Even Vincent had agreed with Anthony that that is what banking is about.

Thus the fall and winter of 1806-1807 was intensely happy for Anthony. He was engaged constantly, early and late, upon a multiplicity of affairs that all seemed to have found a reason and a pole to revolve about at Silver Ho.

He took to horseback again, riding out to the plantation in the early mornings to urge the builders on, and riding back to town about noon for lunch with the doctor at Ba'tiste's and a swift survey of mail and accounts in Sandy's room. Then there was a meeting at the bank or a trip across the river to the shipyard when a new convey of silver came slipping up the bayous from Barataria. There was the infinite exercise of ingenuity in laying out the money in cargoes, in the sending of ships by hook or crook to England or a European port—anywhere, so long as the Hopes or the Barings finally got the goods. There were also schooners to be dispatched to Philadelphia, dispatch boats to Lestapsis at Vera Cruz, and the constant assiduous and often costly nursing of relations with the Lafittes.

Yet with Vincent and the boy in the offing, with the house nearing completion, he enjoyed and throve and grew merry upon it. He sold M'Quiston the flotage, retaining only a third interest. There was no longer time for nor the need of supervising that floating store. The town itself was now eagerly demanding more European goods than could be imported. Purchasing, instead of selling, was now Anthony's chief interest. To be a purchaser of everything is to be persona grata to everybody. He enjoyed the atmosphere he engendered everywhere in spite of the fact that he understood the cause.

He bought and imported all materials for erecting the plantation and for the partial furnishing of the house, in less than a year. There were three separate villages of huts for the slaves and houses for the general and house servants. There was also the expensive strengthening of the levee, the cutting of timber and the drainage of swamps. Not the least of the labour was a plantation road and its branches and the establishing of a ferry over the Bayou St. Jean that formed the boundary of his domain nearest the city.

As fast as he could shelter them he acquired his slaves from the Lafittes. He also resumed correspondence on the subject with Cibo in Cuba. His experience in Africa now leaped to the fore. Even Jean Lafitte had to admit that "no gen'leman in Louisiana knows as much about niggers as Mr. Adverse." Aided by Cibo, the house servants were brought from Cuba.

Carlo also began to write about paying Anthony a visit. It was a pleasant thought as he sat, now a mountain of flesh, on the veranda in the patio looked after hand and foot by Cheecha, who had received everything but her freedom.

And then, quite suddenly it seemed, for the busy months had passed frantically, Silver Ho was finished. The lowlands were green with cane and the uplands white with cotton. The chimney of the house waited for its first smoke. But no fire had yet been kindled on the hearth. Neither Vincent nor the boy had arrived. And with a curiously reminiscent and inconsistent pleasure, like that of a bachelor going the rounds of his old haunts and cronies a few days before his marriage, Anthony returned to taste of the freedom of the city while he lingered on in New Orleans.

The charm of the place lay in its enormous contrasts. He could find the raw and primitive tang of the elemental life of frontier living among the Kaintucks, coureurs de bois, and Indians at the Batture and at M'Quiston's flotage. Or he could saunter along the now thriving mercantile houses of the levee and water-front streets, turn the corner, and by merely crossing the threshold of the Café des

Exilés be in France. There would be M. le marquis de Pierfonds reading *Le Moniteur de la Louisiane* over an apéritif, the chatter of the old régime, and the ardent fluctuating hopes of the Bonapartists. He could stroll, as he so often did about twilight with the dim oil lamps beginning to burn and lanterns commencing to flit about in archways and courtyards, past the candle-lit windows of the shops of Catalans and the boutiques of Creoles along the Rue Ste. Anne, listening to the soft patois, the click of billiards behind closed shutters, to the low hum of cafés that in the summer evenings began to spread out into the half-paved streets. For every ship now brought her ballast in paving stones.

He never grew tired of the sunset on the river behind him, that seemed to be taking place in the south, and of the fires on the deck-hearths of the schooners lying in the Basin Carondelet. He could look up and down the Rue Ste. Anne from one glow to the other, each crossed by a tangle of sails. And he could then go to supper with Dr. Mitchell and Ed Livingston at Ba'tiste's, but preferably with Dr. Mitchell alone.

Afterward, the punch and card room downstairs would fill up with everybody. Vain and loud General Wilkinson, and the soft Jewish voice of Judah Touro were heard there. Creole planters, Philip Marigny who had once been a page at Versailles, Etienne de Boré rich from sugar, Forstalls, Du Fossaus, Fleurieaus, and Duplessis'. Who was there that did not come or go? The silver tongue of Colonel Burr, explaining something, nobody afterward cared to remember just what, had come and gone. The garrulous Theodore Clapp argued predestination with the gentle Sylvester Larned. Members of the territorial legislature framed deals or a bill "by and with the advice and consent of Ed Livingston," as General Claiborne remarked, while Jim Caldwell and Sam Peters listened-in or discussed the new waterworks project. There was no end to what went on in the punchroom at Ba'tiste's. Nobody agreed about anything to speak of, and Dr. Mitchell in a philosophically insulting manner—carrying his liquor and the reputation of his pistol like a gentleman—disagreed with everybody, and was never challenged.

The doctor built the new hospital by the city commons largely by the sheer charm and fear of his delicately impersonal insults. One associated him with the hot atmosphere of tobacco, succulent herbs, spices and peppers of Ba'tiste's; his skill with a probe under the oaks in the morning after a duel with the skill of Ba'tiste and his long-handled saucepan over the fire. One forgave him, too. One remembered in the back of one's mind how he had delivered the baby or— if the provocation was great—one recalled how he shot champagne bottles off the heads of little niggers at fifty yards. "Now, son, watch this picayune on the wall until you hear bang." Those, after all, were great evenings. And if one tired of it—there was the open door, and *La Comédie* in St. Peter Street or the *St. Philippe* on St. Philippe, between Royal and Bourbon, only a few blocks away with *L'Ecossais en Louisiane*, *La Commerce de Nuit* or similar dramatic fare, and loges grillé if one happened to be in mourning.

Altogether one might possibly regret such nights as these even at Silver Ho—with nobody there, thought Anthony. "My God, would Vinc and little Tony *never* come!" Simba brought a family of thirteen into being in an old coach by a moth-eaten mistress, who had nothing to recommend her but fecundity and soulful brown eyes. Anthony sent them all to the plantation with his blessing—and pondered over the empty house. Others were doing the same, he discovered. He accepted invitations. The year ended. No word from Vincent.

One evening as he walked down the Rue Ste. Anne near the corner of Dauphine where the lamplight streamed across the pavement in bars through some tightly closed lattices, he stopped as if he were unable to step across them. He stopped dead. In the room upstairs someone was playing "Malbrouk s'en va-t-en guerre."

He . . .

_____

THE ODYSSEY OF MRS. UDNEY

The Parishes, with Mrs. Udney, who intended to see that something was pulled out of the mess of David's affairs for Florence, had proceeded from Philadelphia to Pittsburgh. "Proceeded," euphemistically speaking. As Europeans they had no conception of the size of North America or what the wilderness was like. Hitherto money, class distinctions, and commercial finesse, in a highly organized society millenniums old, had sufficed to supply their physical needs luxuriously and to confirm their mental prejudices. But Lancaster, a few leagues west of Philadelphia, was the west-limit of this society in the autumn of 1806. Beyond that the chemical realities of nature began.

Mrs. Udney left her bandboxes at Lebanon and David left his temper, the chaise, and most of the rest of the baggage at Lancaster. The track between there and Harrisburg was merely a passage through the forests along the banks of the Susquehanna, accomplished in a German farm wagon that pitched like a '74 off Ushant in a bad gale. Mrs. Udney and Florence wrapped themselves in buffalo robes, which they were at first inclined to regard as smelly, but ended by purchasing for gold, since their own costumes for the journey were such as to have caused the kobolds of Penn's woods, if there had been any, to make lush noises.

At Harrisburg the gentleman for whom the town was named provided them a comfortable night's rest and a drink of white, corn whisky that laid David out long and low. He remained two days recovering, at the end of which time another wagon with some of the baggage caught up with them, and David was enabled to go on in a pair of new boots. His old ones had been left outside his door to be polished and had been "polished off." Mrs. Udney and Florence also found themselves provided with some London millinery that permitted them to look at the Alleghany Mountains in the best form, while adorned in heron plumes. There was nothing else, however, as the man had brought the wrong trunks.

They continued on westward, into the wall of mountains, thanks to the Conemaugh River which had been rather thoughtless of nice people in the kind of desultory pass it made through the ridges. In order to strike the military road to Pittsburgh they went up the Juniata to Ray's Town. Their sufferings were intense, and David, whose feet had swollen, had to be cut out of his only boots. He was also induced to drink of a medicinal spring at Ray's Town, with harrowing results.

The intervention of a Mr. Cessna, who took them into his house at this point, according to Mrs. Udney's diary saved their lives. Cessna conferred upon David a pair of brogues, in which there was plenty of room for his feet to swell, and packed them all off in another Conestoga wagon driven by a drunken Scotch-Irishman who got them as far as Saltsburg on the Kiskiminitas River. A Mrs. Murray, who lived in a log cabin at the forks of the river, took mercy on them, sheltered them, and fed them on deer collops, hominy and sassafras tea.

David was now all for turning back. He knew already that his money was lost and he hadn't had a glass of wine for six weeks in a country which he also suspected to be running over with nothing but laxative springs. He was therefore painfully thirsty.

Mrs. Udney, however, remembered she was an Englishwoman. Going back without having collected what she felt was due her was not in her line. She made friends with Mrs. Murray, patched her clothes as best she could, and pushed on down the valley of the Kiskiminitas. Although she was now sixty-three years of age, she walked. And she forced Mr. and Mrs. David Parish to walk with her as far as the Alleghany River.

That walk was the turning point in the life of Florence.

Hitherto she had been lost. She had sat silent during the trip. She had felt like a demure schoolgirl suddenly plumped down into the midst of the largest continent on Jupiter in order to study botany. Her desire to accompany David on this western trip had not been "heroic" at all. She was bored with Philadelphia, and the tales of the settlements had filled her with curiosity. Confronted by real hardships and some genuine suffering, by large mountains that rolled away north and south like titanic walls aflame with the mad motley of the American fall, she had simply subsided into herself and ceased to listen to her husband's complaints, while her mother supplied the will power.

She was not altogether to be blamed for this. She had led a soft life. The change was overwhelming, and Mrs. Udney always had supplied the will power. Between her husband and her mother, Florence had succumbed.

But the actual physical severities of the trip since they had left Philadelphia weeks before had now awakened her. The rest at Mrs. Murray's enabled her to do some thinking. And the crisp, sensible replies of her frontier hostess to the demands of David, whose mood was one of blind self-pity, as he sat by the fire in the log cabin with his feet in a bucket of warm water and wept, had been an education. Florence made certain resolves about herself and her future attitudes to both her husband and her mother when they should return to civilization. She kept these in reserve, but she intended from now on to act upon them. Along with her mother, she now began to disregard the physical severities of the trip. Between them they got David Parish to Pittsburgh about the middle of October.

They spent a week in that little town while David completed his investigations of titles to certain land grants by the help of General Harmer and some of the Denys' who had participated with him in one of his western schemes. In the meanwhile, in a small brick house on Diamond Street, Florence and Mrs. Udney worked desperately hard making themselves new clothes while they were called upon by the Robinsons, the Nevilles, the Witherows, and the Wilsons, who regaled them with the gossip of the neighbourhood in flat nasal tones.

But if the tone was flat the gossip was magnificent. It was not only dangerous and spicy, it was international.

Colonel Aaron Burr was staying at Blennerhassett's Island. He was making love to Mrs. Blennerhassett. Colonel Burr was organizing an expedition against Mexico. Or was it a revolution? Some said one thing, some another. Some said both. Mr. Blennerhassett was a sweet gentleman who had built a paradise in the wilderness for his lovely bride. Mr. Blennerhassett was a terrible man who had married his own niece and fled from Europe. Colonel Burr's daughter and her husband, Governor Alston of South Carolina, were at Blennerhassett's. Mrs. Alston approved of her father's love-making to Mrs. B. She did not approve. She knew nothing about it. There were meetings at night of conspirators. New Orleans was to be the capital of a new

empire.   Colonel Burr had been heard to say so at Colonel Wilkins'
own table and Laura Detweiler was there . . .

Mrs. Udney almost squeaked with excitement as she heard all this.

"Aw-w," said Miss Lizzie Witherow, looking down her long Scotch-
Irish nose, "and the warst of it is they have music and dancing on the
Sabbath.   I'm not sure you'll be wantin' yur datter to go there even if
she is a married wooman, Mrs. Udney."   But that was where Miss
Witherow was wrong.   When she called next day with a basket of
pop-corn,balls and hickory nuts for the English ladies they had both
gone.

America is full of surprises and nothing in any time or place could
have been more astonishing than Blennerhassett's Island in the Ohio
River in the late autumn of 1806.

In the midst of the wilderness a little below Pittsburgh, and at a
staggering cost, the Irishman Blennerhassett had built himself an exquisite and completely appointed English gentleman's estate.   It was
furnished perfectly, from a telescope in the observatory to the statues
on the lawns.   He brought Adams furniture over the mountains and
wines up the river from New Orleans.   He had a beautiful wife and
beautiful children.   He ate off silver and was served by slaves, his only
concession to the land of freedom.   The scenery was wild and romantic.   The hunting and fishing magnificent.   And Blennerhassett was
still young.   Into this paradise on the Ohio walked the devil in the
charming form of Colonel Aaron Burr, who had come within one vote
of being President of the United States and now intended to be Emperor of Mexico—or boss of whatever he could get from Spain by the
help of the money of anybody who wanted to take a chance and equip
a few western volunteers.

Burr had for years been talking about his scheme to everybody from
New Orleans to Pittsburgh.   And he was talking about it in Blennerhassett's library when Mr. and Mrs. David Parish and Mrs. Udney
arrived from Pittsburgh, coming down-river in a four-oared scow.
The fact that David Parish was Blennerhassett's creditor to a considerable amount did nothing to dull the welcome.   As for Colonel
Burr, he regarded Parish's advent as an act of God in his favor.   He
admitted the first evening that all that he wanted was a hundred thousand pounds.

It was impossible to be in the same house with so many able and
charming conspirators and not be taken into the conspiracy.   In a few
days David was genuinely alarmed.   If Burr succeeded, if he even
delivered an attack on Mexico by way of Louisiana, the flow of silver
from Vera Cruz to New Orleans would be stopped.   Ouvrard's great
scheme and the entire framework in the United States, which he and
Anthony had so carefully built up, would have its life-blood cut off at

the source. For them everything depended on maintaining the Spanish royal authority in Mexico.

As Colonel Burr talked and became more confidential, Parish began to hold forth hopes of a loan in order to draw him out.

He was quite successful. All that Burr needed was money. Volunteers would flock to him if he could equip them. Could or would Parish consider arranging for supplies, say, for a thousand men at New Orleans, and ship them up the Mississippi to meet Burr coming down? Blennerhassett had already pledged his fortune to the adventure, it appeared. He and Governor Alston were heavily involved. The men and boats were to start down the Ohio as emigrants going to settle west of the river. Mr. Jefferson had encouraged that. There would be no trouble. The United States was just on the brink of war with Spain anyway.

"Let the word once get home that Burr has struck the first blow and ten thousand bold spirits will flock to me," cried the magnetic little soldier. "In six months we shall have Mexico and the treasures of Montezuma in our hands."

Parish promised to think the matter over seriously—and he did so. Far from being a madman's dream, he concluded with alarm that Burr's chance of success was uncomfortably probable.

David knew one thing, however, which Colonel Burr had no idea of. He knew that General James Wilkinson, U. S. A., commander of the American forces in and about New Orleans, was in the pay of the Spanish crown. He knew the exact amount of the pension, for he had seen it entered regularly in the accounts marked "strictly confidential—destroy" forwarded him by Anthony from New Orleans. The authority for paying it was a letter from the Prince of the Peace with the endorsement of Ouvrard as the agent for the Spanish treasury.

David's first impulse was to write a letter to Anthony, warning him of the dangerous situation arising from Burr's conspiracy and advising him to apply to General Wilkinson to stop it. He actually wrote the letter. Then he thought better of it. It would be better still to go to New Orleans himself, confer with Anthony, and go direct to Wilkinson. He could arrive there as soon as a letter. Therefore, he pretended to Burr that he was willing to further his schemes and would depart immediately to New Orleans in order to do so. Burr was delighted and gave Parish a cipher letter addressed to Wilkinson who, he had every right to suppose from previous interviews, was favourable to his plans and would further them. Nothing could have suited Parish better. He had a flat-boat fitted up as rapidly and luxuriously as possible, and taking Florence and Mrs. Udney with him, bade goodbye to Burr, Blennerhassett, and the Alstons and started for New Orleans.

Parish had been greatly harassed at the possibility of all his plans collapsing suddenly, should Burr's threat to Mexico cut off the silver shipments. He saw himself returning to Europe ruined and disgraced, for he had involved himself heavily in America along with Ouvrard's investments. In his own name he held vast tracts of land upon which payments were not yet complete. He felt he was doing all he could to circumvent Burr and to anticipate him with Wilkinson. But the slow progress down the river exasperated him. The trip over the mountains had exhausted him. His hands and feet were continually blue and swollen, and he could get no relief. At Cincinnati he dispatched a special courier to Herr Nolte, hoping that Vincent had arrived by now in Philadelphia. In this epistle was a complete exposition of his affairs. The composition exhausted him and Florence had to finish it by dictation.

"If anything happens to me," he said to Florence and Mrs. Udney, looking up during the writing, "I count on you to deliver my own letter with Burr's cipher addressed to General Wilkinson to Adverse at New Orleans." He looked out apprehensively at the banks of the Ohio slowly gliding past the boat as they slid along with the current. "Tell him I count on him to prevent possible ruin. Tell him to act without delay."

"Oh, don't be silly, David," said Florence and went on copying.

But David was not silly. He died three days later of heart disease on a chair in the cabin.

The current of the great river continued to sweep the boat steadily toward New Orleans.

. . . turned suddenly to the door and began to knock violently. The music stopped. He heard a swift scurrying rush of feet and skirts in the room upstairs—and recognized Mrs. Udney's memorable giggle. He pushed the door open and stepped in. The hall was dark, and for a moment he hesitated. Suddenly at the far end of it there was a glow at the top of the stairs.

Florence was coming down the steps carrying a single candle. She was very pale, dressed in mourning, and had a row of black pearls about her throat. In the darkness, shielding the candle with one hand, she seemed to be bathed in fire.

"Is it you, Anthony?" she said, stopping, suddenly aware of him in the shadows below.

"Yes," he whispered.

She drew breath tensely.

"Is David?" he gasped.

"Yes—or no—I don't know what you mean," she faltered.

"Don't you?" said he. "By God, I'll show you!"

The candle rolled to the bottom of the stairs.

For the first time in her life Mrs. David Parish understood what it might be like to be married.

Sitting in the front room at the little pianoforte that she had carefully borrowed for the occasion, Mrs. Udney sniffed. Something was burning downstairs.

"Mercy," she cried, looking over the banisters at the candle-end smouldering on the carpet and smoking away, "if you children aren't careful you'll set the house afire. Now come upstairs this instant. It's disgraceful."

Nevertheless, when they were once seated before her, she looked at them with a satisfaction she could not conceal.

"I shall never let go of her hand again, madame," said Anthony, suddenly trying to recover his dignity in order not to look so ridiculous.

"Lord!" said Mrs. Udney, and the tears came into her eyes.

"And before you go back to father in England next spring you'll see us married and settled, won't you, mother?" added Florence. "I think it's only right to wait for at least six months after . . ."

"Oh, why mention his name *at all,* my dear?" replied her mother, who had not expected to sail for England until autumn at least. She brushed away the tears for a second time and looked at her daughter. Never in her life had Florence given her mother so sweet a smile.

Mrs. Udney understood that her work was over. She seized Anthony suddenly by the shoulders and shook him. "You take care of her. Take care of her, you lucky vagabond," said she crying, and kissed him.

And of course he promised.

They were married in April. Mr. Levritt, the British consul, gave the bride away. Old Sandy McNab was the best man. He never fully recovered from the pride of the occasion and the height of his stock. At least his neck grew permanently stiff. They were married by a Protestant clergyman, for Mrs. Udney insisted upon that. And they were married at the cathedral with considerable fanfare, for Anthony felt that to be not only more comfortable to himself but most advisable in the Territory of Orleans.

At any rate there was no doubt in anybody's mind that "Anthony Adverse, gentleman, and Florence Amanda Colcros Parish, née Udney," were man and wife. They went for their honeymoon to Silver Ho. Two weeks of it. Then it ended. Mrs. Udney came to see that all was going well.

Florence and Mrs. Udney had spent the early winter and spring refurnishing the house. Anthony had given them a free hand. But he was surprised at the way they revelled in it. When they had finished there was not a better appointed house nor a more shining one in the entire region. And that was saying a great deal.

There were a good many changes to make in a house that had been arranged by a bachelor for himself and his only son in order to fit it for a husband and his bride. There were changes in the "schoolroom," which became the "nursery." The unused blackboard and maps were taken down and a more or less complete crèche installed. Mrs. Udney evidently believed in eventualities and in preparing for them.

"You might let that wait, mother," said Florence.

"My dear, you know nothing about it," replied Mrs. Udney. "And I might as well prepare things as far as I can—before I go. Do you agree with me?" She was bending over an empty baby basket as she said that. There was a little wait.

"Yes, I *do*," said Florence. Then she went out to the hall and cried. But she had made up her mind. Already she found Anthony talking over everything about the house with Mrs. Udney. To relent with her mother would be fatal. Her experience with David had at least taught her that.

So Mrs. Udney sailed for England in June.

She was bright and cheerful to the last. Anthony was greatly concerned. He would miss her motherly help and affection. With a shock he realized how much he had already begun to lean upon it. And with a shock he also realized that he had missed just that much in his wife.

As for Mrs. Udney, she waved a dry handkerchief to the last and then went down into her cabin for a brief, maternal Gethsemane over an only daughter for whom she had at last pulled the cherished chestnut out of the fire. "But I know she'll never, *never* forgive me for David," she thought, "and I don't blame her. I suppose we're even." So she forgave Florence—and missed Anthony. "I would like to see that boy of his." Mr. Udney would meet her at Dover, of course, if the rheumatism let him. Lamplight found her still sitting in her cabin with her hands in her lap. There was nothing to do now. "Oh, la," said Mrs. Udney . . .

"Cards!"

At Silver Ho the magnolia shade lay with a peculiar peace on the new lawn as the master and mistress drove up to the door. Florence leaned her head against his shoulder and Anthony knew that they were married at last.

That night he took his madonna from her fine Paris wrappings and set her into the niche by the hearth.

It was the year of the great excitement over the Burr Conspiracy. General Wilkinson had not been slow to act on the information conveyed to him by the letter from Parish and by Burr's own cipher. Anthony had lost no time in placing them both in his hands with the remark that one of the best ways to spurn a Spanish pension drawn upon the Mexican treasury would be to encourage Colonel Burr.

General Wilkinson's patriotism was immediately kindled to white heat. Burr was proclaimed a traitor against the United States. The militia were called out. People were arrested right and left in New Orleans and shipped off for trial without recourse. For a while the Territory of Orleans became a pure military despotism with Wilkinson roaring and threatening anybody he didn't like. Burr was stopped at Natchez and fled east, to be captured and tried for high treason at Richmond. The Spanish troops on the Mexican border resumed a life of sunny leisure varied by pulque and cheroots—and the silver shipments continued from Vera Cruz. Two hundred dollars a week to an American general had delayed the course of manifest destiny at least thirty years.

Anthony took no part in this. He strove in every way to conceal the workings of the Ouvrard scheme which depended upon a total lack of publicity for success. His only touch with the Burr affair after Wilkinson let loose the military was to prevent the arrest of Livingston, who had lent Burr money on his Bastrop lands. For a week Livingston came to live at Silver Ho. After which time, and a call upon the general by Mr. Adverse, the danger mysteriously passed.

"And I wish you would also arrange to release Dr. Mitchell, general."

"A dangerous man, sir, if there ever was one," thundered Wilkinson, "but I'll attend to the matter nevertheless. I am in debt to your own discretion about certain matters, Adverse."

"You can rely upon it, general. But it is contingent upon your own discretion in making arrests hereafter."

The general swallowed. "I hope you and Mrs. Adverse are enjoying your honeymoon at Silver Ho. A delightful place, I hear."

"Delightful," said Anthony—and it was.

Except for this sortie in the interest of harassed friends, Anthony scarcely left the plantation. He turned the management of the silver shipments more and more into the hands of McNab and the organization at Algiers. A watchful eye was all that was needed now to continue a routine. Besides, Vincent Nolte was now in Philadelphia filling the place of Parish. In a business way that was an immense relief.

Vincent had not brought young Tony with him. "I will tell you why when I see you in New Orleans next summer," he wrote. "Do not worry about the boy. He is well, and still with Anna at Düssel-

dorf. In the meantime I must devote myself to affairs here which the
death of Parish has greatly complicated." The rest of the letter was
about Anthony's marriage. Vincent said nothing about his own. He
could not bear to think of it.

What would have been the result if the boy had come? Anthony
often wondered.

He had told Florence about him, of course. She had taken it calmly
enough. "I didn't suppose you had just been living at the convent,"
she said. And so he said nothing more to her about Angela, and she
said nothing to him about David. There seemed to be a tacit agreement between them that the past was to be the past. He burned the
blackboard taken from the "schoolroom" and sold a boy's pony with
*"unused saddle and harness, owner sacrifices for private reasons,
spirited, well-bred, little horse."* And that was that.

Next April, if all went well, there was to be someone in the nursery.
That fact also occasionally brought Dr. Terry M. with the best excuse
in the world for a visit. The room at the end of the wing was soon
known as "the doctor's chamber."

For the rest, the days slipped into one another deep with peace and
contentment, bright with hope for the future, pleasantly busy with the
affairs of the great plantation. But above all, complete with that
double-entity, that hyphenated entirety of existence between man and
wife that makes home—and that makes all other places and conditions
merely more or less tolerable by comparison.

For Anthony and Florence loved each other. He did not love her
as passionately as she loved him. For him passion in its highest sense
could have been complete only with Angela—had been complete. And
for that reason, because it was forever denied him to confer the final
crown of existence upon Florence, he loved her with a transcendent
pity; with a determination to have life make up that loss to her in every
other way. He cherished her with a careful, thoughtful tenderness
that surpassed her understanding—that frequently puzzled her.

Florence had loved Anthony as a girl at Livorno. It had been a
fresh, sweet, and secret affection that *he* had felt and compared then
with the mist upon banks of flowers in early spring. Upon that had
fallen the frigid influence of the cold, rigid years with David and the
worldly-wise guidance of Mrs. Udney. Spring had withdrawn herself
and hidden through that unnatural winter. Then the sun had shone
out again unexpectedly from the face of Anthony. Spring had passed.
It was the summer in full leaf and flower that leaped out of the
unploughed ground.

In her new husband Florence found not only what she had lost but
what she had never hoped to find. In him she had at last found
herself.

This was not a fragile beginning for a union for life for either of them. As time went on it burgeoned in its own way and filled their lives.

The time of the coming of the child passed, a time infinitely close and dowered with peace in which they drew nearer to the centre and core of the mystery of life. Love and tenderness were having their fulfilment. It had not been put-off and starved and asked to repeat and wear itself out. It was taking its natural course and it would soon become embodied and visible.

All that, Anthony felt and shared with his wife when he finally held the child in his arms.

Florence had given birth to her little girl with great difficulty. But she recovered rapidly afterwards and was the better and more vigorous for it. The strained expression and a touch of hardness that had begun to disfigure her expression in the days with David disappeared forever.

It was Anthony's whim, he said, to call the child "Maria." And that name seemed good to both of them. For the first time in many weeks they drove to the city in the new family coach for the christening.

By the hearth in the great living-room the ancient statue of the madonna stretched forth her hands with the babe in them into the pleasant firelight and into the darkness. The figure of the man who sometimes came to kneel before her with a heart full of gratitude and unexpected contentment she may have known. For they had wandered together from the first and in many regions. He on his part was quite sure that he had looked upon the final and most benign expression of her face. Meanwhile, unchanging, she continued to stand there in her niche.

With the birth of little Maria all things at Silver Ho seemed to its master and mistress to be caught up into the longer and more spacious rhythms that mark, for those who can feel them, both the passing and the growth of life.

Spring flashed into summer and summer burned into fall. The sun could be felt slipping down the horizon as the cooler days came. It was "Happy Christmas." Then the jasmine bloomed, the magnolias flowered, the pride of India released its incense and it was glorious June. Likewise moved the body and soul of man responding even to the minor phases of the moon, content to feel them without knowing their cause—as who can? And in this, having her small but infinitely important part as a particular bud of the general seed from which she sprang, the child wailed, walked, talked—and sang.

Summoned from the deep out of darkness by a process apparently inadequate to the result, the child retained in herself, as do all the children of men, the ineffable secret of her cause. She was part of it. Suddenly and mysteriously there was a new personality in the house. There was another soul. Family life began.

To Anthony the science of Dr. Terry Mitchell—and science at any given date was always appallingly modern—seemed to have as little bearing upon this whole process as the doctor's hands and wooden instruments had had at the birth of the child. The hands were willing enough, but the instruments . . . they were like the good doctor's philosophy, a last and desperate mechanical resort.

In a half-bantering way Anthony and the doctor frequently renewed the argument begun that night the nuns had fled. But they never got anywhere logically. The synthesis of their friendship resided in something larger than that. It lay in their mutual humanity, in their desire to do whatever they could do to make the lot of those about them better.

Both had long given up trying to do anything for that myth called "mankind." But they did do the best they knew how, within the bounds of their ignorance, for various men, women, and children they could affect.

And their desire to help was not confined to those within the bounds of natural affection. Their sympathy—or charity, call it what you will—was greater than that. Yet it always remained personal. In a time and century devoted to the acceleration of the millennium by leavening the mass with paper in the form of political documents, money, Bibles, tracts, and newspapers, there was something to be said in their favour. At least they practised their sympathy directly in a scheme of good-doing. With Anthony it took the pattern of a large art of living; with Dr. Mitchell the form of the practice of medicine.

There was, to be sure, the new hospital on the commons in town to which Mr. Adverse gave so generously in money and Dr. Mitchell in service, but one had better concentrate, as they did, in the practice of both their arts at Silver Ho.

Fourteen thousand acres and—before Maria was four years old— over a thousand hands constituted the modest realm of their activities. There was "Sugarville," set in the broad lowlands of the plantation that marched along the levee with the yellow river rolling past them in a great bend around which disappeared into the distance the rippling fields of cane; and on the "heights" above was "Cottontown," where the plateau-levels broke out under the hot sun into a captious winter of blossoming snowdrifts of the plant which clothes man.

And before long there were corn and rice fields, and the fertile tract near the mansion given over to the raising of vegetables and fruit.

Each one of these separate industries employed its own overseer and gang. There were gangs devoted to the animals and pastures; to lumbering in the swampy forests near the lake; gangs on the wharfs and levee, and the rice irrigation. From the upper windows of the house Anthony looked down to the ships landing at the wharfs and to the smoke of his cotton gin and press and sugar works, for the steam engine had already begun to turn even on the banks of the Mississippi.

Faced by the ever-growing difficulty of exporting and importing to Europe, Anthony strove as far as possible to organize Silver Ho as a complete and self-sufficient plantation and to depend more and more for the necessaries brought in from outside upon domestic trade.

As a consequence most of the arts essential to existence flourished on the place in the hands of expert negro craftsmen proud of their place in the community and of the separate shops and cottages which were theirs. There were few things, from carpentry to tailoring, one could not get done at Silver Ho, and done very well. And in this it did not differ so greatly from many another plantation of the time.

The centre of the infinite activities of the place was, of course, the house itself. Sugarville and Cottontown each had its white overseer's house near by, and several other white men and their families were scattered at various places over the plantation. They were mostly men from the North. The chief-overseer had a small, neat house just over the pine ridge from the mansion. He was a Quaker by the name of Josiah Fithian from the banks of the Brandywine. Anthony had obtained his services under unusual circumstances and trusted him, for he was both kindly and just. Yet despite this watchful delegation of authority, the big house was the essential centre of things.

Here before the broad mahogany desk of the master in his library was the court of last resort. Here a careful justice was administered, and here, upon occasions, the overseers met for consultation or the advice and remonstrance of the more trusted servants was listened to and acted upon. Here the great account books were kept by Anthony with endless patience, toil, and forethought. And here also was a book of moral aphorisms, a diary, and a volume of "Philosophical Reflections" frequently pored over and entered upon. On the shelves about began to accumulate the calf-bound tomes devoted to religion, learning, the sciences and fine arts, and a surprising amount of books from London, Paris, and Philadelphia given over to nothing but amusement —especially the "Waverley Novels." On the desk, whenever they ap-

peared, were laid *The Louisiana Gazette* and *Le Moniteur* by a smart
little "jockey" who rode into town twice a week for the news.

Everything built or planted at Silver Ho was first planned on paper
at this desk and marked on a great plot of the plantation which hung
curling from the wall.   All who came there to bargain, to buy, sell, or
steal—and their name was legion—sat in the chair before Anthony's
desk, talked to him, were entertained afterward as befitted them, and
departed impressed by the order and peace of the establishment.

Mrs. Adverse, the mistress, did not make a good "job" of being a
wife and mother.   She had never heard of such a thing as a "job" in
domestic life.   She bore her child in the same way that the magnolias
bore blossoms; i.e., as a function of a particular type of being.   She
became a mother, and she acted accordingly.   Neither did it occur to
her that she had the "job" of running the house and a great deal of the
plantation to boot.   She did not divide her life into separate compart-
ments of unpalatable labour, bored leisure sweetened by frantic amusement, and exhausted rest.   She would no more have spoken of the
duties inherent in her being the mistress of the plantation as a "job"
than Governor Claiborne would have thought that he "held the job at
being governor."   He *was* the governor of the Territory of Orleans.
Florence Udney Adverse was the mistress of Silver Ho.

For the same reason Mr. Audubon, who occasionally came to paint
birds at Silver Ho, was never heard to remark that the mallards in
the marshes made a "good job of bringing up their young."   They
couldn't help it.   They laid eggs and the eggs hatched when they sat
on them.   They brooded over life just as he did.   The result in both
cases was something remarkably like a duck without any "jobbing"
having occurred by either the bird or the artist.

The kind of a bird that could make a "job" out of living was still
rara avis.   And as for making a living out of a "job"—a few government contractors had just begun to try it, with the usual criminal
results.

Melancthon Conant was the bird about New Orleans to do your
jobbing for you, whether it was pickling your deceased aunt in brine,
with a smile on her face warranted to last during her shipment home
for burial, or buying up a few lively gals for the new *Sure Enuf Hotel*
at the American landing—"M. Conant, Proprietor"—or selling wormy
beef and paper shoes to General Jackson's heroes—Melancthon was
the bird for the *job*—and a very good thing he made of it.   But Mrs.
Adverse did not do any jobbing at all.   It was a word justly in bad
odour.   To have told Dr. Terry M. that he was "making a good 'job' of
being a doctor" would have implied either that one was insane or
doubted the doctor's marksmanship.   Neither God nor man was yet
debased by the glorious conception of the "job."   No one had yet sug-

gested that Christ had made a good job of being a saviour. It was still a very backward time. Progress and Fair Science were just beginning to feel out each other preparatory to begetting the factory.

Nor was Mrs. Adverse worried about her position as a woman. She had no doubt of it. Nor did she, when the baby proved to be a girl, try to call it by a boy's name. She acquiesced with the universe in the difference, and in a name which admitted it. Poor woman, her status was too secure and her life too full for her even to have thought of signing herself by her father's name after she was married in order to prove that she was independent of the conventions of men.

Meanwhile, without a "job," and without having insured her domestic importance by inverting the devices of gender, she managed to employ herself a little about the house and place, acceptably, and to while away the time from about six A.M. till before or after midnight.

There were only fifteen bedrooms at Silver Ho and they were not always all occupied. Five or six was a good average. All that was required of her menus was that they should be produced on the place, ample, elastic, well-cooked and dainty. The twenty house servants prevented anything from going to waste. They and she saw to it.

Spinning most of the cloth, weaving it, and making it up into the clothes; hemming all of the imported napery, and quilting; checking various chests and closets full of linen and the hangings used at different seasons throughout the house; seeing that the wash did not appear later at remote parts of the plantation—all this tended to encroach a little on her languid southern leisure, to say nothing of making the soap and candles.

In her room there was a keyboard with a hundred and eighty-three keys on it. With the use of each, and with their combinations, she was familiar. With this "keyboard" she played upon Silver Ho as upon a splendid instrument, providing those complicated domestic harmonies which are seldom even noticed until discord ensues.

A great many articles in the house were imported directly from Europe by ships that landed at the plantation dock, others she drove to the city to purchase. She kept the accounts of such transactions as well as her household ledgers and a little book for each of the house servants. She conducted a polite correspondence of social notes and replies with the other mistresses of the neighbourhood, besides writing long letters in longhand to her relatives and friends in Europe. She kept a diary of sensible and pious thoughts.

Most of the domestic and amatory problems of the plantation were in her hands. In one year there were twenty-seven babies born on the place. She and Dr. Mitchell had arranged a crèche and trained midwives, who needed to be looked after. Widows were to be consoled, marriages arranged, wandering lovers from other plantations restrained, stories to be exacted from black girls in trouble and the child correctly fathered. Such things were merely routine. The depredations of witches and voodoo priestesses were also to be coped with, conjurors discouraged, and the sick and ailing visited.

Every day at eleven o'clock Florence mounted her horse and made the rounds of the quarters, while a thousand tales, requests, complaints, and wheedlings were poured into her ears. She knew her people and she brought them affection, mercy, and justice in the primary relationships of life.

Dinner was at three o'clock, when she saw her husband and discussed the day's problems with him. He had been on horseback since eight o'clock, seeing that every project on the plantation was making due progress. The afternoons, especially as the hot weather came on, were spent in the house. There was a siesta after dinner and then work or play, reading or callers in the afternoon. Six hours of constant activity in the mornings, on horseback, did not require a tennis court to keep the blood moving. But there were bowling, horseshoe pitching, boating, driving to pay visits, and such hunting and fishing as the seasons supplied—and how they did supply it and the table with game.

Gentlemen and their families from up-river passing up and down to the city stopped off at Silver Ho as a matter of course. This was not considered entertaining, it was merely "hospitality." Breakfast for ten—and away they went in their barge.

Entertaining was an entirely different matter. It was considered to be rather light at Silver Ho, for the Adverses had no relatives in the neighbourhood to ride over in parties of eight or twelve to spend a couple of weeks. They concentrated on dinners, dances, and midnight suppers.

At such times Florence shone in her best London and Paris frocks and was more or less the mirror of style and fashion for the neighbourhood. Anthony indulged her in imported furbelows to the limit and for his own satisfaction. Standing on the steps and saying good night with Florence on his arm, as they bowed the Creole gentry, the lawyers and bankers, the American officials, and neighbours over the threshold, marked for them both a certain apex in life.

Some of Anthony's most tender memories of the place were of these nightly parties. Little Maria was greatly excited by the music and he would slip away sometimes to the nursery to quiet her and to sit beside her, while she lay back with her eyes wide in the moonlight. Or they would go to the balcony together to look out into the gardens below, while the couples sat about under the myrtles, and the great house pulsated with the melody of fiddles, the murmur of voices, and the tread of the dance.

He remembered, too, the silver-madness of moonlight nights, the huge, white clouds sailing slowly over the place with alternate dark and shadow upon the lowlands, the sound of banjos and black voices, and the glow of bonfires. How the dogs barked! He let his people keep them. And what is day to an African compared with the warmth and softness and lustre of the southern night?

"Adverse spoils his niggers," some of the neighbours grumbled. But it was universally admitted that he was a most generous and charitable gentleman, and that he and his gracious wife and lovely little child deserved the bounty which they so evidently strove in a hundred ways to share with all about them.

Anthony had no illusions about the system of slavery. He knew its beginnings and its end better than most of those about him. But he knew no other system in the time and place in which he lived. He tried to mitigate it and to alleviate it in every way that he could, using both intelligence and sympathy. He had not forgotten Brother François. The good man had not died entirely in vain. From the little madonna by the fireplace flowed many a mercy that the spirit of Brother François would have approved.

Life was not all dancing, and moonlight, and abundance at Silver Ho. It was also grim and tragic. Among a thousand people not all were saintly characters. Most of them were men and women. But there were also the usual number of beasts—ferocious, lustful, cunning, and all the rest of the catalogue—against which due precautions had to be taken and justice meted out.

Also, there was no way of shifting burdens off onto a general community. They were dealt with by the master and mistress. Silver Ho took care of its two madmen and three simple-minded children, its several crippled by accidents, and the sick and parentless. As yet there were no aged or infirm. But there would be. Anthony could see that. It was his books that made the most profound comment on it, after all. After five years the profits of the place began to decrease progressively. This was due partly to the condition of war and foreign trade. But it was also due to the fact that the natural increase of people on the plantation began to eat up its surplus. "What," thought Anthony, "will the books show ten years from now when many are old and infirm?" He thought this over a great deal. It was his chief worry. He once phrased it morally in a little note left on a ledger: "The earth says, 'In a few decades Silver Ho will be a lie.' Something or somebody else will then have to pay for it—or it will lapse." He thought with satisfaction of certain investments in England and he also began to pull in his horns.

Vincent Nolte came to New Orleans in the winter of 1809 and took all of Ouvrard's affairs into his own hands. It was a great relief to

Anthony. He brought old McNab to Silver Ho; closed his books in the city. He also unburdened himself of the leased lands. Life generally became easier after.

Anthony was now thirty-three and considered himself to be entering upon middle-age. The dates in local cemeteries gave him warrant for that. He and Florence would have liked another child, but none came. Vincent was now much about the house. The table seated him and the doctor almost as regularly as it did Anthony, Florence, and Maria. Old Sandy preferred his meals in his room and followed the child about as faithfully as did Simba, whose muzzle was turning grey.

The memories of these halcyon days by the great river were afterwards to be like springs of water in the wilderness, like the sound of doves murmuring outside a prisoner's cell.

For all things come to an end, usually with portents. There is a certain prophetic direction and gathering of speed and momentum in even very simple human affairs. It began at Silver Ho with the death of Sandy McNab and plague among the slaves.

Dr. Mitchell had vaccinated them and everybody else who was not pock-marked. But he could do nothing against other plagues. There was a sudden outbreak of white cholera. At Cottontown, out of four hundred in the quarters two hundred and thirty-six were removed. There was no question about having to sell the people now because of lessened acreage. That had greatly worried both Anthony and Florence. They kept putting it off. And then a West Indian sloop brought something Dr. Mitchell called "cachexia" that occupied him desperately.

No one at the big house was troubled by these plagues. But in the summer two of Florence's best spinners went by yellow fever. Maria was ill of some childish complaint in the fall. Then all seemed to be well again. But those days of quarantine, enforced by Dr. Mitchell to the point of violence, had brought them all closer. No visitors. Only Anthony and Florence by the fire in the evenings; the child in his lap before bedtime; a sense of dangerous wings having brushed them and gone past leaving them closer. Maria understood that, too.

At last they were released.

He sat by the fire one November evening and looked into the coals. The madonna seemed to be particularly peaceful and dreamful in the firelight again. Later on he was to ride into town for a meeting at the Chamber of Commerce.

"Oh, daddy, don't go," cried Maria. "I want you to stay tonight."

"It *is* rather blustery, my dear," said Florence. "Is it important?"

"Well, rather. Ed Livingston is creating a good deal of excitement by his claims to the land the river is making in front of his holding along the Batture. There is likely to be some pretty hot argument pro and con. He asked me to be there."

Florence made no further remonstrance. It was not often he rode into New Orleans at night.

"Bring Vincent back with you then," she said. "We haven't seen him for weeks."

"Now, child, kiss your father good night."

Maria climbed on his knees, flaxen-haired and laughing. For a moment she lay quiet against his heart, while he promised to bring her something from town and watched his favourite curl over one small ear catch the firelight.

"Good night, good night."

They went upstairs, calling back to him. Simba rose as the horse was led around.

"Stay home, sir."

The dog lay down on the porch disappointed, waiting dejectedly to watch him go.

A window upstairs opened. Florence called down to him, "I wish you'd come and fix this lock on the nursery door, Anthony. I can't get the door open. We're closed in now." She laughed at her ridiculous plight.

"We're locked in, daddy," shouted little Maria.

"Oh, it's all right. Here comes Terry now."

He heard Dr. Mitchell's voice joking with the little girl in her room. The light went out and Florence and the doctor came downstairs. He saw them pass the window in the library—Florence with her high English colouring that she had never lost, her fine, frank, level glance, and the warm lights in her brown hair; the doctor looking tired and grey but as gallant as ever, his humorous mouth just about to say something amusing . . .

He touched his horse with the spurs and rode off into the darkness, leaving Simba staring after him with his head on his paws.

It was quite windy. He wrapped his cloak about him and looped it. He reached town about nine o'clock and found the Chamber of Commerce already in full session with a good deal of shouting and impassioned eloquence taking place. Old John McDonough was booming away as he came in.

"Never covet what is not your own. That, sir, is one of the principles by which every honourable man is proud to be regulated. But how, sir, has my honourable friend Mr. Livingston applied this precept? By fencing in the land which the river has been making. It is land made by an act of God. It rightfully belongs to the city, to the free and enlightened people of this great community."

"Can't God act in *my* favour?" asked the voice of Mr. Livingston from the corner.

"Not always," shouted McDonough.

"The Almighty, you know—by definition," insisted Mr. Livingston.

A roar of laughter, catcalls, jeers and imprecations followed this sally. John McDonough sat down, wiping his brow. Anthony settled himself hurriedly into his seat. Old Cicero went about snuffing the candles, while the wind rattled the windows and the suave voice of Mr. Livingston began to explain the very complicated nature of his riparian rights.

"My friends, far be it . . ."

At Silver Ho, Dr. Mitchell and Florence finished a hand of whist and turned in. Dr. Mitchell was very tired and slept the sleep of the just. The wind bellowed in the chimney. A smouldering log leaped up and crackled. It spat a fat, live coal out onto the carpet. Presently the robe of the madonna, who stood holding the child out in the darkness, began to twinkle with little flames.

The wind in the chimney at Silver Ho and the orators at the Chamber of Commerce in New Orleans roared away till after midnight. The chimney at the plantation now had more than it could do. The windows on the lower floor began to help it out. Between speeches Anthony caught a little nap . . .

He was awakened by a rough hand on his shoulder.

"Sir," said an irate gentleman, "your dog is in the street below raising hell. Won't you go down and call him off?"

"Damn him," said Anthony, taking up his riding crop. "I'll show him—" and he walked downstairs to be almost devoured by Simba, who was whining continuously and had half his hair singed off.

"Fire!"

He stumbled getting frantically to his horse. And it was then as he picked himself up that he saw—just as Signora Bovina had seen it a quarter of a century before in Livorno—a red glare in the sky.

It was northward toward Silver Ho, and it hung with an appalling glow over the river.

"O God!" cried Anthony, and began to kill the horse with his spurs.

With the voice of the hound preceding him like a trumpet, he rushed on through the darkness toward the pillar of fire by night. Already in his maddening thoughts it had become apocalyptic.

At the Bayou St. Jean, incredible as it might be, the ferryman was still asleep. He groaned aloud as he hauled the poor black man out of the shack by his heels and made a note to come back and kill him later. The ferry-boat worked slowly. Simba kept rushing about in the bushes on the opposite bank baying. The light in the sky suddenly died down to a low, pink glow. There were no sparks over the top of the ridge any longer.

Three miles more . . .

He galloped out of the last clump of oaks 'and came thudding over the lawn. The house—

Nothing, nothing was left but a great bed of coals that shimmered like a lake of hell when the wind blew on them and made the spot in the sky above momentarily brighter. A few wisps of flame leaped up with green tongues feeding upon the roof copper—and died away again. Out of this, three storeys high, stood the great chimney white-hot, growing black in places where the cool wind fanned it and then glowing again. It mottled its face at him. Half-way up, the nursery fireplace was growing black. The terrible heat from the place where the great mansion had stood beat up into his face. The ruined horse trembled and twitched under him. Simba sat down and gave the death-howl.

He had no doubt what had happened. He knew. Otherwise they would have come to meet him before this.

He sat on his horse, waiting to go mad . . . .

"Why was there nobody here? The niggers might run away, of course."

"Florence! My baby!—what had Terry done? Why, it *couldn't* be true! It just could not be true. To be burned in the fire; with fire, fire, fire, fire, fire . . ."

The mare collapsed and he sat down on her while she died under him.

He sat there beating his own head with a riding crop.

Someone came up behind and tried to stop him. He fought with several men frantically. A blind impulse to rush down and tread the fire was upon him. Luciferian defiances to the Almighty ripped from his throat.

"Steady, friend, steady," said the sorrowful voice of his chief-overseer Fithian. "We would deal gently with thee." He lay still. He saw the tears running down the face of Fithian. They must have been afraid to come near him at first. He lay still and looked at the stars. The men stood looking down at him.

"Couldn't you do *anything?*" he asked Polaris.

"Thee knows," said Fithian, "that all the doors led into the great room, and it must have been there that the fire started. When we got here it was too late. We could neither get in to them nor could they get out. It is impossible to walk through flame. We tried to see if we could."

He looked at their scorched faces. Smith, the cotton-overseer, was horribly burned.

"Did you hear anything?"

There was a terrible silence.

"Tell me."

"Yes," said Smith, moving his seared face frightfully.

"Well?" He dug both heels into the earth. "What?"

"Three pistol shots."

He grasped the man's hand. "Listen, Smith, you wouldn't lie to me, would you? Not now."

"No! By God, sir, it's true. It was when I was trying to get in through the servants' way. We couldn't. The fire came out at us into the hall. We got the maids out, there. All but two, the smoke . . ."

"And it was three."

"Yes, sir, in the nursery, I think—three shots—about a second apart."

"Nothing else?"

"Nothing. Dr. Mitchell was a great man, sir, a *brave* man."

"So are you, Smith," said Anthony, rising. "And the rest of you." He looked around at the scorched group of his faithful white servants. Someone sobbed once. He thought it might be Fithian.

"God must be ashamed of himself," he wrenched out. They gaped at him in amazement. "But I'll leave Him to Terry. He's up there now." He shook his fist at the stars. "And my baby"—Smith turned away.

"O God!"

"But you *men* will listen to me. I want to tell you something. And don't ever forget it as long as I live." They closed in a little.

"This never happened. It never happened at all! Do you see?"

They stood together for a moment with the glow and heat of the fire on them and then parted.

"Thee will be spending the night at my house, friend Adverse?" cried Fithian, his voice breaking.

"Take me," he cried. "And don't tell anyone except .Mr. Nolte where I am."

Half an hour later a hundred people were arriving at the plantation by both horse and boat.

The news of the tragedy was all over town next day by dawn. Those who heard the tale of the horror-stricken overseers agreed that they had done their best. Servants were pulled out of the smoke just in time. Two girls died, smothered.

"Nobody knew until they saw the light in the sky. And most of the overseers lived a mile or so away. You know how quick a pine-lined house burns. No, it was just too late. What do you think of that fellow Mitchell? Do you think he ought to have done it?"

The discussion about that was quite hot for some time.

"Why don't you ask Adverse?" said a drunken young puppy at the Orleans bar a night or two afterwards.

"Friend," said Mr. Fithian, coming clear across the floor to take him by the throat, "I heard what thee said. I will not strike thee, neither will I kick thee—but I will grind thy countenance in the dirt."

Staid gentlemen voiced their almost tearful enthusiasm over the Quaker's abilities as a grinder.

In the meanwhile Mr. Adverse was in town again—as usual.

No, it was not impossible. It was quite true. The race survives largely by virtue of certain fictions agreed upon. It is sometimes necessary for an individual to do the same. Wise and considerate people, even though they know the "facts," will usually acquiesce in the fiction and even play up to it. That is the part of *common* decency. It is your simple-minded fool who has never had anything happen to him or someone who is too young to understand that reality can have the quality of lightning, who always insist that a perfectly candid peal of thunder must follow every lightning stroke under all circumstances.

Fire had fallen from heaven upon Anthony and crisped his wife, his child, and his friend. The same element also threatened to suffuse his brain with intolerably glowing images and memories; to send him about the streets of New Orleans giving the death-howl like Simba until friends put him away where his voice would no longer trouble the world. Yet—

His heart went on. His body functioned. The event had not stopped them. He was left, left alone in the field of his own suffering, and he took shelter under the only available tree there, his own will.

"This never happened," he had said to himself—although he knew better than anyone else that it had. He was, indeed, the only one who really knew *what* had happened. "Never," he said, and went on living the negative. He left Silver Ho without looking back, because he would have been turned into a pillar of Bedlam if he had done so. He elected to remain sane.

A few well-meaning and curious persons who stopped him on the street to offer their sympathy were met by an uncomprehending stare. They retired, some of them disgruntled and complaining of his hardness of heart. But it was remarkable how quickly, indeed, how almost instantly, the majority of his acquaintances understood not only the rôle he was acting but the temper of the lines he was saying, and how they conspired with him also to be about town "as usual."

In particular there was Edward Livingston whose discretion and tact, whose carefully disguised but boundless sympathy constantly found time in the midst of endless business to devise "accidental" meetings with "my friend Adverse," with "Toni, my dear boy, we must have some ducks for Sunday dinner. They say the shooting at Spanish

Fort is remarkably fine. I won't use live decoys. I agree with you, there's something treacherous about them. But I've had that fellow Audubon daub me a half dozen buffleheads. Man, they're so natural they make the drakes stop to make love to them. It's like shooting Romeos in front of a balcony with a wooden Juliet,"—and away they would go into the marshes for a day or two. And sometimes, sometimes he would almost forget.

There were others besides Livingston who knew. There was Ba'tiste who had received him back into his tower-room as if he had never left it; Ba'tiste who never even mentioned the doctor, who was tactfully merry as only a sad fat-man can be when the pepper gets in his eyes—and yet he must go on cooking as only a Frenchman could in order to convey his ineffable admiration and sympathy pour une pose héroïque.

And there was Vincent Nolte.

He lived in the doctor's old room at Ba'tiste's while he was setting up the working of his new mercantile firm that concealed Ouvrard's schemes for some years to come. It was Vincent alone who really knew the extent of Anthony's confusion. As they sat talking over old times together and planning the future as though Silver Ho had never been, Vincent would find that Anthony was mistaking him for Dr. Mitchell. The "never happened" formula was working perhaps a little too well. "After all," thought Vincent, "one cannot act entirely as if it were just five years ago and Dr. Terry still here."

Vincent thought a good deal about that. As time went on, he began to remind Anthony of the boy and to speak of Anna, "who is like a mother to him at Düsseldorf," of his studies and his life there. "Perhaps you would care to go back some day?"

"Never," he said.

Such talk had but one practical result. Anthony put his affairs in Europe in thorough order for the boy's future. At the end of some months he was able to remake his will. He was able to read the names of Florence and Maria in the old one—and to burn it, too. And now to his relief and amazement he found that if he was careful—if he was very careful to shut out the red light in the sky—certain memories of Florence and the child came back to him with a comfort that was inexpressible.

There was one in particular that sustained him. It was one of those moments of the past, unnoted when it occurred, but cherished by the soul for its subliminal value to the individual just as the great images of poetry are cherished by the race, unreasoningly, with an insight deeper than logic—"die, critics, or we perish"—it was a moment of immortal life saved out of the ghostly ruin of mutability and physical grief.

He would be driving again with Florence and little Maria, leaning back in the comfortable little chaise with his arm around his wife and the little girl held on his knees, her face close to his own. Ridiculously enough, it was along a short stretch of Tchoupitoulas Street. Florence was talking to him. Only her voice conveyed what she was saying. The mere words were lost forever. Perhaps they had nothing to do with what she had been saying then. It was simply (as she looked up at him out of her bonnet with the violets on it) "We love each other and are made one by it. Oh, happiness beyond thought!"—and the child basking in this impalpable warmth and security clung to him. And then—Tchoupitoulas Street led off into the darkness again.

But oh, how warm it was along that salvaged stretch, how the flowers bloomed forever in the immortal light!

As the spring came on with its delicately-untraceable, its unconsciously-reminiscent odours, he must pass that way again and again.

Let the mocking birds and cardinals sing. He could bear them again; bear them even without tears.

Grief is a curious thing. It must reassure itself at last of the reality of the things for which it grieves. Had there ever been a place called Silver Ho; a man who had once been happy there? Perhaps? Almost he had convinced himself "No." Now he must go and see. He *must* see it once again. In some way he must find surcease there, or—

_____

The weeds and bushes had grown surprisingly high about the house. Some swallows were nesting in the chimney. He walked up the fire-scarred steps that led to—nothing. And jumped off into the area of ashes behind. The swallows had made their nest in the nursery fireplace and he blessed them for it. For the first time since the fire he wept unrestrainedly, tempestuously. And after the fit was over he felt an unspeakable relief.

Someone had left some garden roses and early spring wild-flowers at the foot of the chimney. "Probably Smith's wife and little girls," he thought, "or some of the hands. They loved her." He walked over to the chimney and climbed up on the hearth where the blossoms lay. They lay there as if on a rude, fire-scarred altar of ruined stone before the statue of his little madonna.

He looked at her in doubtful amazement, where she still stood in the niche where he had last seen her—that night. And now—there was nothing left but the figure of the woman and the child.

She stood there exactly as she had come from the hands of her maker millenniums ago. Only the fire had glazed her. It had annealed every crack and imperfection. The rivets that had marked them had flowed away and left her whole.   Nothing but she and the child remained.   The golden Byzantine diadem, the gorgeous medieval robe, the heavens of art above her and the pearly steps beneath had sublimed in the furnace through which she had passed.   She stood there, rooted in the stone, still holding her son forth to the man who now lay before her on the cold hearth. . . .

The sun grew hot before he looked up at her again.   What passed was not in words.   He could go now.   A certain patience had come upon him.   He remembered another who had suffered.   One who had not tried to forget and had never been forgotten.

His vision as he looked at the madonna in the niche was peculiarly acute.   The fire had cracked the chimney in places.   An evil mouth of darkness yawned just beneath her.   He caught the glimpse of something moving in this maw.   Out of it, very slowly, as if it were sick of life itself, came a filthy-looking snake.   It wriggled and half-slipped down the brick-work to a level space in the sunlight, where it lay still. An occasional tremor ran through it as though it were dying.

It was this that caused him to withhold his hand.   The thing was obviously in great trouble.   It was a sickly-white colour like an old cocoon. "Poor worm of nature," he thought, "you are horrible, but you are in agony, too.   Perhaps I am not kind to let you live and suffer."   Yet he withheld his hand and kept still.

Presently the snake began to gasp and dart out its tongue as if to taste the sunlight for the last time.   Its eyes looked seared.   Then the skin of its throat parted and a new head came out of the old one.   Its effort had been a violent one.   Like the man on the hearth only a few feet away, it now lay very still.

The man lay there for hours.   The snake emerged.   It stripped itself from head to tail.   It lay in the sun while its new colours became more brilliant and it revived.   It coiled and uncoiled itself, a glorious creature at last, the colour of flame.   It flowed off into the sunlight across the ashes and left its empty husk lying behind it on the stone.

Anthony rose, stiff in every joint, for he had been fascinated for hours.   He took the statue out of the niche from the stone it had been standing on and went back to town.

He spent the whole night arguing with Vincent, who was in tears— and the next morning in a few brief preparations.   And then, embracing his friend for the last time, he stepped into a canoe with four voyageurs, whom he had befriended in old days at the flotage, and started up-river headed for the unknown.

As they passed Silver Ho he lay down and held the madonna close to him.   With the exception of that memento and Simba there was nothing in the craft to remind him of anything in the past.

"It is finished," he said.   "I go."

CHAPTER SIXTY-FIVE

THE PEOPLE OF THE BEAR

JEAN, Pierre, Pedro, and Moosh-Moosh, a light cedar pirogue, Simba, and Anthony ascended the Mississippi above the White Bluffs to St. Catherine's Landing, where about the end of May 1813 they spent a week in making final preparations for the plunge into the continent westward.

At St. Catherine's lived old William Dunbar and one Dr. George Hunter, who seven years before at the request of Mr. Jefferson had explored the country north and west toward the sources of the Red River of the South until they came to the place where hot springs break from the earth out of the mountains and hills.

"All that I can tell you about them," said Dunbar, "is that on January fourteenth, eighteen-hundred-five, while camping at the hot springs I observed an eclipse of the moon and was therefore able to ascertain their exact situation to a nicety. They lie, in a bank of vapour, which can be seen afar-off ascending from the heart of the hills where they rise, at latitude thirty-four degrees, thirty-six minutes, four seconds north and longitude ninety-two degrees, fifty minutes, forty-five seconds west from Greenwich. If you are not sure when you get there, put your foot in the water and it will boil the flesh off. There is no possibility of mistaking them."

William Dunbar was the last civilized man speaking English whom Anthony talked to. He had frequently entertained him at Silver Ho on his way up and down the river from New Orleans, and Dunbar had heard of the tragedy. The good old Scot, who was one of the notable local scientists of his time, seemed instinctively to understand Anthony's desire to plunge into the wilderness. He placed his maps and notes at his disposal and talked engagingly of the nature of the fauna and flora, of the trials and hardships, and of the wonders to be met with beyond the habitations of men. He even wished to press upon him the loan of his mathematical instruments.

"You can return them—in a year or two," he said. "I should then like to see your notebooks and journals, for I am always curious."

"My dear sir," said Anthony. "I am not going to return, and I shall keep no notebooks. As for the mathematical instruments, it no longer makes any difference to me whether I am east or west of Greenwich. You see, I can no longer find my way by mathematics.

I shall follow the moon, the stars, and the sun until I come to the end of the earth."

"Peace to you," said the old man. "The lights of heaven wander but they are at least eternal. Look out upon the glories of the universe and dwell no longer upon the shadows within. That way contentment lies, I think."

Then, in order to distract his guest, he became reminiscent, speaking of his youth in the beautiful country about Elgin, of his long wanderings westward of the great river to the place where the flowered prairies begin, and of his letters to Sir William Herschel, to David Rittenhouse in Philadelphia, and to Jefferson.

"I am sure if you will only look out upon the world you will find peace as I have in merely recounting its wonders to yourself and to other men. I have found peace here at the 'Forest' just remembering what I have seen. Try it, my son."

There was something in Dunbar's face that reminded Anthony of John Bonnyfeather as the old Scot sat before the fire that last night, full of practical advice, comfort, and out-looking philosophy. He received gladly the gift of a compass which the old man pressed upon him as he left next day.

"Even that varies," said Dunbar with a little smile. "But it is the best I can do for you. This will always be the same, though"—and he gave him a warm handclasp.

They went back then to Fort Adams, filled their powder horns, and swinging around the great bend to the southward, turned the bow up the mouth of the Red River where it rolled its red marle in sanguine clouds into the yellow Mississippi.

Jean, Pierre, Pedro, and Moosh-Moosh, a light cedar canoe, Simba and Anthony.

Jean and Pierre were French and Indian half-breeds, coureurs de bois. Pedro was a Spanish Creole from the colony of Bastrop far up the Red River. Moosh-Moosh was an Osage Indian whose real name was Hill-with-Owls-on-its-Head, because he had been born in the Ozarks near a mountain devoted to screech owls. Moosh-Moosh was a nickname given him by the coureurs de bois for the reason that when sleeping he made a noise like the buzzing of many flies. Otherwise he was silent. He had keen, restless eyes and was a hunter and trapper who had been farther up the Arkansas than most geographers of the time would have thought possible. A belt made of buffalo hides and scalps supported an arrangement of deerskin that vaguely resembled trousers. Moosh-Moosh and Simba had upon first meeting prepared for a fight to the death. They disliked each other's smell. A few days' hunting taught them mutual respect. Wounded deer no longer escaped Moosh-Moosh. Simba invariably brought them down. After many weeks the Indian one night emitted an approving grunt and laid his hand on the dog's head. Simba's hair bristled, but he merely wrinkled his lips. On the basis of this working agreement, the party was seldom without meat.

It took them a month to leave the always half-flooded lowlands behind them. Day after day, under the steady impetus of five paddles, the bow of the canoe wrinkled the red water to each side of it, darting forward and forward, always north and a little westward past the low banks lined with scrub-willows and the mouths of swampy bayous. At night they camped on the river-islands or sandbars, building fires of drift wood, driven nearly frantic by mosquitoes that forced Simba to roll in the shallows or to sit with nothing but his muzzle out of water, for he could not take shelter in the smoke as the men did.

Every two or three days they passed flat-boats being poled and dragged up-river through the shallows or coming down swiftly under five or six oars. They were loaded with goods and the bales of traders, for they were not beyond the settlements yet. Here and there on the higher reaches of the banks, or on the islands amid the bayous, were French or Spanish plantations that traded with New Orleans.

They avoided these as far as possible, stopping only now and again for yeast, tobacco, and salt. They passed the occasional flat-boats easily, and began to ascend rapids from time to time. The country now began to lift itself out of the domain of the rivers into higher land where snatches of prairies began; where there were pines, sandhills, and rocks.

At Bastrops they left Pedro behind. It was from here that Burr had intended to invade Mexico by way of Texas. There was a cluster of settlements and plantations, Frenchmen, Spaniards, slaves, and a few Yanqui traders. This was the "capital" of the Baron Bastrop, who had been granted a million acres by the Crown of Spain. Here they drank wine for the last time and Moosh-Moosh filled himself to the throat with rum. Only his eyes moved as they laid him in the canoe. For a time there were only two to paddle, Anthony in the bow and Jean in the stern, for the night before leaving Pierre had blown his head off trying to light his pipe with a powder horn and flint-lock.

"It can be done, monsieur," said Jean, "but one must flutter the thumb rapidly and draw in even at the moment of the spark. Alas Pierre, he coughed."

Two days later Moosh-Moosh arose from the canoe, brewed himself a black broth, confided his trouble to the river, and resumed the paddle.

They ascended into a country of cascades, hills, forests, and uncountable bears. The nights grew colder, the water deeper. All traces of men except a few tree-caches along the banks disappeared. About the end of August they ascended a tremendous rapid and around a bend in the river came in sight of a prairie with some hills in the middle of it from which ascended innumerable smokes. About fifty miles to the northwest tumbled a range of blue mountains.

"These," thought Anthony, "are the hot springs, latitude thirty-four degrees north, and longitude ninety-two degrees west of Greenwich. Moosh-Moosh, do you hear that? Do you know where we are now as well as I do?"

"Ugh!" said Moosh-Moosh. "Boil-um heap fish."

They spent the fall and winter at the hot springs. There was already a bark lodge there where sufferers came out of the wilderness to ease themselves of various complaints, for the healing nature of the waters had long been known to the Indians. It was here that a whole tribe of the people of the Osage had died. Hill-with-the-Owls-on-its-Head remembered. The bad medicine of the pale faces had smitten them with sores from head to foot and they had come here to bathe in the steaming baths that cascaded down the hillsides. Small-pox driven inward is fatal, so they had died by fives and dozens sitting in misty pools. Some of them sat there yet. The rest had been "buried" in treetops. They came across their skeletons from time to time in the woods.

But no one disturbed them that winter. They had the scalding fountains and the country for unknown leagues about all to themselves. Only the Buffalo-people came from the north, drifting through in small herds of a few hundred at a time toward the southern salt pans. Some had arrows in their flanks, which Moosh-Moosh said had been loosed by the Sioux, far-off and westward over the great prairies. They cut off a herd of yearling bulls in a little valley, and largely by the help of Simba stampeded them over a cliff. Without horses it was useless to try to pursue these huge animals. Only a lucky shot could drop them. For the most part they rushed off wounded and bellowing to be devoured later on by wolves.

With so ample a supply of meat they felt themselves lucky and built a heavy log hut with a roof piled high with stones to protect it from the bears. With these thieves the woods abounded and they also were added to the winter larder. Jean, as the cold came on, anointed himself with their grease.

They also built for themselves a log and turf hut with an ingenious floor. Several layers of boulders covered with branches and a stratum of gravel and packed clay formed a kind of platform on a hillside upon which the house stood. Under this floor, and between the boulders, they led a stream of water from a hot spring whose multi-coloured terraces steamed and bubbled only a few hundred feet away. All winter the grateful heat of the water ascended through the floor. Even Jean was lost in admiration of this. Moosh-Moosh hibernated here rather than slept. And Simba made both the white men laugh by occasionally raising his feet and looking at them in surprise.

Jean and the Indian hunted and trapped all winter. When spring came there was a canoe-load of peltry ready for New Orleans. Jean prepared to depart.

And what had Anthony been doing? Exactly what has been related. He had learned to give himself up to being nothing but muscles to paddle with and eyes to search the river ahead; to use every faculty to slay and to keep from being slain by animals; to sharpen his five wits so keenly that the world without became the world within—and he had discovered how to master the world without and how to cope with it.

He had learned how to hunt and fish, how to make clothes for himself out of skins, the ways of a hundred animals and the uses of trees and plants. In short, how to get along in the wilderness without anything but a rifle, an axe, and a knife.

He could walk out on the little terrace before the cabin with the still-steaming water running away in its bubbling channel from beneath the floor, and hear nothing but the water and the wind, and see nothing but the view: blue mountains to the north, stretches of forest and prairie, and the ever-changing sky. He did not think about them. He saw them. And he read into them nothing but the signs of the weather and the messages of the wilderness. As though with the eyes of Simba and Moosh-Moosh he, too, looked and saw only what there was to see without remembering that he saw. He had been helped to this natural use of his faculties by the fact that nothing he looked upon reminded him of man. Every prospect about him was at once unspoiled, eternal, limitless, and new. He looked upon distant mountains; the mountains looked upon him —and he thought no more of them.

The madonna hung in a small deerskin bag tied close to the rafters.   He had made it to contain her fire-scarred body.   With a draw-string he tied the mouth of the bag fast.

When the spring came and the forests grew misty green, the pain of spring did not return again.   He had forgotten it, he said.   If he felt it vaguely, as one who is partly benumbed, he did not stop to recall what it was about.   The woods were turning green.   That was all.   The beavers were starting to build again.   It was differ-ent from fall.   The earth grew warm again.   In a certain way he rejoiced.   He knew now that he was not going to lose his mind.   He had saved it by letting the wilderness flow in upon him.

Jean left in early April.   He took back a few words written on a piece of bark to Vincent and the compass to Mr. Dunbar.   An-thony and the Indian remained at the hot springs, building a canoe.

When the spring floods were over they launched forth with Simba and the rifles and paddled on into the heart of the continent.   Their only kit was a kettle, a small deerskin bag, and blankets.   The to-bacco had gone by this time.   The powder lasted them till August.

By that time even Moosh-Moosh did not know where they were.

They had been following the river for five months.   About mid-summer they had passed through a succession of great gorges and rapids where the stream cut through a range of wild and forbidding hills indescribably rocky and ragged.   They carried the canoe around a roaring falls.   Hunting was all but impossible here, and they had nearly starved.   A fawn that came to stare at their camp-fire one night saved their lives.

Farther up, the river widened out again into a valley two or three miles wide, with islands, shallows, and an imperceptible current.

The valley continued endlessly between lines of steep, clay cliffs with patches of open cottonwood forest.

It was pleasant but monotonous.   The red cliffs faced each other across the groves of cottonwoods and low, sandy islands for hun-dreds of miles.   From time to time they climbed the cliffs to look around them and found themselves always in the same great prairie, an absolutely level sea of land covered with grass from horizon to horizon.   The last of the distant, blue hills had been left behind somewhere in time.   Anthony had lost count of the days.   Only space lay before them in the shape of the endless level plain.

Game abounded.   Down the trails over the cliffs from the prairie above buffalo and antelope came to drink, and herds of wild horses.   The valley was full of the skulls and skeletons of animals slaugh-tered at the fords.   Once they lay hidden on an island for a week.

Horse Indians were hunting along the cliffs above, and they did not dare to build a fire. Simba remained silent, crouching under the canoe as he had been taught to do. The hunters passed on. A few days later the prairie was a sea of fire and the valley thronged with animals that in some places came over the cliff in reckless waves while the flames licked along the heights above them.

At one place they waited for three days while a herd of buffalo passed. They were going south. Moosh-Moosh looked uncomfortable and gave signs of being lost. With a stick he traced in the sand a rude map and indicated that they had somehow taken the wrong fork of the river.

He was sure of it when they came to five isolated buttes that rose out of the prairie like an archipelago from which the sea had withdrawn. He did not know these hills. They lay to the south of the river. A stream drained them and broke through the cliffs into the main valley by a gorge. They turned aside here and followed it up. A day later they were at its source, five great springs that burst out at the foot of the buttes.

These table-top mountains, for they seemed to be mountains in the middle of the plain, lay scattered about in a rough amphitheatre in the centre of which was a large black pond into which the springs drained and where the stream took its rise. This bowl between the hills was two or three miles in diameter and covered with a forest of giant pines. There were signs of an old Indian encampment but of many years past. They climbed the tallest butte and looked about them. From sunrise to sunset stretched the unbroken, flat prairie; from north to south. Across it the river zigzagged like a red gash. Southward great, dark patches like cloud-shadows marked the drifting herds of buffalo. They camped there and soon discovered why so favoured a spot was apparently ignored.

It was not approachable by a horse, the only easy access being by way of the stream, and it was haunted by a grizzly bear of enormous proportions and ferocious temperament. He devoured their cache of jerked buffalo meat and scattered their camp. Without fire-arms they could do nothing about it. An arrow, which Moosh-Moosh launched at him from his short bow, glanced off his jaw and was almost the end of them. They would have become skeletons in tree-tops if Simba had not drawn him off in a hopeless pursuit. They returned to the river valley and spent the winter in a hut made of boulders and cottonwood on an island. It was terribly cold and food was scarce.

As soon as the river thawed in the spring, Moosh-Moosh prepared the canoe to depart for the settlements. He could not persuade Anthony to accompany him and he seemed concerned about it. "No rum," said he, pointing around in all directions. "No rum." Then he rubbed his stomach. Seeing that his greatest argument made no impression, he shoved off. Anthony and Simba remained by the ashes of the fire on the island. As the Indian disappeared around the bend below, Anthony knelt down and blew up the coals. In addition to the fire and the dog, he had a useless rifle and an empty powder horn; he had a knife, an axe, flint and steel, and a certain deerskin bag tied at the mouth.

After that his life, even to himself, became legendary.

He fished and trapped. At the ford below the island Simba lay in wait and tackled the deer as they swam. From the bois d'arc Anthony cut himself a straight-grained piece and shaped a bow. It was some time before he could find anything for a bowstring. Deer-hide parted. At last he took the long tendon from a stag's leg and out of these sinews formed one that hummed like a harp-string and held. The bow was not short as that of Moosh-Moosh had been. It was over two yards from tip to tip and suited the height and the strength of the man who strung it.

That man was taller than his bow and stronger. He now had muscles of iron. His golden beard, a little grey at the temples, fell half-way to his belt and was a continuation of his yellow mane. Out of this bush, above the short bare-space of tanned cheek bones, looked wide, grey-blue eyes, alert, not sunken into deep sockets, still youthful in their expression, piercing now rather than dreamful, whether they gazed over the sea of prairies or searched out the terraces along the cliffs.

He could move like a flash or sit for hours without moving a muscle, not thinking, but like the hound that lay beside him using his eyes, ears, and nose. His outward conversation was now addressed solely to that hound. But it was more extensive in its emotional range and understanding than those who are acquainted with dogs only as household pets and inferior companions might suspect.

When he communed with himself it was not upon the past nor did he always seem to be addressing some dream-companion within his own head. He could now, at times, commune in an external direction as though his whole verbal consciousness were in the mood expressed by that form of address, the use of which has almost lapsed from modern language, the attitude expressed by O.

It is only in timeless solitudes, which the traveller has discovered to be no longer solitary, that a man's lips can learn to shape themselves to the round symbol of eternity which is the crown of human talk and communion, that O complete in itself. And so at last, by becoming utterly lonely, he discovered that it was impossible to be alone. He had asked for comfort, and in some sort he received it.

The physical man busied himself in preparing physical weapons and devices to claim his daily meat from God. He made arrows and feathered them, hardening their points in the fire, for he could come by nothing as yet wherewith to tip them. He took the ramrod out of his gun, and heating it in the coals, pounded it with rocks to a sharp point and set it in a staff. He now had a spear with a bayonet-like point over a foot long. It was no mean weapon. He spent endless hours shooting with the bow and could at last, as both his marksmanship and arrow-making improved, drive true to the mark.

Thus provided, he left the river bottom towards the end of his first summer in solitude, for he had no desire to winter there alone, and returned to the valley between the five buttes, determined to drive out the bear and if possible to kill him.

It was not long before he realized that the bear was hunting him. He found his huge tracks about the camp the first morning after he camped by the pool in the pines. Only the watchfulness of Simba and a leaping fire kept him off. It was essential to find a safe resting place. With that end in view he began to examine the sides of the buttes that rose with faces of sheer cliff directly out of a steep slope of weathered rocks and shale.

Simba flushed a bobcat at the foot of the cliffs. It darted spitting up the slope, and leaping onto a ledge on the cliff, apparently disappeared into the heart of the hill. They followed with some difficulty. The ledge was only about a foot wide. It gradually tilted inward into the face of the cliff until they were passing through a knife-slice into the side of the butte itself. There was just room enough for a man to pass and for a glimmer of sky overhead. Along this cut bubbled a lively little stream through a gutter it had worn in the stone. Simba darted ahead now, and from some distance beyond came the noise of a wildcat brought to bay and voicing its opinion of intruders.

Twenty yards more, and Anthony stepped into the sunlight. The place at one time must have been an immense cave. But its roof had collapsed ages before, leaving a hole in the flat top of the butte as though a rough knot had been extracted from a level plank. The sides were about two hundred feet high, sheer and smooth, and the area at the bottom of this rocky well in the hill was several acres in extent. There was a cluster of gigantic cedars here which had grown in the perfect shelter with an unspoiled symmetry and in the course of centuries covered the ground with their needles and cones. Somewhere beneath this fragrant covering, still faintly audible, ran the stream that drained this little crater, which would otherwise have been a lake.

As he looked about him with satisfaction and amazement, Anthony found himself saying, "This is home." Just then Simba closed with the bobcat.

For a hound trained to tackle a lion, the bobcat was not formidable. Simba broke its back from behind. He then darted into a hole in the cliff and finished off a nest of savage kittens.

Anthony cleansed the place with fire and moved in. It was a cave with a sandy floor that ran back into the cliff for nearly fifty yards. Man had been here before. Near the entrance there was an old hearth with the marks of fire on it. Later on, he found flints, a rough stone hammer, and needles of polished bone. Whoever had lived there had gone away ages before. In the ashes of the hearth he thought he recognized the half-charred nuts of a species of palm. How long ago had that fire gone out? Upon that hearth he rekindled his own fire.

Here he was safe from all intruders except the birds. No one could find him unless they climbed the sheer cliffs of the butte and came to peer down at him. The cleft through which the stream drained was too narrow for the bear. And he soon barricaded it effectually at its narrowest place by a gate of logs. The way along the rocky ledge left no trail. He now slept secure at nights with nothing but the hidden complaint of the stream under its bed of needles, the song of owls, and the moonlight filtering through the cedars as company, for there was not even a wind to sigh in the boughs of the sheltered trees.

He lived comfortably. He set up a rude housekeeping in the cave. He built himself a chair and a bed, a rough log table. He drove pegs into the rock to hang his deerskins upon and stocked the inner reaches of the place with an ample supply of firewood. Best of all, he could now accumulate a stock of dried and smoked meat for the winter, instead of depending upon hunting from day to day.

Some miles away over the prairie, on the opposite side of the butte, he found a salt lick where the deer and buffalo came. By a month's work he was able to evaporate several bushels of the mineral by pouring the brine into holes in a rock and dropping hot stones into it. His chief difficulty was the lack of a kettle or dish of any kind that would bear fire. The clay along the river set him thinking.

After several trials he succeeded in constructing a potter's wheel out of a log end, a stick for a treadle, and a deer thong for a belt. His first efforts at making bowls and pots were weird. But he progressed. He built a rough kiln out of boulders and daubed clay and fired it. The results surpassed his expectations. He could, he found, not only supply himself with pots but with dishes and receptacles of all shapes and kinds. He spent hours at the wheel. He improved his furnace with a bellows and was at last able to melt sand. He made a clay mould and cast hundreds of glass arrow heads. But he was unable to contrive a blower that would work. At last he remembered the rifle barrel and was enabled to make some bottles of monstrous shapes. They were more curious than usable.

Nothing was lacking now but the skin of the bear for a hearth-rug and some grain to vary his diet. And tobacco—

Security had permitted him to declare a truce with the bear. He was not so likely to be surprised by the animal in the daytime but he was aware that when he went down into the bowl between the hills he was frequently followed. Perhaps it was only curiosity, he thought. The animal never left his haunts between the buttes to go down to the river valley or onto the plains below. He was an old bachelor with a temper morose. Gradually, although Anthony saw him only once or twice, he became acquainted with his habits. He lived in a hole in a hill across the pine woods on the far side of the bowl.

Once just as he emerged from the cliff along the ledge, he found him digging for roots on the slope below. They saw each other at the same instant. The bear rose out of the bushes. He stood over eleven feet high, pig-like eyes squinting, his arms falling before him as if he had heavy boxing gloves on. He rumbled out a defiance to his enemy on the ledge above him and made off. Once he heard him roaring and saw him pursued by a swarm of bees into the lake. One night Simba came back bleeding with deep claw marks down his shoulder. After that they both emerged from the cliff more carefully. The "truce" was distinctly over, with one of the parties lying in ambush. About the beginning of winter Anthony got a long shot at him with the bow, but it was too long. The arrow glanced off. Bruin then disappeared for some months. It was not until early March that he was seen again and under most curious circumstances.

The snowfall had been heavy that winter and the little lake under the pines was frozen solid. As he passed it one day, returning from the river valley, he heard a hoarse rumbling-chuckling going on in the direction of the pool. Simba growled and started to creep forward. Cautioning him to keep low, he crept to the edge of the trees himself and peered out, keeping his hand on the dog.

Bruin was there. He looked thin and gaunt after his winter sleep. But he was having a good time. He was sled-riding.

He would climb up a little knoll that sloped steeply to the lake, squat on his haunches, glide down with a terrific speed, and shoot out unto the smooth surface of the ice, bumbling with ecstasy. His remarks and his gestures were those of a bear who had lost all sense of gravity except when sliding, who did not care how far his tongue hung out of his grinning mouth. His little nose smoked rapidly in the frosty air as he scrambled back to the mound and repeated the performance. It went on till sunset and continued into the starlight. In the darkness Anthony finally left, forcing Simba to follow.

Later that night he returned to the pond and reconnoitred carefully. The bear had gone.

He walked over the ice, and taking his spear with the sharpened iron ramrod on the end of it, set it with its butt against a rock and the head slanting up the toboggan slide of the afternoon before. He covered it with snow, and making all as smooth as possible walked back over the ice. He remembered that at best the bear could not see very well. He went back to the cave and slept.

Simba wakened him wild with excitement. He went out and listened and then came back. That afternoon he went down and began to skin the bear.

The spear had been driven clear through him and snapped off.

Anthony was not sorry for the bear. How could he be? He was no longer even sorry for himself. And charity begins at home.

In all that vast region overlooked by the Five Buttes there was not a single being with whom he could have shared sympathy or the peace of God, if he had found it. Not one. For three years he had lived there without seeing a trace of man.

The buffalo swung back and forth with the pendulum of the seasons, following the sea of grass as it withered and bloomed. About the base of his hills broke this spray of the prairie whose tide was controlled by the sun. By this time he had learned as perfectly as might be the implacable laws of the place. From the fish in the pools of the river bottom to the eagles on the cliffs above—what animal so successful as he?

But it was not enough.

It was not enough to be the god of Simba, or to have vanquished the great bear—to walk superior to all things save himself. For he had come into the wilderness for two reasons and he had been only half successful. He had come into the wilderness to let the scars of the burning heal. By living in the present only he had enabled his mind to form its cicatrice. But he had also hoped to draw near to the All-Father in nature by becoming one of his children. And he had become a child again, able to release himself into the world about him and to play there contentedly between sleep and sleep. But of the Causer of Dreams and of the nature of Nature he had learned nothing at all. Nature had nobly sustained his body, and that was all.

It was his custom about evening to climb to the top of the butte where the cave was and to look out over the ocean of prairies from west to east. And he would also rise early in the mornings to behold the dawn. So frequently did he do this that the spectacle of dawn and sunset and of the day between them became one to him in his own mind as he sat by the fire in his cave at night.

Surely, if anywhere in the world without, the word of God might be spoken between those two flaming lips of dawn and sunset a prairie-day apart; a word clear and glorious, a thought vast and stupendous, a great yea-saying between the green infinity of earth and the blue infinitudes of sky.

But if all things from the north unto the south and from the east unto the west combined to praise Him, this was the unconscious music of the spheres and no mere opera for the heart and mind of man.

Who could write the libretto to this fundamental music or choose the words for the cosmic chorus that must accompany it in explanation? His name was Noman. Even the harp of David had not been able to compass the poem to such music, though he had caught the accents of the divine.

Anthony could find no more in it than the feeling of glory, of exaltation, of terror at the coldness of the infinite in this hymn of the prairie. But even Simba experienced the last. In winter when the light failed and the cold stars began to glitter on the sea of snow below, he would sit on the cliff's edge and howl until the quavering answer of the sadness in the hearts of his relatives the wolves and coyotes answered him. In the moonlight the canine people of the prairie went lunatic. An hour or two of their libretto was all that any man could stand.

Anthony would call Simba back with a shrill whistle, and the hound would return to the fire, glad of its cheerful glow and the satisfactory and familiar limits of the cave.

It was on one of these lonely winter evenings, when the cold penetrated even to the interior of the cave, that he undertook to enlarge the area of the hearth. It was simple enough. He had merely to add a few stones. As he dug down in the sand he found that the older portion of the hearth was laid upon a bed of clay. He removed some stones from it to fit on his addition, and beneath one he found, as clear as if it had been made only yesterday, the imprint of a child's hand.

An emotion, too conflicting and too complicated to describe, overcame him, and he sat there unashamed of the tears that coursed freely down his face.

So the place really had been home once! He had given small thought to those who had dwelt there—so far in the past that they had left no ghosts, he thought. But now he could feel them about him as though it had been only yesterday. Perhaps in some such human symbol as this handprint, rather than in the word contained between the lips of dawn and sunset, was the answer to what he sought.

He removed the fire-scarred figure from its deerskin bag and set it above him in a groove of the rock where the madonna held forth the man child to him in the firelight again . . .

How well those who had tried to express the relation of God to man had done to leave the Father understood and unexpressed in the group. For was He not unknowable and inexpressible in human symbols or syllables?

Still, through all, through the fire, and the shadows, and from the beginning to the end, the divine child had been held out to him. Should he let him remain here in the wilderness, or should he take him to his own heart at last and go like Brother François to exhibit his image among men?

The cogitations of the winter were long. Before spring came he had begun to make his preparations for departure.

Simba, who was half-blind now and old and grizzled, seemed to understand that they were leaving. But he showed no joy over it as he would have even a few years before. He crept near Anthony by the hearth, and putting his great head on his knees, wagged his tail slowly and grumbled and moaned a little as if he would say, "Have we not wandered enough, my master? Let us lie down here in peace." And the man did his best to comfort the dog. Amah's friendship had indeed followed far.

Anthony made a warm coat for himself out of the skin of the bear. He used the head for a hood and the limbs for sleeves and trousers. He was most bear-like when he laced himself into it. But he was also dry and warm. Towards the end of the winter, when his supplies ran low, he began to move about in it in the country around the Five Buttes, hunting. And it was thus arrayed that on a bleak March day, with the snow still driving hard, he came suddenly about twilight upon three old women.

They were seated near the dark lake in the pine woods around the ashes of a fire. He would have passed them in the early darkness and the heavy, feathery snow of earliest springtime, if it had not been for the nose of the hound. It was Simba who smelled them out as if they had been so many witches. Indeed, that was what they looked like.

Never in his life had he seen or imagined women so old as these. They were certainly, he thought as he drew near to them, the oldest women in the world.

They, on their part, did not move as he approached them, for they had been left there to die and to be looked after by the bear, which was the god of their tribe. They had been left as all the other old women of their people had been left before them. Their last fire had gone out, and as they peered through the darkness with the final numbness of age and winter heavy upon them and saw the bear approaching, as they had been told he would—they said nothing at all. That was the form in which death came to old women of the People of the Bear; to those who had lived too long. Death *was* a bear. When the bear spoke to them, when a man's head came out of the bear's head and the thing beckoned to them, they knew they were already dead and that they were being commanded to follow to the happy hunting ground of the People of the Bear. But only two of them rose and followed. The third remained where she had been sitting when she last sat down.

Thus, with two all but disembodied spirits tottering after him, the bear and his great cub Simba led the two surviving squaws home to the warmth and ease of the cave. There they drank some hot soup made of deerbones, stretched out their withered hands to the warmth of the hearth, and began to look fearfully about them to see what heaven, where the bear lived, was like. Doubtless it was for her sins in early youth that their sister had not been permitted to accompany them. Doubtless the bear had devoured her soul as she deserved. At any rate, they never saw her again. She was now nothing but a myth for ghostly gossip conducted in whispers in the morning as they built up the fire for the bear.

It was impossible to talk to these old women, Anthony found. He did not know their language, and when he attempted to address them even by signs they fell with their faces to the ground. So he brought them meat and they cooked it. They were careful to see that Simba received his due share, for it was plain from his actions that the earthly smell they had brought with them into paradise irked his god-like nose. It was also plain that their master the bear often laughed at them. His head frequently protruded from his head to do so; at which times they remembered their own sins. Who could tell what the laughter of a bear might portend even in a spiritual state? As for the bear, he was as kind as he could be to them. But he could not help laughing at himself and at the difficulties of even beginning to follow the example of Brother François. One was supposed to begin humbly.

Meanwhile, the two old women grew fat and sleek again. They were well-fed and rested. It looked as though they might live for another hundred years. In the spring they went forth to gather roots and berries. And thereby a change came both to themselves and for their master the bear. Unfortunately, the happy hunting ground still had relations with the unhappy hunting grounds of the mundane plains below.

It was in early May of a certain year, unnamed by the People of the Bear, that the medicine-man of that tribe of wandering red men found the ghost of his deceased grandmother digging for clamus roots on the side of a mountain. Some natural doubts as to her decease passed between them, including the story of the bear. The chief returned to his tepee to make medicine. The result was the undoubted decease of both the old women and the capture of the bear.

Only Simba escaped. He now followed Anthony afar-off, killing such of the Indian dogs as came out at night to hunt him over the prairie. He picked up the trail of his master as best he could. Old bones, wounds, and sores were his only reward and portion.

And with Anthony it was not much better. Only a man in the form of a god could have fallen as low as he had.

He was kept, just as he had been captured, in the bearskin. He was held imprisoned in the largest tepee as the Big Medicine of the tribe. Every article in the cavern had been taken along just as each had been found; everything, except the two old women, who had been left on the floor of the place with no brains left to worry them. When the tribe moved, as they did every few days, southward over the prairies, for they were following the buffalo, the contents of the tepee was loaded onto a pony and upon two poles that dragged on the ground behind him by way of a cart or traverse. This traverse the Big Medicine followed. He had become attached to the thing by means of a horsehair rope. The attachment lasted for three months. By that time they had arrived in semi-arid, alkali country about the head water of certain rivers draining southward into the Rio Grande. No person had as yet taken the trouble to mark these rivers upon any map made in Europe. They flowed quite incognito, but they were of considerable interest to the buffalo which traversed their valleys to the rich southern ranges beyond, and hence to the horse Indians who pursued them thither.

At a certain point in the semi-arid landscape the southward tendency of the Indians became of great interest to the military authorities of New Spain. They had no objection to the wild tribes pursuing the wild buffalo. But they had numerous objections, and strong ones, in the form of regiments of cavalry, to the Indians continuing on into "Texas" and raiding the herds of long-horn cattle on the haciendas or the villages gathered about the missions, whose bells rang never so loudly as when the "Apaches" approached.

That portion of New Spain ruled eastward from Santa Fé was a large one. In the midsummer of 1816 the People of the Bear found themselves halted on the northern bank of the "Bitter River" in pow-wow over a message from their Mighty Father, the King of Spain. It was laconic, written in two paragraphs; the first was a dead rattlesnake stuffed with powder; the second was another rattlesnake which appeared to have died eating bullets. The caballero who brought them flung them into the lap of the chief and departed to his own camp on the other side of the river. There he became the Munchausen of his regiment by insisting that in the tents of the Indians there was a bear who had called out to him in Spanish that he was a Christian man.

This assertion having been repeated to those in authority, and received with the proper contempt due to the sublime credulity or impudence which had prompted it, the Spanish camp settled down to digesting its midday meal, while the camp of the Indians digested the message conveyed by the rattlesnakes. A good deal of dancing, *ugh-ughing,* and *woof-woofing* accompanied the latter process.

From the slit in the door of his tepee, which was tied fast as usual, Anthony could see down the street of the Indian village where the pow-wow was going on. The young braves were for continuing on after the buffalo southward; the eloquence of the chiefs of the tribe was trying to persuade them to turn back. Presently the maker of medicine began to perform a dance. It went on for hours. The squaws, two of whom generally watched him closely, gradually closed in slapping their hands together and moving their bodies to the time. Presently the medicine-man would consult the bear and make up the tribe's mind for it. The dance was merely in preparation for that. They would go north again into the wilderness. He knew. He would never hear the Spanish bugles again.

The heat in the tepee was tremendous. The man sewed in the bearskin sweated and was devoured by fleas. The dance outside went on. In the middle of the afternoon he heard Simba hunting. His voice came from across the river, strong as in the old days, full of excitement. He seemed to have struck an old and familiar trail. He might have come across the spoor of a lion. A remembrance of strength and hope returned to the despairing man in the tepee. Outside the dance went on.

He rose, and taking the edge of his axe, split the bearskin down the front from throat to belly and stepped out of it. He tied the deerskin bag about his neck, wriggled naked under the back of the tepee with the axe in his hand, and crawled down the slope toward the river about half a mile away.

A dry arroyo swallowed him. He continued on down it. He killed a rattlesnake with a stone. Simba was still following the trail. He might rejoin him now. One last hunt together, and they might yet be free. Ten minutes more, and he would make the river without being seen. He listened again, carefully screened by a clump of chaparral from both the Indian and the Spanish camps. The dance above was still going on. He could see the Spanish sentries below him.

Which way should he go? Into the wilderness—or back to Spain?

Suddenly the voice of the hound below him burst into the full hunting cry and began to make straight into the Spanish camp. The sentries began firing. He leaped up and started to run. As he rushed into the river, a fierce clamour broke out in the tepees behind him. The god had gone. The man in the river swam like mad toward the Spanish camp that now lay only a short distance before him. The cleansing caress of the water removed the filth of his three months of divinity and made him feel as if he were reborn. His long golden beard streamed in the wind as he climbed the river bank.

Simba was nearly blind. He had hidden by day and followed Anthony's trail at night. He had not dared to try to enter the Indian encampment. From time to time Anthony had heard him, and so had the Indians, howling in the wilderness. He had lived on what small game he could snap up, and learned to crouch and back off at the whir of the rattlesnake. But he was nearly done now; almost at the end of the trail; gaunt, starved, full of nothing but puzzled despair. The familiar scent of his master's footsteps was the only thing that still dragged him along over the surface of the earth. That odour was the trail of his god who could do no wrong, even if he had abandoned heaven and he heard his voice no more.

Nineteen years of odours constituted the memory of this aged and gigantic hound. As his light failed, and even sounds began to grow distant and confused, he lived by his nose alone. It had never deceived him, and he was never surprised at any of its messages. No matter how preposterous a thing might seem to be to a man, when the nose of Simba smelled it, he remembered, and he knew that it must be true.

It was, therefore, no surprise to Simba one afternoon on a prairie in the middle of America to pick up a trail he had once lost years before in Spain. Suddenly his nose came across it again. It simply resumed. It was the trail of the little man who had once lost his hat to him off a coach just outside the gates of Madrid—and that hat had also had upon it the blood of Juan. In the mind of Simba he now simply took up the chase of Sancho where he had last left off.

As Anthony climbed the river bank, that long trail was nearing its end. The hound rushed baying into the camp. At the far end of the street of tents, "El Gato," seated under the shade of a military marquee, heard him and sat up, his whiskers bristling with alarm. He remembered that voice. Even at the world's-end he could not forget it.

The honours and dignities which had fallen upon Sancho in the new world had not altered the essential nature of the little man. He was still his master's humble and obedient servant. But Don Luis was now nearly eighty-five, and he administered the province of New Spain—of which he had found himself appointed the military governor, some years before upon arriving in Mexico—largely by the help of his still vigorous wife and the ruthless little man who had once been his postilion.

It had been necessary, however, to conceal the humble origin of both Faith and Sancho even from the provincial society of the little town of Santa Fé, which was Don Luis' capital. For that purpose, and to increase his authority, Sancho had been made a colonel, and aide-de-camp to the governor, and had had conferred upon him the star and ribbon of an obscure Italian order, which Napoleon had suppressed years before. The ruse had been highly successful. Mounted upon a piebald horse, with a sabre, high, polished jackboots, a cocked hat, and the order of S. Rosario about his neck, "Don Sancho Armijo" had done his master full credit.

He rode hard and far. And both the regular troops of the garrison and the levies of local lancers followed him willingly. He gave no orders which he did not expect himself to see carried out. If his men always referred to him as "The Cat," they did so respectfully. For it had long been known all over the province and on the frontiers that the Cat had claws and could use them. No one was

.sure just when or where Sancho might pounce. On the present occasion he had ridden northeast clear up into Kansas, burning sundry Indian villages, sacking a pueblo or two, and gathering in several Texan hunters and trappers, who had presumed to cross the vague boundaries of Louisiana into the sacred domains of Spain.

With the Texans it would go especially hard. It was the custom to send them to Mexico from Santa Fé, along with such rebels, criminals, and political disturbers as the governor might desire to be rid of. There was an annual clearance of such rubbish. Once in Mexico the viceroy had his own methods, of which no one had ever returned to complain. Since the expedition of General Pike, which some years before had come to final grief at Santa Fé, the zeal of the Spanish authorities had been especially directed against the Americans. That two of the Texans captured on the present raid had their families with them seemed especially significant. Sancho had burned their cabins and brought them, men, women, and children, along with him, despite the hardships and their miserable plight. His encounter with the People of the Bear was a mere incident. They were not even Apaches, and his force outnumbered them fifty to one. He would give them a few hours to deliberate, he thought, as he sat under the marquee, and then send them flying. He was preparing for a siesta in a hammock slung between two tent poles, when the voice of the dog disturbed him. When it approached the camp the Cat sat up. The dog was undoubtedly hunting.

There was only one hound in the world that had a voice just like that. Fear is a marvellous conjuror. It reduces a situation to its elementals. In the mind of Sancho everything but the fact that he was being pursued melted away. The sense of his rank and authority vanished as the voice of Simba approached. When the grizzled form of the hound, with his nose to the trail, appeared at the far end of the street of tents, panic seized Sancho. There was something almost supernatural about it. The dog seemed to have come across the prairies out of the past from the other side of the Atlantic to bay Sancho's footsteps. There he was, and fast approaching. It never occurred to Sancho to stop him. The thing to do was to flee.

He snatched his feet out of his jack-boots and raced down the camp street toward the picket lines. If he could once get on horseback he might get away. But there was no time for that. As Simba struck the trail of Sancho's stocking feet he burst forth into a hellish clamour. Sancho leaped forward. So did Simba. Sancho now changed his direction suddenly and ran for a clump of trees by the river bank. The dog gained. Before his dim sight he now beheld the ghostly shadow of a cat leaping frantically to escape him, and he could hear its squalls. Simba hurtled forward and ripped the coat off his enemy's back. A sentry's rifle cracked. The cat scrambled into the cruel branches of a thorn tree. The dog sank gasping at its foot. Soldiers were now closing in from all directions.

Just then a naked man with a long, yellow beard rushed out from the covert along the river bank. The dog died with his head on his master's knees. In the branches of the thorn tree above a kind of twittering ceased. Caught on the long thorns, the body of Sancho ceased to struggle and hung limply across a limb with his eyes glazing.

Soldiers closed in around Anthony and looked down at him, where he sat with his arms about Simba.

After a while they led him prisoner into the camp and gave him some old clothing. The dog and the Cat they buried not far from each other on opposite sides of the tree of thorns.

CHAPTER SIXTY-SIX

THE PILGRIMAGE OF GRACE

DUST,—not only clouds of it,—but dust which flowed along the ground like liquid, that trickled into the hoofprints of the troop of horse as they trotted steadily into the southwest, that showered upon the sagebrush to either side of the trail like drops of dry water. Behind the scarves over their mouths the troopers coughed dust. The horses blew it out of their muddy noses. It clogged the corners of their eyes. Over the alkali plains dust-devils rose and twisted like waterspouts, dancing in the quivering heat. Lizards, twitching from stone to stone, left puffs of dust behind them. The long trail smoked with it for hours after the Spanish cavalry and their prisoners passed.

It was a silent land, leeched-out, bleached by the tremendous reverberations of white sunlight, with valleys like the floors of abandoned lime kilns and mountains flaunting dark ribbons of spiny lava along the sky. For Anthony, it was a country that did not remind him of any that he had ever seen before.

At night they camped by bitter, green water-holes that mirrored the stars dully, and wrinkled slowly to the horses' noses when they drank. The cool mornings were brisk and refreshing with the tea-like tang of sagebrush in the air. The distances were incredibly clear. The bugles rang, and they would start. It no longer made any difference to him where they were going.

Although he was a prisoner, he felt free and happy. Physical hardship meant nothing to him any more. The lonely years in the wilderness had both given and tempered his iron strength. He had ceased to try to make things happen. His faith in the director of events was now not only mental but physical. Whatever happened to him was "right." He lived as if he had once died in battle in a good cause, slept in eternity, and risen again to find himself still riding on.

The iron shoes of the squadrons rang on the stones of the dry arroyos, as they trotted on day after day. . . .

From the instant that he had recognized Sancho he knew that Don Luis would be at Santa Fé. Godoy had undoubtedly carried out his intention and exiled the marquis. He had sent him to be the governor of this distant province as he had said he would do. And no

doubt the old man would blame him for that. Don Luis would feel
that a word to Ouvrard might have prevented it. That was undoubtedly what Don Luis had been so anxious to speak to him about
those last days in Madrid. But he had dodged their interview. Don
Luis could never be made to understand how the statue in his patio
had made that meeting impossible. No, it would probably go hard
with him now—after Sancho's death! How curiously the truce between him and Don Luis had been broken! It seemed as though fate
had made it difficult for either of them to keep that truce and yet
still insisted upon bringing them together again.

It was this conviction of fate, plus a heightened sense of the irrevocable direction of time and of the events towards which it drifted
him,—as though they already existed and were waiting for him instead of just occurring,—that marked him as a different man from
the one he had been before; that to a certain extent separated him
from those who now surrounded him. But in that separation there
was also a spiritual freedom, for he understood that something over
which neither he nor his captors had any control was what finally
dictated the march of life.

So the prospect of again meeting with Don Luis could no longer
fill him with consternation. He regarded it as inevitable; but, therefore, with an almost complete detachment. He felt that Don Luis'
judgment upon him, whatever it might be, would be uttered as though
Don Luis were the mouthpiece of what controlled them both.
Yet he speculated a good deal upon their possible meeting.

That event would mark a return to the mysterious influences that
had to do with the beginning of his existence; make visible the curve
of his return to the mystery from which he had come. How little
he had to do with that circle, half of which lay in eternity! Despite
all his struggles and attempts to depart in his own direction, he had
always been brought around again. He was forced, even when he
thought he was flying off on his own tangent, to keep to the ordained
curve of his life.

In realizing this, Anthony did not feel that he was different from
other men. They too must all have their mysterious "rounds." Only
in his own life, looking backward, he could dimly trace his own curve
now.

Yet because he saw fate there, that did not mean he had become
supine and intended to cease to struggle. It merely meant that, like
a good many others who reach the age of forty, he felt the inevitability of direction in existence and the hand of a mysterious compulsion heavy upon him.

These were some of the considerations that let him ride forward
quietly; that caused Major Muñoz, the officer who had succeeded

Sancho in command of the expedition, to describe him as a "tractable prisoner," while they pushed on through the Great American Desert toward Santa Fé.

There was no doubt in that officer's mind about the advisability of holding Anthony prisoner. He regarded him as an altogether mysterious and suspicious character. Although he spoke Spanish, and seemed to be a good Catholic, for he carried an amulet of the Mother of God in a deerskin bag about his neck—still, he also spoke English; his dog had killed the colonel, and his account of what he was doing in Spanish territory was curious, to say the least.

Let him explain to the governor that he had been captured by Indians. Let old Don Luis look to it! He had a way of disposing of doubtful cases. And in these times—with the Yankees pouring across the frontiers into Texas and the revolutionaries out to avenge the shooting of Hidalgo by murdering the Gachupines—one could not be too careful.

Anthony found himself welcomed by the other prisoners, who had too many miseries of their own to be curious about his. The Texans, in particular, were inclined to regard as a benefactor the man whose dog had killed the Cat. The harshness of Sancho toward them had been extreme.

He rode day after day now with one of the white children held before him. He was able to lighten the burdens of the way by sharing his rations and the even more scanty dole of water with some of those who were failing. Remonstrance with the guards about their treatment of captive Indians also brought some results.

But as yet neither his fellow prisoners nor the guards knew exactly what to make of him. They looked somewhat askance upon the powerful man with the yellow beard tucked into his belt, who rode with such a serene look upon his face. What made him so happy? Perhaps, there was something a little uncanny about him? Only the child on his saddle-bow learned to trust him completely; to count on the precious sip of water as the heat and dust of the afternoon began its inevitable torture, and to come and ask for a story at night by the fires.

As for Anthony, he was glad to be back once more among the children of men.

"And there is only one way to live among them," he thought. "Brother François was right: 'Let us be kind to one another.' No man can ever harm me again, for he cannot make me harm him. I am free of everything at last: of all my possessions; of sorrows and hates; of useless curiosity about the nature of God and the Universe. All that I have left is my life and the love of the Divine Child. I sought the Almighty One among the lonely hills for my own comfort and this is the answer. 'Only among men can a man find Him!' The rest is mystery.

"Let the mountains and the oceans that I have seen bear witness to Him. Let me rejoice in, but not try to read the Word between the lips of the dawn and sunset. In me also is the Word, and through my lips and hands, O God, let it be spoken to men. Strengthen me, now that I have found the path at last. Forgive me that not by my own strength have I arrived at this, but because the world withered in fire and in ashes fell away."

Thus he said, riding on through the dust, communing with the spirit in himself, and feeling the weak body of the child before him on the saddle-bow.

And so it was that on a certain afternoon he looked down into a valley where there were a number of flat-roofed, adobe buildings gathered about a plaza. It was a small, poverty-stricken place. The prison would doubtless be none too comfortable. But he looked at it with a serene face.

"That, señor," vouchsafed one of the soldiers, pointing proudly, "is the end of our journey, the City of Santa Fé. We made a great circle when we marched so far into the desert. It has taken us a long time to get back again!"

"Yes," said Anthony, "we have come a great way about."

Don Luis had been military governor of the northern Mexican provinces and frontiers for over a decade. When he left Spain he knew he would never see it again. The Prince of the Peace had arranged his departure with a certain neatness. The appointment to a government in Mexico had been disguised as an honour, as indeed it might have been to any younger man. Don Luis' protests to the king had been unavailing. Both Godoy and the queen were finally determined to be rid of him, and they had enlisted Ouvrard on their side. Don Luis, Faith, Sancho, and a few domestics had, therefore, sailed for Mexico shortly after Anthony had left Madrid for New Orleans.

In a way, Don Luis had already had his revenge for being exiled. While he had been living in his adobe "palace" near Santa Fé, comfortably enough, Napoleon had made a clean sweep of Spain and carried off all those who had exiled Don Luis. Don Carlos IV and his queen, Godoy and his entire régime had vanished from Madrid. They were now exiles themselves.

The canny old man left forlornly at Santa Fé had long made it his study to get along with the viceregal authorities at Mexico, whoever

THE PILGRIMAGE OF GRACE

they might be. He had made himself invaluable to them; to Don José de Iturrigaray; and in due course to Archbishop Lizana. Don Luis was now holding his government in the name of Ferdinand VII. Not that he was enthused with loyalty for his new sovereign; he had instructions from Mexico—and Don Luis' politics always agreed with the viceroy's. He had now only one fixed policy. He intended to die in his comfortable adobe house in New Spain. The ruthless suppression of the rebellion of Hidalgo had taken place some years before. The shooting of that hero and his thirty companions, one a day for a month, had been managed by Don Luis for the arch-bishop-viceroy with neatness and dispatch. He had, to be sure, reprieved the thirty-one prisoners from June to July. But only be-cause July has thirty-one days in it. And he had shot Hidalgo last, on the last day of the month, at Chihuahua.

No one since then had cared to raise the grito of revolution in northern Mexico.

The silver convoys had also been sent south from Chihuahua, reg-ularly, twice a year. Don Luis made it a custom to dispatch with them such persons as might be inclined to trouble him, consigned to the tender care of the viceroy.

The regular arrival of silver and "rebels" from the North was a matter of routine at the City of Mexico. The viceroy knew exactly what to do with both.

Things were therefore peaceful enough for the time being.

"It will last my time," said Don Luis to his wife, while they sat on the porch at the Hacienda de León. He could now look at the distant snow mountains complacently enough. "After all, it *is* better than St. Helena. And I feel it in my bones, my dear, that in a short while you at least will be able to return to Spain with an estate that any widow in Madrid might envy. Taking it all in all, it is prob-ably lucky that we were sent here. It is hard to tell what might have happened to us in the troubled times at home." The news of Napoleon's downfall had only recently arrived and had caused Don Luis to do some philosophic thinking. He laughed to think of the poverty-stricken Don Manuel Godoy still dancing attendance on the exiled queen at Rome.

To her husband's remarks Faith did not reply. For the most part she sat in silence, waiting. It would not be long now.

Don Luis had failed greatly in the last six months. There was no doubt that his end must be near. Faith looked forward to re-turning to Spain and even to Paris for the years of quiet luxury that might still be hers. She felt she had earned them. She had been a faithful wife to the marquis. She looked at him now, sitting in the sun to keep warm.

The lion-like expression of his face had become accentuated. His huge hands, a surprising network of blue veins, lay relaxed upon the arms of his chair. He was a very ancient lion, wrinkled, and white-maned. Only the eyes were still bright and blazing. But even they had to close in sleep too often. On his temples the veins stood out startlingly. His neck had grown thin. His voice seldom boomed now. For the most part Don Luis piped. That annoyed him, so he too said little. Each understood the other's silence.

In his heart Don Luis wished he could die. He felt he had lived too long. He sat and thought of nothing. He appeared to sleep. It seemed to him that he was waiting for something important to happen, but he could not remember what.

Even when the news of the death of Sancho came, his expression did not alter. Perhaps, that was what he had been waiting for. He would not have to miss his old servant long. And there was a certain aptness about the passing of Sancho—as he listened to Major Muñoz recounting the incident—which still appealed to his sense of the fitness of things.

It seemed inevitable to Don Luis that Sancho should have been treed like a cat. So he had died squalling amid the thorns and branches! Hounded to death! Yes, that was what would have had to happen. For generations in Estremadura the family of Sancho had served his own. They were a peculiar race. There had been legends about them, which Don Luis did not believe. But he knew it was a fact that Sancho's people had always looked like cats. There were also pigs, asses, and mules among men. Character in plants and animals has its characteristic shapes. He thought he knew the subliminal why. Don Luis had needed a servant like Sancho to help get his work done. Soon there would be no more of either of them. Perhaps, the kind of work they were needed to do was over? Both their races had run out.

Don Luis stirred a little uneasily. He hated to think he had been used. He looked at the distant mountains as Major Muñoz departed. "What were *they* for?" he wondered. Well, he would probably soon find out now—or know nothing at all.

"It would be just like You," he said, "to send me to hell for it now You are finished with me. Just like You!"

He wished theology were more reassuring. Perhaps it would be just as well to send for a priest? Now that Sancho was gone, the end did seem near.

What an excellent joke it would be to confess himself into heaven! In the sunlight he sat and laughed a little languidly about it. And yet there were tears in his eyes before he finished. "Maria," he thought, "if she is anywhere—Maria will be there." God, how magical that springtime in Auvergne had been—a whole lifetime ago! *That* had been like paradise. That was heaven. If he had only known it then! If he had only had a child by her! It had been a boy after all. "Saints and Angels! When I meet that young Irishman in hell, I will kill him all over again!" He rose, and taking his stick, stumped into the living-room of the hacienda where Faith generally sat, waiting, and the Navajo blankets blazed with geometrical beasts and black lightnings along the walls.

It had made no particular impression upon Don Luis that the man whose dog had killed Sancho had been captured. He did not even speculate upon old trails' having been resumed. That the son of Maria was so near never entered his thoughts. Tomorrow he would go down and sit in judgment on the prisoners that Muñoz had captured. Mañana! In the meantime he sat down to a bowl of atole-gruel and a soft, milky tortilla.

In the afternoon he would sleep.

Faith called Major Muñoz back and entertained him for an hour. She got all the news out of him that she could. Santa Fé had become inexpressibly dull to her. The death of Sancho would make a difference. She would now have to depend upon Muñoz to carry out Don Luis' policies. A great many practical details of the administration now rested upon her shoulders. It was important to keep together a junta that she could depend upon. Major Muñoz was the ranking officer of the garrison, so she strove to make his call a pleasant one and to show him that she took a personal interest in his labours.

"What about the new prisoners?" she asked.

"Just the usual lot," he replied, "a few recalcitrant Indians from the Zuñi pueblos; some Americans who settled without permission in Texas; and the man who owned the dog. I must say I can't quite make him out. He seems to be a kind of hermit from his story. But you can't depend upon that. Educated, I think. Speaks Spanish like a Castilian. But he isn't. It might amuse you to talk with him? He begged some milch goats from me for the children only this morning. I let him have them. It can do no harm. It will go hard enough with those people on the trip south. It's quite a long walk from here to Mexico."

"Poor things!" said Faith. "I'll take some shoes down to them."

"Excellent," replied the major. "From now on they will be on foot, you know. They won't be moving with cavalry." He excused himself and left.

About five o'clock the governor's wife drove down to the plaza. She took along some old clothes. It had been too much trouble to find shoes. She looked through the grating at the prisoners in the patio of the city cárcel.

There were two white women with children. One had a child at the breast. The rest of the youngsters were running about. They looked gaunt but were playing eagerly, although one little girl was painfully lame. The small boys kept shop under one of the arches. Mud pies on pieces of broken crockery were for sale. Some savage-looking men strolled up and bought these childish wares from time to time. They bargained solemnly. The currency was bright pebbles and grains of corn. The purchasers were American frontiersmen clad in greasy deerskin full of rents and falling into naked holes. None of them had had their beards or hair cut for months.

Ten or twelve Indians wrapped in the remains of old blankets sat about like bronze statues in rags, saying nothing. Several squaws were making tortillas at the metates. The two white women were having a gossip. One of them, wearing the remains of a sunbonnet, had a clear, sensitive face. She was nursing the baby.

Faith was surprised to see how happy and contented these unfortunates seemed to be. An air of quiet friendliness pervaded the sunny patio of the bare adobe cárcel. Even between the whites and the Indians there was an obvious comradeship.

For a moment she stood there envying them. The bars which separated her prison from theirs were impassable. She had never really been able to share destiny with anyone. She wondered what it would be like not to be completely lonely—to have friends. Thrusting the bundle of odd items of charity that she had brought with her through the grating, she called out for someone to come and get it. A hush fell on the place and they looked at her suspiciously. She felt it and winced. Finally a man got up from behind one of the pillars and started to cross the courtyard toward her.

He was very tall, with an immense mane of yellow hair and a long golden beard. He was dressed in the scarecrow offerings of cast-off military clothing. A rawhide thong suspended something about his neck. Yet she knew him instantly. It was the way he walked, and his eyes.

"We thank you, ma doña," he started to say in Spanish.

A scream rose in her throat. She choked it and fled.

He came forward and took the bundle she had left sticking between the bars of the gate and looked out. There was no one there. In the archway beyond there was a faint play of shadows and in the distance the rumble of wheels.

"Doubtless," he thought, "it is not permitted to bring things to the prisoners. The lady did not wish to be recognized." In the courtyard his fellow prisoners crowded about him as he opened the bundle and distributed her offerings. Something as he did so made him think of the Casa da Bonnyfeather.

It was Faith's impulse to drive straight back to the hacienda and break the news to Don Luis. But on the way out over the rough road she fell to thinking. Her mind travelled backward and forward into the remote past and into the not so distant future. It was her curiosity to see what would happen that finally tipped the scales for her decision.

"Go back," she said to the young Indian driving her, "I have forgotten something."

They returned to the town and drew up before a house where a bowl hung from a red pole. She sent for the barber and made a bargain with him. The man bowed to her as she sat in her hooded cart with a seat. He was greatly pleased at being given a well-paid commission by the wife of the governor.

"My lady is *most* charitable," he said. "Only a pious mind given to good works could be so originally thoughtful." He would be glad to confer so comfortable a mercy. He would see to it promptly. She could rely upon him.

Faith returned to the hacienda and said nothing about Anthony to Don Luis.

About an hour before sunset the barber appeared at the prison and offered to cut the hair of the men prisoners and to shave them, gratis. It was a work of charity, he explained. He was to say no more about it. Such had been his instructions. Let those who wished to avail themselves of his services step up.

For the first time in years Anthony slept that night with a smooth cheek against his rough pillow and a cool breeze on the back of his neck. His face, left white where the beard had been, looked like a pale mask of himself.

———————

At the Hacienda de León, under a great cotton tree, Don Luis gave judgment on such matters as came before him. The tree was said to have been planted by Coronado. It stood close-by one of the rare springs in that dry country, where the water burst out under a flat rock scrawled over with rude prehistoric carvings. Upon this rock, under the deep shade of the tree, he sat in the seat of justice with a blanket about his knees. At his feet sat a prothonotary's clerk with horn spectacles and a large book in which the decisions of the governor were written down.

The day after Faith's visit the prisoners were marched out of the city under guard and brought before him. They sat huddled together until their names were called. It was thus, with the speckled shade of the leaves of the great tree falling upon him, that Anthony looked up and beheld the old lion sitting upon the rock.

A Zuñi chief from the pueblo of Nutrias, called by the Spaniards "Bigotes" from the long moustache he wore, was the first called. He was accused by one of the padres of making missionary efforts in his region too difficult.

"A subtle heathen, Your Excellency; a sorcerer powerful in the ceremonies of his khiva; an enemy of Christ."

"Does he make trouble for the king?" inquired Don Luis.

None of the soldiers had any complaint against him.

Some of his own people then stepped forward and begged for his release, claiming that his presence would soon be essential in a dance at his village to make rain.

Don Luis smiled. "Do you not think, Fray Marcos," said he, "that in future you might confine your missionary efforts to the tribes in the river villages? I have noticed that in the arid mountains here most of the missions are in ruins. Christianity in order to flourish must be tempered with humidity. You should remember that."

Fray Marcos looked confused. He could not remember anything about "humidity" in the scriptures. Yet it sounded like a virtue. Don Luis turned to the Indian.

"Go," said he, "return to your village and make rain. The priest of the pale face will trouble you no more. But be careful that in drawing the clouds over your pueblo you do not also bring down upon it the lightning and the thunder-birds of your great white father, the King of Spain."

There was a certain majesty in the old man as he uttered this—and the interpreter translated. The Zuñis retired with appreciative grunts, taking Bigotes along with them.

With the rest of the Indians the governor made short work. They were marauders or half-breed malcontents. A brief explanation by Muñoz of the reason for their arrest was followed by the sentence, "To the mines." There was no period to the sentence. No one returned from the mines.

With the Americans Don Luis dealt at some length. He questioned each one keenly, the women as well as the men.

"Jane Chalfont . . ."

"So your husband was killed on the River of Arcansa by Indian arrows, you say?"

"Yes, sir," said the little widow with the ragged sunbonnet, holding her child close to her breast.

"Didn't you wish to return whence you came even then?"

"No, sir."

"What!"

"No, sir, me and Mrs. Johnson and her two boys just stayed on and put in the corn."

Don Luis looked at her in astonishment.

"And we was doin' good enough till your captain that the dog killed come and burned down the cabin and carried us all off into Egypt. I'm glad the dog got him.   Sarved him plum right!"

"Those are 'the boys,' " said Muñoz indicating two very young ones.

"Dios," said Don Luis.   "Why, they're infants!   What are we going to do if these people keep on coming?"

The major shrugged his shoulders.

"Remanded to Mexico," said Don Luis.   "Now then, I'll see this hermit who owned the dog.   Rather unfortunate for him.   A bit cracked, you think, eh?"

Muñoz had purposely reserved Anthony's case to the last.   He had not shot him offhand on the plains for the death of Sancho—which he might have done, and no questions asked—because he had thoroughly despised his little commander as an upstart and owed his promotion to his death.   It was not his quarrel.   In addition, he could make nothing out of Anthony when he questioned him.   With the ingrained propensity of the military man to avoid responsibility whenever possible, he had simply left the decision to the governor.   Bored, he now beckoned to Anthony to come forward.

Don Luis was tired.   For an old man it had been a gruelling morning.   He had already cross-questioned over a dozen prisoners and he felt a little nauseated and trembling.   He sat for a moment with his eyes half closed, watching the play of leaf shadow on the ground. The inside of his head felt like that too.

When he looked up Anthony was standing before him.

He looked at his face.   It was quite calm and serene.   But it produced in Don Luis the effect of a violent electric shock.   For a while he could say nothing.   His own face worked, and he trembled with an access of palsy.   By an effort of will that almost exhausted him he was at length able to control himself.

"Give me your book," he said to the clerk at his feet, "and your pen!"

In a script which appeared to be a nervous caricature of his own precise handwriting, he wrote something in the book and signed it. Then he looked Anthony in the eyes.

"Bastard!" said he, and mumbled something.   No one could understand what.   His speech was broken and thick.   At last he motioned for them to take Anthony away.

Major Muñoz looked in the book. He gave a whistle of cynical surprise and shouted orders to take the prisoners back to the cárcel.

Don Luis got into his litter with great difficulty and was carried home. Faith was much disappointed. He did not say anything at all but went directly to his room. He felt faint and sent the maidservant out for some wine. It was after midday now and very warm. He sat down in a chair before his dresser and took off his wig. Beads of sweat were running off his bald crown. He could see the veins in his temples beating slowly. Suddenly a convulsion shook him. He saw his face writhing, in the mirror. Then, as if cool fingers had stroked him, one side of it became still with the eye closed. He regarded it with the other eye for an instant of eternal horror, while one half of him watched the other half die. Then he slipped to the floor.

A few minutes later Faith was summoned, by the screams of the girl who had returned with the wine, to assume immediately the grief and the duties of a widow. She assumed both equally well. While she arranged with Major Muñoz for a proper military funeral for her husband, she was also able to direct the packing of as much of her own wardrobe and his personal effects as were to accompany her on her return to Spain. The arrangement for her escort and conveyance as far as Mexico was promptly completed. It was remarkable how well, and with what an eye for detail, she seemed to have thought of everything in advance. Both the mirth and the admiration of the major were moved. But he said nothing. For he considered her, despite her age, to be a woman of great determination and the remains of a strange charm.

"Dios!" said he, curling his mustachios, as her wagon and the strong detachment of cavalry that accompanied it disappeared in the dust down the road towards Albuquerque. "What a woman the old girl must have been!" It was only a few days later that he found himself in great trouble merely because of his haste with a lady in trying to reassure himself that he had *not* been born too late.

Even to the end Faith carried with her this power of disturbance. If her intercourse was henceforth purely conversational, it was nevertheless titillating even to the aged gallants who for some years afterward continued to call upon the Marquesa da Vincitata both at Madrid and in Paris—perhaps out of respect for her husband's memory. If so, they had their reward. For her piquant, though veiled reminiscences held fast her many admirers in a mutual regret for the lost pleasures of youth; regrets so skilfully fanned that they almost rekindled to flames. At least she warmed the eternal spark that remains even in ashes.

As for Anthony, time passed monotonously in the cárcel at Santa Fé, and his hair and beard grew long again. The summer waned, and the nights began to become uncomfortably cold.

It was not until late October that Major Muñoz felt it safe to start his now considerable body of prisoners on their long march from Santa Fé to the City of Mexico. His delay was due to the disturbances in the northern provinces caused by the rumours of Don Luis' death, and by the clamorous demands of the intendant at Chihuahua for a full quota of labourers for the government silver mines. So the major had waited well into the autumn, while he "arrested" more Indians and peons, and conducted a brief raid into the Moqui highlands to complete his labour quota to the number desired.

The convoy, when it did start, consisted of about sixty unfortunate mestizos and Indians bound for the mines at Chihuahua as well as the captured Americans, or "Tejaños," whose cases were to be disposed of by the Viceroy Calleja at Mexico. Before the Texan frontiersmen and their families lay a journey over the plateaus and mountains of Anahuac of some sixteen hundred English miles.

There was no logical reason for their being thus dragged into exile. All they had tried to do was to make homes in the wilderness. Unwittingly, they had crossed over certain invisible boundaries into the territory of New Spain. That constituted a political crime, at least in the eyes of their captors, and they were therefore reduced to the status of beings whose existence was an official nuisance. Their only hope lay in what sympathetic help they would be able to extend to each other and in the humanity and mercy they might arouse in the hearts of their fellow men encountered along the route.

Anthony had learned that he was to be sent with the Tejaños to Mexico, but he could learn nothing more. "I am sorry for you, señor," said the major, "Don Luis seemed to understand you well enough! Unfortunately, he has gone where I cannot question him as to his motives, and it is only natural that I should respect the decisions of my illustrious predecessor. I am in command here only temporarily, you know."

"No one commands permanently, señor, one's opportunity for doing good is always brief. But I am not pleading for myself primarily," Anthony replied. "You may think it strange, perhaps, but I find myself just now happy and satisfied"—"God help you," murmured the major thinking of what Don Luis had written in the book—"I thought you might care to share my happiness by providing the prisoners with shoes before we set out. There are old men, women, and children among them. I have done what I could by making moccasins out of the leather fire buckets that hung in the guard-house."

"So that is where they went!" cried Muñoz.

"Yes," laughed Anthony, "but they did not go very far. I could fit the little ones only. Your own heart must be greater than that."

"You are a clever fellow," muttered the soldier, looking at Anthony's bare feet.

"No, no," cried the prisoner, "it is more than that!"

Major Muñoz said nothing. He turned suddenly and walked away. The evening before they left there was a distribution of shoes.

Anthony held up his hand to Muñoz as they passed out of the gate next morning.

"I am glad that I didn't tell him," mused the major as he smiled back at him. "Dios, what a beard he has!"—and he thought of that prisoner no more.

The column of Tejaños and Indians toiled along the rough road to Albuquerque over the cactus-covered hills. They were under the command of a rascal by the name of José Salezar, a half-breed from Tehuacán, who was never at peace with himself or anyone else. In him the Spaniard and the Indian were forever struggling for mastery. His feelings and actions were both cruel and confused. The only abiding satisfaction he found in the world was in the collecting of things. It did not matter what, so long as they were of some value. He was a kind of human magpie. Sympathy was foreign to him, for he could not understand, nor did he care, what the feelings of others might be like.

Hence, the sufferings of the unfortunates in his charge were never mitigated by anything but the fear of future reprisals or the possible indignation of his superiors, which he could not understand. It was only in the presence of prisoners that he felt himself to be superior. He had gladly become a professional route-jailer. He delivered his charges dead or alive, for that was the way his orders read.

With the guards riding up and down the flanks and kicking dust into their faces, the prisoners proceeded in a column of fours to Albuquerque, where they spent a night in an ample jail. Half-a-day's march south of that city they were stripped of their shoes. It was Salezar's intention to sell these at El Paso and he did not want them worn out. From this point on real sufferings began.

There was now no hope of even an Indian's escaping across the waterless desert. At night the prisoners were left for the most part to shift for themselves with only a few mounted pickets thrown out.

On the high plateau northwest of El Paso the autumn cold was extreme. When the sun sank a panic began to develop among both whites and Indians lest they should freeze to death. After the miserable evening meal of half-cooked mush was over, they dissolved into groups which rushed from one dry grass clump to another in order to set them on fire. The grass flared up while they stood about it in circles; wild, ragged figures shivering in the firelight. Then the flames would suddenly die down and they would rush on to the next clump.

They trod in the ashes to keep their feet from freezing. They danced and cried out. For a mile over the flat uplands the weird scene kept repeating itself. Flames leaped into the air and died down again. The circles rushed on. Always herded in the right direction by the mounted guards, by morning they had advanced several miles along the trail and they were then driven in by the mounted pickets.

It was impossible to sleep under such conditions. Those who finally lay down exhausted were afraid they would either freeze or be left behind. The terror of falling by the wayside hung over the column day and night.

On the first of these nights of bonfires and hysteria Anthony had found the Chalfont woman wandering about with her child. She had nothing to wrap about it but the thin remnants of her shawl and wisps of grass.

"My baby is going to die," she said simply. "Feel him. He is turning cold. If I only had something to wrap about him!"

He had already given his coat to one "Grumpa Carlton," an old man who appeared to be dying of a cough, and was then lying under one of the carts. He himself stood with nothing on but a pair of old military trousers and the deerskin bag about his neck.

"And see," said the woman, looking up into his face, as if he could do something. "My son is dying."

They came to him like that now. They seemed to think he must do something about it. At last she realized he was helpless.

"I should think that God would do something," said the little widow. She looked about her in the moonlight as though searching for Him. "But no," she added violently, "no, no! Who cares?"

"Wait here," he said. "It may not be too late yet."

He went to the carts where some of the guards, rolled snugly in their blankets, were sleeping comfortably. There were savage and brutal faces, weak, and surprised and simple faces among them, as they lay unconscious and relaxed before him. But one, that of a full-blooded Indian, bore the stamp of patience and sorrow. He took the image from the bag, and holding it up before him, quietly wakened him. The man's eyes opened. Still in a half-dreaming state, he looked at the figure in the moonlight.

"Madre de Díos," he whispered. Then he saw Anthony, and sat up startled. They looked at each other.

"Well?" grumbled the soldier.

"What is your name, my friend?"

"Pedro."

"Are you a Christian, Pedro?"

"Sí!" The man crossed himself.

"Christ is dying of cold just behind the wagons." Pedro showed no surprise. "Come with me and I'll show you."

The man wrapped his serape about him and stalked after Anthony into the darkness. Presently they came to the woman and child. She was standing, just where he had left her.

"Look," said he. "It might be the Child himself."

The Indian felt the baby's icy feet and grunted. He took off his serape, wrapped the baby in it, and handed the bundle back to Jane Chalfont.

She clutched it to her, warming the child against her breast. Presently the folds of the blanket moved and a faint cry came from it.

"Ugh!" said Pedro, and clutching Anthony by the arm led him back to the carts. He groped in one, and from somewhere produced a couple of sheepskin coats. They put these on and squatted together under a cart. After a while the woman came and joined them. She went to sleep leaning against a wheel with the blanket wrapped about her and the child. Anthony and Pedro passed the Indian's pipe back and forth between them until dawn. They managed to sleep a little.

He spent every night that way for some time. In the daytime he marched bare to the waist. In spite of the coat which he had lent Grumpa Carlton, the old man finally died of pneumonia. As he lay breathing his last in an oxcart, one of the guards came up and poked his rifle in his face. The sick man saw it and cried out. The soldier snapped the lock and laughed. He did this three times. When he strolled on Carlton was dead.

Even the Texans were so exhausted by this time that they merely sat still and watched. A sergeant came and cut off the dead man's ears. They would constitute Salezar's receipt for this prisoner to his superiors, and a proof that he had not escaped. They buried Carlton that night with the ghostly Indians standing around. Some of the squaws started to keen but the guards stopped them. A silent sympathy had developed between the Indian prisoners and the whites.

Finding Salezar happy on mescal one evening, Anthony had approached him and wheedled some tobacco out of him. He distributed the small bundles to both whites and Indians alike. Many brown eyes now followed him gratefully.

Things at last became a little more tolerable. At San Miguel some of the charitable inhabitants supplied them with fresh bread. The panics at evening ceased. They were now in the valley of the Rio

Grande where the chaparral supplied them with firewood. The guards had been prevailed upon to give the women and children a lift in the ration carts now and then. They made so much better time this way that Salezar connived at the breach of his own orders.

Anthony cheered them along with the hope that some help would be forthcoming at El Paso, where he promised, if possible, to appeal to the authorities for relief. He was almost afraid to promise anything, for they were coming to depend upon him utterly. He was the only one who could make himself clearly understood in Spanish, and besides that, he had now gained the trust and fervent affection of every man, woman, and child in the little group of exiles who dragged themselves along toward they knew not what. His great strength, which frequently permitted him to lighten the burdens of the others, his imperturbable serenity, and his tireless efforts to cheer and alleviate their lot had permeated them all with a spirit that buoyed them up even when they were not aware of it.

One of the children was always riding on his shoulders. He became particularly attached to a little girl, Sadie Johnson, who had gone painfully lame. It was the terror of her mother that she might be made to leave her behind. The sight of her sad little face high above the heads of the others, riding on through the dust on the shoulders of the man with the yellow mane gave the woman strength and hope enough to falter after. Her husband, a tall, pale man from the banks of the Ohio, had been hurt when he was captured. He could do no more than march himself. His two young boys took themselves along manfully, but were too small to help.

Day after day on this exhausting march from Santa Fé to El Paso, Anthony heard the half-dreamful, half-benumbed humming of the child Sadie sound in his ears; a formless, endless, half-melodic murmur like the sound of the summer wind in treetops. And to this he would often reply by a little song himself. He did not remember, but it was the song Contessina had once sung to him while he played by the fountain. In the dust and panting heat of the afternoon he sometimes thought he heard the quiet murmur and refreshing whisper of those eternal waters in his ears. The child would sleep and he would plod on mechanically, one foot after the other. On the bottom of his soles was a hard, shiny callous. It was not long, indeed, before those who had been deprived of shoes by Salezar were reshod by nature with horn.

At last they arrived at the Pass of the North and camped. On the morrow they would be in El Paso.

The sunset here was unearthly. In the gorges of the savage mountains to the eastward it lingered in mellow contrast along their black cliffs. Through the dust of the tableland stretching endlessly westward, the enormously enlarged face of the sun sank dark as old blood through what appeared to be a fiery mist. Somewhere a little south of them, he could not see where, the silver vein of the Rio Grande cut through the sombre and ragged mountains.

"El Paso del Norte!" Tomorrow he would pass through its gates.

The premonition of an utterly new and inscrutable experience before him; a flood of memories from the immense and irrevocable past overcame him as the sun sank and cold and darkness rushed upon the desert prairie as though they were one.

For a time that evening, while the mountain peaks still caught the last, high rays of vanishing day, he felt that it was impossible that he should go on. He fell face downward in despair and psychic exhaustion. He must have lain there for some minutes. It was then that a chariot came for him. It picked him up. In some fold of eternity he rode with Florence and little Maria again along that stretch of Tchoupitoulas Street, where it was always spring and the birds sang.

He never saw them again. And this was also the last time in his life that he lay in the dust and wept.

When he rose he was able to stroll back to the wagons where the fires were already leaping as though nothing had happened. And, indeed, nothing in the world had.

There was a new hope, almost a joyful atmosphere about the fires that evening. Finding himself so near the end of this section of the route, Salezar got drunk, distributed extra rations to the prisoners, and gorged his men. For the first time in many days there was plenty to eat. And tomorrow—tomorrow they would be in El Paso!

It is surprising what very small things in adverse circumstances suffice to make people happy—a little food, warmth, and something to look forward to. Already it seemed as though the terrors of the march had never been. Van Ness and Griffith, two of the Texans, actually tried to sing a little. Mrs. Chalfont's baby was hushed. Even the Indians, although they knew they would never come back that way again, passed from mouth to mouth such pipes and weed as they had, together with the magic phrase of change and hoped-for alleviation, "El Paso del Norte."

Early in the morning they struck into the valley and marched through the gorge. The last trial of their strength remained. At a little fall in the Rio Grande some four miles above El Paso they were forced to ford the river.

Several lariats were tied together. One of the guards rode across with the rope, and it was stretched taut. The river was waist-deep in most places, and chin-deep in others for all but the tallest. The Texans took the women and children on their shoulders and crossed over, slipping, floundering, and cutting their feet on sharp stones. In the cold morning air they stood shivering on the far bank, looking back at the Indians who had not crossed yet.

Salezar became impatient at the delay. He gave a shrill whistle, and the guards rode into the Indians, where they huddled on the bank. The sound of hoofs on stones, the sharp crack and dull thud of whips, the terrified cries made a hideous chorus in the quiet valley.

The Indians were driven into the stream en masse. Some of them missed the rope. They struggled with one another desperately. Three of them sank and were drowned. There would not even be any ears to show for them.

Enraged at his own stupidity, Salezar now hurried his prisoners pell-mell down the road toward the town, cursing and swearing. Then he formed them in columns, and placing himself proudly at their head, prepared to lead them into El Paso. Mounted on a baggage mule with silver housings, he curled his mustachios with pride. He was arriving five days ahead of his schedule and counted on selling not only the shoes but the remaining rations. He formed up his guards in as military a manner as possible and sent his buglers forward to announce himself. The population of the town poured forth into the plaza to see the Tejaños.

To find El Paso buried in its vineyards and delicious gardens in the midst of the dusty, cactus desert was to defy all earthly comparisons to do justice to the contrast. For those prisoners who had been born in green countries it was as though they had been dragged for an eternity across the cinder fields of purgatory and had stumbled suddenly upon the first outlying vale of paradise. They crossed the first irrigation ditch, and then, as though their sins had been forgiven them, the lush verdure began.

It was not a city into which they had come. It was far more beautiful than that. It was a succession of luxuriantly cultivated villas that stretched for miles up and down the valley in a wide strip on both sides of the river, sheltered from the withering "northers" by a semicircle of frowning hills. There were broad roads lined on either side by placid little canals overarched by rows of trees and spanned by frame bridges. From the base of the mountains, the place had looked like a green, haphazard chequer-board crossed by white lines on which one might move from a square of vineyard to one of roses, or from a rectangle of orchard to a garden patch. Such, indeed, was the ancient and fruitful game in which the pawns who lived there were absorbingly engaged.

Myriads of birds sang in the thickets, and there was always to be heard, like a constant, whispered assurance of abundance, the sound of flowing water passing over the wooden irrigation gates. Into this bower, which far surpassed all their expectations with its colourful adobe houses gleaming in the midst of groves and gardens, the prisoners were now marched.

The effect upon them was overpowering. The children darted out of ranks to gather flowers and even some of the men wept at the sight and touch of leaves. The day was warm, the sky a faultless blue, and the sunlight sparkled along the hedges. They had been washed in the river and their garments had now dried on them. It was like being reborn. Although some of their wounded feet still left bloody traces in the dust, they marched firmly and with a dignity and joy at still being among the living that only an escape from mortal suffering can confer. They were ridiculous and grotesque in appearance, but they were also sublime.

It was curious how the crowd that had gathered on the plaza was instantly aware of this; how it both laughed at and then pitied them, and called out in encouragement and admiration all at the same time.

The Texans were not shamefaced at their own suffering and appearance. They were beyond that. They could even join in the laughter at their own expense, a little, even when some of their faces were still wet with tears.

By the manifestation of so many complicated and even conflicting emotions at the same time, as when the various degrees of pain and pleasure are simultaneously made visible by a hundred subtle gestures and facial expressions, humanity can best recognize itself as human. For it is in his combined complexity and unity of emotion that man is pre-eminently differentiated from all other living things. Let him once see that this essentially human quality has been outraged in others, and by a touch of self-protective imagination he puts himself in their place. That is where sympathy begins. And that is why it is always most easily awakened by a display of feeling.

Perhaps, then, it was fortunate for the prisoners that they had been so broken down by the rigours of the march from Santa Fé that they could not prevent themselves from openly showing their manifold and conflicting emotions as they were marched through the streets of El Paso. Such displays are infectious.

That is why they were described as "pestilential" in official correspondence—they begot a plague of sympathy—and why the crowd on the plaza went mad over them while it only laughed or hissed Salezar, who was obviously without many human feelings, and therefore a brute. There was no fuss at all over the Indians who were in a much worse way but were quite impassive. Sympathy was concentrated on the Texans. Even the comandante of the district, whom no one had ever thought of describing as sentimental, was touched.

Standing on the steps of his headquarters opposite the cathedral, Colonel Don Elias Gonzales, commanding at El Paso, looked down and saw approaching him above the heads of the crowd a pale, strawhaired little girl with the dark blue marks of suffering under her eyes. The face of that child smote him to the heart. She was holding a small bouquet of flowers in her hand, and her dress, a wisp of faded gingham, scarcely seemed to cover her white form. She was riding on the shoulders of a huge man stripped to the waist whose great yellow beard rippled down over his breast. His ragged trousers with a faded stripe on them flapped in tatters to his knees. As they passed the comandante the child looked up at him, and drawing back her arm in a peculiarly feminine motion of throwing, tossed him her flowers. He caught them and bowed gravely to her. Between the colonel and the man with the beard passed an understanding glance. The man and child were followed by a number of stalwart, weirdly-bewhiskered fellows in all manner of skins and rags, several with bleeding feet. Mrs. Johnson and her two boys, who were waving green branches and had something faun-like about them, came next, with Mrs. Chalfont in her still surviving sunbonnet, carrying the baby in a serape. The two women were dressed in the gowns that Faith had conferred upon them, old court costumes with stomachers, bedraggled and grotesque beyond belief. At the rear limped Mr. Johnson himself, holding his wounded side and looking ghastly with a thin blue beard. Then came the Indians. Their sufferings were indecent and various. A few faithful squaws followed after their captive husbands, hustled now and again by mounted guards.

The colonel-comandante nosed his bouquet thoughtfully and looked across it at Salezar, who sat on his mule with the silver housings, a grin of assured welcome on his face. Over his saddle-bow was a string of eight ears interesting to several flies.

The colonel turned away without noticing Salezar, although he saluted several times. He went in and sat down by a window. Taking a piece of folded paper out of the bouquet, he carefully read some quite minute but very legible writing upon it. It was a diary of the route kept by one of the prisoners. After he finished he sat for a few minutes with his eyelids half-closed. Then he got up and looked out again.

The crowd had disappeared. Across the plaza the prisoners were just entering the gate of the city cárcel . . .

"Sadie, my love," said Anthony, "you threw that bouquet splendidly! How would you like to sleep in a nice soft bed tonight? I believe you will yet."

The child sighed. She no longer believed every cheering thing he told her, although she always responded.

"Anyway, it's a nice jail," she said. "There *might* be some straw."

. . . Salezar batted the flies away from his saddle-bow impatiently. He had been kept waiting for some time. His mule stamped.

"Come up here!" roared Colonel Gonzales out of the window at him. Salezar looked up in stupefaction. "You, *you damned rascal,*" shouted the colonel his face purple with rage, jabbing his thumb at him, "I mean you!"

An hour later the door into the big room of the city prison opened and the colonel, a young priest, and the surgeon of the garrison stepped in. They saw a long white-washed apartment with barred windows near the ceiling, through which the sunlight fell in slanting rays to the bare floor. At one end of it the Indians sat stoically upon the stones. The man with the yellow beard was kneeling down before a squaw seated on a bench. He was washing and binding up her wounded feet. The whites had arranged themselves as best they could in another corner. They had taken most of the benches. The two women sat together. One was nursing her baby and the other holding the little girl with the pale face. The men were already asleep or gathered about a pack of frayed cards.

"Same old three pennies in the poke," said Van Ness. "Well, Falconer, I'll raise yer on this ante. Can't ya hide yer face even with all that chaparral on it?" Suddenly they saw the three strangers at the door and the room grew quiet.

The young priest walked forward and touched Anthony on the shoulder.

"I see we both serve the same master, señor," said he. "Am I right?"

"Yes," said Anthony.

"We have come to help you. Do, leave off for a moment. The colonel wishes to speak to you. Wipe your hands on my gown. You need bandages, don't you?"

"It was you who wrote me the note, señor?" asked the colonel.

"Yes, very hurriedly this morning on a piece of paper I found in the street. It seemed to have been sent . . ."

"It was," said the colonel. "Now where is the little señorita who tossed me the flowers? A most touching thing, señor. I and my wife have been greatly moved. Take me to her. Now what is her name? . . . Sadee? Do I say it right?"

"How do you do, Señorita Sadee. You and your mother are to come home with me. Sí! Explain to them, señor. It is the wish of my wife. What! Two brothers, too! I am afraid—but no, why not? Come, you shall *all* go forth with me. Doctor, you will ask your good wife to look after this other woman and her baby. Look, it is sick. It has puked all over its blanket."

"They usually do," said the doctor looking a little startled.

"Come, come," cried the colonel. "Would you have me send them to the padre's house to make a scandal? Think how the tongue of his washerwoman would clack. Dios de Dios, doctor!"

The surgeon and the priest laughed.

"Now as to these,"—he pointed to the men, "—if they will give me their parole, I am sure we can find comfortable places about town for them. What do you think?"

There was no doubt whatever what they thought. They gave the colonel a cheer.

In ten minutes the place was emptied of the whites and the colonel sat smiling with satisfaction and flushed with the excitement of so much kindness on one of the empty benches.

"I am sorry my house is not large enough to entertain you, too," he said to Anthony. "I am afraid you will have to go home with the padre. I will send you some clothes, and a razor. You will have no objections to that I suppose?"

"None whatever. I wish in some way to thank you!" He hesitated. "What of these Indians?"

The good colonel shrugged his shoulders. "Well, what of them?" he said. "Let the padre look after them. Here, señor, permit me to lend you my cloak. You must go home through the streets. No, no, it is nothing. It is yours." They bowed to each other and he left.

"You see," said the young priest as they walked home to his house a little later, "human kindness is not quite enough."

"That is strange," replied Anthony, "I was just thinking the same thing."

They smiled at each other.

"My name is Ramón Ortiz. As you may have guessed I am the cura of El Paso—and yours . . ."

"Here we are," he cried at last, "sometimes I think it is almost too comfortable for a follower of the blessed St. Francis. But it is just as I found it when I came here two years ago."

They passed through a vineyard and the priest swung open the unlatched door of his adobe dwelling. He drove a hen and her family out of the room. "Shoo," he cried. "Shoo!

"Enter, brother, in His name."

From El Paso to Chihuahua wild mountain ranges march southward with the tablelands—and men march perforce along the tablelands, watching the mountains that now reach into the distance and now close in again.

It was a radically altered band of prisoners that set out upon this mighty road to Anahuac after six weeks of rest and mercy at El Paso. The Indians had long preceded them. Somewhere in the mountains southward they were already labouring in the mines. But they could do nothing about that. They thought of them no more, for the road that lay before them was pregnant with the mystery of their own fate. What it might finally be they considered or sometimes whispered about around the fires, but for the most part they were now content to let this fate unroll before them from day to day.

The panorama of it was magnificent.

In that hour of agony before they had come through the Pass of the North, Anthony had thought he could never find joy or feel the glory in the mystical and unpronounceable Word hidden behind the veils of the outward semblances of things. But he had been wrong about that. It was renewed for him as a gift accompanying the rejuvenation and renovation of his inward being that he had also received. Never before had the Vision of Light been so radiant and yet so revealing. Never had the landscapes of the earth meant more. Now that he had forever given up questing for *what* they meant, now, since he was content to feel them only as vivid words composed at once of thought and feeling in the almighty poem of the universe, his soul leapt up each morning with his body to meet the dawn.

Who has looked upon the world with the focused prisms of a clear outer and inner manhood, washed clear by sorrow and polished, not scratched and falsely angled by the grinding of suffering, might see with him. False rainbows about the edges of things were no more. The perspective was perfected, the light stronger, and the objects bathed in it were clear. He saw them whole, and therefore with a new glory upon them.

There was, it is true, a hint of something overpowering about this, an overtone of an element that was more than light. It was a mental brightness so intolerable that it might turn sunlight into a shadow—as though the light itself were the shade of the thing that cast it, he sometimes thought. So far the exaltation of the spirit might attain—and no more. But he did not recoil from these experiences exhausted. He was not overpowered. He returned with the freshness and strength of them and walked the trail in peace.

That peace was all the greater—perhaps, he only possessed it to the fullness that he did—because it was shared with him by the others who were travelling the same road.

They could scarcely be called prisoners any longer, unless from a purely political standpoint, and none of them took that. They had become, rather, a band of pilgrims travelling in friendship together toward the same mysterious fate.

They travelled in solid-wheeled oxcarts, at least Mrs. Johnson and Mrs. Chalfont and the children did, while the men rode upon mules. But that made no difference. Nor did the hardships and rigours of the route disconcert them. Hardships are, within certain degrees, merely a matter of contrast. What they were experiencing now was like a journey through the promised land compared with the intolerable inflictions between Santa Fé and El Paso.

Salezar and his crew of ladrones and picaros, who so patterned themselves after him, had disappeared. They had been returned by Colonel Gonzales to Major Muñoz at Santa Fé with the suggestion that since Don Luis was no more, it might no longer be necessary to employ wild beasts to convoy men.

The prisoners were still under guard, for the good colonel had in the end been forced to take the political view of things. He could not release them, as he would have liked to do. He was merely an authority. But he had fed them fat and rested them well. Their guards now consisted of the good-natured militia of El Paso, who were also conducting the annual caravan of travellers from that vicinity bound for the New Year's fair at Chihuahua, with apples, raisins, pears, onions, wine, and Paso brandy. The string of carts and pack animals, muleteers, servants, and motley camp-followers—women and children—were now a thousand in number and in marching stretched out for over a mile. At night they camped in a great ring, a circle of twinkling fires.

Indeed, the checks now put upon the Texans were few. At night they were at liberty to wander among the traders as they pleased, going from fire to fire, where there was much amusement to be had. The trip was a sort of travelling carnival for the traders and their families. The excellent, fiery vino del país was broached, and much Paso passed from bottle to lip. There was music, singing, and the clapping of hands and castanets in the dance. There were dice and cards under the carts by the light of horn lanterns, from which Van Ness and Buckthorn generally returned with pockets jingling. And there was also the characteristic sound of lamentation by those whose cart had broken an axle. Half the load of each cart consisted of axles. Lamentation was chronic. These giant wains by daylight staggered, wobbled, and groaned forward upon eccentric courses in a state of epidemic collapse. Yet what could be more comfortable at night to sleep in than one of these great wagons filled with straw, while the meteors streaked down the twinkling bowl of heaven, coyotes clamoured in the distant desert, and the fires died low?

"Listen, big man," said little Sadie one evening, when he came to say good night to her, "do you know what them coyotes sounds like? Like the schoolyard back in Ohio away-way off across the river. I'd like to go back there and play." He sat silent a moment listening. She pulled him down to her. "Don't ye tell ma, will ye?"—He promised—"but I'm going home soon. I know it. Hearin' them wild voices and watchin' stars fall, told me. And I want ye to promise me suthin'. I want ye . . . "—"Yes," he whispered. . . . "I want ye to make ma leave my dolly with me. She might keep it to remember me by, and I don't want to be left all alone. I thought you'd know. It's too bad after you done toted me so far."

He walked out on the prairie a little and came back again.

It would not do to go too far. The Apaches might be about. For that reason the guards had no need to worry that their prisoners would try to escape. By day they even let the Texans range well ahead of the column, for no one had sharper eyes for hostile Injuns than they, but after darkness fell the "centinela alerta" sounded about the camp all night.

It was the night after they had camped at the Diamond Spring that Sadie had spoken to Anthony. The next two days they doubleteamed it through shifting sand hills without water until they came to a spring near the trail-side called the "Fountain of the Star." It was sandy all about. There was only one stone in the neighbourhood. It was called "la puertad de piedra" and weighed at least two hundred pounds. Everyone, who could, lifted it once and threw it over his head along the road to Mexico. One Oacha, a muleteer, explained the reason to Anthony.

"It is for the glory of God, señor. There are many travellers on this road. It is their faith that sometime this stone will reach Méjico and be put in the high altar there. In my time it has moved from the Diamond Spring to the Fountain of the Star. My father told me that in heathen times it came slowly down out of the north. Perhaps, quién sabe?"

So Anthony moved it a few feet nearer to Mexico.

"A fine throw," said Oacha, "that is all that anyone can do."

A few days later they camped at a hot spring that bubbled up out of a mound in a desert of thorn bushes. Here was a great washing of clothes and of naked bodies.

He took the sick child Sadie and laid her in a warm pool. There was something the matter with her hip. The surgeon at El Paso could do nothing about it but shake his head. In the warm water she seemed to revive. He thought from then on she looked better.

"The pain *is* gone," she said.

A few days later they left the desert behind them and entered upon those grassy tablelands with streams lined by trees, and far-stretching haciendas generous as the careless sovereigns who granted them, where the longhorn cattle and the half-wild horses wander in legions over the teeming tierras templadas. Here the mountains receded dimly into the perspective, opening out like the ribs of a great fan. The distances became vaster. They were emerging upon the fertile plateaus of Anahuac.

Not far from Chihuahua, in a grassy valley which is nothing more than a depression in the plain, lies the Laguna Encillanos. Its waters are clear blue, and the prairie sweeps down to it in smooth, curving lawns that about the end of December break forth into untold myriads of nodding, purple flowers. For some reason there are no trees here. The lake lies in the prairie and looks up at heaven like an eye wide-open and fringed with blossoms. It was here that Sadie Johnson died.

They called him to her hastily. She was asking for him, they said. Death had suddenly looked out of the child's face. Her mother and the two small boys, Alec and Tom, stood by the cart frightened and weeping incontinently. Her father, too tired just then to feel anything keenly, sat near by in a kind of dreamful despair.

"Do something, for God's sake *do* something," cried the woman, seizing Anthony by the arm as he came up.

He smiled at her, and putting her hands together, went to the cart and bent over the child.

"Sadie," he whispered. She opened her eyes. They reminded him of the lake. She searched for him with her hands blindly and found his hair.

"'Pears like night's coming soon today," she said.

"In the morning light He will come and carry you," he said.

"Sure?"

"Certain I am."

"Now I lay me . . . " she began—and then pulled him down closer to her. "I want to say it to ma."

He beckoned to her mother, who gathered her child to her.

They were all silent now, even the boys. Most of the men, having heard the news, came up quietly and stood about.

Suddenly the woman gave a scream. She dropped the little body into the straw of the cart, and running out onto the open prairie, frantically began to gather armfuls of the purple flowers.

They all began to do that. That was all they could do. They

heaped the cart. The Mexicans came around chattering and big-eyed.

The father did not move but sat shaking his head slowly in a kind of numb negative.

"Yer no good, Johnson," cried the woman, "yer no good at all!"

"I know it," he said, and went off to borrow a spade.

So they left Sadie with her doll sleeping together by the Laguna Encillanos.

In an inexplicable way this event drew them all closer together. From now on the men went less about the fires of the traders and stayed more about their own. The pilgrims marched southward over the plateaus more and more like one family.

It was not that they had been made melancholy or felt it essential to show their grief in an explicit way. But everybody missed the child. Anthony's shoulders ached for her. Mrs. Johnson trudged on bravely with Mrs. Chalfont beside her. The principal comfort of the older woman now was in carrying the baby. From now on it had two mothers. In a curious way the two boys had been driven closer to their father. Mrs. Johnson had for so long blamed her husband for marrying her that she had come to blame him for everything else. She looked grim when he tentatively approached the fire at supper now.

" 'Tain't pa took Sadie, ma," piped her son Tom one evening.

"Here's your mush!" snapped Mrs. Johnson. "Hush your mouth!"

That evening the boy crept under the blanket with his father and took to tagging by his side during the march. Some of the men winked at one another. They also for the first time took the shy, sensitive Johnson into their midst. His wound began to get better. To their amazed surprise he disclosed a sly, sweet sense of humour that cheered them along the way. Finding herself about to be isolated, Mrs. Johnson relented—and suddenly found her family reunited about her. She remembered how every one of the company, even the terrible Falconer, who was now sweet on Mrs. Chalfont and insisted on helping to carry the baby, had stopped to look back as they left the lake.

" 'Pears like death jes' driv us all together like a pack o' sheep huddles up when they see a wolf," she thought.

And it was true that they were all more gentle to one another because of what had happened. Falconer, Van Ness, McBride, and Johnson took to singing at night. They had suddenly discovered, after some tentative trials while marching, that they were a quartette. At Anthony's suggestion they left off the doleful ballads which at first engrossed them and took to trolling more cheerful lays. One of Burns' songs, then a world-wide favourite, they repeated again and again every night. Apparently nobody ever grew tired of it. The Mexicans themselves took to standing about the Texans' fire at night. The four voices were good ones:

"Green grow the rashes, O;
Green grow the rashes, O;
The sweetest hours that e'er I spend,
Are spent among the lasses, O."

Everyone in the cavalcade was soon singing it—*"Grin-gro, Grin-go,"* hummed the Mexicans as the oxcarts plodded forward. And so it was that the Texans became known as "Gringos."

At Chihuahua, where they stayed in the prison-like Hospital of the Jesuits, they gathered one evening about the stump of one candle that flickered fitfully in the mouth of a bottle, to discuss their situation.

A journey of over a thousand miles still lay before them. To-morrow they would go forward under a new guard, for their good-natured friends from El Paso went no farther. They would be alone. And they had learned that they would have to walk. They tried to organize themselves for the long trail before them. Van Ness suggested a daily leader, "Jes to keep things straight among ourselves."

"'Taint no use doin' that," said Falconer. "That 'ull be like the militia back home. Everybody 'ull jes take his tarn bein' sassed."

"Move we 'lect one cap'n from hya to Mexico," said McBride, a quiet Virginian.

"Adverse," sung out Buckthorn, an inveterate gambler. "He's our most hopeful odd number." There was a laugh.

"Well, what d'ya say, cap?" cried the impulsive Van Ness, springing up and prematurely pumping Anthony by the hand.

The candle suddenly burned out. There was a heavy silence. Out of it after an interval came the colourless voice of the inconsequential Johnson, "I ain't no good, I know. Even my old woman says it. But I'm willin' ter follow the only light I ever heerd tell on that cain't be blowed out. An' I tell you-all it's burnin' right here in the darkness now. Cain't you'ns see it?"

A sound of shuffling and rising bodies greeted this statement. Anthony thought they were going away. But they thronged about him in the darkness, whispering huskily and shaking his hand.

And once more he wept. But this time not alone, and not lying in the dust.

Months later, they marched incredibly ragged and footsore, but still hopeful, into the City of Mexico. It was deep twilight and the summits of the two giant volcanoes hung above the evening already settled in the valley below like islands of mystery floating on seas of sunset. They were all together yet. Even Jane Chalfont's baby, which had begun to walk, was there. It was the sunbonnet that had finally succumbed.

"Ye never can tell," sniffed Mrs. Johnson. "Some goes on through, and some don't."

"I wisht I know'd whar my young 'un was agoin' to end up at," said Jane looking up at the mysterious islands in the sky.

"Maybe hit's lucky you don't," replied the older woman. "But whar we got to now?" she added.

The column of new garrison troops to whose care they had been confided only that morning, had suddenly halted.

"What's the matter?" inquired a mounted officer riding back.

"One of the prisoners is to be left here, señor capitán," replied a sergeant. "The lieutenant says there's a special order about him."

"Which one?"

"Adverse," said the young officer, hurrying up. "It's a special rescript from the old governor at Santa Fé."

The captain looked at it indifferently.

> *"Deposit the body of this individual at the Prison of St. Lazarus, until further orders."*

He heard them calling his name. And it was then, as he looked up at the gloomy building before him and saw the dim faces within peering at him from a barred window, that for the first time Anthony understood the full measure of Don Luis' hate.

CHAPTER SIXTY-SEVEN

THE PRISON OF ST. LAZARUS

THERE is a kind of writing in the forms and lines of things by which he who reads may prophesy. It may well have been the source of the forebodings of Cassandra, for it is a sort of "palmistry" *in toto* of the implications of the future inherent in a building or a neighbourhood. Mrs. Johnson had the gift. One look at the outlines of the grim building confronting her in the now melancholy twilight, coupled with the loud calling of Anthony's name, was sufficient to cause her to scream, "They're takin' the cap'n from us, and we'll never see him no more."

The sergeant was already hammering vigorously with the butt of his rifle at a gigantic, iron-studded door. In the street the prisoners suddenly broke ranks and crowded about Anthony.

He had never realized that he had come to love them as though they were his own flesh and blood. But he knew it now. The two boys clung to him like sons. The baby was for a moment thrust into his arms, as though it also were his, and he must bless it. The two women began that sort of talk accompanied by the kind of noise that greets the appearance of a snake in a parrot's nest. Even the conscripts knew that something terrible was happening. The men came up and wrung his hands in eloquent silence. He found it impossible to say good-bye to them. At the very last he and Van Ness were left face to face, their hands locked on each other's arms.

"Get word to the British consul somehow, Van. It's your best chance. Don't forget the plan I talked over with you. They'll all depend on you now. You're the only one that can write. Never mind about me. I'm done. But I'll see it through, with the . . ."

"Never say die, cap'n. It's not like you. You'll soon be hearin' from us."

"Here, you," shouted the young lieutenant, who had his reputation for indifference to suffering yet to establish, "leave off that English talk."

The sergeant came for him.

He snatched young Tom up and kissed him. He found himself walking numbly between two soldiers toward a small door cut in the large one, through which came a glimmer of lantern light. Behind him he heard the column getting under way. Some of them called out to him—something. They passed. . . .

Overhead the giant iron bell of the Hospital of St. Lazarus began to proclaim the abstract information that it was *one—two—three—four . . . seven*—eight o'clock, in the valley of Mexico. The locks in the door behind him shot home, and he was left alone standing in darkness. The invisible hall that lay before him was so large that gusts of air, wandering as freely as though they were not in prison, fanned his face.

"Well," said the turnkey, coming up and flashing his lantern over him critically, "what the hell's the matter with you?"

"Nothing. What makes you think there might be?"

The man gave a laugh like the grating of a rusty hinge. "We'll see about that tomorrow," said he, and gave a peculiar whistle.

A door opened behind him, allowing a bright light to stream out over the stone floor. Before him was a heavy iron grille. He could see no farther on the other side of it than its own shadows. Two more powerful and morose-looking wardens appeared at the door.

"He's a big one," said the man who had admitted him. "I thought you'd better be near while I chained him up, just in case . . ."

The others grinned.

"Ever since that quite-lookin' little woman pulled his ear off, Pedro ain't taking *no* chances. By God, I don't blame him this time," said one of them, taking a look at the new prisoner and shrinking back a little. "Get that heavy wall chain, Roblado! It's in the old chest." The man disappeared and the clanking of irons was soon heard. On a table in the little guard-room beyond the door Anthony saw several hands of cards face downward amid the remains of a scanty meal. The sour-looking Roblado emerged with a chain attached to a steel belt. The latter they fastened around his waist and the former to the iron grille.

"If you'll not give us no trouble," said the first turnkey, "I'll give you the whole length of the chain." He grinned a little, and then looked ashamed. "Hard luck," he muttered into his beard. "It's orders, you know."

"They don't feed you gentlemen any too well here, do they?" remarked Anthony.

"That they don't, my friend. It's dogs' leavings we get—but you're the first caged bird I ever heard worryin' about what the jailers get!"

"Here's a dollar for you," said Anthony. "A priest at El Paso gave it to me for the love of Christ, and it's all I have. Now go and get yourselves a polio and some mescal or a little wine. All that I ask is that you drink the health of the good cura of El Paso."

They stood looking at him dumbly for a minute. The man Roblado at last bit the dollar. "It's all right," he muttered. "I'll go!"

"And be damned sure you come back," roared Pedro after him.

"Señor," said one of the two ruffians who remained, "in the name
of God, we thank you."

One of them brought him a stool and a pot of water.

He sat down and arranged the chain behind him. The door closed
and he was left in the darkness again. He got nothing to eat that
evening.

Long after midnight the door opened again. The three turnkeys
were all drunk. With great solemnity they approached him one
after the other and left three mattresses at his feet.

Dawn in the prison of St. Lazarus was not like dawn anywhere
else. When he opened his eyes early next morning the white light
was stealing through a succession of high, grated windows along the
entire length of the vast, arched nave of a church. At one end of
it was an altar that still looked as though it were occasionally used
for the purpose for which it had been built. The great dome of the
unfinished church, for such it was, had never been completed, and an
intensely bright cylinder of light poured from the open ring in the
ceiling onto the floor. Through this also poured, as though the
place were sucking in faint wisps of black smoke, an army of bats.
But that was not all that he saw through the empty circle.

Mirrored in the morning sky, its snow fields slowly flushing an
incredible rose colour, was the volcano of the "Sleeping Woman,"
her mighty form recumbent upon a bed of clouds. So beautiful
was this vision floating in heaven that his heart was lifted up in
him out of prison, and he said:

> "The day belongs to thee, O God,
> And the night also,
> For thou hast made the morning
> With the rising sun.
> The sun setteth, and the moon walketh upon the waters
> Because of thee.
> The stars signal upon thy watchtowers by night.
> From everlasting unto everlasting is thy name
> Made glorious forever.
> The measure of the firmament is the depth of thy thought;
> The vision of thy glory reneweth my soul.
> Lo, in thy hand will I lie through the nighttime

Like a lake held by pleasant hills.
The day shall find me there,
And my voice shall be heard among the mountains.
Because of thee I will leap up and rejoice . . ."

After a while the vision of the mountain faded. It veiled itself
in mists, and there was nothing to be seen through the circle which
had framed it but the sky. In the prison of St. Lazarus the daily
round began.

He could see where he was now. The grille was a great cage built
about the region of the door. Before him stretched the long nave of
the unfinished church. Along the sides of it, set in the entrances of
what, if the church had been finished, would have been its side chapels,
were barred gates.

Through these began to come the murmur of voices and from the
one nearest squeakings and husky tones. There were evidently a great
many people in the rooms and wards behind the gates. Once he heard
wild laughter and chains. Some pigeons came through the circle in
the ceiling, flew about inside the nave, and left again with a throbbing whir of wings. The door behind him opened and one of the
turnkeys came out. He gave a grin of remembrance when he saw
the new prisoner, returned, and emerged once again with the remains
of the feast.

"You might as well have it," he said. "Roblado and Pedro are still
asleep. They'll think I ate it. Where did you come from?"

"Sante Fé."

The man whistled and looked at his prisoner thoughtfully. "Got
any more dollars in that bag?"

Anthony took the little figure out of it and turned the bag inside
out. The jailer laughed.

"Well, I guess you can keep *that*," he said. "Looks as if it's been
through the fire."

"It has."

He stood pondering the figure for some time and grunted before he
handed it back. "Feet sore?"

Anthony nodded.

The man began to unlock the chain. "There's a flowing water
channel in the big yard," he said. "Better come along and bathe,
there. Wrap your chain about you or you'll sound like the damned
dead walking. You'll soon get used to it. 'Tain't as bad as if you'd
a ball and shackles. That there steel belt is just one we use on maniacs. I thought you was crazy last night when I first seen you. You
looked so bloody calm and happy. There's a woman here thinks she's
St. Theresa. She's made up a song about a burning rose and the five

Holy wounds. It fair cuts the heart out of you, for she has the face of an angel. But you can't trust her." He rubbed the side of his head. "She damn near chewed my ear off one morning. I was just leanin' up against the bars amusin' her a little. *Ho, ho, ho.*" The ceiling laughed back at him dismally. "Now *you* don't have any cunning tricks, do you?" He hesitated a minute over the lock. "What do you want me to do—bark like a dog?"

"No, no, for God's sake *don't*," laughed the man. "We've got one like that already. Come on, you'll do, I guess." They both laughed. "The doctor will be here in an hour on his morning rounds."

He unlatched the grille, and they walked down the long nave together while the turnkey also unlocked several gates and drew his key jangling across the bars.

"Lepers in there. They're always so cheerful. Make the most of their time.

"That's the plague ward. Nobody there now. Last year they overflowed and half filled the church. We couldn't get them in and out fast enough."

Some nuns entered from a side door and waited until he let them in. Three pale looking sisters came out. One of them held up two fingers. The turnkey nodded. "I'll see to the stretchers," he said to her. "Smallpox. We lock 'em up at night. That's the general ward there without a gate. It's May now and pretty empty. But wait till August when the fever begins! Sometimes we get good clothes off them then. In the spring you can't count on that though. Maybe a hat or a pair of shoes now and then between us. Here's your door." He flung open a door that was not locked. "Come back when you're done. The surgeon will want to see you. I've got St. Theresa and the dog to water and feed and there's a lot of others. Want to see 'em?"

Anthony declined the pleasure and all but fled through the door. He stepped through it into the open air and sunlight, and for a moment felt free again. But only for a moment. As he looked about him he began to understand the plan of the place into which he had come.

He was standing before the unfinished front of a great formless church, one of many left unfinished by the Jesuits when they had been driven out. From its sides protruded the various wards of the hospital which had been built onto it; long, low buildings, whitewashed, and with round barred windows. There were six wards on one side and none on the other. The huge, grey building with its numerous "offspring" reminded him for all the world of a sow suckling its farrow. In the architecture there was something that seemed to decree that the six "youngsters" be given curly tails.

But the front of the church was overpowering and sinister. There were deep, shadowed niches with half-executed carvings; giant saints with square, block faces, featureless, or with the rudiments of mouths and noses; their hands nothing but grey stone knobs, stub-fingered or crossed over their rough breasts, still encased in gloves of stone. Their eyes glared out of rocky sockets left rough as when the chisels had ceased. They were a grisly and depressing company covered with scales of bird lime. He turned from them in horror.

A wall forty feet high surrounded him on all sides. It formed an ample square about the Hospital of St. Lazarus, several acres in area. It joined onto the walls of the church in the rear. There were some spare, neglected shrubs planted in this waste plot that was still covered with the rough blocks and débris of the builders. Through it flowed a water course in a channel of stone. In this he bathed, stripping himself of all except the steel belt and chain. He sat on a great block to dry in the sun. It was thus that Dr. Lopez, the head physician, found him.

"What's the matter?" said he. "You look like a gladiator."

"Nothing," repeated Anthony.

A thorough examination standing on the block—"Now I know how the slaves felt at Gallegos," he thought—confirmed the prisoner. The doctor sat on another block and talked with him for half an hour.

"So the enmity of the old governor at Santa Fé is the only reason you can think of, eh?"

"My dog killed his man, as I said. And Don Luis was a Spaniard of the old school, you know."

"In the time of the old viceroy, Iturrigaray, we had some 'cases' like yours sent to us," said the doctor. "They were sent here to rot. But they didn't. They . . . not that I would encourage you too much," he hastened to add. "Understand me. I do *not* intend to interest myself in your case *outside* of this hospital. I have my small salary here, four children, and a wife with a temper. I do not intend to mix myself up in any political quarrels. I might find myself released. Do I convey my meaning, señor? I am adamant."

"I respect your reasons," Anthony replied.

"Good!" said the little physician. "Inside, I will see what I can do. Let us return. I can see no reason just yet for the maniac's belt. We shall begin by dispensing with that." They entered the church together.

A number of figures walking and limping were busy about the place with mops and brooms. They reminded him forcibly of the statues on the front of the building. He looked at them and quailed.

"You must get over that," said the doctor. "No one knows how you get leprosy. I try to give these poor people something to do.

Now try to bear up, my friend. Let me urge you to do so. In that event—" He waved his hands vaguely, and laughed. "But," he insisted, "consider— Your case is really no different here than any other place. Death dogs everybody—and eventually, you know. Here the process is visible. That is all."

He called to the turnkey and gave orders. "Let him sleep in the vestibule. Give him a new pallet and he can lay it on the stone bench there. That will at least be outside," he mused. "Take off the chain and don't use it unless"—he looked at Anthony significantly—"he offers to make trouble for you. In that case chain him to the wall.

"Do you hear, señor? I trust we understand each other. I am adamant. Perhaps you can occupy yourself by helping a little here and there. You will run no more danger than I do."

The little doctor laughed, gave him a cigar, and strolled off on his rounds.

"Come on," said Roblado. "Give me a lift on these stretchers. You're strong, are you! All right, let's see if you are."

To the prisoners of the hospital time glided almost imperceptibly. It was marked for them in nature only by the slow erosion of certain of the bodies of the inmates and by the sterile blooming and withering of some of the sickly shrubs in the surrounding close. In the open vestibule, where he slept, Anthony saw the shadow of the extended hand of the stone St. Lazarus swing from one joint in the masonry to another, and then creep back again. Into that stone hand the days of his life were slowly being dropped, one golden coin after another, like a trickle of precious alms. Altogether some four hundred of them had now been given away, gratis.

According to all respectable romances, he told himself, he should by this time have filed his way through the bars, overpowered the turnkeys in their drunken stupor, or have managed to scale the wall. At the very least he should have communicated with powerful friends on the outside and arranged to bribe the authorities. There were also several less orthodox methods of jail delivery which he contemplated that at first did seem feasible, but in the end came to nothing. If he had simply been incarcerated as a political offender in an ordinary prison he might possibly have managed to emerge—but the Hospital of St. Lazarus!—that was a different affair altogether.

He did manage through the good offices of one of the priests, who came to bring the host to the dying, to get a letter to the English consul. The gentleman came to see him and talked to him through the grille. He sent him some wine, books, and cigars. He also turned his case over to the American consul, which was exactly what Anthony feared he would do. The efforts of the representative of the United States on his behalf were strenuous enough to call the attention of the new viceroy to his existence. General Calleja then departed to fight the rising tide of revolution which was eventually to sweep Spain clear of Mexico. That, however, did not keep the municipal authorities from preventing the inmates of the plague hospital, and the maniacs who were also sent there, from getting out again. On two occasions he smuggled out letters addressed to friends in New Orleans, but nothing came of them. It looked as though the slow swinging back and forth of the shadowy hand of St. Lazarus was the only thing that would finally bring him release.

Yet despite this, Don Luis had not triumphed. He had meant to leave the son of Maria a legacy of immortal hatred and despair, but once again he had failed. He had merely provided an opportunity for Anthony to understand and to participate in hate's eternal opposite. For it was in the prison of St. Lazarus that he was finally born again into freedom and new hope. He lost the fear of death. Here, where the bodies of men perished and withered horribly, he saw the spirit of love in them working. And he participated in that work. He became a part of it.

When the plague fell upon the city, the second summer after his arrival, he at last gave up trying to penetrate the walls that surrounded him, and looking for hope and freedom to come from the outside. That way lay nothing but hope deferred and prolonged despair. Apparently, no earthly postman could reach his friends with messages. And then suddenly he found that all he had been looking for lay within.

Towards the end of the dog days they began to bring the first fever sufferers to St. Lazarus—and to take them away. The tide grew. It threatened to inundate the establishment. The great nave of the church filled up. There were no more beds. They laid them in rows in cotton blankets on the floor. There were no more blankets. They laid them in rows. A thousand times, in every direction that he looked, the scene in the cabin of the *Ariostatica* was being repeated. There was no scale against which the sights he now saw were describable. None except that of the nature and destiny of man.

A band of devoted nuns and priests, a brotherhood and sisterhood of lay nurses in hoods so that their merit might not be known, appeared, and attempted to administer what bodily and spiritual comfort they could. He saw them sicken, too, lie down, and be carried out. Others took their places. He laboured with them night and day as did the very turnkeys themselves. He lay down and slept, felled by exhaustion. He got up again and went on, his services accepted without question. He understood now that Dr. Lopez, although his science prevented no one from dying, was a sublime little man.

"Well," said that little physician one night toward the end of the hopeless struggle when the nave lay comparatively deserted again, "I see you aren't afraid of a mere leper any more!"

"No," he answered, "I find them marvellously cheerful. I often go into their room now to share that with them. I have friends there."

"So have I," said the doctor. "And I know what you're thinking. No, I wouldn't say that you'll get it. I haven't. Quién sabe? Come out and take a swim with me. That water course through the old priests' garden here is a godsend these sultry nights. It runs into the big canal on the other side of the wall."

"Yes, through a heavy stone grating so narrow a duck couldn't get through after her little ones the other day."

"I dare say you have investigated," smiled the doctor. "Have you heard anything from your friends?"

"Nothing. But somehow I don't seem to care now. After the last few weeks I think, 'What is the difference?'"

"There is a certain perversity about fate," cried the little man, preparing to plunge into the water. His head reappeared above the surface to continue his remarks—"It is just when you are feeling like that, that somebody is likely to appear and insist upon your resuming life again. You see, I, at the present time, for various domestic reasons, I am somewhat inclined to envy you. Believe me, señor, when I return home from this hospital it is from the sublime to the ridiculous. My mother is piously sentimental and wishes me to contribute to her sodality devoted to paying for masses for souls. Can you imagine it? 'Everyone should practice some charity,' she says, and rattles the box with money in it in my face. Two of my children died of the plague. I couldn't keep them in their bodies. And now—their grandmother rattles that box with pesos in it in my face."

"Where are all these people that we have just buried?" cried Anthony. "They are still, and we are alive swimming in the water here. Look, I can move. What does it mean? Without my hands I could not make even a ripple. What do you think? Tell me!"

"Life is like this," said the doctor. He cupped his hands and plunged them in the channel, bringing them up again like a brimming cup. "I now remove the hands. Look into the stream and tell me where the water has gone.

"Do not try to think about the soul after death, señor. It is like talking about a lake without any surrounding land. Now I, as a man of science, have certain theories about the body. It is possible that some day we shall prevent this fever, which you and I have so far escaped. But," he cried, throwing a stone in the water vehemently, "there is only one thing certain about man; that animal has an incorrigible habit of dying, no matter what you do for him. I have just been trying to do the best I can!"

They began to swim about once more and to splash each other like a couple of boys. It was an expression of their triumph at still being alive and also served to cover their embarrassment at admitting an interest in mysteries. They splashed a good deal. They had a good time.

"By the way," said Lopez at the door of the church. "I signed the Yankee consul's request for your release. It didn't do any good. It was like medicine. You're still here in spite of it. But I did say what kind of a life I saw you living here. I . . . I . . ." He stopped overcome by embarrassment. He had never intended to admit it. It was his favourite expression that he was adamant.

"Nonsense," cried Anthony. "Why, I'm only doing the best I can!"

———————

In a place like San Lazaro, where so many came to stay, and were carried away hastily, those who were able to remain for any considerable period inevitably developed not only a proprietary air about the establishment but an intense neighbourliness and freemasonry among themselves. Death was the only stranger, although he visited them often. Yet to the casual observer the cheerfulness and the gayety, a certain intensified nonchalance and *carpe diem* among the incurables seemed incredible and grotesque if not cruelly indifferent. Grotesque, perhaps—in reality it was not hard-hearted. It was merely a manifestation of a kind of wisdom practised only by those who feel strongly that their days are certainly numbered, and who understand that it is a waste of precious time to try to assume for others the burdens which are individual by nature. Thus, when a person finally came to die, he was left severely alone except in so far as he needed or demanded necessary attentions. And it was the same with those in pain, they were not harassed by the constant reiterations of communal sympathy. They received only what could actually be given them.

Casual visitors, of whom there were a few, were shocked and pained by this surface of indifference at San Lazaro. They expected at least to find an atmosphere of dolour, and were bravely prepared to encounter a universal whine. A considerable number of professional cheer and charity mongers departed, therefore, without that which they had come to obtain from the lepers, their own edification. And then there were others driven by a certain morbid curiosity to enter the place in the name of charity, but who could not conceal that what they did was a kind of imaginative alleviation of themselves. "Suppose I were a leper, how brave, how noble I should think those were who came to be kind to me. How horrible they are. How sorry I would-be-am." And they would leave with a certain hastiness, a few running steps and a skip through the door, which they could not conceal. They also went away disappointed; without the admiration they had hoped to get.

Dr. Lopez, indeed, had little use for such sympathy, and these casual visitors were always accompanied by an attendant as they made their rounds. The place took little notice of them beyond snatching their tangible gifts and quarrelling over them. In the presence of strangers the inmates felt they were in a zoo, and they acted like it. "Naturally!" said the doctor in disgust, "but Doña Anna Salledro, and her like, are influential persons, so what can I do about it?"

"Let her come. Maybe she will learn something at last," said Anthony.

The doctor shook his head.

"Not so long as she's healthy herself. Among people who try to practice luxury and charity at the same time the only ones who ever learn to care about other people, outside of their own families, are those who are attacked by a mortal disease themselves. Besides, this is not an educational institution, it's a respectable lazarhouse."

Every three months they were visited by a priest in charge of young lads in training at a near-by seminary. In order to learn humility the boys were each made to kneel and serve one of the lepers from a nest of dishes they brought for the occasion.

There was no escaping this visitation. All the inmates, except those suffering from a virulent disease, were subjected to it. There were more boys to learn humility than there were vile persons to kneel before. So even the turnkeys were requisitioned.

Somewhat awed by the flustered youngster who knelt before him in the vestibule, with the stony saints looking down upon him while he arranged the dishes on the floor with a shy awkwardness, Anthony strove to ease the natural embarrassment of the situation by engaging the boy in talk.

But he did not succeed very well, he thought. He asked him some questions. The replies were truthful, he felt, but brief. He discovered, however, that the youth was bored, homesick, and not anxious to be a priest.

"I am the third son, and my father has only a small hacienda. It would not do to divide the pastures. So you see, señor, the only field I inherit is the church. The grazing is pretty scant there. We bring you the best meal of the year—to teach us humility!" Suddenly the youth put his hand over his mouth and looked up in terror at the man he was serving. He had not meant to say that. Tears came into his eyes and he closed them. He did not open them for some time. He did not dare to. He was being fed from the dishes he had come to serve.

"Not all of it, *not* the pineapple frijole, señor."

"Sí, all of it, Tertio," insisted the big man with the beard, "to the last spoonful. Thou must learn how to share thy gifts with others. It is the essence of humility."

Tertio packed the empty dishes, blushing deeply, and departed after presenting his gift. "It is a horse that I carved myself," said he. "But look! He does lift his feet as though he spurned the dust."

"I am charmed with it," cried Anthony. "Anybody can see that it is a noble animal. It can go."

The boy gravely bade him farewell. Anthony remembered another boy in a long priest's garment and sat thinking.

He dropped the fine little horse that Tertio had carved into the deer-skin bag.

Three months later he found himself sought out and served again. This time, still in the quiet of the vestibule, they shared the meal together and the boy began to question him. Thus at three-month intervals their acquaintance ripened. In all Anthony saw Tertio seven times.

The boy had grown greatly in that time. The man could feel himself reliving his own youth. Inexplicably he felt it being renewed within him. And with it returned something of his old ardour for life; his desire to fare forth again. If there had been a tree in the prison close, he would once more have climbed it. He told Tertio that story—but there were only stunted bushes in the prison yard.

He now began, all but unconsciously at first, to keep an eye about him for possible means of escape. He was even riper for it than he thought. He began to imagine that he might—if he could—go back to Europe—to Düsseldorf. By this time his son would be well into manhood. Perhaps, Angela might . . . and then a terrible sense of the futility and the degradation of returning to them, like a ghost come back to claim their property, would rush upon him. No, dead men had no right to rise.

"Lazarus, come forth."

How *that* would interfere with things! What was there, what was there that he could expect by returning to the past? To return would be to return to all of it, too. It would only be in the end to resume the shirt of Nessus that he had been able to wear—and cast off—only by the Grace of God. He might yet be chained up in the steel belt in the corner along with "St. Theresa," poor soul, if he started to don the past again.

But there was the future to look to, he could not deny that. It seemed as though he would live a long time yet. People died around him and he was left untouched. Even in the pesthouse of Mexico. Sometimes he had hoped—what?

"Never!"

Why, outside it was spring again! From some garden near by, the scent of orange blossoms drifted to him across the wall. He went and lay in the sun and breathed in the odour. The world outside must be mad with bloom. Somehow—he must take his time and consider well—it would never do to be recaptured—but somehow he must see it again. He opened the bag that night and the little horse fell out.

"Anyone can see that it is a noble animal. It can *go*." He heard himself saying that to young Tertio almost two years ago now. "Go!"

At last his own suggestion rang in his heart like a command.

————

The festival of San Lazaro takes place on the eleventh of March. For some days before that event the inmates of the hospital spent their time and ingenuity in preparing for the only visitation of charity which they were genuinely enthusiastic about. It was their own festival they prepared for. Others came to share their joy with them. It was the custom on the eleventh of March for all classes in the City of Mexico to go and visit the leprosos.

On that morning the vision of the great mountain through the empty dome had lifted up the heart of at least one of the prisoners with a renewed sense of hope—and an impulse toward freedom. Perhaps, it was only the unwonted sense of joy about him in the prison that seemed to sweep him on with it. But that morning he knelt before the great altar in the nave, where the festival of the saint of the abandoned and the lepers began, and received the wafer for the first and last time in his life.

The entire company of the prison from Dr. Lopez to the Indian cooks, everyone who could still walk, sat down together and ate with the priests who had celebrated mass, from a board furnished sumptuously by public benevolence and served by masked and hooded gentlemen.

The leprosos had decorated their room with festoons and flags; with bright, pathetic devices cut from all kinds of coloured papers. These were strung about the walls and streamed from the lamps and brackets. Even the bars of the windows were gayly trimmed. The word *caridad*—charity—predominated. Its neatly-cut, paper letters were pasted upon various wreathed baskets and boxes placed where they would most readily strike the eye of visitors. The floor had been stained a bright yellow tint. Strips of red, white, and green muslin were arranged like an arabesque on the ceiling. The cots of the lepers themselves were wreathed with flowers.

They now changed the clothing upon their beds and began to dress themselves in the finery of the world they had left behind them but whose joyful garments they still cherished. No one could gaze upon them now without astonishment. It seemed as though the dead in various stages of dissolution had suddenly emerged equipped in glaring holiday finery; dressed as fearful, flaunting cavaliers and giddy, drawing-room belles. All that was needed was a few skeletons for bailarinas—and the dance would begin. One expected at any moment to hear the infernal castanets and the demoniacal guitars. And there *was* music, the sound of some stringed instrument touched in the shadowy corners of the room by a hand without enough fingers.

Anthony had seen this festival before, but he now looked upon it with a different understanding. It was not a dance of death, grotesque and obscene. Even in these decaying bodies the eternal joy of life, the triumph of the living spirit of man over the matter that contains it was being manifested. He saw past the bizarre clothes covering the grotesque bodies into the tongues of flame that sat upon the flower-wreathed bedsteads, laughing, leaping in the face of death. And within him his own spirit burned with them again mightily.

The big gates at the end of the room had been carefully closed and two small side doors especially prepared for the occasion. They were guarded by attendants, who knew the inmates, so that none could leave without scrutiny, but they were thrown open so that anyone might enter. About nine o'clock the crowds from the city began to assemble outside.

Entering by one of the side doors, the visitors would slowly make the circuit of the rooms, talk to the various inmates, leaving with them such presents as they had brought, and then depart by the door on the opposite side. Yet in spite of the attempts of the attendants to keep the line moving, by noon the throng in the huge chamber was immense and engaged in a kind of carnival in which the laughter and encouraging gayety of the visitors was punctuated by the husky and squeaky voices of the lepers, the rattle of dice boxes, the blurred twanging of instruments, the popping of corks, and the clicking of castanets. For in various places misshapen couples were dancing fandangos beyond description, encouraged by the good-natured shouts of the bystanders.

The beds of the disabled, and the tables of others behind which those who still had discernible faces sat with expectant grins, were piled high with gifts: loaves of bread, cakes, packets of cigars, cigarritos and puros; oranges, pineapples, and mangoes. The constant ring of coins, clacos and medios, silver dollars and gold pieces dropped into the jars provided for the purpose, accompanied the scene with a metallic clink. On the beds and tables of the youngest sufferers piled up offerings of flowers and toys.

"Amigo," said a tall Spaniard whose days were obviously few, "will you receive for me at my table a while? I must lie down for a little. Gracias, may God reward you!" He sank back on his cot, while Anthony took his place on a chair behind the table.

He began to call out with the others begging for charity. His clear voice rang through the room,

> "Let not the humble be turned away with confusion;
>   The poor and needy shall praise thy name."

A peon advanced impulsively and gave him his sombrero. A beggar contributed a silver coin. The voice continued. They understood he was begging for the man on the cot. The Spaniard thanked them magnificently. The gifts increased. In his grey face the sufferer's eyes gleamed with satisfaction.

The room was now aswirl with excitement and colour. The crowd ran the gamut of classes from a city where the diversity of population is as complex as any that exists. There were caballeros with silver spurs, and beggars; priests with shovel hats, and soldiers; girls dressed in the poblana,—short and gaudy petticoats, fancifully worked chemises, gay satin shoes, and no stockings,—girls with hardly any dress at all. There were monks, gamblers, and ragamuffins; ladies attired in mantillas, jewels, and satins; friars and peons, and the families of the lepers gathered about their cots. A party of high-born and fashionable women arrived with a meal which they served themselves.

The second hour of the afternoon marked the height of this orgy of charity. The table before Anthony was now heaped high. He made a last appeal and was about to go,

> "Forget not to the end the souls of thy poor."

A lady disengaged herself from the richly dressed group which surrounded her and approached his table. One of a hundred others who had dropped a coin in the jar that day, he did not look up. He saw her hand dropping a gold piece in the jar. It fell onto the floor.

"Is it possible?" he heard her exclaim.

"Not lost," he cried, "I'll find it for you!"

He got up and found himself face to face with Dolores.

He reached out impulsively and took her hands. She let them lie in his while in each other's faces they sought to read something of the story of the past. Then a look of horror came and she snatched them away.

"Ma doña, I am clean," he said.

They stood for a while in eternity. The room vanished. Then she took his hands again.

"No matter," she exclaimed, "I shall never let go of them now."

And so it was that on the festival of all-beggars he received the best gift of all.

CHAPTER SIXTY-EIGHT

THE STONE IN THE HEART OF THE TREE

BEFORE the death of her husband Dolores already found herself in charge of his far-flung haciendas, his mines, and various mansions. Don Guillermo had for several years been hopelessly feeble. They had no children, but he had long kept a large, hungry pack of his collateral relatives, who looked forward with undisguised enthusiasm to gathering him to his fathers. Some of them, who had more courage than cash, had even proposed among themselves to hasten his demise, should a seasonable opportunity present itself. The skill and diplomacy of the old hidalgo's wife had prevented them, and permitted nature, who is so indifferent to collateral heirs, to take her own tedious time.

And very tedious it was, especially for Dolores. While the old gentleman, to whom she had been joined in matrimony by an allegedly Christian ceremony, sat in the patio of his great house at Guanajuato and played with moonstones and white rabbits, for he had a senile passion for both, she had watched her mirror reflect nothing but the slow effect upon her of the sterile embraces of time.

It was only natural, under the circumstances, that she should at least permit herself some dreams of what might have been, and a more than usual preoccupation with romantic incidents of the past; incidents that under different circumstances she would undoubtedly have forgotten or remembered with an indulgent smile. As it was, her meeting with Anthony at Havana, the golden night in the courtyard, and the few seconds in the arms of her lover there rose like an Olympus from the drab plain of her experience. Her encounter with Anthony at Madrid had only served in the end to intensify her few memories of him by providing a little more reality upon which to feed them.

And yet Dolores was not romantic. Had anyone suggested that she was to the disappointed relatives of her late husband, he would have been laughed at and told, between curses, that she was known to the family as the "Lady Miser." There was also a number of young, and some middle-aged caballeros scattered over the country who would have confirmed the family. They had one and all admired either her person, her property, or both, and found her unapproachable. She was capable of only one passion, they said; a passion for property.

As for the women, while they admired and secretly envied certain qualities in Dolores, which they were afraid to imitate, they were also inclined to agree with the men.

And this remarkable unanimity of opinion in regard to Dolores had, as usual, something to build upon.

She had been married off to Don Guillermo de Almanara shortly after her return from Havana to Spain. The alliance—it was nothing more—had served to cement legally two of the greatest feudatories in Mexico, where the possessions of both her own family and her husband's were immense. More territory, revenue, and people were involved than in many a marriage of minor European sovereigns. But Don Guillermo was sixty-four and Dolores nineteen when he brought her home to Mexico. She found herself confronted with the choice of existing in futile luxury till he died; of idly playing with fire; of enjoying the genuine power, influence, and prestige which the active administration of vast estates and interests might bring her.

Dolores was of a pure Gothic type. She was at once ardent, obstinate, and determined. She had great beauty and a clear, firm mind. She had all the fierce pride of her ancestors, who had harried the Moors from Valladolid to Valencia. She was not inclined to become the mistress of philandering cavaliers even if she had fallen in love with them. She considered her situation carefully, and made her choice. She devoted herself to the administration of her mines and haciendas.

Those who threatened her interests or trespassed upon her property she fought like a tiger with cubs. Indeed, the care of "her people," as she called her peons and dependents, and the improvement of her property became for her the equivalent of a family. She lavished upon this work the tireless energy of a woman who was not barren but childless.

The gradual lapse of her husband into senility provided her with both the excuse and opportunity to carry out her plans. In a short while it was not Dolores but Don Guillermo who spent his life in secluded luxury. She encouraged him in it. She finally sequestered him at Guanajuato, after first having seen to it that his will was in proper order and safe keeping. She provided him with endless moonstones, a platonic harem of white rabbits, and carefully selected attendants. He died in peace, and was buried with that complete manifestation of sorrow which only blue blood and riches can confer.

The reading of his will, however, was followed by a somewhat less conventional and restrained gnashing of teeth. The entire estate, with the wise exception of a fixed income to any viceroy as long as he held office, was left to his wife. Thus Dolores had finally secured what her marriage had been meant to accomplish; the bringing together of certain estates. Because she had paid for this result with the greatest of sacrifices, she defended it passionately.

She gave her husband's relatives pensions in exact proportion to the trouble they were able to make. She encouraged them to live abroad and educate their children there. She held forth the promise of legacies. But she was also obdurate. Once having settled the amount of a stipend, she would not for any reason whatever increase it. She had therefore become known as the "Lady Miser."

Despite the fact that she still desired to complete herself and to have children, she could not easily be persuaded to remarry. She could not overcome her repugnance merely to accepting the necessary man. And besides that, her marriage to anyone in her own circles would have involved immense legal and political difficulties.

Mexico was in the throes of revolution. The Spaniards had been driven out. Iturbide was just about to become emperor. It had taken all the skill and finesse that Dolores possessed to preserve her property in an era of confiscation and dissolution. She had played both sides admirably and she had been lucky. The dictator was indebted to her for his cavalry remounts and other timely contributions. Temporarily she was safe.

But it had been a time of terrible anxiety, and she was tired of it. Even more than a husband, she wanted security.

Yet a marriage with any of the able or influential Mexicans who sought her would have involved her hopelessly in the interests of the particular faction to which any one of them belonged. Upon several occasions she had decided that this would never do, and she had had to say so with all the diplomacy that could possibly be attached to a firm "no." Each of her suitors had easily been persuaded that a man who was as charming as she admitted him to be could only be repulsed by a heart hardened by avarice. Thus opinion tended to confirm itself. Dolores was generally regarded as an able, powerful, and worldly woman. She was received everywhere with fear, favour, and respect—but with nothing more.

And, of course, that was not enough for Dolores. She wanted life. Despite the death of her husband, and her position, it seemed as though she were going to be robbed of it. Desire and prudence threatened to come to a static balance in her and to leave her holding the scales between them without her daring to let go. The worst of it was, she knew it. She was almost forty. It would soon be too late to act, in any event.

Some weeks before her visit to St. Lazarus an amiable but much disappointed man had in the stress of a final interview with her so far forgotten his gallantry as to point this out. She replied stingingly. Don Elyano rode off in a tingling fury.

Perhaps, if he had returned, she would have accepted him. For in his angry reproaches she had recognized the insults of truth. And it must be remembered that this interview was conducted in Castilian; in that magnificent and punctilious idiom that is so capable of expressing the mother wit of fishwives.

For once the poise of Dolores had been shaken. She had almost lost her balance and been precipitated into hasty action.

She had gone about for some time afterward feeling that she would live to regret what was probably her last chance in a decision for life. She was still doing so when she had recognized the voice of the man who had once been her lover calling for charity in the House of the Lepers. "Is it possible?"—her first words to him—had therefore expressed both the supreme doubt and the utmost hopes of her being. She had given him her hands from an impulse she could not restrain.

To both of them this providential encounter provided a way for an escape into life and action. Neither of them hesitated, but they were none the less cautious. It was some time before Anthony was liberated. Now that release was so near, for the first time he began to worry greatly about his contact with contagion. It was possible, even likely, he felt, that he might now be taken off. But fate was even more capricious than he expected. It was Lopez, the little physician, who died.

"When you get out of here, my friend, if you ever do, remember my children," he begged.

In the meanwhile Dolores made her arrangements. She began to take a great interest in prisons in general. A number of other women were also interested. For a while it became the fashion to visit the oppressed. As a result of this, nearly fifty persons incarcerated by tyrannical measures during the Spanish régime found themselves blinking in the light of day again. Among them was a man with a long golden beard from the prison of St. Lazarus. Seeing an excellent chance in this wholesale deliverance to curry favour with the liberals, Iturbide had these fortunate ones marched to the plaza and released after a patriotic harangue and the presentation of a small purse.

The unfortunate prisoner, whose patriarchal appearance had rather tended to fix attention upon him, then disappeared. He aroused a barber late that night to shave him and dress his hair. The next day there was no more reason to associate the quiet, well-dressed and dignified gentleman, who spoke a careful Castilian, but was thought to be an Englishman, with the late inmate of San Lazaro than there was to connect this utter stranger with the name of Doña Dolores. Yet they met frequently.

Anthony lingered for about a week in the City of Mexico, making arrangements for travelling; satisfying himself that certain American prisoners had really been sent to New Orleans two years before, as the records showed, and that the family of Dr. Lopez had a pension settled upon them from a mysterious but charitable source. At the end of that time he set out for the North, well mounted and provided with a small escort.

He traversed rapidly the same route over which he had toiled southward only a few years before. He was received with great respect by the major-domo in charge of a great hacienda two days north of Chihuahua. The hacienda, which belonged to Doña Dolores de Almanara, stretched indefinitely northward beyond the Rio Grande. It was bounded in that direction by a river which lost itself in the desert, a mountain with a village on it, and the somewhat more definite though hostile ideas of the horse Indians as to where their hunting grounds began. Surveying in that direction was too closely connected with the loss of hair to be accurate.

Dolores followed Anthony after a short interval. She closed her great town house in Mexico and made her will, which was so phrased as both to encourage and to restrain her husband's relatives. It was considered a feminine vanity on her part that she still insisted upon certain clauses relating to the heirs of her body. She announced that she was retiring permanently to the country, owing to the disturbed state of the capital, and bade farewell to her friends without permitting them to make much ado about nothing. Her last care was to see that a young renegade by the name of Tertio was sent abroad to study.

A few weeks later Anthony and Dolores were married by the padre in charge of the church at Ysleta, a small village at a ford on the Rio Grande between El Paso and Socorro. Their wedding feast was served by the Indians of the place. And if Anthony remembered another "wedding breakfast," he did not show it. There was a calmness and an assured serenity about him which was reflected in the face of the noble woman who had become his wife.

They expected little; they hoped for much. They rode northward into the desert together, accompanied by a few of Dolores' people, some animals, and a half-dozen solid-wheeled carts. Their objective was a certain detached mountain with a village on it. Dolores had once visited it years before and remembered it as an abode of peace.

It was the season when the yucca was in bloom. Through these candelabra of the gods, hung with delicate white bells as though for a wilderness festival of lilies, they advanced slowly, driving their

flocks before them; some longhorns, extra horses, burros, and sheep.
The beds of dry arroyos, still firm and damp from the recent spring
rains and freshets, were their winding roads. Here and there pools
still lay in rocky holes under the banks. For a few weeks the desert
had become an exotic park, planted, it seemed, upon an almighty
plan by inhuman landscapers for the delectation of stony-faced deities.
The dust was laid; the sagebrush a deep cypress green; the cacti glorious with complex and brilliant, fleshy blossoms inflamed with the
lust of life, and haunted by myriads of bees. Gophers twittered at
them from the entrances of their burrows. The shadows of birds
passed like the shades of memory across the glaring sands. At dawn
and twilight their eery, piping chorus seemed to be the song of ghosts
lost in this peopleless land.

They rested in the heat and glamour of noon under the shade of
the carts, and pushed on again until the flowers of the desert above
them bloomed with light. Their marriage bed was a great oxcart
filled with straw. On this they lay, whispering of the life that lay
before them. Once more Anthony heard the wild coyote-voices as
though the loneliness of the cosmos were giving tongue, and watched
the falling stars, and turned, not this time to comfort the dying, but
to take triumphant refuge in the arms of life. Upon the face of
Dolores gradually spread the deeper shade of the desert and a reflection of the peaceful glory through which they advanced. Through
the day the man and woman rode side by side, reading the promise
of the future in each other's faces.

Westward, a range of bronze-coloured mountains tumbled into the
blinding north. They rose onto the higher and more arid plateaus,
where an occasional buffalo or cow skull marked the trail of the horse-
Indians and cautioned them to build small dry fires in sheltered places
and to keep watch by night. Presently, almost directly under the
pole star, a lonely peak began to show itself above the horizon.

They raised it slowly. At first it was only a glowing mound above
the far level of the plateau. It rose gradually into heaven as they
advanced. Its highest ramparts were covered by a cloud that gathered at night and dissolved in the morning into streaks of rain. These
could be seen, even at a great distance, slanting down upon the forests and meadows that clothed the mountain's forehead. It was like a
giant with green hair. The desert lapped it around and rose half-way
up its side in a furnace of cacti and red lava rocks. The small river,
that trickled like a vein of perpetual perspiration down its face, plunged
through a gorge and lost itself in the desert. El Tronadore, this
mountain was called, because of the thunderstorms that gathered about
it in the springtime.

Four days after first sighting it they entered the flowered meadow which marked the death struggles of the little river with the desert at its feet. The sheep and cattle rushed forward bawling to crop the sweet herbage. They camped that night hearing the bells of flocks far up the mountain. In the morning they began to ascend the narrow gorge toward the grass and timberlands above them.

It was a day's journey to the village of La Luz near the top. Half-way up they were met by the priest and headmen from the town, who gave them welcome, but learned with amazement that the master and mistress of the lands they cultivated had come to make their home among them. Looking at the flocks and goods they had brought, their restrained suspicion turned to unrestrained joy. It was after sunset when they arrived in a great bowl of meadows just below the rain line, where the pine forests began. On one side of the meadow, against a dark background of forest, the lights of the village and the red glow of its doors and windows twinkled as they approached it through a haze of almond orchards in violet and starlike bloom.

And neither Anthony nor Dolores had any doubt that they had at last come home. He lifted her over the threshold of the first house they entered.

The years at La Luz did not deny them what they had hoped. Experience had taught them not to expect too much. They were prepared for sorrows and pain as an inevitable share of their destiny. Surcease, health, and happiness are rare jewels on the string of time. They counted such beads as wonderful, and thankfully added them to the treasury of memory, mindful of the time to come when the recounting of them might be their sole comfort. Happiness came to them not as something ordinary to be ruthlessly used; not as a mere norm always to be transcended by passion, if they were really to feel alive, but like a new gift brought secretly at night by some mysterious and generous spendthrift, who they knew they might find almost any morning had failed to remember them. They did not speculate about it nor spoil it by impossible precautions and useless apprehensions. Like a plant, whose end is sure, they let it grow, blossom, and seed in its own way upon the hill where it stood.

But they were doubly blessed in this: the best of the fruits of time that they gathered together did not come to them as if they were snatched from niggardly hands as wages sharply due them for their honest toil and sweat. They did not live to make ends meet. They still toiled. At La Luz, as elsewhere, the whole daily round of life went on. No one can escape it without having some part of him begin to die—but their rewards came to them now like the two un-expected children whom Dolores bore to Anthony; they came as the result of living as part of a scheme the ends of which, since they cannot be sighted, can never be made to meet.

"At La Luz," mused Anthony one evening toward the end of their third year there, "I think I detect a little overtone from paradise. Or perhaps it is something in the sunlight, a golden reflection from that age which poets can never remember enough about to coin them out of their dark garrets. I am glad that I did not try to live by dreams alone; glad I tried as best I could to pour molten dreams into the mould of life. This is a good mould here at La Luz to let the hot metal of thought cool in. All the shapes of things I see about me are suitable; made beautiful by the sweet necessity of daily human use. Such images are the stuff out of which good dreams take shape—to be recast.

"It is always like that: the dream into the mould; from the mould the dream again. I am glad that I have come to some balance in this flux by living; that I am whole now; that I am neither a mere dreamer nor just a mammal. I am glad that I am a man compounded out of both; that I live; that is, that I can act in between. I have not achieved this just by taking thought and then acting.

"Three things have made me out of a mammal that dreamed into something that resembles a man: Mystery burning in the furnace of experience; Dolores, whom it is pure mercy and good fortune to have found; and a life here at La Luz that changes no faster than a man can change with it. God grant that I be not torn away from this place to wander again, for I am weak, and the grace to prevail might not again be with me. It is for this grace I pray. Life is two things. It is never anything in itself. It is always *like* something else. Only when I compare it with him who is both the dreamer and the thing dreamed can I see that it must be perfect. That is my vision of light . . ."

La Luz changed; that is, the houses and the mountain upon which they stood weathered with the processes of the centuries. The men and women in it renewed themselves and were always there in varying forms. They lived and breathed with the rhythm of the seasons; they experienced slowly, but calmly and to the full, the whole round of life; childhood, youth, and old age. Around them the forests and meadows also renewed themselves with the processes of the years. Between the years and centuries the people of the village remained poised. Their economy for continuing to exist was as perfect as could be invented. It suited the earth; it was not invented by thought alone. If the people changed it was with the mountain. Anthony and Dolores had become a part of this village and its life. Gallegos and Silver Ho had taught him his lessons. He did not try to change the place, to improve it, and to tear from the earth a surplus and superabundance, which exhausts the soil upon which man stands. From too great abundance, he had discovered, came the chief curses to the bodies and spirits of men. So the master and mistress of the place restrained themselves and let La Luz alone. It was beautiful and self-sufficient. "And that is all we need to know about it," he said to Dolores, "that is the sign manual of the approval of God."

They built their house after the manner of those in the village. It lay a little higher on some land they and their people had cleared amid the trees. It was built of stone and adobe. It contained all they needed and only a little more. Here Inez and Flora, their two daughters, were born and flourished through childhood. Only three times in ten years were they disturbed. Once by some Spanish gypsies who wandered from Paraguay to Mexico. They were smiths and mended the great copper kettle of the village that had come down with the first Indian inhabitants from the north. They closed the hole in it that fire had made.

"That is well," said Fray Pedro, the village padre, "I shall bless it, and then whole lambs can be boiled again."

Once they were disturbed by a pilgrimage of Penitentes whipping themselves, walking upon glass and hot stones. They departed for a place called the "Mountain of the Cross" that lay westward over the desert. "Some of them," said Fray Pedro, "may crucify each other. I have heard of it." They took some half-maddened converts from the village with them and left others behind. Fray Pedro did not bless this work. "These are the old devils of the land breaking out again," he said one evening when he had come to call at the house amid the trees. "It is very difficult to drive them away. They even assume the form of Jesus. Do you know what they will do? Just before a penitente dies those about him break his arms and legs. It ensures them paradise, they think, for they say that those who are treated thus have suffered more than Christ who was not so broken when he descended from the cross. Is that not a cunning temptation for simple minds? An enemy has done this!" He sat for some time looking sad and perplexed. "I wish," he said at last, "I had a beautiful image of the Mother of God to hold up mercy before them in the chapel."

Anthony rose and taking the little madonna from the deerskin bag, where he had long kept it, he gave it to Fray Pedro.

"Take it," said he, "I have kept her with me long. I can never lose her now."

And so with due festival the little madonna went home to the village church. She stood in a niche above the altar and the villagers dressed her again.

"How can you part with her?" said Dolores, who knew much of her story.

"I do not part with her," he cried. "Her image still remains in this house." They clung together in the darkness.

Fray Pedro was not entirely satisfied, however. The villagers had insisted on placing their new madonna on a certain stone. "It is a holy one," they said, and would say no more.

"So I have let them do it," he cried, "just as after the Easter services I let them hold a corn dance before the church. What do you think?" he asked Anthony.

"It is well to try to control as best you can, Fray Pedro, but I think it is useless to try to prevent and prohibit. All these things you mention are contained in life. They may eventually lead up to the image on the altar, and beyond."

"And *beyond*, señor?" said the padre.

"Yes," he replied. "One cannot prevent that either."

The padre departed still troubled at heart. He could not always understand the señor.

"But, after all, it was he who gave the image," he thought, and was comforted.

When Inez, the older child, was five years old the Indians attempted to creep up on the village from the plains below. They met them in the gorge and drove them back again. In this, the great event of their lives, the men of the village became brothers in battle.

"These are not my People of the Bear," thought Anthony. "They are wolves," he said to the man next to him, as the smoke cleared away. "Listen to them howl."

"Sí, señor, they go back again. They will trouble us at La Luz no more. Once every generation they try to come up here. They forget. For us now, it will be nothing but peace till we die."

And so it was—the peace of pasture, field, and forest; the peace of the village; the peace of the house—while in the chapel the madonna held forth the image of mercy to all who could see it. . . .

And then one day he took a sharp axe in his hand and went out to cut down a tree.

It was one of those calm, cool days at the close of summer that presage the fall. Dolores had taken Inez and Flora to the village to be present at a little playmate's name-day feast. He raised the axe to them in a happy gesture of farewell as they disappeared over the crest of the hill from his view. Dolores saw the blinding flash of the metal in the sun. There was no one left about the house. The people of the hacienda were all busy that day on the far side of the mountain, building sheep folds in the new east pasture.

The path he took ran west. The great tree stood in the middle of a field. The sun would soon be going down behind it. There was just about time to cut it down before evening. Tomorrow they could cart it away. Its dense shade spoiled the best field he had. He did not like to cut it down, for it reminded him vaguely of the tree in the convent courtyard. But what must be must be. He took a few deep breaths. How sweet the air on the mountain was! Wine with the sunlight dancing through it. He swung the axe up and began.

The tree was very old. In past ages it had taken up a stone, as it grew, into the heart of it. And now it was waiting there—the stone in the heart of the tree.

The hard chips flew; the gash made by the metal widened. Suddenly the axe twisted in his hand as though it had been turned against him. The steel rang. The sharp edge bit into the flesh of the man. He staggered backward, clutching himself. From the great artery near his groin a wide arc of blood spurted into the sunlight with every heart-throb.

For a moment he was only amazed. Then came terror. Then no more of that forever. He struggled desperately to stanch his wound. It was difficult to get at it. He succeeded in stopping the flow of blood a little with his scarf and belt. It would do, he thought. He must drag himself to the top of the hill and call for help. Dolores would hear him when she returned. He could lie still there until she came for him. Already the bright pasture was turning a little grey. "Night is coming," he thought. "How strange!"

His blind determination remained. He dragged himself up the field, his life running away through the grass. He came to the place where he could go no farther. He knew that. "O God, Dolores! Be with her!" he cried.

It seemed long ago. He began to pray to his madonna. He was going to sleep. His eyes opened slowly and wide. Looking down over the slope of the field, he saw the great tree still standing there with the sun sinking behind it. His eyes gazed steadily. He no longer winked. He was in the courtyard again. The light began to stir with strange forms.

The Bronze Boy and the Missing Twin fell in a furious rain of greyness from heaven and strove with each other and the ground. They dashed up flames out of the fountain. From the midst of the fire sprang the great tree. It hung between heaven and the ground. Its branches shaded the whole earth. Through them swarmed the forms of everything he had ever seen. In the midst of lightnings, which perpetually passed through its leaves, he saw himself climbing, and then, he saw himself no more. At the top of the tree the madonna bloomed. She held the child out into the light. Behind her head the sun burned intolerably, shooting forth golden and spiked rays into his eyes. The head faded. From behind a mere shadow of it the light still came. All else grew dark now. Suddenly the rays of light themselves dissolved and began to sweep into his eyes like grey seeds of darkness. He shuddered. All was black now. The . . .

EPILOGUE

THE great mountain continued to look upon the plain. In the springtime the thunderstorms still gathered about it as before. The stream ran into the desert, and the forests grew. But the village of La Luz in the pleasant bowl of meadows near its top was silent. Its dying almond orchards still blossomed feebly but their starry wonder brought no pleasure to men.

Long ago Dolores had taken her two children and gone to El Paso. Some of the villagers had left with her. With how she struggled to retain a part of their inheritance for her daughters; whom they married—this story has nothing to do. It must suffice that all the blood of the man who was their father had not been spilt in the field by the tree which he could not cut down. The tree still grew. He slept in the chapel under the floor before the altar. The madonna still stood above the altar but she was now alone.

The Indians had once crept up the mountain. They did not come by the gorge that time. The roofs of the houses and the chapel had fallen in. Only the wild goats remained to look down from the little hills. Trees grew in the patios of the dwellings where no one dwelt—and the mountain looked down upon the plain.

Like the hill of Gergovia in far-off Auvergne, it too overlooked an ancient human road and seemed to watch it. No one knew how old the trail was. It had been used before man wrote or travelled upon wheels. There had been a good many travellers following it lately. They did not travel as individuals or even as families. They came in great droves and flocks in wagon trains. Their white, rolling tents smoked across the dusty desert and made for the Pass of the North. Most of them went by the mountain, content to water their oxen from the stream at the foot. They looked up and coveted the pastures above them, but the mountain was high. Then they went on in a great hurry. Somewhere else there seemed to be a promised land.

At last a party of new-comers climbed the mountain again. They drove their sick cattle up the gorge to the pastures. They found the old people's road to good grazing. They were from Missouri. "Show us," they said to those who said it couldn't be done, for there were a few people from other states amongst them. They camped in a circle of wagons in the great meadow open to heaven and let their cattle and horses roll in the grass. They thoroughly explored the ruined town.

Something might have been left. You never can tell. But there was nothing valuable. All that they found was the little madonna.

It was some of the children who found the madonna. They came peering into the little chapel, half afraid of the shadows. Who could tell what might be there? They soon found themselves at home, however.

> "This is the church and this is the steeple,
> Open the doors and see all the people,"

they sang, dancing about on the bare stone floor.

Under the stone something crumbled. In the skull of the sleeper was neither music nor dreams nor the vision of light. He was not troubled by anything at all. What was left of him was completely material. He had gotten down to business at last. He grinned. The rhythm of childish feet had only jarred him. After a while they ceased.

It was not much fun playing church. There wasn't as much to it as the old rhyme said. There were no doors and no steeple; the roof had fallen in. There was only the people. So they started to play house, which was much better. It was then that Mary—she wished she had a real Bible name like Esther-Susannah—found the doll. It was splendid playing house after that. The doll had a baby in her arms.

> "This is the house and this is the people,"

they sang. They stopped a minute but no one could make up the rest.

> "And here we are,"

sang out a little boy. They all laughed for some reason. There ought to have been more, they felt—and there wasn't. They screamed.

All went beautifully then until the boys wanted to play store. The altar made such a good counter. Mary Jorham walked off with her doll. She loved it. She stood at the door of the ruined chapel looking at it in the light.

"Oh, you darling," she said. "I'm agoin' to take ya along with me."

Then she covered it quickly with her apron. Abner Jorham, one of the drivers of the wagons, approached. He happened to be her father.

"What you got there, sis?" he said, extending his open hand. "Give it ta me."

She knew better than to refuse him. She put the image in his hand.

"Why, swan to man, if hit hain't a heathen idol!"

"Hits not," she said, suddenly growing pale with anger. "Hits my dolly, par."

"Whar did ye get her?"

"In thar," she said.

"Thought so," said he. "I won't have ye playin' with no sich trash. Now run along to yer mar. She's been callin' yer."

"I'll tell her," she called after him. "I'll tell her ye took it away from me." She burst into tears.

Her father waved his hand a little uneasily and sauntered off. He was quite a fellow with "the boys" from Pike County. They began to arrange a shooting match. "I got the very thing fer a mark. Look here! The kids found it rootin' round in the ruins."

They disposed themselves for the match.

"'Bout three hundred yads, eh?" said Mr. Jorham.

"Make it three hundred and fifty," said a man from Tennessee. "You can stand the mark on the rock there." They waited till he returned, ramming their charges home. Mrs. Jorham came stalking up.

"Whar's that doll you took from Mary, Abner?" she demanded.

"Tain't no doll," he said.

"'Tis," countered his wife. "I don't believe ya know what yer talkin' about."

"Wall, thar she's settin', if ya wants ter find out," he said, grinning and pointing toward the rock at which five rifles were already pointing.

Mrs. Abner Jorham knew when she was licked. She stood waiting for the men to fire.

"Right to left, and a full ten counts between so there can't be no argument," said the Tennesseean. He was on the left and the others cursed his arrogance.

But it took the man from Tennessee to do it. The rifle on the left cracked and the figure on the rock sprang into a thousand pieces.

"Thar's nothing like bar's grease for rifle patches," said the winner.

"Ya might have let her have it," still insisted Mrs. Jorham. "She's lonely, and God knows . . ."

"Aw forget it," cried her husband. "Can't ya see it's too late. I'll buy her a doll at the store when we git to El Paso."

By the wagon Mary dried her eyes and looked about her. There seemed nothing to do. "I wisht we'd get to a home," she thought. "Par, he's alers fer movin'." She fished out her Bible that the Reverend Jacob Todhunter had given her back East and tried to read in it. "Shucks," said she, "hits only a book arter all." Then she looked about her a little scared. She wanted that doll. She needed something to talk to that was hers.

She walked over to the edge of the meadow. There was a gap there in the forest and she could look down upon the blinding plains below her. In all that moonlike landscape there was not even the shadow of a thing to which she could confide the enormous fear and loneliness of her heart.

"Do, God! Give us *something*," she cried.

THE END